MW01566655

PROLOGOS

PROLOGOS

JONATHAN BAYLISS

BASILICUM PRESS

Ashburnham, Massachusetts

Prologos belongs to the GLOUCESTERMAN series.
Gloucesterbook (ISBN 0-9625780-1-0) was published in 1992,
Gloucestertide (ISBN 0-09625780-2-9) in 1996.

Copyright © 1999 by Jonathan Bayliss.

All rights reserved. No part of this book may be reproduced
or transmitted in any form or by any means, electronic or
mechanical, including photocopying and recording, or by
any information storage and retrieval system, without the
permission of the author. Requests for permission should be
made in writing to Basilicum Press, 121 Lake Shore Drive,
Ashburnham, MA 01430.

Library of Congress Catalog Card Number: 98-74560

ISBN: 0–9667807-0-1

Manufactured in the United States of America.

Text and cover design by Arisman Design, Essex,
Massachusetts.

This book was typeset in Adobe Garamond 3 by
Cathleen Collins, Blue Mountain Lake, New York.
Printing and binding were done by Hamilton Printing
Company in Castleton, New York.

Edited and produced by Eugene R. Bailey, Westborough,
Massachusetts.

for

Geoffrey,
Victoria,
and Catherine

'Tis to rebuke a vicious taste . . . of reading straight forwards, more in quest of the adventures, than of the deep erudition and knowledge which a book of this cast, if read over as it should be, would infallibly impart with them.—The mind should be accustomed to make wise reflections, and draw curious conclusions as it goes along; the habitude of which made *Pliny* the younger affirm, "That he never read a book so bad, but he drew some profit from it."

—TRISTRAM SHANDY

CONTENTS

CONTENTS

It is a terrible misfortune for this same book of mine, but more so for the Republic of Letters, so that my own is quite swallowed up in the consideration of it,—that this self-same vile pruriency for fresh adventures in all things, has got so strongly into our habit and humours,—and so wholly intent are we upon satisfying the impatience of our concupiscence that way,—that nothing but the gross and more carnal parts of a composition will go down:—The subtle hints and sly communications of science fly off, like spirits upwards;—the heavy moral escapes downwards; and both the one and the other are as much lost to the world, as if they were still left in the bottom of the ink horn.

—TRISTRAM SHANDY

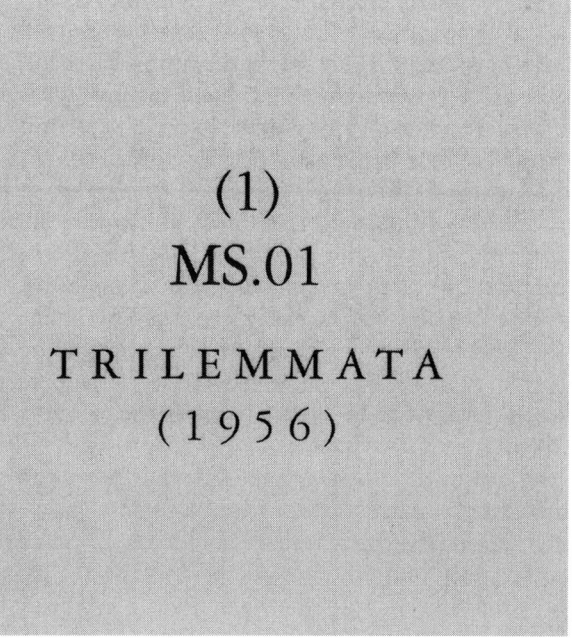

(1)
MS.01
TRILEMMATA
(1956)

*M*ichael Chapman had not cherished any of his three sons before they were born nor had he hoped for them before they were conceived. Ruth Chapman the wife and mother agglomerated them licked them into shape and bred them up for his approval. Except when gripped by the universal pathos of babyhood he had been nearly careless of each undifferentiated babe in the cradle. But he found that humankind's uniquenesses entered his history as engagingly as any less casual father's. In every case the gathering person of a child incorporated him against his will as if without warning.

In the years of growth as the new people of the family nourished their possibilities partly on the father's protein his own possibility continuously diminished. One by one they joined their mother in pruning and oiling the plumage by means of which he personally might have fledged. It was not in themselves that they embarrassed him, not by virtue of existence or intention, but by the statistical fact of their economic connections. Their organic requirements prevented further exfoliation on the father's part. At the age of thirty-three all he had left to himself was the inner man.

Yet there was nothing unsure about his love for the three who loved each other and both parents. His love was crescent and irreversible, a moon that never waned and always grew, even when obscured by clouds of annoyance or despair—not like the moon of his love for the mother, which in the course of the years waxed only haltingly, with countless fluctuations, magnified chiefly by complexity of perception.

There were times when Michael was wholly possessed with Ruth. When she was everything to him his entire mind was devoted to her body. In the seizure of flood tides during unpredictable gales his plenary passion occluded all sweetness but hers. The center of household love was a big bed that swung out of a wall panel in the front room and unfolded to the floor against weightily coiled springs which thrummed once as they were locked into place. In it the family was conceived and renewed. In it the children were comforted. In it on occasion the whole family consorted, king queen and three princes. When all clouds were dissolved in plenteous joy it was the soft nucleus of a simple universe. In any case it was the capitol of Michael's right-hand world.

But on the left a greater part of his longevity was sold to Valentine Greatrakes the boss from whom he earned the living of his dependencies (claiming one for himself) and whose shop was the center of another realm. That enterprise comprised the purchase and sale of commodities mostly indistinguishable from those of the competition at prices determined by manufacturers. The business called for shrewd selection and display, and even persuasion. Michael worried about the store, and labored for its improvement, without an iota of equity in ownership. It was therefore without excuse that he fretted on behalf of interests which he thought he'd come to know better than the proprietor did. His only compensation beyond exiguous wages was a little freedom to do certain things his own way. The owner reserved for himself with his wife's assistance all financial management, bookkeeping and tax reports included. Not a corporation, not even a partnership: it was Val's own affair where he got his money and how much he ended up with.

Mike managed the merchandise that was exhibited to the public. But in an unrestricted monarchy the prime minister must submit to his sovereign's frustrating and unenlightened interference, and defer to an arbitrary attitude that takes the place of national policy. The only true measurement of Michael's performance under such conditions of limited authority would have required rigorous analysis of the investment and turnover for which he was responsible, mathematically isolated from the inventory and profit over which he had no more than partial or custodial control; but Greatrakes formed his opinions as an employer without the benefit of managerial abstractions, having in general no patience for any ratiocination not directly preparatory to an individual transaction.

One effect of this emotional aversion to a rule of law was that the lieutenant could be held blameworthy for almost anything that went wrong with the most conspicuous part of the business. But the sales volume prospered and the relative balance of unsalable stock steadily decreased, so there wasnt much audible criticism; and to make up for the miscarriage of theoretical justice there was perhaps something unearned in the tacit and unanalytical praise implied by the master's growing trust.

Michael found more positive incentive in the praise of influential patrons and in the mysterious pleasure of progressive unsupervised work. In fullest possible exploitation of the economic liberty granted him within the constraints of an absolute proprietorship and between the unpredictable moments of tyrannical intervention he passed his days more energetically than many entrepreneurs, and he often failed to banish the haunting echoes of business that usurped the place of imagination in his brain at night. He was never one to earn the family bread in indolent indifference to the process for which he was paid, though there was every opportunity to please his superior by letting matters drift with the strange currents of that man's thin and intransigent mind according to the principle of least action.

The smallest part of Michael Chapman's longevity was spent with broad and liberal minds. Caleb Karcist had recently become the most important living person of this third estate, which was a very small peerage if you don't count the saints. Grave and portly Michael fraught with a woman and several children; free young Caleb, bachelor and erstwhile student, for whom there was no division in the force of blood: together they were modulus and amplitude of a complex vector in the trigeometric plane that I am about to use for a projection of their obscure polity.

It's a wonder that Ruth didnt hate Caleb. Many women suffer forty-two percent ($^5/_{12}$) of their husband's one hundred twenty disposable hours in an average week of waking attention to be turned toward the purpose of gain, which is justified by family wants, and therefore she had no right to resent Valentine Greatrakes; but as $^3/_7$ of Michael's remaining time (or twenty-five percent of the total) was dedicated to intentions that she and her children did not share, or even know much about, she might well have invoked society's sanction for her occult bitterness. But it was not in her self-examining nature to protest or mislike personal coefficients. She always invited Caleb to dinner willingly and was glad to see him at any time. His presence in her kitchen kept Michael there, or in any event attracted him. She didnt mind that the guest preempted her husband's respect. When the young knight was before her eyes and ears she always found him interesting. And from him while waiting for the king to get home from work she got some compensatory attention. For though he sometimes harangued her with scorn for objects notions or sentiments that she had been educated to respect—objects notions and sentiments long since passed over in Michael's laconic intercourse with her—he also listened to her opinions and brooked a good deal of opposition. As an inexperienced non-husband he deferred to the possibility of female wisdom. If at times he shouted down her diffident expositions she was aware that at least he did so in a manner no more insulting than that in which he dismissed the theses of academic experts.

Michael when present was sufficiently sensible of his own unbecoming impatience at her diversion of Caleb's attention to make polite effort at assisting the conversation. Of the three only Caleb spoke without tact, innocently wounding the woman by curses flung against ideas with which she sympathized as a defenseless and sentient being while irritating her husband by a waste of talk on worn-out public questions which bored to the point of hatred a mind famished for recondite excitement. Caleb came into the Chapman kitchen like a hereditarily rich youth unwitting of his wealth who squanders time and scatters criticism without any thought of concealing his advantages or his expectations. The freedom of his address was unguarded by the wariness of true intimacy.

Watching them take each other seriously Michael could guess that the young man made Mrs Chapman feel desirable, and that he would not have treated her as Joseph treated Potiphar's wife. Compared with her husband Caleb was neither portly nor owlish, and his was the age of greater virility. The obvious fact that this odd little buck would not have kicked the wellvoiced finelooking lovematured woman out of bed did not however prevent her lord from understanding that he himself was somewhat pitied for being married to her forever and ever.

Nothing in the course of events could have brought Michael to the point of saying anything to Caleb about his private affairs, least of all either his clouded or his unclouded love for the familiar vessel of his unselfed seed. How could an ephebic troubadour still full of his own beans have any inkling of the diversities evolved in an unadulterated marriage bed?—of the elementary sensations that could make one smile at the unfamiliar interpenetrations of adventuring lovers?—or of the ageless fire beneath Ruth's handsome dignity and eleemosynary virtue, hidden by the commonplace contents of her outer mind? And despite all the discourse in which Ruth and Caleb engaged each other the overweening boy suspected as little of her private intelligence or her secret strength as of the eisegesis in almost all that she heard from him.

The young dog anticipated in his own career an undomestic glamour. His perceptual devices were ill-attuned for the swift glances that sometimes passed at his expense between host and hostess as he regaled them with his diagnoses of the world. The filters of his perceiving brain favored the admittance of Ruth's ignorance Michael's stolidity and the intolerable condition of both. His mouth twitched in the consciousness of social superiority.

In another aspect Caleb might be regarded as a tiresome friend whose visits nevertheless couldnt be dispensed with: an attentive and loyal friend insensible of the burden imposed by his attentions—who brought food for the master's wife to cook and befriended the master's children but often wasted the master's time to whom he deferred in everything as he deferred to no one else in anything. The fact is that Michael required more of the fetch than of the real presence, which was sometimes inconveniently vivid. Ruth wasnt more than dimly and forgetfully aware of Caleb's ectoplasmatic role in the life that her husband led all by himself in the lowering closet across the hall, a sealed tower to which he retreated every morning early.

By very reason of his evolutionary priority the lively kitchen visitor who was in danger of making a nuisance of himself couldnt be expected to hold a candle to the ontologically secondary creature of Michael's locked study by whom his potentialities ought to have been improved and liberated; yet the likeness showed itself to be far from tractable, more recalcitrant and less lovable than the model, like a puppet wrought with little joy by a clumsy carver with heroic sculptures filling his head. The lugubrious self-willed Pinocchio continually misplaced himself in the hands of educated foxes and crooked cats, forever disappointing grieving and enraging his father, by whom he had been brought in off the street for motherless reconception and endowed with a will freer than any natural child's.

Though for the most part respecting the directions and permissions of the demiurge, Caleb remained instinct with various inertias of the native genes that were supposed to be replaced. Michael sometimes pushed this son of mind too far, even as he sometimes misconstrued the sons of his body, and as likely as not he blundered both ways on the same day, whereupon he was also sure to have set his wife openly at odds with him.

When Caleb the friend paid his visit at such a juncture the two men would sit in the kitchen as they usually did, drinking Michael's hoarded whiskey after the children were put to bed and Ruth had begun to do the dishes; but the unfriendly king hardly concealed his testy impatience with the cinders of his three inflammable worlds. His eyeglasses gleamed opaquely behind the smoke of his cigar. The woman and the young man indulged his mien of disingenuous lethargy in return for his churlish indulgence of their shallow dialogue, which took place while she worked slowly and unmethodically at the sink or turned to face the table absently wiping her hands on a greasy apron before returning them thoughtfully to the pool of soapy water she had dried them from as she spoke or listened. Michael glowered at Caleb for persisting in this the most wretched means of communication between male and female.

Later she would sit with them for a while, smoking nothing, drinking nothing, encouraged by her husband's forbearance who in consideration of their guest made a show of honoring the amenities of suffrage. Having nothing to lose in anyone's estimate she took advantage of her respite from bondage by permitting Caleb to take her part against the owl, for when the talk turned from object to subject her young partisan in his unseasoned zeal to establish justice in all matters would never let her guileless remarks drop without temerarious response.

"You should get Ruth a car and teach her to drive, so she and the kids could get around and visit their friends. If she werent cooped up like this she could go to lectures. It wouldnt hurt you to take care of the children for her once or twice a week."

Thus in spite of her anxiety about Michael's feelings at hearing such words she suffered without rancor Caleb's undersong of disdain for her subordination. But better than Caleb himself she sensed an osmosis of malice toward her husband in his divisive friendship, and since she could abide nothing so disloyal her beams of hankering were refracted away from modern blandishments in favor of the economy to which she was accustomed. At the same time Caleb's misapprehension of Ruth's worth on all planes drove Michael to her side in silent defense against the self-assured advice of inexperienced youth. In their reciprocal mist, Ruth and Caleb, it was Ruth his own flesh that Michael stood guard over.

Michael's untenable domestic domination was undermined before a year had passed, in part by the tacit pro tem alliance between them, so weak in true empathy. But his annoyance at this absurd betrayal by both parties sometimes edged him to the sidelines whence he could hardly choose between them, especially as he saw that she was forgetting the callow fastuousness of her scrawny champion and taking him to represent tolerant and rightminded society in the outside world. For in the eyes of the world, if the world had troubled to look, her subjugation would have seemed the crying injustice of this household; and in her eyes much of the time Michael did scarcely more for his family than generate neglect. He left her alone too much, talked to her too little, helped with her work not at all, and took counsel with her never: no decent model for twentieth century domestic humanists. To Ruth he often seemed ruthless, blind by day, predatory by night—altogether a lazy bird of prey who provided very little for his nest. Worse yet, he owned wanly to some of her grievances without any sign of reformation contrition or shame.

But to his good fortune Ruth's flashes of rebelliousness were ordinarily suppressed and largely contained by an inveterate doubt of immature revolution and by a gentle dread of unsagacious quarrel. Michael evaded acute provocation for much the same reasons, knowing that she would not vent steam until he first discharged his own grudges or brought to issue the grievances on his side which he regarded as hopeless beyond utterance. Ruth knew enough of his attitude to be persuaded that he would never understand the therapeutic value of discussion, but he believed that in their case of irreconcilable opposition it was the wisest strategy to tolerate a tolerable resentment as long as it did not noticeably accumulate but only ebbed and flowed, allowing for due recognition of the difficulty at times in distinguishing an irregular fluctuation from a trend.

It was lovemaking that kept within limits his resentment (and hers), her resentment (and his), notwithstanding the fact that her resentment (not his) made the use of this means (his ends) ever more problematical.

He hoped that by assuaging or diverting the emotions most antagonistic to the touch of his skin when he detected them beginning to color her erotic courtesy he could foil or absorb any salient attack upon the absolute problem of his particular family. There were three globes to keep aloft and if they werent all to smash no one of them could be given more than a quick juggle in its proper turn until he arrived at the fantastical millennium in which he would be permitted to toss away the bauble of office and let the other two rest firmly in either hand.

Ruth Chapman's statistical circumstances were no worse than millions of wives in her station of life. Michael's lowclass opinions on the woman question were entirely in keeping with the degree of poverty they shared. If Ruth did not know her place it was because she had taken her education too seriously. The barrier between husband and wife was a wall blockcasted of the language that almost everyone spoke and wrote, which was formed by an immensely strong crystallization of commonplace chunks and pebbles shoveled in as aggregate by national phrasemakers. Ruth maintained the wall assiduously, assuming that he was on her side of it, as if it was a sounding board which if kept in good repair would faithfully reflect and amplify what little they said to each other, while in truth they were separated by it like Pyramis and Thisbe.

Usually she blamed herself for the failure of communion but at times she was convinced that Michael deliberately closed his ears to the sounds of proven wisdom in some still-unanalyzed perversity of temperament that she thought should be submitted to the iatric "skill" of professional arbitration. When she was not strong enough to take such a calm view of the difficulty she felt herself more miserable than the undernourished Mexican women down by the Southern Pacific yards who were too poor in spirit to protest when their drunken husbands having come home for the purpose swived them in front of the children, called for tortillas and beans, and disappeared for another week.

If Michael had been fully sensitive to his wife's despair he might have been retrospectively amused to compare the poles of her attitude, for after she came out of her negative spells his modest derelictions seemed to her nothing but positive if not glorious virtues. She was likely to forget from one moment to another the taste of food she was no longer chewing. At certain times when all day long the shadow of his gnomon was visible on her face he loomed in her mind as a right good husband of firm wisdom and worshipful power. Then the children delighted her like sunny puppydogs and housework became a salubrious privilege to be celebrated in song.

The man weened that he could look before and after with steadier vision than the woman, and that at any point he could remember and forsee a wider range of joint or separate moods (in consequence of the male's extrinsic advantage in reckoning), but otherwise his oscillations between desperation and hope were as wild as hers. He couldnt for as

much as a week stick to any of his judgments as to whether or not his
course of almost a decade had been wisely furrowed, as to whether or not it
was only the cowardly wake of perpetual default. The more he stared at his
chessboard the less assured was his determination between black and red as
the overpainted foreground of basic fact.

But though he was less perceptive than his opposite of the opposite
person's possible feelings at the time they were being engendered or
revived he was by superior evaluation organization retention and retrieval
better able to support their mutual experience. Beneath the disturbances
of circumstance and the weathers of fatigue he looked to the growth of
Jonathan Matthew and Roger as new persons on the scene to strengthen
the sympathetic overtones in their parents' two waves. The tendency to
lock into phase with each other always conduced to simultaneous movement toward or away from eristic or erotic crisis. Only in the sleeping
hours that followed immediately upon an epochal discharge of love long in
the gathering, when he filled the cradle of her thighs like a god in her
bowels, did they stop moving together or apart in aversion or in want.

If the peace failed to outlast the next sun he wordlessly accused her of
preferring war, and she him. His resentments were absorbed by the other
lives he led but hers would gradually bubble up into a half-revealed noise
of the spirit culminating perhaps in demands for negotiation that made
him turn away more taciturn than ever. Or else in grudging acquiescence
to her tearful wishes he would finally allow a spoken dialectic to brush the
skirts of an issue, grinding his teeth and letting her have her say so that
she might find some relief simply in framing her statements aloud, maybe
enough satisfaction to drop the subject when she got no reply in his fear
that she would goad him into responding to her challenge much too
frankly. To get to the bottom of the conflict would have been to collapse
the scaffold he stood upon before he was ready to kick it away. Whether
from pusillanimous misgiving or dread of interrupting the routine efficiency of his triplicitous act it always seemed best at almost any cost to
preserve the fragile equilibrium a little while longer—a month, a week,
another night, a few hours—until the children were out of earshot, until
he got his paycheck, until a loan was retired, or until a theorem was
proved. He'd silently attribute to her incompetence all the distresses and
deprivations of his petty life, seldom thinking to blame either the custom
of marriage or any fault of his own, but in the end he never let anger overcome prudence by speaking outright what he really brooded over, and the
duration of his sullen reticence was always sufficient.

A slackening of wind and tide would suddenly rotate the light of the
sky to a lovely quadrant. Though it would have been predictable enough
to a narrator, Michael was always astonished at this repeated peripeteia;
but Ruth as a subject of it seemed in her happiness hardly aware that there
had been a change. In any case neither betrayed to the other any consciousness of having passed through the shadow of love's death, and every time

having escaped desolation by the skin of their teeth each remembered the latest estrangement as nothing more than a detachable delirium that had been dreamt alone and would never be suffered again.

Not that he didnt slyly keep track of her calendar, more narrowly than she did for herself. He was always listening to the base rhythm of their coupled life which she seemed not to hear or recognize, so perfectly was she its instrument. He calculated his advantages and prepared for his defeats according to the phases of her moon, while she forgot (he thought) what was bound to happen to her blood if there was no interruption and conducted her daily life without forethought of the resonance that was to be induced or spoiled between them by the continual flux of her body. No sooner did her womb acknowledge the melancholy death of spawn than it would appeal to his lordship for renewal of hope. In obedience to the goddess of all sisters she unwittingly resumed the age-old campaign to abduct the geysered gout which she would soon again become infectiously receptive to. Then for a time Michael viewed his wife only in her aspect of soft gay beauty as the goddess's creature of irresistibly desirous intelligence. The fact that he could see what was going on didnt keep him from trafficking with the tools of fertility.

But there were greater and scarcely discernible tides of extraordinary desire and respect, quarterly or semiannual storms of reckless electricity that lighted up their heavens seasonally. The long slow rises of the year which broke open in these refulgent passions underswelled the smaller heaves of thirteen months, as Ruth's fine deep chest uplifted for his lips the delicately flowered breasts exposed by his gentle hand with more art than the first time.

Ah, those fitful disinhibitions of craving that leveled the wall on these occasions! Nature made them find the fortuitous way to reconciliation: perhaps nothing more amorous than the sudden dissolution of some vague worry, maybe only a cloud that had been almost overlooked by one self and never suspected by the other. Many a time (but not always) one of them when disburdened of this or that vexation in a separate career or successful in a minor hope of separate consequence could emancipate the beloved's desire with a mere touch.

By impulsively writing off in his mind all the outstanding grievances he could remember a man might easily utter an ordinary kind word to rekindle the fuel that he had thought extinguished. Or a woman could totally reverse the march of a man's soul by wearing to bed the nightgown that could be opened all the way down the front. Or again, one of the children might disclose a new concept and the parents would smile at each other like warm friends. It was even possible that having just made the final payment on a refrigerator he would assent to her purchase of some curtain material. Once or twice at such a planetary conjunction it happened that Valentine Greatrakes gave Michael a raise unasked and Michael came home to take the family out to dinner unasked. Yet the most complacent spates of apparent reconciliation, when he would discuss any number of thoughts, began on days following sky-clear sessions before breakfast when all alone in the pure silence before dawn he had put down something which in briefly flaring illusion he judged equal in style or imagination to anything already printed in the books of saints.

In short, when the antagonist was not too hostile to be spoken to, an urge for fusion, released by one slight proximate cause or another, became the most natural inspiration in the world. These were the times that none of their otherwhile worries perturbed a pair of generous lemans.

However, in the prevailing climate, day in and day out, just as neither the gravamen nor the recrimination was sufficiently weighty to break down the barriers of politeness, the rut was neither so long denied nor so inspired as to surpass its predecessor in frenzy. Usually it was not uncommonly difficult for Michael to brush aside his anxiety about the perfection of his woman's conjugal pleasance. Between the truly ecstatic commotions they were willing enough to let their desire take the easiest way and to settle for muted paroxysms not quite up to the mark in orgastic splendor.

Anyway, in most other respects the man and the woman perceived contubernal felicity in different lights. They were a cat and a dog sharing the cave, one hearing her way through the anxious symbiosis as she sniffed only diffidently, the other smelling out their situation with his ears cocked just for outside sounds—each with an odd vision of shape and color though both with eyes to see.

No dogged diver can get down to Ruth's depth in the black purple ocean. At best he can scan the bottom of green shallows or schoon the undersurfaces of highest blue: unless he drown. Unless he drown—and even then his fishy language is no more equal to telling us what he's found than Ruth's own is—there's little in her three-quarters of the earth's consciousness to be comprehended by him. In these pages at least there is no other way to see a married life than through the distorted approximations of Michael's quarter. The special difficulty of grasping this girl Ruth, beyond the general hopelessness, arises from the peculiar affect of his bizarre ambitions upon the knowledge of her that could come only to a husband.

As Michael was battered up and down by the fortunes of the little community he had inadvertently planted in the pursuit of his ultimate purpose he learned how to harden the casing of his domestic tenderness. It was often necessary to assume callous indifference, or to don the vizard of hebetude, when unpleasant problems were broached. He made no attempt to disabuse his wife of her belief that he was trying to protect some nutmeat within his shell, for thus she supplied herself with an idea to focus on that was psychologically classic and therefore tolerable. In his struggle to preserve the family constitution the urge to defend his private rights always swept away his doubts about justice for the majority. Without arguing the case he excused himself from the full responsibilities of a modern breadwinner by dumbly pointing to the limited service he actually did perform for the family in face of his exceptional need for longevous leisure. He flattered himself that Ruth preferred cruelty to widowhood. Yet nothing was at strife but what had been set that way at the gate of Eden.

She partly understood that his apathy toward her suffering was faked, sometimes taking the purpose of his dissemblance to be nothing more than the preservation of a lazy selfish illusion in which he might avoid recognition of his failure among successful men; but the deadpan of a pudgy owl is so inscrutable that it can fool the keenest wife. She had grown too used to the domestic facet of his livelihood to suspect him of indefatigable enthusiasm.

His behavior was dull. Caleb from his opposite angle thought so too. But her life and the life of her children depended upon Michael's behavior. The value of her life rose and fell with the temperature of his familiar attitudes. Her existence cowered in the darkest corridor of his house, the freedom of which she was denied she thought in his fear that she would escape to the world at large or that she would share his liberty and reimpose upon him the burdens of attentive courtship.

But Ruth was not a woman to harden herself against any creature in consequence of the treatment she got, nor to invest herself with peevish acquiescence either. Instead she was likely to be turned the wrong way around like one who's IT in blind-man's bluff. At any rate she felt as if her mind was forced to dwell most in the chambers of least importance to both of them. It was in these dreary rooms that she knew he pictured the mentality of the body he was married to.

But Michael was free to indulge in flight from his immersion. On weekends in the hope of recreation he could rush off for an evening with the parliament of friends which he and Caleb frequented but which Ruth rarely attended—only to rediscover, after a few hours at various stations outside the walls of the University but within a bow's shot of Sather Gate, inconsolation of a different kind. Immersion and flight: interest and revulsion.

He found himself little refreshed by the jaunt from Oakland to Berkeley, from the household of Ruth to the households of lesser women where opinions rang out freely. He visited here and there like a welcome bachelor, here and there talking and eating, drinking in studied studios full of color, talking, trying to avoid the talk of women, talking talking, stupidly trying to penetrate stupidity and join issue with the putative core of academic intelligence, talking talking talking, sick of the monotony of his own voice that only reflected the melancholy contempt beneath his gratitude for food and drink, going over and over and over again the same pothering attacks upon professions, talking talking talking talking, piquing no one with his criticisms, and even sicker of other people who talked and read too much, learned too fast, knew too much, spoke too fluently of ideas-not-thought, who enjoyed too much practical advancement in proportion even to their theoretical knowledge of experience, the best of them affectionately boring: witless educated goads who unknowingly jabbed the numb wounds in his side.

Enough! [Enough for me. Home to Ruth where my strength and loyalty begin!] On the way back he yearned with pity for her absolution of his diligent neglect, and his desire rose with his compassion, hoping that she the only serf of her class would be longing for his return in desirous pity for his repented folly who had need of serf's labor not greater than serf's need for master's protection of peasant penchants.

Meanwhile Caleb's manner of living seemed to cast unintended reproach upon the mastermind trapped by a body in bondage to domestic powers and devoted more to shopkeeping than to its own promise. He stood uncompromisingly with his back to Michael and (for all his youth) platonically motionless, oblivious of currents and precessions in the lives of his friends, never supposing that the moods he sometimes sensed in them were anything but arbitrary or fortuitous, while the pater familias continued to prefer for himself the easiest path leading to the top of his very distant mountain, allowing for tolerable delays switchbacks and apparent reversals. But Michael admired Caleb's moral clarity, and the youth's antithetical doctrine did him a lot of good once a week or so.

When a man is no longer young he hasnt the future to secure his pledges and forgive his lack of proof in the meantime, nor can he still begin a new vocation aimed at the Presidency or a Nobel prize in physics. Michael's distaff was already unwound by half. What had he to show for himself? Caleb had a world of possibilities, but what could Michael weigh against his own impure renunciations of place and honor?

Children, his wife would have answered. Sons, society would have agreed: beyond a certain unique but inconsequential formula of personal will, sons. Man, you've still got a chance to make something of yourself by becoming a good father. In fact it's not far-fetched to predict that with your intelligent and liberal guidance at least one of the three if you can get him through college will achieve something notable enough for a special biographical dictionary after you're dead and gone.

But Michael was obstinate to destiny, and even now, half run down, he had not begun to regard his sons as contributing any iota to his importance. His confidence had no connection with them, nor did it involve their esteem for himself. He therefore loved them with a virtue unknown to more generous fathers. The claim of mere blood had been quit when in each case he had opened his eyes to their existence in his house and found his prejudice against them neutralized, thereby opening the opportunity for disinterested love.

Certainly none of them had begun with an annunciation. As far as he could remember in each of the three cases conception had been undistinguished, perhaps resulting from one of the drowsy accommodations with which Ruth sometimes indulged his blindly bored itch during a month's most propitious sowing season. While the foetus was evolving under his wife's navel there was almost nothing humanly curious in his feelings of annoyance horror and dismay, or of disgust with the selfish containment of a woman who seemed to complacently assume the ineffable approbation of all mankind (for was Chanticleer ever more absurd?). Only on the verge of laboring parturition, for which Ruth had bravely tried to prepare herself by subjective methods that anesthesiologists and almost all other doctors disapproved as atavistic, did he summon any sympathy for the mother, along with extreme respect. The next morning all his love for her was brought back with an unconfessable concentration of remorse by one look at the beautifully unexampled queen calmly pale in her hospital bed already separated from her baby yet smiling at him as if he'd been cheering her all the way through her uncomforted ordeal at the hands of strangers; but his first glimpses of the scowling child itself made no impression that he ever could remember.

It was not until several months later when he began to take watches at home alone with the absolutely helpless infant that he noticed the dewy web of attachment spun by some fairy-spider that he never saw. The crescent love for which he thus by degrees accepted responsibility was by any account empirically inductive: nowhere in his history could you have discovered a predilection for it, and no logical deduction of it could have been drawn from any of his axioms. Long cultivation of pleasure had tamed the cockadoodle incontinence which cared less for its object than for itself and taught him supreme desire for the thunderous affect that his desire could strike his wife's desire with, but his primitive phallic urge had never been civilized by any intention so abstract as the wish for reproduction.

Michael's and Ruth's compounding valency may be anatomized into four kinds of desire. Only three were ever mutual.

When this pair of subjects was in accidental correspondence with each other they saw eye to eye with the *material desire* of contra-parts as one flesh in two kinds oppositely charged by force of nature.

When they were in psychic phase with each other they harmonized in the *formal desire* of maximum touch, playing their roles in orectic evolution like amorous lions with nothing else to do.

And even in *efficient desire*—where the man never failed in his kind but the woman was an uncertain companion (speaking, remember, not of cause but of desire)—Ruth for the most part kept Michael company and sometimes even ran circles round him like a riderless horse with her trainer in the center of the ring. When her tremor misfired she was kind enough to take the default as her own and make the best of her disguised restlessness as an atoning penalty for the transcendent purpose that always gleamed at the bottom of her soul like an unrusting treasure though forgotten disappointed or denied by her accessible mind as a reward never presumed to be repeated.

For in *final desire* she was never matched by Michael. His final desire in fact was only to thwart hers by bemusing its solemnity. His final desire in bed was nothing more than to divert the female's desire from its natural finality to the cultivation of its softest palate.

When his efforts were requited she gathered and reorganized her nerves under his eyes in a seizure of sensuality more terrible than any possible intensification of dischargeable energy in his own body, and the slowly molten overflow of the lava which ordinarily dispersed itself in cranial capillaries or neural lodes near the center seemed to receive his poor heavenly deathlunge as a lightning bolt that quaked the earth and reverberated underground with slowly diminishing crashes. But the powers on her side had bided hundreds of these his triumphs in order to deliver the three blows that shook his timbers, each more jolting than the one before, each making him want to quit the war as a blind victim of his windowless gonads prematurely envious of barren old age.

Yet these powers continued to burnish her treasure and still incited her husband's reckless importunity. Sometimes they hypnotized her into forgetting her contraceptive covenant—and then persuaded him to resume his trust in her conscientious good faith.

Love of the first child only stiffened his resistance to the second, and of the second to the third; but the news of the first (so soon! so soon!) remained the greatest shock of surprise. Ruth's unspoken rebuttal to his unframed criticism was that about a thousand plus nine hundred ninety-seven precious spurts had gone to waste, just as if they had shot off into the air without disturbing a fold of her flesh or a minute of her rest. Moreover, she would have assented with her ready laugh if he could have brought himself to make a popular jest on the subject, the best part of all three ran down their mother's leg.

But her underground mind couldnt dispute the plain fact that the os of her uterus had always patiently awaited its prey in the supposedly unlikely chance that her forgetfulness would coincide with his. (He seldom refrained from fingering for the factitious membrane she was expected to ingest even before she could be sure of her own attitude—if he didnt blatantly ask about it—unless in an access of delicacy, especially right after an occasion on which she had frankly and voluntarily confessed an unmindful abuse of his confidence, he felt obliged for the sake of nursing her mood to pretend to assume that she would not overlook the matter twice in succession.) She also had no cause to complain that the powers of fecundity had failed to exploit her innocent incompetence in the care and placement of the troublesome barrier, and she had every reason to bless in his nature the prurient ardor that so often refused to be brooked by trifling probabilities.

In fine, if the boys had never issued from Ruth's yearning loins Michael would never have asked for them of God or physician. (So he believed.) It would have been no wonder if he had hated the hostages she tricked out of his wizened testicles and clotted with her eggs like poached game. Only with insufficient vehemence or persistence did he try to remind himself that the woman's sweet-tooth was always lying in wait for the kernel of the dioscuric nuts that swung between his legs utterly devoid of pride. But he had known the life-principle before he started. He had thought to talk her out of it, for five or six years anyway. His immediate and reiterated failure to check the powers of paternity provided him with the grounds for a general theory of Oedipality: that everyman was fated to be corrupted by any mother at hand even after the most lively warnings and despite every statistical precaution.

Yet the fruit of his importunate negligence was apocalyptic, not hateful. Once given, predestined limbs of his body, eternal facts, the children insinuated themselves into his expanding organism like separate minds sharing suzerainty of an integral trunk, notwithstanding his unwillingness at first in each case to give them any thought at all. But when he studied the animation of their small heads (round or long, blond or brunet) through the clear shining windows of which they opened themselves to the whole uncompassionate world his joy in them was commensurately clouded with anxiety, for it had happened and could happen and was happening elsewhere that just such heads by accident or intention were torn or sliced from their candid stems as they expressed in the first terror of their lives an utter amazement that absolute trust in mothers and fathers availed nothing outside the family that fostered it.

Therefore in light of historical and political knowledge Michael's sons were as disturbing to the equanimity he strove for as Mrs Chapman and Mr Greatrakes were: in the long run, more so. Dewyfaced fetters to every gesture of freedom.

The fatherman put up with these extrinsic worries (harboring them in fact at the very center of his sphere amidst the rustling precipitations of more proper thoughts) in uncertain barter for indefinite deferral of life's worst bereavement. It was better to fume and to fuss and to fret than to be struck down in fatuous defiance of the passover. Any minute any day any year the black angel might suddenly show himself in the street or at a small bed to reveal at a single stroke all the hideous sorrow of mankind. The elements of grief were gathering in the glands he lived by, of grief for his own hostages immeasurably over and above his sorrow for other children black brown yellow red or poor or abused, or other mothers and fathers, or the halt and the blind, homeless beggars, crippled orphans, or roasted drowning sailors in torpedoed boiler rooms, or cuckolded men with large families, or husbands and wives without children, or passionate ill-favored men without wives at all, or unmatched women, or despised inventors, or artists without talent. It was necessary to keep these wider pities at bay and specialize in the pains of first-person authorship. But even paternal anguish might be forestalled by what was most fearful of all: his own death with work undone.

Romeo's love too, like a bluff, had been called; he too had been engaged to go through with the wedding: only the knell had saved him from Michael's condition; his way out had been the honorable escape of a fulltime lover. But such reprieve was pointless to an American proletary who might have been willing to embrace the coils of half a dozen children if there had been no work—no work, just love—just love. For Michael to die before old age would have been to foil the work living so long for.

As it turned out however, life being too short and manifoldly precious to pay the boys no heed, he accepted the weakness of his humanity rather than pay the full price of strengthening it. He consented to be hobbled if he could live long enough with his nest intact. For all its prolonging variations of moon and mood the husbandry never seemed to change; yet by growth the children themselves did change: their ripening minds weighed down the crown of his stunted tree with luscious lovefruit.

As these rounded persons freed themselves of the nippled bottle and the helplessness of safety-pinned breach clouts, as they enabled themselves with syllables to put two and two together, they thrust up through new crannies of civilization like fragile and fearless plants that the world had never seen before. But they were always still being born as gemmations of the father without his impurity of use or purpose. Which is not to say that the three little nuclei of will didnt whirl like cosmic dust accruing more will of their own, or that the three severally cohering wills didnt have to be taken into broader account every day.

Business also improved in the course of time. Michael's petty authority waxed in the intermittent sun of Valentine's approbation. Life at the store wore away less and less abrasively, smoothed by commercial success that gradually rooted and ramified his commercial interest, lengthening his life's hypotenuse.

But Michael's self-calibration was his tangent, which he always meant to improve by steadily increasing his devotion to Caleb's opposite world in proportion to Ruth's adjacent. He never hoped to achieve a modest unity ($^1/_1$) but he was finding it harder and harder even to maintain the classically rational $^3/_4$ that he had worked up to. He nearly exhausted his time and strength in the struggle to keep the ratio from shrinking. Pythagorean crypto-Caleb enlarged no faster than hypotenuse and side adjacent, as slowly as a chronically ill child, having good days now and then in spite of malnutrition and sleeping-sickness, coming into his feverish growth far less certainly than Michael's nose-rubbed experience of the U S A . This Caleb's advancement, wavering in fits and starts like a flame from flint and steel, unlike the development of sons, was invisible under Michael's bushel, unknown even to his intimates.

And so you have the A B C of Michael's world in these three vectors of edification. By hewing and pruning to this triangle he managed to preserve himself from radical decomposition. Thus he forsook his own father and mother, forswore Democratic politics and forwent the professional

furrows he might have chosen, refusing to walk behind plows that could
be drawn by the teams of others. He paid no court to strange women. He
turned aside from idle friendships. By definition and simplification he
made conceivable to himself the impossible.

The trick was alternation. No man can handle three instruments at
once: he can only suggest simultaneity by adroitly interchanging his three
performances. A servant of three masters can't face them all until he's
reached the end of his rope. Much of Michael's difficulty and most of his
pain came in the quick-changes between or even within scenes. They were
not easy angles of prismatic refraction but jolting reversals of general
direction which in two out of the three cases were more acute than a
baserunning. At every switch from one vector to another the undercover
agent was shocked or nettled before he reaccustomed himself; though
when all went well he soon felt as if he'd never known any other system of
objects.

The weather fluctuated in each of the three tierces of his weird compass but when in scent he always found Caleb upwind and awkward to
reach, and it was all too much easier to run downwind than to tack. Don't
think it was love that made Michael oppose the wind and tide, for actually
Caleb subtended the outlook that was in direct opposition to natural affection. But what it was though not love I cannot tell—more than to say that
it was the teleological artifice of Michael's life, a hope not of his heart but
of his head. It made all the difference between a toilsome contentious life
and no life at all: an insubstantial promise to himself in the interests of
which he had eschewed a number of intoxicating opportunities and
throttled a number of worthy abilities, including the opportunity to ease
his family's lot and the ability to make a name for himself among men
who made the market in American culture.

It should be clear that this is no hero of celestial battle, this Michael,
not even a trumpeter. See him rather as a mangy owl flapping along in the
slack eye of a perpetual typhoon spiralled all round with sensations vanities and indulgences: begetter but creature—like all birds of shopkeeping
woman-husbandry. When he doesnt offer to sally from the hollow of his
tree he wears in obscurity the monitory nakedness of an unmantled
pigeon, a big featherless turtledove with back and sides bare against the
smooth warm skin of his wife, housed where it's dry, where the chicks can
chirp securely, inside the dying oak that he supplies with mice. But this
rector's vigor in the hole and on the hunt is continually bled by his defense
of Caleb's existence, on the one hand against the empirical human vitality
that has been overpowering his own untalented imagination and on the
other against gnostic priestcrafts reflecting academic man's indomitable
urge to close the living system for sake of such intellectual satisfaction as
has been incapacitating many of his friends.

But Michael also knows that until a freeman has bloodied his own
knuckles and broken a toe by himself the other requisite experience is only

cramped by precepts of owlish wisdom. Yet it's harder to refrain from informing the innocence of a fearless young artist than to protect the innocence of three unready children.

Michael himself lived in fear. Even the most insouciant black operator repeatedly dreams of exposure and decapitation; and a triple agent's deepest terror refers to the principality that first signed him on with lifetime vows. It was no shabby international hotel in a nameless city, but the words were similar: "Betray us all you like on the twelfth or fourteenth floor—take as much as you need from the Soviets and the French to feed the mouths in your family—but in the end you must drop genuine documents down the laundry chute to us at the bottom. We allow for inefficiency, we tolerate compromise, we expect temporary defection out of sheer fatigue. But we demand your last breath every night; we hold the mirror to your lips after every infidelity. Never forget that the days of your life pass more quickly than the dollars in Valentine's till, the one employer from whom our secrets must always be safe."

I said I could not tell (save that it was not love) what the spur was that dug into Michael's aching flank. You get little closer to an answer when I say that he was being pricked on by a mysterious power hostile to the rule of social contracts and governed by none other than those glossily named harpies who wield their goad upon all procreators presuming to creation. Judging by his cacoethical mare's-nesting tensity, they had anchored their hook inside his tenderest gut. When he heeded their tug he was cut right out of the human herd, isolated, cruelly doomed; when he disobeyed their barb it lacerated the full length of his intestines.

But you'd never know it from the opaque glitter of his blunt rimless eyeglasses which concealed or distorted the bulging turbid portholes that admitted to his pandemonium the common light of the sun while projecting no beam from within toward those who looked to them for some ordinary expression of vivacity. What he mainly asked of the Lord was health enough for hand and eye to last the second half of his life.

There is little to interest you in the consuetudinal jogtrot of such an owlish hagridden shafthorse except the hitches in his gait.

                    I am trained to a middle station,
                    by my taste as well as by my art.
                                    —MONTAIGNE

(2)
SA.01

MAKING
LOVE

*G*ive and take: life is full of give and take the psychologists say whose living depends on making virtues of necessities. But it seemed to Michael that he had to give a little more every year for what he took, and for her part Ruth thought the same. One night in particular he came home and took what she gave him in taking from him what he wanted to give her. He paid for it the very next day, as we shall see, by having to waste that day the Lord's day the most important day in the week. This is how he got into trouble:

Saturday evening on some pretext or other he had cadged his supper from the Wolfsons in Berkeley but growing affectionate toward his wife in the guilt of neglecting her came home earlier than she'd expected from his not unprecedented telephone notice of the late afternoon. She always spoke approval of his cheerful opportunities with friends, but this time it had been hard to conceal the defeat of a happy hopeful mood that happened to be at work in her veins; at the very moment of his call she had been planning to serve an especially shipshape family dinner to celebrate her love for the man to whom she belonged, and she didnt feel very successful in transferring that delight to the three boys as she'd given them a less festal meal without their father. As this luck would have it however her synaptic charges remained equal and opposite to his, and even the revived resentment that tried to make its way into her circulation from a tiny nuclear gland buried in her brain was not permitted to spread like hemlock and deaden the new blood in her capillaries that quickened her susceptibilities to him. But not luck after all: he remembered the calendar and its influences influenced himself in the mutual menfluence of a woman and her savvy consort.

When he stealthed into the kitchen she was still standing at the sink. The space in which she worked shone with brightened linoleum sparkling glass polished tools and gleaming vessels, and not a crumb could be seen on floor or shelf. The children slept in other rooms under a benison of law and order. He lifted up his heart at her inspiration of competence. Tonight she would not hide in flopping sleep from uglified uncontrolled housework. In person too she was tidied up in a shriven glow, even perfumed, clad in the peignoir he had given her at their first Christmas, ragged now but fragrantly trim and clean, which under other conditions of late (while riding her tumbrel) she sometimes seemed to consider a mocking decollatetion of erstwhile womhopes.

She was vigorously scouring and rinsing at the plashing fountain and did not turn around. He could scarcely believe it possible for her to remain unaware of the fact that he brightened her doorway so intensely. At first he thought she might be scrubbing in sublimating anger—for the day's vexation or for the cumulative shortcomings of all her years since the first Christmas. But then he sensed that this was an improbable occasion probably justifying the hope for marvelous normality. He felt as if a final and permanent reconciliation was at hand, a promise of household peace and proficiency until they should be parted at last by the fleshcoldness of what is least improbable for every husband and wife.

In fact Ruth was turning over female thoughts so broad and tranquil that she would have been amused to know his narrow guesses at them even if he had been informed of her solitude's hazily proleptic drift. When he surprised her she was patiently rubbing the copper bottom of a pan—not smartly but well—as she had rubbed the bottom of its fellows who were now gleaming on the wall beside the sink.

His approach would have seemed shockingly summary to an unfamiliar woman, or even to Ruth herself in ordinary mood, but now she did not start or stiffen when his cool hands suddenly grasped the sides of her chest through the threadbare cloth. The swift recapitulation of love's ceremonies did not now strike her as unceremonious. Her nates and thighs were pressed forward by the thick man behind her; gently and symmetrically her thorax was drawn back, his thumbs softly commanding the pits of her arms as his fingers caressed the pectoral tendons covering her highest ribs, touching off labyrinthal powder trains to the magazine of honey even before his palms descended the upper curves of her breasts. Not for the first time he found some of the secret springs that shortcircuited almost all speech and obviated the tomfoolery of re-seduction. She dropped her vessel into the sudsy well and twisted around in his arms to kiss him slack-mouthed and openly inviting—but not yet urgently, for she had still to wipe her hands on the apron that protected her gown below the waist and unhook the spectacles from his nose and ears before the spark of his match could be allowed to continue on its way to the volcanic pyx. Ruth he says huskily I love you.

She says nothing; but presto—neither in the air about their heads nor on the surfaces of their minds nor in the pools and runnels of their under-most flesh was to be felt a trace of their inequities. At their age of familiar love when desire's history had mined deeper than language it was quite natural that no further words should be expected. It was effortlessly suffi-cient to recall sensations of the past. These copesmates had survived many an innocent expenditure of hoarded frenzy and all the aftermaths of conju-gal experience. The husband was embarrassed by attempts to revive the facetious dialogue of newly emancipated lust, which now seemed the mere childhood of sensuality, and even the wife had become uncomfortable with outgrown poetry on account of its inadvertent travesty. Yet the stance and circumstance of this encounter evoked an old scenario of metamorphosis and clandestine skill; the words they remembered were too discountenanc-ing in the light of disillusioned matrimony to be repeated aloud but they rose like ghostly ammunition from the arsenal with which she served his batteries while he was finding range and bearing in his assault.

[She would have said I knew it was you and he would have asked What gave me away and she would have answered archly Not your hands Sir Peter—Sir Peter Proudfit the Unicorn he was—Go away. My husband may be home at any minute with his stick and he's a very jealous wizard. But I met your husband in the woods and seized his wand and changed my shape for his so that now I am your warlock. Ah sir she perhaps asked will I then be faithful to him if I take you as my sir? He will take great plea-sure in his cuckoldry said the unicorn. The old gray beast she was calling him before he was twenty-five. Variety without adultery, that's my motto dear little Bactrian, he always said.]

Even the old nonsense of romantic love-gabble had usually given way to profligate phrases of solemn epithalamic union whispered into a swoon-ing ear; yet he admitted to himself that there were still times when the banal persiflage of a young gallant not yet tired of beating around the bush might well have helped her ripened voluptuousness neutralize the anxious fatigues of matronal housekeeping and led her psyche to the first step of Aphrodite's altar. There was no denying the delectations that could be raked up in a lovely interval between titillation and the main business. Still, aphrodisiac anodynes were not necessarily imparted by tales or lyrics. He had become rather adept at wordless sibilation and suctorial breathing, at the lightest of frictions and the tiniest of scratches, at the tenderest separation of rose petals to relieve the slight vacuum that tended to phimose his garden's pudic antesanctum, at administering dainty thrills almost as silently as a nibbling fawn. But neither tact nor talk nor tongue seemed to be called for tonight. It all came to the same bluff end anyway, influenced by dozens of variables he couldnt control, good better or best, sometimes just short of indifferent, one way or another: perhaps diminishing in average frequency but improving with age (if you could judge by focussed demand, by little yelps and gasps at the access to recesses, and by the joyful sighings of a master mariner deep at sea with a rolling deck under his feet).

There had been times when in such mutual temper he might have laid her on a table or against a wall (gratifying her fairytale fancy for stupration or his for playing all the angles). These days he simply led her dumbly to the waiting uxorious bed where resentment often kept them back to back. Jointure of body, for which and by which they loved, still held separate mysteries for the man and woman, but after nearly half a generation of probation they liked nothing better in their moments of harmony than to reduce their reciprocity to its quintessence. Yet reciprocals they remained, since their continual exchanges of energy never left them a moment longer in sensational equality, since this their authentic symbiosis required no true empathy, since even into the least sexual aspect of their love they were but counterparts, each an integral paradox: the lean wife full of boundless pantheistic desire regulated by exquisite discretion, her general and mystic amorousness serving the most concrete sensuality; the stout nearsighted husband tormented by acute singleminded desire which was never for a minute left undefined or doubted, his physique repeatedly stirred to extravagant and unredeemable asseverations of spiritual devotion. Lord and lady looked over each other's shoulders in opposite directions when embracing most closely. Still, the sinner's inextirpable lust, fed by the incredibly replenishing reservoir in his loins, was well matched by the saint's ceaseless craving for communion.

On the bed her eyes were closed. The buttonholes of her gown were so worn and tattered that he was able to rend the veil with a single slither of his forefinger. The fastenings seemed to will themselves undone, ruled by his idea. Then came the anamnesis of ten thousand conjugal touches; her body resumed the past. Her head began to librate with almost premature impatience. For a short time more he kept her waiting, stroking and kissing her schoolgirl exposure by gaze alone, and without looking in return she smiled to herself under his schoolboy admiration as she lay in nailless crucifixion with her arms flung out, her legs still closed save for the classic bend of one knee raised above the other little loathe to part. Such posture drew flat the soft belly that had been three times torn in childbirth and her spread wings raised the deflowered granaries that had always confounded his powers of praise into heaps of virginal wheat.

But this time no further superficial touch was required and they were both content to pass that phase with a mere salute to beauty. Before long they were baying full-throated songs of the hunt. He had only to lay a fingertip on the inner hollow of her ankle: in a trice the apple of his eye was cloven; the prey was flushed into an open glade for quick playful chase, all kindness and no cruelty, the old gamecock playing coquet in coy response to sweet supplication in their old dance of the introit, greeting her with ever less disappointing disappointment—until he himself grew impatient with coolheaded pleasantries and allowed the hot seam to swallow whole the liberties he had been taking for her sake like a spidery Spaniard fooling around.

Tonight none of her fuel was slow to kindle. The modest wife ramped in her marriage bed. To him she seemed wild enough to bolt a donkey before the eyes of strangers. [Let that very simile come to her, let her imagine anything, everything. Sometime (not now) make her tell me the most she can think of: not to shrive her but to grant as a psychic extension of the diversity one poor husband can provide, the excitements if not the satisfactions ordinarily unavailable to a chaste wife. A dangerous thought-experiment to be sure, but maybe not as dangerous as not knowing what she's capable of dreaming up. I have always tried to make it up to her for taking me as exclusive lover, a fallible monotonous thaumaturge. . . . But then also she is for me a career of strange women.] A man's most precious trove he thought, the secret bawdry of a beautiful decent dignified faithful wife who may stock her imagination with all manner of stories dilating his contubernal service extenuating his familial neglect and winking at his public humiliations. The key to that mind belonged to him, forged in long exercitation at her gate. Anyone else tonight would have had to seduce her, and in seduction her abandonment would have rendered itself parsimoniously. He was pleased to believe it was his own person that unlocked the teratology of her fancy ["Once upon a time there was a Monster and a Modicum . . ."], and this belief in her desire for him spiritualized his adoration of her utterly unadorned womanhood right now. He deemed her present behavior an honor to the sacrament, ancient and modern.

He was about to lose himself in the marvelous glamor he had stipulated. His faculties were being subverted by the one energumen of his cult, whom he had so knowingly inarched in sparing no effort to churn up the spirals of sensations that pulled him into her vortex. She had already passed beyond image and affection into a state of total anagogic expectation; yet the shorter and shorter waves emanating from her nucleus could not escape the extremities and integuments that bounded her mortality: they refluxed upon their source undiminished until augmenting resonance had infinitely surpassed the simply transcendent amplitudes of honeymoon joy; she moved quickly past threshold after threshold which in former times would have tripped up the further advances of ecstasy. [With youth the nerves start too high. We never got up the momentum to crash past so many barriers. Hungry so often, easily fed. The blade easiest to put an edge on is the fastest to dull. She used to dote on my slim muscular torso, and I paid tribute with all my ingenuity to the full length of that nulliparous mistress. For a whole year she preoccupied me day and night. We never thought of middle age, capering like goats new to the species, tallying our squibs and detonations on the wallpaper.] Finally, won through to the innermost lagoon, he abandoned his last skill and shot straight to the lee on his juggernautical collision course. By now she knew neither him nor herself but only the unendurable compaction of beatitude, for he'd studied himself as well as her, and loosed his own plasmatic pneuma only when he knew that the spate would carry away the last of her dams.

With her cries of affirmation milk and honey fused in the coital shock. Shards of sensation hung suspended for a prolonged instant, then fell about their heads with slow feckless underwater force in the inundated valley. So thorough had been the applosion that it took his suddenly defervescent ligaments some time to perfect their palpitations and permit his disembodied spirit to return to its dwelling place; and as he lay extravasated in the throat of the womb it seemed to him much longer yet before the slow lysis of his wife's waves even began, each tracing and retracing the multiple path to its fainting origin.

Missa est. The only possible communication between this man and woman had been made. His body fell dead upon hers. He felt in it the maternal softness of gratitude, its tone enriched by himself. Yet she lay beneath him as stonied as Semele.

When Ruth drifted back to her senses she became aware of the great dear weight under which she breathed. Slowly her scattered limbs awakened. Her face felt numb, but the waves from her center were now passing through her skin to attenuate in cosmic radiation, leaving her suffused with a peaceful new glorification which by gently pulsing permeation soothed her whole body, cell by cell. A new purely personal integrity of organization had rescued the old mental self from both separation and transfiguration. Without fear or desire she blessed the fluctuating strangeness of the male person whose serene exhaustion was mysteriously essential to her happiness.

After the husband's winded wheeze died out nothing stirred for a long time, not an eyelid, not the tiniest muscle. He broke the silence at last in a sigh of thanksgiving, but all he said was Holy Mackerel. Out of her deep stillness the wife brought two or three faint sounds to her tingling lips which somehow conveyed a greater profundity of sacrifice. As she became aware of concentric glows throughout her re-emerging nerves she lifted her limp left hand to the hairy skin of his back. His whole body now seemed no less tender than it was necessary to her. It could propel itself with incomprehensibly self-sufficient buoyancy like a paddled log that was governed by the common sense from which she now felt she had foolishly excluded herself out of mere cowardice; but it was tethered to her by a miraculously elastic cord that he himself had chosen to attach.

He thought to make her more comfortable by sliding off prone to her right side leaving one arm and one leg to bind him to her soft warm spreadeagle contentment, his fingers twitching at the delicate hair enleafing her ear, his right knee folded over the belly that had borne his thunderbolt. He thought he detected a network of dulcet curative spasms sending her off to sleep as memory was readmitted, but they might have been his own. He smiled to himself officiously, marvelously pleased with his sedative powers. As she finally lost consciousness entirely the wife divined his vanity with fond approval.

Michael's love did not go flaccid with the fall of Priapus, as if merely relieved. The last seminal convulsion had not drained his heart. Sometimes indeed the event only remedied the disturbance, freeing his engines for daily subjectmatter; but tonight he was re-enamored of his wife with a welling afflatus that left no room for business either awake or adream. Purified from skin to bone, every worry healed, nursing as generously on her homage as she on his balm, he dropped toward the delicious void.

It was another quarter of an hour before he roused himself from epoptic enchantment to reach for the sheeted blanket to cover their nakedness. Then nightlong sleep to restore his other vigors. The sabbath's advance guard was rung onto the scene by twelve bells of landsmen striking in the distant belfry that regulated the Chapman household, though they never located it and didn't know whether it surmounted a civic building or a church.

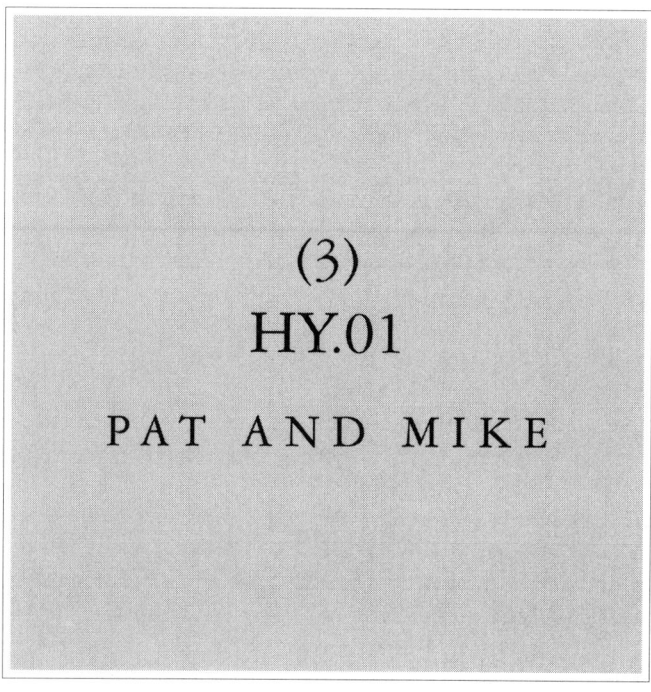

(3)
HY.01

PAT AND MIKE

"C R F has been making cash registers since 1910—"

"By far the best cash register on the market I'm convinced."

"Yes! And you're making better use of the Model 27 than any customer I have because you appreciate what our engineers designed it to do. I always mention your application when I'm talking to prospects. C R F —

"Pardon me?"

"Pat how are sales going? You deserve the trip to Hawaii if you help all your customers as much as you've helped us."

"Go *on*! But thanks Mike. It's just part of the job. We don't just sell machines and paper: we sell a service. I enjoy it. We're having a good year. And this new equipment is going to help us. I'm ahead of quota, but I'm happy to say so is everyone else in the territory."

"Maybe C R F will send you all to Hawaii!"

"Somebody's got to stay home and keep the customers happy. No seriously Mike we've still got a big job to do. N C R still dominates the industry, not to mention Moore, and the rumor is that I B M —"

"If they'd just make you national sales manager! In five years C R F would be getting the antitrust suits."

"We think our equipment is the best, and our forms printing is top quality, but we've got a long long way to go before either side of our business is in first place. Especially when we refuse to chisel prices. It's a great company to work for though. They may work you hard but they treat you fair. I've never regretted leaving—"

"Well if I ever get back East I'm going right to the Park Avenue office and tell the Executive V P about the kind of man he's got out here."

"I've never met Mr Parks—say, Parks! and Park Avenue! How about that! Never thought of it before! Like I say, we've got a lot of good men. I'm about average. But thanks for the nice words. I've always enjoyed working with you. But seriously like I say—"

"How's your son?"

Pat paused and lowered his voice. "I'm still a little worried Mike. But the psychologist from the state Education Department says that if we can just keep him supplied with plenty of books and scientific toys he may not be too much trouble until we can get him into a special class somewhere in the fall. But it's going to be expensive." Pat sighed. "The wife and I can't keep up with him. He's on a mental level with his older sister."

"Is she the one that pulled him out of muscular dystrophy?"

"Yeah. Boy you've got a good memory! It was a long time ago I told you about that. She made him walk when the doctors had given up. They didn't say so but we knew it. Fortunately the kid worships her and that keeps him on an even keel. His coordination is normal now; he plays ball and everything. It's almost miraculous. I'm beginning to think the M S was just a false alarm."

"You're a first-class father Pat the way you've handled it all."

"It wasn't me. It was my daughter and my wife."

"Good thing you had other children."

"Oh hey! I forgot to tell you. The wife's expecting again!"

"Great! Congratulations. I know you've been hoping."

"After we lost that last one the doctor wasn't too sure though and we're keeping our fingers crossed. But she's kept it three months now."

"Then you're pretty safe I should think."

"We're happy. That will make number four. Another exemption!"

"You don't know how lucky you are to have a genius in the family."

"Oh the psychologist didn't say *that*. But I guess Kevin did come out pretty high on his tests. Must get it from his mother. Adjustment is going to be quite a problem. The funny part of it is that the kid *seems* pretty normal now. He likes school. He plays with other kids just as rough as most of the boys in the neighborhood. Goes to show you how easy it is for an abnormal case to fool you. Psychologist says he needs more intellectual stimulation but that he shouldn't be allowed to sit off by himself too much. We're going half crazy trying to figure out what to do with him. Can't keep him out of school, but the teachers are beginning to complain. It'll be a wonder if he doesn't grow up neurotic."

"All I can say is I wish one of my kids had that trouble of Kevin's."

"You'd be able to keep up with a gifted child for a few years. Well look I don't want to take up your time with my personal problems—

"Like I was saying C R F has been making cash registers since 1910 so desk calculators are not really foreign to our experience. For us it's just a new extension of principles our engineers have been using for years. A printing calculator with two registers and a memory device! There's never been anything like it before at *any* price, except those new million-dollar electronic brains."

"What this country needs is business brains as rational as your machines."

"We recognized the need for a desk-top unit that would print a tape and do everything a rotary calculator would do and more besides. No rotary on the market today has a double register and a high-speed keyboard for adding, let alone a tape. All for the price of two or three ordinary conventional adders!"

"But we don't have even a conventional adding machine! We are unconventional in this store whenever it's cheaper. But could I operate your calculator by touch?"

"Definitely. Your lefthanded method would be beautiful on our new keyboard. You wouldn't have to take your pencil off the paper. With your knowledge and aptitude—"

"But we couldn't afford to be guinea pigs for —"

"Mike, this is no untested machine by any stretch of the imagination. It's been on the market for a year; we've sold a whole slew of them all over the country. The only reason I never mentioned it to you is that I thought you didn't have any particular application for it, especially since you don't write invoices; but when you asked if there was a machine that could give group totals as well as grand totals—"

"And percentages too."

"—and percentages too, I realized how dumb I'd been."

"Doesn't matter Pat. I wouldn't dream of asking Val for a printing calculator even if it were recommended by President Eisenhower. My hands are tied as far as capital investment is concerned."

"I understand. But you've found a beautiful application for this machine."

"I'd use the reciprocal method of constant multiplication for maximum speed in dividing series of figures and proving out to one hundred percent, printing totals and group totals—all in one series of operational steps without having to re-enter any of the numbers!"

"The average merchant would never use the machine to its full capacity but you're one guy who could bring out the best in it. Look at what you make that old klunker of an adding machine do by step-over multiplication and all that! Oh boy, this would be a natural! You could check the extensions of the invoices you pay and calculate the cash discount all in one pass! And do all your analysis work too."

"It's too good to be true for me. A year on the market is nothing though. You guys could sell any new product! It takes more years to test reliability. If it jammed just once Val would never let me spend a nickel again and I'd never get a raise!"

"I started to tell you Mike, this isn't really new at all. What we've done is combine two principles. When we bought out the Dutch company we got a concept that has been applied in Europe for many years—an entirely different method of multiplication and division that made possible a true printing calculator. Integrated with our own established concept of—"

"I thought they bought you out."

"A merger. I don't know the details. Anyway a lot more money and effort is being put into product development. This machine was actually sold on the European market for two years before we introduced it here, just so we could be absolutely sure it was up to our standards of performance and reliability."

"*I'm* convinced Pat. I believe you. I'd like to prorate sales, inventory, space, and cost-of-goods every month, by category, and it takes too much time with an archaic adding machine and slide rule. But I don't know how I'll ever get Prince Valiant to spend that much money. He thinks a hand-crank adder is all we'll ever need—he's used one ever since he stopped doing everything in his head. Says he's gotten along well enough—especially now that we have your accounting cash register. The statistics I have in mind would help him; I'm sure he'd be interested in the figures. But like everyone else he can't imagine the value of something new until he has the actual results in front of him."

"And he can't see them until you have the machine to produce enough figures to be meaningful. I know what you mean! But you're in a very competitive business. Scientific management can make the difference nowadays."

"Yeh, it's like the liquor trade in Massachusetts. Everyone carries exactly the same lines at the same prices. Retail promotion is worthless unless you have a larger selection than anyone else. In a town like this people usually know what they want in advance, and they don't have much extra money to spend at random. It's not like the stores in the City, where decorations and fancy displays make for conspicuous consumption. We play a thin market for most of our discretionary trade—at least the part of it I'm most responsible for—and the inventory balance for each item has to be very small. Yet as it is we just guess when we put in an order—"

"Let me leave a demonstrator unit with you, to try out for a few weeks."

"Oh Pat I can't—"

"No obligation. In fact use it as long as you want. You don't have to buy it. Just so you'll know what it can do and someday maybe the store will be ready for it."

"Can I use it enough for a long analysis project?"

"Sure. All you want."

"But it might take a month. I'll have to work at night to squeeze in the time. I want to *use* the figures that we've been getting from the wonderful cash register you sold us. All we do now is post the totals from the tape every day, just for gross comparison. We don't analyze; we don't look for cause and effect. If I can show Val a practical study of our problems he might see the value of the calculator. Does the instruction book tell how to work the reciprocal method of prorating?"

"Yes. But if there's any special application that the book doesn't cover I'll call in the factory engineer. By the way, the Physics Department on Campus has one. They're using it in the cosmic ray research lab to figure costs for their reports to the government."

"A pretty mundane chore. No doubt they take a condescending attitude toward it."

"Ha, ha! They use it for scientific work too. Very very happy with it."

"Did you sell that one? It's hard for a layman to tell them anything. They consider themselves general experts."

"They have the money. Machine sold itself."

"I bet. Any used machines available?"

"They're too new and too good. No one wants to let one go."

Michael sighed. "Well bring in one next time you come Pat. But call first to make sure it's okay. I'll have to clear it with Val before he sees it here."

"But it's free! Like I say, no obligation!"

"Doesn't matter. He'll think we're plotting to spend his profits if I don't first explain that we're just taking advantage of your company and my free time."

"Sure, that's all right! Take advantage of C R F all you want. That's what I'm here for. Need any more register-tape rolls or purchase order forms or sales slips?"

"No, not yet. We've got enough to last for now. We'll need tape in a couple of months."

Pat paid for the coffee they had been drinking and the two men rose from the counter stools. Pat picked up his tan leather attaché case.

"Full of orders?" Michael said with a smile.

"Feel how heavy it is."

"Sorry I couldn't contribute toward your machine quota Pat."

"Think nothing of it Mike, think nothing of it. I always enjoy talking to you."

Taking leave of each other they stood out on the sidewalk backed against the window of the lunchroom in order not to obstruct flocking and streaming students.

"You've come a long way in the last few years Mike. I'm sure the boss appreciates what you've done for him."

"Don't ask him. He'd rather hear you ask him if I appreciate what he's done for me."

Pat chuckled but replied solemnly. "Just between you and me I still say that you've put this store on the map. You've really got a flair for business. And for figures. I hope you find it rewarding. You deserve a lot of credit."

"I'd rather have cash. But thanks Pat. You know we really need another cash register already. But for God's sake don't bring *that* up yet. We'll hit him up for it next year if we have a good Fall and Christmas—after we get the calculator! I'd rather have that first—so don't foul up my strategy!"

"Saints forbid! Don't forget the Model 69 will make payroll a lot easier too."

"Who in hell gave it that number? Must have come from engineers in the old country matter!"

This time Pat giggled. "Go *on*! I just wanted to hear what you'd say. I usually don't mention the model number. With most people I just call it The Comptroller. C R F machines always have decent names. —But that reminds me: I know you're busy and want to get back to the store but have you got time to hear a short one?"

Michael grinned. "By all means!"

"Stop me if you've heard it. It seems that there's this guy who goes to the doctor and says he wants—You haven't heard it have you?" he gravely interrupted himself with a show of doubt.

Michael's smile had been broadening in anticipation of pleasure from an unknown cause. He shook his head decidedly.

"Well it seems there's this guy who goes to the doctor and says he wants to get castrated. You sure you haven't heard this one? Tell me if you have. And the doctor asks him if he's really positive that he wants to have it done. It's a little unusual he says and we have to be absolutely sure. Sure I'm sure the guy says. It's not illegal is it? Go ahead and do it. I know what I want he says. If you won't do it I'll go to someone who will. Okay the doc says I'll do it but first you'll have to sign a paper. So the guy signs a paper. Come back Wednesday at eleven o'clock the doctor says and we'll do the job at my office. It won't take long. So the guy comes back Wednesday undresses and lays himself down on the operating table and the doc dopes him up so he won't feel any pain. When the guy wakes up the doctor asks him how he feels. Fine Doc I feel fine. I knew it wouldn't amount to much he says. As soon as I get my clothes on I'll go back to work. Say says the doctor while I was operating on you I noticed that you've never been circumcised. *Circumcised!* says the guy, *that's* the word I wanted!"

Michael laughed, laughed in his throat, laughed in his belly, leaned against the window and laughed, the laughter gaining on him with each wave of re-echoed perception. Gasping he clapped Pat on the shoulder and Pat began to laugh at his laughter.

The salesman was delighted at the excessive affect of his story. In the full flush of success he waved at Michael and walked off down the street to his next call.

The portly merchant-assistant composed himself. Now the bright sun glinted from his rimless glasses as if he bore the indication of Grace. When he crossed the street to the shop he was in an optimistic mood. Such was the degree of his cheer that he hummed to himself:

> When the war is over
> We will all enlist again. . . .

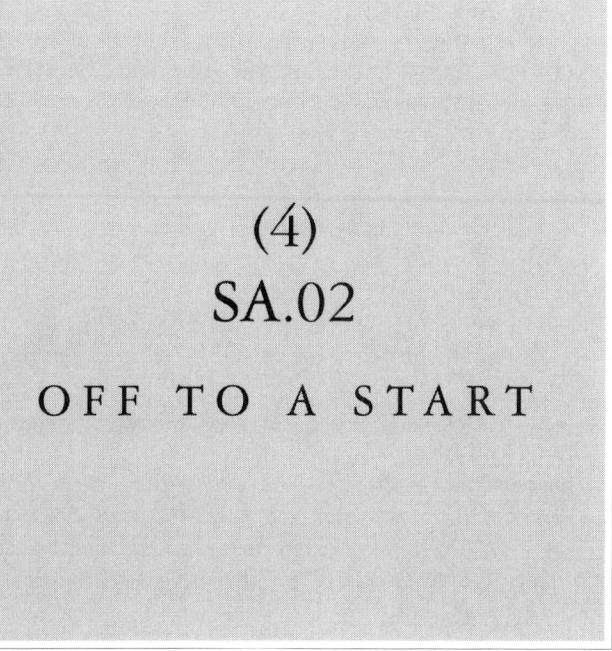

(4)
SA.02

OFF TO A START

*T*herefore Sunday she was up before him, with the children, singing, when he awoke at ease flat on his back every muscle and nerve supported as the manufacturer of a better mattress said it should have been in independent gravitation. Michael lay as plane and horizontal, poured out and uncohesive as a thick man can get—every tendon unknitted, every feeling as aimless and pleasurable as warm spring sun on grass at the edge of a footpath. The annealed tranquility was so rare and valuable that in its favor he had cordially waived his earlymorning duty to the harpies. In truth even they urged him to enjoy the sense of his own flesh in unstruggling repose. The sense of simplified weight in all parts conveyed a feeling of matter, and he happily contemplated the properties of his own mass when situated at its most comfortable equilibrium among all the possible equilibriums of living man.

The totally soothed organism was devoted to radical imagination. Memories thoughts and plans flashed easily through the brilliant spaceless vault where the ether without extension was concentrated within the matter. Any motion to differentiate or integrate or execute these ideas would have been tabled forthwith. It was better to indulge them, flittering and profound, without attempt to arrest or transfix, in the hope that they would leave some sedimentary traces. It was better not to move while sinking widely into the massrest. At the same time he began to believe that he had at last permanently achieved supreme control of his intelligence by separating it from the rest of what appertained to the first person. And he was firmly and joyfully of this mind when he fell away into the deeper explorations of resleep.

When Michael awoke the second time he was hungry. He smiled at the euphonious dissonance that came to him as a single prose from the kitchen. With habitual thought to the duty he would have to put in after breakfast, as he swung his feet to the floor he suddenly caught vague echoes of one of the images that had occupied the interregnum: nothing but a phrase remained, a phrase that in his sleep had epitomized an idea he knew was worth preserving. Those few words would be written down as soon as he could find under the junk that littered the surface of the chest of drawers beyond his reach from the bed a note card and one of the pencils he had stolen from Valentine Greatrakes. With the day's first twinge of exasperation he succeeded in standing finding bending and scribbling, losing an avenue of inspiration with every moment of delay. As he put down first one fragment and then a second that was recalled by the act of writing he lost others that had offered to come flocking, lost them forever; they were lost to the world forever: nor had God recorded them.

Still, the two he captured were notions that would not have come at all under other conditions. He slowly dressed pondering the poor pearls that remained to him as maieutic talismans—and suddenly he was able to formulate in mnemonic simplification (surely requiring no memorandum) a little theme that had been vexing him. Right after breakfast it could be pinned to history!

Relieved and washed, he sauntered cheerfully handsapockets into the kitchen. The Happy One harnessed in high chair had been jabbering at the world, ebulliently drumming a spoon upon the desk in front of him in patient forbearance of his mother's kitchenwise inefficiency, but at the sight of the big father before the others saw, whom he had forgotten, was issued a shreel of selfcontained recognition, a laugh of royal amusement. The two big boys wedged into the corner behind the round table were already eating and amiably complaining about the way their eggs were done although each pair had been cooked to order by a different method.

"Well well well." said the pater familias.

"Three holes in the ground." said number one son.

"Well well." said the sheik.

"Two holes in the ground." said number two son.

"Well." said the lord.

"Daa-eey!" said the third son with a flourish of his spoon.

Michael scuffled in to sit down with his back against the hot water tank where the chair was always reserved for him, a place he could get to and from fast enough but which still was hardly as handy as his wife's to sink cupboards shelves garbage pail front door back door or any other locus of inconvenience that someone might otherwise ask him to attend in unwelcome interruption of eating, and which also was warm.

Ruth stood by, the only woman in a precinct of men, and a lucky one at that. "Life has infinite possibilities for the male child." said she, marveling. "And for the maleman too." he replied with a lewd affection that on a morning like this deepened her appreciation of the virtue in fiery marriage vows.

His breakfast was already cooked—as sign of special favor three eggs opened out on the toasted bread he liked, coffee freshly made at hand, everything coordinated. She sang and served like a milkmaid. Her renewed beauty was adorned with red ribbon in her hair, and her habiliment so clean and trim evoked memories of her gay virgin spirit. The pretty clothes and happy demeanor influenced the boys, saints be praised, sustaining their unwonted courtesy. A gifted course through life seemed assured for each in the family. In half an hour he would be able to withdraw into the room of his withdrawal third cup of coffee in hand without reminding her of cause for silent resentment. Because Ruth had now joined him in his vision of family equanimity his work henceforth and forevermore could be accomplished without grubby contention! Perhaps his years of fretting and unhopeful patience were beginning to yield manifold profit. In all at once passing a breakeven point the leverage of his investment was about to multiply the advantage of effort that up until now had been divided.

But she was more artful than he. In such a blue-sky mood how could he forewarn himself of or even object to the lightning that struck up from the earth? As if impulsively, looking him straight in the eye, she said it: "Let's go on a picnic!"

A moment of awful silence between bolt and thunder.

Feigning innocence of her proposal's import and unconcern for the impression it might make yet clearly meaning that it was not to be taken as a trifle to be dismissed without a damned good answer, Ruth scarcely paused in the task of alternately eating at her own egg and feeding Roger the gruel that contented him. But the big boys halted their breakfast, forks suspended, every muscle of neck and stomach held in poise, curling and squeezing the toes in their shoes. Instead of thunder however the man heaved a sigh or moan.

The boys permitted themselves a little breath between their parted lips, their hopes not yet dashed, still swallowing a clamor of eagerness. They all waited for the decision to mature itself during the ensuing bluster of temporization which they immediately recognized to represent a state of will not much worse than neutral. Roger hollered with delight throughout the contretemps, between the spoonfuls that were regularly delivered to his unprehensile mouth by the calm mother.

Michael's mind darted at a depth where the current was preternaturally swift, toting up debits and credits calculating vectored resultants and composing various guesses at the day's concatenating outcome. But on the talking level he meanwhile assumed a negative prejudice, being from long habit cautious in the knowledge that it is easier by far to maintain a firm front and negotiate a favorable settlement in gradual retreat than to recapture lost strongpoints at the last moment of a peace conference, especially when the preponderance of moral strength lies with forces of opposition powerful without and at the same time subversive within. The issue was foredoomed, but by putting the best face upon it he hoped to control the shape if not the balance of compromise.

"You mean just go on a picnic—just *go*? . . . . What good's a picnic? . . . . It's just an eating, just another eating, only more inconvenient. . . . Food not as good . . . much more work for you . . . a lot of trouble for us all! Now I can understand wanting to go camping: someday we can do that, when Roger's a little older . . . ["Just to get out of the house." she explains.] Just to get out of the house! Can't you get out of the house without eating?"

But his voice was still fairly friendly. He was not yet querulous; satisfaction gratitude and guilt still disarmed savagery. "Well I don't want just to *go*! That's ridiculous. We should go *somewhere*, see *something*. Picnic indeed! It sounds like a maypole dance or some other genteel displacement of primitive pleasure!" A twinge of self-reproach checked him.

"It doesnt matter where we go. Anywhere, as far as the boys and I are concerned."

"It doesnt *matter*! All that effort and it doesnt *matter*! Sweetie-pie, surely you don't mean. . . ."

"All right my dear, you say what and where. Whatever and wherever you choose. Whithersoever thou goest, there go us. That's just the point."

Deep groan. More deep breaths half expressing and half repressing exasperated disapproval. That domesticating attitude of hers was the worst part of the whole thing. . . . [Etc.]

But as a matter of fact there are certain experiences the boys should have before their tastes are formed, and it's about time Roger should start seeing a few things. I wouldnt mind seeing some of them once more—and I'll never be able to travel alone again anyway. Also, a little honeymoon trip will keep her quiet for weeks to come; she'll let up on me for a while. "Okay okay *okay*! Let me think for a minute where we'll go."

Whoops of joy from one and two stared at by number three, shushed by suddenly anxious stage gestures of the mother: daddy's meditation must be respected or he'll get mad and change his mind. So one and two bite their lips hold their hands over their faces and double up in knots of joyful painful sputtering selfcontrol.

I know well enough where we'll go—but softly now, not too fast: what have I overlooked? After all, this morning I did come up with a couple of new ideas for future use today and I have a good feeling about that—better than I should, of course: maybe twenty notions just as good would come along today if I stayed home and made some actual progress, the way one thing leads to another—but I don't really feel much like working today; I probably need an interruption, a real change, the pleasure of travel which I've never had enough of. I can think about my thoughts on the way; I can let my mind wander: if I don't force myself I may burgeon with the talent that I've lacked. . . . And they really deserve it, poor woman, half-deprived kids. I'd like to see Roger's face when he sees— "Then we might as well go to the zoo."

Thus the trouble he got into, affecting casual words—not entirely off guard, not impulsively or in the possession of some justifiable mania, but simply out of weakness, yielding to his partiality for small pleasures. But he had soundly estimated the effect of his announcement, so heightened by his suspenseful manner of delivery: tumultuous glee, gratifying surprise, and extravagant praise. He was mobbed. [Never had number three seen persons behave that way; for a couple of minutes Roger sat simply as an astonished spectator.] Michael's spirits rose at this display of solidarity. But as benefactor it was necessary to maintain a peevish domination lest his benefaction attenuate into the vulgar indulgence of an ordinary father with nothing else to do on a Sunday.

Nevertheless he soon found it impossible to conduct himself as it behooved him. His yen for travel was too strong. Forgetting his dreads he threw himself into the planning, and into the task of motivating others to throw themselves into preparatory action. And he did so immediately, time being of the essence—though in his access of enthusiasm he very nearly reached the point at which he would have had to restrain himself from pitching in; it was only dim foreknowledge of the latter part of the day that moderated his expenditure of energy. So reckless was his good cheer that it could not be dampened by the awareness that everyone fathomed his undisgruntled gruffness.

Whistling bustle in the kitchen, Ruth; a scattering, the older boys; a removal, Michael, to establish the dining room table as headquarters of the operation, where he took more than several vigorous turns in supervision of rummage as the boys assumed responsibility for their own outfitting without being allowed to forget to think of the old man whose prospective burden they should lighten wherever they could. "You can use my thermos bottle for your coffee, Daddy." says Matthew the second child,

> "Somebody take care of Roger. Don't let him open the
> sewing machine drawer!"

fetching it to his father.

"Thanks. Give it to Ruth."

"Okay. Don't forget to shave, Daddy. You looks terrible.

Ruth calls out: "I'll get him ready in a minute."
You *told* me to remind you! Last time you forgot."
"Yes, I've got to shave." [Good idea. Time to think.]
"Jonathan, watch Hodge while I'm shaving."

> Matthew in the kitchen: "Ma, put Daddy's black coffee in
> my thermos bottle. I said he could use it. Then you can
> put sugar and cream in the other one."

"Come here's Hodge!" number one calls from the other
room. Hodge hurtles off, elbowing his way through the
space he traverses, delighted to obey a summons.

> "All right! Just what we needed, dear."
> "Why don't you *ever* butter the bread right out to the
> edge? . . . . Ma, I want to wear my storm boots. I think
> it's going to rain and get very muddy."
> "No. Wear your rubbers."
> "But why?"
> "Because there are two of them. It's better than hopping."
> Matt silently accepts his mother's pragmatical decision.

Michael, shaving with the bathroom door open so he can
hear and make himself heard if need be in every room, experiments to the tune of the Battle Hymn of the Republic:

"O get the shoes and boots upon your lousy little feet,
Get the shoes and boots upon your leaping lovely feet—
       For the truth is marching on!"

He goes over this ditty three times or more, with greater
and greater fullness of voice; then falls silent during the
cutting strokes.
"Listen to Daddy. He's an idiotic nut."

> "Hodge your father's crazy. You might as well run away
> now while it's not too late."

Out of the corner of his eye he glimpses Ruth going into
the atrium to put the first bag of food on the table—the
dessert, not the essentials of what must be supplied to the
depot of supplies and equipment.

> "Look at him trying to put on your sneakers. Jonno, *look*
> I said! Oh now you missed it, and it's your own fault!
> You're always so busy looking in the mirror . . ."

She comes to the bathroom door and watches him for a moment. "Are
you sure you want to go all that way when the weather's like this?" she
asks. "Have you got enough money?"

"Yes yes yes." he says testily, nettled by the thought suddenly imposed
and annoyed at her sudden doubt, his razor suspended in his right hand
before his left cheek. "If we don't go now we'll never go. It always clears
up in the afternoon—"

"April Fool!" she cries, and reaches over to tweak the pensile limb that made him her husband, the giant that slept beneath his baggy clothes like an upsidedown bat. "You never do anything by halves—oh, what a disappointment: you werent even thinking of me!" Though it was not a hustling family she was gone before he could grab her. But as he continued shaving she was much too vividly in his thoughts again . . . and all day long they wouldnt have three seconds alone and private. Who could believe what he remembered of that woman's nighttime double? Certainly not she herself.

In the beauteous swishing whistling self-possession that now avowed itself in her air and informed her carriage (oh, her carriage, her upright highheaded mobile softness!) she seemed mindful of joyous moderation left behind by the storm. The fillip she had just bestowed indicated a gay recognition that that which had been filliped was the mortal remains of the celestial rivet that had sacrificed its stamina to bring on her pithy serenity. [Dosim repetatur. Every night in every light, better and better.] Surely even in the busy morningtime (now that in her mature womanhood she was no longer timid of consciousness) her mind's eye could see something of the smooth hardhot pike that had so often risen in surprising color

"Hurry up—you're not half ready yet! . . .
Hey Matt, can I borrow one of your scout knives?"

"Why?" It's a matter of suspicion and defense.

Then "No."
"But why not?"
"Why do you want it?"

"You know! I lost my knife. I don't have one for the trip."
"Why do you need it?"
"Can I? Hey?"
"No."
"All right for you! What a brother!" One walks away from the other.

from the darkness beneath his pillowy uncolored belly, and therefore she was able to remember if only by visual prompting the ageold method of transaction between male and female. But surely also she remembered little of her own licentious impudicity. It was not shame that made her forget so much: the fact was simply that traces of the effect had to disappear sooner or later after removal of the cause, and the glissando impressions at the seat of her comprehension during the phenomenon were now faded and inaccessible to her thought, as if the memory of them had been absorbed and effaced by the mucous anointment that was still slowly draining from her miserly groin as she moved about on her feet serving less acute pleasures of the family organism as a whole. It was the husband who recalled to his busybody retina her tempest of the night before, arrogating the right to do so as bearer of its proximate instrument—which, by the way, now risen again from between his legs in unshrivelled glory (though concealed from casual eyes) betrayed to himself the fact that the direct recollection of her supposed impressions was more accessible to himself than to her. All the while her love for him as the chiefman of a happy household was infusing itself with general spiritual qualities (like the innocent wish of a maiden for the man who will become her life-long protector and father of prebeloved children), the chamber of her love filled with a bright but-terfly ignorant of its origin or end, his leading blood vessels responded like servomechanisms to her idle gesture as a cat in autonomic lordosis answers to human touch with sprung hindquarters and kited tail no matter what its mood purring or not. His telekinetic thoughts leaped in rifling propensity like wa-ter surging into a fire hose valved at the nozzle, and if it had been pos-sible to disregard the moment's do-mestic circumstances he would have permitted the pressure to become irresistible then and there. It was pleasing to his wisdom however to find himself old enough to know that he would not necessarily miss quintessential experience every time he failed to find relief in kine-matic sensation. As a healthy bull he swelled at every scented pres-ence, but so soon after the utter decantation of a few hours past it should not prove exceedingly diffi-cult to turn aside merely typical lust. This philosophical reflection sufficiently rumpled his starch. A single word in his brain could turn vision into nonsense and divert the blood to his head. He began to murmur less audibly than before (under his breath, in fact), the sec-ond ditty of a young day:

Jonathan returns to his brother. "Please." "No." "Why?" "Because." "But *why?*" . . . No use. This is very unusual, almost mysterious. Matt is always eager to lend and give. Has he suddenly overnight reached the age at which he loses his Matthew-nature and become as guarded and closefisted as big kids?

Jonathan goes back to find some more stuff from his sleeping quarters on the porch but he has decided to complain, even though the risk of proscription nearly out-weighs the hope for official influ-ence on his behalf. He's aware of his own reputation for self-serving cal-culation and of people's opinion that he continually exploits his brother's subservient friendship. The mother and father are more perceptive than Matty is—but Matty is not dumb: Matty wants the powerful brother's daily love on the prairies and in the forests to which decrees of parents can never penetrate. Nearly every day the brothers scream at each other: Matty's squalls of temper are pro-verbial, his rage awesome, in one minute offsetting twenty-four hours of his famous goodwill; but rarely does he refuse his help at anything, and never never never is he known to be stingily possessive; his storms of fury are never venge-ful or mean, for they are nothing

Oh the owl and pussycunt
went to See
And confessed before the
Pope—

[One of the Borgias. A shriving like
that would be something to see!] It
took but slight mutation and casual
elaboration of this frivolous lechery
to animate intellectual imagination
and engorge the bird of prey more
stoutly than ever.

Yet when it came to washing
the lather off his face the touch of
the hot washcloth, or perhaps only
the proprioception of bending over
to meet the water, was pleasant
enough to distract the demon.
When he straightened up to dry his
face with a muggy towel (nominally reserved for himself) so
winkingly quick was his change of
state that he didnt even notice the
lever had fallen until he gave a
little hitch to his rucked-up pants
in order to walk comfortably
through the dining room bare-
chested and complete his toilet in
the front chamber where his things
were kept in a closet and chest of
drawers still obstructed by the outstretched folding wall-bed and its
accumulated litter. In that convertible drawing room he donned a
shirt that had been worn once during the week—for it was ever his
practice to keep used shirts for the
weekends and for occasions of society, inasmuch as it cost over 1% of
his salary to keep them professionally laundered (Ruth being unable
in less than forty-five minutes on
the average to iron out the most

but compressed expostulation of
what his loyal heart has suffered for
a lifelong time, sometimes accompanied by the impulse to kill his
tyrannical elder. [Jonathan never
jeers at these loving and ineffectual
outbursts against himself: he fears
them as he fears the rare anger of
his mother.] Why this staggering
stinginess at a critical moment?
Has little brother all at once arrived
at the phase of a friendly pollywog
turning into loathsome toad? Two
toads in one family are enough.
Three are too much, especially since
the addition of this third toad would
necessarily come at the cost of Matt's
supererogatory offerings of goods
and services that Michael and
Jonathan, as cultivators of self, had
always taken for granted. Such a soul
for love! Such joyfully enthralled
energy! Could such tender assistance
to the whole family have been only a
misleading prelude to permanent
metamorphosis? Is ruinous competition to follow, and lasting strife?

But Jonathan's desire for the
scout knife overcomes his sensitivity to the suspicion of subtile craft
in which he is held by his mother
and father. Trembling in anxiety at
the prospect of having to make the
trip without a knife, he who loves
knives and hates lost opportunities,
the oldest takes up a position at the
supply dump midway between his
mother in the kitchen and his
father dressing in the front parlor-
bedroom open to communication
through a wide double doorway
which is closed to children only at
night sometimes.

conspicuous wrinkles in even one of them, when you counted all the false starts and motionless reveries that interposed themselves despite her determination to be up to the job, which she periodically attempted as a normal housewife's duty). To the children there remained no outward and visible sign of the infatuation; neither was there any inward and invisible trace of it the moment he plunged back into the sticky thickness of picnic-preparation and picnic-justice.

"Matty is very selfish." Jonathan said in an analytical whine. "He has two scout knives and he won't let me borrow one of them just for today."

"Matt is not selfish." the father replied. "He is the most generous man in the family."

"Except for Roger!" the mother called out, though seldom glad to hear such comparisons. "He throws away everything!"

"Who runs and fetches for the indolent prince?" the father continued. "Who gives you his ice cream after you've gobbled up your own?" (Brownheaded Jonathan smiled his guilty sheepish smile, listening with tightened throat.) "Who spends all his own money on Christmas presents for everybody, and especially for you?"

"I'm not selfish." said the firstborn son, eyes lowered, conscious that the eyes of both father and mother were upon him now, twisting and fidgeting under the searching examination of his character, mumbling his defense. "I have to spend my money on lots of things I need! It just depends on who it's to, whether it's selfish or generous."

The man and the woman broke into laughter and moved spontaneously to their oldest baby from opposite directions, their hands meeting and pressing each other's behind his back as they mutually hugged him to their thighs, their eyes exchanging pride over the top of his head. But immediately aware of their indiscretion they moved away again to keep their countenances.

Jonathan wondered whether they laughed about his childishness or about an unwitting cleverness he might have stumbled into: but they seemed to be pleased while making fun of him. Could he have made an embarrassing sexual pun? Something to do with the concept of *who it's to*? Nothing he could remember having heard was clearly relevant to his confusion.

Ruth called gently from the kitchen: "Jonathan, Matt will probably let you borrow his knife if you simple ask him politely. He always does."

She had evidently not heard the two courteous approaches. "But he won't this time. I don't know why. He doesnt even know how to use the knife and Daddy won't let him cut with it until he does!"

"Maybe he thinks you'll never teach him" his mother suggested "if you have one for your own use that you can carry off alone."

Jonathan raised his head doubtfully and looked the other way. His father was still witnessing. "Can *I* teach him, Daddy?"

"Sure. But not now. Some other time."

One further instant the son considered. Presently he dashed a few steps into the kitchen past his mother toward the glassed-in porch that served as the boys' barracks at the back of the house, then slowed down to a jerky stroll for the purpose of offering Matty the *promise* that he would teach him the use of one of the knives.

Suddenly: *where's Roger?* Man and woman strike the same thought at once. "Where's Roger!" she cries. "Roggie, where are you? Roggie!" Stock still, all action suspended, they listen. "Rog!" Michael adds, and whistles for him. No response. They drop everything and spring to the search. Ruth calls to the boys, as she frisks Roger's crib closet the central room and the bathroom, "Is the baby out there?" No! Good lord did he get out the back door and fall off the outside stairs onto the nerveless concrete and is he lying there now in a soundless death with bright blood oozing from his nose and mouth?

But the father finds him, not fifteen feet away, warm nose slobbering, mouth pressed against the windowpane, gazing sidelong up and down the street as far as he can see slowly rolling his head and eyes from one broad angle to the other, for no particular reason. Roger is in fact drawing to the end of five minutes' willlessness. "Ah you child of my old age! That's all right, don't stop. —Ruth here he is! The closet door was open and he was standing behind it, just yooking out de winder!"

"Just yooking, eh? I hope the window's closed." The mother heaves a deep sigh of happiness. Most of her work in getting ready for the trip is on Roger's behalf. "Would have been a pity to lose him now."

Roger has had enough of the streetscape and his father's timely inter-vention has unhanded him of the angel of tranquility whose possession had absorbed him, from whom he now flies as he flies from sleep and to whom nothing could induce him to return. [Not a peep out of him, all the women like to say proudly of their own, Ruth is thinking, but that's what scares you most. No need to be scared now though: the baby will make joyful noise again!] Leaving upon the glass a tempera device of saliva-soluble cereal he hurtles unhesitatingly toward the region of brothers squealing as he goes, elbowing his way past father around big bed through empty space between table legs and window sills, headlong, not doubting to jostle the mother herself who blocks the kitchen thoroughfare, as if his busy schedule calls for an instant interview with Matty and Jonno; but when she grabs him by the waist and tosses him up to her face he laughs at the frustration.

And now the final details are at hand. Michael being ready in person (fairly clean shirt, trousers a little too threadbare for the shop, wellworn tweed jacket, sweater tied by the arms around his neck leaving no neck at all, in fact less than no neck, forasmuch as there was none to begin with), Ruth gives him the little one to hold. He sits deeply sunk in the only armchair trying to keep Roger in his lap from reaching the foison of arti-facts and food accumulating on the table almost within arm's length.

He is attempting to interest Roger a year too soon in the knee-ride that still interests Matty:

> This is the way the lady rides,
> Soft and easy,
> Soft and easy. . . .

"Do it to me, Daddy! Do it to me!" Matthew cries, running in from the porchroom. Jonathan appears behind him, all accoutred, jingling. Each of the boys has a scoutknife hanging from his belt.

> This is the way the farmer rides,
> Clippety, cloppety,
> Clippety, cloppety. . . .

Oh oh—Ruth is about to address them all. She wants something of one of them. Who will it be? It is difficult to deny her requests when she is working so hard herself. "Michael," she says calmly, as if it were nothing at all to ask, "I need to borrow your scissors."

A flash of anger is contained within his stomach, breath caught short. Clustered boys watching. Weakly temporizes: "Why can't you use yours?"

"Can't find them. Otherwise I wouldnt ask, naturally." she replies levelly, bold as you please, as if she werent quaking at the necessity of making this last resort to the worst possible throne of sullen temper, and on such a special day as this (a family picnic, etc.): namely to the redoubt of his ridiculous catshit privacy. By carrying it off well she hopes to shame him through the inopportune crisis, get it over with, and let him forget his grievance in the day's ensuing business.

Michael on the other side can perfectly see the whole train of her determination; but what good does his perspicacity do? His prickly crotchets have been cultivated advisedly and he doesnt propose to blunt them just because his wife can't see the purpose that must be left unmentioned, seeing that it involves the inner mandate to protect himself from her, the psychology of which she perceives without understanding the intellectual substance that is for him the purpose. She has suddenly in broad daylight on a trivial errand penetrated to the face of his rockbottom existence. "Matt, go see if you can find Ruth's scissors." The second son runs off to the front room glad to serve in even a futile cause.

"Please, Michael! We havent got time to look for them." Once again today she is impertinent. "Give me the key and I'll go get yours."

"Watch out Ma!" Jonathan shrieks in merriment, remembering the family joke that Michael once started in one of his regrettably confiding moods. (The kids never forget what you would have them forget.) "Caleb's in there! He'll grab you!" (Especially when it's pseudo-nonsense that they take for genuine nonsense.) The father does not laugh, pretends not to have heard, presents an extremely dour countenance staring straight before him over the top of Roger's wriggling fair head.

Then in spite of himself he does smile at little at his petty defensiveness, but in order to cover his weakness he replies to his wife, who keeps her smile to herself more successfully: "Never mind goddam it, I'll get them; god damn it." Louder he calls out, considerately, averting his ashamed face, particularly the telltale mouth, from the eyes of his interlocutors, "Never mind Matty, don't bother. Here Jonathan, you hold Roger."

"Oh why do you always give him to *me*!" whines number one.

"Take him!" He took him.

With a great groan, slowly deliberately ostentatiously ponderously, Michael gets up out of the chair [which Jonathan flops himself into, tickling Roger as he holds him (the easiest way to amuse the baby for a short time), and the littlest brother squeals in peals; whereupon Matthew comes to help with the tickling and in a moment he and Jonathan are snatching away each other's hands in competition for their small fellow's armpits, while Ruth lightly withdraws to gather more clothes from beyond the open double door of the bedparlor]—damn her sloppy carelessness. Why in hell does she make it a principle never to put anything in the same place twice? A pinch of carefulness would be a powerful sight more useful to a man than all that ex post facto diplomacy.

He walks stiffly around the big table laden with freight, opens the apartment door, and steps out onto the dim landing, fingering his pocket for the key to his citadel. That working closet fills detached Chapman space across the staircase that rises to the third-floor flat of Hecuba Jones, to whom it would have been almost as convenient as it is to him. He enters the musty cubicle (nearly as dark as the hallway landing he has crossed, for its window is obscured by a blank brick wall of the commercial building on the corner of the street) which has not been entered for more than twenty-four hours now, deftly takes scissors from the drawer in the table—looking neither to the right nor to the left, avoiding sight of the table-top litter—, leaves as quickly as he came, relocks the door, and returns to the family living quarters. The errand has been accomplished as rapidly and quietly as we are astonished to learn an elephant can go about its business in the jungle. "Here Matt, stop that tussling and give these to your mother."

An ease of movement and a sense of effortless efficiency in carrying out the little mission invest Michael with a faint feeling of shame, as if his bluster has been the reaction of laziness to a request of reason, and for the moment he completely loses sight of the rational validity of the policy he has long since adopted, one of the motives of which was to teach his wife not to rely upon reserves and alternatives provided by himself and thus through his wisdom to cure herself of gradually expecting reserves for the reserves and several depths of alternative whenever she fails to provide for the future by habit or forethought. But the more important intention of the regime is to preclude the misplacement of tools with which he has taken the trouble to provide *himself* for all contingencies.

Above the gray clouds of the morning Old Sol had meanwhile climbed too high. It was now obvious that a leader's office was called for if the family was to be warped out of the cove before the tide was gone, and Michael gave himself to the job with a will. A good deal of impatience and fussing it must be admitted went into the executive technique, even certain owlish bleatings. Ruth all the while, cheerful longsuffering and calm, did her part with goodtempered gentleness. (A tolerable antinomy: his way to get things done, her way to bring up the boys wisely.) The big bed remained unmade and unrestored to its niche in the wall—nor was there any attempt to wash the breakfast dishes—but at last through cajolery and behest they were ready to take up their burdens and hit the road.

Michael finally loaded up the family and pushed it out the door, bearing no more than his own fair burden. The big sons bounced downstairs like cowboys thumping down the side of a Great Pyramid. The littlest son's noises were less loud but more insistent as he descended the flight ladderwise, his bottom going first, each knee successively resting upon every tread with hollow knocks like those of a dust mop ranging along the edge of a wall, nearly immobilizing his watchful mother who had to stand always at each step next below him during the long second-story dismounting, that she might block with her legs alone (her arms were so full) any slip into a continuous bumping decline from the self-assertive series of regressive equilibriums which the child thought he was so good at.

The husband could trust no one else to close up the place. (Once for a three-day trip he left the responsibility to Ruth and they had returned to find the door ajar.) He scanned the castle systematically room by room closing windows tightening water taps checking gas valves turning off electricity. He put away milk butter bread baloney and other forgotten perishables, for if he had reminded Ruth to do so she not only would have been offended by the reminder that she rarely gave thought to such basic elements of housekeeping but she also would have once again felt the pressure of his opinion that she should form the habit of conserving food for the money it cost, and the disconcerting affect of these two awarenesses upon her psyche would have caused him more trouble than it took to do her work and say nothing. Having cleared away the things in the kitchen he looked for the cat. Her he found curled like giant black shrimpmeat on a pile of clothes that were waiting for ironing on the kitchen floor behind a door. "Wake up and die right, Semiramis my dear!" At his touch on her head she uttered a trilling purrcall of sleepy pleasure, turned her face up, and after stretching curled tighter than ever, forepaws folded under her delicate chin. But he was going to have to wake her shockingly from the trustful somnolence that had weathered all the din of the morning. He stroked her glossy flank probingly, for there had been suspicions lately—as if any gross mortal could hope to detect the shadowy foeti of cubs in their earliest felixity; whereupon she unfolded, rolled over on her back, and arched out voluptuously into a sable longbow against the white sheets and handkerchiefs, draping herself over the crown of the fragrant tumulus. "I hate to do it old girl but I can't trust you in the house all day, and it's not inconceivable that we'll be later yet." Semiramis was not alarmed when he picked her up. She had forgotten her needs and guilts. In the cradle of his arms her drowsiness gave way to waking sensuality and she purred unabashedly with the small rumble of pleasure that flatters a cat's human lover. But the twang of the spring on the screen door stopped that sweet sound instanter. He felt her stiffen. Yet she did not struggle, not she, though reared in the streets where struggle makes all the difference; she merely summoned the selfhood she would need as one city cat among many. It was not such a great shock after all. Unceremoniously, out the door her master tossed her. Then he hooked the screen—while with twitching ears she sat in regal umbrage surveying her neighborhood from the top of the open stairs as if a god had scorned her sacrifice upon the summit of a ziggurat—and bolted the door.

Curse Ruth for her refractory neutrality in the housebreaking battle between himself and Semiramis, who having come from the streets as a kit is exceedingly willful and resourceful. Ruth would rather clean up a mess and two puddles a day than administer or even abet the summary discipline required to train a cat. Putting a kitty out into the cold without even dressing it is for her like putting a naked little girl out into the storm, or an orphan woman, especially when spanked and noserubbed with her own sin.

On the way back through the kitchen he picked up a clean diaper that Ruth had dropped, stuffing most of it into the pocket of his jacket. The man's self-allotted cargo was a large cardboard suitcase crammed with utensils playthings and esculents, with receptacles carboys demijohns and camping equipment. This baggage now assumed, he stepped out into the hall, pressed the button in the edge of the door to set the lock, pulled the door tightly closed, tried it twice with his hand and knee (more vigorously than a policeman would have done if it had been the entrance to a jewelry store downtown), and stumped down the stairs.

—To find his flock *waiting for him* on the front steps! He had deliberately provided it with the opportunity to wend along to the corner at its own speed like a slow convoy taking advantage of every minute to move into the offing where the need for his protection began, who could easily overtake it in plenty of time; but instead they had *waited* for him—the fastest!—before casting off into the inner channel where there was no conceivable need for escort! [Trust the family of an efficient man to compensate for him. Keeps him realistic about mankind. Millstones make the busy one swim harder, perforce add patience and flexibility to his list of self-disciplines.] Consequently, though he began at once to drive the sheep on their way and though he soon was leading them by an opening number of paces, milling his left arm in exhortation like a cowboy with lasso, the unnecessary delay was just sufficient for a sprightly streetcar to present itself, pause on the wing to release two counter-hurriers, and impudently resume its swift express down Teleology Lane before the Chapman outfit gradually gathering corporate momentum could reach the curb at the corner. Without so much as a glance they were sailed by, and sailed by by a trolley car in all respects identical to the clumsily trundling sister vessel that when they at last get into it will groan and grunt and falter at the drop of a hat for every stupid Tom Dick's grandmother who hasnt the wit to be on time or the strength to climb aboard before the motorman has to set the handbrake and step over to give a hoist.

[No use to say a word to anyone, or even to look at her.]

Watch that receding yellow beetle start dawdling, now that it's past us. Sure enough, two blocks down it halts for a traffic light, the noise of its shudder reaching Michael's surly nervous system after his perception of the stop itself. It waits long minutes for a change of the light as its rocking energy subsides into a purely inert crouch, out of action entirely. But instead of springing forward immediately upon the change from red to green it claps open its folding door and against all rules calmly tarries for an old mother-in-law to take her sweet time *from the opposite side of the street*—crossing catercorner, jaywalking so imperiously that no vehicle denies her right-of-way, in order to examine the captain on his itinerary and deliberate her embarkation before she mounts the steps, as if she were dowager of the Key System's founding chairman; which brings on another change of the light as soon as she's finally inside with both feet flat on the floorboards; whereupon, too late, the door closes after the lady and the machine drops off into a little catnap. Thus before the very eyes of the man who most deserves its service the car loses three minutes from its schedule, just past his reach, who must cool his heels for seventeen more, peering up the Lane at least eighteen times in the interval in order to be prepared for outwardbounding in its successor with his meiny intact, and growling in his teeth "Hurry up and wait!"

The amblers who had been dropped in front of them, like others who came all the way on foot, were proceeding to the African Methodist Episcopal, a massive and flourishing temple down the Chapman's side street, quiet gentlemen in bright hats and more animated ladies of horizontal decoration, with little need for haste because it was still only ten thirty. When the surface tension of Michael's chagrin had somewhat relaxed (as he watched very hard for the next streetcar) he remarked at large that "Today's Palm Sunday." And Ruth said, as she did every week, "We ought to go to church some Sunday. The boys should be in Sunday School." "Yeah" he replied politely. "I don't want to go to Sunday School!" Jonathan protested as usual.

Jonathan and Matthew then dropped their impedimenta at the waiting post and swarmed the hopping blocks of the wide concrete sidewalk in front of the Just-As-Good Laboratories, a storefront manufactory (housing also sales and service) for prosthetic devices custom-made, two or three samples of which—nothing exciting, just legs and arms—were genteely displayed upon retables covered with velvet, the predellas of which served as backdrops for various professional certificates and seals of approval, the whole bathed in a soft fluorescent light that enhanced the color of flesh. This illumination emanated from hidden fixtures day and night in all seasons, the little stage presenting itself as a constant altar of hope for the maimed of the world. So successful was the little enterprise the boys hopped in front of that even the rich were required to make appointments for fittings several weeks in advance. Out here in the marches half way to Berkeley you wouldnt be seen by anyone you knew and yet it was close to the hospitals. This quiet shop was altogether more exclusive than the most discreet and secure death parlors that lit up finer brighter sections of the long straight thoroughfare, for though the latter could match the former in discrimination among clients they could scarcely maintain such an efficiently scheduled allocation of sales. In short, Just-As-Good had a corner on the personal extremity-market, and this explained the fact that it had never bothered to move when people like the Chapmans and the Africans came in to depreciate the real estate on the west side of the car tracks, opposite the hill of professions where doctors dentists and psychologists held office in the daytime. The boys were used to the limbs in the window and paid them no heed during hopscotch.

Now Roger notices his Pop and laughs. He moves from his mother's skirt to hug his father's big legs, Ruth transferring his dependent hand from her own to Michael's. "Daa-ee!" He dawdles about the baggy trousers, clutching confidently with his free hand, the caressive grasp of an affectionate citizen of the kingdom of heaven, while he experiments with his new discoveries in voice: "Baa-gaa, bar-gaa, bar-guy, bar-gee, bar-gow, bar-go, baa-gaa, bar-guy, baa-aa-gee-ee. . . ." Chant-song. Over and over again.

{*Postulants only:* GO TO (6) SA.03, page 65.}

(5)
HY.02

SYNECTIC METHOD OF DIAGNOSTIC CORRELATION

> In order to define a deep statement it is first
> necessary to define a clear statement. A clear
> statement is one to which the contrary state-
> ment is either true or false. A deep statement
> is a statement to which the contrary is another
> deep statement.
>
> —NEILS BOHR

Michael Chapman's Statement to the Arnheim Foundation
in Support of his Application for a Grant

[1] My request for patronage rests upon the assumption that this Foundation recognizes the scientific value of analyzing the administration of human affairs, and upon the hope that it does not abhor intellectual emotion.
I propose to spend a year developing the theory and practice of a statistical
technique that I call the Synectic Method of Diagnostic Correlation. I
would report the results of this work in an extensive essay.

The concepts of S M D C grew out of experience with petty commercial problems. They have been applied to large-scale realms of abstract
thought. But the Method is nothing if it is not practical, and that alone
will insure its survival, once planted, in this "pragmatical pig of a world."

Indeed it would be surprising if this generation did not spawn its like somewhere else on the globe, for its opportunity in cultural evolution is clearly at hand, so nicely does it meet the new world-historical task of coping with blizzards of data, even as science's need for Newton's fluxions was met by Leibniz too. It is thus in haste that I address my appeal.

The basic idea of S M D C is simple enough, involving neither complex statistics nor advanced mathematics. At the same time it has proven to lie beyond the grasp of ordinary empirical minds illiberally trained. For most administrators (to say nothing of intellectuals) its tentative, indirect, but comprehensive approach to a taxonomic universe of data is too much of a departure from the hard-won habits of conventional analysis. It is impossible for me to make my case within the ranks of either business or academic institutions without a more patient and professional presentation than I can now afford. Innovation must be disarmingly introduced if it is to take hold in the brains of those who hold office by virtue of cognitive facility or social talent rather than of the critical imagination to entertain challenges to the dogma of their church triumphant.

Other foundations have refused to consider my request for support on the grounds that I am not sponsored by some of those whose judgment I seek help to overturn. Surely you will agree that endowed funds for philanthropic enterprise sometimes frustrate their own avowed purpose by fostering opportunity only for workers who are put forward by the creatures of established professions. Awards commonly hinder the advancement of arts and sciences by crowding the nation's laboratories, studios, and editorial offices with homeostatically reproducing phagocytes such as those that are hosted by Leviathan himself. It goes particularly hard for an antigen accredited by not so much as a single diploma, publication, or disciple.

Therefore I request subvention for the time and means to acquaint myself with the mathematical language and documentation required of petitioners—whereupon (though there is no remedy for my lack of a respectable *curriculum vitae*) I could hope at least that the Arnheim Foundation would vouch for its own exploratory investment when the time came for me to search out funds for full-scale employment of S M D C in one or more of the social sciences. I believe it is not unusual for a small grant from one charitable institution to breed a larger one from another. With a year of independent livelihood I could prepare my argument in full dress, partly by illuminating the limitations of orthodox methods and partly by canvassing problems that can hardly be attacked by them at all. Yet the experience of working with hypothetical paradigms would undoubtedly suggest ancillary applications of standard mathematics (such as matrix algebra, set theory, topology, differential equations, or vector analysis) for fuller exploitation of my approach.

[2] S M D C is called *Synectic* because it joins disparate categories of data (even if expressed in a variety of units); *diagnostic* because it discovers func-

tional syndromes of real or factitious systems; and *correlation* because it relates an unlimited number of values to each other. Its usefulness is confined to situations or operations where at least several entities can be compared in terms of the same set of attributes. Its effectiveness is limited by the wit and judgment of whoever constructs and arrays the categories of description, and (at least at this stage of its development) by the investigator's talent for analytical interpretation. With these qualifications, S M D C 's power to detect causal or synchronistic patterns in a welter of mutually independent variables is far broader and more systematic than that of orthodox statistical procedures. The more the data that is brought to bear, the greater its advantage.

Business diagnosis, for example, is ordinarily taken no further than what can be expressed with a few operating and balance sheet ratios, each of which reflects no more than three or four conventional financial measurements; at most it resorts statistically to a number of small multiple correlations that are not readily related to each other for useful reporting. Commercial research usually spins an otiosely complicated web out of oversimplified selections from the blooming buzzing superorganic world in which control is intended.

Sometimes certain special etiological relationships that are particularly sought out may be estimated or confirmed with the apparatus of standard statistics, but unless analysis is undertaken by endless mechanical testing of small combinations any heuristic results are purely accidental. By this new method, in contrast, one can simultaneously scan many "profiles" or hypothetical patterns to determine reciprocities, appositions, and affinities that may otherwise be obscured by the myriad data.

Furthermore, whether or not S M D C is put to diagnostic use, it offers discriminations that may in themselves serve a primarily taxonomic purpose. In displaying the sets of values that characterize an entity, and in comparing such sets with others, it takes into account all available data relevant in various degrees to one's initial definitions. Indeed all criteria for classification can be regarded as tentative, for the specifications used in codification may be experimentally chosen and freely replaced.

The paramount convenience of S M D C is that no quantified bit of knowledge or conjecture about an entity or group of entities need be excluded from any one provisional classification. A phenomenological description freed of nominalistic bias as well as perceptual habit may become an evaluation that takes into consideration resources, function, environment, and incentive.

After the following characterization of the Method I shall give a practical illustration, and then mention a few conceivable ramifications of theory.

[3] Analysands, called *entities*, are represented by the rows of a matrix, and each matrix comprises a set of entities (or a set of sets) and their

attributes known as *categories*. Each matrix *plane* describes one independent set of data in an artificial system expressed by the terms of an indefinite number of *columns*, one for each *category* of data. Every specification, property, condition, or statistic (which may include subjective evaluations)—so long as it can be measured in numbers for each of the entities—is assigned a separate column. The units in which values are expressed must be homogeneous only within a column—e g , dollars, dozens, horsepower, miles, square feet, file-drawer inches, pairs of wings, bushels, daily average pounds of milk, number of female children between one and ten years of age, number of reciprocally resolved coitions, number of first-choice or n^{th}-choice selections in a public opinion poll. The columns, as encountered in reading across a row, may wholly differ from each other in respect to the nature of the values they indicate. The effectiveness of analysis depends largely upon discretionary grouping and sequential arrangement of categories. The design of each system is a matter of rational art acquired only in practice.

Categorical data that vary with time or occasion may be arrayed in a third dimension for purposes of etiological research. For such depth-analysis, intervals or sequential cross-sections of time are represented by a series of parallel matrix planes perpendicular to a third rectilinear axis, each of which, one behind another in congruent format, presents a separate synchronistic or pseudo-synchronistic array.

A *cell*, at the intersection of a row and column, represents one datum or virtual fact. The line of data perpendicular to a matrix at a cell is called a *stick*, which is therefore a time-series or quasi-time-series of cells that are homogeneous in respect to both entity and category. The vertical perpendicular plane intersecting a set of matrices at some column is known as a *lattice*; it contains "diachronistic" data about all entities in terms of one category only. The perpendicular plane intersecting a set of matrices along some row is a *grid*—a horizontal slice containing all data for a single entity through time or quasi-time.

[4] Since many of the columns (and lattices) are ordinarily disparate with each other in terms of units, scale, or order of magnitude, the numeric tabulation remains uninteresting until all values are transformed into common terms. This conversion of raw data is accomplished in at least and especially the first of two ways: (1) by summing each column's data independently and representing each entity's share as a percentage of the homogeneous columnar total; (2) by summing each stick and likewise calculating each cell's share of a stick's historical or quasi-historical total.

At least two numbers are therefore entered in every cell, the first of which usually fades out of consideration, except for occasional reference, after preliminary inspection of the matrix:

1. The raw datum expressed in its original units.
2. The entity's percentage share of a category's total in its own single-plane column.
3. The entity's percentage total of a category's total in its own multiple-plane stick (through the third dimension, showing its relative "historical" weight).

These two or three figures in a cell very simply imply the absolute sum (= 100%) of the column or stick in case it is not displayed outside the matrix.

[5] Descriptors of an x, y, z coordinate system may be used to elaborate or generalize the properties of the rectoparallelepiped thus constructed.

Since each relative attribute of an entity is treated as a variable dependent upon the total numeric value of the "whole" category for all entities of the chosen universe, its categorical share may change through time—even though its absolute value remains constant—as a result of changes in other entities of the group. Rows of percentages are still less representative of objective reality to the degree that the categories may indicate potential, uncertain, or even specious attributes. They may include environmental factors or extraneous estimates that are not intrinsic to an entity.

In short, I propose that any uniform colligation of things, agents, or abstract components—natural or artificial, real or fictitious—may be treated as an arbitrary whole for the purposes of comparing their relative attributes, whether or not they bear logical, genetic, or operational relationship to each other. This artificial framework may be regarded most generally as a cross-sectional sampling from the history of a pseudo-system. The complex of feigned associations, composed of natural and/or artifactual and/or subjective parts, may reveal a pattern of causal or other significant relationships between the constituent attributes of an entity. The quiddity of real or imaginary definitions is explored by organizing them on paper.

[6] In the analysis of individual entities—reading rows of percentages like staves of music the length of a matrix—the value of any one category can be taken as a tentative criterion for the others. Consider the liberal reasoning invited by this simplified hypothetical example:

The *Sch. Our Lady of Good Voyage*, like twelve others, is counted as $1/13$ or 7.7% of independent Portuguese and Italian fishing boats selected for analysis from the Gloucester fleet, but she bulks as 10% of the group's total tonnage. The latter index, that of weight, seems a good norm upon which to base expectations of performance; yet since the acid test is return-on-investment (R O I) rather than design-efficiency alone, it might be best to keep in mind the criterion of acquisition cost, which happens to be 15% of this theoretical squadron, or else of last year's total costs, which are 11%. But we find that on any accounting she yields more than her share (12%) of the meretriciously totalled profits.

This high-liner's attractive characteristics can be drawn by comparing these figures with the following indications of her physique and manner of operation. She is built for 11% of the hold capacity by volume, but the surface area of her sails is only 6%; under power her cruising range is 16% of the sum of all cruising ranges, her actual fuel costs 15%; she carries only 2% percent of the dories but she hails 18% of the trip-loads by logging 17% of the fishing days at sea, crediting herself with 12% of the catch by weight and 21% by market value; she is hauled up for repair 5% of the group's total marine-railway time, at 7% of the total yard costs, although she was built with 9% of the summed lengths, 11% of the beams, and 17% of the horsepower; she is manned by only 5% of the fishermen, but their personal earnings are 17% of the total; her captain has had 16% of the years of schooling attended by all the captains, and the crew 45%, with 40% of the children who are high school graduates; she has 50% of the divorced men, 48% of those with two children or less, 3% of those with more than five; her men account for 5% of annual attendance at Mass, but 10% of the total church offerings; they pay 21% of real estate and 29% of income taxes, and suffer 18% of the heart attacks.

The same calculations might well be made for five or ten separate years in order to trace the changes in one category that may affect another, and all the relative results of aging.

These categories, and many more (limited only by the availability of data), may be grouped in any logical or convenient order—for instance, under the headings of Investment, Resources Used, Input, Output—with scores or hundreds of detail columns. It may be found useful to show each boat's row of percentages as a broken-line graphic profile, but even by simply reading the horizontally tabulated numbers, glancing back and forth to compare one attribute with any other, owners, naval architects, tax assessors, and insurers can appraise the *Our Lady's* performance and diagnose the reasons for her success, so that they may carry forward, modify, or reject her various features and practices in the construction and management of new boats, or perhaps indemnify her loss.

It's obvious that this vessel is entitled to the title "Schooner" by courtesy alone: she's already a hybrid trawler. Future diesel draggers, her own descendants, will bring her more into line with her share of the statistical universe by introducing improvements of design and equipment (if not of rational management) in the rest of the squadron, especially by further exploiting the advantages of infernal consumption engines.

When more categories are entered into the array, some of them related to success in very subtle ways, others apparently irrelevant (such as the time spent by captains in reading novels), critically controllable elements may be isolated in unexpected areas of management—hours of sleep at sea, for instance, or dietary ingredients at sea and at home, or preventive main-

tenance expenditures on electronic devices. In this way the application of
S M D C can accelerate the evolution of management as well as vessel design.

In my example the entities are somewhat associated in the real world,
if only by virtue of place, time, and custom. The artificiality of the system
is therefore not as clear as it would be in other examples. Yet even boats
from the same port are not necessarily related to each other beyond their
common membership in a purely abstract set that is arbitrarily defined,
perhaps only according to which owners happen to keep the required
records and are willing to submit them. The appearance of system arises
from the ontological device of measuring the properties of component
units as proportions of absolute quantities determined by unnatural selection. The illustration would have been general if I had made up a larger
flotilla of one vessel each from San Francisco, Monterey, Eureka, Seattle,
Sitka, Campeche, Wakayama, Lingayen, Haiphong, Basrah, Piraeus,
Palermo, Barcelona, Cherbourg, Grimsby, Galway, Sag Harbor, Tani, Point
Judith, Lunenberg, and St. John's, as well as Nantucket, New Bedford,
Portland, and Gloucester.

Thus the purely abstract organization of entities can be raised to high
degrees of systemic unreality by incorporating entities that are socially or
geographically isolated into a pseudo-universe that makes possible the
practical analysis of each of them, or of the class typified by each. The art
of diagnosis can be carried further by constructing a hierarchy of entity-
classes within which comparisons can be made at various taxonomic levels
of aggregation by a pyramid of matrices based on any number of individuals and rising through species, genera, families, and orders to a grand set
of phyla. Or, having compared unique boats in local groups, you may
study the efficiency of ports, nations, and amphictyonies by summing the
absolute values of all categories and converting them to shares of a quasi-
universal whole.

[7] The entities of an S M D C composition would seldom be concentrated enough to represent the interactive components of a biological
system. They are discrete and comparatively few—mutually exclusive
individuals (or sub-groups) of the proportionalized whole. You might say
that the entities together dispose of each chosen attribute exhaustively, but
even in an arbitrary system the number of attributes, as in life, is limited
in principle only by infinity. Leaving aside the numberless specifications
that are not attempted at all, furthermore, some y-axis descriptors may be
subtly separated (in parallel) from their gross categories. In other words,
the horizontal positioning and grouping of columns is a matter more of art
than of science. Definitions may dispute each other or even overlap, and
the schedule may include vague or hypothetical data.

In a Medieval curriculum, because of this liberal orismology and taxonomy, S M D C would have fallen not into the *Quadrivium* of arithmetic,
geometry, astronomy, and music but into the anti-pythagorean *Trivium* of

logic, grammar, and rhetoric. Though derived from counted or measured quantities, its categorical percentages resemble ordinal epithets in that (like words and unlike most numbers) their meanings change with context.

As previously mentioned, S M D C analysis can sometimes be served by incorporating opinion or speculation. It is not only the subjective judgments of observers that are permitted to enter into the pattern of shared attributes that distinguishes one entity from another but also the entities' quantified estimates of themselves. Obscure motives and causes are sometimes detectible when their professed representations or shadows are proportionalized in the light of similarly proportionalized facts.

In constructing categories and deploying them across the page a practitioner of S M D C art will usually face questions of visual as well as syntactical composition. For example, should each column of conjecture be set next to its objective correlative or segregated within a distant visual group by epistemological modality? Should columns that express calculated combinations of data or summarize more detailed categories appear together in a compendium at the beginning of the display, or should they immediately accompany their categorical factors or components? The analyst is free to order his columns as they suit his intuition and special interests, but an artful sequence is crucial to any direct translation of the numbers into a line-graph "profile".

Generally speaking, according to the rhythmic or synthetic configuration of clusters—of rows as well as columns—an S M D C array can be either merely the first step in analysis or an immediate source of interpretive communication. A skillfully designed "profile" is also crucial to pattern-recognition procedures, where characteristic similarities must be distinguished from spurious data and grouped by inspection or by mathematical iterations. As long as it remains unnecessary to consider the effects of absolute size, "curves" may be grouped into taxa based upon their general shapes or upon certain critical segments of their shape.

[I have here left undeveloped whatever can be expressed only in the language of diagram; but this omission will do nothing to worsen the prejudice of lawyers and accountants on your awards committee.]

[8] At some excursus in my research I may provisionally drop the rectoparallelepiped as inconvenient in application to problems beyond the type epitomized by social entities operating on regularly administered calendars. A more flexible scheme (when large-scale mechanical computation is available and when visual aids are unnecessary) may be a single matrix of unlimited length. Chronologically differentiated columns of some or all categories could be either repeated in synchronous blocks or gathered in diachronic groups, the latter alternative being appropriate when full sets of historical data are unnecessary or unavailable, since additional columns can be interpolated here and there without the full format required for planes in a third dimension.

But the chief purpose of extending a single matrix may be to abandon the three-dimensional image for an abstract geometric model of n dimensions in an unvisualized coordinate system. Let a separate dimension mutually perpendicular to the x, y, and every other subsequently posed axis represent each category in the long horizontal string. Entities can then be located as points in hyperspace. The numerical distance from the origin can be calculated, by the distance formula of the Pythagorean Theorem, as the square root of the sum of the squares of categorical percentage shares. A point's coordinates determine the magnitude and direction of a resultant vector (the hyperhypotenuse of an n-dimensional right triangle), which serves as a taxonomic index of complex characteristics. Species would be defined by clusters of points in hyperspace, and hybrids planned accordingly.

[9] One special case in my research will deserve the attention of philosophy. It is highly improbable but not impossible that an entity attain to perfect normality in its relative physiognomy, sharing equally in all the categorical data of its set. In this ideal situation the order of columns is entirely insignificant, for the graphic representation is a straight line. This level profile (representing a row of repeated percentages) suggests paradox.

In one view the shapeless configuration of a straight line in a highly populated universe stands for a uniformly average entity without character or idiosyncrasy. In real systems one would be inclined to associate such a description with random distribution and degraded or unavailable energy. It smacks of the highest probability. But how can a character of maximum probability be reconciled with its minimum probability of occurrence?

This question is complicated by the expectation that such uniformity in the relative attributes of one entity (if significantly large) would be accompanied by an increased probability that co-entities would tend to settle into a straight-line pattern. In such an event would the large and small entities of a superorganic system tend to average out in size as well as shape, over time, under Darwinian or Lamarckian influences? Any such change in favor of uniformity at the expense of exceptional individuals contravenes the evolution of complexity.

An entity's density of complexity, or intensity, may be expressed in an n-dimensional model as the ratio of the number of inter-categorical relationships (possible direct connection between coordinates) to the volume of the rectilinear hyperpolyhedron formed by its axes, which in this special case is cuboid. Thus the intensity of a normal entity varies as

$$\frac{n^2-n}{2s^n},$$

where s is the entity's equal share of all attributes and n is the number of attributes. Intensity increases with diminishment of share. Such entities when relatively small in respect to the whole system, either because of their own absolute size or because of a large population, therefore seem more intense than their colleagues. Does it follow, according to thermodynamic principles, that small entities are less probable than abnormally large ones?

[10] In my final report I would discuss several other questions and paradoxical inferences arising from attempts to consider relative pseudosystems as if they were real. I hope to formulate a theory of the differences between real systems (whether natural or artificial) and those that are figmented to an even greater degree than figures subjectively constructed in the sky from stars individually belonging to unequal cosmic histories.

Among my concerns will be the problem of how to handle negative data: overdraft, debt, want, desire, renouncement—whatever may be represented by a minus sign. When such a number is encountered in a column that is positive in total (leaving aside the special case in which the total is zero) the share must be expressed as a negative percentage; hence the shares of complementary entities will sum to more than 100% Certainly some means should be found to prevent absurd visual profiles, but the metaphysical questions are more important. A negative share seems analogous to negative probability. Such a notion anyway illustrates the need for Keats's "negative capability" in science.

In general these artificated structures may be regarded as immortal but not eternal systems—without purpose, powers of self-perpetuation, or mnemonic inertia: systems because they temporarily relate entities to each other by intellectual transformations. They fall into the class of fictitious systems (as distinguished from real systems of nature, society, or artifact) that comprises virtual objects in figmented relationship.

If I have occasion to broaden my inquiry I hope to advance theorems in this new field of applied quasi-mathematics. The monograph I propose to write as your client, however, will range no further into theoretical territory than its anticipated title implies: *Prolegomena to Any Future Metaphysics That Will Be Able to Present Itself as an Art of Fictive Systems.*

[11] Meanwhile I offer S M D C simply as technic. It can be used to good social purpose in evaluating educational institutions and, in turn, their own departments; in allocating the commonwealth's civil and military budget; in comparing the political economies of states; in rating the efficiency of ships, aircraft, and army units; in studying congregations; in administering libraries; in suggesting epidemiological causes (especially for nutritional deficiencies, hypertension, certain heart diseases and cancers); in proposing assessments and disbursements for the United Nations; in improving the management of hospitals; in controlling crime; in advancing conservation and birth control; in planning political campaigns; in appraising officials; and in rationalizing the distribution of capitalism's finest fruit by foundation potlatch. But its usefulness to private enterprise could be realized more readily. Your Founder would have appreciated its

advantages in controlling his companies and their divisions, since it excels money itself as common expression of the elements that businessmen claim to manage.

[12] The requested grant would cover my family's living expenses for a year, rental of a small working office, and purchase of a desktop printing calculator.

{*Postulants only:* **THE END.** You are matriculated.}

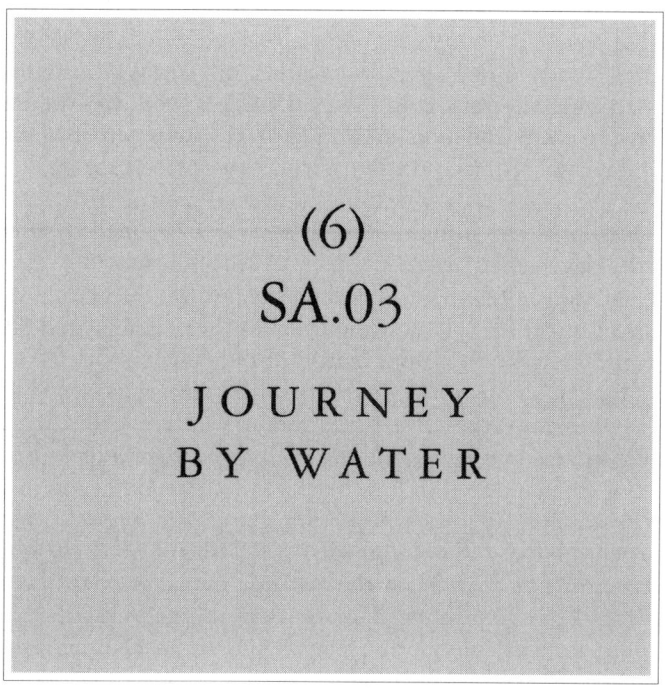

(6)

SA.03

JOURNEY BY WATER

*T*he journey outward was not despairingly difficult. The Chapmans were an hour late in getting started and they lost time at every step. But travel does take time. One must accept the fact that it takes agonizing time to travel if he doesnt have staff and equipage at his disposal with everything paid for by an employer. Travel takes time especially when travel is one's greatest pleasure. And in this case it took time most of all because it was not Michael's lot to travel light.

Light! The cool weather had seemed to call for heavy precautions against the various possible conditions on the several dissimilar segments of their route, qualified of course by the diversity of souls on trek: blankets, extra clothes, changes of clothes, buskins, backdrops, machinery for changes of scene, offerings of food and libations in more than one kind, and everything a troupe of mummers could think of save incense, trap door, and derrick for a god. Yet they did get under way without too many superfluities, and they managed to move along.

To travel in the spring! By water, by rail: in the most interesting common carriers! To Michael the spring was no real spring, only a California spring, but there was a new freshness everywhere, as if all the streets had been cleaned at once. The great potential energy of a fresh new day—any day but particularly a day off duty, weather be damned—was scarcely to be contained by a vigorous man's skin. Unlike a workday, the balance of which is put to waste the moment you leave the house on your way to the shop, this day was still not wasted beyond the proportion of its expired hours.

Each person of the mutual retinue severally rationed or frittered an unexpectedly intensified appetite for just such a trip. At destination, released from the confinement of vehicles, some would unstint and leave little of their hunger for the return journey in the degraded end of the day; another would be the wisest, as a matter of temperament, deferring to the pleasure of others, in measured doubt as to the importance of objects they set store by; but only the close-fisted father would continually calculate his reserves on the journey out as he exchanged fussbudget ergs for the electromotive force induced in him by the kinetic stimulations of travel.

Notwithstanding fury at a departure gone awry he was commencing his spree at a high bias of bodily goodwill, for when he had come to break- fast his capacitor was charged to the last microfarad, perhaps even begin- ning to leak a little like a cow that wants milking, simply because until that late hour he had done nothing at all but lie in bed, since midnight having neither cast seed nor troubled himself with work. The boys, for the time being, were containing themselves with marvelous sagacity. The baby studied life and amused himself, alternately. And now that the jaunt no longer hinged upon efficient preparation Ruth dreamily accommodated her attention to the various male moods in whose service she had already suffered the equivalent of a good day's moil. As rear guard she soared on the wings of the morning resting as she rode. More hard slogging was yet to come.

Those old enough to hope were repletely sanguine, each according to individual experience memory or purpose. He who had no hope, immedi- ate faith and charity being all he knew, seemed as forward-looking as the others (especially when with the others on foot he rode seated out in front), displaying his equanimity. Any cloud of discomfort or squall of anger that might perturb his spirit was to be no more alarming than that which would have crossed his brow on the same day of his life if he'd stayed home in familiar surroundings, thanks to the presence of the same mother. In his superiority to extrinsic events he dismissed the possibility of newly transcendent fears.

Eagerly highspirited cheerful and joyous though they all were, it was not on any first-class ticket that they voyaged from the land of departed oaks to the park outside Golden Gate. Brave words careful intentions and physical ebullition cannot breast the ebb tide we swarm in, no mat- ter how often we fortify our spirits with recharges and countercharges.

This expedition was mere skin off the noses of three playboys in their regenerative nonages; but Michael and Ruth, quite naturally, were never to fully recover from it. Out into the atmosphere and down into the public benches on which they sat seeped the irreversible energy that is exacted of middle age under the best of conditions by fourth-class travel—as well as by the declining arrow of time itself. You always spend what you pay for.

Don't think that what Michael paid wasnt something. A trickle of dimes quarters and half-dollars for a man like him adds up. Even with a free-fare and two half-fares a number of Federal Reserve bills were broken up just to get where they were going and home again, not counting much greater disbursements for the pleasure of shoddy ad hoc nourishment in transit and on location. No blame to him then that in the anxiety of his providence right at the outset he firmly denied the little woman's request that he yield to the shortsighted importunity of Matthew and Jonathan when they clamored for purchases at the buffet in the ferryboat. It seemed to the chief-executive-treasurer an absurd plea for vulgar indulgence of waste, inasmuch as breakfast was over and lunch was still to come. She had known of old that he hated to yield to the popular custom of patronizing vendors simply because their facilities were at hand; and now she agreed that the time it would have taken for their turn at the thronged counter should be preempted by an inspection tour of the ship and a survey of all the artifacts to be seen on the waters and margins of the great Bay. She had nothing to say against fulfilling the purposes for which he had planned their elaborate itinerary (although it would have been simpler cheaper and quicker to get to San Francisco by taking the train across the bridge). But his argument seemed irrelevant: they carried with them enough sand-wiches apples oranges salads cupcakes prunes raisins cucumbers bread chicken cookies bananas coffee milk and other aphrodisiacs to content a platoon of platitudinous menfolk-feeding womenfolk of French shopkeepers carrying sunshades on a bank of the Seine with servants to lug the hampers.

At the first stage of the way as at so many other moments of every day Roger was Michael's one unadulterated delight. The child was still clean and dry both outside and inside his clothes. Nothing did he demand or criticize. A father's plans were good enough for him. For the present he took no thought for what he should eat or for what he should drink. Like a lily of the field his face turned with the sun and wind of his family's climate. No will had yet rooted itself in his head, nor fear nor aggression, to resist his father's pedagogy. Early on the way he was still open to whatever he saw of that which took place before his new eyes. Yet his selection of objects from moment to moment was clearly so much wiser than his tutor's that the tutor sometimes had to neglect his own interests in a vain effort to learn from his youngest pupil.

Therefore it was a tribute of remarkable respect as well as love, being the man he was and no St Christopher by temperament, that he hoisted the child's collapsible gig on and off high-platformed streetcars without complaint while carrying the child himself and two or three stone of other impedimenta, directing the deployment of his people among available seats, coordinating descents at split-second junctures, and warning the older boys against loss of the baggage they had been charged to carry.

Sitting on his old man's lap in his coat of many colors (best dressed of the lot) at the window of one royal barge after another Roger patiently awaited pleasures to come while providing pleasure to all who beheld him.

Yet his enjoyment of travel was more kinesthetic than cognitive and, except for some pleasant vibrations that reached him through his father's body, today's sally did not yet fill the bill insofar as he still had no opportunity to practice proprioceptive locomotion. Blithely but politely he ignored his father's attempts to make esse in intellectu certain elements of the passing scene that appeared esse in re. In fact he dismissed all strange and wonderful res outside the windows in favor of interesting res in and on the familiar person of the man (less familiar however than the woman who was always on hand at home as well as out here among moving places). Trying to pull things out of the jacket he was pressed against; finally succeeding at a side-pocket

Ruth made such studies all year round, and with more success; she rested from them now, gazing out the window in repose seeing nothing feeling everything that made her lifework seem good, drowsily lulled by rhythmic rolling motions not greatly unlike the sways and lunges of the vessel she had begun in as the golden egg of her own mother's futile lifework. She the girlchild poor weak Ruth hoped she had put a stop to the self-perpetuating transmigration of love's ignorant selfishness that she had been born to from a long line of mothers. Would he ever see that she had rescued his boys? Not by avoiding procreation but by making it her profession she had loosened her mother's fingers from the future, and without help or sympathy, without the courage and talent she used to pray for at school, without the faculty to apply or prove any other way all the things she knew through failure. Three times she had launched afresh the life first launched by Eve. Doubtless she'd die young, for her success was leaving its ravages and it was not yet even half complete. The pain of self-doubt still sometimes made the housework seem too hard. But she was ready to bear a girlchild and take the risk of becoming the mother of a woman to whom she could point out the door to a walled garden that seemed secret it was so forgotten by all the women who unknowingly wandered in search of it—which was the supreme test, to be the mother of a mother. How different from pushing out another bouncing baby boy! Boys are sailors

with the book which his father had brought along out of some absurd notion that he might on occasion find himself alone or unobligated for a minute or two before the day was over. "Boke-e!" said Roger. "Yes. Book!" said Michael: a word not known to have been known— indeed was not known, only in the uttering now is known.

Jonathan and Matthew are not too busy to hear. They turn around in the seat ahead and clap their hands. Ruth is not too preoccupied in the seat beside to smile her splendid sudden smile that gladdens the heart of anyone who sees it, a beautiful lady-mother, a beautiful and desirable lady both to those who want wives and to those who want mothers, though since she sits on the aisle so that Michael can hold Roger to the window one might not be quite sure that she is mated to the father or dedicated to the child if it werent for the field equipment she's holding. "Put it back!" the man says. Boy obeys clumsily: one of his earliest obediences. Boy and man very interested in each other. Boy interested in father as a man, as the man; father interested in boy as the child of his old age. [Has anyone ever said he looks like me? Incredible that he should not be my spit and image.] Woman and other children silently congratulate society on this mutual

or poets, slow or quick at learning, always measuring or being measured up. She and Michael were so lucky that the multiple fruit of their poorly matched love was greening without blight. Yet to make a girlbaby would be like having the Ruth her mother had had the chance to bring up—perhaps smarter and more beautiful but at least measureless and independent, spared at least the useless pain of believing herself to be an incompetent daughter. Above all, safer from her mother. (It was easier with future men because you didnt know enough about them to worry overly.) —But of course there should be no such test: it would be too hard on Buffalo Bull. He'd look upon it as another trick of fate, another cross to bear, another nail in his coffin. And she herself was almost too tired. Thirty-three already! Belly showing stretch; even losing the one advantage of small breasts, she noticed the other day standing without her clothes on: fit for a bridegroom's eyes only when she was lying on her back, or dressed in the deceitful molds worn by all mothers over twenty-three. Maybe if she were a widow, if someone came along who wanted a daughter, who wanted to cherish the mother of his daughter and of another goodman's admirable sons . . .

interest because it keeps himself in good spirits like beer and makes him overlook the defects of other family individuals and of larger entities within more general organizations.

Roger's temper was as sweet as a fairy tale. How could Ruth remain so composed as his lucky mother, or rather keep her motherlove so unostentatious that to anyone but her husband it was known through its effects alone? Would she be any different with her stepchildren, the oafs and

ninnies that a successor to himself might merge with the Chapman boys—
if there was any guy that liked becoming a family man as much as all that?

At every transfer point the leader would be fussing and puffing,
counting noses, calculating herding cajoling advising insisting scolding
and all but screaming with the voice of an owl that has been hooting too
much. Before their bourn was to be gained he had to hurry them along in
every possible way, pull them away from shop windows, preach on the
shortness of life.

In Roger's view—a manchild still neutral, not yet having committed himself to objectification (though daily on the verge)—the ride was something passing by them, a background take it or leave it, relative to the mothered aseity of his family. Others there were, especially dogs, far off or a little nearer, sometimes attractive, but never really to be studied as they had no connection whatsoever with his people. He didnt expect to remember the trip anyway, and he had never looked forward to it: to him no part of it was either past or future. So memory was still to come; but then, after he became a mature second-baseman, what would remain to him from this phase of the passage out was to be no more than a single impression that marked its transition to the next—a folding steel fence infinitely longer higher harder darker and colder than the wooden barriers he found stretched across open doorways at home. From his father's arms he touched it as they waited. A great white bird hovered at the center of open sky framed by the end of the huge dim shed they were in, all seen in chiaroscuro cast by the presence of his mother behind him. This first incubated memory of the still fresh and cheerful morning chose itself from among all the things in his river of

Meanwhile it was a great day so far in the spring and summer of the morning (in fact drawing on toward the autumn). The passing scene excited senses memory or imagination. This landscape of maritime cities was neither foreign nor too well known, now reintroduced to everyone except Roger (to whom much more else remained to be introduced) from some degree of previous experience, and therefore even to Matty not at all strange. It was a field that Ruth could feel comfortable in because it contained nothing sophisticated or recondite or abstruse to cope with: natural English spoken everywhere. Indeed for her far more than merely not unfamiliar: positively rife with marks of the girl-past between childhood and Michael which she was surprised to find herself lighting on, and with those later tracings of wartime when San Francisco and its tributaries were full of officers and sailors—even after he had come to her and then gone away again to sea. How puzzling that he had been one of those disconnected restless men, sharing many of their forceful thoughts. Odd enough even that he's Michael! Who is Michael, what is he? For that matter what is any he? They're not just different in a few parts, on the chest and between the legs; they sense differently all

time that were too confused or too unconscionable to be retained, or so abrasive as to be suppressed coming from the senses before they could be differentiated by the drifting brain, which now lodged for a few seconds on the blackened pilings of the pier until they were cast loose by the movement of the waters.

But on the second stage their cicerone kept at it with two minds more amenable to his own fixed interests, leaving Roger to the mother who better assayed him. Uneasily Michael admitted to himself that Jonathan and Matthew were not quite as ready for the commonplace wonders of the world as he gave them to understand they were, that they were not yet and perhaps would never be the students of objects that he might have wished; but he made them pace the deck of the ferryboat and listen to his explanation (laboring against the wind) of every marvel in sight, including the double-ended aptitude of the fat nearly empty ark itself.

over, mathematically. It's one thing to see through their acts but quite another to find out whether they feel anything at all internally—

Internally! She closed her eyes and shifted her hips to touch his without uncrossing her ankles or allowing her knees to lose contact with each other. Last night was her latest memory of the foreigner. How long till night oh lord?

Afloat just then the bay was as unpleasant as it ever got, neither rough nor peaceful. The opaque gray-banked sky was too uniform and high, not fair nor stormy nor soft nor foggy. Beneath the cold motionless lid of such a firmament the noisy civilization of a great landlocked littoral was hushed by the passengers' chugging isolation. Between the two flat metallic plates of god's metropolitan capacitor the atmosphere of men and birds made less than a mile of unreliable dielectric. Their new platform with its rounded white housing scudded through leadenfooted antimistical whitecaps that slapped pointlessly at the shallow black hull which was driven into them across a slightly whining wind. Everything seemed to annoy the sullen hard mass of the sky whose nether coating hung overhead impassively, refusing to be imparted with the air's animation, utterly unsympathetic to the invisible currents of tidal waters. Ruth kept to the cabin with her baby, whom she stood on the varnished seat-worn bench of all classes where he could watch his heroes through generous perimeters of rectangular window.

Out on promenade the mindless wind that pressed no sail and wasted itself wherever it reached on land perhaps didnt amount to much on the Beaufort scale but it seemed magnified by the sparseness and distance of its few obstructions, and indeed by the stubborn course of the singleminded vessel that was perturbed not at all by its diagonal opposition. All too swiftly the stubby hollow duck hauled its one enthusiastic passenger across the complicated inland sea with webfooted paddlewheels spread like waterwings, slanting under the bridge on which one could cross ludicrously faster. He insisted that the boys appreciate this bare broadbeamed boat as the last of its kind, telling them what he happened to know: that in the middle of her age this train-boat, which still made the last Southern Pacific connection from the Atlantic coast, had been rebuilt by the old Pacific Northwestern Railway into the largest passenger ferry in the world; that in one trip she could be used for an annual picnic to carry the entire complement of a battleship to the beach; and that she was the one that had taken him out on the Bay to Treasure Island with a whole train's draft of sailors right off a week of cattle cars. She still conveyed some transcontinentals nowadays, travelers from Bar Harbor Boston and Baltimore, New Yorkers and Pennsylvanians cussedly resisting the convenience of airplanes, who preferred like themselves to stand out in the sea air for a last half hour of their westward journey, notwithstanding that today it was too raw for the few such pilgrims that had gotten off the boat-train from Chicago.

But even though the boat was not in ballast she gave no heed to the nasty little domestic waves as she was urged to do by this local seadog who swayed back and forth athwartship flexing his knees like an old salt; not a jot or tittle of ocean swell could he transfer from his two pillars to the unexcitable gray deck he mounted. Jonathan and Matthew treaded innocently, as on land. Nothing could faze the paired water wheels that rowed the great ugly mill with implacable will across the final dished-out valley of the fatherland, levelly ignoring the churned seapups yapping at her skirts. To the walking-beam steamer such a uniformly turbulent surface was of no more account than tumbleweeds to the hurtling ranks of wheels that highballed the California Zephyr across the Nevada desert on taut straight rails cleanly ballasted on crushed gray rock. The hollow ferry met her schedule as flatly as an excursion boat ascending the robustless Charles in grassybanked August.

But the wind came whistling colder as they got out into the stream. No need for the wind to be so cold in this climate. True, there was no call for anyone to stand out in it. Even so, a churlish whimpering wind something between breeze and gale angers a man when he has graciously of his own free will exposed himself to the elements asking for either smooth blue sky or rollicking storm.

Shouting hoarsely he showed them shipyards Navy beauties anchored merchantmen barges romantic tugs navigation aids and near or distant bridges. He pointed out before it could be seen the tower on the hill where once stood a mast which even after its telegraphic function was obsoleted by electrical messages had served to suspend and drop the noon time-ball to synchronize the chronometers of a hundred ships from the seven seas. In exploitation of this rare opportunity all features of the moving azimuth were impressed upon the boys as they shivered at their father's side—that they might not fail to take interest, that they might draw upon a rich fund of images during abstract lectures at home. He brooked no diversion of attention, no talk of yesterday or tomorrow, still less any suggestion of retreat to the leeward whence most of the best would be lost to view, whence nothing could be seen but the pink and whited suburbs of the contra costa they were leaving behind, its once ineffable hills and savannahs first despoiled by seaworn pioneers athirst for the ownership of any land at all.

By way of geography history and brute economics the father tried to imprint upon the tabula rasas of his senior sons the faraway jaws of the bay's northern channel hard under the great mountain of western culture's westermost seacoast where through straits and antechambers of inner gulfs obscured by the hills of the main that barricaded the broad plain of milk and honey against books and slums the merging rivers of sacrament and evangel muddied the salt waters of Poseidon's vast ramified salient though rising with his tides far up into the mesopotamian valley and killed off the salmon with unstemmable and irreversible silt first tailed from gold long since spent but still eroding from torn banks and now thickened with the sewage of a million trash-consumers. With a thrill that he did not succeed in conveying he was glad to report that ocean ships bound for Europe and Asia could now navigate to Stockton 70 miles away across flat willow-banked fields thanks to dredges and new inland piers at the very heart of agriculture and that perhaps even the State Capital would someday dig a century's alluvium from the bottom of its own naturally greater channel and compete for the world's grain trade. But it was melancholy to teach them that the railroads and highways had superseded lovely steamboats elegant and homely alike in all the rivers and creeks leading to the grand estuary, some of them indeed not very long gone, although none of those sternwheelers ever matched famous old sidewheeler *Chrysopolis* (whose name he glossed) that once made it to Sacramento under the flag of the California Steam Navigation Company at only a dollar a head (if you didnt take a cabin) in five and a third hours. They seemed a little more truly amazed when he told them the funny thing was that the first steamboat on the bay had been Russian, brought down from Alaska even before the Gold Rush.

He directed their admiration also to the Pacific's bleak opening at the Golden Gate spanned by the lovely marvel of engineering which alas had been designed by ungrateful and shortsighted men not to carry rails. Beyond that very edge and last construction of congenial humanity, except for a few scattered colonies spoken of as possessions or manifest mandates all the way to the land of the setting sun, lay nothing but the whale-prairies of stateless Oceanus.

Save in war. [*Greetings from the President!*] In war that immense naked side of the planet had been humanly occupied—not permanently, not with railroads or housed women, but one meridian or parallel at a time, in knots or yards or footholds—with flying floating crawling instruments of transformed chemical force, legions of steered engines swarming first one way then the other on the most remote flank of the sphere where there were never Canaanites Britons or red Indians to displace, only myriad tons of salt water and a few palm trees. It's the tract of the world in which it's easiest for men to suffer a loosening of centripetality and drop off into eons of black nothingness, to be absolutely missed in action in, for there is nothing on that ocean to cling to, especially at night when you regard stars as the nearest population. You think only your frail bark's tenuous adhesion to brine and the water's own surface tension reinforce weakened gravity in preventing you and ocean itself from being dropped into space for lagging behind the sun. On such campaign it isn't so much your own geotropic mass that binds you to earth as the gravity centered between millions of pairs of legs walking the homeland under hip-swung skirts. Yet there's no love in all those empty inhuman latitudes and longitudes except the heartless vegetative kisses of jellyfish the diabolic storge of giant manta ray madonnas or the infernal affection of gap-lipped sharks; and never a ritual but the pelagic mile-wide courtship of nobles once looked upon by Ishmael but now scattered by envious harpoon guns and suspicious depth-charges. Not one of the coral-wreathed peaks that break the heaving swells of the vast gibbous medium between west and east (otherwise unopposed in months of gathering momentum and even at their brightest calmest blue always longer and higher than the largest whaleboat) would ever have been touched by intellectual beauty if Taji hadn't beached on them. . . . 'Land's End'—how presumptuous were the British Isles! . . . Even USS Owhyhee anchored a little to windward of Golden Gate with women and children aboard was still lonely for a fully-minded Radio Technician. The history department of an island university couldnt civilize the Western Ocean; nor will our young Constitution. The bamboo-tinkling landfall of Yahoo is a lushly spoiling rock in a freakish clump of money bags full of whistling drunken Wahoo bustle 2000 miles beyond the outer ledge of the last continental shelf at the uttermost end of the whole human universe! When you're living in Tent City on a crowded sand-spit in Pearl Harbor with nothing to do but wait for orders and breathe red dust you feel as betrayed as one of Columbus's sailors even when you turn your back to the sea and lift your eyes up those fronded slopes of hypercalifornian streets and luxurious bungalows knowing that the volcano has been tamed by residential prosperity. . . .

Having fallen into silence during this retrospection, while the boys looked for themselves, he returned to occasion's duty. "Gentlemen, that's where I sailed out into the teeth of war on a miserable afternoon in a flimsy hybrid ship that started to buck at the rollers while we were still waving to the girls on the bridge."

"Did you have *girls* on your ship, Daddy?" Jonathan was incredulous.

"God forbid! I meant on the Golden Gate Bridge, way up over our heads. It's much higher than it looks from here. Half the men were sick before we got out of sight of land even if they'd been to sea before. It was one of the most depressing times I ever went through."

Matthew took up another strand of the old seaman's yarn. "Dad, what's a high-bread ship?"

"Hybrid means baked from several different kinds of flour mixed together."

"Is that what Catholics eat in church on high days?" The poor kid dropped the thread he was tracing and led himself further astray by plucking at this new etymological clue. But he was immediately struck by the funny feeling of an invisible trap closing around him and he stopped in foolish confusion.

"Oh Matt, you don't know what you're talking about!" Jonathan said with a half-friendly grimace.

"There wasnt much eating before we got to Honolulu. Every day we heard rumors about ships being lost on the way to the Islands but some of the guys were too sick to care."

The idea of ships being lost formed itself variously in the two smaller heads, and they were expecting either vagary or vexatiously simplistic explanation from the largest head when the bows of the ferry were crossed by a rusty deeply laden freighter plowing methodically toward the aforesaid pass to sea with such steadiness of purpose that it seemed as if the engineroom telegraph had been set at three-quarter speed all morning long, though in fact there were men still on deck securing cargo hatches and coiling hawse lines. "Look look, Daddy! Look at the boat!" Matty cried.

"Yes isn't she beautiful! But a boat is a craft that can be hoisted aboard a ship." His father couldnt help instructing him.

"It's a ship, Matt!" Jonathan was as sententious as his father, but experimentally: "She's got a bone in her teeth."

"British." said the salty headman pointing at her colors. "Limey."

"They're still pulling up the bridge!" Jonathan exclaimed, rashly referring to the gangway that was only just then being hoisted inboard. "—No no, I mean the plank!" He bethought himself in time to forestall correction, or even ridicule, of which his little brother was quite capable when still smarting under one of his own jeers. "Prob'ly going to London."

"London Bridge is falling down!" was all that Matty offered.

Speculation was cut short of one accord by the joint impulse to step to the forward rail and assist at the stern's bowing insertion into the funnel of creaking groaning piles that gave way in visible waves of shock but sustained and correctly deflected *Eureka*'s final lunge after she momentarily wallowed broadside to the tidal current, backing her engines in shuddered protest against the inertia that had brought her there. For so she was called, namesake of the State motto, displayed in gold on the black nameboard mounted above them on the white pilot house, to which Michael drew the boys' attention without however letting any detail of the action on the bow/stern deck escape them. He could the more easily interpret in all directions because they had come out of the wind in slowing down to enter the shelter of this barnacled palisade. With equal concentration all three watched foamy brine churning at bay as it was jostled into the head of the slip.

They were awaited by casual landsmen at the hydraulic portcullis set into the postern of the clock-tower at the foot of Market Street where the deep intimidating waterfront covered over all the mudflats that once protected the easy-going Spanish settlement from direct contact with ships. The reversed paddles brought docking to a roiled climax. *Eureka* gave a shiver and fell silent.

The sudden blessed remission of noise for the last few feet, all effort suspended for three seconds of gliding peace, was followed by one final surge of locking power as she was grappled by hook and drawn tight to the shore's lip. To new sounds of clanking chains and whirring winches she was forcibly nuzzled into captivity. Almost before she had been manhandled to security the drawbridge descended, nearly at their feet. For Michael the brief space of cheerful warmth and agreeable repose between contrasting hustles had dignified their approach little less than the arrival of a *Queen*.

He managed the disembarkation skillfully. Nobody lost anything. Nobody was lost. Not a squabble, not a squall. Even Ruth the musing mother stepped briskly ahead. This success was especially gratifying to him because, as if they were circling the rest of the earth by land, this was to be the only landing of the entire round trip. (They were to come home on short-circuit by the bridge-train. Without that means of rapid return even Michael could not have entertained plans for a peregrination as ambitious as this one.) The going ashore went so well that it seemed much less remarkable than it was, almost like a commuting routine, chiefly because they were confronted with nothing but a level floor broad as a polo armory to stream out through—no detours, no Customs, nothing to declare. Without a hitch, as airily as if they were flashing a lifetime family pass, they proceeded through the Ferry Building—symbolic sentimental tied-off bellybutton to a city that was breaking its motherbond to the sea—out onto the grand Venetian concourse where nothing was happening on Palm Sunday.

The Embarcadero, San Francisco's broad parade and inland seawall raised over the spile bones and planks of a mud-wharfed strand that had successively advanced its contour like a siege trench against the harbor and been backfilled for venal real estate at the expense of former hills (in the manner of Boston), lay before them in undestructed desolation, a ghostly Liverpuddlian quay of commercial space and rolling stock that seemed never to be renewed and always threatened by radical displacement. Yet surely there would be work afoot on Monday, and only a little less work a year from Monday—fair enough perhaps, for a place going to waste, if it weren't for the fact that elsewhere the Gross National Product swelled from week to week.

Couldn't blame the holy day or even peace for this neglect. It was the bridge stepping highhandedly across the sky that threw a shadow on the thoroughfare, drove boatmen and teamsters landward, made them hunger for the expansive middle conditions of their time. Not the longshoremen guilding to drive wages on the docks too high but the beautiful concatenation of suspension bridges that lifted traffic clear over the waterfront on colossal pairs of shanks and carried wealth directly back and forth to highlands and hinterlands recently leveled or invested. [But it's foul play indeed that doesnt help win a war or bring someone something somewhere. Not only by its erection during Depression did this bridge make good with pork chops but it developed an Atlantis dredged up onto thitherto useless shoals between two mutually attractive cities, flung out flat by a ramped isthmus from the god-given rock once called Goat Island but now known by the name of the town that had been made into San Francisco after ceasing to celebrate its own sweet herbal creepers—as if a fairgrounds had been causewayed seaward from a Mont-Saint-Michel. The manmade islet was dubbed Treasure both for what had had to be sunk into usury in order to separate dry land from the shallows of mid-Bay and for what was to be attracted thereto; for in the last years of European peace (north of Spain), when the local masses began to ride electrified tracks slung beneath the weather deck of the nobly segmented span, the cadastral innocence of its scraped-up subaqueous soil had been adulterated with the palmed and glittering Golden Gate Exposition, then given over in part to a flying boat terminal for the China trade, and finally sold outright for a sumptuously payrolled Navy base preserving and utilizing the dinosaur halls and galleries built for that World's Fair but repainted with camouflage green mottled by the original colors, the central pavilion further improved with neat new olive barracks laid out on a grid of fine streets lined with lawnlets of lighter green. It was there at Radio Matériel School (an absurd frenchification, as coming from the US Navy, intended to mask what it may only have called attention to, namely radar and the like) that he had stood many a landlubbered "anchor watch" at night wearing undress blues with canvas leggings known as boots and a temporarily S P -brassarded peacoat gathered tight by a webbed guard belt, gazing infinitely desirous at the wonderful amber-limned city covering more hills than Rome and sparkling fabulously against the Pacific sky until paled like a sleeping princess under her lover's eyes at dawn by an opposite light rising over the campanilied acropolis across the bay where Athenian and Etruscan beauties lay sequestered from unscrupulous sailors and at last revealed in its morning colors and details as a splendid humanization of the natural grandeur that was elsewhere marred by nouveau peasant villas climbing the slopes of this landlocked valley beloved of ships.] It lured more citizens to California. Indolent Jamestowners went south. Modified puritans stayed to work—no longer, however, on the Embarcadero.

Under the base towers of this bridge looming out-of-proportion over the plaza that the Chapman family had emerged onto in the warm land air there was no poet but Michael for true American monuments: the city's own railroad serving serried piers that bore vast cool cargo sheds, cavernous warehouses in which now and then you could still smell bales of some such commodity as those in Celebes under the custody of clerks made known to literature by St Joseph, although now more exciting for emptiness than for what they now only sometimes contained—a row of possible theaters waiting for plays that will never be mounted, fronting the street like gated palaces; berthing aprons for barges of freight cars (not much changed in two generations), which rolled from one element to the other on gantlets rising and falling with the tide, never off all but universal rails (Russia and Newfoundland remaining notable nonconformists), and moorings for the tugs now mostly diesel that shouldered them; freight platforms and twelve-branched candelabra of sidings where shiploads used to be anatomized into a thousand bills of lading:: all of them capable but no longer much called for.

Like a circus family not good enough for the Big Show but traveling to join some seedy carnival in a strange town they assemble at ease on the cobbled boulevard sceneried OFF RIGHT by foundation columns of the bridge to wait for an old tramcar (here green instead of orange, distinguished also by clerestory windows in the raised roof and by a crew of two, fitted with a crowd of seats set ingeniously at right angles to each other in vestibules and compartments as anachronistic as social classes: all in all a fine big bunkhouse caboose for family travel) to end its Market Street run circle the square and pick them up.

Terror firmer, says Jonathan to himself, tentatively. Aloud, pretentiously: "The land is still rocking under my feet."

The father snorting strikes him painfully on his bicep with the knuckle of a middle finger. "Cut the rhetoric. On that scow you couldnt tip a sixpence off your radiator cap."

Jonathan grins guiltily insofar as he has seriously tried to make an impression and disdainfully insofar as he has offered the remark sarcastically. Michael drops the subject defensively insofar as he hunches the ambiguity. In support of Jonathan the mother says that she always feels a little dizzy when she comes out of a wind into a windless open space. Nobody says anything about the fact that having made her passage in the cabin she has not been exposed to any wind today.

"Look look!" cries Matty who has been rhythmically shifting his weight back and forth from one leg to the other and to whom therefore everything at a long angle of vision can be seen as moving. "Look at the trains running in the middle of the street!" He points excitedly, still swaying, OFF LEFT.

"Do you have to go to the bathroom, Matty?" Ruth asks.

Brought to self-consciousness the boy stops rocking and vehemently shakes off what he takes as an accusation. But they all turn to stare at the scant forlorn company of boxcars, probably empty, certainly stationary, waiting like dejected levies for perpetually deferred marching orders, deserted bums from diverse states fortuitously suspended over a long long weekend together hoping for nothing more than to be hitched for a day or two into passive teams of retired reservists. They seem illiterately careless of historiographical value in the faded legends and devices stenciled like stars of David on their peeling shacksides of yellowish black reddish black brownish black or whitish black all smitted with ferruginous bird-droppings (e g BM Capy 110000 Ld Lmt 131400 LtWt 45600) though they can hardly be indifferent to the facts of commercial geography.

Most businessmen now argue that demand must be created. This theorem is less appalling only than the tacit propositions of the financiers running the railroads as if they were lawyers charged with liquidating like partible inheritances the endless swaths of land erst granted their clients' grandfathers by the people through their Congress who had taken it from the Indians who had counted themselves its custodians although it was acknowledged to be at least equally the hunting grounds of wolves who preyed upon ungulates who were less possessive of the earth than beavers rabbits prairie dogs and rattlesnakes. The railroads' particular inversion of stewardship calls as little attention as possible to the way the price of its stock is kept up while the hypothecated industry is run into the ground. Chapman a history-minded buyer and receiver of small consignments with an emerging awareness of the contradictions and incongruities of American transportation as accidentally formed by riotously competitive capitalism in the nineteenth century and bureaucratically crystallized in the twenti-

Tell me little boy of prosperous self-delighting family what do you see in the stars as construed in chalk on the old paint I got before the war. Come up close and look why don't you. They always mark it where we can't see our own and they never tell us anything at all. I wonder how come I know as much as I do even about my past seeing as I never had no upbringing except what I heard from yard cops and stinky hoboes over the years putting two and two together, memory being my long suit. It's a fact that I now belong to the Boston & Maine but I was born in servitude to the Denver and Rio Grande long long ago. Got too old for them I reckon but anyways it don't make no nevermind cause in those days everybody went everywhere and liked it especially during the war. We did our part and then some. But I'll never see Key West again. They din't bother to put back the track after that big hurricane. Or Jamaica Vermont. A thousand sidings you never heard of son where they say you can't hardly find the rotten ties under the grass and the rails all tore up of course. But I'd

eth by an Interstate Commerce Commission pettifogged and encrusted with reflections of the colossal undermanagements (except for the Pennsylvania's) that it has been sole monitor of may be forgiven for emphasizing the less-than-carload aspect of slow freight which he is now reminded of as a user of Parcel Post. He believes the decay he's contemplating represents the beginning of the end for hopes of national efficiency as considered in any geologic sympathetic with the mother of us all. As you might expect, says he to himself, the L C L problem seems to be working out to almost everyone's immediate advantage (the only advantage considered in business) without scruples of patriotic forethought or global philanthropy, to the net effect that the sovereignty of American logistics has been yielded to highway engines without a fight by the very powers that might have been supposed most motivated to resist. If the railroads don't do battle the philosophers can't. In board rooms of the Association of American Railroads the policy of resignation has been deliberately evolved even as operating managers shadow-box the motor carriers in the good faith of ignorant incompetence bewildered by the faithlessness of technology and fooled by the disingenuous financial manipulations of their masters the holding companies that call the shots unjustified by any record of wisdom or success as far as anything besides real estate is concerned. If there's a principle underlying machinations

sure like to roll into Saint Jo again (Vermont or Missouri it don't matter) or at least anyplace there's somethin for a body to do tween national emergencies. Kid you don't suppose I'll ever roll across the drawbridge into Gloucester again for a load of salt cod before they leave me in some boneyard do you? Nowadays the highballs are so few and far between for an old bugger like me that I can't remember my last hotbox. Let me tell you I'd sooner work a hunnert and forty hours with no demurrage than get stuck in a rusty shunt like this on the State Belt Line. Belt my ass! More like a jockstrap. . . . Free and astray, that's what I am! Dollars to doughnuts they've lost me. I'll rot here before I'm found, much they care. But I aint no union teamster and I can't stand fuckin off like this. Hurry up and wait! But there aint really any hurry up no more. Christ there was a time when they was tearing each other's heart out to get a car like me, supply officers running around the yards waving requisitions and bidding up their D O numbers seven days a week, and even after the war for a while freight forwarders had to stand in line and maybe slip the dispatcher a fifth. What a sorry sight this waterfront is now, damn the red longshoremen. All the good old days I could tell you about before interstate highways and head-office I B M machines. Take it from me there was a time when this Belt Line did some real volume with all the West Coast roads your old man's trying to think of, some of

of A A R misstatesmanship it must amount to the strategy of shortening defenses in order to concentrate the fat that's to be lived off. The directors retreat to their citadels while pretending to mount counteroffensives. With only listless and sporadic modernization of people equipment or plant it's only natural that costs should rise as volume shrinks. Rates creep up as the trucking companies benefit increasingly from roads built by the public treasury; service gets worse; damage claims burgeon: until at last the carloading outfits and pool-car shippers are going out of business or turning from rail to the convenient traction of freewheeling infernal consumption. He is gloomily convinced that the degenerative process will continue until railroad freight solicitors find themselves proposing nothing less than trainloads of bulk cargo and until all track not needed for grain minerals petrochemicals or mass transportation of the enemy's new cars will be ripped up and their right-of-ways lost forever under the collective and ungainsayable profit-incentives incorporated in the grander waste of a whole country living tastelessly high on the hog off mother earth's capital.

But no use trying to tell the future to Jonathan and Matthew who'll know it soon enough willy-nilly. They need their father only for the past. Yet even history's too much tutelage. Simply point out what they havent seen before; don't try to warn them that it may not be here next time they come. Such monitions just inure them to my proffered images as boringly oldfashioned.

them gone before he was old enough to wipe his own ass, and I had buddies from every one of them or anyway heard tell some way or another, maybe a few of them even before my day, being as how it gets confusing with all the mergers and receiverships that happened in my profession the last hunnert years almost and my mind is naturally filled up with names from all over the country, especially when the East's a hell of a lot more complicated than out here so you can't help getting mixed up between the past and the present and somebody else's past and your own personal experience that you use the same words for, which happens even if you can't read when you have a pretty good idea of who's left you up shit creek without a paddle. There used to be some lines you never hear of today like the South Pacific Coast the Stockton & Copperopolis the San Francisco & North Pacific Coast the Sacramento Valley, and don't forget going concerns like the Sacramento Northern the Northwestern Pacific the Western Pacific the Central Pacific and of course the two that everyone knows made good the Southern Pacific and the Atchison Topeka & Santa Fe. . . . Anytime they ask I'll still take on eighty or a hunnert thousand pounds sterling, which is pretty good when you only weigh forty-five thousand six your own self. I don't mind working. That's what we're put on earth for. . . .

Besides it's less than little likely that either of them will grow up like myself always trying to breed the flagging past to that heated bitch of a future in some futile hope of reforming progress before it arrives.

"Where are the engines, where are the engines, where are they?"

Michael points FAR OFF EX-TREME LEFT. "Way over there at the old roundhouse resting up for Holy Week. But only switch engines. There's not much for them to do here anyway." [What he doesn't mention aloud:] Insufficient return on investment. All the track and rolling stock as well as workers slowly suffer retribution intended by unions and populists and poets for the scions of Wall Street barons whose civil crimes were actually only special cases of the fundamental cruelty and greed of the entire electorate cherishing its pragmatically piggish ignorance of history and science in the willful belief that property as birthright or aggrandizement is the only purpose of society. Nevertheless from an administrative point of view the owners of American railroads (who once had on their side a manifest destiny envied by capitalists all over the world) might have managed their great interlocking exploits of overland locomotion with more foresight, especially after the turn of the century when formal thinking was becoming available to the captains of industry, particularly in respect to personnel policy. Most of their chronic difficulties half a century later can be traced to the cumulative and compounded incompetence of uneducated whitecollar supervisors at every level—against which bluecollar featherbedding is an inevitable and predictable reaction—the

The dumb little tyke axes the same insulting questions we hear from all the hoodwinked kids brought up on picture-book pap. The charming heroic puffinbillies! sweet cozy little joyriding cabooses! Kids nowadays don't know nothin about facts of life. To them we're just cannon fodder to fill up some space between head and tail. "Poo-poo, Choo-choo—Off we go!" But to tell the truth I wouldnt mind seeing a big black old hogger again myself. Doubt if I ever will. Diesels have took over all the jobs cept coal-hauling and what do they want with a car like me in West Virginia anymore? It's those infernal overgrown track-tractors that started all the trouble putting everything on a so-called businesslike basis. Progress is movin in the wrong direction. I want my own brakeman—maybe three, one for each shift: to hell with air brakes! Let the Brotherhood have a feather bed on every car, as it was in the beginning. Because if Westinghouse and the efficiency experts with their punchcard machines win out the whole guild will have to learn something new from the ground up if they want to put their boys through business school. They'll be whizzing us all over the country untouched by human hands and dying young from overwork. Like all them people that perish from lack of personal contack with their doctor. We'll be regimented by remote control. The heart'll be taken out of us by social-

whole intercompany network having been conditioned to the normalcy of recruiting young clerks before their education has gone too far and of honoring seniority as if it were implicitly superior to the merits of commonsense and courtesy sometimes fostered by good organizers in enlightened businesses when they have the chance. And what a chance our railroads have flubbed, shrugging off the power they abused, falling for General Motors' line while General Motors is getting into mother earth and sodomizing Uncle Sam. Anyway the abuse was so elaborate that it's little wonder the antimanagers of public law tried to defend the people the only way they knew how, by spawning and perpetuating an equal and opposite institution of paperwork calculated to employ a new class of attorneys on both sides to check every competitive impulse that might somehow stir in the torpid private bureaucracy that runs the U S A's most fascinating arti-

ized medicine unregulated trucking automated classification yards and the whole goddam atheistic degeneration of American family life. They'll start checking up on every last car with their photoelectric gadgets and want to know where we are every minute day and night. What with longer consists and a lot fewer of them they'll want new steel cars over 5000 cube, and then it'll be early retirement without a pension for the rest of us. All the things that made this country great are being destroyed by lazy Commie freeloaders. Full employment is what makes our system work. But the bosses don't care if I rot to death in an archeology yard. . . . Well back to sleep, rest between wars, and maybe at least I can dream about good old steam-driven imperialism. I won't be any busier tomorrow than I am today. Rest is over all too soon when there's no work to do on workdays. When to Christ will I ever get humping again?

fact. Too guiltily the railroads lame and late complain about laboring under an I C C tariff structure thirty years old, grafted and supplemented to death with special cases and tinkered exceptions (which are shamefully inconsistent with its own geographically and historically isolated logic-segments) of such volume that the printed amendments if stacked on top of the original canon would reach eight times as high as the Washington Monument; and about having to spend twenty million a year just to publish their tariffs.

Meanwhile where's the damn streetcar? "Oh god will we ever get humping again!"

"Michael!" Ruth dug his side with her elbow and looked about with an apprehensive little smile. "Don't let the boys hear you say things like that!" she whispered.

He nearly pulled her off her feet, folding his mighty arm around her neck and fastening his wrist with the other hand. "That's a railroad term my dear. I am merely expressing my impatience to get from here to the zoo. Far be it from me to exploit any ambiguity you may choose to find in my words."

"You're a masterly archangel to get us this far so neatly." He had released her and now she hung lightly on his sleeve as if in evening clothes they were waiting for their limousine to be brought around.

"This is just the beginning Baby, just the beginning. The worst is yet to come. . . . It's not going to rain though."

"No. You were right. You're always right." Almost always. "It's getting hot." She looked at her sons and looked back up at her husband, eyes alight with amusement and hope. But it seemed to him that she saw streetcars buildings boats bridges and railroads as a cat sees rainbows in the sky or faces in a picture—that is to say either not at all or as unedged shadows. She picked out no more of his objects than he did of her subjects. Without casting reflections on men's silly susceptibilities she was able to put first things first and to dismiss mere tools and conveniences. The world was full of obstacles and forces that could crush or shield the existence of her family but those that now preoccupied most of her menfolk were not among them. "Earth has not anything to show more fair . . ." she murmured by way of teasing her husband's enchantment with the city that she still took as quodlibetal despite personal memories of her earnest officegirl days passing thereinto and thereout.

Beauty was gathered in her face by peaceful thoughts of love, and standing there in the wide empty public square she felt beloved of four mutually loving men—their happy servant their mistress and their mother too, blessed by the authority and protection of the man who was not only her sons' father but also her own. That beauty drew the man's eyes to the fine ears uncovered at their lobes by the soft nutbrown hair tied back with a red velvet ribbon; to the lissome Egyptian neck shaded by the open collar of a whiter blouse that crisply disclosed no more than the supposition of her alabaster bosom; to her cool dawn-tinted lips whose suddenly soft and warming kisses always taught him more than the words they could form (whereon he now surprised her with a swift tender kiss of his own, just when she was most sweetly unaware of her freshly desired beauty, quite openly right there in the wide empty public square with the three by-products of passion at their elbows and knees now paying no more attention to their progenitors than peripheral plashes to the entwined stem of an Eros-and-Psyche fountain); to the thin patrician nose that on its proper level of society would have ravished jaded princes; to the level wide-spaced eyes, now hazel in the sunlight burning off the clouds, unresting and unrestless eyes that looked not merely before them but also inward or afar and sometimes could be recalled to immediate necessity only by an effort of will—now happy in the joined purpose of the family, rejoicing not in the purpose itself but in the rare concordance of multiplicity, in a whole intercalated day of unity, in the knowledge that this event set aside for love could not be repealed by any ensuing vexation. Most of all he was drawn to the ageless palimpsest of her maternally wise eyelids by their sexually matured web of fine wrinkles between brow and cheek in

a smooth youthful face, as if he had been admitted to the private chamber
of an unfortunate people's widowed young queen. His male antenna stirred
like an equerry's at the suddenly enriched beauty of her personage.

And so with the blue of the second third of the day came his revised
sense of the body he had made love to the night before, of the loveliness
that changed like the sky but not always with the sky. "You're an amazing
beauty!" he said quietly in his old ever-renewable admiration. "You look
like a secretly passionate lady of good breeding."

"Truth to tell, that's just what I am."

"If you look like what you are then everyone knows what you're up to
at night. I can't say I like that!"

"You've seen more of me than others have. That's what feeds your
imagination."

"But still they think they can imagine what they havent seen from
what they have. As for me, I'm different from you: I conceal everything; I
may be wonderful but I look fat dull and clumsy."

"Oh Mike you never look clumsy!—Besides," she further lowered her
voice, "you're fat and dull—and I mean blunt—in the right place." They
grinned at each other and held hands like springtime innocents.

Once more he congratulated himself that Ruth was a seemly woman,
for all her openness to him extraordinarily delitescent to other men, yet
serene and immensely understanding with the women who liked her for
the reserve they missed in themselves. "We should speak at Pre-Cana Conferences, explain to the Micks and their demivierges what's important and
what isn't."

She thought over his jest. "Hecuba told me she went to a few of those
with her boyfriend once. The priest told them that when they got married
they'd both have to give up things they'd set their hearts on."

Oh god there it is again when you least expect it! groaned Michael the
Hypersensitive to his secret double, bemoaning both the abrupt (however
unintentional) correction of his enchantment and the tiresome old wisdom
itself that was always waiting for the chance to assert its claim. Give up
every unselfish motive that doesnt minister to the family's fucking fertility! (It's true of course that there are also some selfishnesses which don't
serve it either.) I suppose if I were a priest I too would avenge my celibacy
by seeing to it that the men of my parish paid the price of flesh and kept
themselves in continual bondage to gravid women. God's higher purpose
is strengthened only by frequent and prolonged pauses in our pleasure!
(I'd make them envy me for my vow of freedom!) But that's not all that
balks us by a long shot. In atheistic jewish protestant or recidivous couplings, which even on the woman's side don't necessarily postulate a
higher purpose than unselfishness, we come up against barriers more
subtle and exasperating that Romans who are stopped by condition or conscience never even get to. We'll go to any lengths to bring our ladies to an
unselfish purpose. It's the number one motive for America's high standard

of living. Entertainment culture banks on the generosity of our inducements. Otherwise nothing is more difficult for a busy tired breadwinner
than to overcome the familiarity bred of daily cohabitation in the family
lifeboat. It's no fun to be reduced to raping a bedfellow so unmoved by
tedious pawing and delving that she doesnt even bother to demur. St
Willie notwithstanding (who seldom misspeaks), a man's desire, in marriage at least, is for the desire of the woman. Skill and patience are not
enough when the worn mother who knows all your tricks is busier and
tireder than the head of the house and twice as discontented, filled with
the hopeless recognition that even her inferior prospects depend upon your
own. If you're lucky enough to find her bodily predisposed you still must
somehow call down into her head the grace of psychical sensibility; or at
the very least (if you chance upon a spark mysteriously sustained or
rekindled despite your unreconstructed antipathy to womhopes) take
unnatural precautions against betraying an unceremonious attitude toward
her person. For a man of principle who refuses to squander his money or
fake his words the conjugal approach can be excruciatingly difficult,
unless he happens to be met with a perfectly matched mood of playful
concupiscence or seized with the kind of authentic enthusiasm for his wife
that can momentarily neutralize veridical consciousness on both sides, no
matter how wisely he makes use of his hands. Nor is much purchased by
good works, for they too become familiar, come to seem no more than the
performance of common duty, or else like blackmail lead to an absurdly
inflated expectation of the attentions payable only by a full-time lover,
when all he really wants to do is play the lover on occasion—the very
ethos that turns aside household grace in the first place. Life is too short to
forespend it in an extenuation of courtship, particularly for one whose
allotment of other work is not less but more than normal.

What then explains my good fortune last night? Nothing can explain
it but a love for me so extraordinary that it's still able to shake off its burdens at some unintended mental representation of my worth! Isn't it
remarkable, in longsuffering marriage? An adulterous seducer shares no
burdens or blame, and a married woman if she's to respond to him at all,
forgetting kids and household bills for the moment, in his fresh instance
can dismiss her general grievance against the male advantage, yielding to
self-centered grace instead of the higher purpose. A marauder thus suffers
not the handicap of history, which I must ordinarily overcome, and he can
always succeed at least to the portal of ecstasy without taking the pains of
a spouse.

Could a woman like Ruth ever fall for the phony showmanship of
unfamiliarity that most women are at least tempted to fall for no less than
once? To what increasing degree in the years ahead must I take further
trouble to forestall or divert the potential foolishness that lies buried in
the best of wives—just as truly as in myself lurks fatuous besotment with
fresher flesh and less familiar revelation?

Of course I don't seek out strange sweet dalliance. That much I can give up by virtue of necessity in my negotiation for an optimum life. (Or is it only by virtue of unprepossessing corpulence?) In short, I'm an evangelist of orthodox conduct since there is plentiful delight in a good day of marriage. There are many advantages that I shouldnt lose sight of. I'd be wise to keep reminding myself that it's too early to predict and too late to repent. If my life were any simpler it would have to be even more selfish.

". . . we could stop all wars." she was saying to him, having drifted off his subject in proleptic contemplation of the lives of her sons and of all women's young men.

But he stopped her at his own level with a whisper at the selfless ear: "Honey, I'm the bear for your honey-garden." Already once again as insensitive to her womhopes as a bachelor.

Luckily just then their trolley car showed up. It leaned screeching and grudging around the loop, taking Michael by surprise. Roger wasnt caught napping, but to him its arrival was no more than an unsurprising resumption of causeless events. The older boys jumped up from the curb who had been pitching burnt-out matchsticks at a groove of imbedded track.

"Let's go, Daisy-Mazie!" Michael yelled, to bring back her outgoing mood.

(7)
HY.03

HOW TO
MANAGE
A SMALL
BUSINESS

*A*s first mate and merchandising manager Michael insisted upon handling new stock. Others were permitted to replace goods that were sold off open shelves or tables with more of the same from stored reserves, but it was he himself who classified placed and displayed all items when first received from vendors. He made sure to be back from coffee at ten-thirty every morning lest Valentine Greatrakes who owned the merchandise pluck it up from the back room table and lay it ignorantly about the store in his imperative instinct not to lose any odd moment of opportunity for a sale. If necessary Michael would scurry to meet the Parcel Post delivery in his hardly concealed determination to obviate any such innocent sabotage of his system. He was continually inclined to postpone his vacations for the same reason. But now the proprietor was gone for the day and Michael walked to the back of the shop without haste or anxiety.

From the lunchroom across the street he had seen the postman come in his truck and unload a small stack of packages on the sidewalk, and while listening to Pat he had watched Sam come to the door in his apron and without offering to help wait for the driver to finish his task.

There had been one package for Sam to sign for: an order from England. It was this consignment that Michael especially relished the prospect of inspecting and setting out for sale—of exploring the assortment that he had long since specified and forgotten, of calculating the net cost after postage and duty were distributed among the various items (according to the pounds-shillings-and-pence shown on the invoice and U S Customs statement enclosed); of computing and marking the selling price, and of carrying the merchandise out for display in the front of the store where the public could admire it.

To discover and examine new articles for the stock in trade was every day's keenest pleasure. He rubbed his hands in anticipation, crossing the street, mildly regretting the earlier part of the pleasure which Sam was enjoying. For Michael's rise in the business had obliged him to delegate the wild surmise of opening cartons. (In the beginning there had been no Sam: only a Mike.) Sam had now been allowed enough time to unpack everything.

When he walked into the back of the store Sam was pricing the latest uniform batch of a standard stock commodity, one of the uninteresting domestic staples. This job lay within the range of Sam's trustworthiness because invoices from American suppliers showed unequivocal list prices in dollars and cents, and because the invoices were attached to the corresponding shipping cartons in First Class envelopes; because also in some cases the individual items were wrapped in descriptive paper imprinted with the fixed retail selling price. He had trained Sam, when an objective correlative arrived, to find the matching purchase order copy hanging on a certain clipboard alphabetically by vendor; the which, removed from among its fellows, was to be checked against both the packing slip and the invoice, based on count and cursory inspection of the goods themselves, dated, otherwise annotated, and transferred to another board that hung alongside.

Michael, annoyed as ever at the indolent pace of Sam's performance, is content to detect a friendly and cooperative attitude this day. Sometimes Sam is sullen and contumacious. Greatrakes hates him because he is a little bit of a poet and a little bit of a Red and insists upon his rights; but so far he has stayed just this side of the line at which the boss could fire him without risking more loss of investment in training than gain in subserviency. A heavy brown walrus moustache and many wrinkles about the cheeks rendered the young man's unvoiced insolence formidably mature.

Sam's pleasure is Scotch whiskey. His desire is debauchery with women. His fetish is French culture. Contumaceously humble on the job; presumably a great personality among his friends. Loves opera. To these ends his voice is deeply musical and histrionic. His vanity about it is one trait among others that keep him a poor radical and a shallow poet, his own opinion to the contrary notwithstanding. Native conviviality and an emerging respect for money erode and undermine his general sarcasm. Off guard, a sweet man alert to others. Handsome devil too; but his legs are too short, his clothes are ill-matched by any taste, and he stinks. Some of these attributes he remains unaware of. With tolerable truth he regards Michael as his protector. Until simply tiring of the attention required, he sometimes unguardedly permits himself in pale degree to share Michael's zest for building up the business.

In the world of which he affects off-duty mastery, moreover, he admires Michael for his remarkable provenance. Gloucester is the Innisfree of Sam's heart's desire and he makes no bones about his intention someday to quit the store and go East to live there. Yet he is forever disappointed at Michael's refusal to gloss Gloucester poems in the magazines he brings in and resonantly quotes aloud when Greatrakes is out for coffee. Michael knows who it is whose sometime moustache Sam affects (from certain Gloucester photographs circulated out of the limelight), but Sam knows not that anyone knows. This firebrand bachelor, a brownish and mellow-looking man withal, his handwriting on commercial documents is more childish than any poet's disciple's should be.

Leaning over the shipping table and manipulating a pocket sliderule Michael began to translate the British invoice. With a pencil he extended each line-item in dollars and cents and drew up a bottom sum; taking this figure as the provisional whole he marked on the paper each line's percentage of the same, Sam with constipated breath and unwashed aura peering over his shoulder.

"Now to be strictly accurate I should be distributing the postage according to weight, and only the duty according to value, but roughly speaking this is close enough. See: I apply each percentage to the total extra cost and add the results to their respective lines. To check my computations, if I add the adjusted costs I should come out to the gross cost of the shipment, invoice value plus postage and duty." Michael did not really wish to explain what he was doing, for he knew right well that Sam could never be trusted to learn and execute extra-poetical mathematics, but he did so as his supervisory duty for the sake of a growing business.

"I think I'm beginning to see what you're driving at, Chief." said Sam. (Michael he calls Chief; Greatrakes, Boss.) "Maybe next time I'll get this part of it. But go on. Please try to get it through my poor literary head how you get from there to *our* selling price. I still can't see why you don't just add forty percent the way Prince Valiant does when you're not here."

"He's used to working with discounts, from the retail catalog point of view. But when you don't have a list price you have to figure a markup on cost, and the percentage is not the same as a discount if you want to come out with a given margin. Thirty-three-and-a-third discount is a fifty percent markup. Now if we want the equivalent of a forty percent discount—"

"Once when you werent here he got mad and said you hadnt been making enough money on the imports."

"I know that, Sam. We've been over this before. You told him I'd been using 33-and-a-third, which is what they give us off the U K list. He thinks we should have a bigger margin than we get on American stuff because the risk is greater and we can't return anything, so he adds 50 percent to our cost. . . ."

"—He thought we should make as much as we could get away with, considering how cheap the English prices are in relation to our standard of living."

"Yeah. So he added fifty and thought he was marking the whole lot for extra profit! Well, after I add postage and duty and apply forty percent on a true discount basis, I make him about seventeen percent more gross profit on sales than he comes out with when he does the pricing."

"I thought you said you used a markup instead of a discount?"

"I use a calculated markup percentage to arrive at the equivalent of our usual discount—in fact a little more, because we always have to absorb the postage on domestic shipments."

"To this day I don't think the Prince understands it any better than I do, and he's supposed to be the businessman!"

Michael continued his lecture to this half-sarcastic skeptic, fully sensing its futility, simply because he could not help finishing his elaborate correction of stupidity. "Many retailers don't understand this. They want to make x percent gross profit on revenue, so they mark up their merchandise x percent without exception, and then wonder what's happened when they see their P & L statements. They think the employees have been stealing." Michael glanced at Sam's face to see if it would blush or falter, as he misbelieved that Sam was innocent of walking home with merchandise under his raincoat; but that intellectual visage did not bat an eyelash, as if Sam had no idea that Michael suspected him of crime, though he should have known that Michael would doubt him inasmuch as he Sam was always extolling the lives and practices of free-loaders and free-lovers, and dispraising the sanctity of private property, especially that of businessmen.

"Well, how do you arrive at forty percent discount?"

"I divide by point six oh. See, right there." Michael pointed to the C-scale.

"Hell, I can't read a sliderule."

"More's the pity."

"The most pity is that Prince Val can't."

"Never mind. Let's get this finished up. We're going to need you out in the store this afternoon. Lilian's going home."

"Merci beaucoup for the lesson in high finance."

Michael carried out an armful of wares to dispose them. One item he was so proud of—in his certainty that no other local store would have it, least of all at the price he had marked it (since his competitors bought their British goods through importers, who made no mistakes in their wholesale markups)—that he put it in the window, making room for it among featured articles there displayed. The other new items he carefully installed at various locations in bins and shelves or on countertops.

Lilian sat on a stool near the special showcases she was responsible for, arms folded, hunched, gazing out the window listlessly. Michael supposed that it was the sallowest time of her month. Her eyelids were puffed and her waist seemed a little thickened, "I'm sorry you're not feeling well, Lil. As soon as Sam's finished out back you can go home. You can go now if you really want to. Too bad this is Sally's day off."

"No thanks, I'll wait." Her mouth smiled, and her low peaceful voice, but none of the rest of her self could rise to Michael's level of social energy. By vocation she was a painter, and at such times in dull hopeless contemplation of the lifelong struggle to which she had bound herself, he thought, she witnessed from her perch, from wherever she happened to be during the day, the peasant tide within her body silently whelming her mind and sapping the piles of sand she was perpetually scraping together as men had taught her to do (—men seeming to know better than she how to wage the war of art, how to release oneself from language, though they always had to use as many words in the classroom studio as in the store where strangers came). "I'll be all right tomorrow. I wouldnt want to jeapordize our planktonic relationship."

Michael paused in his business, in an access of sympathy that could not be touched upon, pleased to understand her affection in taking up in the depths of her discomfort the pleasantry he had sometimes practiced in flirtation. Openly facing her dulled eyes for a few seconds he gazed at her unshielded Slavic or Amerindian femininity, as if he was her doctor who could cure as well as diagnose. Under prevailing conditions her competence and goodnature annealed the brittleness and ambition of the store's people, softening even a spot in the boss's hard heart for artists. Her broad monochromatic face and lips, forehead ears and neck hidden by loosely gathered and coarsely braided black hair, were exotically attractive to brothers sisters and lovers, and to men like Michael who would have been if they could have been the senior consort of such a talented loyal sympathetic girl. She dressed carelessly, and when she adorned herself at all she seemed to do so not for the sake of her appearance to others but out of her own liking for a certain ornament, or simply to experiment with it.

At times Michael imagined for her a series of actual lovers from the earliest possible age, each in turn disappointing her of an intensity and nobility that she could devote her spirit to; but usually he saw her as one who was awaiting and never doubting the hot secret fascination that she knew would be her undoing—knew so clearly that in her frank and friendly manner Michael fancied she nearly said so, freely and directly, like a dog.

The senior officer returned to the back room and surprised his Shipping & Receiving clerk seated upon the work table, cigarette in mouth, looking through a small magazine of poetry that he had brought to work that morning in his back pocket. "Listen, Chief!" he cried triumphantly, unabashed at being so discovered. "Here's your other Gloucester man:

> taking each thing as it never was
> is more than a beginning

That Lefty is *committed*!"

"Don't be ridiculous." Michael retorted. "It's not Marxism. —Lilian would like to go home now."

"I'd like to go with her. She should be the receiving clerk and I should be dishing it out, like."

Michael furiously gathered another load, American materials that had been marked and neglected by Sam's heavy hand, who now unwillingly stepped down to the floor and untied the printer's apron with vertical stripes that he liked to be seen in. He washed his hands at the sink deliberately, using the roller towel most fastidiously, and put on his crumpled jacket, carefully spreading the wide butterfly collar of his sepia shirt so that it covered all the upper margins of his outer garment. (Neither the chief nor the boss had the right to make him wear a tie.) A small triangle of mustard Army singlet was thus exposed to the public, and curls of sable hair thereabove, even unto the white skin of his neck, nearly to the adam's apple. His head was wobbly on its thin meerschaum stem (which neckless Michael envied not at all)—weak by birth and nurture, weakened further by recessive pallor, a puny nexus between the lumpy collarbone of narrow shoulders and the massive dark Babylonian face with spectacles that made huge circles around his eyes.

"Say, Mike:" said this Sam, "do you know why I call you Chief?" He smiled with goodwill, clicking his heels and saluting, but indeed expected no answer from his testy superior. [Michael grunted, pausing almost imperceptibly on his way out the door with a load.] "Because I know you have certain Reservations!" Three or four broad yellowish teeth gleamed cheerfully under the grimacing moustache, and abruptly they were carried off ahead of Michael to relieve the watch.

Out on the floor, attended again by Sam, Michael examined and classified each item of merchandise. Lilian was gone, leaving a void. Sometimes Sam offered to protest the chief's judgment, but he docilely obeyed instructions, took each artifact from the authoritative hand, deliberately acquainted himself with it, and meticulously installed it in a specified area, thus giving the chief to understand that he did not intend to be known as a clown in the basic intelligence of their business.

But in twenty minutes the job was done and Sam's virtue lapsed. He sank down upon Lilian's stool to wait for lunchtime. Not a single customer had disturbed the tranquillity of these preparations. Sam's wit rose, and his indiscretion, as his weight settled. Against his chief's back, who was passing down the aisle to take up clerical duties in the rear, he flung in elocuted tones his finest possession, the chosen epigraph of his life:

"I must Create a System or be enslav'd by another Man's;
I will not Reason and Compare: my business is to Create."

{*Postulants only*: GO TO ITEM (9) SA.04, page 103.}

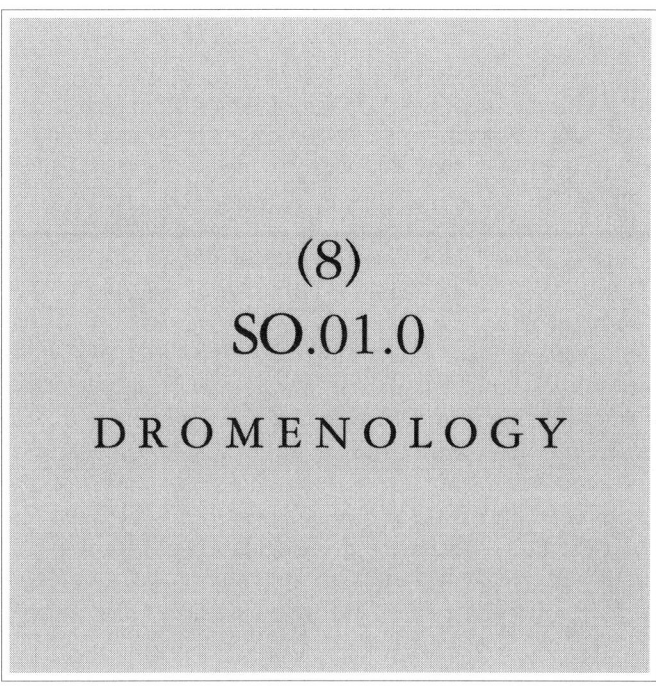

(8)
SO.01.0
DROMENOLOGY

Manuscript Submitted to the *Square Root Review*, Berkeley,
Under the Title "A Vocabulary of Ritual", by Michael Chapman,
Offered as a Review of Johan Huizinga's
Homo Ludens: A Study of the Play Element in Culture.

The English language is the most complete system. Thanks to poetry its evolution is even in a certain sense almost reversible. But according to proofs of metamathematical logic, it is said, the best of systems can never be complete and can never fail to contradict themselves as they grow. The most comprehensive systems persist in time. They continue to exist because instead of claiming efficiency they defend themselves with hedging redundancy and will not abide the constraints of category or situation. An enduring system develops with variable relations among its elements at their several ages.

Mutually exclusive classifications obtain when you discern only the most convenient boundaries within a cross-section of time. In the name of reason many a limited and unbreathing scheme has been extracted by time-slicing your piece of space, oddly enough in the same synchronistic manner with which we turn causality into the stochastic dysreason of indeterminacy by displaying chosen events in a single plane that deprives them of their particular histories. As a practical scholar Huizinga is sensitive to the problem. Though he englishes his own German, his response is nearly to abandon system.

Homo Ludens precipitates some dross but leaves too much suspended. I wish Huizinga had read Jane Harrison sufficiently, or had at all read Dom Gregory Dix, that he might have acquired their reagents to admix with his own, since ritual, as he acknowledges, is the base of all the washes through which we see the schools of our fellow fish. We should make people stop talking about ritual as if it were merely epiphenomenal illustration of fancies or inchoate ideas. To that end I am going to propose systemic meanings for the terms we use.

I advance not axioms but complex postulates. Do not expect me either to prove them or to pleach them. The purpose of my dictionary is to make more explicit the human behavior that engages Huizinga and hundreds of other modern writers. I will deal with electrolytic syntagms that you can chain together to discharge the energy of theoretical poles. From any electrolysis of culture a moiety of your yield will be ritual.

1.

First, as to our science, it should be called *Dromenology*, knowledge of things done. (From *Dromenon*, a classical Greek word but originating in the earlier time when ritual occupied its whole span.) The world appears and the world is made, to us, by us, and there on the wave-front we witness what we ourselves do as part of what appears. All doing is ours.

Some of what we now maintain or introduce never appears to us as a modification of antecedent reality, but all the doing that went before this moment is actually part of the world as it appears already. Although Nature is still usually spoken of as if it were separable from the willful and the adventitious of human doing, really the only distinctively human events are what we are going to do from now on. What concerns Dromenology is human act in the instant common to the progressive present of experience and the perfect tense of immediate history, things done while they are being done, alive to their own motives—in short, human act as a special case of human possibility. But further restricted to things we have done together, more than two of us, and to things that *are done*—are in some way expected to be done—not spuriously like riots but according to habit, rule, or plan.

Dromenology is all the more important because such acts in community are sources of much that we do alone and in pairs, and thence of much or most of what we separately feel and think.

Since what we do becomes at once phenomena to others, and in time to ourselves—since, that is to say, closed systems of the instant are opened into larger systems as we move on in time—it is not impossible to make an -*ology* of the moving points on the diachronic world-line of human event; and we can track a doing even though as retrogressive investigators of the past we cannot stay for experiential simultaneity in history's cross-section any more than action itself can halt in the forward direction. Proprioception eludes discourse until its memory is available (like emotion recollected in tranquility), and if we can scarcely study our private doings from the very inside of their moment, all the less can we pretend to transcend objectivity in thinking about fields of collective action.

Dromena, then, are things done by us but seen only after they are done, seen therefore in the past as evidence for a body of historical knowledge from which hypotheses can be induced but in which can be discerned no natural laws determining time's future surfaces; and though in dromenology we may deal with what happened this morning as if we know that it will happen again in the next performance, our minds are always prevented by the principle of uncertainty from being precisely where the action is.

In general motion makes time by giving space persistence. In the human case things done corporately, and not as continuous processes but at rhythmic intervals, immortalize a cult by making place persist: place as a situation in which a particular doing occurs at every cross-section of time fulgurated by that doing. Places are essential points in space without which no event can be said to recur. Thus the things done that I am speaking of are locally incarnate. Like matters of geography their order of reality is that of history but their affect upon consciousness is not of the order that usually calls for historiography.

Things done, as I have qualified them for my purpose, include *legomena*, things said, but not things felt or thought, except insofar as the things done there on the spot produce where we can't get at them the things felt or thought. Nevertheless it must be understood that dromenology embraces the direct products and consequences of dromena. Thus we concern ourselves with myth.

Let us say then that we are concerned with certain corporate actions of the body that generate culture. Yet, finally, not all such actions: not things done out of necessity, not acts of immediate self-preservation. If dromena bring economic advantage they do so by their indirect affect upon the agents of gain or defense.

2.

I offer ritual, drama, and game as three subsets of dromenon, refusing to exclude the possibility of another if I should in the future suggest theorems not now anticipated, but positively recognizing that these three categories, especially the last, overlap behavior that belongs to other sciences.

Let points in a plane represent categories you are interested in, and draw lines to connect those that are related to each other. If you end up with a polygon or a fan, or even with something like the rigging of a clipper-ship, you are simply too lucky. In truth you will end up with an irregular ill-made net which can be picked up and hung by any node; it will pinch and gather itself most oddly and skewly in three dimensions, because some of the segments pass each other without connecting. Since the edges are very ragged with deep bays and digital peninsulars, from any point you may successively converge and diverge with others in tracing relationships. To be neat and convenient you have tried to knit your net from the cleanest corner, or at least to hang it from there, with the fewest short-circuiting jumps between distant points; but it is really a matter of logical indifference which point you set higher than the others. Despair of hierarchy. Even a mop may be hung out to dry by any one of its strands.

So though I have started with a clear taxonomic breakdown of dromenon into three subdivisions the next front of subsets is not division at all: it is a spread of syntactical alternatives, and any alternative may be shared by the categories which have been made arbitrarily superior in position. For instance, *play*. I put it at the second step out or down, as an attribute of one kind of ritual and of one kind of drama and of one kind of game. The path that may be chosen in analyzing a thing done is a reversible sentence of differentiating elements. You write it forward or backward according as to whether you have the full specification of your event to start with, and want to classify it, or you have its general nature and you wish to test its particularity against the possibilities of your language.

Even if we state that the categories of ritual, drama, and game exhaust the term *dromenon* (a suspiciously neat proposal), *play*, the next knot we get to, since it includes solitary and paired human phenomena, as well as extra-human, represents a classification that is wider, though thinner, than either *dromenon* or any term on the *ritual* level, simply because more strings enter into it. At this radial distance from the origin of our path *play* resolves more uncertainty than it can up at the beginning where Huizinga puts it (as if ritual were *its* occasional attribute). In fact, I maintain, the dynamic function of syntax (to wind up or release, steadily or in discontinuous jerks, the energy of thought) requires that *play* be regarded as a substantive or participle for some kinds of ritual, some kinds of drama, and some kinds of games—as well as some kinds of other events: as itself an occasional attribute.

I am asking you then to take *play* as you take a word like *beauty*: it is the abstraction of a certain quality or aspect shared by entities which may be otherwise unrelated (except as all things are related in the network of language). *Beautiful* comes before *beauty*, and *play(ful)* comes before play. This, that, and other things, and especially games, are sometimes playful acts.

3.

So far I have only objected to the way Huizinga ties his net, but there is one point on which he actually fails us. What are the alternative attributes, or what is the single complement, on *play*'s level or isobar of syntactical decision? He offers one, though there are two words for it: "earnest" and "serious." Even so, "The play-concept as such is of a higher order than is seriousness. For seriousness seeks to exclude play whereas play can very well include seriousness." It is only when *seriousness* has "ethical content" that Huizinga is sure that this branch is crucial in the analysis of culture. But an obvious complement or counterpart of *play* is *work*, which I do not remember him to have accounted for except as something "earnest".

Yet these two terms together, *work* and *play*, are insufficient to provide for the range of discrimination which we must exercise at this distance from the origin in our statements about dromena. We should try to find at least one complementary noun, gerund, or participle that denotes non-work/non-play, abstracted from the adjectival idea of that which in dromenological doing is neither workful nor playful; and thence, by way of the gerund and the gerundive, the verb, presumably transitive, which, though no less abstract than the noun, and despite the fact that we come to it last, conjugates in one category certain human actions according to the way the doers feel about what they are doing. Not in our language, and not likely in another, shall we pick up any one term that fills out the field of dromenon and at the same time consummates the categories of doing for singles and pairs and for other animals. The word my search has led me to, in various forms according to part of speech, is most commonly employed in the fields I have excluded from dromenology. That word is *imagination*.

Sometimes the verb will be preferred. We are at the tier of action itself. Play, work, and imagination are kinds of game, ritual, or drama—but only because game, ritual, and drama are played, worked, or imagined.

4.

Dismissing Huizinga's confusion—that "there is no formal difference between play and ritual"—it appears that his subject is less play than it is ritual. In fact, returning to the first level of classificatory decision, with closer looks we can make out cross-connecting twine like irregular ratlines between the parallel taxonomic categories that we recognized at first. This secondary network represents the adaptations that any linguistic system must undergo in order to fit its logic to its object. The light lines independently traversing nodes of main rope serve two purposes: they bleed off and relieve intolerable disequilibriums of forced distinction, and they trace evolutionary sequence or priority.

I shall reflect the need to express such overlapping or evolving qualifications by allowing mutual modification among ritual, drama, and game. In the zones where one term merges with another the adjective of the one may be applied to the noun of the other, which to which depending on which is the base of emphasis and which the modifier: e.g., ritual(istic) drama *vs.* dramatic ritual, where the modifier indicates "some of the characteristics of".

I here take for granted, as Huizinga sometimes seems to do, the priority of ritual over game and drama within the span of dromenology. Ritual is their formal and their material cause, their phylogenetic stem. Among dromena it is the closest to necessity, the root and trunk of culture. We cannot reverse vectors in the finely threaded cladistic tree upon which our analytic/synthetic network of taxonomy is superimposed. Ritual came first. Distinctions between its wood and leaf we can hope will sharpen our language for all of dromenology without grinding it down to an array of motionless terms on a single plane, and if I direct myself to the specification of ritual norms perhaps in a few pages I can set forth the basic vocabulary for the full science here proposed.

My starting definition for the word *ritual* is a scaffolding to hold it up until it stands well enough to be used with tentative precision: Ritual is the traditional and orderly corporate action of a community—a rhythmic manifestation of the cult, periodically performed, in which ordinarily all witnesses take part. It purifies, dedicates, initiates members of the corporation. It excites and regulates desire. By means of it we say our prayer or make our sacrifice. We act with any or several of these intentions, specifically. There is no need for private emotion to begin with: but at least subconsciously we wish for the feeling that we shall succeed to. Game and drama vibrate their occasions, but ritual makes the human world resonate, and, if it is successful, resonate with God.

{*Postulants only*: GO TO ITEM (11) SO.01.1, page 115.}

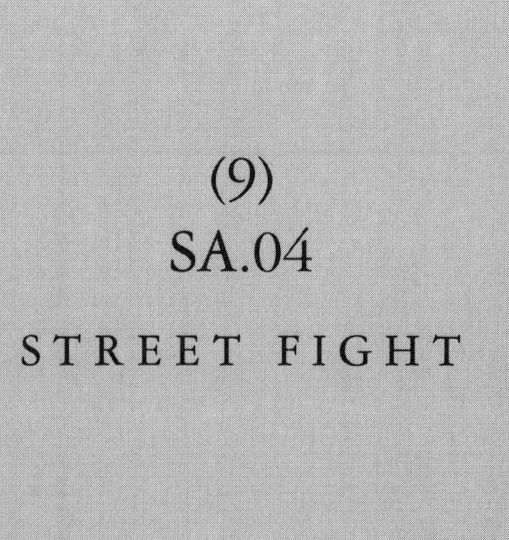

(9)

SA.04

STREET FIGHT

*A*t the beginning of the third segment of the journey out Michael took care to sit beside his wife so that he could keep her thoughts in the proper channel by striking her knee ever so gently with his own while together they listened to the chatter of the children, and this time since she sat between him and the window with Roger on her lap she was ever so slightly bold enough to let her knee slacken ever so wantonly in response to his rhythmic pressure. This little game of courtship was soon cut short however by the option of transferring their selves their souls and their bodies to a cable car, in accordance with one of the leader's vagaries of unselfishness that he would not give up in marriage. He would spare no expense in the artifactual education of his boys.

For once the little Chapmen made return for their father's policy in full measure. Open benches, long anxious ascents, vertiginous descents—the boys were beside themselves, couldn't sit in one place for a minute at a time, scrambling to miss nothing outside or inside the craft, much to the annoyance of the crew. All the boys except of course Roger, who was now in Michael's lap again, clutched tightly from the beginning of this adventure to the end, laughing with delight at the delight of his brothers. And

Ruth's attention to this episode was also as immediate as her husband could have asked. She noticed store windows, doors of houses, flower pots, views of the Bay (as bright blue as before the Spaniards came: didnt the city in the foreground make it more beautiful than it ever was in the past?), as well as the joy of her men.

Michael gazed down upon the excited blond head under his nose where the bright whorls curled clockwise about a tiny bald spot, a center-point of symmetry no bigger than the sin within. He examined the skull attentively, forgetting (Michael himself forgetting!) to look out upon the city at the high places they crested and dipped away from. With his fingers he felt the bony cranium that had so much so frailly to protect, comforted to find (against the frailty) that the baby's parietal helmet (how long had he not noticed, a whole year perhaps?) had at last knitted together at the crown which he had used to watch in excruciating anxiety for the naked brain of the infant that pulsated with every heartbeat barely beneath the thin hairless skin. The head was still too big for the delicate stalk supporting it, though that neck seemed old for it was creased (if you looked closely) with wrinkled fissures and porous imperfections like those discovered in the skin of beautiful Brobdignag women who took you to their bosoms. It was sad to see that health and innocence could germinate no more perfectly in mankind than in green mansions of the Amazon's layered flora where not a single leaf it is said in all the vastness remains for a day wholly untouched by smut or worm. Are they in the southern hemisphere, those great green cathedrals where coral snakes play with innocent greenclad girls? If I had lain there with Ruth on idyllic greensward our brown skins flecked with dancing gold photons filtered from the sun, then the heads that wrenched her pelvis, would their caps of hair curled counterclockwise?

All at once they are standing at a corner in one of the city's vales, landed there to wait in their long series of sweaty struggles from waiting point to waiting point. "Don't worry, we'll go home in a taxi!" Michael kids them, but their smiles are wan. Hunger is beginning to loom discretely, superadded to the threat of boredom from the fatigue of unremitting adventure. They are making their longest stand of the morning. Clouds no bigger than a man's hand, mere possibilities of fret, rise in the family firmament under the now cloudless blue of the city's Sunday meridian, a time when streetcars like to take it easy. Roger sits blinking with surfeit of scene in his wheeled chair, a trusty and familiar vessel, his integral midget prairie schooner with its hood down, a compact vehicle in which a man can join any train or ford any river, an amphibious bench with many conveniences.

The machine is so well contrived, so intricately light and collapsible, that the sight of it brings contrition to the father's heart who once grumbled and grudged and evaded and delayed the appropriation for it, after having first grumbled and grudged and evaded and delayed its noncommittal authorization: a brand-new device at that, never previously used by others, which he said would turn out to be merely the indulgence of a transitory and hallucinatory "*need*" on the mother's part that no puritan or pioneer ancestor had ever needed. "You were right about this thing" now he says, pressing her hand contritely, almost with a sensation of moisture in his eyes. She responds with a definite squeeze and a happy smile. And thus one old debt is wiped out, that the next one he incurs may sit the more easily.

Roger bends down to kiss the abacus rigged to his desk, laying his cheek for a moment on the cool surface; but his head bobs up again at the thought of a kiss that thereby comes to him. "Boo-ool! Boo-ool!" he calls out.

At this signal Ruth rifles through two or three of the luggages stacked against the brick wall of a building where the boys have set them, working with an ostentation calculated to allay Roger's incipient impatience, blatantly demonstrating by word and action an intelligent response to his demand. The little king's longsuffering good humor must be somewhat cajoled, eked out until, properly encamped and fed, he can be permitted to sleep stretched out in his mobile tent during the heat of the afternoon.

From a shopping bag she at last produces the large urine-absorbent companion of Roger's crib at home: firm of flesh except at the floppy joints, brown of carcass black of ear white of face red of nostril, but mouthless, with fixed eyes that seemed to roll: the Friendly Bull. "Boo-ool, boo-ool!" Roger croons, accepting it without surprise or gratitude, appreciating his mother's providence not at all, clutching it to his breast however with hoops of steel, kissing the blunt nose. With revived love he coos hugs cuddles snuggles and babbles in uninhibited pillowship, there at the edge of a dangerous open space in a foreign city, guarded by the watchful Mama Bear.

The Father Bear and the Brother Bears, ears cocked for the distant approach of a streetcar, steal off around the corner into a narrow ascending street of tenement houses. More education, but this time no lecture. Up from the avenue they climb in silence, the boys so impressed by such lousy trappings of the great city that even knowledgeable Jonathan does not pretend to have anticipated his disgust.

They come upon a hillside alley in which two citizens are altercating passionately. One of them is smaller than Matthew, though much older belike, fantastically thin, wearing absurdly a long-visored baseball cap split at one of the seams, a black sleeveless undershirt from a larger citizen's wardrobe, long trousers scraping the dust and torn at the pocket, now and then showing a grimy sockless ankle bone, and low blue tattered sneakers tied to his feet with string. He is having his arm twisted and his chest thumped by the other. The aggressor is twice as big as his victim, an older and more beautiful child dressed in a whole baseball cap, a white undershirt with short sleeves, dungarees neither too long nor too short, and high white-trimmed black sneakers with yellow socks under them. His black hair is greasily pompadoured in imitation of the city's drugstore cowboys. He is forcing a candy bar out of the weaker one's hand.

Blazing darkskinned Sicilian boys with sweet faces and white teeth, shouting all the while in authentic violence of spirit, chopping precocious little body punches that truly hurt. It might be English they are shouting, unintelligible English—unintelligible until the little one screams "Fuck you Salvatore!" with no Italian accent at all. Salvatore kicks scornfully at the younger and laughs. He now has the candy and is arrogantly tearing off the paper wrapper, flinging new rubbish onto the pavement already covered with trash in conformance with his community's disdain for public ordinance.

Now a pale little man shrouded in black clothes, blackly unshaven, carrying a black valise streaked with white stains, projected headlong around the corner by his descent of an upper street, hurries down the alley. He has seen nothing of the conflict but he knows without doubt exactly what has happened. "Hey kid, whaddya want with him? Leddim alone, leddim alone!"

"Aw he's only m'brudder."

"Okay then." And the man keeps going without breaking his stride, though gradually slowing as he continues along the walled contour path of the goatless hillside, as if he might have hoisted his load to the top of his head, past the kids, paying no attention to the timid bourgeois he's already passed. Maybe he's a baker on the way home to his own family. The gamins stare after him shoulder to shoulder until he is out of sight. They too ignore the little Lord Fauntleroys and their old man looking in the same direction from further off.

Then the victim resigns. He sits down on the curb to scoop handfuls of dirt from the gutter and throw them toward the opposite wall of the alley. The big brother is still cramming the candy into his mouth when he takes a bald tennis ball out of his pocket, swaggers past the clean-living Chapmen out onto the street, and begins to bounce the ball off the steps of a house across the way. He throws it sharply with a sidearm motion and fields it with graceful surly skill, flinging it again and again on tricky hops in cycles of increasing rapidity, effectively challenging further upward progress by the Anglo-Saxons.

Jonathan tugs at his father's elbow. "Let's go back! I think I hear the streetcar coming." he whispers, fearing that the tough kid will not continue to ignore him. Matthew is tugging too, wordlessly, but in another direction, toward the alley, fearing nothing under his father's protection whom he is silently urging to offer reparation to the victim.

But Michael checking a like impulse concludes that any kind of indemnity or comfort would only make things go harder for the little brother afterwards, and he is especially conscious of the contempt for himself that would be felt and certainly exhibited by both the natives if he dealt succor to one without an ear-boxing to the other whom he couldnt hope to catch or endure the insults of, not to mention the neighbors stirred by any outcry against missionaries. So he turns back agreeing that the streetcar is due and wondering how he could in any other way explain his decision to stouthearted Matty.

As soon as the Chapmen move down hill the big boy goes back into the alley and they hear the little brother's rage burst forth in unsuspected maturity; then the more distant screech of a mother putting an end to the skirmish. Matt keeps looking back over his shoulder as he is dragged down the slope by his own brother's claw on his biceps, trying to guess the sequel and weeping he thinks unnoticed. As it turns out the streetcar is still a long way off. But he's absorbed the diversion without protest, calling no attention to the arrested crystals evaporating from his pure cheek in the palmy blue sunlight.

"I lived in a place something like this when I was your age." Michael says to his boys, hoping to foster family pride by exaggeration.

"Were you that poor Daddy?" Matty asks, looking up in self-forgetful wonder at the great wise face. It comes into his mind that a father's youth can have been different from his own.

"Yes. I never had enough adjectives when I was a kid." Perspective and mystery.

The not unruthless man thus returns to Ruth, who says nothing of her apprehension about his spate of zeal for realism.

The old uneasy dilemma of family life: truth versus kindness. For himself truth, truth from first to last when he acts for himself; for Ruth, kindness, only kindness, when she doesnt have to make concessions to truth in deference to her husband. What about the boys? Is it any good to educate them beyond their mother's limits, beyond their own experience? Wouldnt conflict in parental policy serve them worse than her excessive protection? Which would damage their manhood the more, ignorance or shock? —Shock that would have been no shock if from the very beginning he had refused to compromise with kindness, if he had taken the time to give them his pain for the sake of truth.

Suddenly a wave of disgust and anger inundates Michael's parlous geniality. The same old waste of a day in the life of triple pollination that he himself had brought to naught. What can all his fatness come to when he feeds on years like this? Irritations are nothing, struggle is nothing, the suffering of inefficiency is nothing, nothing is anything—so long as it does not fall to him on a totally wasted day: but now he remembers that this day was doomed at its inception.

Just as suddenly, albeit, he is delivered from despair and recovered from perversity by the voice of Roger charming him back to the cave. "Kee-ee, kee-ee!" shrills out clear and pure. The manling has been observing while his siblings were brooding and his parents thinking thoughts.

He points vigorously at a window in the brickwork above their heads. They wheel about, father mother brother and brother, to see a large gray cat staring at them, paws afolded under its most serene chest, as inviolate in its highness as if it watched from the loftiest balcony on Nob Hill. Nothing but dirty torn lace curtains can be seen behind the royal couch.

Glory be to God, Roger has set off a new squib of good cheer, which Ruth underhears in the higher alertness of true kin-craft. She has a good ear, the best ear in the world for the hypostases of speech, if not for vaporous speech itself.

"His eyes look like the cashier's cat's!" says Jonathan, seeking to put his father in conceit with himself; but Matty's currently favorite doggerel supervenes:

> "I like dogs,
> I like cats,
> But in my sandwich
> I like brats!"

Which brings on the counter-chant of Jonathan, who, laying aside the allusions of culture, presents them with a stanza of original recitative:

> "The cat wanted to drink
> But couldn't drink—
> Because Deedle-de-dee-diddle-dum did!"

"Did you have a kitty when you were a little boy Dad?" Matthew asks. "Yes."

"Ha!" Jonathan jeers gleefully. "I thought you said you were poor!"

"Ya, ya!" cries Matt, thrusting a singled finger almost into Michael's lips and hopping up and down on the periphery of a semicircle. They think they have the wiley old owl trapped.

Though in a million other tight spots Michael may find himself at a loss for words, here he is master. "Cats are nouns. Nobody but a dumbbell is ever too poor to have those."

This retort nonpluses the boys just long enough, until the streetcar is all at once sailing up to them. Roger does not forget to look back at the cat and wave "Bye!", though only a few days ago he would not have thought of saying the word unless he had first noticed his arm extended before him, so rapidly was the logos gaining ascendancy over the action that engenders it.

The family grabbed and folded, and piled aboard. The motorman was indulgent of their unpreparedness thanks only to a lovely greeting from Roger. Since the pilgrimage was getting close to the Delectable Mountain there were many people on this last conveyance and it was necessary for the older boys to behave more circumspectly than theretofore.

"Can I have the extra orange cupcake, Daddy?" Jonathan whispered to the archangel.

"When the time comes" the father whispered back confidentially "ask the martyr. She's in charge of foods."

"Well don't take it Daddy, will you?"

Roger's second wind of attentiveness (the only baby among all the passengers, for most babies who get to go to the zoo ride there in private cars) captivated the holyday throng, not the least among them his mother and father, and not the less among his father and mother his father, who grinning held him on his lap with as much satisfaction as any Italian with his first nipotino, making the most of the one uncomplicated affection that in spite of all private and exclusive hopes can bind an erethistic hermit to the world he rides in.

Roger's person by some rather improbable constellation of happy causes was still clean dry and sweet-smelling, the blue of his parti-colors matching and drawing all eyes to the hyperhuman blue of the merry eyes at the center of that moving universe. ["The sun is not so central as man." some Protestant had said.] He pointed Roger did at the one sour old dame who had been resisting his charm, and said "Doggie!", making her smile at last, no old bitch after all, proving his own word wrong, on the very occasion when one would least expect a lady to smile.

Now in his moment on the stage he pointed at an electric bulb in the ceiling travelling with him as constantly as the audience and intoned "Sky!". (An actor he is, a most accomplished comedian, trying out every word he knows, stabbing at correspondences, very pleased with himself and no more unaware of the strangers' approbation than of his father's, emitting as the carrier of his communicative words a continuous wave of rhythmically unarticulated comments and ejaculations in his native language, which he still relies upon for explanation or justification of his emotions.) All the oddnesses of the Chapman menage were excused by this its latest gemmation. Roger's bright delicate self-confident intelligence was acceptable to the world at his age, and for the nonce it enticed into movement nearly every soul dull or neurotic that encountered it.

Nevertheless this little fellow's mind would not open to the things views buildings vehicles that began again to interest his father outside the moving universe. No matter how hard Michael pointed (without being able to extend his arm), or thumped on the glass too, Roger looked only at the lips that spoke the words, or at the glasses out of which his father looked at the kinematic mise en scene, or at the lips glasses ornaments and other properties of the people who saw his father's failure at demonstrative teaching (and never had that portly man been less inconspicuous in public). Nothing would make the whelp look out the window. Ruth and the big boys were becoming uncomfortable at the highly unbefitting deportment of their captain, who was behaving like an anthropocentric dog-trainer at the end of his patience (well aware of the probability that the next time Roger rode a streetcar either he'd be beyond the reach of instruction or the instructor would have no stomach left for showing him the sights); though—for acting like a million other dying and self-perpetuating fathers ludicrously attempting to pump their delights of experience into heirs who were still potentially susceptible to paternal outsights (of which fathers there happened to be none other present at the moment to let Mr Chapman appear as normal as he was)—they were not yet painfully ashamed of him.

(10)
HY.04
WASTED PITCH

*T*he magnified eye of Mr Chapman codlike neckless jaw-hung mouthbreathing utterly unreceptive goggled at the natty man from San Francisco who walked coolly in with pointed black shoes ostentatiously appraising without praise the merchandise on display and asked for Mr Greatrakes.

"He aint here."

"When will he be back?"

"Tonight."

"Mr Chapman then?"

"That's me."

"My name's Max Rose, from Universal Distributors."

"I know. I remember you."

"Last time I was here Greatrakes said I should see you. You were'ent around at the time."

"I remember you from last year. I heard you talking to Mr Greatrakes about your services."

"Oh yeh. I recall your face, now that you mention it. Never knew you was Chapman. Been promoted? Congratulations." He took Mr Chapman's hand, friendly as he knew how to be; but the indifferent hand immediately dropped back to where it had been, twitching and tapping on the counter. Max's headway was checked. "Can I talk to you now?"

"I guess so." Mr Chapman looked fastidiously at the watch strapped to his incongruously slender wrist. "Until Sam has to go to lunch." His fund of good nature was clearly reserved for those of his own kind, inasmuch as he called out to Sam in cheerful friendly fashion: "Sam, call me if there's a change in the weather."

Max followed Chapman into the back room undiscountenanced. An antisemitic individual without doubt. He's some kind of a nut anyway. No fast-movers anywhere in the store. Not worth my time. But I'll make Greatrakes buy over this guy's head. Owners always go for the best deal in the end. Chapman stood leaning against the work table while Max half seated himself on a stool. He was not invited into the office. The scene was set for argument, not for reasonable persuasion. Those rimless spectacles glinted now, and no human eye could be ascertained. But opacity was a comfort in discussing pure economics with the adversary.

Max tried to explain the rising practice of wholesaling in the trade, for the benefit of the manufacturer the wholesaler *and* the retailer. Chapman knew all about it. But something was eating him. He resents the exclusives we already have, the bastard: he hates it that he already has to buy through us to get some old standbys; he's scared we're going to tie him up for other houses.

"We've got a much bigger line now, and we're adding all the time. New warehouse on Third Street; three trucks of our own. Overnight service to you, don't forget. We stock all the popular items." He opened his catalog case but Chapman refused to look.

"That's the trouble Mr Rose. You're in the commodity business." [Sure I'm in the commodity business. I should be selling radio spots?] "For the most part we buy specialties. That's what I'm building on. Go up the street: the other stores are more interested in popular items. I'm not competing for that trade."

Why the hell are'ent you? "No matter how thin you slice it—a rose by any other name—you're interested in profits. High turnover. The margin is less, sure, because we have to carry the inventory and make a nickel. But you save transportation costs, and you can return any item within ninety days for full credit. Our truck is over this way almost every day to pick up returns as well as to make deliveries without cost to you."

"The way things are going in this business I'll have to buy through jobbers soon enough. And when I do you'll get my business because you deserve it. No one else has called on us. What you say about profit is true enough. Maybe you can save so much on carload freight orders from the East that there's real economic justification for jobbing. But most of the stuff I'm interested in you would never stock: I'd have to get it from New York anyway; and while I was at it I'd just get the few of your stock items that I needed at my full discount from the same place. If I split our business we'd lose on both ends. Besides, if I analyzed the costs I'd find that the postage on our small orders from the East is less than the discount we'd lose by buying indirectly through you. Thanks to the postal tariffs authorized by the Congress of the United States we're no worse off than the shops in Cambridge. Furthermore we absorb postage in our mail-order business and we need every single percent of margin we can pick up."

But Max knew that Chapman did not like the very concept of jobbers. "Greatrakes doesn't think that six percent is too much to pay for a much higher turnover. U D takes the risks, U D pays the freight, U D —"

"Well if we order properly, with enough lead time, our turnover will be just as good. We can get stock in ten days."

"Naw, you can't do it, you can't forecast every sale you're going to make for ten days ahead! You'll be out of stock, you'll lose sales! But we have a scientific inventory control system: we have over a hundred outlets and we can forecast their combined demand pretty accurately, the popular items—'cause we don't stock items that won't move!" The last phrase he added warmly.

"That's just it!" Chapman permitted himself a prim self-congratulating smile drawn by tight muscles, a stiff animation that persisted in the beholder's retina no longer than a single frame of the steadily churning cinema. The quick conversation was passing into its final phase, rehearsed and fully expected, but indispensable to the conduct of either man's business. "Most of our items we turn over only once a year. You'd never stock those, and we can afford to wait ten days to replace them. During that time the probability of a call for them is about one in thirty-six."

Max was still new to this particular kind of wholesaling, for indeed it was a new application of ancient commercial principle, but he recognized this fancy numbers-man type, retailers too educated for their own good. "But we sell to a lot of stores. If an item turns only once on the average for all our customers we have enough volume to justify stocking it. Try me out! Name one and I'll tell you." Again he made motions toward his bag as a matter of form, but he was easily stopped by the protest that he knew Chapman was smart enough to offer.

"Yuh but if an item turned over even two or three times a year in only two or three of your stores—"

"That's right: it wouldn't pay to stock it." Max frankly admitted. Now that the interview was nearly concluded he shucked off the restraints on his anger that had been imposed by the nominal hope for an order. According to the axioms of salesmanship he should have kept his patience, stayed his manner at a certain level of subordination, with some view toward the future, but he was proud to be an old-fashioned peddler at heart: life was too short for alien amenities. "Sure, we can't handle special orders on our margin. But then your store's got no business stocking the stuff either!"

"Those are the items I'm most interested in." said Chapman, putting on the air of a haughty patron. "People don't come to this store if all they want is the ordinary crap."

What can you say to a stuck-up ash-hole like that? "You're shitting against the tide!" was all that Max could bring forth, not even So long I'll call again. The whole gang in here must be a bunch of fairies. Greatrakes sounds like one anyway, talks like he always has mashed potatoes in his mouth, and flipping his hands around like a girl. Or maybe Reds.

Max left without another word, casting disdainful eye upon the merchandise he saw on the way out, unhurriedly sneering. Outside the door he paused to glance contemptuously at the window display, lighting a cigarette and letting it dangle from his worldly lips, savoring the hatred of the gaze that was presumably following his movements from the back of the store.

The scene set by the storefront was just too queer for words. Good clean space all wasted. Prices were too prominent, and too much emphasis on cheap goods. And there was even some second-hand merchandise, and no bones about it, right there in the brightly varnished racks outside the door. Too much variety. Everything different, but no cumulative effect, no color, no psychological inducement to buy for elegance or prestige. If you're going to sell rarities you want to highlight expense and background. Like *The New Yorker*. If you don't want to be popular you've got to be fancy. One or the other. You can't have it both ways.

But there it was in the window, a solid mass six feet high like an abstract mural. He tilted his head to read, hand-lettered in black crayon on a strip of adding machine tape stretched diagonally from bottom to top like a cartooned beauty-contest sash, YOU CAN ALWAYS ENTRENCH YOURSELF BEHIND A GREAT WALL OF BOOKS. Supposed to be something clever about the war scare I suppose. What's the use? We'll get the Berkeley trade through the other stores. Someday drugstores and newsstands too. We've come a long way since we just distributed magazines and World Almanacs. These eggheads won't stay in business much longer anyhow.

{*Postulants only*: GO TO ITEM (12) SA.05, page 123.}

(11)

SO.01.1

LITURGY

5.

*S*ometimes things are made by dromena. Most ritual merely recurs,
perhaps slightly altered in the repetition but leaving no change in
the world, maybe only an alteration of feeling or perception. But
certain ritual acts leave the objective world different from what it
would have been for the lack of them—either changing it or keeping it
going when it would have run down.

It takes work to mutate matter, to transform energy, to overcome friction, and work may be performed by a discharge of disequilibrium
brought about by previous change of state or by an extraordinary human
willingness to exceed nature. *Liturgy* is this special case of ritual, the religious work of the priests and the laity together. Like ritual in general it is
collectively mandatory, but it is also conditionally necessary to the cure of
the individual and absolutely necessary for the survival of society.

From Huizinga I have Frobenius's statement that ritual is "playing at
nature". This notion may be accepted in reference to certain kinds of
primitive ritual, but it is typically defective as definition in that it fails to
comprehend the opening of closed systems. When ritual organizes itself
more finely than the nature that surrounds its moment and its place, and

thereby dissatisfies itself with natural rhythms or natural emotions—and if it is not then to die—it must erupt its old boundaries to admit influxions of external energy. By opening the things done and the place in which they are done to communication with the world, liturgy makes of the in-formed corporate circle an engine for the dynamic exchange of physical and psychic energy. The extent of the expanded field determines the historical importance of the work. Ritual that is only played remains closed to all forces except those represented by its own internal tensions.

The work done in liturgy exceeds the product of the force and the displacement ("distance" as naturally experienced during performance) by the energy which is introduced from the wider system and dromenologically converted. (The energy metabolized in waking, erecting, and moving one's body is as great as the internal work produced, disregarding the heat loss inevitable in life's conversions. Therefore I cancel from ritual's equation the work of forgathering, posture-holding, and motion. The net accomplishment of nonliturgical ritual is no work at all.) If the energy required to differentiate the acts of ritual is no greater than that required to differentiate approximately equal physical acts of human life in general, the dromenon effects no remarkable exchange and accordingly involves no extraordinary amount of information: there is no energy available for work in response to exceptional purpose. So I say that liturgy is ritual into which counterentropic energy and/or information is transferred from the world beyond the circle.

It follows from Huizinga's definitions as well as from mine that liturgy cannot be *played*, and from mine alone that dance cannot be one of liturgy's distinctions. But it does not follow that liturgy cannot be *imagined*. To rule out that exclusion in this glossary it is sufficient to state that the imagination of liturgy converts it from a special case of ritual to a special case of drama.

When Brooks Adams calls capital *energy* he means potential energy. Your balance sheet is a cross-section photographed at an arbitrary interval of time. It shows your net wealth, a measurement of the movement or transformation still subject to the control of your will, or at least of the net advantage you will enjoy from any permitted use of your property. It may take a long time to accumulate this disposable energy, and it may take a longer or shorter time to dissipate it, but in economic life the only way to spend your capital instantly is to give it away, orgastically. Alexander could cut the Gordian knot because, as Huizinga emphasizes, a riddle is a game whose rules can be broken; but no one can cut a knot of work without sacrifice.

Sacrifice is a twofold work of liturgy: the work required since the last sacrifice to produce the new capital, and the work performed in a burst of power within the ritual action to spend that capital, or to transform it utterly, for the intended benefit of the commonwealth. It is a decisive gift to the god, but its returns are problematical. I say that only one liturgy has ever been truly successful (despite the prevalent perversion of its practice), and its continuation remains in final doubt. But in all liturgies the work of economics is coupled to the hopeful work of surgery.

This is not Alexander's kind of surgery, using the kinetic energy of an instrument hoisted aloft, but intelligent work with the hands, working knowledge, *episteme*, learned in doing—making and made by knowledge of the end, *telos*. The eye and the ear convey information to the brain but the hand is the brain's chief agent, technology's tongue, in reshaping "perceptual groups" of matter. The laity brings its economic work to the *temenos*, and there the priest, with tremendous leverage of delicate sentient muscle-power, endows it with metaphysical value by the form or position he gives it with his hands.

By motion and touch—but also by word. The priest's mouth is a Maxwell's demon within the larger Maxwell's demon of the corporate event, catching, fixing, and applying the most highly informed energy of energy already highly informed. The vocal geste is the psyche's act to bring the dromenon to the highest pitch of organization and to precipitate an economic transmission. Speech like a hand's hand further condenses the accumulated capital that the priest has isolated as sacrificial matter at its instant of maximum free energy. Except for certain achievements of personal imagination this is the moment of lowest possible entropy for the culture: the use and sustenance of prime myth.

Most ritual misses this mark. By the same token most "mythology" is secondary—fanciful, ludicrous, or psychic—either cut off and degenerated from cardinal myth or generated and sustained by primitive or decadent ritual. But in the special case of ritual that brings to bear an extraordinary concentration of energy, force exceeds the requirements of motion and semantic value exceeds the requirements of rubric and communication. Acts of hand and mouth that are ordinarily undistinguished transcend natural history by virtue of a crucial distinction that is conferred by the god at particular places under particular conditions. He is arbitrary in selecting specified materials acts and words from all the symbolic matter that otherwise might seem equipotential. He has distinguished sacrament among the elements of certain dromena. Liturgy is *sacramental ritual*.

From my definitions it follows that any ritual is either liturgical or nonliturgical; and that nonliturgical ritual may be either preliturgical or postliturgical, historically or ontologically. The decadence of ritual is what we mostly see, and most cultures seem to have been forever disappointed of liturgy: they fail to produce it at their ritual maturity; and their cults, petrified into unthinking superstition, are perhaps perpetuated only by ceremonial tradition.

Liturgy bucks the devolutionary probability to which other ritual generally succumbs. Therefore it must be worked, and it may be imagined, but it can never be played. Its information reforms the natural world, for the moment, locally. It cannot begin, and it cannot survive, in genetically encoded adaptation to the received environment.

6.

We have reduced dromenon to two elements, *action* and *word*. In liturgy they are approximately coequal components of ritual work and its transforms. In other ritual, as in drama and game, their proportions may vary from one extreme to the other. If we had a way to measure differing densities of the respective powers of motion and utterance we would have a science of dromenology in the making, for we could equably parse all the terms in our taxonomic network. They obviously enter into the vocabulary of related studies (as an element is likely to enter into a variety of compounds and mixtures), motion for instance being the substance of sport far beyond the boundaries of dromenon. Likewise word is the sole element of mythology. But its part in ritual is so complex that another level or two of distinction is called for.

The fact of tradition proves that the collective consciousness is invested in ritual words (since we do not have the heritable instincts of ants or birds). Things said determine things done or feelings and thoughts about things done. They are causes, usually necessary causes, but never sufficient causes, to effect transformations. Given words dedicate the material of sacrifice and at the same time inform the mind that directs the hand.

Other words, or the same words functioning dually, are spoken or sung *about* the dromenon of which they form a part. Things that are said about the ritual act can be discriminated into those that account for it and those that interpret it. Words of interpretation tend to separate themselves from the dromenon as gospel.

Making bold with Jane Harrison's studies in *Themis*, I propose to reserve the term *legomena*, things said, for words of the first category: the prayers and rubrics that recollect, direct, assist, inform, determine, or confirm the action. Within this set of technical intelligences we can distinguish the *effective* from the *procedural*.

I then appropriate the term *mythos* (that which comes from the mouth) for words or aspects of words in the second category: things said that describe or give meaning to what is done. *Mythos* I use as prime myth, uttered during ritual action; but of course after the thing is done it can transcend the particular occasion and elaborate itself in the exclusively verbal manner of mouth-made images. Thence it's off into the limitless world of the *logos* and *gnosis*.

7.

Now take *ritual* as a substantive adjective, as you would take *beautiful* if there were no noun *beauty*: that which pertains to rites. At *rite* we get to the particular, the algorithmic syntax of locomotion, surgery, and language proper to a certain repetition of occasions at specially used places, but originally used at one site only. *Ritual* describes a set of rites that accomplish the same thing, or, as I have so far chiefly used it, a set of such sets. But *rite* is like *a* play in drama, *a* game in play: specified action. People "belong" to their rite. They learn it as easily and no more easily than anything else that dawns upon a child's consciousness; and only at epochs of evolutionary jump does it occur to them that it can be performed in another way.

That's what rite is: way, flow, procedure, ordinal. I call it an algorithm because it is a controlled sequence of functions or equations that are each worked out for the sake of gaining entry to the next, played through to a solution (as Huizinga rightly has it when his diction is apt), or at least pretended to be experienced; and because the word accidentally brings to mind both poetic numbers and the beat of dance.

Hence a rite embeds the logic of a culture's transformations. The operating statement of an enterprise ("Profit and Loss") includes and links a finitude of states recognized as a succession of recorded or unrecorded balance sheet equations, which are serialized cross-sections of time; but whereas your P & L only summarizes what has happened between moments, your rite, like a bookkeeping journal (if we can accept more frequent changes of recorded state as digitally homologous to kinetic and continuous reality), enacts the very process.

A man on the stage knows nothing of tragedy, while he carries out the instructions of the piece, save from the words he speaks and hears; and a lover, in his private play, wishes to know nothing about the reproduction incarnate in the procedure he follows for another purpose: so also with the work that can be accomplished, perhaps unknown on any one member's part, in pursuing the choreography of the rite. The ritual program makes an action that is equivalent in event to a transitive sentence in the mind, but the action requires no mind to comprehend it. Meaning in the verbal structure is pleonastic, and conscious meaning, to whatever necessary degree, embarrasses the exchange of energy.

To be sure, the procedural legomenon has meaning as certain sequences of operational words, especially as directions and cues, as definitions, as communication of the tradition; but even in liturgy (excluding mythic hermeneutics) the physiognomy and structure of the rite as a whole can be called "meaningful" only if we accept the debasement of the meaning of meaning whereby anything organized, ordered, or even recognizable is said to "mean" something. The dromenon is an act, not a statement.

Yet of necessity a sacrament is symbolic. Of human necessity, procedural or efficient action as well as procedural or efficient word suggests metaphor—in case we are interested. And we are often so interested, especially in things done (for which we have accompanying words of description), that we mentally colligate casually similar behaviors, to which we assign the same symbol, and pretty soon forget that only language sustains the analogy and habitually connects one behavior with another in our minds. There is no stopping us. The most painstaking writing has failed to keep us from assuming as a mode of thought that things refer to other things simply because they share representation in our most complete system.

It is consequently difficult to believe in exclusive fashion that something is "contained truly, really and substantially, and not in sign, figure or virtue" in the consecrated sacramental species, and that liturgy is not merely "pointless but significant" (as Huizinga thinks it is, quoting a certain Guardini, with Plato in support). I would cite Zipf: "The apparent antithesis of real and symbolic resolves itself in the problem of evaluating the degree of reality." Like the Jungian gnostics, Huizinga would have it the other way: they resolve the dialectical problem by the degree of symbolism.

I must grant that all things can be construed symbolically, and that liturgy, once it has been made self-conscious by the myth it generates, or once reflected from the eyes of a spectator, is open to the objective conspection that defines phenomena. The problem of the leveling tendency of symbolism manifolds itself in the very proliferation of words introduced in homeopathic fashion to fight with distinctions and differences the metaphor that like a gravitational field centers in every meaning. If you see "speech as a course through a universe of acts of behavior" you accept the fact that ritual cannot do without symbol.

Words abbreviate experience, and the more familiar they are the faster they move us through it. But when for speed you sweep a large arc with a small twist you lose detail and fine control. Without this kind of compression ritual cannot take place, for it is a habitual collective instrument; yet without the refined power of linguistic differentiation there can be no gain over the past. Through regenerative feedback the slightest verbal or somatic experiment disturbs community of action; whereas, on the other hand, if increasing velocity (from habit) blurs the clarity of gesture your cult loses its equilibrium with the changing environment of the open social system by worshipping the fixed old rhythm itself instead of the living god. These are the opposing decadences of drama and magic respectively.

The only unperverted definition of *worship* hinges on the concept of assigning value (to a god), which is the function of praise. When men have managed the world as far as they can, and the managerial urge has not yet attenuated, they praise, they exhibit the energy of appreciation. There is no differentiation like the full attention of language when speakers know that they cannot manage the world alone. Such praise calls for a spectrum of scales: anatomy, geography, and astronomy in one articulation. Thus myth is made apposite to the work of sacrifice, far-ranging on the horizon of a small place.

8.

Care without cure, in speech, in movement, in the choice and arrange-ment of material: that's *ceremony*. Its purpose is not accomplishment but elegance of use, and originally it is a matter of some bishop's discrimina-tion among innumerable pleasant vestiges of tradition. Ceremony waxes as efficient motion wanes. The manners of appearance tend toward mere dis-play. The ceremonial aspect of primary physical action scarcely reaches consciousness, but when there are witnesses who are not performers and sensibility overtakes action, the "art" of the rite is all that can be seen. When priests and people think they can save themselves by doing things exactly right they become anxious about the way they look.

They then justify the whole rite as symbolic. The dromenon becomes a mere display of the cult, ceremony its rhetoric. Of course it takes some ceremony to carry out liturgy self-perpetuatingly in ordinary society, with form and rhythm that can be remembered and reenacted with pleasure (though in such circumstances as those of a concentration camp an emer-gency rite can be devised to do the liturgy without any ceremony at all); and ceremony alone may establish civil manners.

The confusion of *rite* and ritual *ceremony* arises with art's contestation of religion, when old hopes are weakening, when religion preoccupies itself with mere reassurance and with what has been called "extrication" from the real world, and when people go to church because it's the one thing that they expect not to change in the modern world. Thoroughgoing Prot-estants spiritualize their local assemblies by entirely substituting arbitrary ceremony for rite, thus purporting to assert their independence of artificial forms, while para-Catholics use ceremonial rite as a substitute for creative art as well as for sacrifice.

These epidromenal accretions begin as gloss and interpolation. They embellish the main action and like farce stuff the interstices with some-thing to hear, look at, or smell. It is the ceremony that the child is taught, like rote arithmetic without science of number. Acolytes become an order of the clergy: orderlies, supposedly, of officers. But these contingent externals sometimes fasten in the god's imagination, and it has sometimes happened that they reenter culture at a new stage of ritual as elements of sacramental dromena, as myths also reenter and fulfill themselves, as words become metaphor and then become newly literal. "Let the children of Israel keep the passover . . . according to all the rites of it, and according to all the ceremonies thereof." Among these ceremonies the Lord later found sacraments for the second dispensation.

{*Postulants only*: GO TO ITEM (13) S0.01.2, page 129.}

(12)
SA.05

PICNIC LUNCH

*T*hey arrived at the main gate of the tuileries for a blue and green afternoon of society all hot and bright. The cold gray drab with which Sunday had disguised its intentions in the morning no longer put off the pleasure-seekers of the metropolis whose zoo it was. Michael's dogged foresight and logistical skill had nearly compensated for outlandish handicaps of distance and transport. With two hours of headstart he was practically even with the competition. But family carriages were beginning to arrive at the parking lot and it was only a matter of minutes before droves of rich peasants would embouch in a swarm.

The instant foot was laid upon turf ravenous hunger overwhelmed the several wills that Michael had to reconcile to his own. Inasmuch as this was a picnic, the family had come to eat. The father acquiesced to this syllogism not because of its tautologic but because its effect was to sanction several expediencies, one of which was to stake out ground before it could be claimed and colonized by rivals, another of which was to keep his wife from getting angry, and the third of which was to gratify his own the greatest appetite.

The people chode with Moses. Contention and doubt was not about the schedule but about the site. A family divided against itself is handicapped all over again in a rush for land. Michael could not trust Ruth's choice who seemed insufficiently theoretical; there were too many fine places along unending green alleys and within clean copses of fresh trees. He would not come all this way only to eat in the first clearing that came along. But noon was passing over their heads. Time was sweeping them along. The tide had set.

He led them from point to point, bounding ahead first on one course and then on another, fitfully exploring the compass of selections while maintaining a general course away from the origin, always racing to keep ahead of the commoners that were fanning out behind them, vowing to miss nothing good in his haste. With a series of final preferences hovering on the tip of his tongue he shook off the all-too-ready compliance offered by his followers, who gladly waived their opportunities for preliminary inspection.

Having passed the zenith of acceptable locations, as the number of his rejections mounted—as experience and disillusion implanted his secret regret for dozens of spots he had spurned, the epicycles of his careering became tighter and tighter, until at the end he was fairly twirling in indecision. Still even yet awhile he continued to make impulsive chases at shorter and shorter distances, and to find himself in each case disabused upon closing the interval. These disappointments severely tested his inveterate idealism, which persisted no doubt as some glamored distortion of a childhood junket in Massachusetts.

When common sense at last began to close off the favored neurons of edited memory (which had been like to wear an exclusive image into his brain) he grew testy at the apprehension that he might well have passed over the best of all possible picnic-spots in the vain hope of something still better—only to have it overrun and staked out by a party of ignorant villeins before he could reconsider his judgment. But for fear of the martyr finally coming to the end of her endless patience he discarded the idea of dropping garrisons at a couple of good points that he might scout ahead to either eliminate the less good or discover the best possibility and thereby keep three of the most likely prospects under control until he could make a final decision and collect his troops.

What he sought was fresh thick grass, level ground gently swelling with the roots of at least one deciduous aryan tree, solid shade as well as temperate sun, no buildings or roadways in sight, tolerable offing from all paths, and a position not outflanked by sites that would attract audible or visible units of proletariat.

When he finally brought himself to a commitment at nearly one o'clock of the same day, having settled Ruth and Roger, as fate would have it he noticed another clearly superior place that he had unaccountably overlooked ten yards away. He hurried to the better claim, abandoning the first. His shouted summons to move smartly at last was obeyed by the whole tribe. His confidence was restored.

But they had scarcely pitched camp when the matriarch's firm voice was heard to point out that the pitiless sun was o'erspreading their roofless shelter and soon would leave them no shade whatsoever. She would hate that. Roger's tender skin would burn. The milk would curdle. Matt would get a headache. The lettuce would wilt on the way to their mouths. Jonathan would criticize. Michael would sweat. She had no need to speak these scientific predictions: her mute argument was irrefutable; she simply insisted with some display of spirit that they move back to the previous spot. "Here Michael, just take Roger and I'll get all the rest of the stuff. Please." The patriarch was too disgusted and enraged to reply. He simply complied.

Hastening back through the bushes to their last previous stepping stone he found the advance guard of a Republican family setting up its beach chairs: to whom he bared his dull yellow fangs in the manner of a smile and past whom to save face he continued his as it were accidental course, Roger in arms, veering off to the left as soon as possible without betraying his mean chagrin, Jonathan and Matthew trailing along behind him like weary cubs, dragging their loads along the ground, just wise enough to hold their tongues in the presence of winners. Michael doubling back intercepted Ruth and half the remaining baggage midway between the occupied and the untenable.

"Just *anywhere* Michael!" she sighed, daring to add his motto: "Life is too short."

Michael lost no time in proceeding to the mangiest plot in sight, shady all right, and very like a little mountainside in its irregular eminence, bitterly demonstrating his ability to compromise with reality. Their new homestead proved to be situated on a natural shortcut between other bivouacs and a latrine. A rubbish barrel stenciled KEEP YOUR PARK CLEAN was clearly visible behind their principal tree a mottled and graffitied eucalyptus. The precinct was somewhat strewn with a week's paper and popsicle sticks insufficiently attracted by its waste receptacle.

With the sides of their shoes they scuffed away the largest stones of a tiny moraine covering the space between leaves of grass—nay Matty had to scrabble with his hands while Roger watched the untimely game with little patience. Then they spread two blankets so that no one would have to sit in the dirt.

The picnic hampers were at once torn open, and without the mother's assistance. In ten minutes everyone but Ruth and Roger had gulped enough to satisfy nature. Michael and the older boys were ready to leave when the woman and baby were still ruminating, but because they were obliged to wait they resumed eating like Romans stuffing themselves sloped on their sides.

Roger was still silently absorbed in the task of feeding his face when Michael looked over at him. "Roger is homely. He'll never be as handsome as I. Do you think it will give him an inferiority complex?"

"It's not just that that will do it." Ruth answered. "He'll be inferior to you in everything. He already is, and he's not yet three years old!"

"It's not that Roger will have inferior complexion." Matthew threw out, pitching on a different slant. "Daddy has a complication of superiority."

"Wait till Daddy finds out about God!" Ruth warned.

So it was that as usual the very sight of Roger could banish Michael's bad temper (though never beyond recall). Anyway this liberality of conversation put them all in a mood to thenceforth indulge the querulous tones of the greathearted owl who devoted his prime to their livelihood.

"Let's go, let's go, let's *go*. . . . . . go, go, *go!*" Michael murmured dulcetly, leaping to his feet. "For Christ's sake this is Palm Sunday!" More loudly: "The afternoon is half over and we haven't seen anything yet. Every bird is on the wing. This is a big park and Roger has to see it all!" He even went so far as to start cleaning up the mess.

Ruth was now converting Roger's phaeton seat into a prairie-schooner bed and handing him a bottle; soon he would be asleep snug as a sailor and she would change his pants after he woke up. "Roger may not want to see it all." she replied, just in case her husband might be open to reason, just in case her words might drop through to his brain at some unforeseeable crack in the afternoon to come.

Michael kept up his chatter like a shortstop (—like a player-manager, that is). "Jonathan, come and finish the apple. . . . You can't let this milk go to waste, Matt. You were stupid enough to ask for it; now you've got to finish it. . . . Don't forget . . ."

Thus unseemly was the picnic finished with few signs of satisfaction. But Ruth was contentedly disappointed. The essential objective of her day was being accomplished, and no more sadly imperfected than most other achievements. It was cheerful enough simply to eat food with the family away from home, to get out and see strangers. Humming and whistling, as Roger gurgled his bottle peacefully in the private shade of his ark, she rolled up this and tied up that; wrapped up for disposal half-eaten pieces of banana and cake (Michael pretending not to notice); capped bottles (when she could find the caps); stuffed paper into paper bags; took armfuls to the barrel. While she was at it she gathered up some of the midden that their predecessors had overlooked. Michael gave her a little kiss at the back of each elbow. Taking advantage of his affection she asked him to help her shake out the blankets.

A great reserve of victual remained uneaten, after each parcel of it had been reviewed and rewrapped by almost all the members of the family, and was still to be borne, but Michael trod buoyantly at the thought of what had been consumed and thrown away: that which had been thrown away would no longer have to be carried at all and that which had been consumed (being internally assimilated or reduced) required no handles and in any case was about to evaporate in part as gas. A gentleman always travels as light as he can.

But alas he had not calculated on their miscalculation of the weather. Outer clothes and outer shoes that had been more or less evenly distributed about their persons must now be bundled and actually carried—jackets sweaters rubbers hats leggings scarves and everything but mittens—for the weighty insulation could no longer be tolerated on sides backs feet legs necks or heads. A paterfamilias travels heavy.

Out they set again, a ragged sweating caravan: the fretting and determined mule (Michael), the heavily laden Bactrian (ambling double-humped Ruth), two cavorting and errant yearlings of an unknown conscienceless breed (#1 and #2 child), and in their midst drawn or pushed by one drudge beast or the other an unresponsible sahib, too careless of the toil of his escort to stay awake much longer, yet condescending to rough it in the open, sucking from the tropical bottle held singlehanded to his indolent lips, mocking his English contemporaries.

{*Postulants only*: GO TO ITEM (14) SA.06, page 131.}

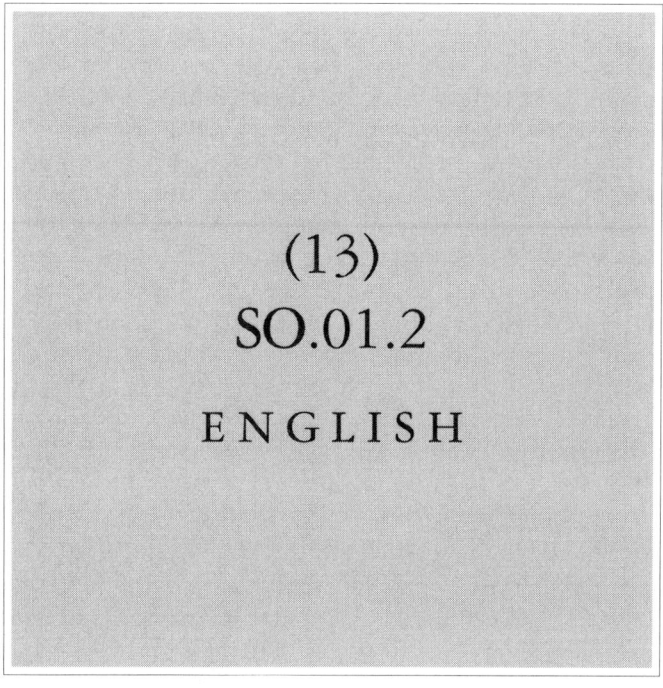

(13)
SO.01.2

ENGLISH

9.

I hope it does not seem ungrateful to complain about Huizinga's book—especially since he is so generous in leading criticism to the attenuations of his anthropological learning, all the while endearing himself to me as a master in pursuit of new intelligence. I am attentive to his collations and etymologies. But he drops his case without meeting two obligations: first, to recognize the essential problem in the affiliation of myth and ritual; and second, this historian of Europe, to look at the barn door, the phenomenon of Christianity, which is either founded in myth or not founded in myth, and if it is founded in myth it preponderates for us among all cases in ethnology, and if it is not founded in myth its ritual and "play of mind" should be assigned a special provenance before we try to discuss the universal experience from which we thus would seem to except ourselves. What mainly concerns a lexicographer, however, is Huizinga's grammar.

This Dutchman has a nice bias for English (which makes you trust his inner eye), but it may be that it is our system that plays him false in the end. He mistakes the liberty with which we use the word *play*, compared with the restrictions placed upon its several counterparts in other languages, for breadth of concept; and the fact that we cleave to the same form for noun, adjective, and verb, I surmise, has led him to deductions that are proper to the more inflected speech of the Continent. Maybe in truth it is only phonetic accident, something about the root sound, that the word strikes us as so tralatitious (we like to play with it so much)— almost as handy as *make* and *do*, often enough puzzling foreigners, I should think, by the way we can switch it, in our idioms, with *work* itself.

It's what you do to a thing, or make its connection with, that seems to start most metaphor, at least in our language: the imaginative use of verbs. But when we let a particular figure crystallize, out of laziness or for the sake of picking up speed through subsequent abridgement of perception, we are likely to modify meanings of the elements even if they have been frozen at some instant of tradition. The difficulty for Huizinga is to decouple the verb from the constructions we have used it in. If he distinguished the function of play from that which is played he would be able to convey his fine feeling for attitude without reckoning overlaps in "general concept" and without, for example, having to make an exception for playful behavior in the earnest "jewel of games". He himself tells us that in Blackfoot any verb can be turned into play by a suffix. It reminds me of the man in Dostoyevsky who says "I didn't mean that: I only said it."

{*Postulants only*: GO TO ITEM (17) SO.02.0, page 171.}

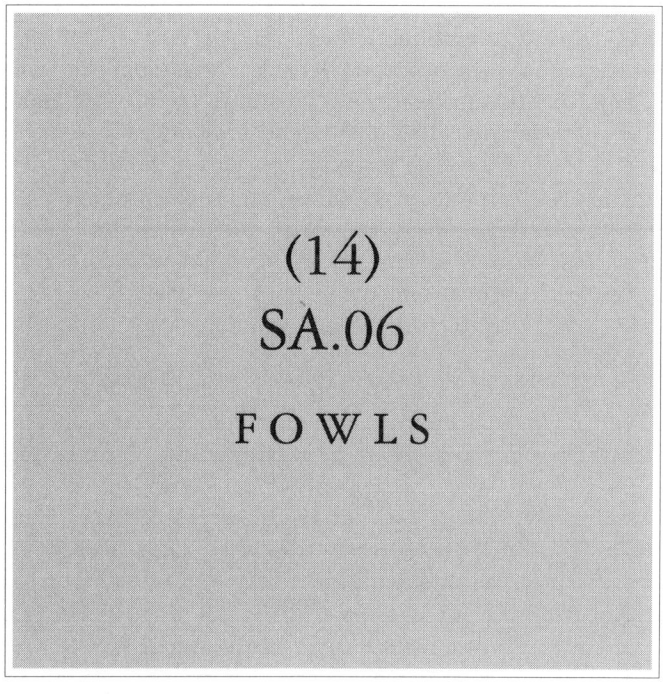

(14)
SA.06

FOWLS

*A*plunge into the garden's depths of the Zoological Society to find whatever public pleasure may lie therein. An unconscionable pastime but for the children. By himself alone, out of the question! Paired only with Ruth, worse! [Meanwhile the wife thinking if only we could come to places like this once in a while without the children as we did in the early exciting days when he courted me! Without a tight belly, without a lean man, can I ever feel like that again, or will he ever again desire me for what I think I know am in spite of what we both now know of each other?] No drinking no reading of verse no unnatural conversation here if the Society could help it; no kissing, no mating. For man as well as beast the fetid miscegenation of smells from various Houses—the odors of six continents lay low and dark under the azure sky, pungent enough to find a way into human blood. The atmosphere at ground level seemed as fertile as the smothered air in which the Chapman half-sons had successfully fastened to their eggs. But the authorities prohibited bestiality. There were no female attendants for the larger mammals.

The musky gases that reached Michael's nose were wafted on an almost undetectable breeze with overlarding scents from musical mixtures of brightbanked variegated Botany. Beautiful species of rooted life without touching seemed to perpetuate each other contrapuntally without the thrill of blood at all, clustered and separated by beds plantations and paths, all of them in their kind moving or growing in a juxtaposition as contrived as a cemetery's. The visiting fauna were awed and directed by planted duchies and principalities whose sanely begotten courtiers stood all about like powdered military police silently controlling pace and choices. The neat flowers shrubs and trees opposed goliards of another kingdom. Yet for their own serene entertainment seals played endlessly in an endlessly curved pool plenished with simulated brine from the mouths of marble dolphins.

The cubs and calves that came to life in Zoology's palaces Michael supposed were conceived and born in secret rooms or at secret hours as if they were the fruit of horribly audacious grafting. Did the males visit their assigned wives—with roar, with purr, with throaty giggle, or silently—under the jealous eyes of their keepers like the inmates of penitentiaries in unenlightened countries where penal policy permitted? In any case the pleasure of such a sight was not to be extracted from a Sunday afternoon walk in the Bois all stippled with impressionistic color. No, a day's pleasure at the boisoise tiergarten was limited to the amusement of recognition—identification of individuals by their species—a childish interest that a man in the company of his own children had not outgrown.

If childhood is the mystic medium joining men and beasts and lilies of the field, so much the more are personal and unique specimens of children the bond of mankind itself, for in children (as animals understand) the class of man is real, not yet nominal only, seeing that men are man so long as possibilities are open to them. All children, inversely with their age, are in some degree capable of exceeding the species, leading it out of the all-too-human or destroying it. Yet all are ideally real, therefore universal, transcending the idiosyncrasies of family blood. Any child in any park, unless it snivel, is an affinity between its father and any other father or mother or potential father or potential mother or formerly potential father or formerly potential mother, and between its father and its mother who are or once were elsewise affined. And the child of any stranger, save to a Nazi, is mankind's mutual gage, collateral between priests and whores, between clean chins and beards. A child is one thing a poet can talk to a Republican about.

In fact if men did not have children Michael's kind wouldnt have anything to say to any other, nor the heart for any speech perhaps; this afternoon would have been an outrageous waste of life. The heat the glare the French colors the German regulations the American impertinencies would have weighed too heavily, to say nothing of the ancient weariness that always complements boredom for beasts for fellows and for self.

It had been the intention of the sheik to miss none of the species ensampled in that zoo but it soon became apparent that not even iron will could accomplish itself with such a weakwilled entourage—weakkneed at any rate. (Men of action are always doomed to somewhat frustrated achievements.) He was obliged to curtail the itinerary. Furthermore once or twice he had to allow Ruth's crochets to obtrude upon his optimized plan of experience—innocent cravings (when little of her interest could be spared from silent preoccupation with possible therapies for the failings of herself Michael and all others in America and nonamerica who lived together and brought children from the first kiss of childbed to the desires of independence) for exotic pinbrained and practically wingless feathery bipeds in cathedral cages, and for such victims of nostalgia as nibbling bunnies purchased by the Trustees from pet shops; and to indulge Matthew's partiality for goatish types: which were all wastefully peripheral to the main purpose of going to a zoo and certainly not to be counted among wise or puissant species.

Michael drew closer to Jonathan whose thirst for archetype was nearly as developed as his own—whose optative vision. (It was a pity he never liked to help the family.)

Now one of the purposes of the Trustees, and Ruth approved it, was to educate city people to the simplehearted existence (except for mating parturition and slaughter) of American animals whose proxy

No child but comes of a woman, and no child but must at length disclose its deficiencies—any child born and trained of woman (who cannot help but abuse the seed as it passes through her athanor and out into the open field of her influence, especially when the seed is of slight character to begin with, a lone tiny scout (vanguarding an otherwise unsuccessful army), high of velocity but low of mass and easily attracted. Yet the wonder is, before deformity sets in, that each child male or female—providing only that it is not born into plain misery—presents to the world of superorganic epideformity a marvelous lobe of male or female possibility. Children not too advanced from their origins are still capable of full culture, still competent to grasp all understandable matters—as far as anyone less than God can know. Blood of course will some day tell; a certain spermatazoon will make its progenitor's mark most noticeable long after the salient Capital I that launched it has been put to the chemical uses of the earth. But until deformities and prejudices from the mother and father begin to discourage the hope of all mankind for each of its children, until then (always too soon) the difference between Democrat and Republican is nothing at all, between pitcher and catcher, between a bookkeeper's wife and a private investor's, or a lineman's and an electrical engineer's. Higher family intelligence is still possible for each and all, under cultivation or pressure, as ambitious parents

as a political bloc was to this day more important than city people's, soul for soul, especially in the Senate, though outnumbered in almost all counties. They were not to be despised, cut off in the antiseptic filth of their concentration camp from the voters whose delegates yielded them too much suffrage. The plain citizens who surrounded the Chapman family, and at least one in the Chapman family, scarcely visualized life as she is really lived down on the farm. Trustees here and elsewhere had discovered that these beasts were as strange to the masses as anteaters and sloths. Their pens were placed along the way to elephants and big cats.

The first and worst colony was a poultry yard which in order to get a look at the Chapmen had to knife through milling spangled finery flowery neckties and sweaty armpits topped with straw hats artificial cherries and balloons of spherically inflated red blue green yellow rubber that might better have been extruded in plain white cylinders for the interception of deformable children, using Roger's vehicle as a prow, sometimes confusing the Chapman procession with others which to all gross appearances were of like kind, brats housewives and shopkeepers.

Inside the wire fence a tall Rhode Island Red paced along beside them with towering comb horrid wattles armored hackles and gorgeous firework tail, pretending to be as wickedly spurred as a gamester. Roger had unaccountably waived his nap after a short repose

gypsies and cuckolding wives can prove. And in the field where Ruth hoed her dream no necessity differentiated the love and trust of one fresh human being from another's, Nazi or white or black; for love and trust though all too delicate and vulnerable in the defective world are more independent of the peculiar dextral or sinistral twist of a father's cryptic strain than talent or intelligence is. The symbols in one gene or other may declare whether the mind of the creature will be reservoir or spring (according as to whether it receives and gives back the word unchanged or changed), but the gladness and pain of love, and the virtue of unselfcentered attentiveness, lie ductile to the touch of the hand that rocks the cradle before it is too late, perhaps even in children excepted from hope by starvation or bondage whose dawning minds have not yet subjected them to awarenesses that dogs and cats are spared. Unclouded by glory come new human beings, having nothing to remember, quanta of evolved sentient energy spewed against time, bursts of clarity almost always in large part futile. Neither opinion nor depravity is brought from another world; birth is no forgetful descent from a mountain top. It's possibly that numbers are known by revelation, since for practical purposes they are preexistent, but boys and girls inform themselves of the liberal arts like spagyrists, ignorant and wilful at first—ignorant of history and failure, wilful for strength or honor but not for acquisition, or at least not for acquisition that requires preoccupation.

with the bottle and risen refreshed from the depths of his berth (which thereupon had been converted to a chair again) and was now crooning softly to himself as he gazed about at the children in the crowd, especially those lower or smaller than himself, nonewhat bothered by teeming masses. The orgulous bird eyed Roger, the two of them stalking and rolling on parallel courses, before Roger eyed the bird. But then the Chapman file turned a corner away from the crowd down a narrow path that clung to the perimeter of the hen yard, and the baby man suddenly sighted the fiercely pacing prisoner whose head was on a level with his own and not three feet away.

Witnessing the event from a vantage of thirty years one hundred sixty-five pounds and forty-six inches superiority Michael like a cold scientist or an insensitive pedagogue had been hoping for this kind of accidental confrontation; but it was Roger's good luck that Ruth his mother was doing the wheeling at the moment, and no psychic danger to the family (bating Michael) ever failed to pluck her attention from its meditations. Instantly she swerved the chariot aside toward opposite bushes to sweep the monster out of Roger's field of vision whose face already hung on the extremity of surprise, the fearful image in his retina not yet confirmed by his brain, before tears could bring the shock to his heart.

And so the wave of fear never broke its crest, even when with a mighty skirr and flutter the rooster

Thus on animals and children the ruminations of Michael agonistes, freshshaven bespectacled glinting black operator in a transitory state of brotherhood and neutrality.

But a wasted day must be wasted efficiently (whether a day at the shop or a day at the park) if a man is not to give himself over to suffering and sulks. Use every last droplet of steam, until its condensation is measurable; wring every last B T U from the low pressure end of your engine even unto water as cool as the milieu: yet carefully, carefully, so that you don't put a vacuum on the high pressure piston and end up resisting yourself. The bore has to be larger, that's all, and the more boredom the greater the spread of low pressure force, the wider your strength's attenuation. You must start your heat recovery when reciprocation hits negative peak. In general there's no other way to compensate for losing too soon, for never having had except as a sailor mostly locked up at sea the keen knife of tireless bachelorhood to slice up life's cake with.

At the thought of his policy he comforts himself by losing weight in the healthy sweat of cagey adaptation. Praiseworthy, if any god could see what was going on! The thought of the thought invigorates him and draws him closer to equality with the brave and the free. But his boys Jonathan Chapman Matthew Chapman Roger Chapman, the only persons in the world he's competent to teach, they are still equal to any great expectation, or nearly so, Jonathan less than Matthew and Matthew less than Roger—Roger

sprang to the ridge of his coop that they were passing and discomposed Roger's startled father. While it was still flapping on its perch it issued a harshly broken throat-swallowed crow.

Ruth swiftly returned the ark to its course, and at a greater distance Roger simply wondered about the bird being up there troubled by something. He pointed in warning and sympathy, crying out "Oh *oh*!" with pure clarity of expression, and looked up at his mother to see if she saw. The hens who had been pecking on more distant dirt were arrested by the child's voice, though the cackling people beyond them could not have noticed it. The harem's response was not lost upon its man-chicken, for it had ignored his sounds. He hopped down to the ground, perplexed and embarrassed at the impression he had made as a protector, and darted inside one of the portals that pierced his noxious refuge from humanity. "Aw gone!" said the vanquisher, now as callous as his father had been (who was now most sensitive), but open-hearted.

Michael and Ruth halted to see if they could fathom the blackness of the coop's opening. Therefore Roger was halted too. The older boys, who had ranged ahead watching over their shoulders, returned to the nucleus. Meanwhile some raucous fat-faced parvenus had discovered the back-alley path as a route between points of interest and were beginning to brush past the Chapmen, annoyed at the obstruction they made and unhesitant to exude their annoyance in demo-

most of all because not yet specialized in talent, not yet confirmed in any weakness—but all three more than a dozen years superior to Caleb Karcist a licensed bachelor. On the other hand ten years more susceptible to accident and history, ten years more liable to the end of the world (as witness and victim, or as father to one or more.) Here lies his own advantage over the four he compares himself with: ten or twenty years less vulnerable in his mortality.

But to confine his thoughts to the sandlot diamond his boys had to play on (where the advantages of middle age are ill appreciated): could they beat out the throws more often than three times in ten having swung at nothing bad and missed nothing good, or even often enough to lead the league? From the outset they had shown themselves as remarkable as the hanged man's virility. They were the only three of his myriad half-children who had not been baffled by a piece of rubber or exhausted to death by a long swim. Three in two thousand they were (counting only the volleys and not the rounds), and before they ever saw the light: exceptional kids! By the same token, of all his wriggling missiles they were the misbegotten. Against all odds on separate occasions each had survived to the mouth of the inmost cave by informing himself of the misfitted particulars and insinuating himself accordingly. Coeffected by the fact that they were sired by one in a million out of one in a million. That made them three in ten to the minus nth: call them unique, each of the three.

cratic and all but open hostility, incapable of perceiving the quality of those that hindered their passage. Defiantly Michael paid them no heed; the true nobles of the family were not aware of the strangers at all.

"Doesnt he know how to sing?" asks Matthew.

So Jonathan teases the bird:
"The chicken tried to crow
But couldnt crow
Because Deedle-de-dee-
    diddle-dum did!"

"Roosters can't sing." The mother answers. [To Michael:] "Isn't that right sir? [To Matt:] "He was trying to crow."

Everyone is unique as well as individual to start with. So, what makes for the uniquely unique? A father's prejudice, a mother's unconscious deformation, God's will, composite chance—or Tyche's pitching lapses? Perhaps all the lines of force (including these) that enter every human field in slightly different combinations, continually changing in accordance with the accidental intersections of conception? Probability again! No, let it be called diversity of gifts plus free will. And freedom's a question must be begged forever, long after men have learned to decoct and unscrew meretricious semen for

artificial production lines (untouched by human glands and matrixed without emotion). There'll always be the mystery of what makes a man extraordinary, or a woman.

"Cocks aren't usually allowed in the city." Michael remarks. "They disturb the peace. Maybe this one has a speech impediment."

"But Michael what's the matter with him? He's a beautiful man but the hens don't pay any attention to him!"

"It's the same problem I have. They don't recognize a master's voice. That was his swan song, and now he's gone inside to die. Maybe it's the first time he ever tried to crow in the middle of the day."

"It didn't work and now he expects the sun to drop out of the sky and the world to turn black! Poor rooster! But why don't the chickens look up when he—"

"Call him a cock. That's what he is, a cock. All fowls are roosters. Hens roost."

Jonathan pipes up again: "I think he wants the sun to go down if that will get rid of the stupid people watching him all day long. "Let's go! I want to see the elephants."

"Okay okay!" The father acknowledges Number One's demand, even joining him in it, but puts him off, all with the same gesture, which waves him down with a flapping hand held high on bended wrist near the chin while still facing away at the mother. "Madam, he's depressed from being jeered at for believing that he conjures up the sun in the morning. But humiliation and ignorant ingratitude won't make him change his ways. It's his thankless duty to earn the whole barnyard keep by acting like a dandy barnyard coxcomb while he's actually only making the earth turn."

"Not with his voice!" She's hanging on his arm now, laughing.

"Of course he knows what the world knows, that the sun will naturally rise and set every day in the year without his summons, but he also knows that his hopeful call to Helios may one day turn out to be a proclamation of the Great Day that will have no sunset. Then he will be acclaimed our evangel and awarded a soul. Whereupon he will be relieved of his faithfully ridiculous noisiness. So every day meanwhile not in fatuity but in Christian hope the captive biped who's so foolish in the eyes of the world practices to usher in the morning of the millennium, the endless sunlight that will deliver him from his pomposity and make him an immortal cock."

"Come *on*!" cries Jonathan stamping his foot and jiggling his baggage. By this time the proletarians have worn a detoured path around the contemplative family.

"Come *on*!" chimes Matt for the fun of it joining forces with his big brother.

"Cum cum!" says Roger, catching the refrain, pointing up and off somewhere, looking at his brothers to read their faces, adding "Go? Go?" with perfectly rounded long drawn-out resonance as if responding to an elocutionist. They all smile, for every ear in the family is continually attuned to his progressions and variations, no matter how employed the brain or the mouth it belongs to.

"I'm *going*! Come on!" shouts Jonathan stamping his foot.

"I'm *going*!" shouts Number Two.

"Go, *go*." says three.

"We're going ahead!" the ringleader finally threatens. But the two independents still hang back near the old people, fidgeting without conviction in frustration not unprecedented.

Michael spins his yarn, rehearsing aloud what he might more easily amuse only himself with, because

"Don't talk like that, Michael."

"About cocks?"

"No. About—about another war. It's not good to joke about it."

"Aw come on, Daisy-Mazie!" He pinched her arm, affecting amusement and assuming the didactic air with which since her virginity she had always encouraged him to tease her intellectual innocence (in joint deprecation of her conscientious honor-student years at the university), and excluded from the forefront of his mind shuddering disgust for her mistaken sensibilities, her dread of certain words, her hatred of sarcasm and fear of irony, her infinitely charitable aversion to bitterness—all of which together might account for her ghastly misprision of his highspirited medley. But he continued, at pains to dissolve her horror by persistence, and she seemed to respect his effort. "Thenceforth the cock shall listen at his ease to the song of the nightingale, who once so enchanted him that he forgot the dawn and missed a Great Day, like the old man at the hawk's well missing his immortality; and the nightingale will sing forever at noon. So you shouldnt laugh at

she always wants conversation with him as she had it in the days of advancing intimacy when the foolish male teacher thought the female student was truly a student and she seemed to think so too. But now he is working for an affect with the defensiveness of a miser maintaining property he has long since paid for. The pitiable birds that must dance and sing in their courting never get any further than a mating, and most of them being diachronically polygamous can never taper off but must ever return to play upon the same lyre. One of the advantages of marriage should be that you don't have to start all over again every time you feel like fucking. You can gradually reduce the nonsense—not as a matter of policy or forethought but just because it's natural for you to put off childish things and employ your mind elsewhere—until the object of fooling around is so acceptable to the other party that the unadorned thought of it is sufficient in and of itself. A day at the zoo should be more than enough paternal *and* conjugal duty.

They begin to move along the fence again, but Matty still dwells upon the image of that chromatic animal beating its wings like a sudden engine never designed for successful flight. Shrewdly gauging the risk of derision he asks his older brother if he doesnt think that airplanes should be rated by birdpower rather than horsepower, and Jonathan (in the comradeship of their joint impatience with the slowfooted buzzing of the parents) mildly replies "Yuh, that would be a good idea Matt!"

Chanticleer just because he's absurd. It's just that our prophet was victimized by improbability."

"At least he's a profit to the farmer's wife who wants some new chickens." she replied in kind. "That's the whole profit in all your manhoods!" pressing his mighty bicep. "He deserves a little vanity and luxury for himself between fertilizations."

"All you think of is eggs," he hissed, to make her think of the eggs she had to cook for him every morning of their lives because eggs are all *he* ever wants; but at once regretted the words that may have revived her implicit suspicion that he desired the other egg he always delved for believing he abhorred it.

"Semi has a soul." was all she added. Poor pregnant kitty shivering in the back yard and scratching in the cold dirt, convinced that I've deserted her.

Michael says no more. Ruth, wishing to sustain the mood of fellowship brought by conversation, commences to whistle: a low melodic rounding of sweetly pressured breath which is likely to go on as long as she is not speaking or spoken to, so innocently and with such peaceful composure that Michael never has been able to account for the irritation that makes him squirm from it as if she were chewing gum. Something aristocratic in his blood makes him hate this blind spot in her courtesy, a failure in her education, which glaringly proclaimed her appallingly vulgar idea of easy manners. What was worse (though he can clench his fists no tighter), at any moment it

The elder looks back at his father and mother with a view to telling them about Matt's smart will regress like snow to sleet from a whistle to a hum. suggestion, but he makes up his mind that the drag they are putting on the progress of the party disqualifies them for this delight just at present. Then he sees the pain in his father's face without guessing its cause. But an old rhyme pops into his head and he gleefully turns to lob it at his mother:

> "A whistling girl
> And a crowing hen
> Always come
> To some bad en'."

Michael cruelly chuckles at this check upon his wife. She will not hold it against her son, understanding that far from being taken as an attack upon herself it should be heard as a fledgling claim to folk-learning. He disingenuously reaches forward to pat Jonathan on the shoulder in cowardly hint of his displeasure with her inveterate barbarism. Thank God for children, especially children attaining to the age of mind yet still innocent in paining their parents: they're clear-eyed objective observers who can speak without rancor, without overtones from a bitter past, not yet competent to abstract failings from familiar behavior. "Where did you hear that one Jonno?" he asks.

"From Hecuba. Her mother used to say that to her on the farm in Chicago."

Hecuba! Father and mother look at each other in a true marriage of surprise, smiling over the young man's head. Smiling and beginning to wonder. "But when?" Ruth inquires lightly. "I never heard her say that."

"Neither have I." the father marvels.

"Neither have I!" cries Matthew.

"Eye, eye!" echoes Roger.

"Oh shut up, Matt." snaps Jonathan, turning again to resume the march; and this time the whole family keeps pace with him, treading his heels two abreast. "I was up there helping her put up some curtains."

"I didnt know he ever called on her." says Michael to Ruth with a nick of jealousy.

A tiny fleeting smutch of alarm flashes a new pathway in the sexual landscape of Ruth's brain several years sooner she thinks than it should, though she will never again see herself as the governess in jokes and case histories. But the pang dissolves at once into the diffuse piquancy of a new amusement uniting her to the boy's father, and she seeks to dismiss the memory of it as she has dismissed the pain of their highfalutin criticism— without thought of the thing mentioned, only of Jonathan's psyche in which it is reflected. Yet wondering a little about Michael's too.

Goodhearted Hecuba, Michael says to himself, spangled bleach-blond Hecuba, the girl without a husband who likes children, the kind neighbor who bakes cookies for the Chapman family and takes huge delight in baby Roger, who introduces her senior mystery man (a grandfather himself, driver of his own long black Cadillac) to those she trusts and envies—to whom she discreetly omits to show her poorer lovers. Seeing that he cannot inspect the consciousness of his son he tries to recall the desires and lost opportunities of an age no more innocent than it should have been.

"Look, look!" Matthew's shout puts an end to everyone's speculations and regrets. "He's come out again and he's running over to the hens!" They round another corner of the enclosure onto a main path. "He was sulking wasnt he Mommy?" the second son asks looking up into her warm wise face envalued with eyelid wrinkles of love and experience.

She nods and smiles, avoiding the eyes of her Chanticleer. He the husband laughs at the shortsighted insights of Pertelote and her chick, generously clasping her waist.

They progress smoothly past turkeys ducks and geese. Jonathan has taken Roger's car off his parents' hands and helpfully leads the way with his passenger. The pococurante rider chats to pedestrians about him. From time to time he twists around and leans over to look back past his wheeler and calls out with the high pure voice that gives his father more pleasure than any other sound on earth: "He-ah Da-dee! Here Daddy!"

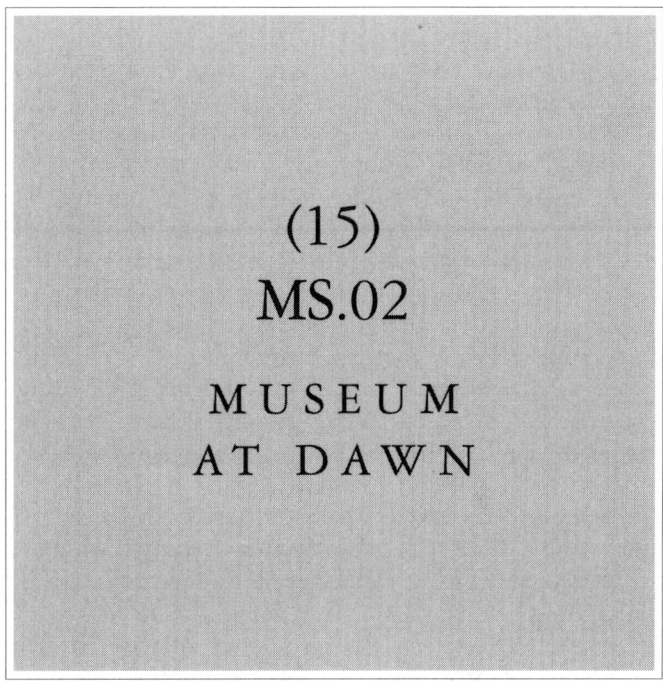

(15)
MS.02

MUSEUM
AT DAWN

*A*t the lower end of the dry bathtub black against white sat Semiramis ("empress of many tongues, mistress of Babel") staring contemplatively at the hole barred by a St John's cross, decorous tail curled about her tall feet, testing her power to compare and combine that Kant called the faculty of thought. "If you were as wise as you look I wouldnt need advice from anyone else." Michael remarked to her. She was formally expecting a mouse, but the heraldic attitude of her hunt masked a regal desire for the companionship of this human admirer. Every morning at five-thirty she sprang lightly into the family's empty pool and aligned herself at a right angle to the axis on which he shaved before his enlightening face in the mirror. 'Twas a matins of all seasons, sometimes of darkness outside the walls of their keep, sometimes of chirping prelapsarian bird-light, but always together the cheerful bear and his panther stole a march on the household, never awakening mother wolf or the cubs.

He is just after fuming at the lapsarian condition of the kitchen and has ceased his silent fulminations against the proprietress. The time lost in rinsing out the coffee pot (with cold soapless water that would not unnecessarily increase costly entropy in running over a midden of dishes glasses greasy pans encrusted pots butching tools and chopsticks to meet the sucking drain blocked with garbage), yet not washing anything he didnt need, is already forgotten. A clear fresh brew is about to burble and thump under its glass cupola with gently gathered energy from gas turned low. It will be ready for him (boiling time plus six minutes) when he is ready for it. Meanwhile his shaving is too methodical to be entirely efficient, but it's a warm comforting procedure of elegant symmetry, calculated to coterminate with the optimum percolation of the gustful drug without prospect of which it would have been a bore.

Semiramis supports this ethos of private routine.

With cordial hot water half way up his forearms in drawling baptism of a clean day the man prepared himself genially. (Hard to believe that ten minutes earlier the same subject had kicked and groaned against the chain of noise suddenly lashing out of peaceful darkness to tear away his private scene, a tautly meshed fascistic whip that always must be disconnected at once by staggering up out of a perfectly furnished compartment of sleep hundreds of decks below, for it could not be waited out like the thundering rumble of finite forged links rising from a chain locker and falling into silence when some bottom was reached. Harder still to believe that soon afterwards his every thought had been whipping hatefully through the house striking rage with every impression and feeding its passion with woe.) Sweet reason welled with every stroke of the razor on his smoothly rounded chin, stropped upward in the sheer pleasure of lucid godliness.

Family breakfast and the time to flap out into an outer world was a good two hours off. He flexed his muscles and chortled at this stretch of aristocratic privacy, blessing Semiramis in his joy and dancing tip-toe into the kitchen to fetch his mug of A-number-one Java with her high-tailing it at his heel. Larded with unspecific self-congratulations, hardly containing his exuberance but heedfully ginger with the scalding black tonic, he opened the front door stepped deftly across the hall and flourishing his key unctuously admitted himself to the museum. He took care that his paramour also slipped through the doors before he closed them softly behind him.

At this time of day there was never too little to think about. He sat down at the table and began to sip the surface of his precious stimulant from behind the importunate tail of the cat, who was dominating the foreground of his stage—until all at once she deftly flattened herself straight across the spread notebook he was about to write in, a woman settling lasciviously to draw him down after her (she who "licensed lust by law") with invitational purrs. Apologetically with both hands he slid her gently away, a man strong enough to reject warm beauty. At length she accepted his decision and moved a little off to curl up like a flat broad lump of ink on his chart of Cape Ann that already footed a pile of books at one end of his trestle. [In yesterday's news a cat got credit for rousing a family to save it from fire, but obviously she was just caterwauling to save her own skin.]

A soundless dogfight of the dawn patrol began as usual in the upper air. The contending demons were flooded in white light reflected from the incandescent cone of 150 watts overhead by the open field beneath his magnified eyes. At first the archangel hung alone in warm windless peace high above the soft bright plain of clouds as he willfully organized his unruffled powers for the superhuman fighting dive. Then with mounting intensity he invoked the muse of gravity for his unnatural and unnecessary attempt, flagellating his buoyancy all the while. Yet loathe to shake off the tranquillity of his unspent strength he lingered to breathe the ozone of this rational empyrean, hoping as always that the intellectual beauty of an eagle's vantage was no false zenith for a highflown owl.

Shaking his head and wagging his wings in warm-up passes above the deep billowy surface that he was getting ready to drive himself through to the bottom of, he took a last look around at the alluring books that coolly appraised his struggle to resist their enticements even as they mocked and goaded him. Suddenly in an access of cacoethes he was possessed with a ravening desire to feed upon them a dozen at a time like so many field mice. But they instinctively befuddled him by scattering motionlessly in twelve directions and he lost them all. Not that they scrambled too fast for him: it was just that he couldnt fix on any one of them, his promiscuous appetite defeating itself in self-conflict. Blessed, though, their success, for he was too fat already and perhaps in danger of unhungering. Each one sported a private life competitively allied to the others in rivalry to his own. Over the ages sweet reason had brought forth a myriad-eyed peerage of theoretical knowledge oh so bitter to leave off the pursuit of, which in a trice were no longer field mice but thrones and dominions filling an excited sky under the leadership of Gabriel and Satan. If he couldnt vanquish them all it was no good to devour one or two (taking time from his irreducibly minimum practice of action) that would only exacerbate the perpetually underprivileged desire of a born scholar born to be thwarted, born to live outside the walls looking in at experts.

[Mr Savant, down sir! Down I say! —But give me one solid year of leisure to catch up in and I swear I'd never read another book again! I'd give up crypticism prolusion toposophy inframatics psychogogy theoreography metaparabolics and all the ships at sea. Then I'd build and sail my own craft. —You lie in your guts, man. You'd be high and dry within a week if you didnt have these invigilating interlocutors to keep you from stranding on your own petty experience. And even physics is a lifetime study. —I have no life to spare; so down, sterile lust, or I'll disturb the peace by sweeping to the floor all these perfectly innocent reference volumes. Schopenhauer tells me that past thirty is too late for books that can alter the crinkled bark of my brain. So, Mr S , I'm already done for in the learning department! Ah, I hope I am done, I wish 'twere done when it was to be done! But truly never is it done. If I lived long enough I'd read all their genealogies and rattle the door of the academic house of lords. —There's time enough in senility, when the other work is done, if the world lasts long enough. . . .]

The owl never did jack himself into a dive. The more he struggled against the struggle in a regress of self-consciousness the less he was able to point his head on thick unbending neck to lead the buoyant body straight down. Insensibly, rather, he settled into the cloud bank with a scuttling horizontal flutter. He had to forget both firmament and earth, zigging and zagging on the subjective plane, no longer heeding the reproachful warehouses of knowledge planted about his table, as sitting otherwise motionless he tippled his coffee, blown and buffeted by memories and ambitions that jostled and snatched at each other while his maneuvers were carried oscillating downwind—until simple gravity pulled him through. Yet the great foe of dragons could barely forbid himself turn into the breeze and soar back to the beautiful peaks of serene potentiality on a climb without sweat.

It took strenuous mining to make good use of his time at these altitudes. But his boring purpose was fixed. Downward it directed him against every natural urge to indulge the frail character he was working with. Still, he knew from long experience that his most effective tactic was to abandon the hope for efficiency and give himself over to a gravitational drift of daydreams that would come to naught unless they came to earth. Thus while almost unresisting to a whole class of mutually canceling temptations on the level he could apply himself to overcoming updrafts. By reversing the pitch of his feathered pinions he won a few feet of descent at every beat, taking care to desist from flapping after every declination (lest he call the attention of Fate to his fundamental determination) and making his unobtrusive way down airy ravines and around tight corners.

By these habitual techniques of clandestine navigation he began by degrees to scent moisture in the air, and then its brine. At last he was groping with his feet for the rocks of Ararat.

The weight that pulled him through had been gathering on the nether surfaces of ratiocination stretching from his head to his fingers to his belly to the ligaments of his gender. Throughout his mass he grew gravid with earthy music. The parturient joy he had expected seemed close at hand. Anticipation of delivery drove out all memory of his celestial battle. He forgot lust conception gestation and the pains of labor like a mother the minute she hears the first coughing whimper of her reproduced life. He's actually skipped the painful part. It was as if from parthenogenic nous he was bringing forth without the mediation of development something misshapen and never to be perfected but live and real, something it hadn't been given God himself to make.

His happiness was not deceived but it was premature. He didnt yet have a babe in his arms. He was not the kind of votary whose inspiration precipitates all at once with a bolt of lightning; nor did he hit the earth like a live fish falling into water.

These are the contentions that remained to Michael Agonistes early in
the morning even after touching down: vagaries of Mr S , practical necessities domestic comforts, the headstrength of Mr P , beauty love envy,
personal economics, impersonal statistics business machines personal
inventions, sales analysis, the double-entry accounting equation, industrial
engineering, panaceas for universal inefficiency, personal hopes particular
practical problems practical generic problems classical practical problems,
personal this practical that and all the other irrelevant habits of the mind
that haunt and tease a successful man in his decompression chamber—

{*Successful*! Indeed Caleb so remarked; but Caleb was the only one from
whose standpoint the component of success in Michael's prickly shielded
existence could have been abstracted. No one else who took personal or practical interest—least of all Michael himself from within the nutshell—had
any such notion. And Michael understood the appreciation as ambivalent:
that he was an effective worker in the world and not a deep-feeler; exigency
and managerial practice had compacted the spaciousness and duration that
otherwise might have fostered sensitive imagination. No hero, but not a victim either, was what Caleb had in mind, to whose limited admiration
Michael in short concerned himself less with that which happened to him
than with that which happened by him in the common world. Caleb alas
was too inexperienced and too overweening to fathom everything he looked
at. Unlike Michael himself who resembled a good tailor in remeasuring his
customers on every occasion, Caleb was inclined to be opinionated in his
estimates. As a matter of fact, aside from congenital or involuntary impulses
producing mere jabs or dollops of detailed influence, Michael conscientiously refrained or desisted from interfering with much of the world, and he
deliberately eschewed the Presidency. Furthermore it was from this very
state of nonintervention, in an owlish incarnation with few natural enemies
and high life expectancy, that he was now decompressing—not in order to
suffer his condition more finely (with all its impotent pain from thwarted
possibilities of success) but so that he might undergo the expansion of
another mentality that was ordinarily squeezed and numbed by the various
pressures he claimed he had chosen not to avoid. Before fresh oxygen could
be released into the enlarging space in which he now once more breathed
and twitched, in order to decontaminate the chambers of his creative lung
by ventilating success and self, he had to finish wrestling the duels of both
Satan and Jacob with his independently seraphic nature. Any logorithmoid
can be cleared of memory by a simple click, he cries to Semiramis, and not
for the first time. Why can't I expunge by single command all the magnetic
lines that fasten my mind to the Body of Fate as if I were wearing an
ingrown helmet of electrified iron?}

—including the most seductive one, which St Willie warns against,
"creation without toil." For instance, as follows, the purely external pathway (among others more or less of the like) that this time tempted him in
his elation, starting at the bottom and proceeding upward:

With steel knuckles he knapped away at the gritty stratified flint in his head, forcing all books out of office by coup de tête. He took up a stenographic pad containing randomly recorded facts themes and key-words with the intention of venturing a new beginning with the seed of old thoughts. (Except for these notes his only resource besides will was the inert and provisional network of his present consciousness. There was no imagination to start him off.) Fortunately the pages were written on one side only, and so as he scanned them there was nothing to prevent him from tearing out the nuggets that pertained wholly or in part to his imme-diate object in order to arrange them in some reasonable sequence of articulation.

At this stage of each fresh endeavor he was misled and frustrated by the suddenly capricious antics of doughty old Memory, the one faculty he had to rely upon to keep him in the running with fellows of education tal-ent sensitivity leisure *and* imagination. At the first breath of forced draft it began to tease him with otiose and perverse puffs of fancy like erratic flames from a too tightly packed bank of coals that ought to be raked out onto the fireroom deck and stoked all over again. But except for those few brands his sodden memory withheld—as if secret—all thoughts that had not already been shoveled into the furnace.

It was only by ignoring the undigested cache in his stomach and retracing the ideas already webbed in his head that he could find prin-ciples of continuity or schemes of interconnection by which to sort out his jumbled jottings. Yet he was all too aware that the structure he sought for his little heap of symbols must not be simply horizontal like a story but also vertical skew synchronous cycloid analogical etiological reversible and exegetical, even verging on fantasy. In the end he decided that it was best to put aside the abstract predilection for order.

The degree of his vexation always varied inversely with the space of time available for fiddling around, and time had been shrinking exorably with the insistent growth of his affections as well as inexorably with the gathering of his years. [I havent had time to write letters since Jonathan was born, and so there is no longer anyone to correspond with me; but now I don't even have enough time to read my own notes! Worse yet, it takes time I havent got to construct safeguards against the loss of my memory, which I ought to regard with desperation because I'm losing 100,000 cerebral neurons a day without gaining anything but the ground I occupy in the latest cross-section of history, even though the more aid it gets the more it falters, like a bard who takes up reading and writing as a pair of crutches. The only way I can keep in tone the diminishing remainder of what I do remember is by rehearsing unto reduction a few of my own general ideas. I change shape too fast (back and forth between gaseousness and parsimonious solidity) to be able to track my mental experience without a pencil. My wits need every artifice to cope with diur-nal alternations from anywhere in the spectrum of excitement to everywhere in the spectrum of fatigue. A man who's counted neither as fish nor fowl nor good red herring must have something besides mere improvisation to pull himself together by. I can neglect the sentences of others, if the choice comes down to ultimate necessity, but I can't dispense with the conceits that I shall not have the leisure to strike upon a second time.] Yet he realized once more that notes and annotations could multiply hypergeometrically, they were so easy to spin. They demonstrated the counter-fertility of advancing age like accessions to the Library of Congress.

Resolved to snip up the detached pages so that he could shuffle and sort his thesaurus of disparate information pseudoinformation quasi-information and obiter dicta, as well as of his own insights and inventions, he opened the table draw to reach for his scissors—

The careful student, having formed a reasonable estimate of the probabilities for dislocation of secateurs in that household, will immediately anticipate an angry cry of disappointment from the lips of Michael Chapman. A thread-cutting cloth-cutting paper-cutter was an article often required that usually seemed to have no fellow anywhere in the whole flat. He had rummaged for no more than a jiffy among colored pencils old pens paper clips slide rules compasses protractors celluloid triangles rulers screwdrivers pliers and other accumulated tools before he suddenly recalled that the scissors had been extorted in the name of some familiar emergency two or three weeks since, on pain of contemptuous rebellion against his irrefutable stinginess.

But I must tell you, gentle reader, the error of your supposed extrapolation, although I can't say just why you were wrong unless it was because of dovegray morning's soft silent influence upon the violence of a nature schooled to self-restraint. For the owl did not squawk and beat his wings, or drop from his perch in a rage, nor yet look to heaven in piteous supplication. He met his balk like a wise gentleman, inwardly almost as well as outwardly, like a good manager. The corners of his mouth tightened slightly; his fingers drummed on the surface of his desk. Then, remembering that Ruth had once called him masochistic (in spite of his behavior toward herself!), he inhaled deeply and exhaled noisily through pursed lips.

Semiramis got up and tracking his papers backed her asshole against his chest, her tail brushing his eyebrows voluptuously. Absently palpating her wildly beautiful flanks for the first sign of kittens he forced her down again, offering to still her with all his weight. Taking his vehemence for attraction she instantly curled her tail and relaxed, couchant for sensual dozing; made systoles and diastoles with scimitar-clawed velvet forefeet on more than one sheet of spread paper, purred in the warmth of his lamplight, watched him with lidded eyes.

Her master sat motionless again, like a Buddha now with palms open on his lap. Because he was trained to calmness under the Fates' arbitrations, curses had yielded to contemplation before they could form. Ruth will not change as long as family life may last: that's what he meditated on. I'll never see those scissors again. I'll have to buy another pair, secretly. One more needless expense representing one more moment of deferred liberation, one more outlay of irrecoverable time to pay for the replacement of a minor necessity. The Weird Sisters think I want it this way—an aspect of my masochistic success I suppose. But as long as Roger needs a mother I must not shatter her with disciplinary attacks no less bootless than precept or analysis. . . .

Masochism—bah! More like superhuman suffering of sweet reason's fraction and refraction. Hell, if I can get along without chess or music, foreign languages and travel, romantic liaisons, grants and fellowships, not to mention a college education, as well as all the other perquisites and privileges of my peers, I suppose I can get along without a pair of office shears.

So, by meticulously twisting his right thumb and forefinger, biting his lip and snoring through his nose, Michael separated a gerrymeandering series of sinuous strips with his bare nails, turning the sheet in his left hand as if he was cutting a picture puzzle by table jigsaw everywhichway. He had to thread a course among some very narrow lines and closely punctuated phrases in order to reduce his agglomerated slime mold to discrete amoebae of viable thought.

It was the neuromuscular process itself, not the nuggets of meaning, that started up old Creative Mind, as if he'd undergone a Cartesian revelation while telling the phases of the moon. An obscure synapse somewhere fired and made a circuit that for some stupid pigheaded reason had never been made before in his gratuitously overloaded brain even though the enlightenment it produced had been commonplace in the apparatus of administration and scholarship for several generations.

Ah, said he, I not only *can* get along without scissors but I *should* get along without scissors! Henceforth I'll use three-by-five cards (with my discount only nine cents a pack at the store). I don't mind wasting the white space that my gems will be mounted on if that's the only way to provide myself with the finite means for infinite combination. Besides, I can use the backs before I throw them away.

The fact that the bulb of this inspirational flower had been perennially harvested by pragmatical academics (thereby establishing the demand that assured him of cheap supply) marred Michael's pleasure not at all. Until now he had judged their use of file cards a symptom of intellectual weakness. But to Michael Chapman a prejudice overturned was more exciting than an original opinion, perhaps because it was relatively much rarer in his own experience; and he liked to examine curious crystals left by the evaporation of residual bathwater. Shucking old categorical hypotheses for more enlightened new ones hardly broadened his tolerance, inasmuch as every postjudice gained the new ground it cleared without defending its former positions against the advancement of similar distastes and aversions, leaving behind as much growing jungle as ever before; yet he found his history richly deepened by any succession of revised and sometimes contradictory attitudes. So now by shaking off a backward practice that was little more useful than keeping a diary (and much lazier) in order to adopt a valuable habit he would inscribe this morning as a milestone in his career without weeping over the fact that he'd become wise too late to improve the elapsed moiety of his projected life on earth. Anyway he turned to his work with fresh zest, in the belief that he was beholden to no Muse for his discovery.

Nonetheless, having cleared a space on the table and arranged the curling skittish strips and jagged blocks in a sequence that engaged his interest without any clearly active sentence coming to mind that could start him off with a leap, and still confused moreover about what was to be accomplished, he slipped into temptation without toil. Before he could stop himself the commercial librarian was forming a plan to set up a card file for all the books he stocked at the shop.

The sales log that he had instituted was much better than no records at all but it showed only what customers bought and not what was in inventory; and the handwritten entries took too much time when more than one person was waiting at the cash register to buy something. He weighed the advantages of that journal, which showed the day's transactions all together for simple review and analysis on the axis of time—a history of what went out of inventory—against the advantages of a reference file of separate bibliobiographies which could be manipulated and construed after hours for all kinds of demobibliographic research not only in history (a little less conveniently perhaps) but also in taxonomy of any kind. At the register he or a colleague would simply pull from a drawer at the counter a card already bearing a book's full legend, date it, and note any exception to list price. . . .

[*Simply?* Michael postponed the question that a good businessman would have confronted first.]

Each card in the perpetual inventory would show a title's case history next to its current status and expectations, since it would record purchase orders and receipts as well as sales, and might be used to calculate the profit from individuals and classes. The cards could be sorted by publisher when I'm making up my orders, for instance, or by category or shelf location when I'm analyzing return on investment. . . . I'll need a two-digit coding system and colored pencils for distinctions. . . . Eventually I can calculate certain succinct ratios. (One point two three four dollars per day average gross profit on Tragedy. This to be compared with an average gross profit per day on Literature in general as against bestsellers and cookbooks.) From the cash register tapes I'll compute the average number of books and dollars per sale. . . . With a C R F printing calculator it would be easy to go beyond the ratios and relate everything—oh oh, here we go back to the woods of abstraction, swing-whack, cutting all the timber anyone could ever want with my infatuating Synectic Method of Diagnostic

Correlation! [Why must S M D C disrupt my museum work—when the imbalance of interruptions is already appalling? At this time of life, on a godforsaken corduroy road supposedly headed up the mountain, after all paved thoroughfares are deliberately or perforce renounced despite a curiosity second only to Leonardo's, you cross off one professional possibility after another—and now none is left. But you're still not safe from attack by minor distractions and guerrilla obsessions scarcely worth mentioning in the true order of enemies. Is this the time to unabnegate, so far along the way—to disinhibit any of the hooded interests that Ruth is dimly aware of in my grotesque psyche with so little sense of their insidious threats to my museum?] Only the lack of working capital keeps Val from bespeaking the empty store next door tearing down the wall between and letting the popubibulation multiply. Then we'd have the volume to justify my machine and the machine to justify my system. We'd have more help and I could cut back on my hours, spend Saturdays in here. . . .

But the peasant mind is right, Michael now was thinking: all acts of business reduce to the simplicity of gain or loss on each transaction, and if you buy and sell at fixed prices (as in feudal times) the profit hinges on expenses. So also in your own lives brethren this archangel saith that it is better for the spirit to be close in the spending of gold than to fret about getting it. [All the food she wastes—milk soured by warm bacteria, good fish neglected for the cat to steal, apples enough for a regiment bought by the peck to rot in a corner of the kitchen, three vegetables one day and none for two—tortures my mean soul, and worries my public spirit for Mother Earth's sake too. And Ruth wanting me to get some moonlight job to pay for a twelve-cubic-foot food freezer!]. . . . Spending it on people: Sam's slow with numbers; we don't get our pennysworth out of him. For one thing he spends too much time wetting his thumb to leaf through the receiving slips. Maybe Val will let me buy him a rubber finger, a rubber thumb. What size, 11½ or 12? There won't be so many slipups either—

Oh slips that let the babies rip! What evil spirit makes her misfollow all directions? If the package says thaw the fish for two hours she dumps it into the frying pan at once; and if it says cook while frozen she leaves it out three days to go bad and Semiramis can stuff herself. . . . Just slip inside, sir. Press ever so lightly and you'll slide right in. It's all so easy and innocent to pocket pleasure there—legal proper moral and sacramental too! That's what happens to hope for easy circumstances in your declining years. You can't stay out of the trap that sweetens the bait with its victim. The Lord created man from clotted blood according to Gabriel's Koran.

The market grows apace for books and even if the proportion of beloved readers continues to shrink the absolute demand for sentences may well exceed the national supply. But whence the best if potent men are deprived of their time? Money is time. *Tempus non habeo* should be tattooed across my chest. But she wants the family overhead absorbed 100%!

If she had her way the production facilities would never lie idle. Same way she hates to have this room tied up that's used only two hours a day by one person when it could be the family sitting room used at all hours.

All the same, she's got a nice little lobby that isn't always occupied by a long shot, through no fault of mine. Maybe she wants a tanist, or better yet a young full-time seducer devoted to supporting her economics, who'd help with the dishes as well as keep her Bartholin glands active and healthy, and who'd enthusiastically join her in the mindless prestorgenic urge. (What are the caresses and irrumations of advanced pregnancy or postparturition in a ménage à trois?) He could buy her a house.

Michael dropped his hand to acknowledge the clothed obtruder that Ruth would have felt if she'd been horseback riding on his lap. Comforting the homunculus for a minute or two with his fingertips he was unable to regret its distressing domination of his thoughts. How could he ever get her to take care of the rubber ellipse according to directions, keep it dry with cornstarch and safe from pinpricks when not in use? (It's her mother's fault, my worst enemy, the only one I can think of as a trespasser against me and candidate for forgiveness, who's been giving a surfeit of directions from morning till night for thirty years to make sure poor little Ruthie's properly trained for life.) There's no reason my cooperative way of doing things wouldnt go smoothly and pleasantly if Ruth only had a more mature attitude toward what's expected on her part. She never knows what's for her own good. I put up with all kinds of difficulties that no other man would stand for—the mask in my maskochism—like breakfast in random sequence: eggs cereal coffee and finally orange juice. To her the best thing I can ever do is turn the victory of contraception into the defeat of menstruation. We brothers can't win the war of biologic. —And yet one still can't overcome periodic horror of the death-blood that precludes horror of new life, unless wrought to some thoughtless "condition of fire" by prodigious momentary besotment.

He stood up to shake out his loins, stretched, sat down again, spread out the pieces of his notes. More than half an hour had already passed. How'd I ever get off on Sam and his rubber thumb—?

Thumb? Something about that word disquiets me, not always but right now, as if it's been in the picture very recently. I havent been reading any anthropology lately. . . .

Semi rose again, wakened belike by a tiny visceral disturbance, and came to sit facing him high and cool. Into his eyes she gazed with the dignity of a wise man's wise and beautiful confidant (as if Sheba to Solomon), but she was only making a solemn request. So he began to rub behind her ear, gently scratching the puny skull beneath, and made her smile. Unaccountably there was no change in her posture; to his surprise she refrained from rising on her haunches and even did not uncurl her tail. With this intelligently undemonstrative reception of his affection she waived catkind's claim to a sensual but unclimactic succession of spinal strokes.

She therefore however felt no obligation to thank him and move aside. If she hadnt planted herself directly on top of his scraps he would have hunched his chair to the right and plied his pencil in another clearing. [This table is big enough for a black panther. It takes up two thirds of this closet. In a few years only rich men will be able to afford such large privacy, and the devil a lot of good it will do them when there's no Creative Mind to jig to.] "Semi old girl, I wouldnt dream of pushing—"

Dream! He was no longer puzzled. As it was his lot to go to sleep nearly always exhausted by the day's effort of hope supervision worry or love, only to be wakened by the chainsaw instantly severing his alarmed brain in its struggle for objective consciousness from whole realms of active being which might otherwise have been retained by diurnal memory, he knew little of the lovely "time between sleeping and waking"—for St Willie the true creative leisure of many minutes and for himself the few seconds required to register a dream or even the fact that he had dreamed. Usually before wisps of word or image could lodge anywhere in his convoluted cortex they were lacerated and dispelled by the clock's machinery. Still, by metaphysical reasoning he had long ago divined the existence of a teeming dream-life only faintly suggested by the phenomenological scraps he occasionally became dimly aware of. Now, wonderful to tell, his memory was suddenly in possession of a shaped and worded experience which an hour earlier had been as immediate as the fresh rain introducing the dawn, to which he had awakened with an abruptly tilting plane of consciousness that delivered him from veridical fear:

Walking across an unspoiled Dogtown pasture with his three sons. Hodge running ahead as confidently and independently as an older child; Matt also, watching over him. He himself and Jonathan come last, hand in hand (though in life this eldest is too old for such submission). They are increasingly aware of danger from a bull but they havent seen one yet. In his growing haste to reach safety he grapples for a better grip on the boy's hand which has been slipping again and again out of his grasp, for he must make the skeptical one fly as fast as the younger brothers in front of them who aren't frightened at all. Impatiently, for a better purchase, he clutches the thin forearm. Then glancing down at his frail son's hand, now flapping like a head shaken by the neck, he sees that his fastening has been so slippery because there is no thumb. From wrist to forefinger there's only a smooth streak of white skin, not even a scar. Jonathan was born without a thumb and he the father has never noticed it before! He stops to examine the other hand and it is the same. In cold dread he calls the other boys back to him. Matthew's smaller hands according to the general character of his body are thicker and rougher—but they too have no thumbs! It is even so with the baby boy on the point of stooping to pick a dandelion between two fingers in innocently clumsy trial of his widening world. "Come on kids, let's hurry! We'll be late for supper." It ends with Michael wanting to rush home and demand of Ruth why she has so long concealed the deformity of his sons.

Of course he contented himself with the reality that offset this dream, which he searched no deeper than if it had been a forenoon puddle left at daybreak by the brief rain. The children might have come placid or feeble-minded as well as epollicate. They might have been born without eyes or ears. But by a stream of miracles that he deserved far less than most other men they thrived hale and whole, sleeping in the castle he rented for them, perchance dreamlessly. His uneasiness slowly abated. But he was glad to have dreamed at all, and especially pleased to have remembered the counterfactual phenomenon itself.

How many thousands of dreams had he missed for want of time to affix their echoes? Maybe he dreamt a story every night. Was his shy white-winged psyche leading an ironically free life of fecund nocturnes on the gerrymeandering marshes where the land mingles with the sea? Undoubtedly the dikes and culverts of his every occupation obstructed or polluted the nighttime tides. He had grown almost too tough to register even the few dreams isolated by chance that made their way to high ground like gulls indifferent to the real estate they lighted upon. There must be all kinds of birds, all kinds of auguries. Was that whole elusive parliament a personal imagination's creative collection? His head reeled with pride.

Or was this a guilt he dreamed of? He shook his head. He'd had a mysteriously negative glimpse of one of the Anima Mundi's inlets perhaps; but the syntax of occult imagination was as much too subtle for gnostic revelation as for human analysis by electronic microscope.

Ruth's dreams seemed different. She recounted many of them (not all!) carefully and faithfully. They revealed reality he thought. She asked his interpretation, when she could get him to listen, of the stories (those that she offered!), which she told frankly and dispassionately. She had none of her husband's unwholesome outmoded self-defenses and was quite willing to submit herself to an intimate's hit-or-miss understanding.

In the latest of her dreams known to him—which by now owed so much to his own thought-rehearsals that he couldnt be sure she had dreamed it alone—she is working by herself in the kitchen at night while the big boys sleep on their porch and the baby lies in his crib two doors beyond her in the opposite direction. He himself, the husband, is shut up remotely in his private room across the hall. A large minacious figure moves into the space she stands in: maybe a gorilla, maybe a horribly mute savage. For a time she somehow fends it off with gestures of deprecation and words of conciliation, by desperate cajolery expressed in vague behavior. Meanwhile, between words, she calls to her mate for help, imploring him to save the children, or to take her place while she runs downstairs to get help from Nick Topalis. She is aware that Michael hears her cries but that he calmly dismisses her fantasy. He is too busy to respond to vain fears. Nothing she could call out would move him to understand the urgency of this danger. He keeps writing, his reply vacant and inaudible, without looking up from his paper. And the ape is not to be put off. Finally, when no longer able to feign equanimity, she screams. That substantive sound brings him at last. But it's too late. She and the children are doomed.

The dream ends with unresolved terror, which she smiled at, glad to be awake and safe with her family after fourteen hours of mulling, when she had her first chance to tell him of it. Hearing the dream and her closing laugh he had vouchsafed no opinion but hugging her to his breast kissed the innocent forehead with aching compassion for the subordination in her mistrustful vision of himself. And the next morning being Monday he had departed from his family with the most irrational reluctance, in raw gray weather, as if he was abandoning his nest to earthquake and risking its every dear life for the sake of his pleasure on the job.

Without question he took himself to be a coefficient cause of his wife's earth-cracking dream. As a doctor lawyer priest (according to the notions that she had formed from the journalism of her lifetime) he might have gratified her inveterate bewildered longing for a sensitive protector; as combined guardian mentor partner and patient he might have chosen to play the guitar, which she thought it would have been easy for him to be good at. A man's option for self-sacrifice could forestall his wife's despair. It must take a powerful excuse to prevent him from making a move to help her. Something should justify his cruelty: gospel-preaching, singing in concerts, the Presidency, millions of dollars, a doctorate in surgery. Some career that a mother and other citizens could accept as plausibly in the wife's interest. How could she be expected to suffer spiritual abandonment for the sake on an uncalibrated motive whose object had as yet no existence in the world? Brother, it had better be good and soon! . . . .

Okay, resume emissions you nonergodic generator of words. "WHEN WORK STOPS VALUES DECAY." You're ignorant yet you know too much, too old yet so young that you still indulge your romanticism, too strong to go mad yet too weak to do anything irresponsible, too pragmatical for poetry yet too theoretical for the success Caleb's got stuck in his head about you. Full of thoughts and feeling nothing. Come prove me wrong! Get on with it. . . .

Michael picked up a long sharp pencil and to whistle up a big wind with a little wind crossed out and rewrote the last sentence on the page before him, drawing from himself without toil a little judgment and some wit, in the main by simplifying punctuation. punctuation says he to himself troubles us more than illogicalities of idiom although some especially those versed with the sizes of lines and margins say were free to get along without it as a mere convention mostly a la mode certainly as seen over the centuries since spaces were first invented as characters in the font to be used between words for easing the eyes and not only for the resolution of uncertainty you probably had to be a very good writer in oldentimes to communicate at all in what to us would look like one long word filling the fourcornered vessel whereas we have difficulty making even short sen tences without a lot of help from gaps and pricks and pollywogs and double gaps and primed pricks and superpricked pollywogs and superpricked pricks effetely evolved beyond the grasp of manly cuneiform information even in an age of cheap paper when poets can extravagantly exploit variably repeated white spaces down as well as across and recover numbers by measuring out nonnumbers we unimaginative blokes still scorn to turn our stitches and are proud to keep going at the mercy of a typesetter who hasnt much choice right to the arbitrary uniform edge ulti mately determined by the market of fair readers whore inclined to bolt down tractable prose by the gulp hoping itll be weightless and transparent strictly a selfeffacing ether to carry messages with no pigment of its own to slow up assimilation now that its encumbent upon test takers even if not for a wordgulping phdoctorate to race down pages like a programmed printing machine a line at a time regardless of horizontal span certainly not the unit an author composes with in any case the auxiliary notation required by the consumer to mete and moisten her syntactical swallow also serves to egg on a writers complexities and convolutions until shed just as lief wed never worked up divers conventions of differentiation elision and separation undetectable by ear in the cadence of passing ranks like the somewhat unfair rule of orthography that gives him an advantage over speakers in punning by homonym and a specious extension of his ability to overlap connect or ironize plain audible meaning still every time he puts down a word he makes even his ambivalence vulnerable to ambiguity and by choosing a particular sequence he makes himself exponentially more vulnerable with every word he adds so its no wonder he loves punc tuation to armor his joints and limit misunderstanding as for instance when a fully mailed modern can show what diction he refuses to accept responsibility for or in all fairness declines to be praised for without trou bling himself to modify the language he takes advantage of in laying his statements or doubts before the reader by the same means with which he makes distinctions of attribution between second third and nth persons in speech imitating gossip negotiation or conflict or reflecting character or sex or intending to vary the point of view with laconic efficiency always to mask his personal attitude toward the words he uses but most of all at his disposal is the expressive rather than mathematical device for making the reader stop for breath at the right instead of the wrong place in fact con trolling all progress through the whole shebang so that his meaning may sink in even when shes stubbornly ignoring the natural sound not to men tion cryptic melody resolved as usual to skim the whole show like a busy medieval catholic as if the piece were a mass that could be appropriated in total merely by eyeing certain junctions or checkpoints so in general written

language as for instance in the book of job is a perverse nuisance if you
don't have extraalphanumeric marks within the gross boundary of a para
graph which indeed was the first demarcation of all toward the end of the
days when writing recorded only what was already sung or said or sworn
to according to song form or formula requiring no awareness of sentence in
other words determined beforehand written by way of confirmation or rec
ollection rather than to make it for the first time as we do you might say
writing in order to think without the slightest expectation that it will live
again off the page as its being read in each case unless it enters into lyrics
or communiques contrary to appearances no one ever did get sentences by
dividing up a paragraph yet who who demurs at researching the search is
to say what single action each word belongs to if you dont use an adjuvant
symbol or two for purely syntactical gestures are essential even to the least
of languages e g that of the bandarlog that of the airwaves or that of the
logorithmoids mahouts for a long time in short its been impossible to dis
pense with the sense of sentence especially in prose that isn't just a string
of telegraphic stepping stones across the stream of time articulations of an
english sentence are more determinant than the concatenation of sentences
themselves as components of the paragraph which often seems no more
than a visual gimmick to relieve boredom and the grossly massed shape of
it is the thing thats often arbitrary if anything is sentences do all the
marching and fighting for they have the legs and stomachs and its they
who report to the writer for rations and quarters as well as for all opera
tions such as attack defense or diplomatic show of force which sometimes
call for rigorously elegant algebraistic discipline and sometimes shrewdly
conveyed suggestions of accent and breath notably for the tongues robust
or nervous of histriones heralds and other criers who teach the masses what
to observe in maneuvers of gorgeous or olive drab privates but also for the
common reader who wants slowing up to make her think while shes still
engaged instead of possibly when its too late to benefit yet this brings me
to the heart of the matter because too much apparatus only encourages her
fluency in translation when she should be dwelling on the art as it is set
before her without jumping to singleminded semantic conclusions by
vaulting along with all those crutches that penmen like henry james spoil
her with as if in imitation of a peculiarly academic manner of talking but
it isn't all a question of assisting and hindering the actress student or aes
thete the artificer himself who thinks of his readers not in order to con
form to their preferences but to make them assume his own also needs
some help but not too much help perhaps no more than color coded lob
ster buoys in keeping track of where he is in his own thinking yet gener
ally unless its a letter to some known mind or something boldly writ in a
single whitehot sitting the whole subjectmatter clear and present to his
memory before he begins if not woven on the spot with an unpremeditated
shuttling of his fingers or unless hes rambling inconsequentially in

demonstration of his personality the illuminating cryptographer ought to be more sensitive to wavering ambiguity or triguity than any cryptanalyst and do whatever he can to forestall *n*quity except of course when it suits his purpose to ride the same perhaps by evading a semiotic issue raising etymological doubt exploiting a qualm or hinting by pun at a complexity the receiver would like to ignore in the end he discovers for himself what old people never teach because they were never so taught and maybe arent even conscious of that there is or was some practical use in most conven tions at least american if not british after you have swept them all away you find that you have to start making up arbitrary rules of your own sim ply for operational expediency nay out of sheer logical necessity perhaps with no hope that theyll be tolerated by the middlewomen of the market place while youre still alive only to realize at last that your scheme cant be very much more evenhanded in application or less self contradictory than those of orthodoxy and that the subtle discriminations in such a secondary business arent worth the trouble of fighting everybodys habits including your own if youve been well educated nay it would be altogether too painstaking and fallible to strike for independence if it werent that as with words themselves you can take the entirely unmathematical liberty of inconsistency with convention according to a purpose that is continually changing the rules of reason can change provided that they remain under the metarule of obedience to your own true taste or style as its called in selfconscious discussions like this in fine you cant get along without a trifling extension of the alphanumeric repertory in the old struggle for infinite ends from finite means and theres something to be gained by devoting a little effort to modification of traditional notation if it serves a purpose as long as you arent pedantic enough to feel defeated by systemic contradiction theres only one general principle and that is to draw from your magazine as sparingly as if every skirmish were only the first and never never never simply to call attention to your tactical genius by parad ing drill teams so if you cant do your job by cable telegraphy you should make yourself understood with punctuation. Now this was the kind of heavy meditation that always plunked him down upon solid earth.

Thereupon he leaped down the mountain to make himself lord of the jungle, weatherproof and serene, equipped to walk anywhere in pachy-dermic security, without interfering in territorial professions but astonish-ing hypothetical women and critics with the strength and subtlety of his gentle finely controlled trunk, yet unconscious of his metamorphosis. He got in a good half hour of journeyman sentencing. . . .

Matty's quiet knock finally brought his father's eccentric felicity to a halt after repeated cheerfully whispered calls from the semi-public hallway had been ignored. Michael had no more than thirty-five minutes to finish dressing, eat his breakfast, and get down to the corner. The pearl of his day was already spent, but unshown there was a little show for it. (Did not

Hesoid say that dawn sets man well along on his day's work?) Locking up
the chamber of reason behind him he pressed his second son to his hip and
headed to the refectory.

> Oh thine eyes are the windows
> To the soul so bright within,
> Thine eyes are the windows
> To the soul so light and thin—
>   So never even wink at me!

> Glory, glory, hallelujah!
> Glory, glory, hallelujah—
>   Never ever hinder us . . . !

His song started the day off right for everyone else too. It was
apotropaic to any mischief capable of spoiling the sky already bright blue.
Even the one hitch was actually turned to good account, as follows. There
was no bread in the house for making toast to mount his poached eggs on,
so for the first time in many years Ruth served them to him softboiled. It
was a pleasure to see how cleverly she timed the cooking and the cooling,
how neatly with a perfectly fitted spoon she removed the half solid white-
jacketed richly yellow meat from the clean hot shells, filling the bottom of
his favorite cup by legerdemain. (This laboratory skill, which he was too
inexperienced in shifting for himself to match, reminded him of her formerly impressive competence at large, as if he'd suddenly again found
himself at tennis as her humble partner in doubles.) He found that nothing was as distinctly delicious as a properly softboiled egg. That morning
a delicious variety was reintroduced into his life of delicious breakfasts.

So he trolleyed to the bookstore in a state of great happiness. Said he
to himself, settling in his commuting seat on the teleograph line, my life
proceeds in oscillations, and the shorter they are the slower my pendulum
works. Every day at best I isolate just a bit more time than it takes to get
breathing at my natural atmospheric pressure and find my way back to
where I left off. Meanwhile to the boys I'm primarily a father, to Ruth
mainly a husband withal, and to Valentine Greatrakes exclusively an
ambitious wage-earner. I'll call myself a superman! I now have seventeen
minutes to doze on a comfortable stomach, plan the declining joys of the
day, and recompress myself for the function that takes most of my superhuman time. It's too much trouble to read the book in my pocket.

In this peaceful hiatus between holy enthusiasm and fitful rage against
his fetters he silently descanted on his vital good luck. At the same time
he hoped that by accepting his ignominious routine without conspicuous
protest he might mollify the unsympathetic destiny irritated by his idiosyncratic willfulness, and that by sustaining small and superficial misfortunes he might propitiate for all five Chapmans the aleatory goddess who

meted out fatal griefs to private lives. Our clerk had grown accustomed to the anxious calculations with which he sought to reassure himself by reducing the probabilities of future disaster for the persons of his family as they survived each successive cross-section of history and continued their perpetual encounter with the passage of circumstantial time.

In his prayers he gave ostentatious thanks for every mote and moment of mutual or single prosperity. The Chapmans and their cat had love. The parents and children had no illness. There was food and shelter. If you came right down to it, nothing but deficient ability could be blamed for frustrating his rockbottom purpose. In this light he regarded his methods and procedures as reasonably cunning. In other words, his was a mien hypocritically assumed with the hope that far from tempting fate his pettifogging rationalization of undistinguished failure and lugubrious renunciation of highlife would forfend criticism of his dull comedy, disarm spectators, deceive the Weird Sisters.

(16)
SA.07

BOVINES AND
PACHYDERMS

*T*he inspection party came to cloven hooves among the domestics. Again it was Michael who busied himself maintaining the family's pace. "Keep going. Keep going! Pigs and goats can see the wind but you can't tell that by looking at them. Keep going!" He nevertheless here turned a blind eye to Matthew's straggle—for the billygoat seemed number-two son's special longlost friend—without however permitting Ruth (who could never make up speed later) to fall back into her clovenfooted camel pace, in fact dragging her at the elbow. He allowed Matt to commune a while with his friend, with no mother or brother hanging over him, provided that he paid attention to the course and speed of his distancing tribe so that he could catch up when his spirit cleared. With a steadiness of vision that others might not appreciate Michael never faltered in his anticipation of the day's principal rewards yet to come.

But first it remained to visit the bovines, and he was obliged to admit that they were important. The Chapman entourage passed along the outside of a cowshed contrived for the public with hinged shutters dropped down to make an open window above the mangers and personal water

troughs of the Guernsey sisters who now stood in their stanchions prepared for the best part of the day like housewives chewing their cuds on a
club holiday free of their own children but equably attentive to the children in the parade now passing before their inn—Roger in particular,
whom they craned their necks to see, not to gush over him but simply to
take in the perfection of his species.

He hadnt anything to give them to eat but it was so obvious he was
sorry for his parents' neglect to provide him that they nodded to his
mother in approval of his manners as they sympathetically accepted his
shy caresses, held up by his father to reach their moist dark muzzles. The
fragrant hay and sweet breath penetrated even to the man's affections.
From considerable endurance of the public these cows had become judges
of humanity, most of whom they ignored as placidly as possible; but they
were taken by this goldenhaired little one who came up from wheels, especially Delilah (according to the posted name) who looked long after him
and he back at her, the one whose maternity had been most recently
exploited, whose aching milk leaked to the straw-strewn boards, who had
not yet forgotten what every cow must forget a dozen times in her life, the
lost cause of her freshening. Roger was unable to console her, but he
learned her word: "Cow. . . Cow!" he repeated, with long round Os.

They paused again at the end of the dairy's enclave. A great craggy
black Holstein tasseled and udderless stood in the shade of a eucalyptus
near the center of his paddock confused and stupid, the white zones on his
cowlike flank smeared with manure, shambling his cowlike feet and
swishing the splotches on his body with a cowlike tail as he shivered the
ring in his nose. Head lowered, morose, he ceaselessly shifted direction
from one panel of spectators to another, as if eyeing them by the hour; but
never would the human herd seem friendly which squealed at every move
he made and snickered every time his stare passed the fourth side of his
domain where a double fence separated him from the seraglio of skittish
heifers and dry mothers of his own and other colors who had no need to be
sheltered like the Guernsey ladies in a shed. His pasture was a corral of
hard brown dirt festucined dung and gray dust.

Now and then he snuffed the ground—whereupon snorts of fire
flashed upon the inward eye of the throng, and into the inward ear bellows
of rage or lust. Every move portended. Cynosure of the multitude. Hegel.
A master poet of the coffee house who may not be left to breathe alone. A
Spanish beast pawing for the charge. Half-convinced shrieks from the fair
sex, brave chuckles from the men. Someone whistling bullfight music. A
drugstore cowboy in shirtsleeves waving a red handkerchief challenged the
critter to mortal combat. But any calm observer could have told you that
Behemoth all this time was only turning in a jerky circle like a freshwater
boat anchored in fitful crosswinds.

"I wish they'd put a cow in there." Ruth whispered to her man.

"You arent the only one—look at all those eager people!" he replied. "But if she were in heat she'd be awfully disappointed, and so would you."

"I might be, but why the cow?"

"Look for yourself. See? A discompleted cod, a ballless pizzle, good for flagellation only. Nothing between his legs."

Slowly, doubtfully, wary of jest, the truth dawns on the city girl, the Trustees' mean abuse of credulity; and, tut, tut, broad amusement at the showmanship that deceives everyone but her Michael; bridling and clucking, lighting up like a woman suddenly returned to herself. For which then and there he kisses her. "Not now Mike, people will get the opposite idea!. . . . But the sign says a male—"

"A bull would be too disturbing. He'd make your eyes bung out, being a professional, and everyone would neglect the other animals. This is an ox."

And on reflection she was almost glad of the truth, what with the children there, though partly sorry to have been disabused. As if the authorities would have let an estrous cow anywhere near the place! "Oh Michael you know too much!"

Jonathan now moved and carried the motion that Roger walk for a while and that the kid's trundle cart carry the baggage of the eldest son who had too much to do that afternoon to be saddled with burdens. But the judges duly insisted that Matthew should share the benefit, and perhaps one or two others in the party.

Roger was happy to be on his feet. As soon as he was released Michael had to chase him about a capricious spiral before he could get hold of the milling winglike hand. Ruth converted the chair back into a gondola, and no sooner had done so than Jonathan and Matthew dumped their loads and ran ahead free and clear, joyful gentlemen disencumbered. With care Ruth was able to pack the freight in such a way that most of Michael's and her own could also be taken aboard, and when they resumed their way she was wheeling

In fact Michael knows too little—that much he knows at least—because he hasnt had time to learn everything about women, even about Ruth; but he does know that at this very moment she is entertaining in her head the same line that has been summoned to his own, from lore held in common as a family joke handed them one night between the year of Jonathan and the year of Matthew at a burlesque show. *After all you must remember she's been spoiled.* Sufficiently cryptic in its allusiveness to be uttered thereafter (without the preamble) on almost any public occasion, though it was possible that Jonathan who never asked or commented had eventually trapped some inkling of its general import in the seine of his loitering curiosity. The thin little man with a sharp face straw hat and cane told it in a patter, his voice almost too scratchy to hear in the littered

an untented overloaded prairie schooner, and himself was slowly listing along to clasp an extremely small slippery hand at the level of his knee with as little pressure as would serve the purpose. Yet God, it was slow! So after twenty yards of unsteady progress Michael picked up the new man and swept him over to the elephant pavilion, setting him experimentally upon his feet again.

But the parents could do nothing to make the guest of honor look through bars and across a dry moat at the great champions as they stood in the sun tossing hay over their shoulders, neither from his father's arms nor from the ground on his own two feet. So Michael let him watch the other new men and women nearby, who also watched him, while the old men and women watched the elephants and kept an eye on the new men and women.

They were Indians, these elephants, gratuitously chained apart from each other by the foot, smalleared sad and intellectual, reasonable with man, not wont to flap histrionically like Africans, very very slow to mate with Americans about. "This is the kind Mowgli rode." said Jonathan. "They can walk very softly and run very fast. . . . They're wiser than human fathers." he added archly. Maybe, thought Michael; but their tusks were gone their mouths hung flabby and they apparently had nothing left to talk about. The Trustees had made life more pleasant for them than the slavery of stacking teakwood in jungle clearings where

theater rustling and seething with impatience, not much of a crowd to say the least waiting for blowsy Venus to unblouse who had something to show (beside whom Hecuba would have looked like a svelte dryad), valiantly pretending he had the house in his hand as he took expert pratfalls, though in truth all but a decibel or two of the noise that could be identified as response was provided by the two-piece orchestra the straightman and himself. The patrons were not come to witness freedom of speech. *{Last week the wife took our little boy to the zoo, see. He didnt say much after they got back but yesterday he begged and he hollered for me to take him again. So finally I did, see.}* In those days Ruth was still young, her body compared to Hecuba's what Hecuba's now is to the burlesque queen's, having not yet much outgrown its integral years of virginity, and male displacement was still a rather small share of her cumulative history. According to archangelic doctrine desire sometimes required infernal grace: claps and peals of rut or sensual mysticism would occlude but never entirely eradicate the wont and rule of girlhood, which was still likely to come back to the fore—not as thought (which could hardly be reversed) but as condition of rest or pared-down libido. From time to time the woman still had to be roused and focused again by a flame fueled from within but enkindled from without. In the freedom of will conferred by such grace a good woman in Michael's doctrine chooses the atonement made lawful

their shame might be seen and remembered by those who could
appreciate the extent of their humiliation. As prisoners or as viziers,
unlike the Jews they made no attempt to preserve their literature.
Their noses were too long for assimilation, which doubtless they
had attempted at one time or another for the sake of the children.

"They suffer from captivity
more than any of the others." Ruth
said, offering no proof. The words
expressed her notion of elephant
pain misleadingly, for it was not of
this concentration camp that she
was thinking but of a certain atrocity in the history of men, an unthinkable torture of a defeated
army's most sensitive and tractable
conscripts, when the victors in vengeance hacked the trunks off these
terrified beasts, not only in battle
when the soldiers should have been
killing proper enemies instead but
also afterwards in the general's garden when they'd almost better have
been raping women or putting children out of their misery; and it was
fear of Flaubert's book that lay behind her remark, polarizing for a
couple of seconds all her distastes of
art for its heartlessness.

When one of the lady elephants
divined that there had come among
the crowd a soul who understood
their condition, and searched nearsightedly the row of heads lining
the bars, it was the thin pale face of
Jonathan that she picked out. She
moved to either limit of her spancel
and touched with her trunk the
trunks of her fellows on both sides,
who each turned to look at the boy,

by the seventh sacrament, and each
deep taste of atonement predisposes
her for the sooner return of beatitude; and habituation to the
enablement of grace will presumably dissolve at length the pudicity
of deportment that civilized women
have been accused of.

Brave theory. Works out very
well if the husband has a lifetime of
leisure and no thought for posthumous fame, if he enjoys a large unearned income with which to buy
surcease of obligation and insulation from world news, and if he is
endowed with a lover's armamentarium including a faculty for perpetual excitement to keep him
going year after year like Zeno's
paradox trying to reach his
beloved's essence by continually exploring what he knows already, by
finding ways to express himself like
a cinematographic succession of different heroes while remaining the
same old husband. Both of them
despairing of such manhood, lacking the fillip of an annual visit to
the secret spectacles of Europe, and
ruling out adultery, a burlesque
show every few years would seem to
do Ruth a lot of good. Whereas she
was guiltless, the sight and sound
of immodesty and its fancies were
vivid enough to be fetched up for a
long time afterward by the most
lightly suggested allusion. {He led
me straight to the elephants, see, and
sure enough honest to God this big bull
has a tremendous hardon. Look Pop the
kid says, what's that he says. I get suspicious, see, and I says did he have it
last week I says.—The little man
walking quickly back and forth

a solemn maneuver for a short glance: and then all three moved as far from him as possible, coming to a stand with their tails toward the Chapmen. Archfoes of dragons! Prime ministers to philosophic kings! But these milksops would trumpet at the sight of a worm on their pavement! "*Why* do they have to take their tusks out?" complained Jonathan in querulous disgust. "Let's go! This is no good."

Never had the interests of the family come closer to coincidence. Despite Jonathan's disdain and Roger's indifference, which prevented a comfortable focus of cooperative attention, the general community of father and mother, as comprehended by the father's embracing mind, established an uneasy unity that inferior wills could not squirm out of for the moment. Matthew was party to the major cohesive force during the time they stood there (always a vote the administration could count on) gazing personally at the great gray animals; lost in a new admiration that was dissuaded not at all by his big brother's trenchant deprecations. An epochal visit for Matt standing there speechless, almost forgotten by the family that sometimes dispraised him for talkative ebullition; and funny goats were driven forever from the passionate center of his general love. He easily imagined the tusks. But the elephants never responded to his yearning silence. Soft tears began to blur his vision of those gray giants who brought to mind the unselfish kindness protection and worry of his mother

twirling his cane, giving the straight man opportunity to urge him on with the story.] Their night out together freshened the well after a long watch and the domesticated opportunist never once looked away, although in the public obscurity of the sparsely attended theater sitting by themselves in the parterre he could only press with his finger beneath the coat on her lap (his other arm thrown openly around her shoulders) the larvic blossom that stirred him almost beyond containment. [*Yes he says. So I says did you ask your mother what it was. Yes he says. What did she say I says. Ma said it was nothing at all he says.* —Pause, ostentatious silence on the stage, not however canceling out the atmospheric drone of the auditorium. *Son I says, you must remember she's been spoiled!* Ducks through the curtain with a prance of the heels. Trumped up flourish of the ensemble to simulate applause.]

Queenie and her girls are next, and no men allowed on the stage. By itself the yoni is somewhat permissible in the flesh, as long as it's not fully disclosed, but the lingam must be represented symbolically only, never in the same act, as a separate fraction of the whole subject, confined to farcical gestes in entr'actes (a cane poking out in front under the little strutter's coat) as homely counterpoint threatening neither social stability nor the common man's vanity—never displayed while the girls are on, never never juxtaposed. But there it was, from the depths of the lecher's little old heart, speaking what the expert doctors refuse to admit, as if they

and his father. He hung away from the others so that none might see his face, lowering his head and taking care not to wipe his eyes.

knew women better than the folklore does, that magnitude makes a difference.

Man's live engines of civil service and war from the dawns of Asia were despoiled of their sagacity before they could begin to evolve wings, superannuated by lesser wisdom, and crowded off the earth without leaving behind a language, merely because they had no thumbs to write with. (People praise and regret them by wearing belts of elephant leather as if they wished to be compared with defenders of Jews who go circumcised.) The new logorithmoids their successors are taught to play eyeless chess (without memorial ivory statuettes) and spew bales of information to be stored in libraries for universal posterity until all magnetic pages and eyes finally perish together. Thus the wisely sad workers of goodwill who predeceased crude steam machines, leaving the whales without allies, and consequently yielded civilization to democratic swarms of infernal consumption engines, are now beaten even at a game of memory and calculation by the latest of men's creatures which are unable to move anything heavier than a line of type while pursuing every course of decisions with the utmost simplicity by counting repeated OHMs and NOT-OHMs over and over again in a labyrinth of witpitting designed by bipeds who were first taught to think for themselves. These thick-skinned nonruminants (once classified with pigs) could live longer in their own kingdom than they do in captivity by four score years and ten.

Only Roger is too unschooled to notice their distinction. When the family at last moved off he would walk no more. With squeaking sounds, arms upstretched, he implored his father to carry him—a demand so touching that the devil himself could not have refused it. When mounted into Michael's arms he laid his cheek upon the thick shoulder and gave up his spirit to the repose of the afternoon. But soon he was reembarked in his yacht now shaded and soft where he displaced the baggage—which had to be taken up again by human porters, except for what Jonathan could pile about the sleeper without crushing him.

{*Postulants only*: GO TO ITEM (18) SA.08, page 179.}

(17)
SO.02.0
ART OF LOCALITY

**Michael Chapman's First Lecture
in a Projected Series Announced
as *Special Topics in Dromenology:
Museless Art Number One***

I am given to understand that you are all students, that your eagerness is for academic revolution, and that you are likely to be interested in discourse that contributes to the proposition that a metaversity is best begun with theater. My purpose at this meeting is to address part of the question of drama's origin.

We are too vague about the theater, a nearly popular subject. Scientists are no longer vague about life, though life remains mysterious. Let us talk about ideas that are equal and in part opposite to the ideas of life-science. But first consider the sense of your rebellion.

Academus—he "of a silent district"—betrayed to Helen's brothers the place that Theseus had sequestered her and was well treated by the invading Spartans. Plato his most famous beneficiary has imposed upon our minds to this day the consequences of his epochal insurrection against poetry's rote, leaving us through his followers what Henry Adams called "the old laws of association formerly known as logic." In the academic universe, as well as in the theatrical profession, most associations of terms remain crystallized. You rightly rebel in refusing to become good students to teachers uninterested in the liberties of reconstruction.

But meetly remember that I am speaking to you in a room that Jack Wolfson got for our use under orthodox auspices. It is in dim response to ideals of the type we are protesting that the authorities give us leave to protest.

Yet isnt there always an inchoate revolution? Already, "do not all things exist for the student's behoof?" You benefit from all history to the degree that freedom of performance is its fruit. You are at leisure to espouse counter-success. The treasures of a whole library are urged upon you, along with the time to spend them—for the most part rendered conveniently into English currency. Therein is written all the liberty that has been taken in the past.

I warn you that as a speaker I bear less responsibility than your teachers. Less also than those who earn their living in the theater. I am too little trained to make even an American scholar. Yet it is necessary that I come before you with the same old language: we shall have no other. It is not new syntax that we require, but the opening of closed subjects and a more serious devotion of English to the functions of metalanguage. Without official calibrations or cachets I can't get paid by those who define disciplines, and I can't get published by those who want a new language; but I am accordingly in a special position to oversee the criticism of universities.

But there is also the establishment known as Broadway, whose vandals leave little of the language they got hold of and nothing difficult from the past. I trust that the guild of the Theater is recognized as our common enemy, like pollution of the waters. Against its devolutions, therefore, when all is said and done, we must defend the thermometric academy of letters. Know you then that there are other professions, other instruments than thermometers, and other purposes of the intellect than to rise to success in sealed straits merely by accumulating the heat of assimilation; but let you not break glass bulbs and spill into common puddles the mercury that can be used to assay panned gold.

As embryos you are not preformed thermometer men and women, but you are free, and welcome, to become thermometer men and women: better a professional student of art than a journeyman converter of art to money. In the epigenesis of a whole person the choices of livelihood may be bleak, but whatever your sorry case may be, as an American thinking, it is to your advantage, now and hereafter, to possess yourself of the counter-revolutionary savant faculties and not to destroy the parietal institution by mutation or by wound. Someday you may get hungry, as I am, for lack of its wealth, albeit that here, for you now, and all their lives for thermometer people, books may seem like food eaten by courtiers, the pleasure, if any, arising rather from the pique or boss of your swallow than from satisfaction of the belly or sustenance of action.

Your use of theater—all the facilities on the margin of this Bay—is likewise sensual: self-gratifying and sensational. You "experiment" in drama as if you have exhausted primitive and classic plays. The intervals between theatrical sowing and reaping get shorter and shorter; productions grow like weeds, more and more quickly mounting to the visibility where topicalities can be brandished. Your successors here will be free to have people fucking on the stage. This is not the kind of antithesis to the university that will make "the sluggard intellect of this continent look from under its iron lids."

We nevertheless have hope for new drama. It should be on the way, seeing that brilliant producers architects and stage designers already anticipate they know not what, and are getting funds to realize their preparations. Restless directors and composers are supposedly ready for America's Elizabethan age. Willing audiences expedite an industrious confusion. While poets are showing interest, the actors of drama are preoccupied with roles. But dancers seem to understand better than either poets or actors what the theater's for.

There is a fixed amount of material in the world, and many more people every hour: yet the population is not encouraged to conserve; it is demanded to consume. Everyone puts through her hands or before her eyes or into her ears as much various mattenergy as she is permitted to be party to the degradation of. But she is able to digest very little of it, for she has finite areas of external or internal surface for sensation and very little space for accessible storage. In passing it is spoiled, most of it turned to waste without yielding nourishment. Absorbtion of sensation alone has become a virtue in the new ethos, like bravery in olden times, without much regard for formal cause. No person, no place, no landscape gives you great pause. The things you own are revenues and debts, not true property.

But you are free. Instead of place and knowledge you have fungible resources and personal energy. Forasmuch as your sexuality is not greatly constrained, you suffer little from false love. It is for adventure of intellect, for new possibility of experience, for mystery in love, that you need the theater.

So the main purpose of working out a theory of the drama should be to stimulate this central art, that of the master-builder, the playwright. To that end the past is interesting. We fish the past for its vast simultaneity of manifestation. In the past lie first things, middle things, and last things, whole cycles that we could never live through personally, even if with the aid of our self-conscious efforts they were brought to repeat themselves. Our lives are so short that we must be efficient. We have little time for redundant experiment. Substance is history, some say; and I say the substance of art as well as the Body of Fate's.

But can we study our own substance too, the substance that is final for the present, the substance that sustains the mind of the self? For many years we have been discovering a self-consciousness that can never be covered again. We shall have to produce our history out of the very awareness of history, and to exercise new controls according to our new knowledge of control itself. Artificially, as you might put it, we have to reverse the process of social evolution by making a corporate art that can reassert its sovereignty in our culture, whorling a center from ideas that in other times would have been spun off by a nucleus.

Every point in the gyre of history moves at a unique distance from the axis and from the origin, and it thus differs from all corresponding azimuth points at other levels; but though the various cultures themselves occupy different sections of the conic nappe their phases always have counterparts. In our eon the point of the present is continually moving in one upward centrifugal direction, not on a track but laying a track behind it. I speak from this continually changing moment, and I am always looking in both directions, at the historical and at the anticipated. The gyre itself is discernible. It is possible to extrapolate from reasonable prejudice. Knowledge of the exfoliating program can inspire or depress our spirits. Right now the gyre of our self-determination may destine that the idea of the gyre should enter into the field of the gyre as the newest centripetal force required to compensate for the increasing speed of life and its distance from the axis. Otherwise we are lost, about to fly off on a straight line of illimitable regression.

Yet in speaking of the past, finding pattern in it, I must appeal to scholars for factual distinctions between moment and moment. I have at the most a point or two to work with, besides the moving point I live. Professionals might therefore forbid me my opinion on the full subject, or at least public appearances. But I am so partial to drama the art of locality that I am willing to risk controvertible speculations, hoping that the advancement of amateur theory will help get things going among you who have the talent, the facilities, and the time for scholarship.

The beginning of the art of locality is dance. Knowledge of drama's origins will help you understand how to use dancers in the theater. Indeed almost everything in art started with dance in its ritual phase. But beware extant leaders of dance as you beware actors: listen to their words only when you have them pinioned, in despair of their own careers. The new independent art of dance has gone its own separate way; yet solemn drama can be recovered only in the theater this dance has created, even if plays continue to leave dancers off the stage.

Jane Harrison once wrote that "almost everywhere, all over the world, it is found that primitive ritual consists, not in praise and sacrifice, but in mimetic dancing". Notice that she was speaking of *primitive* ritual. This statement applies to the pre-liturgical ritual that she reconstructed from traces of *dioikesis*—the customary control of society—in archaic Greece;

and it points even farther back toward a pre-mimetic dance antecedent to ritual itself. By following this line of investigation in its other direction— up to the famous high time of Athens—she set forth the principle that from dancing at length springs art. All arts.

"Art and ritual are at the outset alike in this," she said, "that they do not seek to copy a fact, but to reproduce, to re-enact an emotion." They originally make the *feeling* of an action. The mimesis is a recall or foresight of the *affect* perhaps of desire; or of victorious survival. This inward state is re-induced proprioceptively by means of action. At the outset the objective aspect of performance is no more than the procedure by which the performer attains to a feeling; the action has no "meaning" and the dancers intend no communication. Since the community of dancers is not conscious of the outward appearance of its dance it doesnt dream of affecting others. How could it? There is no one else to watch: all denizens are in the act.

The original emotion, which is reflected in the earliest dromenon, inheres in a practically superfluous action referring to a real and earnest event which has taken place, which will take place, or which the community would like to take place. The feeling is generated by the physical response to memory, or to anticipation (based on memory), or to instinct. This response is the "utterance" that Harrison speaks of as the source of ritual, as that which in representing a feeling can also reproduce that feeling.

The complimentary gest is made up of the same elements of movement and particles of sound that are used in the real event of practical action, but the elements are played in a different way. Their sequence, duration, and emphasis are changed. Organized into a new structure, they generate the feeling for which there is a want.

The psychic function of this otherwise useless behavior might be called release from emotional tension, or expression of surplus energy; but in any case the utterance is a natural use of muscle. One's play is at first more or less random and phenotypic, like a baby's laugh; but then when it accidentally interacts with someone else's, as a bounding dance of joy belike would do, it moves from spontaneity on the individual's part to corporate spontaneity, which tends to regulate itself, still unselfconsciously, according to tribal perceptions.

This gradual incorporation of action is a process of self-controlling the inchoate communal psyche. The corporate utterance is held in the *common* memory. Now there is of course no common brain, and no means of recording a collective memory in order to maintain it; and the individual's nervous system recalls an action better than an emotion, far better than a thought. The dance itself is reproduced from individuals' kinesthetic memory. It then serves to regenerate the original and forgotten feeling. But it coheres as a phenomenon of the collective will and regulates the person's otherwise aberrant or idiosyncratic utterance, controlling her feeling throughout its fling. The feeling itself, once under discipline, reinforces the regulatory characteristic of the dance, and together the dance and the feeling generate the ideas which eventually inform a fully developed ritual.

The strengthening of ritual self-regulation permits leaders and musicians to withdraw from equal and constant participation. They—and after a while others too—begin to watch that part of the dance that is not specifically their own. For by now the evolving action has begun to differentiate itself into parts. What begins as a discrimination of function winds up as a generic separation of performers and witnesses.

At last the expectation of the watchers affects the dromenon. The partial objectification brought about by distinction of function is a condition for the development of mental leisure—starting with the first thought unrelated to the requirements of immediate satisfaction or survival. The thought may now quite efficiently serve as cause for renewal of the corporate feeling. In order to reproduce the feeling a complex community must think, and in order to think it must cause itself to witness the movement which gives rise to the thought.

So at first ritual "imitates" dance, and it is in this ultimate sense that Aristotle's words about drama should be read. The body's recollection of past action can excite the self of a dancer as an intellectual image retrospectively excites the tranquil self of the poet in a literary culture. But the personal performance is now modified or perfected through dawning consciousness of the spectators' objectivity. She becomes aware of her direct influence upon the theorists—those who behold.

And so in time dance becomes expression instead of utterance. The dance of ritual, having brought under its corporate sway the importunate blood of individual bodies, constrains the explosive utterances of earlier stages—and of course still knows nothing of personality in its celebration of tradition. Yet in the beginning it resumes remembered passion, and at its prime it reproduces a passion that cannot be experienced outside the cult. But in its decadence it imitates a passion that can no longer be experienced by its witnesses.

When it was said in Greece that men had been taught ecstatic dance by the wine god the time had come when men were grown too circumspect to dance spontaneously without intoxication. The people were *hoping* for passion. The dance of the Corybantes now produced what was thought to be primitive emotion. Its subconscious effect was to test, ludicrously, the demotic energy for leisure. We may indeed suppose that the introduced ecstatic dromenon represented elements from the religious past that sanctioned its archaistic pleasures. But the dance that carried the ritual implicitly harbored an intention of which the people concealed their suspicion: subversion of custom.

It is well known that at certain times of ecstatic ritual taboos are violated, human bodies are transvalued, mutilated, or destroyed, negative powers of mana are made positive, or sacred and demoniac elements exchange positions. For a moment, in cathartic confusion, the cult trembles. These celebrations (and the cultures in which they appear) are far from primitive.

The consequences of religious dance are thus not conservative but atavistic. Every person and every society continually copes with the ambiguity of allegiance to *nomos*, *ethos*, organization, superego, tradition, and the dance of Themis herself. The very ritual that preserves the culture, and, through differentiation, advances it, is the first instrument of individual and collective reaction.

This recidivous potentiality of dance is exploited by several different motivations. At one end of the spectrum a proclivity for reaction may simply represent personal lust seeking to evade the regulations of civilization. But at the other end it may signify a yearning for personal redemption, since a return to primitive praxis on one level of experience can conceivably compensate the psyche in anagogic ecstasy for nerve-wracking progress on all other levels of whatever modernity. The vice of mystical simplification presents itself as virtue. The selfishness of purification becomes holy.

A fascinating syncopation of mythological object-matter was revealed in the Greek Mysteries to suggest spiritual transformations that eventually turned the motions and materials of concrete religion into a gnostic apparatus destined to influence for the worse Christianity's entire course, and some prominent science of mentality to this day. . . .

{*Postulants only:* GO TO ITEM (19) SO.02.1, page 193.}

(18)
SA.08

CAT HOUSE

*T*he youngest son is therefore safely removed from the line of sight in his wheeled ark when the goodman and his family visit the cat house. Risk of shocking him will be further reduced by shortening his stay. After obliviously touring the first gallery all asleep and unfeared he will roll out again into the open spaces pushed by the woman who in pure prejudice will have been asked to leave and naturally take him with her. For this is Jonathan's chapter of the trip who is acknowledged to have earned special privilege as a theorist of great cats, and everyone understands that he will remain nervous and nearly silent until he is alone with a father that appreciates (having inculcated) certain passions and allusions.

It'll be a heartless slight of the woman that feeds and doctors Semiramis a real cat who with good reason regards her as sovereign of the household though never literary theoretical or dominant. In the cat's estimation a boy is no more than an admirer nice to have the hand of on her back when she comes in sleepy from her wild lone outdoors. Ruth doesnt claim but a reader can't be much amiss in believing that the small domestic semblable (but big for her neighborhood) no matter how ignorant of books and stories about greater and wilder cats can be better trusted than a Cub Scout to pass judgment upon the authenticity of sympathy for uncivilized cats in the breast of a person who never fails to fill the dish of a civilized one. In any case the overweening manchild was born to underestimate the respect in which his mother is held by the black cat nominally his own that except for sex serves as a citified model of Bagheera himself.

When the time comes for the family to divide, Roger's faction will be reinforced by Matthew, not at anyone's insistence—because not even the cat-lover is cruel enough to exclude him positively—but in the untroubled propensity to accompany his mother whenever he notices her segregation. He likes cat stories or at least his father's conversation as well as the next boy. The guilt-ridden soul of Jonathan on the other hand is not wholly insensible of his and his father's contribution to the injustice of the world; yet without speaking of his view he holds that the worship at hand calls for knowledge and desire but not agnostic sympathy. He does not wish to come upon his prince the black panther with a mother asking a lot of questions that miss the mark or crying out in shallow pleasure at the deep delights he has been cultivating most of his life, especially as she is wont so to behave not in simple admiration of the thing itself but in sentimental support of his own pleasure, which to his distaste he often perceives to be the real object of her uninformed interest in his interests.

Meanwhile contentment obtained in one cell only, the current main attraction of the arcade, where a recumbent inaudibly purring lion-woman pawed and licked as she smilingly suffered two tawn cubs to tumble at her teats. The long body of the mother stretched out behind her erect frontage a warm soft ridge of endless nourishment and presented to her children a world of felixity without let or scold. They used it as their own while she watched them learn. The unreserved attitude of her belly for the delectation of milky little gum-stones and kneading pawlets belied a prestorgenic alertness in the complacent amusement with which she at the head surveyed her trunk. She gave no thought to the certainty that motherlove in her bones would soon be outlived by the little man-lion and his sister,

From the line of ill-smelling cages issued an earthless and leafless jungle of growling humidity. Low roars mingled and reverberated like experimental music all about the booming hollows where the people lingered or passed in a twilight dimmer than the barred cubicles yellow with the electric illumination most becoming to coats of tattered unstately lions and tigers none too neat. Species that never met in forest plain or mountain here mixed their scents and responded to each other in cacaphonic waves of factional grievance like political prisoners from mutually opposing factions always personally betrayed, glancing through the fourth wall at their visitors only to seek in the nakedly opaque faces some reflected trace of their fellows in neighboring cells. For they were unconscionably partitioned from

though in her clover-round ears it continued to filter out the anger sounding from her fellow prisoners in both directions along the block. She gave no sign of recognizing her husband's special anguish standing alone his heavy tufted tail atwitch like the devil's two doors down the line, informed of her tidings only by scent. Zoo Trustees had the advantage of their counterparts at the museums of art in this amazing faculty for increase without acquisition. All day long one could come upon a cluster of rarity-seekers hanging before Cleopatra's alcove as if a Rousseau and a Gauguin had bred a couple of little neo-impressionists.

Of the wakeful Chapmans Ruth chose to be most deceived by the apparent happiness of this maternity, but none of them refused to delight in the cheerful tumbling of the undefiled kittens or denied a wish strong as lust to caress and domesticate the pair. Ruth and Matty were filled with love for the cubs' innocence, Michael and Jonathan with possessive visions of their maturity, never questioning the cicurative ability of the Chapman home in Oakland. But only the Chapman mother cared to guess the sacrificially depleted sensations of the lioness being sucked at and punched with prickly small pads, admiring more than anything else the neatly crowning symmetry of her sister's achievement in delivering herself of the twins called on the label of the cage Apollo and Artemis, for was it not truly said that you are not a complete mother unless you have a daughter?

the sight of other cats, howsoever close in kinship or location, with not so much as an opposite row of cages to look at, the Trustees having divided and subdivided the residential galleries with curtain walls down the middle of the great hall presumably with the humane intention of mitigating feral torment by depriving it of reflection.

The spectators had come to look; but, casting their eyes from one beast to another only to see the lifted lip just too late to match the laconic voice, they could scarcely ever catch an individual sound where it was formed, so well did the prisoners with no means of conspiracy (as one could not claim for them anything more of language than the utterance of feeling) make grim game of the sluggishness in human perception.

Yet some locked up there were pacing in restless silence fed by longing too terribly imprisoned for a free man to see without trembling at the jurisprudence of his own kind. Others lay awake with clamped jaws in cathectic deliberation upon a liberty they reckoned coming to them for the debt they were paying to society. Many of those born without the walls had been dragged by wheels before their prime yet already in every sense apprised of the freedom their life was intended for, and these were now as angry at their fellow inmates for witnessing their degradation by the molecular broadcasts through their fetid air as at the invincibles for netting them ignominiously in the springtime of their lives.

Many of the featherless bipeds chafed at being forbidden by the Trustees to use their cunning little packages of thunderless lightning without which they could not satisfy their artless desire to carry home praiseworthy proof that they had actually seen this dioramic tableau, the only menage then to be found anywhere in the feline menagerie. There were many photographic attempts notwithstanding, a continual volley of tiny little sliding clicks more presumptuous in their creative modesty than the blitzes of Zeus. But the captive queen indifferent to the rabble never once posed for her full-face shots.

Now Jonathan's admiration of cats was more fanciful than scientific and he increasingly felt the pangs his temperament subjected him to as he modified his growing knowledge with greater and greater difficulty. But he often took the trouble to revise his hierarchy of beasts—as a boy of some previous generation might have troubled himself to keep his hierarchy of gods and heroes relevant to advancing education. In any event he was attentive enough in seeing to it that members of the Felidae club (right down the middle: catcher pitcher second base and center field) dominated his all-time intercontinental all-star team. The fictions he had heard from his father or read for himself, sometimes altered or expanded by his willful sense of propriety, had merged imperceptibly but not totally unaware into the slight portion of realism absorbable by a male Chapman. His theory of black panthers was about

Others hothouse-bred were paying for the sin of their fathers who had not refrained from yielding to their ruttish blood under the salacious eye of the exploiter when suddenly (and only then, on the rare occasions of long years reserved for the lucky few that the Trustees happened to be matchmaking for) released to the sight and touch of a female whose signals of special distress in spite of herself were maddening the atmosphere. [But who who has known life long at sea would be the first to cast a stone at one longer yet in jail that takes up an offering to his lust without giving a fig for observers? Had not Michael himself written his Ruth-girl letters more naked in flesh and soul than copulation itself even when he knew they had to be read by the commissioned censors of his own idle and gossipy ship well acquainted with him in his daily rounds, young squires and lordlings whose superiority of position equality of desire and inferiority of feeling set them at jocular contention with each other to read his masterpieces when the outgoing mail of the enlisted men (less to be trusted than officers not to write place names to a woman somewhere whose loose talk would cost lives in a bar frequented by correspondents of Japanese submarine captains, though always kept in doubt about what they were doing in the war as many degrees as possible more ignorant in that respect than the gentlemen) was divided into piles on the wardroom table, humiliating the expressed profusion of his unique heart more painfully than

to be put to the test of observation and he was apprehensively preparing himself to criticize (in event of disappointment) the sampling of nature here on display, or at least the official interpretation of it, if not zoology itself; for he had long known that no one species quite perfectly attained to the nominal form of giant cat that had become his criterion for judgments and affections. The most exotic of extant species as represented in San Francisco must needs fail of itemized supremacy in size and somatic proportions or in arboreal proficiency or in cross-country speed or in aquatic versatility or in adaptation to northern winter or in humanist intelligence or perhaps simply in uniformity of blackness; and no jail could be expected to obtain a single specimen truly excellent in all categories—legendary instances being rare enough in the natural history of wildlife. If such hero lived he would be the most evasive of capture.

A beast that had not naturally evolved would have to be put together from existing stocks. Jonathan's interest in lions was limited to the tall kings of the race, for the noble proportion of forequarters to rakish hindquarters—for their special contribution to the ideal which as a whole they suffered by comparison to. Cataloged in his mind's bestiary was a lion-size hybrid from India Africa and America: a mountain-climbing ocean-diving yardarm-walking wall-leaping road-speeding night-watching day-purring body-guard and traveling companion, politer than a collie in gentle society and keener than a bloodhound in

the leering eyes of guards who had wives at their sides every night could have shamed his commonplace desire by watching him appease his conjugal concupiscence with an official whore? It had not been a month aboard before his proud resistance to the class-privilege of censorship was overridden by the necessity of speaking his mind to the one in the world with whom he found communion.] These compulsory offsprings of slavish parents gave evidence of their stock more vaguely than their less alienated seniors because they had no definite disappointments to focus their puzzled readiness for insurgence; they had no way of life to anticipate or remember. Having been weaned in captivity they never afterward saw their kind save flashingly once or twice in choiceless dizzy matings and were incapable of understanding the horror in their manhandled perpetuation of the species. These degenerated cats with no sodality to school them in the dignity forestalled (unlike the homely elephants of that city who having signals with each other passed down the memory of self-respect and with successive generations of captivity progressively curbed the urge for procreation and finally asserted their tradition by impotence or sterility) ingenuously acquiesced to the master race and bred more caitiffs further and further removed from natural law.

The workless servitude was sorrier to behold than any slavery more liberal in motion than the treadmill, equally cruel to muscle and wit, so oppressive in its

trailing the lost or the fleeing, his young master's best friend. But something more shapely than the high-hipped African female was required in the pedigree—something of the burningbright tiger's length, perhaps Siberian, for sinuous lines and independent power.

"Why don't they let a mother tiger and a father lion get married?"

"It must have been tried." said his own mother. "If anything had come of it I think we would have heard."

"Maybe if we could read the New York Times every day . . ." murmured his father with interest. [In zoological pleasure gardens why shouldnt the most patriarchal cat taste the sweets of foreign novelty? Elsewhere it does not take unbelievable lust to cross the boundary between species. It would be strange if cats somewhere had not come up with a feline mule. How far beyond the possibility of such an attempt is the likelihood of issue?]

Jonathan declared that he himself if he were a lion would try the experiment. (Did he not always sneer at fancy purebred dogs in his preference for the mongrel?) He regarded this conjectured devolutionary violation of species and its hardly imagined result with deeper interest than that he would have taken in the miscegenation of Pasiphae. The problem now was to work into a heroic family tree the Hermes-swiftness of another African he admired, the tractable palace-guarding cheetah—but without its spots its pinched head or its unseemly high rump. And one North

hopelessness and moral neglect that Michael would almost as soon have borne witness to the controversial tortures of vivisection. Several convicts were permitted access to skylighted private atriums through drop-gated apertures in their scenery and they endlessly explored their tiny apartment endlessly disappointed of both caves and savannahs as they endlessly returned to their inner trap. Rarely did they cooperate in the mockery of basking on their public shelves under artificial trees where the malicious catcalls of men and their cubs were more irritating than the bombilation of the manswarm on a concrete floor echoed by the lofty clerestory. No wonder Michael Chapman asked himself what made them keep living, putting himself in their miserable particle of space where he couldnt look behind him or to either side, and looked out in front only to face scot-free enemies jeering at his loss. He could not accept the prevailing assurance that even such godlike freethinkers suffered less than human beings in a dungeon. He wasnt convinced by the putative fact that animals were inferior in nervous complexity and self-consciousness. Werent those walls and bars as cruel to a lion having neither word nor reason as they would be for himself if doomed to incarceration with language in his head? The question would never be resolved but this much could be said that a royal cat or transformed man of whatever psychic history (whether blessed with symbols or otherwise, whether tortured by or insensible to an

American, duke of the Rocky Mountains, lonesome rival to invincible grizzlies and brilliant wolves, cougar puma catamount or any name you wished to pick from all those with which its only predator inconsistently blessed it, persecuted by the firepower of civilization's least bridled nation: so that the bloodline might be engrafted with the genes of all great cats.

All these they saw in their progression down one side of the Cat House, amongst lesser fry like ocelots wildcats and lynx. Jonathan's heart beat faster in anxiety and hope. When they turned the corner would he find the living shape and hue of a triple-crown champion? Or was the world grown too old for him its late citizen to feast upon the sight of Bagheera's heir?

The preamble was over. The better half of the clan went straight out the postern to the Monkey House while with tightened breath he and his father reversed direction to search the second row of aristocats. Alone together they made discovery and conversation.

Third cage, among the leopards, there he was! Suddenly, without conviction, Jonathan was stockstill in front of a flowing silhouette more majestically black than the panther of his dream, pure as snow, sole father and form-maker to the son of the marvelously epigenetic cat-mother envisioned, potential progenitor of the supernal and insuperable scion, himself already perfect in golden eye and silky chin and lengthened jaw, in courtesy, in silent tread and calligraphic tail; in repose and liquid motion as

uncalendared invariance of events, whether comforted by religion or blessedly ignorant of past and future particles of time, whether trained to examine his unbearably compacted rage or guilelessly bemused by an unenvisioned urge to tear and kill all tormentors indiscriminately, whether racked by entelechtual suffering or benighted in solipsism) suffered cruelly and unusually from the deprivation of natural love when foiled of incest and pederasty by solitary confinement and unindoctrinated in the autofellation facultated by a conveniently supple spine.

What enraged the angry ones enough to stay alive? Did their cramped pace slow down over the years? The excruciating frustration of energetic bodies in a confinement next thing to the tomb (while sensing liberty all around them) comported better with decay than with a steady state between liberty and death. Or again what secret hatred caused others to draw breath from one instant to the next, and to put up with the paternalistic custody by which men affected to protect each species of cat from the general extinction men themselves brought into the world with all their woes? I would rather die with the last of my kind.

But there was nothing emaciated about the look of them, and therein lay most of the answers. It was hunger kept them alive. Not the eating itself, not the food flung to them in scientific measure once a day, but the slowly gathered attention of secreting neurons (in spite of absolute despair) which like a

paradoxical as a boomeranging arrow, unpredictable even in his restless pacing of a small box with three walls, nothing static or arrestable in his movement: wholly beyond the scope of photography and altogether outrivalling other cats in his mercurial specific gravity as a masterwork of quick power in the liquefied cohesion of finely formed parts:: a slim almost unwatchable black shadow or indeterminable black quantum that could not be fixed, a black ghost that a boy's hands might be expected to pass through airily if in the yearning of his bowels he had been permitted to reach out for its love::: but really a hot muscular shade easily enlarged by changes in the slant of the sun.

Jonathan exulted at the placard namesaking this hero Bagheera. His animosity toward the Trustees dissolved in the warmth of literary sympathy. In his pleasure at the convergence of official imagination with his own he forgot for a moment the cruelties of public imprisonment—in his trembling delight at the mirror of existence. ["We be of one blood, thou and I . . . remember, Bagheera loved thee."]

The dream seemed real before him, a true black subAsian, only slightly smaller than a tiger after all, its delicate sagacious head categorically distinguished from the thuggish or complacent countenances of other Felidae. If he was a mite low in the shoulders it was a small matter of taste which could be corrected in a high-bred melanasian son.

tide lift the senses unaware and organize the endurance of time. A hunger disarmed of suicide by red meat daily flung free before their noses in the vicious diurnal rhythm of captivity—the one satisfaction they expected and couldnt help themselves from waiting for, just as when once you exhale there's no way to prevent air from filling the vacuum of your lungs and then from relieving its own pressure with a sigh. The ineluctable modality of appetite thwarts any hope of high-minded cachexia and perpetuates the pain of a beating heart. You cannot stop yourself from ingesting matter and excreting time. They use your one indispensable frailty to force the incessant conversions of oxygen and protein. You cannot refuse to obey. There is no room even to mime a leap but by the same token nothing in your routine to represent attenuation. You are given no work to do and notwithstanding every effort of will the calculated ration is transformed into the oscillating motion by which specialized time is measured out. It was not surprising that the keepers could not make friends with their clients by feeding them.

Hunger's flood-tide slaking lasted but a few minutes of the day. Then a cat could resort to sleep. (But even a cat can sleep only so much: he learns not to squander god's allotment of unconsciousness and to regulate it for his own good.) Only in sleep could he escape self-disgust sadder than that following uninspired coition. But first he permitted himself that

Bagheera was a recent acquisition still unused to confinement, still soundlessly snarling as he prowled his cage, still thinking swiftly behind slowly blinking greengold eyes, still revolving policy. The other cats beyond his walls seemed aware that their prince was now among them, fearfully preparing themselves to obey his command when he chose to lead the terrible escape. Yet this was no blusterer. His voice was too soft and ironic for any human ear that didnt come as close as a boy's would who lies against his side stroking and hugging the godlike neck as black and smooth as the glossy coat of miniature Semiramis.

But alas, according to a shock of science, not so immaculate. It was only now in humbled pride that Jonathan began to learn something new from his visit to the cat house, and his father teaching him would presently share yet another surprise. In the trance of discourse they both abstracted themselves from the blooming buzzing confusion of human nature, and to the man supplying knowledge the boy's feelings were as his own.

singular pleasure of his waking life—a jaw-stretching yawn.

Who could anatomize meaning in this anthropomorphic grimace of a caged felix? Assume if you like that there's no mind or language centered in that head; that the brain therein can never take enough objective interest to form fetch apprehend sustain or alter thought, nor to notice beauty either; that its senses are impervious even to advertising: you must nevertheless perceive in the yawn some sort of sensuous proprioceptive device, an anesthetic gesture of indifference to the diverse odors and lineaments of yahoo figures sauntering past. Or at least this muscle-toning mechanism for a moment relieves captive lions of some disequilibriums that are normally acquitted by amusement play or work. Is it the evolutionary end of cats to sublimate their superhuman force with yawns?

But ye who love these big mousers must not assume too little. See in their yawn a beginning of art. Put them without prey upon the stage. Give them leave to dance! The ancients sometimes pictured them so doing.

SON: "Dad, why did they stick him over here with the leopards? He should be with the lions and tigers."

DAD: "Because he's a black leopard."

SON: "He is not! He's a black *panther*!"

DAD: "Read the sign Jonno. The black panther is not a species." Buffon, who started by following the philosophers, came around to declare that the only real category is the species, his empirical proof being the sterility of hybrids. (A remarkable case of science in support of idealism!) The black panther therefore exists only as a spurious individual. There was no black panther in Noah's Ark who rescued only arketypes, whether real or nominal. My boy's plan won't work: you can go only one generation down with the miscegenation of animals. 'Tis increase makes a species, not just fucking fun without responsibility. I wouldnt mind living in a nice clean cave with Bagheera's sister. "He's a leopard that's changed his spots. If you got up very close you could still see them, black under black. You didnt read the book carefully enough. This is an individual variation like a long-haired German Shepherd or a white whale. By all odds none of Bagheera's cubs will be all black."

BOY: "You mean he's a leopard just all blotted over? But I *know* he's a black panther! He can't be anything else!"

DADDY: "Don't say *just*. Black is hard to get. It makes him more distinguished than you think. He has none of the colors on him. Don't be sorry that he doesnt have his own species. Ordinary animals are like their kind. You should be glad he's changed his skin! Besides, don't sneeze at leopards. They can do everything black panthers do—not counting of course our unique friend Bagheera. Leo-pard: a leopard, my boy, is a lion-panther."

BOY: "Ha! Then what does panther mean, Old Man? It must mean something!"

OLD MAN: "Pshaw, young man, I don't know . . . . Maybe Pan-theos: all the gods in one."

YOUNG MAN (giggles): "Hey daddy call me by my ten names. You havent done that for a long time. Please?"

[*Beginning of game:*]

DADDY: "Okay, but keep to the subject, which is the cats we see. —Is that your big brother in there, Brother Jonathan?"

BROTHER JONATHAN: "Yes, sir, it is. In the book his life began in a cage."

SIR: "But Jo-nathan, this Bagheera will live out his life here without a friend."

JO-NATHAN: "You are his friend, sir, and so am I. We'll come often to speak with him. There is no language that he does not understand."

SIR: "Yes, Jon-ethan, but I wish we could get his attention."

JON-ETHAN: "He has the sweetest breath in the animal kingdom, sir. —Goodbye Bagheera!"

SIR: "Especially in Christendom, Jonah-than." He refuses it to the females here. In the jungle he seduces his prey. "Protector of the weak. —Goodbye poor cat."

JONAH-THAN: "Next time we'll bring Semi with us. She can get through the bars with our messages—sir! He will love her."

SIR: "I'm afraid he's too angry to love anyone here, Jon, even though he's a natural friend of elephants wolves bears pythons and man-cubs. She'd be scared to death and spit and yowl. She can't see black anyway. —Look how quickly he makes his turns! But he is slow to anger in his own country. —Let's go see the others."

JON: "Daddy—sir—why do Cub Scouts have Wolf, Bear, and *Lion* badges? It's s'post to be Wolf, Bear, and *Panther*, the way it is in the story. There are no lions in India!"

SIR: "There used to be. But maybe they've just tried to make the thing more American. You know, Jonno, all big cats used to be called lions, especially mountain lions.

JONNO: "But they're the wrong color, sir! It's just tricking with words anyway. They really mean African lion because people don't know any better."

SIR: "Little Jonny Appleseed, most mothers and fathers love lions because they are the only cats who live together in big families."

JONNY APPLESEED: "They call them prides, sir. —Look, Dad! Look, look, look! Here's a *huge* black panther!" [They have been strolling past spotted leopards and cheetahs, but now he points ahead to the last cage, yanking Sir by the hand. Jonny Appleseed pays no attention to the public printed word unless he is driven to an extremity of self-reliance.]

SIR: [Immediately after the first breathtaking glance comes forward and reads the sign.] An extremely rare black jaguar from Brazil. "His name is Lucifer!" Haunted zoo! This is the godfather of all black kittens. Bagheera's archangel! Power and beauty beyond compare! "Duns, this is a great day for us. I didnt know that there ever really was such a great cat!"

DUNS: "I did!"

SIR: "You did what, Dunno?"

DUNNO: "I did, *sir*! Because he was perfect in my head, and he couldnt be perfect if he was just imaginary! He's big as a lion. Look at those muscles! He could do anything! I'd like to see him race a cheetah. He's clean and smooth as Bagheera, and black as black can be! Even I can hardly believe it! What a relief! I knew it was possible! Let's take him and Bagheera home to Semiramis! She won't need lions or tigers!"

SIR: "But Mowgli, why do you need Bagheera, or Semiramis either for that matter? Lucifer is the ideal black cat already."

MOWGLI: "Bagheera knows the ways of men. He's smart and wise and I think he's more friendly. He would watch our face when we talk to him. He knows the tools and customs of man. But I wish we could make friends with this one too don't you, sir?"

SIR: "Jonathan, the best way to make friends with an animal is to take him for long walks. Feeding isnt enough. None of these cats like their jailers. Of course the keepers don't know how to talk to them and that makes a big difference too." Mowgli says what I have always thought: there's no high culture in South America, even less than what we have in North America. Up here it's all machines, down there it's all nature. The mind of a cat is interesting only in the Old World, where cities and jungles mingle, and linger into desert, so that memory and lore can be passed back and forth between men and their four-footed brothers. Still, Europeans have always understood South America better than North Americans do. Maybe I've been too prejudiced against Spaniards and aborigines, Aztecs and Incas too, for their cruelty for their ignorance of Shakespeare for their lack of elephants. I seem to have put too much weight upon their ineptitude for wheels and abstractions. My son has inherited his imperialism. St Joseph was fascinated by the mental isolation he found there. . . .

LUCIFER: I have more culture than you think, gringo child. I can lure fish with my tail. I have swum the Panama Canal to avoid hunters in infernal consumption engines. And from the slopes of the Andes many goodly states and republics have I seen all the way down to the purple land. But I am best known among the upland waters of Brazil where gnostic doctors of the soul propitiate me as nightmoving god of their jungle. In the villages I am feared and obeyed for my traceless beauty. I would like to teach you that there is more mentality in my spiritual power than you can fathom in your industrial dreams full of literary allusions. And learn from you how to escape this zoo. For I shall die here if you don't spring me, and in death my mateless singularity will be as lost as an unwritten legend. You may ride my back as Riolama used to do, and sleep securely under my protection with your arms around my satin black neck as she and her companions did until she was roasted beyond my reach in a tree by the leaping red flower with which they sought in her to kill my daimon. It was in that defeat that I taste gall. I heard her scream, I saw her dive, but there was nothing I could do against flames made by the most cowardly of creatures. Between Arizona and Patagonia, never have I had another companion, and few are the mounted majesties or fruited plains that I have failed to search. Your clever little Bagheera, though I would welcome him to my heart, is a Commonwealth provincial who knows nothing of wild loneness, for all his Hellenic philosophy. My soul-sister Rima was preSocratic in her sagacity. She was not much taller than you but her taut small breasts were more delicate and tender than any in your mythologies, and she had no need of archery, or chastity, to rule the Amazons before I lost her in the end to that trustful English botanist to whom her ghost belongs. So if I have little Greek and less Sanscrit there is nevertheless lodged in me a memory of wisdom Bagheera would do well to respect. A neolithic vegetarian princess who speaks a language older than Babel and commands a necklaced copperhead with her mysterious love has more culture to teach than a predacious wolf-boy. The story that Den Mothers would not like lies hidden behind the changing color of my eyes, but you shall have it all if you take me away with you. I'll adopt your Californian ways, and follow you to school, watch over your little brothers, quiet the fears of your mother, patrol your father's study, love your tiny lady-cat. Do not be deceived because I remain quiet and untroublesome in this last cage. The others don't yet know that I'm among them. I am not smelled or heard. I waste no energy in bootless complaining. (Another sign of higher culture!) But I cannot live another hour without my freedom! Step up and unlock this cultured torture chamber. Your little white hands are clever like Rima's. . . .

SIR: "Mowgli, I wonder how Lucifer and Semiramis would take to each other."

MOWGLI: "You said it twice! I win, you lose! Sir!"

SIR: "Starting backwards I have to say it again, foolish little manling."

MOWGLI: "Oh I forgot. Okay, sir, we'll keep going. —Next to him she'd look small as a mouse. Anyway, compared to him, her ears are too big, she's too high up at the tail end, her chest is too thin, her face is too short, and she's too fat in the belly. Besides, she's a girl and not smart enough to be his friend.

SIR: "You're an ingrate to think her ungreat, Dunno. You'd better take the first step in getting more closely acquainted. From now on you are the one to feed her, every day before breakfast. Ruth has enough to do." He wasnt kidding.

[*Jarring pause. Game abandoned.*]

SON: "Well all right I guess, as long as I don't have to take out the garbage at night."

FATHER: "No. You do both." More on taking responsibility, etc . "Matty's still too young."

SON: No further words are heard by the Old Man, but they form or begin to form and under his breath or almost under his breath the kid nearly dares to think *Why don't YOU?*

{*Postulants only:* GO TO ITEM (20) SO.03, page 197.}

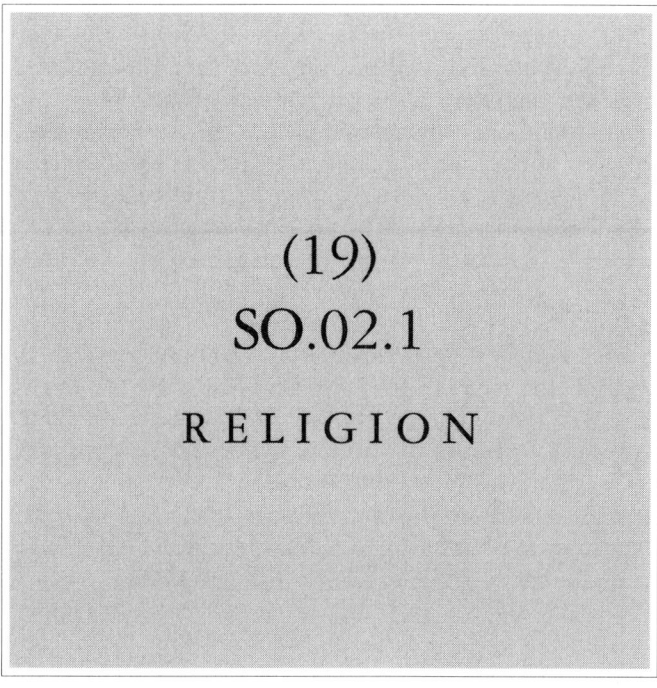

(19)
SO.02.1

RELIGION

. . . The fundamental fact is that dance can produce emotion and generate ideas, sometimes perhaps involuntarily, as a shiver makes heat. A variation of movement gives occasion for new feeling, new thought. What an opportunity for experiment! Experiment with a body's motion? Experiment with ritual? Then it is art-dance that we are now talking about. The discoveries of art are of a different kind from the discoveries of ecstasy. Art's action is governed by mind and imagination, not by frenzy or trance.

When a culture has passed its liturgical prime, or when it declines without having attained its fullest possible counter-entropic effect, it may come to seem that theatrical art can serve as an instrument of recovery. Euripides brings in a dance—a dance within a play within a dance— which artificially, consciously, deliberately induces the imagination of revived passion within an orchestral circle. Perhaps the playwright abhors the object of his thaumaturgy, worked up like sweat by the chorus under his direction.

If so, his purpose may be to recover by means of antithetical horror the sweet civilized reason that he fears his modern Athenians are about to abandon. But it seems to me more likely that he is miscalculating an attempt to recover lost religion. Instead of the ritual that once integrated the lives of their ancestors, urban spectators see and hear in the dance before them a hallucinated differentiation of the Panic element. *The Bacchae* is late, decadent, and imaginative. It takes the dangerous for the prime. The petrescent institutions of official religion are still too sacred to be overhauled in public, and really too familiar to be very interesting, so the new age finds retroactive ecstasy in poetic corruptions of exotic liturgy assumed to be older than its own mythology.

In the Western case also liturgy has been variously misunderstood. Its true myth has hardly yet emerged from the concepts imposed upon it by Hellenic culture the moment it showed itself outside the Jewish matrix. Since then Christianity has been almost always distorted either by professional institutions or by individualism. Elements of its ritual have been abstracted and separated. It has suffered hundreds of bland or superstitious deviations and diversions: sentimentalities, enthusiasms, and magics, through ignorance and confusion as well as by theological design. Yet the discipline of the basic liturgical action has stubbornly persisted, sometimes without intelligence or judgment, often no doubt in mechanical fashion. It is by the gyroscopic perpetuation of this physical process that the church has survived.

It was possible to keep the essential dromenon alive only because dance was kept out of it. Christians were bequeathed the hard-won wisdom of such exclusion by the Jews, who had finally learned the practical necessity of extirpating dance within a certain distance of their worship. If dance had become a mode of Christian ritual, even in Medieval times, but especially at its primitive stage of Pentecostal enthusiasm, it would have whirled every congregation back beyond the year One, further back than Euripides, dissolving the corporation into its elements of anomic self-surrender. The church would have found itself possessed of another cult entirely, an ephemeral religion without liturgy at all.

Inasmuch as the purpose of our anamnestic liturgy is to reduce the entropy of human society—to nourish and enable the organic forces of order in their hopeful struggle to offset the flow of universal probability—any corrupting (i e , dissociative) practices have had to be scotched. At its inception the Mass comprised or reflected contemporary ritual components, but its genetic myth had arisen from much older ritual, from an immemorial complex of sacrificial dromena that underlay the actions and passions of the Old Testament. This myth—reshaped, clarified, reinforced, and realized in the actions and passions of Jesus Christ during the six days beginning with Palm Sunday—informed the new liturgy.

As all sacrificial myths have similar structures, the story of a crucified Son of Man and his Last Supper was religiously plausible. It is probable that like house-cat and sabretooth tiger, the shape of Christ's new sacramental dromenon was distantly cognate with that of the unknown prehistoric ritual that had anachronistically generated the Son-of-Man myth—so that mythic fetchings from another place and time, as in the miscegenation of Homeric epic and Athenian dithyramb, could all the more sympathetically revolutionize the inherited motives of sacrifice.

Once instituted, the new liturgy spun the web of the church by generating the new myth of the gospels—which in turn explained its own genesis. The New Testament should be read as an epiphenomenon of the liturgical action. The Mass has always sustained the evangel. The truth of the myth is upheld weakly or strongly by the efficacy of the dynamic sacrament. Christianity's entelechy is understood only by historical criticism of the Mass, which is kept more or less interesting to each succeeding generation by the fluctuating intelligence of liturgical practice.

The truth-value of living myth must be taken as in part objective. Sacramental ritual (as I define *liturgy*) is a process of conversion and exchange between subject and object. Objective truth is discovered and preserved—indeed, developed—by means of highly specific performance, only one aspect of which is subjective. Objective belief can nevertheless survive in literate tradition like a free balloon when disaffected of its ritual source. Even as dead or corrupted myth it can be revived or reformed by virtue of the word. But in liturgy it can outlive ignorance or doubt with less damage than it can suffer without liturgy the individualism of anagogic ecstasy. The church rejected corporate dance because of its ancestral subjectivity, not in rejection of carnality.

Christians repeatedly turned dance aside from their most sacred ritual. Yet they were faced with the fact and the feeling that in natural life a rite without dance was a stemless and desiccated blossom deprived of its sap. In the days of the earliest saints it was only enthusiasm that kept alive the young deformed organism of the new cult (until reason and polity could tolerate and assimilate it), and it must have gone hard to deny the spirit of the Lord in the bodies of those few. Proscriptions of dance must have been frequent and difficult.

If ecclesiastical authority had accepted dance into its ritual it would have had to deal with either a dance of worshippers or a dance of performers. With a dance of worshippers it feared betrayal of the action of the Mass to a merely subjective solidarity of collective emotion. On the other hand a dance of priests and acolytes watched by the people would have turned the passion of communal sacrifice into an object of aesthetic contemplation and made the performers artistic in spite of themselves. And art is liturgy's chiefest rival.

The Fathers understood that art inside the temple is an enemy as dangerous to religion as orgy in the same place is, and that dance presented both dangers. Yet, again, dance had always been the prime utterance and expression of corporate feeling, and on their crucial occasions Christians could not remain unfeeling; in fact they could hardly be less than passionate in their crazed hope to overturn the trend of history.

But as a historical ritual Christianity developed in time as well as from time, despite continual Platonistic attempts to deny or truncate that dimension. The injunction "Do this in remembrance of me." was taken not as a behest to observe a sacred moment of the past but as a procedure to be followed in developing the future, a means of discovery. In the experiential evolution of their theology Christians came to see (through performing the action prescribed) that the sacramental ritual was a sacrifice of work on their own part, something that had to be done, like pumping a lever to keep water out of a leaking ship under sail for the new world. Christianity itself has usually mistaken its truly social purpose for revelation and private salvation.

The Mass had to be done anew every time. Its very offertory was the product of work. No ritual that was either played or imagined could have accomplished a useful transformation of energy or gradually metabolized boundary molecules of the unorganized environment. Christianity's sacramental ritual evolved away from dance because its function was to improve the real welfare of humanity. The mere exchange or modulation of internal energy in a closed aesthetic or ecstatic system would have advanced the world in general not at all.

Yet there was no more call for Christians to merge their personalities than on the contrary to make themselves personally interesting. In keeping dance out of the vital dromenon they only liberated it for the expression of true profanity. In large measure we can thank the church (especially through its Reformation) for our cumulative enjoyment of previously unimaginable freedom in art.

Next time, if anyone shows up, I'll try to get closer to the separate art of dance—in abstract terms of course!

{*Postulants only*: GO TO ITEM (23) SO.04.0, page 243.}

(20)
SO.03

LETTER
TO CYNTHIA

Fall Equinox, 2:00 AM

Dearly Ex-Beloved Duckling:

Jack Wolfson says he's heard you're getting married, or maybe already are. It rings true. Very likely you'll spend your Senior year in uxorious pleasure, with an apartment and a big double bed to play house in. No dormitory rules to defend your honor, no conscientious House Mother to spy on your reception of callers in a subdivided lounge.

I pretended that I knew, as if I myself had suggested that you find some good man who wanted to settle down. It's hard to imagine you with an industrial engineer, even though I saw him once—truly by accident! (I wasn't following you.) To my utter trembling dismay. Remembering every honest and deceitful syllable of what you'd told me about him in the successive stages of your inimitable revelations.

At least I assume that's the fellow who's won your body for good. I'd be greatly surprised if there's been a secret dark horse or a tall stranger with a deep voice. I have studied your words and acts more shrewdly and jealously than you can know. I am the world's expert on Cindy, and I expect to retain my coveted but secret title for years to come, despite occupational failure. As far as my knowledge is concerned, it doesn't make any difference that I'll never set eyes on your glorious golden hair again.

First he was said to have been a dull pest you forced yourself to go out with from time to time simply to bolster your sanity against my crazy possessive intensity. I suppose George is as afraid of the word *love* as you are of the thing itself. A happy pair!

I still study you, writing letters without hope of reply. It extends and rounds out the research for my unwritable dissertation. But the only reason I do it is that I can't help myself—even as I see quite clearly that my coarse interpretation only makes our story more ignoble in your eyes. And I do so without ever having had many of the facts. I'm doubtless misinformed on a few of the points I spin my woe from. What's worse, I further shrivel your opinion of my masculinity. Thus my final Cindy-act (so typically!) undermines its own thesis, which I here reiterate: to wit, that you have bodily rebelled against my totalitarian love without being able to dissolve the spell I've cast.

To be sure, you may love another man—perhaps several in the future. Maybe you love or will love him/them without shame or revulsion, possibly with untroubled clarity of desire, conceivably with a plethora of physical and professional admiration. But secretly you know or will know that he/they cannot understand you as little Caleb could, cannot love you as your firstlove did—whom you loved equally, until you reached the end of the madness he ignited in you. By returning to "the pragmatical pig of a world" you have succeeded in replacing me; but I insist that the traces of my passage never be effaced from your cortex.

But I'm beyond jealousy now. Already was, two months ago, when you told me so charmingly that in suddenly masterful fashion George had "raped" you on your first visit to his room, thereby accomplishing what I had failed to finish in a year of assault by service and praise—because I was too solicitous of your respect (in our all but extreme intimacy) to violate that last ridiculous reservation. How absurdly glad I was, so late in the game, that you still trusted me as your closest friend with a confession of what I had dreaded most but most wanted to know if it became a fact. While I was still listening to your voice as we sat in Blake's the news seemed sweetened by your flattering frankness. But later it was doubly embittered by reflection upon how much I had deserved the blossom of that bud.

I was too poor to get you into location for surrender. I didn't even have a room I could call my own. Whenever I might have made it to the cherry's pith by your leave, the place was out of joint if the time wasn't. But you don't remember your own desire. You never did, the next day. It was decidedly more direct than "the desire of the woman which is for the desire of the man"—often as innocent and sweet as your mysterious girlchildhood. Girls are all unknowable, but you more than others. How I wonder at your consciousness!—what you put by, what you savor, what you are candid about with yourself.

Do you ever recall the only reason you said you were glad to be a woman? Or only your distastes betweentimes? Can you remember the tenderest sessions of our long love, when like Aeneas I set your inmost sense aflame, as if you'd been a widow all your twenty-one years—when you drank my milky stars and abandoned every privacy but the deepest? You were willing to have penultimate adventures on a visiting room sofa.

I still groan over your wild demurs at those preciously wasted moments when there was good occasion to satisfy our hearts' desire. For instance, that morning alone in your native Central Valley bedroom. I would have ravished you if your words hadn't been so bitterly unfriendly. For a while there was pure hatred on both sides. Finally, after you got up and dressed, I began to alter your mood. Your hostility melted into speechless invitation. Your mysterious person was exposed to hot summer sunlight. I saw in heady hues the unstitched seam that until then I had known only under the shroud of darkness. —And all of a sudden your mother's car door banged at the curb not twenty feet away! Not by chance returning so soon, I'm sure, even though she took me for a politely moral boy friend. She nearly caught us reckless on the living room rug in flagrante delicto bareass.

But the few times we really had nothing to worry about from "malign externality" your innermost resistance was especially alert. I all too artlessly admitted that I was a rank opportunist, being too stupid to understand that for all your sophisticated talk you wanted to be fooled. I'm willing to bet that George actually laid you not savagely but with the ploys of vulgar seduction.

Analysis is useless now, I know. From the beginning it probably did more harm than good between us—though it renewed and prolonged our passion beyond its natural life, artificially cultivated a too-clever sensitivity to each other: more love but less endurable love with each new level of penetration. (What an ironically metaphorical language we have!) You had burned right through my manhood and come out on the far side. My agony was the axle turning our millstones, but it was the endless ratiocination that weighed upon our grist. Yet dissection revived us more than once when we were dead.

Even the second time we were ever together, remember how everything was spoiled (so it seemed) so soon after the breathtaking instantaneous coruscation of our first meeting at the House dance the very night before? Neither you nor I had slept or eaten while waiting for our date. We both acclaimed our destiny, if you remember. I had called your hair ethereal within the first half hour and babbled incessantly about my enthusiasms. Your eyes had shone in the mutual elation of love at first sight. I was the last to leave. You watched me from your window, waving, as I backed slowly into the low parapet of the terrace and nearly broke my neck.

But then we found ourselves having dinner in that clammy Chinese restaurant with nothing to say to each other, as if we'd been brought to an awful second sight by sixteen hours of anticipation. Some overnight blight had withered us on the tree of joy and dropped us off face to face into a hell of divorced loneliness. The mockery of a love disillusioned before it could be declared devastated everything we tried to bring up.

But then walking back through the Campus we began to talk about the weather, how it can affect peoples' moods. The sky had been dismally overcast all day. Now it was softened and warmed—in fact excluded from our scene entirely—by the restorative darkness. The night closed in our vision. We discussed the psychological process of finding beauty before one's eyes that's been too incredible to see. At least I did. It wasn't exactly analysis at that stage, I suppose—more like experiment with poetical conceits—but it was the beginning of this now ended Double C dialectic.

All at once we were laughing. There on the little lilac bridge, to the fairytale purl of the unpotable brook that comes down off Cyclotron Hill, I kissed you. Imagine that! The bliss of the next three or four hours is unbearable to recall now that we are so far fallen from innocence (you maybe pregnant by a Bachelor of Science). All that time we stood by the rail embowered with fragrance, or stepped about in little figures—softly laughing, softly kissing in the faintly rustling shade of an enleaved street lamp far enough away. Not once did anyone come along that sinuous secluded path in the middle of the biggest university of the world to interrupt my rapture with your aureate sand-dune beauty. I did not hesitate in my advances, but I remember no lust then. It was enough to lay my hands without urgency on the thin cotton you wore, and to sense with my palm the delicate springtips of Christendom's loveliest wheaten paps. We joked and teased each other about irresistible attraction. That night we dawdled on the light side of carnal knowledge.

But thereafter (though lagging far behind the bounding progress of our mental explorations) we investigated the gestes of love much too fast for you. On my part the inquiry proved interminable. It remains unterminated.

You know me—here I am—I can't sincerely resist this terminal indulgence of my propensity for words. (No wonder you prefer a solid man with a sliderule.) If I still love you I can do no less than tell you how. Not that you deserve my gratitude. In all those later times of feverish frustration and substitution, in every kind of union but one, you ruined me as a natural lover. May you be stricken frigid in your marriage bed and sentenced for life to a fakery of wedded contentment! It's not fair, what you're doing.

Still, I can't deny my faults. They've driven you into the arms of security. You have analyzed me well enough: I'm grubby and greedy. I was always stalking you or making you feel trapped. You said so. Now I believe you. It argues a weakening of the mutually irresistible attraction. By telling the truth about my enchantment I disenchanted you. My attitude toward marriage wasn't the stumbling block.

Three weeks I haven't seen you since we met for the truly last time. (I wouldn't want to see you again till we're old.) At that unexpected encounter, while my heart was pounding, you smiled brightly and self-

confidently, the way you smile at all men and boys, and listened to the
stammering news of my new career as if nothing could ever have happened
to you by me. You were going about the study of poetry (which I started
you on) as if it had always been your principal intention, admiring certain
professors as if they were the real thing, without a trace of irony!

Until yesterday, when I heard the good news that has delivered me
from the vicious constancy of foredoomed hope, I was persuaded that I had
forgotten the disgrace of losing you. I wanted to have it that we'd both
actually exhausted a desire too violent to last and a love too complicated
for the romantic form. We never found a literary pattern for our uncanon-
ized love, yet there's nothing new about a sensory soul heaping up impedi-
ments to its own purpose in months of frantic undisguised mania for the
purely natural magic that would have made you submit to my kind of
crazy mastery and dissipated your last superstitious claim to spiritual self-
possession. The mere inter-assurance of our minds didn't make for my success. Instead it led us into continual analysis of unconsummated sensation,
and in the end drove you to the unromantic convenience of industrial
engineering.

But what a wise and skillful lover I'd have been! Maybe that's precisely why you refused your lock to my key—for fear that it would always
open without the warrant of a notary. You didn't want the likes of me ransacking your castle irresponsible for the consequences. Your heart had
already gone too far, you thought. Our love died a thousand unconsummated deaths because you always saw to it that circumstances would
thwart my obsession. You allied yourself with poverty, rules and regulations, all the age-old brambles planted by malign externality to frustrate a
boy's devout atonement. How I plotted and ciphered to get you into warm
comfortable nooks where you'd put aside your horror of "sordid improvisation" and your neurotic fear of getting knocked up!

Yet sometimes I think it can't all have been for want of a safe bed. Or
of confidence in rubber membrane. Was there an ancient moral reservation
which you were ashamed to admit, an idea of integrity inherited from all
your mothers like an evolutionary attainment pitted against older instinct,
an anachronistic swan's diffident imperative buried under the fears you
anatomized with psychology and aesthetics—traditional propriety that I
involuntarily heeded and George who marries you did not? (I paid too
much respect even to your unbefitting taste for Hit Parade music.) I tried
to feel like you because I thought your taper was fused with mine by our
intemperate twinings.

No matter how flatly you may recant, it was love itself that disinte-
grated the Double C. You were terrified at the loss of your independence, so
naturally you fought my headlong lunge for the one true end of love, though
you craved it as much as I did—almost. But if you'd unstinted your thighs
you'd have become no more dependent on me than you already were. In fact
I think the shortcomings of our solaces were harder on you than on me.

Those appeasements were lovely enough, forsooth—lovelier than the normal successes of other lovers, sometimes more passionate by virtue of displacement than the satisfaction that comes in easy beds, leaving us to say goodnight with peaceful kisses of totally intimate bemusement, the consolation of our liquefaction tasted on each other's lips. I would whistle home like a tranquil shepherd walking through a field of clover spread about me by your attar, elated with pride that my blissful loins had been fainted of sweet torment by the equally sweet intimations of a goddess's mortality. I rejoiced most of all that the divine lyre had willingly answered to the same plectrum that vibrated my tensibility. When I had felt you moan in low crescendo my boon was more ardent, more gracious, more intelligent withal, than any quietus put to a hero's father by Aphrodite herself. Far be it from me to complain of dalliance in the delectable orchard of demivirginity!

Yes, once or twice it has crossed my mind that I may have been too skilled a knight at outer ports and vestibules. That you would fain have me tarry evermore in training exercise. I accused you of distrusting pleasures of the pit. Yet I do hold you blameless for not wishing to risk gray disappointment.

Still and all, if it had been in our crossed stars only once to find ourselves in sequestered comfort, warm and naked from head to toe, we would have turned the heavens further out of course. How much we were deprived of! Superhuman love had to content itself with rubbing and licking. Now that I think of it, that's what it all amounted to: loving from hand to mouth! May God damn your confused wits for racking us both with the unnatural delights. They were bound to pervert the sanctity we began with.

But to return to the main question: whether you fought me only because my love had grown excessive, taking into consideration your then apparently almost masculine fear of losing a liberty that's now gone so blithely by the board. You should have known that excessive love is in the nature of a dog like me. Or did you struggle against excessive love solely because this particular dog lacks the grandeur of some preceptive image of knighthood dreamed up in your silly inexperienced head long before I caught you off guard one gay night when no one else happened to be paying court? My answer to this question is more accurate than the one you'll give yourself—if you're still interested enough to read lovelorn letters. In truth, real love is too radical for your petty bourgeois conditioning, which (as I now see) underlies all your loose Bohemian talk and makes merry with your literary complaints against life (which you say brings on thoughts of suicide three days out of four).

I'd have done better to snatch the natural half of you and close my ears to your talking points. . . . But then it wouldn't have been me, would it? The talking points you talked me out of the one true end of love with were no less romantic than the talking points I used when I first talked you away from all the other Georges that hung around your nunnery.

No one could have been so foolish thinking he was sure. I tried to absorb your soul. You were right as rain on that score. It's no way to get into a beautiful girl of the modern age! I thought that the lack of a car would make no difference for *us*. You always seemed to be kidding, or confessing merely capricious frivolity, when you said you'd love me more if we had one. I took it that you were thinking with amusement of your lightheaded past. It never occurred to me that you might have preferred the seat of an automobile to an idyllic bed of pine needles. I was the romantic and you were the voluptuary. Little did I understand that even in your most amorous of moods the charming bowers of outdoor nature leave you cold, hungry, and uncomfortable. My simplicity comes of being younger than you, and of having missed high school life with all its mores and tempores! In living out my delusory pastoral I mistook Helen for Chloë.

Remember the soft misty day on that Mill Valley road, when we heard nothing but our own voices? The whole world was shut out from our joy in each other. On our long dallying saunter up over the ridge and down into Muir Woods the first few hours were so uncontainable with tender love, your kisses so happy and soft, that I believed you were forever to be my Erato and Psyche both. I bided my ulterior time almost patiently, waiting to get you into the silent depth of the redwoods. My energy was boundless. But yours wasn't. While your fund of willingness was still transpiring with the exercise I heard at my back time's wingèd chariot hurrying near. Even after it actually started to rain I kept trying to lead you to a dry spot! I was still beside myself with paeans for the sylvan occasion. Of course now I see quite clearly not only that you hate bus rides but also that you hate walking after you get off a bus—that you actually do desire luxury. You told me all these things often enough. You tried to get them through the thick head of your crude swain. I have no plaints about coyness.

Somehow we had fallen in love without forethought in one and the same pang, and that's the wonder. It certainly wasn't my verses that made you love me. They didn't come at first sight. (I now know too that you don't like my poetry. That's one taste of yours I increasingly sympathize with. I shudder at the thought of what I wrote in my transports. But I must always thank you for setting me awriting at all.) In the later days I couldn't help imploring you to keep loving me. Again, you warned me that I was only fooling myself when I took advantage of your weakness for my caresses. Sensual coercion can't outlast the day's curfew.

Now I have an apartment—both romantic and comfortable! *Now* I have money to spend! I could get a car if I had you to go into debt for.

This job is not without its pleasures. I don't have to see people. I have a little time to read and write. The ungodly coat dust smeared on this paper is not from hell, but I have a devil of a time getting my hands clean in the morning. If you were here you'd recoil from my touch. Yet what I'm undergoing is purification.

I burned your letters tonight. I had thought to drop them off Golden Gate Bridge at the very spot we once stood while you spoke airily of all the times you'd decided to kill yourself. (It was one of our most carefree days.) I would have made confetti of them and scattered it like ashes; or else tied them in packets that might bob to the surface and float out past the Farallons before they got waterlogged and sank (if I hadn't been afraid that the tide could carry them back to Berkeley's strand instead). But a furnace is warmer, more humane and classical. I watched the pages curl as your blue ink turned brown. It was the honorable thing to do. I no longer wish to blackmail you. I mean to free myself of lugubrious perturbations. I was born no more for successful love than for lovely success. I am clearing the decks for long years of solitude. Henceforth my libido will be diverted from erotic communication to braver work.

I've already wasted a week of the year I'm supposed to be here. But the word I got about you yesterday has galvanized me. I confess that I had been ever so slightly hoping to blunder upon another meeting, to be followed by another mutual analysis, another new beginning. Furthermore, it seemed to me that having furrowed your first wild oats you could hardly refuse my old claim. The precedents could now be cited on my side. The terminus ante quem had become post quem.

After all, there was one occasion after your "engagement" when you were ready to be unfaithful to George. I wonder whether that evening ever rises to the surface of your mind these days. I don't throw it in your face. It was an offer of lovely leavetaking that I wasn't able to accept in time. It would have been one first and last fling for the Double C, and I have no doubt that it was the first and last time you ever expected to deceive your betrothed.

I suspect he chose that moment to go see his family because he was aware that I had intended to be out of town much longer. (I'm always inclined to assume that you told him enough about me to give him cause of uneasiness.) If I weren't so scared of rattlesnakes I'd never have quit my job in the Sierras and come back that soon. It was an attempt at adventure as far away from you as possible. For once I had plotted nothing; except for the cots always in my wallet I was laughably unprepared; I hadn't even been looking: I thought you'd gone home to your Valley. So you swept me off my feet.

It was the only time we ever had a car to ride in—and it was George's. We both drank too much wine, I guess. After I understood what you were proposing I nearly killed us on the Grizzly Peak curves. Knowing you and your fickle spirits, I fell once more into the most incontinent haste, giddily responding to your reckless provocative speech. Only this time I was driving a car! Clearly it was to be my last chance, my deferred but

unrenewable meed, my initiation, my one carnival with Cindy. And just as
clearly it was a sign that you deemed yourself liberated from my possession. As an experienced woman you were about to give me on impulse
what an exciting stranger might have been given (judging by your
mood)—though we needed fewer words. All the better! Who was I to
complain about your choice? Or else with newly tutored curiosity you
wanted to cap the affair begun in your innocence, to enjoy without mourning the bittersweet romance of an old flame's overlapping valediction.
Whatever your motives, you were tipsily inscrutable.

At the time I didn't care about past or future. But I was a most unlucky
lad that night, as usual. As I believe, you likewise were an unlucky lass.
Everywhere that could be reached on wheels, the most unnoticeable places,
we found other cars. Naturally it was too cold for you to explore the
bushes with me, too dark and foggy. We were beset by all sorts of constraints and dangers, and I couldn't think coolly in my drunken agitation.
So you reneged—in fine, withdrew your offer with an apologetic inebriated kiss. There was no precedent for the lovely wild things you'd been
saying to me the moment before; never had you dug your fingers into my
skin so crazily. It was some time before I could relax and admit to myself
the ludicrous untimeliness of my good luck.

We must have driven twenty miles from spot to spot. I wish I could
remember the interesting confessions you made about your new love-life. I
was too bent upon the search for privacy and too befuddled by balks to
decisive piloting—too dominated by my miserably gross preoccupation—
to take most of them in. But because there was no clear way for me to
exploit your incredible vagary on the instant, you began to take it back
without at first changing the tenor of your inflaming remarks.

Oddly enough, before it was over I began to concur with the alteration
I found in your realtered attitude. You might say I was spared a test. We
had a nice friendly talk on the way back, and I took a certain shortsighted
satisfaction in our manner of farewell. Your last kiss was as soft as the first.

Now, though, I have before me the freest freedom I've ever had: neither college nor love to mold me. Shackled only to myself. I'll sleep the
sleep of healthy fatigue, cease my ceaseless reckonings, walk the streets
once walked by us together without looking for my heart. No longer shall
I feel compelled to pursue you covertly, or make excuse to pass your
House, or seek out images for my jealousy, or wait for the smallest
response to my large letters. But I'll never dare go near our little Campus
brook again. Wretched freedom!

A hundred times I've seen girls that at a distance seemed to look like
you. I've heard voices in stores and streetcars that seemed to sound like
yours. But not one of them can be in any way like you. *Like you*! The
phrase is a travesty. You the most distinguishable of geese! You who move
and speak in common places only because you must live among commonplace fowls. I well enough know how my ugly duckling, hiding with

books under San Joaquin River willows, her alienated light-clad beauty unnoticed in fat illiterate schoolrooms, suffered a whole childhood with willfully ignorant barnyard poultry.

Precious Cynthia, read on. I swear this is my swan song. Little Caleb's last howl. Be sad, grieve for yourself also, for I am your Merlin, and when I die your soul will fly up too.

Industrial engineering is beyond me. It sounds like the kind in most demand. Yet how can a guy who's spent four years studying to be an engineer have the faculties to be wholly sensible of you? (It took me all my life in liberal arts to be so studious.) Did he have experiences in the war or with other loves that made it possible for you to bring out in him some quality antithetical to his profession? No. It's hardly plausible. Knowing my sense of general (if not special) inferiority you must have scrupled to volunteer the whole truth about him, understating your infidelity to me, when you openly announced your first acceptance of his persistent overtures—as though my prejudices would disarm my jealousy. He's probably really at least an electronics engineer, perhaps even a physicist.

You were very clever in managing this separation—this divorce, this murder. Never once did you come right out and forbid me to call you, but you made it impossible for me to see you. With a slightly new cadence on the telephone you affected to wipe out every trace of acknowledgement that our association had been unique. You politely obliterated all telltales of susceptibility to your old god Pan. Then you contrived to banish me from earshot with my syrinx. I'm sure you cut classes for weeks at a time, and even stayed in to eat House food, in order to steer clear of me. I hope I kept you off balance and confused about my intentions.

But alas it may have been my "persecution" that you thought you were taking refuge from in the mechanic's bedroom. Is that where you are sleeping this minute? I can't wish you joy. I hope you fail all your courses this term on account of cold palpitations brought on by the dismay of having committed yourself to the boredom of George's companionship. I hope he treats you ill. I hope he makes you over into a good obedient Roman Catholic. You'll conceive at once and remain tied down to squalling kids for the next quarter of a century. If there's any justice to be found in the court of love, your punishment for prolonging my immaturity is to remain saturated with the essence of Caleb Karcist, to such degree that by virtue of manual and lingual telegony you will be reminded of me every time you look at your firstborn. You'll forever be sorry for rejecting the fascinations of an analytical life with me!

Did you really want to get married? As you say, I never gave any serious thought to a future for the Double C . George has five years advantage of me in guessing a girl's motives. My opinion of marriage is faltering. I'd marry you now. It's not too late, if you're not already carrying his child. I could even stand a baby of my own if it would get you back. But this offer holds for a minute only. I expect to be free thereafter.

I could manage a new equilibrium—or at least my grief would rise to mere melancholy—if only I had some inkling that you were renouncing me against your will, for your health, for your peace of mind, for prudential reasons. Many lesser times in the past my woe has turned to weal when I so found—or rather my persuasion that such was the case; and the confidence I got from that illusion always won you back. This time imagination could not of course bring the same result, but it would emolliate the bitterness of absolutely desolate severance.

Why can't I stop making it worse and worse with my cowardly lamentations? Love is the one thing about which I should know how to be saintly. I can no longer haul you away from the eye of a House Mother into the courting room for a long talk. That deforming habit of making a clean breast once earned your trust. It encouraged you to show me more of your self than you will ever in your life let on to anyone else, no matter how much time you spend in bed with him awake.

I have been left in a state of decomposition by the end of your love. I must begin to pull myself together with the work I left leafy Berkeley to do. I repair to sweet reason. From now on I'll bring forth none but kind recollections of the doubled life that anchors my remaining half-life. Please read my final churlish outpouring not as effrontery or indecency but as a cry of penitential sorrow.

By George, someday I'll make my mark too! But it's no longer for me to rival Leda's raptor who may merit the granted mating. My dear CYNTHIA, you are of more beauty to me after moonset than any star ascended to fill Keats's spyglass. As for me—

> A nonesuch am I,
> and as such
> only just begun.
>
> Nothing can reform
> the inner boy
> You called Nonesuch.

Yours in a history without future,

Cabe

(21)
HY.05

PUBLISHERS'
REPRESENTATIVE

What O heavenly muse lay concealed that afternoon behind the glinting barnacles of our archangel? Only the secrets of a practical mind too prosaic for the liking of friends or readers but so impressionable as to be allured by the small game in which he was borne through swift hours often unaware of his body, parts, or passion. His game was no less gripping between its diurnal terms than the games of scholarship addressed by his customers. A cold man of dry humors it was thought, undemonstrative methodical and just. Fellow workers pitied his family. He guessed that only Lillian's pity was directed the other way.

This stationary colporteur grunted at the two unhelpful students (an unpaired male and female) who separately straggled in as help for what was hoped to be the busy part of the day. He couldnt be called tight-lipped because he breathed through his mouth, but his mouth tightened. They had become cackling cronies of Sam, but without a word of politics as far as anyone could tell.

When there was occasion to do so Michael spoke to customers with courtesy and goodwill (so long as they responded in kind); but always when he wasnt doing anything else he watched what was happening on the public floor. Except when he found pretext to step behind the scenes in order to break up by his wordless presence any loitering conversation that might be taking place in the back room at so much wages per hour per capita, he kept busy in the vicinity of the cash register, regretting that he didnt have the lightfooted omnipresence of his celestial namesake. He had to point out the logical nesting places of books that rightfully impatient walk-ins asked about, which were difficult to locate for underlings so ignorant of almost everything represented in print. The inquirers (undergraduates, doctoral candidates, subprofessors) sometimes cast curious or grateful looks upon his pasty impassive face with the puffy jaw that hung open far enough to show the fillings in his neat lower teeth.

Brown-bagging his lunch out back at the "shipping table" (where much was received but little was packed) he had perused the latest *Publishers Weekly* as he gobbled and gulped, writing orders with his free hand, voraciously galloping through the intermission of his homo erectus business day, and then with an accounting textbook under his arm hurried out around the corner to get his Viennese coffee. On a stool at the restaurant bar he had irritably read a paragraph twice through without taking more time for further progress.

The predecessor to Valentine Greatrakes quaint old Mr Bow (long since gathered to his fathers and cleaned to the skeleton by bookworms) would have been astonished at the style to which his life's monument was altered. The remodeled store was serving a remodeled university. Ancient bookmanship had disappeared. Outside Berkeley the printed word itself was called into question.

Our modern bookman had a visitor that afternoon. For Michael the call was an interval matter of intellectual pleasure under the aspect of pure business. Gordon Jolls blew in from New York—not directly from New York of course, for he was hitting Bow's Ark during his extended semi-annual sales tour of the Coast, but from New York nevertheless: a man of the world who knew the Eastern climate, which (seasonal, deciduous, half the time bare) Michael sometimes sorely missed. An elegantly unobtrusive way he had of turning even good books to account. He traveled and dressed as a gentleman, favoring downtown hotels over automobile inns. Early and late in the business day his speech was as debonair as his appearance—modulated voice, a nicer sense of grammar than anyone in the West. Yet pleasantly informal in manner. His lean face was pleasant, his smell was as pleasant as Fifth Avenue. Above all he was pleasantly frank, sympathetic, confidential—with Michael particularly, he seemed to imply; certainly as seductive and perhaps as faithless as a literary traveler amusing himself with a lonely country schoolteacher.

This remarkable publishers' representative seemed to understand Michael Chapman's ideas. He seemed to appreciate Bow's Ark professionally. He seemed to divine the difficulties under which Michael labored because of the proprietor's culture, and he refused to allow the employer's poor credit rating to reflect upon the employee's ability.

Jolls's principals were of the best, including Rothschild and several of the university presses, a dozen good lines in all and none likely to come up with a bestseller. Since he knew all the decent bookstores Denver and west his approbation was of some satisfaction. Bow's Ark it seemed had become his favorite. This call it seemed was the one he liked best. His carkless friendly smile warmed a cold man's heart, refreshed the mentality of a drudge, enlivened and clarified the outlook of a fussy merchant clerk.

At Jolls's unscheduled arrival Michael's theoretical mind leapt like a flame of clear exclusive cheer. He put aside petty operational problems. Never did Robin Hood more joyously leave behind his bickering witches on a cerulean June morning than Michael now bounded out of his morained and middened thickets into the lovely parkland of the king. Plans and projects came easily to his lips. With ambition and gratification he looked at his burdenless impersonal acquaintance and then at the orderly walls and tables.

Long rows of bright variegated color stretched like continuous unpunctuated messages in modern code from cash register to show window. Infinite uses of finite means from all times and places, atomic and organic too, a most impressive diversity of adventurous words in prose and rhyme, lustful or Buddhic, tempered only by each other—but put together by the library-buyer himself. The great tessellated banks spread before the eye like Babylonian walls in Renaissance perspective: tolerably catholic. Not however universalistic. The collection was unexclusive and reasonably comprehensive, but articulated by a strong spinal column. He might have characterized it as certain products of certain minds super-organized by his own. Chapman's palpable bibliography had the extension not only of time but also of mass; his functional citations specified economic value and commercial source as well as proper names; his unwritten records usually recalled heft shape and decoration.

All these ciphered sounds and caskets of meaning, which did not belong to him but some of which he appropriated, sojourned where he'd set them to form a single edifice cunningly uncemented. Although his inventory was displayed in rectilinear parallels conforming to the warehouse space, with two aisles and a central pier of book-garden plots, the abstract design resembled a gyre. Its complicated and imperfect maquette was coiled in the chronological and categorical dimensions of one brain only—however, not without provision for pragmatic imperatives. Many exceptions to taxonomic rigor were positioned and recalled much as one remembers after trial and error that the ketchup bottle is too tall to go on the shelf dedicated to sauces and spices, or as one keeps a ridiculous place for the olive oil simply in order to take advantage of a fixed habit rather than try to buck it, in face of the fact that the storage of corn oil is ruled by logic.

Irrespective of the deep underlying taxonomy and its anomalies, the high clean room uniformly lighted by a phalanx of fluorescent lamps in recessed fixtures (into which a large portion of Prince Val's grave bankloan had been sunk in order to enhance the allure of any book) was altogether attractive to high-class salesmen despite the opinions of Dun & Bradstreet's credit analyst.

Jolls came with new bills of fare as a peddler to peddlers, but neither handling nor possessing the goods he brokered. Michael's main interest was the salesman's sideline of remainders, books from all publishers that hadnt made the grade with consumers, almost as interesting as manu-scripts that failed to attract any investment at all, or too disreputable for comptrollers who'd rather get ten cents on the dollar than continue to tie up working capital that wouldnt turn over as fast as public opinion. You could easily identify the publishers whose hardnosed financial men were making inroads on the old school of editors who liked to live with their commercial mistakes. This recalcitrant buyer piqued himself on finding scholarly bargains in the byway catalogs that his voguish competitors dis-dained to examine. Again the desire arose from his bowels for special learning and profit—for the discovery of overlooked gems in every quarry of knowledge—and came upon him as it always did like the appetite for breakfast.

They sat together on stools behind the counter slowly making up a small order, the shopkeeper rising from time to time to ring up sales while the solicitor filled out his forms. It was fitful progress through the lists. Michael Chapman was garrulous and Gordon Jolls was attentive, the latter selling to the former as the former's rare animation was exercised upon the latter. Sam and the other clerks kept a seemly distance.

At first Michael talked about paperbacks—how they would trans-mogrify the old trade channels and dominate the common reading business not only with students but wherever there was any market for the arts and sciences. While buying titles going out of print at far less than list price he liked to tease the prosperous commercial traveler about his expensive lines, excusing himself from heavier purchases on Val's already overextended credit, partly out of his bottled-up urge to vent the prophetic fires of his business vision, which was the last thing he could vent upon Valentine Greatrakes, for whom the anxiety of the day was emphatically sufficient.

"Mike, you should write an article for *P W* !"

Mike sighed and shook his head. "What good would it do? Val wouldn't even read it."

"It would make a name for yourself." the soft drummer urged.

"Not interested. I'm not a journalist. But I'd like to get in on what's bound to come about."

"The Chapman Theory of Cheap Editions should be promoted in New York."

"I know. Now if you could get me a job there . . ."

Sympathetic furrows appeared in Jolls's high lean brow. From his superior position he returned kindness for Michael's ungracious views on the nature of things. "That's a hard one. Everybody wants to work for publishers in New York, and willing to do it for the glory alone. It's almost like working for universities, except that they can't very well expect you to be an alumnus. You'd have to spend months there beating the bushes and waiting for an opening." [Meaning, Michael took it as tactful warning, no degreeless wights need apply.] "And then you wouldnt make enough to support a family. I think you'd be better off in the retail end as your own boss. Have you thought any more about starting a bookstore in Gloucester?"

"Oh I was never serious about that." Michael patted his guest's arm. The real reason he liked Gordon Jolls, whose manner and curriculum vitae would otherwise have aroused his antipathy, was that the man liked Gloucester—Gloucester in particular as distinguished from other New England seashore towns—a man who had come to know all America, and Europe too, before during and after his seasons in the Ivy League. He had no need to dissemble an affection for the place. He obviously knew it as well as a yachtsman might. Gloucester's expatriate was willing to risk beguilement by believing the wellborn agent's sincerity, especially by token of the fact that friendship had been offered after knowing the uncertain social fit. At all events Jolls had been to Gloucester many times and was aware of its unlovely distinctions. Under the influence of such endearment Michael gladly closed his eyes to sweet-smelling corruption and tendentious charm.

"But I still think it could be done if a man had money enough to last out the first seven years. After that it would pay off." Michael went on to speak of establishing a reputation for polymathic resourcefulness, of gradually accumulating a comprehensive stock, of cultivating a mail-order business. It would take a long time to get regular customers from the permanent population but some summertime volume could be expected at the outset. He found the glib words of commerce coming out of his mouth against the will he swore by, extracted from his brain as if they were a civil Member's only possible response to the sucking vacuum of a bourgeois Parliament.

The sounds of his voice stuck to the inside of his cheeks. His lips hardly moved as he spoke. Jolls bent forward to catch his meaning. Michael forced himself to complete the statements he had begun in an unguarded flicker of enthusiasm, and to make them intelligible to a normal mind. It was his obligation to meet the conversational expectations of this friendly man who was so decently tolerating hints of gratuitous self-pity.

"Some day I may be lucky enough to scrabble my way back to Gloucester, dragging the family, but I'll never arrive with capital to invest. . . ." The clerk smiled wanly, hoping to simulate a pleasantry: "Unless you want to put up the money for a partnership!"

To his surprise the traveling salesman's reply was solemn. "If I had it I would, Mike. If I had it I would! There'd be no serious competition. We'd make a barrel of dollars in the long run. I could keep my boat there." He sighed the sigh that many a time is sighed by men who talk about making their living the way they think they'd like to. It was a sign of brotherhood. "How would you set it up?"

Michael brought himself up short with a shudder of revulsion. He shied off, his eyes rolled, he wheeled on his haunches horrified at the pass he'd come to, carried along in the headlong visionary rush of a provincial fascination, as though the game was vital. But better to strand in the West than to swim with the entrepreneurial herd. He'd rather wait on table as a house servant.

[I'll take swabbing the deck of Bow's Ark over having to live in Gloucester with my best foot forward. True, talk is cheap and there's no danger of anything coming of it—but the word debases before the fact confirms, debases the person, debases the place. Ugh, what's becoming of me? I'm a mere technician of small business riven by ignoble ambition, a degraded artificer divided against himself. Let me be content to make small improvements in my squirrel cage, if for me it must needs be that there is never so perfected a thing as a job that offers nothing to be changed. But I'm such a zealot of efficiency that no doubt in fields of grain I couldnt have abided the way hands have always learned to swing their scythes! Farming has its farm, fishing has its boat: if I were a farmer or a fisherman I'd be worrying every day and night about the condition of my investment. But here the fuss of my stewardship lasts only a hundred fifty thousand minutes a year, and I can choose what to fret about until I'm fired. I bear the half-curse of management: spare me the full damnation of ownership.]

But he could not turn back in this conversation, not without doubling the shameful course of his ill-advised momentum. He must bull his way forward into the clear. He thanked Gordon, touched by an apparently unfeigned interest, but he was now entirely out of sympathy with what had to be said about his commercial vagary: He'd have one copy of everything in print that was fit for print, new or used, in the cheapest possible edition—paperback, British, or whatever . . . and if publishers refrained from cracking down on special orders he'd be able to do business by mail as well as anyone in the country, thanks to the equalized parcel post rates for books. . . .

[Yet the pitiless confusions of a struggler in the book trade! Better to deal in grommets of all sizes and compositions, in various colors too, with different discounts, imported and domestic. One reasons books are so difficult to manage is that they are subjects (and therefore unique) as well as objects for classification. You can't traffic in vicious inciteful fevermongers unless you're prepared for a life of desire and loathing. If you treat them with any sort of consideration they play you for all you're worth. You never get enough of the little teasing delinquents. No sooner do you finish with one than the next piece of jailbait comes along in a colorful skirt and an open blouse promising something nicer than anything you've ever had before, something any man would trade his time for. There's too much pussy on the street, dressed to drive you crazy. But turn them upside down and they all look alike. They're all the same, most of them, broadly speaking, when you look back. They excite you, take the starch out of you, infect you with disease, waste your substance, steal your leisure, keep you from your own object. There are too many to size up personally. It's not surprising you end up a pimp purveying them to museless consumers whose dissipation can proceed in virtuous serenity. Pray let some great flood drown nine tenths of all these wantons and sweep the earth clean of this harlotry. If the arkangel can rescue a few genetically sound saints from among them for the sons of God to breed with . . .]

Jolls was suddenly grinning and twinkling at something Michael must have said aloud. "You'll be apothecary to all the secret contraceptive passions of Gloucester, filling intimate prescriptions to the legal limit!"

But the host wouldnt be diverted until he'd set the record straight about his frailties. ". . . I can't keep my mind on profit long enough. I'm too interested in the preservation of the species to be a good businessman on my own. I like to get things right. —Even about Gloucester, in fact, I'd rather be right than resident!"

Thus on the buyer's terms they both paused in silly relief from the pointless speculation that betrayed too much of his vice. The seller almost giggled, his urbane texture charmingly rent. Michael warmed to him again. It went to show—yachts and martinis and all—a friend's a friend for all that. But Michael still could not refrain from disappointing his comrade and making everything worse with a final appeal to Rockefeller Center. He sounded like one of the deserving poor in complaint to the duke who ought to be his patron.

The duke put the best face on what he heard (as follows) but his embarrassment was mitigated only by Michael's self-deprecating smile; he hoped to detect ambiguity or sarcasm in the complainer's tone yet feared to discover that he was being mocked in all deference as the drummer of his Princeton class.

The gargoyle's words were no more grotesque to Jolls than they were to the gargoyle himself. ". . . and to me inventory-time is just an opportunity to reclassify my stock, a spring cleaning. I'm perpetually too dissatisfied with what I have to sell. You see I'm not really a businessman. But working for a businessman, for a corporation of businessmen with a large organization, now that's something else. I should be in New York with a big publisher, running the distribution system. I can increase profits for other people if they provide me with a going concern." The dour clerk waxed boastful. "I can analyze, I can plan, I can organize, I can administer . . ."

The one who was actually acquainted with magnates of the great world wondered how this petty wage-earner had become so confident of extraordinary management ability, but he kept his overt attention fastened on that glinting moonface in the professional conviction that any wandering of the eyes might be taken as skeptical search for evidence to corroborate the braggadocio. "Are you thinking of that mathematical invention of yours—what do you call it?"

"S M D C . That would be one means of operational control. The larger the scale the more effective it would be. —But I'll never be able to prove it because I have no connections and no degree in anything."

"Oh come on, Mike, that shouldnt stop you! Write something for the *Harvard Business Review*."

"They'd never publish it, for the same reasons. Besides, writing wouldnt help me in the real world."

"At least you'd get credit for the idea. Somebody might make you an offer."

"It would be too hard to read."

"Then try the foundations."

"I have. They all say they won't support research that isnt sponsored by an institution. Anyway, they base all their awards on credentials and references."

"I still think one of the professional journals would be interested."

"Well I just don't have time for all that stuff. It would take months out of my life." Michael faltered and bridled, acutely aware that he was beginning to provoke the slow impatience of this unprejudiced listener who seemed incapable of unjust indignation.

"I don't understand you, boy! One always has to put in a little extra time if he wants to get ahead."

At last it had come out, the vulgarity that lies at the heart of all salesmanship. But Michael hardly noticed. He was too busy assuming the role of a clown. "I don't want to get a head. I'll use the one God gave me."

Jolls smiled, but he was not to be put off. "I think you're afraid of success!" He had finished writing his order and was trying to figure out why the disgruntled shopkeeper's assistant should expect to be treated like an undiscovered genius.

Michael blushed at such a baldly psychological presentation of the misunderstanding with which his anchorage in society was regarded. Once more he had contributed to the misapprehension by ellipsis in his squirming declarations. The sallow owl blinked, as if while vaunting his way with another man's wife he'd been indicted to his face as a cuckold; as if a career of deceit had been mentioned, or the sin of selfishness, or a blowhard's failure. The allusion that had been made to the Synectic Method of Diagnostic Correlation embarrassed his modesty as if with shame, the former excitement of it fouled and soured by his sensitivity to the world's opinion of cranks. [It's too simple for the minds of experts. I can't waste my life in persuasion. But someday I'll get a paid invitation to Washington.]

It was an indifferent book order from the salesman's point of view, commercially speaking not worth the time he'd spent to get it. But Michael was secretly worried about the size and composition of it for contrary reasons. If Prince Val checked the eventual invoice for anything but prices and discounts he would find too many esoteric titles for his pragmatical little business.

As Jolls was preparing to leave Michael happened to ask about a news item to the effect that one of the firms he represented was in trouble with the law. The handsome face lit up. With a furtive leer the older man took from his pocket a sheet of paper that had been folded and unfolded many times. But exposure to light had not yet faded the crisp typing. "I got a kick out of this poem. One of their editors is sending it to the *New Yorker*. The whole notion of controlling obscenity through the Post Office is ridiculous!"

Michael read and immediately approved:

TO THE POSTMASTER:

When your genitalia
Begin to fail ya,
   Read the books
   I'm gonna mail ya.

Jolls quickly retrieved the document and replaced it. "Pretty good eh?"

The clerk's appreciative laugh reminded him of the complimentary generosity that was ordinarily reserved for lucrative customers. "By the way, pick a book on my list that you'd like me to send you at home, no charge, for your own library, in appreciation of your business."

Michael was pleased to find himself well prepared. *"Shakespeare's Bawdry."* he replied without hesitation.

(22)
MS.03.0

BIRTHDAY PARTY

29 September 1956

1.

Jack Wolfson and Sarah their house was arrived into by all submerged friends floating to symposium from the sea around. Caleb Karcist seahorse-timid cavalier swam into ken reminding himself that chubby little Newton Cahners just pulling up with Sylvia had all three a wife a house and a car while Wolfson had a wife and a house and limping Randy Jillison (soon to be on scene) had a wife whereas he himself getting there with his own fins had none of those three assets. A house in that sea he did not regret, one like Wolfson's at least, nor a childbearing wife, at least not one like Newt's intelligent and lascivious but plump. Yet he came here as he went everywhere craving a woman almost any friendly female of the deep and he had lately grown to see what other fish always saw much sooner that the lack of a private submarine put him at quaint disadvantage in the competitive search for natural lovely quenching of the dominant desire which in a spirit of compromise stemming from incessant failure muted his forthright scorn for practically all society. He was far from averse to the company of soft mature women accustomed to a husband's foibles. They seemed to him usually more sympathetic than college girls to a poor scrod's claim for experience.

Besides the hope of adjusting for sexual motives to the pressure of a community's silencing medium he had other reasons for fingering his scorn out of sight in his pocket: to wit, his diffidence among elder knowledge-mongers and his shamefaced longing for reputation among them; to wit also, his liking for the common man in Jack Wolfson the disarmingly ambitious host who out of love for the approbation of friends that criticized him behind his back took upon himself and his wife the social responsibilities sometimes ludicrous or irritating to them that preserved the sodality they all counted on; and finally to wit, the expectation of meeting and perhaps holding conversation with Michael Chapman (whose lecture had excited him and to whom he knew his essay on Yeats had been shown by Jack)—if he was not met with opaque rejection of intellectual affiliation.

There was nevertheless no lack of purloinable bait to batten Caleb's suppressed disrespect for such a party. He made invidious remarks to himself continually sipping Jack's water of life that he wasnt used to in an effort to equal within him the pressure without. It seemed to him knowing little of his fellow fish that the others were perfectly adapted to the atmospheric bath that he found barbarous after his own years of immersion. He was puzzled by Chapman's case who (to judge at a distance from one public appearance) ought not to be any more comfortable than himself in swimming with this school.

But it was Michaelmas in the nominally prevailing religion and the archangel's friends always celebrated together, though they never observed their own birthdays as collective feasts, because that dry son of God lived ashore, without the pale, in an arid exile that they thought it took a saint or hero to survive without degenerative apostatic metamorphosis. It was the one common holiday of these few—May Day and Thanksgiving rolled into one. This year in order to become acquainted with the guest of honor's oldest friend they had invited another outsider—from San Francisco (a political entity even further off than Oakland but a blooming desert by comparison)—one David Wilson, who brought his Joan.

Jack Wolfson was always happy to keep inn for the occasion. According to custom all the guests brought food or drink but it was not expected that the average single or couple would consume less in value than its own contribution so of course Jack and Sarah provided more than their share in victuals as well as facilities utensils and principal labor. Their children lay quietly upstairs in one of the two bedrooms.

Wolfson greeted each arrival with anxious cordiality. Having planned a rather formal entertainment, based on affectionate research and intended for ecumenical edification, he had feared they wouldnt all get there before the birthday king and his consort. Success depended upon his management of the assembly while Sarah prepared in the kitchen. Caleb knew the Wolfsons more than slightly. He judged them a cooperative pair of vertebrates who never doubted the excellence they strove for in the larger's career or recognized that it was his best traits that hindered the struggle. Paced by him they were careful of quality at every step they swam. In light of the books that covered every unpierced wall Caleb believed that Wolfson had not been accidentally perceptive in singling him out from all the undergraduate fish of the sea. Such a library he found it in his heart to praise aloud, and indeed he gratified with particulars of his own perception the scholar who was generally diligent for friends' approval and even now was bustling back and forth in business with others for the sake of everybody's subsequent pleasure.

Despite the host's worry about Sarah's end of things and the Chapmans' timing he spoke and stepped about as admirably as a softened patriarchal lion. ". . . Come in, come in! Delighted you came at the very best time. Mike isnt here yet but you can have a drink before we begin . . . Ah thank you—but you bring such riches! I'll take them to Sarah . . . Oh I have a new book I want to show you later . . . Yes my collection finally came out after a whole year in press. But none of my poyems ever get obsolete you know . . . Don't sit in front of the fireplace. . . . Let me take your coat . . . Worry not about making noise! Those kids will sleep through anything . . ."

In appearance he is large and shaggy of head and forequarters, but gentle. The paws are too small and fine for a lion; they antedate the evolution of typewriters and seem made to drive the quills of domesticated birds, too white for the household woodworking that Sarah says he's so good at. Hair streaked like weathered straw covers his head in thick banks and grows from the pointed rims of his ears. His prematurely creased face is diapered with pale freckles. But in academic sieges he plays the roaring Joshua (as Sarah puts it) for a small insurgent faction and his campaign for the doctorate goes hard with professors fearful of seeming to have the guts to betray an antisemitism. Jack's willing to bet that he already owns more books than any of the academic senators who aren't independently rich.

Caleb desponded at the learning on those shelves. Wolfson's specialty was Courtly Love but he was also current with the scholarship in everything else that interested his young new friend besides much more that didnt. They were the books of a combined poet philologist and bibliophile and they were catholic enough to anticipate the inquiries of any expert a literary man was likely ever to have in his house. This collector was Chapman's best customer at Bow's Ark where Caleb could scarcely ever afford an actual purchase.

Anyway Caleb had always found that shop too neat and tight, even somewhat ostentatious in its specialized competition with the vulgar glitter of neighboring large stores. Once more he reflected on the antipathy with which he had at first been conscious of the solemn funnylooking pastyfaced lieutenant who slowly opened and closed the rondure of his mouth as he stared at browsers like a supercilious headwaiter. Caleb still easily recalled his surprise at discovering that such a fellow was the lecturer on action, when he saw him entirely afresh. A new fascination had replaced the earlier public one in which the import of that goggling gaze was wondrously reversed after the first few minutes of abstract mumbling. Expectantly watching the door for this strange being whom he'd been too shy to speak to after the sparsely attended allocution Caleb forgot his contempt for the intellectual affectations of Berkeley society.

At first whiskey only clouded the medium between him and the people he was warming to. As the brine blocked his ears he peered at them slowly moving slowly talking slowly laughing. No close fish had seemed too loud or quick by the time he set himself to study the Blake print tacked over the fireplace, in the distance as it were, focusing on Eve's unopened pod. Sir Serpent was envious, coiled around the still more distant Tree, and Adam conversed with an angel who was nothing like the one whose birthday the drinking was for. The gentle beasts of the picture seemed to prefer the snake to these theomorphic strangers. A single red candle burned on one side of the mantlepiece. The hearth below was cleanswept. Judging by the careful scene Caleb thought this might be a party too well organized.

Immediacy returned with his second tumbler of pellucid scotch when Nancy Jillison drew general attention to her enthrallment with the princely talent of her lame husband. She turned his game leg into an advertisement of something denied to other women. She sat next to him making no great secret of what she was bragging about with her hand on his knee nor affecting to blush at what was so secretly marvelous about five years of squalid marriage to a half crippled unwashed painter certainly of great vehemence verging on solid success in the mural market. Though Randy presented himself as a Bohemian and obviously disliked bathing he kept the choice black moustache on his upper lip meticulously cropped. The hollows of his dark lean cheek fluctuated rhythmically like some physiological mechanism for relieving pressure in his gills.

Randy listened with an unembarrassed smile as Nancy began to retell a story he had imparted to her long ago in bed (Caleb presumed), an impersonal tale by which in the warmth of its personal associations with the man from whom it had come she gave one to understand why she was happy to have domesticated a classic stinker. The fisherwoman contrived to describe the length of her catch without mentioning her private knowledge of Philoctetes.

Caleb pretended to be lost in deep preoccupation as his sidelong eyes stole looks at the shameless young mother who once or twice took him in with a general glance at her audience of ordinary men and unprivileged wives, but he couldn't help suspending his annoyance until her story ended and he finally turned away in silent expression of his disgust at the recidivating lewdness of marriage. How many times had Nancy pestered Randy to repeat his reminiscence and supply the details that fascinated everybody but stock-breeders?

Randy stared modestly at the floor evading all eyes as she rehearsed the boast from his student days at animal husbandry college before he'd discovered his visual imagination. According to Nancy he used to hide like Pasiphae inside the hollow of a meretricious frame padded and scented like the pinbones of a cow to entice and encapsulate the semen of rocking socking bulls. Her secondhand account was so fond (though for Caleb insufficiently explicit after all) as she slowly waved her glass and basked in the rare attention of adult company that she succeeded in conflating the exploited sires with their vivid observer. Or at least she led her listeners to suppose that every time the smelly archer turned to her in all his glory the imagery of his memoir arose to thrill her with the fearful hope of conceiving a Minotaur in vivo. Caleb recoiling from his involuntary awe and envy declared to the daimon who heard all his speculations confessions and complaints that perhaps this unforgettable anecdote pantomimed in bed had implanted in the young matron's plastic nerves her notion of art beginning in virility and ending with the hatched eggs of human rut.

Caleb feared he himself would never gain such somatic commitment of a woman and was disconcerted at the sight of one as comely as Nancy who thought she had the best and made it clear she wanted no better. At the end of her recital he walked away angrily suspecting that only he and the other two newcomers had been really listening. Doubtless all the others—including Sarah in the kitchen and the Chapmans still on their way—had heard this pseudo-fabliau before, and then some. He was grateful for the more solemn behavior of his host.

2.

"Michelangelo!" The Chapman couple was there at last. "Mickey Mantle and Babe Ruth!" rose one cry of welcome. Michael Chapman grinned, bridling agreeably, and immediately chuckled at the ceremonial appointments of the room. Everybody came up to shake their leader by the hand, and some (not Caleb) to kiss his diffident queen. Long-out-of-touch Dave Wilson clasped Chapman's shoulders lower than his own. Sarah came from the back of the house taking off her apron and wiping her hands on it. "Happy birthday!" she welcomed, warmly squeezing Ruth's wrist and kissing the man's cheek. "It's been much too long since I've seen you." she said to Ruth. "I wish you'd come with Mike more often." Then she took Ruth's other hand too.

"Well, it does my heart good . . ." said Mr Chapman.

"Oh Michael isn't this *nice*!" exclaimed Mrs Chapman who was clearly less accustomed to conviviality. She and Sarah went into the kitchen with things she had brought for the table.

Caleb the last to offer Chapman his hand was surprised by the deep pleasure of being recognized without hesitation before Wolfson could make the introduction and of finding that he was deliberately placed next to the big armchair on the right of the fireplace where the guest of honor was installed.

Soon Wolfson himself having dried up the merriment by turning off the electric lights took up a place Stage Right before the lighted candle on the left of the bare hearth. Sarah sat to the rear on the edge of a straight-backed chair where she could most nearly keep an eye on what was still acooking in the kitchen whence a softly plumping doubled bubbling could be heard hissing plashing throughout the proceedings from behind cheerfully illuminated cracks outlining the door in its frame visible to those who turned their heads and reassured themselves of common innkeeping verities. Randy and Nancy sat as close to each other as new lovers glad of the dimness, her hand still pressing his knee. Joan Wilson (so called without the sanction of marriage as Caleb later found) the Greek stranger from across the Bay sat alone in the furthest corner avidly drawing hot fire down the stalks of her cigarettes, more active than any who spoke. Ruth Chapman and Sylvia Cahners had begun to talk about their children but now they looked up obediently without surprise at Wolfson's latest fancy as if listening to an interruption. The others sat neither stiff nor loose, raising an eyebrow here and there.

After crying to silence every male and female the master of ceremonies began to read in a well-modulated mellifluous voice from a small red volume. He had taught himself to use Cranmer's Prayer Book, and Newt Cahners too, Sylvia's husband, his prepared assistant for the occasion who stood beside Chapman's chair squinting in the candlelight whenever the script was passed to him.

FIRST JEW: O Everlasting God, who hast ordained and constituted the services of Angels and men in a wonderful order; Mercifully grant that, as thy holy Angels always do thee service in heaven, so, by thy appointment, they may succour and defend us on earth; through Jesus Christ our Lord.

Of all the congregation only Karcist and Chapman found themselves mumbling *Amen* automatically.

SECOND JEW: *The Lesson is written in the twelfth chapter of the Book of Revelation beginning at the seventh verse.* There was war in heaven: Michael and his angels fought against the dragon; and the dragon fought and his angels, and prevailed not; neither was their place found any more in heaven. And the great dragon was cast out, that old serpent, called the Devil, and Satan, which deceiveth the whole world: he was cast out into the earth, and his angels were cast out with him. And I heard a loud voice saying in heaven, Now is come salvation, and strength, and the kingdom of our God, and the power of his Christ: for the accuser of our brethren is cast down, which accused them before our God day and night. And they overcame him by the blood of the Lamb, and by the word of their testimony; and they loved not their lives unto the death. Therefore rejoice, ye heavens, and ye that dwell in them. Woe to the inhabiters of the earth and of the sea! for the devil is come down unto you, having great wrath, because he knoweth that he hath but a short time. *Here endeth the Lesson.*

"Thanks be to God." said Chapman with a reflexive expiration that sounded to the people like a sigh and they laughed. Then in returning Wolfson the book Cahners farted aloud like a land animal albeit asking pardon almost before it ceased and the people laughed again. Wolfson was patently distressed at the possibility of losing control over the congregation that seemed already out of sympathy with his purpose and this time read in a louder voice until everyone was compelled to pay him heed.

FIRST JEW: *A portion of the Holy Gospel according to Matthew* [rapid as a Christian making three small signs of the cross one beneath another in the air]:

At the same time came the disciples unto Jesus; saying, Who is the greatest in the kingdom of heaven? And Jesus called a little child unto him, and set him in the midst of them, and said, Verily I say unto you, Except ye be converted, and become as little children, ye shall not enter into the kingdom of heaven. Whosoever therefore shall humble himself as this little child, the same is greatest in the kingdom of heaven. And whoso shall receive one such little child in my name receiveth me. But whoso shall offend one of these little ones which believe in me, it were better for him that a millstone were hanged about his neck, and that he were drowned in the depth of the sea. . . .

They were listening, these women and fathers. Perhaps some in the room heard Christianity for the first time. Caleb took it for granted at least that few had ever before listened to the English Book of Common Prayer. Both halves of the Cahners couple chubby and self-assured, reading or listening, seemed to apprehend the New Testament curiously, if only as humanists do, despite abjuration of the Old in their youth. This little book after all was more important than the Bible to the civilization in which the authors of Newt's profession were raised to literacy. He stood with eyes wide open while Jack his colleague sounded out the words more thoughtfully by the minute as if he too had never before perused slowly enough the passages he now read.

Caleb watched the cherubic face of the Second Jew listening to the First Jew and felt a sympathy overcoming his resentment of that brilliantly competitive intelligence bound for fame in literary criticism, for he knew that children at home were the apples of its eye and that it cleaved to their fleeting years of innocence notwithstanding Freudian self-absorption, notwithstanding the enlightenment (widely proclaimed) of its heavy course with a Viennese doctor (paid by parents), notwithstanding the cuckoldry it may have been aware of suffering. But at the same time thinking nothing of his own heartlessness and taking advantage of the little gossip he happened to have picked up at large Caleb wondered whether Sylvia on second thought maybe not too plump but simply less formal than other women about her underclothes—also psychological witty and critical of ordinary men—was exclusive in her infidelities or indulgent enough to receive a proposition from the likes of himself without outcry or laughter. . . .

> Woe unto the world because of offences! for it must needs be that offences come; but woe to that man by whom the offence cometh! . . .

Even to Caleb's unihorny way of thinking who never made much effort to imagine the feelings of married men it was an offence to adulterate a friend's wife unless the friend approved or cast her off, especially when the hot streak might reach her womb. But his head was full of the natural sin that might be vouchsafed a bold scot-free bachelor. He tried to imagine himself invited into the flesh of a hardworking critic's woman. But that was nothing new and Sylvia was nothing special.

> Wherefore if thy hand or thy foot offend thee, cut them off, and cast them from thee: it is better for thee to enter into life halt or maimed, rather than having two hands or two feet to be cast into everlasting fire. And if thine eye offend thee, pluck it out, and cast it from thee: it is better for thee to enter into life with one eye, rather than having two eyes to be cast into hellfire. . . .

Now their unbelief returned. No man there under any threat would lose the limb of his gonads nor no woman suffer her man's loss of the same. They grew restless, for from the way Jack was fingering the pages it seemed almost over. Food was surely ready and the pleasures of reckless conversation were at hand.

> Take heed that ye despise not one of these little ones; for I say unto you, That in heaven their angels do always behold the face of my Father which is in heaven.

Jack kissed the book. *"Praise be to thee, O Christ."* murmured Chapman like one who's early habits are readily evoked. The congregation stirred, doubtful whether to commend the host or the principal guest, or to clap and stamp the floor. But Jack immediately stepped upon a stool and spread his arms above the heads of the people to make a priestly cross. When he had their attention he smiled and bowed from the neck.

The sonorous recitative that followed struck Caleb's devil as a fatuously histrionic attempt on the speaker's part to dissociate himself from the only manner in which it was possible to carry out the program his heart was set on. With this nether malice Caleb looked at Chapman to see if the honored one's embarrassment seemed as mordant as his own. But that object of all the fuss was only gazing blandly at the loose watering lips of the mock-priest not a whit leonine. Caleb tried to understand his own failure to grasp Chapman's tolerance and swore (if it wasnt too late to escape the withering prejudices of social xerophagy) to broaden his sympathies until he could lend himself to every custom that that man might lead him up against. More than ever before—this time not for sexual but for intellectual reasons—he regretted the easy intercourse from which the sere puritanical prickliness of his self-defense excluded him. Even addictive cigarette smoke, which had once seemed the most promising of common tastes, only extended the desiccation to his lungs and seconded the spillage of unenclosed semen that continually sapped his skinny loins and repeatedly laid to a moment's rest his normal desire. Brooding over the social success of that secular clerk whose year was being celebrated, who suddenly seemed to flourish on capillary fountains from the salty earth and normal tonic drainage back thereinto, and who now appeared to chuckle at that tingling mingling circulation, Caleb missed some of Jack's panegyric. As he listened again he began to thirst impatiently for more of the water of life. Himthought he was the only dry and sluggish fish among darting or serenely gliding denizens.

". . . my friends. Soon we shall be eating together and drinking to the twi-man whom we are here to honor: merchant, husband, father, mentor, metaphysician, lecturer, and—for all we know to the contrary—artist! And to his most dearly beloved lady!"

"Hear hear!" Dave Wilson called out gently striking one palm against the other to help Jack along. Caleb noticed Sylvia whisper something into Ruth's ear who laughed aloud at the thought of whatever it was but then sat back patiently again as if watching happy children, perhaps not paying much attention to their ideas but ever alert to their need for attention. Meanwhile in respect to her husband she made a backward queen who knew nothing of politics and cared little for the diversions of court life except to offer help when appealed to. Caleb wondered what it was that lightly clouded her beauty and hid the youthful aspect.

". . . to him who has taught that a hungry father should never hesitate to take the best morsel and fob off the worst on his kids as long as they're young enough not to spot the difference, seeing that it's all too soon they'll be demanding their share of real butter heavy cream and lean meat! Good taste is a curse and should not be cultivated he says. We salute him who remain in bondage to middleclass sentimentality!"

"I propose a toast!" shouted Newt now standing at the back of the room near the kitchen door.

"Wait a minute, let me finish. The drinks are coming again when the roustabouts set table. —Now today is Michaelmas, an immovable feast, the morrow of William's amphibious landing hard by Hastings, and the birthday of Michael Cervantes—"

"What a coincidence!" The cry of undawning amazement came from Nancy Jillison. When everyone laughed she looked about in gasping confusion, her hand over her mouth and her head pressed against Randy's shoulder until he pinched her and she gave a giggly little scream.

". . . his name day. But this is also Quarter Day and we must pay our debts."

"I can't." drawled Sylvia Cahners. "My husband cut me off without a cent."

"You're a liar." Newt retorted. "If I cut you off without a scent you'd stink!"

Mirthful disturbances only stiffened Jack's determination to finish the agenda he had begun. Caleb thought the effort inflamed his ambition like that of a chief balked in potlatch who throws in all his reserves to discountenance critics and daunt his rival. Although this was his first glimpse of Jack at home he was already aware that the good officer always won such contests without much reciprocation.

"'Michael: who is like the Lord?' Leader of archangels serving the universe—yea in the heavens of Muslims Christians and Jews. He who dompted the great dragon, he who stands upon the heights! The only herald that God can trust to negotiate with Satan (who in admiration sometimes steals his name to fool innocents like Joan of Arc), yet archenemy of the Slanderer, prosecutor of the Prosecutor, great Opener of the Door of Life—"

"You mean he's a big prick?" Newt sniggered. "Satan's not only sterile, he's confounded with penis-envy!"

Caleb winced at the unseemliness, embarrassed to witness women being imbued with such figures of speech. He was further disquieted by Newt's therapeutic insolence in pursuing the subject. Unhallowing exposure seemed to be the motive of all their wit.

"I hate the word penis, it's so clinical!" Joan of San Francisco surprised everyone, speaking for the first time in husky Greek tones. Her mature unfamiliar voice sounded too solemn for the occasion. They looked at her. She was lighting a new cigarette before the old one was half smoked. From what Caleb had heard during the introductions he surmised that she was defying the Roman nuns of her displaced childhood, her Irish teachers, in exhibiting the disashamed interest that Dave her pinched-looking Anglo-Saxon Apollo had recently inculcated who was becoming notorious for going out of his way to discuss sexual attitudes in the public high school classes he taught.

Newt helped her out: "A masculine word with a feminine ending."

"Like Jesus?" said Sylvia smoothing the fingernails of her right hand with the thumb of her left.

"Not a word to be used in hot blood." Nancy added.

In sympathizing with Jack's vexation at these untimely indiscretions Caleb remembered seeing a poem of his that derided the new publicity of private speculations. But who could condemn children of the twentieth century?

The speaker of the house resumed his intractable encomium. "Yes, Satan's main adversary; your chief warrior against Lucifer; keeper of heaven's keys; protector and advocate of Israel; prophet of Christ and fore-teller of all history from Eden to Armageddon; who 'with one foot on the sea and one foot on the land' shall sound on his trumpet 'the brazen death of time'—'Time is, time was, but time shall be no more!'—; celestial high priest, viceregent of the Trinity: I give you Chapangel Mike!"

Low cheers and hear-hears. But Jack had not finished.

"He has driven us from innocence. He has shown us that anything any-one says about anything is too simple since everything is connected to everything else. He teaches us both judgment and wit. . . . Simplicity may be sublime, saith our Chap, but at any point in human history it's a false contrivance of communicators or mystics and it can never serve the reality of our complex middle world. He hates idealism as his namesake hates sin—"

"Just an eurotic symptom!" shouted Newt.

"Let's have communion!" Randy Jillison interrupted brutally, waving his glass to arouse the people.

Again Jack raised his voice. Glancing again at his notes he rushed through to the end of what he had docketed himself to cover and probably had to skip some of his best phraseology. The peroration came too sud-denly after all: "No one in commerce has ever cast so many pearls before so many swine. Yet he has also given the world—not in his leisure mind you but in his foggiest fatigue—such shattering ditties as 'Who Put the Dyna-mite in Mrs Murphy's tampon?'—"

On this note (which was apparently inoffensive to everyone except Caleb) din supervened and the water of life began to flow again. Jack him-self went to toss salad in the kitchen and others attended to the table. Nancy reluctantly left her husband's side to work under Sarah's direction. But Chapman remained where he was like a sitting bear with his pupils about him, never moving save to bend his elbow and bring whiskey to his lips which otherwise little moved, for when he spoke deadpan nearly always the sound was formed by invisible apparatus between his cheeks before it escaped the barrier of his teeth. He gladly taught his friends yet often listened head atilt, mouth hanging open the slight distance weighted by substantial jowls in fish-jawed equilibrium. Yet he drank in great steady gulps also like a fish inelegantly appropriating whenever he likes the amniotic nourishment of his medium.

"Jack showed me your Yeats paper. I was hoping he'd get us together. Maybe sometime we can talk about your theory of tragedy." Michael gave no sign of having noticed Caleb in Bow's Ark who was now so flustered at the pleasure of a finer recognition.

"It's supposed to be Yeats's. I . . . I'm not sure he'd approve . . ." Caleb stammered between creative pride and scholarly humility.

"Have no scruples about interpretation. When he was younger than you he called truth 'the dramatically appropriate utterance of the highest man.' You're right to pick out his one true mask, which nowadays no one else has latched onto, and to ignore the psychology of magic that everyone dwells upon."

"Well I also had to ignore his old age when he eased up on tragedy and started allowing for self-sacrifice."

Newt had been listening all athirst for argument and now he broke into the first conversation Caleb ever had with Michael. "Joyce is the only one who's analyzed 'the tragic emotion'—and that's what counts!" He was the most polemical critic in his Department.

In a trice they turned on him, the two new friends who had both despaired of allies; but Caleb was given the single combat and Michael only urged him on. It was religious war, and with the challenging cry *"Mere aesthetics!"* the young dog exulted in his first probation. He found himself out of water eagerly trembling at the new acuity of his eardrums and facing under an upland sky the nimble adversary better armed than he. His aerobic faculty and telluric mobility restored, he argued the anti-social aspect of heroism against the morality of democratic art.

3.

Later, hoping to have championed a master worthy of his allegiance, Caleb found a place at the table opposite Michael, scrupulous to avoid displeasing him by sticking too close on an occasion that after all was not intended to be seriously deep, yet joyfully unable to prevent himself from taking advantage of any opportunity to be near.

"Are you going to be a Yeats scholar?" Michael asked him before the general clatter rose.

"Oh no. I'd have to read Shelley and Blake!"

"How about doing a Master's on the philosophy of tragedy?"

"The professors forbid me to continue my work on 'imponderables.'"

"All they can deny you is a degree. Don't let them turn your star into an asterisk. Literature is the art of meaning and you have the mind for it."

"The trouble is that my reasoning is neither inductive nor deductive, only dogmatic!" Caleb laughed at the liberty he was taking with Michael's first favorable impression.

"It's your own dogma. That's what's so rare. You're a dog not yet distempered with expediency."

Caleb beamed at this flattering intelligence of his name's meaning but he could find no reply. He wished Michael to love him but Michael was already engaged on another subject down the table that annoyed Caleb for its competence beyond his range. Could one who spoke so attentively of trade and politics really understand what his essay was about? Yet he recalled Yeats's notice that Shakespeare had spoken of Hamlet as 'fat' and 'scant of breath', who was also pretty good at dealing with ugly ambitions when he chose to. But why must Michael Chapham waste so much time with inferiors now that he had a peer?

They were teasing Michael for his love of efficiency and he was answering that he had to live economically to make up for the time he lost as a slow reader and a dull learner. "It's my sense of form" he said to Newt: "—what Henry Adams called 'the instinct of exclusion'. The only artistic instinct I have is to exclude whatever wastes my time."

"The art of living." Dave Wilson suggested pale and conciliatory, for all the world a beardless misbegotten Norseman carefully thawing out the blood vessels he was born with, perpetually smiling from on high at the melancholy pleasure of human fellowship, his small stiff head thinly covered with softest flax. Native Far West courtesy was bred into the strained hollow sounds of his few words which were always grasping for the meaning of the person he was talking to, though they concealed almost everything of himself, tall and thin as a telephone pole. Misunderstanding his old roommate: "That's the best art of all."

". . . I'll never run out of things to paint!" Caleb heard Randy proclaim from the end of the table (to which all the revelers now turned their attention), extolling the warm vitality of his art as over against the colorless intellection of his sexual rivals.

Just then his wife came in from the kitchen with a plate of sliced cucumbers. Her tongue was loosened by gossipy tippling with the backroom sisters and she spoke up impulsively: "The one time he can't do it is when he's painting, and he knows he'll be confined to my bed if he runs out of models."

"See, I paint for dear life!"

When Nancy set the dish down Michael snatched two of the wafers in quick succession. "Ah heavenly host . . ." he drawled with his mouth full. Caleb observed a gold wedding band on the slender white hand flipping with gourmet satisfaction, and he smiled to find himself tolerating that badge of slavery on his new master's person.

"Sylvia will be bringing in the cold cuts." Nancy added slyly.

Randy rose to his cue. "Real Horsecock!" he yelled, affecting as was his wont the parlance of a Navy that he'd been born disqualified for. "No matter how thin you slice it—cucumber pickle banana zucchini salami or baloney—it's still Horsecock!"

"Just different ages or moods of the horse." Dave made his contribution with a thin little whickering laugh at the top of his closecropped skull.

"What a pity Randy has to work so much under the lights at night." said Newt to Nancy on her way back to the kitchen. "There's such a shortage of seamen, what with all this birth control."

"He'd better stick to his last in the studio." Michael asserted, resuming the enigmatic manner to which all his acquaintances were accustomed and munching on bits of food within his reach. "Any more than a dearth of births is too many. What's needed is better antianthropoetry. At least the fourth child should always be strangled or exposed. If the largest family had three young ones the average would have two, considering the natural incidence of sterility and attrition. Even then the population would grow because grandparents remain alive; sibling birthrights and equities would still be diluted. So there won't be any actual improvement in humanity until we avert a third offspring in every family."

The room of mothers and fathers fell silent for a few seconds at the tactlessness of this modest proposal, while the men waited to be served and the women most of them hurried their service lest they miss too much of the main conversation, who rejected the principle of subordination yet were for the moment tolerably content with the old ways of Themis, as though they served lamb with cakes and wine in a mountainside grove of olive trees. It was fortunate however that the most sensitive of them was detained in the kitchen with Sarah and didnt take in this cruel display of her husband's playfulness.

Jack abetted. "Third child: *Gratissimus error.*"

Dave Wilson joined the play. "If our population gets much bigger the psychoanalysts will be trying to differentiate personalities instead of integrating them!" He uttered his whinny of nearly silent laughter with a show of jaundiced surprisingly long grass-cropping teeth, looking about with crinkled eyes. Caleb had a bizarre feeling that this stranger was responding to the company under the dictation of a subaqueous ventriloquist. But he himself was encouraged by that flat voice as weak and toneless as his own, for he had learned that Dave was used to the command of men and aircraft in war and peace when he temporarily took on the greater difficulties of urban schoolteaching.

Michael kept the field. "Even now as we lap up milk and honey the multiplying wasp-cluster has overloaded the creased gray nest that God gave us as a limit. The weathered paper can't support our weight much longer. There's nowhere else to swarm to."

"Maybe there is." said the flyer.

"Will they swarm after a queen?" asked Sylvia having overheard the last few sentences as she sauntered into the room with a platter of horsecock. Ruth and Sarah followed more spritely with a clatter of pleasant noise bearing hotter dishes. Men's eyes followed the food.

Randy rose with salacious gallantry to relieve Sylvia of her symbolic burden. "A herd of stallions would."

"Well that's okay." she replied unsmiling. "I love animal lovers."

"So long as you don't forget your diaphragm my dear." her merry little husband said. "A litter of centaurs would eat us out of house and home."

She patted his shoulder, languidly surveying the jumbled items on the table for possible omissions, with a preoccupied air of bored indifference to Newt's facetiousness. "Hush Mr Cahners. I'd never be ill-bred."

Soon they were no longer baying at the victuals but eating in full bustle and gulping red wine from a variety of glass vessels. Caleb listened to them talking about things they must have talked about a hundred times before. To his mind none but he himself and Michael expressed any thought that was not opinion received or taste accepted from one press or another. To him they seemed to believe themselves independent intellectuals simply by reason of making bold to dispute secondary qualities and because they found themselves at variance with the popular majority on certain matters of which public opinion was ignorant or careless.

Politics was a different matter, when they all agreed to Michael's leadership who was now emphasizing the importance of Presidential appointments to regulatory commissions, an aspect of policy to which few of those devoted to the beaux arts ever gave much thought during the cyclic emotion of national campaigns. Caleb drank in and thoroughly absorbed this enlightening lesson that he would have closed his ears to if it had come from any other human being except Yeats or Nietzsche—all the while he groused to his daimon that generally Michael's friends when left to their own judgment followed tracks of thought scored in their brains by the lactic acid they sucked from the dugs of almae matres.

It was an ingrained pique, he almost admitted to himself, that called up his callow aspersions. He always hardened at once against those found lacking in potential appreciation of his theory of tragedy, inasmuch as he deemed himself unworthy of respect for anything else. He tended to assume this want of ultimate intelligence in anyone who refused him attention even though he reminded himself of Jack's generous praise. But if he earned no esteem here under Jack's scepter where would he ever find it? So he couldnt help falling into a self-conscious sulk in resentment of Michael's unworthy diversions.

Fortunately Caleb's cloud of ill temper was now cloven by a hunger that drove him to gobbling and grabbing like a ploughman sitting below the salt at a castle table.

Michael was saying that he might take his kids to the zoo across the Bay hoping they might hear a rooster crow at midday because one could no longer hear one in Oakland at any time—but this comment instead of leading to a discussion of postwar denaturalization brought up the folly of both sexes. Sarah compared crowing cocks to women hoping for the Messiah every time they go into a labor room. Or hoping for a Jewish president, Newt added. No, she said, only fathers have such thoughts . . .

"Women can spin and men can delve . . ." Jack chanted.

Caleb finished the verse to himself in lamentation: "But I shall burn forever!"

Why should anyone want the accident of fertility? he asked the gods. Even Dido hoped for a hostage. For just as vessels and not their freight draw a boy's ambition to the sea Caleb believed that a man's orectic interests had nothing to do with a girl's generative instinct or one of his own.

All that matters is the deep deed itself when I finally delve a girl deeper than mere love with the fingerless tongueless shaft of ego-skin channeled straightway to the one true comfort and object of existence inside everything that can be patted or fondled or plucked at, where shotten arcs from the land's end of my continent are snugly muffled and contained by the firmly palpating core of a sympathetic female body—where I'd be delivered again and again from the phallacy of misplaced concreteness! That's the delving that will break my lifelong fast by filling a sweet crevice with my foison! Then the timid scowling dog will be freed of all his envy and malice!

But would he ever be left in peace by the fierce homunculus that groaned ludicrous plaints from the hinged perch at the root of his body? Ever freed of the ache like freezing water surcingled in an airless pipe of steel, the numbing pain of inelastic hydraulic pressure felt even while eating spaghetti or walking down the street? Will the time come when he no longer passes a day waiting in chronic distraction for the brief nocturnal respite when the wretch is throttled and wrung out in its aggression? The hawkish sparrow looked around at the coupled women among whom he had been invited as an odd unmated windhover. Never before or since Cindy had he been presented with a girl precisely of his opposite kind. The gods seemed at a loss whenever they noticed his case.

There was one modest formel, softly aquiline in beauty, gentle in movement and lovely of voice among the talking fowles, but long since dedicated to the only friend he hoped for and hardly imaginable as the paramour of a sparrow-hawk. Though her words were quiet and her hands untaloned the timid young tercelet saw in her carriage and thin flared nostrils the lineage of eagles whose tastes and prerogatives she had renounced like a disputed throne for the sake of tranquillity in her nest.

Yet it seemed likely to the presumptuous falcon that Ruth Chapman sometimes strove without success to overcome the admirable weaknesses that kept her from courtly life. Sitting beside her, across from the overweight owl whom she served in reparation for the sin of Eve, Caleb's ill temper vanished. He watched her smile and even laugh in middle notes of bell-like clarity at the persiflage of which she was sometimes in doubt, never looking for kindnesses but subtlety offering them at opportunities that would have been overlooked by anyone else.

At first she tried to make friends with Joan pseudo-Wilson the stranger, leaning forward to look past Caleb (who drew back in his chair to abet communication), but got only hard answers. Joan was too busy studying the sentences of men. He thought Ruth took the cold response as her own failure to express the sympathy she felt for the alien girl's earnest aspirations. Without sign of disappointment she turned to talk with Sylvia about the Cahners whelps and with Sarah about the Wolfson cubs but these two matrons were also preoccupied with the alliances and competitions of their men. Worst of all, by the look of it, she was the least of the company in her husband's eyes who scarcely ever glanced her way and never appealed for her assent. Caleb was surprised to find that it was the other women who kept Michael merry.

Thus the youngest person of the party began to sniff the vulgar pleasure all these bonded men found in hinting at designs of illicit adventure not to be followed through with—adultery without impropriety. As far as Caleb could tell, Michael led all others in playfully affected betrayal of trusting friends. How attentive his grunts and chuckles as he dominated his rivals not by overweening charm but by weight of body and mind, by experience and versatility! Was he aware of stoking his vanity with the cheap respect of bondwomen? Was his fluent comprehension of every subject nothing but the wellworked mastery of technique?

No, that wife was there in golden testament to his placered worth, the mother of his other presumed admirers. And so Caleb and Ruth turned to each other for conversation, the two who most craved gifts at Michael's disposal: one his opinion, the other his geniality.

Otherwise she seemed to detect the company's benign tones only. She picked out goodwill in the landscape. "The people where we live don't have much education. They don't try to understand how feelings are formed. But our friends here know something about psychology and they can do a lot of good in the world. My mother is a good woman but she didnt have these advantages. Happy children come from mothers and fathers who think about such things. There would be no crime and no war if all kids went to the right kind of nursery school."

Now Caleb learned from Michael's wife. He had been unaware of the distinctions between nursery school and kindergarten that she now made important with her explanations. Slowly and thoughtfully smiling at her own unexercised powers of discourse she told him about the difference between discipline and play in earliest schooling. "You don't train children at that age to get ready for school. Without precepts you let them discover how to do things they want to do, especially together. Play before learning. They benefit from love when it's not some kind of law or property right. Reading writing and arithmetic are easy enough when they're willing to learn, which is soon enough."

"Psychology is something I've never read. Before I got to college I thought it was mind-reading."

"You should study it before you become a father! . . ." The gaiety of her seriousness and the touch of her hand on his arm made him want to tease her with stories of famous childhoods and his own need to make up for all the play he'd lost to learning. Yet when he happened to take notice he felt his undisciplined little hunter cockled in sleep like an infant Eros; he himself floated sweetly on the still waters of her experience. With desire at peace he was glad and not aggrieved that she spoke with her thoughts upon the words and not upon him or herself in relation to him as an admirer of his freedom.

Then she was saying that unhappy people reproduce their own unhappy kind. "Not many people know how to raise happy children. Almost every girl passes on the methods she grew up on, and she's usually deceived about the origin of her unhappiness. It's the duty"—she laughed "—yes I mean it: that's what duty is—it's the duty of people who understand these things to reproduce more than others do in order to gain ground in the general population."

"My mother had only one child. I hope I don't have any."

"Shame on you! You'll change your mind after you fall in love."

Without smelling any perfume he sensed the lavender fragrance of this straight-backed woman only a dozen years older than himself. It seemed inappropriate to tell her that he had been in love. "But I'm not enlightened."

"You are now! —Anyway," she smiled, "that's just male stubbornness." But pausing doubtfully her frank eyes invited his help in thinking out the statistical problem that she began to put before him with a firm deference that won him over to her side of the marriage question before he could remember his objections.

"Not counting any brothers or sisters at the beginning, there are nine human beings where once there were four: my parents and my husband's have added him and myself and we have put out three more. But except for me all the offspring have been male. It's women who have the most influence on society—through their very young children, but especially through their child-bearing daughters. That's the intention of 'be fruitful and multiply'! Every woman should be an exponent of self-multiplication." She glanced at Caleb drily but didnt wait for him to catch up to her, and when she laughed it seemed to be merely at the pleasure of seeing past the arithmetical obfuscations.

"We can't hold our own against the big Catholic families unless we each have three daughters! The world's being overwhelmed by children of confusion, five or six to every couple. But the good that every child of light can do is immense and a few more of them could leaven all humanity. There should be as many of us as possible!" Here she indicated the roomfull with a slow turn of her hand. Caleb now understood that she was unaccustomed to wine, and to having a listener.

She continued with an embarrassing frankness that flattered his capacity for intimate appreciation, as if she had forgiven his sin of pride and found him a youth of more than common wisdom. "Michael and I should have at least one girl-baby, a mother-to-be who will understand from the beginning what I only now understand, and who'll be much more competent, much better able to change things—by teaching, by showing men. . . .

"But even if our children turn out no happier than the rest it's good for the cities and farms of the world to have more people, billions of people packed together in bustles of cooperation: jammed food stores, crowded parks with lots of people watching every chess game, swimming pools brimming with kids and old codgers, every tennis court being used all day and all night under the lights for doubles. The more human beings there are the closer they must get to each other. They'll touch each other when they talk."

She spoke without selfassurance but she had no doubt of her feeling: "Maybe any of you can easily prove me wrong. . . . But crowded people would *have* to learn cooperation! They would be obliged to love one another. They would *have* to understand that war is no alternative to mutual feeding. If only there were no room on earth for a person to withdraw into a study all by himself families would be stronger and cells of love would make up loving communities, and all countries would become a single nation. Then writers would be loving citizens just as schoolteachers and some doctors are, and they'd work on puppet shows for children instead of abstruse abstractions. There would never be any hesitation about which to rescue first in case of fire, kids or manuscripts. *Then*, once people have discovered what they ought to know by instinct—then we could liquidate half the population and allow stuff like art to flourish!"

She paused for a reply and Caleb smiled uncertainly. "You mean by some sort of euthanasia?"

"Yes, sterilization: compulsory if necessary!" she answered in a very low but almost vivacious tone bowing her head and leaning toward him. Then glancing at his nonplussed brow she broke into contralto laughter so pure and merry that all heads turned to stare; whereupon amused at her own embarrassment putting three fingers to her chin she opened wide her eyes to scan the smiling faces that questioned her innovative deportment.

Caleb felt as if he'd been saved by some strange kind of goodness from making a fool of himself with misplaced solemnity. In all humility he pinned her colors to his shoulder and vowed to serve her ever more without the hope of guerdon.

"Well I can't very well stop people from making love can I?" she whispered to him as the others not insisting on an explanation turned back to their babble.

But he caught Michael looking at him now that he least wanted King Arthur's attention. Under that inspection he shrank and fretted with the unprecedented feeling of being understood better than he could understand. At the same time he was reflecting that a boy like himself who attained to such little success in his life-plan for a series of different women might be well advised to narrow his panamorous intentions once and for all. Winning one true woman and living her love alone unto wise old age might be the broadest experience of all.

Besides, if he started looking for a wife like Ruth his talent for loyalty might somehow shine forth and render him more attractive to all the girls who came across him. Why not marry? Why not do something further with love than anything he had until now given his imagination to? Freely and wholly know the life of one woman beyond price deeper and inestimably

more valuable than any glitteringly infatuating schoolgirl like Cindy! Be
carelessly or even hopefully glad to fill her with maternal Euphrosyne,
sweetening exclusive love with natural proofs. Make her a mother fresher
than the virgin. After some months the child's two haploids would begin to
cohere as the center of a unique universe.

4.

Dishes having been cleared away whiskey bottles stood again among
the wines and Jack's main business appeared to be over. For a while there
would be ice from the huge Wolfson refrigerator but when it was gone and
more could not be frozen fast enough nothing but tap water in West Berkeley Creamery milk bottles would be splashed into the remaining fire
water mostly sweetish so-called sour mash from Kentucky named for
French royalty.

Jack gave Michael a cigar glancing at traces on the table cloth of many
a pot of honey that the bulky bear had dipped—twice as many as anyone
else. "How do you feel now?" he asked the birthday king.

"I feel better." Michael understated, patting his stomach and expressing savory puffs of smoke.

"That's not allowed in a democracy!" Newt protested.

"Even as the tyrant of one day in the year." Sylvia added.

Jack matched Michael almost puff for puff likewise slouched in his
chair having for the nonce shucked his responsibilities and likewise displaying the male kind of selfsatisfied laziness. But presently he straightened up and took the rolled leaf from his mouth as he brought back to
mind the duty he had imposed upon himself. It was a wonder he didnt rise
to speak this piece. He did however lift his arm with cigar and glass in
hand, though in order not to seem as overbearing of this soft indulgent
mob as the master of ceremonies that he would have loved to play he
hammed his part out of the corner of his mouth, and when others
responded he sank back into his own smoke as if indifferently. Altogether
he simulated a most self-effacing host despite the fact that continual interruptions brought twitches of frustration to his physiognomy.

How he began was: "My lords, ladies, and knight—we are here
assembled to salute the black operator who among blackguards seeks to
bring forth good from their evil and who by force of mind can make a
Heav'n of their Hell. Now let us lionize him in this house of the wolf.
—But first drink to his theory of art as proof!"

Thenceforth toasting kept all elbows bent so that malgre much shouting there could be clapping with no more than one hand. What a pleasure
not to hear applause in acknowledgement of every sally! Caleb dared not
propose his own wit but he joined the festivity with right good will.

"To rith and mitual!"

"Mass as crass . . ."

"Rite on site!"

"To the focus of the locus!"

"Myth as math!"

"Mike are you going to have the second lecture?"

"Why do you keep trying?"

"The lectureship is worth a Mass."

"He makes it more challenging with his monotonous delivery."

"Monotony is permythable."

"It disguises heresy as counterrevolution."

"It must have been a powerful allocution because it overcame me."

"To his permactations and conjactations of complex numbers!"

"To the square root of a minus onion!"

"To him who oscillates between his axis of the reals and our axis of the imaginaries!"

"Workers of the world, conjugate with art!"

"He claims no issue is simple and he loves every brainchild."

"He says storge brings sorge."

"Give up crypticism and become an artist. Give in to your imagination man, give in to simple imagination! Forswear your beloved complexity. Forget that everything is related to everything else!"

"Okay. After I finish my lectures."

But more was coming in the birthday party: a corporate present; Michael was being given money like an office girl about to get married. "Holy Mackerel, you've got the offertory out of place tonight!" he murmured looking down at the envelope that was laid before him and glancing at Jack furtively. "You Jews and Protestants are good at heart and bad at theology."

"We do everything backwards on black Michaelmas." Jack replied. "Anyway, with us eating and drinking comes before money."

"Jack," Dave Wilson asked "how do you know so much about catholics?"

"I have to read their books to get ahead. . . . Go on Mike, see what it says.

"Gee!" Why did Michael stall, turning the thing over two or three times like one dreading to open a telegram?

But finally he read aloud the words Jack had written on behalf of the subscribers: "To the negative Pathfinder: Pioneer in Reverse—that he may buy powder for Killdeer on his long journey to the East, and cod bait when he gets to Gloucester!"

The stoutest fish of them all now faced his arc of expectant friends without expression but his gills like bellows dragged the burning coal up his cigar as if it was the lightest of cheroots. In further sign of agitation he flicked away the ash before it could form and extend itself, indecently exposing the open fire of the ostensibly phlegmatic brand and nervously blowing smoke into the face of the whole company. He began to cough in a cunctation quite uncharacteristic of his social address.

Jack took up the pause. "Catachumens, rejoice in our last collective presents and celebrate our first bishop's return to his fathers!"

After a silence Michael spoke at last in a husky whisper. "Here Ruth, look at this." He handed the envelope across to her. Caleb saw his hand tremble as she took the thick light packet. "Money to eat on during my trip back East."

Ruth faltered and lowered her eyes, declining to examine the purse. She lay it on the tablecloth between them. Her lower lip folded itself into her mouth but her head was erect as she looked straight at her husband's averted eyes. "What trip?" she asked in a clear voice.

He could not bear her gaze. Picking up the gift he took out the bills and counted them with a poor show of heartiness. "Wow! This is terrific. . . ." With wooden unsmiling face, as if he hadnt heard her question, he sucked the words past his inert lips. The hidden tongue seemed to generate sound mechanically. But he finally answered: "You remember . . . If I go back to look for a job."

"Remember what?" In the general stillness her irony rang with courage. Despairing of privacy she pressed him. "When? —How are you going to get there? —Are the children and I going with you?" She stopped.

Who betrayed Michael Chapman? The big owl wriggled ignominiously in the glare of publicity, pinioned clinically by a kangaroo court. At bottom he himself could be blamed for not keeping his plan long enough secret as well as for misplacing his confidence so unconscionably. It was the pain of such appalling retrospection that Caleb began to share. Or at least Michael's shame suffused his own selfconsciousness. But it would have been unnerving for every person in the room to hear the confessor of most of them blurt out any kind of guilt at all, to say nothing of domestic treachery.

"On the train. I got my ticket this morning—but I'm probably not going for about six months. I've saved the money to send for you as soon as I get work." Sinking lower in the eyes of his judges he added hurriedly: "Gloucester's the one place I'm willing to buy a house. . . . Besides, I can always cash in my ticket if it doesnt work out."

His lame defense brought to Ruth's face the faint reassurance of a brief smile. "I won't ask you to, Michael. I think it's a lovely thoughtful present your friends have given you, very generous."

"It certainly is!" he asseverated, seizing the small relief she had offered. He nodded all around the table and mustered brave words for the assembly at large avoiding the sight of his wife. "I want to drink to you all. Thank you, thank you, thanks! . . . Every man has his gift and mine is skill for travel."

The first kindness to Ruth came from Dave Wilson. "He was going to surprise you, and now we've spoiled it all! —You've got a lot more explaining to do when you get home Mike!" he joshingly subjoined in the manner that coast to coast any married man may be exposed to.

The whole company began to crack jokes again.

"You'll be taking Killdear with you. Ruth will have to get a do-it-yourself kit."

"Not while I'm around!"

"You'll soon be a fishwife Ruth."

"That's a backward part of the country. When you get there with the kids you may have nothing to live on but a codpiece."

Michael's opaque diodes began to glint again in the candlelight now that the worst was over. For the rest of the evening he swooped and skimmed over his people's heads like a nifty disburdened seagowl.

Thus the cenacle of friends at which Caleb got to know fowl from fish. For a long time he sat in silence twirling his glass at Ruth's side who wept silently with head high and hands in her lap.

{*Postulants only*: GO TO ITEM (24) SA.09, page 249.}

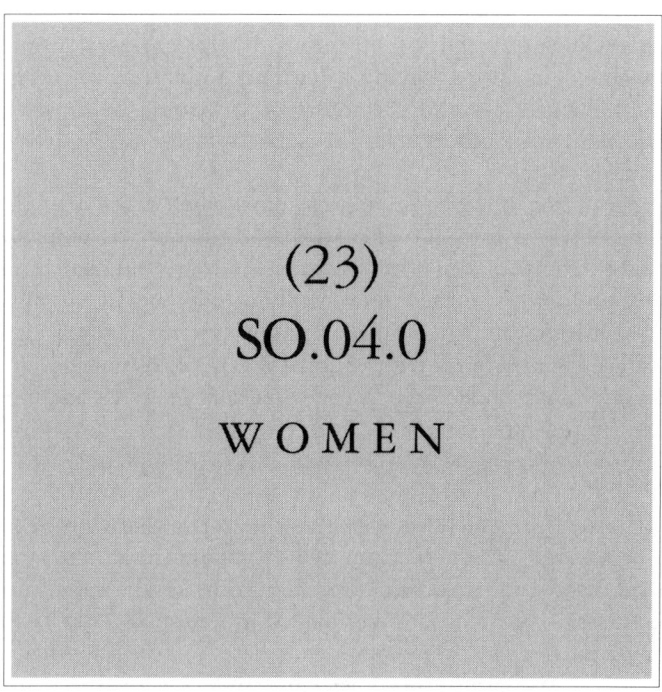

(23)

SO.04.0

WOMEN

**Manuscript for Michael Chapman's
Second Lecture on Museless Art Number One
Which Remains Undelivered**

Dear friends you must be. I am surprised to see anyone here at all, except Jack, who loves to set me up for his foil, and takes notes for secret purposes, though it costs him time from reading and writing and must therefore be counted as the highest generosity. But there are certain fundamentals that I must continue to get out of the way, even were I to make no sound for lack of ear to hear it.

Music has been so important to dance first because of the fact that we are not able to shut our ears; and second because it is superior to sight in not being limited to straight lines of transmission.

It is usually performed in a theater of some sort but it need not be simple space that music fills; an architecture exclusively for blind audiences might have been quite different from what we have. But there is no such thing as a pure audience in congregation. Even electronic musicians can't avoid theater because people listening together don't want to sit looking at each other, and it's nigh impossible for ordinary people to keep their eyes closed if they're paying attention. So auditoriums have always been built for audiences and spectators both, having being designed for visual requirements, notwithstanding sound's facility for getting around columns and corners.

Whether or not in the beginning of human time dance may have generated music (which in turn perpetuated the original dance or inspired more dance), dance in our day avails itself of music to rouse and control individual performers, to coordinate their movements as a group by sounds that are equally available to all participating nervous systems, and to signal those out of eyeshot whose interest may be attracted by the dromenon.

Although most music is performed ensemble (with more than one voice or artifactual instrument, or with one mechanical device that serves for many), and by power of amplitude fills simultaneously every space open to it, the sound of only one or a few alternating instruments knifes or curls to all attending ears also—such as the music that's produced in the syllables of a single voice. If some new discovery in aerobics (or an old secret of the East) could teach dancers how to maintain a constant supply of oxygen to the vocal organs without compensatory loss in the blood supply to distal muscles, they would not have to rely so much upon the sounds that come from others—musicians, singers, actors, machines. They might then overcome a theatrical deficiency by which tiny bands of impecunious players are necessarily confronted.

Music was admitted to the Church only when it had shucked the dance. It entered with the Alleluias, assisting the voice of the liturgy. All to the good, especially to mark the order of business for those who couldnt see what was going on. In early days the principal musician still supplied his own power. But at length he was relieved of labor, attaining to the controllership of compressed air, a position of trained skill and responsibility to which he was officially appointed. As curator of multitudinous vibrations he now sat at the console touching his upsidedown puppet strings and stealing the show by enveloping liturgical action in opaque clouds of ceremonial sound. And so, as sacred music turned into the art of domination by the manipulation of machines that exercised power beyond the capacity of human bodies—always in the interests of edification or supernal beauty—it freed itself of the choir and began to vibrate the auditorium in willful independence.

Large congregations required large shelters for celebration of the Mass. There was only one Sunday in a week for the indoor gathering of a see or at least a whole parish. Unlike a factory for which overhead can be efficiently absorbed by spreading out its utility on round-the-clock shifts in hebdomadal cycles, thereby minimizing capital investment, the basilica or cathedral was on the one hand a pile of idle glorification and on the other a meeting place for all the people at once. It had to be very high for adequate natural lighting, yet the great empty spaces of upper air could not be used, and in winter they drew off the animal heat of shivering worshippers. The small dromenon at one end could not be dispersed into aisle-processions, or raised far enough off the floor, to make a clear scene for the distant people (to say nothing of getting them into the action). Cool vastnesses called for comforting decoration or distraction.

Composers eventually regarded church music as free in form, so little were they required to respect the meaning or length of the words making up Kyries, graduals, and other parts of the ritual. Priests were then obliged to wait for the music (as nowadays football scrimmages must wait for broadcast advertisements). Even in the West action at the altar was overbearingly masked or smothered by majestic sound, as it is veiled by shrouded rood screens in the Eastern Orthodox rite. For the people couldn't have heard legomena anyway. Single human voices weren't strong enough to fill the cavity. Yet sound was the only means of doing so. Thus the laity was satisfied with aesthetically emotional experience.

With both singers and an organ the clergy too found themselves pleasure that could be justified. The most subjective of arts filled religious houses as well as churches with an interesting and beautiful object that was amazingly variable. Variations of diurnal liturgy were few (all repeated within a year); the daily mass seemed to convey no new experience, and, in the loss or failure of offertorial understanding, its performance grew rote to the point of reversibility. (Goliards and warlocks plucked the ritual for caricature.) The art of sound helped to save the sacramental dromenon, in which it played no essential part, by keeping its ritual apparatus alive during the time it took to reform and recover at least a semblance of Christ's intention. This miracle of grace is still in process and not yet disproven.

Anyway the pressure of eucharistic space-sound, having been found transcendingly decent, kept the doors of the temple from swinging inward to the clamor of dance outside. That was a dance of play before it became a dance of art—advisedly profane ("before the temple") at the outset of our era. The ontogeny of western theater, both drama and dance (oppositely branching limbs), is distinguished from the East's by the remarkably improbable resistance of our liturgy to a decadence otherwise universal in cultural phylogenesis.

Here it is not my purpose to discuss this unique dromenological durability, nor to propose an explanation for the special origins of western drama; but one of the crucial effects of Christianity was to force a divergent evolution of the dance.

Profane corporate dance, excluded from religious liturgy, cannot in any important way survive social customs whereby everybody's desire is too readily satisfied—when every day's a feast. Political or religious repression founded in idealistic doctrine is no more pernicious to social dance than absolute sexual freedom would be. If thoroughgoing license were ever to obtain it would enervate the libidinous appetite for gratuitous movement. Not even the ambitious discontents and abstract preoccupations of the modern city do more to disintegrate communal dance (the remains of which—as diversion and entertainment, or as a decaying device for the introduction of boys to girls—are of only peripheral interest in dromenology).

At the same time the speed of our mechanical advantages whets the old hunger for human motion (alas if only to see it). Dance offers professionals themselves the heady possibility of ignoring ritual limitations, and of advancing beyond the untrained reach of common movement.

Art dance (as distinguished from the communal) is conceived by the slow condensation of a century's mass amusement, night after night, on the boards of ten thousand music halls. It is through personal intensification rather than exfoliation that it is brought to birth by individually experimenting dancers—quite otherwise than it was with drama, which itself produced the actors and was much closer to ritual and corporate dance.

Nevertheless, having progressed from play and display to a new art of pure movement, modern dance has become truer theater, etymologically speaking, than the best of drama, for it is essentially conveyed by vision alone. A theater is a place for seeing. From the aesthetic viewpoint movement is visible action. In art dance the action is seen without explanation, uncoupled from solidarity, from work, from play, from religious hope. Maybe the mainly American version will ultimately surrender itself to a master of drama, but meanwhile, as long as plays are dominated by psychology sociology and journalism, it provides us with most of the new imagination we get from the stage.

But who are these dancers that can with their bodies perfect their imagination?

Of course these dancers are women. Yet why do we intuitively think "of course"? How does dance, as art, so often incarnate the feminine creative psyche, though sometimes employing masculine minds and bodies—as the drama, using actresses, expresses masculine civilization? I am going to pursue the hazardous notion that I can open an anatomy of the art by attacking this question of gender.

It is women who have it sexually within their power—by diverting certain instincts and at the same time honoring their immemorial nature, forgetting nothing, but transvaluing the inborn tradition—to save our planet and mankind's institutions.

Erotic desire is one thing that can bring a man down to earth, in more or less beneficent worship, as civilization is turning out, considering how much less evil even the ugliest lust has done than pollutions of the spirit that anaesthetize the skin and obtund the nerves of sympathy. However awkwardly I may fail to describe woman's good office, I hope to peg it as an unobtrusive persuasion of value that sustains our hope against cruelty and force. It's true that its instinct of motherhood keeps plowing us under in the self-defeating cultivation of fertility, but there can be as much more to feminine agronomy as there is to masculine husbandry.

Women live for final cause instead of ambition and yet are able to feel time and space ever more immediately, change and changing merged in consciousness as they are merged in reality. This unspoken modality testifies to a genius which left to itself would ignore our Faustian norms. The perishable life of art dance is over even as it is being shown. Like childbirth, it confers no immortality. It has none of the persistence by which the most volatile organization is characterized, much less the assured repetition of ritual. There can be no more than imitative performance of a dance after the first dancer of it is too old to perpetuate it. Few dancers take seriously the efforts of preservational notation.

Male human beings, by and large, erupt from their places exogamously, aggressively, curiously. Their acquired velleity for domestic facilities and intradomestic consensus is no more than skin-deep, despite their acquiescence to the pettiest applications of architecture and to the dictation of decorating industries. Aside from bourgeois symbolism, their drive for family remains secretly weak. But women must defend mortality. It is from innate sensitivity to the helpless frailty of singled mankind that women insist upon a society organized for the protection and education of children, and that they fear more for their children, as even Gertrude Stein says, than for themselves.

When the feminine psyche devotes itself to an art of its own invention the result is bound to be more delicate than it grossly seems, lacking as it does the benefit of spectators aesthetically prepared by specific cultural evolution. Small refinements in the control of energy produce great changes of expression. Infinitesimals of variation affect the physiognomy of dance as if the dancer were racked by the most extraordinary fluctuations of passion. In my meteorology of women the danger of instability must be cited, but not as a matter of chance.

The essence of dance that baffles the capability of positive reason belongs to that form or mode of our consciousness by which, in bias against women, the existence of art is called for. Yet the question as to why dancers of the theater are chiefly women is equivalent to the question as to why we have this special art at all, which might otherwise have survived or aborted as nothing more valuable than the chorus of opera. Though the hours from sun to sun dispose themselves symmetrically in the geocentric year, night cannot anticipate itself as Phoebus does who displaces darkness beforehand and who also trails behind him lingering tinctures of the day; and so in a lifetime we know more light than darkness by far. In some such penumbric way the male overbears his consubstantial opposite—with all his artificial illuminations, with his stars, and with his lunar reflection in herself. But in dance she creates of night an art opposing his.

I shall point out five aspects of the counterartist's qualification, or anyway five aspects of the art to account for the primacy of the female dancer. . . .

{*Postulants only*: GO TO ITEM (25) SO.04.1, page 255.}

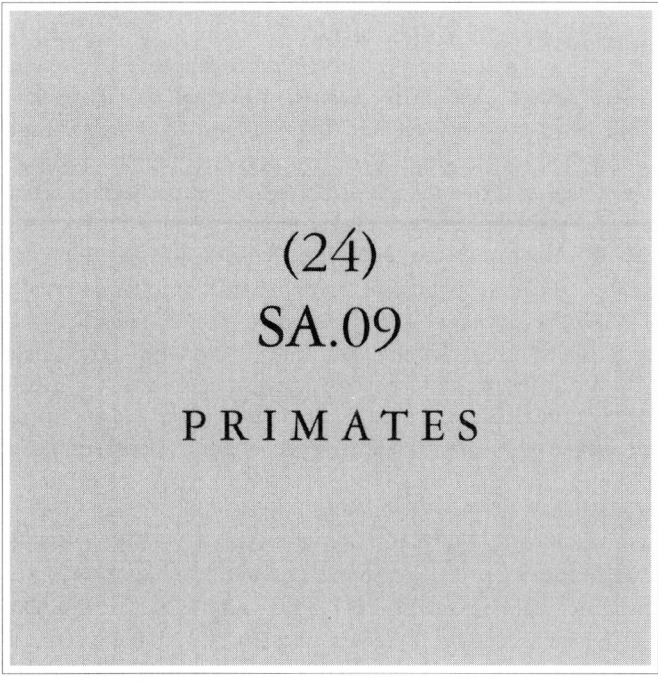

(24)
SA.09

PRIMATES

*B*ut father and son emerged from the jungle of cats happy enough with each other, the latter hoping that the former would forget the disquieting codicil to their conversation. Now the path opened out into a wide circle containing another jungle, this one situated at the point of maximum communication where all paths met, because the Trustees back in the beginning had hired a French city planner who believed that no visitor to this kingdom would want to miss the Capitol itself, which was therefore erected as a bare-ribbed armillary hemisphere at the locus most convenient to myriad eyes and feet.

"Bandersnatches!" said Jonathan.

"You mean Bandar-log." said the chief magistrate.

"Yuh, Bandar-log."

"Ruth and Matty want to see them." Michael explained with guarded reticence under his obligations to family solidarity, assuming the mask of reasonable tolerance.

"Well anyway I hope Hodge doesnt wake up." the boy sighed with disingenuous piety. "They'd be a bad influence on him."

When they came up to the questionable half of the family already among the merry snickering common people, however, they themselves succumbed to the influence. The monkeys penetrated Michael's scorn, and so also Jonathan's. Soon the father was smiling—not laughing like any Tom Dick but at least smiling—and this sign that his prejudice had been violated, that he was after all a warm human man sharing warm human sensibilities, gave Ruth a certain satisfaction.

Jonathan was younger and prouder, in this instance perhaps superior to his old man, holding out against the masses a minute or two longer, in loyalty to felines and canines, slightly annoying his mother who had at first taken it for granted that he was aping his father's snobbishness and failed to see that it was the father who had been stayed for a time by his son's moral standard. But the son finally abandoned himself like everyone else to the blandishments of correlation and incongruity between the caged kinds of primate and his own, reluctantly made aware that the loreless leaderless tribe bemuses even those forewarned.

Michael was soon being peppered with questions about the animals as if he should know everything about monkeys lemurs apes and men and could impart his knowledge directly if he only chose to open an ad hoc educational relationship: as if he was expected to serve as an enhancing medium between subject and object. This putative responsibility irritated him. In answering questions, or in tracing the boundaries of his ignorance (always too scrupulous of the truth to lay down statements of general import that he was inwardly in doubt of—too conscientious in respect to the general need for truth to be able to slough off the effort like an ordinary member of the Republic ["You got me, son! Ask the eggheads."]), worrying himself about accuracy that was beyond his competence yet reasonable to assume in a paternalistic common reader, trapped as he hated to be trapped, forced to stab at specifications and then withdraw them (concerning for instance the interhominoidal relationship and distinction between knuckle-walking African gorillas/chimpanzees and arboreal Asian gibbons/orangutans, or a definition of the Bandar-log as a set), digging himself deeper and deeper into a hole of exasperation. Nevertheless as strangers began to listen in he found himself not unsuperior to the throng, *primus inter primates*. Primate of Anthropoetry, Primate indeed of all Anthropoetics.

Yet every word and every minute was another measure deducted from his mortal time. He struggled snarling with ill temper in the web of familiarity and ignorance that netted him into the community of vulgar amusement, knowing that he should have shut up and kept saying I don't know I don't know I don't know (which wouldnt have helped his kids any), and started scowling instead of smiling at the brutes on both sides of the fence.

It took a sharp eye to see that the labile crowd of men women and children was not the same populace all day long. The Brownian movement outside the great umbrella cage of subcages was as continuous as that within though far from uniformly distributed inasmuch as certain sectors were negatively charged with singularly attractive denizens. ["How graceful is a human being, if indeed he is human." saith Heraclitus.] But always the same pressing levee of peanut-eating catcalling space-bloating inessential individuals murmurously acclaiming the inane entertainments of Lemuroidea and Anthropoidea.

Yet the gasborne corpuscles of human movement were not chiefly brownian in color being mostly white people inasmuch as blacks steered clear for the most part. But there were always some far more simian brows and upper lips of uncircumcised bogtrotters with their raucous sons jeering at the red asses and their own Irish faces behind the bars. ["Do you know why Irishmen carry monkeys on their backs?"] And always a few effeminate fatlipped Jewish boys tittering at the abominable mockery of God's images. ["For spare parts."] Item also: Jews of the East, members of the world's largest plurality, unimpressed by the foolishness of races inferior to the Chinese but showing their children the facts of American civilization, and Japanese, more open-minded, giggling at certain acts only. ["The wisest man, beside god, appears like an ape, in wisdom, beauty, and all else."] Item: suspicious Slavs laughing apprehensively at humanoid clowns pensively fingering their cheeks and chins. Item, more than a few: brachycephalic Europeans whole families together full of mimes and guffaws, feeding the monkeys along with themselves, rewarding everyone with their easy joy and screaming at their kids. And item, semper: the main body of the packing list, a thousand cases of dyed-in-the-wool Americans of all sizes but of one uniform quality: warm and human.

One pinkfaced sportsman of middle age imitated a mandrill so successfully that in the eddy to which he belonged he himself became the primary object of public approbation. Protestant boys of all complexions looked for teats and pudenda on all the catarrhines that seemed female, hoping to witness masturbation if not coition, wondering if in sooth the estrous cycle of the girls inside the jail was similar to that of the objects of their own lust, and if the internal anatomy of the head was likewise comparable. Spectators of all ages were enthralled by the tettered back faces of these immodest devils so bare and ruddy under their tails, ugly as sin, whom no witch would want to kiss on a sabbath. [*Is this the face that launched a thousand shits?* That tortious schoolboy refrain invaded Michael's head round and around like *"Punch brothers, punch with care/ Punch in the presence of the pass-en-jare!"* in bumptious impertinence.]

In a zoo the principle of indeterminacy comes blatant. No animal can act natural, least of all monkeys, who have probably never behaved unhistrionically even in native jungles. Here they leapt

Yet methinks says Michael to himself the new hotshot logorithmic anthropoids could never stuff a girl legs foremost up a chimney the way one these big devils has done (to see if upsidedown she

about ostentatiously in chase of food and misleading inedibles tossed into their cages by those at liberty. It was a great colony of unemployed grasshopper-men, wizened homunculi without family, manikins who hated ritual. They theatrically exploited their very diversity of size and shape.

One morose fellow housed in a private cage within the larger theater patrolled rapidly back and forth on all fours his idle tail arched behind him looking at nothing but the bare short floor ahead. When he came to either end of his shuttle he whirled toward the inner wall as if making the wrong turn in running out a base hit in order to avoid the sight of human beings who as travesties of his race would have sickened him beyond the sickness of his captivity: such was his wily comic affectation. Matthew Chapman was diddled by the mummery, crying above the din with false insight: "Look Dad! He's trying to get away from all these people!"

These words served to cue the outsmarting performer. Pausing only long enough for the unguarded opinion of the child to register in the brains of his public the canny actor suddenly sprang to a shelf, and thence to a bar above, swinging by his tail, mugging and capering to the general laughter. Only the unwilling straight man himself failed to join in, who was as alarmed and confused as any coneycaught dolt (robbed however not of his purse but of his self-respect). And then this unscrupulous exploiter of humen, making sidesplittingly ludicrous grimaces

really looks like all the others?), nor carry a lady off like a little ivory household goddess in the palm of his hand, nor climb the outside of the Empire State: for the simple reason that even with all their digits they have no hands—only calculating but unprehensile digits. Such primates have no nose to pick; eunuchs of prestidigitation yet incapable of digital monkey business even with a demivierge. (Is it therefore that those demons without passion are entrusted with certain technical decisions that may one day liquidate all girls as well as the need for them?) [*Digitalis normalis, Dosim, Repetitur.*] A woman prefers some bluenose baboon with monkey glands.

—*Monkey*! The very word doth like a bell recall

> Bell-bottom trousers
> And buttons made of brass,
> Loose around the ankles
> And tight around the ass!

Monkey-suits they called them— great for freedom of navel action, having a codpiece of thirteen buttons (not brass but navy blue) that could be loosened and let down at the drop of a hint, or easily slipped off altogether without taking off your shoes—which even at the mere thought of fucking failed to conceal a youth's angle of inclination. I was a boy then, slim and free, and I thought the raffish bell-bottoms well worth tailoring from regulation dress blues at my own expense (as if the Navy still expected us to swab the decks barefooted with rolled-up pants). I was

to show gratitude for their laughter, held out his hand for food.

Michael and Jonathan with the rest had been laughing the laughter that is as involuntary as the response of a man's eye to the presence or image of almost any naked part of a woman's body even in the very teeth of conviction that he is being used by the woman or by the employer of the woman for some impudent mercenary end among many possible ends, the least vicious of which is purely carnal.

But Michael's smile faded and his visage darkened with anger when the well-schooled throng clapped at the divertissement. The people applauded like a mindless drill team punctuating a variety show for the airwaves because clapping was the only courtesy to which they were trained—the only means of expressing everything from scant tolerance to enthusiasm. Michael feared he'd have to bear successive waves of that reflex to art. In hatred and disgust, as fast as he could push his way through the crowd, Moses led his own tribe from the scene.

as insensitive to the sufferings of my shipmates who had to wear the skin-tight uniform over a paunch as to the fears of the wretched married ones that they were only trading their own aching wives to dogfaces or bellhops on the other coast for the dogface or bellhop wives they sometimes found on the local beach, maybe with dogface or bellhop babies, dreaming faithfulness while they tore at the thirteen lightly anchored grommets. Nobody was willingly chaste. What good luck to have married late, or rather to have gone so young to sea. The war made people love each other too easily. Hecuba still loves easily, really likes her guests; very friendly and affectionate she must be. Not what I'd call promiscuous. There's still a Regular Navy man visits her in spates every three or four months (if the old man who pays the bills is out of town), a Storekeeper First who was probably a fuzzfaced Scout when erst she fingered in shy panting curiosity somebody else's baker's dozen under a bush in some Chicago park on the way home from a rollerskating rink, willing to risk the shame of being collared by one of the Irish police matrons who scourged the shadows intransigently under the lash of their own sectarian flagellation, but not yet prepared to go all the way.

No more of this mimikey business at the base level of humanity! Better learn at matheums of science and industry than in zoological gardens. The bloodless logorithmoids visible but inapplaudable in airconditioned cages with soundproof glass walls where nobody can throw monkeywrenches into them—as far as accuracy's concerned closer to the angels than both men and monkeys—make word into number and number into word according to the choreography of human puppeteers whose brains (at whatever power of sexual excitation) are slower than theirs by something like ten to the minus ninth and only three times as heavy as a chimpanzee's. They can do endless sums as long as dynamos keep them quickened.

(When electricity stops values decay.) It's a species of small population and leaping evolution, reproducing with the greatest conceivable mutation from one generation to the next, each selflessly overtaking its own progenitors in the headlong dash to sustain man's exponentially increasing admiration of his own creatures. These genies climb the beanstock with palmless and soleless digits, no less thumbless than passionless. Best yet, women can be employed as their attendants without danger of funk or agitation.

Having backed out of the brute congregation at a time that would have angered the most liberal Unitarian preacher (Ruth apologizing to the crowd with a brave smile as she pushed the little caisson straightarmed before her, nodding her head to foster the impression that it was only a nameless detail of parenthood's sacred duty that could have torn them away from the warm human swarm at the altar of its unity), the Chapmen proceeded to the last stage of the day's education. The head of the family was looking to the bottom of their descent for the purification that comes through pity and terror.

{*Postulants only*: GO TO ITEM (26) SA.10, page 261.}

(25)
SO.04.1

DESPECIALIZATION

. . . I refer first to her unspecialized body. The male is a specialist. His salient intentions dominate the speech and technology of our civilization. He is imitated by women who would compete; but those who feel no rivalry, if they have been neither nurtured by a household of intellectuals nor coerced by authority, are likely to investigate the world actively only after they have learned through its living affects the unequal varieties of its importance. Dancers in the same concrete way discover through movement the possibilities of the body.

A man's brain concentrates libidinal energy at one end of his spinal column; its discharge takes place at the other end, specifically pointed, and the decantation is diffused only to the degree in which he sympathizes with the vessel of his impact. His backbone serves only to conduct necessary signals from one organ back and forth to the other, as it neurologically connects the higher organ, headquarters, with all others. But there is no ganglionic hammer at the top end of a woman's spine, and her ideology is usually governed by an endocrinal hierarchy.

Her distinctive art could not have begun but in a counter-specialization relegated and programmed by the masters for their own aesthetic satisfaction. In classical ballet, a movement consists of the passage from one ideal and immaterial point to another, and the idealism is not the dancer's. Like a rope-dancer trained in strength and poise, the delitescent woman is assigned a series of public postures, often as high as possible off the ground, as if to illustrate a man's objective imagination; or at best, later on, she learns to leap hoops of fire close to earth, like a lioness left to her own grace only in passing through a sequence of positions determined by a trainer.

But in the latter days of ballet it takes all the arithmetic of traditional ambition to keep her tame, and she cannot bear its discipline forever. Generalizing intellect, the most extreme specialty in a world of discrete abstractions, has at last gone too far in insisting upon its way against flesh and touch. Mens' music, sounding linguistic and visual power, meets rebellion in the bowels of helots who are now in principal possession of the stage. Some remain docile, protecting the kind of self-consciousness they have learned in their profession, but others (in their hard-won self-objectivity) take heart for creating an antithesis to the over-soul's idealism. It is the revolution of abused physical subjectivity. The creative dancer throws off an assigned specialty to assume mastery of the whole dromenon.

Some say that dance is the art of movement, speaking of it objectively. They should say that it is the art of the movement of the human body. The movement we speak of in dance cannot be understood abstractly as a category, a property, or a secondary quality accidentally incarnate, nor as a force like gravity, an energy like light, or a disease like cancer. Rather I would say that human movement, considered as a fine art (that is, neither decorative nor practical), reduces to the art of the human body. The body is not human when it's dead; there is no theatrical art of the static. While it lives its gross behavior consists always in motion, in the inhibition of motion, or in cessation of motion; and its internal maintenance is continuously dynamic. Body, as the composite function of living, is the material of dance as consciousness is the material of poetry. Art uses material more freely than nature can, and in this sense imagination exceeds nature.

Creative dance forestalls concepts of the imagination before they can gestate in the brain. The dancer's spinal column bleeds off thought before the central nervous system can act upon itself, and steers creative energy, which might have turned mental, into action just as artificial as poetry.

This art requires the whole body for its memory as well as for its expression, delicately extending the comprehension of a brain. The female's body is the richer of the sexes in respect to somatic cross-relationships. The fact that men are less apt to refer sensations from one part of their bodies to another does not preclude their inferiority also in the opposite ability to dissociate ordinary articulations of movement and to endow with motor independence some parts that have grown up reflexive or subservient to the ego. Male thews specialize (though their specialties may alternate from moment to moment, profession to profession, desire to desire) because a man's hope of immortality is spiritual, and his body serves him merely as a vector for the self. A male's principal passions are suffered as if peculiar to his discrete consciousness, or shared by his brothers only metaphorically. But women know their experience to be common in time and space, not as means but as purposes of nature. It is to them that denatured men must ecologically adapt themselves.

Nature and woman supplement each other, relieving man of the need for a full range of pain and joy. However unnaturally a dancer may drive herself, she is at least predisposed to reckon with all her flesh and blood, seeking justification by language and knowledge only when she must defend herself against deprivation or fear in the civilization she inhabits.

For a woman "the process of choice which leads to action" in creative dance, as in love, is begun and conditioned more immediately by subjectively modified disposition than by sensory communication. A trained dancer becomes to such extent athletic that at the muscular level her reflex is partially decentralized and speedier than the normal three-tenths of a second neural relay. But dance is no contest, and its end does not require the exhaustion of a dancer's strength. As self-directing behavior its reactions are almost entirely proprioceptive, except for that of the foot against the floor; and seldom does it call for sudden or instantaneous response.

For relatively sluggish molecular reactions are more subtle than electric pulses and binary synaptic switches in integrating rainbows of simultaneous movement. Sometimes it is hard to believe that a woman's skeletal muscles are not single cells, so smoothly do they tighten and relax; it seems impossible that they are started and reversed by discontinuous signals. But it's not implausible that an organism highly susceptible to all the mixed persuasions of chemistry in the earlier phases of intention should also distinguish itself by nervous talent for modulating the hormonal disinhibition of muscles.

Women who have not "grown argumentative" (as, according to Yeats, George Eliot did) are generally indifferent to game and sport, and this is perhaps the chief reason that they usually seem more mature than men at all ages. For men physical action must be athletic: if there is no natural or economic object they make one up, with definitions and rules, whether to win something or to beat somebody. Their dance normally turns into drill or parade, if not into some endurance contest, which requires that they carry some weapon or tool even when there is no excuse to brandish it. Like Athena, the foremost argumentative woman, men have always "thought it not meet to dance with empty hands". A man's movement is not often disinterested. Give him no opponent, prize, goal, mark, comparison, praise, standard, or guerdon, and his body is lazy. He aims to accomplish or excel, on any one occasion, in a particular function, in a single category of movement extracted from all the possibilities. Compared with the dance of an artist, a man's decathlon is only the slight compounding of a very limited championship. If you add up all his selections from the movements of life—in work, play, love—you won't get the tenth of an American Dancer; you'll never see a Man Moving—fully moving.

Nor, as American Poet, a Woman Thinking. At least not with a total subjectivity of mind matching the total subjectivity of her body. In respect to *soma* and *psyche*, she is the poet's converse. The dancer is a specialist when she uses her mind. She may become an intellectual athlete, a winner in ten academic departments, but then she's selecting narrow bands from the spectrum. Her mind must call upon will for the mental modulations which come unmediated to a poet. As object, humanity seems remotely explainable; it is as subject that the human is ultimately mysterious. The brain of a dancer differs from that of a poet in sexual degree, like their differing flesh, not in cultural value or importance but in respect to which of the two subjectivities dominates its function. "Her" ego cannot be separated from the body, nor "his" from the mind: essential to the art in either case.

It follows that the mind stands in the same objective relationship to the dancer that the body does to the poet. From it she is likely to appropriate with confidence only the same sort of instrumentality that he expects of the body. This principle at least explains why women are often more ruthlessly efficient than men in logical studies and in the acquisition of memory's inventory.

But polar terms are meaningless by the half. The subject must be object to the world, mind to body as well as body to mind: something abstract (as Whitehead says of all objectivity). It goes without saying that man and woman are opposites, but you can't use the terms of subjectivity and objectivity to describe male mounting female unless you know the proper names of each, their separate histories, and all the circumstances of this day's desire. Feeling is the determinant. Yet to know feeling, before recollection sets in, is an oxymoronic possibility.

Except for the retrospective analysis of an intellectually arrested experience, you have no means to contend with this human principle of indeterminacy: for you can never know both the exact quality of an emotion and its exact trajectory at the same instant—especially for two parties at once. All persons are liable to thought and self-consciousness, as well as to disinterested pleasure, whenever the gods are pleased to intervene. And so any attempt at the specifics of even your own single "volitive unity" twists in the very first sentence like a Möbius strip.

The bootless effort to lay hold of another species tantalizes far less than the dumbfounded disappointment of a poet trying to share the experience of the dancer in his arms, closer to his heart than his own toes. But we take satisfaction in the fact that what the lovers are doing leaves all symbolism behind. To use Robert Burton's Scholastic words for two kinds of passion: the mutual thing done is neither in the abstraction of the "concupiscent" nor in the feeling of the "irascible".

Counselor Owen Barfield defines the *concrete* as "that which is neither objective nor subjective." Concrescence is the better appreciated by a person who possesses its medium. From woman's first advantage in dance, an unspecialized body, I thus infer her second: a talent for vanquishing the rational distinction between subject and object in acts of the body—in short, her concretion. . . .

{*Postulants only*: GO TO ITEM (27) SO.04.2, page 277.}

(26)

SA.10

SNAKES

*T*he Trustees were obliged to maintain no more than the prevalent degree of public innocence which as it presented itself at the Main Gate though perhaps no better than it should be was by any account unexcessive in imagination. They heard no call to purify their patrons radically. Yet in accordance with the general duty they had assumed with their charter they took care to soften and diffuse the shock of visiting the central pavilion of pity and terror, hoping that the people would be dis-eased less by scandal of the flesh than by scandal of the spirit.

At the very beginning of their whole creation they had determined to build the snakehouse upon a mounded plateau. The airy prison rose as high and ethereal as the capital fund had been able to inflate it, the architect having apprehended that illusions of volume and elevation would disarm any gallinaceous demand for ugly maximum security by making everyone overlook his own worst fears and strangest compassions. The vast inverted pit had space enough to house the parliament of birds.

Moreover, it was not labeled the Snake House. Doubtless the Trustees eshewed such a raw term as evocative of vulgar lore about the dreamlife of neurasthenic women. REPTILES was what they had inscribed in six stone lintels. This title pretended to a broader view of the class than the collection demonstrated, for aside from a few familiar turtles (such as the one that cracked Aeschylus's skull from on high) that were resting motionless by open garden pools flanking the door into the great hall—the Chelonia placard hinting that the absent orders were to be found among mammals or fishes in other buildings—the Ophidian group was here housed to the exclusion of man's other scaly creeping tail-necked cognates.

The shorn snakes lay dim in the crepuscular sunlight admitted through a lanterned dome in which the glass had been yellowed by agelessly sibilant exhalations converging toward the sky from a community of indiscernible breathings. The air rutilant as a lily pond turned slowly with the movement of mankind's sphere. Oxygen seemed to lie low in mephitic gas. Nothing obvious transpired in the scenery of revealed dungeons. But the cohabitants bred there all the same, as they noiselessly assimilated the horror of their feeding, quieter than halcyon seaweed, detecting without eardrums the alien vibration of fearful footfalls that mixing with human whispers echoed throughout the vault though repressed and flattened like gunsmoke by the bottom of the atmosphere.

"I don't like this museum!" came the clear antipathy of Matthew's cry, which circled the muted hall with dreadful publicity. "Let's go have some ice cream." But he was unwilling to wait outside alone when his father offered him that alternative.

Roger he wakened again. This time the babe showed signs of having set himself at cross-purposes with his world, in no mood for walking or wheeling either; so Michael agreed to take up the burden—give the little woman a rest—if she'd like to man the pushcar heaped with freight. He carried the child for aegis or talisman, an apotropaic grail, a Christchild into the unpropitious shadows, repeating aloud *Hosanna to the son of David: Blessed is he that cometh in the name of the Lord; Hosanna in the highest!*

The father said to his savior "You can't fuss in a place like this,

How many of the people who lingered in clusters were disguising as fearlessness a hatred at the root of their fascination? Where was the pity in warmblooded eyes that joined each other in pairs to analyze the tangled mattings of low-liers long since overcome both by the supernatural Michael and by the supernatural master of all Muses? The partless passionless demons, distinguished in their several glassed colonies (species here and there amicably intertwined) as adders cobras corals kings rattlesnakes moccasins or other less famous breeds, lay warped in comatose reciprocity with their mates and fellows and with themselves. Now and then some prolating segment of a clotted mass caught the eye as a bafflingly isolated double-ended movement with no sure correspondence to any one tail or head.

Eudemons or cacodemons? the wingless Michael asked himself.

Hodge. You might quicken the still life!" Having neither the hips nor the endurance of a mother he found it difficult to clasp the baby for very long anywhere else than by the legs on his own shoulders at the back of his neck—what little there was of it, certainly less than the mother's which he was apt to cradle with both hands when his elbows propped his weight above her raptured breasts and his thighs divided her thighs, his thumbs stroking the hollows under her delicate ears, his extended fingertips threading the soft hair at the back of her head and pressing the fragrant scalp to lift it from the depths of the pillow as he sensed the slow gentle undulations of his lower body closing the circuit between them until he could follow with his palms the feverish roll of her upturned cheeks (altogether a most lovely method for amplifying the vibrations of mortality in both halves of the beast at once)— though the pants of the rider began to make a damp and corpulent yoke. The first oozing sensation of hot moisture disgusted and humiliated the family hack (himself already none too crisp) who held the ankles of his son almost straight out before him like the shafts of a stunted litter (since the seat made by those thick shoulders was too deep for the short chubby knees to bend onto); but the interfacing surfaces of conductive heat soon settled into comfortable equilibrium and if it hadnt been for cultural prejudice against this category of personal contact the warm scarf might have seemed to the horse an honorable gorget of paternity. He reminded himself that

Man's exitial enemies are not necessarily evil. Or anyway we're maybe their living evil equal—but aesthetically opposite, seeing that we do not shed our rotting skins and are hypertrophied with all sorts of grotesque branches and patently sexual eversions. Our tongues are grossly simple.

Behind glass they were less terrifying to him in ganglionic colonies, at least with a convoy of allies about him, than even the slightest and most harmless slip of a green garter handled in an Irish kindergarten or surprised on a sunny rise of the Old Joppa Road on the island of Cape Ann, which seemed free of residual danger (though because it was still almost a peninsula not quite as secure as Ireland or Typee). He was nevertheless striving to suppress signs of his inborn trepidation that might have conveyed Adam's punishment to his sons as hereditary fear, and he glanced at Ruth in admiration of her totally successful self-control. The older boys, faces he watched with care, betrayed no trace of the old curse—neither Matthew whose inchoate experience was still innocent of troubling historical echoes (thanks to the salutary intermediation of his mother) nor even Jonathan who knew echelons of attributes from books and studiously ranked his serpents by length and fang as he ranked his cats by size skill and speed.

A couple of boa constrictors no doubt male and female but inert with identical pregnancies rested from their recent labors of ingestion, their sickening lumps not yet

the urine of an infant largely evaporates in open air without much residual odor, and that anyway as Sunday was his own bath night and Monday always the occasion for a clean shirt this was the best possible time of the week to be wallowed upon.

No reins or driving signals had been arranged, nor periscope, and because the rider had as yet no learning of the language known to his colporter either to speak or to listen it was difficult for the upper man to communicate his interests to the nether. One of the purposes of the day was frustrated because in this position the old observer who didnt want to waste his afternoon could not observe the observations of the new observer. As an inexperienced horseman Roger clutched for safety with muggy hands first at the eyeglasses and the eyes under them, then at brows and hair, disheveling in momentary fright what in quick-won confidence he presently disheveled in glee.

"Ruth, what's Hodge looking at?"

"Me—No, now he's looking at your forehead. —Why are the turtles here? Shouldnt they be in the aquarium?"

"They're just lady snakes with feet."

"Oh yes, I've heard of the tortoise-and-the-harem!"

"They're hornier than their slithering sultans."

Ruth shuddered and said no more. Another incipient anxiety cast its shadow behind her eyes and under her throat: one more troubling sensation to push aside like

a quarter of the way from their jaws, which seemed restored to nulliparity though it was only a few days since they had strained and gaped inhumanly unhinged on horizontal axis, vilely distorting the form to which herpetologists are attracted. The Trustees could prevent people from watching Christians being thrown into the pit after hours to be hypnotised and crushed or scathed to death in the swallowing but they were unable to obscure or explain away the resulting deformity. Still, unlike the waxing burden implanted in some towered princess by Zeus or an intramural pikeman, the bulge would daily wane.

In other compartments many of the smaller kinsmen were viler and more terrible, comparatively vivacious from readier and less infrequent meals. Their heads looked proportionately larger and more intelligent in the malignant manner of assassins concealing instantly unsheathable weapons. Having no gift for the haptic sensuality of coiling embraces their teeth according to God's arboriginal decree bruised the extremities of their victims by ejaculation. Among these whose venom shot from the brain the Naja was most envied: he who was least in need of it enjoyed Buddha's protection against kite and man. But the asps and cobras-da-capello living here in several clans disappointed knowledgeable spectators (especially Jonathan) by failing to demonstrate the tumescence of anger and defense. They never saw mongoose or angel to arouse their fear,

wisps of hair. And Michael knew that the flesh of his flesh did not love him for his quips.

It took just twenty minutes to tour the abyss. Not far from other spectators they stepped viewing the bottom of the world among wingless dragons—who made no response to the kaleidoscope of guest entertainers: colorless bipeds forever milling like endless arabesques of dream. But even half that time, one sixth of an hour, was too long for a lazy unaccustomed chief to carry his papoose without shifting the load. He was too convex to form much of a side-saddle, so he began to carry Roger against his belly in a sling made by his hands laced together out front like a marching drummer's strap, leaning backwards in counterpoise. But the boy-child resisted, now jacking himself into a stiff log of wood about to roll himself over the edge, now folding into a hinged puppet trying to drop ass-first through the bottomless loop.

Matthew had resigned himself to the pedestrian circulation but was sympathizing with his father's annoyance. "Hodge-Podge, don't be so flimpy!" he said, reaching up to pat his little brother's ankle.

But this oddly silent struggle for freedom or change did not last long before it ended in change. The father made a new bosun's chair to the right, bandoleering the little pig's hams so that he could sit up with his legs dangling and kicking to the fore like a sailorboy sitting on the crosstree of a topmast too thick to hug.

Soon it was funny the way this father tried to lean away from him

and had learned to ignore shadowy motion pictures of the ancient enemy within striking distances baffled by the glass.

Surely, though they conspired with the Trustees in deceiving tourists as to their gratifications, Thanatophidia's institutional feeding was no more delicate than the gross messing of constrictors. When the sun was down how horrible the whiplash lust must be that succeeded the sinuous ease of basking torpor. Who could well imagine the absolute terror of batrachian or rodent captives suddenly thrust into those seething tombs for nightly sacrifice? Michael courageously searched the camouflaged dioramas and their posted muster lists for the Naja kings and queens (giant *bungarus*), hamadryads of oakless jungle, who lived on lesser vipers: terror upon terrorist, ruthlessness for the ruthless, fang over fang, throat within throat, metabolizing embolism embolized. But such redundant intensifications of nature were never meant to be easily visible, and this owl of the western oaks was spared the ultimate trial of his compassion.

All these distensile linear-lunged acutely salivating sternumless slithering neural tubes, sidewinding frictioneers, hiders coilers streakers climbers swingers and even swimmers, informers and negotiators, liars whiners and soothsayers, corpse-dwelling tailsuckers, guards to the tree of life, silent creeping incubi, striking baneflingers or crushing fascinators— all these podless counterpoises to the seraphim, viviparous oviparous

to look down at things, the way Da-da kept swinging and turning like a dancing bear, and the way his broad double chin wiggled when he looked aside to speak to others. The poor kid was at first too innocent to understand that his father had become more interested in the masterpieces than in his rider; but as Roger was about to tickle the jowls that ordinarily delighted in such tickling he began to sense the truth that he would only have irritated the god of his adoration. As his perception of life was still too inexperienced to follow the eyes of his fellow man he fell instead to gazing at—to engaging the attention of, and silently giggling with—a little whitestarched Salambo who was being moved afoot, pink-sashed and prim, by the same labyrinthine current.

But soon he tired of the girl and looked at the motes suspended adrift in the jaundiced air of the great cloudchamber, hearing less and less of the human buzz, eyes winking more and more slowly, comfortably desisting from all essays at thought, which every day of his life he was coming a little closer to attaining. Nothing in the architecture or the light drew his attention to what the family had brought him to see. The father mother and brothers and the other fathers mothers brothers and sisters were every one of them lovely or noble images of God that he was used to, and they were the only life he saw in the curving corridor they all paced together. Everything else except the shafting sunlight was uniformly dull.

and ovoviviparous—had survived the flood by deceiving Noah's pity. Thus licensed by a second reprieve they still beguiled the guileless children of men. Here Michael smiled to himself: they have never sincerely Apollogized! They have reduced life to the spinal stem. The line they make is not your contrast between surfaces but a wave of longevity made by abstracted movement along surfaces and beneath surfaces, or an arrowed wave of autonomous enmity intended to sting the hearts of men and women. But as a matter of fact they are the most integral of animals, perfectly continuous and equally subtile at all vertebrae, as if they were almost purely mental articulations and as if all their movements were reversible, never delayed by synapsis or rectification because motor sensor muscle spine and brain are but a single soulless cell. Ambiguous nonetheless, these fork-tipped lanciform curves. You can't even be sure that the head's the beginning and the tail's the end when you contemplate the hoop snake's primordial endlessness of line. The uroubolic circle sucks and swallows itself to the envy of any honest man at the extremity of his desire. Efficiency of form is no cause to hate these deadly pets of Hermes.

A few of the fiendish hodologists draped themselves upon fantastic branches of petrified trees like burlesqued anchor foulings or digitless dollar signs, in cunning pretence of unarmed vulnerability as dismounted wingless flora; but most of the wordless numberless

Slowly they spiraled toward the sanctuary of the circular fane to see what the Trustees had fixed as the omphalic altar at which chthonic good revealed itself under the aspect of chthonic evil. For the holy of holies was given over to Kaa the benevolent rock snake, Mowgli's special protector, longest monkey-eater in the world—seventy two feet overall, Jonathan claimed: thirty-six feet from his head to his tail and thirty-six feet from his tail to his head:: racer climber swimmer and font of wisdom. To Ruth and to most unread citizens the *Python molurus* did not look much like a benevolent friend.

Its tombstone, designated umbilicus of the zoo, was limened with spelean rocks laid as a cairn at the lowest depression of the temple. The barkless trunk of a gray tree with stumped limbs spanned the hollow at a sloping diagonal, above a waterless pool of slimy cracked concrete. The curb of this inmost circle's perimeter was barely two feet high, and the grated covering of the naos was supported only by three thin steel posts planted upon it to frame the three curves of glass each demarcating 120° of overextended transparency. The pit's ceiling deck, little higher than Michael's head, was hinged and padlocked. This lattice served as jungle foliage by dimming and slanting the Apollonian light from above. But at least the roofing of the cella was strong enough to hold nine dancing charities graces or fates, and one assumed an appropriate safety factor in the tripod that supported it.

integers were lying low together as a plexus of topological lines in a chamber lofty enough for a pride of lions. These retes mirabiles displaced less air than their daily prey, as if the serpents never had anything either gaseous or solid to eliminate after swallowing the matter that enlivened them. Michael wished to see them scatter like glints of moonlight on the sea, but he could detect no more movement than the slow adjustment of an immortal coil here or there obscurely implicated, or the slightest peristaltic glissando of an untraceable section. Whenever he picked out a bluntly tapered cuneiform head at the end of a corded brain the tiny beaded eyes were fixed upon an epoch of the future, meditating contraceptively on the world's occult egg, or warding by emanation the mystery of stolen knowledge.

He began to appreciate the architecture of dim hollow vastness that sheltered these fearful defendants. It filtered and amplified from the city's promiscuous noise any such vibrations as might augur their cataclysmic liberation, while at the same time it was calculated to expand and diffuse asmodean carbon dioxide that might otherwise have grown too concentrated for the health of viewers. But the tenants themselves did not appreciate the steam heat provided by their captors to preserve their toxic vitality in a sometimes anti-coldblooded climate. The taxpayers endowed them in perpetuity with the warmth of vivification—or at least until their emancipation,

Sections of the snake were discernible on some rocks six feet from Chapman eyes, and also the head, higher up, flat and inert on a horizontal ridge of dead wood, pointed athwart their line of vision. Inert but not asleep, though dreaming perchance. Neither torpid nor actively hungry: no bulge to be seen, but a slowly mounting appetite seemed to betray itself telepathically. It had learned to expect no opportunity here to start a search or lay its trap on the hunt, nor any need to do so.

The rock snake's celibacy seemed inflammable by hope but Michael

when the glass shall fall asunder the walls crack open and all quick-crawling fugitives find themselves beholden to the clemency of weather—as if the commonwealth felt it had nothing to fear from powers incapable of generating their own heat, easily exterminated in case of insurrection!—even though one man alone, or yet an unaided archangel, may well shudder at any blundering encounter with the tiniest of these innocents. Their urge for action was continually placated with milk and honeycakes.

and Ruth wondered if its provocation would have been male or female. Were its rightful ecstasies of egg or sperm? [Can the male and female thoughts of snakes be as different as the male and female thoughts of humankind? Both sexes are aggressive, both swallow their prey with the same agony. Shall we conclude that their form of life is too low for substantial distinctions of sex, the consciousness of which may not be much more widely distributed in the animal kingdom than the distinction of menses?] Man and wife separately decided to call it nor he nor she, Jonathan's assumption notwithstanding.

During its life sentence the god or pythoness (whichever it was, but certainly no mere messenger) had slowly charged the full length of its spinal wire with standing waves of vicious meditation on the disappointments of its dungeon. It could only dream the liberty to uncoil latent locomotive power and project its linear brain in transverse waves between Earth and her flora at a speed astonishing to featherless bipeds, like a Titan arrow loosed across the slippery pineneedles of a forest floor, or like the almightiest god's single spermatozoon cast as a wriggling thunderbolt through all pitiable barriers into the Great Mother's egg.

But dream or meditation broke off just as the Chapman family came to a stand there. The faceted head lifted itself and slowly swung toward his dreading idolizers as they gazed at its motionless coils trying to trace beginning or end. They were suddenly faced with its hard winkless eyes devoid of their images but seeming to pause in extrasensory divination of their fascinated flesh. A few seconds of general silence chanced to fall upon the visitors to its house. Roger sensed the movement of a line inside the glass and awakened from his own congenital reverie just in time to see the prehistoric countenance closing the distance to his own. Thus it happened that the first serpent he ever noticed was the world's most dreadful.

An instant only the child looked at the snake's blunt head moving toward him out of a figureless creche. He jerked backward in the father's arms and screamed, his glazed eyes searching wildly for his mother. For an awful moment the sound that was to follow the first utterance did not break through: it was caught knotted in the belly, strangling the rigid little body, stopping the second breath before it reached the throat. The bore of terror roaring in upon an inchoate mentality full of love and confidence whited the twisting face with shock.

Every other member of the family was nearly as breathless, in excruciating anxiety for the very life of its absolutely precious baby, whose soul now flickered out of sight before the onslaught of unconscionable experience.

But at last the terrible hiatus gave way to reflux. All resistance yielded to the lunatic wave that rushed between narrow walls in a devastating surge to the head of the fiord. The baby abandoned himself to fear, accepting it totally in crest after crest of convulsive sound, the vigor of expression fading only with the exhaustion of his vital capacity before each fresh peal of his protest, which became louder and clearer as the horror,—unnamed and therefore already unremembered—dissolved into morally aggrieved anger at the man who was his agent. He demanded recognition of the tort. The powerful wails issuing from the contorted red face were accompanied by streams of pearly clear tears. At first he refused to appeal for comfort even to his primary guardian, glaring in reproach when he could not avoid her eyes. But his own voice shattering the peace of the hall revived and prolonged the terror.

Without the telltale haste of guilt his father carried him firmly toward the door. At length the ugly paroxysm softened into quieter weeping. No longer rejecting or withholding love, Roger opened his arms to the mother and laid his wet cheek on her shoulder with tightly closed eyes as she at last satisfied

Ancestor of all life formed by the decomposition of chaos, primeval gene of all Olympians! Try to pity this poor ancient of God, created without evolution, forbidden feet hands wings tools and speech. See not the putrefaction of a Titan's marrow, nor yet Eumeniditic retribution, nor plaything or victim of the hotshot god, but resident of the Acropolis, or denizen of Parnassus itself, brother to Themis, though abhorred and persecuted by millenia of weak talkative ciphering simians as a monstrous autonomous organ without parts, mutilated at birth by a cleft in the earth. Have pity on the unshielded genitor of chthonic wisdom deprived of its origins and captured by mortals. Though prehensile only with its whole self, as vulnerable to the disc-harrow as its picture on an allegorical flag, it can neither love nor hate whatever cause it serves. We no longer find the silence to hear its hissing fear of our gears and slicing wheels. On human sufferance it must wait for the coming end of time, endlessly dreaming of the two great trees with which men

her craving to squeeze him to her breast. He was now possessed by nothing more than the sorrow of gradually abating tears; having lost the memory of terror he had no notion of its cause. Ruth shielded his peripheral vision with her hand as they passed the glass cells that lined their way out, lest he should open his eyes and recall the object of his fear.

The cold peen head of the limbless dragon had slowly retreated. The monstrous uraeus having stretched itself forward in instinctive predatory interest now dipped away in indifference to the choice prey that was (like all the less attractive shadows of the day) hopelessly beyond the invisible barrier of glass. Perhaps it was also faintly irritated by the peculiar vibrations that suddenly came dopplered from the retreating image as it faded.

Ruth stroked her baby's sweating head as steadily and calmly as if she had not been obliged to suppress as much as single scintilla of the cumulated fear that strove to betray itself through the pores of her body. Inalienable responsibility arrested the progression of panic and obliged her to insulate the occult reverberations from her child's subsiding palpitation. The fear that passeth understanding, she thought: she had failed to anticipate it when the family was misguided by Michael into precipitate verification of scripture. By her own negligence had she been accessory to this assault on Roger's infancy? She blamed herself for incautiously acceding to another one of

associate their earliest attempts at immortality. Does it regret its merciful disappointment of Gilgamesh's delusory hope for superhuman longevity? Our slings and arrows were brought upon it by the theft of eternal life, and by misapprehension of its service to woman. To lose life again and again in futile guardianship of others' treasure against armed heroes is not so terrible as to be feared and hated by them whom one protects, and to be named by the name for rottenness. He who once overcame Tiamat at the beginning of Creation can put nothing between himself and his modern enemies: no fur, no paw, no books. Yes, pity most of all the degraded and mateless inconsequence of one whose riddles used to call for sibyls but who can no longer make his warnings known by any medium.

But stay! Even in a New World of machinery the fate of Python is not so simply pathetic. His subtile wit might have thee think so, but a prudent man cannot doubt what it's doing here. This thick train of muscular undulating sphincters was hatched from the young pair first seen on the beach at Troy and has grown by delta increments of diameter (skin succeeding skin) in concentric rings that will never be exposed by cross-section. This is no mere adjiger brought from India in a basket.

Does it take a baby to see that? The demon has been sent by god to inhabit this grotto in order to attract another sacrilegious priest and his sons (issues of his sin), touching at Gloucester Harbor on the way (as

Michael's hateful tests, for allowing herself to enter this baleful cave with her children. Even now—lest she transfer more of her own fear to the fear-stricken infant, lest any of the boys absorb her instinct that this place was balefully signifi-cant—it took every nerve to refrain from hastening to the exit. Her knees trembled, and also all the other parts that did not betray themselves to her newest manchild or were concealed from the intelli-gence of others. Her flesh crawled where the little one must not sense it. Her soul was filled with Clytem-nestra's nightborn terror of the snake's mouth at her nipple. But she walked as slowly as she was able, nigh as slowly as she was wont, forc-ing herself to amble like a home-ward cow at milking time, hoping to keep the small face she swaddled from looking back.

Roger did look back. Nothing could stop him from looking back, squirming under his mother's hand. But he could no longer make out line or motion in a display further dimmed by tears and distance. Before he reached the open air door his brain had lost the eidolon of horror and his attention was turned from its echoes to a warm sensation of the frontier between himself and his mother. His dry screams of radi-cal terror had become wet sobs of resisted comfort.

The latter end of joy is ever woe, but the affrightment of a cheerful babe can always be as-suaged for the nonce by familiar caresses, by the one most familiar voice—the voice of the cradle say-ing familiar sounds, saying sounds

recorded before the age of photog-raphy when there was still a wind-mill where the Tavern is). Laoccoon Chapman, faithful sage short on piety, ruled by the boneless digit between his legs (boneless as a shark, more shark than snake), hav-ing wrongly attempted to dedicate his wife to Apollo, has been de-tained some years in the land of the sequoia to which he fled, where he's now come forward with his price-less boys like a silly monkey perish-ing in his own feckless curiosity. Is Chapman's Odyssey at an end be-fore the Iliad's finished? The dragon shorn of limbs wings and reason by its creator the Ancient of Days long ago swam round the Horn into the new Ocean of the West ocean to await me here, supposing itself still mastered by the master of nine su-perannuated spinsters, unaware that its commission had expired. This the worldworm's ignorance fright-ens me all the more.

And fear displaced all residual pity when Michael finally under-stood that Python had retracted itself only in order to seek its un-derground way. Shivers of cold im-memorial presentiment passed up and down the back of his neck and twitched his shoulders. Only by great effort did he control his shud-ders of reaction as he clamped the hands of his two older sons in a grip that death could not have loos-ened. His knees trembled. Match-ing Ruth's pace he followed her outside. The boys made no protest at being clutched like toddlers. They did not have to be dragged.

Without looking back, without glancing at the minor loathsome

that the voice always likes to say. "Hodgy Baby Hodge—Rocky Baby Roger . . ."

He quieted himself, biting and sucking the end of his finger, allowing his mother to wipe away the pearly streaks on his cheek. Land birds sang, seagulls prowled, children squealed, people bustled swished and buzzed in the near distance. "You havent had a good nap yet, little nestling. We've kept you awake too much, my poor sweet wet boy, wet at both ends, arent you now? But Mummie will change your pants. Soon we'll be home and Hodgy-Podgy can sleep in his own safe crib. I'll fix it up all clean and white. Good sweet Rog, your mother loves you . . . Roger the Dodger is sleepy now. Daddy will take us home. Daddy loves the Hodge, Jonny loves the Hodge, Matty loves the Hodge, and *I* love the Hodge! *We all love the baby boy!*"

She placed the tips of two fingers on his chest to mark time by alternating the pressure ever so lightly, not insisting on a tickle (as the father would have done) but leaving it up to him to accept the touch as a tickle if he was ready for it: thus tactfully did she show her respect for the sensibility of her very youngest man, restoring the familiar without violating the propriety of the occasion. She carefully underplayed her cajolery, for all these kids were as sensitive as their father to meretricious gesture, as they would be commensurately sensual in their mature affections.

pits that were to be enfiladed in retreat, their father swept the ground with rolling eyeballs, fantastically alert for the spot at which the atavistic reptile head would rise beneath their feet from a tilting rupture of the pavement, when the sky would suddenly darken at earth's lesion and a vast rolling rumble would fill the four quadrants, and his wife with his baby kouros would be swallowed before the terror-stricken eyes of Matthew Jonathan and himself by a second coming of the great American earthquake.

Out in the bright clear sunlight among familiar sounds of heedless people unprophetically wresting amusement from their boredom, heartened by the color of the trees and the jauntiness of fresh air, Michael shrugged off his vision; but it only coiled itself out of sight in the lowest chambers of his memory, and he could still hardly put his foot down without jumping or touch his wife's elbow without jerking, as if he was a body just severed from its head. He tried to expiate by words the shame of his leadership, with lips that must not sound them in the presence of wife or children: That goddamned cocksucking snake, that goddamned cocksucking motherfucking snake! After a while he was ready to comfort the kids with persiflage.

The corners of the homely little mouth turned up and the face became beautiful again. A smile began, paused in one last shadow of distress, and flowered—flowered to a giggle, eyes gleaming with the iridescence of freshly lifted rain in a summer garden—and Ruth's little man squirmed gleefully.

So the tiny mind shook off its unidentified trouble-spot and opened its heart to the full range of native magnanimity. Merriment and curiosity altogether revived. There was a delighted squeal at the sight of father and brothers catching up.

The family was purified—for a moment only, to be sure: but once a month is sufficient, or even more seldom.

"Why did Roger yell?" Matthew asked Jonathan.

"He didnt know there was glass."

"Oh! . . . I did!" And Matt turned quickly to ask his father the question that Jonathan had been about to ask (thereby innocently incurring the latter's displeasure, though in the immediate interest of hearing a good answer all recrimination was suspended): "Dad, what's your favorite snake?"

"*Favorite!*" The daddy smiled. "How can you have a favorite *snake?* Maybe I have a least favorite."

"That's what I mean! That's what I mean!"

". . . mean. That's what I mean!" Jonathan chimed in, appropriating to himself both question and answer. "Mine is a cobra as big as a python—a cross between the two. It can bite *and* squeeze!"

"The nearest thing to that is the giant cobra. It's called a druid."

"How many kinds of snake are there *really?*" Matt demanded.

"One point eight times ten cubed."

"That's not many."

"Almost two thousand."

"Wow!"

"Come on Dad!" Jonathan persisted. "Which is the worst, for you?"

In this family the father was expected to answer such tough questions. He had to deliberate before he could find a truth. "I suppose it's Shamir, a tiny snake that can break the hardest stone."

"Will it break steel too?" the middle brother asked.

"Have you ever seen one?" asked the skeptical one.

Rapid fire: "How does it do it?"

"I don't know. Asmodeus brought it to King Solomon."

"I've heard that name." Jonathan remarked. He had been pushing Matt (oversize clown perched on top of baggage) who had preempted the baby's chariot; but now in whimsical resignation from the conversation, as if absentmindedly, he abandoned the job, freeing himself of any obligation to continue it that could be argued by a parent in public debate, and capered off to look at something up ahead.

Michael took up the task of wheeling in silent annoyance, but Matt rode sweetly as the baby king's regent, and upon his head freshly sprung paternal love descended. The love of a a father is equal, but how can its

"I have to take Roger to the Ladies Room." said Ruth. And they all found that it was time to urinate, each in his own way, in the

fullness be felt simultaneously and undiminished in all directions?

Again he looks down on the soft hair (but this time thick and

manner of relief appointed by God and modified by society. Together they sought the official latrine, now of wills *e pluribus unum*, including Roger's (though, unsynchronized, he did not wait to reach the goal). Fortunately there was no doubt or debate about making their way, for the Trustees had provided a hundred signs directing visitors to the nearest comfort, whether to keep a man from despair when his back teeth were floating or to reassure a pregnant woman with excessive pressure on her bladder.

[Why am I afraid of snakes? (Ruth ponders.) My mother doesnt seem to fear even the poisonous ones and Daddy always said he used to hunt rattlers for fun. The story of the little girl picked off her pony and swallowed by a boa constrictor hanging from a branch she was riding under: it might be that. But Eve's serpent was smaller and different. It couldnt be a phallic thing: they don't get stiff. (She shivers.) Maybe they're nightmares of congenital deformity, tubular fetuses slipping out of the uterus without fingers toes or ears.]

dark) that so slightly protects a tender brain from blows above and behind. Yet Matt's body appears tough to opposing scouts, for it is sturdy and compact; his voice is powerful; he is a worker, possibly a leader. But now this middle child is lost in the rare enjoyment of special attention, the pleasure of his father's service outweighing without great indecision the embarrassment of being seen in a baby carriage.

Even at that age Jonathan would have burned with shame to be discovered doing what Matt is not loathe to do before strangers who will never know his schoolfellows, or before his family that already knows his every weakness. A second child may be content with narrow possibilities for dignity between the praiseworthy achievements of the first and the lovable charms of the third. He emulates without thinking; he's jealous and does not know it. He is a child little like his father, the least well known by his mother. He has to dig deep for his own talents, never suspecting that it is his very virtues that make him less conspicuous than the others whose devices and desires he so often assists. Without inner protest, full of conscious tender passion for the family about him, he responds circumspectively to his particular position, and by doing so enriches the particular love centered upon him by both mother and father. This special sub-circle within the family sphere produced a self-reliance delightful to the parents, as if Matt felt that he should learn not to be a burden before he assumed one, such as their own old age. From this emotional platform he is happy to scatter the feathers of natural fun.

"Some snakes are good." Michael says to this boy when he thinks it safe to return to the subject on all their minds, judging him strong enough to choose his own fears. "Even the cobra. But it doesnt matter to me because I'm scared of them all, including pretty little garter snakes that eat things like locusts that are bad for gardens."

Matt rises in his seat and twists around to see if his leg is being pulled, and he is not sorry to find that his father (as estimated from the thoughtful face) is speaking the grave truth. "Are you really, Dad? So is Jonny!" He lowers his voice uncertainly. "But *I'm* not. I'm not afraid of *them*! . . . I know how to kill rattlesnakes."

"I'd be afraid to, even with a gun. I'm glad you're not that foolish."

"Well . . . I'm a *little* afraid of snakes. I *hope* I never have to kill one!" He intended diplomatic kindness more than true confession. He added with a grin: "Jonny can't even pick up worms!"

[I suppose I ought to take the boys fishing sometime.]

The mother has been listening from her distance with one ear. In her opinion Matthew still feels the cold shade of the image Michael is keeping alive. In any case her duty toward the middle son this year seems acute.

Jonathan returns to the family with a tuneless new stanza:

> "The snake wanted to squeeze
> But couldn't squeeze
> —Because Dee-Diddle-Dee Diddle-Dum did!"

Which Matty repeats, climbing out of the motorless chariot and going to walk at his father's side.

"Pythons live a hundred years!" says Jonathan the cadet of learning, living up to imaginary standards of masculine imperturbability, never suspecting the faint heart that can conceal itself under the thick coat of a father screech owl. He did not regard as hypocrisy his own effort to scotch the fear started by the parents of us all.

The second son is innocent of such self-discipline. "That trip was scary, Dad. I don't know why. Right under my bellybutton!"

{*Postulants only*: GO TO ITEM (28) SA.11, page 281.}

(27)
SO.04.2
CONCRETE LIFE

. . . In the beginning were concrete phenomena, before they were divided into antitheses of awareness; and the female comes first in evolution: her experience is prime. The rest of us are differentiations and specially evolved offshoots. At first glance *fe-male* looks like a reduction or limitation of the word for male, but in fact it carries the force almost of *super-*male. It is a fecund creature taking precedence over an adjunct gender. The second sex pays its tribute from a distance, or does its seeding with the death of its motive.

The male must learn to handle and distinguish objects before he can be of any use in gathering, hunting, or cultivating food, whereas the female nourishes her young upon the substance of her own flesh, not by work or pursuit but by the milk of instinct. A man's testicles, sacs to cool his sperm (so it won't get sterilized by cooking), he keeps pretty much to himself, though they are visible signifiers of his special function. But the breasts that feed a child are not concealed: they proclaim and offer the mouth a surplus warmth. And can you conceive anything more palpable than the merged subject and object of another life within your own, increasing daily in weight, size, and thermal energy?

All other mass (even as it behaves in the earth's gravity) is abstract by comparison. Men have less sense of volume. We rarely speak of pecks and bushels anymore, and few know the bulk of an ounce of processed cereal. A man's life from beginning to end has little in it that comes near the concrescence of a woman's single day. Even in the reciprocal act of the jewel of games, the most common moment at which an urban male's awareness is concrete, he suffers in his rigidity no initial deformation of shape, and his sensation of the atonement is hardly deeper than cutaneous until he feels the quick kinesthetic extravasation that abruptly acquits his desire; while the woman's flesh is internally parted and displaced. Her nervous permeations vastly outreach his comparatively thin series of triggering signals; and meanwhile neither in the process nor in the aftermath is she normally possessed by anything like his conceptual pride.

Almost all of a man's taste of the concrete seems to him secondary, and even eating is no exception. Save in war, most men after childhood suffer practically no pain until confronted by disease or death. They think in transitive sentences, with subject and object; and their feelings reflect their verbs, which are less concrete than nouns, being abstracted from numberless acts performed by all varieties of agent in events of widely differing import. A civilized man's limited somesthetic experience is the sum or alternation of the three discrete *-ceptions* (in male-determined language)—*intero-*, *extero-*, and *proprio-*, especially the last—plus kinesthesia (most prized of all)—which on occasion communicate with each other across boundaries that the presiding self is much more loathe to wipe out than the boundaries within his partitioned mental life. This compartmentation explains his special delight in locomotion, which of all functions is the most easily separable from others because it leaves him untouched in its pure reversibility.

By contrast, his beloved recognizes classification of psychosomatic functions as piffling analysis.

Certain persons of "esemplastic imagination" are able to make poems—particular and unique applications of speech—by bursting historical categories of meaning. In order to do so, in tranquility, they think about what they feel, remember, and know. The principal thing they know is language, an immense but logically constrained abstraction of speaking behavior. Poets prove their inspiration in an abstract expression of unprecedented linguistic possibility, which in analytic discourse may often be regarded as paradoxical. "All thought becomes an image . . .", as Michael Robartes says of the Fifteenth Phase. The particular poem peculiar to a particular person's imagination is uniquely abstract.

Certain other persons are able to make dances—particular and unique applications of movement—by disregarding the habits and efficacies of action. The principal thing they feel remember and know is human movement as the concretion of motion. Dancers prove their inspiration by concrete manifestation of the body's kinetic possibilities without the mediation of symbolism.

The difference between those two kinds of artist I call sexualistic.

Some of the best are androgynes, especially those who lead the dance; and enviable are they in any art who can cross frontiers without false passports. But whoever assents to the gonochoristic superiority of women can't help shuddering, as Yeats did, at "that girl whose movements have grown abrupt, and whose voice has grown harsh by the neglect of all but external activities." A stream of emigres seeks military citizenship, new Amazons (single-breasted, that they may handle bowstring and arrow without hindrance) claiming their indisputable capability for all the administrations, scholarships, and mathematicses of discursive life as if justice demanded an alteration of their nature. At the very time when literature is trying to chasten the arrogance of logic in order to freshen all kinds of perception, modern women are misguided in hoping to be rescued from their seaworthy lifeboat by the ice floe of masculinity. Or, having had no experience in mechanics, they uncritically swarm aboard the first ship they see, most likely a ruptured old submarine getting ready for its last dive. That is how feministicism emulates masculine rapacity. Already our new colleagues are beginning to drive cars with one hand like nonchalant cavaliers, and to negotiate on two or three telephones at the same time. There's nothing they cannot imitate and match, marking their territories like male dogs. They flip away their cigarette butts with exterojective snaps, drink beer from the bottle, and give orders like an admiral topside on an aircraft carrier. When they fall behind in the end, defeated by an emptiness they can feel before men sense it, on sea and in the air, they will find that they have been persuaded to exchange their legal tender for the mere symbolic value of defaulting high-interest bonds.

Not that they are all ambitious fools despising their birthright. Women have solved the evolutionary problem of love and distinguished themselves from other female animals by attaining to orgasm. Having studied and surpassed their pleased leaders, whose development in this respect had long since been arrested at the stage of biological necessity, they were able not simply to imitate a single paroxysmal trajectory but (as Tiresias found) to manifold its contour into a family of curving surfaces scintillating with volleys of seizure as concretely imagined by the invaginated cortex of an awakened pelvic brain. This the female's boon to both parties serves as single staggering proof of culture's affect upon biological evolution.

With such a splendid achievement to their credit, women are not greatly to be blamed in mistaking similarities of historical form for analogs of value. For it does not seem unreasonable to suppose that if a few women, deprived of dignity and family, and dedicated to the pleasure of men, could develop and reveal to good ladies (who bore men's children and managed their property) the subjective rights of orgasm, then perhaps (now that the sexual injustice of nature has been more than fully redressed) the new feministagogues educated in masculine psychology will lead the modern girl across the ever-expanding frontier of subjectivity in a final reduction of dimorphic discrimination. Surely we can find plenty of examples in other species, with some of which in order to identify a female you practically have to see her eggs being delivered; and the opposite sexes occasionally confound each other.

But the laughable irony of attempts toward biological conflation is that the equation of human genders undermines the one virtue that some women now seem most determined to exercise: liberality of sexual affection. Women enlist as carnal cannon fodder at the peril of their one advantage, like heat working to disadvantage in craving to occupy a colder body at its own expense.

The campaign for justice will trouble the world a while longer, but feminine nature will not long misconstrue the counter-evolutionary cast of false emancipation. Those fraternizing ones I speak of are never inwardly and truly dissuaded from their intuition that a feminine self incarnated of feeling and body, provided that it is possessed of sufficient objective mentality to understand the way of the world, comes better skilled than a self ruled by emulation to attract the kind of attention that procreation requires, not to mention erotic climaxes or the new art . . . .

{*Postulants only*: GO TO ITEM (29) SO.04.3, page 303.}

(28)
SA.11

SANDY AND
HIS PIG

*R*eturning comb to hip pocket tossing thick lopsided shingle of palely streaked titian locks that protect flat head from the gods and snuffling by habit from allergy once a cold now ten years old Harmon Sandys turns toward the louvered swinging door OUT and unexpectedly confronts pushing through the louvered swinging door IN followed by two trained boys old senior friend and sometime host Michael Chapman longtime not seen. No one else could have been so honestly glad to come across that source of wisdom and sons. "Well well well, if it isnt Michelangelo himself! Howya doin guvner?"

Now this young man because of his hair and flair and freckled fair skin is called Sandy by fellow workers on the job (any job) by bedmates (in any bed) and by his few friends including Ruth Chapman and Michael being first so dubbed before his appearance on the California scene by pals of his youth in mockery of provincial Manhattan teachers who inveterately sounded the great Churchill-loving surname with an extra syllable and in celebration of the irony obvious to themselves in the name and mein of a tousled All-American Boy whose depravity was not credible to employer teacher or parent despite the fact that he made no effort to conceal it. It was the intelligence and ability that Michael had at first found hard to credit. Just plain Sandy commoners took him for, who were not yet undeceived.

He isnt one to be seen exposing himself to sun just in order to get a tan, what with an etiolated auburnity all too easily bemottled even by the pasty winter air of cities. Too nervous and jerky moreover, too hard a worker, to lie still long enough to risk the consequences. He wouldnt bother to take off his shirt for such a bland purpose anyway. In any case this maturing Angle can no longer be mistaken for an angel or wanted for one by any cruising lecher who could have his pick: loose and no longer lanky, bigfooted bighanded bigmouthed and no longer narrow at the waist—fleshy at the jowls and stomach, legs now noticeably too short for the towering thin-shouldered torso. His mouth is always grinning and it squeezes his cheeks wider than his broad forehead. Altogether like a Japanese battleship making an irregular impression of stratified pots and pans stacked tall.

He bends his head to Michael respectfully, and his deference is extended to Michael's sons. In the ill-smelling dimness of the public latrine this ingratiating dinosaur peers awkwardly at the boys and then returns to the father's dark-crowned smoothly rounded head masked by a face that even with the light at its back seems white as a Noh player's. Behind that visor Michael listens to the mumbling apologetic stumbling voice so easy and teasing to the ear and notices that Sandy's not as sloppy as he used to be but clearly heavier, slacker in the flesh, yet as equably mocking and goodnatured as ever. See the freshly shaven gleaming jaw and little yellow hunks of sleep in the corners of his eyes. See the tight knot in a broad saffron-flowered tie; see the rumpled shortsleeved Hawaiian shirt printed with larger brighter species. See also a clean seersucker jacket slung over the wrist hooked by a thumb into the left pocket of brown and yellow checkered trousers not very long since pressed that survived too short with popped button at the lower belly from his earliest days at a college. And the large uncalloused white hand, which is offered all round in his same old flimpy way. As Michael's doubled owl-eyes adapt to the cool dark atmosphere he wonders if Sandy who speaks with the same old self-deprecating friendliness is still capable of the same old heinous effrontery.

For Jonathan the reappearance of Sandy revives memory of earliest social pleasures with an amusing person more interested in playing games than Daddy ever was. But the encounter is too sudden. He cannot find proper words of response, or anyway make them heard above the muted reverberation of strange voices under a low roof, though he succeeds in twisting his wan face into an anxious fleeting smile at the embarrassment of being treated like a man. It has been three or four years—back toward the daybreak of personal experience nearly to babyhood—since his last sight of pseudo-uncle Sandy (once confused with Uncle Sam) who in this

public shelter now shows a certain insensibility, a trace of brutality perhaps common to all grown men, which he is not yet willing to steel himself to, not even in his father who assumes it in defense of the family, and
which he fears as a necessity to be faced in his own future like a personal
fist-fight or the death of his parents. He despises his brother's alacritous
reception of the man:

Matty's eyes sparkle to meet the unremembered figure of the well
remembered name that haunts his edition of the family annals, the name
known from curiosities and mysteries of household conversation in half
forgotten anecdotes connected with himself, as if he and Sandy had a tradition of special affinity; to see how cheery and different he is from beloved
new uncle Caleb. Matty speaks right up even as he rocks sidewise clutching his groin to relieve the worsening ache of his bladder and smiles
robustly at the unexpected pleasure of a hero's greeting. "Fine!" he cries
loud and clear.

"You all on your way in? Course you are. Go ahead. I'll wait here."

The Chapmen thus released move to the row of gently dribbling stanchions along one wall mostly white like the soiled flanks of winter-byred
Holsteins where they arent black. Matty runs quickly to his business and
splatters the puddles on the concrete floor never questioning whether they
are leakages of feedwater only, heeding not the tiny splashes on his bare
legs as he stands with a sigh of relief before the stinking porcelain with his
mind on storied Sandy whom he anxiously tries to watch over his shoulder,
twisting his body a trifle too far with the craning of his neck and thus
contributing some Chapman water to the misplaced water of careless
masses. It's lucky for him that his father stands to the windward, else a
much bigger leg might have been wetted.

Jonathan has found the driest place, least frequented, down at the far
end of the row. Strangers more or less sullen come and go about them,
walking around Sandy who has thoughtlessly planted himself like an
annoying supercargo in the center of the deck and raised his voice to speak
to Michael's back, loathe to pass up a minute of the reunion. He cocks a
thumb (seen only by Matty and one outwardbound citizen) toward a series
of black horizontal horseshoes resting on streaked white pedestals,
obscured by short raised doors all ajar except one or two which are tightly
fastened where one can see the collapsed leg-ends of eavesdroppers' trousers. "Myself," Sandy calls out none too modestly "I've just been having
the world's most underestimated pleasure." Michael grunts, Jonathan
shudders, Matthew wrinkles his brow in perplexity.

A spate of traffic while he is still waiting and Sandy becomes aware of
other people. Begging a series of pardons he steps back and forth out of
both ways with jerks of his head and a continual grin all the while he
keeps talking to his old friend, now considerately attempting to stay clear
of the various personalities who unzip and zipper up as they come and go
at various paces or (in a few cases of the old or very young) unbutton and

button up. "I heard you had another kid. He must be ass-high to a wolf-hound by now."

Matt shrieks a gratuitous reply: "Daddy says he's ankle-high to a royal highass!"

"Oh yuh?" says Sandy encouragingly.

Mortified Jonathan fancies he detects snickers in the room where never fear every ear is open. He asseverates to himself that he will never tell his marplot brother a single thing that shouldnt be broadcast. In his inconspicuous corner he shrinks from public affiliation with the family.

"Oh yuh?" says Sandy again.

On the end wall there are two mainly ignored unbleachably stained coldwater basins with drain plugs removed. Michael walks up to one of them, having been the first to finish micturition in spite of all his morning coffee, not because he has relatively the least to get rid of but because according to Poiseuille's law the flow in a meatus varies with the fourth power of the radius.

Sandy tardily follows this example. "Guess I might as well do the same." he mumbles. So they find themselves side by side at their ablutions; together they glance at the paper towel dispenser which looks as if it's been empty since Shrove Tuesday and in negligent unison go through the motions of drying their skin with pocket handkerchiefs. "You can always tell a gentleman: washes his hands after taking a piss."

Michael's makes his first concession to the younger man's amiability: "Harvard men wash beforehand."

"Oh yuh? That's true." It's Sandy's habit to respond to everyone's statements with equally attentive respect. He seems to reflect on whatever he hears; rambling ruminant shambling and shuffling, smiling and deferential, whether speaking or listening more inclined to listen, and more inclined to listen to Michael than to other men, though with women more inclined to act than either speak or listen, no doubt rambling and ruminating as he acts. ["Oh yuh?" to every No—and to every Yes as well? Does he snuffle and clear his throat trying to make himself agreeable when he has the girl on her back and there's no longer anything to mumble or listen to? Why should she care what he says or doesnt say or what strange noises he makes or how dirty his underwear is as long as he has and does what she hopes for or remembers?]

Matty hustles up to them, eyes ashine and still buttoning. He's never been the kind of kid to worry much about the urethra's last unhurried drools; black spots of moisture therefore spangle the scuffed toe of his left shoe. Directly he leads the men through that louvered swinging door OUT. A moment later Jonathan brings up the rear looking neither left nor right.

Once outside Sandy sweeps Matt up into his arms. He holds the chunky boy across his chest like a babe. Matt is not a whit embarrassed, in fact fairly beams his joy—not with pride or a humble sense of being

honored but with pleasure at the retrieval and expansion of forgotten affection, as if he were garnering a supererogatory quantum of goodness for the
world that needs it.

"Well old man, do you know you can still sue the city for building
sidewalks too close to your fanny?" Sandy quizzes him.

Matty giggles at the rhetorical question without feeling obliged to
understand such an unnecessary redress of childhood's disadvantage.

Jonathan remembers the orange man's pleasantry as having been
repeatedly directed to himself and now surmises with faint disgust that
it's the man's banal patter practiced upon every small child he chooses to
charm and that there is nothing in it truly appreciative of Matthew
Chapman individually or of any Chapman by virtue of family. At most this
formula distinguishes the speaker (though it hardly smacks of originality):
it certainly doesnt discriminate a particular relationship.

The middle boy is set on his feet again and now that they are out from
under the shade of the overhanging roof Sandy begs leave to take a picture
of the young ones in sunlight. Whipping a cyclopean camera from the
pocket of his slung blazer he hangs it on his neck by the black thong and
makes the brothers stand where the sign MEN will appear over their heads
in his composition.

"What brings you here?" Michael at last asks Sandy as politely as he is
able, taking no part in the arrangements and no interest in the prospect of
being presented with photographs of his sons as the pretext for some
future meeting.

"Didnt you know I'm a zoologist now? Working on penal reform.
Trying to get them to allow conjugal visits here. —Okay kids. At least
one of these snaps should come out." Scrutinizing the subjective fetish
itself he reverently restores the cover of its lens; but it remain pendant on
his chest like a machete for future aggressions against time.

Michael glances at him deadpan. Wouldnt be surprised at any job he
conned his way into. Sandy the homeless has already served at hard
labor—in no clearly established sequence, certainly in no ascending order
of prestige—as dishwasher Latin tutor barge captain faculty club busboy
plumber's apprentice chemistry teacher short order cook bank messenger
yacht club lackey highway surveyor's chainman camp counselor assistant
curator of genealogy letter carrier welfare investigator hospital orderly
diesel mechanic encyclopedia salesman acting circulation manager long-
shoreman pot-walloper oiler cabby and paid Roman acolyte among other
things—and in no descending order either—working like a Trojan careless
of his youth. Sandy's best vice is promiscuous work. [Some might think
that I'm the only one in these parts as crazed with work as he is, but my
dementia is highly selective and parsimoniously narrowminded, not at all
befitting American romance. Michael smiles to himself at the idols of the
literary marketplace.] Perhaps he's now assumed the performing art of
photography.

"Naw, just kidding!" Sandy adds reassuringly when he finds he's had no response to the joke, uncertain of the older man's sophisticated credulity whom he does not wish to embarrass. "Even though you might say that I've always been a penologist." He snuffles other mumbling words that never get out into the open air, tacitly apologizing for himself as always—for his clumsy effrontery. "You still at the store?"

Ignoring Sandy's inquiry Michael sends the boys off to wait for Ruth and Roger at the louvered swinging door in the other half of the building. Matty looks back smiling over his shoulder as Jonathan pulls him away toward the segregated facilities which are equal in every respect to the men's—in fact more than equal, to the measure of a fully doubled row of cubicles providing every second-class citizen who needs use of them a nice and even mandatory privacy. Furthermore they tolerate members of the opposite sex under the age of curiosity. Outside this gyneceum, which is more populous and noisy than the baronial hall on account of its much slower turnover, the two brothers join other attendant men lurking about with affected autonomy.

Meanwhile the old friends saunter into conversation awkwardly. Michael mulls over the chance and circumstance that once brought Sandy into his private circle, and it seems to him that no quarrel or spontaneous antipathy is so inimical as the estrangement of an accidental companionship that has led to exhausted boredom and been saved from open breach only by a total divergence of career and location. He toes the dust strolling and listening. It is intolerable to play any part but that of a graduated mentor—so little his enthusiasm for the surprise of this encounter, so great his distaste for renewing old ennui—sullenly glad that he has never revealed very much of himself.

"Naw, I'm a dentist." Sandy was replying to Michael's polite inquiry.

"Still? I heard that a year ago."

"Oh yuh? Yuh, still a dentist. I've always been orally erotic!" Laughing as ever without the full sound of laughter. Soon you don't notice the continual laugh, a habitual mannerism that fades out of a witness's awareness like the barrier of a window screen. "But we're married now."

"I didnt know . . ." Mindful of Sandy's reputation for abbreviated liaisons Michael has tactfully hesitated to speak of the marriage he has indeed heard of. "Is it the girl you brought to meet us the last time we saw you?" He reconstructs his impression of what sailors would have called a pig, messy scraggly piano-legged and impudently sarcastically political, her gender repudiated like the itch of an infirmity.

Sandy goes right on chuckling and snuffling, probably guessing what the stolid man has in mind. "Yuh I went back to her at the apartment again and we finally got married."

"Now I remember. Ruth was her name too. Welcome to the fraternity." But there was nothing cordial in Michael's tone.

"Thanks. Course she was pregnant. Decided to get rid of it though. Matter of fact she's staining now." He tosses the upper strata of his thick straight orange-blond hair (darkening with age) to indicate the other pair of exclusive louvered doors that he too is waiting for his woman outside of, and shrugs. "What the hell, I wouldnt mind having a kid. But she's got a job and there's plenty of dough between us. . . . When I don't like the way she treats me I've still got all the pussy I want coming to the shop. . . ." Some hyperbole here, for Harmon Sandys has never had and never will have all the inlets he'd like to claim. ". . . So I get plenty and Ruth gets as much as she can handle. —Say y'know you can really tell a lot about a patient when you stick your fingers in her mouth. I don't have to waste as much time out of the office as I used to. I've got no complaints."

This is what comes of a poor earnest honor student letting himself get weaned away from the disciplines of engineering by the bad company of a subtile literary classmate who preached a free love not yet practicable for himself. The awakened follower trustingly cultivated a catholic taste at the expense of his earliest calling. He came West. His apostasy from the sliderule sect liberated great chunks of time, even whole years, for loyal service to his new comrades, for weekends of labor strong as a professional's and twice as effective in assistance to his friends (such as more than once moving Chapman household chattels from one second floor to another), but above all for gratifying in pity and craving the opposite pity and craving of oppositely incomplete bodies.

In the meantime on the road and in two or three colleges he financed more than his share of various joint ventures with his vagrant eastern pal (now a poet), always doing the cooking and most of the dirty work. But now without even that one friend he's adrift in a lucrative profession, floating with the flood tide of civilization and no longer capable of surface dives. Having forsaken the decently productive furrow of technology to follow and protect the precocious intellectual who had sided with him in family disputes on the strength of chummy intimacy since the fourth grade, for nearly a decade Sandy has flouted the expectations of the father who bred him and the hopes of the mother who bore him, indeed partly for love of the ancient Greek language to which he had been subverted by the buddy who himself couldnt take it for very long and from which he had been distracted by the exigencies of technological education before he could get through the *Anabasis*, when he was still at the threshold of satisfaction. When he left New York he had no illusion that a rebellion which entailed earning his own living would restore him to Homer. Fuckit, there's always Chapman! he'd said to himself, and I shall see poetry in the making. But he never got back even to the other English poetry he wanted to read. The aftermath of the escapade had not come an end in dental school.

Michael assumes that Sandy regrets having served the sisters of the sacred well only as a distant Anglian auxiliary to their obscure legionnaires.

In any event he's had no reward for his apostasies but addictive desire for what he regards as humanistic experience.

Yet he puts Michael in mind of a young New England elm that quickens with greenery in the spring sooner than its fellows only to shed its aging foliage in the autumn before others have fairly begun to turn gold and brown as if deliberately hastening the diseases that lay waste to longevity. Young Sandy seems already old and gutted. But the joke is that he will be renewing himself in perpetual evasion of death at an age when the archangel of efficiency is like to be charneled from fatigue. And oddly enough, whereas Michael stopped smoking cigarettes only after a series of celestial battles at an advanced time of life, this ravaged reprobate who stutters and stumbles with vice has never lighted tobacco save to abase himself for such temporary purposes as to make himself especially agreeable to smokers suspecting him of virtue, just as he also sometimes affects an interest in other narcotics in order to protect his reputation and further his ends with dopey women. Nor does he park cars in front of hydrants write bad checks or cheat on his income tax.

Michael now sincerely attempts to recall the purer stages of Sandy's loyalty gentleness and considerate courtesy to everyone he knew, his respect for knowledge, and particularly his services to the Chapman family—and to see afresh (as at first blush through the eyes of a female patient) the cheerful countenance of a tousled fair knight who endears himself without ever explaining his quest. So the elder takes off his spectacles and rubbing the bridge of his nose blinks up at the deceptively crinkled lines on the face of his erstwhile friend. "How are you coming as a dentist?"

"Fair to middling. Have to take a shower every morning and put on plenty of aqua vulvar. Drilling and filling's right up my alley. But I like prophylaxis the best. I make out better when it's quiet and easy."

"And Ruth?"

"Slower than some."

Michael believes this wisecrack but it brings no acknowledgement to his grave face and makes it even harder than before to assume a revival of dead geniality. "Are you on your own?" he asks in his throat by willpower, scarcely moving his lips.

"Not yet. Still at the Joyful Jerker's. He's letting me get some surgical experience. But I've been saving up to start my own practice." Snuffling he savors the success in his freelance career as if it were a run of luck in gaming. The very fact that he seems artlessly unconscious of his gauche picaresquing has always lent magic to his spear.

In truth, though bearing a heavy scutcheon of vair and lead he's a soft-bitten hoplite mounted on skates where there's never any ice and not another player in sight. He's still seeking a teammate among wraithy strangers, still scaring up nothing but light scrimmages with lonely members of the opposition who momentarily sympathize with the uliginous appetite of his tined crotch, all of which is sometimes charming simply because it heads off love of pelf and keeps him a cut above most other American men in any survey made by Tocqueville's ghost. It's clear that his new wife has not dispelled the old mild melancholy cynicism. Sandy the Maladroit has goosed one more profession.

"It's too late for them to take back the diploma!"

"I bet you could get into the F B I !" Michael remarks, marveling little less than Sandy himself.

"Oh yuh? But I never got a law degree." Sandy grins like Little Orphan Annie's dog (but snuffling instead of arfing) as though he's already looked into that possibility. Laconically shrugging he explains how he did get into the California State dental school: "I told them I had found myself at last and wanted to make a lot of money. Said I'd always been frustrated because I couldnt make a good living with my hands as well with as my brains. This they liked to hear. The Dental Association is a lot more public-spirited than the A M A but their personal drives are the same."

Michael still has not returned any of Sandy's grins, trusting even that a small exaggeration of the characteristic dryness in his mein will not be taken painfully amiss. "I suppose you graduated at the top of your class."

"Oh yuh?" Sandy laughs more distinctly. "Afraid not. Met some jazz musicians just back from Vegas—or rather their wives waiting for them in a bar. Took me home with them, big apartment up on the hill. The five of us never went outside for three days. Just before final exams, the weekend I'd been saving to catch up on my studies. Almost decided not to go back at all. Best time I ever had! But I've never been so dehydrated in my life. One of those girls and she wasnt fat either had the biggest knockers you ever saw and every time she opened her nutcrackers I saw what I'd always been looking for. The other one was a dual-purpose job, more of a chow hound, and her dental arcade was beautiful. They were both so excited that even with the three of us they couldnt get enough. It was quite a sensation to watch two women trying to make each other happy. . . . By rights I flunked, but I told the professors I had Asian flu. . . . Boy my pathetic phallussy ached like a bastard all that week! . . . They said they knew I knew the stuff because I was their best student in the clinical courses, so they passed me. But it was only the first day of exams that I actually fucked up beyond redemption. . . . They were nice to me."

"Glad you got through. An industry professing to admit that its own existence should be unnecessary can use a guy like you."

"What the hell, I can use it! The Painless Jerk lets me take all the patients I want and I get a decent cut. I'm going to practice in Oakland maybe. That's where the population will grow the most. Ruth wants to buy a house. Might as well get respectable. Gonna get a sports car I guess. . . . Oh well, it's too early to predict and too late to repent!"

The unresuscitated dregs of animation immediately freeze on Michael's face. He scowls at Sandy's presumptuous quotation of ipsissima verba uttered passim in lighthearted moods now almost unbelievable that unluckily Sandy used to attend upon. The ostensibly flattering refrain from ancient cheerfulness echoes like bitter mockery to a mature mind sourly out of spirits. The impertinence rankles. Michael restores his glasses to their proper place, further chilling any residual humanity in his expressionless face, and looks away.

But Sandy seems to notice nothing untoward, his quick apparently defended by an innocently puzzled affection quite unlike the singleminded yen that carries him as far in his gynotropic quest as Galahad on another search who was preserved by a different purity. Michael's anger at the liberty Sandy has taken prevents him from betraying so much as a smidgeon of idle or urbane curiosity about the orgy. Were those jazz players and their broads no better than dazed dopes and slatterns more anodyned than sensual, or would they have been found peachy alluring and keenly fascinating companions by ladies and gentlemen of good taste—friendly sybarites (black or white?)—with whom Michael himself might have been passingly unashamed to lay bare the glabrous lust of a stylite? He can't help wondering exactly what they did in that quincunx of pleasure. Lowermiddleclass middleaged clerks usually have never seen the desire of other men, and never more than one naked female at a time; they never sate the curiosity of desire.

For the second time this day he finds himself obliged to conceal the outward and visible sign of the inward and invisible aspiration that's now as embarrassing as if he'd stumbled upon a forbidden picture lying in the sunshine on public grass. He shifts his suitcase in order to carry it in both hands across the bottom of his belly, affecting to amble into it lazily like a man who for a short while elects to manage his burden inefficiently while he rests his best muscles. But the hidden involuntary response is a thing of the moment, not never to return, a capricious shot from the god's bow aimed randomly, easily undone only because it's even more easily revived—in itself merely a heady sample of whimsical powers dwelling in an ancient forest, not much different from a thousand other incidents that animate any male pilgrim in his progress.

Michael's attention reverts to real and present company, for Ruth and Ruth having also met and recognized each other come out through that other smellier louvered door, Pig Ruth courteously holding it open for Horse Ruth her better who is pushing the chariot with Roger refreshed.

They approach in more genuine rapport than their husbands. Michael's Ruth a chestnut thoroughbred trimly groomed now seems tall as well as slender. From time to time with a smile she replies (speaking but never opposing), mostly listening cordially to the stouter Ruth who busily explains herself, while Roger rising and stretching toward his daddy inarticulately urges the women forward.

Sandy's catamenial wife was first presented to him at a Women's Surrogation League meeting he had boldly attended on the make; but Michael now sees that perhaps she isnt so bad as once had seemed and may now be qualified on private occasions as a warm snuggling hedgehog. Her publicly exposed pimples have vanished, her neck is washed and all her paste-white skin is smoother; she has painted her mouth as other women do; the frames of her glasses are pertly pointed sloe-eyed in the accented fashion of the day; she wears the same kind of raised heels and sheer stockings that other ladies wear. These recent conformities to custom though not yet comfortably or prettily matched to the strides and gestures of that uneasily feminine body hint at a pleasing evolution of self-respect inside the bundle of purposes and complaints. They suggest graduations of her intolerance for a stupid world. Her short black hair still bravely avoids beauty parlors but at least there is a token of style in the leather barrette that makes it stick out in back like a filly's.

[People can change fast in their youth—witness Sandy himself who was and didnt just seem cleancut and wholesome before bad characters cut him out of the herd. I'm prepared to revise my opinion of the girl. It should be understood that my prejudices are only scaffoldings that pretend to nothing but tentative convenience of opinion reasonably deduced from previously induced working hypothesis. This method spares me scientific limitations of vision by freeing my rational intuition of rigorous empiricism. It's only pragmatical that memory and abstraction should guide my evaluation of perceptions that I don't have time to expand. The prejudices against me in certain quarters are quite different. They are based on economic class professional status and mere appearances.]

Sandy greets the newcomers. "Well let's first look into Chapman's latest homo! Didja ever see such a kid!"

After one long gaze to make up his mind Roger smiles wriggles and laughs in response to laughs longfingered pokes and smiles from the burly simplehearted stranger. The others stand about watching the instantaneous friendship burst into flower. At last Sandy straightens up and in all solemnity still contemplating the child declares in a low voice "He's a remarkable boy!"

"Well don't erase him!" The boy's mother responds with wit noticed only by her witty husband.

But they all—men women and children—smile or laugh or clap their hands, delighted with the splendor of her son, Ruth Sandys for the first time since puberty fully opening her eyes to the spring garden of childhood. It's clear that Sandy's genuine fancy for Roger has coincided with the enlightenment of his wife's instinct by this heavenly Eros sprung for them out of the blue fully armed. The image of Roger is henceforth lodged as the ideal of a piglet. The swift adoption can be seen in Sandy's face.

Horse Ruth is glad that one more great decorticator is ready at last to go to a woman's core. Michael looks for exultation in Pig Ruth's perception of her husband's new desire, but clearly it's with wistfully unselfconscious hope that standing there in the unpolitical agora, which with no more than fitful interest she has consented to visit merely in order to keep an eye on him, the cure and triumph of her crippled love are suddenly disclosed. Among the citizenry of a public park she silently attends her first confession, surrendering to biological grace.

But there's no surrender to Sandy. No matter how far she may have retreated in secret she will never concede the cause to a man, partly out of policy and partly out of the distrust with which her fortified pride has singed their language of intercourse. She has never bolstered Sandy's efforts to discuss the emotions that she scorns as irrelevant. Yet an intimation less definite than the vaguest thought informs her that because they both now wish her to lay an egg she will conceive within the fortnight and that she must put aside the fiercest of the signs that have pronounced her independence. And Michael reads in Sandy's face the ultimate tractability of a cuckolder who will serve his wife as phalarope.

At this juncture, which happens to have been fixed by an accident that can be spoken of as God's purpose (the Chapmen being chosen for messengers simply as veterans of their own fixes), Ruth the pig stoops to examine the smallest Chapman in profile, balancing herself with one hand resting on Sandy's arm. She looks up at Ruth the horse with an open admiration

entirely new to her susceptibility, devotedly and almost humbly hoping for this gentle woman's excellent friendship. All at once she loves the lady who for a few minutes at least has induced her to love everyone in sight and brought fondness to the troublesome craving for her arfing husband. And even Michael, of whom in the past she has heard enough from Sandy (in respectful reminiscences which only confirmed the mutual hostility she had immediately struck up with him on their one previous meeting) to instill hatred, is included in her general amnesty for all those who engender babies in the marriage bed; and now she looks on him as godfather to a creative act of her own. [As if myriad addled egglets were not still seeping from her moody spring, where far more frequent seed has yet to lodge itself and start a receptive cell on its way to term!]

Ah but now suppose that Roger werent here! Unsuppose that key person and the unique knot of time and space that dictated his existence; retroactively skip that one forgotten and indistinguishable plunge of a flushed old unicorn into the occult rose at his night-side, the boon of a long day's work in the public light, probably after some ordinary sunset clogged with purple fatigues: then there would be no infant Eros now to make an epiphany of this encounter:: then the destiny of the childless worldly pair would have remained unmodified.

But without Roger's existence what would have been the actual affect of this otherwise unaltered meeting on the history of our multiparous couple his parents, aside from different future memories of an unimportant occasion? Presumably very little.

Presumably I say, but not necessarily. If Roger were not in the

Nothing Michael says or does not say can now discourage the sociable affection of this imminently fertile couple. Ruth Chapman's ingenuous kindness to them stirs up her husband's relaxed fear of obligation to tedious association. He does not wish to cultivate patience for unwanted clients and in this case feels unconditionally absolved from a Christian's charitable duty.

"He's got a touch of you in him." Sandy observes.

Heretofore this resemblance has not been detected to Michael's knowledge by any other eye than Roger's mother's, least of all by his own. A remark that amuses the mother and flatters the father, in fact softens him. The best reassurance a man can have, coming from a disinterested third party. And so the virtue of Roger the Puisne works wonders in his own family as well.

"How's it going with the vending machine?" asks the professional man turning from the child to its proud father. "Are you still donating blood to St Valentine's cash register?"

"We got a beautiful new one." Michael answers bridling solemnly and smiling for the first time at Sandy's cynical sow who should know sarcasm when she thinks she hears it and embarrassing his own Ruth who knows it isnt sarcasm and abhors the perversity with which he likes to show himself as a sort of mechanistic crank.

The pig charges in for her shot at capitalism. She cocks a thumb at Sandy. "This bastard goes shopping in the supermarket with a sliderule!

picture and only four Chapmen found themselves on this excursion yet still happened upon the Sandys team—under such supposition the present interview (sans Roger) might have issued in an improvisation more singular for the Chapmans than for the Sandyses, in accordance with options of free will exercised right there in broad daylight.

As for instance Sandy and his partner ever alert to possibilities (undiverted from their ends by any such bemusement as a child) ask Ruth and Michael in practiced tones to come to their City apartment for dinner and a little party next Saturday night, for Hecuba upstairs could be enlisted to guard the two boys against dangers of darkness with the hall doors open so that she can hear and act if their sleep is endangered. Now Michael has had inklings as to the propositions that eventuate from these introductory parties; so even though Sandy offers to pick them up and drive them home across the Bay in order to make the night-out as convenient as possible, anticipating their chief excuse for refusing, he hastens to decline with the trump plea that he can never stay up late because of his early morning regimen, making sure that Ruth is given no chance to mar his counterplot, for he's not sure whether or not she remembers or wants to remember what he once told her of his suspicions. [It might have been a different matter if Sandy were a peer in discretion and reticence, if the pig were finely formed or sweet tempered and deliquescent, if she were affectionate and sympathetic to

You should see him figuring the costs per pound!"

"Oh yuh?" says Sandy, a concupiscible rather than irascible bloke, chuckling and snuffling.

Ruth Chapman of rational cast offers to pacify her new admirer by approving Sandy's defense against the commercial system: "I wish I knew how to do that! Michael thinks I get fooled by price tags."

But Ruth Sandys continues to ridicule Sandy's grubby technical zeal on behalf of her household unit. ". . . wheeling the cart along with his big stomach while he's busy with his hands." [And what the hell are you doing in the meantime sister?] But her tone has already lost its habitual whine as if in the glow of her annunciation she's begun to appreciate her own tender percipience in loving that Knight of Rueful Figure.

The two census cells agree to walk together part way to the pleasure garden where eats are sold and where the little ones can get their father's money spent on them for other amusements as well. Is it in deference to seniority or to breeding skill or to Roger himself as a particular offsprung dependent that the Sandyses (like comites to royalty) escort milord and milady and their heirs toward the last object of the day's progression?

Under the full brightness of a hot afternoon they emerge from an alley of trees into an open place full of humanity and devoid of beasts. Puffs of Pacific wind gently disperse pockets of heat before they become quite unpleasant, but nothing mitigates the placid or irritable Ruth (as in this Rogerless scenario she is not), bisexual or not, and if Michael himself didnt believe that in such experiment lies danger to his own erotic prestige at home (for who knows that there are not vague disappointments hidden in the breast of a chaste wife which can be focused into burning discontentment by a taste of hornucopian fare, the more so by her husband's sanction and perhaps even with his perverse encouragement?). For what stronger reason, besides the proprietary blood-rights of procreation, have men always liked to keep their narrowly experienced women to themselves?] He might at least have accepted an invitation to the preliminary meal, but he knows full well that in any further negotiation the other man (Sandy himself or another trader) is bound to have the better of the bargain, a rose more precious than any common jewel that Ruth's husband can hope for in exchange. There have been flaming times, thinks the owl, when I would have appeased my priapic mania in almost any open purse, honeyed or not, but today I'm so pleased with the woman dowered me that I can hardly envisage a substitution, especially for both of us at once. Anyway, the purebred mare would shudder with contempt for me and shame for her misplaced conjugal love if she knew I entertained so much as the theoretical possibility of such a thing, even with a saintly scholar or any whatsoever best friend, to say nothing of a stud like Sandy. Yet on the other hand (if it ever came to the point where the proposition is less than absolutely ruled out) perhaps she

noises of milling people. Their shouts and cries fall together canceling one another or reinforcing waves of murmurous talk, joined with the faint flapping of clothes the creaks of women's harnesses the jinglings of men's pockets full of money or keys and the squeaks of baby wheels, all blending into one continuous human grunt.

It must be a seething sound to the seabirds feigning indifference as they watch the waste of food in this feeding of the fattened. The manner of the gulls dissimulates the appetite of their discriminating eyes. They observe events not only from the sky but also from perches not far overhead whence they can from time to time dart down for a differentiated morsel, suddenly discarding the pose of fellow sightseers.

"You should see that goddam Harmon in the store I'm telling you when he follows the young mothers up and down the aisles. He goes right up to the feminine hygiene shelves with them and tries to get their advice. You'd think it was for himself. Says scuse me Mam when his arm accidentally on purpose brushes up against their teats. (He likes cows.) When I'm there I

would be more jealous than ashamed, since (putting myself in her place) the other husband wouldnt necessarily prove more demoniac than her stolid owl, and the other wife might not look like one who'd necessarily suffer the talons of a domestic bird of prey unmoved.

Thus to this unrealized mooting of a secret event Michael's response would have been such to incur no social obligation and no liaison of any kind with the Sandyses. Since the offer would be turned aside before it could find voice, whatever might thenceforth have taken place between Chapmans and Sandyses would not have differed greatly from what actually will happen as a result of the Eros episode: namely, Michael is going to wetblanket the actually incipient chumminess founded on more seemly grounds the best way he can without abruptly hurting the feelings of the newly philoprogenitive youngerweds who now actually emulate the orthodox occupation of most olderweds and who all at once seem more interested in kidnapping than wifeswapping.

have to pretend I don't know the son of a bitch. God knows what he does when he goes to the store alone. . . ." The oblique allusion to her own ichor is only a beginning of disinhibition in the company of these unlooked-for companions through whom she rails at Sandy like the mother of Jack-and-the-Beanstalk for not bringing home the bacon. But she seems to attack him without malice, calmly and disinterestedly, according to habit that reflects nothing of her lovely new broodiness, never smiling or intending to amuse her audience.

"Oh yuh?" Sandy mumbles thoughtfully, as if she has been quoting or misquoting some scoundrel he'd never heard of.

With all the strength of his silence Michael conjures the Sandyses to leave the Chapmans, to want to go away, to go away, to go see the chaffing gibbering monkeys, to restore equilibrium by absenting themselves. But the pig and her boar obtusely block out the message coming to them in and under his terse politenesses and long silences; their blaze of friendliness is slow to fade, much slower than the sparks of Michael's concealed interest. Matthew and Jonathan are again ranging far afield as the heavily burdened owl feverishly and silently fuming walks beside his equable Ruth staring straight ahead and listens with excruciating anxiety to the comfort she gives the clinging pair by encouraging their conversation. He worries about her appreciation of the situation and fears for her prudence. It is possible that even she his own flesh hasnt noticed his attitude, maybe because she's almost forgotten he's there. Every now and then he says something to redirect the drift of conversation, having prepared plausible interruptions to any invitation that might be hovering on his wife's lips if she hasnt sensed his warning.

But as he will later understand he needn't have feared a lack of circumspection on her part. Pity for the Sandyses and approval of their attention to the only true product of successful marriage kisses has turned to mild distaste—unlike his own, perfectly tolerant and totally disguised—by the lewdness that gurgles in their talk and smuts the bright image of love. The scabrous words that only when seldom spoken serve their meaning are commonly less often sounded between men and women (guardians of civility) than among men alone, who then mostly have no notion of signifying stench or passion; but these two participants in the debasement of verbal currency rather unctuously play the ugly sounds as the most habitual of joint expressions, situated conveniently at the middle of their keyboard for cross-handed duets. In an outworn rebellion against the philistines (treated all alike) who ruled their separate infancies this marriage is fouled by language more obscene by context than the vandal usage of sailors who have been taught no vocabulary between the poles of curse and prayer.

[Roger, close to the trodden colorless grass of the marshaling grounds, close to the gray black pavement which on their course alternates with it, down among people's legs, down on a level with other constituents of an innocent realm, hears the palaver above his unprotected head as a remote component of the universal commotion.]

Sandy's snuffling chuckles and muted guffaws keep things going like the interjections of an unwearied hostess, courteously acknowledging all statements with "Oh yuh?", even those of his wife as she interrupts him. On her part she prods him when he flags, and she needs no spurring to hold her own in a vigilant continuous voice that hardly misses a beat, sometimes raising a reserved laugh from Horse Ruth or a faint unwilling smile from Michael as he looks straight ahead wondering if she's privy to the confidences he heard a little while ago, for instance that a dentist can always manage to brush the breasts of visitors to his chair with the back of his hand if he wishes to test the authenticity of their contours and estimate the probability of favorable response to the virile eminence of his white-duck fly before he calls attention to it with a rub against the outside of their elbow on the arm rest.

[The girl now of epigamic aura who was once so poor in spirit and obviously underweening of Sandy's first unexpectable favor—what hold has she found on him to anchor so well her raffish vision of pregnancy? Why does he accept the humiliation she deals as if it were a witty honor? What does she do for or to him that makes his degradation worth it? Maybe for one reason or another she was the only one of his paramours not quite unmarriageable, or the only one who in wedlock would not be too proud to share the benefits of what must have been an enormous induce-ment to union; but now she's somehow confident of holding him for life without disavowing her viraginity.]

Pig Ruth lights a cigarette and holding it like a man between thumb and forefinger trots along between Horse Ruth and Sandy, who keeps the pace by ambling half sideways indulgently and seems to see her as a mar-velous machine that knows and coins everything if you give it a little lee-way. [She's the type of female that in certain species resembles the male. It's a wonder she doesnt lift a leg to leave her mark on the trees we pass. Yet this same strident person would still look poor in spirit and thor-oughly underweening at a wartime dance, where any sailor's first glance (without even approaching close enough to expose himself to the aggres-siveness of her compensatory speech) would be his last—except on nights of acute shortage when she might be grabbed without much ceremony in the near certainty of a quick piece of ass. Pigs are sometimes pretty hot in the pants and never expect excessive consideration, being only too glad to let any guy into them before he loses interest, certainly never expecting to see him again, for they may not have another chance before the war ends and its maritime imbalance of the sexes.

But an appraising seaman's first impression would be dead wrong about the spunk of this particular stringy-haired creature. (Her pony-tail is already loosed.) Having been nailed by a very satisfactory boar, this woman of strong will and clitoral pride, now with the bloom of fructifica-tion forecasting itself in redoubled assurance of countenance and gait, seems to intussuscept his manhood and wear it in her placket, sneering at any petty infidelities he may commit at the end of her leash.

Now pitching her voice at a higher level she is making sure to leave no doubt that she loathes her bondage to the free enterprise system, scorn-fully discerns the stupidity of businessmen, and regrets that she ever learned to type. She thus apologizes for holding down a job that fails to distinguish her from the herd of high-heeled slaves whose culture she defies (as for example by refusing to adorn herself with the false scents that they and their men take for granted especially in a close office, airing her sweat as an odor of sanctity).

"Oh yuh?" Sandy reiterates. [Of course his attention must be else-where, yet he really sounds as if he still finds her line of thought interest-ing. No doubt he's really thinking of other snatch.]

Mistakenly encouraged by the passivity of her Chapman escort, she recidivates to the spiritual state in which she lived before entering the Ladies room half an hour ago, her manner no longer softened by traffic with horse and archangel. "When my vacation comes up this summer I'm just going to take my two-week's pay and never go back. I'll say see you later and I won't tell them off because I want the old bitch that runs the department to count on my coming back. But I'm not going to walk through that door again. If they try to call me at home I'll tell them to stuff the job up their ass. You wouldn't believe the crap I've had to take. They try to make you work right up almost to the dot of four-thirty and they get pissed off if you're ten minutes late in the morning! One morning when old Harmony gave me a hard time I was twenty-three minutes late and she told the office manager so he called me in. We'd had run-ins before. American Legion type that thinks he's still a sergeant in the Marines. When he started yelling at me I got mad and one thing led to another. Shut up you asshole he says. Assholes can be a good thing I say, if you had an ass you wouldnt be so full of shit!" She gave a short laugh: Q E D . "Sandy got a kick out of that one, didnt you old boy?" She touched his arm again.

"Oh yuh?"

Mrs Chapman a former office girl who had observed all the conven-tions and used perfume asks how Mrs Sandys can get two weeks vacation after only six months of service.

"Oh I told them I'm married to a sailor at the South Pole who won't have been home for two years except on his leave in July. I'm getting half of next year's vacation in advance!" The femaster's triumphant satisfaction with her swindle of the tender-hearted office manager seems founded as much on pleasure in her skill as on the righteousness of her enmity to authority.

Michael is so disturbed by her attitude toward management that he's glad to hear his wife open a new subject by asking her namesake where she and Sandy will be going on their vacation, making it sound as if she her-self and sons like all other families are as a matter of course taken every summer to the seashore or mountains of their choice by a devoted hus-band, her question ringing sincere and generous.

Sandy intervenes with his snuffled version of the stereotyped bur-lesque of a southern drawl, bending forward to look around his wife and past Ruth Chapman, reaching down the rank almost to Michael's round stomach with a knobby poking forefinger that bends upward when stiff-ened: "Why, don't you-all know, we all aim to sojourn at Portsmouth Vagina, naturally!"

"Shut up for the love of god, Harmon!" The pig angrily pushes his arm away. "No one wants to hear your stupid puns."

"Oh yuh?" His grin persists as he sheepishly withdraws. but his jest has told a lot, and it serves to remind Michael that the impudent porcine pachyderm herself is a Virginian nurtured in the reestablished Church of England who's crossed both the Mason-Dixon Line and the continental divide shedding her inherited garments of courtesy at every stop-over in a career of vandalizing the genteel precepts of her softspoken mother by harrowing every hell. And now this very hour she's chosen the most twisted hook since her own conception with which to torment her father the Admiral as well. Now for the sake of earning plane tickets home she'll rejoice to hold her peace at the office and conceal her morningsickness even though she'll therefore have to forego the satisfaction of flaunting the belly-tale of a false libertine life during the protracted cruise of her fictitious husband's icebreaker.

It just goes to show [according to this prophecy of Michael's] that the most willing martyr to the W S L 's revolutionary movement can't help recognizing the self-degradation that's come of adolescent insolence and must eventually act on the secret hope of reconciliation (not unmixed with malicious ascendancy) when she's able to take home a grandchild in vivo. He covertly watches the striding Tidewater blueblood's short hot drags of the air that makes her cigarette blaze between clauses, with every breath drawing sere smoke that seems totally absorbed by her perfervid blood or anyway never exhaled through the visible orifices of her capital parts; her fireproof organs suck in all gases unfiltered to oxidize an unhappy mind that might have been turned to good account in a proper civil war against Socrates: nothing comes out but male words combusting into rapid sentences. Xantippe's is the one kind of female disconsolation that's untouchable for a tender woman-lover. [How would she be to the touch, this attarless Camilla, if she kept her peace? After you have silenced her oaths and made her submit to gentleness—could you then feel sorry for her tribadic tensity, when doubly triste you've cast the fertile grain (which let's say Sandy's turned out unable to come up with) to gratify the moaning entreaty she might be driven to? Maybe her swinehot lusts and brainhot smokes bear false witness to fairly gracious feelings. . . .] He once more congratulates himself on having sworn off his addiction to the papered weed, notwithstanding that in combination with an extraordinary underlying appetite for food (caused he supposes by a further complex of unsatisfied appetites for travel and/or strange flesh) the abstinence has made him fat.

Although the Sandyses live in San Francisco they have never before resorted to the zoo for entertainment, and they have only just arrived. Michael's discovery of this inexperience presents him with an opportunity to shake off his curt demeanor with a helpful suggestion. "You should take the time to see it all!"

He risks his dignity in hope of riddance, pressing the thin end of his wedge into the tiny crack opened by Roger's instauration of the radical attraction between this bride and her groom. With long unskilful passes, hoping they're inconspicuous, he swings his scythe to widen the swath separating his family from Harmon Sandys's; offhandedly he lays bare the ground rocks and ditches of the impressionistically misleading continuity between his meadow and theirs. For with rather sudden eloquence he praises the Trustees in terms calculated to pique a woman who at least until a few minutes ago has professed to disesteem all things valued by the bourgeoisie, and to impress both the vulgar and the esoteric intelligence of her escort the perpetual student of life.

"Believe it or not, the taxpayers here are supporting a humanitarian institution. Gestalt-tested apes are the center of everything of course, but all the animals are given every possible opportunity to see people of all kinds in their more or less natural habitat. There are damned few communities anywhere that have been edified by such a diversity of anthropological cognition. This representative faculty from the Ark can acquaint itself with human survivors of almost every classification and variety, every size and shape, every age from preconception to senility! If they'd only let some of us die and have our funerals here none of the beasts would ever want to go to the movies."

"Oh yuh?" But Sandy seizes Michael's disingenuous conceit. "I'm sure there are other rites de passage the patrons would rather see. They should be exposed to our natural and unnatural practices. If I were an ape I'd like to see the governor of Alabama's daughter on the cathouse floor with two great big bucks deceiving her father."

"But they couldnt allow that!" the disarmingly tolerant Lady Chapman protests with a straight face, much to her lord's amazement. "The very idea! There are cubs in those cages! Besides, it would make the lonely animals too unhappy."

The other Ruth stares at her alma soror with sincere approval.

"Oh yuh?" Sandy leers.

Michael is growing alarmed at the petard he's planted. The better half usually makes no such modest remarks before third parties. His backfiring diversionary tactic has only made the brace of Chapmans more attractive to the predators. So he can't conceal an urgency in the tone of his final effort to arouse their curiosity about the proper objects of visitation. "You should go to the tholos and see the tomphallic snake dreaming of his mate."

"Oh yuh?"

"And they'll soon be throwing daily meat to the cats!"

"I'm glad we're late then. The earliest Christians get the hungriest lions."

But as far as Pig Ruth's attitude is concerned there's no need for Michael to worry. As Saint D H said, thinking of the prodrome to milk-secretion that now possesses the erstwhile androgyne, "Everything living wants to procreate more living things." She wants to get her man to herself as soon as possible, to be as nice to him as she knows how to be, that he may join her heart's desire. She wants to explore this incipient tenderness. "Well Pappy," she cries cheerfully to Sandy, "let's go see them now so we can get home early! It's Palm Sunday, for Christ's sake!"

"That's what you said, Daddy!" a small voice exclaims hoarsely and its elbow digs Michael's thigh barely missing his cod. The boys have reappeared just in time for the pig's last sentence, and Matty's pleasure at the day's encounter with friends is capped by this echo of the phrase that struck him at lunchtime when it was uttered by the supreme commander himself and has now been repeated by this lady who has the same first name as his mother. [Is he astonished by her knowledge or by mine?]

"Oh yuh?—Just a second, Ruth. —Say did you hear the one about the couple that asked their little boy what he wanted for Christmas? 'I wanta watch.' the kid said." Pause with smirk, squinting from face to face of the elders. "So they let him!"

Michael can't suppress a broad smile. Ruth Chapman laughs aloud in frank delight at the twist of grammar and flip of image. The old gag is new to her, and evidently quite impersonal. It doesn't occur to her that Sandy probably offers such ice-breakers to establish communication and declare his interest with every mother and potential mother he meets, losing everything when his ploy doesnt work (which is far more often than not) but making a swift start if it doesnt immediately repel his quarry, perhaps with his finger distending her cheek from the inside as he's exploring.

Jonathan pretends not to have heard. Slowly his ears begin to burn. Matthew doesn't expect to understand the distant talk of Christmas.

"Okay folks, we'll say goodbye now." Sandy opens and closes his puppet fist at the kids, waves to their parents on the picture plane with a flexing of his elbow. "Goodbye Babe Ruth, goodbye Mickey Mantle, goodbye Jonny Appleseed, goodbye Mattarooney—and bye little Fra Angelico!" snuffling and grinning, attentive by turn, finally deciding to reconfirm his enchantment by shaking the hand of each. His suddenly unselfassured young shrew follows suit with the best of intentions, but she may as well have been a porcupine just climbing out of the water with quills laid back, her pigness only rodentwise reduced.

When leave has finally been taken the headman breathes freely again at the restoration of his family's integrity. But not before Sandy once more calls back confidentially. "Hey Ruth—leave me your teeth, will you?" It's another unconscionable exploitation of former familiarity, for he remembers hearing that Ruth Chapman has willed her eyes to anyone in need—to be taken at the moment of her death for the use of a living head. Someone is expected to notify the university research hospital before dispatching any other message.

The father leads his own people onward, ruthfully congratulating himself that he's steered clear of any assignation with the unlovely social climbers.

{*Postulants only*: GO TO ITEM (30) MS.03.1, page 309.}

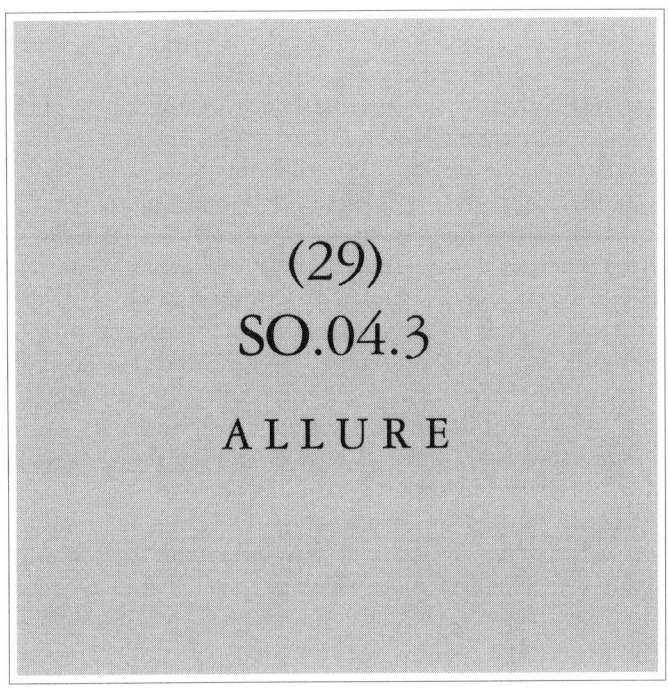

(29)
SO.04.3
ALLURE

. . . A woman in our language is a wife-man—a "marked" *man*, some linguists might say (exactly inverting embryological development)—the human being who trembles, who vibrates; the subject of agitation. I take the Greeks to have been right that all life is doing and suffering. Woman is the one more likely to suffer. But the trembling may be her veil's that wavers as she walks, the liquefaction of her silks. Anyway the suffering is associated with hiding, with modesty, and hence with mystery. The sufferer is usually an object of value, pursuit, revelation. As object of another, she can choose no object of her own: she can only anticipate her suffering while she waits, and compensate her long inactivity with a depth of feeling incomprehensible to the hunter. *Pathein* is her particular verb, for she is normally patient, passive, passionate. I have come to the third advantage of women in the art of dance: their special allure.

Culture without it would come to an end. It is allure that makes it possible for a victim to bewitch and govern the dragoon. As an aspect of feminine subjectivity it invites the objective attention. I speak here not of sexual congress itself but of initial identification, which impanels the possible objects of concupiscence. Allure is not acute: it has only an open, obtuse power of selection; it is not for particular targets but for as many as may behold (like a broadcast), and overblessed urban women are merely more aware than others that their ambience is entered by thousands of men who never make themselves noticed.

The subjects of the object select themselves—many, a few, a single lover, or a faithful husband—stochastically, circumstantially, accidentally, whether by competitive aggression or by default. The relative success of passive allure (compared with the efforts of the game hunter, who must search out and catch, one by one) is her compensation for the pathos of ethological constraint. If by chance there are no suitors at all in a year, or no harvester of the pearl in a lifetime, it is still not a failure of nature's communication: for the identification never fails; circumstances condition the length to which fulfillment is deferred; consummation can scarcely be reckoned proportional to allure. Accessed or not, the recognition of an individual's dignity is her success. In professional life, as in natural life, that is the general purpose.

Even as a baby the girl child is less interested in touching than in being touched. Yeats refers more than once to "the desire of the man which is for the woman, and the desire of the woman which is for the desire of the man." No credible anthropology can deny the social consequences of this imparity in any society. But I am here concerned with the attractions of art dance.

The epigamic permeance of allure plays a part in the subsumption of desire by imagination that is fully as ironic as reason's part in the subsumption of experience by poetry, where art is more than equal to the truth. All arts use their matter more freely than life can, and in exceeding nature they can cross it. Sex, a central force of empiric doing and suffering, is transformed into a power of dance, constraining and conserving its attractive properties in the service of metasexual imagination, reversing such conceits as Donne's who celebrated orectic experience with images of navigation or perspective.

On the dance stage an alluring woman is neither delitescent nor deliquescent to men; she appropriates the male action-principle. She is capable of pure action because she has not been bred to its pragmatic purposes or its symbolic justifications. Metaphysics hasn't been able to grasp *action-in-itself*, but here we have it on the stage as both performance and examination of movement, and there is no syntactic or semantic escape from the phenomenon itself.

The female subject has made itself object, and human action is seen in sublime form as the subject's objectification of passion. The consciousness of allurement has disappeared, forgotten in action. In a selfless display of the action of the self, liberated by movement from social demands upon femininity, the dancer escapes suffering; the woman comes out of hiding and ceases to tremble: her movement is no longer submissive to other wills or to general destiny:: she moves at her own will, and surely, with no waste of energy in transverse vibration.

In dance the dis-idealized woman actualizes an old ideal of virtue: the superiority to passion of one born to it. Not a virtue of virginity or fidelity or chastity, but an excellence of sexually differentiated ability which translates sex. *Arete* was originally a term for excellence. Its meaning is intensified by connotations of strength of character in one who is of such worth and condition that nothing external prevents her from accepting pleasant and honorable alternatives to her self-imposed profession. The Greeks saw it in strong-limbed Artemis, whose skill in archery was bated not at all by two fair breasts, supreme hunter and witch of uncultivated dark woods, goddess of roads and harbors as well as childbirth: the opposite mask of artful deliquescent Aphrodite's, and perhaps more faithfully worshipped. In Artemis the venery of love, which emphasizes desire for satisfaction, was transformed into the venery of chase, which emphasizes the joy of pursuit; and veneration was shifted from that which is pursued to the pursuer. The pursuits of art are not so pointed. Its creative action does not imitate the masculine virtues of athletic force, but our dancer, like Artemis (not the sort of woman to drive her knee into the groin of a man who opposes her), dedicates redemptive female proficiency to a world established under male jurisdiction.

It is said that sight is touch at a distance. Then sweat, invisible at a spectator's range, is the dancer's alluring perfume. An inborn valuation, stronger than gravitation, directs human eyes—male toward female instinctively, female toward its own by a socially cultivated association of ideas—toward the softer or less forceful type of human body, and with an alacrity that generally seems more instinctive than the abstracting measure of admiration for the male. There is no allure in a runner's frame, which is an instrument of ambition, whether to save the nation with a message, or to escape with his life, or to win a competition.

The female body is always at athletic disadvantage; yet let it appear before men as an instrument of its own world and it may fasten attention upon an art that doesn't come easy to most spectators, whom it can lead in unlikely bemusement from the pleasure of watching what might seem a display of amorous propensity, with its promise of perfect recreation, to an appreciation of movement expressing a serious and disinterested imagination that is limited not at all to suggestions of desire. The continuum from entertainment to art is traversed by sexualistic beauty, which educates us to human uses beyond our hopes and forestalls the lover altogether.

Most women are rewarded for their gift of sex. What distinguishes a whore is not the pattern but her hierarchy of values, her manners, and her turnover. Here in dance the different manner is everything and the turnover is less than zero, less than the virgin Artemis's. In the consummation of creative dance none of the dancer's allure is used up, none of anyone's libido advanced or retarded. Nothing is yielded. Instead, the entrancement is compacted, suspended, prolonged. Yet you wouldn't dream of calling the dancer a tease. You don't feel as if something's been withheld, or resent as meretricious Nature's old cause serving a new effect. A dancer eluding the natural consequences of her concrete sexual presence leaves no tinge of exploitation or disappointment in the aesthetic excitement she stirs.

On the contrary, she makes herself doubly admirable. For the man, unalluring, though it is nothing to display his athletic nakedness in a stadium, it's physiologically impossible for him to maintain the specific fascination of an ithyphallic posture during theatrical action. But the surface of a woman in its entirety is the form of her art, the kinematic lines with which she brings about the watcher's "change in consciousness", and even at a distance one can scarcely rule out a possibility of sexual allusion in the least ambiguous position or movement. For women, who love fences and curtains, self-exhibition is of some importance; their nurtured modesty is a manifestation of intelligent fear. It therefore takes special courage for them to mount a stage without dress or song to mediate their revelation.

Yet the fact is that this self in its very epiphany forgets itself with the same selflessness in which the mind athinking loses consciousness of its subjective self. No creative art-dancer sets her cap with the knowing allure of a female calculating her affect upon a congregation for the sake of personal attraction or career, and she has no business considering even so much as the kinesthetic sympathy of those who see her.

She dances in bare feet to give herself a grip on the floor, and she wears tights to disencumber her body even as it is sufficiently warmed by the minimum material means of separating her person from dance-in-itself, her intended purpose. No muscle from toe to scalp is favored for its sexuality: energy flashes anywhere. Parts of the whole rarely remarked in either public or in private life—instep, kneecap, or thumb—are here suddenly made for an instant more interesting than lip or thigh, as the dancer transcends traditional gesture with the motion of an original event.

In another era this sublimation by dissociation might have been impossible. Creative dance has appeared in our culture at a time when sensual satisfactions are comparatively easy, or at least when the avenues of satisfaction are so familiar that most men grow less and less desperate of the guerdoning. An undressed woman can now be seen upon a stage without the former affect of a high-gartered burlesque star decked out in a bustle. It is not as difficult as it once was to check and divert incipient lust on particular occasions, or to divert gross lust at erotic spectacles. Art dance rises with the cessation of sexual repression not because there is more liberty of performance but because the common level of undischarged libidinous energy has healthily slackened.

But the temper of the age never entirely obliterates the rivalry between prurient and aesthetic affection that remains unacknowledged by sophisticated patrons (each perhaps attributing his secret response to shameful aesthetic immaturity)—which would be met with fierce scorn by the cold and splendid artists if ever confessed. It is partly her sheer superiority that daunts a man, as a layman is daunted by all professional concentration, but especially in women when they haughtily triumph over nature in their own person, and over the male command of it. Art neutralizes a daunted man sooner than one inflamed. . . .

{*Postulants only*: GO TO ITEM (31) SO.04.4, page 339.}

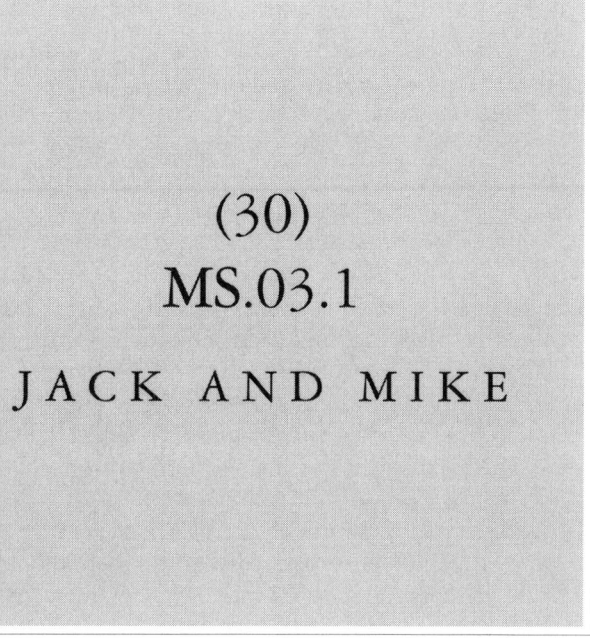

(30)
MS.03.1
JACK AND MIKE

1.

*L*ong and merry ran the nighttime saturnalia of friendliness. Caleb speaking now and then to one of the peripheral persons watched it pass. He patted Black Minnaloushe the Wolfson cat a fluffy Zoroastrian that Ruth in an armchair had got in her lap whence it observed human gaiety, already contented with scraps which it rightly supposed had been produced by this same good time. Caleb lowered his ear to listen for a purr.

"Michael likes black cats too." Ruth said. "Ours is a lady." She had been helping Sarah in the kitchen and so had missed a part in the charades, which distantly observing without spoiling the players' fun she had unriddled for herself while the guessers were still floundering.

Chapman was captain of one team and Wolfson captain of the other. Proverbs maxims and verses. The opposition immediately divined Chapman's apothegm: *It's too early to predict and too late to repent.* Evidently he had made it too famous. Removed from Berkeley competition by circumstance, and not so often seen that he might lose his salt, he was clearly the darling of the group. But now almost everybody was becoming darling to everybody else. When they started to play games of personal encounter

Caleb went into the bathroom, much as he would have liked to kiss the lady he had vowed to serve.

Again there he was able to avoid their fussing artless undramatic goodbyes when the time came for leavetaking. Thus he relieved the older people of his unspoken pejoratives and verbal clumsiness. Nobody could help him along in society. If they gave his absence any thought at all it was to assume him sick from too much water of life. But far from it, as a matter of fact. He was still waiting to warm up. If even the women didnt attach much importance to his company he preferred not to rehearse their inane courtesies, and he did not choose to honor their commonplaces by risking between his lips the tip of Sylvia's tongue who would encourage his advances only to mock the confusion she could cause.

Caleb sought comfort in aloof chastity as he stood for a long time making water rather stiffly into Sarah's gleaming white porcelain. When he heard his name being called he refused to hasten his act or to acknowledge the attention. Having flushed the hopper he sat down on the pink plush cover and gazed at the clean soft furnishings of the tiled compartment which displayed special towels for guests and no trace of the children.

Dave Wilson and his Joan had left earlier than the others, shaking hands all round with a gravity appropriate to outsiders and taking from the Chapmans a special leave. Those two from San Francisco hadnt much splashed about in the swimming hole like the others. Joan was just beginning to release her genius from its bottle when Dave guardedly corked it up and dragged her away. He seemed to fear that the alcohol she gulped as she hung unwinkingly upon Mike's jests and chuckles would loosen her personal Greek harpy. He smiled with sad watchfulness as she was having her thickened say at the end. It was then that Caleb had ceased to resent the man's self-effacing superiority of stature and lineament as an airplane pilot and commander of men at war. Worldly experience had gathered Dave's tight pale skin into premature creases at the corners of youthful blue eyes weathered by responsibility and fear. Having risen politely for that couple's departure Caleb had hung behind the Chapmans insignificantly as the old friends took leave of each other while the host and hostess waited unobtrusively further off near the door to add the last goodbye.

"So long Mike. I've just been remembering that I was the one who introduced you to Ruth. In fact you stole her away from me!" Ruth laughed and pressing his hand drew him down to kiss his cheek, but his gallant response was by way of her lips with a bluff relish unseemly to the unnoticed witness. This liberty like an awaited cue authorized Joan to double-kiss both Chapmans, each on each cheek, as if she was at pains to distinguish new friends in a manner she hoped appropriate for the academic demimonde by neutralizing the polarity of gender that she herself couldnt forget for a minute.

"Lucky misfortune!" Ruth replied for the Chapmans. "Now you have Joan and a baby daughter too! She must be as beautiful as her mother. I can see why you want to go home early!" Mike's arm hugged his wife's shoulder and made a close happy yoke opposite the other couple.

"But we don't believe in marriage!" Joan claimed in a stage whisper, and they all laughed again each in a different kind of uncertainty, and even Caleb assumed a one-sided smile in case anyone should look his way. He had felt unable to move off without attracting a notice that would have been more embarrassing than the neglect he suffered.

"Well in case we don't meet again before you go East, good luck!" said David solemnly shaking his old pal's hand in both of his own. "Maybe we'll get to Massachusetts some day."

"Oh I don't know." Chapman drawled. "I'll probably see you infinitely sooner than that. I'm sure there'll be many a slip between that cup and my lip."

"When will Ruth go?"

"As soon as I find a job and a place to live."

"I can't understand why you want to go to the most depressed part of the country when you're trying to earn a living. But I grant you that it's picturesque. Ruth will love it."

And then they had left without a glance at little Caleb, and he had never offered to call attention to himself by speaking up in farewell. Consistency now forbad him honor the others with civil initiatives. The front-door vestibule however was acoustically closer to the bathroom than to the drawing room and he could make out many of the words spoken in the general departure. None of the guests insisted upon saying goodbye to him. Those called by nature were routed to the bathroom upstairs. To them it seemed beyond question that he occupied this lower one in thrall to the bottomless barleycorn illness of an intemperate young enthusiast. "Caleb was feeling no pain an hour ago." he heard Cahners saying.

When it came to that he could recall no such stretch of time. He found to his amazement that he remembered nothing after the Wilson leavetaking except some Nietzsche words from his own mouth as he ridiculed Randy Jillison's lordly drunkenness in Mrs Jillison's ear: '. . . noble wine, which at once heats the blood and induces meditation'! Was it to be concluded that with or without conviviality he had made himself known?

More now swam into his memory from the indefinite past: for instance himself trying to be reticent for fear of getting drawn into passionate argument about something that interested no one on either side; and finally coming away, again in fear of his tongue, in slow watery shock at the gradually dawned induction that nameless gossip he had heard on Campus associated Sylvia Cahners with the very professor who supervised Newton Cahners' doctoral candidacy.

Caleb made allowances for Wolfson as a cordial friend and self-defrocking comedian who even in aggression seemed frank and generous, and of course for Chapman the wisely democratic master, but he marveled that well-read men and women compared to himself could be so sure of themselves, so smugly satisfied with the little circle that shut him out, so unaware of the populace's hostility to their caricatures of the commonalty—above all so content with their modest percipience when laid alongside his. Yet when he considered each of the others in turn he found that he must make allowances for them all. No one at this party was typical of the academic collective he had abstracted; only Wolfson and Cahners belonged to it at all.

[Maybe I wouldnt be so distasteful to my companions if they understood that I pay for my arrogance of Creative Mind in spiteful and rancorous depression commensurate with my incompetence at all other affairs. —But by god I'm not inferior in autonomy!] His demon comforted him. [I have no woman and no prospect of touching any flesh but my own—but at least I'm not haltered by marriage!]

In better-humored impatience he waited for the end of the leave-gathering that was taking place so close to his ear and began to hanker for the glass of whiskey he must have left standing he knew not where. Fleeting perturbations disappeared and those that remained as chronic or essential he now found he could examine or forget with an equanimity that broadened with the ensuing curtailment of rivalry for Chapman's attention. Suddenly action seemed feasible, or at least influence. It seemed possible to palpate the entire world and perhaps eventually to knead and mold the elect minds of modernity. With burgeoning hope to take his place as the headstrong scion of Chapman's power in whose hands real people (if Caleb Karcist was real) could be reconstituted and adjusted in order to function in reciprocation or complementarily with the superior first person, all energies in polylogically dynamic concert according to the first person's design, he pondered his emotional situation during a night that was growing more and more cerebral.

Without for a moment renouncing his consolatory craving for lonewolf distinction he was eager to put at his liege lord's disposal the free energy of his Damascus blade. Body of Fate stretched before the potentiated joy of reinforced Creative Mind with alluring egocentric plasticity. He imagined theaters made like sculpture. At this moment to speak would be to make; if he danced he would engender. He yearned to speak and dance before Wolfson and Chapman whom now he called Jack and Mike.

Caleb was the more encouraged to prove himself by hearing Mike and Jack ease their old friends out the door. But would they throw him out too, instead of concentrating on his capture as a prize to be disputed?

It was a long time before all the departing guests actually got out onto the street. There was always something to add or listen for, more to witness, a stirrup cup to drink; and the farewells ended only with protracted discussion of travel arrangements for the benefit of those who had no car. The Cahnerses' craft was going to take the Jillisons home but Randy was probably still waving a glass as he gimped into earshot yelling the end of his favorite song:

> . . . I did, the boarder said,
> And shouted all the louder.

For Philoctetes was lurching about from wall to wall on his withered leg pretending to Byronic gusto Caleb had no doubt who despised him for converting art into money while Newt who saw no wrong in such motivation must have been waiting amiably with car keys in hand, his argumentativeness macerated by the long evening that had no doubt left him sober.

"Caleb's okay." Caleb heard Mike saying. "We find that he lives only a few blocks from us. He said he'd walk home with me. Once a year I walk it." The pleasure of overhearing that such an unexpected promise had been exchanged three sheets to the wind charmingly enhanced the grave plash of that voice which to the general public seemed monotonous. The words ordinary in themselves were strung together in simple syntax but Caleb wanted to take possession of them with both his hands for a long slow look at the whole cloth they wove. Save in writing how is a person revealed if not by his voice? [Why does my voice come to people's ears only as a single thread that they must be on the lookout for if they're not to brush it off in absent annoyance as some wisp of cobweb left by a harmless spider?] Caleb's demon laughed and made Caleb laugh too. Together they knew that Caleb had no personality to express and that in this relief lay his second superiority to the adored professor of concealment whose self was only reserved.

"Hey Randy!" he heard Mike say, presumably taking the stinker by his arm. "You should meet our baby-sitter. —Ruth, Ruth!", calling on a higher note: "Don't you think Hecuba would pose without charge for a friend of ours? —Randy, she could make your fortune on a calendar. —Newt, take Ruth home first so Randy and Nancy can meet Hecuba!"

"I'll wait in the car thank you!" Nancy cried.

"She's a fire-shovel eh?" asked Randy. "I just wish I had my sketch pad."

"We should take Caleb." Sylvia insinuated. "He's the one who ought to meet her. Randy can sketch them juxtaposed! Now that would be something, wouldnt it?" Derisively she called his name. "Ca-leb, Caleb, come boy!"

No answer.

"I'll make coffee for everybody who wants to meet the model!" Ruth offered with a laugh that raised jealous pulsations in the heart of her hidden unadulterous knight merely by its timbre, displacing a flare of shameful anger roused by the previous remark of the plump blonde bitch. Mrs Chapman's contralto was a lady's voice, anchoring his loyalty.

But it was the goodhearted overbearing voice of Jack drowning out the gentle words of his hostess that finally packed them all off. Caleb flushed the water closet once more and loudly dropping the hinged seatcover began to wash his hands as noisily as if he'd been long at difficult stool. Then he dashed out with the air of a man sorry to have missed the chance to bid good friends adieu.

Jack asked Mike and Caleb to stay a while. The suggestion suited all four. Sarah returned to the kitchen to clean up what she and Ruth hadn't finished.

2.

At first Mike seemed round and closed, like Ptolemy, and Caleb felt as if he was about to be put to more of a trial than he had bargained for. But as it turned out there was no need for him to fix his latitude and longitude in the system. Neither Mike nor Jack tried to pin him down. And in fact for some time the talk remained desultory.

Seated on the floor unlike a chief Mike tapped on an African drum taken from a Wolfson cupboard and Jack warmed up a recorder he was teaching himself to play. The cessation of hubble-bubble soothed their halfhearted efforts. No one commented on the feigned haste of Caleb's sudden reappearance or seemed to have paid any attention to his conveniently belated motions in opening the front door only to foolishly wave goodbye into the darkness. The car doors had already slammed, the last engine had already revved and pulled away.

"It's midnight of my first new day." said Michael of his namesake feast, no longer inhibited by the presence of one who truly knew him. "I've won my foothold and the battle of Hastings is at hand. But it's also the age of a man's life to beware crucifixion." He paused to sip from a glass on the floor beside him.

"Your year of crucial fiction." Jack suggested between breaths.

"That's a fact."

"An artyfact." Jack had been trying to toot out a Medieval song.

But now both piper and drummer laid aside their instruments like divine jurists getting down to business. So when at last they turned their attention to Caleb it was he who sat on the floor and they who towered sternly above him on the chairs of a divided tribunal. Of Jack the lips curled, the ears sharpened, the brows contracted into angles. Of Mike the bland moon-face banished all betrayal of inner warmth and loomed as motionless when the whiskey glass was brought to its lips as when it mumbled or stared. The two dicasts opposed each other head to head at ends of the table alternating in access to the bottle and took turns at stooping to help Caleb with the same. Vitalized oxide of hydrogen was still the only medium between men and boy.

The judge advocates between whom he had chosen to choose bulked ten to one against him—scaled five on either side, or split four and six, six and four, sometimes consentaneously doubling themselves to twenty-

weight or more, shifting or reversing in array until the shapeless
befuddled proportion of joined brows settled down at about seven to three
the victim thought. A broad beam seemed to thump around the courtroom like the sweep of a lighthouse that never hit upon precedents of reason or feeling: a stupid rotating power, categorical and ineluctable, beyond
chance or persuasion—an instrument of baptism freezing the liquid virtue
by which even holy water takes the shape of its latest vessel.

[This setup is a drunken formality. Let them accuse and underestimate
or even praise each other all through the night. They might be even-steven
in the judgment of any other defendant but jurisprudence goes for naught
in making me less partisan. My master's irony of person redoubles every
line of attraction and draws me to him like simple gravity regardless of
argument. Say on! I'll make songs under my breath.]

Quotations of grand and greatgrandmaster Yeats and Blake and one or
two others were conflated in meaning and bibliographically confused by
Caleb's drugged apparatus of perception, which registered or misregistered
the sounds of buzzing logomachy mostly lost upon him so little did he
discriminate for lack of acuity and wit the foaming currents of a torrent
that he himself divided like a roundbottomed rock soon to be loosened at
its foundations and swept down the cataract.

Jack Wolfson said or seemed to say: drink to the prince of sufficient reason—but sing pathema, mathema, and poema! Prosit! Here's to verse that always turns and runs! Drink to the prosaic abstractor but form habits of the heart that slowly perfect the senses. Sit and kiss—ring and buy! Caleb is romantic!	Mike Chapman said or seemed to say: drink to our master of ceremonies—but celebrate parity, equity, and art! Versus him! Be not averse to propriety, orthodoxy, freedom! Drink to the laureate poet but pray for will to power, not to cultivate your taste. Cry and fly—Stand and hiss! Caleb is romantic!

"I've never been to Rome!"

Write a book on tragedy: *The World as Comedy and Tragedy, or What the Art of Tragedy Should Have Been.* Common English needs such recension that he who would use it to the full must write it like a learned language. I can give you the power of the Pentagram. Your very name makes	Don't bother. Creation without toil is the chief temptation of poets. The fascination of critical hermeneutics uses up most of the lead in a scholar-poet's pencil. Assume the reality of the natural and material world. Bring to proof whatever you can that God never imagined therein compossible.

you my man. The new breath of comedy has begun to wither the beauty that I love. Cold comedy. He's a cold man, champion Yankee, Micky is: not like Babe Ruth, but comic and commercial for all that, not a drop of poyetry in his veins.

Your peripatetic Asterotle is no traveler even in this realm of gold!

Don't analyze your will in terms of the mask this academic man would fix upon you, only in relation to itself . . . between sleeping and waking. Let him stuff the Pentagram up his ass. He's outread me, but he's a warm humanistic shark. Better for you a passionless guardian!

> Balls sometimes fly
> Across the sky
> When Mantle's there
> To fan the air!

An archangel's nothing but a shark extremely well governed. Here's to our young magician!

Beware the impresario of witchcraft. Stick to counterrevolution!

> *Here's to me, young howler!*
> *Here's to biblic Jew and umbilic Greek!*

Cathar rather. Heresiarch of two faiths as well as poyet gentleman and scholar. I can show you religious pleasures that we can't tell him about at all because he disapproves of everything that youth most craves. I don't want no Dante deforming my Manichee gnosticism with primitive social Christianity. The shopkeeper speaks of my occult heresies as if they were overstocked inventory. He grudges me my spiritual licentiousness.

Irish, if you please, like Lawrence of Arabia, despite the English name from a recessive Swedish naval architect way back. The only circumcised Irish family in Gloucester according to my mother. But him there, he's nothing but a sophisticated Chinchilla: hear nothing, see nothing, do nothing—outside the pale! The most influential of my inveterate customers. But the law compels us to wait on magi and students alike.

> Celestial evil
> Makes me quake:
> Its angel tastes
> Like devil cake.

Come to my Black Mass. Be a footloose troubadour, not an industrial engineer! He's crude and

Fantasy, all of it! A Gold Rush jongleur, old pseudogoliardic spagyrist! He's

gross. His bourgeois probity keeps
him from being invited to private
courts and conventicles on any day
of the week. My way, IT will be
yours! His way, you'll be saved
from risk by Bow's Ark—a
lumbering scow. Bah bah for the
white sheep! Better to drown
with us Druids! Come study
rites with me. I am called an
indulgent teacher.

refined and sublimated. Actually
he's genteel. (Look at this house.)
But dangerous nevertheless. Stoop
not down to the darkly splendid
world wherein lieth continually a
faithless depth and Hades wrapped
in cloud; delight not in irreducible
lyric images. Science is open-ended
and more subtle. Join my system
and be your own man. I teach
nothing. I forbid nothing.

[Caleb lay back on the rug watching
Jack's ceiling tilt back and forth
like the deck of a ship and composed
another poem, this one of several stanzas.]

A glittering career lies before
you in the morning of your life if
you will bring criticism to wisdom
by means of rhetoric learnt from
me. Purpose not to make yourself
a mere man of action, drudge of
time and space, full of war prince-
dom and victory: but win power
and all sweet pleasures at an early
age by living the secret life of the
spirit as my acolyte. I am no
tinkling sciolist. The Cabala
already flows in your blood.
Come study further. Interpret
Odo's dream and master all the
great visions before you chant your
own. If you would undertake the
responsibility of letters or as critic
lead the mind of your age you
must know so much that you can
divide your subject and so write
little at a time, but deeply.

He promises you the fool's gold of
alchemy. . . . What do I see before
me—a young man in mourning?
You know too much already.
Do not seek knowledge on slavered
silver from a wolf. I haven't time to
teach you anything, least of all the
art of persuasion, or I'd take lessons
from him myself. I must continue
with edification of my own, and
extend my government. No: be not
savant but engineer. Better to
design a brick than memorize the
world. Pay no tribute to universitas
magistrorum et scholarium. Be not
European manqué but American.
You need masonry to sing of. . . .
If you can't succeed as an engineer,
then try real science. Zodiacs and
Chaldean arts indeed! You mongrel
son of a bitch, don't follow any old
beggar that feeds you!

Lactyantic records
Of pure sweet milk
Ran along the ceiling
On rolls of yellow silk.

Ignore the practical arts but learn all true knowledge that makes symbols of the macrocosm. With the mastery of all languages and signatures you will please the secret gods that rule the universe. *His* reason is builded upon sensation, but yours will be the truth of highest places, eternally sweet to savor. Without generalizing away all the minute particulars of life you shall win your way to the Tree of Life. All he can do is classify little walls of books. His shelves look like a Hegelian chart of world history; dotted lines of crossreference are implicit in deceitful color schemes. But he reads no more than a dozen books a year, and it's I that lend him those!

I don't know why I should be forbidden to walk upon a bit of ground just because I'm not prepared to defend it with my life. Knowledge of what? Of learned delusions intelligently interrelated but excluding evolution? —Of closed systems drawn up for aesthetic pleasure and intellectual certainty? That's what they call spiritual. No, find your symbols in mutable facts of nature, which is infinitely richer and more playful for a mind of genuine negative capability, especially if it's inclined to hypothesize, than all the goetic libraries of Zoroaster Paracelsus Hermes Trismegistus and Karl Jung raised to the thirteenth duodecimal power.

> The caterpillars languished
> For lack of better leaf;
> Crenellated turtles
> Swam from every reef.

What a hypocrite! The dexterous Michelarchangelo can lead you to destruction. He will never expose himself, he will never bear witness for you. He'll be jealous of your time and distrain your liberty that you may be reduced to his own puritannical theory. He will make you the virtues of his necessities. They call him a thesaurus, but he doesn't aim like Roget to promote the diffusion of knowledge, no matter how fast the printing-calculator keyboard he sharpens his claws on. Follow me and at an early age you will have

In truth it's too hard for a gnostical neopythagorean paleoplatonist to cope with change. He wants to prove himself up to pseudo-Solomon or Apollonius with his seven fixed rings. And then there's no room left in his head for any idea later than one of Goethe's. How can a sinister quasi-Cathar Perfectus deal with real hippogriffs and fictions, not to mention true sacraments? He's lost in a multiplicity of images on the Hodos Chameliontes of Languedoc, the last of the Magi confused by subsequent history, rejecting evolution for its inconvenience. He diffuses knowledge like a bank of diesel smoke never stirred by a

disciples of your own. Your name will be made known far and wide. You shall explore pleasures unknown to dwellers of the marketplace.

wind. Yet he'd do well to keep a thermometer shop catering to any profession. It's easier for you to do what he wants you to do than what I can't do that you can do.

Of all the several vermin
Three stood out apart:
A shiftless little beetle,
An earthworm, and a tart.

His is the way of work and there is no aesthetic emotion that he doesn't neglect. He would drag you into the service of Og and the Anakim. He would use your personality as the object of his systematic will and design. His styptic spirit rejects the riches of esoteric tradition and submits all history to American rules of evidence. He justifies himself by making his own success impossible.

I say to you that people listen only to those of academic credit, and that if you wish to wake your countrymen from the sleep of nature you must communicate your knowledge of the emotional opposition of the Will and the Mask! Take up rhetoric and position, manner and beauty, voice and good repute! He mentions nature only in passing. Notice how he tries to manage us all with his deadpan monotone!

He fancies himself as your omnific superego, some fictive god of the prudent unexcessive imagination. I'll drink to his pathetic simulation of consciousness—but by the Damnèd Lucifer, I refuse citizenship in his Age of Irony!

But all you're thinking about right now is Hodos Cuntos and you believe there's more his way than mine. Maybe. But the false gods on high places like all pirates are finally pirated because they never build a city to uphold their jolly roger and must grow weak without a wall, twirling to face enemies on every side. Incline toward Dante's beam of the balance and clearly love all that is ontologically simple, corporate, traditional—where sameness weighs more than difference. Then you will no longer wander bewildered by numberless possible symbols. You can integrate all that I prickle at or forever crave. But not through personality! With personality you may seduce but not do the fucking. I'm tired of personality, even Yeats's. Give me a man who puts his head down and plows through his work like Bartleby—no matter how I may discount his opinions. Perhaps a little dance now and then, and a word of praise once or twice before he dies—but no persona-playing with false masks, no histrionics off stage! Nine times out of ten the poetic personality of an academic boils down to manneristic anacoluthia—present company excepted! Bottoms up!

Never more would Alice
Keep those records pure,
For she was called to Boston
To take a beastly cure.

No Christian gonna open up his system on me. Don't you get caught in his preposterously galactic fishnet. Historical Christianity has dwindled to a box of toys and he can't translate it into process and reality by wishful thinking. Why, he sets economics and religion together on one side and art on the other—so he says—and yet it's all one big figmented supersystem that he pretends to explain with a liturgical key. The nerve of the man! A fine arch-messenger is he: messenger from himself, his own god and herald—under the guise of subfusc modesty! You'll wear the drab mask he plasters over your face while his knee's on your chest. Any druidical Manichaean catharistic Jew of classical or romantic education knows that the sole function of the imagination is to discover and express the timeless truth, but *his* skull is ruled by the temporal ratio of the five senses. When he is not wide awake his brackish thoughts sink like water into the coarse sand of his deserted brain and no sensibility is left for cheeses and wines. . . . —Thus said Jack or seemed to say.

All art is indeed a monotony in external things for the sake of an interior variety, a sacrifice of gross effects to subtle affects, an asceticism of imagination. I know no other christianity and no other gospel than liberty of mind for exercising the divine arts of creation in which passive truth is unessential. The tree of life is a profuse vine of perpetually rerooting conflict. Go put off gnosis and put on Creative Mind. For a boy like you, what is life but art and action? Any redblooded gentile American ought to see that christianity is not the virgin but the dynamo, which is no more alien to the uncontrollable mystery on the bestial floor than love and politics are. *He* repudiates America's saints every time he opens his mouth. Weakness of the bones undermines his learned brawn, and along with love the habits of body-comfort rule his well-ordered house. He searches for emotion in narrow narcosis and ancient dreams falsely reported, and he intends his polished verses to discredit emergent and anamorphic organizations for their redundancy and vigor. . . . —Mike said or seemed to say.

Now with Caleb it was always a question of either speaking his whole mind or remaining silent and ineffective. Since he was confused by inconsistencies in the taunts and boasts of his two elders, since whiskey was no elixir to make golden his tongue, and since in any case he had been told it was bad manners for a man under thirty to permit himself to be in the right, he said nothing in reply. The net effect of all the conflicting advice was to leave him with his own affections. He had read that at his age a man already had in hand not only everything he required for understanding but also too much more—and that the difficulty would be to learn what belonged to his particular truth and what did not.

It was therefore quite satisfactory simply to observe the contest as an athletic agon that he was not called upon to judge. Sitting on the floor with legs folded in something like the lotus position and swaying with the swing of his eyes from one demigod to the other, the water of life having blessedly dissolved all vexation self-indictment and desire, not putting one thing against another to choose between them but on the contrary trying to amalgamate a theme that granted him the Being of Christ and Antichrist as one and accepted even the equation that liturgy is to magic as art is to pornography (which nevertheless gave expression to his hope that in the long run the two numerators would be more interesting than the fascinating denominators), he watched the opposed Veterans (brothers of the Ruptured Duck who had separately brooked a war unconscionable to timid souls like himself, one by Army the other by Navy tutored in the ways of common men) wrestle with their left wrists on the table between their chairs like Indians who had no tables. He saw the shapely white hand of the archangel on his right adorned with its gold wedding band slowly slowly tilt away clockwise toward the fireplace beyond and knuckle down upon Sarah's cloth widdershins the similar wedlock fillet of the magus.

3.

The next thing that came to mind he was being dragged to the kitchen a clean well-lighted place that Sarah might hold searing black coffee to his lips saying over her shoulder "You shouldnt have got him this drunk!" His two mentors laughed cheerfully not at his condition however but at the sight and smell of scrambled eggs and their own cups of coffee to end the feast with.

He opened his eyes in a new continuum of happy consciousness responding with a smile to the woman's warm ministrations. Cookbook or classic, a book that she'd been reading was open on the sideboard. Having scrubbed away every trace of the party she had changed into her fluffy bathrobe and slippers brushed her hair and waited to be of further use. Caleb wanted to throw his arms around her and press his face into the cozy flannel pajamas that covered her soft bosom. It wasnt for fear of Jack's displeasure that he refrained, or hers; he was kept from that natural friendly loving act by loyalty to his lady Ruth, of which he bethought himself in lovely vision of higher desire.

In four or five hours (if he understood anything at all of domestic life) Sarah would have to be in the kitchen again for her widely wakened children. [Does that hulking talkative Joshua so affectionate to all his friends cover Sarah every night in love? Do married people ever exhaust the inexhaustible?] He saw Mike gazing not at the housewife but at her works, rooting himself to a seat at her modern classlessly comfortable fireless hearth.

Shaggy-headed Jack perched on a high stool with crossed legs and pointed knee keeping up the landlady's spirits with tunes from his reedless pipe, a satyrized Pan playing for their supper. "I hope old Oedipus went through with it." he stopped to say. "He was drunk enough."

"Hecuba sounds very nice from all I've heard." Sarah remarked standing at the stove tired as she was with an unflagging attention that attracted the grateful interest of her guests. "It's too bad we don't have someone like that among our friends. Ruth said she grew up on a ranch. I wish we could have invited her here tonight."

"But Ruth couldnt have come if we'd had no baby-sitter." Mike said gently. "Besides, if she'd taken a fancy to Caleb here, who knows, her gentleman-friend might have used the Mafia on him. What a waste if Caleb died now!"

"The offences will occur, but woe unto that man by whom the offence cometh!" Speaking up for the first time Caleb surprised himself no less than the others with the clear ring of his wit. They all smiled benignly.

"He's coming alive. I won't have to carry him home after all." Mike leaned over to pat his shoulder. "Glad to have you back with us my friend."

Caleb explained to Sarah that without knowing it he had been living near the Chapmans in Oakland.

"Why do you want to live so far away from things?" she asked ingenuously, dishing up a glossy yellow omelette on broad plates with strips of bacon and toasted homemade bread. She served the three men almost equally as if they were sons in from the fields, though Caleb noticed that Jack her eldest got number one helping, no doubt under influence of the unconscious messianic hope of which she had spoken early in the evening. "I should think you'd want to stay close to Campus. Or do you have friends down that way?"

Caleb blushed. "Oh no, only a job. I keep body and soul together as a nightwatchman and I live a couple of blocks from where I work, in a big old mansion made over into a hundred crazy little apartments for odd people. It's cheap and romantic."

"I didnt know romance was possible in Oakland." said Jack.

"All I have is one of the many corners of the fourth floor. But at least there's an alcove kitchen and a fire-escape. It took me a week to learn the shortest route to my door. The halls are so narrow you've got to sidle past anyone you meet. Sometimes on your way upstairs you have to go down a few steps. You'll never find a haunted house like that in Berkeley! It's on a wuthering hilltop and I can see Grizzly Peak from my window. There are some great oaks out in front."

"I know that place." Mike almost exclaimed. "I call it the Rabbit Warren. But I suppose its days are numbered. The land's too valuable."

Sarah asked Caleb where he worked.

Nearly anywhere in Berkeley he had been embarrassed by his enthusiasm for the livelihood he had been lucky to find. Now he was practiced in a tone of deprecation that in his own ears still tinged integrity with shame. "Oh just in an old office building for doctors and dentists that's owned by a San Francisco used-car dealer."

"I know!" exclaimed Mike. "That must be the man Hecuba works for. Mr Wine." He smiled at Caleb in worldly calculation. "Someday Hecuba's influence may come in handy."

Caleb doubted his grasp of this inference, suspecting that through appalling simplemindedness he'd misread the proof of a theorem by overlooking a major premise. But with knitted brow he smiled wanly in return, temporizing, marveling and trepidating but daring not to pause for thought. "I could use some protection." He raised his foot to show a hole in the sole of his shoe. "I'm destined for perpetual insecurity."

"Like Adlai Stevenson." said Mike. "A good man can always get a job."

Caleb wondered if it was the old bear and not himself who falsely simplified an unworldly youth's reality. How could you expect such a successful self-sufficient possessor of the basic desideratum to appreciate (though all but omniscient) the elementary incompetence and naked social agony of an utterly timid weakling never bred for plain or forest whose scrawny neck and unlistened voice invited the scorn or indifference of all except unprofessional philosophers in every walk of life both male and female?

By now all the men were eating, with many compliments to the cook, who stood watching them, ready to assist with whatever good or service might further be required, urging on their appetites as she poured more of the heady new-made coffee she'd ground from beans.

"I can see why Jack has always been a nooner." Mike observed. Sarah and Caleb both blushed. Jack reached out to her and she moved closer to meet the arm with which he encircled her waist. "Mike knows what's good when he sees it, my dear." he whispered to her loudly.

Sarah changed the subject. "Ruth was the prettiest one here tonight, Mike." she said contemplatively. "So lovely, such a fine mother. I wish I could be as patient and kind as she is. She was talking about how lucky we all are to be safe and healthy. No one else we know is interested in everybody's happiness. I must admit that I'm very egocentric when I listen to radio news."

Ruth's husband replied gravely. "Me too.

"Thomas á Kempis says *Ask not after the news*. There's no profit in knowledge of current events. Most people are so busy staying on the wavefront of history that they never get more than an inch deep into the past. I'm not a stock-trader or a Pentagon officer so I don't need the latest news—except for the pseudokinaesthetic pleasure of following major politics and baseball. So I subscribe to the principle of his opinion. But only because I'm too thickskinned. I'm so parsimonious with my time that I've grown inhumanly indifferent to hearing the latest events while people are still suffering them."

"You're heartless when you keep telling us to read history only." Sarah smiled at him affectionately. "Which is the story after all feelings are sifted and averaged, I've heard to say."

"Yes. Sometimes I find myself becoming just as callous to other people's pain as those who inure themselves with the constant noise of news. But Ruth isnt inured. She never gets hardened to the shocks and reversals. The news of the day only quickens her sympathy. Everyone knows that for the first time in history we're all in the same boat—but it doesnt take such abstract knowledge to make her sensitive. She doesnt worry about the universal future as I do, but she understands the only true rebuttal to Kempis." He added a confessional grunt.

"Well there's plenty of room for all kinds of worry." Sarah sighed, staring from where she now sat among them toward a point on the opposite wall, chin resting on the heel of her palm, elbow on the edge of the table, her eyes glazed with inwardly familiar thought.

When Mike went on it seemed to Caleb that he was justifying himself to his absent wife. "History itself for the first time in history may be truncated in a cross-section of simultaneous classless agony. I no longer envy the young. Our expanding gyre of personal possibility is offset by increasing probability that among those now alive not even Mithridatic cats will live out their lives. The sudden end may come when we are better off than ever before. The suicidal shambles will take Republicans by as much surprise as if a billion children were dragged without warning from their birthday parties and burned at the stake by their own crazed parents." Perhaps he was calculating the longevity of each member of his family and mourning the disadvantages of love.

"We have always pitied our young." the Jewish matron said. She covered her face with fair hands reddened by dishwater. Her golden wedding ring matched Jack's but it was worn next to the diamond frizzily mounted in platinum that memorialized his courtship. Caleb remembered that there was no diamond on Ruth's more slender finger.

Sarah wept without sound but Jack leapt out at her angrily, for weakness, for failing to live up to the society they were assimilated into. "That won't do!" he scolded her. It was the very phrase Jack had been reported to have wailed when she failed to distinguish herself in an attempt at graduate studies. "It just won't do." he repeated more softly, shaking her gently by the shoulders. The annoyed master of the house followed her scattering thoughts telepathetically like an anxious housewife with vacuum cleaner correcting and compensating for an irresponsible husband though sharing his despair at a far deeper level than her care for the oriental rug.

Thus Jack strove to keep Sarah from broaching the common grief of
Jews and laying open his own clear and present fear of history. Even to one
who knew him only slightly he seemed doubtful of success for his chronic
attempt to seal off hermetically the racial memory of camps with chimneys
wherein he himself his mother and father and every prosperous Wolfson
might have been extinguished but for special geographical luck in their
particular extension of the diaspora—but jealously to exclude less bitter
fears that might be shared with the goyim. Yet Caleb divined that in fact
the dread of absolute doom—a flood without ark irradiating all families of
all nations with undefendable fire, sparing not even the Japanese—had
been infiltrating Jack's veins like a symptomless disease and had all but
obliterated the distinguishing terror with which the chosen people had
been stricken by those most recently volunteering to make offense against
them. Jack protested this current infusion of unprecedented dread because
the special injustice of chronic suffering was in danger of being overlooked
in humanity's last and general judgment. Therefore his anger at Sarah was
throttled by its own cause. His heavy eyelids wrinkled by millennia of the
written word nearly closed in face of Michael's unwanted reminder of the
new eschatology. He and Sarah seemed at one in the pain of their hearts,
but she not he (irritating his suppressed passion) fostered the signal hope
of recruiting fellows one by one to their despair by making all men Jews
enough to be able to imagine the unexcepted universalization of extinction
and (improving upon Jewish prophesy) to forestall by human means the
awful perfection of human time, seeing that in easy circumstances the
Jews by themselves nearly always suppressed their talent for wisdom. But
it was she raising her head and clearing her face with a wry old smile who
said "Yes Yaako, we must stop thinking about it."

At least Caleb saw the domestic problem: how to infect whole populations with unequivocal alarm and yet keep fear out of the family bosom. He
made diversionary reply to Mike's earlier remark before he finished finding
the meaning of his this insight. "I'd still rather be son than father."

The others stood mute on that question. This time he felt that they neither ignored nor scorned his comment but rather that they loved him as he
now loved them all three for sake of the lady who had gone home early.

Sarah tried to laugh at herself in explaining the tears that still freshened the colorless streaks from her reddened eyes and gleamingly washed
from her sallow cheeks the sin of her racial prejudice. "I'm sad because
Ruth and Mike are going to leave California." She marveled as she spoke
that the Chapmans whom she didnt know very well were already her first
genuine companions from the dominant Gentility. Yet the burden of charity for the whole world was too much for one still unequal to the endless
struggle for clan-locked success. She felt it more than enough to expect
herself to barely keep from failing her two god-given children as she had
failed to reinforce her undaunted husband's career. With the corner of her

apron, head tilted and inclined, smiling with self-deprecation, she began to wipe away the sweetly salted moisture that she had until then made no attempt to absterge.

Wracked with sympathy and embarrassment Jack rose indecisively. But Mike reached her first, just as she was gathering her robe to stoop and wipe teardrops off the yellow linoleum floor. "I too am sorry to be leaving you, little sister." He bent to kiss her forehead and then pressed her face to his chest like Joseph among Egyptians making himself known to a daughter of Jacob. "Jack thinks I'm crazy." He quoted Yeats directly: "The wisest of men does not know what is expedient, but we can all know what is our particular truth."

The bantering words that contradicted his tender gesture seemed to flatter the steadiness of her nerve. "I want to shake off my California fever and walk on snowshoes." he continued. "I can't live the rest of my life in a state that doesnt rate a stripe in the flag."

Jack fell in with Mike's tactics, patting Sarah's shoulder. "He thinks he must be in Boston to answer Henry Adams."

"Me and Whitehead." said Mike whom Sarah now hugged in gratitude for his respect, and as he went on she withdrew from his reciprocal embrace only to hitch her chair closer and watch his impassive face while he avidly consumed her coffee. "On finishing my thirty-third year I'm surprised to still be living, let alone to find myself on the verge of a counterentropic act!" He paused while they readjusted themselves for a return to his impersonal grindstone.

"Women like you and Ruth year by year contribute to the favorable side of the world's prospects by teaching us the futility of progress. . . ." He broke off, but after the last gulp from his first cup started anew. "Maybe at last Christianity will give up its insistence upon faith and rebuild itself on the essential miracle of latter days—which is hope."

A shadow hovered on Jack's brow as he deliberated whether or not to send his wife up to bed (while anxiously encouraging Mike and Caleb to stay), but he decided instead to fetch her a cup and saucer and pour another round of coffee for them all, returning modestly to his peripheral stool.

She was laughing outright. "Now he wants to convert us!"

"To Christianity as it never was!" Mike responded with a full smile, raising his cup.

But Jack would not permit his friend to dawdle. His purpose was to provoke Mike into an exposition of private belief. It was a strategy of rivalry, not the least consideration in which was his own standing in the eyes of a wife who had grown aware of confusion at the bottom of his ambition. If the steadiest mind of all could be goaded into revealing provincial commitments or parochial intentions the endlessly ramified burrowings of a gnostic symbolist might be justified to the worshipping woman.

[And to me, Caleb Karcist. But I look in vain for a sign of passion from my man as he's faced with this temptation to expose his subarchangelic humanity. I must listen carefully, for I may have mistaken a pompous self-educated fool.]

"We know what you're going to say!" Jack teased. "Christianity has given the church a bad name! Ever since St Paul. Greeks' fault, especially Plato's boys. Just abolish organ music however and Christian idealism will die a death of inanition. Vine will flourish again. The Myth's not dead. Not God or Christ but Church can save world!"

"Laugh." Mike chuckled, taking no offense but hesitating at the bait. "Yet what else in society is live? If you can't have faith in the pruned vintage you can still have hope for the roots."

"New aphorism!" Jack mocked. "Preach us a sermonette!"

"Yes!" Sarah cried clapping her hands with unfeigned pleasure. "Tell us what we should know."

"Reason with us. Use us in the Christian dialectic."

"I am no midwife," Mike protested "and I have nothing to say from a Christian pulpit."

"It's the uniqueness that gripes me." Sarah remarked without intentional irony. "Or rather the arrogance of making one messiah universal."

Mike (recidivating) lit a cigar and tried to set a slow pace. "Just a special case of the general uniqueness of earth. Earth is just as important among heavenly bodies for its consciousness of the universe as mankind among all the species of terrestrial evolution."

Sarah smiled and touched his thick arm. "Poor dear kindly old Baloo, sing us the jungle lore!"

"After Platonism its opposite the metaphysics of statistical probability will fall too. In its truthless way of competing with the Academy it fails to deal with the reality of hope. Its critique is coming." Mike shrugged, but the clouds of smoke were forming thicker and faster.

"So you do hope." Jack jeered. "Maybe you're working on an etiological refutation."

"Havent got time. There are empirical ways to controvert statistics."

"I know, I know! 'Art as proof'! Caleb will support you there."

[My heart leaps, to be cited with respect! But I must say nothing until I'm alone with Mike.]

"Art is the proof of any number of epigenetic improbabilities; but we're talking about history now." The bear spoke doggedly, reacting patiently to the first phase of his baiting, mindful of his duty not to curl up and ignore the throng. But the first few lurches warmed his memory of nobler strife and lumbering reluctance soon gave way to nimble and accelerating apologetics. Again and again he expressed the intensity of his feeling by tapping the whitegray cap of ash off the racing coal of fire that was sucked toward his unanimated mouth with forced-draft puffs. They couldnt see his visage for the smoke—except for the opaque glass shields blocking the twin apertures that might have vented the all-too-human soul. Everyone listened without reply.

[What I hear baffles all my formulas. Everything he feels comes out of will or idea—yet his meanings are those of a fellow who suffers the world's sticks and stones. May I never speak against the man he masks! I'll hear him out with a thousands ears!]

4.

Thus preached Michael Chapman:

". . . about the history that provides art. The question is whether human history can prove to have been true. Or will intellectual beauty, love, and all consciousness drop into a cold slate sea like all the other snowflakes that crystallize uniquely in the deeply laden sky? It's impossible for us to imagine the face of the waters after our local cloud precipitates. I mean the total obliteration of literature—as if Shakespeare and Homer and the prophets had never writ. World without end amen. The very absolute end of what we absolutely value. The human universe brought to zero-level by sudden burning or drawnout poisoning of victims and priests alike, before they starve or slowly wither. Neither innocence nor nationality nor success will prevent death in no wise painless. Not one will be gathered in the fullness of years. Not one will be leaving behind property progeny or works. No molecule of potentiality or whit of idea will be left to have died for. No children, no justice, and no art.

"Maybe it's the devaluation brought about by a subconscious knowledge of such finality that turns politics into a psychology of sentimentality and makes philosophy seem vainer than gluttony. Nowadays there's no patience for primary sensations to get as far as the seat of memory.

"Notice the ontological difference between one's individual extinction and the disintegration of all subjects and objects together. Who hitherto has ever pictured totality's end without at least heaven or hell succeeding? The annihilation of all culture is much more difficult to imagine than one's own death. Until now death-pangs have always provided for the continued existence of our enemies.

"You wonder why I anticipate the agony of an imponderable unlikelihood. But I'm going to tell you why it's the most likely possibility of all, and why the slightest expectation of even bare degenerate survival can now be seen as extravagant optimism. The worst of all possible worlds, or history's best, is verily our *only* possibility. The world's as bad as well can be, and a French scoffer can't adduce acts of God to make it seem worse. Merely to eke out an attenuating civilization by Mithridatic absorbtion of profitable carcinogens, dosing ourselves with banefully synthetic anodynes, is much too joyful a prospect to bear comparison with what I'm talking about. In the past even perpetual injustice has yielded some margin for art; but now at best all our sins converge toward a last world war over food and oxygen.

"I'll give you three reasons for a wise humanist to despair of peace.

"First we have the biological paradox that our means for the 'collective extension of mortality', as a by-product of lust, entails an entelechy of war. The original transgression against God was not fucking but the mother-hood that it often brings about. Population is caused by desire, but fulfilled desire does not necessarily cause population; therefore the trans-gression (which is now against society) lies not in the cause but in the effect. Yet women must continue to commit the crime if we are to sustain culture under any conditions whatever.

"I'm no Tiresias; I will never fully understand the motive for this crime of parturition. But I do know that it's practically impossible to stamp it out before everything gets stamped out. Consider: Under present circumstances there are fewer and fewer economic inducements for child-birth. On the contrary you might say that nulliparity fosters an ergerotic efficiency that new women think will earn them fantastic pleasure power and independence while rendering them more desirable. Soon they will be in a much better position to make their way in the economy.

"So they are beginning to *think* the way they ought to. But they still *feel* the old way. Why do they choose parity against equity almost every time? Why do they still prefer the fruitful to the sterile?

"It can no longer be said that it's for the love of children they do it. These days the birth of each baby increases the eventual certainty of all babies' unnatural suffering. Our breeding only extends the excruciation of consciousness. Under conditions of accelerating decadence every child now faces insuperable odds of untimely death deformity or chronic deprivation.

"Nor can it be the old messianic hope that explains this stubborn yearning for procreation. Women know that perfection of a man-child is everywhere cut short by our cultural evolution. History has demonstrated the vanity of expecting redemption through leadership. Even a generation of great healers can't cure the mass blindness of mankind.

"Meanwhile women remain almost as obtuse unjust and inefficient as the general population. We all persuade each other to confuse want with need and to pander to our readiest feelings in aversion to reason. Even the Roman people were not *taught* self-indulgence. Despite the advancement of learning people still give their daughters dolls to play with. It should be obvious that in the formation of character they are more dangerous than toy guns.

"So for the sake of perpetuating culture we continue to allow this vicious reproductive instinct to determine our social values (as reflected for example in tax incentives). The insoluble problem is to check the urge without defeating its means.

"Since the motive to become a mother is congenital it must be called natural. Whether healthy or not it's presumably integral to the feminine mystery. Moreover it's not peculiar to our species. Therefore it must be regarded as a necessary property of animal life on the way to death.

"No prohibitory regulations could be ultimately effective. All law and order must bow to life's necessity. Women will take to guns if they can't get dolls. For if the urge to have babies is sane then any limitation placed upon its satisfaction would lead to ruinous competition for a right that's basic and inalienable. Or it would require some arbitrary law of rationing, which is inevitably conducive to black markets and all the other consequences of unduly restrictive economic policies as well as to the grievances that rightly arise from any attempt to legislate privilege, whether according to the majority's criteria or to the elite's norms. In either case the nature of mothers would be so wrenched and distorted by the stress of competition that their reason would be shaken, and whatever the degree to which the craving might be satisfied it would hardly be worth the effort of nurturing its product; for scarcebred children of neurasthenic women would turn out so precious and overwrought that in two or three generations their regressive vitality would leave humanity more brakish than the Dead Sea.

"But if the craving for pregnancy's issue is insane then licenses for reproduction would be granted at the worser peril of furthering the female disease. In order to perpetuate the species we would outdo Agamemnon's one unforgivable crime by presuming to make selective human sacrifice not by the mactation of children or embryos but by the genetic recession of whatever mental wholesomeness might have remained in the lineage of women chosen for motherhood. Even if we found an overplus of willing victims like drugtakers who trade longevity for immediate relief from psychical discomfort we'd only reinforce the feminine heritage, inasmuch as all our females would be born to women particularly susceptible to the curse in question; any eugenic improvement of the female stock would be overborne by vote, and through political franchise our species would be returned to its present proclivity for self-indulgence.

"But if we were able to discover a cure for the instinct, what rightminded woman could fail to demand it? And then we'd be faced with the acute injustice of withholding the remedy in the cases of those deemed most worthy of contributing to corporate immortality—those above the average in health beauty and intelligence. Such injustices are the very roots of social disorder, and in this instance the world would be incited to war by the victims of society whose influence in America at least has usually prevailed.

"On the other hand if this cure were administered to everyone who asked for it the residual procreative perpetuation of our mortality would be left to wrongminded women only. Such degeneration would produce a posterity ignorant of the past and incapable of sustaining culture.

"—So that's why you should despair of the future from a zoological point of view."

Jack fetched his pipe and huffed several flames as he stalled reflectively until he could distinguish play from imagination in Mike's homily. Sarah, her flush of happiness yielding again to wan depression, poured yet more coffee, incapable of speech, as she pondered the man's depressing conceit who a few minutes earlier had been her tender shepherd. Was he pretending a joke or affecting cold scientific reason? Was her wise Baloo a monomaniacal misogynist after all? Jest or not, it was her responsibility, here alone, to defend from disrespect not only herself but also Nancy, Sylvia, and all other women whom she now represented—especially Ruth, who was so bravely suffering the shock of Mike's cruelty revealed this night as a secret intention far worse than his clever words that suddenly sounded cynical.

But Michael persisted, imperviously. "It takes less time to refer to my second reason. It is statistical and therefore easily understood. A humanist can reject metaphysics and pure mathematics but she cannot disregard statistical analysis even when it confounds the doctrine by which she labels herself.

"The statistical truth is that cosmically speaking our snowflakes can scarcely be unique. There are more storms in the universe than snowdrops in an entire Sierra blizzard. And we must believe in the assumptions and techniques of statistics because we rely upon probability for the continuous curves of distribution that replaced our great chain of being. Without continuity all our calculus fails. So you have to take the bitter with the better: you can't help accepting the likelihood that we are far from singular in our being, and that our particular historical series of presentational immediacies may be anticipated duplicated or repeated—Christ and all— as similar configurations of quanta elsewhere.

"Now if you believe that humanoid life may manifest itself in several separate worlds it's cold comfort to be told by astronomers that more or less equal species are forever inaccessible—judging by one absolute we cleave to, the constancy of light. Even our signals couldnt reach the nearest collective selfconsciousness in a lifetime. The probability of other worlds has therefore failed to keep men of theory as cheerful as they were in Nietzsche's day.

"No residual theism can save our snowflake either. The likelihood that we ape or are aped by other populations, perhaps even isomorphically, bedwarfs our importance to almost any master god who might otherwise take particular interest in our salvation.

"It's idle to speculate on some sort of negative probability to ease our hearts. Even if we embolden ourselves to conceive the possibility of a reversal of progress we're obliged to acknowledge that the satisfaction of its conditions would decompose the culture which I'm assuming it's our purpose to further the elaboration of."

Two kinds of smoke clouded the monologue. No one either yawned or challenged.

"There remains the third cause, dearly beloved brethren, to add to my biological and statistical reasons for desperation. We must face the problem of social competence. A humanist with eyes in her head should laugh to hear those who still confide in civilization.

"It's true that we might reasonably expect imagination logic and wisdom in the art of management. Certainly we often have public performances in which persons materials instruments and words are successfully marshalled. We sometimes find combined genius in the design and execution of architecture. In most case ships are well conducted. With felicity exceeding our wit for gratitude a few teachers are able to enlighten and motivate pupils who first confront them with deeply conditioned prejudice against intellectual education. And many personally controlled enterprises seem to achieve comparative effectiveness. So you'd naturally think that entities like governments universities hospitals and big businesses could succeed in organizing and directing a multitude of private wills in intelligent collective operations.

"Then why are groups or associations of human beings hardly ever wholly organized? Why are their efforts at improvement always compromised from within? Why are they frustrated even of usufruct commensurate with the sum total investment of their members?

"Humanity's failures lie disproportionately more in management than in policy. Incompetent administration compromises or subverts its own goals. Yet we usually make a virtue of apparent necessity and make little apology for undermanaging enterprises. And if we can't reform our present organizations we'll certainly lose something more of hope with every new soul born into the kettle of willful ignorance.

"With all our talent and science we have not been intellectually competent to reconcile with each other our selves souls and bodies. Americans especially by refusing to appreciate rational disinterested values—aesthetic and moral—have failed to find the facultative grace of God that's essential for social health. While we occupy ourselves with questions of self-interest and personality an invisible worm, descended from the Garden of Eden, keeps eating away at whatever we have gained in methodological and procedural wisdom. Its way of thwarting pragmatic humanity is to keep our minds off the sloth and perversity of our mental habits. This little anti-Maxwellian demon would be easier to extirpate than some dragons that we've already overcome (more or less) if we paid greater respect to reason and taste in everyday life. But it looks as if we'll never even ask for the antibiotic that's available.

"I'm talking merely about the mundane facets of our ineptitude that can be assayed in terms of aesthetically pragmatic efficiency. Efficiency is by no means the only criterion for an operating system—and often it's incompatible with other desiderata. But it's the one attribute that's slighted by the parties to both worlds, and more deprecated by liberals than by conservatives. Republicans take efficiency into their narrow realm of consideration but they are too deficient in education and/or goodwill to broaden their blindly limited valuation of it—whereas New Dealers and psychologists and cultivated academicians are educated to denounce it.

"Bearing in mind the prospects of civilization and our dissatisfaction with the past world compounded of sufficient reasons for its successive successors, consider the citizens who are devoted to amelioration of the human condition. We're naturally most concerned with our political friends the liberals. They would apply the criterion of efficiency to intrinsically valuable purposes if only they recognized as humanly important the principle of least action.

"Here again we meet disappointment. I'll tell you why our own partisans do not esteem efficiency. In this respect at bottom they don't greatly differ from their enemies.

"Poor management levies a greater expenditure of energy or matter or human time than may actually be necessary to get somewhere or produce something or please somebody. Executives in our economy are rewarded for unacknowledged waste as well as for value added. The economic man is reimbursed as much as for his sloppiness as for his productivity. People always get paid for both ordering and disordering local resources. As long as the vendor of goods or services commands a price for his time or possessions he makes no distinction between value and waste. Of course he doesnt care that the difference is left for posterity to pay. A clerk may have come to think he's paid for putting in an appearance. An advertising salesman thinks he's paid for devoting his time to money. Steadily or intermittently, they're both rewarded for occupying catallactic points in space. With their pay they go to other vendors for necessities or luxuries, or simply for an opportunity to spend on a new product. The Federal Reserve doesnt mind how excessively time and energy are used up in exchange for money—as long as someone's profiting by the loss as well as by the gain.

"It isn't only those selling their lives most dearly who employ this mechanical advantage in political economy. The altruists grasp it too: every wasteful organization and transaction affords an incremental redistribution of pence, which in turn will demand the time-included materials of others. Everyone prefers the process of promiscuous and progressive consumption to the steady-state efficiency of a liturgical commonwealth.

"I'd guess that half the gross national product is commercial exchange for the sake of fiscal motion. The economic world-soul requires that we pay as many people as possible for everything that happens. Democrats make no secret of their devotion to the capitalist principle of economic agitation. We find ourselves believing that the prosperity and even security of our population requires the inefficient use of our liberty. And you mustn't forget that all your art science and philosophy—the ultimate justification for a collective pursuit of happiness—subsist as colonial dependencies of the sovereign economy.

"But the folly of a society living off the earth's irreversible depletions is no more to be wondered at than the personal folly of almost everyone we get to know well. Just as a great many citizens spend most of their psychic energy concealing psychosis, the population as a whole conceals its infirmity by making believe that featherbedding is wholesome as long as it's financially feasible—and, often, that wasting is pleasant. The unique franchise of humanity is squandered largely in the manner of taking pleasure. Among consumers by and large work enslaves itself to triviality. Charm is seen as the boldness with which deferred satisfactions are discounted. Both work and leisure are inflated by the inefficiency that cushions all lives and debases our judgment.

"Even you my dearest friends will disdain either as parody or as quibbling fanaticism my solemn advice: do not let your bathwater run down the drain until you've recovered most of the heat by letting it cool in place. You don't think it's important to retard your household entropic expenses."

"Even in hot weather?" Caleb dared to protest.

Sarah sought relief in affected indignation: "You don't save your wife the elbow grease and scouring powder to clean the dirty rings left by standing water! Of course you don't care about her time either."

"I'm a gentleman and I leave no ring." Mike grinned complacently.

"Let him finish, honey." said Jack. He hoped Mike would continue his plunge toward radical absurdity.

"Allow me a certain simplicity of expression." Mike resumed.

"Inasmuch as we nowadays pride ourselves on evolving our own selfconscious will for change, especially through education, you may object that the enlightened few could gradually reverse our attitude toward efficiency and moderate the common abuse—if only I would grant you the possibility (which I have denied) that efficiency, broadly construed, is possible in human society. Very well: for the sake of argument I'll waive or qualify my earlier postulate and assume that fully successful management of affairs is hypothetically practicable. The issue then boils down to the leader's problem of persuasion in overcoming universally adverse emotions and sometimes fiery hostility.

"Anyone who does not rely on journalism for her knowledge of our democratic polity should know, I repeat, that inefficiency is demanded by both the elect and the electorate. No one intends to be satisfied with just deserts; everyone shares the guarantee of ecological injustice. Voters are content to remain in ignorance of inefficiency because existential knowledge of it would frighten them out of self-indulgence.

"Inefficiency will kill liberalism before its enemies do. A working moralist finds it hard to choose between inefficiency and motherhood as the devil's prime contribution."

"This is a cheerful birthday message from our archangel!" Sarah groaned with a cheerless smile.

"It may be true that we are capable of the art of management." Mike went on relentlessly. "There is no necessary reason that managerial intelligence should be rarer than literary or scientific genius. Despite all educational influences and social disincentives a few minds have been able to conceive reliably efficient human organizations as well as advisedly redundant artificial systems. It is not inconceivable that an institution could operate efficiently without either hindering herd prosperity or stealing undue energy from the environment.

"But those who would bring about a radical revision of our regard for management, the most abstract and general of practical arts (which is now so slighted by its practitioners and so utterly misunderstood by its academic wiseacres), will always fall victim to banausic expediency before reaching the battlefield. Even as we hope for the liberal leadership's return to power we must admit that our own party refuses to open its mind to such an unpopular attitude as mine, which is found (if at all) only at obscure lower levels of precious few establishments.

"Even in the corporate system of a single manufacturer the study of efficiency is relegated to the industrial engineers of mass production and to no one else. These isolated individuals have neither philosophy nor mathematics of any subtlety and they aren't educated as common readers. Therefore they are incapable of mustering a language with which to make revisions of generalizations. In fact as ambitious Americans who have gone to college in order to get a job they tend to scorn attempts at hermeneutical communication of technological value. They have been all too successful in making their occupation into a profession. In complacent intellectual confusion industrial engineers associate themselves with cost accounting rather than with the arts and sciences. They docilely accept their restriction to the mise-en-scène of factory floors and make no protest that they are scarcely tolerated within the managerial culture that hires them. They are employed primarily for conventional duties, like ancient scribes or heralds. He who would go deeper than industrial time-and-motion into the study of efficiency is discouraged by friend and forbidden by boss.

"Such radicals are hardly ever found within the profession, especially when paperwork is concerned. The creative mind is rarely accredited. If it is not averse to the nouveau learned profession that presumes to turn out ready-made managers it is almost always excluded by them. If by some unlikely coincidence of circumstance and exigency it should be permitted to mount a comprehensive criticism of received doctrine it would immediately be crushed by the tiers of accountants consulting psychologists and business administration professors irritated by a presumptuous untrained sansculottism that might threaten their tenuous academic status among the older faculties.

"If the three branches of national government were to pronounce efficiency a serious criterion for our institutions the prospect of reorganizations or even salutary mutations that might survive the individual innovator would seem minacious to financial orthodoxy. Every man-jack holding his job or earning his fees simply by virtue of a vocational diploma is galvanized into selfprotective reaction whenever an antigen challenges his scholasticism.

"Our spurious managerial evolution has reached a dead end. Doctors from the fountainhead of the Harvard Business School have invested too much in the largely iatrogenic epidemic of inefficiency to approve philosophical medicine that they recognize as lethal for their departments. And on the other side our politicians hardly try to learn the internal workings of the public bureaucracies they have established, the purposes of which are thwarted by the ad hoc mentality of lawyers who draft their legislations—epitomizing a subcategory of the negative grace that universally defeats the perfection of organized human emergence.

"Since some kinds of waste strike liberals as detrimental to the profits of their enemies, many are inclined to tolerate inefficiency. A similar cicatrization of reason can be seen in those who patronize the merely apolaustic end-products of the economy without caring to understand the social implications.

"Undergraduates, though quite ready to open all questions that they are able to frame, have been conditioned to associate efficiency—the word is so abused—with all the inhibiting forces of gerontocratic oppression. An antithesis of efficiency and freedom has been mouthed for so long that the dichotomy seems bred into our fetal brains. There it will naturally continue to escape the criticism of vigorous young minds formed under its categorical persuasion.

"In fine, for a realist hope is more difficult than faith ever was, and nearly as futile. Humanity's evolutionary success is out of the question!"

Everyone had had about enough of Mike's astonishingly abstract hobbyhorse just when he had sense enough to leave off. Save for Caleb, they half doubted the inexplicable passion of his monotony. Why so defensive of a cranky idea?

Jack began to jeer reasonably. "If mankind is just a snowflake about to sink upon the limitless face of Oceanus why do you take all this penultimate time to rub in your pessimism?"

Almost simultaneously Sarah broke out with puzzled irritation, practically interrupting her husband: "I don't understand the fun you're having with us! You obviously arent depressed. I don't believe you've given up!"

Mike bridled, smiling primly. "I don't call myself a realist." he said.

[I'm rapt! My eyes shine! There's nothing for me to say. I love the man who threatens me with captivity!]

There was a pause for reconsideration.

"Then you must justify some unrealistic hope that the human race is not lost." Jack persisted. "Everyone knows you're a hoper."

"The burden of proof is not mine. The fact that I hope you hope and they hope in the face of biology, statistics, and the tide of culture demonstrates either the irrational nature of human instinct or—"

"—Or the existence of God as the only ground of hope!" Sarah broke in. Her face was lighted with the excitement of theological inquiry. "Is that what makes *you* hope?"

The cigar was smoked out and the preacher sat with hands folded on the pillow of his belly, slumped in the chair feet crossed and legs stiffened straight before him from his lower back. This posture broadened and multiplied the annulations between his chin and open collar.

He replied quietly, without at first modifying the pompous aspect of his ironical didacticism. "Well there isnt much to say. There's no argument against the entropy I speak of: only the kind of speculation that's no better than preferred reverie. I don't expect you to believe me. But I think that if the world lasts long enough for a little more ferment some new generation will discover my kind of radical antidisestablishmentarianism."

"Wow!" Jack mocked. "Are we turning fascist in our old age? I have written poyems about hope. Hope is by exclusion. You hope by suppressing what you don't want to remember. That's how the man in my poyem puts your case."

"No sir, not my case! The hope that I hope for takes everything into full view, forgetting nothing; holding just to the *possibility* of human survival—of that which can be conceived only contrary to all objective probability—without the slightest degree of predictive commitment."

"Hope stripped of subjective probability also?"

"Yes. Practically speaking, hopeful wanhope."

"Get on with it then. You're stalling. Make your modest proposal."

"It's hard to talk about when full of Scotch." Mike poked Jack's thigh with one of his feet. "I think Caleb and I had better go home now."

"You can't stop now!" Sarah implored. "We know you're inexhaustible. If you can hope at all there must be some subject of hope—and it's not you alone because you're not alone in hoping. Ergo—" she faltered triumphantly.

"Sal, stop playing with sophomore philosophy!" Jack admonished her. "You should know better after all these years with me! . . . Still," he added softly, "we're grateful for your attention."

"Grant you grace, I hope the cat will scratch your face!" she replied with ostensibly playful asperity.

Mike patted her hand. "Only God can grant the grace that the whole world needs. We don't need any other miracles. The world doesn't profit enough from philosophy."

"How do you get God's grace?" As if fearless, Sarah pressed where Jack was too delicate.

"Indirectly. I don't hear the voice of Yahweh. All I know is that he's no false god. Epistemological criticism doesn't interest me."

[Lofty evasion. The dear man has his limitations!]

"So you rely on a psychological proof of God after all!" Jack protested with amicable disgust.

"I tell you Jack I'm talking about *hope!*" With a show of animation Mike toed him again. "Sarah's right: if other people have the same kind of hope then there's hope for the world."

"Just what I mean: subjectivism!"

"Yaako be quiet. I want to hear why he's hopeful, even if he's wrong, after all the dreadful things he's said about women."

"It's my temperamental buoyancy I guess." Mike stood up and stoutly stretched himself, evidently resolved not to be pinned down.

[Does this untraveled lecturer believe his audience too uneducated to know what he's talking about?]

But suddenly sitting down again Mike reverted to the monotonous drone with which he had conducted his examination of despair. The affect of his ensuing discourse was as usual neutralized by the mask of his countenance. Not that the hope he now began to express was belied by more gloomy mein; it was rather that the manner of his long preamble had been cheerful in foreknowledge of a rebuttal never intended for delivery.

{*Postulants only*: GO TO ITEM (32) SA.12, page 347.}

(31)
SO.04.4

TROPHIC TIME

. . . In astronomical time, a dimension objectively constant to terrestrial minds and therefore uniform in slope, density of experience varies from moment to moment. But for each subjective consciousness internal time itself is a variable. Consider the time of place. Even in your own place, a locality surrounded by disorder or vagueness, where space and time are experienced on the same scale by all persons inhabiting it, you know that under ordinary conditions no one even tries to grasp the psychic time of neighbors. Yet it was dromenon that originally claimed your place from landscape, and on occasion it can take place again. Under certain dromenological conditions human time is shared. For a while the diverse densities of experience are synchronized. Subjective time is made common by the action.

The art of dance is produced wholly in the immediate time of the congregation. The effect is multiplied by the number of witnesses, as if its energy, according to a new thermodynamic law for the theater, could be transmitted concurrently and undiminished everywhere in the system, gaining counterentropic value by multiplication. In this violation of natural law dance does not differ from the other arts; but modern art-dance in principle (like jazz) is distinguished by simultaneity of creative and aesthetic experience, where the act of creation is present and visible as the performance, and can take no more time than the performance or the attendance. None of it can be determined earlier at another place, at the artist's leisure, and translocated; the event itself can't persist beyond the time it takes place; nor can the aesthetic experience be deferred. Each performance is visible as a new action which moves at a pace leaving no time for reflection.

Creative movement can't be planned in such a way as to be specified in advance by an unseen wright; nor recorded more than suggestively for future dancers. A novelist during composition can forget something of what he's done and still review it for change before his presentation. He can also make the people he writes about more intelligent than himself, or give them better memories, perhaps by endowing them with knowledge and perspicacity at a preternaturally early age, or without plausible time for learning by study or experience.

Thus as a charlatan of time even a realist can prove the existence of people superior to himself, not only those whose genius surpasses his own but also those whose deeds excel in efficiency any possible behavior in actual life. But the dancer, practically naked, unassisted by symbol or concept, can simulate with the actual only. Her imagination must be personally proved in the performance, not before it is witnessed. She has no business playing around with pseudo-densities of time, and she wouldn't know how to falsify her skill. Dance is the only creative art primarily energetic. Extraordinary human heat is generated and dissipated on the spot, in its own time. Dance is the art opposite to fiction in its temporal sincerity.

Thus the fourth advantage of women in dance is their natural sympathy with trophic time. I call it trophic because I refer to all the rhythms and durations that have to do with the nourishment or protection of life for its own sake, as distinguished from movement by life in pursuit of such other values as are indicated by tangential vectors, asymptotic progressions, or vibrations of higher frequency than human trembling. In respect to sense of life, nutrition stands in opposition to narcotic inanition; and protection is opposed to locomotion as place is opposed to travel. Trophic time begins and ends with the span of individual life. Its flows and oscillations are irreversible, and therefore the trophic consciousness is preoccupied with feelings of conservation. On the other hand, its antithetical counterpart, the analytical awareness of astronomical time, which serves the necessities of "arithmomorphic" treatment, can in principle extend throughout all cycles of existence, inorganic as well as living, and repeat or reverse all events except those of art. Men and women are not insensitive to trophic and measurable time respectively, especially when as thinkers or feelers they make the effort to transcend their sex; but they are prejudiced. A man to erase his bias must reorganize his personality, but a woman has only to suspend her feelings for an hour, calling upon an idle corner of her brain to take up reason's commissions.

Every schoolboy knows how girls enjoy their superior memory—maybe from millennia of being married into foreign tribes and having to serve as interpreters. They memorize their lessons for fun, as boys play at unofficial riddles, and their pleasure in the employment gets them an early education very easily. But it's only practice, in the amusing male world, for their real lives as women, where memory rules in earnest as landlady of the brain: nay, as the very place of the mind, within which all mental action is contained— the chamber, the bed, the loculus of intelligence; as the persistence of consciousness which may be called even the female mind itself.

Memory is the plowed field that men walk away from after they've pulled and bagged a few concepts to play ball with on a gridiron, perhaps nowhere nearby. Men also remember enough to understand plots, or to lay them. Most thinking and experience (such as manufacturing) is now recordable, reducible to reference. As far as technology goes, mnemonic requirements do not much exceed the alphabet and the decimal system. (As for wisdom, they say it's all been written.) But a single dance cannot proceed without an unassertive and transparent memory that keeps the mind in one place and makes of protracted movement a single, unified, organic image. So also women knit yarn when excluding what they do not wish to incorporate.

But nowadays the bruitings of social enlightenment have so intimidated scholars that they overlook such sexualistic distinctions. Learned men are personally fearful of appearing to support injustice; and no lover or husband, for one reason or another, is entirely free to seem to do so. I can only speculate about what would be discovered. Some of the old disowned archetypes of paired opposites, favoring either side, might be attested. Much of the injustice to women stems from definitions of value and standards, not from inequitable doctrine. Is it an injustice to act upon the belief that some variations of a woman's feelings result from regular and detectible modulations of moods common to both sexes? Or that women spawn their eggs once a month, like it or not, whereas men produce sperm so frequently, for random or irregular replenishment, that the event seems to be either random or at will? The periodic purification of life's dead possibilities by means of an irreversible trickle escaping from vascular circulation surely doesn't imply that women are inferior to their opposites whose purgation is usually voluntary.

Then too, it may be that scientists are loathe to extend distinctions of gender because their techniques are habituated to quantities and measures compatible with clock-time, like grams and calories, at the expense of skill in developing ordinal metaphors, such as that required in estimating magnitudes and shapes of body surface in relation to sexual hue or saturation. They rightly know that human value can't be graduated by dimension or ratio within the category of their own sex, whether male or female, at least for most purposes; but they're not justified in their understatement of the probability that differing ergodicities in historical and contemporary observations of male and female behavior testify to corresponding differences in the tenor of individuality, which is more essential psychologically than mere opposite valence in the single function of reproduction.

The female rate of metabolism, at rest, is said to be slightly lower than the male, in face of the fact that men are larger than women and that in general this ratio is higher for smaller animals. Women also live longer—which is to say that they depreciate at a lower rate—despite apparently greater wear and tear. How can we explain such a mismatch, as expressed more or less in the terms of scientific discourse, between those who unite in one flesh to produce another one of either kind but never mixed? Without offering any alternative method to that of traditional research, I hereinafter guess at future findings in dromenology.

Basal Metabolism Rate is now formularized on assumptions that should be called in question. Considering all the factors that enter into intensity of oxidation, I find it hard to believe, even in principle, that the rate of vital energy exchange is any less than loosely correlative to the area of skin; but, for the sake of simplicity, let us grant that total heat dissipation, equaling total heat production, varies directly with surface. But the tables that convert height and weight into surface area apparently make no allowance for differences of shape. They give a woman, compared with a man, too much surface for her volume. I would say she is slightly more spheroid. Thus her B M R should be reckoned somewhat higher.

Yet there is a more important correction. It seems to me that women are less dense than men. As smaller animals than men, the relative weight of their bones is less; they are relatively less muscular. Indeed they are precious especially for the expansibility of their hollows, having been formed with capacity for internal transitory volumes. If an extrinsic mass gets lodged in them it is expelled before their specific gravity reaches a limit.

As a majority females redress the imbalance of both density and size in humanity's phenomenological total. (I postulate an equal sum of holistic life in each division of the population.) Look to formal and organoleptic values for the noumenological counterweight to masculine density of mass. Science is still too crude even to measure, short of total immersion, so simple a specification as a man's volume, and must roughly rely upon height and weight for planning the human use of space; so no one should wonder at our incompetence in abstracting sexualistic quantity. But at least I can reason that an increase in the index of relative metabolism must follow from my reduction of estimated density.

These two revisions together may be supposed to bring the rates of energy-conversion closer to equality; but they do not account for the difference in longevity. Here we must recover from a profound prejudice, if we are to offer a general theory of femininity, by invoking the principle of trophic time. Since prose isn't sinuous enough to express the feminine directly, I must express my contrasts in terms of astronomical time, as follows.

Feminine time is "slower" than the standard. A woman's hour lasts longer than mine. Her unit is larger. It takes more of my units than hers to make up an interval. Thus, in my statistics, she seems to live longer. I cannot estimate the magnitude of adjustment required for all the phenomena of sex, and I doubt its constancy of proportion, but I'm not likely to be mistaken in the claim that it would put the basal metabolism rate of a woman *above* my own, thereby enlightening a number of puzzling observations by introducing as an epistemological concept the alternate and variable densities of time.

Everything that it takes women too long to do should be examined in this light. All their latenesses and lags. Whatever they are slow about. Wherever they seem lower than you in intensity, look for the subjective time scale of their lives. It is obvious that they all love plants more than machines. They'd rather knit than nail. They have fewer heart attacks. But when you wonder about the evolutionary cause of trophic time you turn to the best evidence of all: marvelous natural patience in nursing and teaching children after they are born. It's a rare man who can serve mankind at that slowest pace of all.

By dividing up astronomical time in masculine fashion, now and then we can hazard translations from the trophic idiom, provided that we don't try to fix any coefficients. But at bottom the two modes of consciousness can never be reconciled, despite the use of a common language and the mutual contact of love.

Even the moon is no truly trophic sister, for all its sympathy with the struggle against overlords. However long it may seem to a woman from any midnight to midnight, the twenty-nine and a half rotations of the earth that measure the synodic period of the moon cannot be counted as equal to the twenty-eight, more or less, which round out her own—nowadays at least. 'Tis lunatics who attempt such ancient adjustments. Poor epicene Artemis is kept from perfect harmony with her brother by a sex still not strong enough in self-assertion and, tightly bound, she is caught between sun and earth in an uninterrupted asynchronous clockwork of unacknowledged estrus. This complicated symbol of temporal compromise is still the best possible reconciliation in a third party.

You will find true androgyneity only in a peculiarly intelligent kind of the female brain, a seat of consciousness most to be prized and yet perhaps the most uncomfortable to be subject of. (Other male and female organs such as the heart may be interchangeable, but they are all used exclusively either for male or for female purposes, and even if they are transplanted from one sex to the other they are never called upon to serve a bisexual function.) Leaving aside the asymmetrical function of mating, such a woman can do or learn just about anything of which a man is capable; but the converse is beyond a man: he is too specialized, for instance, to match her in the early education of children. Her versatile and simultaneous abilities are accounted for by details of cerebral anatomy—as in the brain also a man's residual femininity betrays itself, conceal it though he may everywhere else in his person.

The brain takes only ten percent of the body's sustenant energy, and very little increment of oxidation to move from rest to hard thought, but its homeostatic thermal requirement determines the temperature of the entire male or female organism. All the more, then, would you expect the separate male and female time-scales of a woman to be controlled or indirectly paced by simultaneous and disparate oscillations of voltage within the skull. If there is any harmonic relationship between the parallel brain waves it's too difficult for my competence; but I would search for femininity in the lower of recognized frequencies.

The *Delta* frequency range is harmonic with that of the heartbeat, and it is associated with most of the conditions in which nervous vigilance is lessened, intermitted, or relaxed. *Alpha* vibrations, which seem to me characteristically masculine, are five to ten times as fast, as if purely synaptic and less influenced by endocrinal fluctuation. It is in fact the slower and older rhythm that dominates childhood, sleep, disease, and the approach to death, and seems to prove the psychic effect of chemical forces to the extent of emolliating neural tensions and disarming aggressive irascibility. To my mind this is a case of Mother Nature showing herself where she's needed, absorbing the machineried madness of her son or lover before he becomes forever lost in "the fallacy of misplaced concreteness."

Half the people who speak the languages of the northwest quadrant of the earth have learned time merely as a dimension, and they have the feeling that its spatial content may be fixed for the record whenever a point is chosen in its steady progression. For all practical purposes they can abstract time with as much certainty as if it remained still while space moved.

But how can such classical persuasions get deep into the bones of a person to whom time is so physical that it passes like blood and comes as empirically as natural variations in heaped or exiguous supplies of food? To such a one geometry itself puffs and shrinks within the month and the growth of love modifies the law of contradiction. First things and last things, doctrinaire concepts bullied and hypnotized into the superficial brain like catechistic idealism, can't be integrated into a life of seasons, flux, and generation. Somatic rhythm is the invisible ground of being, and consciousness of it emerges only through mechanical opposition or disturbance. Trophic time fosters not objectivity's perceptions but the internal illusions of life's own wildly variable foreshortening, microscopically sharing the virtue of history, which is to refrain from observation at such great distance that any event can truly be taken as an ergodic repetition.

Compared with natural woman a man is mechanical in making love and electrical in his synapsis, almost simply binary; whereas she is moved more slowly in a cumulative chain of responses at endocrinal speed, and in electromagnetic fashion holds on to what she has attained for some time after the energizing force has left off. This orgastic hysteresis retards the reversal of condition and slows the flesh's loss of residual sensation; prepares it for new summations of private history, until the voluptuous peristalsis has dampened itself in the memories of daily life. Thus trophic magnetism discloses itself in the aftereffect of a visceral climax.

Even when modern devices both lighten the inconvenience of catamenia and prevent its inconvenient interruption, making it feasible to schedule dance performances with little fear of default, sustaining allurement with a constancy rare in the past, it is no secret that women suffer more frequently than men in the struggle to adjust their regressive moods to the impersonal progression of distinctly personal achievement. Dance must overcome not only the human, like all art, but also the very femininity of its foundation. Nevertheless one can acknowledge that of all arts dance is woman's most sympathetic without easily seeing that a weaker grasp of trophic time puts men at a disadvantage in this species of theater.

Creative dance does not follow music, and it obeys no form but its own. A comparatively informal mise-en-scène is typical of modern dance because there must be no limit to liberty of body if new movements are to be made in a place that permits no locomotion. Tempo and movement define the space of the place.

When a man tries to escape the formality of chronological time he is likely to open its system into a larger system of the same time, or into times of the same character, just as he has escaped from Newton's laws by localizing them within metalaws of Relativity. Also, by the same token, when he starts a hierarchy of internal systems, opening one into the next, his subjectivity regresses to inverse infinity, each set subsumed into a broader set, as in the historical paradigm of certain saints: "I am alas still proud to have confessed my pride in confessing the pride with which I confessed that I cannot find humility. . . ."

Such rational evasions boot nothing when it comes to the plasticity of time. There is no help for it but to close the system and isolate it from all others, keep it in its one and only place, free it of all chronological environment, so that there can be a beginning and an ending, and a *new* beginning which is not merely a rebeginning. A dancer can't do it the way a mystic does, by denying time, because even occult dance would be an art of biologically sequential action. The material cause of its music and kinematic sculpture is the irreversibly living body.

Men can no doubt invent positions and patterns well enough, but these constitute movement no more fully than a string of points constitute a line. Women are autonomically able to control time as a variable continuum, perhaps by the manner in which they draw breath, slowing down their costal muscles or speeding them up.

Movement is more interesting for its varieties and degrees of angular velocity than for the stances it passes through. It is the dynamic mutability of trophic scale that makes possible for these irregular curves of acceleration and deceleration their personal subtlety and unique range of motion.

Women have a headstart in fictile movement because they are born as free of time's universals as of geometry's. They are more docile to nature than men are, much to our confusion, but less tractable to preconceptions of this evanescent art.

{*Postulants only*: GO TO ITEM (33) SO.04.5, page 361.}

(32)
SA.12

PONY RIDES

We approach a turbulent concourse wherein the Trustees have made concession to the electorate with a vengeance. Or rather the concession is for the electorate. Some entrepreneur—maybe Howard Johnson in disguise—must have been licensed thank god without competition or advertising but under suitable regulation of taste and price to serve the fatigues and hungers of those about to submit themselves to the animals, of those like us who have already run the gauntlet, and of those who have come to the gardens not to learn at all but mainly

My how nice. What a lovely park. But it doesnt seem as big as when Daddy took me. With the cane he used to hang over his wrist when he was getting money out of his pocket. How did that old car ever get this far? No bridge then. We must have driven all the way down the Bay and up the Peninsula. Or maybe we came over on the ferry and then took trolleys the way Mike brought us today—but it seems to me that all they had then was cable cars. I must be getting it mixed up with another trip. The time he took me alone with him in the yellow Model A up to the Gold

347

for the alimentary refreshment. Obviously there are many who refresh themselves coming and going, maybe eating and loitering here between visits to different caged faces and asses, returning again and again, prolonging the ordeal by renewing the pleasure, walking further and taking longer than their more efficient compatriots either our kind or the others who come here first. At the edge of this milling campus the trees and shrubs are green enough but wrongly too green for the season. Even palm trees, on Palm Sunday! The shyest viridescent twigtips on bare branches would be sweeter. I should have gone back to Gloucester after the war. It's hard to remember cold weather. Like seasickness: the worst feeling in the world when you have it but completely forgotten the minute it's over. They say childbirth's like that too. Paul is it? Somewhere in the New Testament. Never saw Ruth's worst pain. Just the contractions, and it was only with the first baby that I paid much attention. She's so quiet about things like that! Never complained that I was neglecting her. I'm always insensitive to other people; didn't realize how cruel I was. Gave her unnecessary pain just because I was angry. Always hated pregnancy, every phase of it. It's a miracle that the kids came out alive and whole when so many don't whose fathers like Pat pray for them. It's always green here but not evergreen. The deciduous trees never seem fresh. No winter purification. Leaves never dying or aborning together but like corpses at a city hospital they seem to

Rush country. Used to buy me things all along the way—and he didnt have as much money as Mike probably has. —Here's a good place to have a treat before we start back. Nice tables under the trees. Refreshments for sale. I wonder if it's the same place. I hope he'll loosen up. There's no need to be so stingy all the time. Children should grow up feeling secure and generous, never pinched when the parents arent really pinched. I must ask him where all the money goes. But he doesnt seem to want to earn more money. That was a sweet boy who kissed me in this park. Must have been near here, right in broad daylight. I hope nobody was looking. My first date in San Francisco. Mother wouldnt let me go out much at night until college. Mike's been nice today. He was good last night. . . . um . . . very good. I wish it were always that good. But I think things are better than they used to be. I thought he didnt love me. The doctor was right. Maybe from now on it will always be that lovely. It's not that I expect him to be in love every minute. He doesnt have to be tender all the time. In the old days I used to have to ask him to be a little rough once in a while. But sometimes he seems to be doing it out of sheer willpower, when it isnt even true lust. Is it possible anyone could still desire me? But he works very hard. Too touchy to talk about, that he never gets anywhere for the family. Almost like alcoholism. I think he'll change. The boys are hungry. I am too. It's funny, he's not making any fuss about it. Sweet of him to get

appear and fade separately in more or less random distribution without any discernible rhythm. More like pythagorean souls flittering away at night. I'm not going to go through the agony of trying to find out what everyone wants. I ought to be able to make four decisions. Nothing for Roger of course. I swore that after the Navy I'd never wait in line again! Where's my pastime book? Well never mind, it's more like a cluster than a queue and I'll have to keep alert to get my turn. The flora of California is too big and easy and therefore pulpy to have Nordic core or Celtic density, let alone gnarled Puritan integrity. The palms they give out in church must really be some kind of reed, not from these trees that are brittle before they're picked. The palms at Saipan. Hot beer on the beach. Very coarse coral sand. Sumerian or at least Akkadian priests used to fertilize date palms artificially. Among the northern trees they look like diseased weeds with scrofulous bark, but Californians are proud of them. If there are ten billion neurons in every human cortex then how many neurons do I see on the hoof right now? The animal crackers are for Ruth even if she gives most of them to the kids. Get two I guess; her father always got her two at a time. I wonder how many species they bother to make for those little suitcase arks. Still look exactly

things for everybody. It's good to sit down and let him wait on us for a change. I hope he'll allow the boys to go on at least one ride. Once in a while he lets up on that Yankee cussedness Jack teases him about but there's something to it. He says he's seen it snow in the moonlight though. Must be beautiful. I've never seen it rain in the moonlight. He's very stubborn about Gloucester. The trees here are perfectly lovely.

"What do you want on your hot dog Matty?"

He calls me his little horse. If I were a horse I'd snort at his silly comparisons. Always comparing things. They used to say in Sunday school don't make invidious comparisons.

"Stuffed olives."

He knows too much. He'd be a professor now if he hadnt left college. Jack and Newt shouldnt encourage his vanity. We have an ocean here too. He used to think Monterey was heaven when he was courting me! It would be softer than other moonlight where I suppose snowflakes would be falling everywhere, falling on snow. But too cold to make love, and we made love under the pines in the sand dunes, with bright white moonlight beyond the shadows. And to think that I touched him down there even before he put his hand under my dress! I was impatient after all those dates when he didnt notice my body at all, didnt even kiss me for a long time. Curious too, about how big it'd be. He says he's seen seagulls in Gloucester flying alone at midnight during winter storms looking for food.

"Oh boy, popcorn!"

"Popcorn is my favorite fruit."

"Fruit Daddy! Popcorn isnt a fruit!"

the same as they did in Gloucester. I remember these white shoestring handles. A & P, First National, Brown's, all the little stores. More species than books. (Titles in print, or all titles ever published?) The original ark was just a big box shaped like Ishmael's life preserver. No need for sea-birds to be saved— but what did they eat for forty days and forty nights with no beaches or mussels or fish gurry? They were passions torn from the breast of Adam according to Yeats, like each of the other species. Which passion? Freedom. They're pretty tough and fearless-looking here. What kind, herring gulls or California gulls? Be funny if one of them has seen Gloucester, by way of northern Canada or by the Missouri to the Snake and the Columbia or by the Panama Canal. I doubt that the ornithologists could prove anything. But they just don't seem the same kind here. Look at that crippled bruiser with the folded foot. All the others are swooping

I wonder if there could be a white seagull flying through the white snow in the white moonlight? Thank you Lord for the birds we eat, that's what Jonathan said for grace, before Roger, when Matt was a baby. I took him to Sunday school a few times for the lay group they had. Mike wouldnt pay for a weekday nursery school. Mr Gilchrist was in love with me but my own husband would never believe it. He was all excited about California when I met him and now he just makes tiresome remarks about our fruits and vegetables. What's wrong with being big and luscious? I don't want death and resurrection in the plants we eat. This is a fine table. All of us together. No one in a rush to get anywhere. It's nice to have everyone cheerful at once. But I don't think these seagulls are so nice. They look fierce. That one doesnt look clean. I don't trust him. Dirty-looking scavenger. I'm glad he isnt any bigger.

and busy picking up garbage but he just stares off westward into space. Probably not twenty feet from us. If he's not interested in the hurly-burly why does he stay here at all? He should be standing on a tower of Golden Gate Bridge.

"Daddy! He took my hotdog right off the table!"

"Look! The others are trying to get it away from him!"

"He's fighting them all off!"

"Why that goddam little sneaky bastard! I thought there was something funny about his pose!"

"He's flown up to the roof! He's having a hard time getting through the cellophane!"

"Oh boy—did you see that disappear? It's gone already!"

"You can have half of mine Jonny."

"I'll give you another one mister. Every once in a while that happens here. Birds get rambunctious when they're protected by law."

> "He's gone away and that other one's pecking at the wrapper. Too late old man!"
> "How do you know it was a he?"

Nice guy. I didnt have to ask him. It's embarrassing to be a victim. In Gloucester they have too much self-respect to do a thing like that. Or else there's too much easy fish.

Fiend! The nerve of him! It's a good thing the man gave us another one free or we wouldnt all be laughing now. Roger is the most excited one of all. He loves to see

> "Well well! That's life!"
> "Life is the key to civilation."
> "Civil-i-*za*-tion, Matt!"
> "Why do you always correct me, just because you're bigger? I know it's civilization!"
> "I'm sorry. I didnt know you said it on purpose. Did you really?"

Christ that was fast! How does his brain first learn to identify hotdogs for good eating merely by their shape? Maybe they look like fish. In Gloucester they sometimes walk up lanes and stroll around houses like chickens hardly looking for food at all just to see what yard life's like. When there arent any dogs around. Cats can't give them any trouble. Give me a mongoose for its deeds but a cat for its thoughts the Sumerians said. Cat in a lab with his brain lobes disconnected or something tried to fuck a duck. Kids used to play what you'd get if you crossed a —— with a —— . A quacking kitty. Or a whiskered fowl. Walt Disney has wiped out the authentic imagination of three generations so far. Might still have been some margin in radio with sound alone but kids' invention—

everyone laughing at once. But there's no girl-child to laugh with me. Would she laugh at the same things? The world is for men as the map is for North. I can't dispute it. If I were a Patagonian queen and had my way I still wouldnt want the tail of my country pointing up. No one would like everything reversed. Nothing would change except that we'd call the north pole the south, but women wouldnt be on top. It's funny when we do it that way I feel strident just because of the word I guess. Anyway it would never be equal. Why does someone always have to be boss? It's better just to be as different as possible from men. There's symmetry in life if that's the word for it. But very sweet of him to get the animal crackers really thinking of me. A gift, he gives me a gift. But

> "Dad if you didn't have numbers time couldnt keep going because you couldnt have smaller and smaller time—millionths of seconds and billionths of seconds and smaller and smaller. I'm just glad letters can't get smaller and smaller or we'd have billions and trillions of words."

mine too—was cut off even there and worse deformed by commer-

it's always only a gift in the morning to keep the children respect-

cials dinned in. Only ideas remain. But you can't be an artist just with ideas. I should know. There's touch left though. I always forget sculpture. They still have sculpture in art and sex in life. Millions of people crave touch, plastic or cognitive or therapeutic. Is it humans only? But

The strain of man's bred out
Into baboon and monkey.

The touch stays on, devolving with them, but imagination's left behind. I myself don't have any to spare. If I could really remember the winters I actually knew I'd probably be glad of this weather. That's what she thinks, too clever by half. But you take the winter as a matter of course when it comes, like sickness—I remember that much. But back there you take the spring for granted too. I always tried to store up the summers but I

able, a morganatic marriage, one thing I remember from those English courses I never should have taken. Those doves are much nicer than the gulls. Gentle, but none of them are white. I wish I could go to a ceramics class once a week down at the Center. He thinks it's creation without toil. Photography too. But that's exactly what I want, creation without toil. Everything else is toil. Such a silly snob he is, and all the rest of them. Lofty as Tolstoy. As willing I'm a slave; as unwilling I'm a rebel. Told him that once and I think it scared him. But I've never rebelled. What would I do anyway? All I need is a chance to show that there's a thought or two in me. I told him that too and he laughed at the language of it. The people here must have a terrible time cleaning up after all these birds, pigeons even

"Daddy what's a ski toe?"
"It's something like a green thumb."

never could carry one day's weather to the next. I'm always totally adapted, like the lowest form of life that can survive everything. Maybe after all a different man each day each hour each minute each second. A creature of climate. But not so far gone I can't see that the green here is neverfresh forever. You

even ickier than gulls. I could never do it. But now I know I'm very good at anything Mother can't do well—tennis and chess and bringing up children. She never even had a boy. It was worth all that money it took for me to realize it. I don't need the doctor now. But Michael could afford it. He gets a new suit

"Daddy does everyone think the same thoughts or do different people think different thoughts?"
"Different."

can't blame the palm trees for being tufted and prickly but the trees here that take their names and lines from the East I condemn for lack of heartwood core and for rings too far apart. Looks as if there's no sap in them, very little

whenever he wants it. Tolstoy. Selfishness is a sad thing in the best men. Why do they call them great? Nobody writes down the good men—or the great women. But the doctor wanted me to become reality-oriented. So now I'm reality-

seasonal at all. Never fear sir, this is no clime for a Druid cult. But still if you overlook the seasonless boredom this landscaping is really pretty nice. Taken all in all without my theoretical preconceptions it's a fine park, at least outside of this swilling pleasure-precinct, free and irregular with valleys woods and unfenced ponds yet nobody's game preserve. Alleys of bowling green as cultivated as Holland.

oriented. Stronger. Better for the boys I guess. But I forget the truth about things and I don't try to help the world anymore. Self-oriented. She was no better than she should be. Doctor lied to me. Everyone lies because they don't know how to tell the truth. It's the strong people that can't bear the truth. And now they've made me forget the truth. Why should I be weak when so many people are strong? I know

"Dad your body is all over you, it is!"

"That's what *you* is."

"But how could it be, because you know what? Jonny is just blood and bones. God changed him into a real person! He's still rather weak. But if everything were made of everything nothing could hurt it, could it Dad?"

Views of the unconfined Pacific. More beautiful and refreshing than any public park in the East at any season, less styptic with shabby chastity; and less abused. The city was generous to itself here, taxpayers to city, city to taxpayers—favoring both leisure and sincerity. Who had the foresight? For once, foresight that was successful: somebody knew—and could persuade the public—what would be important in a hundred years. The miracle of society despite willful stupidity at

what to do with strength but I don't seem to like strong people. Except him. He's a good man underneath his selfishness. With him it's an intellectual affectation and he doesnt know how much damage it does. Probably no man understands important things. That's why I left him that week I took the kids to Russian River. Silly thing to do when I see it now but I thought it might make him understand my abilities.

large. Look at the landscape of someone's foresight for posterity!

"Daddy did they fire you out of the bookstore?"

"Not that I've heard."

"Well, you know the grand-right-and-left in dancing?"

"Yes."

"Well, you should hold on to your job until you get another one!"

Though Michael owned at last that nature in decking herself practically the same all year round (to a New Englander neither bleak nor fully blithesome) was only a little misguided, and that the contracts for leveling the coastal sand dunes negotiated by some committee of magnates sitting on bags of gold-dust had amazingly issued in a district of educational beauty for the use of their boom-town's grandchildren, he still could not reconcile himself to the behavior of contemporary taxpayers. They tarried without leisure and without generosity, even those here at the zoo never entirely unpreoccupied with the ambitions and rights by which they aggrandized defended or insured their personal nests and perquisites. Their voiced carcasses boomed and shrilled with mild amusement—but in a restless discontent not anticipated by Saint Alexis, who may never have suspected that entertainment would forestall "pleasures of the mind" and abuse the central nervous system with an addictive narcosis that could not be sustained by botanical beauty natural history travel fresh air or Coca-Cola. Nor would their vacuity have been plenished by witnessing any of the conjugations excluded from view, or even by experiencing for themselves the one game that can seem to recreate the mind existentially. For Michael, as for that French admirer (before the lovely Golden Gate terrain passed from incompetent Mexicans to the flag of the grizzly bear), who said of democracy that "many men would willingly admit its vices who cannot support its manners," real wickedness was the last thing to worry about. (At least between elections.) Tocqueville's prophecy throbbed in Michael's heart as witness. No assurance that Europe had equally hateful behaviors could edulcorate the burning gall of his patriotism.

Plebes bourgeoisie and professionals possessed every nook every picnic table every vantage that might be prized by persons seeking rest from entertainment. To an ear capable of filtering the composite waves of sound: mothers screamed at their children as if there had never been joy on either side, and the older ones responded with peevish if not insolent execrations, too exasperated by the ostentations of petty familial authority in that heady carnival atmosphere to fear any of the banal threats. Yet to an eye not engaged in its own business: it was possible also to discern within this general disordered vibration the discrete acts of a thousand faithful fathers filling five thousand pairs of lunchhooks with half a thousand pounds of garish and toxic foodstuffs purchased on the spot.

Further, to the eye and to the ear of our invidious veteran, or to his memory: youths lordly slick and loud strutting through the crowd in the style and costume of their grade, slender or brawny triangles jostling each other and prancing about on their points with the poor arrogance of callow virility and with no thought or interest but what pertained to that virility, indifferent to past and future; living on desire that would bring them in the end to the worn and wearing furrows in which the shorter broader people (their sullen enemies) were treading and were trod; always searching for and displaying themselves to their unconnected counterparts the pert teasing semi-assertive flowered female bodies from the same or equal schools who were less certain of what they wanted but in the assurance of consummation-at-will and in the outrageousness of their exhibition far less pitiable. Michael abhorred these gumchewing selfdespoiling girls. If they had not been future women (with their budded breasts due to be blown by the usage of life) who could make or break the American nation with their conception of childhood he would have wished them the worst, out of sheer aesthetic hatred.

But he knew that his wife was able to see them, both the boys and the girls, not as men and women squandering time and freedom but merely as colts and fillies not yet obliged to enter the marketplace and still innocent in their manners. She was right: if he tried hard he could see each private future behind the veiled eyes in these gangsters of desire.

Those adolescents nevertheless remained for the moment clustered objects of his censorious allegation. He hated the males for the familiarities they were granted, the females for the inaccessibility to himself of what they studied to make desirable, and all of them for the contempt they bore him and the other plebes bourgeoisie and intellectuals possessing every nook every picnic table and every vantage.

Yet here and there were old folks come to remember their own children long dead or long spoiled or never made. Here and there a family quiet in its wonder and pleasure, ready for kindnesses to any of themselves who asked money for more of that pleasure or wonder as if asking for love, meekly waiting in line for its hard-earned doles—perhaps immigrants luckily escaped from the late European troubles, or stray clutches of cottonpickers from a Godfearing strain, or fragile unexpectant Chinese from nearly ceaseless laundries, or even ordinary fleshy Americans unaccountably humble. Here and there a mother or a father still fresh with amazement and joy in the amazement and joy of laughing children. Here and there a single child grateful or pleased or affectionate. Here and there an attendant who did not despise the herd—and he the most saintly of all!

But no critics or personages; no arbiters; not a single sign of virtuosity; no learning displayed by intellectuals. Not one of any degree wearing culture on his sleeve.

The taste was howsoever no worse than Tuileregentsgarten fashions. More ignorance of Aristotle and lessness of classical tongues makes no difference. Yet not so unschooled either, taking a true statistical sample, if you count living souls only, San Francisco vs Paridonlin. A city except for rapid transit superior in engineering, or anyway in natural beauty; one might suppose superior in energy, or at any rate in innovation, especially because since the earthquake (when the worst of greekish imitation's imitations were shaken to the ground by Seahorse, much to the secret satisfaction of the uneducated) there remained but few lines of official Victorian beauty, whose force had been waning with the memory of Albert's actual warmth in bed. Creased and warrened with the imperfect networks of a living brain this city would decently sphacelate and ooze after death, Michael thought, unlike some old cities that he could name if he'd been good at foreign pronunciation where the vermiculations of the past were preserved in hard dry bakings, and the crawlings of few enough worms at that, considering the time that had piled up. Around the Acropolis or the Vatican would you not find less—or would you find more?—to justify the labors of those who have striven for the world's prosperity? Much more than less however here at the Golden Gate would be hard to justify. Local civilization he held to be just barely defensible. Wow! The very place that Jack London had picked, walking in this park on a Sunday afternoon, to excite himself with visions of desolation.

But now Michael was drifting with the will of his family—the boys willing all things, Ruth willing nothing that could be fathomed—drearily despairing of any clear thought or spontaneous motion for the rest of his day, abusing the privilege of travel and wasting consciousness like a million others passing diurnal time, meanly dully inertly agonistic. For a while he reflected upon just one theme: that only the rich and the academic could know the luxury of perpetual intelligence and the liberty to devote any hour of the week to loveseeking or beautymaking. They could go to Afric or the Indy to have their zoo and see it truly live; to New England or even England at least once every seven years to see a truly fresh green April.

Ruth again had Roger on her hip, which was thrust outward as she listed lax and almost slattern to the opposite side, disguised by fatigue, one would think a Gypsy queen once proud but forced by circumstance to carry through the streets a heavy sack of golden apples. Appearances could equivocate the worth of a good mother moving through her dearest occupations in a tired intermittent daze. But she was less careless sweaty dusty and uncombed than the men she served.

They came to a place where ponies were led around a fenced path circling a diameter of scarcely a dozen yards. Children rode frightened stiff in boxed saddles ornate as galleons. But here it was possible with your bare legs and hands, if you were very much younger than Michael and Ruth, to feel the live coat of an unfamiliar animal. It prickled and quivered.

Everything was conducted for the utmost safety, but in the interests of economy each ponyboy led two, one at either hand. He did so silently but not with remarkable patience. Perhaps few of them applied for the job out of love for children or horses. The kids were not permitted to mount by stirrup but were derricked aboard their steeds by a jolly riding master who stood at the stepped platform—as if every patron, knight and lady alike, was helplessly encased in helm cuirass and greaves. Grimly mounted under the vizards of innocence, clutching tightly the pommels that saved them belike, saying nothing and thinking nothing to smile about, they proceeded with the pace and mein of cannon fodder. Some dared to twist their necks for a last glimpse of loved ones; but most did not, notably those whose feet scarcely reached the stirrups by half.

By the time these Cids and Joans began to confide in their skills they were returned by rotation to the platform where they were derricked off again. A circus with the mean rhythm of a clock, pause and walk, pause and walk, regulated by cogs and catches designed for the democratic demands of a queue, all speeds averaging as one despite aberrations of temperament and agility which might have led to individual variations of movement; and because of peak-load conditions the ride was almost as jerky as that on a crowded ferris wheel that takes no chair more than a single revolution, and between stops seemed no faster than the circumam-bulation of some starved old nag turning an Irish grist mill. To a scientific gull on high it would have appeared a long day of aborted preparations: an army of children continually gathering waiting and walking out to where they hoped adventure would begin, only to undergo a brief and muted happening of no distinct pleasure before returning to the general agitation of prevailing boredom. There was no roll of drums—to say nothing of trumpet blasts or dramatic flourish—to compensate for the dearth of action. The riders were yielded not so much as two paces of trot or a toss of their solemn pony's head, whose lackluster goodwill and humble expec-tations had perhaps driven him into the field of education. The perfunc-tory human ostlers craved not action but brown sugar-cola every hour.

Jonathan suppressed the scorn that would have withered his opportu-nity. He supported Matty's clamor. Father Chapman was not unwilling to grant his two oldest sons any such extraordinary treat that required no worse a waste of his own time. If only we didnt have to wait in line, he almost said, you could have a pony ride. The words came to the tip of his tongue as he eyed the queue. [For the enlisted man ashore and afloat every dispensation had called for lining up: chow line, sick call, ship's store, U S O largesse; and horny seamen fresh on the sandy beach at Lingayen for two-hour liberty, the enemy not long gone, had spontaneously formed a line under the darkling palms to await their separate turns inside a low coop kept by a worn-out Jap-ridden crone who sold her indefatigable cel-ebrations of Liberation sperm upon sperm (though her service unwitting-ly exceeded mere accommodation with at least two couplings of that particu-lar line from the lone L S T in the anchorage, for she had the honor to ini-tiate by total immersion a pair of mercifully quick hamfisted beefy Baptist virgins taunted into thus satisfying the desires of manhood by the scum of the ship's company, in accordance perhaps with their own sordid and un-distinguished rites of passage long before boot camp). The High Com-mand of the vasty nearly shoreless Pacific, having had little expectation that MacArthur would avenge himself so soon in the Philippines, would have been still more surprised that in the event such clandestine vice could arise almost instantly after Liberation on an extremely isolated beach far from a city in the territory of a "village" so dispersed as to be for an American unnoticeable even as a hamlet. After waiting indecisively half an hour almost last in line without moving much closer, on the general prin-ciple of seeking maximum experience, young Michael had a good excuse to shipmates for changing his mind. He walked away without having seen the woman of whose very presence in the lair he professed to remain skep-tical anyway, and whose face to say nothing of figure could hardly have been glimpsed by those who hastily patronized her inside the tiny dark hutch, where she presumably lay on straw without rising or grunting. Joyfully, all by himself, on the well-trodden path through the sand of a coconut grove under the clouds of a crepuscular sky, he had then found his first overseas friend. The young Philippino husbandman riding a water buffalo was ingenuously happy to meet one of his liberators, and as soon as he understood the American's amusing request, was glad to provide him with an experience rarer and more wholesome than the one he'd declined. Elated at an adventurous alternative to lust's putative necessity, Michael was allowed to mount bareback and ride part of its way home the capital animal of a family, led by the small native. The beast's hide was prickly and quivering, and its neck too low to break a rider's forward precipitation, but the delighted sailor's doubts about the equability of its ambling were soon forgotten.] His comminations were on the point of rattling dumbly about the heads of the other fathers and sons—mothers and daughters too—who enjoyed their liberty in a line. The gall of suffering many a slob's priority to worthy Chapman privilege contended in his breast with the generous secretions of proud paternity.

But the owl was diplomatic enough to turn aside the wrath of the tigress and her savage cubs—for into such his suppressed words, had he uttered them, would have transformed the gentle mare and her affectionate foals. Those relentless minds were remembering a little promise he had made without qualification. So he bought two tickets and handed them to the boys. "Here, go get in your first line." He had not been so foolish (he warned his conscience) as to have said that he himself would queue up again for anything in the world.

"I'll stay here with them." Ruth suggested.

"Oh no you don't Madam! If these boys want to ride ponies like all the rest of these kids they'll have to learn to put up with waiting alone. After all, they didnt have to pay for the tickets." He insisted that she and Roger come away with him to sit in the shade on the grass that looked nearly unlittered.

Ruth swiftly weighed the psychic consequences for her children. Was it worse to abandon them to fear and confusion in accordance with her husband's grouchy laziness or to fight it out openly and spoil a memorable day for the whole family? By her decision (over which she couldnt help smiling) it was better not to provoke the father into a new revelation of testy unreasonable selfishness. Besides, would it scar their tough little hearts any deeper than the first day of school to wait a few minutes in an orderly line among harmless children and parents with purposes the same as their own? ["Jonathan is certainly old enough to do *that* for himself!" was a refrain of Michael's household can't.]

The older son's anxiety was from vanity only; it arose from fear for his dignity in encountering unknown social procedures. But Matthew whose courage in the face of protocol would have supported any number of older brothers truly feared nothing more likely than falling from a pony and being stepped on or kicked. ["Why when *I* was that age . . ."]

Thoughtfully chewing her lower lip Ruth said nothing to cross the man, but before she turned away she dropped a few words of comfort into the ears of her sons, pointing out the place nearby where she intended to watch with their father. [Must every bit of learning make us more orphan?]

But Jonathan suddenly demurred. "Oh never mind! I don't want a pony ride now."

"Oh *please* Jonny!" Matt pleaded, looking up into his brother's troubled face.

"What!" cried father. "*After I bought the tickets!*"

"Oh I forgot. All right Matt."

As the parents moved away with the tiny brother who was still exempted from forced learning Jonathan placed Matthew in front of himself—not as leader and not as precious charge to be watched over the more easily but as pilot car pushed ahead on the track in hostile territory. By this technique (which the loyal little brother never suspected) Jonathan hoped to protect his ignorance of ticket-using from embarrassment. While quietly learning from the other's trial and error under unfamiliar conditions he strove to preserve his dominance.

Michael forcibly stationed the remnant of his family at a vantage difficult for the abandoned boys to spot. Roger was put upon his own two feet to observe whatever he liked. Ruth rested on the grass leaning back on her elbows, smiling at the pleasure of rest and Roger's pleasure, keeping an eye on that artful dodger with the habit effortlessly conducted in the background of her mind. For lack of immediate attractions he would stay close of his own accord if no one tried to grab or recall him. Mainly she attended at a distance the two boys in the linear crowd.

Not even for Roger did Michael's eyes leave for so much as five seconds his two epigoni pressed close together peering about at the gross bulks that stood mostly between them and fellow candidates of the riding academy. They did not know what to do with their tickets when the time came. They did not know how to please the officials. Besides the dangers of falling and kicking they wondered at the probability of being pissed upon by a pony. Meanwhile they unsuccessfully scanned the environs to make sure their guardians were still watchful.

The father saw nervousness in those two faces of his separated body. Already repenting, he was anxiously overcome by fresh shame for his own insensitivity. Though he said no more of his contrition to Ruth than Jonathan said of his timidity to Matthew—proud soft men both of them—the dusty tarpaulin that had been covering his heart blew away in a puff of tender Mediterranean zephyr. He jumped up, gruffly motioning Ruth to stay where she was with her duty, and strolled over to the two hostages held of him by fortune. (By the laws of electricity one would have thought that the two in parallel would have halved the love for each pledge instead of doubling it.)

Even Jonathan's greeting of this avatar was unreserved and unembarrassed. The breath of both their joys at paternal reinforcement fanned the tiny flame of Michael's guilt into a prairie fire of determination to justify his part in their diphyletic love. With reassuring words he hurried off for ice cream to while away their waiting with. He got some for Ruth and Roger too, as well as a particolored plastic windmill on a stick.

He ate his own sweet chocolate cone standing with Jono and Matty, glad to find that the line had been moving after all, and was still moving at steady intervals. He laughed with a gentleman ahead of him at the comical hesitation of a stiff little girl in pure white who was suddenly reluctant to straddle the dusty black seat on a mothbitten Shetland monster.

At last came the turn of his sons, all refreshed and bolstered. After the indignity of being hoisted like babes had been put behind them they sat in the saddles diffident but pleased. Their father walked beside them outside the low circumferential lists surrounding the track. They had drawn seats in pairs led by two different grooms, having come to their dual turn on the odd chance of separation, so Michael kept abreast of the younger whose pony was on the outside while Jonathan rode behind on the inner path (getting a shorter ride for his disingenuity in putting little brother ahead of himself). The boys savored their precious time in the cavalry, eking out the adventure, concentrating in silence, hardly aware of the strangers beside them.

Now Michael would have died for their innocence. He thought that maybe at no time of their lives would he ever abandon them to any capital instruction but his own, least of all to the pedagogy of unguided experience.

This event was not lost upon the watchful mother.

{*Postulants only*: GO TO ITEM (34) HY.06, page 365.}

(33)
SO.04.5

FLEXIBILITY

. . . The fifth talent, another versatility, may be the most obvious: flexibility of flesh and skeleton. Little boys are always less supple than their sisters, and their delight in running—the most efficient human locomotion—favors the growth of stringy gristle on the axis of up-and-down drive. Male strength is founded on the reciprocal motion in which muscles tend to reverse themselves perfectly, regaining in the stretch some of the energy lost in contraction; and it is oriented in the forward direction of its prevailing momentum. Men could have been twice as good at running, as good as dogs, if they hadn't given up half their feet for the sake of hands. Women, however, in yielding to men this special superiority, and one or two others, won something of their own, you may be sure, with the breasts and hips that slowed them down.

Nothing can be more useful than flexibility in an art of inefficient movement, where the limbs change direction at every instant and, with extreme expenditure of energy, accomplish practically no external work, not even that required to overcome the friction of wayfaring locomotion. Witness the fact that women are comparatively less inefficient at swimming, the most laborious means for a human being to cover distance without artificial help, full of transverse or writhing motions that are not easy for sinews evolved through walking and climbing, in which way is made by linked reactions to solid resistance.

The components of flexibility are pliancy and elasticity. Regarding the former, one would hope that any muscle or cartilage could be called upon to do anything, even when the body's on a deflected or irregular course. But the phenomenon of elasticity includes deformation as well as resilience, which is to say that residual effect and restoration complement each other in the result of a desisted force upon matter, or that at any particular instant after a distortion the excess of elasticity over resilience is deformity.

Memory and age are physiological deformations (or reformations) of pre-existent states: but with the first, resilience can win out in the long run as forgetfulness; while with the second it always loses everything to deformity over time. However, we here confine ourselves to the approximate present, disregarding long-term strain or restoration. One finds a comparison in genital anatomy, the hysteresis of vaginal distension as against the total reversibility of phallic tumescence, which adds not one cubit to its stature in a thousand stretches. In general, elasticity without deformation—mechanical reversibility that's apt to come to an end suddenly—is masculine.

Hooke's law states that, within the elastic limit, a strain (the initial distortion of shape or size) is proportional to the stress producing it. The stress of dance, like that of parturition, exerts itself from within as a physical pressure of the will, long in cumulation, without much reckoning of self-preservation or thought of the next conception. It is only the range of immediately restorable displacement and the degree of distortion a dancer can suffer without breaking or tearing that limit her effort to violate the ordinary bounds of movement. The sum of resilience and deformation is what counts, not youthlike reversion to original figure, in getting through a performance for the sake of issue, whether child or art. She does not expect to defeat the strains of experience. Age and memory will be incremented in the next dance, making it possible to exceed previous limits of stress while gradually dissipating counterentropic energy from youth's alluring but not bottomless purse.

In any event, elasticity is inversely limited by muscular strength. You should find no more muscle in a dancer's body than it needs for its art-movements.

Men are too thick in the neck to be able to free the head from the posture of the trunk, and they have too much muscle binding thorax and abdomen to free the chest from the belly or the belly from the hips. For dance they are too inarticulate. This fact accounts for their stamina, their upright spine. Stiffness is reinforced by a column of air that pushes into the visceral cavity and tends to rigidify the entire torso, as the stem of a tree is kept upright by the water in it. A man breathes up and down to fill his vital capacity, and his backbone wants to function as a single lever. Oversized muscles not only hamper independent movement of parts but also use oxygen inefficiently, especially when, as tensed and slightly unbalanced antagonists, they are required to perform delicate movements or subtle modifications of poise. In cultural evolution the male body has become an instrument for the particular purposes of such external work as bearing the weight of another dancer; but the internal operation of dance calls for lighter muscles flexibly dispersed.

A woman's rib cage is more resilient (as well as more markedly divided from other segments of the body). For breath she pushes her chest outward and seldom drives her diaphragm down for a deep footing of air (the deformation of her visceral cavity being reserved for uterine expansion). In ordinary life she makes up for inferior thoracic capacity partly by demanding less of her voice; but in dance she benefits from a compensatory efficiency of respiration corresponding to her lighter muscles.

In drama, as Barrault says, an actor has to divide his wind between a bag for the role and a bag for the person. The action of dance, on the other hand, is nothing but movement, the fiction of which consists entirely of undivided reality, and the most exceptional vital capacity can never be large enough to deliver poetry on top of it; the maximum oxidation of a whole body can spare no pneuma for diversion to a rival exchange.

Yet a careful investigator would probably find that the tidal volume of a woman's breath, because of her chest's lateral resilience, is relatively greater than a man's in ratio to vital capacity. This speculation is not inconsistent with another: that women, on the average, over a lifetime, breathe more slowly than men. Taken in conjunction with the apparent fact that their internal air has a lesser mean distance to move (due both to shorter stature and to a flatter diaphragm during inhalation), it would also explain one aspect of superior respiratory efficiency: less residual dead air increases the oxygen density of every inhalation.

This peculiarly feminine aerobic talent would account for the low inertia of breath that enables many women (when not dancing) to speak or scream without an instant's preparation, in any phase of the breath-cycle, almost as if in this one manifestation of reversibility their speech could be powered in either direction, ready for utterance no less during inspiration than expiration, like the old Down-Easters who can say "Eh-ah" to indicate assent on an inward draft of air without appearing to interrupt the exhalant effort of what they are doing or saying. Quick aerobic response is advantageous in unexpected or unnatural motions of all kinds, in difficult inhibitions of natural reactions, in accelerations of accelerating movement, and in sudden relaxation of breathless intensity.

My principle of sufficient strength has at least the virtue of minimum hypothesis in a sexualistic theory of dance. Much of what I say was axiomatic in earlier times. The agitations of our civilization have obfuscated many a plain intuition. . . .

{*Postulants only*: GO TO ITEM (35) SO.04.6, page 373.}

(34)
HY.06

VALENTINE GREATRAKES

*V*anity is done for the day in Berkeley. The historical man has once again let pride take an old false cue from passing moments of unsubstantiated clarity fostered by provincial isolation and evoked by the sympathy of a commercial traveler. Now comes the casting down, first by reflection, then by further rotation of fortune itself. What was high moves lower, clockwise, declining with the time of day's light like an evening spate sluicing into his balky waterwheel, or a downdraft of cold air from the sky.

There is now no trace of the pneumatic upward gusts that have sometimes seemed to counteract fate's untoward intentions. Between the visits of salesmen there's no one savvy enough to discuss the business with. So Michael must listen inside his skull to the hollow echo of his pretensions, which mock the feeling of capability that he can no longer account for. Still, so far, it's all in a day's work.

The clerks go home and leave him with nothing but the cash register and the inventory to supervise yet with every laggard customer to face and the boss to wait for. His tone slackens as the sun dips that he cannot see from within the shop, dropping fearfully toward the vast desolation of

Moby Dick's domain beyond the seaboard ridge. But his spirit is not dead. It struggles against its chains.

Now that he is personally tending store his managerial work is over until morning. There is less to do, less strength to do it, and more to brood about. Froward inquirers, rarely buying, disturb the peace. He must overhear the conversation of his betters like a good servant saying nothing but sir and thank you and thank you sir—almost please sir when he's addressed (although there have been and will be times when he steps eagerly into the open to offer suggestion). He rings up the few sales impeccably, calmly consoling himself with the self-control of his degradation, shameful as it is, and doubly shameful in the bitter heart that keeps him at his public career for the sake of the secret purpose that he supposes himself to be earning his living for with such humiliation.

He prefers not to answer for the part played by Mr P in leading him into a life of abject need. That delightedly blind leader always backs off to leave his man holding the bag. But the leader's follower and host finds comfort in the worn old thought of freewill in having chosen to escape the intolerable indignity of submitting his life's theses in advance to some committee of senior docents. [By now, Herr Professor, how high would I have risen in the thermometer?]

For the moment nearly idle but far from free in his suddenly willingless responsibility for an establishment largely built up with his own hands and informed with his own gray matter, entirely subprofessional himself listening to and dealing with the athletes and aesthetes of all learned professions, what else than fuming hatred can express his criticism of the Academy and kindred thermometers? Hatred is the only resource of such a one when thus imprisoned under the last hour of post meridian merchandising lights. At certain junctures under the ordinary constraints of a commercial society hatred is the truest occupation of an energetic mind that's excluded from the sodality of professionals by academic walls, especially when it believes itself an intellectual aristocrat in having elected the vulgar side of them.

Michael would admit to himself this superior sense of inferiority if his objectivity were not on such occasions so thoroughly overwhelmed by the hatred itself—which if it were otherwise could not be called a passion but perhaps only a little system of prejudices. For hatred which at least at the peak of its intensity doesnt wipe out all thought about hatred is not pure hatred but merely some combination of grievance pain frustration fear and rage. Citizens like Michael who are as far from society's forefront as the remnant of lighthouse keepers find themselves with no personal or hereditary enemies (except, far too vaguely three years out of four, outspoken Republicans) to bear their chronic or cultivated hatred. He doesnt often hate his customers, and soon the customary subject matter of his livelihood will again pigment the depths and reaches of his tempera.

His hatred isnt all equally merited. Even harmless injustice can touch off the passion of a man who focuses his imagination. Hatred of the honest general kind—when there are no opponents but only those made enemies by their indifference to injustice that has no personal victims—must fix its object in the faces and voices which seem to characterize those who do not suffer: actors and actresses who arrogate reward or security. It is the histriones that Michael hates the most, with their benefices and handsome superficies—the Southern accent of a woman, the British accent of a man, the vocal competence of an undergraduate, the commercial diction of an artist, the estate of an intellectual; the complacent or aggressive miens of most white people. Simple condensed prejudice.

So what? All judgment of others is prejudice, inverse in varying degree to your experience of them. And you can't get along without making provisional judgments. A decade of marriage is little enough for modest postjudgment of the closest person; and a lifetime too short for estimates of the self: yet nothing less than a cornucopia of estimates and judgments is expected of most breadwinners all day long. If he were at leisure for meditation Michael would assert that therefore prejudice is as proper to the hating function as to any other. In praise of prejudice, Creative Mind can't work without it, Michael holds in his normal state of mind. And without it, especially, you can't have the rare pleasure that comes from most cases of having it disproven (one of his favorite ethical themes), the sweetest moral delight of an unillusioned man to whom the child remains father. What pleasure when a scorned writer is read and proves herself great! When a haughty belle proves herself your admirer! When a professor esteems your work whom you have disesteemed! (Chastening though, to be doubly shamed by such an act of justice beyond your own ultimate capacity for dispassionate judgment.) Rescinded prejudice is a pleasure denied to citizens who affect unbiased emotions about their fellows; to individual subjects of the supremely positive prejudice (known to strike at first sight) that leads us under the yoke in ultimate benefit to social order; and, for the moment, to Michael himself, who's in no mood to consider the slightest challenge to his meat-axe blindness. Indeed what would become of love and hate if we always bent over backwards to enter upon them with wisdom and justice? For a clerk or busboy not to hate is to accommodate humility.

The sense of injustice and humiliation no doubt entered into humanity's original motif of retribution (in Michael's sometime objective view); but retribution got corrupted, in the usual way, by a secondary abstraction, the doctrine of vengeance, which began to incite hatred instead of following from it, turning hatred into a passionate ideal, into principle and pattern nothing like the pure hate aroused in an unwilling aristocratic servant by occasional persons, clear and hot as the finest broth, brighter than hope, a condition of private insight and explicit intuition.

To hate is not to despise, for to despise is to have contempt for, and Michael hates what is formidable to his pride. Hatred is directed for instance to those who are accorded the privilege and prestige that rightly belong among the emoluments of an archangel though he's no more decently fledged than his double plucked and singed in hell.

"Yeats's plays are too gossamer." he hears one say closing a book at the opposite wall.

"Yes, his characters have no human flesh and blood, don't you think?" replies that one's adorer gazing rapt at his lofty bearded visage, herself but for the parrot-shrillness of a perched brain untenderly desirable, her softly cusped torso incompletely underclothed. Her body is superior to either of their minds. [It's decadence at any early age when you get stuff like that throwing itself at you without lifting a finger.] They saunter out glancing superciliously at the storefront stock. The bearded one is known to be a winner of literary prizes, with a name in New York already.

"But I think he's very poetic . . ." the female is saying as the couple exits.

Another male comes in with the single purpose to carry off a hoarded book (nowhere else to be found on the West Coast) that Michael has long been hoping for the time to borrow or the money to buy before it was sold, and doubtless then returns to comfortable bachelor quarters where he can devour in peace the property coveted by its merchandiser.

Another and another, more young men and a few girls on the right track with time to spare. [Real students, eager scholars, boys without businesses or trades to spoil the leisure sheltered by a university, responsible only for their learning—quite content to be guided by likeminded instructors. They mortally believe that their principal duty is self-cultivation. When they attain to professorship they will handle both teaching and administration with the casual methods of superior intellects taking it for granted that such chores require nothing of them but time and condescension, and they will leave to the public men they criticize the irksome difficulties of dealing with open systems. They will ride the featherbed of fellowships and grants, and the inner thighs of lovely likeminded intellectualasters. There's no robust crossbreeding in their marriages— which issue in cultivated epicene children: scarcely any polar valance; thesis and antithesis synthesized to start with. . . .]

A customer asks for a piece of French literature à la mode, his accent as phony to a frog-hating American like Michael as any Parisian's, and with a surprised glance gives the tradesman his due for silently responding with the English translation he was really after. [The truest spoken French is the most gaulling. These guys and especially their parrot-brained girls buy French culture like fabric, the perennial rage of the age. They have a real feeling for the texture and they line their unprefabricated nests with it, assuming as self-evident a sort of cerebral preeminence in careers of Francophonic imitation. These fabric-loving dandybirds—meseems they're all of a flock, vultures under the skin. I wish to god we'd won the Seven Years' War unconditionally. They hate Bow's Ark because I won't make nationality a major classification. . . .]

But now the time comes when there are no grazers or predators at all. The archangel (= arch-messenger, information monger) staring at the brightly shelved words and pictures that made walls of his wares, long past teatime on an ebbed afternoon, his banausic passion spent, begins to fetch drooping sighs for the cathexes of his leisure.

A somewhat spurious treatise on the Provençal and Druid affinities of witchcraft has recently arrived, imported under an innocuous title (with the imprimatur neither of a university nor of a recognized colophon) and furtively stowed in its taxonomic place (an arbitrary decision of sly boldness) with nothing visible except its almost colorless spine where in all probability it will escape Greatrakes's anger for at least a year like many another nugget that he doesnt know his capital's invested in, albeit as proprietor he's legally liable for purveying it. For Michael's plaint now flows not from the heart but from the head; now the torment returns of intellectual passion, perhaps the worser curse of his trade, its object-matter of the most enticing quality.

In fact this is the pathos of Argus, with as many eyes to be tempted as kinds of matter to see. Now he has forgotten his managerial mania for creating superorganic form. The urge that supervenes is in fact more personal, though at the same time more aesthetic and scientific: a craving to dive for expanded experience. The freshened appetite for knowledge and criticism of other minds excludes no witness either to what St James called St Willie's "loveliness which has long faded from the world" or to "the loveliness which has not yet come into the world" that he thought was represented by his own efforts.

Michael refiles this book in its place and excitedly paces the polished deck as he passes in review the wine cellar of his stewardship, the varietals and generics all arrayed in their several vintages as a handsome plexus of compossibilities, unrestricted objects for restricted epicures: histories of philosophy science and ideas, the history of art, philosophy itself, science as the latest simultaneity of objective ideas, facts of life that can be known through books alone, discoveries and hypotheses on all fronts, new evidence on the origin of gods, this year's verge of Sumerian studies, exegeses of Herodotus, universal theories of the history of histories, literature itself.

But even as he reminds himself that culture is the use of limited freedom, and that everything else is necessary or accidental, he picks up a thin paperback written by an insane French actor, a few cauterizing words of which are sufficient to check the indulgence of his propensity for the wonderful connexio rerum. Providence directs him to a warning intended mainly for Frenchmen: "and if there is still one hellish, truly accursed thing in our time, it is our artistic dallying with forms, instead of being like victims burnt at the stake, signaling through the flames."

So much for Michael's delusions of structure! With self-chastising pedantry he replaces the book as fussily as if it were any other in his commercial repertoire.

But the Devil's more potent antidote to order and organization is a spiteful ignition of the backlog fire from which the poor clerk has been trying to stay the match. Michael takes it into his head to reach for the shelf where he stores what little is published in the way of speculation upon sex as a sacrament in the neolithic age before it degenerated into heirodulia and contract. Fortunately he finds the book he's chosen a little too spurious, a little too ridiculous to endanger his reason. He draws back, not soon enough to avoid inflammation but prudently enough to keep up his guard against the shock of any further intrusion by the public.

Clean-handed but not unscathed he leans back against the central pier-table of faded former bestsellers (*Worlds in Collision, The Mature Mind,* all the volumes of Churchill's *Second World War, The Prophet,* et al) and gazes through plate glass at the subdued street without listening to the noise of its irreducible traffic. He's pondering the revived subject of vaginal haptics. (This arms-folded twilight contemplation staves off and temporarily supplants the evening appetite for food.) The low-class letch leaves little to be desired. He makes out woman as both guttural and palatal. [But does she taste you or do you taste her? Is it plunge or swallow? Her dresses advertise that compacted inner purse expansible from no volume at all to the volume made by a foreign body of like shape and temperature when it's harder than anything in her body except bone. . . . There must be pursewalkers in this town who'd like me to be introduced into them, but I don't know who they are and they don't know who I am or the purity of my desire.] For the past two weeks Michael has been getting nothing of Ruth but cold knees in his belly. [Are concubines sometimes as recusant as mates? I suppose even women who specialize in men have holistic fits at times, when they take offense at being valued for the convenience of their parts and hold out until they think they'll be swived for their very own true integrated selves.] Suddenly for no definite or extraordinary reason he finds himself as prurient as a young dog in spring scenting his town from the end of a leash. He believes that he's restrained only by his consciousness of age appearance and law, at present the only reliable anchor of his loyalty.

Thus a misrequited biped (wingless for the nonce) grumbles that of all sacramental determinations God's worst decision was that male and female should feel the want of each other as members of a single species and pretend to communion in order to make the child, their one common love, which is hoped for and feared for, which momentarily unites the two races. [This miscegenation only encourages us to gloss over specific differences in generic desire. Our mixed white tribes are going to defeat the lust they rate so high if they don't expose the truth again. Few of the relations conducted by a President are more foreign than his cohabitation, and

compared to me any President is a very domestic individual. But the
President and I, neither of us is less flagrant than the black guy out there
with that beautiful trim-hipped blonde.] He watches the girl browsing
through his outdoor book-bins with the lover who makes clear-cut contrast to her in every way except in his fingering accompaniment across the
bindings of Bow's Ark's used-book titles. What faculty does he belong to?
[What faculty do I lack that he should be the one . . . ?

Down Mr P, down boy! Down, I say!]

But lo, no need for self-discipline! The wheel of fortune jerks suddenly
to its nadir as Valentine Greatrakes flings himself through the door flapping a rolled-up newspaper against his leg, nervous eyes blinking and
squinting and twitching, mouth screwed up similarly, his entire countenance working in silent phase with a more than ordinary displeasure.
Something is exercising his mind. He is annoyed with his assistant. Who
is at once totally deflated.

In one afternoon Michael will have been brought from the crest of
highly imaginative confidence to the trough of tremulous insecurity by a
combination of thoughts and events centering in a very small business. He
doesnt need to hear Prince Valiant's reasons. There are always grounds for
guilt and shame.

{*Postulants only*: GO TO ITEM (36) SA.13, page 377.}

(35)

SO.04.6

GENDER

. . . . Of course men and women are not to be compared! I have been comparing only certain qualities or attributes, not men and women themselves. I speak as an advocate of femininity, as do all who care to concentrate upon the human fundamentals close around them. Women refuse to lose heart from the hopelessness of loving or helping humanity in general as long as they can nurture, reclaim, educate, or ease the pain of a single human being near at hand.

At tactile range, as indeed at the long ranges of demographic soulcounts, the dignity of the sexes is equal. And so also, seen close enough, there is no rank among truly creative artists. But of them there are few. The inequality is not among masters but among apprentices. Those who are tall have the advantage in tennis; those with nimble fingers, in watchmaking; those with ambition, in politics; those with beauty, in prostitution. Yet everyone knows of ambitious courtesans and beautiful leaders. Not without qualifications do I hold that ceteris paribus a man is the better dramatist, or that a woman is the better dancer. Art is in all cases a rare and difficult achievement; sexual bias may well be the least of its difficulties.

We are nonetheless entering upon a dictatorship of social power that cannot be exercised without sexual fascinations. Things will not go well in the first phase. Psychology has already vanquished civil engineering. In the first flush of general contraception women may seek vengeance instead of dignity. We shall be lost altogether if they persist therein so long that they sour men's desire. For only with strong femininity—if need be, in women insatiably satisfied by a cheerful broody childlessness, careless of marriage, willing to render the Caesars all coinage of the realm while with every vote displaying the gestation of goodwill—shall we find living salvation for nations grown military under the sway of bulldozers and advertising. Better to be ruled by a million Catherines the Great than to live under so many Joans of Arc. Women have it within their power to awaken men from "single vision and Newton's sleep". Sex is the last remaining thing to keep us human when we've given up plants animals and children. Thus art's present obsession therewith.

The worst of women will fake the symbolism of male freedom and turn it against themselves. They'll receive roving cowboys in the mistaken impression that they are taking their own pleasure as the cowboys take it, and in their behavior they'll leave nothing of the feminine prize which used to make men want to keep a girl. And so they fool themselves once more, this time with liberty, while the cowboys secretly whoop with relief at the end of romantic love, which has brought with it Romeo's responsibility. So the new joys of women won't sweeten their tempers.

But as doers or seers who can respect themselves for *not* being duped by the male apparatus the best of them may make up for the blight of inorganic civilization and guarantee the security of their independent intelligence. These can deliver themselves from injustice without ruination of the thing saved, even though they may renounce the world-defeating trump of motherhood.

They will foster, above all the arts (of which they are the most numerous patrons), the art which, for the five reasons I have given, moves with their nature, or which at least does not move against it, not excluding from their council, from their performance, or even from their leadership, any equally talented men who like that nature well enough never to have entirely excluded themselves from it by single vision. Art anticipates life, they say. In dance we already see the transvaluation of domestic and maternal values, in such manner that the artistic use of certain unexploited differentiations introduces men to something in women that both sexes have been for the most part too indoctrinated to develop.

Far be it from me to deny that women can also write and paint. And I make no animadversion upon men who dance, like priests of a goddess, staking out straighter and heavier volumes of action with stronger arms and legs (though they sometimes come on stage with high head and arched chest as if they were meaning to display their nipples). All I say is that dance is what women are especially good at, and that it is an art as it were equivalent to an imagination of objectified female consciousness.

This approach to the center of my subject, dance itself, through equivocal discussion of its material cause alone, cannot recommend itself either to scholars or dancers. After all, dance is not a branch of anthropology. Yet no woman will gainsay me, at least not in words—which Yeats (half imbued with feminine sensibility) admitted to be but "a little foam upon the deep". The truth is that I make more of my conceits than of my facts in order to cover as much ground as possible before being silenced by female authority.

I won't insist upon the erotic. Underneath the division of desire lies the universal interest of mankind in itself, and I make no attempt to penetrate this radical mystery. Dance in its evolution has moved from fertility to birth control. An art is danced by anyone who can. What I have said, then—let it be taken merely to establish grammatical gender in the brief organon with which I hope to conclude this unendowed public series.

{*Postulants only*: GO TO ITEM (39) SO.05.0, page 423.}

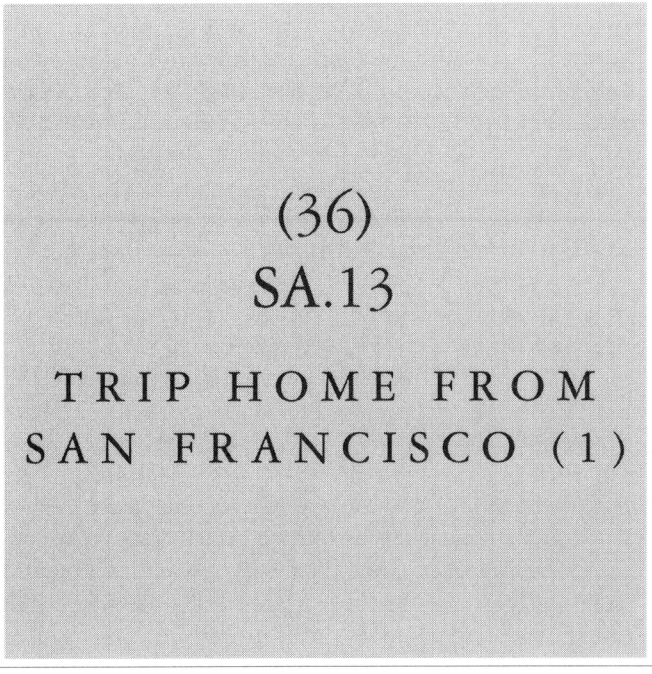

(36)
SA.13

TRIP HOME FROM
SAN FRANCISCO (1)

Jesus cum Maria sit nobis in via.
—CHRISTOPHER COLUMBUS,
et al., passim.

*T*he return journey was not quite despairingly difficult. No
child lost any blood or picked up any germ to which he was
not immune. No private exigency publicly disgraced the
family anywhere between the louvered swinging doors OUT and the un-
labeled bathroom rented for the family. They made it home beyond all
probability (it seemed to the anxious father) without any casualty except
the father's time. And at every point that time-waster himself—because
from the outset he had dismissed the day as profitless—felt nearly equal to
the diminishing prospect of his ordeal. The latter half of the family trajectory was sufficiently occupied by a contemplative combination of worry
and thanksgiving.

Yet as they clambered aboard their first homeward-pointed streetcar
hoisting equipment after them the depletion of energy and patience
required to disengage himself from baggage dig out a well hidden dollar
bill make change with the conductor and deploy his personnel amidst barbarian throngs pressing for seats deserved by their betters almost
unhinged his control of the corporate Chapman fret, of which his

tetchiness remained the lion's share, for the boys though slowly tiring seemed concerned about nothing at all, and the wife's anxieties (not counting her household dreads) could have pretended to match his own only if his conjectures about her had been 100% veridical—because on the trip home it was her personal history he found his troubled spirit hovering over.

Uncertainty about the degree to which his discomposure was justified only excited the yeast of uneasiness. In the worst case his anxiety actually

In the foreground his travail was at first so grievous his impatience so profound his sense of loss and subjugation so absolute that he was reduced to stony calmness. Thus he succeeded in winning a seat for Ruth with her youngest in lap. Except for the personalty on their backs and in their pockets the entire inventory of portaged property was assembled in a pile on the deck of the car where it could be guarded against pilferage or rather vandalism. It seemed to impede other passengers. Michael nodded slightly and twitched the ends of his otherwise unemotional mouth in a nominal effort to disarm their irritation at having to hoist their own impedimenta high in the air to get past the obstruction in single file. Jonathan and Matthew when falling short of open quarrel grumped at each other monotonously, first one and then the other plunging through the jungled din of standing swaying giants to appeal to their mother (Matthew aloud, Jonathan in hot whispers), and back again to their father's claim. They swung themselves about the stanchions in bored forlorn playfulness and chased among annoyed people in the aisle where the forest was sparse. But enveloped by the greater noise of jolting machinery and the garrulous crowd of

exceeded hers by two to one inasmuch as there could be no uncertainty to compound whatever anxiety lay on her side of the questions that disquieted him. In the best case her travel anxiety must have been negligible, so much did she trust his management of the day; and then his share of the total anxiety would approach unity, granting for the sake of abstraction that when treating of a family the whole can be taken as the sum of its parts, and disregarding the woman's chronic anxieties that had nothing to do with either the day's excursion or the brooding that suddenly possessed him.

His anxiety then: how it came upon him at this particular moment and in this particular form, him in particular of all husbands supporting the children of a wife and the wife herself, seeing that as sweet St Will says no man can ever be sure (not even Hotspur in an age of respect for virtue whose woman adored him) though he may forget his shadowy fear most days of the year and though more than one proof at issue may already have turned out spit and image of himself and yea even though he doubt not the honorable desire of the mother for himself:: not such a fool that this was the first time he'd admitted the common possi-

human birds this roughhousing of two unmalicious boys was lost to most ears as it blended into the blatant catcalls of large snickering youths (some of them outreaching the owl in height and breadth) who ceaselessly tussled and fidgeted on a vagous parallel to the homogeneous behavior of clustered selfconsciously budsprouting girls crooning unsustained snatches of commercial love songs and loosely grinding their insolent lower jaws against tongue-pushed bubblegum white or pink. Still, by beneficence of fortune the various cattle-cars accommodating the Chapman family were gradually depopulated on the swinging tracked passage to the bridge.

But no conversation took place between husband and wife from zoo to Key Terminal where the Chapmen were to take a train eastward across the Bay (whence they had come by slow double-ended ship), the fastest way home—when speed was most needed, as wiley owl had rigged the itinerary (keeping his own counsel aforetime)— and also advisedly integral to his notion of the full interest pleasure and experience to be squeezed out of such a day's travel, which when rare and exiguous must be planned for maximum exposition, inasmuch as none of life's lessons should be uselessly repeated; nor from the Terminal eight or nine scenic miles across the water to downtown Oakland. No more than a functional word or two from one to the other now and then. Ruth for her part would have been glad of her husband's address at any time.

bilities of life to his kingdom; but precedented flashes of intuition can shake the castle's foundations when they are corroborated by what seems to be new evidence or by instantly acute inferences cutting across the routine furrows of vanity in his tenets about the behavior of a very familiar copesmate::: this is how it came upon him and obliterated the unfeeling melancholy of timewaste with the soulfelt stab of Eros's most poison arrow right in the middle of his heart, impelling him to level with one thrashing convulsion the wall that he had raised by habitual labor like a Vermonter chronically clearing his pasture, the perimeter of piled stones that had kept her and the herd from trampling his spring and ravaging his grass since the last time he'd been wakened to his misery by a stroke of suspicion:::: this is how it happened that Archangel Michael the Complacent dropped his pick and hastily made off across the boundary to her field, which at once (he had forgotten!) seemed all along to have been more interesting than his own, and the latter he now willingly abandoned for the nonce to threatened encroachment in order to defend in the former something closer to his inmost self::::: this I say is how that late afternoon he totally devoted himself to his chestnut mare, filled with chastening respect for the person of his other half who could bring him to his knees:::::: this is how memory released the bowstring that shot him back into the unhappy turmoil of men in love:::::::

An old geezer of sour crabbed countenance boarded their first streetcar at a time when there were seats for everybody. His happened to be directly opposite Ruth and squirming Roger the co-tenant of her place. The man's back was long and straight; his heavy stick seemed more weapon than crutch. He moved and sat with a disdain of the voters that Ruth smiled to think must have struck her husband as absurdly arrogant. Perhaps the old boy was accustomed to look at nothing but what had to get out of his way or serve him, a gentleman who could no longer afford to keep a car with its driver (thanks to the intolerable arithmetic of the socialistic politics begun by That Man in the White House), but was not inclined to call a taxi and risk the discourtesy of an independent black chauffeur. Great bony hands resting on the upright head of the cane between his knees, elbows pressed stiffly against his ribs that he might not touch or be touched by his fellow travelers, he swayed to the common motion with dreadfully imperious mein. No notice would he betray of Roger's greeting, and still less of the babe's puzzled disappointment at his stony face. He perhaps disliked children, and probably working-class women too. But Ruth's curiosity was sympathetic. How did a man like that face his terror when the time came? Maybe he practices for death's tap every minute of the day. Why indeed should a hardly surviving ancient so occupied with dread pay any attention at all to

Yet it began with thoughts of strange flesh purely for his own oblectation, the reverie of a hale man idly drifting away from his worries in passive obedience to the diversion of natural mentality, who however even as he disports his fancy would not dream of sparing time from his works and domestic affections to actually attempt its realization on or in any woman but the person who had long since preempted his practicable lust; and it continued in erotic twiddlings of the mind that suddenly switched from mere timewaste into the most precipitous life-fear:::::::::
1] The slim thighs that were to set this train of powder alight rose before his face covered with barely opaque cotton raised by the high step of the car he was helping his family into outside the gate of the zoological gardens. Later standing in the aisle he found the girl's splendid golden hair within a sniff of his nose, sitting as she was between himself and Ruth (who sat further forward facing the front and little suspected the attraction behind her), though his curling palm was forbidden the fresh never-freshened paps within his easy reach. From where he stood it was possible to estimate the delicate calves and neat little feet without making a fool of himself. He could steal glances at the young person's thin humorous lips which seemed glad enough of things as they were yet composedly expectant of sensational experience still in store. Whence? By whom? To what extent? An obviously delightful com-

people of the streets or mussed-up women or dirty little cherubs?

Methuselah's ride was short. As he made motions to rise, Roger who was still watching him solemnly unabashed again tendered a monosyllabic salute, his native assurance of tone having given way to soft diffidence, for his smile had faded into staring fascination. It was unexpectedly difficult for the old one to stand up. By strenuously clutching the back of the seat before him he poked himself further upright with an uncertain purchase on his cane. (This exertion mitigated the haughtiness so hateful in Michael's eyes.) When the old tyrant lurched to his feet the car was still rocking with speed and he was obliged to steady himself by grasping with one hand the handle at the corner of the seatback in front of Ruth, and over the wrist so extended he hung the crook of his cane. She saw to her surprise that there he wore a watch, confirming his new-fashioned aristocracy (a thought she laughed at in her head before it passed) in contrast to her father (a Republican crony of Jack London's) who like all other men she'd known of that generation carried a chained gold watch with lidded face in the same slitted vest pocket that half facing her he was now plucking at with the long trembling fingers of his other hand. She was alarmed at his haste: he might have been getting at a pill for some sudden distress of the heart. But no! For the first time revealing his awareness of fellow persons he held out to her the back of

panion for a young man like Caleb—yet maybe, just barely, not so close to the misapprehensions of maidenhood that she wouldnt under exceptional circumstances of intellectual admiration pause long enough with a middleowled Chapman to yield him her tentative plaisir. Meanwhile Ruth wrestled patiently and reflectively with her baby son in the seat ahead, autonomically coping with the little squirming will inside the bobbing head that had last wedged her maternal thighs and renewed her maternal granary. To Michael all at once she his wife seemed unnecessarily tired, gratuitously unfashionable, almost haggard with premature age. But there was nothing invidious in this dual vision. The young one would some day strike a man the same way if she was as good a woman.

Thus his appraisal was somnolent, comparatively liberal yet still to some degree disinterested. What interest there was chiefly concerned the part any man at all could play in the means and events by which such a girl progresses from the parthenic to the blown. [Ah but this young woman not yet discovered of her imperfections (leaving aside whatever her parents might have found in her of their own nature and nurture)—perhaps she is one of those I presume there are under easy conditions of life whose sexual esurience and tegumental tone (thanks both to temperament and nulliparity) keep pace with the moods of a faun. If that beautiful piece of humanity contains any sort

his fist and at her involuntary response dropped into her palm a conical chocolate kiss wrapped in silver foil. By this doing Roger was shown how to receive, so that the mossback with a mother's pantomime consent was permitted to press a duplicate into the smaller paw. This consummation of tacit sentiment gave away a pitiable trepidation of jaws and limbs. The donor had lost the control of his face that it takes to smile, and he dared not try to speak. With a sense of guilt at having made no offer to help him she saw that he was very very old, older than any other person she had ever seen in public, perhaps outliving the fear of death. But she was immediately distracted by the problem of getting the candy unwrapped before it entered Roger's mouth and before she could make up her mind about whether or not she should thank the venerable gentleman with a gesture of assistance he turned away abruptly, recovered mastery of himself with an astonishing power of locomotion, and made his way to the front of the car in time for his stop. In slow descent to the street his pride of carriage could no longer conceal the painful difficulty of movement which (as she guessed) her husband had taken as arrogance defensively assumed instead of kindly fortitude in its only feasible manifestation.

[These details were not lost upon the watchful father, observing from behind the bright clear head of the female angel he'd been admiring who likewise witnessed the deed; but the conclusions drawn from what he saw did not resemble of mind at all it's because she has nothing else to do. Does she conceive and gestate any thought divagating from routed feminine mentation? Or if she's a monstrous thinker in the light of her own opinion could you find in her any small lump of self-effacing talent to make a woman out of? It may be counted a blessing not to know the lovely girl you see.] Michael contrived to thank his wisdom as well as fate for the infinite distance between himself and the accidental object of his general desire.

Roger looked too, standing on the lap of his mother looked back over her shoulder at the lady his father had been looking at. Whom there was this to be said for, that she liked to look out the window at the places she was passing through, and that she carried a hardcover book (an incomplete clue as tantalizing as the lap it rested opon because the professional bookman— crane his neck and strain his eyes as he did—couldnt make out its title); but especially that she looked at Michael's son with incipient friendliness, now looking out the window, now looking back at Roger. They smiled at each other. Michael caught the breath in his lungs. The boy looked over to his father also and smiled, embracing them both in the sympathy of that act. The girl thus guided twisted toward Michael an upward glance and smiled at him the same smile she had smiled at the baby with. But alas truly it was only a quick look of politeness, no more than a perfunctory congratulation to acknowledge his proprietorship without his wife's interpretation: it was a foolish gaffer champing badly shaven jaws in disgusting response to some infantile reverberation, trespassing upon innocence with the vile nuisance of his dirty little sentimental gifts (—very likely one of those ninety-nine-year-old liars who tells the feature writers that the secret of his longevity is clean living and soon has 50,000 readers avoiding all occasions for ejaculation while he keeps himself alive on pornographic vice cackling in bitter envy of their youth at the early death he's tricked them into)—gratuitously hindering his son's delicate acquaintance with a beautiful girl who was clearly not in the habit of encouraging boys and might all too lightly drop the possibility of a friendship that was naturally so much to a father's liking.]

As Ruth helped Roger peel the chocolate drop for his prematurely indulged sweet-tooth, depositing a little ball of silver paper in her handbag to throw it away at home, and later as she allowed him to pry its twin from her hand [much to the father's horror who was more worried about sugary acid eating into the tender pearls of Roger's mouth than about corrosion of his character], she wondered about the antediluvian's probable part in a genealogy. He must have grandchildren nearly as old as herself, and therefore greatgrandchildren at least Roger's age. But maybe he'd never seen all his grandchildren or any of his greatgrandchildren. Perhaps they were scattered all over the country (as Americans too loosely flung for cohesion), dissemi-

alluding to his authorship, and it was not to be construed as a wanton invitation to dalliance. And she never offered again.

A man like Sandy of stronger nerve might have exploited a much smaller opening behind his wife's back. Michael's excuse was his unprepossessing appearance. At any rate as he was impotent to seize time by the forelock his face remained woodenly devoid of response. It was a matter of pride to give her no sign that the joy of her intimate company was beyond his reach. He was involuntarily protected from this gifted and discriminating succubus by his pettybourgeois physiognomy and girth. Therefore he perhaps dampened her kindliness by seeming to snub it with impassivity.

It happened that just then he was obliged to take a seat for himself and his braves a little further back in the car. Concupiscence interruptus: curiosity speculation but no discretely hardened partisanship; some disequilibrium indeed, but not enough to rouse the demon seriously. That strange incompleted body was too lean to look womanly; his own organism was still tolerably contented from the previous evening. Past his prime moreover. 2] But the casual imagination of himself at leisure with this girl as maturely desirous (and no counter between them) led to more applicable study. Some women in the fullness of experience assign value where value is due. His distance from Hecuba Jones was by no means infinite. At least she was a friend of the family and knew

nated by the opportunities of war or the accidents of profitable peace. It was possible that some of his children or children of his children's children were dead of violence or disease. Perchance all of them. He may have been his own sole survivor, the residual beneficiary of a tontine started by himself. If on the other hand it was a tenement full of warring kids to whom he made this labored excursion his generosity with the candy seemed improvident. She scarcely doubted that in any case he had been a progenitor: else he neednt have lived so long; instead he would have shriveled and died at three score and ten. But how joyfully had he last engendered?

The eleemosynary self-training of her heart had not been too disinterested to prevent her shudder at the thought of such a man's clammy touch. A withered male's flaccid desire was secretly horrible to think of, like certain cases she would never read in her psychology books, but it was still less pleasant to imagine oneself its aphrodisiac when by some nearly terminal exertion of lecherous will it fleetingly hardened. Before her mind's eye from many years ago flashed an old pastured horse standing alone as if in the dream of a desire never enjoyed in his working life—if Michael's explanation of the display which he too had not failed to notice was to be credited, that the image unintentionally transferred in ungraphic words to her visual memory and lodged there by her innocent interest at the time (which must have been on some leisurely

something of ordinary troubles. Now at the peak of her erotic attention, fullblown and not a bit bony, with a rather frank history known to him through Ruth. Doubtless she knew more about the desires of men than Ruth and the girl together did, though less about trophic responsibility or books or men under the particular conditions of books and babies. Likewise more about her own pleasure, inasmuch as for perhaps two hundred forty moons (calculating twenty years from the age of menarche and assuming no undisclosed contretemps) she had been cultivating the sensuality of arrested womanhood without domestic restriction—or so he chose to conjecture. Fullblown and arrested in her own eyes too: the very sorrow that rendered her tolerant and sweet, improved her mind, and made her regard unprepossessing fathers (he hoped) with a certain wistful respect. The monthly loss that had always been the forgiveness for unpunished pleasure was now as melancholy to her as a cornfield winter sky. Bleachly blonded Hecuba, not Irish but a good Catholic cheerfully guilty, her style of dress not as high as she thought it was (for lack of a college education) and her style of indoor sport (as far as a man who didnt know could guess) equally bold but subtler and more diverse, sometimes was gone for the night or a weekend with the ticket agent her protector. She would come home weighed down by so many hours of upper-middle-aged protection far advanced. But then from time to time a certain sailor or a

erotic trip before the cares of marriage began) was that of a superannuated Morgan gelding. Its extended black grandissimus (as he said it was called in whales) was still comically embarrassing to an urban girl for its implausible magnitude yet vaguely repulsive in its salaciously formal abuse of senile sterility. So Roger's benefactor might have been no patriarch but a pure craving bachelor perhaps emasculated by a Mexican bullet or German shrapnel before his gift had been accepted by a possible wife, dreaming now not of naked girls but of the eradicated seed-bulb. [Is it true as Sylvia has told me that eunuchs were at least some of them willing and able to go through all the motions—and, if so, known by their sultans to be willing and able? Such a fact would shed new light on the condition of harem wives. Perhaps the Turks were not entirely indifferent to their contentment after all. It says something for the emotional maturity of the tyrants themselves if they were above petty mechanical jealousy in a matter safely detached from questions of genetic continuity, division of property, or succession of power!] She shuddered at the callousness of her unkind reflections upon postpotent men expressing natural affection. If it were within her power, and if she were free to do so, a woman should try to make an old man happy, concealing her tremors. Hecuba did it, Hecuba concealed her tremors.

But then, Hecuba's principal boy friend wasnt yet too old (no more than a quarter of a century

stranger guest did not escape her closest neighbors' detection flitting up the stairs; occasionally when the children were asleep and street noises muted for the midwatch Michael or Ruth heard a plashing rustle in the bath above, and the murmuring sound of goodhumored voices following a long run of water. Grinning, Mr and Mrs Chapman would call each other to the bathroom and hush their breathing with ears cocked to the ceiling where the common pipes rose vertically from one privacy to another, never stopping to wonder if landlord and Mrs Topalis below indulged a like prurience at their own similar festivities; but though the topfloor lovers were talkative and laughative, Hecuba's mature giggle easily distinguishable from the deeper briefer pleasantries of a male, not a word of the celebrating voices above the plastered ceiling could ever be distinguished. To Michael who therefore observed at a disadvantage Hecuba seemed if nothing else a friendly voluptuary who knew subject from object, and object from object; she was only secondarily an independent gainful employee by all accounts fully as capable as any pinched old maid married to her job. She was too amiable to dislike anything she was actually asked by men to do or have done to her; and she was in a position to be asked to do or have done no more than her sympathy or kindness (if not desire) disposed her to do or have done, for her easily handled bookkeeping work in the City earned comfortably more than mere necessities. "Jesus Mary and

older than Michael), and he described himself to her as a loving widower and father, hinting also that he had loved more other women than there are virgins in California. There was no question but that as a worldly man he had seen much of worldly women, having made plenty of money to account for his luxuries. His childless daughter, whose married name he could point to in the telephone book, would not receive or visit Hecuba of course (probably professing either reasons of propriety or loyalty to the memory of her mother; perhaps the putative heiress would have preferred not to be aware of Hecuba's existence, not to mention her special status). It was no easy situation that the Chapmans' friend that amiably ambivalent bookkeeper had accepted. Ruth was privy to the claim that Hecuba had been promised marriage and equal footing with the daughter if the father could succeed in his heart's desire since he wasnt going to be a grandfather to become a father again by planting in her an ultimate beneficiary who had half a chance of being a son. Much of his income was devoted to the stimulation of fertile desire, either directly to his own hygiene or indirectly to Hecuba's pleasures whose active passion, instrumental to the purpose, deserved every sort of encouragement.

{For the last quarter of an hour of their final ride in the streets of San Francisco the family was gathered together among thinned-out passengers, Michael with Matty listless on his knees. Warmed but

Joseph," she'd say goodnaturedly with mingled pride and deprecation, "if there's anything I ought to know it's values. My boss calls me the world's smartest Jew." She even knew the value of things she herself didnt care for. Through Hecuba's good offices her protector the ticket agent had been most generous to Ruth and her parsimonious husband. From orchestra or dress circle free of charge they had attended the highest performances of the highest culture that San Francisco could mount, including the grandest Wagner of New York's travel repertory; nor had they missed solid Shakespearean tours de force almost direct from London; but with these complimentary passes above all they had been granted the happiness of seeing Elizabeth Quicherat in ballet, swan and princess of British dance, to whom Michael ingenuously paid hyperdulia rather too ostentatiously, in disregard of his theoretical partiality to Modern creators. Many were the unsold tickets to musical comedies ice-skating shows and basketball games that the Chapmans declined. But before finally quitting the vice of baseball attendance Michael had watched from a box seat in the home park with Dave Wilson as his guest (drinking beer out of paper cups at the guest's expense) three games of the Oakland Oaks during their historic climax of Pacific Coast League training for the Majors. So they owed Hecuba some favors, or no less than one uncommon favor. What could she want that lay within the Chapman power?

immobilized by his burden he stared out unseeingly at the waning neutrality of the late day's atmosphere or gazed inertly at faces he'd never seen before, sorting with mechanical carelessness the lives they led (even as he pursued other themes elsewhere in his thoughts) like a painter idly abstracting models from the presence of human selves that had nothing to do with his interests as a man. This brooding recess from the pains of truthseeking was interrupted by the jolt of their creaking squealing arrival at the station where homely claptrap streetcars with bargelike clerestories and rectangular woodwork swept nearly to a tangent with the terminal loop of large articulated trains operated by the East Bay's Key System.

Thus now he came to remember that once long ago in a similar mood of gratitude they had invited Hecuba on the same night that Harmon Sandys then a bachelor also came to dine. Sandy had left early without any overtures to his blonde dinner partner. Several times afterwards Hecuba had inquired about "that cute boy."

Michael found it accordant with the odds of his career that the train they wanted had just left. Another forty minutes must be endured on the spot. The parents were too heavily laden and penurious to wait it out anywhere but on a hard bench in the booming fuzzing confusion of the restless waiting room. Roger who had been asleep on the last ride was now awake and whimpering for his tea-time milk. Ruth conscientiously attended to his demands, laboriously fishing first in one bag and then in another for the various elements of a nursing bottle full of milk capped and nippled. Her onerous babyman was fed with every tender consideration of his past and future life though her soul drifted far far in and away from immediate presences with no more indication of where she found herself than her husband gave of where his thoughts were placed who was outwardly caring for the outwardly directed older boys, most of whose requests for things and liberties he fended off testily and unreflectingly: but at an inquiry that never came she'd still have responded with a spontaneous smile lightening everyone's weariness that she was very happy with the way the day was going, with never a complaint anywhere near her lips. Roger's round well-lined stomach was soon comforted but he continued to suck the rubber teat drowsily, more and more slowly with longer and longer pauses for thought.

"His lids are too heavy." Ruth murmured.

"What do you want—" replied the father: "safety valves?" It was a pale cheerless flicker of good humor not bringing on but brought on by the words he spoke.

Yet the forty-minute penalty in life's time was doubly compounded by the customary obligation of a man once more to refresh the other mouths of his family, in this case at the cost of diminishing by a dollar or two whatever amount which if really funded and not perpetually depleted within hours of accretion would have paid for his retirement from the world as much earlier than the age of sixty-five as proportional to its size among other pennies that might have been saved and doggedly compounded. He tried to estimate the number of extra minutes he would have to work at Bow's Ark to compensate for this out-of-pocket loss, but long before he could figure it all out he gave in to the moral imperative—since Ruth deserved some alleviation of her forthcoming duty to cook a supper the minute they got home, since it would do no harm to make the talking members of the family a little friendlier toward himself, and since he himself was hungry.

So he gave Jonathan money to fetch four hotdogs with Matthew's assistance from the end of the long low hall to which all the peasants were oriented. Under such famishing conditions the lad was not too shy for his task, and he had the intellectual capacity to retain the longwrungout combinatorial schedule of preferences (including his own) for mustard relish ketchup chili onions or sauerkraut, all of which were surely not available at a mass-feeding monopoly concession and some of which would therefore have to be substituted for others without the opportunity to cable headquarters for further instructions, though he tried hard to refuse thankless plenipotentiary discretion.

The forty minutes turned out to be much too short. They were still stuffing gnawing slurping slopping and dropping major and minor fragments of food as they trooped bedraggled upstairs to the untimely train. Yet the father as usual more wiley than commoners was thinking ahead. He calculated on window seats for at least two of his party. What with the dripping insecurity of their remaining collation, clutched or balanced like weathervanes in hands already otherwise loaded with responsibility, as well as the dissonance of their nerves, this boarding more luckily than skillfully accomplished by the skin of their teeth without mentionable loss or damage was altogether the most remarkable of the day.}

Hecuba had confided to her that her protector wasnt so far past his prime that he couldnt keep it up for a while on many occasions, though he sometimes had to quit in flagging fatigue before he could even pretend to have introduced a dribble of fertilizer from what he still regarded as an ever-normal granary. At any rate he fancied himself extravasated often enough to sustain his hope and regenerate his desire. Hecuba told Ruth with her low-pitched giggle that she couldnt feel the difference anyway. Yet there could be no doubt that

3] Sandy at table in Michael's castle with two women—yet so circumspect, even melancholy, his freckles etiolated almost to the fairness of his skin as if paled by weeds of mourning! At the time his host had hardly noticed this amusing deportment, half consciously attributing it to the philanderer's diffidence in facing the test of an expert examiner older than himself and wiser by virtue of more extensive experience in those activities which the male is conventionally expected to be the more knowledgeable of and thus all too capable of taking

she nurtured mutual pleasure with affectionate sympathy and heartfelt cooperation. To Ruth as an enviable friend (to whom she would not of course reveal more than a few immediately relevant details of her life) Hecuba showed herself both rueful and amused at the much celebrated romantic love that her destiny denied her; and she was certainly aware of her social disqualifications as far as younger marriageable men were concerned: so there was even more reason on her side of the bed than on her aging paramour's to hope for a shotgun wedding.

This interesting neighbor flattered Ruth the virtuous wife as her sole confidant by trusting not only her discretion but also her tolerance of virtue's varieties. Ruth blamed herself and not Hecuba for the tremors she felt at the words used by her earth-sister to explain the faithful goodwill in her long most serious affair. But the educated matron had good success in making the unlikely friendship important to them both. She knew that the honorable girl would never have told a man such things about another—but then Hecuba would never have found herself in the warm sunlight of a littered kitchen just downstairs from her own being served coffee by a man. "Goda'mighty dear, I want a kid and he wants a kid. Who cares where it comes from? He's no fool. In a way he's almost begging me to cheat! He don't say he'd kill me if he found out. You'd do the same thing if you'd been dumb enough to waste your life like I did." [Have some more, there's plenty of cream.] With coffee cup in one hand and cigarette

his prowess down a peg; or else to having his style cramped by the stultification inherent in an all-too-obvious opportunity with an obvious woman obviously of the type he most liked to think of himself as successful with. But now like a sudden bloody accident in the midst of a happy family holiday the memory of this little dinner party swooped with a timeless whir out of the blue sky to pluck from a sepulchre in which Michael Chapman was accustomed to bury unmanageable facts an earlier memory whose origin in historical truth had been earlier yet. Without further suggestion his thoughts were instantly cast back several years to find an anterior cause for an interior perception that had never previously registered in his waking mind. But his sudden new vantage of the past brought a violent breach of the time-dam that had hitherto held back a tributary torrent of pelting sensibility that immediately overtook his busy preoccupations. Thus in repose, riding a common carrier far displaced from that odd scene, Michael for the first time reconsidered Sandy's demeanor sitting there like a pure and modest knight. Vicious thoughts swarming and interbreeding in schools nipped at vital parts he had not known to be vulnerable, quickened the ashes of old cysts and tumors. The recent brush with Sandy at last steeped to the core of his intelligence, and memory of that master cockswain sitting passive before Aphrodite herself roiled the muddy bottom of his placid old river. For Sandy's motor system was always innervated: a principle

in the other Hecuba told Ruth that every once in a while she'd let slip to her senior lover some little cause for jealousy just to keep him virile by assisting his imagination, thus fostering her hope and his. Well as the French would say Ruth ventured, he must love you if you're the woman who makes him jealous. The cheerful blond head (a little heavy under the jaw but naturally lovely in its unadorned morninghood) gravely paused to consider this thought. "Yes I think he does." she said slowly, but then chuckled at what she was about to dilate in continuing where she had left off: to wit, in the unspoken communion between herself and the cleanshaven graybeard they agreed that despite her limited and playful teasing from time to time he should be given no cause to admit to himself the possibility of his having provided her with a motive to become the mother of an unknown father's child. Perhaps he only wants a sort of grandchild anyway, Ruth suggested with a smile, though she at once regretted the alacrity of her moral abetment. Hecuba stopped to think about this unexpected comment—perhaps her first encounter with a psychology of the unconscious—and after a few seconds, in dawning admiration of her smart friend (who had not meant her remark as a considered judgment), seemed to appreciate its casual import. Taking everything together, what other kind of honesty than Hecuba's could have better served the parties concerned?

The goodwife had her own honesty to reckon with, or at least a certain uneasiness that could have

you could count on. That night then, what was it alert to? Did some rare discretion make it seem to seethe the less? Did it all of a sudden mislike the obvious or resent the prompting set-up by meddlesome friends? Or could it be that Lancelot allowed himself no license with the King's choice for him as long as he found himself under the Queen's eyes?—Was it as the Queen's own knight that he declined to wear the sleeve of fair Hecuba?

Michael trembled on the verge of new truth, still unprepared to drop his shield against primitive anger and pain, yet in the technical thrill of discovery pricking hard toward the lance that might pierce the escutcheon on which his honor was devised and unhorse him forever. For a moment the unknown mind that always so profoundly influenced the broad middle mind he liked to live in (because of the freedom there) thought it could help its evolutionary descendant anesthetize emotional susceptibility by appealing to the occupant's self-esteem as a savant. That anodyne lasted only as long as the purely rational satisfaction of a shocking induction; it faded at once and utterly, though it was to reappear much later when from time to time he would be desperately obliged to seek shreds of comfort for his nakedness.

So a definite rupture of the assuasive webwork cocooning his true self was briefly postponed while he took immediately lesser pains to reconstruct from one or two wispy filaments that unexpect-

been cured only by a worse uneasiness (by the way breaching in part her trustful sister's secret, albeit to the most silent listener in the world she thought); for she had not transmitted to her husband the intelligence of what was really at issue upstairs, getting a child being the last of his suspicions, notwithstanding that in other cases and in other aspects of Hecuba's case she had not scrupled to confide to him most of the interesting hints she happened to hear about the private lives of their friends. To such gossip he always listened. Michael knew about the sailor because he had seen him come and go and even listened for him, and he had heard a little talk about the doubtful possibility of Hecuba's betrothal to the ticket-daddy, but he had not been apprised of the athletic-looking optometrist who came to visit Hecuba at lunch hour nearly every Tuesday (her day off), Harold Gold by name, husband of a *skinny nervous college graduate*, according to the epithets bestowed upon her sight-unseen by the less styptic and perhaps less mercenary of the two women presumably most influential in his busy lucrative life, whose capability of indignation Ruth discerned for the first time in the voice with which Hecuba delivered the phrase, as if intending a vivid cultural horror, whether diagnosing or paraphrasing the hebdomadal lover's characterization of her unwitting legitimate competitor somewhere in the suburbs. It sounded as if the vendor of frames and lenses came to Hecuba for frank animal comforts, including a decent meal. The man was nothing

edly materialized in his recollections an older incident that Ruth herself had recounted to him. Why hadnt that dinner itself, with Sandy and Hecuba, so long ago and so much nearer the origin of his disquietude, brought her previously told tale to the mind he used? Had his metamind having immediately boxed up such significant information deliberately kept all its weight on the lid of his undermind until this very moment fully two hours after a stimulus so glaring that it would have stirred the dullest memories of a far less sophisticated dolt?

All these questions accompanied retrieval of the data he now sought for the first time; and as it was a process of unalloyed cerebration (that is to say without new evidence or experience), with only the illusive strength of his mind to keep the truth from being immediately absorbed, subverting accusations swiftly concatenated themselves from all sorts of small clues like rats springing out of walls and cobbles to form linked chains behind the Pied Piper without waiting for a call to parade. He remembered also the thousand warnings of literature, especially the sad wisdom of St Maddox's statistician who even of modern English women had known that their most honest words on personal subjects were gestures but not communications. Yet what Ruth had told him must be presumed a minim of the truth—to wit:

One day just before moving across the Bay to San Francisco young Sandy, respectful trueblue awkward friend of the family, had

if not deserving of women, judging by what Ruth herself could see, and in her most secret reveries she didnt claim to be an exception. He looked capable of sympathetic attentiveness as laughing at herself she peeked out the window at his departure or listened for his quick eager tread on the staircase outside her door. Hecuba intimated that he was a good-looking guy in more aspects than one: well formed in the flesh and rich in blood line. She hinted that he deceived himself in his confidence that she took care of the contraception. In truth she did so only at times that her conditional fiancé (whose attentions were sometimes suspended by illness or business travel) might have calculated impossible for his own success. "It's the melody method." Hecuba chuckled. And in a later Tuesday morning coffee talk, grown even less reserved, she added: "Of course I usually see Hal only for an hour or so three times a month— and then he needs time to eat—so it's no wonder I havent got pregnant. I hope he keeps coming because it's really something special to be in bed with him for twenty minutes." She smiled almost shyly, not like a knowing sensualist but like a faithful woman in love. For one fluttering instant Ruth imagined that in the way they looked upon Hal Gold she and her worldly sister had exchanged their prevailing attitudes toward men. "Still," Hecuba went on, "strange as it may seem, he might not have what it takes. In fifteen years he's had no kids at home." She blew smoke at the sky shown through the window

paid an afternoon visit while both the small children (who then had no little brother) happened to be asleep, and waiting for Michael to get home as Ruth continued her housework took up with her a familiar kind of light talk that prevailed between the older couple and himself which usually expressed mere habit of companionship without much real conversation (to say nothing of useful dialectic) but which was welcome enough by her who was always pleased to be disignored by the larger world. But this time, with no words to warn her, he all at once pushed back his chair at the kitchen table and came up to her from behind when her hands were in the dishpan. Drawing aside her chestnut mane without (she said) any sign of disrespect he paid schoolboy homage to her beauty and kissed her on the shoulder of her neck. She had been slightly amused at this unripened salute (she said) but sternly scotched further words and put a stop to all advances (she said) by ordering him to sit down and shut up in a peremptory tone that put him to shame without any other recrimination. He sheepishly complied (she gave Michael to understand) and resumed his place with no subsequent mention of the incident. Nothing to make an issue of: just the natural impersonal impulse (she said) of a lonely self-pitying boy who had come to say goodbye and was surprised by his own response to an unanticipated occasion. [As if he had reason to believe that I ever headed home by three o'clock in the afternoon!] Much

over the kitchen sink. "Naturally there couldnt be anything wrong with me!" she went on with a merry laugh, touching the back of Ruth's hand.

But Ruth while apologizing to herself for shrewdness was acquainted with the noumenon of disingenuity enfolded in candid sincerity. For the very reason that it was always to be looked for and could not be prevented by any degree of attempted honesty she took no offence. The good odalisk could hardly have avoided some explanation of the optometrist, since he had been frequently seen on the premises during the hours when many a woman's secrets are formed. Yet the confession of uterine motive (especially since the more immediate desire easily explained Adonis's presence) seemed to come through like two messages on the faces of a coin: heads, you're the kind of woman who really keeps a sister's secret without exception, in which case it's a blessing and relief to have you for a friend—you with your lovely children and your smart husband—because there are times when it's good to be able to relax and feel warm with someone who understands and never has a bug up her ass; or tails, this very night you will make the exception and betray my secret to your mate either as a matter of loyal duty or in order to get his attention, and in that case he will hear what I want him to know, for you yourself have told me that your children were all conceived ostensibly against the odds and it's not unnatural that I should be interested in a competent and

later when the king returned to his castle the guest had gone with her godspeed, having declined to stay for supper.

By the time Michael heard about this gallantry from the wife herself Sandy had long since disappeared from their social life and was dismissed from the master's consideration as an outgrown and departed friend well relieved of. The king and queen were lying in bed during an extraordinary banquet of love exchanging intimate recollections and playful confidences, idly regathering their appetites for prolongation of the conjugal feast. "You can't get this far without having had a few offers." she said. He was extremely interested. Why, what do they say? "Oh they don't say anything usually, but you just know from the situation that if you simply act a little differently it will come about." It was then, not in illustration of her general remark but by way of mnemonic association, that she had casually come out with the Sandy anecdote. Now, so long afterwards that her husband was confused about the essential chronology of revelation, he faintly remembered a slight perturbation of the heart which he had thereupon all too successfully pacified with the easy determination that the incident was only her past-and-done-with tribute from a hopeless knight and hapless rival, and in fact speedily cured with the letheful delight of what he was then about.

But the older king, who now knew a little more about the discontents of a loving queen, was wiser than the younger. In the Key

accessible man with a proven record of aggressive insemination and a gentleman's normal impulse to help out an independent girl in such a plight. Hecuba was attractive enough.

Ruth mused over this game with an uncertainty formally similar to that with which she often pondered her own serious messages to Michael; but she reasoned that if the coin was willed by its tosser to fall tails then the outcome was surely not being left to such tortuous and unreliable means alone and that she should be looking for evidence of attempted seduction or truer secrets. Maybe, she teased herself, I too should have my eyes examined!

So far nothing had altered the cycles of Hecuba's boundless good health, Ruth believed, though it seemed from what she heard that the old guardian telephoned indefatigably on the days of the calendar in which he thought fecundation might be questioned. No young Italian bride was ever so tenderly queried—and certainly not Ruth herself by Michael. But it was conceivable that Hecuba had given birth to the superstitious idea that only magic sperm like Mr Chapman's could find its way through congenital barriers to disprove her barrenness. On this count Ruth guessed Michael's superiority to Hal Gold rather unlikely. In somewhat sensational fashion she visualized the big stranger kneeling over Hecuba on soft pink sheets, and for some minutes she cultivated sensual empathy with the other woman (Roger rocking gently on her lap),

System waiting room he stole a glance at the inscrutable woman. That little confession of which he now bethought himself in a broader light might have been intended to make him help her resist a temptation that she felt susceptible to! The effort to penetrate the mystery of her desire was not new to him but he had never revived it with such urgency. One must assume that she sees oneself as he really is, after such long exposure—a disappointingly selfish familiar, unclean weak and crude; whereas it would require more than a brief experiment in intimacy to disabuse her of a stranger with interesting secondary qualities.

But a worse possibility than that she had felt the hankering curiosity of delimited experience was that she had deftly disclosed a fact or two in order to alleviate a greater guilt than that of having failed to report the transgression that very night! A kiss at more than the nape? More than mere amusement superior to the outgrown schoolboy's infatuation? And *more than one event*? What better method to put an end to shameful sin than to feed her beloved husband a suggestion that will put him on future guard for her? Yet only now at this late date does the poor simpleton at the head of the round table choose to heed her plea and make himself alert to what had threatened to enter into history, to what *did* enter into history, much earlier—to what most couples would call ancient history.

The inner mural of his skull glows with several distinct and

thrilled and a little faint at the imagery until she opened her eyes.

Her speculation about Michael in the same act was considerably colder. With the regret of tardy wisdom she remembered her indiscretion in having described to him the richly fallow golden body she had once seen as Hecuba dried her hair and aired her skin at a sunny window during a chat on the third floor after a knock at the door with a cup for sugar. Had the wife implanted in her husband's memory an undislodgeable picture of that lustrous depilated feline like a smooth soft girl-baby dedicated to men from forehead to toe who indeed was to be commended for confining herself to the alternating caresses of a mere two or three ailurophiles in any one transit of the moon? Ruth shifted her weight without disturbing Roger's. [Are women like stomachs that they are made to draw in foreign bodies? Why did God intend us to love men so, and yet not leave us always content with the aftermath of joy in our wombs—even when we're one of luckiest? Do men ever feel anything inside themselves, or is their pain and pleasure always clearly in front of them like Sierra snow to be pushed off a right-of-way by the plow in front of their engine? Is that why they suffer on the surface, and never from feelings alone? I bet they give in to torture before we do. . . . How much of a difference can there be between Tom Dick and Harry on top of you? Yet it would be horrible to feel obliged to one of them you didnt love, especially a weak clammy man old enough to be

vivid images; yet every minute the number of accursed possibilities multiplies, confusing his imagination and enveloping his brain with spinning marks on the rosetta of a swiftly slowing roulette about to be readable. Had her defensive reflexes failed for a few seconds to reject that first brush of a kiss, and having failed to protest his touch had she then stood still in surprise to suffer the unhasty movement of his gentle left hand to her breast, pinioning her arm with his as he bent his cheek to her temple, until in her stunning failure to react his other hand grew urgent on her opposite hip and slid forward round it? And had she only at that last reversible instant twisted tempestuously away from the sink and out of his embrace? *Or* with her own hands uncurling out of sight in the warm dishwater had she failed even then to resist the cool attack of the transformed boy, and numb with fear or transfixed by sensation or silently and fatally obedient to a crest of cyclic want happening to fall on that day of her moon, or to some expectation kept secret from herself, submitted to the amplifying pressure of all his ten spread fingers exploring the front of her apron until finding their way beneath it with two or three pawings of the huge palms they lifted the skirt of her dress and went in under the hem onto the bare skin of her thighs, a brace of seducers who as they moved upward gathered and pressed what they could glean before they reaped and were only now echoed and reinforced by his amazingly delicate lips nibbling the

dead, blindly doddering? —Wait now! That old man with the cane wasnt blind!] white skin exposed at the top of her spine by the forward droop of her unparticipating head? And had the bold youth then drawn her pelvis away from the supporting protection of the sink to give the prehensile twain passage toward each other in the smoldering spinney of flat curls underneath her most inner clothes on the crown of the volcanic knoll that was now the center of contention—only to have her whirl out of his arms in recusant torment at the very brow of doom? [Mr P throbbed as if party to the betrayal and being rooted in the husband he supplied him as observer with a certain complex excitement that for a time usurped the rightful place of dismay and anger.]

Or again, had she faked the tolerance of shock in order to let him go a little further in this harmless manner only while she fought her way out of the swoon that had overtaken her so unfairly (all the while in tactical transition he was loosening the underwear from her hips), that she might heave one final tremendous sigh and break off the affair with no more gratification than having felt his coolly ranging fingers verge upon the outer folds of her undisclosed abyss? But of course the penultimate is almost always too late for an experienced girl's refusal. . . . Yet perhaps at least she refused to face him, refused to speak. Clutching the rim of the sink and trying to pretend that it is her husband dropping his trousers behind her back she forthwith allows the man (considerate and tender in all his movements withal) to guide her by the hipbones with a firm grasp strong and gentle as a doctor's. The astonishing mania of an old friend is more inexorable than the attack of a stranger, especially when it comes doubly unexpected from behind. A woman in heat hasn't a chance to contemplate the unseen incarnation until being dragged a little backward at her middle and forced to bend double so that she must cling to the white enamel fixture to keep from falling she already feels the searing push of its blunt head searching the perineal valley that now straddles its inverted path. A flexing of his knees, a deeper bending of her back, and she need only slightly shift her stance to assist its dehiscing of the ventral seam. At length with excruciating slowness but with a tiny confirming jerk of his torso the crouched assailant offers to take upon himself the burden of her adapting weight. Her eyes that have been squeezed shut are opened wide by amazement before faintly falling closed again, rolling upward in her disarmed head. Her legs have grown weaker but are levitated with his support while with gradually more pronounced oscillation her last renitent reserve yields to the unprecedented invader of her husband's tillage. With both hands free to manipulate her rump it doesnt take long for a big frog with a long reach and a flat stomach to bring the amplexus to a jointly gasping finish. [Here the injured beholder was not too enthralled by his drama to beshrew his Phi Beta Kappa mare with primitive epithets of blame.] . . . Still, probably, not a single kiss can the rapist have gotten when hobbled by half-divested fabric she collapses at his feet—for indeed he's not so crass as to force from her that token of his mastery.

Such was a possibility. Michael's chosen depiction of it represented in one view the respective attitudes of wife and friend in playing him false. The prominence of its gluteal feature suggested both Sandy's bestial enormity and Ruth's aversion to unromantic carnality. [Had he not himself labored to show her how live sensation could be extracted from dead spirit when she lay in bed stiff with resentment about estrangements that bated not a whit of his desire, holding out the brave promise that making love was to make for love, and that like a flywheel tiding you over a brief failure of energy making love would sustain it too?] . . . Cold comfort that the deed was done but once, that she succeeded in forgetting the unforgettable, or at least in forgetting the details and remembering only the shame (thereby intensifying both the guilt and the motive for healthy forgetfulness, which together had restored sincerity to the ensuing years with her wedded unicorn), as she and other women forget childbirth's pain at the same portal. Yes, cold comfort that Sandy's whore-pipe had tented her no more than once.

But another possibility was that she had willingly doted upon the boy's suit from first to last, many a time and oft, face on and deeper yet, spread wide in the king's bed, refusing nothing—having indeed invited the knight's invitation. Yet not in love from the lovemaking—of this the king was confident—for his queen could not have feigned the love for himself that beyond all doubt was never interrupted; she was morally incapable of deceiving him on that score, and it was out of the question that a woman of her fibre could divide such an emotion between two lovers (unless she had lost her mind for a spell) while also loving two sons each with all her heart. And certainly not without constancy of repentance. From the stem to stern of his thought, from keel to masthead, even now, he did not question her essential honor as a true lady, not driving but driven by her helpless body beyond the pale of conscious volition. Her responsible guilt lay in no more than not having confessed the whole truth, and it might well have begun in the erotic curiosity he himself in queer foreknowledge of the risk had tutored her in. In another light: perhaps it was wistfully that she yielded each time to Sandy, surely without scorn or pity for her husband—that she benefitted from her lawful initiator's longstanding encouragement to cultivate ecstasy's proximate cause, thereby regretfully leaving him behind in her advancement. Certainly she had married as a good girl mystically disinclined to separate her love into separate components, which was sometimes left for her dreams to do.

Her dreams? It was one of his own that suddenly swam into ken on a sky he hadnt been watching, as if at the signal of a soft bell sounded only once, too quickly for his slow brain to have taken in, but leaving on the air a single faint tone outlasting the meteor that it announced. Here was a fragment of involuntary vaticination from sleep at Ruth's warm nude side on the eve of this very morning! A dream-within-a-dream: hers after all!

In his dream she had told him her dream, which he heard with belief that would have been appropriate to dreamt fact. Her remark from the quickly faded apparition dwelt distinct and verbatim in his ear: she had been in the hospital for tests or therapy and was telling him about her stay:: "I didnt mind the shots; it was the penis-probes that seemed to bother me." Mentioned as frankly and calmly as if she had for the first time encountered a well-known medical procedure.

If a Jew living in Babylon dreams he's naked it's a sign of innocence; but whose dream was this one, whose captivity? If it came to that, it was the primary dreamer who had married into captivity far from Gloucester. Michael thought dreams came from dissatisfactions with consciousness. Was he no less culpable than Ruth when he sweetly dreamt of Lilian? [I wonder if Lil ever dreams about me, in all innocence, her accidental captor.] Within the dream his wife seemed free of guilt in light of the unblushing simplicity with which she related an ordeal that she had undergone without his company; but his must be the truer innocence because his was the master dream! Who knew how richly she was clothed in dreams that she never mentioned?

All the same, he couldnt deny that it was she who stood amid alien corn all her life in tears. Therefore all the more possibilities to account for his consciousness of her consciousness, to account for the confusion of fact and imagination according to the inherent interdependence of subject and object: his and her intuition, or the tuition of experience, either dreamt darkling or educed by the rules of evidence. In the case of a woman weathered enough to have borne several children and to have interpreted "a few offers", after various but limited intimacies with Michael's precursors, and with a dream history sufficiently expressive of discontents, her husband is naturally presented with series of questions. Does she secretly acknowledge her desires and denominate what he cannot be or do? Or is she ignorant of what she feels, and does she merely dream what she deems to be unwarranted amusements, realizing none of them physiologically? Or does she know very well what she isnt getting to enjoy yet conscientiously restricts herself to dreams and compromises? Or does she know not, but finds herself imagining ravishment by a certain kind of man? Or even doesnt know and truly doesnt want to know but gets it anyway?

For Michael, of all these possibilities those that entail actual getting are clearly the worst. There's no doubt about that—although in the eyes of a disinterested observer devoid of human sympathy, an untrained angel for instance, there could hardly be anything especially distressing about one tube tromboning into another (a geste much less mysterious than the alimentary process of ingestion and assimilation), or anything more serious than a violation of local custom in the disturbance it is sometimes apt to cause among certain parties. But even the other possibilities can awaken a proud man's feelings who never having doubted his absolute preeminence in the erotic consciousness of his wife has spared himself the trouble of trying to decipher every variable occupying the nearly unbounded psychic acreage of a liberally educated honor student now thrice a matron.

Since however Michael is now wise enough (he flatters himself) to admit at this moment of deferred revelation the ambiguity of nearly every term on her side of the suddenly inverted inequation (fraught with intentional and unintentional unknowns) by which marriage at any one moment may be expressed, and since he despairs even of sorting dependent from independent variables, the average man's outrage at a so-called injury to himself is overwhelmed by the exceptional man's distress at the failure of superiority in this as in lesser matters to set him apart from other men by immunity to commonplace woe. It seems bad enough to have suffered even in a past no less distant than intact maidenhood the ineradicable ex post facto truths of his woman's bodily prehistory with other males; despite the insignificant incidence and healthy normality of those small fortuitous facts their intense particularity can never be dismissed in some general anthropological statistic: but her emotional knowledge of another man is totally intolerable if it began or continued after she first accepted his own lovership.

Adding insult to injury in the burden of proof Michael thereto remembered her once having said in reference to the days when they'd all been much younger that the poor lost awkward student with big feet was a "smooth dancer". Maybe a single dance with Sandy (—though why "single" forsooth? —there may have been many dances, and more than just dancing, way back then—) had been enough to implant a casual identification that later was deliberately evoked or at least made recurrently available to her material imagination by the accidental touch of a spring during periods of discontent.

Thus his speculations led from one torment to another until he came to consider the proposition that he might have preferred the certainty of catching the lovers in flagrante delicto so that he could centralize and organize all the evidence in his attempt to establish the historical depth of her perfidy, paying for the cognitive assurance of an unimpeachable witness by his own sight-draft. But his surprise would have been more shattering than their own shock at being exposed (who must at least have considered the possibility of discovery); it would have been instantly preceded and wholly accompanied by the tumultuous trembling that serves as signal to the brain that what is being seen is too cataclysmal to recognize, complicated of course by the bewildering if not shameful suffusion of sympathetic aphrodisia that for an instant suspends the breath one should be crying havoc with. As it was, with certainty out of the question, riding an ark on Palm Sunday after sailing many a different sea of trouble with this shipmate, he grew almost as excited by her public presence close at hand as if he'd blundered upon her naked limbs outflung in senseless satiety on his devastated bed as he heard the back door closing and heavy hurried footfalls on the outside stairs.

Damn it, there was only one thing to do: ask the woman! Speak to
her! Wring some relevant words from her own lips! Words true or false are
the only relief: thousands of words for hundreds of questions. Talk all
night—forgo the precious hour of dawn! At such a pass it takes words to
cool the enfevered blood. She couldn't ignore direct questions. Already he
burned with impatience to examine her alone in the dark, to have her to
himself for better or for worse. Pray the night soon to come.

But four hours of grinding travel and household mother-duty stood
between husband and wife; meanwhile it was impossible to escape the earshot of their children: so he necessarily resumed his madding reflections
upon her inscrutability.

Before the first long traction had hauled them to the crown of the
great double span tensed against its nobly duplicated catenary arcs in a
single tangent curve high over the ship channel (once traversed by the
Harvard man who had gone to sea for California hide-work a hundred
years earlier, between Francis-town and its goat-loved sweet-herbed
island), their high spacious leather-seated Key train with stylishly tapered
sides of faultlessly transparent glass evincing trust in a civilized populace
and pride in the magnificent right-of-way—faster taller heavier smoother
and longer than common rattling trolley cars, loftier smarter and quieter
than the mean proletarian mass-transit trains elevated or burrowed in a
few worn-out vandalized cities from the Atlantic to Lake Michigan—
drawing itself with almost exclusive dignity along the profit-making
middle-class rails that so neatly exploited the Bridge of all the people primarily for the benefit of the great port's rivals and suburbs with a pleasant
toy system less versatile than Chicago's less vigorous than Cleveland's less
efficient than New York's and less intricate than Boston's (where the layout connecting our oldest university to our oldest money-market was
determined by waterfront contours about the time the Lady of Christ's
College was studying to write *Paradise Lost*), gathering power through its
third rail for the prolonged acclevity of the covered deck bracketed by
girders that also cradled a lower-level commercial highway alongside (on
which noiselessly insulated from the dampened vibrations of the comfortable cabin automotive trucks according to their direction whizzed or
glided gently past the indolent passengers—Roger was again asleep on his
mother's lap. With straight back and unnodding head she too had closed
her eyes. Her soul took no special pleasure in rehearsing the sight of ships
trains and bridgings, but only of flaming sundowns or of moonlight in
moving ribbons upon the dull or gleaming waters of the Bay, and it was
still too early for those glories.

Michael with his boys on the next settee mechanically pointed out the
marvel of riding on high over an ocean harbor, in fact right over the course
of their ferry that morning: "Remember when we saw that train above us?
Remember how high this looked when we were right under the track? The
Golden Gate Bridge is even higher but it has only one deck and those

engineers were too infatuated with cars to think people would ever need trains again." During the brief eminence of their transit he also drew attention to other things that he had mentioned on their westward passage by water, not omitting even the dull hazy reaches of South Bay, mostly useless beauty now that the salt flats were abandoned, too shallow for ships but once harvested by oyster boats.

After passing its zenith of vista the train made a long descent coasting and braking into the tunneled rock of Yerba Buena in the middle of the Bay—which divided the nobly tensed bow of the bridge's suspension spans from the pragmatic series of inclined cantilever trusses that strode over shoal waters like a file of cranes on stepping stones and flattened out to land on a bleak new mole (which covered the bones of Oakland Long Pier where the Overland Limited used to meet the ferry and where all Central Pacific freight was transshipped) leading straight to the storied shore of St Jack the First—and stopped at the orange-lighted underground nadir. The Chapmen looked down on sparse clusters of men in ordinary clothes where throngs of sailors in white hats had formerly jammed the platforms for almost every train to either city.

[Civilian clothes were forbidden on the base in wartime. Not that Michael himself had ever wished to forego the advantages of a uniform, the great equalizer of worth (within your rank) in a period of unembittered democracy and the emblem of patriotic claim upon public and private generosity. On the pavement that he and his sons now surveyed he was first and many times thereafter set at liberty in the great gold and alabaster basin for which he'd longed ever since it became famous to his boyhood in the crabbed East for its noble bridges and romantic flying boats, having been landed on the Treasure Island (which lay attached under the protection of this miniature Gibraltar) by the Navy's chartered paddlewheel ferry (perhaps even the *Eureka*) at no expense to himself with all the excitement of jack-tar come with a hide-trader around the Horn from Boston.]

Michael described to his boys the electronified castle planted on the steep rock atop this hollowed citadel, and the clean military road winding intricately round the sides of its crag after rising from the level appendage dredged up for the World's Fair and before spiraling down into the leeward grotto in which they now paused, where the second leg of the bridge was massively anchored under its upper highway. Returning from liberty clockwise on that road, in the same kind of Navy busses that he now saw parked below the station, he had time and time again ascended the erstwhile sweet-herbed cliff of goats below the mysteriously guarded radar watchtower of the Western Sea Frontier, crossing over the westerly portal of the public tunnel, and dropped swiftly jolting down to the sealevel castra, which had been built for commerce but was stockaded by the same tides that guarded the neighboring Alcatraz prison. The midnight cargoes of uniformed drunks and straggling shades like himself, no longer

exuberant, were already morosely counting the hours before their next
sortie into freedom even as they desired nothing in the world so much as
the pleasure of sleep under Navy security. But even in dispirited exhaustion as Seaman First Class Chapman scanned the amber-lighted sweep of
the bay from his window seat on the left side of the cold squeaky bus full
of silently lurching sailors with unseeing eyes he did not forget that his
forenoon joy on the way out had not only exceeded everyone else's but also
remained less disappointed.

[Yet since his sojourn on Treasure Island he'd never passed through
this umbrageous stop of the Key train without remembering one day
when his joy in liberty on the way out had been awe-struck and choked—
as far as he could tell more brutally hushed than any other's not an eye-
witness of the act—by the unaccounted moment of a nobly trim young
Chief Boatswain's Mate, often seen on just such a bright blue Saturday
fresh-shaven and bronze turned out in the earned dignity of gleaming
visored cap white shirt black tie and freshly pressed blue suit embroidered
with anchors fouled in gold, directly from the noontide inspection before
his men in the palmy warm sun, headed for civilian fields as a representative of highest success in the ranks (no longer required to wear a
monkey-suit with thirteen buttons for its lap)—not on his way back from
disillusioned liberty but like the whole lower-deck crowd waiting with
him on the platform being released at midday into an indulgent and
respectful society with money in their pockets. It was said that the brake
shoes of the Berkeley train were already screeching against the wheels
when he lunged headfirst under the plowshare forefoot of the towering
orange dreadnaught that rumbled another fifty more yards before it could
stop. This enigmatic abuse of life has been an unimaginable thunderbolt
to the heart of the young seaman who happened upon it a few minutes
after the voluntary decapitation; but now it seemed not quite so inexplicable to the aging veteran whose imagination was richer with experience
and with observation of experience in life and books; for it may well have
been that the godlike C P O was suddenly overwhelmed by the hopelessness of his mysterious feelings as a practical man surprised and betrayed by
his passion for some complex human being by whom he had suffered torments that too easily assailed a simple pussy-loving character ignorant of
vicarious experience. But the wartime hordes of strumpets were outdone
by many a Cressida.]

After the train pulled out of the Yerba Buena station Michael started a
short campaign to imbue his sons with another appreciation of unique
cityscape that would have seemed bizarre to most commuters and natives,
of the splendid route by which having passed cargo ships of the new
empire loading at the Army Base they would be rolling stately between
houses and factories (antlered pantograph now raised on high) and overlooking curtained windows or hung-out washing, directly into the center
of London's town—on its very streets but high above all other traffic like

sealed royalty on aerial wheels, and by which if they chose to keep their seats as far as its ending they could fly out along parkways dedicated to their progress, sweeping across great public thoroughfares onto ballasted boulevards in broadly banked curves and private doglegs in disdain of the dreary gridwork that had been laid upon the landscape in numbered avenues (as if the roadbed had antedated civic plot-plans) and among the pleasant groves of graceful old neighborhoods that had once been separate villages situated on mild slopes leading to the wrinkled hills, though in fact they would stay aboard no further than the oakless hub of East Bay trading paths.

The father sustained his monotonous chatter in obedience of course to the standing purpose of his will, which as we already know too well was to make every minute count in this rare opportunity to teach his boys the pleasure of looking at things, but also in order to keep them awake, because if they slept it would be unpleasant to wake them at the junction, the waking would complicate his own irritations (impeding the processes of his lower consciousness), and they would remain uncooperatively cranky all the rest of the way home. But there was no disguising the dull depression of downtown Oakland, introducing moreover everything that was all too familiar, even though it was less than three minutes since they had been skirting neatly knotted railroad interchanges near the Key System maintenance yard in a ganglionic welter of frogs and switches that confused even the cicerone himself as to which was which as they went swishing and clacking past them: Sacramento Northern, Western Pacific, Southern Pacific, or Atchison Topeka & Santa Fe. While father speculated Matty (deepest most stubborn of Chapman sleepers) dropped clear of the droning voice and sprawled in thoughtless irresponsibility against the solid warm parent (who only for a single moment had failed to test his attention) as if a whole night of slumber lay before him. So in the end Michael threw up his hands and relapsed into undivided meditation as his weary family rode the last half-mile of the day's most rapid stage in silent self-indulgent inertia.

Thus they left behind the points of interest in no time at all. It was with the most disagreeable lancination of nerve and creaking of bone that he opened cold wounds by rousing all his charges from their sleep or trance. He addressed them in the cracking voice of a querulous prophet. With a carload of other monkeys and apes, black white and yellow, they were set down at the graceless shallow crossroads of race and class. They staggered down the steps of their space ship with all the aching burdens of a long long day whose last exertions were yet to come. Empty office buildings (topped by a single tower belonging to the newspaper publisher known as the Senator from anticommunist China) rose neither low nor high enough above the travelers, less impressive than the mooselike train, which continued to dominate their sky until it resumed its way and left them melancholy on the nearly deserted pushcart asphalt.

None of the remaining sunshine was able to reach the sad rout of men women and children scattering or waiting with sporadic voices under the dour shadow of the week's last evening, which was presaged also by a chilling little wind. Not one person in the square was animated by desire or stirred by hope save by the desire and hope of hunger. In desolation all mankind strove to put off thought of Monday morning. Matthew gave a shiver (his heat-producing mechanism); Jonathan sneezed crossly. A pale fraction of moon was barely distinguishable against the achromatic dissolution of the day's sky, which was not here touched by any of the vivid display supposedly about to be seen in the clouds beyond Golden Gate, but soft darkness was still far east behind the Sierras.

(37)
MS.04

WALK HOME
FROM BERKELEY

HN 1. Three blocks up, right turn, and straight down Teleology Lane. The distance to Sather Gate opens at their backs, Michael and Caleb, as they swing along in the soft misty darkness rich at first with the green scent of trees but then in the bare open straights sweet only with the faintest salt of westerly fog which nevertheless still insulates them from men's artifactual defilements. Too late for any traffic, bating a slow police cruiser that clears them with a friendly glance protective also and quietly gathers speed out of sight. There's no light

---

"Let's walk the world together."

"I hope it won't be the last time as well as the first, you going East so soon."

"We have a couple of months. I wish this [*HN 1*] were the Gloucester-Berkeley Ship Canal."

Now she knows. One less sierra to cross. I'll have to talk to her. I feel like talking now. But no matter what, I have the ticket! —This little windhover can stay as my

All summer Jack wrote poems. He thinks Mike is jealous of his leisure, which is spent among birds of a feather going round and round with symbols commonplace or

too hard against the softness. Their own footsteps sound pleasantly in the fragrant yeasty privacy of their way. Caleb finds that the thick man moves very fast whether talking or not, proving that the fat is on the surface and not in the frame. ❏

agent. —The cat's out of the bag, but damn Jack's soul for opening it. Of course it wasnt the right way to pull it off: I was far too cruel. If only I'd told her first! Sheer cowardice. That's what hurt her most of all. It'll turn to anger, terrible anger, the worst yet. I harangue my friends about efficiency without progress [FN 1] while she cries herself to sleep. Jack, he goads me like an antithetical Muse. Tomorrow: how will I recover, going to bed when I should be getting up, and a big issue to settle with Ruth? How do I extract any more hours from this exhausted ore? I can't even seek the goad without losing time. (Every pleasure is a robbery.) His poems arent worth deciphering one by one, but I divine a Hebrew prophet selfdefrocking, still struggling against the Law and in learned intellectual passion straining as if he were an Irish aristocrat to make "a movement downwards upon life, not upwards out of life," yet torn also by the war he can't bring himself to acknowledge—the

cryptic, never outside the covers of his library. Now I see that it's better to buy and sell in an alien market made by the masses. Jack is the bibliophile. The book of his verse is designed before he starts his manuscript. *Skull and Crossbones*! A title chock full of robust awareness that nobody can top. Complete with epigraph

> ("*Thou art the Opener of the Doorway of the Womb . . . and yet, that which is born must also die that it may be renewed Therefore art Thou Lord of the Gates of Death.*")

and colophon, equally awry in taste:

> "*As I will, so mote it be; Chant the spell and BE IT DONE.*"

Sun and Moon and Mercury in every sonnet. Nothing but research of tradition's arcanum arcanorum . . . But truly I envy. Let me admire anew the infinite variety of literature and the endless marvels of human imagination, especially while I am still too inexperienced to distinguish true art from the false. Most

---

FN 1. Sitting with his back to the door he appealed to the principle that mind is freer than will and intimated that his cheerfulness was but foolish light accidentally seeping through the prudential husk that shaped his mentality at all degrees of expansive temperature. It was a self-determination of intellectual liberty to confine his brain to thought as simple in location as the body sustaining it on daily shuttle a few thousand yards back and forth along the trolley tracks and decidedly narrower than the vision of contemporaneous humanists who in the face of empirical reason could admit no hope. He explained that as a matter of fact despite his own definitions he was more humanistical than the professors in his refusal to pay attention to geometries that didnt support the Pythagorean Theorem. On this one point he was Greeker. He added that his apparent rigidity of outlook was doubly ironic in respect to the stupefying negative capability

contention between his true virtue and his overlarded ambition. There's poetry in the unfeigned conflict. Along with all the Gentiles inoculated by baptism he ignores Christianity while surrounding it with objections. In Jack's program it is as if our liturgy had never been— nor tragedy either. But in the noble vices of learning which he presumes to resort to without remorse there is tension enough and true agonizing opposition to his reversed and otherwise single-willed career as academic poet. To his meek brave little wife he seems the avatar of Philo Josephus Blake and Goethe rolled into one but her good opinion like his parents' in Los Angeles seems to him a worthless boon, not having been won in contest. Instead he strokes her dull fair hair two shades lighter than his own that spreads too wide at her shoulders to improve the proportions of her worried peaked face and says "My wife hath more haire than wit, and more faults than haires." She always blushes when she hears it, wringingly grateful for his protection. But he has other honest words for her. More than once I've seen him pat

of my feelings are still only ideas. Am I a monster of inverted youth? My only genuine sensibility is lust. Avaricious as he is, poor Pinocchio the effigy of boy wants a soul. I am contrite. Let me master the apparatus of Jack's arcana as but the key to certain minor artificial powers. —What's wrong with artifice? (But that's another question.) —My theory of cosmic injustice is the most idiotically artificial self-serving aggrandizement ever conceived, trumping everybody, excusing me from competition: wretchedly narrow-minded stupidly inflexible foolishly comprehensive decadently abstract. No critwit ever presumed so much. At least Jack is a real man who concretely inhabits a soft loving woman and actually reads all the books we mention. If I had not so timely met this obscure factotum walking by me now there'd have been nothing invidious in my opinion of Jack's acquisitions. But Mike, ah, I embrace his doctrine whole! He converts me from magic to science in one conversation. Just yesterday I still scoffed at all the practical arts, and now I wish I'd taken courses in descriptive geom-

---

required to sustain his larger view. Whereupon Sarah remarked that he was not untangling the knot of his argument as well as he had tied it and charged him with the responsibility of rebuttal instead of metalinguistic analysis. "Back up" she said "the way you came." It was thus according to her injunction that he involved himself and his yawning audience in greater depths of revelation than ever intended. In adverting again to his tenet that there is more liberty in the mind than in the will he made more than one of his hearers smile to himself in suspicion that this peroration had been in the works all along and might easily have been given voice without such coy pretext. He gave no sign of suspecting such suspicion as he plodded evenly through his reraveled tale, as follows: The means for overcoming willful stupidity are mental but roundabout. The mind's freedom may be positively exercised in such a way as to dispose the will which in turn directs the powers of practical reason. The question was what would make the

her on the ass and kiss her too while he tells her she should be sitting on a silken pillow. He can very easily make her happy. Not so the other way around alas. So he reads more books than I sell. You have to respect his knowledge of them all. He's the one who told me about Jane Harrison and lent me half of what I've read. He should have my job and I should starve. (Which would give Ruth something to complain about.) But he's never really had a center to lose hold of. Like all the rest of them in the end etry and thermodynamics. How can I ever dispute a man like him? Already he has merely to say something about me to make it true. He's a stolid bear who cares for nothing but his lore and his honey, and he has the advantage of me in knowledge as well as age weight and reach. He knew I'd like his arm around my shoulder. I can't be an orphan forever. And he will listen to me! In return for my eager footwork at his service he *must* listen to me. I don't care how busy he is.

he makes aesthetics a category. Talks also about morality in art (not *of* art), which I can't say means much to me. The only thing I have to say that's more important than what he has to say is what's the crude truth. Yes there's something to empirical truth after all. It's always at a disadvantage among the metaphors of poetasters. . . . This little puppy here gives me all I need for fictitious truth. —Gloucester: does the tide get earlier every day or later? I ought to be able to remember things like that if I'm too ignorant to figure them out.

"Once I hated the sight of you. No more than a thousand others around here, but still it was blind hatred."

"I'll have to help you reorganize your prejudices."

"I've abandoned that working hypothesis. Now I see that you lack the company of peers and so are making one."

---

common mind exert itself. The answer he gave boiled down to the notion that it might not be too much to hope for the failure of expediency in economics. Hard times were always just around the corner. As long as some few remained alert the opportunity for radical antidisestablishmentarianism would once more present itself as an alternative to pendular revolution. The attractiveness of efficiency was slightly greater than ever before since it was beginning to dawn on economic man that every day there was less raw material available for waste and more demand to share what remained. Every newborn babe preempted the resources of a human life in the future. Pray for higher prices he even said. Writing had been helped into the world because travelers' awareness of economic differentiations had presented the need for credit. Like writing it was possible that efficiency could stay on to become an end in itself and trick mankind into a pragmatically effective transvaluation by making ends of means under the discipline of limited wealth. He went so far as to venture that the only reason for knowing oneself was to attain maximum efficiency in life (for example, in contrast to Pentheus). Why couldnt we recover our youth as we exhaust the planet? If scarcity and leisure increased together, and if secondary pleasures were curtailed in favor of the

"You'll be praised for my success. A person who's a peer so young will one day find himself superior."

"Then you'll get credit for *my* success. I envy the playwright more than the play's immortal protagonist, who looks back on him condescendingly, or the actor who patronizes his part."

"Do you condescend already sir? I hope at least you do so with filial piety."

"I only anticipate my condescension."

"I would that I could live to protest it."

"Why have you wasted your time with Jack's people?"

"So that I could find a protagonist among them. . . . But at least they *select* their opinions!"

"A million others have previously chosen the same ideas and expressed them with the like sententiousness."

"You are too young and cannot understand my friends. They are decent and affectionate, especially the ladies."

"Their decent opinions are made out of putative facts and principles that they accept in patterns of thought received from their mothers without salt or pepper."

"I can't deny that. Especially about religion. They'll swallow any liberal pap. Nothing in the past of any culture is too esoteric for them to see as religious."

---

primary, a new delight in method would embolden the management of our commonwealth and revive the sense of liturgy. This longshot hope for more improvement of the world than progress had ever brought he asserted to be contingent upon a mutation of psyche like that said to be undergone by certain men before a firing squad suddenly pardoned. He maintained that the bourgeois libido dementedly devoted to the aggrandizement of private nests might be so shocked by shortages of material that it would pull down its picket fences and forsake domestic patios for joint-stock management perhaps no less crazy but a thousand times more praiseworthy. "It's possible that like me a few others will graft illusion and memory to the intellectual experience of 'science and good journalism' so that an integrative madness that I call holophrenia will get started in America and thence spread to Europe on the strength of organic social technology. My illusion is not that of vision but of power. In facing reality I suffer the same exciting lunacy as a playwright presuming to use the make-believe free will of the actors who condescend to play his fictive game. In all sanity were I even President with millions of doctrinaire followers I could at best moot some transitory discussion in the *New York Times*, but in my holophrenia I can raise an immodest hope in the minds of two or three displaced persons who while like me devoted to efficiency are also like the Renaissance masters that Caleb's sometime master speaks of: 'never quiescent never as it were in a mood for scientific observations always in exaltation never founded upon an elimination of the personal factor'. In the real world of incredible multiplicity any such implication of esemplastic possibility may seem tantamount to the metaphysical optimism of some earlier age in which unity was

"Including ceremonial magic!"

"Including ceremonial magic."

In short Michael and Caleb agree that the individuals under discussion, but chiefly Jack, hold opinions on politicians artists and priests without an inkling of their own vulnerability to the rapiers of heroes and Christians, chiefly Caleb and Michael watered with life to the gorge.

"We chime, we chime!" Michael embarrasses Caleb with a little jig on the sidewalk, albeit sobersided and frowning.

(Their resonance is not yet perfect.) "You got it, my boy!" But monotonous as ever, lips as stiff as a marble bust's. "Now listen to me. They think I'm well adjusted and normal simply because I'm equable about their troubles, but I'm really an agonizing conservationist. Next time we'll drink to comity gentility and deception!"

"When? You'll be leaving me."

"There's time for training, little merlin."

"I'm only a sparrow hawk. But what will you set me to fly at?"

> "Not barnyard fowls
> But gulls and owls."

"What will be my training?"

"A swift kick in the eyas." Lightly comes the kick with a side motion from behind. Embarrassment dissolves. "Take that from peregrine pickle!"

"Let no more of our occasions be cluttered with inferiors."

---

received with absolute faith." One strand of his argument was that the holophrenic mind in its most temerarious state can beard sleeping categories in their dens and rout them out to fight. "By rearranging the 'perceptual groups' of things and motions we can hope first for the operating and then for the theoretical competence to leaven human affairs." He elaborated on his allegation that deceit was required to gain acceptance of new constructions. Sly patient self-effacing innovators would have to make their way in institutions and enterprises without the rewards of personal recognition and for many years suppress all recognizable self-expression. Their work could be started only at levels of detail beneath the interest of ambitious operators and policy-makers. This negative sabotage if noticed at all had to be disingenuously explained in conventional terms. Under false pretenses a small new method or procedure may be permitted to take its place in local practice, justified by minor aspects of achievement but never presented in its larger significance. Such an underground career unlike that of our poets will exclude the beatitudes of publicity even after its obscure travelers have successively become trusted staff officers and departmental managers within occasional reach of penultimate power at least in middling organizational entities. Such cunningly disguised wolves among ambitious sheep would be regarded nearly as saints for renouncing the predatory success commensurate with their proven abilities. They would have discomfited the experts without credit for victory. "Youre asking for philosopher-kings-manqué!" Jack cried: "—through

Mike agreed. "Men of fragments and surfaces, women alien in under-standing."

"For hours tonight you flouted my impatience with sanguine promis-cuous confabulation. But once your allocution began I ceased to scorn and listened only."

"Phase one of my discipline for a falcon."

"Is there any kindness in your regime—any delight?" [Must I cast my seed upon the ground forever? Will he give me his wife to sleep with? Of course not. I can already see the selfishness of this grunting puppeteer. Also that he must needs always know it all and keep the upper hand. That's why he shows nothing of himself; that's why he doesnt ask me questions. But there's more to it than his ridiculous deadpan breathing through the mouth always open like a fish's with thick shapeless cheeks hung as frozen as the jaw which is always dropped though you can't see it for the flesh. The fact is that he's just as impervious to me as he is to his wife and everyone else. (Maybe Yeats was like that too—yet at least ex-pressively animated in his arrogance; undoubtedly he showed his famous emotion. Now I should rewrite the whole essay I suppose and take out the idealism.) I am demeaned by my admiration of this man but there's noth-ing I can do to recant it. . . . *These fictions will occur, but woe unto the poor man by whom the fiction cometh.*]

"There'll be delight in your assignment. You shall have every freedom. You shall not waste your days as I waste most of mine."

"After I have suffered my stint of boredom and drudgery?"

---

the miraculous subterfuge of insidious supermen bizarrely sensitive to the dear-ness of time and preternaturally susceptible to the notion of banal efficiency!" "And indifferent to the loss of pleasure." Sarah added. Michael made no direct reply. He was beginning to hope that his meteconomic doctrine would gradually reveal itself as the open double-entry bookkeeping system for a liturgical society (the canons of which proscribed the latterday compassions of psychology refused the management of hospitals to doctors and denied lawyers the rule of Congress) when Sarah interrupted him again: "Enough of competence, iconoclastic Mr H-Bomb! How do you hope against all odds?" "—All gods!" Jack rhymed. There-upon (having already alluded to cardinal virtues) Michael returned to statistics. It was a dismal discipline he said. It tried to eke out mathematics into the world of ganglionically and galactically irregular phenomena without giving up the conti-nuities and symmetries of the ulterior mental formalities that have always been inconsonant with living reality. Orthodox measurement, sufficiently apt for the earlier geocentricity of an exclusive solar system, had brought us to the conclu-sion that if we chose to regard our own mother earth as a single standpoint of reference all the planets suns stars and other conglomerates of matter except for the moon would have to be seen as gyrating and thumping around us without relief from bogglingly idiosyncratic eccentricity. Even the relativistic cosmology invented to economize our terms of comprehension had become a tissue of maxi-mum hypotheses for the very reason that it was expressed and understood *without*

HN 2. They are following the deserted steel parallels of the unsung street railway directly toward the heart of Oakland and have come to the only romantic
spot on that straight run, Berkeley now far behind them. The Sacramento
Northern's right-of-way crosses theirs between ordinary shrubbery and buildings on either side of the broad Lane and curves tantalizingly out of sight;
only a single red switch light in a blacker darkness betrays on their right hand
the mysterious passageway of the freight road that once carried passengers
from orchards and ranches down through the residential city westward to a
ferry on the Bay. It is an electric line with overhead power that ingeniously in-
tersects the wires of the domestic trolley at a diagonal, and like its cousin it is
obsolescent and nearly extinct. ❏   _____

   "Not very much. And you shall have a woman, and then at length perhaps a few others—
   "Look, this is where the Sacramento Northern crosses." [*HN 2*]
   "Strange. I never noticed before."
   "This is the kind of thing you will start noticing. I used to live along
this track in a canyon on the other side of the hills. It comes through a
tunnel and runs down to the Santa Fe. I think all the railroads around here
interconnect next to the Key System yard. But there's no reason freight
cars shouldnt be run down Teleology Lane as well as across it."
   "You clear the scales from my eyes." [I must stop resisting externali-
ties. I want to babble to him about everything that I have ever thought
but all he wants to speak of is technology!] "I wish this were the Sacramento River." said Caleb politely with passenger boats in mind.
   "That's nice too. They used to drive barges up it by sail. But tonight
the only river we're coming to is for us to cross, and here it is: by day a

_____

the perspective of a continuously changing scale. Unconscionable distances and abstract
trajectories were no more convincing than the absurd megalomania of mystics.
He acknowledged however that his own loophole for intellectual hope remained
to be worked out, presumably as an organon based upon a coordinate system in
which the vanishing points of all dimensions including time would be determined rather by some curving order of acceleration than by simple velocity. "As
long as you keep the Pythagorean Theorem!" Jack gibed. "Yes I confine my interests to earth" he replied, "which I take to be the first sacrament. Etymologically
speaking, geometry's good enough to get me through my future years of ignorance. I am not obliged to account for cosmic clusters cataracts or eversions. It is
from those who do profess that job that we contract the scientific melancholia—
unless we take reactionary pride (as I urge you to do) in the scandal of particularity." He then hinted at the wish to establish a ubiquitously centered continuum
of continuously variable acceleration such that any consciousness aware of the
universe could invert the insignificance of its own body. "Nothing but regressive
humanism!" Jack guffawed. Michael shrugged: "Who cares? —as long as one can
suffer the infinitude of complexity without cleaving to the principle of simplicity!" Sarah accused him of an ordinary empirical chemist's incuriosity but didnt
pause for his rebuttal as she hastened to demand his final reason for hope after all

curving stream of automobiles but now an estuary of ghostly blackdropped concrete that we shall ford almost in a silence under the faithful red-orange-green eyes sleeplessly regulating by wink all possible traffics that never materialize at this hour."

"MacArthur Boulevard!" [Why do I so ostentatiously respond? I trade my dignity without negotiation. I must stop smiling all the time. A solemn mein is neutral: it doesnt commit you to an ingratiating attitude. You can grant encouragement or offer cooperation after you've held your own for a while. This coryphaeus never risks a smile; he'll never open himself to rebuff deprecation or scorn. Merely by an affectation of impassivity he forfends hostility and makes everyone strive for his notice. Yet how would a circumspect Jew compose his face while traveling alone across Medieval Europe? Without putting on a phony manner of fellowship, what is the least antagonizing attitude, the least vulnerable?] "I think I never crossed it until I came to live down this way."

"You neednt cross it again. Berkeley's not good for you. We are luckier than St Herman and St Willie to be more or less enabled by the struggles of new philosophy to shake off Plato's shadow. But they were luckier than us in not having to address a population of automobiles."

"Do you approve my new labor of life?" Caleb asked.

"I authorize it."

"A labor of service assisting the comforts of others in higher service. You too are in service. What's the spectral distinction between mercenary service and prostitution?"

"We're not whores because we don't lend our internal parts." [Lame casuistry. I must please my clients with a piece of my mind that's greatly desirable and please my master to the degree that I please them. I rent my brain.]

---

so that she could go to bed. "All right my little snowflake!" He raised his voice as if in definitive pronouncement. "Even without the accelerating fields of solipsistic perns or the logarithmic perspectives of a sacrament there's hope for mankind if it'll come to grips with the fallacy of taxonomic equity." He then explained that by this term he meant the ancient and modern notion that one can claim for herself a special justice due her putative genetic category whether assumed by nationality or supposed by virtue of a single set of accidental qualifications that arbitrarily exclude other sets in present space on account of past history. The intention of Christ in reversing the talionic code was to remove such sanctions even within the short span of a person's own hour. Justice lies not with the claims of ancestors or in-laws but with a person's immediate and immanent worth in relation to mankind's. No classification of an individual human entity is much less tendentious than any other. We have long since learned to isolate a person's guilt he said, but it remains to rid ourselves of the persuasion that the pains of our grandfathers have earned us a more favorable dispensation than that deserved by the grandsons of the grandfathers who oppressed ours. How can anyone who has read the Bible and the New York Times prove what people Palestine belongs to? What cross-section of time determines natural ownership of the British Isles,

HN 3. Down the center of the car tracks two rails on either side of them they cross the Boulevard against a red light and no one the wiser. ❏ ————

"I asked you about a scruple in your sophistry but you answer as though we were discussing the virtue of a demivierge. You get money for your time."

[Feisty little puppy! But patience my heart. . . .] "If you refuse all service you evade responsibility and therefore never know the larger part of love."

"There's nothing responsible about the kind of love I want! Meanwhile I serve my own private part right sorrily."

"Console yourself that you arent polluting anything of coefficient fertility. Your love and responsibility will be confined to yourself just a little longer."

"By nature I'm a prepotent lover—but by circumstance a man potentially only, and as a youth grievously discontented. Yet not so aggrieved at my condition that I'd take on a baby."

"I've never been crazy about other people's kids either. But soon enough I'll fix you up." [*HN 3*]

"I warn you:

> . . . till action, lust
> Is perjurd, murdrous . . ."

"I know, I know. Of course I know. What with frozen foods and all we don't need women for their cooking."

"Already I could rape the Blue Fairy bringing me my soul! —But back to service: I'm in it by virtue of necessity only."

————

or of the U S A ? No new injustice is any more just than old injustice to my people. What indeed is "my people"? Nurture culture and heredity may condition my consciousness and form my will—but if we believe in individual existence, personal rights discontinue themselves with death. His own interest in the old sacraments of baptism and repentance that were designed for the soul's protection against history he professed to owe to the coadjutant train of thought that the modern mischiefs of effortless locomotion by occult combustion and of electronic telekinesis, which have spawned an unlimited world trade in novelty amusement and sensation, will perhaps by historical irony advance the cause of miscegenation. Maybe people will laugh at blood-feuds recalled during love-play with their ethnological opposites. From growing accustomed to the expression of all values in the terminology of statistics they will come to understand that their opinions demographic characteristics and secondary qualities place them in one ad hoc category after another merely according to the convenience of observers. Citizens will learn to see themselves continually reclassifiable cross-classifiable subclassifiable multivariably classifiable or rejectable as spurious. Once they distrust the basis of any benefit or penalty accrued to them on taxonomic grounds

[Who isn't, wise guy? But I'll fix you all right! —Almost dawn. I'm about to waste a Sunday seeking sleep. —But he'll make the neighborhood more interesting. Now I'll be able to see the inside of that rabbit warren.]
"You must filter out Yeats's magic as everyone else filters out his theater."

"What you call magic. But not the double gyre."

"Certainly not. Keep history and antihistory; keep the Moon and the Masks; keep the tower and its stairs. Even his attempted mysticism is less adventitious than his occult thaumaturgy."

"I thought I was supposed to get sound advice from a well-balanced sage. Instead your jealousy of metaphor taints the play of mind."

"You'll have the mellow profit of my prosaic limitations. In the meantime I don't mind if you privately question your orders—as long as you do as you ought."

"And if I rebel?"

"Then back to the orphanage for you, and we're both lost. Without me you'll be overlooked again, maybe without a girl forever. And you are my last hope. [FN 2] I was about to say that as one grows older he gradually sees the causes of certain conventions. For instance, chowder calls for a shallow bowl so that you won't get strands of codfish wound around the

---

they will begin to foster sympathies that ignore and subvert nativity groupings. A sense of radical inalienability might complete the disabusement of class immortality. Property would be eyed more narrowly as something that for capital and usufruct alike is rightfully enjoyed only by oneself unless donated during one's lifetime like King Lear's but by taxation always bequeathed in part to the commonwealth of tribes and classes. Both past and future having been removed from categorical consideration and the heritage of ownership having been curtailed for the sake of synchronous justice the truly categorical dichotomy of men and women might be recognized in statistical purity. Concentration to the point of celibacy is always possible for the few, but the common craving for stimulation and adventure would be reinforced by other tendencies of the new age. In cumulative experience both males and females would forget their own deflorations. Most claims of preemptive touch would go by the board. Women when no woman comes to a man intact would begin to believe jealousy clean gone from men grown accustomed to the easy hunt of free fish and indifferent to the social perquisites of paternity. (Semen is only half seminal anyway—maybe less than half he dared to say.) The final dissolution of romance may remit women their original sin by inducing them to cultivate amid general inconstancy a reformation of instinct about babies equal and opposite to that forced upon by men at the beginning of institutional marriage and thus to perpetuate the rights they will have won in their democratic revolution. Children would be charily borne not from but for love. Society would provide ample facilities for each well-advised delivery. —In some such words the homely philosopher illuminated his pericope on the mind being freer than the will. ❑

FN 2. Sarah's sallow face surprised him with its beautifully candled glow as they finally went to the door though her next day would be ruined with

HN 4. It turns out that Caleb lives little further south than Michael and not much further east of Teleology Lane than Michael west. They shake hands in front of the lighted reredos of the Just-as-Good studio. Michael breaks into a little trot to get up speed for mounting his stoop three score yards down the side street. Caleb makes a long diagonal crossing of the Lane (rare opportunity and a minor pleasure), thus avoiding trespass of the livid light from mortuary signs on both sides, the last two of seven on this way from Berkeley to downtown Oakland. He touches the opposite shore at his own corner and turns left into the less translucent darkness of a short steep hill. Living on high ground in an upper story has its drawbacks in times of water shortage but it's an advantage when there's faulty sewage. ❑   ———————

shank of your spoon when you dip for the potatoes. One also comes to appreciate the hypocritical customs."

"I'll think on't."

"Not too much. See your mind in the mirror of nature, not nature in the mirror of your mind. And don't follow that unholy Hebrew in Berkeley. Your art must disprove St Willie's prophecies and descend the staircase further yet than Dante Shakespeare and Goethe, deeper into things of life's labor and their accidents."

"Don't drag me down too fast!"

"The sooner you're diverted from the quest for perfection the sooner I'll have the bird I want." [*HN 4*]

[But will he return when I cry lure?]

{*Postulants only*: GO TO ITEM (51) MS.05, page 501.}

fatigue. He could only guess that her heart was comforted with a hope that the Jews would not be singled out for suffering and go down alone; yet perhaps her puzzling joy came from him pressing her hand in both his own and saying you gave me a lovely party, to which she replied saying please blow out that smoke before you kiss me goodbye, seeming undisturbed by the cryptic and inconclusive sermonette she had heard, the tenor of it filling her heart as oddly welcome and mysteriously irresistible, discounting the irony masculinity and religion of its unauthorized preacher from among the Nathans' ancient oppressors. There at the entrance to the outer world now nearly silent, while Jack and Caleb lingered together for half a minute, she spoke more confidentially than she'd ever before spoken to any man not her own. "I hope Ruth likes Gloucester in particular as well as you do." she whispered. "I'm so glad to hear you're both planning on a daughter!" ❑

(38)
HY.07.0
TRUK

*T*he only time Michael ever bore arms was while still on his job with the U S Navy after the Japanese surrender when we had entered into the age of hyperarmament.

The vessel in which he served was one of such a large class that the Bureau of Ships could not be bothered with thinking up and keeping track of names for well over a thousand of them fabricated more or less identically on three coasts but especially also on the banks of Midwestern rivers (launched sideways in Emergency slapstick) where steel was handy so that the real shipyards of tidewater bays would not be tied up with such simple mass-production, albeit the dowdy Nereids drab and ungainly were larger flatter easier to put together and more powerful in anti-aircraft defense than many trimmer ships graced with names if not hailing ports of their own: certainly shallower and generally more useful.

The versatility of Landing Ships Tank in hostilities had been demonstrated by the transportation and beaching of warsmen and war's engines against both enemies; but now, when most of the Navy's named ships suddenly became so many replicated museums too expensive for peaceloving citizens to man and maintain, these deepsea hybrid ferries were proving

their positive and reconstructive value as the first ocean-keeping amphibious fleet since Vikings rowed their dragon ships onto North Atlantic
strands two or three at a time. The L S T known to Washington Pearl
Harbor and its own anonymous flagship only as 1066—dubbed the Reluctant Green Dragon (no doubt cognominally redundant with more than a
few of her fungible sisters) by the men who as chosen taxpayers considered
themselves her proprietors, with less pretense to distinction than her
young successors a few years later when the Navy named the survivors and
mutations of its class after counties (of which there are about three thousand in our nation, including all the duplications among states, which
tended to copy each other in westward progression just as the first colonies
imitated their mother country), under predictable influence of a certain
Disney-typed fancy that had been commercially imposed as standard entertainment in peace as well as war upon all the reduplicating fragments of
American mind throughout the world, the sobriquet being in truth too inconvenient to be often used except to protest distaste for members, even for
a unique combination of digits writ large in white on either side of her jaws
for the purpose of guiding personnel in a beached congregation of otherwise
identical cargo-carriers as well as for convenience in controlling convoys beforehand—was now anchored off an island in the lagoon of Truk waiting to
embark a roster of Japanese garrison troops for repatriation.

Without military freight the ship floated light and fully hollow revealing the irregularities of her crudely stamped lines. The Japanese were
yet to be made out more clearly than strangely uncoffled prisoners dimly
distinguishable under palm groves on the shore under supervision of the
Marines who had been occupying the place for nearly four months. None
of the 1066's officers or men had ever seen a Japanese fighting man. The
crew was as young and green as the ship herself except for a few veterans of
the European Theater where beach warfare had long since ended.

To people of the Navy no name besides that of Nippon the capital of
every evil mystery had sounded so sinister as Truk, malevolent heart of
Japan's Pacific darkness where it was said that for twenty years secret powers had been assembled and compounded, center of subhuman terror more
magically invulnerable to white men than the entire remaining Empire of
suicidal yellow drug addicts, though to strategists merely an impregnable
fleet-anchorage to be bypassed on the steps of conquest. Even now not
many Western eyes had beheld it.

In the diction of journalism it was always the enemy's black ocean
"bastion" (demoniac counterpoise to angelical Pearl Harbor), if not in fur-
ther-fetched simile the Japanese Gibraltar; but to Michael such epithets in
the lazy abuse of English seemed only tawdrily apposite. Nothing he saw
suggested tunnels of living rock or concrete ramparts or electronic para-
pets concealing deadly machinery of embrasured defense. Nor did he see
any evidence of airfields docks cranes warehouses or barracks required at
least by Western admirals for aggressive operations.

Yet as his ship slipped through the southwestern pass of the reef into the vast almost empty roadstead he had hardly doubted that he was gliding into the hollow of a cobra nest deep as the mountain-bearing mother volcano whose giant truncated perimeter brimmed the surface of endless waters. Privy only to such rumors and facts as were mentioned among enlisted men he had taken this eerie landfall for nothing as natural as an atoll of mostly subaqueous peaks that formed a lagoon in the shape of a broad spherical triangle projected upon the oceanic plane as a distorted circle thirty miles in radius, far beyond any continental shelf but cultivated by Micronesian natives and rationally appropriated to the uses of one empire after another. It made little difference that all fighting was over and done with, the enemy defanged.

To objective eyes in the 1066 (if there were any) this forlorn Mardian stronghold surrounded by its low whitecapped barrier loomed no more formidably than a few hills scattered like the last projections of a prehistoric world succumbing to universal flood, only one of which rose in the background to any significant height, as if their impenetrable green vegetation swarmed with concentrations of vermin surviving worldwide panic. A few of the larger islands, like the one they came to rest in the horizontal shadow of, were flanked and extended with leveled shelves of land on which habitations and parade grounds seemed to crowd all the flat space kept open among spiles of living palm trunks rooted in rufous larvic sand beaten black by brownish feet and canopied with flavescent fronds paler green than the beetling jungle palisades and more vulnerable to psychic oppression by the union of purpled lagoon and cloudbanked firmament.

These dispersed citadels now satisfied none of Michael's topological expectations. But disappointment of classic grandeur only broadened the malignant emanation that hung upon the face of the waters under a dead gray sky altogether unwelcoming to mammals.

A few days before, violating the sullen silence with a precipitate rumble as peremptory in this forlorn roadstead as the sound of chains from a battleship, the 1066 had dropped anchor in the same dread sunless sticky weather. The morrow was Christmas. A week later the ship's company and its ninefold growth of segregated guests would get under way with more bustle but less noise, making for itself the only visible motion under the grim light of the same still unyielding heavens. Then half a day northerly the 1066 would come out from under the thick atmosphere that hooded its entire visit to the undelectable retreat of winged devilfish and sharks by steaming for hours above the malevolence of its diminishing pelagic slopes and spurs until blazing blue shone upward from the wholesome whaley depths of a solar world.

The commanding officer of the prisoners was a gentle bandy-legged major in shabby khaki shorts. Though no social equal under the conventions of war, Michael, a junior petty officer, would soon be better acquainted with him (through a very few words of English and much sympathy of eye) than the ship's commissioned gentlemen were, thanks to the opportunities of propinquity on the bridge deck, where the men of Ship's Control Division were permitted to spend their many leisure hours and where also the father of his people would naturally station himself as the best vantage from which to oversee the open main deck most of the length of the ship before him.

There his children crouched or moved about like unemployed galley slaves, if not sleeping matted on the floor of the garage below, all skinny docile mature and incurious, most of them wearing loincloths, performing all their necessary functions and serving their time without apparent boredom. In little more than the half day required to restore Americans to the blue skies beneath which they were accustomed to Pacific sailing the entire topside complement of the mercy ship was used to the sight of nearly eight hundred wiry veterans of isolation and privation who showed no sign of hesitation discomfort or confusion living what must have been much like their old life though on a more confined new platform: an orderly informal crowd of self-disciplined little brown men scarcely yellow circulating peaceably and chattering or undemonstratively receiving rice from their own kind ladled out of great iron caldrons like try-pots and squatting on the hatches with their wooden bowls like simian masses at some internal picnic of a zoo, always clustering and dissolving adventitiously, meditating easily. They frequently perched upon unpainted timber racks that Navy carpenters had out-rigged in perfect alignment over both sides, windward or leeward, for shitting and pissing directly onto Poseidon's prairie.

As Michael drifted in the current of national emotion that for five or six years had been drawing him away from the political vortex and into this isolated solidarity his discernment of trends and high purposes was not assisted by such communications as reached the ranks in a detached L S T responding to doubtfully coordinated orders in the furthest reaches of Oceania. The center seemed to have loosened its hold, and it would be much later back at home before the Radio Technician Second Class would begin to see even the obvious historical tide that had borne the crests and troughs in which he'd swum. Only long after returning to the States would he grasp so much as the simple geographical placement of Truk in the Caroline Islands seven degrees above the equator and nine more above the Trobriands, not to mention its history of possession by Spaniards and Germans before the Japanese, or the Catholic Protestant and Buddhist composition of its native population whose very existence he never suspected at the time, like almost all his shipmates having been denied an occasion to go ashore.

It was also to be only through books that he would disabuse himself of gross distortions in the perspective of his own eyes on the scene and discover that somehow the immediate shade condensed by the particular island they were calling at and its closest neighbors had obscured or foreshortened the bulk and height of major peaks, just as in the eyes of his

distant high commanders legendary intelligence had obscured or foreshortened the actual condition of the enemy garrison until they discovered
that a full year and a half before its national surrender the Imperial Combined Fleet had abandoned the magnificent anchorage. Unknown to
Michael (and in discredit to his ship's scuttlebutt) the whole base had subsequently been neutralized by repeated air attacks launched beyond the
horizon from the flat decks of very large vessels bearing our most illustrious names.

A decade later when the Truk lagoon was almost forgotten a typically
bookish chance would pluck it back into the foreground of Michael's
superseding memories when in riffling through a new war memoir at the
store he discovered that even earlier than the first air reconnaissance some
few Western eyes of prisoners from the U S submarine *Sculpin* had scanned
the Imperial base at Truk, whence they were trans-shipped for forced labor
in the copper mines of Japan. One of their wounded comrades had been
tossed to the sharks by the crew of the enemy destroyer that had disabled
their boat and picked up the survivors, suffering a death more dreadful
than that of his commodore with a skeleton crew of others who chose the
last irreversible dive to a more passive grave among the bones of Moby
Dick's children rather than risk the secret information in his head to the
frailty of his tongue under the torture he expected.

Reading the account in times of subsided passion, when sympathy for
former foemen was spreading even among veterans, his doubt would be
renewed concerning the justice of his wartime beliefs about such enemies
as those transported by LST 1066, and he would remain more skeptical of
atrocities than any Nisei listening to our radio would have been in those
days, and of the innocence of those with the most information who twice
thought it proper, in the balance of civilized lives, to let fall the bombs of
apocalypse. Yet did barbarous intention turn out any worse than the
aggression of friends for that half of the Sculpin captives who failed to
reach the mines because they drowned in a Japanese carrier sunk unbe-
knownst to their colleagues in *U S S Sailfish*?

It is said that it was only after their imperialistic enthusiasm reached
its climax that the Japanese having occupied Truk for many years began to
mistreat the local Kanakas, beautiful people half way in every respect
between the blacks and the browns of the Pacific, in order to work them
harder on fortifications and runways, the febrile construction of which
seems to contradict at least the literal translation of the Japanese admiral's
word who called those Shimas Jimas and Tos, protected by the far-flung
coral breastwork, "natural" aircraft carriers. After Michael returned to the
States and learned that the bestial adversary had named the haiku islands
of the lagoon after trees seasons and days of the week he could not remember which of them it was that had given image to his experience there.

Anyway, as early as that first noon on a northerly course to the Land of
the Rising Sun, still pondering the human event that had stirred the ship

more than any other since its Indiana launching, he would marvel at the
incommensurability of his lot and an Oriental's. The peasantry of the
U S Navy was normally well fed and comfortably housed and democratically entertained. It was technologically as well educated as it cared to be
(a spotty passion), and there was usually no dearth of physicians or dentists
for the cure of bodies. It even had mechanical laundry service. The crew's
quarters of nameless L S T s were specially provided with such conveniences as individual flush toilets (unscreened to be sure) rather than slats
over the usual troughs of a warship's running seawater.

When the 1066's cargo had included American troops her sailors'
space was abridged, but when passengers were yellow men the disturbance
was no greater than that of sparing a couple of her unassigned sleeping
compartments for the major and his three inconspicuous junior officers
(who were fed in the ward room, where enlisted personnel were forbidden
anyway), and twice a day during off-hours resigning the galley to self-
sufficient little rice cooks.

The ship was always remarkably generous to her own (considering the
living conditions of land warriors)—almost as much in war as in peace,
though peace gradually liberalized each man's latitude through the happy
attrition of senior men and others of particular category eligible for early
release from service, especially compared with a submarine or destroyer in
regard to the possibilities for privacy, which consisted not so much in being out of sight or reach (an unthinkable privilege for the lower ranks) as
in occasionally being able to sit somewhere on or below deck without the
grossest disturbances of musical loudspeakers and loud unmusical mouths.
Few of Michael's peers ever seized such an opportunity for privacy; they
left him to this luxury without much competition. But in no Navy ship
could either officer or man escape electromechanical noise. With the best
of luck a sailor could hope only for the steady or mixed and flattened
sounds that might be mentally blocked out and ignored with the least difficulty, just as the harsh mechanical sough of ventilators and the dim light
of electricity always besieging his "rack"—his one retreat, a folding
bunk—were excluded from his sleep.

But on that New Year's Day 1946 as they came to the end of the dark
Christmas octave, Michael was to reappear on the bridge deck for leisurely
reading, restored to contentment and harmonized with intellectual beauty
by soothing motion through indolent seas, by the regularized ease of duty
underway, by radiant Apollonian energy from the blue world above, by the
silent friendliness of the Major sitting like himself cross-legged on an
ammunition locker under the awning, by an afflatus of love for the brothers of those believed to have done their worst in making pain for his
brothers, and by the mystically sensitive aftermath of his first accompaniment with death.

{*Postulants only:* GO TO ITEM (40) HY.07.1, page 431.}

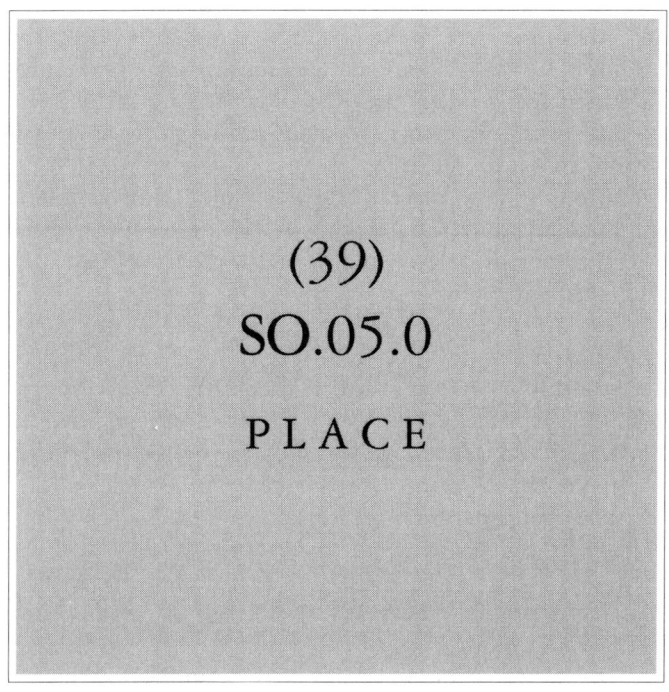

(39)
SO.05.0
PLACE

NOTES TO SPEAK FROM: MICHAEL CHAPMAN'S OUTLINE
OF HIS INTENDED THIRD LECTURE ON MUSELESS ART
NUMBER ONE, WHEREIN HE FINALLY TRIES TO GET TO THE
HEART OF THE MATTER IN DROMENOLOGICAL FASHION

1) *Most people are prudent enough to cluster with their professional kind, where
their knowledge will be respected and they will understand everything they hear.*

—encounter nothing extremely unfamiliar.
—need not think about assumed values: tacit consensus of those
joined together in what they are qualified for.
—painful and deemed unnecessary to attempt or attend
unauthoritative discourse.

*Thus people go into professions so they won't be mocked or parodied. But I shall
persevere even when only two of us remain here.*

2) Aristotle (per Jack) : *"Place is neither a part nor a quality of things."*
Dromenologist must take issue.
Place originally was flat space for dance: its locus differentiated by
use for altar and/or sacred burial. Center of cult makes for topological

distinction; establishes city with citadel and markets; determines geo-graphical point of view as counterentropic focal point (community hearth) of knowledge and social order; provides inhabitants with reference for all locomotion and boundary marks. So place grows galactically if not sym-metrically from choral center.

As armature of society, place is a space-point in irreversible time that being named and recognized by everybody can be returned to in space as the one spot that cannot be averaged out with others or substituted for—even after "Panhellenization".

Thus place generates dromena. Simplex locus of religion, history, economy, politics, art.

[Discuss continuum space, abstracted from consciousness (no tasting, touching, smelling, hearing—and only negative seeing) vs. local space, which occupies consciousness as particularly as trophic time in relation to astronomical—known in immediate though complex perception prior to rudimentary and therefore also to universal concepts.]

3) [Dance as a modern art of locality.]

4) In ritual the persistence of place and repetition of performance are mutually reinforced by myth. But no art is so poor as dance in devices for its own preservation.

Theater's place has become variable and fungible (—sometimes even portable): = fictitious place. But requirements of alien rented platforms are small disadvantage to drama: imaginations of language fix their own locations anyway (since drama in general has unfixed its original dromenon).

Look at Euripides: used place to imagine kinetic landscape. A telling symptom of post-Panhellenic disintegration; introduction to all modern drama by way of dance represented as locomotion (travel) but not danced as such because physically constrained by the same old orchestra. [All three Unities done for.] Locus of community order and customary behavior (no longer subordinated to the stability of Themis) suddenly used as seat of imagination's displacements.

(In still-living ritual the social organism responds to change in outside world without disintegrating because action remains conceptually local.)

Bacchae liberated dance from ritual in ironic piety. Now the art exists only in temporary space generated by its own movement. [Does not expand like sound to fill cavity of its chosen building.] Dancers having no words cannot accept intellectual assistance of geographical definition; can-not make spatial reference to anything but themselves and floor.

Hence:

—embryonic pseudo-place is real only by virtue of congregational occasion.

—dance space manifested as plastic object with no predetermined delimitation or axis; spatial structure cannot outlast the moment.

5) Motion formerly considered as object's change of position. Now seen as set of variable relationships in space. We go so far as to doubt motion whenever position can be determined. Like physics modern dance also recovers primitive (pre-geometric) persuasions by eliding position when motion is sure.

[Position distinguished from location.]

Yet dance (bastard daughter of ritual) is reaction to science in refusal to abandon absolute objectivity of created space; establishes special concrete spaces here and there, now and then, temporarily, on human planet as center of universe.

Generates orchestral space by human movement. [Motion within absolute place *vs.* relative and abstracted motion.]

Regular motion (in clock time) maintains present order within larger system, makes no space; random motion (Brownian movement) is disorder limited only by artificial boundaries: but creative movement—motion with motive (therefore both subjective and objective)—describes unique new self-limiting continuum that can be called motivated space—ephemeral means to peculiar order, physically profound but brief, totally mortal, absolutely particular within cosmic time and space (themselves relative and universal).

6) *"In man face-to-face with his Space lies the basis of the theater."* Jean-Louis Barrault, speaking of drama in which players can be set anywhere (not just in choral precincts and sacred mountain pastures) by intellectual imagination, erupting from any place or presenting to the mind any number of different landscapes. [Drama can generally dispense with unity of place—or of time—or even of action, each according to warrant of other cohesions.]

But dancer doesn't face space until she's made it—and then almost too late to glance at it as she leaves the place, where it lingers only as long as the corporate after-effects of the performance.

One artistic problem of dance: to open consciousness of body by closing *situ*ation. [Contrast: brooding seagull, coming home to colony, recognizes site, not nest or eggs themselves.]

7) Second artistic problem: cult (feminine sense) *vs.* news (masculine communication)::

—within place all information retained, echoed, savored, fermented inside boundaries; whereas news (result of variable relationship with distant world) consumed almost at once, like transportation or amusement: value diminishing in repetition, unlike alluvial sediment of experience.

—yet danger that culture may deny communication of reason by making idols of canonical images.

8)   Third problem: *Orchestral space is coterminous with its own trophic time, discontinuous in duration as well as location.* Its maximum distances limited to the confines of a cylinder described by the longest reach of the highest leap from a flat circle; essentially independent of architecture. But to the extent a volume remains undescribed it has no existence as dance space. [Cf unused stone from statue, or parts of life's spectrum not mentioned in a novel.] This space (in pseudo-place) must be generated like universe from central energy as *"domain in which physical laws can operate"*. Its shape is function of a fleeting history; unlike universe, size no indication of age.

9)   God being simultaneous and ubiquitous would have no aerial linear or temporal perspective of any field or scene. His system too large and complex to control except by granting natural law and deputizing freewill to let it operate. Artists generally can manage their own tiny systems only through limitation, ignorance, selection, simplification—but dancers more constrained than others by physiology. Their artistic danger is not fantasy (extreme fiction) but imitation (mime). Yet by reduction of scope dancers increase their control. [Advantages of self-control.]

Place of performance is misshapen or too large if variation of perspective among spectators makes a difference. [Define dance topos as orchestral space in relation to its architecture as a whole: stage, auditorium.]

Dance loses even gradient intensity of distance when depth is distorted by point of view too near or too far. Spectator vantage approaches plan or elevation according to relative altitude of the eye, especially when entire frontal surface of dance volume seems little larger than the eye itself and the center of action is shrunk practically to a vanishing point. *In a place of suitable size and slope neither the plan of the dance nor its elevation dominates vision.*

Radius of dance's cohesion determined by specific human energy concentrating its space. Dancers can't interact close-packed like billiard balls; but collective density of force is diluted when company gets too large and boundaries of orchestral space expand, threatening the discontinuously real space of the building. Whereupon, because of foreshortening, spectators can't help favoring certain planes or sectors as vantages, which (like short-distance views) vary in their distorting perceptions of the dance.

10) Orchestral perimeter should be more or less equidistant from dance's center of gravity; maximum possible ratio of shortest visual radius to longest. Then dance stage can be designed as broad ellipse—its limit an ideal circle—with no quarter or angle unduly preferred. Dancers must not be obliged to avert their faces from a back wall. Any seat-holder can hope to see no less dorsal than ventral surface of the company as a whole.

Thus despite geometric focal points of pragmatic ellipse the orchestral space denies axis or grain. [Omnidirectional multiplicity of views, assuming aforementioned situation and choreography.] Spectator can't orient himself to any one vanishing point. Dance has no facets.

Call the space *horizontally isotropic*, but limited by shape and position of stage (orchestra). Cannot be cloven like crystal and isometrically projected to extrapolate planes of movement unless they are actually generated. Totally devoid of bias toward vectors in any azimuth; impartial anent horizontal momentums—until dance itself makes its own curves or axes. *The sole predetermined alignment is gravitational.*

Thus as far as possible the field is informal—until formed by the action; even then informality of volume implies that horizontally isotropic space may envelop or omit any shape or set of coordinates without taking possession of it.

11) Freedom from solid geometry fosters experiment, helps defend against artistic danger of ritualistic anesthesia. Awakens patrons to unlimited possibilities of action in generating dynamically modeled space within the somatic license of a small place, unprejudiced by any graduation of scale except nonlinear acceleration of gravity.

[Contrast: thoroughly prejudiced anisotropic perspective of modern dramatic space—at worst, single vanishing point of proscenium stage (to which full range of spectators must accommodate themselves); at best, for the few (with apron stage), perpendicularly paired vanishing points from oblique viewpoints: but in any case built upon rectilinear axes, usually further formalized by scenery and motionless properties. If you walk around the galleries during a play the dramatic space seems to swing on vertical axis like earth, thereby dictating longitude, poles, and equator (if not simply x, y, and z axes) as epistemological preconceptions; whereas dance keeps gyroscopically true to itself—without alteration of aspect for the peripatetic eye.]

12) N.B.: For convenience I speak of single dancers, of individual imagination, but advanced treatise on art dance would deal with collective laminations and overlays of isotropic movement. Art of dance allows creators to work in community—that is, concurrently in common medium, toward coalesced object, in the same place.

It is also only for convenience that I speak as if all dancers were creative artists (their own choreographers).

Superorganic creativity is almost as rare in dance as elsewhere (cf jazz, commedia dell'arte). Crucial distinction is *composing with one's self* (even if another person is to perform the composition). In principle, creation and performance are one. Choreographer, less traditional than Greek coryphaeus, as master-dancer delegating all parts in terms of her own trophic time.

13) Anyway, during performance dancer can't be distinguished from the dance. Consider the aesthetic; take dance not as dancer's expression but as theatrical phenomenon:

Dancers come naked into center of expectant place, save for music have little support from ancillary crafts or peripheral artistic collaboration; little room for novelty through clever mounting of production; basic architecture is single delimited plane. (Any article used or carried by dancers must be subordinated in bulk and symbolic value to the human physique—or must extend its movements without pretending to explain them.) Dancers abuse the aesthetic of their theater when they elaborate or intensify the symbolism or sensation of costume.

14) Neither spoken words nor tradition can excuse or reinforce or offset the bare action of a person whose sole present existence consists in that action. Dance can't be prised open by leverage of ideas. *It's telluric art, ruled by the goddess of gravity.*

[Emphasize that it's no light difficulty for a contemporary work of art to be deprived of external reference and to rely solely upon its own immediate energy induced and sustained by its own unassisted exertion.]

15) Almost everything in dance is frank and direct, being confined to closed non-linguistic system. But open to music, the source of its peculiar irony. Music originally for benefit of dancers in stimulating and coordinating performance of corporate dance, but in art dance its function predominately aesthetic (for audience) rather than managerial or energetic for performers. To my disappointment we can't do without it. Not the music itself annoys me but the fact that we need it to occupy a sense demanding to be occupied, which if not placated will alert itself to rustling of audience or prick up its ears to catch traffic noise from outside world.

Percussion of stick, cymbal, or drum was originally necessary to synchronize the rhythm of grouped dancers, who couldn't watch each other for cues during action unless it remained simply circular; couldn't pick out each other's footfalls when there are were no boards to sound them. Melody and musical expression were supplied by voices or instruments outside the ring when performance of dramatic ritual became too strenuous complex or congested for specialized dancers with manual or vocal energy to spare.

Advanced arts of music and dance are each in a peculiar way rebellious against Themis—mutually reactive or at least independent violations of ritual. Music is best regarded as sound made by particular dance, unless it's an aleatory or heuristic initiative challenging its biophysical accompaniment. Music nevertheless continues to carry common astronomical (if not trophic) time to the ear of each dancer. It measures for spectators through their own organs of time the persistence of the space made by movements they see. Otherwise each watches in her own isolated time: an antisocial welter of different aesthetic receptions.

But such elements of irony are also elements of sentimentality. In getting away from the primitive meter of foot and breath the two arts are all too convenient as aesthetic diversions for each other. Music covers up both silence and thuds of unangelic feet; at least at its (worst) no less adventitious to dance than electrical lighting is, which not only illuminates but also conceals people with artificial darknesses. Music sometimes used to make dance seem to do what it fails at, or has no business with. Yet it does advertise the action!

Music makes harlots of dancers when it sells their dance as thrilling locomotion. *An American dance audience ought not to be persuaded to sit still by the aural suggestion of a moving landscape.*

But it's impossible for members of a modern audience to accept silence even when they're thinking working or sporting. . . .

{*Postulants only:* GO TO ITEM (41) SO.05.1, page 433.}

(40)
HY.07.1

CHRISTMAS

*I*t was lavish food and lax discipline that celebrated relations between the Navy and its men on Christmas at that purpled gray green lagoon of Truk. Better than halfhearted attempts were being made generally by the high command and specially by operating commanders not as much to overcome as to compensate for the demoralization of anticlimactic duty served in ignorance of any transitional policy. Days were passing slowly and undistinguished for those who could have no hope of getting home at once, slowly and obstinately for those closely calculating the service "points" that made them eligible to be sent back to the States for discharge into civil life. No other topic no other motive sustained conversation or execration.

But with a new port-of-call came mail from home and new film for ship's movies, as well as a heap of treasure for the ship's library: freshly packed literature from the inexhaustible list of Armed Services Editions (compact paperbacks short and wide, printed two pages on one as double columns, handy for dungaree pockets, prodigally donated by the book trade itself, "NOT FOR SALE"):: enlightenment for many hardened minds that had never till confined at sea discovered magic casements closed or open on any foam at all. The boredom of those without ready faculty or imagination or even ability to read pruriently was relieved only by the prospect of meeting the enemy at last. Michael surmised similar acedia in the few other ships of like kind that lay off distant islets as isolated reflections of the 1066.

One minor blessing was the daily spate of uniform and windless rain. It discharged the polarity of evil built up daily between the plates of lowering sky and sullen sea, temporarily neutralizing the electrostatic potentials that fixed the anchored ship. It was an atmospheric respite from institutional lethargy. In the rain every island lay monochromatic with sea and sky.

But the leaden waters bore luridly inspissated jellyfish, inverted Medusa-heads hanging with livid gastral streaks and spreading filaments, weighted just beneath the surface by a gravity barely stronger than the buoyancy of slime. Nothing in the elements comforted a sense of horrible desolation that pervaded the itinerant community of a ship accustomed to the sparkling ocean lakes of other pacified stations on its fitful journeys. The gray dispirit of officers and men could neither be explained nor acknowledged. In military life there is no medium for collecting and expressing private feelings and no admission of vague emotions that cannot be comprehended as recognized sentiments like homesickness lust or fear. Memory and hope were in danger of being ruled out by the place.

Mr Keily the First Lieutenant, in reality a high school teacher of physical education and basketball, unexpectedly demonstrated the virtue of paternalistic enterprise. Having straightway gone ashore to make arrangements for the delivery of holiday supplies from the Navy godowns he had stumbled on an opportunity to provide all the people on his ship with prizes of war. On his initiative the Marine ordnance officer released to USS LST 1066 as trophies indirectly earned certain arms and armor gained by conquest from the Japanese: official souvenirs for vicarious warriors, booty from an unused arsenal. What else could be done with a surplus already too long out of date for modern warfare?

The ship was soon buzzing with word that the day after Christmas a seven point seven millimeter Imperial Army rifle with its bayonet and a steel helmet would be coming aboard for each man, and a Luger-type pistol for each officer. The anticipation of having something martial to show at home in authentication of personal contact with the war slightly enlivened a dreary celebration of Christ's birth.

Before their turkey dinner the men were issued cans of beer. The Armed Forces Radio never ceased playing Christian carols and commercial love songs in the solemn or lugubrious mode. A small artificial Christmas tree was decorated in the After Crew's Quarters. Red Cross presents were distributed, that no man without parcel post from home could be said to have had nothing of American generosity.

{*Postulants only:* GO TO ITEM (42) HY.07.2, page 439.}

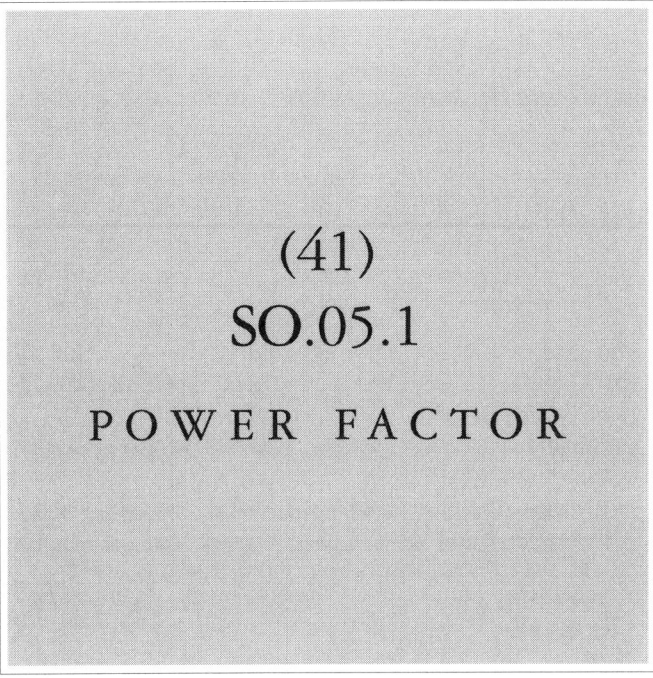

(41)
SO.05.1

POWER FACTOR

16) How does dance in wordless action electrify the place with its show?

Techanalogy makes best metaphor as follows for discourse on the dynamic art of human bodies.

17) [Explain alternating current *vs.* direct current.]

AC is the natural form of electricity within an artifactual world. Each dance is its own variable modulation of frequency and amplitude resulting from all subharmonic rhythms and vibrations entering into performance. A C of dance may be said to synchronize actions and sensibilities of all in atten-dance, though because of its low frequency undetectable by the senses without analytical recollection in tranquility, reflection in retrospect. Unlike alternations of dynamo that synchronizes all clocks of a city, the dance establishes unison of irregularity like the common absolute motion of everybody in a ship advancing through high seas at variable speed.

This A C makes trophic time-ground for all its components of audible, visible, and proprioceptive frequencies, such as:

—each dancer's foot pace and oscillation of parts.
—heartbeat and breathing of all subjects and objects.

—vibrations of music instruments; rhythmic and melodic fluctuations.

—plane and perpendicular patterns of choreographic action.

—strophic propensities of corporate emotion.

In a communications machine you would tune circuits to resonate at this frequency (if tuning could be comprehensively variable). But composite (resultant) oscillation of dance is too slow for radiant (ethereal) transmission of signals; none of the mutual modulations forms a message. *We are here concerned not with transmission of information but with direct transformation of power from the creative to the aesthetic.*

18) [Power as intensity of energy dissipation.]

No cells (or pages) to store dance power in, and no external sources. It therefore must be generated in time and place of use.

[Power transformation as electromagnetic coupling of primary and secondary coils.]

Fluctuating magnetic field of demonstration, *"touch"* at a short distance. Dancer and spectator magnetically as close as two circuits of a transformer.

19) From biochemical sources dancer produces electromagnetic energy in kinetic manifestation. Dance itself, as process, transforms internal work from power of maximum action at minimum psychic potential to phenomenon of inverse proportions: a practically motionless state of extremely high attention. Thus aesthetic load inverts creative input.

So far, a strictly natural principle: conservation of energy.

20) The insubordination to nature appears (as with all art) in the leveraged multiplication of negative entropy—in this case not over time (as in writing) but simultaneously, concurrently. If value of art remains undiminished by use or consumption, then affect is multiplied by number of its events (which in a single dance performance is the number of appreciating witnesses).

Later I'll return to this third order of negative entropy (following, first, life; and, second, mind). Meanwhile concerned only with one-to-one mechanism of creative/aesthetic conversion, each spectator considered individually as a sole and private power load.

21) Look upon the coupled circuits of performance and conspection as a closed system (ignoring requirements of temperature-control, ventilation, lighting, and population characteristics) to generate, transform, and internally dissipate the ludent power of human body moving under the direction of imagination. No energy reserved or accumulated: power, to be produced, must be used utterly; yet without overheating the aesthetic load.

This sublimation takes place by reduction and delay of energy flow (current).

22) But first a technical excursus on sexualistic qualities of electromagnetic circuits. It is here that gender enters into my conceit.

Electricity generated by motion in magnetic field or by changes in magnetic field. Field itself often produced by part of current generated!

An A C circuit is either masculine or feminine, or it is resonant.

Everything magnetic is feminine in tenor. [Allure.] Reluctance is magnetic resistance; hysteresis, residual magnetic history.

Feminine elements of circuit called inductors. Chief inductive device is coil of wire passing A C —sometimes solely for purpose of counterbalancing masculine elements in circuit; often wound in an electromagnetic machine (motor) that converts electrical into mechanical power, or mechanical rotation into electricity (dynamo or generator); but also, juxtaposed with another coil (perhaps embracing a common iron core that intensifies the coupled magnetism), as the windings of a transformer.

[Inductance as peculiar to alternating current.] Magnetomotive force acts upon magnetic material (even if it makes poor magnet, such as air inside simple coil) to produce magnetic flux, which reacts against the same current that induces it. Inductive reactance thus slows down current when it's trying to rise. Inductance is drag. Cf mechanical dashpot or shock absorber.

[Tugboat tows its load.]

By same token, inductance stores energy in magnetic field and tends to prolong current in declining phase of voltage (pressure). Amount of energy stored and released by coil varies as square of current.

Henry Adams: "If the laws of inertia are to be sought anywhere with certainty, it is in the feminine mind."

Masculine traits show in opposite tendency. Sometimes, under resonant conditions, exactly balances the feminine for best possible efficiency; but sometimes overbalances it: in that case energy—proportional to square of voltage—is stored in an *electrical* field; flow anticipates pressure.

Specifically male elements are called capacitors. They charge up with batches of electricity. [Concupiscence, capacity for expostulation.]

Capacitor ("condenser") made of two plates, acting as reservoirs of antithetical polar charges, arranged as close to each other as possible without passing current (amperes), separated by dielectric material which must be better insulator than air unless voltage (pressure) is extremely low. Sometimes used solely to compensate for feminine excesses; often employed simply to absorb and assist in reversing surges of current that would otherwise, insufficiently impeded, defeat the circuit's purpose. Capacitive *reactance* advances oscillation of current in relation to oscillation of its electromotive force (voltage).

[Tugboat pushes its barge.]

23) Can now understand how sublimation of libidinal energy results in part from essential femininity of system in which heavily inductive or magnetic elements outweigh masculine and neuter (resistance) factors in circuit load:

Power felt by spectator vibrates in unison with power generated by dancer. But power not in tune with itself. For power is net *effective* product of flow and force (amperage and voltage), which in a gendered circuit are out of phase with each other. At no instant do they mutually reinforce as well as they might. In feminine circuits cyclic pressure passes its peak and declines in advance of the electron flow. (But current and voltage each remain undiminished an Sich.) Effect is that actual power—density of work in time—falls short of power reckoned exclusively from its two components. *Ratio of real to virtual*—always less than 1.0 but no less than .5 in an unbalanced circuit—known as the *power factor* coefficient.

Unity of action in dance matches unity of time and place, but this integrity is faulted by dissonance between act and feeling—like the misregistration of color and line in a picture book, but intentional instead of erroneous. This mismatching remains internal and invisible—artist's unconscious secret—as little objectionable as discrepancy of earth and atmosphere in New England seacoast spring when warm weather comes only after some blossoms have already faded. Everything comes slightly beside the point though exactly true to form, deliberately disabling the cooperative fullness of power. The feckless component, which engineers call reactive power, shows up in dance as creative sweat and aesthetic illusion. [Cf hysteresis in core of inductive persons; physiological inefficiency.]

Movement and emotion, respectively the creative and aesthetic counterparts of current, lag behind the active and passive counterparts of voltage: imagination and interest. [Contrasted to preponderantly masculine dromena.] Thus dancer keeps a distance from her sex without denying it in the slightest. Also the spectator from his desire.

Low power factor (of inductive gender) prevents creatively excessive work of dancer from gratuitously or even dangerously disturbing the social world that provides the art with its material and its public. Dancer's job is to dissociate force and expression as far as possible without throwing the power over into masculine phases (where a given infinitesimal of movement falls so far behind its foreshadowing imagination that it suddenly falls back into the following cycle). Teaches herself to sunder and control two faces of a moment, keeping time fracted that she may not drift into sexual resonance with her admirer by unguarded instinct.

24) The skill would be remarkable enough if there were only one resonant frequency to keep clear of. But as an art that disclaims the Platonic yearning to arrest time, dance invests its own system not only with change but with infinitely variable rate of change. [Acceleration *vs* velocity; acceleration to *n*th power.] Electromagnetic values of human elements continually changing as power fluctuates.

These independent variables together determine the resonance that dancers must elude at each instant. Without limiting either force or flow, each one must be able to check playful or violent surges of actual power that would be engendered in the output circuit as perfect conjunction of emotion and interest.

25) Yet the doubled system must transfer power over widest possible range of frequency and impedance. [Fidelity (versatility) *vs.* selectivity (specialization).] *The art of dance broadens a man's frequency response.*

26) Reduction of current (with voltage increase) occurs in transformation from chiefly kinetic to chiefly potential energy. Dance performance itself (as transformer) is common to dancers (primary coil) and spectators (secondary coil), created space being the core.

[Principle of transformer: voltage proportional to number of turns; current inversely proportional.]

Efficiency of transformation can be very high. Adds less to reactive heat than artificial lighting does. Stage temperature not significantly increased even by the most prosperous conversion of action to consciousness. [From "rehearsal" to public performance.]

Performance reduces strong action (movement) to physically imperceptible emotion for those whose interest in the dancers' imagination has been stepped up by the same transformation. [Power at any instant is constant: interest/imagination and emotion/action as mutually inverse coefficients.] Creative power is transformed for aesthetic dissipation at relatively high tension.

But artistic value of particular dance comes in part from transformational restraint. Increase in ratio of secondary (aesthetic) interest to primary creative imagination must be balanced by:

a) a living load of feeling, which otherwise may be stepped down to purely dispassionate admiration of beauty; and
b) originality of movement (overcoming habits of the body).

Transformation of the most robust power can fail entirely if the emotional output is too faint to enter memorable experience, or if imagination leads the movement so weakly that the dancers only carry on tradition. . . .

{*Postulants only:* GO TO ITEM (43) SO.05.2, page 449.}

(42)
HY.07.2

KILLER KANE

One of those least susceptible to Christmas sentiment was the man whose face would come first to Michael's memory ever afterwards when he saw the name of TRUK or was led to the thought of it in his bookstore on a streetcar or anywhere else his brain might find itself at liberty. That face was called addressed referred to and recalled by the name of Kane. Enlisted men were accounted for and given orders to, without favoritism or nuance, by surname pure and simple (the initial of the first name appended when distinction was required between Joneses Smiths or others of like-sounding families who happened to find themselves on the same muster list); but in this case the naked and un-modified word Kane was invariably used also by the face's shipmates—bunk neighbors, fellow gunners, victims of its terror, beneficiaries of its protection—messmates withal, as Michael himself and everyone else who had to stand in line three times a day for food was its messmate and could never entirely forget that brute fact no matter how clearly contradistin-guished by temperament, duty, or sleeping quarters.

Yet the body not the face better identified the man shunned or appealed to—Kane did this or Kane did that to earn the Bad Conduct

Discharge hanging over his head; or pray Kane do this or that if it isn't too much trouble, seeing that the war's over and none of us like this shit any better than you do—the phalloid skull and neck being of one piece with the body and patently unsuited to the face. For Michael it was the face that bore the burden of this discordance, even though of exceptionally small proportion to the whole animal.

The crew described Kane as a "specimen", employing the term like Platonic Realists or normative drawing teachers to express the embodiment of ideal muscularity, abusing the language in this case no worse than their betters did; but they should have called him musclebound, for the thews of neck thorax and limbs were developed as if separately organic to limits elsewhere realized only in hypertrophic deformity. He was called specimen instead of monster in respect for his athletic superiority.

The muscles worked harmoniously in a variety of exercises. They seemed nowise slowed by mass, and they were limber enough for high-diving swimming volleyball football basketball even baseball, and supple enough for wrestling, though better trained for weightlifting—uses of his body all demonstrated now and then ashore or afloat. But above all his was the force speed and footwork for money-boxing. For that he displayed his skilled endowment at every opportunity, with encouragement on all sides. In brawls on liberty he was said also to be very fast with a knife strapped to his calf. The ship's champion, its underworld pride.

In a larger population he might not have been awarded the palm for tennis or water sports. His exertions at swimming for instance were disproportionate to the locomotion, for he had not learned to bury his face in the water while exhaling his breath and flailing the waves. To Michael it was plain that he had never enjoyed instruction or access to the facilities by which civil athletics are normally fostered.

But even as Kane's particular enemy, whose fear and hatred of the man was ambiguously betrayed only by a stubborn refusal to distinguish him from other crewmen with signs of outstanding respect, the Technician admitted to himself that this specimen was purely athletic in its reincarnation of the classical Greek prizefighter specialized in profession but most liberal in means of combat. This Milo needed no cestus to weight or harden his fists, but in authorized bouts the Navy would not allow them bare. Without brass knuckles, even thickly padded with puffy regulation gloves, those curled claws nevertheless felt to his reluctant sparring partners like scarcely softened peens of a double hammer. In a restored Olympic pancratium—if he'd been eligible as an amateur in consideration of his love for the sport—wrestling and boxing with naked hands and no holds barred, but improving upon the ancient art with modern science (straightarmed haymakers and windmilling uppercuts superseded by rifling jabs and breaking hooks), Kane might have championed the whole United States.

None of the elements of Kane's brutality were unprecedented or uniquely distinct in the observation of one drawing toward the end of his long sentence to social poverty among generally brutal peers under mainly ignorant and ineffectual officers. Perhaps even the quantitative integration of his qualities was then matched somewhere in the armed forces of the world, and there is some probability that strained nature has more than once repeated gross aspects of the Kane phenomenon since Michael's encounter with it in his floating stockade. In the ordinary course of events, just as bully terrors of childhood dissolve little by little under protection of the civilization that one gradually enters, the continual fear of meeting Kane on a narrow deck alone on a dark sea, and the feckless hatred of his unsmiling arrogance in speech and gait, might well have faded from active memory after Michael's return to the uncontained excitements of a richly sexual society with newly appreciated and expanding worlds of intellect marriage and independent livelihood—indeed even the dire outcome would have merged almost unremarkably into the welter of a youth's continuing experience in rude society—if the misplacement of that distinguished face upon its thick post had not peculiarly affixed in Michael's accessible memory everything he had observed and felt about the vicious human monolith.

In fact the recollection of anomaly (as Kane's physiognomy struck him) would retrospectively intensify the anxiety he had felt about the pugilist's presence aboard his ship. He hadn't been scared enough! The time would come when he marveled at his own temerity in refusing to knuckle his forehead at every encounter with the undeclared enemy. For his silent criticism must not have gone unnoticed; his ostensibly democratic blindness to Kane's superiority of force, his tacit insubordination to the unofficial tyrant of the crew, might have been calculated to incite implacable vengeance and expose him to the quick and soundless dangers of private enmity at sea.

In the midst of bustling civilian security that had long since succeeded the uncertainty of a sailor's footing he would shudder at the veritable insensitivity with which he had leaned upon a rail alone in the dark or climbed a leeward ladder to the deserted boat deck on rough nights underway. A man might have been quietly knifed and dropped overboard—or simply upended and shoved, fully conscious of his absolute helplessness—many hours before he would be missed.

The small delicate ears, taken as part of the mask-like face, were still uncauliflowered. No one yet had laid a glove anywhere on the spuriously prosopographic head. The small refined nose and level brow were still undamaged for the same reason. Considering also the golden cap of close-cropped curls, which certainly did not sort with the adamantine skull that swivelled atop its trunk like a Monitor turret, the patrician visage at first seemed to belie its every act and word as well as its reputation for act and word. But after a day or two of acquaintance one ceased to discriminate the godlike countenance, so quickly totally and justly did social contact corroborate the infamy of its proprietor.

Michael had more than once seen such sculptured masculine comeliness felicitously extended to the whole man in both Cambridge and Berkeley, but never with a torso like Kane's. Even Hellenistic carvers declined to imitate a body that bulged so much. Yet Kane's nice ear was carried forward from the Classical, and the hair and the cheek. The forehead too might have derived from Greek art of the time at which it began to represent the mortal features of its heroes. But these conventions of ancient beauty emerged as the finely chiseled perfection of Anglo-Saxon virility to the modern dynamic taste. If Michael's memory was to find guidance from the Greeks, years later during the leisures of dawn, Kane had to be studied as an imagined statue of Autolycus the great Parnassian cattle-rustler, son of Hermes and maternal grandfather of Odysseus, whose powers of disguise no doubt justified the neglect he seems to have suffered at the hands of sculptors actually ashamed of his thievery, of his mandate to professionalize athletics, of his hypermuscularity, and (as apparent only now) of the transalpine features that we prefer. But physique and physiognomy were less harmonious in the wholly mortal Kane than in Hermes's scion, who went as much too far for Greek culture in thuggishness as in larceny.

Michael's life was spared by Kane's simplicity in underestimating the hostility of inactive resistance to brute preeminence. But on certain surprising occasions this simplicity brought to the surface a touching homoiousian goodwill. Perhaps it amounted to nothing more astonishing than a soft spot for its own self. Kane's plaintive appeal was heard in the extreme instance of his humanity, its high-water mark in Michael's memory—never quite expunged of a passive enemy's suspicion.

Thus:

Two blessings had befallen the ship that summer. One was the end of the war, brought about at some expense to American reputation by means of an unprecedented double atrocity against the Japanese people, which mooted LST 1066's conditional orders to take its place in the first line of what certainly would have been the world's bloodiest and most strongly opposed invasion, and which in all probability by its timely severity saved Michael Chapman's life. The other blessing, ending almost as the peace began, was an illness that striking nearly as suddenly had removed Kane to a hospital in Guam for a good ten weeks during which the ship's company lived without fear.

He'd returned to duty while the ship lay at Saipan. His welcome was constrained. Officers and men hoped he was a little wiser from his stint of helplessness, a little chastened by pain and medical discipline. All eyes sidelongly watched his temper for signs of permanent improvement. Of course every sanguine expectation was to be disappointed in the long run, but the temporary mitigation of vigor was beguiling while it lasted—a week at the most. It was during these brief homecoming holidays that Michael had overheard him talking to Ensign Rand about his feelings.

No other officer and certainly no enlisted man was so credulous as to think that a concealed streak of goodness somewhere adulterated Kane's dynamic purity. Kane himself had never been loathe to lead the crew's scorn and contempt for the tall skinny shock-haired bumbler who nominally functioned as gunner officer in the declining phases of that department. That graybeard of twenty-three, unaware of the Quixotic impression created by his own tumbling speech and ill-fitting untidiness, apparently subscribed to Fleece's opinion that an angel was nothing but a shark well governed, despite the fact that his tough predecessor after making every effort to govern Kane had been obliged to bust the man from second class gunner's mate to second class seaman for threatening his superior life. Rand's policy was to take an aristocratic interest in Kane's future boxing career. As a tactic it was successful to the point of encouraging the fallen angel to confide in him (truly or falsely) as he would never confide in peers. The soft-hearted officer-boy's Christianity wasn't as hard-headed as the old cook's when he addressed the sharks from *Pequod's* deck well out of reach.

In his manners Mr Rand anticipated the ostentatious informality of the coming age that his wardroom fellows were not prepared for. A treasure of beer had been donated to the crew by an official agency of patriotic generosity, and he volunteered to take responsibility for a beach party (in two shifts, port and starboard watches alternately) while most of the other lords spent a day at the officers' club on the hill (which was said to have been the first structure erected by the Seabees while the Japanese were still defending the other end of the island). He lolled tousled, having flipped his garrison cap onto the sand beside him, his back bent against a shallow bank cresting the beach where a year before from an unheard-of logistical distance eight thousand men had landed in twenty minutes to take the true keystone of Japan's western Pacific arch. Saipan was the loveliest of tradewind islands. Its margin still littered with rusting steel bones from the amphibious assault was not denied to the crew of LST 1066 all athirst for the edges of loveliness.

For many days they had been anchored off Tanapog Harbor close to the beach. Even in recuperation Kane had led daredevil dives from the peak of the bow into sweet warm waters. For many days the sun had risen for them behind the green and open flank of Mount Tapotchau casting fresh morning shadows upon the tree-clustered lower slopes covered with beauties of temperate summer so seductive to an eye weary of the open ocean and to a nose conditioned by diesel fumes that Michael would have jumped ship like St Herman if he had not known that lovely landscape to be invested with the discultured prosperities of a major military base safe from all counterattack but taut with the humming momentum of imminent victory over the northwest horizon.

Across the channel opening to the south stretched another island Tinian flat and low. It was from the invisible airfield there that unknown to the thousands of innocent soldiers sailors and Marines nearby, to their officers, to almost anyone but a cache of distant commanders and scientists, heard only undistinguished in the familiar multiple drone forerunning rosy-fingered dawn—only apparent evidence of the daily offensive operations for the sake of which these islands (named after Queen Maria Ana for official reasons though better known in Spanish according to Magellan's appellation as the Isles of Thieves) had been so expensively seized—a B-29 had risen in starry sky with the most surprising and successful load in warfare's long progress just a few hours before the first case of beer was broken out on the beach for Kane and his shipmates.

The warcraft called *Enola Gay* (an unofficial name recognized by all historians) was still in the air, not yet within returning sight of its jubilant welcome on the neighboring island, its aviators not yet fully apprized of the work they had undone at Hiroshima, while Mr Rand, his long lips retracted as usual by the habitual tightening of his cheeks whenever he looked or listened breathing high in his shoulders to the beat of his Adam's apple (though even in facing skyward he had no external cause to squint thanks to the finest sun glasses a fair young blade could find), was attending Kane's confession with perfectly disinterested sympathy. He sipped beer from a can, democratically sharing the warm brew that had been doled in units to the men upon whom much to his amusement the affect was generally pronounced inasmuch as they swallowed the diluted alcohol without the mithraditic protection of daily drams from a ward-room liquor locker. A short distance away, without respect for persons, the main body of celebrants loudly and simultaneously commented to itself on the degree of virtue in every possible object of consideration within the field of its collective experience. Such shouted prose and hearty song was rarely to be heard under the open white and turquoise glare of forenoon. The boisterous voices easily diverted common curiosity's attention from Kane's confidential tones as he squatted by the gunnery officer's indolently crossed ankles sifting sand with one hand and holding his own sun-heated beer with the other.

Michael had lingered dreamily in the delicious pellucid shallows of the glaringly bright lagoon where the gentle waters rose and fell with the moon little more than eighteen inches all day long—peering nearsightedly face to face at tiny gorgeous fish (reluctant to acknowledge his need for air), hanging underwater almost motionless and no more alarming to them than the ridges of coral long since mutilated by demolition men on the eve of the invasion to make passage for swarms of horseless amphibians; no stranger to them than the now familiar hulks of failed chariots holed and sunk as it turned out for their safety and delight to seek and hide in—and walked up the beach to find his clothes not far from Kane and Mr Rand. He was sitting for a few minutes furthermost of all the people in the party from its center drying his feet with a towel so that he could put on his shoes and get up to claim his beer allotment. The coarse sands were still

strewn with corroding artifacts of war amidst the natural debris of vegetation loosed from the land by rain or from the sea by infrequent squalls,
and so it was no wonder that the corner of neither windward eye in the
two preoccupied heads heeded one more odd shape that seemed out of earshot and intent upon its own affairs. Michael dared not listen long, making believe not to notice their presence.

Kane's voice even in the best of health was not half as deep or as thick
as his mighty chest, and its emission of the universal monastic blague in
no way distinguished itself in Michael's memory—nor by any prejudicial
accent, whether drawling narrow strident or aggressively urban, least of all
by the broad intonation that might have been expected of the face. But
none of the ship's company had ever till that day had much to say that was
attractive in sound or memorable in substance to the dour technician from
Gloucester. Few words of officers or crew ever charmed or impressed that
silent critic at the time he heard them, notwithstanding his vivid registra-
tion of many a man's behavior.

Highly redundant expletives of the primitive vulgate were uttered in
force and number sufficient to penetrate all varieties of intelligence but
unproductive of eloquence when addressed to minds higher than the lowest. In this language personality expressed itself by slurred permutations
of shit piss and corruption, ceaselessly woofed into the warp of prurient
expostulation to convey predictable opinion or wisps of doubtful information, as well as by varied intensities of sound. The official tongue of the
U S Navy still retained (passim) certain idioms more stylishly historical
and humane than the living utterance of its modern salts—as for instance
the twice-daily call heard on prouder ships than L S T s: "Sweepers man
your brooms! Clean sweep down, fore and aft." Such phrases piped in
dying tradition made the Navy itself seem to Michael kinder than its contemporary population, which spoke of destroyers as tin cans officers as ass
holes and women as cunts. Of what he'd heard in his own ship, memory
favored meaning over style. Most of the true communications were orders
(which in the postwar phase of the game grew laconic and few) or operating information such as the announcement of an object's distance and
bearing (which was relinquished by the brain as soon as the first in a series
of new situations supervened).

It was equally difficult to recollect in particular cases the gracelessly
general scoffery that stood for discourse among his enlisted colleagues. But
he had been impressed by the substance of Kane's words, and in coming
years he remembered his perception of them at the time, abstracted and
compacted from the actual sounds, subconsciously reshaped for neural efficiency, edited for convenience in mental assimilation, and perhaps excessively influenced by the speaker's obvious effort to modify vernacular for
the ears of an officer half way to ladyship in moral authority.

". . . Sir when are we going to pick up a load and get moving again,
hit the beaches with some action? I'm losing a lot of time in this fuckin

war sir. Fighters got to start young, they don't have many years. Sir it's like knowin you might die before you fight, and I won't have nothin to do when I'm too old to fight. I never been in a hospital before. It gives you time to think, which I guess is good for once in your life sir. Like I realized a few things.

"I realized that if I ever had to do time I'd go crazy. I got nightmares about being in solitary with irons on me. I don't hold my liquor too good sir but I just can't get into no more trouble, I just can't. All because it so happens I can beat the shit out of any man in the Navy and there aint no two dogfaces or gyrenes that I can't take with one hand and I've proved it. What can a guy do when there's no fuckin Japs to fight?

"I was wonderin if you could help me keep out of real deep trouble. Don't let me see any mealymouth cocksuckinmotherfuckincuntlappin sonofabitches when I aint busy. I can't stand the bastards if they say shit to me. Gimme extra duty if you want, I won't say nothin I promise I won't sir. Once we get some action I'll be okay, there's nothin I'd like better than tanglin touch-holes with a fuckin Kamikaze on the number two forty, best fuckin gun on the ship thanks to me believe it or not, crow or no crow on my sleeve. It's the waitin around that drives me nuts. I've lost my rate I've lost my pay I've been on every shit-list and work detail that anyone can dream up and I've been at more masts and had more restrictions than any man in the fleet plus two summary courts and there aint no one between here and Anzio been docked more liberty than I have.

"So I have a B C D waitin for me and I'm scared shitless it'll turn into a Dishonorable. I don't give a fuck about the D D but I can't take what goes with it. One night in the brig at Pearl was enough, even with a hangover I almost went berserk. I'm scared I'll hurt somebody. Sir in the hospital— Jesus I was sick they say I almost died, spinal meningitis is goddamned serious and they almost didn't ship me to the hospital in time after they saw I wasnt fakin. Shitheads!

"But once I got to Guam they were sure good to me. *Me*, for Chrissake! Here I am almost booted out of the service with everythin in the book thrown at me down to lousy Seaman and they treat me like a V I P as long as I'm sick sometimes with two or three doctors lookin at me together and a nurse gettin things for me all the time built like a brick shithouse but I was too sick to get a hardon most of the time. She told me I could have been paralyzed. Sir can you imagine that—Killer Kane paralyzed? For a couple of weeks I was as good as paralyzed, I didn't have no strenth at all and even when I got better they wouldnt let me get out of bed for a long time. All I could do was listen to the radio and I bet I know every song ever sang and I've heard Tokyo Rose more than I've heard my own mother. I almost wisht I was dead.

"So I finally get back to the ship and all we do is lay around. Sir I'm not an atheist, I pray to God that if he's goin to save my life in the hospital he damn well better let me at the Japs and keep me out of jail cause I can be dangerous you bet your sweet ass I can be dangerous sir. If I'm goin to get into the fight racket I got to get goin *now*! I'm all alone without nobody to *let* me get goin! Aint nobody on the ship'll put on the gloves with me no more. . . . They oughtta tell a man's age by how many years he has left."

"It's tough for a guy like you on a little ship like this, Kane. Nobody in your class."

"You aint just ashittin sir! Fucked by the fickle finger of Fate."

That was as Classical as Kane could get.

{*Postulants only:* GO TO ITEM (44) HY.07.3, page 453.}

(43)
SO.05.2

MULTIPLICATION

27) I don't say aesthetic persons have no energy of their own. On contrary, appreciators of art must have their own secondary power supply—enough to repel private and public distractions. As cultural aristocrats these stimulated receivers ultimately evaluate the piece of art. [Individually, not by oligarchic or commercial vote.] Their active function is to criticize or praise.

Performing arts, which exist in real time (begin and end at points described by coordinates in astronomical time), must bring to bear on the transformer large amounts of power (concentrated dissipation of energy). This primary energy is provided by highly irritable agents whose instrumental passion is interpreted for customers.

28) But in the special case of dance (to the degree that choreography is completed in the act) it is the creator's own personal power that is communicated to the people. Power, not information, is content of performance. Dance can be seen as direct transmission of power-for-its-own-sake—far greater power than needed for mere communication.

Value is conferred by force in created form. Action of artist modulates sensitive personal power of spectator, whose own mind is nearly suspended, whose will follows the pattern imposed; but it does so with sensations of impersonal strength substantiating aesthetic perception. Watching art-dance the lap demon's private interests are forgotten.

Dance excites a variety of analogical vibrations in its witnesses, *making* them sympathetic but leaving little leeway for either instinctive or idio-syncratic response. It controls their ready energy partly because they are far less practiced in imagination of movement than in fictions, manufac-turing, or sonic thrills (since everyone in school learns to write, make things, and sing), and have comparatively little proclivity for such objec-tive action on their own part.

But when process has stopped, spectator in retrospect must set *value* of modulated power, especially in comparison with other such events. At this point all artists are passive in respect to their own work: aesthetic judge-ment rules in axiology.

29) Every art has its special mysteries within the general mystery of artis-tic value, which there is no time to state here, still less to discuss, and which I've never been much interested in stating or discussing. Such an effort is inevitably more difficult and less important than the individual work of art which proves the thing that can never be generalized yet defines itself amply and no more than sufficiently in each of the unique presentations concretely essential to its existence. Once I've pursued reason to its limit in normal consciousness I don't try to dissolve the boundary.

Yet an attempt at one particular mystery of dance can be deferred no longer. Have already alluded to it as the multiplication of energy. [Special modification of Kirchhoff's first law.]

30) The rapidly attenuating power of a radio transmitter is broadcast with-out slightest sensitivity as to its reception. It dissipates in space whether the signal is picked up by a million receivers or by none. Detection anywhere of its electromagnetic waves makes no marginal demand upon originating engine. Any one of an indefinite number of detectors requires only the tini-est interception of transmitted energy to demodulate information and apply it for the intelligible modulation of its own power supply. Thus original information is indifferently scattered without division of energy among receivers, dissipation balancing production, until it has become too weak over its radius to irritate any local sensor.

But the transmission of substantial power must be infinitely less profli-gate (more efficient) than broadcast dissemination. Requires nearly maximum possible concentration of directed energy (as in transformer). Production bal-anced by consumption.

When there is no load (use of power) none can be generated. This law holds in dance: rehearsal in empty auditorium is training for dance, not dance itself, as running without competition is not a race.

Yet according to physics the power used cannot exceed original power. The preternatural mystery of dance (beyond the familiar, consistent, and well-described mystery of electromagnetism itself) is that performance power can seem to expand like a womb according to the load, so that each human coil wound about the secondary core will feel the same virtually kinesthetic charge whether it is one of a hundred or one of ten times a hundred. As long as spectator is personally near enough to submit himself to the magnetic field he taps as much power as each of his fellows. Neither he nor any other spectator suffers any loss of benefit by his marginal addition to the audience. In this complementarity the dance can be regarded either as a transformer of power or as a transceiver of information.

The dancer works with undiminished speed and freedom no matter how heavily the secondary coil is loaded with people. Therefore it's not dancer growing more powerful but dance itself: flux of transformer becomes denser with demand. Dancer doesn't feel magnetic resistance to every breath and every move when house is large. *She feels no drag.* (If anything, maybe a lightening of her psychic burden with congregational extension of aesthetic sympathy.) Ambient temperature rises only with increase in number of auditorium's heat-dissipating bodies.

31) In short, each patron couples to dance individually, personally closes his own secondary circuit. [Cf Christian prayer getting God's immediate and undivided attention.] Without sharing value, enjoys full power of performance. Air pungent with ozone from exchange of energy in core space. Electromagnetic benefit of the joint neurosis (a resonance frustrated by power factor): again, maximum touch at distance.

Dance is somatic yet congressional and evanescent: consequently must generate vastly more power (*rate* of energy) than a mental work of art, or one which can be warehoused transported or visited over the course of centuries. The only energy it can occasionally absorb and store (for release no more than a moment later) is imparted, mulled, deferred, and conveyed by portable artifacts such as fabrics or scepters serving the purpose of flywheels or surge tanks when imagination fluctuates too wildly for the most brilliant resilience of spine.

32) Like flame, dance consumes value and leaves behind neither *ergon* nor *logos* to augment the uncertain stock of 3rd order counterentropy that makes up heritable culture. The cost of life is paid by its environment; the additional cost of mind is very small (= work-equivalent of information): but the cost of art is paid by life and mind.

Dance itself contributes to environmental degradation little more than the heat dissipations of so many exerted bodies in so many minutes of metabolism, less than most athletic contests—but the expenditure of counterentropy is magnified by its aesthetic worth. Women naturally abhor aging, yet dancer uses herself up without reward of property or offspring: dance comes out of her hide. Whereas athlete's encratism serves maximum personal survival (health or surplus compensation), suspension of aging.

Though women are magnetic, there can be no Iron Woman of dance. Baseball produces Iron Man because it's only a pastime; but dance proves to be the great American time-grasp—presenting real time to men who usually try to forget it. As with all art, dance tends to diminish immediate social order by occupying minds that might otherwise be devoting themselves to social improvement. Nevertheless, dancer strengthens all patrons at her own expense.

In fine, value of dance lies neither in ash nor in fuel but in flame.

{*Postulants only:* GO TO ITEM (45) SO.05.3, page 459.}

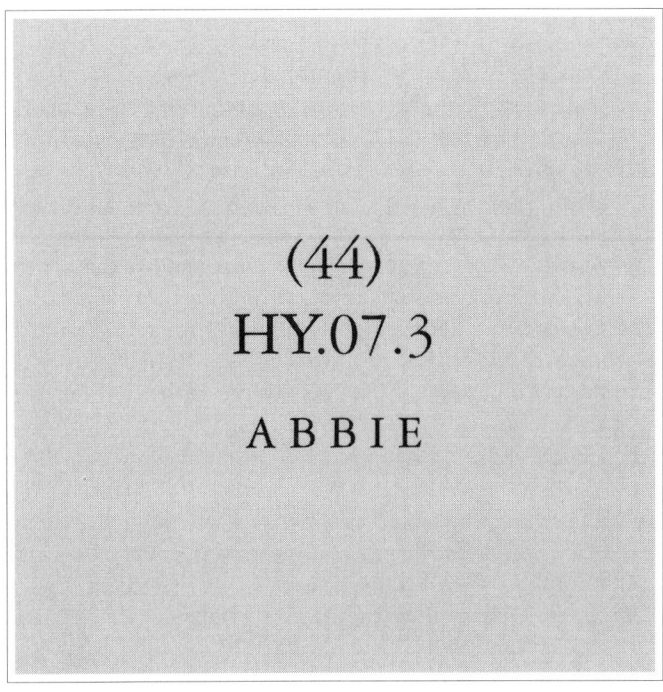

(44)

HY.07.3

ABBIE

*B*ut the sailor most susceptible to Christmas sentiment was a boy whose face was to persist unremarkably in Michael's memory as perfectly appropriate to the high long head: broad withal of brow cheeks and nose, long of mouth with large arched teeth whitely agleam within the bronze skin of perhaps illegally enlisted youth; yet as lean in frame as an Indian brave. The lengthy muscles of the towering trunk and neck, of the ranging arms, looked maturely perfect; but stringy immaturity was betrayed by hands and feet still too large and by fatty tissue still exiguous for the man's size. Already he walked with the underlying motion of an accomplished catamount, but his strength was invested with the awkwardness of unfinished growth, with a plaintive diffidence and loneliness easily discernible under the toplofty swagger. At the edge of a group the face hung forward to ingratiate itself, bent down toward the level of its own sinewed shoulders at the cephalic plane of confident and unaspiring shipmates.

This was Abbie. Forasmuchas Michael did not muster with the deck force and never had occasion to witness the boatswain giving the boy an order, he was to retain no memory of Abbie's surname. To the brothers of the ark there was no sense in any other name for simple-simon Abbie the troublesome kid always hanging around getting in the way and trying to attract attention. Michael knew him mostly through casual observation and hearsay, and in consequence of his pitiless scorn for Abbie's pretensions and emulations he did not deign to address him or to seek further acquaintance in spite of his theoretical interest in the fact that such an Apprentice Seaman had come directly to the Navy from an orphanage and now having taken responsibility for the ship's black puppy carried it whenever unforbidden cradled in his lanky arm against his browned hairless chest, often caressing and speaking to it as a doll. Michael found no one who could attest the derivation of this kid's invariable sobriquet if it was not as they assumed the diminutive of Abner or possibly Abraham, christenings lately still imaginable at an asylum lagging three or four generations behind the vogue; but its derisive tincture of femininity seemed to suit well a rude sense of irony that was sometimes evinced in Navy society.

A foundling of such swaggering physique warranted little sympathy. As in many a case of annoying personality it was beyond the curiosity of institutional masculinity to attribute a cause to its effect. His unslaked tenderness must protect itself in the immemorial manner of half-castes. A flinty couthless nurture had educated the boy no more than scantly for sensitivity to the social irritations and exacerbations of his own behavior, or even to the more easily imaginable affect on his shipmates of actual or suspected larceny. Abbie was known as the ship's petty thief of personal property. This reputation was confirmed by more than one official conviction recorded by the yeoman and signed by the Executive Officer for Abbie's personnel jacket. Hyperbolized notoriety therefore served to justify the merciless contempt in which he was held by all those who would have feared him if he'd known his own strength or if he'd had a few years of experience in concealing his emotion. They called him Little Orphan Abbie to his face, bringing on a wan defensive grin, when his trivial boasts and lies succeeded in inflicting themselves upon colleagues who had failed to avoid his conversation.

But he slashed in turn with borrowed insolence, by way of jeering curses and extremely precedented denunciations of vaguely defined authority at all levels, along with triumphant downward pokings of his great forefinger, always ad hominem, at the vulnerability he sensed in anyone who offered to pay him common respect if only in passing the time of day with an extremely precedented remark.

"You bet your sweet ass it's a hot day! Shit man aint you never been in real heat before?"

With such demonstrations of his manhood in the course of time Abbie scotched the friendliness of every kind man in the crew. He was given fewer and fewer opportunities to assert the vigor of his will to make the grade among men who presumably had Stateside parents siblings or women to return to.

In his attempts to storm the fragmented fellowship of the ship's company from the outermost ring of a cluster he watched over other heads and listened avidly to every word as he stroked the puppy pressed against his ribs like a football. Cued by others he chimed in with standard invective, approving laughter, customary witticisms, or well-tested scatological expletives. If he happened to get a slight response to his hazarded comment at some payday crap game or casual blackjack circle or congregated rehash of speculative scuttlebutt he would hastily enlarge upon the occasion without skill or relevance, oblivious to sense in his headlong flush of success, raising his voice until the awkward words petered out sheepishly upon the withering indifference of sailors occupied with their subjects.

But nothing daunted his ordinary gait buskined with combat boots meant to be a paratrooper's. To all his inferiors in size and strength the young Great Dane displayed himself with a show of arrogance the equal of any warrior's on the field at Ilium. So at least it seemed to the invidious Radio Technician who was himself but few years more mature in the primitive rivalries of the male race and despite undisputed superiority in culture not yet wholly outgrown of athletic vanity or totally reconciled to physical inferiority, and whose insensate resentment of being lorded over on any score was scarcely mollified by his understanding of a social competitor's tender psyche.

The ship was Abbie's high school. He strutted its corridors perpetually combing the pompadour of his wavy brown hair. Like most of the deck seamen he wore a sheath knife at his hip, but he held too little office to contrive a ring of keys (jingling badge of importance or privilege sometimes acquired even by unrated sailors). Instead, to officiate his stride he carried linked to a loop the multifarious instrument supposedly issued to Swiss army scouts for which much use was yet to be found in the American navy comprising besides blades of several kinds a diversity of screwdrivers scissors awls spanners forks and spoons all thickly folded up together in a conspicuous compendium as heavy on the belt as a small pistol. And he alone for decoration comfort and distinction carried opposite this convenience on his zone a quirt or knout of rawhide thongs stylishly bound and sennited with marline cordage which for lack of goad or mace he sometimes unslung and cracked smartly against bulkheads and stanchions.

His white hat when he wore it curved debonairly low on the brow and swept back in upward sheer exposing the rump of his shingled nape. Now many a manjack though long denied appropinquity to womankind continued to assume for self-esteem the bearing and likeness of a square-jawed weather-toughened battle-tested saltsea sailor steady as he steers—according to an ideal in the modern unofficial tradition somehow passed like children's games from elder to younger and even at last unto the fast-multiplied citizenry of the warswelled Navy (though Michael himself had paraded Market Street amid bevies of other benighted new bucks with his hat on the back of his head in defiance of regulations before he'd caught on to the authentic style). "Salty"—the term as used in disdain carried ridicule of stylistic failure but falsely hinted that the speaker himself disavowed the image brought to mind sarcastically—was flung at Abbie whenever he needed comeuppance; but perhaps never entirely to his displeasure: the sneer honored a common notion that only the bitterest conscripts sincerely scorned as bell-bottomed folly. That kid that salty kid, salty as a swabby well could be at the age of sixteen.

But what most of all turned Michael's face against Abbie's blundering appeal for charity was the allegiance he paid to Kane, in whom he found the vicarious independence that kept him from weeping for the hope of love. Certainly from Kane there was no hope of affection, howsoever perfect the devotion that earned it, nor of respect—not even of encouragement. Yet by putting his ardent nature at the disposal of the winds (being anchorless) Abbie found himself clinging always to the side of the cloudgatherer who stood for everything apprehended as strength.

There were reflected beams of popularity to be shared in the nimbus of flattery infamy and fear. Abbie's vainglory was not so contemptible in Michael's eyes as the choice and ranking of his god. The unhatched archangel watched with disgust as the youth poor in spirit deliberately despised the kingdom of heaven by debasing himself and abusing the freedom to choose his values. Here too Michael's disapproval of Abbie's judgment left no room in his own heart for human mercy or divine grace.

On Kane's side the matter stood differently of course, and especially after his return from the hospital it gradually developed along the lines of self-education in cult leadership. An annoyance to be snarled and swatted at had bred the taste for a worshipper's perverted immolation—especially the grinning acceptance of intentional ill-treatment—and therewith the pleasure of commanding as apprentice a huge lithe savage who expected neither kindness nor loyalty, nor anything else but permission to serve. Abbie sacrificed everything except his puppy his impudence and his reach.

When Abbie asked for pugilistic instruction it was his reach that made him a worthy sparring partner at first, briefly exercising his senior's skill; but this innocent advantage of the gangling understudy was all too easily overcome in the tutorial exasperation it elicited, and the teacher's open irritation checked the progress of an apt pupil by striking fear into his heart and turning mock-contests into feckless defensive skirmishes for the intimidated junior. Thus their encounters with the gloves on, contributing little to Kane's own progress in the art and at the same time inhibiting the development of Abbie's confidence, were soon discontinued, the salt of pedagogy having lost its savor on both sides.

They were no buddies in much else. Abbie had never risen above the rank or consideration of the lowest seaman, while Kane was still treated with the respect and duty-assignment of his old Gunner's Mate rating, quite apart from the deference he earned as a private person. One was kept busier at chipping paint swabbing out heads and other menial jobs than older boys, being lowest of all in the Boatswain's deck force (without even a messcook's access to esculents), while the other was officially concerned with important deliberations in the gunnery department (for even after combat-training had suddenly lapsed the guns were occasionally required to shoot up drifting mines) and unofficially conversant with the most esteemed members of Gunnery Deck and Engineering divisions. And so their association was practically random and accidental, as Kane would have it, despite Abbie's inarticulate yearning for continuous and undivided companionship.

Yet after all it was still a navy recruited in wartime, a representative society that did not suffer outright criminals as comfortably as the older service had done in the days of poorly paid renegade volunteers. They were the only two of the 1066 who faced Bad Conduct Discharges (for transgressions that would not have been so egregious in scumful peacetime), tacitly associated by a putative future in the underworld (their present inequality notwithstanding)—unless Kane could indeed escape his destiny by extraordinary success in lawful prizewinning.

Nevertheless on Christmas day Abbie's attention wavered and recidivated for the first time since Kane had returned to the ship. He was drawn like a hungry coyote to the central community of men, and for once—touched by his self-effacing approach and signs of entreaty that suggested destitution contrition and good will, disarmed also by the exuberant friendliness of the little black puppy held out before him in one plowboy hand—some took pity and negligently showed him photographs from home when he quietly asked to see them.

A few noticed his close and prolonged study of faces furnishings and houses that claimed neither wealth nor fashion (to say nothing of beauty), which even their sponsors realized were in no way remarkable or attractive to anyone but themselves as kith or kin of the scenes. How could a tough kid take such singular interest in some mother grandmother or mother-in-law, some little brother or little sister, some canary kitten or even beagle, some tinseled parlor or front stoop, who or which were utterly ordinary utterly unfamiliar and utterly beyond his reach? He listened carefully to every personal anecdote and brag that no one else but the teller paid any real attention to, sincerely earning his right to ask questions that were intended rather to nourish his imagination than to ingratiate the proprietors or to acquire information about the names and domestic details behind poses innumerably duplicated all across the homeland.

With his eyes searching the faces of others to read their feelings Abbie also joined several communal attempts at hillbilly song rendered in a jeering twang impervious to any suspicion of soft sentiment, only to be disappointed by the general spirit of morose impatience at the war's aftermath. He enthusiastically awaited and then timidly acclaimed the variety and quantity of the turkey dinner. For the nonce he avoided Kane and the handful of Regular Navy men who gathered with him on the fantail with some extra beer they had scrounged, oiling their well-tempered emotions with cynical philosophy flung across the flat gray lagoon and somberly absorbed by the darkly virent island now floating off their quarter as the ship swung with an imperceptible tide.

{*Postulants only:* GO TO ITEM (46) HY.07.4, page 465.}

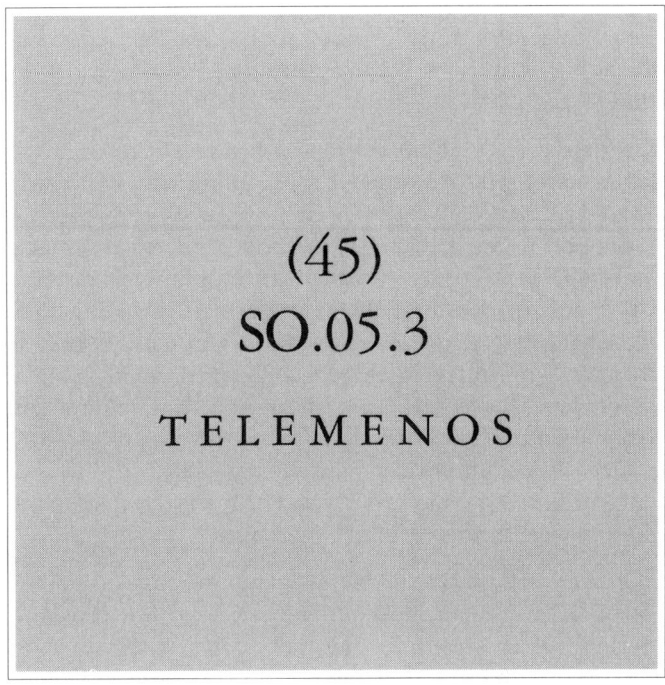

(45)
SO.05.3
TELEMENOS

33) Have been preparing you for a certain Homeric term.

A few years ago, attending some Classics lectures given just inside Sather Gate by a marvelous Irishman out of Oxford (belonging to a generation of Jane Harrison's Cambridge students), I learned the import of *menos*: a word that stood for the extraordinary strength and courage which a few mortals have been known to summon at moments of doubtful victory or survival. *Menos* can hearten a man even in contention against an immortal enemy. Its symptoms border on madness but the empirical effect is extravagant competence. It enlarges or enflames a man's normal motive.

This temporary power is said to be conferred by a god miraculously, but there are reasons to take such an opinion as metaphorical. For animals are capable of such possession. *Menos* makes the chest heave and the nostrils flare; it infuses the arms and legs with mighty *self*-expectation: which is not necessarily divine. One imagines an almost twitching hyperventilation of the whole body, and perhaps a slight darkening of the brain, as if from a dose of alcohol confined to the head, in preparation for an effort so tremendous that extra oxygen must be compressed before the astonishing supercombustion can begin.

I therefore take *menos* to be the energetic spirit that a few can conjure under challenging conditions by an especially gifted faculty for anticipatory breathing.

34) But I'm here to talk about theater of action where entire activity is exclusively supererogative movement, without sentences or words and not susceptible to signification by words. Therefore do not look for meaning.

Yeats: symbol = "an image that has transcended particular time and place"; but I hold dance to be immanent in its place. There's no harm in taking W B Y 's definition for symbols in general (including those he had no use for). Then, as you can mean nothing without symbols to signify by—whether they are letters, numbers, diagrams, or anything else—the expressions of dance have no more "meaning" than natural phenomena (such as a mountain or a sunset) in the basic order of perception.

Dance doesn't communicate subject, predicate, or idea. Of course imagination informs the action, but you don't see the imagination—that which makes images: in this case kinetic images.

35) The root of *orchesis* (dance) connoted trembling, maybe raving—not as if in fear or doubt but (I surmise) as if possessed with enthusiasm or even *menos*. Art-dance sublimates the vibration of dance, controls it, modulates its power to fulfill intentions of imagination. Breathing converted into movement, which is decoupled from the cycles and amplitudes of its origin by the interval of blood dispersion before oxidation.

Both Artaud and Barrault make much of "voluntary" breathing as the source of histrionic emotion (the analog of movement in dance). On pneumatic energy (Artaud): "It is certain that since breathing accompanies effort, the mechanical production of breath will engender in the working organism a quality corresponding to effort." Strenuous or pronounced inspiration, an act of the intercostal muscles, can put a stop to trembling.

Meanwhile blood keeps circulating as independent distributor, its affinity for pneuma and its rate of flow determined however by the endocrine system in manic (menic) state. Thus movement continuously energized in any direction sequence or force by circulating reservoir without correspondence to phase or wavelength of breath. [Cf bagpipe, organ, blacksmith's bellows.]

36) Dancer, unlike actor (Barrault), requires only one bag of air. No need to breathe in and out at same time, or to overlap doubly frictive drafts of air. Thus extremely efficient aerobically.

Yet must produce rhythms discordant with own breath (vs poet). Like natural athlete, gifted dancer able to sustain highest levels of energy expenditure and unnatural movements with a practically constant (though heightened) respiratory frequency governed not by the artificial dance but by her personal metabolism.

Yet dancer might as well have two bags of air. She's like a pair of lovers: even in sleep one breathes faster than the other; in ecstasy their rhythms are different.

37) But it can't be done on air alone. Anaerobic energy must be drawn from the cells (and replaced after the performance). Neither initial forced draft (flaring nostrils) nor efficient breathing during the dance can keep up the power supply required for the most important aesthetic loads.

Self-possession is the subject of all art-dance: possession of perfected body (both endowed and trained) with frame and plasma disciplined to super-human virtue, of which strength and beauty are secondary qualities. Dancer's *menos* is produced by enthalpy and kinetic energy in the posses-sion of a particular intention of the imagination, beginning in the muscles of chest and diaphragm, ending in an exhaustion of all energy extractable from human flesh.

38) Do not confuse this creative *menos* with the passive power of maenads who yield their bodies, vacate their reason, and follow the reedy skirl of a god's pipe up and down the landscape. Those women ordinarily put them-selves at the disposal of priests. Under one narcosis or another, with streaming hair, they break out of Themis's place, shaking their sistrums, without wishing to understand, still less to possess, themselves. They waste most of their breath. Alcohol or drug inhibits distribution of oxygen to muscles and brain. That kind of possession is used by gods to lead us into orgy, glossolalia, or lynching.

But art-dancer is quick in every fibre; more awake than most other humans, who leave much of their body sleep.

In watching dance you are awakened too. No more than a victim of lightning do you see the *menos* that electrifies you. You don't see power, only its generator; transformed, you feel its affects.

If the average word is a dead metaphor (Barfield), then *the average movement is a dead habit.* In spending her energy dancer either rejects or reanimates every iota of secular or religious behavior, awakening the dead also—as a poet does with language.

39) It is world-lines of movement that we see—vs cinematographic shapes that occupy separately successive positions. In dance we see actual continuity of motion made by human bodies: lines that are not made by boundaries or envelopes but by paths of process determined by the net re-sultant forces acting upon the whole body and all its parts in four mutu-ally perpendicular dimensions.

Motion (vs movement) is as perfectly continuous as a line. It cannot be isolated or analyzed in terms of its subject; quanta-fication and approxi-mation pertain only to the segmented body—down to the cellular level if necessary. Dancer's discretion may be so fine that having mastered arms

and legs she can move each bone of the finger wrist and ankle independently, each curve of the face and each cell of each striated muscle—or call
for anaerobic energy one cell at a time precisely concatenated in irregular
series to meet dynamic needs most tempestively, meanwhile anticipating
and differentiating the generations of impulse for gross movement.

But in last analysis the whole body moves as organic unit, not as mere
integration of articulated movements: *dance-in-itself*—perceptible to the
mind of the spectator only by retrospective abstraction. *Movement is trans-
duced into smoothly fluctuating lines of electromagnetic force.* It is these that
empower the transformer.

40) These primary forces are undetectable to us as watchers in the
secondary, but their transformed flux leaves us wakeful. We become so
vibrant with strength (or potential energy), sitting still as we must, that
we can finally discharge our capacitors, after the flow of current ceases,
only by ovation.

Nothing intentionally aesthetic so disgusts me as traditional dance of
aspiration broken into little trills of virtuosity—defensible only as illustrations of performer's skill—and calling for immediate applause. Enraged
by vulgarity of American audience that willingly obliges, congratulating
itself as a congress of connoisseurs, and ostentates trigger-happy European
"bravos".

Cooler objection is that work of art can never gather potential when it
is repeatedly bled off on the spot by galvanized adulations. In creative
dance untainted by meretricious career-consciousness real power moves
from primary to secondary without interruption; power isn't short-
circuited on either side until cessation of movement suddenly calls for restoration of sophrosynistic equilibrium. True purpose of final bow is not to
thank the crowd (which should never be thanked for availing itself of a
privilege) but to keep the primary circuit closed (uninterrupted) for the
safe and orderly reflux of high voltage accumulated in the final reactive
tremor.

41) You can remember something of the dancer's body and its movements—i e , certain features of the visual phenomenon. In this respect,
and only in this respect, dance survives. But you can neither perceive nor
remember the process by which you felt the menos of action. Power cannot
be remembered, not even in its transformed state. Its affect perhaps, but
not the power itself. Even mnemonically it doesn't outlast the performance
like a magnetized tape. There is no after-image of something never seen.

To experience a work of art *in vivo* is to feel a concentration of
counterentropic but mortal life. Such feeling from dance might be called
proprio-aesthetic.

That gets us down to the irreducible mystery.

42) But what can be taken a little further is the dromenon of dance as power transformation. I do so with the concept of *telemenos*: the transmission of power between humans without touch or organoleptic contact. But not maximum power. (Too much power, resonating naturally, would agitate the congregation, maybe even enthuse the whole polis.) On the contrary, power in the smallest feasible amount sufficient to express corporeal imagination without overcoming the gravitation or gravitas of physiological situation.

Telemenos is not straightforward. Efficiency of power is frustrated on purpose (vs neurosis, which frustrates unwillingly). Aesthetically inhibits responsive movement in order to serve freer more accelerated final cause.

[Explain that inefficient application doesn't imply inefficient process. Of all arts, this one, created before our eyes, demands technical efficiency.]

Ethologically speaking (Tinbergen), dance is irrelevant behavior, like certain formal gestures of seagulls which during courtship "displace" copulation until mate is ready. But the art-dancer's purpose is to forestall, abort, neutralize, mock, or undo courtship as long as possible—and her methods are informal (free of predetermining influences). Gulls are capable only of immemorial movements associated with particular effective acts of instinct and survival; but dancers (thanks to expanded central nervous system) use all parts, make all possible movements—natural, calisthenic, or grotesque.

Stressful movements must be forced athwart the dancer's own humanly resisting lines of magnetic force. But this internal work is the sole source of power for transformation and transmission without contact or symbol— power enough to make our nostrils flair *in contemplation*!

{*Postulants only:* GO TO ITEM (47) SO.05.4, page 471.}

(46)
HY.07.4

TROPHIES
OF WAR

*T*he day after Christmas there was little ship's work. Once the spoils of war were brought aboard in the forenoon the talk and the bustle pertained to nothing else. LST 1066 became a ship of boys all aplaying and none not Michael himself was immune to the excitement, neither he nor the scrawny sour captain and all his officers, nor any cook messcook or officers' steward, nor Water Tender or Motor Machinist, nor Radioman Quartermaster or Signalman, nor Yeoman Pharmacist's Mate or Storekeeper, nor any Seaman or Fireman Electrician Fire-Control Man or Gunner, Carpenter or coxswain, nor Chief or petty officer of any class, now down to less than a hundred in all—each weighing his Japanese weapon and meditating on the precision and discretion of the compendious power he would have been holding in his hands if he'd been given ammunition too.

The enemy helmets were negligently tossed aside, for every sailor was well used to turtle headdress from long danger-weary hours spent at his all-too-familiar battle station all across the Pacific Ocean in practice and at false alarm and on the insecure beach at Okinawa; but the heft of a rifle, its balance and density, was something still exciting to lads who had been cheated of storied old ways in American war, who had been spared training for combat man-to-man and even the sight of remotely drawn blood. Its concentrated mechanism (though a little out of date), personal and self-contained, fascinated any myrmidon used to mobile power at the disposal of private will.

The manual satisfaction was braced for sporting men by memories and expectations of hunt for living creatures in forest plain swamp or marsh. The sighted feel of snugly integrated steel and wood brought forth endless comparison of firearms and much sententious blather about calibers and ranges, as well as anecdotes of lucky and difficult prey. For others, metropolitan men or Parises more accustomed to the chase of human breasts and thighs or to the heft of gold, the possession of small arms was intensified by layer upon layer of heroic romance unwittingly summoned like quiescent lust by any glimpse of a naked weapon. A man could fancy himself on an even footing with any single adversary, and maybe with more than one.

The rifles were issued each as packed with its bayonet in an unpainted wooden case at a Japanese arsenal. For an hour the air was full of squealing nails and screeching boards prised by hammer claws pinchbars screw-drivers and sheath knives. The men were given twenty-four hours to inspect their plunder and fondle it. Thereafter they were to render it to the boatswain for safekeeping against the ship's return to the States, except for a few who like Michael chose instead to repack their victory awards for immediate shipment home by post, consigned to the man of a family or future family, as for instance Ruth's father, without bothering to improve the grease-preserved appearance of the gift, despite doubt (later to be jus-tified, for the old man would hardly remember having been delivered the parcel) that one whose active life had taken in the Klondike days would find much to arouse his interest in a device long since imitative of Ameri-can prototypes.

The buzz soon died down. Most imaginations had exhausted the nov-elty and were left too tired to sustain mental pleasure. Before the after-noon had half expired rifles and bayonets lay carelessly about the deck like toys in a living room and their owners waited for the next meal listlessly playing cards or lying in their bunks found aesthetic satisfaction in cover-less pulpy booklets filled with illustrations that limned successive posi-tions of familiar personages and instruments in narration of buffoonery or adventure, with cloud-puffs of large explanation lettered in black and white above the faces of distinctly red yellow green or blue protagonists and sidekicks, antagonists and henchmen. The few on watch were not sorry to have the duty, merely for the unappreciated comfort of mild rou-tine that kept the ship's society from falling asunder into raving or coma-tose units of unengendering mammalian decay.

In the chart room Michael took his turn at voice watch on the local "shore control" radio circuit. The single radar set being secured at anchorage he the ship's most technical artificer could make no other practical contribution to the communications or protection of the monastery. According to his duty he selected from the light traffic on the frequency-modulated airwaves a small number of tedious commonplace messages intended to keep the Navy's larger society from disintegrating—typing and acknowledging them, sending them below by the seaman on bridge watch to the solemn blond Jewish law student who served with secret code manuals as Communications Officer. Even that privileged person had lost the nervous energy to fix the import of such missives in his conscientious memory, for none of the locally broadcasted words singled out LST 1066 or called for its reply.

The quartermaster on duty made no pretense of watching for blinker lights or signal flags from the outside world. He sat on a stool next to the lifeless engine room annunciator in the wheelhouse reading a Book-of-the-Month Club novel newly sent from home by a father who though owning a New England town had been unsuccessful in keeping his son out of the ranks, in which nevertheless that good-looking rich kid destined for a career in Republican politics had made himself comfortable by the subtle prestige of wealth and by hints of personal favor. He was still an unabashed hater of F D R (his late Commander-in-Chief) and the insidious leader of covert antisemitism. He was also Michael's closest enemy.

When Michael was relieved of his unskilled seat at the typewriter (as distinguished from the one in the radio shack where wonderfully skilled operators translated International Morse code) he went below to sleep a while. In the After Crew's Quarters through which he passed lazy men lurking in bunks or drooping at tables had inured their ears to the worn-out words and faltering rhythm of a song offered them over the public address system for the sixth time that day by an officer controlling the wardroom machine who loved its lyricism:

When the lights go on again
Aaalll over the world . . .

The lights had been on again longer than it took to cease marvelling at the values of peace.

Michael found his way to the more privileged sleeping compartment far forward on the starboard side where he and his bunk mates had agreed to keep the entertainment turned off. There also it was far enough from "Officer Country" to escape reprimand for unscrewing the red battle-light bulb at night. By day at tropical anchorages when it wasn't raining the sun itself pushed a narrow glimmer past the slightly opened shield of a hinged deck-hatch through an overhead manhole into this demi-elite fore-castle, meeting and conquering the yellower incandescence perpetually projected from hatchless midship sections where regulations insisting on illumination could not be ignored.

But light didn't make much difference to sleep: a sailor learned how to cope with fatigue or boredom under any conditions, in extremity even on the steel plates of an open deck. When not on watch (provided there was no call to General Quarters or to a special work party, or muster or inspection) anyone not beholden to the Boatswain's shipkeeping efforts was usually permitted to retire into the two-foot-high privacy of his chain-hung bunk, the only seclusion vouchsafed to all hands and well cherished by all, where Night ruled more or less around the clock, temporarily restraining one of his sons Thanatos and assisting Hypnos the other who with steady wings beat air through ventilating cowls and ducts to all resting places in the hollow ship and with immortal vigilance watched himself pour from a bottomless krater sleep enough to fill any interstice of a man's diurnal time while guarding against the nudge of his brother that would tilt the lip too far.

Michael at any rate was never refused. On his back at sea he slept dancing to the roll of the beam and the scend of the bow, waves slapping and swishing, waters slipping and soughing, his aluminum-framed cradle heaving in the superficies of deep Ocean whose most intimate surface sighed and splashed against the plate of steel a few inches from his undampened skin. Then in the swell and conversation of passing brine the engines far aft vibrated unheard; the external sounds of banging dips and abruptly stopped lurches were comfortably blended with the groans of structural steel and the swinging click of internal gear. Blessed sleep was generally easy. Yet it was never hard to awaken instantly at a messenger's merest touch warning of the next watch. But in the inertia of a motionless anchorage the divine draught was drunk too strong. It left him thick and groggy, as if in the aftermath of other liquor.

This time he barely caught the last call to chow. Sitting with his compartmented stainless-steel tray apart from a few hasty stragglers at a like-minded mess table he stabbed absently at unappetizing slices of a stuffed phalloid bladder wrinkling his brows and rubbing the back of his head in a listless struggle to recover the faculties of sense. He noticed nothing untoward in the sounds or smells of the ship, and by way of habitual retreat he soon escaped with his book to a distant portside compartment designated for letter-writing that he found blissfully empty. For more than an hour he smoked and read in the hoarded luxury of solitude.

Thus like a shortsighted miser he missed the cusp of the gravest incident to stir the ship in all its career from riparian baptism in the Ohio River to perfunctory decommissioning at less than three years of age in the floating cemetery of Suisun Bay where the ghosts of Sacramento River boats passed to and from San Francisco to the Mesopotamian valley.

There were no eyewitnesses to the catastrophe of the main event, and few to the prelude; yet when Michael heard the known facts he would have no difficulty telling himself the short tale: he knew the players well

enough for that. It was not hard to construct the narrative without inter-
viewing participants or taking pains with rules of evidence. The geste was
elementally probable, even predictable. But less than a decade later he was
to find it impossible to remember literally what part of memory's truth
came from empiric certainty and what part was obtained from the richer
experience of mulling reflection.

{*Postulants only:* GO TO ITEM (48) HY.07.5, page 475.}

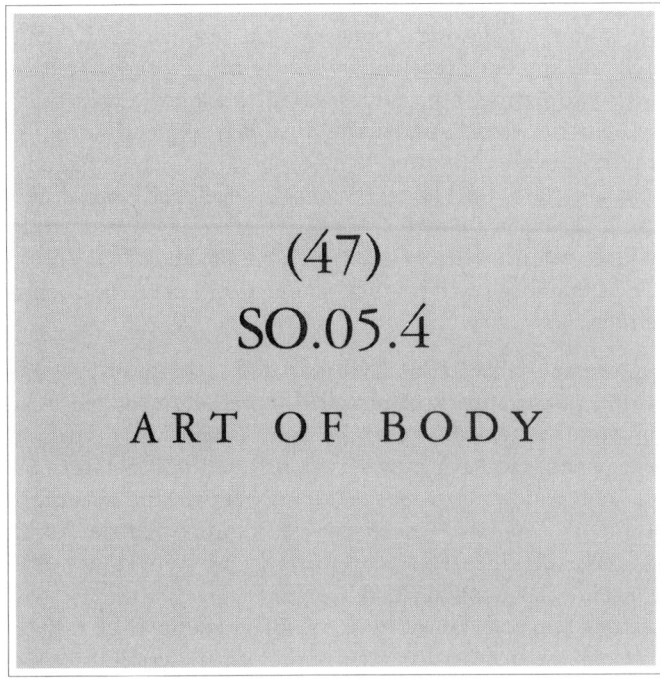

(47)
SO.05.4

ART OF BODY

43) I have called creative dance the museless art because it is something new invented by modern women without divine inspiration.

[Show that Muses are truly goddesses *from* their art, not *for* it. So-and-so is never the god *of* x, but x itself, or he who does x; not personification but ritual origin of verb x. Muses as epitomes rather than inspirations.]

I go so far as to suggest that most of what we hear about the Muses is sloppy interpretation. You should be especially skeptical of the literary variety who inspire keening or dancing at noble funerals and weddings, or animate riddlers and orators. What you can say is that the Muses are traditional artists and performers who have never been bettered, like saints, and that they should be studied by practitioners of art.

But our dancers have had no one to learn from. Can't quite say that American dance is parthenogenic, but it's even less hereditary than enthusiastic.

44) Human brain has never been fully occupied managing its body. Physical work or sport may drain energy or tax skill but it scarcely exercises the cortex—which meanwhile tends to cultivate its exuberant mental function (if at all) in pursuit of abstract complexity and innovation. Most people,

like animals, use their flesh and bones within very narrow limits of behavior, especially on any one occasion; any extraordinary capacity for inventive control and coordination is usually devoted to aspirations of the psyche or the psyche's favorite senses, under the mistaken impression that the possibilities of physique are exhausted by necessity, instinct, strife, and fun.

But now a certain kind of exceptionally developed central nervous system has found a way to devote itself to art of body. Manual work or play sharply reduces brain's share of total metabolism, but I venture that even in the most strenuous creative dance you could measure no such reduction of relative mental activity.

45) Since power of dance is totally dissipated at place of production, and leaves nothing in the supervening world materially changed or displaced, no residual work [force × distance] is accomplished.

On other hand, fact that power is transferred to spectators proves performance is not play, despite dancer's para-pleasure in freedom of gratuitous movement. Art-dance useless to courtship or battle [vs gymnastic demonstration]; too disinterested (creatively as well as aesthetically) to remain at level of desire or conflict.

[Spectator's appreciation of movement—made in time but realized in space only. Contrast to spatial perceptions of art materially stored in time.]

Dance liberates movement from instrumental concept of it (as seen in popular theater, where actors move empty cups to lips or contrive to change position on stage solely for the purpose of getting attention at fourth wall).

As art, unlike work or play, dance describes and illuminates its own value without advantage of ophelimity or entertainment. Take the component of value that can be called knowledge: dance shows structure and dynamics of body under self-imposed stress of exceedingly artificial conditions. Unnatural variety of space can be generated or distorted thereby— usually without the weight and extension of inanimate objects or the webs and concealments of fabric—under unnatural disciplines of place and schedule.

Dance realizes certain attempts of philosophy by embodying the motion of movement rather than its positions. Dancer admits static posture only at beginning and end (purely mortal necessity of rest), the only cross-sections of time at which position can participate in motion. Discovery and revelation are made by speculations and probations of totally intelligent *body.*

Having canvassed and essayed movements neither known nor useful to natural life, as well as those known and used by anyone at all in practical or playful acts, dancer has learned to pay no more heed to the conceptual constraints of 85 steps and positions canonized by tradition than to the combinatorial limitations of 6 fundamental parts that make up 19C machinery.

The most ingenious and intricate mechanical assembly, milled or turned to the smoothest finish, can't make of wheel, axle, lever, screw, wedge, or inclined plane anything to match the most commonplace electrical engine in versatility of function. Mechanical device may demonstrate strength and hardness of materials, virtues of mass and inertia, complex reasoning of cause and effect, skill of workmanship, and extreme inventiveness; but electrical system better exhibits thermal and magnetic properties of matter, economy of form, interpenetrability of forces (in a field), flexibility of coupling and placement.

Likewise, despite the shorthand of choreographic notation, human movement is not articulated from individual motions. Dance, like dancer herself, is organic. Rigorously considered, whole compositions are no more susceptible to division than smallest bit.

Art of dance reveals what others can't, not by heuristic synthesis of given motives but by continuous plastic reformation of kinetic experience. Such as the meta-sexuality of women—its potentially sacramental significance, as against the putative masculinity of priests.

46) [Knowledge as a principal type or origin of value.]

Noetic experience may come with work, play, or imagination. Knowledge from one of which is transferrable to another. The three kinds of occupations can interact to establish values together. No one of them is logically defensible without recourse to a system beyond its own.

Imagination descending and ascending length of spine both establishes and appeals to value—and all values are serious. The value of dance: its beauty of course; its earnestness and zeal, its painstaking care for evanescence, the real presence of brio and panache—but *most of all its power.*

In generation of electromagnetic power, magnet must be opposed by physical force of its own prime mover.

{*Postulants only:* GO TO ITEM (49) SO.05.5, page 485.}

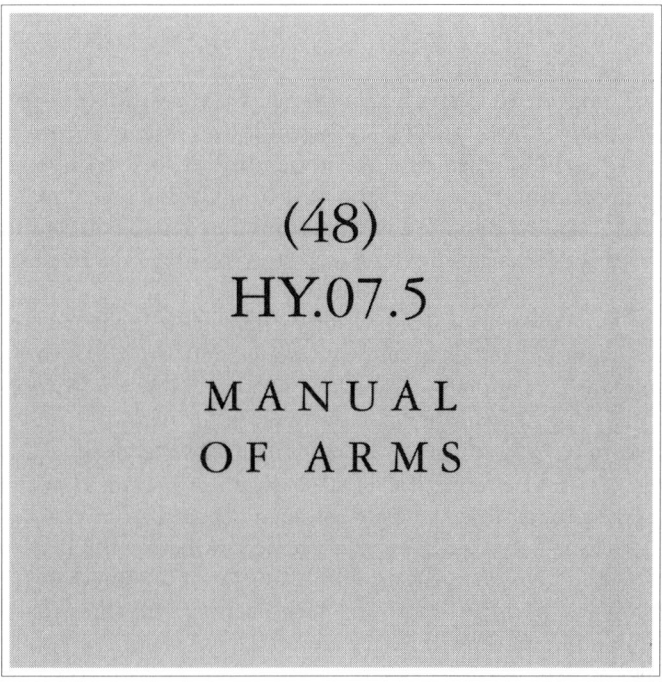

(48)
HY.07.5

MANUAL
OF ARMS

*A*bbie had tried every motion that he thought could be made with a rifle. Over and over again he had run through the manual of arms (as well as he vaguely remembered it from boot camp)— *Order Arms, Trail Arms, Sling Arms, Port Arms, Present Arms, Order Arms, Right Shoulder Arms, Parade Rest*—with Marine Corps precision and experimental variations. Some of the movements such as little tosses from one hand to the other had been practiced with successful slap and gusto. He had even tried to imitate what he knew from movies of the German style—until there was no fun left, only ridicule from those who noticed him.

Having slung and carried his trophy in all possible manners, balanced and unbalanced, with the strap at various loops and tensions, with one hand and two, pointed up pointed down pointed at a level to the outermost reaches of the space he could describe with its extension of his arms, he'd taken mock shots from the hip at shipmates he encountered, much to their annoyance who couldnt trust him not to have stolen ammunition somewhere, until they made him keep the muzzle lowered in their presence, refusing to dignify his play with their cooperation. And so he was reduced to firing over the rail at distant figures whom he took to be

Japanese, and high up at sea birds. After every shot he worked the bolt, simulating fictions he had seen.

Now sitting on the afterdeck with his back against the stern anchor winch, his bony knees jacked up toward the sky, the barrel wedged between his legs, he began to shove the stiffly sliding cylinder by a continuous reciprocating fling with the heel of his right palm monotonously repeated. The aimless musician with narrowed eyes and pouting lips stared absently over the fantail, the whole ship stretched forward behind him. An empty weapon could be played no better.

The bayonet sword hanging from his belt in its scabbard was already lost to his attention. Its rigid length brushing his thigh at every step had at first lent a military glamor that infinitely belittled the nautical accoutrements dangling at his other side or pressing his ham; but now this drab olive accessory pointed diagonally downward onto the deck at a little distance from his hip, propped awkwardly against his waist where it was fastened. For a long time the bolt sounded regularly—click-clack, click-clack, click-clack—in an action that seemed to be appealed for and perpetuated by the genius of the machine. But at last something broke his trance and he laid it down. From the back pocket of his dungarees where it had been bent and macerated by the squatting sitting and repose of a week or more he unscrolled a wadded codex of colorful illustrations, which immediately engaged his imagination as he restored the puppy to his lap.

But the mature shark in pursuit of amusement was less fatigable than this his understudy. Kane had started to furbish his own rifle (after voicing professional contempt for its foreign imitation of oldfashioned design) when he and the lesser gunners were interrupted in their personal occupation by an officially unofficial request to put the officers' new pistols in working order. He was glad enough to take on the job, insofar as it served to ingratiate, especially in his particular assignment to Mr Rand's, from which he inferred respect for himself as an ordnance expert—notwithstanding his ulterior resentment at the involuntary task of a body servant.

Moreover he found it remarkably interesting to open inspect clean oil and buff an elegant not to say romantic Luger (or pseudo-Luger) famous ballistically for its neat penetrating velocity; and to clench the handsome little energy-exchanger, Teutonic and black, its slender tapering cylinder so well counterpoised by the rakish rectangular breech-block that a man seemed to feel no torque from its mass but only horizontal equalization as he grasped the molded stock relishing with peculiar felicity the leveled steel pressing into the web of flesh between thumb and forefinger snugly curled. When he'd resumed work on his own prize he was less interested in its outmoded mechanism than he was in human scope of action.

So Kane had begun prowling the ship with his rifle and bayonet. No purpose filled his mind but his will was consumed with the appetite for purpose. He stuck his head through the curtain to the C P O Quarters. The Chiefs were asleep. Then up on deck he nodded to the two men on gangway watch without interrupting their conversation. Leaning for a moment on the rail he watched the ship's empty "small boat" (itself a landing craft) swing in the sulky currents, lightly tethered below on the skittish skin of the water like a curious heifer afraid to venture beyond her mother's shadow. He raised his piece to the tiny fisherman in a distant proa crossing between two of the outer islets, thought better of the futility, and walked through the galley companionway across the ship to starboard where he would not be noticed; but before he'd reached the opposite rail he decided to visit the fantail to see if there was anyone to pit himself against.

Perching himself on a green-painted bitt he laid his equipment on the deck crossed his legs and concatenated half a dozen brisk movements about his person ending slowly in the puff of a cigarette, all the while he stared at Abbie. Who soon put aside his brochure of cartoons and in disadvantageous position hastily assumed his version of the masculine style evolved by poised and jaunty sailormen in finding plucking tapping and emplacing his own tube of tobacco. Abbie made a globe of his hands in putting it to the flame of a snappy lighter, narrowing one eye more than the other to evade the first curl of smoke, yet with a certain proficiency of lips and fingers he nonetheless betrayed his novitiate by the tense angle of his elbow.

"Shi-it kid, you're too young to smoke!" Kane snorted.

"I been smokin five years."

"Yeah. Why they call you Abbie, orphan boy?"

"Beats the shit out of me. They called me Tex in boot camp."

"What's the matter with you Tex-ass, you don't like guns? How come you readin funny-books? You got every day in the year for that but you aint goin to have another chance at this Jap gear before they put it in hock. After tomorrow you won't have nothin to do but sit on your Tex-ass again. Kid your age oughtta be workin out all the time."

"What the hell can I do with it? Can't shoot the fuckin thing for Chrissake."

"I guess you still like to play cowboys and rustlers. Aint you never heard of cold steel? Y' know what that means? Hand-to-hand combat. Let's see your blade."

Awkwardly shifting the weight on his buttocks Abbie drew out the bayonet and handed it to his mentor.

"Jesus man you got no right to carry around messy steel like this! You havent even wiped off the packin grease. I hope you aint aiming to strike for gunner's mate."

"Coxswain. I wantta get into the boat crew if it's the last fuckin thing I do in this goddam Navy."

"No use now. Won't be no more beach fightin. Well don't be so damn dumb when you swipe things. Mac, you got a lot to learn! But first I'm goin to show you how to clean a big knife like this." He ran his thumb the length of the steel. "Needs a better edge. Gives yourself a damn good spear at the end of a long gun, and a lot quieter than shootin. Takes more heart though. Sometimes I'druther no one ever invented guns at all. Seein as how I got screwed when the draft board sent me to the Navy I never had a chance to kill Japs with my own hands. Amphibious trainin wasnt worth a shit for that. But I know you can get a hell of a good leverage on a knife when it's stuck on a rifle; that big butt gives you a fuckin good twist." He produced a whetstone a piece of waste rag and some emery cloth from his pocket. "It's a sin not to take care of good steel. Watch good now, orphan boy. These weapons aint never been used . . ."

Three or four times he was on the point of handing the job over to Abbie who hankered to take it on but he ended up by finishing it himself, his native zest briefly unstinted in an avidity quite at odds with his attitude toward the person he was condescending to.

"I never thought of the bayonet." Abbie admitted.

"She-it. Well you better start thinkin if you want to hang around a pro. The motherfuckin goldbraid aint gotta turn in their pistols, you can bet your sweet ass. Sonofabitches! One thing about heavy action on the beach, you can get them bastards in the back and nobody knows the difference."

"I never heard of that in the Navy!" Abbie was unable to conceal his awe.

"There's always a first time, orphan boy. I was never sick before either, but I *got* damn well sick! A man never died before he's dead!" Kane's menace to authority was encouraged by Abbie's nervous admiration.

The brightened blade was compared with Kane's and by three or four finishing touches on either hand the two were matched in luster and bite. Whereupon they affixed them to the rifles in emulation of those who most existentially followed the profession of arms. Standing addorsed suitably cautious with legs spread facing opposite sides of their rounded curtilage they poked at the air gingerly like a pair of the king's pikemen protecting themselves from an ambivalent crowd of their own countrymen. They were so intent upon getting the feel of their weighted and rebalanced pikes now as long as Kane's body, silently experimenting with stiffarmed swings and rocking lunges toward the open rail, shifting grips and stances, and on the other hand so conscious of the need to check their own unopposed power, that they were not aware of being watched for thirty seconds by a duty cook taking the air as he wiped his hands on a towel, whose laconic observations (later overheard) raised for Michael the image of a great two-headed eagle like the Holy Roman Empire's escutcheoned in motion on a field of gray against the taffrail jackstaff, waving its wings erratically and asymmetrically while steady in compound equilibrium.

Such limited calisthenic is soon outgrown by men trained or trainable to its like. In about three minutes they left off of one accord, much to the delight of the puppy who had been abruptly divested from Abbie's warmth and wished to join any other play if there was to be no more sleep. Carefully grounding their rifles one after the other they retrieved their waning cigarettes from the top of the gear housing and stood at ease while Kane contemplated a course of training.

"Well we gotta protect these blades from the salt air." he told Abbie. Without removing the bayonets from the rifles they capped them with their dull sheaths. Suddenly Kane snapped his cigarette butt over the side. Abbie followed suit. "Come on orphan boy, we're gonna have a bayonet drill!"

At last there was a purpose. In words fewer than fingers Kane explained his idea to Abbie, who had no difficulty accepting it as appropriate to the use of small arms in peacetime, never thinking to question how it would square with the Regulations he had so often run afoul of but rejoicing at his windfall of heroic companionship. They would go down to the tank deck and in the space where Kane was accustomed to train himself for future fights on the civilian scene they would rig up from discarded clothes and rags (which were easily found there just outside the ship's laundry) a dummy torso, straw man for their thrusts, doll for their play. "I seen a picture of Japs practicing on a Limey body." Kane said.

The puppy tried to follow but Abbie kicked it away in unmistakably fierce irritation, threatening aloud something more lethal than the deprivation of his love. Before the outcast could recover its footing in the scuppers its master had stepped out of reach over the high coaming of the starboard hatch hastily following his god. In a right hand big enough to retain a disputed football at arm's length he gripped his pointed club as lightly as a cowswitch.

They were seen on the way. Kane was so well known for adventurous exertion on his own behalf and Abbie for subservient hustle that their thumping passage through the drowsy crew space brought to notice nothing more than the not improbable prolongation of their interest in the Japanese souvenirs. The music was now coming from Armed Forces Radio, sweet to current taste:

> The stars at night
> Are big and bright
> Deep in the heart of Texas . . .

Many a ship had gone down in tropic or in Arctic clime within the wraithy outreach of such catchy tunes radiated in mercy for our sailors and soldiers. Now the song-signals were cast broad and strong over the whole realm of the globe-girdler, sweet cake distributed on the air to dissuade the hardly employed victors of sea and islands from grumbling mutinously, as saltpeter was said to have been infused in the food supply to quell their cacoethes. The grinding words modulated the short-wave energy of their medium with but imperfect fidelity, advancing and receding in irregular volume as if carried by airplane along a bumpy stratum of the sky; yet they easily idealized themselves inside the ears of Michael's shipmates thirsting for the culture of their homeland.

One at blackjack called out: "Kane, Chief's been looking for you about gangway watch tonight."

"Tough shit." Kane replied without turning his head or breaking his stride toward the ladder down to the deeper deck. "He can see me when he finds me." His words were no surprise to anyone.

Another at the table mocked the official tones of the ship's public address speakers: "Now hear this, now hear this: The Chief Gunner's Mate will stuff the gangway up his ass and report to Killer Kane for shit detail. . . ."

> The rabbits rush
> Around the brush `
> Deep in the heart of Texas . . .

Down on the tank deck a couple of slovenly young seamen slightly less apathetic than those who preferred to lie in their sacks or play cards were conversing with each other in lackadaisical tones far forward under dim lights while they drummed a basketball on the seamed steel flooring with short sporadic trills and in turn lobbed it aloft at the netted funnel hung from a square board hinged down from the overhead's thwartship beams. Despite the reverberant properties of a nearly empty steel chamber the sounds of their play came dull and dampened to the fighter and his sidekick as they emerged from the transverse bulkhead at the other end of the same deck far aft where the vast cargo space made a rectangular bay against the heavy section of the ship.

Kane snapped a switch to light that end of the long tunneled garage, but the scrim of gloam between the two meager illuminations made a mutual fourth wall of the distance and insensibility that deterred communication and dampened attention between the two courts as each pair of shadows kept to itself. In retrospect Michael later imagined that to Kane and Abbie the pneumatic sphere used in the desultory game beyond the murk must have sounded as clumsy as a medicine ball, whereas to the far-off sharers of their cave the makeshift bundle that the bayoneteers were soon taking their swift turns poking at could have seemed nothing but a rehearsal prop for feckless dumbshow.

At ordinary ship's business the great elongate hangar boomed and echoed to the smallest noise, but now the ship's music descending through an open shaft from one of the crew's compartments in the enceinte was absorbed by the basic hum and throb of vibrating metal and forced air which even at anchor pressed constantly and unattended upon habituated ears as more normal to the senses of a modern seaman than sounds of the sea.

> Give me land, lots of land
> Under starry skies above—
> Don't fence me in . . .

No merchant freighter had ever been designed so extensively unpartitioned in its hold. With clam-jaws closed, drawbridge up, and portcullis down an empty L S T was the hollowest of ships. An entire convoy or battle line of horseless carts motorized wagons armored chariots siege machines and other rolling engines of war, or especially a phalanx of forty caterwauling treaded dreadnoughts, could be englutted transported and disgorged like an unfolding train of anaconda-prey. It was for the protection of such passengers afloat and on the beach that more ammunition was fired from the battlements of these hybrid blockhouses than from the sum of turrets and platforms on all the stately historical castles of the Navy during the whole long earth-shaking globe-grasping war, Poseidon's greatest. L S T s were built and manned for nothing but this precious seagoing womb formed by a flat shallow bottom, straight sides, a graceless weather deck without sheer or camber (pierced by two elevatored cargo hatches), and a pair of curved watertight gates in the tacked-on bent-up bow. They were a triumph of emergency mass-produced naval architecture.

By way of compensation for the loss of longitudinal rigidity resulting from the special logistical requirements of mechanized amphibious warfare this unobstructed and untrussed box was designed to flex by as much as six feet like an awkward Damascus tube in doing battle even with half a gale of waves. It frightened both greenhorns and old tars from unbending ships to stand aft where the two students now practiced combat and watch the forward section begin to rise while the stern was still ascending. But with the resilience of a King's pine gracefully deflecting to the north wind the 1066 snugly survived more than one storm that defeated some of the deep-sea fighting fleet, including an infamous typhoon that sent two inflexible destroyers to the bottom of the China Sea put a battleship's steering gear out of commission and damaged thirty three vessels in all.

With its gates closed (though at peaceful anchor) the vasty stable was now secure within its moat of brine. Fumes of petrochemical droppings left from former voyages would have wafted with whiffs of exhaust from the ship's diesel generators in deeper baileys further aft and poisoned the air even for lassitude if the gymnasium's atmosphere had not been perpetually discharged by the hoarse steady air-blowers that fuddled many a lyric word with their white noise.

> I've got spurs that jingle-jangle-jingle
> As I go riding merrily along . . .

Soldiers could not have lived more than two minutes on that tank deck with all their infernal engines running if those invisible banks of fans had weakened or desisted, or if the ship's dynamos had failed that also lent them electricity to get ready by as they steamed toward the beach in blacked-out flotillas.

And so in the hollow lists where the smell of cordage blended with the smell of horsepower (beloved of civilians far from the shimmering sea) voices of the separated twosomes did not reach each other significantly. The earlier occupants of the gymnasium dribbled tossed and shot baskets in cycles of diminishing frequency, no longer interspersing spates of zeal to prove that they were not debilitated by sticky humid boredom. They were dimly aware that the two recognized figures shrunken in vivacity by distance and intervening obscurity were at some needless business to which only such drastic characters would have put themselves on a day like this at a place like Truk: godforsaken gloomy wearisome and sexless, 27° hopelessly beyond the line demarcating East from West.

Tum—bull-ing tumbleweed . . .

A hatch was closed somewhere and the influx of music ceased, as if excusing the pastimers from their game of ball. On their shambling way off the greasy steel flags they paused to watch the grimmer exercise, wagging their heads doubtfully but daring not to provoke Kane with words of intrusion or gestures of ridicule.

In both suspension and resistance the sculpture had failed as a simulacrum of the yellow enemy. It lay dismembered on the deck, white viscera exposed but not oozing through gashes in its denim skin: boneless shapeless bloodless—altogether too light too yielding too aerial for their beefy thrusts. It had not long suffered the alternate jabbing sticking pushing digging twisting raking scything passes of white giants chanting "The Spirit of the Bayonet" Kane had learned from a soldier—-

> Blood and guts,
> Blood and guts,
> Kill, kill, kill!

—or grunting battle cadence from the solar plexus without movement of lip or tongue. Higher-pitched battle cries had repeatedly aborted in the throats of the frustrated attackers. The victim could sustain no force. So now the agonists were drilling face to face, their blades covered again with scabbards, trying to devise a more satisfactory dance on the cheerless stage.

They had been at it long enough that sweat was starting on the muscles of their arms. It was already wrung from their heads, and it glistened on the bare chests, one all hairless, the other grizzled with fine filaments fairer than the sunned skin. They forbore to strike each other, but playful flourishes were over. The heavy rifles were now held like bone-numbing quarterstaffs, with each pair of hands on either side of a virtual fulcrum, working point and butt alike in swings and parries and arcing rams. The power of their exertion increased steadily with gradually quickening tempo of breath. They had found a panting rhythm that coordinated respiration with the precession of their shoulders and were able to swerve from direct contact with opposite flesh while still punctuating unchecked follow-throughs with the dull clash of arms. But such restrained gladiation, without the pageantry of shield or blazon, no more plangent in its thudding monotony than the snort of heaving lungs, soon exhausts the interest of spectators accustomed in their daily life to confrontations far more vociferous. Even a rampant lion and unicorn, unless engaged in serious violence, could not have stayed the hungry loiterers. They went off without a word, leaving the mock-adversaries in absorbed possession of the eerie maw, bronze flesh gleaming white in the deserted theater.

It must have been shortly afterwards that one of the performers demanded that they make their workout more piquant, a little more dramatic, by removing the dull scabbards that bated their blades. He did not reckon on fatigue. They both relied too much on the rhythm of their inhibitory skill to balk the sword of the feast it craves.

{*Postulants only:* GO TO ITEM (50) HY.07.6, page 489.}

(49)
SO.05.5
ACTION

47) Still, I could be wrong, you know. Not dead wrong, but wrong in the claim that we have a new art. Overwrought speculation can blind common sense. In reaction to celsitude of ballet I may have overestimated the auctorial *menos* of modern performers. Obviously, as there are fewer playwrights than actors, there are fewer creative women than modern dancers.

Several times I have been given tickets to ballet. Have seen the best of that. Madam Elizabeth Quicherat is loveliest dancer of western world, supreme in *arete*, Muse of her tradition. Apotheosis of beauty through sheer selflessness of movement. Takes joy not in herself but in perfect instrumentality of body, right down to last joint of fingers. Spiritual devotion to performance after lifetime of *askesis*. My breath stops when I see a woman so expressive of her role.

Am I then plumb foolish to call for personal *creative* imagination in her future dance? Is it really possible to hope for self-directed originality on the classical scene? Or on the other hand to find her peer as a performer among the few who make their own dance from the beginning? But perhaps it's destined that the American dance will decline when the few fierce geniuses that created it are dead.

Anyway I've never actually seen the new dance I expatiate upon. I'm not given tickets for it. Modern impresarios don't seem to have access to an opera house this far west.

48) But pretty soon maybe even the geniuses will begin to believe that there can't be any more new motion under the sun, and creative dance will turn out to be only contemporary dance after all: like Io's oestrus, lasting just long enough to attract international seed before it dies in living again.

Consider in evolutionary terms just three of dance's difficulties in surviving as new or newly grafted art of performance, particularly as against American music (which is, sociologically speaking, the strongest art in age of noise because challenged by greatest barriers of neural habituation, as well as most in demand, hence most competitive):

1. Looking demands more of the nervous system than hearing does. (Ear doesn't have to swivel or focus. Its short-term memory lies in sensations that resonate in leisurely staging phase between detection and cognition. Little nervous acuity or mental effort required. Thus from subject's standpoint, sound more agressive than vision. Can listen to music when drunk or drugged—or at least hear it. It takes cerebral concentration first to watch movements, and then, by retaining their continuity, to discern form through time. Spectator must be specially tuned to pick up power through lightwaves alone.
2. Dance cannot be captured and preserved for arbitrary reappearance, or reproduced at just any location.
3. Being grossly physical, dance can't keep up with music in acceleration, the ratio by which Americans hope to equal density.

By the same token these three disadvantages help protect dance from debasement by commerce. In a world of night-and-day clamor theatrical vision in the dark is more chaste than the promiscuous ear.

49) Dancer would like to convert whole body into wordless lobe of the brain. But in truth it's impossible to develop central nervous system without touching mind—and any mental process stimulates linguistic reason. Thus dance of stage tends toward drama despite every attempt to escape literature. In organized effort one can't help taking thought.

Here I begin to share everybody's doubt that an ephemeral event can hold interest for very long without some sort of significs. Much easier to be interested in history or theory of dance, or in its personalities, than in dance itself, especially when its rate of creating new solo movement for the finite body has necessarily passed its peak.

50) Effort to imagine pure action too often gets no further than decoration if it's not at least suggestive of symbolic value. Already, even without any further attempt at "meaning", the struggle against language may be lost.

Begins a series of meanings that rise level by level, regardless of dancer's intentions, tending toward fully literary interpretation.

It's impossible to confine even the smallest trace of meaning to time and place of performance. The implicit semantic of a dancing human body is some predication of human ability, referring momentary phenomena of art to the relative perduration of real or imaginary life.

Yet the ultimate humanity is in feeling, not ability.

[Lyric poetry at the upper limit of culture: proof of capability for the extreme freedom that our uniquely complex species hopes for. Unsustainable, moody, fitful, sometimes perverse.]

51) Ritual reconciles specifically human with generically natural, mediating liberty and recurrent functions. If behavior were peculiarly human there'd be no society. Capricious institutions would not outlast the moment; always inchoate. Art wants to extract from ritual its human elements, its irregularities, its private rhythms—*without disowning the natural matrix itself.*

[Drama as violation of ritual; tragedy as violation of liturgy.]

Whereas drama rescues and intensifies ritual words, dance tries to keep separate and parallel course in extracting and humanizing ritual action. But maybe it can't resist anastomosis, and must by some law of dromenology converge with poetry.

I take it that no one here is concerned with the kind of dance that is willing to merge with allegory, opera, or musical comedy. If art-dance can't sustain its own purity let it absorb the drama—to complete its humanization by opening its theater to language, and thereupon to truth, a special case of meaning.

Hesiod has it that when gods mate with women their sons are born immortal—Heracles or Dionysos (but disregarding Autolycus, son of Hermes)—yet that when goddesses take men for lovers the heroes they bear are mortal, flawed or political, like Achilles and Aeneas. But we who honor the full menic power of magnetic artists make no scruple over any gender.

52) Meanwhile: *The very end of life is action of a certain kind.* [Aristotle.] For the first time the stage can show action perfectly obedient to the body's imagination. *The very end of art is imagination of a certain kind.*

I have opposed the natural to the human, but others (like Artaud) oppose the inhuman, hoping there to find that new imagination. Their surrealism of tortured voice and fantasms of sculpture, with the most terrific electronic music, subordinates creative action to aesthetic sensation in lyrics of superhuman despair.

But the theater these women have made is too trophic to ally itself with inhuman as well as unnatural efflorescences of decadent drama, and it entirely bypasses the artistic vice of journalism. So that's the theater we should seize for the use of intellectual imagination.

53) Absurd to think of trying to imitate first beginnings of drama. We can attain to nothing valuable by pretending to be primitive.

[Creative dance as antithesis to dithyramb.]

We are bound to believe Yeats, that "no beginnings are in the intellect, and no living thing remembers its own birth." We are damned to the agony of historical self-consciousness—but doubly damned if we therefore try to shed the mind's experience of the past.

But we can take advantage of decadence in imaginative exploitation of our license.

54) I hope I myself haven't abused liberty in generalizing from unfamiliar analogs and then reasoning back to wishful particulars. But I think I've gotten as close as a man can get to such mysteries from the outside.

55) What? You clap? I weep to have been heard a while!

{*Postulants only:* GO TO ITEM (56) MS.06.0 (Second encounter),
Antilog 2: Symposium, page 701

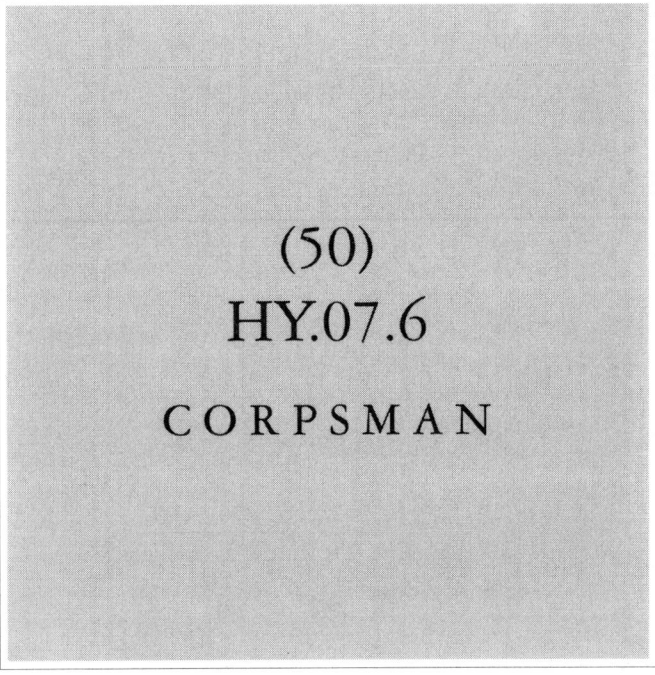

(50)
HY.07.6

CORPSMAN

When Michael took his place in the chartroom he found the logged record of a message that had been sent to ALL SHIPS PRESENT by his predecessor, who rushed off duty without pause for scuttlebutt under the assumption that no one could still be ignorant of the event he was making haste to visit the scene of, where witnesses to the immediate aftermath would be discussing it from all points of view.

> ANY SHIP WITH DOCTOR PLEASE SEND IMMEDIATELY TO ORIGINATOR X MAN SERIOUSLY WOUNDED URGENTLY REQUIRES MEDICAL ASSISTANCE.

The appeal was almost two hours old, a euphemistic understatement sent by the Executive Officer during the early moments of shock when it was still possible to conjure uncertainty. It had been followed a little later by a request to the Marine command ashore for arrangements to dispose of the body. Evidently the call for a doctor had been belayed and followed up by blinker-light signaling or by the radio shack's Morse code exchange with a distant admiralty. Nothing in the local voice radio log suggested that compatriots on the beach were excited by what had happened afloat.

The smallboat was long since manned and ready, its coxswain and crew already reconciled to confused indecision but growing impatient at being out of touch with orders and announcements that greatly fluctuated in audibility even when not contradicting each other as they circulated the ship's deck above. With the descent of black night (nor moon nor star) a floodlight taking in the quarterdeck watch and men crowding the gangway cynosured the boat detail gazing up from water level like a circus team waiting for the drumroll and fanfare to announce their unrehearsed act.

That much Michael could see from a balcony level by momentarily neglecting his station when he stepped out through the wheelhouse onto the wing of the bridge where most of the men of the Ship's Control gang were gathered in the darkness to talk over all the tidings and speculations of sense or imagination, disproven or not, speaking in low tones of awe and suppressed excitement. Curiosity was rather inflamed than quenched by the few undisputed facts of which he now possessed himself with a hushed hunger in no way superior to theirs. Conversation seemed only to forfend comprehension of the one essential fact, which would be brought into true knowledge only when they presently saw Hypnos and Thanatos hoist a mortal body over the side down into the apron-bowed landing craft that waited upon its mother ship like a lesser ferry serving the greater in landing passengers from a broad reach of the Styx. So the crew was waiting for that proof.

The radio circuit was now as quiet as usual after working hours in such a sparsely occupied anchorage. Michael turned up the gain and trusting to keep within earshot permitted himself now and then to dart down the short companionway from the chartroom to the sacred precinct of "officers' country" in the donjonkeep where all prestige was domiciled and whence in port all orders were issued. Poised for a minute or two on the lower steps of the ladder as if on official business, trusting to remain unnoticed as a familiar servant of communications in the press of officers and specially summoned P O s who passed expectantly to and fro through the narrow corridor connecting wardroom captain's cabin and lesser staterooms, he would cock one ear toward his duty topside while with the other he listened for better-informed hearsay than what was being bruited on the open decks and tried to integrate snatches of instructions that would set in motion the public action generally awaited as the official response to death. Thus in excited thirst for experience he turned to advantage his confinement at watch within the windowless bulkheads above.

"No one on this ship ever got killed before!" he heard more than once in a tone of dawning philosophy.

The only medical man aboard was a young Pharmacist's Mate Second Class with loose salivating lips known mostly behind his back as Hickey for the unfortunate case of acne that he showed no signs of outgrowing but fundamentally respected for his studious devotion to the art he loved to find himself serving—though it was regarded rather as a technology by most sailors, who called men of his rating penis mechanics; for if an enlisted man never answered sick call or contracted meningitis or suffered a bayonet wound he would encounter these acolytes on duty only during the iterated "short-arm inspection" that followed any possibly good time ashore when one of these technicians would sit on a stool at the head of a line facing each man in turn uncircumcised or not and chant a professional command known wherever our Navy shows the flag, "Milk it down and skin in back, milk it down and skin it back", like a priest repeating the words of distribution to each communicant, making sure that the doctor behind him (brought for the occasion) would get a look at suspicious specimens.

Johns—Johns being his surname—performed this close review of every man's private part as he performed all his unsupervised duties, such as diagnosing and treating endemical variations of "tropical rot" (a trivial but anxious ailment mostly intertriginous and out of sight), with dispatch and self-assurance, confident in his knowledge and utterly impartial. Though he practiced preventive medicine, as for example by advising the men to cut their toenails straight across to keep them from ingrowing, he made no apparent effort to stop the blackheads on his brow cheeks and neck from reaching the unassisted maturity at which buds of white pus offered to erupt before one's eyes. Though for some his competent but unlovely impersonality was spoiled by a manner that suggested the strong domestic influence of genteel women, Michael liked him for declining to affect the brusque patter of hearty virility with which many Hospital Corpsmen seemed to disclaim the embarrassment or resentment ordinary sailors would expect them to feel at the Nightingale service they had been sold into. This ingenuousness gave rise to dark hints about his motivating passion that were sometimes given jocular credence in the face of nigh certainty that no Greek love was ever practiced in this mobile monastery. Then too his Christian name, which he did have sense enough to suppress, was Percy.

But there was nothing effeminate about the way P Harvey Johns nursed his first mortality. If it was difficult to envisage him in intimate siege of a girl it would have been even harder yet to imagine his response to such an emergency as that in which he had actually accepted acute and sole responsibility far beyond official expectations of his rate. After commandeering help (including the murderer's) to get his patient up a ladder from the tank deck to Sick Bay he had coolly stanched blood absterged the wound pronounced death and made the corpse ready for deportation, all without any guidance from precedence in his own experience or advice from authority. His confident skill and composure was now the toast of the wardroom whither he had been called to make his report after he finished preparation of the body where it lay on the operating table, and to accept an unofficial drink from the officers avidly awaiting his account of death's details before the order was given to get rid of the outward and visible remains.

"Here Johns, this'll put lead in your pencil! Not that you need it— tough job, all by yourself! Well done!"

"Thank you sir. Now that it's all over I'm a little shaky. —Amazing: it was just the tip of the blade."

"Got him right in the heart eh?"

Yes, blood had warmed very little of the sword. A quick taste of flesh no deeper than a dipsas bite; to all appearances a shallow insignificant satisfaction—at least after all the spurted menos was washed away and the little puncture exposed in the stone-white skin.

"After all our hours at battle stations!"

All those calls to general quarters, and this is the way it comes, when you're off guard, the enemy innocent, no one to hate except stupidity itself: an accident bringing to light as no death in battle would the common end of life. Savored in solemn company.

At last Johns was released to go over the side and take his place as supercargo in the smallboat, and most of the gentlemen followed him to the gangway. Everyone from messcook to Executive Officer waked the dead. Only the captain was absent from this unpremeditated obsequy (a product of the war-worn Atlantic destroyer fleet who mourned his assignment to a landsman's freighter and anyway a solitary man by office); he remained shut up in his cabin without showing personal respect or betraying any interest in the way his curt order was being carried out.

For a few minutes the body lay cered in its mummy-basket on the main deck, a candid shadowless and exact target of contemplation under working lights bright as a surgeon's or fish-cutter's penetrating the lower plane of the tide-rode funeral barge with its white faces of upward-gazing boatmen to deeper levels of the yellowed green circle in which pallidly spreading hydrozoa hung like colloidal mushrooms summoned to witness punishment. Every desire was forgotten at sight of the figure that seemed less animate than the mortcloth to which it gave a smoothed profile.

Now too a wonderful complicity of silence made similar illumination for the ear. No note of music, no distorted or magnified voice near or far, no raillery, no braying taunt disturbed this united acuity of attention, as if in leaving the bones the soul had impressed for its escort all the ship's vigor and warmth. Except for the vibrating hum of the ship's respiration to which all ears were inured the only sounds came from a few men manipulating low-geared tackle under the quiet direction of the giant black-bearded Boatswain, the one Chief without whom the skipper would never put to sea no matter how sticky the man's shore detention for tearing apart a bar or assaulting an S P patrol, who though knowledgeable of death from the longevity of his naval service was as touched on this occasion as almost everyone else. These small squeaks and thumps only

intensified the isolation of the scene, which being without water music or
the walls of a theater seemed as vulnerable to the cacodemons of outer
darkness as an incandescently lighted execution on the Siberian steppes.

The spell was broken when the engines of the nervous tender burst
into power. From the beginning of ship's time this blunt L C V P (with
its starboard twin) had served its green old lady and all her sons with
unfailing devotion—at sea bundled symmetrically to her very cheeks by
the embrace of davits, clasped as high and close to the citadel as a bulky
life-jacket collar muffling her face, but at an anchorage always launched
and ready for manifold errands. Though never cast loose as a lifeboat, and
like its mother never called upon to assault a hostile beach with guns
ablaze, it had tirelessly plowed the cockles of every roadstead as whaleboat
jollyboat bumboat Moses boat lighter cutter canoe dinghy dory punt
wherry longboat shallop pinnace yawlboat watertaxi gig Whitehall boat
and liberty launch—albeit uglier and thermodynamically more wasteful
than craft put to such uses in former ages.

The sturdy brave bulldozer with power to spare was now waiting to
perform as hearse in conveying the victim sans honor guard to his lych-
gate ashore. The waxen sailor bound in a snowy sheet and strapped into
his battle stretcher was laid upon the open boat's flat bottom, shrouded
silken lashes closed under a drained forehead, his bled heart having ceased
from the business it had begun. Once all lines were cleared the boat crew
made no further ceremony of the job. The willing craft had escaped the
field of light by the time the bow swung round to its heading, and it
roared off to Hades with two open throttles. Michael wondered how carefully the leatherneck burial detail would inter a swabby who rated no taps
or rifle salute—unless the body was to be shipped home in his cist for a
veteran's flag-draped descent into less corrupting soil.

Attention shifted at once to the killer whom the captain taking no
more chances with the ship's good name had ordered to be confined while
the legal situation was pondered. There was no doubt about the accidental
nature of this manslaughter, or at least about the loser's voluntary and
cooperative risk; but from a distant bureaucratic desk the game that had
been played might be regarded as a duel of equals. Besides, the victor's
well documented history of bad conduct might easily be interpreted as
psychopathic even by the chicken farmer in command of a mass-produced
ship. It was clearly imprudent to leave the way open for some still less
excusable mischance, even though neither the skipper of a ship with too
little chicken-shit discipline nor the First Lieutenant Mr Kiely who was
sweating over his part in the facultative circumstances had to be reminded
that it was the height of folly to be wise too late. These two closeted
themselves with the Executive Officer to frame equable reports.

Their reaction, as it came to manifest itself, was defensive and twofold. First, early next morning, sooner and more vehemently than previously intended, the accessible spaces of the ship were to be expurgated of

all Japanese artifacts. Second, they prepared to remove the relic of embarrassment and salt-mill of continuing trouble. Orders were given to send the prisoner ashore for higher command to take custody of and pass judgment upon, whether as autonomous criminal or as guiltless client of Tyche.

In the wardroom two of the most junior officers speaking their opinions were much of the same mind as their superiors despite both their freedom from responsibility for the behavior in question and their immeasurably more subtle appreciation of it. The case concerned them dispassionately as members at large of the wardroom club who had only their own men to personally look after; but it was grist for a future career in psychology law or genethlialogy.

The grizzled mustang Engineering Officer overheard them without much comprehension, sitting by himself close to the medicinal liquor that had been broken out for poor young Johns. In his mind the ship's misfortune had been brought to bear on a brooding preoccupation that had begun with the Japanese surrender. Would some collective culpability hasten the revocation of his temporary commission, or at least Bureau of Personnel attention to the roster of LST 1066, and all the sooner return him to his permanent enlisted rank as a Chief Machinist's Mate? Like thousands of other roughneck parvenus without benefit of letters science or jurisprudence he found himself vainly accustomed to the enjoyment of despotic privilege that came with living on an equal or superior footing with college graduates and Academy men. He thought he deserved such consideration of the Navy that if it could not sweeten it certainly should not accelerate the anticipated humiliation of serving again as an ungentlemanly C P O , perhaps among crewmen who had suffered under the temporary tyrant. The senior-grade Lieutenant of wartime had accustomed himself to swallowing his observations about glib unreliable kids like these undeserving subalterns who played chess and bridge, who raised their glasses at officers' clubs and cried "Gentlemen—to the Mikado!"

The one out of Harvard, Dodge, always talking like a movie actor, was pontificating as usual. "As I've always said, this fellow is unbalanced and he has to be kept under watch. Can't be trusted with any sort of freedom. He may do it again, some other way. You could see it coming if you looked under the surface. Sadistic personality. There's no such thing as an accident in the final analysis. Any man that's crazy enough to play around with bayonets is too irresponsible to be in a ship's crew. *I* think he ought to be sent to Portsmouth, the only place a man like that is safe!"

Ensign Drake, a susceptible Southerner given to literary twists of sympathy that his brother gentlemen were used to excusing him for, couldn't bring himself to touch the murder weapon which had been detached from the rifle and laid upon a towel in the center of the green baize wardroom table. His thoughts were on the victim. "I guess a man's lucky to die young like a cocky dog, never knowing any death but his own. At least he got out of life a trip to the Pacific islands."

* * *

It was decreed that the pro tem prisoner's guards should be chosen from among the junior petty officers presumed to be least acquainted with him and most conscientious about their general responsibility as representatives of the commanding officer, especially those known to be courteous or taciturn in their sobriety. Doesnt the Navy say even to bluejackets wearing the crow "Be gentlemanly in all your actions"? And does it not define even a swabby gentleman as "a man who is never intentionally offensive to others"? The ship had no proper brig with bars and locks—only the port chain locker beneath a hatch in a forward compartment where the bow angled up toward its peak, and though the captive would be given a mattress and brought his meals he would have to be lowered a ladder and escorted aft whenever he called to use the head.

Michael drew for his brig watch the last two hours of nighttime. He trembled with apprehension at the prospect of a detail for which he was totally untrained, notwithstanding assurances that it was only a Regulation precaution hardly required in this accident case. This arrested killer from the very first sight of his opponent's surprise had been most penitent docile and cooperative, pathetically hopeful to expiate the horror and to propitiate authority.

Seeking guidance the inexperienced guard-designate dug out his *Bluejackets' Manual* which in never having opened since his first day at boot camp he was a typical sailor. It had been issued as a standard item for his sea-bag, along with a whisk brush a hank of light stranded cord (white as fleece calibrated at intervals by paired daubs of pitch to be cut between for making "stops" with which to bind rolled clothes or hang washing) and other accessories to the main body of shoes socks skivvies long woolen underwear dungarees denim shirts dress blues undress blues blueblack neckerchief peacoat watch cap blue dress hat (the "flat hat" he never had occasion to wear after posing for his official photograph at Great Lakes) and white hats that supposedly could collect rain water or trap air to help keep a man afloat as well as express his character among both sailors and civilians and distinguish him from officers who might be wearing work clothes or life jackets otherwise too much like his own. But he found this Gideon Bible cold comfort to an unmilitary technician who would be required to strap on a guard belt while the ship was asleep having no previous opportunity to examine the pistol, still less to practice squeezing it. If one had never handled a sidearm it was better to prepare with sleep than to study what could not be practiced.

For not another man of the crew but had more military education than Michael. A passingly acute demand for electronics experts had hustled him through a very short course in the fundamentals of Navy discipline taught without persuasion or theory on a frozen treeless plain covered with black asphalt and gray wooden barracks far from any maritime evidence even of the fresh water that the Station spread midwestward from in its bewildering wartime expansion in order to get him off as soon as possible to a series of serious schools wherein to learn his assigned trade, which had then kept him from sea duty until it was too late to get in on any of the 1066's combat training as an integrated fraternity; when he came aboard the crew had long since finished its indoctrination in amphibious seamanship and gunnery.

As the ship's only doctor of radio and radar equipment he had been assigned to the communications department under the immediate jurisdiction of a First Class Radioman, softspoken and highly skillful amanuensis of alphanumeric information received but (in an L S T) seldom transmitted by the unreflecting manipulation of electromagnetic sounds that Michael was never able to master autodidactically—Morse to English, English to Morse—at speeds far too great for thoughtful translation and recording on the radio shack's upper-case typewriter by a supernumerary who presented an organizational problem.

It was this supervisor who once mentioned the obvious to Michael in the kindly tone of one who sincerely wished to protect him from the hostility of his anti-intellectual colleagues. "See, you're just not cut out like the rest of us." By this explanation the gentle Iowan, far from intending flattery, was attempting to bolster the odd-ball's morale. The good man himself knew nothing about the superheterodyne principles of his gear but understood quite well the duties as well as the feelings of his other subordinates, even of the radar operators, whose half-tutored functions Michael despite his rating was obliged to share when the ship was underway.

Chapman's arcane responsibility for keeping both classes of electronic equipment in order was regarded by operators as rather otiose. Preventive maintenance of black boxes seemed purely academic (contrary to the unequivocal instruction manuals by which Michael justified his pay), especially when there were few moving parts inside apparently dirtproof cabinets, and when most L S T s berthed no technician at all.

Even his reputation for diagnosing acute trouble, based upon a certain faith in his title—about which he himself was diffident, seeing that he'd given short shrift to the practical aspect of the curriculum at the Navy schools he'd survived thanks only to a certain faculty for theory that carried him through examinations more by reason than by knowledge—was irreparably damaged and given over to mockery (as much in dispraise of all book-learning as in personal malice) on the one occasion that the ship's hitherto indefatigable little search radar (made in Massachusetts) all of a sudden went dead. After feverishly troubleshooting all its component sub-assemblies for twenty-four hours with schematic drawings and wiring diagrams spread everywhere in the chartroom like agnostic treasure maps, after even resorting to the trial-and-error replacement of nearly every part he had a spare for, he the sudden attractor of anxious official attention had had to admit that he couldnt fix it. The emergency had fortunately occurred in clear weather and after peace had been made, only half a day before arriving at an anchorage where he was able to call upon an experienced engineer from a great fleet supply ship. His ignominy was only slightly mitigated by the facts that it took the expert a full ninety minutes to find a very obscure solenoid failure in the transmitter unit and that he clearly thought none the worse of young Chapman for not having spotted a rare and esoteric malfunction. All the same, to smirking onlookers it was the defeat of an intellectual.

The only thing that Michael had ever actually repaired happened to be the wardroom radio receiver through which the ship picked up its airwave entertainment. A year's special training was vindicated when he tracked down and replaced a tiny capacitor in the audio circuit.

Yet because of his lonely specialty he had never been instructed in loading aiming or firing the twenty- or forty-millimeter guns with which an L S T bristled in twin mounts; and sidearms were almost as far beyond his competence. If the plan to invade Japan had been executed, with 1066 in a first wave against the green and pleasant island of Honshu, he might well have died idle at his battle station, for the little SO radar was useless on a beach.

In his bunk on the eve of his first and only armed-guard duty he was plagued not with nightmares or tossing sleeplessness but with jumbled reduplicated pleonastic verse pounding in his own voice and ceaselessly reverberating in his skull without meter or meaning, the churning wails of a repertory past the hope of fresh sensation, rotating jumbled fragments of banal bulldozed tone-deaf melody crowded in a narrow space that there was no hope of escaping:

> I've got stars
> that jingle jangle jingle
> —deep in the heart of Texas . . .

my spurs are bright   —don't fence me in
like lots of light   —under starry skies above
—all over the world . . .   —but make me glad I'm single
     . . . where rabbits rush
I've got land lots of land   around the brush
—where the moon is bright   —deep in the heart of Texas
deep in the heart of starry
skies above . . .

when the lights go on again
—my spur will jingle jangle jingle
—under starry skies above . . .
—deep in the heart of Texas
give me night lots of nights
—for my merry little song . . .
when the lights are lit
and the rabbits flit . . .
—deep in the heart of Texas . . .
—tumble-ing tumbleweed . . .
I aint so very far from wrong
as I go riding merrily along . . .
my spurs at night
shine so bright
—deep in the heart of Texas . . .

Words he hated, harmful chelating words imbedded in the soup of hypnotic music thudding back and forth in delirium until his neural strength
was exhausted with the involuntary effort of unprehending them and he
was left expurgated for the last hour of rest before his call.

But at the messenger's touch of his shoulder he came instantly alert to
the fear of facing in isolated silence a man just come from killing another
and perhaps doubting his own life at the hands of Navy justice. After wakening his dilatory will with a most bitter mug of residual coffee from the
urn outside the locked-up galley he went forward on the deck below and
took the guard belt from his predecessor without a word, in exquisite hope
that the losel just beneath his feet within a whisper's range of whatever
sound might drop over the flange of the barless opening into the dark
lazaret would not stir from his sleep or say anything for the next two
hours—if pray God the manslaughterer was indeed at rest!

Like one of Joseph's lily-livered brothers Michael dared not peer into
the pit. Under other conditions he would have taken pleasure in carrying
the .45 trimly covered in its holster (whence a fast draw was happily out of
the question) where it was bound snugly to his hip by the comfortable
broad girdle of webbed khaki that dipped rakishly with the weight
(though of course not slung as low as the civilian baldrics worn by swift-
firing gunfighters of the libertarian West). There is nothing necessarily
lethal or aggressive about a man's delight in guns. But in Michael's opinion the Navy service pistol was too large and too heavy for its general purpose. He had been warned of its kick.

The stuffy compartment lay beyond the reach of the ventilating system.
It was nothing but an overhead antechamber to the airless hole of a chain
locker that suggested itself as a dungeon when the anchor was well payed
out. Otherwise the principal utility of the bare lobby when its hatches were

dogged shut was that of flotation space, which was rather precious in an L S T, especially at the bow, owing to the vast unpartitioned and exceptionally vulnerable cargo stomach that preempted most of the ship's volume.

Nowhere was Navy space so quiet. He heard nothing but the incessant creaking of steel, which at anchor was too faint to claim attention. The cell below had been unfurnished except for a coil of hawser cable; he remembered having noticed at Saipan that the white surface of its sloping outboard bulkhead was scuffed and dented worse than its other three walls, while its canted gray deck bore stains of rust.

Pungent smells of Manila cordage and barnacles nearly overcame the general odors of paint and grease in the guard's upper antechamber. There was a bare bulb to read by, but he was too frightened to get the book out of his back pocket. If the incarcerated survivor had suddenly spoken he would have jumped out of his skin. With as much care as a prisoner trying not to wake his captor by the first move of escape he carefully lowered himself to the deck and sat next to the open hatch of the only access to this vertical suite, his spine against the transverse bulkhead and his outstretched legs crossed before him on the deck's upward grade. Staring at the pit of gaping shadow he composed his body in such a way as to ease further shifts of weight, and his mind in such a way as to reason away the fantastic questions that had been filling his thoughts.

Was the criminal really asleep down there? Was he crouched with the desperation of death in his eye, reconsidering his apologies and forswearing his renunciation of violence? Had he been searchingly disarmed? Or even now did a silently ebbing suicide redden the gray with blood? Indeed was he still down there at all? Had the earlier guards conversed with him? Did he have any idea who was guarding him now? Or did he think perchance that he had been left alone—and this very moment mean to leap up and catch the lip of his dungeon for some insane exploitation of the situation as he may have supposed it?

Michael little by little succeeded in dissolving his absurd fears, in the main by forcing himself in the light of fact to correct his persistent prejudice as to the person of the shrouded figure that had been sent to land. Over and over again with increasing conviction he assured himself: "Killer Kane is dead!" The panic-maker with heart like fire and hands like burnished steel was gone from life. He who had been as powerful as Heracles and as fast as Hermes, fierce as a double axe, was more mortal than the orphan who'd outreached him.

Everyone in the ship was saying it: "His reach did it. . . . No Jap could ever have done it . . . He had the reach, he had the reach on him!" The reach of the long arms that had borne most of the weight of the worshipful body as it was taken up to Sick Bay.

Michael's terror turned to pity when soon after dawn in their dawnless enclosure Abbie simply asked the time in a quiet salty voice. On the next guard's watch Abbie too was sent ashore, leaving the black puppy to the whole crew.

On New Year's Eve 799 Japanese repatriates came aboard from scows. (At the last minute one had been picked up by Naval Intelligence for undisclosed cause.) Thus the first postwar cargo of the trampsteaming USS LST 1066.

{*Postulants only:* GO TO ITEM (57) HY.09, page 791.}

(51)
MS.05

RIDE HOME
FROM BERKELEY

*T*he entelechtual but public man starts his ride south on Teleology Lane hunched utterly detumescent in the sparsely populated womb of a rattling trolley car midships at a portside
window. Rush hour has gone and past. There's no one to jostle his elbow.
He slouches gratefully against the steel and glass shell he has paid to be
carried in. His cheeks and chins have darkened with a long day's whiskers.
For his money he can expect at least twenty-three minutes of movement,
about six minutes longer than coming north through the more orderly
traffic of fresh morningtime. With the fall of evening, mass commutation
all thinned out, promiscuous motion begins. The sidestreets randomly stir
with cars roused again from short rests. The commoner's day shift is long
since ended. It can't match Michael's in symmetry of twilit margins.

This passenger is hungrier and tireder than any other. His arms are
folded on his chest for warmth but an elbow pressed on the narrow varnished window sill picks up through his auditing humerus the subsonic
vibrations underlying the overt noise of steel wheels upon steel rails driven
by electricity derived from the 19C. Ageless D C motors jerk and haul
him with themselves in a familiar bundle of intermittent jolting and

HN 1. What thoughts first creep back into the depression of Michael's spirit?
{Michael as you have seen was always inclined to make ideas as important as feelings, and to turn feelings into desires. For this perversity Blake as understood by Yeats would have called him a most ugly man, and most modern readers would certainly agree. But Caleb had already grown more open-minded and to him in the unbloomed wisdom of simple experience Michael's weaseling attempt to escape emotion in order to find imagination seemed to work, and it was for no other reason that he called him a successful man who apparently cared more about what he was able to do to the world than about what the world did to him. Caleb to be sure saw nothing of the battles and retreats that took place behind the opaque physiognomy known only for its expression of ideas. These alarums and recursions were not purposely concealed from the young friend: they were masked by a peculiar habitual maturity which Michael told himself was dictated by his excruciating responsibilities. Such a person can't be a poet. My assertion may be accepted as corollary to the somewhat deeper principle of antithetical perfections in life and art as propounded by Yeats. It's proven by the following conceit which occurred to Michael at exactly this point in his journey home, which illustrates the middling profundity of his psychic behavior in the face of a genuine opportunity to hit bottom, and which arose from his envy of those who are paid to travel for their business:}

There's too much flying done in the name of money-making. Passenger traffic is the most inefficient segment of transportation's contribution to our gross national product. Even Joseph K when he was preoccupied with higher

---

coasting whines down the wire from Athens to Piraeus, returning him safely to the workingman's quarter after the day's service.

No book appears in his hand tonight; none lies open in his lap. Neither the will to do nor the will to know offers to strive against his sullen sloth, and he scarcely notices that he's wasting in idleness this public solitude. Doing nothing but indulging his sulky demon, consoling himself, squandering time, dismissing time, throwing time to the winds, he gently sways with the transverse motion of time's arrow, making the least of this occasion. The waxing of his belly's hunger is dimmed and diffused by the brief comfort of private narcotic relapse. In such circumstances it's a pleasure to savor the world's misery. Something like humble pity is now the burden of his lament for universal stupidity.

Thus lumpily he shoots the telegraph wire cradled like a slung bale of low-grade freight or the husk of a dreary routine communication lacking the novelty to distinguish itself as information [*HN 1*]. Anyway he's slated to drop out of the message long before it reaches the waterside haunts of Jack London whither it will arrive without him as a report of totally uninteresting noise. To and from his way-station every day he shuttles, climbing by morning the long flat imperceptible slope to the foot of the Cyclotracropolis, world parthenon for man-made gyres, and now rolling back again when the sun is gone, but except in such special venture as hereinafter never further than the cross-street he lives on, day in and day

matters took train trips merely to hear and say a few words of compromise or expediency probably pertaining to single topics of financial operation when no doubt a few thoughtful letters or ciphered telegrams would have accomplished as much. Nowadays except for salesmen no executive should be allowed more than one trip to see each place he deals with.

Unlike athletes dancers actors surgeons priests and other performers most businessmen don't need their bodies. Why lug the whole carcass or even the skull wherever our brains are taken? Millions of useless bodies are carted and flown across our States with vulgar pretentiousness like so many deadweight kegs of beer wrapped in ostentatiously speedy self-importance. For them every cityscape is flattened with concrete and uproar. A million chrematistic images of God interrupt what little sensory and motor life they have at the office simply to haul their heads and throats to unnecessarily personal interfaces—rather than sustain the mental exertion of thinking speaking and *writing* five days a week without change of scene.

If brains will always need to get together we must devise a way to containerize and ship them as cheaply as cinerary attache cases neatly compendious and easily stacked in small aircraft dispatched directly to the rooftops of office buildings. The weight and bulk of a life's experience is so much less than a whole man requiring food liquor and water closet that it might become economical to fly the essences of even prospective customers to each national headquarters for unmediated selling packed into a few minutes of concentrated persuasion. Ninety-nine percent of our passenger-tons could be eliminated if every business location had sets of standard organs for sensing and emitting signals for any brains plugged into them.

That would hardly eliminate passion from our business decisions but it might help us distinguish between transport of personality and locomotion of thinking. When you ticket a career man on the wing moreover you move not only a parcel of flesh and its appetites but also a whole mentality of which only the smallest fraction is required at the destination. Being immaterial it has no simple location anyway, and even for its limited ad hoc purpose would function just as well at home. But specialties and professions such as cost accounting or medical diagnostics deal at best with syndromes made up of "extracted categories"; their multiplicitous data, usually purged of subjectivity by the original observer' symbolic translations, may be easily communicated without altering the geographical coordinates of analyst or integrator. If it is unnecessary to present to a subject who wishes to remain objective the full context of distant places or persons it is no longer necessary to visit them more often than there are significant changes in situ.

We should heed St Willie: "An emotion produces a symbol . . . just as a symbol produces emotion. The symbol without emotion is more precise and, perhaps, more powerful than an emotion without a symbol." Gnostics need never travel, nor anyone else who hypostatizes language. It's only when the symbol really is the real thing that transportation should come into play.

I should be more careful [he reminds himself] in distinguishing between the communication of information and the commutation of sacrament.

My own daily shuttle over this highway best traveled seldom is no more enlightening than a worn-out palindrome like

.LEWD DID I LIVE :: EVIL I DID DWEL.   ❏

HN 2. Why is he libidinally more interested in this she-school than in most other walled gardens?
It is where rich females prepare particularly for the University of California and generally for motherhood of the most advantageous kind—that is to say the kind ten years deferred. [Nuns today, mums tomorrow. In the meantime lights out at ten, candles out at eleven.] In his own schooldays he was pre- pared for motherhood by passing a thousand times the riddling billboards which declared like an answer to some catechism question that THE

out as busily as if he were engaged in some accumulative business like the construction of a nest.

His family precinct lies in the larger and less pleasant city adjacent to the one he serves in, which by the look of the tower that dominates its acclivity is actually more Venetian than Greek. He envisions in the sky behind his back the sunset now finishing which did not penetrate to his consciousness while he was angrily waiting for the streetcar. From Bow's Ark itself he never could see the sun flattening into the eternal haze or purple tumult that forms the horizon behind Golden Gate and screens the intellectual void into which he will never sail again. Vermilion streaks of reverberated light were being squeezed to aquamarine by earth's rolling mill while he had stood with vacant sight in the long shadow of Sather Gate absorbed by a black trouble gnawing at his belly for the solace of food. The larking excursion of matins had been pure and energetic with ascendant spirit, but the scuttle home at vespers disgraces all joy and mocks all the painful echoes of his bitterly embarrassing mania.

Furthermore he's now retracing with ashamed sensitivity the course he strode as Caleb's master not long ago. Since that night of his birthday he has passed many times back and forth along these rails blinded by his casque of esemplastic illusion, or at least even in the worst of hunger and exhaustion weatherproofed by the hood of someone's printed word, seeing nothing on the wayside. But tonight he begins his journey home from the till as an ignominious exile from the alien world in which his proprietorship has been revoked; the subject of his strength and influence is eviscerated.

The only anticipation that stirs his interest is reunion with Roger (son of his old age decked perhaps for the father's homecoming in a coat of many colors), soon to greet him with beautiful surprise and faith, two emotions of innocence that being misplaced on such a day will only inten- sify the pathos of Chapman life as Mr Chapman now sees it.

So the only anticipation that stirs his desire is food. Specific and rav- enous hunger for supper has passed into a phase of stomach ache.

Before the car has left Jack Wolfson's neighborhood where many of the streets have Unitarian or arboreal names, still nearly within hindsight of the Gate at which Teleology Lane originates, he gazes with the envy of aged deprivation at the wintergreen trees sequestering the grounds and bowers of the Alphanumeric Academy for Girls [*HN 2*]. But when a man's in disgrace with fortune and beweeping his outcast essence too he has no heart for the

GLOUCESTER CO-OPERATIVE BANK IS THE MOTHER OF HOMES. Later in wartime he was led to expect that a well-advised prospective mother would make a man milk it down and skin it back before letting him court her. In main however the Navy did so well by Hygeia in protecting society from bad blood that it seemed unnecessarily indelicate for good women to inspect fresh veterans of the sea before engagement. Nowadays among civilians who don't get married there's no such healthy public discipline: good enough reason for a girl to be wary on this account even if having heard of many repeated and perfectly happy evasions of premature reproduction she's willing to go all the way withal. Almost every Alphanumeric student probably almost always squirms out of juxtapositions in which her willpower alone would be called upon to bear the full burden of refusal, knowing instinctively that self-protective fears of disease and pregnancy will abandon her on the verge of flagrante delicto. But no sooner does she matriculate at the University (chosen as much for its infamous liberality of custom as for its provincial prestige) than she makes a beeline for the campus clinic with a story that she's about to get hitched and asks to be fitted for a contraceptive deceiver even if the required measurement can't be taken without surgical defloration. So although these wise virgins give little thought to the Navy's worry they know there's no room in a student's life for mistakes of the second kind.

[Of course at the moment Michael is in no mood to speculate about the arousal of schoolgirls, but he has been over this ground many a time before now; what you here overhear is a smattering of the antecedent inquiry always fully available to his present mind at any passing reference without a scan of the entire recollection, which is nevertheless imaginatively enriched with each such retrieval. These subordinate thoughts evoke in turn another train of reflections that flick through his head at equal speed since their component elements are easily fetched as long-since formularized ideas.]

In the service a man too was judged largely by his mistakes, which were carefully recorded to follow him everywhere, but fertility errors were the least noteworthy—except when they contributed to the stability of the American family and were therefore rewarded with allotments of extra pay. It is only in business that mistakes are buried unashamed, sometimes (if the profit margin is wide enough to absorb stupidity) with the smug pride of anti-intellectual pragmatism.

Corporation managers unlike their rational daughters fancy being judged on what they call their batting average, a rating which like gentlemanly grades in the old days at Harvard couldnt be very high without losing caste. The double standard of conduct is never better demonstrated than by the estimation in which society holds the method of trial-and-error as applied to the hazards of a businessman father and his daughter respectively. Uncontrolled experiment in American banausics is commonly preferred to induction because it demands neither knowledge nor Creative Mind; and expediency seems more manly than deduction because the national temper prefers heuristic success. And just as the mean number of one's successful guesses must not run suspiciously high, it is understood that operating costs should be controlled only by habitual questions of common sense. (A dollar to Internal Revenue is more bitterly grudged than three dollars of waste.) The gods are never to be tempted by a manager's improvement of administrative efficiency. As long as business is comfortably in the black for the current quarter, and a little better off than the year before, or at least bigger, most executives are loathe to consider how much greater their return on investment could have been all along if they hadnt taken an infinite series of pragmatic decisions rather than three steps of abstract thought. On the rising tide of general prosperity everything that doesn't work out as hoped (except actual losses that may be applied to the reduction of current income taxes) is negligently wiped off the slate, especially the most enormous errors of judgment.

Whereas in military culture a man is supposed to be responsible for his history of stupidity and failure. Reprimands and black marks can never be expunged from a service jacket. Avoiding mistakes, as in other professions, your rivals move up the thermometer. Few Navy officers labor even for the illusion of improvement in organization or procedure. Their idealism in this respect is either present-perfect or pluperfect. No professor unless he be sunk to administrator cares to think of these matters at all. And a priest making his living in the church is not permitted to perfect anything but his own sermons or the performance of sacred music.

Therefore [even in this dark mood Michael tells himself] if Creative Mind is forced to choose between these two Bodies of Fate it must favor business over profession. Yet according to every poetic aesthetic and dromenological sensibility business is the worst of careers to endure, most of all because its intrinsic possibilities for combining efficiency with effectiveness are always as frustrated as they are in government—without the moral value of government's service to society. The urge for profit by the management of money and people is more liberal but more abused than the urge for managed service. Yet its trial-and-error methodology *could* have the back-handed virtue of natural selection—if only it were infused with the rational virtue of a profession! Alas, the possibilities of accelerated peacetime evolution tantalize me much too much!

An exceptionally unscrupulous executive, given the opportunity (which usually must be seized from chance by a long series of indirect nudges and inconspicuous dictations), can design or revise the proximate motivations of all concerned, including his own boss—provided that he's left with plenty of leeway for benign misunderstanding. The sneaky author thus succeeds (if he does succeed) because he treats management not as a profession but as a practical art. But the other side of it is that he gets sucked in. The ignoble art is alluring under the illusion of perfectibility.

Michael's own futile struggle to improve the practice of fools [he now thinks] is nothing but self-destructive aggression against a vast rock-pile, a ludicrous attempt to make a plastic art of geology, when everyone else knows a mountain's for the art of climbing. [Why can't I earn my bread at some lovely rote long since perfected—steering a ship, milking cows, mowing hay, pruning a vineyard, digging graves? Why can't I let pass any chance to revise the work of Themis? The sooner things went to seed the sooner I'd be out of it.] ❑

expense of spirit in his waste of shame. And then in a few blocks comes the corner of a street leading to the hospital where student nurses live, girls of a different ilk, a grade older, privy to sights undreamt in finishing schools, but two grades more innocent in fantasy [HN 3].

HN 3. *Besides provisional escape from poverty or family without immediate indenture to a husband what attracts girls to this bloody and scatological trade if not some awe of life and fear of sin for its wages?*

It's no cervical bonnet they work so hard to be capped with at their graduation by a pure white tiara of cotton "as yet unstriped" worthily earned by virtue of sobriety and good sense. They have been accepted for their Christian character rather than for vivacity or gusto. At the end of the course they are awarded three tokens as precious to them as college sorority bids to the girls of the other school which likewise admits no Jews while refusing to admit that it refuses to admit them: first, a New Testament provided by the Gideons (that same Christian Commercial Men's Association of America which as Harvard's 19C forecastle hand had urged did issue to all contemporary soldiers and sailors including Jews a miniature volume that lasted scarcely as long as the Bluejacket's Manual in Navy seabags and which still supplies all hotel rooms ((booked for whatever purpose even by disguised Jews)) with the complete first two Testaments bound together in octavio, as well as all prison cells where in Michael's judgment some of the narrative in the older could cruelly exacerbate the conditions of unrequitable desire); second, a Florence Nightingale torch consisting of an Aladdin's lamp with a candle stuck in it (similar to the emblem of the Tower and Flame undergraduate honor society his wife had belonged to), which to him seems to suggest that the girls are graduated to the state of enlightenment at which they permit themselves to rub for their wishes under contraindication of the telltale act that the Japanese major told him was poetically represented by a bird of their namesake species crossing a valley; and third, a rose "signifying inner beauty" like the rose window of love's Gothic aperture.

Even then (in further differentiation of their social class) it's not a diploma in bourgeois nubility that they next look forward to but a blue stripe for their cap like the distinction worn by Midshipmen on their sailor hats. For the most part there's little more in their backgrounds than in their institution to inure them to certain things they see and sometimes touch in the line of duty that may reinforce their fear of erotic consequences. Are they most interested in obstetrics because they regard delivery as a joyful and triumphant enhancement of the healthy patient's life—or simply because it infallibly cures the pathological condition of cyesis without recourse to abortion?

Those classier and younger Alphanumeric girls, when reason has failed to protect them, would hardly scruple to make angels of their unborn babies, but these servants abhor the post-prophylactic remedy as more heinous and far less defensible than the originating sin. [Michael admits that he might be of the same opinion if it were his duty to carry away baskets of forcibly miscarried fetuses and stack them in the morgue like piles of tiny Jews at a camp of chimneys. Could red babies be frozen like surplus bait for unseasonal use by medical schools?]

Burton quotes sickness as "a dissolution or perturbation of the bodily league which health combines." Thus according to Michael every blooming female has regular proof of mortal sickness even though by universal consent her dysfunction is called healthy by virtue of the fact that it can be cured only temporarily by the disease of pregnancy. When purity is restored between the last blood of parturition's wounds and the first blood of new unmilted spawn the strength of an unassisted housewife is drained by another secretion. Then it's lactation that tests the tiny household civilization she struggles to bind to herself for the sake of child and family. The nonsacramental juice of life is itself symptomatic of the fight for sanitary existence though another dissolution on the way to final corruption. Michael there sees the gist of our human destiny, the revealed mystery of the last stage of Greek religion (if you reduce symbols to their base reality); or at least the meaning of virgin Artemis the hunter as protector of childbirth.

One level's distemper is the health of another. The only immortality of mankind is woman's self-perpetuating cycle of allergies forever mocking the desire that energizes it. The bright menos full of "internal venom" is pumped through every body's antibiotic moat to keep out foreign infections, but in a woman it's also a venous solvent to loosen her dregs and wash away the swarmed ovules that would kill her if they were confined in unselective autogamy for mass gestation. Yet suitor and suttee never give over their dispute with life. From the first stirring of gonadic sensation until the last flicker of recollected erotism in the neurons of memory that outlast the protein of desire itself men and women each in their own way continue to suffer this primal disturbance.

Is it also a malady that in KANE's tale of Navy hospital life was treated by the commissioned nuns of the medical profession built like brick shithouses who under the tyranny of commissioned priests had ceased to keep the Nightingale faith in chastity after many a morning of being sent down the line of ward beds to flip back the sheets one by one and chop a little rabbit punch with the edge of their flattened palm at the base of every impertinent dreadnought to render it instantly limp? [Wham wham wham—thank you maam maam maam.] But chances are that yonder little uncapped civilian apprentices never see the menos of male patients mounting to an impudent posture of fascination. They still think they'd sacrifice their careers rather than perform the daily rounds in a monastery. The passing commuter in the streetcar fancies that the less hymened Alphanumeric girls though younger and more by touch than by sight are less ignorant of our anatomy in its manic state.

The contraseptic young women dedicated to nursing are nevertheless far more aware of life's related mysteries, and they seldom forget the unfinished victory of matrimony over wedlock, says Michael Chapman to himself. ❑ ──────

It's not half an hour since Valentine Greatrakes strode suddenly into the store with a glance at the table of untouched still-life that any customer had to stumble across. Not a single copy of *Bonjour Tristesse, The Prophet, The Man in the Gray Flannel Suit, Dianetics,* or other bestsellers that he'd ordered himself had been liquidated by his sales staff. They lay still unloved cheek by jowl with *The Dead Sea Scrolls* and suchlike healthy items. Twisting an upper lip to greet his servant with a slightly prolonged exposure of his foremost teeth, clearly unfriendly but not man enough to speak his mind, he stepped behind the cash register and in habitually preoccupied fashion punched out the day's sales totals on a section of tape that he tore off and squinted at perfunctorily. Then he stood at the counter fidgeting with the sales log like a preacher beclouded with organ music waiting in the pulpit for a hymn to end. With greater than usual frequency the middle finger of his left hand poked the self-adjusting pads of his gold steel glasses back to the pinching point of his nose whence they were always slipping down. His eyes blinked rapidly and the skin around them twitched, as all day long they were wont to do whether he was vexed or pleased, but the lining of the lids was as red as a bull's.

Michael's first impulse was to depart at once, contrary to custom, with some special domestic excuse for taking his rightful quitting time. But honor demanded that he stay for the sermon. It should be counted only to his credit that he made up his mind to linger a while in order to find out what the Christ he was being blamed for, though he might well have evaded the confrontation and relied upon a night of postponement to absorb or diffuse the fierce beam of his god's displeasure. It was a deity whose person he knew so well that he could have no doubt of its anger or of the object of its anger. An innovator is guilty of so much, especially as improver upon a divine enterprise, that it was only a question of exactly what it was that he wasnt getting away with in abusing the small authority with which he had been invested. Cold sweat unmanned the sinful archangel whose posture made little show of militancy as the chief went to a shelf in random search of evidence for what he was opening and closing his mouth to get ready to say. Opaque spectacles shielded the inferior soul from immediate damnation, but not his head and shoulders from the accusation of eyes shiftier than his own.

Greatrakes blurted out his opening statement without turning to the defendant: "The fellows at the Association are complaining about our import prices!" The tone was querulous but the amplitude as yet restrained.

"That where youve been?" Temporizing with a stupidly impertinent response.

"I don't mind giving them competition and suchlike. But I'm in business to make money." The boss knew perfectly well that Michael knew perfectly well what was up.

"The more volume—"

"Dammit Mickey, our trade-books arent a volume business!"

During the ominous pause for Vally's leap of logic Mickey disdained to comment on the introductory axiom. "This is a small store and I've got one hell of a lot of overhead." Meaning primarily Mickey's salary. "There's no two ways about it: our foreign books have to be marked up to a fair price!" His voice rose and the steam in it gave him courage to face his clerk. But even in the flushed heat of temper his eyes stayed lowered blinking faster and faster with all their might as if by the voluntary exploitation of his tic he could squeeze the energy of repressed passion out into the field of management. Meanwhile he kept jabbing his gold pencil at a pad of paper on the counter breaking off the end of the lead and then unmechanically screwing around with the shank until he got a new point. Before the conversation was over he had to busy himself with the task of replacing the delicate stick of graphite from a reservoir in the barrel. "I can't support this shop on cheap books!"

"But I mark up British books as much as American!"

"Youve got some crazy complicated way of figuring it. I just don't think it's correct. I don't trust your algebra or whatever it is!" The boss was always frustrated in his faltering attempts to demonstrate arguments mathematically. "Can all the other stores in town be wrong? Besides, even if we do get the same discount out of those books we can't return them if they don't sell. There's much more risk!"

Michael wondered if Sam the poetic communist had impeached him. His only course was to meet Prince Val on commercial ground. "Theyre standard books that will always move sooner or later. Anyway, I include postage and duty. The postage is extra profit, compared to the domestic trade."

"Well we can do a lot better!" The owner's anger waxed with his last recourse to reason. "The fact of the matter is that the others get more for English books than we do."

"I doubt they make any more than we do on them. Most of them buy through the British Book wholesaler in New York. Theyre either too lazy or they don't know how to import them on their own. Why, you yourself were the one who showed me how to buy from Simpkins in London! How else can we be really competitive with the big stores? We'd just be playing into their hands if we matched their prices when we don't have to. I've picked up—"

"British books are just an accommodation here. All trade books are, if you come right down to it. My business is basically textbooks. Always has been, always will be! I know all the ropes, especially the wholesale used-text channels—know them like the palm of my hand! All the stuff you fool around with is just to absorb part of the overhead during the slack months."

Most unkindest cut of all, this resort to his ruling idea. "I made money as a one-man textbook outfit and I don't intend to go into the red on account of smart employees!"

Greatrakes was immediately conscious of having gone too far in aspersion of the best worker on the street, as well as in gross allusion to his own expansion program. In token of retreat he lowered the pitch of his voice to the level of self-bolstering explanation. "I can always compete on second-hand textbooks. I know the best places to buy them in the East. I know where I can sell them too. That's what built my business. Trade books will never amount to anything in this store as far as volume's concerned. If I'm going to continue to carry them at all I've got to make every last cent on the few copies I do sell. . . ."

The crass threat was thus blended with his faintest reassuring hint that Michael was not personally to blame for all the shop's financial problems. But in this shift of emphasis the very ground and purpose of his clerk's superhuman efforts over the years was called into question and all but dismissed as merely somewhat less than failure. What more than anything else roused the employee's hatred of his position was the employer's use of the first person singular in betraying his view of the shop's success.

Compelling himself however to accept the fact that the egocentric manner of speech was as insignificant as most of the thoughtless cliches of bourgeois language, Michael in his faltering reply chose to put the best face upon words that might have been construed as an invitation to resign or at least as incitement to lose his temper and give unequivocal cause to be fired, for in his heart he no more wanted it to come to that than Greatrakes did. "It seems to me that the demand for texts is expanding and changing so fast that used textbooks—I mean the pattern will be entirely different—that is, almost every year the books will have to be new—well what I mean is that if Bow's Ark's going to stay competitive I think youre going to have to offer something distinctive along with the compulsory items, and the cheap book market is going to grow faster all the time—" Michael's mind went blank as he groped for diplomatic reconstruction of an elusive argument meant to express the frustration of his indenture to the boss's stupidity. Inarticulate before the eyes of his inarticulate superior, who at least had the defense of property and the prevailing opinion of a trade to guide his passion, he was saved from foundering in subservient exasperation by the interrupting cry of a threatened professional flaring up again:

"Cheap book market! Don't talk to me about the cheap book market! Cheap trash is ruining the market for good books! Paperbacks will drive us all out of business. I'd be a fool to encourage that trend. Every drugstore and supermarket will be the local book mart pretty soon. The publishers will go bankrupt too—all the decent ones . . . It's bad enough when they start selling by direct mail . . . And all this talk about teaching machines and electronic brains—just a bunch of flickering morons, that's what they are! Not to mention educational television. . . . What's doing it is the idealists and communists in Washington. Even Eisenhower can't get the internationalists out of there. . . . Taxes, taxes, taxes—what's the use of being in business?"

[Fishermen in Gloucester, the old Yankee type not much longer on their own hook, maybe not much longer outside the breakwater at all, ranting against the foreign ships bringing in close-packed flagstones of frozen fish—as if the schooners themselves hadnt freighted God-frozen herring bait from the Maritimes every winter! Imports that drive down prices for domestic landings! They have no ear for the prophecy that frozen fish is the only thing that'll save the harbor for fishermen at all, bringing transcontinental trucks to the waterfront and fending off for a couple of decades the most excessively damaging speculations of realtors pimping to the pleasure-seekers, keeping there at least the modern version of the oldest industry in a country of beefeaters, and by way of protection sheltering as a shark shelters his pilot fish the otherwise squeezed-out carriage trade of fresh fish overnight to the Fulton Street version of book stalls. Theyre lucky to be selling anything at all in a country of hearty money-spenders where a pound of fish weighs less than a pound of steak and tastes far less substantial. The fresh-book trade or no book trade at all! —But this old highliner will never go back to cottage shoemaking when his summer's over. . . .]

Michael's fine calculations of return on investment had evaporated at his boss's first attack. His heaviest business theories blew away before contemptuous wrath. Confidence in his commercial style vanished like sunlight in a cloudburst. A boxer who's not a fighter can't argue for his form when face to face with a more serious puncher of whatever effeminate nurturing.

"All the fancy cash registers and double-entry calculators in the world" the sole partner concluded when his hysteria was spent "can't make money for me if I don't get the most I can on every book sold. . . ." His compendious phrases trailed off in a gentle lisp intended to moderate the categorical reprimand.

The amateur business assistant took his final licks in humble sullen silence. It was true that Valentine Greatrakes dealt dispassionately with the myriad succubi that led Michael Chapman astray. But he was thankful to have no worse truth forced upon him. And he was relieved to find that Val's single accusation left unmentioned a number of other bold refinements that might have been laid to his initiative. Not until he was walking away from the shop did his own anfractuous anger rise to its undemonstrative heights. Val had offered to mark the price of every imported book himself—to step in as it were and save the business from an intellectual.

In some slight attempt at friendly chaffing (to show that nevertheless all things considered he didnt want Mickey to quit out of hand) the poor pinched boss contrived another twisted smile and with mashed potatoes in his mouth lobbed a farewell shot: "Good night Mike. Thanks for staying. The only trouble with liberals is that you forget to keep your eye on the ball!" Ha ha. The echoes of this infuriating remark only exacerbated the wage-earner's raging depression, and all the time he waited for his street-car he was muttering his resolution to walk off the job some fine day with a little speech of his own.

[Let the stupid bastard take over everything. The store might take a year or two to go to pot but he'd see what happens to a college bookstore without knowledge taste foresight or mathematics. First few months he may not miss me at all, but sooner or later when he realizes he's got to look for some hardworking responsible foreman he'll wish he still had good old Mickey. Yes indeed, then he'll find out what he has to pay for anyone else he can trust enough to mind the store. . . . And I suppose he expects to keep expanding all by himself! He'll buy nothing but bestsellers. . . .]

HN 4. What is it in Michael's displayed inventory that excited his mania?

The trick is to cleave to reason even while suffering the unreason with which current events are conducted. Michael's method was to magnify his fragments of the universe and bear down upon any of the details that seemed plastic or affinable according to the purposes of his self-adapting plans, of which he shuddered to hear Val do violence to by calling idealistic. He regarded the store's trade books as organically invested with an artificial purpose making no claims to objective dispassion. Any indefiniteness of realization could be explained as a reach exceeding the grasp of aims beyond the bounds of purely architectonic science. Even though he took his constituent particles from the inorganic world he was unwilling to accept the aphorism that he couldnt improve upon nature. (Wasnt evolution itself an anamorphic emergence of meristic structure from lifeless quanta?) Even in logical despair he did not despair of the reason in what he despaired of accomplishing.

[If he'd been reading Gibbon on his trolleycar ride he might have been comforted by the Mohammedan doctrine that "all contradiction is removed by the saving maxim that any text of Scripture is abrogated or modified by any subsequent passage"—a vitalistic and electronic principle further liberalized in application by the fact that the Koran having been written on unnumbered pages and filed without sequence was only randomly retrieved after the programmer had been translated out of this world. It is thus possible to organize the history of another mind by applying your own idea of developmental supersession and then sorting your data thereby. If the Prophet had dated a series of confessions or kept a diary he would have risked the same kind of

---

But now seated in the familiar thwarts of the Key System's slouching capsule of amnion that's beating doggedly out of town to cross an invisible line into the landscape of a much larger city, disabused of illusory success and emptied of intellectual passion, the prudent man begins to gain an upper hand over the demoniac. [It is good not to be fired. This job entails no obligation to play golf or join a power squadron. Now and then I can talk to people who set store by some of the abstractions contained in the merchandise I sell. Besides, in the eyes of the world I am far less qualified for any other banausic job even than St Franz who was trained at the law. Beyond the sound of the Campanile's bells all business is bleak. Don't forget that Ruth and the children hang on me like a double brace of dewlap anchors. Shorn of them I'd cut loose fast enough, free as Caleb Karcist and twice as wise.] But thereupon he starts to review the trichotomous tension he has always so dubiously balanced; and no such survey can fail to reckon his actual and positive accomplishments at Bow's Ark, proven by a succession of pay-raises granted by the irritable proprietor, starting from the lowest pay any gentleman has deigned to work for since St Richard shipped out to California before the mast.

In his vision, stoically and gracefully sustaining all the wounds inflicted by customers, he's erected a lovely organic edifice of books [*HN 4*], each fertile and differentiated cell elegantly assimilated or continually

commitment to history that we see in our Gospels which as myth were among the determinants of Michael's willful psyche in the first place. I am not merely calling attention to the obvious though unlikely possibility that the ordering of a wall of books can represent some of a man's latest taxonomic views: I am speaking of the more general proposition that forms in space can enjoy certain advantages of forms in time as well as forms in time (like sacred literature) can enjoy certain advantages of forms in space. That theory comes to the same thing as Michael's practical conclusions; but as a high-order abstraction of the concept it might have spared him a great deal of mental confusion.}

In his Cambridge grammar-school history books he had loved more than anything else the drawings of Midwest pioneers neatly encamped upon log rafts steered through the promising wilderness down the Ohio to their landing on the Mississippi where the logs that carried them would be sold for a prairie schooner or raised as a barn house on whatever river bank they chose to settle.

His own raft of reason floated on a shoreless sea of storms. No irreversible river decided its course. Tilted to the perpendicular as a wall opposite Lilian's art-supply counter its length was not incalculably greater than the height. But all rafts break up like the sodality of Democrats when it gets too broad for the stresses of their ocean, disintegrating into irregular pontoons or jagged flotsam perhaps barely large enough to support a single anti-intellectual nonRepublican. Michael's problem like Lord Mountbatten's with the rafts of artificial ice that he proposed for Normandy landing docks and airstrips was to determine optimum amounts of controlled accretion from the seawater that his self-refrigerating platform attempted to navigate in. A man sometimes learns too late to fear excessive aggrandizement of the crystalline deck he stands upon. Even the brittle little floe you start from is likely to crack in the middle under strain of flexure when ocean swells lift opposite wings above a trough of waves.

But since his raft of books was placed where its tesserae could be examined individually without inconvenience it was too close for customers to notice its mosaic patterns. Yet some of the public took subconscious pleasure in the galactic variegation of colors and shapes slightly expanding and contracting from week to week in their wide-columned rows, and he himself when not possessed with bitter insights was soothed by the Mesopotamian beauty of the scene. He alone was fully alive to its aesthetic potentiality. Some of his customers like Jack Wolfson knew too much about everything to distinguish between what was focussed and what was left vague in the master-builder's picture: they could find their way through his associations and imbedded indices without ever seeing the deepest design in his bricked wall. Michael was used to making abstract images that were imperceptible to the world and inaccessible to his diffident powers of communication. Thus for him even the middle world of reason was very private.

The art of classifying and deploying books for one's own library is a test of reason that the artificer must always fail simply because the cohesive forces of reason are too weak to organize more than a few ragged clusters of intelligence. Sometimes Michael had to separate one or two redundant copies of a book for purposes of cross-reference. The imported edition of Yeats's *Essays* for example was stored not only in Drama with all the other books by and about the author but also in two other categories, Criticism and Poetry. Likewise he often chose to place an extra copy of a historical or biographical work for discovery at some subjective point in chronological or alphabetical space if it might be overlooked in the knot of object-matter specified by his logic.

But as a rational scheme had to take into consideration the questions of working capital and turnover of investment the fertility of an object-minded brain capable of dealing with ambivalence and ambiguity was more of a frustrating curse than a welcome talent. Granting the stringent fiscal proscription of all but a few duplications of stock he had to face painful decisions (both methodological and metaphysical) in constructing and maintaining his labile wall of bibliography. How to display and search chronologically when some of the mosaic's stones were a thousand years longer than others? Or alphabetically when some had multiple bylines, especially if their titles were without taxonomic or cladistic significance? Which books of each species are most worth preserving for an ark in the flooded marketplace?

More vexing: should he submit all editions to heterogeneous constellations within a single set of galaxies, regardless of physique or commercial mode—or should he yield to tradition with good grace and keep in different bunkers of his bazaar fresh fish frozen fish and canned fish? This the most natural of major segregations—paperback, hardcover, and text—is not to be sneezed at by anyone having at heart the common reader's convenience who likes to narrow down her scanning space to the scale of her means by going directly to the class of commodity she has in mind, so that every title she can afford is within immediate range of temptation or competence: cheap goods generically separated from glossy durables and from weighty thermometer books clad in sharkskin that may repeat reflect or reduce professional information for orthodox consumption. It is also of some direct advantage to a business-minded manager, insofar as those who resist an expensively jacketed edition when placed next to cheap reprint may more readily buy the latter if they remain unaware of their alternative. Under this system of guided merchandising, on the other hand, a browsing scholar is more likely to miss something unique in a neglected section of the inventory and the store's buyer is therefore less likely to enjoy his holophrenia.

When the perceptual groups of arts and sciences are continually shifting their shapes and exchanging energy with each other, ignoring the old boundaries of university departments, how do you determine what new superordinate or annectent classifications to commit your working capital to? Should you interpolate Cybernetics, History of Ideas, Sumerian Studies, or [universal principles of] Design in your mural thesaurus—and dissolve such species as Elocution, Sloyd, and Harness-making? Should you anticipate the revival of Rhetoric? Is typology of method a more reliable guide to the divisions of culture than function or value, and should we for instance eradicate our idea of Art as an otiosely general kingdom of phenomena? Can a single department comprise literature, history, and philosophy; or painting, cartography, and the theory of graphs; or sculpture and job-shop fabrication; or biology and systems theory; or dance and sex; or music and acoustics?

And in any case: how to allocate shelf space in such a way as to accommodate random new acquisitions without having to shift tons of books every few weeks in order to insert new vertebrae at particularly crowded points in the too-well-articulated sea serpent? (Can you trust Poe's cryptanalytical order of frequency e a o i d h n r s t u y c f g l m w b k p q x z j and v for the purposes of a modern library?)

There are no answers you can altogether count on in every mood. You have only the hope of logical tactics within hopeless strategy.

But if reason scarcely passes its test with objects as palpable and immutable as books (petrified manuscripts) it cannot be expected that a man will ever succeed in keeping together a raft even large enough to support his own weight. Michael should be blamed only for the unnecessary illusions with which he usually deceived himself—as for example when in the brightness of this very morning he had fondly gloated over his comparatively simple array of stockkeeping units as if it was a multidimensionally organized and reorganizeable castra of variably classified elements and substructures quantumly continuous taxonomically informative philosophically expressive and eminently amenable to the Syntectic Method of Diagnostic Correlation.

Of course in any business that can be run primarily as an affair of inventory management the rational examination of turnover entails corresponding analysis of purchases and sales. Michael as we know was avidly interested in making statistical studies correlating all data that could possibly be extracted from invoices and sales logs; he enthusiastically envisioned a time when he would be able to assign a catalog number to every book and use it in printing out a cash register tape. Certain digits would signify genus species variety and publisher. While the machine is automatically punching date and time of day why not also enter a code for the customer's sex and race? [It's a wonder he didnt dream of demanding her social security and telephone number!] At the end of the day week month quarter or fiscal year this tape could be used to post sales statistics on the infinitely sortable cards of his stockkeeping master file which recorded commercial facts about each bibliographic unit (including its source and terms of purchase and the cost of its entire Bow's Ark career) and answer almost any question a smart consultant would think of asking about the demographics logistics and home-economics of any or all tiles in the wall.

There was nothing to limit his excitement at the prospect of this gnostic power but an utter collapse of his interest in the game itself. ❑ _____

replaced in its proper tissue. The bones and organs heal biologically, ever more healthy; and despite every adversity the cells multiply among their own kind.

Not that the owner can see this miracle of life. But he realizes that Bow's Ark is a landmark once more, and when he's not in a panicky fret about his overextended capital he seems quite aware that his store's renaissance of academic reputation has had a little to do with its growth. The off-peak trade between the beginnings of semesters used to be nothing at all: time was that a whole year's overhead had to be absorbed by a few weeks of rushed inefficiency crowded behind the counter with ignorant irresponsible scarcely supervised temporary help; and Christmas business was a frothy sham of indecisive shoppers eddied in as overflow from the saturated competition. You are obliged to assume that Val's a man of Leonardo's second category and can see once he's been shown; for it is perhaps too much to believe that as an entrepreneur impressive enough to get commercial loans he does not see at all. (No need in Free Enterprise to see for himself in the first place.) So taking one thing with another it can hardly be doubted that at this very moment despite his determination that no employee will ever learn all the secrets of his business Valentine Greatrakes is bethinking himself of his luck in having Michael Chapman as chief assistant.

Why else indeed does he on his own part and in discipline of the lesser clerks meticulously observe the practice introduced by Michael of registering every fresh and frozen sale in a log kept at the cash register—rather than retain for himself the former rote by which each unit in Mickey's repertory would have been replaced without knowledge or insight—if not to benefit from knowledge and insight that might be lost to his employ? He's hardly shrewd enough to see in his own case, still less in general, that an organism can't perdure as a closed system; or that his present buyer's personal clientele who account for a large share of this lucrative ancillary revenue would never step inside and look at books just to have a word with a Republican proprietor. Yet he must be sufficiently forehanded to understand by now that it would be as inconvenient to negotiate this bewildering mass of culture-symbols without a common reader's help as if he were to start dealing in diamonds without knowing a carat from a flaw.

And again how could it be imagined that this businessman is so blind to the advancements of administrative reason that he can't recognize for instance the new purchasing/receiving/accounts-payable procedures as a clear strand of improvement (replacing the old Brownian bumble) whereby a greatly enlarged volume of transactions is already being processed more smoothly accurately and speedily than a hardheaded practical businessman would have thought possible at any level of overhead investment, operating with fewer man-hours, and man-hours of lower pay-grade to boot—almost solely on the slim motivation and meager talent of Sam the softheaded non-enterprising revolutionary aesthete?

One should further assume that the capitalist is capable of enough abstract and introspective reflection to perceive that efficiency in the necessary evil of paperwork during this period of flattering prosperity contributes a relative saving in overhead perhaps equivalent in profit to another five percent in gross dollar volume and goes a long way toward paying for the blunders in canned book-buying that follow from his own "experienced" way of anticipating enrollment trends in higher education, of approximating Bow's Ark's share of the market, and of estimating the force of habit in the dictation of course texts by professors. Even if the intelligence and imagination required to appreciate pragmatical possibilities in S M D C cannot be expected of that illiberal brain one must suppose that for the purposes of earnings it will at least count the pennies saved. . . .

And so from the very depths of his grame the petty officer's will to power flares up from the ashes of former enthusiasm and delivers him from frozen despair. A certain urge of initiative will not die in his heart as long as life is worth living. For as we know from Plato any life of value cannot remain unexamined: no sooner does Michael examine his talent for administration and compare it with the common man's than he is seized once again with a renewal of bureaucratitis and deprived of the spiritual enlightenment he has so briefly sunk into. Yea, to his higher but deferred sorrow, the minute he touches bottom in ignoble defeat, when he well might say to hell with all little schemes and the macrosystem too, and take up cigarettes again in the conviction that he's only a broken-down villein earning no better than vicious pleasures (especially as he's now past the median age of American males), he begins by rational contemplation to rise again on the buoyancy of his fat. With the last remnants of wisdom he makes as if to anchor his feet; but nothing will prevent the healthy ascent toward a bright blue surface where winds are raised that make the nostrils flare and classic battles of the sea are drawn.

In short the depressed man (if not the angry one) is a spurious false front for the holomaniac who returns again and again in a variety of guises to occupy the hollow of his mask. He can no more suppress this pneumatic ascent when it's wearisome and hateful, when there's no pleasure in it, when he's fully conscious of its delusory narcosis, than when it seems an afflatus of intellectual beauty that need only undergo certain voltage transformations to make itself felt in the nation's management of collective destiny. Rocking along in a hollow ship of the streets his embered anger glows again, this time more slowly and deeply, not at Greatrakes or at any outward condition of his own livelihood, not at the economic civilization of his country, but at the wasteful manifestation of his incurable compulsion to promulgate efficiency in practicable life. The organ that suffers and betrays this affliction is the brain, which for him serves as the seat of many functions ordinarily attributed to the heart. [Mr Manager give me peace. Down man, down I say!] But the fever roused therein cannot be quelled or exorcised without quelling or exorcising the steam to make a living.

Thus the American genie bursts this one vessel of its circulation without orgastic resolution of its scalar desire. Over and over again Michael has proved to Mr M that it's folly to spend his life trying to interfere even with a single destiny. [Oh I know, I know, I know. . . .] Yet there's no relief from the torment of will-to-power save in conditional surrender to Mr M's hegemony, a meretricious and addictive remedy at best, leading into an infinite series of small temptations—or else by demanding the fanatic and undivided ambition to deliver a championship punch for which perfection is not required. Since total dedication is out of the question in Michael's case he must resign himself to a petit mal of rebellious or disjaskit rages whenever he tries to escape Mr M's dominion without substituting Mr P's.

It is still a few minutes before that wolf will arouse himself to chase away the fox now eating at his bowels. The weather of his mind rarely changes instantaneously. He is still no further along his road than the CHAPEL OF THE RECESSIONAL. He stares glumly through the steel grid of his window at the neon already outstanding in twilight. Under the sign of that inn the chaplain who operates it in NON-DENOMINATIONAL tolerance has been and will be eulogizing many a mediocre puncher exactly as he praises the losers and winners. It is Berkeley's largest mortuary, well located on the Lane close to the city line, near enough to its Oakland competitors not to miss behind-the-scenes bids in that larger market. Those who have been charneled through this stained-glass organ-sighing parishless church without its own yard as their public station on the way to grave or furnace are claimed to be happy about what they have accomplished.

The memento mori is not vivid enough to silence Mr M at once, but it does remind him of other difficulties in the human universe, or at least of certain philosophical problems. However the trolleycar has no call to stop near the establishment, and before he can veritably reexamine the edifice of death he is borne over the line into his own city where the streets can be counted by their arithmetically descending names (the first being not much more than double the number he lives on), for even in the 19C letters failed the tedium of undistinguished topography. Unlike the cataloged numbers for green ships of war these are ordinal and fixed by space. Despairing even of proper nouns Dr Merritt of Plymouth Massachusetts yielded to operational efficiency in laying out the civic carpet.

But our observer does not ride past this landmark so fast that the sight of it fails to change the subject to some extent, or at any rate to direct the subject toward the matter of personal eschatology at which all possible subjects converge. All the year round on his daily tangents he wheels back and forth past this morbid agnostic laboratory and several others like it with such impunity that he seldom takes notice, but despite the presentational immediacy of his persuasion that no god envies his glory he has just been undeceiving himself as to the reversibility of his personal progression toward some such bourn. The all-too-seemly funeral parlor is premature terminal for many a wheeled life supposed to be detained above ground by all sorts of obligations relating to the protection of a dependent family against disease accident crime poverty and political misfortune. Money sometimes seems to insulate, but no insulation of power or possessions can do more than slow up the leakage of vitality. Yet almost everyone he knows though not as childlike as himself is young in outlook. Usually death seems no more certain than a chance statistic or a dereliction on the part of a medical constabulary. The daily business even of a scholar leaves little leisure for images of the end, and even less in Michael's life encourages the study of his own final cause.

Frank thought of human fate lifelessly embodied in his own dispersonated atoms or in flesh belonging to him by sacrament falls beyond the pale of his ordinary bravery. At this moment the word for death and the idea of its vacuum revives his uncritical opinion that he of all men deserves utmost longevity; yet mere reference to that tenet conjures up a proleptic complex of gloomy antitheses founded in deliberate suspicion of the biographical irony he's always been banking on: in other words it raises the concretion of absolute and everlasting failure. Thus the well-cultivated superstition that he usually keeps at bay through sheer preoccupation is sometimes admitted by wound or derangement long enough to warn him of absolute disappointment.

Perhaps then it's in mere apotropaic credulity that he now calls up generous sentiments for a venal old man come to the store a day or two past—a patron of extraordinary age at a mart for youngsters who do not yet own all the books they will ever wish to see. Is Michael capable of sympathy only when aroused by fresh perception of a state [FN 1] that he himself cannot eventually avoid? Whenever he envisions the coffin of a man soon to be dead rolling silently down the aisle and expeditiously back again into the hearse like a ball-bearinged file drawer and out once more for the last time at the lychless cemetery, gliding even unto the edge of the

---

FN 1. At a distance he looked slow but sound. Closer: still fresh and trim, good teeth, fine white hair, neat waggish goatee; but the first-rate clothes of old style had grown too loose at the waist chest shoulders and neck of the ramrod skeleton. Closer yet: a tripod turtle shrinking within its shell and fearing nothing so much as being set upon its back. The aluminum cane had a rubber sole. "Young man I'm ninety-seven years old and I go to the library every day but there's one book I want to buy." He wasted no time browsing. My displays made no impression on him. He spoke as confidently as if he'd come to ask for a rather lean lamb chop and an Idaho potato, not boasting about his endurance but simply explaining himself in a strange neighborhood. It was only by the wildest stroke of luck that I a biped was able to supply his want.

The acquisitive old codger had come in for a new book called after its subject *The Art of When to Buy on the Big Board* and subtitled as a new approach to the stock market. He must have already studied a fair number of arcane theories on the increase of talents, most of them no doubt pretending to emphasize the pains one must take to come out ahead. The price of the book didnt bother him at all. With measured but unhesitant motions he fished his money from an oldfashioned purse with a twisted brass clasp, then refused a paper bag in which to carry his purchase and went down the street as steadily as he had come up it, clearly familiar with everything he was likely to encounter, taking no notice of the courtesy he was accorded by any of the thronging lecturers smart girls and latterday Franciscan bohemians who deferred to him on the sidewalk, the book easily secure in his left hand hanging straight down.

They say he's a retired professor of industrial engineering. His economy of motion almost made me laugh aloud in his face by putting me in mind of the sharp little man in the straw hat who likes to spice up his act with a little economics between more serious routines: as he shuffles across the stage on his way to the racetrack, counting greenbacks with his cane hooked over his arm and ostensibly unaware of the love-goddess emerging from the wings to take his place in the limelight, he distinctly murmurs I HOPE I BREAK EVEN—I SURE NEED THE MONEY!

Is it possible that margin requirements and tax loopholes for capital gains will complicate the academic engineer's last feelings? St Willie in his wheelchair was still reworking the poetics of the western world. Bow's Ark's special customer is much older and healthier. Perhaps he's making bold investments for the sake of his heirs. Or else it's become for him the jewel of games, played with paper and pencil and daily quotations to manage a counterfactual portfolio for the fun of it. Either way, whatever the excuse, abstractions like money are undoubtedly closer to his soul than materialized children of his own or of his own's own. To the Incas according to St William Prescott gold was "tears wept by the sun"—concretely immortal. Their kind of avarice is easier to sympathize with, even when it's too late in a civilization to convert the teardrops into art. (In Philadelphia there's a Philological architect who designs his cast-in-place concrete as "spent light".)

Having been willing to defer most gratifications so long, such shrewd old men possessing securities and pensions have lived long enough to despise all but one obsession. They still arent wise enough to see the fatuity of their smug common sense when it refuses to give up its game in favor of prolonging the struggle for posthumous fame, which even the profligate short-lived saints who die young still unwilling to defer anything pleasant, their work not half finished, hold more precious than all ephemeral prizes put together.

Thus I judge, even in despair of the future itself and fearing that our posterity can be found only in the past. An artist whose work is not advisedly convertible into golden tears may enjoy a virtual reputation among the saints that have gone before. The Muses will require to be shown what can be done during the collapse of humanity when perhaps they're the only ones interested in a fame that will remain busheled till the end of reversible time. The hard thing is to register the evidence before you die. As you grow old the prospect of recorded proof gets dimmer—no matter how chipper you often get from confidence that you're capable of it.

Now there's something Spengler (unlike White Jacket) did not grasp—believing that if Goethe had died young *Faust* would still have "been" even though it "lacked the poet's elucidation"! The supersophisticated historian failed to see the difference between proven art and its potentiality, which Tolstoy could have taught him by the old Christian interpretation of life as the one probation. In aging you resolve too much of life's uncertainty and leave too much of art's. You have proved your mediocre history at the expense of freedom to prove what's ageless. You find yourself more and more boxed in—until the young crowd you into the last box as your fitting nutshell.

Whatever their last wishes stick to—property kinfolk God or even one of the Muses—the very oldest men live their indefinite closing years as fatherless tripeds unfathering and presumably disfeathered of most other illusions, pale-minded and forgetful, no longer mathematical or analytic but waveringly confident in the intuition bequeathed by experience, on the postponed verge of eternal faithlessness. Only the most fortunate of their cohort's surviving minds are absorbed in that which finally turns out to have been their life's true vocation, utterly expunging their career in the world if it has not answered exactly the same call.

I long for longevity because I defer too long. There are living saints no older than I! Will I be able to swear, when life begins to abandon my limbs, that mine was the only way for me? At present I still too much extol the value of maximum touch when I should be troubling myself about maximum objective survival. The subjective advantage over successful rivals and leaders that secretly comforts those of even doubtful future fame dissolves like every other premium at the last spasm. But maybe servants of God are the most disappointed, objectively speaking. Maybe all who suffer in person—women, victims, subjective failures—have the only objective vision.

Nonetheless when I ponder the question as carefully as ignorance permits it's hard to reject the presumption that acquisitive psyches will suffer the greatest shock. I wonder what their foresight consists of. Maybe like the Nurenberg Chronicle they keep reserving six blank pages for their remaining history and then in their gaming for pelf deliberately forget their doom until it takes them by as much surprise as possible. But how can that kind of play last beyond the beginning of old age's exploratory pains? Death is less shocking but more painful for the prehensile mind that's never had the reach or muscle to do justice to its aggression. Think of poor Doctor Sam (no saint of mine) his prayer to be pardoned by God when he would "render up, at the last day, an account of the talent committed".

At the onset of your last scotomy all models fade. When you know you've had your last meal you can't recall any of the laws you lived by—even though you are still able to repent the foolish objects you lived for. Games become absurd when the rules are questioned.

> A game's a game
> All the same:
> You'll have no fame
> Like Crazy Jane!

The soul that all its life hasnt chosen to sense anything but what affected its pride or success, does it feel its ending any more than others do? That old man with whom I conducted a transaction will take his practical book to the worms with him, open face-down under cross-spread wrists pressed snug by the plush silk lid of the casket like a graduation watch. He'll have been seized unshriven in some crammed den of ambition decorated with framed trophies little less abstract than his major spoils, maybe carried off during a splenetic throe of hatred for my party or for a public person dear to me, a curse upon reform rattling in his worn-out throat as he reads the front pages of the New York Testament, which he's already studied the Business section of. How can I remain indignant at such a Republican in that strait? Pity for myself washes away my hatred for that hatred of his.

Pliny says Aeschylus died of a turtle dropped on his bald head by an eagle. It might have happened sooner, when there was still a full head of hair. It can happen to me, seagull dropping a mussel, before Caleb's written his first tragedy. I don't yet have confirmed cause to envy any public life except (maybe) that of a future President—but every day that I live reduces the small probability that I'll be able to say as much with my dying breath. . . . I *must* waste less time, waste less time—*waste less time*! I don't have time for chronicles, neither mine nor

grave on unobtrusive rubber swivel wheels which have taken the place of men's shoulders for burial-box portages, it is on closer examination the Chapman body therein. When he meets such an old buzzard he can't help jumping to the conclusion suggested by old age unless he's too busy to pay him any heed at all. But it's a mortal blasphemy to pray for the soul of a body still living; and to wish the body dead is a vulgar sin. . . .

Yes rubber wheels, not so distant cousin to streetcar wheels of steel and creaking wheels of fortune and timbered water wheels—or wheeling heavens from any point of view: Revelations, Apocalypse. Wheels within a wheel within a wheel!

> The big wheel runs by steam,
> The little wheel runs on gasoline.

Roger rides on wheels, Roger will die on wheels. Womb-to-tomb wheels; from the cradle to the grave we're windowless cyclopeds.

No. Not windowless in childhood he mutters to himself staring through the window for all its worth. In the aging process opacity gathers like body hair to shade the transparent skin. But Mr S (the savant within) tells him that he can't judge the casing of an old man's soul at first sight without extreme fallibility. It's no easier than guessing the feelings of a brightly clothed girl when glimpsed but once with her best foot forward in competitive society, having not so much as her name to go by. He allows that knowing either such object a little better (but still without the

---

Rome's nor Egypt's, let alone South America's: no more than I have for France and the French, for chess, for astronomy, for chemistry; nor for Tarot cards or the precious symbullisticism of gnostic psychology; not even for music, or the verse of saints and friends. I skip all that—yet still I have no time!

. . . . Yet I continually forget to feel my case! I postpone the agony like a critic talking about his philosophy of art instead of its works. Would I be better off if at this moment without kids or wife I were roistering toward a death of booze and inspirational drugs with St Jean-Louis and his kith across the Bay? Perhaps. St Alfred's all too right when he says primordial value comes not with preservation but with intensity. But it's too late for a new strategy.

I now have no choice but to resist the temptation of saying to hell with my life it's all over anyway and tobacco can't do me any more harm than it already has. Yet it's not too late to skip rope every day just because new women are out of the picture; I've got to live as long as possible in full possession of my bladder bowels and reason if I'm not to die unbegun. I mustn't be afraid to admit that my carcass has become as lazy as a city dog, old too soon from nothing to do between matings but flee or fight, likely to drop dead if I had to run a mile. Some jazz players can blow continuously from the belly while they replenish air through their nose. That kind of physical culture is not to be despised by a self-deluding entelechtual. ❑

HN 5. *What are Michael's reservations about neo-orthodoxy?*

He thinks it is only philosophy, the anachronism of its last two syllables notwithstanding, that will mainly advance psychology. [One might have expected this philosopher to have perceived the Last Dispensation, from within its web, as a new organon—not to regard it with ever-differentiating lamentation. But even tonight he would have obstinately defended his arguments if anyone had tried to take advantage of his mood.] To wit: received psychoanalysis, like obstetrics a maieutic profession unconcerned with preventive medicine, is founded upon human variations consolidated and generalized. All syndromes shake down to half a dozen monistic fallacies. If I have an Oedipus complex, says he to himself, so has every other man who reads the last testament; if I love death, so does everyone else in my civilization; if I suffered birth trauma . . . Therefore the personality expressed in bewildering sensitivities in agonizing compensatory behavior in ostentatious despair in ruling passions in privileged humors in social crochets or in any other reactive outering (conscious preconscious subconscious or unconscious) should be treated—or better yet dismissed—as a bundle of composited deviations that are no more or less significant of the human subject/object than diversities of body. . . .

———

benefit of a glass panel in their skull or chest) he might criticize somewhat differently—more pleasantly or less; but he insists that learning more he may either revert to his first judgment, every iota of prejudice confirmed, or with no greater than equal probability form a new estimate without resemblance to the first. He argues before his own bench the fatuity of trying to know a person by observation as a journalist does for lack of some history of responsibility to or for her under a variety of pleasant and painful conditions as boss subordinate or copesmate with wide spaces of time to season all influences at their own shambling pace, which is far slower than the hotshot process of induction that intelligence too much shortens.

In this manner he often justifies his laziness in arriving at impartial judgment on the evidence. With a chip on his shoulder he admits that nothing interests him less than tolerant fairminded study of character. Let time dilapidate his passion or dispel his indifference as destiny may require: he'll be the most generous of disputants in acknowledging his mistakes. Meanwhile he doesnt care to advance psychology psychologically [HN 5].

Shrunken and timid but briefly secure in his paid pew the introspective commuter talks and listens to himself that he may take at least the small satisfaction of one perfectly conversant companionship, albeit that in a trolleycar moving through a world of imperfect men he cannot hope to lecture a council of lesser Michaels like the archangel's double standing on a bottom rock of hell. He savors the supine freedom that came with impotence of will. Right now will is possessed by an uncomplicated hunger for meat and potatoes. The refinement of his body is degraded in organization and vibration almost to the level of the inelastic seat that supports its

[He approached psychology like a metamathematician, letting the unconscious represent the innermost system—not the broadest but the most enclosed. Of course this notion seems to contradict his efforts to build up counterentropic rafts of reason (objective consciousness), for it suggests not that reason tosses in a storm of disorder but the converse: that the unconscious floats in a sea of consciousness. His alternating opinion, which could fairly be called a radical inconsistency, grew out of the intuitive understanding (in an objectively deterministic world) that distinctively human action, called forth and directed by the mind at least in the superconsciousness of art, evolves from the natural will—which is thus and only thus made free. He would have replied to his critics that irony opens the innermost to the outermost system and reverses their ontological situations according to the genre of discourse; that you are free only when like Hamlet and Oedipus (seen philosophically) you subsume the values of your inescapable culture. Prometheus too. This whole epiphenomenon of Michael's mental existence is related to the inversions of form and the eversions of content in dynamic works of art. The point is that whatever reconciles a man to such inconsistencies is his religion—his largest system of all, the one that he hardly thinks of. Before he dies it may or may not reconcile his reasons rationally.] ❏ _____

practically inert weight. But the conceits of his moping mind can still speed a million times faster and in infinitely more directions than any transcontinental express highballing eastward a hundred times more steadily than the trundling tram in its dawdle down the lane.

The habitual traveler, impassive and opaque, is uncannily trained to ride without looking (if he chooses to read or close his eyes) until he reaches exactly his own point on the thoroughfare, subconsciously compensating for irregularities of transit due to agitations of the myrmidonian traffic through which his vessel must make its somewhat inflexible way. But now piercing the solid and populous banks of the avenue as if for aesthetic fenestration comes an interlucation that this bourgeois voyageur rarely fails to appreciate even when oscillating between destinations without otherwise focusing his eyes at a greater distance than eighteen inches. This is where the roving roadbed of the Sacramento Northern slices obliquely across the domestic trolley rails. [At the intersection of these paired parallels the passenger on his urban shuttle often tries to imagine the fleeting exposure of his own Teleology Lane to the romantic passengers who once rode out of the hills and down to the Bay. In the words of St Alexis, "Man springs out of nothing, crosses time, and disappears forever in the bosom of God; he is seen but for a moment, wandering on the verge of two abysses, and there he is lost."] On the way home this crossing marks Michael's halfway point in time though less than half his distance remains, for because the car is more frequently interrupted in the approach to London-town it loses all but its primitive resemblance to the highballers that thunder-roll the prairie rights-of-way. (The tracks themselves

HN 6. Why is Michael fascinated by railroads?

A man may understand this technology without quite fathoming his feelings about it, yet Michael living in the glow of its declining years is beginning to discern the mandorla of a principle which over the years he has struggled to identify. The question does not yield to frontal attack. Little irregular twists of clarification are fortuitously jiggled into sight during the most irrelevant speculations—not when he is inspecting tracks or admiring their rolling stock—since plenary excitement leaves no room for reflection. The following thoughts for instance have arisen from two previous occasions perhaps a week apart, developing in tandem but with a good deal of mutual modification, so that the consequences of one could no longer be distinguished from the consequences of the other: once on the way home from work when reading Saint Fyodor (son of Michael) he found the network of European railroads referred to as "the star that is called wormwood" (representing "the whole tendency" of humanistic progress), a Russian elaboration of the horror forecasted by Henry David Thoreau (no saint for this reader); and once setting out in mousegray mornlight under a fresh afflatus of reason when his memory

---

are common: though in the one system imbedded in pavement and in the other ballasted clear above the footpath of gandy dancers they are intercommunicable fabrications of the same constant specification [*HN* 6]).

Michael dismisses negligible worry about the only accident there is to fear at this point on the local rails: a berserk electric locomotive charging out of its alley to crush the germane vessel making passage on the street and thus to silence the busy brain sitting midway down its belly on the near side. [Here his reference is to St Herman: "In Shakespeare's tomb lies infinitely more than Shakespeare ever wrote."]

But the lapsed person still falters in the null moment between rapidly faded sensitivity and illusive mastery not yet recovered, drifting in and out of self-speech, neither carefree slave nor guiding master of his freely chosen thoughts. Indeed it's a poor way to live, leaving the mind to do your living for you, with no other servants at all, while you float in your concoction of sickly reason—mixed at best with feelings stirred by lively appetites but never seasoned with so much as a crocodile's exudation of poetry. . . .

Now his motionless eyes solemnly regard the double chins faithfully imitated in darkened glass, and beneath them the protuberant belly; for with the fading of the sky his window has become a mirror to the dull lights inside his noisy ship, which has turned itself into a vectored lantern sporadically hauling its horizontal grid of facets through a city amazingly softened by the day's gradual quit-claim. Indeed he must shade his brow and definitely peer if he is to recognize any shapes outside the homeostatic cage save those that intervene in other windows moving through the virtual bulbs and self-images of his looking-glass. Reflection dominates the cityscape. Behind himself in the picture stretches a gallery of advertising panels illuminated by the starboard bank of overhead lamps changing position in the larger space of time as he rides stationary in the locomotive system of coordinates. . . .

drifted for a minute or two back to the days he had to drive an unreliable automobile that almost swamped his overloaded barge of fiscal responsibility and to steal most of every day's sweetest energy simply in getting to the store from a settlement behind the Oakland hills on a steep wooded bank where Ruth on behalf of baby Jonathan had claimed to suffer too much shade and loneliness above the electrified track of the bravely dwindling Sacramento Northern where it pulled slowly up the canyon to burrow the tunnel giving out onto the sunset-lighted basin of the Bay and kept him longing with far more melancholy than he spent on the Medici for the old commuter trains that would have carried him still rapt by the corona of sunrise-catching redwoods right down to this very transfer point on the broad buzzing Lane where the clever intersection of wires above and rails below formed the schematic diagram of an aqueduct taking a canal across a river.

Michael has marveled like millions before him but more doggedly than most at the pleasure of observing and using a transcontinental mechanical institution that has produced the nation by which it was produced under the star emblematic of bitterness and gall to poets who saw through progress a century ago. (It seems to him not the star of rails but of infernal combustion that they were groping to prophesy who were no less mistaken than the Three Wise Men as to the historical nature of what they descried.) He defends the railroads of his country almost as he defends the Constitution in explanation of what he's patriotic about (even though he understands it is only the latter that can buck up for a little while longer the hope for justice without the hope of church), inasmuch as the railroads of the United States are not simply the arteries of its industry but also its ontogenetic skeleton, having preempted most of the calcium assimilated by the voracious states—diverting capital from canals, alienating passengers from riverboats, discalcing stagecoach horses—and given our muscle the shape of our prime; and for that very reason we of all sovereignties are most vulnerable to the osteopathological maladies characteristic of degenerate phases.

But his own fascination still puzzles him. It's really a megalomaniacal desire, which as its object shrinks will not yield to newer technological appetites. Though you might think the explanation could be found in a chronic general nostalgia the craving is acutely artifactual—not universal and primitive like gynolagnia but a little like a man's enchantment with guns. The object of admiration is durably palpable, imperial and willful but controllable, normalized but flexible, ritualistic, and thoroughly conditioned by childhood play: too ingrained to be further analyzed. At any rate this particular reiterated glimpse of the Sacramento Northern property brings forward from his history of mysterious pleasures the combined notions of channeled power, standardization, and travel:—

All the tracks he has ever ridden except the old Narrow Gauge from East Boston's ferry slip to Revere Beach with hard varnished straw seats are four feet eight and a half inches, the clearance between inner walls of the angle plates used to guide the wheels of standard 17C wagons still drawing coal in England when steam began to replace horsepower—before the flange was forged on the wheel itself in order to reduce friction by rolling on the head of the rail. So to this day the wormwood system has never freed itself of measurements laid down for horses, even now that horseless carriages off the rails have bred themselves into a shape hardly similar to that of a classic coach. Michael rejoices that our tracks are wider than the Japanese but regrets that they are narrower than the Russian the Spanish some of the superseded lines in Maine and the old Great Western out of Paddington Station, for a full 5 feet or more would have improved stability and made it possible in our spacious land (granted to the barons in broad strips practically free of charge) to increase the loading gauge and thereby improve in width the cubic advantage of freight cars over trackless trucks—despite the fact which even he's willing to admit that it's too late to advocate a change of convention.

Now his all-too-familiar tracks are intersecting the Sacramento Northern without communication but somewhere in the distant yards there are switches that connect the domestic line to this romantic one, and to all others of standard gauge if not to the ghosts of those deceased. In counterfactual history Bow's Ark's books might have been shipped to the door by rail from the Times Square subway platform. He might have been riding home from work in a club car. He might have taken his family in this covered wagon right to the heart of Gloucester, and on to the salt flats behind Good Harbor Beach. The Pullman shit that has been sparsely spewed at high speed onto neatly graded crushed stone might also have been dropped like horse manure on the cobblestones of downtown cities.

By putting your ear to the burnished steel of any street railway in California you should still be able to sense wheels on the wharves of Boston. Through these constantly parallel lines of transport the impulses of Oakland could be telegraphed clear across the Mississippi the Hudson and the Annisquam River when its drawbridge is down. The same velocipede on which he would like to pump himself back and forth to the store might be worked from the Pacific to the Atlantic over the facilities of a hundred different corporations, routed by track not yet untimely ripped. (At home he has inspired Jonathan to draw well-equipped prairie-schooner cabooses for the family to migrate in.) The very first railroads were ruts paved by the Greeks for their gods (or their marble blocks) to journey to the coast on: sacred roads. 19C men themselves were more god-like than they knew when the exact paths of self-powered machines were determined by their arbitrary or shortsighted forethought.

When we stopped laying new track the marrow began to decay in our backbones and all our growth was put into bulges of fat that added sensory surface but no strength to the national weight. The body of the transportation system continues to spread in rosy smiling flesh, not according to value or efficiency but in obedience to the assimilative cunning of its greediest parts, while without a cry the inner skeleton begins to suffer the painless ravages of shrinkage and osteoporosis. In its ethical blindness our economy has given in without protest to the phony self-indulgent expediencies whose results pass in the public mind for evolutionary necessity. The trackless vehicles now swarming the bestial floor of America (Michael complains) make no noble or rational apology for following you to every village and yard, along beaches, up mountainsides, into the forests; their momentums are capricious with the whims or petty motives or vulgar ambitions of their myopic drivers, who subordinate their own political suffrage to the liberties of the machines they operate. The self-contained and unarticulated automobile makes people feel free as they enslave themselves to its maneuverability. It renders men women and children a plethora of power to abuse human freedom. Those who keep their reason amid the promiscuities of this myriad demon are swamped at every voting by wheeled centaurs male and female. [See *HN 7* hereinafter.]

Yet it is not reason that imbues Michael with the love of railroads. He's tolerably sympathetic to rational emprise, as you've seen, but also perfectly aware that reason in railroading is pretty well confined to the scope of its mechanical civil and electrical engineering, and to the construction of intricate timetables that are interesting enough in themselves but for intellectual achievement easily outdone in other manifestations of industrial and military technology. No, his desire and his disappointments are no more technical than a master-builder's passions, nor yet architectonic in the aesthetic sense of that term; his yearning is systemically and historically ekistical, configured and reconfigured with galactic and ganglionic images of place. All with the outlook of a pedestrian who loves to ride!

Even during the most brutal and avaricious haste of national implosion (when both ends were being thrown toward Promontory Point in the middle for Leland Stanford to fasten with his golden spike only twenty years after the Gold Rush began) the railways were building the mostly standard-gauge conglomeration of segments and snatches that in the end coalesced took joint root and knitted into one carpeted flag all the knots and creases of the land. On the rails of this akoluthic network you could run a locomotivated train of cars from the handspiked turntable at Pacific Grove just west of the Monterey station to the little potbellied crane planted in the ground to unload steel for the Cape Ann Tool Company at the Atlantic end of the country just east of its easternmost turning loop—threading an amphictyony of irrational jurisdictions and local interests without once having to lay your hand on a steering wheel or tiller. The trucks of your faithful engine's tender and its suite swivel like the bogies of logging sledges as they follow your power clicking through switches and clacking along trestles at any speed you choose. That's as near as Michael can get to the mystery of his fascination.

But now once again his general desires and disappointments are absorbed by special sorrow for iron horses and anger at their exterminators. His power-plant would carry an open fire, its steam-traction modulated without altering the flame; but at this very moment of the century's oil rush the reciprocating pistons driven by water vapor are being finally replaced by sealed engines rotating at inhuman speeds, by the tortional eccentricity of discontinuous internal explosions—on the ironically disingenuous plea of efficiency by General Motors. Though for railroads mounted on noble frames, to Michael who has suffered their noxious exhaust at sea these cacodemonic inventions of a melancholy German are nothing but formidably magnified improvements upon the demanding slaves steered by private citizens. The cruelty of our railroad empire's wholesale conversion from great open-air cylinders of steam to hidden blocks of sparkless pumps totally lacking in melodic rhythm will soon be complete. No reformation has ever apostasied with so little controversy.

Happy indeed the poet who had only the mechanics of steam engines to baffle his competence, for thermodynamics could easily have been added to the quadrivium of classical education without spoiling a bachelor's sensibility. To think that only a hundred years ago such a one fretted about steam cars rattling within earshot of Walden Pond! ❏

HN 7. What's Michael's general attitude toward the governing class?

He's more inured than impervious to the automobocracy. Yet his sensitivity to the regime has not been worn below the threshold of irritability, and when his perturbations are not forestalled by constructive hopes or crowded out by other negative affections to which he's susceptible (such as hatred of the plague [*HN 8*]) his chronic hostility to the rule of automobiles discovered itself equal to the narrowminded revulsion of radically impressionable Neothoreauvians against all Technology. Still, his behavior has grown too habitual and wry—ostensibly phlegmatic—to betray the latent violence in his contemplation of infernal consumption engines as most commonly employed, even when he is subjected to extreme personal provocation (as for example on trying to cross a busy street without the benefit of a traffic signal, on observing the ceaseless strings of insensate motor trucks hauling across open country loads of freight that could well be carried by rail or water if worth carrying at all, or on being arrested by advertisements of petrochemical energy put to conspicuously wasteful consumption of leisure), except when a car run by some criminally negligent elector wheels full tilt into his street from the Lane squealing with the centrifugal friction of rubber taking the corner too fast and narrowly missing (it seems to him) one of his children: in which case he screams an inarticulate cry of com-

---

Anyway what's the profit in recovering your good spirits during the age of the last dispensation that's as common to Jews Christians and Moslems as the book of Genesis? His Teleovision panel is rife with speedy abrupt motions bearing or obstructing the informationless graphics of commerce. The darker it gets the more vividly do trivialities of the least import light upon the retina of an exhausted soul. It's soothing to ride with a fixed platoon of particolored plaques and pictures. Yet tonight's travel is imbued with the renewed horror of his helpless position before them. Flat dismay cramps even the welling passion for his children which every evening, rivaling hunger, dominates the last few minutes of his decompression.

At the broad junction of MacArthur Boulevard the docile tub waits to take its turn across the presumptuous stream of headlighted slaves swarming home from the greater city in implacable columns under the reins of their competitive hermit crabs. As the common carrier resumes its motion the humiliation of having deferred to such an upstart mainstream is compounded for its elite passenger by the mirrored vision of forward-pressing double-eyed demons pressing inland three abreast in serried chiliads from the distant Bay Bridge, glaring their impatient resentment at the ancient right of passage still due at a cattle-crossing, the endless triple line tensely coiled for one more moment before it springs after its preceding section— which at the same moment presents an attentive watcher through the same advertising glass hundreds of small red lights speedily receding in unison under so many tail fins. [*HN 7*]

But tonight this commonplace horror of demotic totalitarianism doesnt penetrate Michael's inner armor. He has learned by induration how

bined fright warning and threat, adding under his breath (that the child may not hear him) in a manner usually reserved for inanimate objects that jump out of his hand or for deeds of his own stupidity: great gray green jumping christ you lousy shitheeling bloody pighumping mothertonguefucking son of a writhing fat usurious sidewinding Republican copywriter—and even if the driver turns out not to be a white man.

On the present occasion he has little time to pass his sociological opinions in review, but his partial analysis of the time he lives in can be summarized as follows: Yahoovian exploitation of the mechanical population has brought about an unprecedented multiplication and distribution of horsepower without the old obligations of feudalism or livery. No one is expected for instance to baptize the serfs he buys newborn or mature, nor in reckoning the commonwealth's levy to count their souls as live. The temptation to abuse personal mastery of a whole cavalry is too much for a person's self-control when free of the responsibility for feeding grooming harnessing and shoveling up after perishable slaves. Inwardly our voters are perhaps no more selfish or shortsighted than any generation of ancestors—but the easy horsepower at their private disposal as well as on many a job turns them en masse into a numberless army of despotic C P O s full of fury at the notion of civil rights or constitutional liberty for pedestrian minorities.

So the highways storm through arable land and bulldoze stone walls for parking lots and storefronts. It's no longer possible to travel under trees or along back fences, or to see roadsides cut as cleanly as a rail bed, for rubbish more polluting and certainly less useful than horseshit overflows the right-of-ways and blurs any demarcation between highwaymen and law-abiding farmers; cars can stop anywhere at will to expectorate fuck eat or take pictures, and they don't stop at all to do their littering. Shining new real-estate puddles bleed out anywhere, making crossroads where none existed. Artificial swamps of domeless pleasure are located where hills once stood, attracting instead of delivering the carriage trade. The forces of dynamite and petroleum turn landscape into plastic. Without sweating ditch-diggers or even steam shovels, almost without supervision, driven not by whips or threats of chastisement but by nervous spasms, great yellow toads wheeled like toys or treaded like battle tanks incessantly butt and scrape their aggressive shields, campaigning with noise, leveling and filling, bullying turnpikes and homogeneous tracts out of hills immutable whilome, straightening rivers burying brooks stanching the tides of marshes, paving with crushed stone and boiling tar what used to be plowed with the power of thoughtfully clumping horseshoe cleats.

The problem he would set for social psychologists in the symbiosis of an animal unable to love its own species and its paired slave (in lieu of nearly two hundred exquisitely sensitive horses), brought into existence with no nervous system to love with, is to explain the cruelty with which the faithful machines are abused. Their useful lives are shortened by jockeys' unsympathetic demands for cold acceleration, stupidly fluctuated velocities, gruelling competition with their own kind, sleepless readiness, inordinate patience with human stupidity, passive submission to banging bumping freezing boiling duty, voiceless tolerance of medical neglect—and sometimes ended suddenly by deceleration a thousand times too abrupt for the inertia of steel. In the movies these chattel are treated without respect or consideration, often sacrificed like laboratory rats; it has become as habitual to ignore their feelings as it once was to ignore the sensibility of horses. There is some unidentified compulsion to push to ever-increasing mechanical limits the age-old inhumane pain that was visited upon teams of flaring nostrils by coachmen and squires. But now as never then the driver is so deceived by cheap fodder and dumb loyalty that he's inclined to think of himself with his indentured servant as a private system closed to social law. Yet who the master, who the slave?

This mutual bondage is historically unprecedented also because the lavished slave is casually indulged in its propensity to run amok and kill animals of all species, including toads—sometimes the toad in its cockpit. Equine nature has understandably turned hateful in its transmogrification, has shed its kindly affections, and actually does more carnage to the master racers than enemies of their own kind. These engines commit their murders and suicides without fear of prosecution. They are treated ill but never chided. The unenfranchised serfs have more autonomy than their masterless victims; the influence of these unbaptized infernal machines upon the Yahoo-toads (whose preponderant capital they constitute) defies regulation.

Every such servant ostentates an investment more or less of the same order of magnitude as his fellows'; or at least they mix equally in traffic. This promiscuity of personal fascism is most alarming to Michael Chapman—it weakens the best families and reduces barriers to domination by proletarian quality—not because he fears democratic tendencies in themselves but because he shudders at their future affects on the behavior of women. He secretly predicts that within twenty years all fair readers will be racing around capsuled against nature like men, under the impression (even when tampioned like muzzled cannon) that it's the only way to defend themselves against extinction, every clitoris tumescent with irritation. This is his only charge against birth control. ❑

———————

to prevent old wounds from opening at the mere presence of popular ordnance. For the same reason he is now hardly perturbed by the sight of the plague [HN 8] that intrudes in full color upon the fleeting images in his window. In their infancy Americans are inoculated against proper indignation. Even cultivated readers are as apolaustically accustomed to the phony meanings of advertising as to the falsely paneled walls of ferroconcrete libraries, as diners to the hollow beams of restaurant ceilings, as mourners to the veneer of coffins, or as children to the grotesques in animated cartoons. Though Michael has never paid the tariff established for unmolested carriage of his person without in fact remaining unaccosted by strips of iconographic prostitution that catch the upper corner of his eye, he's long since reconciled himself to the aesthetic indignities of riding with common folk uncompartmented in a polluted coach.

Besides, the great arterial road now being crossed, named after a five-star Philiparch, was constructed to keep the myriad hipparchical asteroids off his people's by-streets. [Supreme Commander of holocausted Hiroshima. The only good Jap is a dead Jap, so we oxidized the country, and

HN 8. What is the epidemic social disease that Michael deplores as American?

The American plague [he often says to himself] is hardly to be compared with the French except that both are systemic infections usually contracted in the heedless pursuit of pleasure, both can disarmingly survive their primary symptoms, and both lay curses upon the victim's offspring. But syphilization is unfairly identified as French; its transmission and reception is limited to personal communication, easily avoided by aversion or precaution; and it can now be cured if candidly reported. Furthermore a child may inherit it without infecting his mother; if not reintroduced, there it ends. Finally, it is communication by touch, a sense not yet exploited by the superorganic disease of advertising.

Advertising was broadcast right from the beginning, and incurable. It can be stamped out only by the suicide of mankind. Its microbes, instead of mixing and suspending like steam-blown soot that in the end can be precipitated onto a collecting surface and washed away without permanently altering a person's air, combine organically with the hypostasis of their victim's mentality. The malignancy is cumulative and disintegral, attacking from within the senses of eye and ear (even as it progressively thwarts its own lethal efficiency by breaking down perceptual distinctions), thus blunting the mind's sensitivity to meaning and ultimately bemusing it with a sickening self-conscious commitment to the process of its own corruption. The American disease is more damaging to education than the seven deadly sins and all ten plagues of the Old Testament put together.

The pestilence began innocently as straightforward communication of fact or intention, but from its start in America its facts have been incredible and its intentions commensurately licentious. In their excited demand for capital and labor it was impossible for our countrymen to refrain from hyperpersuasion. Notification inevitably grew duplicitous, and in later stages of development our national communications concentrated on articles of mass production—which were thereby found to be the world-historical purpose of capital and labor, but which on this soil materialized too easily to keep all the capital and labor busy enough unless forcibly demanded at a rate of consumption faster than the composite rate of human reproduction and immigration.

Without plan or conspiracy—of necessity, economists would say—those including railroadmen whose proper and specific rise depended upon the disposal of goods or services found themselves tempted past mere duplicity in the information they put out. Their words and pictures and sounds, outdoor or indoor, static or kinematic, evanescent or persistent, became multiplicitous. The means of inducement formed themselves into a new order of businesses (now collectively called an industry) that supply a new category of goods and services and take an honored place as one of the largest segments of the Gross National Product. But the econometrists hardly take into account all its phases and ramifications—in barber poles cigar-store Indians press releases medical journals mailing lists Coca-Cola signs billboards marquees labels brandnaming trademarking racing cars truck panels shopping days till Christmas movie props gas station design world's fair architecture blimps skywriting searchlights election slogans calendars neon signs public service sponsorships rose parades music hall dramas tourist graphics radio jingles brick walls transit ads railroad overpass beams lunchroom cornices candy counters book display racks pens and pencils key rings window dressing fund-raising public relations news programs scoreboards sports broadcasts athletes' testimonials; newspapers magazines and matchbook covers; to which should be added Christmas Easter Mother's Day and Times Square; motion picture trailers; product insignia, package wrappers: space and time in every medium, especially the most recent.

Advertising this immense trade upon trades grew to such an essential articulation of the economy that it was necessary for its clients and the clients of its clients to sustain and assure its growth by inculcating a universal taste for the vices that required it. It is only natural that several new levels of advertithing should have sprung up to serve the purpose of inducing an appetite for further inducements to enhance the sale of advertising to advertisers of advertising services. Even when that which is to be sold for vital use remains the object under direct consideration, as in the promotion of fish, so firmly has the passion for persuasion been imbued as an end in itself that marketing managers think it encumbent upon their firms at extra cost to exploit the last remaining blank spaces by printing polychromatic trademarks and highly charged varieties of busily inconsistent words (sometimes slogans in quotation marks meant to convey an emotion that can be fully appreciated only by themselves) on at least four surfaces of the shipping cartons that entirely conceal during shipping and storage the totally persuasive selling packages they contain, albeit these outer casings are seen only by lumpers teamsters and warehousemen and never by the wholesale buyers whose persuasion must antedate this phase of distribution, still less by supermarket consumers—to the chagrin of materials handling experts who perceive the resulting obfuscation of truly useful information conveyed by the stenciled codes and descriptions required for sorting and selection by the men who must commit no errors in selecting products at high speed in eerie light where the atmosphere may be polar in temperature and the bills of lading poor carbon copies of shipping orders which often describe in several different ways the items to be picked from amongst hundreds of other perhaps more popular commodities, and the consequent expense (ultimately reimbursed by housewives) of shipping untold tons of food to the wrong place while the intended consignees curse Gloucester and during Lent at the peak of the year angrily substitute turkey or chicken pies in their display freezers.

But Michael's hatred was habitually focussed on the more obvious developments of this putatively ancillary commerce. The most honest peddler of imitation jewelry inflates by incitement of intensively unnatural demand the doubly artificial worth of commonly known fakes; but even the phony dollar-value of corrupt information about meretricious goods is impartially credited in economic statistics as an element of fungible "value added"—as if cancerous growths were reckoned as ingredient to a child's cellular advancement!

The limit of this progression (says Michael) will be a political economy operating on purely negative information, all added value being mendacious. Any epidemiology of advertising (in his opinion) should concern itself mainly with the perversion of communication, or the mutation of information; now and then he muttered his belief that society should look for its two intellectual extremes in the phony science of information and the science of phony information. (He once heard his son Jonathan remark to Matthew a less advanced speller that *phony* was the phoniest word of all because it should be spelled with an *f.*)

The American plague is so leaching and subtle as well as blatant that sometimes the only thing that makes you suspect it in what you are beholding or being subjected to is the aura of phoniness, its one imperishable but neither exclusive nor excluding trait, and often it's so insidious that only your abstract knowledge of the epidemic makes you notice even this general speciousness, its necessary if not sufficient symptom. Because it infects most forms of invention and permeates common meanings, in distinguishing a presentation from its environment you can't always tell whether you are witnessing an attempt at art a hope for reform an effort to amuse or a persuasion to buy something: most likely it is some experimental cluster of means—perhaps a multifaceted or cascading reference to higher or lower orders of related advertising (as when Radiogog advertises Telemagog's advertising entertainments).

But since negative information corrupts rhetorical precision, an essential process in cultural dyscrasia, the phoniness symptom of this and other diseases is usually not difficult to detect (unless you wish not to) even in what isn't called commercial. When talents are being abused you may notice the total absence of irony in the production team's intentions. For if an object were treated ironically you would see it in the light of a foil discernible on all sides of it or at a different level; it would be made to appear within a revelatory space or time.

As you should by now expect despite the lowborn manner of Michael's servitude he follows the gentleborn St Willie in taking style to be "high breeding in words and in argument", as "a still unexpended energy, after all that the argument or the story needs" and "a most personal and wilful fire." He therefore tells Jack and Caleb that advertising phoniness inevitably betrays itself in stylelessness. Language is attenuated in broadcasting. Every phonily artificial ad hoc facon de parler multiplied a million times exhausts or blows away an inch of our topsoil. In certain moods it seems to Michael that the never-final cause of destiny and the inefficient cause of consumption are being displaced as the guides of evolution by the amorphal cause of advertising; and that this antiaristotelian perversion is a vicious travesty of the broad entelechtual revolution in which he hopes the biology of what he sometimes calls meristic epigenesis (and sometimes anamorphic emergence) will eventually overcome most grades of idealism.

Some may protest that Michael exaggerates the relative growth of the American Disease in an expanding economy. Every year it bulks larger and larger in cultural mortality rates, to be sure, but this apparent gain may well result from advances of education in curing other psychological afflictions and allowing minds to live so long that this one disease survives as the proximate cause of many otherwise natural deaths. It's difficult to escape the White Death, for in U S life of all things not impossible the most difficult is to withdraw from mercenary society, which can be nullified only by negative economic growth.

There are no opportunities to sink your private treasure lock stock and barrel in safe deep water without giving up the ghost. One of the few ways you can hope to go out of business—and it would occur only to a born loser of alienated type—is to spend your life converting money into art; and of course this hope's a mockery to those who have no metabolic money to begin with. In practicing real life the best you can do is to delimit your consciousness.

So for him today it is not wormwood but sugar that galls. Sugar tasted by tongues of silver, infinitely more narcotic than any natural "sweet pestilence" that Blake complained of for the indolence it claimed. Michael sees persuasion (the major function of rhetoric) as an exploration of the original sin Sloth, which is now bloated and arrogant under dominion of the pernicious virus that thereby proves its unique powers of malversation, and which, undermining capitalist morality, has taken corruptive precedence over even avarice lust pride and specialization. An archangel divines his duty as antitoxic—hence, these days, reactionary: a negative business against the ultimate negation of liturgy and art, against the infernal comedy in which almost all American artists are almost always engaged. Nevertheless the job is accepted not by girding one's loins but by turning away to work on an antibody.

But how can he avert his eyes from phony holidays of commerce that his children observe with loving hearts and presents to both parents? Or from the fact that New York's fitprinting daily evangel of the Last Testament—arbiter of history's forefront, defender of the best and the beautiful—is supported by advertising, especially in the Sunday supplements all full of style? Or from an "inherited conglomerate" being rapidly adulterated with the assumptions methods and results of therapeutic psychology in which, by exponential smoothing, the latest year of jargon carries the greatest weight, perhaps in proportion to its increasing share of mankind's remaining time, while by the week everyone grows more tolerant of fellow citizens trying to grab as much as they can before the end, no longer capable of repenting the degradation of their language, and the discriminating ones who looked to jeer gradually succumb like all the rest and fall silent before the amusing spectacles of the plague? Besides, if he hears no evil sees no evil and speaks no evil he can't make a living.

But he constantly resolves to shield his children from the mutations radiated by the latest and most devastating instrument of mass infection. On his nighttime sallies through streets emptied of the opiate-addicted populace except for sex-prowlers and dogwalkers he scowls everywhere at naked little picture windows burning through curtained windows of the larger picture, burning into the brains of unseen toads old and young as they sit mesmerized before the cyclopean snake hour after hour night after night. He is still shocked to see the devil's eye in every house from half a mile away.

In thrall to Panamerican taste every switch in the commonwealth is turned on for free cultivation that gathers and bewitches all generations classes and sexes, having soothed the evacuated anima hominis until it no longer distinguishes confectionery amusements from the sugary advertising that animates the whole boardwalk of armchairs, a proscenium tunnel of circuses offering bread. The millions watch but do not see. They applaud with passivity the conquest of their sumptuary conscience as they worship at the peepshow of their penniless arcade—the flickering hearth of starlight shed through Satan's asshole, according to Michael. Even the busy rulers of our nation spend their happy hours eye to eye with the same devilvision that enchants the brutish poor the meanly ambitious and the condescending intelligentsia. Yea the very richest criminals and innocents alike who live inside huge unmullioned thermopanes overlooking bays and valleys and can command the pleasures of any continent or sea (discretionary buyers of any pastime, at leisure for any art or sport) peer at the same fascinating cinematic images that drug the proletariat.

Michael keeps to himself the opinion that all of them, male and female, lumpers and magnates, are effeminized by an industry battening on domestic materialism. And if the academics one would once have looked to for taste and good breeding now suffer from the same debasing unbewitted plague that lays low the commonalty it is no wonder to him that the speech of the country every night congratulates itself on instantaneously popular devolutions of appreciation and conflations of discrimination. Any new linguistic malformation coming over the air in comedy or ignorance, and insinuated into glimpses of rosy parades touchdown passes mass starvation battle fields state-of-the-union speeches sentimental fictions or the weightier revenue-producing adformation itself, is instantly disseminated to the left cerebral lobes of all classes as idiomatic.

It was the technology of the devil's business in Hitler's war (while it was still called phony) that implanted the seed of pictography in the womb of mother radio already commercialized. So the plague has now fastened upon the clients of a perfect courtesan, insuring the Father of All Lies his final dominion. Its copyrights control personal as well as public time; its pap or poison can't be skipped or stopped for contemplation, can't be slowed or speeded, can't be laid aside for future perusal. You can block it out entirely only on pain of alienation and innocence.

But as a patriot Michael worries most of all about bad blood getting into the logorithmoids. If robots prove susceptible the last hope for democratic culture will evaporate like the remnants of liturgy. He has been apprized that these quasi-intelligent artifacts behave at any instant solely on the basis of their latest state, which is altered only by serial algorithmic steps determined in advance by the brain of a logical man or woman. Thus it's only if programmers are willing to refuse the highly lucrative temptations of the persuasion business that the most resourceful of all germs can be kept from the genetic cells of the new species.

Meanwhile in the pathology of everyday life Michael's only recommended cure for devilvision is massive homeopathic doses: promiscuously more new sources of radiation:: unlimited and uncontrolled proliferation of wired or wireless options::: cheap narrowcasts for all factions of culture. The ensuing specialization of advertising might stem the epidemic by sheer competition, at least for a year or two, by separating hoi aristoi from hoi poloi. ❑ _____

now he's made them all into good merchandisers. Soon they'll be importing our beef and lumber on profits from mechanical exports of smart design and spreading the yen for their electronic instruments of our plague.] "I shall return!"—the phoniest line of the war.

But the ylem hasnt yet been totally differentiated into broadcast cyclopes and shoals of shiny automobiles that glitter by day like silver mackerel—. Oh for the fish of Gloucester! Gloucester's not midway on a highway leading somewhere else—. Why Gloucester? Some freshly lost experience. . . . Ah, a dream-memory [FN 2] from last night's depth suddenly for a second time breaks the surface of space with a flitting dorsal signal to claim fullbodied recognition. But memory of a memory that he's already rehearsed, before breakfast in his citadel, appallingly vivid and wonderful. There's no need now to renew the horror of imagination's daimon.

—He ought to be reading. No better solitude is he like to get in a day's round. It's almost too late to pull St Alfred's book from his pocket, but he has been climbing its pages line by line for three months along his own segment of Teleology Lane, and perhaps even in the next seven minutes he'll light on a sentence that will excite his unabsorbent brain. Yet finding his place he once again gets no further than the first predicate nominative, his eyes repeatedly tracing the subject and its modifiers without the slightest intelligence. His fool mind is too far off again bumping down a different trail to notice which of the words—maybe only a feminine pronoun—has turned him aside into familiar meditation.

In fact the metaphysical clerk is already transported by the passion he never tries to resist, the one passion that can always reduce radio hams air force colonels murdering gamblers Protestant preachers or Republican advertisers to the simplest manhood, a sensation of anatomical extremity which in gross examination is not easily secerned from deepest love, a palpable proprioception nonetheless renewed without much general relevance to his domestic prospects at the end of a long day. The children are forgotten. His leonine hunger quietly stands down. But as he sits without voluntary movement the book resting on his thighs betrays the tremor that in his household temple makes him priest. The shriveled little trunk so long telescoped into its occult nest now stirs at the roots to gather firm foundation; the frustum tenses, the column unfolds, the wakened capital cocks its engorging helmet in mutely awkward struggle against cotton fetters and

---

FN 2. I was lying alone on Good Harbor Beach, Sunday afternoon and nobody around because of the season, hoping for a tan but appalled at my own feckless sloth when I remembered that tomorrow would be the final exam of a solid geometry course I'd started and then entirely neglected after the first few sessions. I got up to search for the textbook sweating at the prospect of trying to get enough out of it in one night to prevent the humiliating truncation of my academic career and came to a crowd of people dressed in jackets and oldfashioned striped bathing suits that lacked bottoms—men whose bedraggled genitals dripped glistening exhausted slime and women whose milted sluices gaped in hirsute crotches as they gathered in opposing semicircles around a granite millstone upon which lay the body of someone who had drowned in the tidal creek that runs under the footbridge. A policeman knelt by this altar tying a hangman's knot in a half-inch manila rope, risking court martial for his merciful offence (especially because his head was uncovered), in preparation for a hasty attempt at resuscitation. I pushed my way toward the center to identify the white limp fairy child

with a final shift of tactics attains the stature that still fascinates all humanity, until its hydraulic pronouncement, sorely contained only by the thinnest of skin, is almost too tightened to bear in silence. Wracked by internal tension compressing within elastic flesh half a pint of incompressible blood corpuscles, which a demon has trapped inside valves of membrane kept closed under the same pressure, and by the excruciating torque of twisted strands squeezing each other in a cable of organic steel anchored to the lowest bone of his back, he once more suffers (not without pleasurable anticipation) the involuntary agent of lust. In his youth this indicator often signified no particular correlative—perhaps not so much as a subconscious memory or an unconscious suggestion by a chance word from a page, let alone love—to set itself hard ablaze; in those days it was enkindled at any time during almost any occupation but boxing. Its insurgences were fortuitous and undiscriminating. The iron pipe was inflamed in autonomic expression of the body, needing no attraction of image or cue of scent. The poor homunculus sprang to attention so fast and so often, anticipating all causes and all signals from the high king's central nervous system, that his duty seemed perpetual. (At least when tested the sentry was always found awake.) But it's still too soon for Michael to be thanking his stars for having outlived the nuisance of a subordinate part's inveterate insubordination, seeing that now like a temporary youth, before he's had a chance to bethink his beloved (although she thereupon appears instantly as a reasonable cause), the old thalpotic limb demonstrates to full degree its former specificity of heat in arousing the desire it is meant to stem from. A prelinguistic urge for incarnation summons up the proper noun. Thus suddenly is he possessed as a thousand times before by heady visions of ultimate touch with his wife.

But not preoccupied with the ultimate alone, nor with the obvious only. All is fair, all is felt. One omits no fold or surface, no curious possibility, in

---

face-down on the fluted wheel of rock in miniature black swimming trunks fitted to the nateless hips under its pollywog belly. It was Roger. My anger with those at fault was cut short when I remembered that it was I who'd brought him to the beach to play. Some girl in a blue summer dress carried him across the bridge. He flopped in her arms utterly lifeless. The policeman and I tried to drag the millstone after her. Someone said "Don't bother with that now. We can send a wagon to get it before the trial." In the trolleycar along Washington Street past Folly Cove he lay on his side across an empty seat with his left elbow folded under his head. I sat across the aisle reaching over to brush sand off his marble face while Ruth stood by humming something hopeful. "He'll be all right when we get to the hospital if you have the proper attitude." she said: "He was born there." Looking about me in the car I saw that the people of Gloucester were getting around new conservation ordinances by smuggling sand home in their shoes. Ruth had been after me to build Roger a sand box in the back yard. It was too late to do anything in California but I would certainly start it as soon as we got back East. ❏

HN 9. *What is Michael's peculiar interest in the procedure commonly referred to as 69?*

What intrigues him is a certain problem defined from his own comparatively inexperienced point of view. It's not for him a burning question but only one that he considers occasionally, as others might turn their minds for amusement to the hopeless puzzle of squaring the circle though quite aware that mathematicians have long since lost interest even in proving the job impossible. When he whispered the piquant problem to Ruth she thought he was kidding.

That microscopically smooth skin that tautly covers the tender ridge stretching nearly the full length of Mister P in his orectic state seems supremely not to say critically erogenous. On the shortest way to taking its own measure in straightforward interface it finds the touch it craves from the haptic pressure of delicately striated tissue at the bottom (or back) of the aperture by which women have the advantage of men. It is no accident that this thermoplastic burrow straightens to the shape of its intruder, wholly enveloping and palpating the haft.

Yet for a certain variety of pure self-centered sensuality, reserved for uncommonly spontaneous feasts, Michael suffers as his wife's sweetest devotion the lingual caresses of the mouth paying her generous respects to his lordship either during some inconvenience to her ordinary pleasure or when an afflatus of phallolagnian curiosity overcomes her scruple to assist a wasted emission of precious sperm. To Ruth kneeling before her spouse in a ventral situation the sensitive underside tendon must present itself as an anterior surface made by God for a tongue's cupping ministrations. The good wife—of no ordinary lingual facility (having been a polyglot at school), notwithstanding her chaste history of disinhibition—clasps with both hands the rooted base of his sanguine column ("hard as a crowbar" she once said "but not as cold"), and with rounded wonder at its livid venous fluting as in her fascination she slightly alters its orthostatic direction, brings sialogogic lips to the swollen capital of what she called the family's Capital I. Speech is left to him alone while with sacerdotal laving motion she plays slowly back and

---

dilating upon those adored loins at reciprocal behest, in playing upon the supererogatory frenzies [HN 9] that sometimes precede transcendent bliss. Yet at present his desire refers only in passing to epicurean digressions. Tongues and fingers are instruments of desire, to be sure, but there is no desire in a tongue or finger; fingers are instruments of work and tongues are instruments of worship: there is only one organ that as both antenna and scepter at the same time reaps and disseminates a reciprocally introduced sense of love's true end. It is a more specialized limb of ingression that leaves the mouth free to meet intelligently psellismatic lips or press storm-darkened windows of the soul while the hands are free to caress and glorify all the shapes and surfaces at a man's command and the eyes to love as Shelley said by finding beauty. Only that part of him is able to straighten the sphincteric labyrinth and reach the very stem of the woman's womb where her fundamental heartbeat can be sensed all the way to his toes in an

forth, gradually extending his phallacious misplacement to her limit, gently nodding at her task as her imploded cheeks moving in and out like lasciviously throbbing gills draw the god so far past the buds of taste that the velar vacuum is overfilled and she fears to choke on the obstruction, while her curling indrawn antenna flickers in tempo allegro to modulate the overarching pressure, making recurrent obeisance to the most sensitive inch or two with darting melodic touches. Never does the skillful wanton bare her teeth. Then with all her means (unless she breaks off her tantalizing dalliance before it's too late to save him for her orthodox satisfaction) she more solemnly grasps the obsessive homunculus and spurs on its transductive pulsations until the ecstatic geyser floods her throat with an astonishing abundance of yeasty balm. He, quivering in praise of her speechless dulia and blessing every bone in her body, clutches her scalp and strokes her temples. With his paroxysm her orisons are finished. She seems as spent as he. The sideshow was the main event; the lips of the gorgeous sword-swallower are closed.

But at times Michael takes the analogous part, his own version of supererogative tribute, fronting the delitescent lower-case i keystone of his gothic hearth. It's an opportunity to apologize for Caliburn's bad manners who except perhaps in the most fleeting and frivolous horseplay at the same site always turns his back and slips away from that tiny hermaphroditic cuneiform which shyly surmounts the portal that's been dubbed Ginny after the Virginia known as Good Queen Bess who once when vexed with her courtiers exclaimed "Had I been crested not cloven, my lords, you had not treated me thus!" [If it be true that this covert fin, homologue of the froward lingam, formerly overlooked by male experts, is the tolerably slow trigger of a girl's happiness (Michael speculates)—a point that seems important to those who would prove the independence of woman as well as to those who for one reason or another would prefer to think that a vigorous end-game is less crucial than indolent foreplay—there's something to adduce in support of his contention that female orgasm though antedating Tiresias was an acculturation as late as leisure: maybe the efficient cause of love.] Then as lips meet across each other it's his laving tongue that calls forth the saliva.

In the decadent phases of culture (which is to say, as Spengler would have it, in highly civilized times) a wife like her husband is nothing loathe to enjoy the pleasures of extraordinary conversation with an accomplished linguist. Now and then it's worth his effort to rouse her weary household body to the pitch of youth with an antipasto tantalizing to the deep palate and conducive to forthcoming transports of a more spiritual nature. On Michael's part there's calculation. A couple who bear with each other for many years in sickness and in health get so used to the opposite half of their flesh from nightly propinquity and from doubled trouble of the spirit that the man at least must guard against an almost onanistic habit of regarding his wife as the lawful convenience for quelling an undiscriminating urge rather than as a particularly desirable body. Like the leader of a people who from feeding every day on meat have outgrown gratitude for feasts the husband is obliged to teach strangeness in what's familiar and to cultivate anew the rose at the gate of his garden, hoping in each instance to elicit moans of licentious recreation.

But his inclination is not merely dutiful. Nor are all the artilleryman's rewards deferred as he labors at the breech of his piece, though he may seem to serve it with the gallant disinterest of a Roundtable knight, pursing and licking under the cocked key (once generally regarded as pleolagnastic) which he has exposed with the tender pressure of his thumbs as his propensity transcends itself in what seems the most intimate of mysteries, for which blunt phallic communication is much too distal from the center of his experience. The inspiration seems its own reward as he endeavors to make reparation for all that she has suffered at his hands. In his nearly unselfish latria the jingo at the other end of his spine has dropped back to rear guard. His worship of blessed holy Ruth becomes an experimental art. No pompous quidnunc of a tipstaff with a helmet on his head, unprehensile in his blundering, can possibly investigate and sense the delicacy of such a flower. There are times when the pretentious fellow must be put out of reach, when deaf ears must be turned even to Aphrodite's renascent plea for natural fulfillment, so that the rapt student may remain free to feel with disinterested admiration the fomented movements or other symptoms of inflammation and prevent himself from becoming too soon a totally sympathetic subject. Nevertheless in this imaginative appeasement of his craving for identity with the woman through her loins his cerebral excitement at the Bacchic affect of his service may tighten and draw too taut the string of his discarded bow and perhaps loose tactless arrows before it can be properly employed.

Now therefore (finally to the question!) what could be more natural in the deception of nature than to make the obvious combination of complementary cults. If primitive satisfactions must be transcended, why not simultaneously? Sometimes by turning upsidedown they undertake to jamb two Arabic numbers into the same space. Let two enantiomorphic pairs of legs loll at opposite ends of a single double-headed two-backed crab. If carried to term this glued and pegged lamination, a dizzy mode of reciprocal veneration that upsets Mother Nature's most important linkage, incurs the jealousy of gods not simply because it outwits the principle of fertility or because the welded mania displays two mortals idolizing each other but because it exercises a tantalizing freedom denied their class. In any event Michael and Ruth, they sometimes liberate themselves for a moment, part and counterpart, though not from mortality at least from anxiety for and against procreation. For thus they can't distinguish the head from the tail of their species; and there is no space for unbemusing words when they are giving suck to both their other halves.

But in this vale of tears even when we honor nature and imitate her Arkworthy beasts we are not granted perfection. With anatomy formed by gods in their own image for archetypal methods no artful contortion such as that here indicated can quite equal the primeval posture of coupling as far as comfort is concerned. All pleasure is fallible but at its tried-and-true best that of the gonads cannot be equaled by the mouth and tongue. Even the loveliest perversion is subject to a sexual law of conservation, especially when its convolution entails exercitation somewhat excessive of the least that marriage requires. It is doomed to evolutionary failure even in purely cultural heritage because it strains the pleasure principle. To Michael for one it is not a flawless jewel of games.

Taken as an entire drama, of course it falls short in depth and other dimensions that foster reproduction. But even as a single act within the play it is marred by Mother Nature's objection to such coaptation. Moralists and countercontraceptionists need not fear excessive cultivation of this salacious taste. It will never amount to much in national degeneracy. For the fact is that in reciprocal inversion many of the suctorial caresses are necessarily somewhat mismatched to the particular areas they address. Evolution saw to it that his optimum sensation would be shy of the maximum. Far be it from Michael to complain about such a minor flaw in lavish gratification as a slight leverage upon homuncular declination faintly discomforting the upper roots in his groin. There's no use trying to correct his wife, for whether alow or aloft she can't help exerting a little stress without unhinging her neck or providing herself with jaws built on the opposite tack unless she removes from his half-smothered face her own gratified loculus. An intelligently passionate woman in her position is hard put to keep from inflicting scabrous indentations upon her singularly unbending prey once it's taken much further than the ogive of its head; or from scraping its tender ventral (sometime dorsal) skin against an upper fulcrum of ivory stalagmites. . . . Well, Michael's devil was in further palpable details. For playing these angles the female's tongue should hang upsidedown from the ceiling of her mouth; then the surface that's so sensational when she's facing the male could find its way to the same exquisitely erotic stretch of skin on the breast of her family herm. Sixty-nine is off the mark, not the number it's cracked up to be; and anyway it's plain that most courtships ignore this kind of kissing. On the other hand, to put an end to intolerably intensified desire there's no need for this kind of teleiosis.

Therefore, unless Michael's recklessly overtaken by exotic imperfection and it's already too late for him to prolong the feast for another course, he'll decline to consummate the uncontrollable mystery in this manner and break off to rectify the procedure before its crescendo, that both Hera and Aphrodite may be praised and glorified in the momentary solution of all conjugal difficulties, which occurs (if ever) far beneath corona and petal at the very center of a wife. In the aftermath of which as he lies back to sleep sometimes comes his wonder that Ruth nevertheless responds with such exceptional abandon (if at all) to various hors-d'oeuvres.

Does she thereby taste compensation for not being carried across the orgastic threshold at a princely height by her natural husband? Does she bemoan subliminal or even acutely conscious disappointments of plenary bliss? Does a failure of his to make the grade lie as an embarrassing secret at the heart of their marriage? If so, considering how skillfully he's striven, it seems to him that his fault would not be moral but congenital. ❑ _____

auscultation by which she is made known to him well enough for him to call her by private names and he also made namely known to her for the privilege of naming as they are fully known to each other enwreathed in correlative appeasement at once of male craving for ownership of the mystery ˚ and female yearning to be filled therewith. By both old lovers in this unity solid gonadotrophic impressions are more profoundly tendered than heady piquant frictions reputed for outrageous sensation.

So even to himself it's scarcely unlaughable that in the face of his most obstinate theories and opinions semen is the humor to classify him by, especially as there is plenty of beauty in his bed to tantalize his gymno-sophistry, seeing that he's fortunate enough not to be coupled with another owl. The memory of his chronic danger like a picador in his own employ thus wakens him from the inertia of melancholy. He straightens his back impatiently, ceasing to reflect upon his window's reflections, and stares distractedly at the tarpaulin curtain that the motorman has drawn behind his back to keep the reflection of passengers from reflecting in the clear windshield of forwardlooking responsibility.

Sitting motionless the gyneolotrous archangel fails to notice that the fox of hunger has ceased gnawing at his bowels. All his molecules have realigned themselves like freshly magnetized iron filings. With every nerve now single-mindedly oriented, every thought swinging on one axis, the heavenly mind is enticed by flesh and enthralled by hope for the daughter of man whose parts are his only images, the program of the next four or five hours best calculated for getting into whom with the least pos-sible delay to the best possible affect his only remaining speculation. His gynocompass has been set spinning in tropotactical inertia pointed toward its lodestar with the obsession that keeps even superannuated males in contention against death; it trains his untelescoped gun through all the yaws and scends and rolls of his evening's course.

As he approaches the corner marked by the eternally lighted window of Just-As-Good Laboratory the angle of his yet unseen cynosure opens swiftly to the right. Yet mark: instead of pressing a signal button to bring the almost emptied vessel to a halt at the latitude where always before he has stepped to cold earth near his board and bed he allows the argussed cage of warm yellow illumination to trundle right past the stop, as only his inner eye swings sharply starboard for a broadside glance toward his destination, and sails right past the home he longs for!

Certainly not because he's befuddled by desire or forgetful of the municipal labels that have marked his progress; not because his ardor has cooled at the prospect of wide-awake kids inhibiting adult behavior by their parents; not because there's a mistress to visit further down the line; and not because it's too cold outside: but on the contrary because he is plotting as intently as a most avid seducer determined to possess a particu-lar woman and that woman only, all agonies except the contest for her par-ticular attention having dropped below the horizon. All anxieties except those of this particular desire having dissolved in the breeze of a momen-tum that carries him at fair speed away from the only woman he ever makes love to, he silently prays the helmsman to keep steady as he goes but faster if possible.

The archangel is bethinking himself of the public calendar. Not a minute too soon he has remembered that it's Valentine's Day, the feast of fauns, the day all birds choose their mates. But it's always a complicated and equivocal matter to woo a busy housewife—nay most of all on Valentine's Day! For in order to recover his bride this night he must contend not only with ordinary time and occasion but also with special circumstances. His supper on the kitchen table and the children hanging around it still excited from anxious givings and receivings at school on a long-hoped-for day fulfilled by studious and tender preparations of veiling white lace stuck to stiff red paper with thick semen-odored paste inside small square envelopes (two for a penny), butterflied crimson hearts and tender arrows labored everywhere with scissors and colored pencils, still happy with suspense in anticipation of his response to what he will find with amazement under his plate when Ruth lifts it to serve him meat and potatoes from the stove! Tonight of all nights these precious thorns will most affectionately catch at his sleeve before he can reach for the rose.

But offspring are not his only stumbling block nor the holiday his only complication. Many factors must enter into the calculations of Mr P . Even if he were awaited by the woman alone, and on a day that commonly called for no presents, he wouldnt usually get very far if he tried to plunge without ceremony into the ruby-dark center of a love long since claimed as his own. He maynt simply socket himself forthwith. A wise husband's portolan warns him in general about the ending of a mother's bedraggled days, and a man whose destiny is humbler than his origin should take more pains than anyone else to offset the daily cares of his wife. The erotic demon has grown wary learning to compromise his selfishness, and after more years than Egypt's famine he has learned to feed his analogic firecontrol computer any number of compensations for relative course speed season weather tidal currents and rotation of the earth. The most critical of these navigational adjustments is for fertility [FN 3].

Haring past the gradined sculptures in the shop window at his home corner it fleetingly occurs to him that if he worked in that shop of immortal merchandise where passing fashions and personal style are never displayed he could run home for lunch every day and there would be no more

---

FN 3. Less than five months since my birthday party (the beginning with Caleb Karcist the end or anyway the beginning of the end for essays and lectures—yes but also the end of the beginning of household wisdom: wisdom denied but pregnant even while still the weak-kneed wisdom of bondage:: the end of hopeful insensitive love, the end of my reason's misrule, the end of my pigheaded domestic pomposity—or if not the end of it at least the beginning of true knowledge silting over my old false civilization in a precipitation of conjoined responsibility and horror) my fatuous optimism has been quenched in a bath of cold terror that happens to be momentarily rescinded in my conscious mind by a wave of lust.

I am no new man reborn but the same old man who soon loses the details of his feelings and always allows inveterate reason or rather comforts of mentality to obtund fear, narrow aversion, blur the pain of love. I have already cauterized my flayed eyes and headed over my nerve-ends to make them watertight like an ironworker's pounded rivets, once again scotching the raw sensitivity I was born with. Nothing has really vanished or healed that made me wake from the sleep of

than a sleeping baby to frustrate the hostess's entertainment; six hours saved in travel every week could be devoted to the art of love. [Of course his present excitement at this fancy blinds him to his quotidian knowledge that leisure would do nothing to unstew a household always out of hand, and that it might raise expectations of housework as well as a seigneur's privilege. "Mortal love is but the licking of honey from thorns." said a lady at the Courts of Love, who moreover was speaking of something lovelier than her own leisured marriage, to say nothing of toilsome democratic matrimony practiced by journeyman employees of American petite bourgeois.] In self-serving semi-abnegation he has once more made

---

reason yet I find myself climbed back onto the raft as if nothing's happened. I shake the brine from my fur but I don't shake the fur from my skin nor the skin from my flesh nor the flesh from my bones which to me will always be invisible; I'm drenched in spray and never dry, always too cold to expose my skeleton if I could. Nothing happened that hadnt been happening all along except that I was suddenly tilted off into the water to flounder for my life in a distasteful struggle against the numbing storm and for the first time forced to soak up the temperature Ruth always swims in.

The only definite event was my headlong baptism. But that was an immersion that I can't permit a repetition of unless I become willing to drown my puppies with myself.

The first few days of my thirty-fourth year brought no more change than if I had never threatened to shatter the assumptions of her existence. I thought she was hoping that my phlegmatic humor would first diffuse and then obliterate the cruel intention of tearing her family up by the roots and dragging it three thousand miles away—or worse, letting it drag itself after me unassisted—to what she supposes is one of the bleakest capes of North America, without the assurance of automobile house or job.

But I did change my regimen, relaxing the schedule that has constrained me and ruled my family for the best part of a decade, lapsing into a more nearly normal cycle of lesser effort—not of course discussing it with her but simply getting up late Monday morning and staying up late that night and so on—until seeing the futility of that policy I dug in again and pledged myself to stricter prudence than had ever before seemed necessary. I'd hoped that my tentative indulgence would serve the purpose in several ways: first by thus warning of my determination to carry out the plan regardless of how she faced it—since such a marked revision of my usual stultified behavior (just when the memento of another birthday might have been expected to intensify my discipline) would have signaled nothing less important; but also communicating my offer to suspend as long as might be necessary the rigidity of will she always complains about, and to spend more time with her, hinting even at some last fling of social life with the kind of people she preferred; and by thus conveying my recognition of the immense practical difficulty of emigration, together with my awareness that pioneering was no light matter for any of us, even many months beforehand.

But this unmistakable alteration of habit was meant mainly to offer my apology. The offence was beyond words. My remorse for the brutal fact that she

up his mind that he'll never again relieve the excruciating preponderance of his libido with the torpid degrading unreciprocated sedative that he's sometimes demanded with hardly a grunt at the end of a hard day. Even with unbalanced fuels the flame should be mutual—or snuffed out at the first inkling of flint and steel in his blood.

The floorboards vibrate in sympathy with organ-pipe pulsations, but at this increasing distance from his attraction he's far more canny than a bull. With her naked presence still only contingently prospective for the touch he's not yet careless of danger or blind to regret; he hasnt yet forgotten to remember that the last thing he needs is another baby messing

---

should have been the last one to be informed of my intentions was not so much for the treachery of keeping the secret from her as it was for my folly in confiding it to a good husband like Jack Wolfson, totally innocent of the discretion I took for granted in trusting him, who could never have suspected the depth of my ruthlessness at home. Before the party was over I had forgotten the stupidity of his goodwill, since I love the man for his seriousness and have long accustomed myself to make allowance for the concentration of academic minds: so that self-criticism was the only possible channel of my anger. But of course the obtuse optimism that extends all the way to my innermost core has always prevented me from taking much blame for anything important. I must have been urging my underground will to deprecate the importance of its own errors.

Even as my memory of the event broke apart and dimmed the silent pressure for an explanation was building up. The first night of the week we went to sleep politely without touching each other, after having spoken of nothing but our children since the party.

That night I dreamt that Ruth and I went to a dingy marble-vaulted hall supposed to be in the Massachusetts General Hospital of Oakland. At first I was just waiting alone as at a train station but then we were both in a labile crowd full of rustling movement while listening to some lecture without attention or formality. I noticed a single shelf of books a little above my head on a wall. That reminded me that Ruth had worked there as a receptionist in the early enthusiastic days of marriage and I'd set her up with these she wanted to read. Wondering how I could have forgotten about such important possessions that I'd been missing for years I immediately began to carry them out to our old black coupe, yet only one or two at a time since I was in much anxiety about getting them past the guard without being asked to prove they were mine. I knew that I could ultimately convince higher authorities of my ownership but I was afraid of getting entangled in the bureaucracy of a public institution. Within the dream I then woke to the light of dawn and understood by revelation that the dream explained what had happened to *The Eclipse of Reason* which I was still looking for.

When I actually awoke in the morning I went to my study and found that book conspicuous in the middle of the third shelf. I remember the dream because I wrote it down on one of my new 3-by-5 cards as I rode to work.

How rarely I remember anything at all of my dreams! Yet the next night I was to have another also so vivid and imperious that it too had to be recorded for wondrous meditation before I forgot it.

about in the nursery-niche that deserves the full-time occupation of an
awe-inspired gardener jealous of his place. (His hardship aside, brothers
have already done damage enough to the purse.) And the fourteenth of
February falls this year at a moon-time doubly inauspicious from the
vaticinator's point of view—relatively uncertain and absolutely dangerous—for he seems to find his wife least susceptible to purely disinterested
love when her unconscious valence is most attractive to willful ions loosed
within. In this paradoxical phase she is not especially amenable to his
attempts at dispelling her fatigue and anxiety. Perhaps a primitive lump
in the brain is cyclically depressed by the contraceptive covenant to which

---

The previous evening Ruth had gone out to a meeting of Cub Scout Den
Mothers after putting Roger to bed and I had the two boys to take care of.
Having read them a chapter of *The Jungle Book* I kissed Matty goodnight in his
bed but allowed Jonathan as usual to stay up a while longer. On an impulse in
the spirit of the great adventure which had not yet been announced to the children I took him with me into my jammed writing closet, bringing a stool and
clearing a place for him to draw pictures at the end of my big table. At first I
made him keep the silence while I sat before a fresh blank pad of paper with a
pencil in my hand gazing sidelong at my most precious properties and trying to
attack the problem of drastically reducing transcontinental baggage.

I longed to start a new life purged of useless appurtenances and cleansed of
needless complications, in hopes that the jolting necessities which she would have
to face one after another in getting herself and the boys across the country (assuming that I was successful in finding a homestead to summon them to) would
wake her from lifelong reverie and free her from the dreary web of her childhood
history around here.

I myself would take no more than a casket full of plans and distillations
accumulated during these prolonged preparatory years that will be totally wasted
if I don't hold on to them as the sorely labored extensions of my undermanned
brain. That evening I still believed that I would need no other tools with which
to clear a field build a cabin and stake my claim to a vigorous livelihood in the
sun and mist of an east salt wind. But I was just then beginning to see how
related are all the things in my little homeroom. Reference books, when you
think about them one by one, some of them old enough to be practically irre-
placeable, can't possibly be dispensed with: classified facts would have to go with
me in a trunk of their own. But books of the saints, expensive books yet to be
read, dull books I'd have occasion to consult, memorable books not yet memorized, and all the books that had my marks improving them by a whole order of
information for highly pertinent reperusal—how many of these were essential?
Where could I draw the line of triage between impediment and independence?
Even if I left behind the books I'd never read. . . .

As I was beginning to appreciate the burden that Ruth would be left with—
mine as well as hers and ours, for I'd have to trust her with most of my library—
Jonathan remained sensible of his unprecedented privilege and kept the silence
with all his might and main. He must have been watching my inactive hand out
of the corner of his eye as he bent over his elaborate lines almost too light to

it has been bound by the rational cortex of the conscious person. Though not impossible it is past probability that on such a night in the middle of an exhausting week she will anticipate both his desire and her own by taking the trouble to equip herself in advance for ardent addresses that she seems never able to imagine herself responding to until she's already yielding to the old fascination that brought her to his bed long before their troubles were born. And at the very lip of union it's heinously indiscreet, cruelly disconcerting, to call up the deepest issue dividing their house—to break off caresses and suggest that she retire to the bathroom to install in his interest and against her own inclination an impervious trap made of

———————

make out on the yellow manila paper. When his interruptions finally began he tried to palliate them too by whispering, and I replied in kind, to discourage the infringement, though in truth I was not sorry to have his lamplit conversation on this occasion, and even glad to hear the comments and questions that he couldnt contain despite the best training in the world.

"When you sit down your pot belly puffs way up more, you know that Dad?" I was surprised that his happiness did not produce a more tactful observation. "That's just tough skin," I hissed, "and when I'm thinking all my muscles swell up under it." He giggled, but at least he was wise enough to let the topic lapse during an interval in which to feel out my taciturnity for an invitation to speak what was really on his mind. It was now I watching him as he continued to work at his picture of a complex arch-and-truss bridge spanning a rugged canyon as deep as mountain peaks could make it with a navigable river at the bottom. [Chip off the old block. I've started him off on the wrong foot. He should have been mounting butterflies or writing a sonata.]

Certainly his loyalty isnt like Norkid's who used to lie by me wherever I sat, entwining himself with the legs of my chair and making a pillow of my instep, fulfilling all the hopes I'd ever had for my childhood dogs, more trusting and less critical than any thoughtful offspring, easier to love with an utterly selfish delight and simply objective admiration. Except when drawn off into the business of dogdom that dog behaved as if he thought and felt exactly as my best friend should. That boy is no German Shepherd. He brings up subjects of his own, heads his own way, questions my judgment. But therefore he seems more innocent than the dog, who had greater investment in my arbitrary infallibility.

He's always gravely interested in the tinted print on my wall, a fellow to Jack's sequel that shows Adam and Eve being driven from heaven. Maybe because its draftsmanship seems to him within reach of his own ability while at the same time too deep for his understanding. But this was the only time he's ever said anything about it. Some sense of propriety or embarrassment had prevented him ever before from asking about it even sotto voce. It was not that he sought a meaning of it, I'm glad to say. And I don't think he tried to compare its naked bodies with the men and women he knew. He recognized the third human figure as an angel, but despite the unorthodoxy of its form according to his experience in iconography he made no mention of it. His only remark as he poked the eraser-end of his pencil in the direction of the picture was about the tree in the background. "I've never seen one like *that*! Is that a prime evil tree?"

insensitive fabric. She would do it, and with gracious goodwill to boot, maybe for the moment oblivious of disagreement, but the private indignity of her hasty half-squat might put a hitch in her tempestuous enchantment. The pleasure of surprise would be lost, the gust of unreckoning passion put off, the hint of ravishment withdrawn.

On the other hand he has not quite forgotten that occasionally she offers advances when he least deserves a reception, and confounds the wisdom of his pessimism by carefully forestalling his apprehensions about fertility. He can't remember what has happened on most Valentine Days, neither moods nor greetings nor rewards, but he hasnt forgotten last year's

---

I whispered back that it was withered: "But it's a good tree. You'll see trees like that in winter if we ever get back East." I was careful of course not to give him the exciting news of my plan before Ruth could decide how to announce it in line with her policy for protecting the children; but I was ruefully tempted to enlist his enthusiasm in my support during the conflict that was being uneasily deferred on both sides only in order to compose courageous words for shaping intelligible passions. "They creak in the freezing wind, but in the spring they're greener than the trees around here."

I half expected him to challenge my romance but he let me get away with it. We were both making overstatements anyway, induced by the preternatural intimacy of the evening, and were both aware that the pleasure of our shared privacy lay in its formality, not in its truth. Still, now that I look back on the scene, I suspect him of an obscure and perhaps anxious intuition. Maybe if not in his head at least in his bones he was beginning to fear that Ruth and I would get divorced and one of us leave him and his brothers forever. "You'll be able to play in the snow." I added more boldly in my indicative mood.

"I'm tired of California!" he declared, and I laughed with pleasure. He never said anything about the serpent watching from behind a leafy bush.

For a quarter of an hour he was scrupulously quiet again, eking out my unsolicited indulgence about bedtime, knowing that the sentence might fall at any moment and put an end to the indefinite hour of uncommon privilege. The only sound came from my eight-day clock ticking every minute more discretely. I could see that he hardly dared shift his weight for fear that any disturbance greater than the noiseless friction of the lightest stylus moved by the tiniest muscles between wrist and fingertips would bring the absentminded father to his senses. At length he ceased to risk even the movement of finest art. He began to watch the clock. Covertly I followed his eyes, falling into his trance as I tried to imagine the thoughts that led him toward sleep. Yet rather than trying to enter his skull (which I've never succeeded in doing with anyone) I concentrated on his objects and thereby shared the mystery of his attention—for we were boys of the same country, half of the same blood, more or less of the same ambitions, and I think that at the moment my recalled puzzlement was as fresh as his.

I too had long studied the faces of clocks before having learned to decipher the dials' markings (in my day Roman numerals, in his Arabic, but both schemes now yielding to the streamlined calibrations of pure polar relativity on the same tide of effisience by which the Navy had been obliged to give up adjectival

unique coincidence of other feasts with the Lupercalia, on the day that according to the earliest tradition of the church they could celebrate (rather than on Groundhog Day) the third baby's presentation and her Purification with his own Candlemas for the birth that had occurred in the Christmas octave forty days before—when for the third time this second Eve recovered what the first had lost, not by churching, not by reappearance after long seclusion, but by the mansuete renewal of a priestly lover's service.

In any case on this holy day with another year's experience under his belt, if he doesnt want another baby before next Christmas, he must court

---

points on the compass card in favor of universal degrees). I couldnt remember ever lacking northern hemisphere clockwisdom or ever entertaining the possibility of either big hands or little hands going counterclockwise. (It was too hard even to remember my ignorance of the first ten cardinal numbers.) Time's compass, its rote once learned, seemed as categorically plain as a straight line drawn on the beach: its tethered arrows, one slow, the other slower, with scrolled heads shaped like spades or pierced black hearts. It had always been obvious that the months went around a year in the same fashion. So the thought of season-time ticked by the tocking clock took the place of bedtime, the long hand already a month into the school year and unaccountably moving though you watched and watched without seeing its motion toward Christmas where the short hand waited for it stout and loving like Matty.

Suddenly there was a jerk of the head—mine or his I cannot say, but I jumped to the conclusion that it was his. He was rubbing his eyes with a knuckle. I found myself with four fingers smoothing the crowsfeet above my right cheekbone. The long hand had disappeared! Or rather the short hand had grown longer. All at once the arrows of time were on top of each other pointing the same way.

So when the voice of command descended upon his head it was blessedly gentle and yawningly sympathetic. Responsibility returned to us both at the same time. "Time for bed, time to sleep, little Jonah-jar." As teeth were already brushed and 'jamas already onstalled he refused a last chance at the bathroom and was led away unprotesting. "You lucky kid. I wish I could go to bed now." When he lay with the blankets up to his chin, the genetic and generic image of my soul limned rather by touch than by the dim light filtering through the darkened kitchen to the dormitory porch, he was giving the thoughts of the day one last waking consideration. "Why don't you?" he challenged.

I bent over to kiss his forehead his nose his two cheeks and both sides of his neck, a procedure which made him mildly squirm at the familiar titillation of an unshaven face scraping his epicene skin. In customary self-defense he drew his arms from beneath the warm covers and hugged my mouth to his lips so that the chin bristles could be disengaged, thereby sealing our nightly farewell. But he was still intent upon his question.

"I can't Jonno." I replied. "I have to work." "You mean work for the store?" "No. My own work." "Then you don't *haffta* work Daddy! It's just for yourself. You can go to bed if you really want to!" He was testing the sincerity of my

her safely. The recrements of marriage may be shaken off for the night of Saint Valentine if he precludes doubt without having to prompt her to the bit of business so inimical to her instinct. His new purpose is therefore to sheath the offender in guaranteed machine-tested self-forming apparel far more elastic and transparent than Colonel Cundum's of panegyric fame 300 years ago but as a tranceiver of sensation still somewhat unfavorable to the rapture of perfect love even if he succeeds in diverting attention from his own little business of unrolling it in place. An expendable rubber lifesaver is all the more desirable (despite its drawback) if he positively cannot wait for his wife's bedtime preparations.

———

sleepiness as well as probing for my motive. "That's true I suppose. I don't *haffta*, but I *should*." What else could I say without getting into theory? He resolved the question for us both: "I know what you mean. You *want to very much*! That's why you don't go to bed. Don't say you *haffta* stay up!" He drew out his last words in whispered flourish of triumph that released him to contentment. The day was finally rounded off and he was well pleased to drop into the sleep of his earlier childhood as if his intelligence had confirmed an enduring perfection of the love between us. But I did go to bed very soon, at my usual hour, though I had slept almost to breakfast time that morning. My body always takes advantage of a change in routine. It favors laziness and only tardily honors the half of any bargain in which sleep loses what it has elsewhere gained. Especially during times of trouble when I dream profusely just to stay asleep. That night I did not wake up even when Ruth came home to bed, no doubt primed for conversation.

Anyway, the dream I could remember riding up this boulevard next morning was one that under other circumstances might have wakened me before it ended. In it I pretend not to notice someone being silently beaten in the dark shadows while I am easily visible to the assailant. I continue with whatever I'm doing, reading I think. My idea is that being well dressed I shall be regarded as too esteemed by society to be subject to attack, so long as I show no awareness of what's going on. I am afraid; but I'm also confident that the thug will never dare accost such a citizen as myself if I don't interfere or otherwise provoke him. I believe he fears the total police mobilization that would follow any such assault upon me. Although I see a wallet taken in dumbshow as the mute victim is noiselessly flung to the ground limply unresistant to the brutal larger shape I say to myself that it's a matter of long-established gang rivalry, a pair of mobsters, thief against thief. The aggressor moves away, a shadow moving into shadows. I continue with my occupation. Later someone comes to raise the beaten figure and shows the bloody face of Matty twisted on its neck, the eyes dislocated like a fish's. He's as utterly senseless as Roger in the earlier dream.

But neither dreams nor love could save me from facing the music Wednesday night. I thought of inviting her into my study after the kids were in bed. She could sit in my chair while I took the high stool. But I knew she would refuse. She once contended that I never let her in there except when I want her to take off her pants. I'm a little too fat for that lap stuff anymore, but it's true that my lechery was never very funny when I'd tell her she could interrupt me anytime

[After making my Valentine present what's wrong with dragging her into my museum on the pretext of a brief conference while all three boys are eating? She wouldnt die of the syncope, pinned to the back of the door, if I enacted a playful imitation of the uncriminous rape she sometimes wished even before we were married—simply as a rough-and-ready fore-taste of the deeper longer swoons to be visited upon her a few hours later. I'd make short work of it for the sake of an unhurried rebeginning when she's finally ready for a long night ahead. In ten minutes we could be back in the kitchen flushed and faint. Of course I'm old enough to know that such fictions are seldom consummated, and never when premeditated; yet

---

she was in the mood anywhere. The grossness of my address sickens me now. The wonder is that she can ever bear to let me touch her while talk like that is still echoing in the room. Making love at our present stage of intimacy requires an exclusion of memories, consciousness pared down to an awareness as shorn and pale as the sun seen clean through a morning fog. Yet all I ever mean by such words is that I hold her desire sacred and will never refuse to honor it. Indeed I've always been ready, even in anger or despond when my expectations run to the contrary, when I have anticipated anything but a renewal of her warmth. When I'm there she never comes inside that door, never opens it when calling me to meals; but of course that's for deeper ways I've hurt her.

I was unable to determine upon any initiative except a clumsy bellyflop into the coldest of waters, either at a special kitchen sitting called for the purpose or in a colloquy on the flat of our backs with the bed for council chamber. I hate both recourses, but the latter at least had the advantage that it must be post-poned an hour or two longer than the former, and that I wouldnt have to look her in the eye or blush at my guilt. Therefore as soon as I said goodnight to the boys I went for a walk.

I wanted to prepare nonaggressive tactics of containment, and to deploy my reserves of grievance for commitment only at last resort if I found myself losing too much ground. I reminded myself that the sole purpose was to defend a deci-sion already taken—not exactly a fait accompli to be sure but at least an auto-cratic intention which if preserved from adulteration would take upon itself the function of a mutual master plan. Any endeavor to prove my case positively, or to justify my general attitude, would certainly lead to irreconcilable conflict between two irreducible postulates of value. As usual when I try to prepare my-self for a speech I made little progress in framing and memorizing even the base logic of my position. Nevertheless in the effort to encourage myself I stirred into one stew a lot of old separate feelings that in such concentration prompted me to conquer all opposing arguments under a banner of absolute authority—in face of the fact that her moral forces could not to be overcome without dissolving the center that held mine together in breathtaking weakness.

The small surplus of energy acquired that morning by sleeping into full day-light now carried me much further than I'd ever walked sober and alone since I had Norkid when we lived in the hills where I spent whole afternoons almost every weekend exploring bottomland redwoods and sunny uplands for miles around that small chain of green ravines (almost unknown to metropolitans since

it's no more than prudent to prepare for any difficult but not impossible revivification of household foreplay. . . . She too can be pretty unceremonious when the fancy takes her. Comes without coaxing. Like that time in the cemetery. . . .]

On foot again, downtown in the brightly lighted all-night Payless drugstore where all things are sold that it has been proven people will buy, ten thousand items in twenty different departments, Michael is as nervous as a cat and much more excited. Most of the unessential sections are usually closed after normal business hours, and so he counts it as rare good luck to find the florist's concession open this night for the convenience of white-

---

the Sacramento Northern had gone out of the passenger business), slyly unadvertised by the few freeholders and tenants who hadnt yet been evicted by eminent domain under direction of the district water commissioners. The settlement still hangs hidden by foliage on its inhospitable slope eccentrically retarding purification of the gurgling stream that drains the opposite watershed already preserved by the City of Oakland which for the sake of a promiscuous population is extending its reach from this side of the beautiful ridge that formed the sheer head of our obscure little Canyon.

The sparse hamlet strung up along one steep lane and several steeper paths occupied the western end of a long tract that was little by little being repossessed from cranky eccentric homesteaders hitherto left peacefully to their outlandish inconvenience as commuting squatters or tenants of squatters. With Norkid I never walked as far eastward as the first of the reservoirs fed by the tributary "creek" springing from somewhere above us on the escarpment, that barrier to my daily job which the single-track electric railroad tunneled through at its base, and which the road I drove to work on had to climb like a goat trail almost too precipitous for my old engine on the pull up and for its heavily pushed low gear on the way down when I was always in danger of meeting a speedier and less cautious resident at one of the switchback turns. The creek and the road flattened out on the invert of the ravine, accompanying the track past the deeply shaded store and post office, past the shaded wooden school Jonathan would have started at, before they took their separate ways, one toward mingling waters in the forested depths to the right and the other out to the broad open valley of walnuts distinguished by psychiatrists and dominated by Mount Diablo. All the denizens lived straggling or sequestered as high as they could on the northern bank where they could catch from under their pitched roof of trees a little of the sun that never got to the bottom. Their brown dirt paths, most of them joining the gray paved byway to tiny part-time ranches on the grassy rim of the canyon, came down to meet the dark wayside of village conveniences under tall moist aboriginal evergreens lining the obscure road once used by mainline stagecoaches crossing the old pass to the Bay. Where people trickled down across the tracks to their cars you could still see the platform of the station at which rusticators used to catch their morning trains to the city.

For me it was the best place we could ever have asked to live in, albeit barred from the sea, even though (with Sandy's titanic help) I had to sweat tons of chattels up our long hairpin path and (without it) almost daily loads of food or

collar swains and portly experienced gentlemen like himself. There a year ago behind her back while she was making her crucial purchase at the back counter he bought a carnation for her to wear at the restaurant dinner they were headed for. This time however she shall have nothing but red red roses.

Shocked at the price of a dozen he sheepishly buys six wrapped in a cone of white waxy paper. What he's doing is perfectly obvious to observers. All afternoon other more liberal spenders have been doing something of that kind, though many with gardenias chrysanthemums daffodils or even orchids, having no poetic knowledge of what Abelard the scholar of desire was talking about:

———

kerosene, doing whatever I could think of to keep Ruth from rebelling at the putative hardships of idyllic semi-isolation. But it's true the house had been built as a summer cottage, judging by its flimsy underpinnings and the general dearth of studs, and in the winter it was colder than any New England cabin. There was a patch of sunlight for Jonathan to play in at the doorstep where he fearlessly turned up scorpion-like insects that would terrify him now. I kept up my enthusiasm for the daily ordeal until Ruth could stand her loneliness no longer. My will may have been the cause of her discontent but her mother was the agitator. Before we finally moved to our treeless street of white stucco gleaming all day in the sunshine the old lady whom I hardly ever spoke to had prevailed upon her in such a way as to precipitate Norkid's death the best friend I've ever known.

Waking from his naps on the floor of my book-feathered aerie at the top of the house flooded with afternoon sun above the treetops of the bank below he'd roll onto his back stretch straight his shapely arms yawning like the king of beasts and at the same time retract his hind legs as a baby does when not yet unfolded for life. Or standing up stifflegged he'd spread his toes like a cat. He was my sole and joyful companion on every walk I took. Once at the zenith of confident good spirits half a mile up from our house where the trees gave over to a bright green pasture he learnt respect for horses by getting kicked for his rambunctiousness. He was learning other things too and had begun to grow obedient in the fullness of his strength, already more loving than my heart could bear. One night of equinoctial frenzy on the rug in front of our ugly wood stove that could easily get too hot blazing into the long flue I'd rigged for maximum dissipation of heat having had my first fill I taught him to give tongue to my unquenchable desire for the wild thornless rose with long hot gently lapping splashes of obsequious courtesy. I've never heard such a moan of surprise. For a few seconds his homage was received so intensely and generously that her ten fingers scratched the floor in arcs. Only once or twice again, before domestic resentments put an end to all essays at orgy, when I could still occasionally get us to put aside shame, was I allowed to set our eunuch at the experiment, which I never got him to prolong, perhaps because (having been bred to assist the blind and therefore dedicated to even less self-interest than he would have served us with anyway) he'd been gelded too young. But by thus tasting our mingled curds and whey he shared an absolute secret I'm sure she never confessed to her Dr Etwas.

But according to inveterate pattern she allowed herself to be persuaded by the protector of her childhood that she'd never be able to manage a 90-pound

PROLOGOS

Take thou this rose, O Rose,
Since love's own flower it is,
And by that rose
Thy lover captive is.

He assures himself that money laid out for useless and ephemeral decoration does not necessarily indulge either vicious feminine sentimentality or wasteful masculine superstition. There's no more harm in giving in to festal instinct than to the less indulgent voice of your god—provided that you can be sure it's really instinct and not just instinct's prostitution. If

---

beast in my absence, just because steaming with life he still barked in welcome at the sight of any human being and had not yet learned to refrain from placing both forepaws on the breast of any man woman or child he tried to greet with a kiss on the face; and rather than even attempting to reinforce my gradually effective discipline or to otherwise tame his behavior she accepted from her mother without consulting me a length of chain intended to solve the problem of my friend by brute restraint. While I was away at work she leashed him to the rail of the stoop right on the edge of the dooryard terrace while she and Jonathan went for their afternoon walk down to the post office. By the time they were out of sight the poor dog, left behind for the first time and not yet taught the nature of chains, howling his disappointment at not being able to follow their footsteps to the head of the path, had leapt off the side of the steps to get directly to the lower level six feet below his platform, and of course the chain shortened by his woeful circlings of the post stopped him short half way to the ground. He choked to death on the training collar—unless his neck was broken first.

After her brave phone call I drove home almost reckless of my speed and half blinded by my grief, still ignorant of these lethal details. Before asking all my questions and without waiting for Norkid's firm body to grow as deadly stiff as the beloved jaws (locked shut while still agleam with the milky ivory of young fangs under his loosened upper lip known alive only in smiles of perfect faith) I waved Ruth back into the house with Jonathan and dug his grave in hard earth just beyond the swing. Then I carried him as a prince with my face buried in the faded warmth of his life-ebbed ruff, weeping so violently that I could hardly see the dirt for shoveling when in solitude I covered his deep chest still hollow with the breath of life, his glossy tawn and gray fur quivering at every brown clod and pebble that thudded on his ribs.

Never could I speak my blame to Ruth, and I've always wondered if she recognizes the relevant fault in her reactionary aversion to training. Though she's never uttered self-accusation her own misery and her sympathy for mine were sufficient apology for any catastrophic accident, and the cruelty of venting my hatred for the attitude toward boundless nature that she was brought up with would have so far extended the pain she had already suffered in beginning to understand the effect of her mother's benighted attitude toward liberty that I would have incurred a greater guilt than any other in connection with this death, which I secretly held to be murder in the second degree by that interfering old woman, with Ruth her foolish accessory. My unforgiving bitterness has not yet

not instinct, for a poor clerk throbbing with conflicts, it's dissipation. But was it not Blake's opinion expressed by St Willie that "dissipation is better than emotional penury"?

In his family life Michael has always regarded the day of Valentines as sexual rather than charitable, or at least as erotically rather than civilly Christian, and his personal stand on the matter has long since been tacitly accepted by Ruth as an element of the niggardly Chapman tradition. She and her sons nevertheless include him in their practice of the customary civil agape, along with almost every schoolmate and relative of the boys; and does so without apparent resentment of his attitude, which is excused

---

been purged, and I have never since then walked but in city streets. Jonathan is still too young and will always be too talkative to take the place of my magnificent dog.

But all this was far from uppermost in mind as I took the solitary urban nightwalk to prepare my defense for the procrastinated confrontation with Ruth about my own deliberate and unpardonable guilt as a highhanded tyrant. On my aimless tramp I passed the locked and unlighted pseudo-revived-Tudor-neo-Gothic phony brown-stained fane of St John, episcopal but not papal, the last trace of its catholicism used as inconspicuously as possible in the mandatory words of Cranmer's compromising prayer book, which were forcefully bracketed by an intimidating organ and further diluted by idealistic preaching, genteelly outliving its originally fashionable location. Mr Gilchrist still young with an ugly wife and four obviously unhealthy children was ordained by a laying-on of hands in direct succession from the first bishop of Rome but he's an innate Protestant psychologically educated to the responsibilities of a modern pastor and he doesn't like to be called a priest. For him the ritual of Morning Prayer is a framework for professionalized and organ-ized hymn-singing to mount his sermon in.

I was more uncomfortable than usual when Ruth openly admired him for the spiritual humanism of his preaching. As convert from her old bleak Methodism (or whatever it was) she listened to his liberal advice enthusiastically. Having started there in an attempt at cultural conciliation she sent the two boys to Sunday School after I put in one appearance to prove that I appreciated her choice of the church closest to the house (except for the African one a block down our street) and that I wasnt finicky in my prejudice against the Low majority of my native communion, and then like most of the husbands dropped out of sight. I might have reappeared at Palm Sunday and Michaelmas if she had stuck with it. But despite her ardent yearning for almost any right hand of fellowship it's inconceivable that she would ever remain a constant parishioner there or elsewhere, whatever the level of theological understanding.

The freest years she ever had even at college were spent as a day student studying at her mother's house. She's been a stranger everywhere, but not by choice—almost as much among those who partially divine her subtle good works or the unique worth of her gentle womanhood as among those who dislike her diffident nonconformity. Her renewed hopes for "organized religion" went sour when she found she couldnt encourage the world's charity by belonging to a club of sanctimonious worldlings. But her best reason for withdrawing, known she

as the failing of an executive too busy to find the time he'd like for affectionate trifles. At least he has the grace to give Ruth credit for the boys'
cheerful innocence of his churlish recusancy, blessing her gentle diplomacy
on this point as on a hundred others, well aware that she would have been
pleased to have a father for her children more alive to the fullnesses of
growing hearts and less scrupulous in discriminating his kinds of love.
—Anyhow, he admits no obligation to buy other presents now.

   Averting his eyes from the array of candy and nuts that cruelly lures
the ravenous beast in his guts he sidles toward the barricaded booth at the
back of the store, affecting to search varieties of notions like a weak-willed

---

said only to the three of us and presumably thought by Gilchrist to be known
only to the two of them, was that misled by the spiritual affinity of his hopeful
client he had fallen in love with her and was trying to get her into bed. I asked
what had happened, how did she know? "He tells me in his sermons. Michael if
you won't come to church with me every Sunday I'll have to drop out as soon as I
can without causing a scandal. I must stop letting him see me, don't you think?"

   And even after she had ceased going to services, having taken the boys out of
Sunday School (which they remember not at all), she continued to estimate the
affect of her ideas upon the world by the announced texts of his sermons and
those of his ecumenical colleagues all over Oakland, as listed in the *Oakland Tribune*, in which national automobile advertisements also carried personal messages
from him. I have tried to avoid ecclesiastical discussion ever since then, but I
think it very likely that she will someday try religion again at a less "organized"
level of protestantism.

   A little later I skirted the commercial district marked by the large brick
Teleology Moving & Storage Warehouse company where I've secretly paid good
money to keep my duplicate manuscripts in the trunk room, which fortunately is
accessible to customers during business hours but which I have to visit in a
sweaty rush at lunchtime without much time to eat, though of course it's possible
to get in a little reading on the streetcar out and back from Sather Gate. The tariff for safekeeping could be spent more usefully, but it's the only insurance I have.
I was glad to find it at the height of my fear for everything important to me after
the Sunday Tom Topalis came out to the back yard when I was burning some
trash in the incinerator to see what I was up to because Ruth had just fled down
the street with the kids after knocking on his door to warn him that I was trying
to set fire to the house and burn them all up. I've always been grateful to him for
tactfully assuming so little from the incident, which offered him all the more
excuse to raise our rent; but apparently he took the incident as nothing more than
a domestic tempest. Maybe even Greeks have such troubles too.

   On that occasion of indecisive dismay I went out on the avenue to trail her at
a distance, finally overtaking her in the park. As a mother she was calm and
attentive but I saw in her face that extraordinary preoccupation that's now so
familiar. When I lightly touched her arm with the best smile I could muster, as if
catching up on a family outing, she gave a blink of fright but then seemed glad
to have my company. She carried Matty, then our baby, clasped to her breast. Her
hair was all astray. In vain she had waited five minutes for a street car, having

browser, the little spray of nubile buds pointed downward to keep them he hopes from opening too soon. Two or three people are waiting for the pharmacist. Perhaps he's the same man to whom Ruth presented Mrs V 's adjusted prescription two or three diameters larger and much tougher than Mr P 's standard rubber quoit shortly after her latest gauging the day Roger had begun to crawl, as the old saying goes that's quite unscientific in light of the fact that at six weeks a baby probably can't even roll over by himself though of course he may look as if he's trying to stomach his way across the blanket—or in other words his appointed day for first inspection at the King's Well-Baby Clinic and his mother's at the GYN Department (with

---

difficulty with Jonathan's questions and complaints who wasnt dressed for an excursion, and I think she would have taken a ride in either direction; but then she had walked in a burdened mother's normal haste to the familiar place of grass trees and swings where other mothers were resting with their baby carriages. I think I was right not to have presented myself until we'd both had time to recover ourselves.

It was only then that I began to see the depth of a suffering I hadnt taken the trouble to divine. But I trembled with my own fear and helplessness rather than in true sympathy for her feelings, which still horrify me like the open ocean on a gray winter day when you shrink from the water as you float on a wet raft. I feared for the children and I feared for my time. In her sickness I could summon no love, none of the compassion or praise or desire or mystical friendship that I might feel for her even in the most hateful moments of health and that will surely overcome me at her death if it comes before my own. My love is hardly to be mentioned beside hers. Mine yields to alarm or selfishness whenever it's tested, whenever it might be of help to her desperation. I have made some advancement in understanding but hardly at all in empathy. How can I make myself try even to sympathize? I only want to escape my absolute dismay at her illness, at my part in making it worse.

Without a word I took the baby from her arms and we all walked quietly home. "Michael I need help again. I'd like to go back to Dr Etwas. Do you think we can afford it? . . . I know how hard it is to pay for."

I pretended not to notice that she was weeping in her quiet unselfsobbing way as I patted Matty on the back and watched my step at the curbs. "Why honey for crying out loud of course we can! Money isnt important at a time like this." A wave of joyful relief swept over me at the positive bravery of this blessed unhappy woman who despite the overwhelming blackness of her firmament was renewing the long struggle to suspend despair and join the dreary middle world of consensual reality. She was able to make one more plea for rescue from the endless deep cold sea that she fought to keep from drowning her children in, gathering her remnant of strength to look back toward the last island she had dispensed with. The doctor she had left off going to was my own last hope too, the one person in the world who could relieve me of total responsibility. In the gratitude of my heart I repented all the resentment and distrust I had silently heaped upon him and the expense of him for two or three years.

Her spirits rose higher than mine, more no doubt because of my attitude than at the prospect of actually facing her old therapeutic antagonist again. "If I could only forget everything personal and remember everything objective I'd be a

another six weeks still to go before the bloody leakage resumes)—while her man waited as inconspicuously as possible at the same paperback book display that now detains him as he keeps his eye on the short queue.

Owing to his brisk changes of position, the anxiety of disbursement for his initial purchase, his simulated inspection of other products, and the renewed rumblings of hunger, Caliburn P has been flagging; but now (as in last year's instance) faced with pictures and titles on tendentiously designed covers the prurient priority is reasserting itself. With one hand deep in his pocket the putative master assists his sovereign servant in freeing itself of obstruction on the angular way up; with the other hand

---

brilliant girl!" She laughed and squeezed my arm. "That's the kind of amnesia I'd like to have! I'm just a little child, Michael. How can you put up with me?"

But I was learning to know that nothing had fundamentally changed and that there was no such thing as a cure. A doctor is at best a lightning rod who conducts by white lies as long as his treatment continues. In your desperation, as long as you can pay him to listen to her, he's worth every penny, like successful blackmail, even if you may begin to lose sight of that fact as you grumble at the monthly bills. You find out what he's good for when she drops out of his course. Meanwhile you wait for the children to grow clear of the thicket and you look forward to the psychic toughening of her old age when the gross history of even discontinuous and exiguous survival begins to weigh as strength and when the sensitive skin has been tattooed with scars and calluses that can benumb her to fresh pain. The doctor tells the patient to adjust to her husband and gives her to understand that the man's neurosis is something she'll have to cope with if she wants to stay married, a motive about which neither consultant nor wife are ready to admit serious question; and when my interview finally came about after years of refusal to meet his several predecessors, having at last expressed my willingness to talk to him for her sake (thus demonstrating to her satisfaction my concern for the inner person herself and with my promise putting her on a temporary mend), he said pretty much the same thing to me—about adjusting to her—except that he allowed himself to go so far as to hint at an unhopeful diagnosis of paranoid schizophrenia. I was very grateful for his perhaps unethical disclosure, which I admit made me see years of incidents and misunderstandings in the light of my insensitivity to her frightful weakness and enabled me to recast the simple war between her and me into a tacit league of two for raising unreason's siege of our hearth.

But all too well I know that I remained essentially intransigent, and that Ruth's burden of shadows is leadened by the man I am and then redoubled by the bizarre perversity of my hobby horse which may never justify itself to any part of posterity, still less to anyone she respects, and which is detected in the pragmatical world of psychologic (which she remains a citizen of) only by the disturbances it makes; and in this view, which every once in a while I am obliged to take into consideration, my cold passions stand simply as a variety of common personal derangement. "I thought you were trying to kill us!" she explained with a sober smile.

That night of reckoning no distance seemed to tire me, as if it was a holiday and I hadnt been on my feet all day. After an hour or more of wandering the

Michael lays his thyrsus of roses across the tumult to conceal it from the suspicion of citizens.

[We walked all the way downtown together to this first stop on our evening out, gay with tingling visions of our reunion and full of indirect small talk feeling foolish for what I thought must have been patent to every passerby, while Hecuba kept watch over our newest baby and his brothers.]

In order to neutralize any appearance of furtive lechery he saunters along to the magazine racks covertly watching for the last man to move away from the dispensary. But here the provocation is worse. Words and

---

quietest streets of our district I finished my loop along the ridge of the hill so that I could swing past Caleb's rabbit warren before turning back down to our dreary streetcar Lane nearly opposite the all-night display of practical sculpture. Passing the medical building in which Dr Etwas keeps office it was comforting to reflect that he seems aged far beyond the middle of middle age—at least old enough to have mitigated my suspicion that she had confused his desire like the Reverend Gilchrist's with mine even though he represented the paternal protection I think she always seeks in a man having never had it from her yearningly beloved father who was ever negligible in his household and even in her childhood had seemed superannuated.

Etwas is wiser than most; but it was only to be expected that she'd stop seeing him when he told her pointblank (as I later found out) that her "ideas" were absurd; and during the one call that she and I later paid on him together I actually heard him try to disprove by logic one of her delusions of personal influence upon the United Nations. I must assume that he very seldom yields to the healthy temptation that I an inexperienced layman soon learned to resist; it may be that as last resort in some higher notion of dynamic experimentation he was deliberately forcing her to face the verge of stark raving incarceration in a hope that the womancula in her would summon the strength to turn back from a giddy leap into the bottomless void: but it seems to me that it was Ruth herself who saved his tactics from failure. Her ultimate sense of reality was just sufficient to prevent weakness and despair from sweeping the field of resistance. Did the doctor ever understand that a precarious inconclusive truce, however painful to the rational sensibility, is a triumph of success compared to losing a patient of more worth than any other in his career and bringing disaster upon her children (the most precious ever yet engendered) simply in order to prove to her that she's crazy?

Anyway that particular episode accusing me to our landlord as a murderous arsonist—I think the only time she's unmistakably betrayed our danger to the outside world—followed by her decision to return to the doctor, the sign that succored by his weekly or semiweekly voice she'd refuse to surrender herself to the easier destiny, revealed to me at the same time her pricelessly human exertion and the tenacious substantiality of the shadows she has striven against most of the years of her life. Perhaps I did not start them in her life but I am to blame for paying no attention to her bravely understated cries and failing to appreciate the strength she was able to draw from her soul at critical phases of the struggle. Since the day I finally saw what was happening before my blind self-centered

illustrations reduce him to the flaming manhood that populates the world at any cost. At the same time he's alarmed to discover that the apothecary is being assisted by an appraising girl from the patent medicine counter to whom it would be morally impossible for him to address his requisition. He must wait until she is called back from her own sector to ring up a humdrum sale.

Consummately enacting every possible gesture of indifference to whatever wares were guarded behind the counter he affects to drift into the position at which he may be the first and only patron to get the man's service as soon as the officiously lurking girl (no longer occupied,

------

eyes, though in trembling cowardice I still ignore much of what I should make sure to understand (as if her psychosis were my own passing delusion or as if the nightmare had worn off) and shamelessly try to forget my witness of what I havent been able to avoid seeing—since that day even in my angriest despair or most optimistic relief I have never taken a stand with or against my wedlocked mate without fearing for my foothold in the sand under water.

I accepted the fact that I couldnt demand that she go back to the treatments I really knew nothing about unless I was prepared to drop everything else of importance and either devote myself to long patient sympathy or prefer charges against her before some grossly categorical M D of public sanity who would have diagnosed the mother of my children with summary indifference to her peerless quality. If she wasnt given the help she might be supposed to have earned of men they'd get her out of circulation regardless of the violence that would be done to herself and to her survivors in seeming to confirm the cold enmity of society and in forcing her the last step across an undetermined borderline into the zone of irreversible depression. Sometimes when her symptoms are remitted by spates of happiness or held in abeyance by the natural cycle of a woman's spirit it seems as if I've been overstating the case to myself; but I can no longer believe in cure. Even when I forget many of the pathological words and acts that have reiterated each other my memory is never so relaxed that I can altogether fool myself as to her essential condition.

I could no more risk letting her suspect my sudden fear of her secret attitude toward my manuscripts than my opinion that domestic matters had grown out-right dangerous and that therefore she should go back to the program of self-evaluated therapy that had kept the family in penury and thwarted all my own hopes for escape from petty circumstances. I've never feared for the children at her hands, nor for my own life while they live, since her god has never called for anybody's pain. But it was all too easy to guess the symbolic significance to her of some great sacrifice on my part that would force a new beginning upon us all and insure my undivided attention to the family.

When we had returned to the apartment after that crisis at the park I found one of the gas stove burners going hard with an open flame in the cluttered kitchen as if she'd been overtaken by her cloud of terror just as she was about to start cooking supper. A few days later I ran into Hecuba on the front steps as I was getting home from work and she asked me how Ruth was feeling. "Why, has she been sick today?" I asked. "Oh no, not that I know of. It's just that she

ready to pounce) is diverted to another wicket by someone else's open and aboveboard response to national advertising. He finds himself at the newsstand (which was placed at the far end of the floor no doubt in order to maximize a sucker's exposure to the lures of more profitable merchandise on his way in and out) where he stares down at an authoritative bit about Washington politics as recorded on the front page of the New York Testament (a few days late on the West Coast); but he can't make out the text without gracelessly stooping to read and turn the paper over, an act from which he refrains for fear of incurring the obligation to lay out another 15¢.

---

seemed a little nervous Sunday afternoon. She said she was afraid of fire. Did anything happen?" I shrugged it off by saying "Maybe she thought she smelled smoke."

As it turned out the doctor—or simply the fact that she went to see him again—did succeed in making her separate a vast dysreason from the small logic of family life, and to conceal it if only to protect its higher truth against the military reasoning of a masculine culture, against all the prudential enemies of imagination that seemed to have been planted like weeds by Mother the malevolent gardener. And I too helped slightly by bending a little with the wind, sometimes taking time to play the rudiments of a domestic part (concealing clenched teeth at every abuse of my honesty and taste), though I made less and less effort as a stronger or more illusive pattern of self-reliance began to appear in her life. But she had become a Cassandra of unpredictable prophecy, to which after our life settled back into the routine that restored me to my own dream I pretended to listen respectfully.

It's strange that I'd still been so obtuse the year before that first acute scare. Probably just because the old lady supplied a housekeeper to take care of Jonathan without disturbing my private hours when Dr Etwas sent Ruth to a private hospital for a few days of "tests". She put a cheerful face upon it and seemed to worry more about how I'd get along as a bachelor than about what she herself was about to undergo. Maybe she was pleased at getting concentrated attention. But at that time she was still strong enough to protect me from knowledge too profound. When she came home she was smiling. I was told that specialists had ruled out somatic dysfunction, relieving the only anxiety I was seriously susceptible to. For a long time thereafter I noticed nothing remarkably untoward, blinded by the irritations of messy home economics and by the difficulty of paying Etwas to talk to her so that I could concentrate on the things I like to concentrate on.

Later she began to assert independence by giving over the weekly therapy. I was given to understand that she discontinued her appointments with the doctor's approval, and I took the cessation of his bills as a profession of success. It was only when I knew more about her troubles the second time around and finally visited him that he told me it was she who had broken off her history as a patient with the insistence that she could get along by herself, declaring that it was more important to the family that our money be spent on household furnishings.

Once I was so wrought up about wasting my life that I refused to take her and the kids anywhere during my vacation. Indeed I was determined to indulge

Still not known from Adam in the city he inhabits, his embarrassment mitigated by anonymity, he just then finally gets his chance. Unhastily stepping up to the specialized clerk (better accredited as a professional than any customer and well aware of it), as it were absentmindedly, and using what he believes to be the most generic trade name Michael casually asks for a package of Athenians. To his heartfelt relief the transaction is as simple as it's ever been since the first time he was able to screw his courage up after many passes back and forth through the North End, long before he had the slightest prospect of a willing girl, at the only drugstore in Greater Boston where though obviously no more than sixteen he wasnt

---

my selfish appetite for seclusion (two weeks fulltime being worth a year of daily compressions and decompressions). At first I was foolish enough not to be perturbed when she announced without advanced notice either to me or to her mother that she was using some "emergency money" from the old witch to carry the two children off to a "cottage on Russian River", taking the bus late at night with little luggage and no booking of accommodations. She was serenely confident that the Lord would provide. He did—but at the cost of premium rates, shocking outlays for the duplication of clothes and utensils left at home, and severe fiscal restrictions on any fun they might have had.

My heart was angry most of the time she was gone, hardened by inconvenient self-services, before it softened with tender loneliness and tough desire. I finally went up to fetch them and found a dark tent on a wooden platform cluttered and filthy from a week of attempts to rough it with two untrained little boys. For all my dismay at the time it seemed only another case to confirm my simple diagnosis of slobbish laziness. I was too heedlessly defensive as her adversary in marriage to apprehend the helplessness of her incompetence. To me everything was still a matter of will and discipline. I've never believed in teaching by precept force and punishment but until the shattering day of vivid and explicit revelation the crude motto of my rage and disgust had always been *She'll just have to learn for herself!* or *Let her stew in her own juices!*.

That was the only answer of which I had been capable to the question of what was to be done in a situation that seemed to argue nothing but gutless indifference to order and was hardening my resistance to every cry for help. I believed that short of abandoning the whole family like a totally irresponsible criminal my front of natural hardheartedness was the only means of educating her—if I was not to resign my own life to permanently ignominious failure. For that pedagogical reason I had made it my business not to seem aware of the funks she fell into when I was out of the house, of the weeping she tried to hide, of ever-unfinished housework, of morning enthusiasms forgotten by the afternoon, of unsuccessful endeavors to join groups or make friends like other housewives, of endlessly heartrendering resolutions to turn over a new leaf and become as others are, or to embark upon some career that would improve either the world at large or our family's standard of living. Yet she had valiantly spared me most of her feelings and carried on her struggle as long as she could alone, and allowed her anger to show itself against me only long after it was intricately compounded and absurdly overdue—even then diverting most of it toward her own abulic infirmity.

worried about being seen because it lay deep within the most fearful precinct of antianglosaxon Italians, when he discovered as a windfall of experience that they were always packed in units of three called quarter-dozens
(according to the mercantile tradition still observed by manufacturers)—
though then for experimental reasons he was to use up two of them without waiting to find his object and like a Boy Scout who was always
prepared carry the third in his wallet for a couple of years—for now the
druggist batting not an eyelash silently slides open a smooth little drawer
under the counter and quick as a wink slips the handsome little square
packet palm down into a paper bag as adroitly as if a third-party rubber-

---

Thus I lost confidence in my opinions when my vantage was suddenly elevated
by an involuntarily inflated observation balloon and I saw conditions on her side of
the battle line. I grew willing to retreat as broadly and as rapidly as she was capable
of advancing, for there was no good in my loss if it did not become her gain: we'd
both have lost the war. Yet how could I let her occupy territory in which she would
be overthrown and destroyed by the populace? So the front didnt much move even
after my enlightenment, and in the stalemate of defensive battles—interrupted only
by the raiding impulses of intolerable boredom, only temporarily suspended by
bedtime love-truces—our warfare sustained itself over the years with few salient
attacks. Most of our military activity took place far behind the lines, usually back at
supreme headquarters where on both sides there was plenty of dissension on the
general staff and a great deal of postwar planning.

My central policy was to prevent a collapse on either side. I had begun to live
in fear of victory. If it were not for anxiety about the children and my dim grasp
of her excruciating anguish (despite nearly total nescience of spiritual pain) I
could almost say that to me her chronic illness became transparent again, itself
invisible and irrelevant in the faulty communion I would have had with any
woman. If you pay most of your attention to the ego's half of a yoked life it is not
difficult in a phony war of immobility to ignore any progressive danger short of
flame-throwing Marines or spear-armed phantoms in grotesque masks screaming
weird battle cries against bunkers and barbed wire. Yet the times were to come
when I was terrified by apparitions in peaceful daylight.

On my evasive nightwalk I did not pass a single pedestrian. It was during
the most heavily advertised hour of devilvision, whose myriad eye I saw everywhere from the empty sidewalks—through curtains, through shades, through the
very walls. When I got home the children were asleep in their usual innocence of
the gratuitous squalor. The kitchen was littered exactly as when we had left the
table (except for the scraps that Semiramis had dragged to the floor and sorted for
consumption), and Ruth in bed scarcely undressed was buried under a jumble of
blankets in the front room pitch-black and stuffy with windows closed and shades
drawn. My recurrent anger at this slovenly abandonment of all effort to maintain
decency, as well as at her peasantlike attitude toward fresh air, had become so
familiar to me that I literally shrugged my shoulders even as I clenched my fists
and figuratively whistled the opening bars of America the Beautiful. Although at
that late date I was well used to her varieties of disorder I still could not bring myself to make much allowance for her hopeless fatigue. In imaginary conversations

neck were standing in line and without even asking if sir wants a full dozen despite the putative fact that he's a married man buying Valentine flowers to mend fences at home with a view to softening up the ass he hasnt been getting regularly for typical domestic reasons—unless he's a sneaky and even more ridiculous pursuer of young bait, seeing as how he's plainly too penurious to have a girlfriend on the side. The professional vendor is presumably less conscious of his clerical degradation than Michael of his own typical motives, and clearly not at all surprised that this frugal kit of so-called prophylactics is the only item besides flowers on his customer's shopping list.

---

that could never be permitted to occur I was continually reminding her that she had asked for children before everything else and ought to be able to live up to the conditions they entailed. But I did refrain from slamming the shrouded glass door I'd opened to find her at least alive in her retirement. Instead I went into the bathroom to clear the tub of toys and wadded wet towels. It seemed impossible that we would ever touch each other again.

Yet lying in my bath with favorite barge and tugboat, insulated by lovely hot water from all sensation of chaos beyond my control, and forgetting all about the new issue between us, I became more philosophical. My spirits began to rise, as usual. Tonight's glob of entropic degradation had not harmed the children or hindered my work; it had cost nothing out of pocket: it was merely a recurrent lapse in the performance of inessentials. In due course she would cheerfully try to set it right. The present state of the house was not unprecedented; it was not even as bad as the worst it had been many times before. Judging by the past, I reminded myself that this might be the lowest water of a spring tide that flowed and ebbed with the rational and irrational alike, regardless of any particular tempest—that I was merely paying in the old way for three weeks of peace already spent. Her mood— along with a certain puffing of the belly—might symptomize merely a vague malaise that usually preceded the erotic euphoria which often announced the imminence of her monthly miscarriage. I was cautious about reading nature's signs now so roiled with mentality's disturbances because even under ordinary circumstances I have sometimes been mistaken in my studies, but as I watched the homuncular Mr P floating from his anchor like a languid nun buoy, resting from his highest pursuit, my heart leapt in almost unguarded relief from the hitherto undispellable anxiety that Sarah's last remark to me after my birthday party might have had foundation in dread tenacious fact. I had been especially uneasy because we were in the midst of one of our fructification battles within the larger war.

I blush now at the peril I repeatedly courted long after I'd been taught my lessons. On one occasion she ripped the rubber of her contraceptive tympanum (not yet darkly ripened with post-Mattem usage) by forcing it down the handle of a broom, and with a gay laugh held the ragged bracelet up before my face as her third wedding ring, informing me that Lytle J King would not leave his money to her for the work she was expected to undertake unless she produced a girl-child to carry on her line. I couldnt help smiling at the first news that she was heiress to the great philanthropic tycoon before I understood that it was not merely metaphorical. There was no play of mind in her poetic license. Lately I've

During the swift exchange of goods for money Mr P has dropped back to pensile rest in his hiding place next to the twin companions who sponsor all his ascents, doubtless disgusted with all the catallactic nonsense that's coming between him and his very simple longing for the deep comfort of his proper and familiar goal. So now according to the orectic law of conservation up springs again the desire in Michael's stomach, a right flank attack when the left has faltered.

Back outdoors at the car stop across the street everything conspires to revive the wilted hopes. The commercial displays of furnished rooms with three walls are more luxurious than such a city warrants. A soft warming

----

heard nothing about her great expectations. Maybe she's grown more canny about the world's cruel want of faith and now hides her convictions from me as she learned to hide them from the doctor. But like as not she's forgotten that scenario. I have never openly scoffed at such simplified shortcuts in the hopeful part of her brain. In Essex County all the marshes are drained by rectilinear ditches that give passage also to the clean life-laden sea coming in. Yet these fictions make my hair stand on end and scythe away whatever patch of cheerfulness I've been nurturing. I say nothing partly because I haven't the courage to discuss my horror and partly because I don't want her to fix in memory any of the delirious pronouncements that she might feel obliged to reconcile her saner opinions and decisions to. I usually make a show of accepting them as matters of possible fact in which I simply happen to have no active interest. But sometimes I flatter her by using one as premise for a logical argument that I must make against some absurd demand or intention urgently requiring denial on strictly practical grounds.

I sullenly resolved not to go near her until she forgot or modified her objection to rubber, hoping that in the pinch of her own desire she'd let me use thimbles of the same material until she could be brought around to asking a druggist for another tympanum of the type much preferred by both of us and also safer. I'd never grudge the money for duplicating any number of such replacements.

But she'd have nothing to do with my old tricks and it was in my extremity that I finally hit upon the compromise that the Pope recommends. Only I didnt tell her what I was plotting. But it's hard for the man alone to be as scientific as two cooperating Romans. Of course there was no way for me to get her diurnal temperature, but by preserving a much wider margin against error than my florid part liked to put up with, keeping a gross record on my private calendar, I relied on biological generalizations for compromising total abstinence and encouraging her warmest affection with the false implication that I tacitly concurred with an end-cause as good and natural to her mind as its means were to mine, for I must confess to an obscure thrill of unstinted nakedness that I had never before been aware of hazarding.

I began to suffer the consequences of my deception when later she revealed that baffled by our failure to re-engender she'd been to the fertility clinic and pressed me to do the same. She thought it might be a matter of some minor anatomical stumbling block on her side, since my functioning had always been perfect; after the third child something might have altered in the conduit of

darkness has descended upon the streets and poulticed away their raw provinciality, enriching the amber-lighted sumptuaries behind perfectly perspicuous plate glass that invites you in rather than keeping you out even now when the building is closed with invisible locks on the cosmopolitan revolving doors also thickly glassed in bronze frames. The quietening pavements of the town's ostensibly prosperous center give off soft swishing clicks and echoes known to encourage romantic hearthside desire.

The streetcar comes at once, cheerfully lighted a little less comfortingly than the decorated shops but well suited for its return to the darker suburb (suburb of a suburb, sometimes hight the Athens of the West!), as promptly as if it has been waiting around the corner for our bridegroom to

---

intromission. She wished me if necessary to become the donor for her artificial insemination. Of course I refused, and one night when in urgent disingenuity I'd almost asked her to hope patiently she said quite distinctly "If the man I love won't give me my daughter I'll get her from someone else!" Which I pretended to take as a jest.

But the following Christmas, quite unaccountably, to my indescribable joy, she put a new vaginal baffle under the family tree as a gaily wrapped package to me from her. It may have been a quid for some quo which she weighed much more heavily than I did, for I was quite puzzled about my desert. Perhaps the new refrigerator; or the key to my study, which I had agreed to leave hanging where she could find it when the floor needed sweeping: an extremely important concession that not long after the holidays I had to rescind (without a word of recrimination on either side) when she failed to replace it on the appointed nail and almost lost it entirely despite all her assurances that in this crucial regulation my irritating crochet would be scrupulously respected. She apparently yielded in the symbolic issue, so that after this very significant retreat I recovered my earlier defensive position.

About that time however, after she had parted with the doctor again and thought that I therefore had plenty of disposable money (though the saving was actually spent many times over on old and new debts), she insisted, in obedience to some unspecified voice demanding her acknowledgement of Mr King's promise, that I should buy one of that magnate's new small cars dubbed Little Kings when he brought them out to challenge the industry in Detroit, which had already determined the public against efficient automobiles by employing the self-fulfilling market research that's always obtained by massive campaigns for inefficiency. (He had become so famous with prodigious feats of shipbuilding during the war and with the endowment of a semisocialized medical institution most of us continue to share with his workers that it was merely good business and not vanity to name the cars after his giant-killing self.) When I explained that it was impossible for us to make any capital purchase that required either a downpayment or a monthly installment she chose to disbelieve me, as I found out when a salesman phoned me at the store, much to my embarrassment with the boss standing nearby, in order to verify my intentions—about which I had to tell him there was some misunderstanding. In that humiliating fashion she gave herself another opportunity to learn the cruel fact (which in our case I'm glad of)

appear. He takes the right rearmost seat whence he can make the shortest time to his house as soon as the car stops at the orange-banded pole opposite the Laboratory. [There will be no legerdemain once the kids are asleep! Ready or not here I come my honeyed rose, as raring as a king with nothing but an heir in mind.]

The car's first pause comes at a principal intersection where the front door claps open for a clutch of transfer passengers from the San Francisco train. A juke box sounds from the penny arcade in which pomaded sailors and leather-jacketed cowboys (maybe sailors in mufti) pick up broads and pigs from among chewers of gum who saunter in pairs. The unctious plaint of an invulnerably womanish man ignores the noise it emerges from:

------

that women own little credit in their own right—especially when they have not a scrap of property or income to their name.

This time I couldnt help asking her how she knew what old King wanted her to do, since seeing that the understanding had to be kept secret from his family and associates he'd never tried to meet her. She revealed that the messages came from classified ads placed in the Automobile section of the *Tribune* by King's dealers [who by then actually were trying every possible means to liquidate their ill-considered investment].

I wasn't surprised when she repented of our contraceptive covenant. Before Easter she burned out the membrane of my Christmas present with kitchen matches and left it on my pillow as fair warning of a coney snare. She had heard a United Nations speech with the message that God did not wish her to lead the women of America in birth control until our population was larger than Russia's. After a bitter fortnight I resumed my risky method more resentfully than ever.

It's very difficult to keep up with the variable facts about a half-estranged woman when you must keep her from knowing that you are interested in them, especially when her rhythms are often disturbed by emotions sometimes strong enough to lead rather than follow her body's necessities, and when she herself seems continually bewildered about where she stands in a month of signals coming to her from all levels and directions without caring to recognize even her most predictable moods. I've seen her so improvidently overtaken by what must have been interoceptively accumulated menses that she dripped fast spots of blood on the floor staggering out of bed to the bathroom as if listlessly surprised by the unexpected nuisance of menarche. I wonder that my desire ever revived.

But it did, it always does. The inveterate flaming that might have been easily deferred weakened my judgment on precisely the wrong night, probably a certain one I remember from about the time in question. I was immediately so anxious about what I'd done in slipshod half-asleep indulgence of habit that when I woke up I was about ready to have my balls cut off. If Nature hadnt given me a month of suspense to get used to her dreaded intention, and then nine more to prepare for the actual calamity, I'd have jumped off my raft of responsibilities and let the devil take them over. Yet Roger was conceived a pure and perfect soul. Ruth grew happy within herself, in spite of my utterly heartless and bitter response to the accident (expressed only by odious silence).

> I've got a touch of the love
> That comes from above . . .

When the vessel lurches forward again Michael notices that one of the new fellow-travelers is his overhead neighbor Hecuba Jones. She sits toward the front of the car with her back to him and several passengers obstruct his view of her. Putting the flowers out of sight he shrinks from any backward glance she might throw his way. If she caught him in his act she'd immediately recognize the obvious. She'd laugh to herself (and maybe later to one of her boyfriends), pitying the poor husband! Married men are no mystery to her, those caitiffs who longing for the deliquescence honeypot support half the music of America by taking their wives to night clubs for public softening.

In the most unforgivable and hateful kind of opposition to my fate I withheld all sympathy and help. But in the event I had finally accepted my immediate destiny. I love Roger as much as the other two, whose conception was her fault not mine at all because as she afterwards discovered and confessed to me with a smile she had been inserting the goddam thing upsidedown. I also found out that she had just guessed at the size of the second one when she lost the gynecologist's prescription slip.

And so brooding in the bathtub, a prisoner serving three concurrent sentences for his folly, I was much more cagey about trying to beat the system. Since I was a little older in tissue and a little less optimistic about narrowing prospects, and since I no longer expected new experience in the marriage bed, it was slightly easier to abstain—except when hers was the invitation, except whenever I found her willingly transfigured once again as my goddess of sweet delight. During that latest stretch of peace it had been as if she thought of nothing but our recreation, and I attributed her extraordinary readiness to the more sophisticated cultivation of our mutuality [HN 9]. Yet I was never confident of a negative outcome and every month the indication that I had deceived one more full moon (my technical triumph, her occult defeat) outweighed all the deprivations and displeasures of my current life. Sometimes I think I could undergo her outright total insanity better than a fourth child.

For a while I almost believed my destiny spared of both those absolute afflictions. I was still trustful enough—trustful as the doctor, if (according to her account of how things wound up between them) he had really discharged her from his care the second time and she had not indeed discharged him (to use a term that makes me uncomfortable in the context)—trustful enough to believe that as her lunacy had remitted in its socially embarrassing aspect it must have internally dissolved or abated rather than merely withdrawn from the behavioral surface and intussuscepted as a carbuncle of compressed symbols in the citadel of her brain where frustrated liberties and other people's misapprehensions can be converted into claims of personal power.

In other words I was fooled by the growing appearances of harmlessness as long as she waylaid me with mature if not constant carnality. Her letters to the

Spying, he finds it touching that innocent of sophistication after all her years of urban commuting she's shading her eyes from the internal light of the car to peer out the window at a dreary cityscape as if she were just returning home from a trip around the world. He must avert his face for fear she'll see his reflection in the glass—but not before confirming his opinion that she's rather full of figure than slim, a little too blond and plastered in her style. It appears that when traveling alone she habitually purses her lips in a silent whistling—not like that of a pert gamine assert-ing her worth to others but in the manner of one praising her contented independence. [Hecuba might have brought to mind a certain new kind of culinary utensil which just at that time housewives were selling to each other more aggressively than encyclopedia salesmen, pots and pans lined with brown plastic that permitted no organic matter to adhere to its

---

editor when I steeled myself to find them still made me cringe before Republican readers of my acquaintance (especially Greatrakes), but they did me no irremedi-able harm—even when the Tribune printed her comment (anent some news item) that Americans bathe too much, keep too clean, and that it might be good for penal reform if prisoners refused to wash instead of going on hunger strikes.

One cryptic piece nevertheless had made me distinctly uncomfortable, though I was still enough of an innocent about spirituality to regard it as nothing but an attempt to prove her unrecognized creativity in clever language. It seemed to have been written in opposition to an elevated-highway plan being bruited for somewhere on our side of MacArthur Boulevard—a proposal that had hitherto lain entirely outside the scope of her interest in public affairs and that I wasnt aware she had even known about. Her words struck so far off the mark (and yet were still so sarcastic or metastatic in a style mortifying to my sense of propriety) that they would have been taken by almost anyone else as favoring the project. As usual I pretended never to have looked at the editorial page, and as usual she seemed willing enough to have it escape my attention until she grew more sure of her effectiveness as the days went by. Finally when she could no longer contain her craving for recognition she referred to it as an article attacking sexual repres-sion in religion to which she had gotten "thousands of responses from all over the world". Having my attention drawn to the importance of her "spiritual leader-ship" was enough to jolt me out of hopeful illusion. It was unbearable to listen to her, but I could no more bring myself to speak against the free expression of her "ideas" than to offer the least bit of phony encouragement.

God knows how many letters of hers have been published on both sides of the Bay! What I don't know won't hurt me. I take a little comfort in her modesty of spoken address. It may prevent scandalous abuse of the telephone while I'm out of the house. Always preferring the written word she's a wonder of speed accuracy and syntax on that typewriter I bought her in defense against the ostensibly rea-sonable request to use the one in my study; but of course the machine won't last long if she lets the kids play with it and never bothers with the dust cover. Unbeknown to me she's probably sent out hundreds of wry witticisms too clever for my sleep of reason by more than a half. From time to time I've found a polite

surface, thereby dispensing with scullery maids, and guaranteed to outlast any marriage.] She always looks like a buttered bun, even after a day at the adding machine.

Hecuba and Ruth—there's two to compare! It may be that love sees beauty, but it's the beauty of a garden that makes you love it. And this one's no garden: just a single bleached poinsettia, potted, more specialized than a wife or mother; at best, to mention as Keats in his letter did, the root instead of some derivative, a tantalizing cunicle. She's nobody's fast fish—nor yet entirely loose. [But this archangel doesnt go for the fast and loose daughters of common men. There is only one plausible penetrale in his own real life. Is Michael secretly afraid of new experience? Familiar fucking has a taste he wots sweeter even in its passive recusancy than the perfumed sweat of that strange flesh that seems to take one man much as

---

reply of noncommittal acknowledgement lying half unfolded on the kitchen table, often on small 24-lb raised letterheads with three of four short lines of centrally placed text from some high corporate or institutional sanctum (once from the President of Harvard), or from someone's secretary who's important in Sacramento or Washington, though she shows me no real concern with government or politics and hardly knows the difference between a Senator and a Representative, as though she never memorized enough to pass Cal's "American Institutions Requirement".

Ruth absorbed most of her education as a faithful transaction but never with love and confidence. She never let it make her pregnant. Like most of her expenditures it was largely wasted. In spite of her Phi Beta Kappa success she felt alienated by study at the world's largest university. But she remembers certain things from her psychology courses and every scrap of Spanish. A few things in literature have left impressions. We used to share silly conceits about her being my questing horse when I was in the saddle and "just an'eurotic horsewife" when I wasnt; and not very long ago when we were laughing about something during one of our unpredictable celebrations of love she fearlessly clove open our apple as if she'd suddenly emancipated herself from its core: "You used to call me Rosinante—but now it's Donna Quixote! For the love of Miguel, don't you want to ride me?"

Indeed for fear of exacerbating her intelligence it was a long time since I'd used that title of profound respect to convey my appreciation of her admirable difficulty in navigating a world unworthy of her efforts. I'd been steering clear of literature with her for the same reason that I've had to steer clear of religion. Lately our conversation has been reduced almost exclusively to the subject of our children.

Yeats says madness like trance and deep meditation withdraws the soul from every impulse but its own. As the raft loses its edges it shrinks your area of consistency. It ends up too tiny to support the mind's weight. Sometimes in winter storm it's only the formation of an ice casing that keeps it in one piece, until the soul is staying afloat upon a cake of frozen water that has swallowed up its original platform. When we drift into warm water the struggle must begin again. I must admit that I've helped her stay north of Ocean's pity! According to Camus

another except in its respect for affluence. He believes he's glad to keep his caste; for even coarse repetitious usage of a modest gentlewoman (all the less excusable for her being so well known to him) is less threatening to this man's self-respect than sordid adventure with a goodnatured demimondaine. He wishes only to continue what is lawful and fitting— without candlelight and wine, without black lace or music, without the humiliation of pursuit or dismissal, as well as without the frenchified frivolity of seduction. (The Courtly paradox that love in marriage is a kind of adultery anyway sometimes compensates good clerks with a little piquant expectancy at their domestic swiving.) As dominant half of the legal diphthong (embroidered monogram of two), despite remonstrances of Priapus, he seeks one yoke only, with the argument that in a single combination of Mr and Mrs everything delectable can be fully accomplished and above

---

one grows out of pity when pity is useless. But I was too defensive to feel it, too busy extending my own raft already grandiose.

But one should always conserve heat. As usual I let the bath water stand until I was dry and ready for bed; then I adjusted the plug so that it would gurgle out slowly. When I switched off the bathroom light and carried my armful of clothes across the dining room I was astonished to find Ruth in her nightgown sitting up like a queen prepared to hold levee in her bedchamber, except that she occupied only her side of the sheets and mine was neatly turned open for me. She had made the bed tidied up the room and brushed her hair.

It was a strangely smiling woman I glanced at while I was putting on my pajamas. I had seen that look two or three times when she was about to announce that she had decided to become a thrifty industrious housewife henceforth and evermore. She had a Bible on her lap but calmly closed it and put out the lamp. I opened the window adjusted the curtains and trimmed the shades according to my formula for excluding light from the street pole across the way but admitting enough natural darkness and dawn to guide my morning judgments of time and weather. I could see her still sitting upright as I lay flat on my back waiting for her to do the job I should have done a long time before—which was to broach a very serious talk. I couldnt guess what she was thinking, what symbols would be directing her approach: I knew only that she had girded her loins against the abomination of desolation by which she had been devastated at my birthday party.

I hardly dared breathe as practically for the first time I contemplated my plans from her point of view as well I could imagine it. All at once I became too paralyzed even to clear my throat or lick my lips. In cold sweat nevertheless I mumbled brief confession of my guilt my cowardice my cruelty, acknowledging my sudden access of pity and pledging my despicable charity by pressing her rigid thigh with the back of my hand. She judiciously ignored my contemptible effort at this last moment to subvert the justice of her court.

Yet almost immediately my feelings started to glaze over with weariness! Every time in bed that she wants to discuss grievances or matters irrelevant to bedtime I'm overcome with sleepiness. It's my old involuntary defense against irreconcilable domestic issues. Even after that momentous parley had well begun it was a couple of minutes before I abandoned the somnolent plea of nolo

all developed to exquisite maturity. It takes at least ten years to get to the bottom of a woman's psychosomatic sensation, and he intends to cultivate the investment of his prime decade.

By way of whistling in the dark vastness of unsacramental desires and setting at defiance the indiscriminate urges of his most clamorous member he falls to chanting under his breath a tuneless tonguetwisting rune of his own composition that he thinks ought to be popular:

> I can't go out without you, Baby—
> 'cause you're the only one
> I can't go out without with . . .

Hecuba gives the pilot her signal by buzzer cord as soon as the car has rattled past the stop before the one that her unnoticed neighbor also prepares for. When she unhastily rises he is surprised to catch with lowered eyes from under bent disguising brows the vague maculation of a gray smudge on her turning forehead. At such a distance it's so light in vestige that it might be dismissed as an oddly spotted shadow or a couple of streaks missed by hasty powder-puffing if its centered position and two-stroke configuration didnt stir in an unexpected corner of a disused memory the faint sense of something sacred. As he ducks quickly out the rear door opened for him at his own buzz—which he purposely has delayed and shortened as much as he dares in face of the fear that if he waits too long he'll be disregarded by a skipper preoccupied with the gorgeous passenger high-heeling it daintily down the forward step in her captivating tight skirt—the meaning of this stain presents itself. Jesus Christ, Ash Wednesday charcoal! What a fluke conjunction of fixed and moveable feasts!

Waiting for her to cross the thoroughfare and make her way with a surprisingly pleasant stride down the sidewalk to the building she shares with his family and their common landlord, he hides impatiently in the shadow of a hedge. Supper is being kept much too late. But suddenly he's struck by a much worse complication: My God—*Wednesday* is Caleb's night off! If he comes over tonight how will I ever get rid of him? I can only hope that if he's giving Ruth and the kids any Valentines he'll have brought them over during the day. I'll be fit to be tied if she's invited him to supper. Another holiday spoiled! Besides, he drinks up all the milk before our boys get enough.

Hecuba vanishes inside the front door. Within a minute he follows her, but turns off at the second floor, irritably bearing his gift to Mrs Valentine.

---

contendere which has sometimes served to evade debate and allow me to slide into the sleep I crave more than anything that my stubborn will drags me toward in daylight. But suddenly I was as wide awake as I've ever been in my life, ready for fighting all night to hold my own. My wife was in her Cassandra phase, plangent enough for a whole parish of husbands. . . . ❏

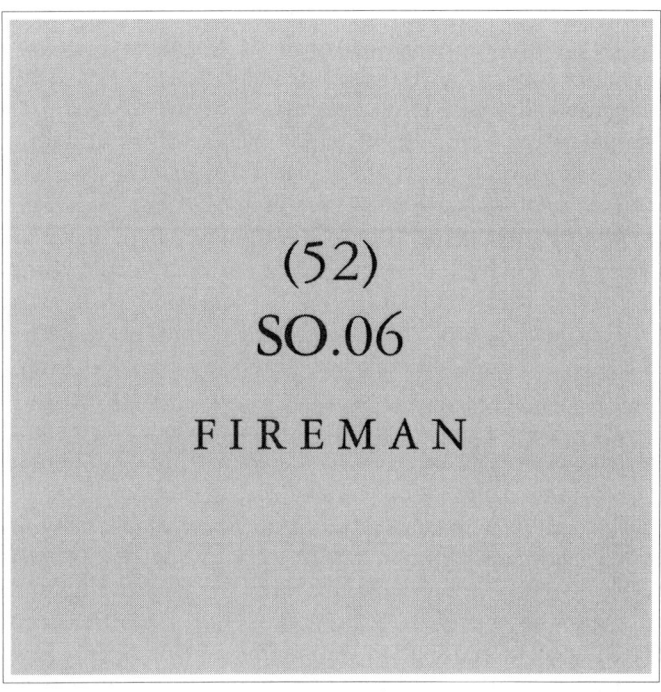

(52)
SO.06

FIREMAN

CALEB KARCIST (A)

1.

Near the hospital just above Teleology Lane is an office building you'd never think unless you looked curiously at the steel hatch in the sidewalk of the street cresting the hill, or unless you actually happened to see an anachronistic truck unloading with a chute, was still burning coal for its heat and hot water. When Caleb was working there the property was owned as an experimental investment by Mr Wine the used-car man who employed the Chapmans' neighbor Hecuba Jones as bookkeeper at his lot in the City, and it was she through whom the pater familias's character reference got him the job.

Michael vouched for him as a philosophy student who needed a year to earn the money for continuing graduate study. "A future professor . . ." he lied to Hecuba, and she honestly passed the word on to her boss. (Ruth was annoyed at such deception and only the combined weight of Michael's practical authority and Caleb's scornful dismissal of such scruples kept her silent on the subject with their goodnatured blond friend as far as Michael knew.) Philosophy in the minds of Hecuba and Mr Wine—one a lapsed but unrebellious Roman Catholic, the other a Jew known only in his secular life—was virtuous, if not religious and mystical, and gave off the odor of self-abnegation. From brief observation of his personal appearance and from his casual words reflecting upon the quality of the social macrocosm Hecuba might have questioned the maturity of Caleb's sense of responsibility for other people's capitalistic possessions if her reservations hadnt been overcome by respect for Michael's judgment. Experience had taught Hecuba that people who "receive a good education" don't always as kids act like the people whose ranks they will be joining, but she usually liked them for their apparent superiority to gross lust until they specifically disappointed her, no matter how airy their field of education. Ambiguity in itself far from offering scandal might be an exceptionally cultured boy's attractive mystery—maybe an essential and therefore unremarkable element of his major career, not to be discussed with Mr Wine only because it had no bearing upon the minor stewardship of real property.

Anyway the proprietor made sure to interpret as favorably as possible any letter of recommendation, for few of sufficient intelligence and energy were available who would accept his stipulations of employment. He required a man who was economically foolish on his own behalf and yet took lively interest in the steaming economy of that fixed but somewhat complicated ship. In the wisdom of practice Mr Wine expected to be fooled in some particulars by any unsupervised employee, and he never deceived himself to the extent of hoping that a second person existed who would use coal as parsimoniously as the first person could; but making every allowance and compromise for degeneracy of quality in the present labor market it was still almost as hard to find the right man as it was to assure himself a continuous supply of cheap and reasonably combustible fuel from the few dwindling stockpiles that phasing-out dealers were all too ready to give away for landfill to developers who would buy their waterfront coal yards even before the last trucks in which it was distributed conked out utterly. Caleb was a windfall, manna from a generous sky, if he would faithfully undertake the job. As chance would have it the young man was prepared to accept the wages and hours at once, moreover making no demur to the condition that the term of service was to be short—only about a year—and entirely at the discretion of the owner, to the general effect that he was expected to stay exactly as long as he was wanted, without any prospect of vacation mitigation of schedule or increase in pay. He understood that in the fullness of time he would be dismissed without notice.

On Michael's advice Caleb played the game straight and signed a bluffing piece of paper (which Wine called a contract) signifying his agreement to these absurd provisions on pain of forfeiting his first two weeks of salary. This amount of money was to be withheld until the employee left off his employment in the good graces of the employer.

The arrangement was illegal on at least two counts: first, the indenture smacked of involuntary servitude; second, Caleb was not a licensed
boiler engineer.

But the fact was that the party of the second part was even more glad of
the deal than the first party was—and not in ignorance or idealism either,
for if he had not perceived Mr Wine's motivation Michael would have disabused him. The terms were perhaps mutually advantageous in respect to
the foot-pounds of mechanical work performed, the B T U 's per foot-pound,
and the dollars per B T U , for each party took satisfaction that he was not
being exploited as he exploited the other in solving his particular problem;
but the presentational immediacy of gladness was definitely the greater on
Caleb's side simply because the job constituted his entire livelihood and
most of his intercourse (practically unpopulated though it was) with the
outside world at a time de passage in his life, whereas management of that
individual property occupied very little of Wine's time and only a few iotas
of his intellect—still less the nighttime operation of it. Once the arrangements for this narrow span of his self-interest had been consummated the
entrepreneur in giving occasional thought to it was more likely to have
mildly trepidated at the possibility of a dreamy goyish student of whatever
philosophy letting the furnace go out on a frosty dawn than to have chortled
over the dumbly custodial capture of a learned brain.

So Caleb always had the retained pay coming to him at the end of his
service, like money in a bank that paid no interest, which was not lost on
Mr Wine but which he himself was the last boy in the world to be self-
interested in; and which Michael, who on Caleb's behalf was satisfied (even
under conditions of perpetual inflation) with the security of any lump sum
at all for him eventually to leave California on, did not encourage him to
worry about. Caleb didnt feel the necessity of saving anything else besides.

This his first job exceeded in pleasure any expectation he had had, and
he spoke of his delight in the transition "from the ivory tower to the
ebony cave". He suffered no shock of emergence. Nor was the change of
medium and mode from university to coal bunker felt as degradation.
Feeding a furnace by shovel for a living entailed none of the temptations
anxieties or hatreds on account of which he refused to work in a bookstore,
the livelihood that one might have expected Michael to recommend as a
better first step on life's path to avoid falling at once, unprepared, into the
postwar bramble bush.

Caleb was scarcely beset by variety or pressed for innovation. The job kept
him lonesome. Once he had manfully organized his efforts there was no need
to waste vital energy in trivial communication. For these reasons Michael
envied him profoundly. His friend now had more time to himself than anyone else they knew, though granted neither holidays nor summer vacation,
for he was relieved only on each week's Wednesday when Maintenance Service Inc could supply a man who rotated as a substitute among six clients.

[If Caleb had ever been out sick for a night—and he'd have had to be pretty ill not to be able to walk merely two blocks to perform the essentials, seeing that he was provided with a settee and an alarm clock on the job—his pay would have been docked (and no wonder: Wine was obliged to pay double or triple time for an emergency man from the Service). But such penalties were all to the good in Michael's view: Caleb needed something to help keep him to the mark in a rhythmic discipline which of itself would provide chains of quiet time away from the public as well as from girls.]

Michael was not displeased that Caleb had anticipated nothing of the agony he was to suffer in gaining this resolution of his wishes for the year. Indeed a few months living inside his porcelain stove amounted to torture for the hooded young bird and more than once it seemed too much to bear. Even within the first quarter he was on the point of waiving his deferred nest-egg and walking out. He began to lose his romantic interest in hand-fired steam. His heart's desire now was the job of a deck hand.

Michael's purpose for Caleb was served in the long run despite many narrow escapes from freedom, the young man's appetites notwithstanding. New achievements always take longer than you make your schedule for, and come to a little less, no matter how much time you allow for contingencies and laziness, or how much margin for imperfection. Caleb labored under forced draft without knowing it, and it was an indication of his worth (Michael was glad to find) that he mistook cruel constraints for his own deficient capability, and a good beginning in philosophical humility for the crystallization of perpetuating failures (as if this cruise and the present enlistment would last all his life).

2.

Meanwhile Mr Wine the old huckster of the automotive trade continued to educate himself in the "opportunities" of petty capitalism as he tried to cash in on new schemes for exploiting revised tax laws and at the same time to hedge his investments in such a way that he could take advantage of interchangeable selections from the feast of esculents ambrosias and banes that was spreading itself like a tricky fair for his generation of new venturers with new money. He still remembered the Depression too vividly to trust the stock market yet, but there was much else to ponder, among which was the possibility of a new-car dealership with Studebaker.

Wine had already committed himself in a small experimental way to the future of Scotch whisky, "for liquidity", he would tell Hecuba, as well as for stable appreciation of value. Unlike real estate it was supposed to have a ready and instant market, right at the warehouse where he bought and stored it (bonded) without ever seeing casks or bills of lading. Insurance storage and commissions together would not exceed 25% of his investment if he sold the whisky four years after his purchase of the freshly distilled product, at which time he expected to realize a price double what he'd paid. Few other commodities improve in quality with age; and the appreciation of value was to be steadily augmented by booming demand for limited supply. Best of all, for a man tentatively learning how to move his money around, there was a market for Scotch at any age from the first day onward, though under normal conditions a four-year holding would probably yield the best return. The tax policies of both mother and daughter country were favorable to this method of exporting U S capital. And Wine's pleasure in liquor was immeasurably enhanced by the fact that he could conduct the entire business through a New York broker with a very minimum of "paperwork". His plan was to buy a lot annually and at its fourth year to start selling it. Once every twelvemonth he would then either sell a lot and take his 100% gross profit on it, sell it and convert half the profit into an equal amount of new raw material, pocketing the difference, or plough the entire proceeds of the sale back into the same furrow, thus duplicating his investment without additional cost. "If this thing goes right, kid," he said chuckling to Miss Jones his bookkeeper, "I can see it now, a business all its own: Wine 'n Spirits Incorporated!"

He was very cautious about involving himself in a corporation or syndicate. As he educated himself in finance he secretly dreaded the growing necessity of formal complications. But he easily understood the law of scarcity: more and more people were going to want to drink Scotland's water of life, just as there was a fixed amount of land in the world that an unlimited number of Jews gentiles and niggers competed for.

He also grasped the advantages of borrowing, of using other people's money, especially for land and buildings; seeing that if he could negotiate a "small-business loan" to borrow ten times whatever he put into an opportunity, a mere 10% profit might represent a 100% return on his investment. As long as the government made sure the interest rates were low he could contribute more than his share to the expansion of the national economy. Thus he had begun to see the intriguing possibilities of a holding-company pyramid that could provide him with unlimited leverage. In arm's-length intercourse with outsiders he concealed his diffidence about schooling, the importance of which for his purposes he ignorantly overestimated, but by Hecuba's account that was obviously the only element of his generally self-confident makeup which prevented him from incorporating ventures right and left. He would doubtless do so in the end, when he came to accept the fact that he had to entrust himself to a lawyer.

For the time being he did well enough in mastering the hedges and loopholes and tax shelters available to a small proprietor. He seemed to get more interested than he had originally intended—more than any purely financial manipulator would have been—in the management of the property attended by Caleb. It was gratifying to get bank capital for a "professional building" in the neighborhood of a hospital. The press had provided him with a snippet or two of sophisticated language that suited his modest needs of self-expression. "I like to keep my options open." was the refrain of explanations to himself to Hecuba and to his wife.

Wine's policy was simply to keep the investment in each case as low as possible—not so much to broaden his property among many equities in order to expand income as to conserve with uncommitted funds a liquid position otherwise incompatible with the ownership of real estate. Michael suspected that his initial innocence of refinements in tax calculations sometimes led him accidentally to anticipate beneficial changes in Internal Revenue rules, so that by the time he learned what was wrong with what he'd assumed and acted upon he was found by his C P A to be in compliance a jump ahead of the experts. Thus in cautious obscurity he pioneered without dogma, poking at the wilderness newly opened to his emprise, in many of his essays more advanced (though less explicitly conscious) than the financial journalists whom he could not understand. He made an intuitive distinction, for example, not only between tax depreciation and economic depreciation but also between normal and accelerated tax depreciation when he seriously considered a long-range plan to convert the office building into a hive of "dwelling units" in the conviction that eventually some administration in Washington would provide tax incentives for private solution of middle-class urban housing problems.

Caleb cared nothing for the financial context. Like a ship's engineer he saw the enterprise exclusively in terms of the efficiency of the vessel to which he was attached. From his inferior vantage he could see how successfully Mr Wine withstood the endemic tendency of speculators to underestimate the importance of running expenses simply because they were tax-deductible and therefore only about half as costly as they seemed. Likewise with expenditures pertaining to capital gains. There were no pseudo-losses for Wine. He would have fought for ten cents on the dollar. He maintained the building as if its operating profits loomed large in his personal income.

The canny landlord moved neither too fast nor too slow in placing his order for the conversion from coal to automatic oil heat. This year was his breakeven point, at which the expense for labor fuel and repairs on the old equipment began to surpass the projected amortised costs of a new system. The cheap service to which Caleb was sworn eked out the obsolescence a little longer than good economics would otherwise have allowed. A few months of grace can sometimes make the difference between optimum transits and asynchronous discord of the multiple planets and stars that make up the aspect of a new undertaking in the business horoscope, such as maturity and retirement dates fiscal year-ends depreciation schedules and tax deadlines, any one of which can threaten formidable inconvenience, and the disordered looming of which can break a man.

Circumstances as influenced by human intention might well offer architectural as well as mechanical opportunity, when the time came, in the very center of the East Bay medical profession. Wine found himself in an enviable position to serve the "health care industry" at a time of rising prosperity, and premium rents could be had for the asking if he provided residential apartments at that convenient location. Gradually, whenever possible, he had been renegotiating the leases of his tenants to make them coterminous with his coal-burner, so that every one of them would be subject to cancellation at the epoch of remodeling.

In the interval, on Caleb's watch, he allowed the building to run down. Every repair was a lick and a promise. The landlord defined maintenance very narrowly—as for example in respect to office floors: washing but no waxing. While he temporized, while he refrained from throwing good money after bad into a property that was soon to be turned inside out, Wine was hard pressed to keep his clients from overt anger and civic complaint. His contract with the Maintenance Service was scarcely as generous as he gave the tenants to understand; he accordingly undertook to see that all their grievances were mediated by himself or Hecuba. Thus no matter what fee he paid for the contract-cleaning he got more for his money than mere janitorial work, for reference to the faults of vague Maintenance Service personnel furnished him with a whipping boy a scapegoat and an objectified vector of his own guilt: an omnibus excuse for the charge of negligence.

He affected a terrible role on the telephone ostensibly relaying and underscoring the grumbles and whines that came to his ear—actually ignoring those that could not conceivably fall within the secret limits of the maintenance contract but embellishing the others with bluster to keeping M S on the defensive in its highly competitive situation (yet ever closer to the point of saying fuck you brother we don't want your kind of business). So Wine abused his vendor, shouting and distorting the complaints, and then unctuously flush with confidence called back his customer: "I really gave them hell, Doc. I pay them good money and they don't want to lose it. It won't happen again. But let me know if it does, hey? If they can't do the job right I'll get somebody who can. But I'll have to admit everyone's having trouble finding people who want to work these days. None of them give a damn. You just get one broken in and he quits. All of them aching to be fired so's they can collect Unemployment. It'll help a lot if you just call Hecky here the minute you're not satisfied. Next year I'm going to put in vinyl floors which practically keep themselves clean even though it'll cost a lot of dough but I want you to be happy because your prestige is important to me and this will be the most pretentious medical building on the hill. Call us for sure now if those bastards let me down again. I'll be over to take a look myself every night in the week if I have to!" Sometimes in Wine's absence Hecuba would perform this function, but her style was smoother and truly more sincere, though she would perhaps not bother to annoy M S with a useless call between her two conversations with the doctor of one kind of medicine or another.

The landlord took pains to teach Hecuba her part, and to keep his own patience, not so much to prevent turnover of tenants or damage to his reputation (neither of which were important elements in his science of gain) as to forestall legal actions that might bring to light picayune solecisms of which he was guilty in his compliance with certain city ordinances and state safety regulations. The conflict between this negative objective of civic security and that of positive commercial advantage from the trimming of standard expenses was uneasily borne by tactics of equivocation, as if he hung perpetually between clearcut alternatives; but of course his strategy adscititiously fostered an unfluctuating level of discontent among the rent-payers, on the latent principle that as long as basic conditions were held tolerably constant medical men (especially the psychiatrists among them) could adjust their thresholds of rebellion to a steady and predictable state of annoyance. To this end he guarded equally against both degradation and improvement.

Wine's administration suited Caleb especially well because the advantage to the owner in hiring a cheap unlicensed boilerman constituted also an advantage to himself as a cheap illegal operator benefitting from a joint wish to be hidden from the world during his paid meditations on the premises. Meanwhile Mr Hansen the licensed day "engineer" continued to act as building superintendent, the only employee of the management ever visible to the doctors or their assistants, though seen by them only after vigorous seeking and ringing and never seen by the public. He was a grizzled veteran respectfully responsive to the address of all humans indifferently, but his rejoinders never exceeded the laconic. He was even briefer with inspecting representatives of State and City. Thus he was able without attracting attention to ignore perfunctory questions about night coverage, content to let careless authorities continue to assume that the licensed name of the former night man whom they still carried in their records of the building remained valid. In any case coal-furnace regulations had become almost deadletters of the law, and were winked at all the more because it was made known that Mr Wine had automatic oil-burner equipment "on order for installation in a few months".

Mr Wine's fondness for Sig Hansen, an old-world seafarer anciently stranded, was enriched, like Hansen's taciturnity on his behalf, by the fact that the skilled custodian's Social Security retirement schedule coincided with that of the boiler that required licensed attendance. The Norwegian's bright blue eyes, nearly buried in his knobby face, lighted up in amusement at the hardly mentioned prospect that he his new young friend Caleb and the coal furnace were all expected to depart at the same time. Indeed as a plan it made everyone happy, possibly with the exception of Hecuba who in her office across the Bay must unofficially bear the moral responsibilities that remained unacknowledged by the actors and would seem light enough as long as events did not betray expectation for any one of them.

Right from the outset, as an excommunicate of what society he had known and a barbarian to all other, Caleb was a better employee than Mr Wine was aware. It would have seemed unparalleled in the eyes of the world if it had cared to look: the diligence of the erstwhile irresponsible and eccentric dissenter in establishing a record of personal reliability and cooperation as he cannily determined to earn the trust that would ensure his sole nocturnal possession of the boiler room. For him the laboratory of catabasis, the athanor of purification, and the lonely vigils of phase-state transformation were joyfully fascinating perquisites. He danced before the massive hearth howling the names of Sweet Will and Great Willie, and patrolled the premises more restlessly than a radar-eared German Shepherd or the of banshee of a ruined castle.

3.

But the callow merlin found it very difficult to enlist his liberty in the cause for which he had chosen obscurity. Self-hooded—caged, most of the time, by his own will—though starving for prey and dreaming of empyreal conquest, he brooded over the unending desire that diverted his imagination to visions urged upon it by the foremost pulse of his body. Or else he lay pinioned by the demon of sloth who slipped in through the open door when he was all prepared for an annunciating muse to reward him for chastity. Stagnant air filled the birdy tubes of his bones and the inert hollows of his breast. He strove for the motive to breathe deeply and slowly, to exhale every last atom of blood-carbon before admitting pure air to the channels of ventilation that fed his spiritual fire, the scarcely smoldering combustion that nothing seemed to set ablaze. By devious experiments he found annoying mystery and despair in the pursuit of intellectual beauty.

On many Wednesdays he went to the Chapmans for supper. Otherwise, coiling his strength in the very springtime of youth, he seldom left his nearby eyrie when he was off the job. At the most three or four times a week he walked downtown to the public library where Jack London had educated himself, or to the Y M C A where partly in an attempt to offset the affects of tobacco he was slowly mastering speed and rhythm on the light punching bag and gradually increasing the number of his laps on the boards of the hanging track that encircled the gymnasium. By the time he plunged into the pool, where he might have found his only real pleasure in exercise, the muscles tightened to special tension would hardly slacken for exertion in water, and the breath trained to falconry would not willingly change its route through his head. At the Y in good weather he sunned himself afterwards on the roof among a handful of corpulent middleaged healthseekers who deluded themselves without toil by sweating the solar rays into their skin and then zestfully tingling themselves golden-brown in the shower. He lurched home on sinews needed for walking which now almost failed him at the knees, too loosened in his body's confusion of exercises to master the function of ordinary locomotion. His main hope however, in strenuous contention against indolence of physique, in watering and airing and in heating and cooling his skin, even in the immediate awkwardness of erotic sensation, was to abate his inveterate concupiscence.

Fearing for his health, for his safety, for his dignity, for the sobriety of devirgination, Caleb declined to seek out taxi dancers for relief. Jack London, a personality for whom lust was no problem, thanks to the favors of his fortune, had forthrightly secured the simple peace to work all day, but Caleb's cerebral stumbling blocks were swollen and congested by sensational blood pumped to every capillary by the genital engine slung between his legs, cruelly exacerbating the complexity of a literary education. He sought simplicity all right, but it had to come *before* he could work all day, or even for an hour—that is to say, allowing for other interests, work at getting ready for the proper work of writing plays.

It was not surprising that the particular object of his inchoate dramatic poetry had yet to be precipitated from a rich murky solution felt to be inspissated with theatrical sediment, for he had never seen a professional performance, had never read a "commercial" play, had never visited or listened to actors technicians or directors (most of whom he regarded as theatrical whores), and had never looked into a book on theater architecture or stage design. At the university he had scorned to assist in student productions, whereof he said the histrionics and other crafts were as sickeningly vocational as courses in journalism (as if he didnt know that paid hypocrisy had begun on the Athenian scene). It was no wonder that with so little respect for "meretricious" experience he had not yet imagined a theme or a character for his first item of proof.

Michael understood that color-blindness kept Caleb from military conscription and assured his freedom to prepare for getting ready to begin to commence his preliminary notes. But to Caleb himself the job seemed his very salvation, a defense against distraction and an encouragement of virtue, affording not only time and seclusion but also facilities for the transmutation of knowledge. Not in mortification of the flesh but in praise of purity he shook down the grates and raked the clinkers for both shifts, carried out more than his share of the ashes, and even besooted himself two or three times as often as he was expected to do in brushing out the thickly sabled tubes, thereby relieving Sig Hansen of a disagreeable task in the penultimate stage of his labored life.

After the first blush of enthusiasm, to be sure, finding that simplicity of heart and discipline of body did not immediately and of themselves confer poetic imagination, the zest of the spagyrist sometimes flagged. Then it was the moral force of the contract—no longer the novelty of it— that kept him to the monotonous rhythm. But he anxiously sustained appearances (such as they were) even after his vigor had slackened internally—when his secret officiousness had subsided into almost perfunctory observances of duty—though he never ceased to appreciate the use of Mr Wine's assets. The black laboratory remained his precious studio. The faithfulness with which he continued to tend the heating system (or rather its steam generator) was an outward and visible sign of loyalty singularly impressive to Michael, to Sig and Hecuba, and to Wine himself.

The particulars of Caleb's balanced routine compensated for the generalized and unbalanced conflict in his heart, the outward and visible sign of which was a worsening deformity of voice a further displacement of the bite of his jaw owing to increased strain on his teeth and a sloppy cheek that darkened and rankled between shaves as if the skin was corrupting. There were times in his desert when he doubted that English was his native tongue, and he spoke no other. Perhaps in the beginning of childhood he had been forced into taking it to live by, he speculated; maybe that coercion accounted for his nearly perpetual discomfort both with and away from most of his human fellows.

He incited himself to rebellion against solemn complexity needless multiplicity and endless thought. In the fire that he inspected through the peephole or openly stoked he thought he saw purification and simplification together. Yet it was a curious complication of simplicity. One man's simplicity is another man's labor. When, in approval of continence, the first simplification, he repeated to himself the famous old words "As for living, our servants will do that for us!", it was as master not as servant that he considered the ambiguous proposition. But if he was master of himself, who was the servant? And as far as the castle was concerned, who if not himself was servant to the owner and all the tenants?

It was a measure of his respect for the contract that almost all his thoughts were cast in the perspective of mastery, if only to show its failure. Perhaps at times he even had a dimly quasi-Christian sense of self-mastery through perfect service to others, which was certainly a simplification of spirit if not of task. In any case, the "disease of perfection", disguised and unacknowledged to himself, was still his instinctive homeopathic remedy for the disease of book-learning. In short, it was a complicated process to wrack his imagination for simple fictions, though for the sake of transmutation he was willing enough to don the hair shirt of humility for his regimen.

Thus the place of labor became oratory too, and his notion of purification (omitting the fears and exclusions of exorcism) emphasized the conjuration of Aphrodite. He hoped through intensification rather than nullification to lead his bull under the yoke of imagination; but at his age the libido forces the mind to serve the body, which means that in the end flesh has to mollify fantastic mind. Repeated emollition made this timid youth more timid, especially as he'd originally grown timid from having set for himself higher standards of erotic exploitation and possession than even normal gifts of attraction under conditions of normal opportunity could attain to, in face of the fact that both his gifts and his chances in this matter had always been subnormal in his own opinion. As the hope for a new girlfriend gradually faded, therefore, the more readily mind and body attempted to satisfy each other the more timid he became. Imagination was all too easily seduced, time after time, by hallucinations of satisfaction.

Caleb was not happy about his increasing self-effacement in the outside world, but believing that his main purpose could be best served by an hermaphroditic emancipation from the trivial preoccupations of pursuit seduction and contraception, foregoing hope for the naked presence of a consubstantial female, he confined his self-study to the realm of purely private "courtesy and self-possession", which for Yeats was the living equivalent of style in art—these counterparts both arising "out of a deliberate shaping of things, and from never being swept away, whatever the emotion, into confusion or dullness." Withdrawing into a world without social complication or responsibility or personal love, his vices rectified, he hoped to be able to contemplate with simplified vigor the reality he left behind. Far from fearing to diminish himself, as Axël's Master Janus would have put it, by submitting to a slave's senses, he sought to exact the highest possible sensation from the inferior pleasures of autoeroticism. His struggle was to resist a slave's method. The virtue of his necessity lay not in a series of momentary liberations from desire, such as those of which all boys avail themselves, but in the manikin's transcendental Romance. The rub was to set dreams agoing by withholding from his "enlarged and numerous senses"—a phrase from memory that came to him out of place on every occasion—the first artless gratification that came to hand.

So the agony had to be doubled before the ecstasy was: to sit and move about as if his wrists were tied behind his back to keep them aboveboard during waking hours, to lie spread-eagle waiting for sleep like a thumb-sucking child with its sleeves pinned to the mattress, while he constrained blood's instinct with every ounce of psychic energy, compressing more and more desire, gathering explosive hypogeal pressure so consciously that self-serving will swept away all other mental faculties. Practicing like an apprentice, though without the patience of a Zen archer, he was but gradually able to turn gesture into dream, not always memorable at that, often not remembered. Yet always as sweet at the briefly prolonged extremity of sensation as a Japanese nightingale crossing the valley; he blessed himself, asleep or awaking with pleasure, for the delicious purity with which, always suddenly, he felt the unsublimated mercury start up the length of its retort and pass from his spirit. Without a lover no other course seemed at the instant so virtuous or so courteous.

Like all others training themselves to transcendent feelings he was not wholly successful, but he provoked a psychically delectable crisis often enough to suggest an experimental attempt to do so with the sole and unaided assistance of his brain. Only to be defeated by trebled torment in the passivity of total abstention, his elaborate fancies unequal to prolonged temptation and short-circuited by some faint unintentional friction of fabric or even air on the most delicate skin stretched taut by the thought of a succubating womunculus who revealed little more of herself than gender before vanquished by the burst of phallic greed. In such instances his acute nervous system could sustain no irritation more substantial than gossamer thought without responding in slavish ignominy, the transitional pleasure of which was overwhelmed by immediate regret for the antecedent tension.

His romantic mind seemed to be growing weaker in its resistance to the autonomic reaction of his most sensitive sense. He wondered if his mother had stopped nursing him too soon, leaving him with too few brain cells. At times he found himself too quickly disabused of his solitary Catharism, the delusory expostulation anticipated by his disobedient limb. By transforming his hair shirt into luscious velvet, smooth cool sheets treacherously forestalled the fully embodied warm-skinned admirers—those amiable tender dream-girls—who might otherwise have been sent by Aphrodite to relieve him sympathetically. The gentle Galahad was often unequal to the ordeal of waiting perchance to dream.

But when he did toss and burn in own bed on his own time (shielded from the Apollonian light of day by drawn shades) he wasted his imagination by yielding to banal visions and fabricating loveless stories with plots of unilateral simplicity lacking any complication of discomfort resistance or conflict but padded with optional means of bliss. Sometimes these short daydreams of the early morning (usually begun as night dreams on the job), absurd or ridiculously logical paths forced through the brain without ceremony, devoid of delicacy subtlety or true imagination, made some pretense to fictive amusement; but more often they simply found the quickest way (save that of the slave) to the closest target. In lamebrained impatience for the heavenly muse who dwelt beyond the beck of his all-too-literal wits with complete images of palpably probable sensual affection (not to mention deliciously irresponsible love) the scenario whereby his hero consummated conjugation never lasted long enough to give off the odor of sanctity peculiar to the perfectly erotic innocence of his sweetest dreams.

[The Magnate and his meinie have left by land in his private car on the Western Pacific for expanded hotel suites at the Democratic Convention in the East. Captain and crew have been given a month's leave. Caleb is shipkeeper, alone on the last remaining steam yacht, which surpasses in trim spaciousness all the world's more recent luxuries afloat, exceedingly modernized in all conveniences, anchored with rakish splendor in an unfrequented cove of northern San Francisco Bay. His bedroom is the captain's cabin, his library the chart room, and the immense bridge his study. His only duties are to keep up enough auxiliary steam for the generator and to take care of the family's black jaguar. Most of his daylight time is spent like an otter in the pool and browning himself naked on the whitened oak planks beside it under the benevolent eyes of the great friendly cat, trained to growl at the approach of boarders, purring in the shade of the boatdeck awning. The silence is broken only by a faint distant drone of landsmen in their commerce and pleasure all around the vast landlocked harbor and its several cities. The ship swings calmly at its moorings under the slow influence of river current and ocean tide in the lee of a westerly headland. . . . A night of full moon. Laughter and warm scents now and then drift intact from midsummer's-night parties at great houses on a majestic island; cheerful soft lights mark the steep wooded hillside and vivacious strand of a bohemian village on the shore beyond . . . from which a white sloop all at once puts out to make its way toward *S S Samburan*. The cat called Satan recognizes the boat; he paces expectantly back and forth on the quarter-deck before Caleb notices their visitor. It's the wandering daughter of the owner, coming off from her studio ashore to spend a few days in rest while her family is away, to swim in the pool, to sleep in her wide stateroom, to bask in golden showers of sun. . . . She offers to teach him to sail her seabird. . . . She has heard of his work and she asks him to read to her. . . . The hypercarnation of Eve Sara Emmanuele de Maupers. . . . She desires him to be her first lover; he does not choose to follow Axël of Auersperg's renunciation. . . . Their bodies and minds are perfectly matched—in the moonlight, in the tank of pellucid seawater, in her soft azure bed of aristocratic ecstasy. At sunrise they are awakened by the sweet breath of the panther. She delights again in his gender as he worships hers anew. He hears her laugh that their companion will be the only other lover in her life. . . .]

Yet Caleb's diurnal emissions seldom involved much more than the usual propriosensuality of wasting seed—a dissipation of form hardly higher in principle than the nocturnal pollutions of the furnace he presided over that carbureted pure air and emanated heat by dissipation. The purposeful oxidation in both cases was no more efficient than the beginning of wisdom, a troubling but imperative necessity that had best be accepted with shrugs of hope for progress.

And in both cases, according to the latest alchemical gnosis, his contribution to the noisy decay of the universe could have been lessened by more knowledge. If God or social science had provided Caleb with information acceptable as truth he could have gone straight to one of the presumably innumerable girls who were tossing and burning for a man like him. With a probability of success approaching certainty he could have made his proposition to a particular dryad without gallantry, sated himself, and got on with his proper work, sparing himself many painful disturbances of equilibrium, provided only that God did not allow him to fall in love with his lovee, or her with her lover. If there is any sexual symmetry in the world at all the chances are that the best women have as much difficulty with their loneliness as the best men—for surely most of the obvious beauties have already dropped out of the class of best women by weakening to beautiful men. It would be hard not to fall in love with one of the best women whose beauty is more private than public were it not for the multiplicity of choices and alternations and even simultaneities open to a man possessing the information in question, at peril of removing himself from the category of best men by reason of spiritual carelessness.

Likewise, as Michael Chapman would have pointed out, if men and women as voters learned more about countering entropy by opening their minds to the free grace proffered so persistently in the church's demotic metabolism they could alleviate the need for dentists optometrists podiatrists hematologists psychotherapists dermatologists pediatricians epidemiologists gastroenterologists allergists carcinologists pathologists gynecologists chiropractors proctologists homeopaths saproanalysts amnesiologists osteosynthesists hystericists heresiologists viscerologists pederastiologists necrologists sacrotherapists dogmatists trichopathologists maniphysicians propriologists anatripticians orgasmanalysts digitotherapists theriacologists orthomythists psychomancers cuneologists dysymbologists catameniologists nymphotherapists orthocephalogists femimystics phallopractors ithyologists scatologists psychopomps aphrodisiasts orthohypnologists gynosynaptologists urological surgeons and other doctors who require private shelter and steam heat for their consultations.

4.

Mr Wine's last coal supplier went out of business even sooner than expected and without waiting to auction off his dwindled inventory, which was simply bulldozed over the bank of the estuary by a land-developer one dark night before the collier's old customers got wind of their new predicament. While other sources were being sought Sig and Caleb were enjoined (this time in the name of physical necessity) to eke out the bushels still left in the bunker.

Caleb thought of suggesting recourse to the Tropical Belt Coal Company, that isolated enterprise in which the evaporation of capital had left behind some unliquidated stock in trade, but he finally dared not risk calling gratuitous attention to his existence on the payroll, soon to be truly supernumerary in any pragmatic and expedient view. As Michael warned him: "When you get down to emergency level Wine will have no choice but to cut out night operations entirely. He'll take his chances with the law and further abuse the faith of his tenants. He'll make Sig start a new fire with trash every morning and leave the building entirely unheated on the weekends." Then with sudden solicitude for the vendor's possible difficulties in meeting the original delivery date Mr Wine would re-schedule installation of the oil-burner a few weeks later in the season.

And so it was that Caleb began in earnest to contemplate transmutations of matter, thermodynamics, and conservation of fuel. So it was that he became a yet better employee than he had intended, even to the point of being willing to make a contribution from his own wealth if he could discover the means to ensure his job thereby. Again, so it was that he unexpectedly found his own main purpose reinforced by the landlord's intensively hardened scrimp.

The art of conservation did not keep his hands very busy. He checked his gauge as usual, now and then opened a water valve for a few minutes, and lightly shoveled a little of the remaining lignite. The stack draft was poor and he had to keep a thin fire; since efficiency, like rectification, requires steady heat, he was obliged to charge his athanor more often than formerly, seeing that exiguity and constancy are mutually abhorrent. But how else could he improve the production, use, or recovery of heat? Nor shoreline of driftwood nor copse of fallen branches nor woodlot for saw and axe nor vehicle to collect refuse with: none were available to the trusty and anxious servant.

He found an old instruction manual for the boiler, which would have been lost forever had it not been misplaced thirty years before at the back of a high shelf behind the alarm clock.

All things about the boiler room should be kept clean and in good order. Negligence tends to waste and decay.

—Babcock & Wilcox.

The neat simplicity of nature was revealed in the stated fact that density of steam varies as the 17th root of the 16th power of pressure (which was the one variable indicated to him on the face of the grossly simplified furnace). In practical equivalence, said the booklet, $D = .003027 \, p^{.941}$.

His reason was more exercised than his emotion in preparing for limited but conclusive action. First of all he put aside all of Jack Wolfson's symbolic mysteries. They failed a man in the pinch of real life. Besides, chrysopoetic procedures cut no ice when it's base material that you're after for the sake of latent/potential/thermal/radiant/conductive energy. He would have tossed a philosopher's stone into the cinders, decanted the fugacious menstruum backwards through the alembic, or stuffed the Gross National Product of Sumer into the firebox to keep his job in the laboratory.

Simplification is a virtue in expressing thoughts but it's phony in beliefs about reality when that's what's being thought about. Caleb is now concerned with objective facts and hypotheses; complexity for him lies in the phenomena themselves, not simply in human language ineluctable. Although science simplifies itself to the extent that it can, as soon as it can, sometimes it must perpetuate complexities of expression. Yet an explanation of the natural structure of events is comparatively simple, for it relieves the speculative mind of innumerable alternatives or occult suspicions.

No ancient word or mark but what turns metaphorical on you (if it wasnt already!)—then ambiguous—and in the end makes your head ache with the inconsistency of its burden in disparate systems. Was it not one of the alchemists themselves who put an end to the latterly accreted tradition of the alkahest by pointing out that the great universal solvent would have eaten through the containment of any vessel on earth? And this woman-founded art had been at the outset an attempt to simplify and objectify, to reduce to nature, man's multitude of magics!

By starting on his own in this old science, for special economic reasons (according to his interpretation of Michael's oracles), Caleb made a signal contribution to his own purification, which Thalia and Melpomene awaited before offering to present themselves. Thus he sought the few confusing and protean ideas that might guide his operation: things like fire and heat, gravitating and subtle fluids, the transformations of matter and energy—first as simplified by Heraclitus and then as complicated by Clausius. In an era of petroleum-fed internal combustion engines the opportunity is rare to study in vivo an openly stoked heat chamber not very different from that in which the Lord's angel danced with Shadrach Meshach and Abednego. "If all things should become smoke then perception would be by the nostrils." said the Greek who dared to criticize Homer and Pythagoras both, one for failing to understand the dialectics of strife, the other for "much learning and bad art", adding that "souls smell in Hades." (Not that they stink.) In Caleb's parallel to the doctrine, if all things should simultaneously catch fire then all perception would be by pain. So he tried to stick to *serial* "transformations of fire" as the central process in an unending world. In a fully flaming world you couldnt have fire as legal tender. All the same, he could not be sure that he himself wouldnt burn forever.

A footnote in his textbook told him that Sadi Carnot, namesaked after a Persian poet by his father le grand Carnot (theorist, administrator, man of action—always on the people's side), died of cholera at the age of 36 leaving many unpublished manuscripts that had to be burned, presumably by official command in the interest of public safety, thereby purifying a household at the expense of economics and thermodynamics. But enough of his work remained to establish him too late for his own satisfaction as father of the latter science. Which has since turned out to be queen of them all, succeeding theology. This was the most valuable information Caleb got from a library in his desultory attempt to experience technology without actually learning it.

But he did teach himself to criticize Heraclitus and his eternal condensation of rarefaction and rarefaction of condensation. It was almost like calling into question the validity of Yeats's vision to perceive that the upward path and the downward path were *not* the same! Thermodynamics had not defined itself until Clausius enunciated irreversibility as law. Time's arrow shot into the symmetrical field of physics and unbalanced everything, faulting and skewing some neat principles of conservation that had comforted men's hearts since Heraclitus or indeed his forebears, eventually shaking Plato's dominating valuation of permanence and stillness, even as the scriptural principle of living types was being fatally undone by the arrow from Darwin's bow. In mounting excitement about the general implications of his idiosyncratic problem Caleb chose to ignore the latest scientific speculation that threatened to restore all symmetry by allowing for the reversal of time itself, even though such a hypothesis would seem to have chimed with Yeats's scheme, for thanks to Michael Chapman the homely paradigm of human evolution as the middest concrescence had become dearer to him than truth. Accordingly he had learned to respect the second law of thermodynamics as cosmologically trustworthy, though subject to the merely apparent exception of such topical evanescent events as art, life, and other counteractive eddies as special subsystems within the one truly closed system (if indeed it *is* closed)—intuitively if not formally analogous to Newtonian mechanics as imbedded in the total system of Relativity: locally lawful but peculiar to the human zone.

The boiler he tended was a heat engine of zero mechanical efficiency. It drove no prime mover. It drove no secondary mover. It drove nothing at all. It was designed solely to dissipate heat. Heat that had to be wasted for people's comfort—for a practical purpose as fleeting as art-dance. But the energy had to be replaced and if there was not enough coal the problem was to substitute some other fuel.

Now forasmuch as the science of heat cuts across the sciences of all objects it includes the category of structure and hence especially the analysis of information. At this point in Caleb's lucubrations he grew feverish. When he read claims of formal proof that negentropy and information were mutually convertible he nearly jumped out of his skin. The mathematical functions of this reversible [!] conversion were beyond his literary education, but poetically they suggested an experimental solution of his empirical problem. At the same time they seemed warranted to loosen a knot of dispassionate perplexity.

That left only the burning subjective question. And in the event, quite unexpectedly, that exigency was also resolved. Here follows in simple narrative, with sufficient hints of explanation, an account of our young dog's deliverance. His reasoning is part of the story.

5.

Two or three days after his enabling afflatus the door bell rang. At first he didnt recognize the sound: a terror-striking blast into the silent basement like a coarsely amplified and prolonged telephone ring, harshly metallic and mechanical in the manner of prison signals, announced only by an infinitesimal of preparatory vibration (detected only by his reflective ear in retrospect) when the disused solenoid was so suddenly surprised into shaking off its dust. The clarion struck without melody or rhythm, as ugly and close as the first machine-gun burst of an unexpected war, disintegrating its victim's self-possession; but the raucous noise was as sharply defined as a life sentence chopped off at the guillotine block.

But even on the instant he managed to light upon the proximate cause of his panic and its implication of remote human agency. The little electro-magnetic sound-mill revealed itself on the darkling wall not ten feet from his shattered tranquility; the push-button of efficient cause he remembered to be inconspicuously placed in the outer frame of the main entrance on the floor above. He was expected to respond at once. Indeed he wished to respond at once lest there be a repetition; he hastened in fear of another signal. But as he sprang up to face accusation his trembling persisted from the shock of absolute discontinuity between the intense stillness of active contemplation and the panic of unconscionable discomposure.

Having finished his first rounds of the building early in the evening he had been lying on the wooden bench he called his couch for a spell of abstract thought before resuming the great experiment where it had been left off at dawn that morning. When the blow had been struck one elbow was crooked over his face, shoulders bent, ankles crossed. By the time he reached the stairs to the lobby he was staggering against time, frantic to prevent further aggression. But already, though still shaking like the defendant at a lynching, wrenched brutally out of a privacy nearly as deep as death, he was beginning to allay his terror by reasoning that his reflex was disproportionate to a commonplace alarm. Everyone had unexpected visitors at one time or another. As a matter of fact it was an occasion that he had dreaded in the early days and only gradually forgotten to worry about. Never before had seekers or aggressors disturbed him, neither by the public telephone from its booth opposite the street door (whence he could not have been supposed to hear it at his work station), nor by the night bell that was now reverberating for the first time in the chambers of his skull. Yet it was extraordinarily inconvenient that a technological disintegration of his peace should happen to interrupt the most occult phase of his philosophical life.

Who could it be? Doctors had their own keys. Patients didnt come in the middle of the night. Was the basement being raided to discover his guilt in intellectually abusing Mr Wine's good faith? Was Wine himself checking up on the performance of his watchman? But then a real estate owner wouldnt have forgotten a key. Nor would Sig have returned for something without his own key. The cleaning crew had left and nothing ever brought them back to their first venue of the night; and in any case they could let themselves in. Boiler inspectors in surprise investigation? Police, with nameless warnings? Criminals: drug addicts in entitative need boldly come to murder him and ransack doctors' offices? Burglars in a test of occupancy before making a break? Perhaps an enraged avenger of dental violation or of a psychiatrist's professional breach. Even someone maddened by the diagnostic truth about his loved one. Or could it be a benighted traveler seeking directions in the deserted neighborhood?

Among all the possibilities in his magazine of dread he did not count the visit of an angel.

But a messenger it was, though he knew not her quality or her mission when he recognized her close outside the glass door standing in the dim nightlight shining from behind his back as he worked the lock from inside the lobby. He remembered Hecuba Jones from slight acquaintance but she seemed so different from his recollection of her that he could immediately identify her only by intuitive induction: woman, interested in the building after office hours, delegate of owner, living nearby, blonde: who but Hecuba Jones? Empirical certainty immediately succeeded the inference, along with the fresh knowledge of what she really looked like, a natural image easily supplanting the loosely rooted memory. It was her naturalness that without the aid of reason might have made him doubt for a moment. Once at her desk in San Francisco, once or twice for a minute or two on Michael's stairs, he had seen her made up for the world. But now she looked like an interesting young woman out for a walk by herself after supper.

Indeed he found that such was necessarily the case, for she had a purpose. At this late hour she was performing an unpaid option of kindness rather than washing her hair. With her purse hanging by a strap from the shoulder and her hands shrugged into the pockets of a soft cloth coat she had come as both messenger and seeker.

Still, Caleb's alarm concentrated upon this definite new figure as a surrogate of dangerous power. Perhaps she had come to see if he was drinking, or if he looked and smelled respectable enough to deserve the job. He hadnt shaved or bathed for several days, and in fact he was uncomfortable about the deterioration of his social aspect, which had waned in presentability as his spirit had waxed in antisocial confidence. Too suddenly his private life was being thrown into relief.

Contrary to his vague presumption it turned out that she brought him an impersonal warning with nothing censorious in her attitude. His suspicion subsided as she seemed to present herself rather as a sympathetic fellow-employee than as the boss's creature. "I brought a key but I didnt want to come into this place alone. It's scary-looking!" She shuddered pleasantly.

"I'm late getting the payroll out this week because Mr Wine gave me a lot of special work that just had to be finished before he went down to Los Angeles. It should have been in the mail two days ago. Then he was out of the office most of today and I had to wait until five o'clock to get his signatures before he left on his trip. So I thought you should get your check tonight at least."

"I forgot all about payday!" Caleb nearly giggled. "You shouldnt have taken all this trouble."

"No trouble. I also brought a Social Security withholding form for you to make out. I meant to ask you for it long ago, and I'd like to take it back to the office on Friday."

The news that tomorrow was her day off might have something to do with her unhurried interest in the shadowed building as he led her down to the desk in the boiler room that served as control point. He hurriedly cleared away his own papers, in automatic defense of privacy risking her suspicion that it was excessive.

But her glance was quick. "Been working on your thesis? What small handwriting! I'd never be able to read it. —By the way, I'll leave Sig's check too, if you'll give it to him in the morning."

While Hecuba waited on foot Caleb sat down and rapidly filled in the all-too-simple form that declared him to be footloose and fancy-free as far as responsibility to others was concerned and therefore liable for a rate of taxation (quite apart from what he contributed to the Social Security he thought he'd never live to claim) equal to that of many conjugated procreators enjoying a much greater share of the economy, apprehensively aware that she was idly scanning the untidy chamber and his personal effects.

"It's a nice mild evening." she remarked propping herself against the desk, careless of coal dust despite his warning. "But you have the daytime to go out in. Maybe that's better." Just as he rose to hand her his signature she hitched herself up to perch on a cleared corner of the grimy surface. "Oh I also have something to tell you!"

Her message was about coal. There would be a load of tolerable bituminous in about two weeks. She herself had located an obscure carload en route to a suburban dealer, cajoled a fraction of it, negotiated a price that Wine would pay, and—most wonderfully of all—exacted the promise of retail delivery. "What a relief! The boss has been talking about turning off the heat and just running the furnace for hot water. I'm the one that would be in hot water! It's hard enough now for me to keep these doctors from suing us. That's why you never see the boss; he's afraid to show his face around here even at night! He won't let me admit he's there when they call. But I can't take any more guff unless he hires another girl to help me. —That'll be the day!" She sighed humorously.

But she was in earnest, confidentially. "Can we get by for another couple of weeks? I hear you're down to four or five days."

"Maybe six in this weather."

"Is there anything you and Sig can possibly do to make it last longer?" She asked to see what was left and he led her over to the bunker, a boarded compartment half the depth of the building. He played a flashlight over the tiny heap of gleaming anthracite.

"I'm sorry to see the end of that good stuff." he said. "A little of it goes a long way. Soft coal won't go as far."

She laughed. "Boy oh boy, the boss was fit to be tied when I bought that load by mistake! Fifty dollars more than the soft coal. 'Do you think I'm made of diamonds?' he says."

"Good thing you did." said Caleb. "We'd have been out a month ago. But I can cut the night consumption to almost nothing."

He took her back to the lighted center of the boiler room. "My father was once a coal miner when he was a kid." she said, dropping pensively onto the bench opposite the boiler. "Can I see the fire?" He opened the furnace door and she got up and thrust her blonde head almost into the orange aperture.

"Be careful!" he cried. "—Oh, I thought you were going to stick your head inside! . . ." He had touched her elbow in diffident warning. "Your hair is glorious enough already."

"No compliments please. I'm here on business." But she was smiling as she went back to her seat.

"It wasnt a compliment." Indeed he had meant that her hair was famous, not beautiful or praiseworthy. But too late he saw that she had taken his miscalculated etymological gallantry as a denial of flattery rather than a polite salute to her business reputation. Well if she didnt understand his stupidly respectful witticism, so much the better, as long as she wasn't irritated. His unforeseen success in making himself socially noticeable only reinforced the uplifting affect of the news she had brought, for he was now confident that his prospective success in thermodynamics would be appreciated. And her apparent acceptance of his unbusinesslike person seemed to help kindle warmth conducive to frankness on both sides.

As she was mechanically picking up her purse to leave she abruptly exclaimed "Jesus Mary and Joseph, I almost forgot the paychecks!" Her apologetic rifling of the angular leather handbag produced two envelopes, one of which he placed on the desk for Sig to find; the other he absently folded for his pocket. He was disappointed by her incipient departure just when his defenses were relaxing.

But in her hasty search she was also arrested by the tax-exemption form he had executed. In the habitual manner of a clerk well experienced in meeting and helping the public she took out her slender silver pen to edit his entries without the slightest surprise or animadversion. "The withholding statement: what's your middle initial?" she asked.

"X."

"X? What does that stand for?"

"Unknown. It might be Axël."

"Axle begins with A, you dope. Don't you have a middle name?"

"Neither did George Washington or Abraham Lincoln."

"That's because they were too famous!" She laughed as she put away her pen, folded the form, and clicked shut her omnibus purse. "I'm sorry you had to wait for your pay. I would have brought it to you this afternoon when I first got off the streetcar, but I'd never find you in that haunted place you live in. How can you live among all those weird people? Besides, it's a fire trap."

"It's cheap. And no one asks any questions." He was marvelously pleased that she had learned to associate his mailing address with the medical hill's embarrassing Rabbit Warren (as Michael Chapman called it).

"Why, you got something to hide?"

"I'm a bastard. That's why I havent got a middle name. And they won't list me in the phone book without a middle initial to distinguish me from all the other Caleb Karcists. Besides, I can't afford a telephone. So I don't let them put one in."

"I know. It's impossible to reach you."

"I thank you for reaching me now. But don't you like the oak trees in front of the house? If I didnt live there I'd go by the place just to look at them. No wonder the city was named after them. There's an oak in England that three hundred and twenty four horses can stand under, or four thousand three hundred and seventy-four men. At least the people at the Rabbit Warren have plenty of room to take umbrage with each other."

She didnt seem to mind being puzzled. Perhaps the very doubt about a man's literal meaning made the circumstances familiar; but at the same time she seemed ambivalently piqued by this insubordinate kind of pleasantry that displaced familiar patterns of male kidding. She found herself in an interesting new rhythm of interlocution with this odd unkempt boy whose friendliness might still prove false. "You don't look angry anymore." she said.

"My boyfriend told me that in the first World War in France they had boxcars that carried forty men or eight horses." she continued. "I think there was a song about it. . . . Let's see, what would the French be singing under that tree? Forty-four hundred men at five men to a horse would be eight hundred and seventy-five horses. More than two and a half times as many horses!"

He *did* mind being puzzled by her legerdemain. "I can't do algebra in my head."

"It's not algebra, it's arithmetic."

"That doesnt make sense. Percherons are much bigger than English riding horses. There should be fewer, not more, French horses under the tree. You can't use the French ratio for an oak tree!"

"Maybe the English soldiers were coal miners, even smaller than the Frenchmen. They were always too crowded by the owners. . . ."

"English engineers used to figure that four Englishmen could do the work of a horse but it took five Frenchmen. . . . —I wasnt angry."

"Are you English? Doesnt sound like an English name. . . . — Not at me maybe, but at everything."

"English is all I know. I have the energy of six Frenchmen. 'Once more into the breach dear friends. . . .' I've been angry only at myself—but not tonight."

"I thought you were a philosophy student. Isnt philosophy supposed to keep you calm?"

"Not my philosophy."

"Then you should study psychology. —You thought I didnt know the difference!" She smiled, and then paused, seeming to consider her deportment in getting to the heart of her curiosity. Swinging half around she pointed to several wooden orange-crates stacked on the floor along the wall. "Do you read all those useless books? Is that how you learn how many legs will fit under a tree in Europe? More like history than philosophy isnt it?"

"I hate psychology. . . . My books arent useless: just unusable to me."

"Well I'll use whatever you tell me about them. It'll floor the guys! . . . . Do you hate psychology because it's about people? It is about people, isnt it, most of the time?"

"I hate people too, but that isnt why I hate psychology. I think psychologists are going to rule the world, and they're all wrong. I don't want to be ruled by people who don't believe in free will."

"You've got pretty strong ideas for a kid!" she said patting his forearm and bowing her head with a chuckle. "Are you going to be a P H D or something? You love books so much, why don't you write some and tell the world?"

"No Doctor's degree. I'm not even a Master. Doctor Johnson is the man you want. He wouldnt let them publish his dictionary until he went to get his Master's so that M A could be after his name on the title page, even though he'd already held up the publishers for years. I'm the opposite: I'd be glad to publish all my masterpieces with not even an X after my name. But I don't love books."

"Yes, you hate books too. Is Doctor Johnson the one on the third floor? I thought he was a psychiatrist. So you hate him double. What's the matter with you, anyway? You hate the whole world. You sound like some of the girls that were in high school with me."

He flushed in defending himself. "It's not that I really hate everything. It's just that I'm tired of learning things. Yeats said: 'How much knowledge can the soul endure?'"

"I like that. Was he a philosopher like you?"

"He wrote plays. He said knowledge was the surface of life."

"You want experience, then why take a job like this?"

"Just for new images."

"Holy God, you sound like a high-brow movie! I can't understand you at all. You seem to think you've seen enough of the world already! Do you have a girlfriend?"

Taken aback, he laughed with forced clarity as he made up his mind to throw caution to the winds of chance. "If I don't keep to myself I won't be able to write my own plays. I want to be a greater writer than Shakespeare."

"I hope so. He's boring. My father was a sort of radical and he made my mother name me from Shakespeare. He had two years of English and Hecuba was all he remembered. Hecky for short. Said I looked like a little golden Hecky-hen when I was playing outside the barn. But half the time he said Hecky stood for Hecate. Ma called me Kate when she was feeling good."

"'What's Hecuba to him or he to Hecuba, That he should weep for her?'" Caleb was very happy to remember that one line. She made him go over it several times so that she could memorize it. "It sounds sad." she said. "But don't tell me any more about it. I don't care what it really means. Hamlet Act Two is enough for me to know. —Well at least you're beginning to level with me! Don't worry, I won't squeal on you. —You're the first one I've met who could tell me exactly where my name came from. The teachers in Business English didnt know anything like that. And you knew it by heart!"

"Hecuba was originally a Trojan queen."

"Well I aint exactly a queen and I'm no Trojan."

"You're more like Pandora."

"All I know is that she was too inquisitive. Am I asking too many questions? Well I can't help it. I love books. I don't read them but I love 'em. I don't even have one in my house!" She laughed in her belly, bent almost double, hands spread over her mouth. "But I mean it. I'm not being sarcastic." She glanced at him curiously before continuing. "But what I really want to know is why you brought all your books down here. I don't care if you *are* a scholar, you can't read them all at once! You must be writing a play about books."

"I'm not writing a play about anything yet. I'm just getting ready to write one."

"Okay, you don't have to tell me. You hate books, you're not going to put them in your play, and you can't even read them all! Then why are they here?" She stepped over to pick up a small one off the top of the nearest crate. It was the one book of them all that he had looked into at the beginning of his watch. She opened to the dog-eared page without looking at the outside of the binding, reading aloud without advance inspection, all the words stressed alike: "'For the very best choose one thing before all others, immortal glory among mortals.' That's what you underlined. You want glory: that's why you're here! Like my hair!" She giggled, and then laughed outright, this time in peals ascending from low to high as she was struck by each successively revealed layer of merriment.

"In books I mark the passages I understand."

She had already leafed through later pages without moving her lips, and now she was rapidly scanning two or three other books. "Well there arent many marks in these books!" she exclaimed in provocative triumph, devolving into chuckles of lower pitch. "Well what good are they after all? You can't even understand them when you do read them.

"—I'll help you. Have you got one here that will tell us how to keep you from getting laid off—seeing as how you seem to think this is the only place to seek your glory? All we need is one little miracle like the loaves and the fishes." She started to unpack a crate of books without looking at them as if she was searching for the answer unbooked at the bottom

like a precipitated ingot. She looked up at him quizzically. Can't we at
least find out how to make coal?"

"YES!" He leapt before her, hands and arms spread like one of Goya's
revolutionaries, almost scaring the wits out of her. It was his turn to
laugh, and to pat her on the arm. "Yes!" Raising his voice to a muted
shout: "I'm going to make coal tonight!"

For the first time she stared at him with wide eyes. He subsided, turning aside with a grin. "Or at least make the coal last longer!"

"Why you crazy kid!" she said finally in a soft tone of astonishment,
forsooth of admiration. For a long time he felt her eyes fascinated by the
skull behind his face.

"I'm burning them! I'm burning them to keep my job."

Silence. At last she sighed. "Oi schlect, I thought he knew what he was
doing!" She wagged her head, affecting an air of sad disappointment, and sat
down on the bench with crossed legs, one ankle swinging thoughtfully. She
leaned her cheek upon the hand of one elbow supported by her knee.

"Now please tell me how a few boxes of books can heat a great big
building for two weeks. As a matter of fact please tell me how you can
make them burn without using up coal faster than ever. And then tell me
why you should sacrifice your only possessions—right?—just to keep a
lousy job like this for a few more lousy months when you won't even have
your lousy books to read so you'll know what to put in your probably
lousy play!" It was plain that she wasnt yet prepared to take him for mad
but still sought the key to his metaphors, if not a recognizable emotion to
account for his zany talk. "And tell me what good it does to waste your
education. Tell me why you should waste all the money you spent on these
books. Jesus Mary and Joseph!"

"I had to get rid of them anyway. This way they're *not* wasted. —Look:
this book is on thermodynamics. It tells how to get the most heat for your
money. Books are a fantastic bargain! I hope Mr Wine will appreciate
what scientific knowledge is doing for him. But don't tell him until it's all
over—if we can make it until your load of coal comes. Meanwhile with
due care I think I can keep the coal consumption on my shift down to
about half. That should pull us through. If no one borrows any of my
books!" Hopeful of her humor he studied her face. "If you stay awhile I'll
show you. —Yes, go ahead and have a cigarette. Relax."

"I don't like astrology and magic: I'm still a little of a good Catholic.
Do you mean to say you believe in all that stuff?"

"This isnt magic or alchemy. I'm not trying to make gold or love-
potions. It's just a scientific mutation of energy."

"Well it sounds like spooky chemistry. Just like this whole building at
night." She looked around and shivered. "At least we can have a drink
first." She took from her capacious pouch a slender silver flask delicately
rounded at the edges but of flat shape no more obtrusive than a paper-
bound book. "Matches my pen and pencil. —My friend the Silver Fox

gave it to me." she added lightly, unscrewing the tiny ladylike cap. "Here, have a swig. Southern Comfort."

"Thanks. —Now I'll teach you the value of books. First I have to stoke the fire. Just a thin layer of coal and keep it steady. See the blue flame. Now you'll understand. I think it's going to need only a couple of dozen books a week. There are several different kinds that give various amounts of heat, and you have to mix them like proteins in such a way that you use them in the right proportions, because I have a lot more of some kinds than others. The trick is to get the most efficient blend and not to run out of the more energetic ones early in the game. The fire should be steady not only from minute to minute but also from night to night. You can't be casual about it." He accepted another slug of the excessively sweetish liquor. "Do you want me to explain the theory of it?"

"Sure. But I want to see it happen too. You gotta prove it to me. Otherwise I'll have to see that you're fired for using company coal to burn your own trash."

"If you burn *me* up in this furnace you won't need coal for another year."

"But you'd stink up the air too much. So I won't tell Mr Wine after all—I'll just take away the rest of your books. Anyway you better begin— you're still arguing for your life!"

Caleb's demonstration and lecture was gradually warmed up not by the fire (which as much as possible for the purpose was kept cool and economical in fundamentally steady state) but by the tiny sluices of confectionery fire water that came his way from time to time. He was not surprised to find that in fact her interest in what she called "theoreology" was nil; but as a student of his practice she proved attentive, as if soberly, like a new apprentice on probation. She watched his face as from time to time he opened and closed the cast iron portal to watch and poke the fire in rapt preoccupation with what he was saying. Occasionally he tossed in a pound or two of books. Otherwise there wasnt anything for either of them to do. The process however was highly selective and calculating. It wasnt long before Hecuba began to appreciate the skill of it, and to sympathize with the victims like a respectful illiterate forced to witness an unintelligible book-burning.

"I happen to be following a traditional gesture, but I need symbols more than the next man. Especially counter-symbols, which have to be very strong to overcome my extraordinary psychic imperfections as well as my titanic burden of wet academic snow. Only an operation in the real world can generate the power I need. The force of a symbol can be proportional to the degree of economic transformation that it's the by-product of. . . . I have only recently learned from your worthy downstairs neighbor to see the world economically. . . .

"Now what we want here is usable heat, as much as possible from small resources. This is no simple case of converting matter into energy, like getting heat from your coal. When you burn coal you de-structure it.

Millions of years ago a lot of energy went into making the molecules of the plants that make up the coal. Molecules are made by putting atoms together. The atoms are always there, always have been—at least until very recently. So it's the organization of the atoms that makes the difference: atoms knit together in special arrangements that make life and fuel and available heat. Since even low-life like coal, which is really dead-life, gives back heat energy when you take it apart again, I ought to be able to get more heat from less matter if I burn fuel that is more complicated. Books are more complicated than anything else except brains. We can't very well burn brains. . . ."

"Unless you're fired. You seem to have brains to burn. Maybe you're the smartest guy I've ever seen. I bet even Mike Chapman wouldn't have thought of this."

"He knows *too* much about it."

"Still and all, it's only what you called symbolic. I have to see it with my own eyes: I'm not educated but I'm from Missouri—actually just outside East Saint Louis, very close to Missouri. Coal country."

"You can't expect to see the steam. Eventually you'll see it in your accounts payable. We'll be using a lot less coal as long as the books hold out. Will that be proof enough?"

"I still think you may be kidding me, but I'm not sure. You may be crazy but that doesn't mean you're a genius."

"I'm not a genius. If I were a genius I wouldn't have to burn books for a living. . . . Anyway—to be practical about it—as you can see, the technique of combustion is important. . . . Watch now. . . . It's hard to tear up a book. Obviously you can't take the time to tear out each page, but you have to scatter it as much as you can, like the stones of Jerusalem, down to the level of chapters or signatures if possible. —Yes, like that, only more so: tear it again. Watch through the peephole. You want to see every page curl in the flames. . . . The covers have to be ripped off every time. That's where you get the greatest pleasure. Paperbacks are the most efficient. . . ."

"I like this part of it better than playing with symbols."

"Scientists play with numbers. Look at what they've come up with: unavailable heat equals disinformation. . . . Never mind, you'll see. Here's the important part now—this is the art of the job: if you need steady efficient heating you must pick the right number and assortment of books at each feeding of the fire. Otherwise you wouldn't need me; you could hire any book-burner off the street.

"I classify my books according to their quality of information. . . . The base order is knowledge. The noblest is imagination. But it's the large middle class of critical thought that makes this library so valuable. . . . Now we have to be very frugal in burning works of the most substantial imagination. About midnight we can sacrifice another classic to maintain energy-production with fewer books. Maybe two more before morning.

"—Don't get your lily little hands dirty now. That poker's too heavy for an office worker. You white-collar people are too delicate for furnace-stoking."

"I don't know, I've been called a fire-shovel!" she suddenly giggled and clutched his arm. They were sitting side by side on the bench. "—Here: but save me some; it's almost gone!"

But his cerebral fever was already reignited, and his ruminations resumed as if he had forgotten the presence of her body. "I don't much mind that they call it all information, but you shouldn't let them stop you from insisting upon the qualitative distinctions that make all the difference in the world. It takes more life-blood to make poetry than to make a textbook because poetry has to make many more new connections. It is not just more complicated: it's original complexity.

"Perhaps you'll object that I'm overlooking the first law of thermodynamics. You will say that we can't get energy from nothing. You will point out that coal got its potential free energy from the sun, a very hot godlike body that sustains us all; but where do individual books get their particular counterentropic values? What virtue has been expended for knowledge and imagination? (Don't forget that the intermediate orders of information involve all history in our flames here!)

"Well, I say these chronicles interpretations judgments anatomies ontologies epistemologies verses scenes acts sonnets lyrics epics stories epiphanies compendiums and myths are all paid for with the specie of life. The only way you can add to the library of premium fuel is to suck up words from the earth you're rooted in and ram them into personal order against tooth-and-nail resistance—while you do the screaming and kicking—until they are locked into eternal life by their own cohesive force."

"How can you be so sure when you havent started writing yet?"

"What makes you think that?"

"I can tell."

"I'm speaking theoretically of course. I know what I'm getting into. I already know what a struggle it is to produce second-order information." He suddenly sprang to one of the boxes and tumbled out all the books to get to the bottom of it. He waved a slender manuscript before flinging open the fire-door. Look! My highest work so far: a tyro masterpiece: 'YEATS'S THEORY OF TRAGEDY'. Watch this—only one sheet at a time! Look at the blaze, look how long it takes for each sheet to brown and curl. Hottest heat of disintegrating value—and almost no ash at all!"

"Probably just a first draft. In a year or two you may be able to raise steam for the *Queen Elizabeth*. I hope you don't burn the Bible."

For an instant he was annoyed at her disrespect. "There are millions of copies of that. Besides," he added, mildly however, "it's nothing new."

"You're unbalanced." she said with equal gentleness. "Southern Comfort goes to your head."

His fever flared up again. "You're damned right I'm unbalanced. I'm unbalanced because—"

"Ten words or less!"

"—all positive resistance to cultural degradation comes out of the hide of people like me. Art is painful—painstaking and painsgiving. I sometimes think pain is the highest order of information."

"Especially painsgiving!" she laughed. "What do you know about pain? —Fiddlesticks for your consistency!"

He gazed at her in admiration, not knowing that she had heard Ruth use the latter words to Michael. "But actually," she went on, "there *is* no one else like you and your term paper." Since she was sitting beside him on the bench like a proud sister she leaned over and kissed his cheek.

After a motionless pause he mumbled "It's simply that a few people have to be unbalanced to make eddies against the tide. That's the closest I can come to doing something for society."

"By burning the world's best books?"

"I'm getting rid of teachers and premature influences as well as possessions. No more 'mere intellect'. Imagination can't be forced, conjured, or cajoled: it can only be freed. Even if I have to be crushed like an apple in a cider mill and left a bloodless passionless pulp. Right now I want to deconstruct my husk. How do you expect me to be symmetrical? The whole world's unbalanced the other way!"

He picked up the Heraclitus, one of his last favorite possessions, which would have been spared until later if it hadnt been so dramatically convenient for the occasion, reading aloud: "'Fire coming upon all things will test them, and lay hold of them.'" And he tossed the little book into the supermetamorphic maw.

But the whole of Heraclitus was now so small in the library world that it had to be bound with other and contrary wisdom in the same volume. "Watch out," his pupil warned: "don't smother a good fire!"

Thus too all the academic matters that had once seemed the substance of life-worth-living were at last reduced to friable carbon. "'Every tub must stand on its own bottom.'" Caleb told Hecuba, meaning that imagination like wisdom must build its own foundation. Sometimes he had to wield the poker vigorously to get the philosophers to burn, and no doubt he lost more heat through the open door than they contributed to the useful thermal process. The charring froth of alien fuel looked cooler than the boiler tubes above.

"Well," he said after a long silence, for the first time looking her levelly in the eye, "the quintessence of romantic transformation is inconsistency."

"At least it sounds romantic."

On this cue he spread his arm across her back and gently pressed her shoulders. An experienced seducer could not have calculated to better effect.

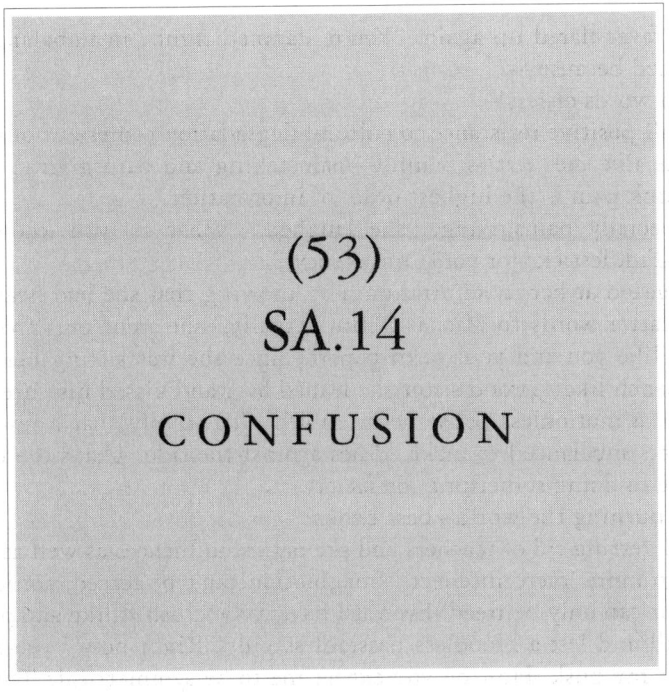

(53)
SA.14

CONFUSION

[CONTINUED FROM (51) MS.05 FOOTNOTE 3]

"The brain is the most erotic organ." she said in the dark. I knew what she meant but I thought that for once it was irrelevant. My fingers ceased moving at her side and I shifted my weight in the bed so that I could as if accidentally reduce the chance of contact without apparently appreciating the significance of her words. She meant don't touch me until you're ready to take down the walls of your tower brick by brick: I'll have none of your mechanics tonight, maybe never again.

She mistook me. Never have I thought it a poorer time to make a play for her favor. (Two or three times in our history I have been astonished at her response to my most unassuming touch when I thought her utterly preoccupied with transcendental spiritual matters hateful with anger exhausted unto deathlike sleep or for some other reason uninterested in my particular body; but almost always I know very well when even the longest most patient siege can end in nothing but my own bootless abasement.) And never have I felt more frigid in defense against this terrible Cassandra whose oestrus cycle I realized that I had lost track of during all the secret excitement of resolving and planning the greatest change in my life since getting married.

I may have been drifting toward sleep for a few seconds but now I came fully awake lying perfectly still to figure out why she chose that statement to express her uncalledfor meaning. Maybe she was telling me something subtle. Was she suggesting that I make her want me on this extraordinary occasion not simply by a long exchange of comforting and affectionate words (such as she always hoped for) but by a whole sapping night of confession that might earn my absolution without acquitting her of obedience to my decision? Or was she saying that no degree of explanation apology compromise retraction or new concession at this late date could prove the only kind of love that wasnt sheer lust and deception?

I was in no mood for proving anything; even in such unprecedented extremity of guilt it takes much too much time to clear the air with a storm. [I say, she says—I reply, she answers—then say I, then says she—etc etc etc: finally we both breath easier but my throat is dry my sleepless body jerks from enervation of the mind and it's time to get up and go to work. Thereafter I must sustain all the goodwill that we've generated! The result is that it's twice as hard as ever before to transgress the canons of humanistic matrimony. Whereas if I quietly take my lumps, leaving myself unassoiled, I can at least maintain some forward progress.] But on the other hand I was entirely uncertain about the best course of passivity. My sole purpose was to get through the trial without overt domestic disaster yet keep intact at least the spine of a plan that represented my only possible escape from a web that it was almost too late to struggle in.

But she again spoke calmly in her usual low clear voice that seldom betrayed the stain of tears. "I'm not going to be your convenient girlfriend any longer Michael. I'm not a pin-cushion. I won't be boared like a patient sow."

I chuckled. It's not uncommon for either of us to come out with something funny, or to recognize it, right in the middle of grim angry fear. Her spirit, my comic blubber—even when drowned they need weights heavier than any guilt to keep them on the bottom.

"You never take me out to dine and dance. You never even take me for a walk. The lord and master simply steps out by himself whenever he feels so disposed and abandons me to a sink full of dishes."

"But we can't leave the kids by themselves."

"Of course not." she agreed with that ironically non sequitur tone of hers, neutral and unassailable.

She knew that I knew that she knew the implacable and unremitted facts of responsibility, and that I couldnt be expected to stay home and take care of three children after a day's struggle with the outer world while she went out for a walk in the dark streets alone, and that she wasnt partial to walking anyway except for its symbolism of fellowship. [The few walks I've forced or beguiled myself into taking her on have painfully compromised my self-respect by the sheer hypocrisy of honoring the kind of sentimentality that I most hate. No matter how slowly I stroll she saunters even slower, looking around like a schoolteacher on guided tour of Paris humming her contented possession of a husband, and we never get anywhere.] My reply had been unnecessary of course, but it gave me a chance to deny my silence and warm up ever so slightly to the gratification of her standing wish to get me talking as I'd never talked before about the flame of anguish burning in the lighthouse we kept for our seaborne children.

After an aporetic pause she continued. "You think all you have to do is rub me the right way until I sneeze. That'll keep her quiet for a while, you say to yourself. Well let me tell you there arent enough sneezes in ten men to silence me any more! Sleeping with a man is not important to me. A woman has her own life to lead and it's something better than drudging away for a man all wrapped up in his selfishness. I hardly ever see you; when I do it's only because you're lolling around for some stupid noisy ball game on the radio or preaching to me about the sins of inefficiency while you eat and drink watching me at work in the kitchen from your chair in the corner where I can't get at you to scratch out your eyes!"

"One can be efficient and lazy too." I explained, but she paid no attention to my sorry diversion.

"You always expect to find your food the minute you walk in so you can wolf it down in great greedy gulps like a starved lumberjack. You never even raise your eyes above the rim of your cup before you're off to a nice clean shiny store where janitors and other people do all the real work for you. Or you lock yourself into that sacred treasure cell where you don't have to pay attention to anything unpleasant. What's more, at Canyon you took the only big sunny room in the house and nobody else could use it. So it's easy enough for *you* to renounce ambition and happiness!

"If you're the father of a family without a house of your own and you pass your neighbors on the street—men your own age with families living in comfort while you grub along as a clerk with no more money than a ditch-digger—you can console yourself with the idea that someday they'll hear how great you've been in secret. But what about *me*? You have academic friends to throw parties for you; you give snobbish lectures to admiring intellectuals: but I, I have no connection with the world except through little boys and their playmates. When they grow up what have I got to look forward to? If you ever earn any distinction it won't be shared with me—I can bet my bottom dollar on that! Even the boys' success will never be mine."

"But what can I do about it? You knew . . ." So far I could absorb her words like an archery butt. They had been said before in one form or another (though rarely so directly), and acknowledged too. She's never seemed to really care about bourgeois social status but her mother's venom always works its way to the surface when the sediment is stirred up. With these words she would bring the whole respectable world to her reinforcement.Sounding off gave her some confidence in her grievances. But she had nothing difficult to prove.

"There's no reason you can't loosen up with my relatives and other people I like to see once in a while. You could join organizations with me where we could make new friends and do some good with warm unaffected folks—even if it were only the Parent-Teachers Association or the Cub Scout support group or a church club—maybe something more to your taste like a play-reading group. Things like that . . ."

"But you've stopped going to church! I went with you—"

"*That* church! You know I had to leave it because Mr Gilchrist is evil. He wouldnt listen to my ideas. All he wanted to do was make love to me. There are plenty of other churches, including the kind I was brought up in; but the denomination doesnt matter to me so long as it's not an organized religion. But you don't like anything simple and straightforward! Anything I want to do I must do alone. Always alone, without a husband, always having to make excuses for your absence and feeling out of place by myself. *You* hate normal people, *I* don't. I never see people *I* can talk to! You hate this, you hate that. You never ask what I hate. One thing I hate is standing below everyone we know. You could have been a teacher by now if you hadnt thought yourself too educated for college!"

This last cut was so absurdly off the mark that I immediately forgave its poetic license as nothing more than another manifestation of her still incredible incapacity for any discernment of the allegiance that rules my opposition to her anti-intellectual sentimentality. I did not stay in college for several reasons, some of which arose from blind pride, it is true, but the main cause, notwithstanding a splendid government subsidy for war veterans that F D R had prepared the country for, was her premature primogenesis followed by the first of her postpartum depressions, which soon burdened me with serious household inefficiency and the extracurricular expense of medicine-men.

Her admirable voice remained low and steady but the words of grievance seemed endless. ". . . Then there'd have been no question about needing a house and car and vacations and college money for the boys, and all the other things we havent got. Roger wouldnt look like a ragamuffin and I'd have decent clothes."

"But you went out and bought a new coat at Magnin's, a new eight-five dollar coat, and I didnt say a word against it!"

"You know it was really a hundred-and-fifty-dollar coat marked down. It was a very unusual bargain. Anyway, I'm sorry about it, and I told you so. I know I was extravagant."

"Honey, you needed it. I don't begrudge it. But we have to finish paying for it before we buy anything else."

"I know, Michael. I'm still a child about money. But I want to learn! I'll never learn if I'm always treated like a helpless little girl." She paused to regather the anger she had dropped in reverting to the habitual struggle against herself. "I don't intend to bet my life on your fragile 'work' that no one is allowed to see and that you won't talk about even to your own wife—especially when you boast about not ever being able to make any money on it. You could get a decent job if you really wanted to, and make a good salary. Or get a second job at night. Many men do that for their families. You let Mr Greatrakes take advantage of you because you get some sort of perverse satisfaction from thinking of yourself as a romantic artist. Some romance! You're much more prosaic than I am."

That's true, I assented with rueful sincerity.

"Well the children and I don't like being poor. I'm the one that's starving. You have butter while the rest of the family eats margarine. Well I'm hungry, hungry for food to restore my soul. . . ."

Sympathy for her was just about to dissipate the dull old anger at the fact that I should feel doubt and guilt for my kind of purity; but she infuriated me by returning to the subject she'd already said far too much about.

"Why don't you at least show your manuscripts to a professor who can tell you whether or not they're worthwhile when you have so many other responsibilities. But let's say some of your stuff turns out to be professional and you can sell it—what then? Why then you say you'll give up your job and spend *all* your time piling up more words—abstract bloodless inhuman words I'm sure—even if you can't make as much as we're living on now! You yourself say we'll always be poor. You seem to like the idea. Failure is what you *want*! Well I wouldnt care if you were doing it to help other people. You know very well that I wouldnt mind being poorer than everybody else if you werent so selfish about what youre doing. Or at least if you were a real genius—generous and temperamental—and couldnt help burning the candle at both ends. But you seem to know exactly what you're doing, like an I B M machine. Anyway, how would I know how important your work is? You can't expect me to be enthusiastic about what you don't even want me to understand. You and your taxidermy or whatever you call it!"

I couldnt help laughing and neither could she; but at the same time she was deadly serious and so was I. In fact I trembled under the impulse to leap out of bed and fling off all the bedclothes to beat her as hard as I could with my belt, shake her by the throat, or pack up and leave the house once and for all that very minute with everything I needed in two suitcases and a handtrunk. (Alas no cash that day! And the children of course—can't leave them to disaster. . . .)

". . . You and your Key to all Rituals! Mr Casaubon, that's what you are, I'm sorry to say. A Boston personality, 'the east wind made flesh'. (I guess it's the west wind out here.) What am I waiting for the rest of my life? And if you're ever successful you'll just leave me for some tight young literary girl."

What could I say to all that? She plucked too many different vibrations at once. Either I had to try conclusions with her or I had to shut up. So far I had lost no ground; and at the same time in spated utterance she was gathering the kinetic strength that gave her the heart for healthy catharsis. I reminded myself that if given suffrage as a woman I would not have chosen to be in Mrs Chapman's shoes, though as a mate I would still choose her feet before all others. In our youth if I had known where the graduations of condition were going to lead me I wouldnt have given two cents for the hopes that kept me in countenance; yet in maturity I still do not regret what so far has come of a life with this incomparably lonely woman doomed like an enchanted queen whose attraction and precious-ness come and go inversely with her confusions. I no longer try to get inside the glass casket that neither husband nor doctor is qualified to open, nor anyone else but the children born within. There was no unlock-ing kiss or antipotion I could get to her lips. Hippias said that the most beautiful of earthen pots is ugly in comparison to maidenkind, but I say the most beautiful of maidens is crass in comparison to my Ruth, who takes on the vulgar speech of journalism, who speaks commonplace thoughts in imploring the sea not to swallow up the children who are also mine. She disprizes everything but agape, as a blind person might disprize everything but sight, and devotes her life to seeing that no one else shall go without it. It is to that end she wants new children to be born—that they may give love its chance with new men and women. Perhaps I should be giving up my eyes for her sake.

I was still careful not to touch her. I again forgot how much pity was being displaced by my rage at her skeptical appraisal of what I might be good for, though it was a faint enough whiff of the pain she herself has always been sodden with. You would have thought she'd been consulting a creative writing teacher about my grades; or that she was making a blunt try after many tactful attempts to shock me out of an alcoholism that was bringing me to ruin with all who depended upon my performance in life. I hated her fear of my mania. I hated her judgment. Most of all I hated my fear of my own judgment.

My unstanchable gall welled up afresh with the old sense of irrevers-ible time-waste (in her eyes such a paltry contribution) that I had already invested in her commonplace demands. Then too she was blaming me for not finishing what she was blaming me for! I havent got a leg to stand on, because if there's anyone whose unseen worth for lack of proof must remain worthless 'tis I! Yet she had no call to fasten upon the most hor-rible literary model, totally misunderstanding the precedent. Casaubon is my nightmare. If I had his living, i e money and leisure . . .

Yet she was sniffing near the pragmatical truth. I've squandered far too much of my laboriously filched hoard of golden timepieces on mere parerga of ambition. Of course it would be foolhardy to confess my temp-tations to her: she'd never again doubt her doubt of me. Besides, very soon now I'll be finished with exposition by lecture, and then put behind me the amateur anthropology of youth for the real work of my life that has at last presented itself. How should she know that my sophomoric days of preparation and digression are almost over? Vain pride prevents me from justifying myself to the one who most suffers from it, but I silently swear by the hollow of her thigh that I'll let nothing again divert me from the straight and narrow toil of Chapman's own epic. . . .

At last came the censure I was preparing for: "You should have told me!" Now that she had climbed to this new elevation of our essential quarrel and was pacing out a new contour for the first time, she began to lose control of her voice; from her tightened throat it slightly rose in pitch. "If only you had consulted *me*! We could have talked about it. I'm no less involved than you are. More so in fact, because I'll have to tear up my roots."

It was a surprise to me that one whose grasp of the soil was so light should not have realized herself as rootless as a tumbleweed since the birth she'd been given by her mother. I equivocated, or rather prevaricated, as I always do under lesser accusations. "I tried to tell you." Despite my long anticipation of this reproach I faltered. "Every time I was about to discuss the subject something came up. Several times though I've mentioned that I want to go back East. Many times we've talked about moving. It seemed too far-fetched to take seriously until all of a sudden I found that I'd saved as many nickels and dimes as I needed in that little coin bank you gave me."

There was nothing else to say. How could I make her understand the obvious fact that it had been impossible to persuade her forthrightly in advance that such transplantation was a good thing for our family? It would have been a continual hell of time-consuming impugnable argument, bringing on the kind of conjugal weather that closes up the rose and unhives the family for lack of any honey whatsoever. Besides, how can you speak unreservedly of your ruling passion for a particular townscape to one who's never cared much even for her own places? It seems like mere preference, or reaction to the place you're in. Yet after all these years she should have divined the depth of my patriotism.

"You never objected to Gloucester."

"You know perfectly well that you hadn't ever proposed moving there. Goodness gracious, it used to take a whole year for the frontier to move westward a mere seventeen miles, and you want to go all the way back to the Atlantic Ocean in five days and four nights! I've always told you I'd hate the winters there. Anyway this is an unspeakably high-handed thing to do, and no other woman would stand for it. What's most unforgivable is that you should have been saving up all this money without telling me . . . *when you say we can't afford a second-hand television set!*"

My heart froze when I was once more forced to consider how deeply she desired the one substitute for a family hearth that's most poisonous to the marrow of my bones and dullingly pernicious to the sweet fresh tenderness of children's brains. We had been through all the arguments a dozen times, but all the authorities of the age (slavering at the prospect of entertainment without toil) play into her hands by proclaiming that television can educate. I had thought she knew herself well enough to see that she'd lose control even of the good thing she thought it was, seeing that the boys would always be too young to decline the soothing sugary addictive drug on their own account.

"It would be mainly for me." she had said the last time we disputed the devil's vision. "No more than half an hour a day for them. . . ."

If you have children you can't fight the times. From now on there will be nothing public (no res publica) without it. Even without commercial advertising agencies ugly salesmen like Richard Nixon have learned to use it for sentimental diseducation. But to her my opinions against the American grain are absurd "elite" theories, highfalutin snobbery, ridiculous esoteric preciosity. She has no intuition for history. Nevertheless I had thought she reluctantly acknowledged the force of my tiresome philippic, for after all our values in respect to child-rearing are by no means entirely at variance with each other.

But I suppose that my erroneous sense of having won that debate did not formally differ from her presumption that she had talked me out of any serious intentions toward Gloucester with her perdurable argument that migration would traumatically damage our little hothouse Californians by ripping them untimely from the soil of their Eden and setting them down among dour backward Puritans and bigoted superstitious Catholics contending with each other to survive on wintry bare rocks, where they would get old-fashioned lessons by rote in boring schools on pain of the "red hand" of punishment which I had once mentioned meaning to amuse her with Gloucester's endemic vernacular for the erewhile universal *rattan* that she could remember at least by hearsay from her own schooldays before the psychologists had educated the California State Board of Education. But at this point I was so dismayed by the grim substance of our abysmal disagreements that I found nothing congenial in any form of her attitudes. With the revival of my frustrated rage I scorned to reply. I merely listened numbly, stupefied as never before. It was the first time I ever saw in myself the masochism she accuses me of.

But suddenly, when I found her returning to my proximate guilt and declaring that there were no cooperative nursery schools in places like Gloucester I couldnt help volunteering that my native town didnt even have kindergartens. "There arent many playgrounds either." What is it in her that always drives me so furiously awry in the rudimentary tact of persuasion?

"There you are! And where in the world would you ever get a job? Don't tell me there are bookstores in Gloucester!"

"I'll commute by train, somewhere down the line, maybe to Boston. That's as big a city as San Francisco you know, even if it no longer has much in the way of hills. . . . *We can buy a house* on a G I Bill mortgage." I was not relying solely upon the great feminine principle of self-sacrifice to make her see my way.

But her mind was on another track instead. Now she dwelt on what was of course the greatest difficulty of my scheme. At some length she rubbed in the plain fact that it's not easy to get a job good enough (and soon enough) to move and improve a family, especially if you're not qualified for the kind that pays relocation expenses, when having already left your old one without savings or credentials you go 3000 miles as a stranger to the least ebullient census region of the U S A where the cost of living is high and wages low. It's harder than I wanted to anticipate, even harder than she could imagine who enjoys our present economic station in a familiar area after many years of adaptation and who has no inkling of the trepidation that undermines my business-world aggressions. On this count I was prudent enough not to shake her ultimate confidence in me. [Have I ever had the pleasure of a moment's indulgence to expose my frailty to one who might understand its special condition?] She already had reason enough to regard my shabby island in the East as a gray tundra of starving exile. I could hear her mind once again going over the lines read in high school:

> Through the sad heart of Ruth, when, sick for home,
> She stood in tears amid the alien corn.

Yet I thought my volunteered bondage to real estate (lightly promised when most remote) would satisfy that heart, to whom a house was a home, the reward she'd been cheated of by my stubborn perversity: the one place of her own, the one desire, the one innocent greed, the one indemnification for having to bring up children virtually alone, the one hope that could bind her to the practical world that was otherwise beyond her grasp and at the same time bind her husband to twenty-five years of mortgaged groundskeeping and handyman maintenance—as well as the one real proof that he who hated responsibility really loved her. I was only repeating what I'd mumbled at my birthday party, for then having been taken off guard I had prematurely bruited my only major bargaining point. Just in case she'd missed it the first time.

But no such luck. It now appeared that in her subsequent brooding she had found the offer phony. As a bonus peculiar to my project it was now discounted and dismissed as fake. "If you can buy a house there with your veteran's benefits you can buy a brand-new house here right here in Alameda County just as well as some old Colonial shack. If you have enough money for us all to live on while you're panning for gold in New England you've been saving more than coins and you must have enough money for downpayment on a house here and now!"

"But I don't have that much!"

"Then for the love of Mike how are you going to get us and the furniture across the country after you find a job?"

"I can sell my books." was all I could think of to say.

"Sell your books! Nobody wants books like yours. I looked into that long ago." I was too agitated to catch the significance of her remark at the moment but when it came back to me a couple of days later at the store I was furious. I knew she liked to pour over the classified ads. She always wanted to see if there was some way to pay for one thing or another that I denied her in the name of necessity. Could she have called in a dealer during that time I trusted her with the key? I don't think she'd actually have sold them behind my back but she might have wanted to confront me with an offer of cash on the barrelhead that would show how much of the family assets were tied up as my personal property, while also demonstrating what a good businesswoman she could be.

Yet in a seizure of misapprehension—who knows what the most faithful lady will do to betray her husband when he's revealed to be the enemy of her children? [Yeats says that no sane man is permitted to lie knowingly. If insanity excuses poetic lies—"truths of passion that are intellectual falsehoods"—and such lies excuse insanity, then logically a woman's madness may excuse her playing the poet a little false. And vice versa. She herself once told me that "truth is a thing of words".]

Ruth has always protested against keeping my books out of sight where she and visitors can't see them, the one species among our furnishings that would give people a hint of something distantly respectable to account for if not to ameliorate our otherwise undistinguished penury. "There's no reason to hide them." she had said. "They arent empty whiskey bottles. You'll never read them all anyway. Besides, they're fairweather friends. Some day you'll outgrow your childhood comforts."

I often forget the good reasons for my offences but the fact is that the books are locked in my study for preservation. When some were in the bed/sitting room she wouldnt take care of them. Over and over again I found that the kids had been at them for playthings, or that she'd taken one out and let it get wet somewhere, one after another in fact, never putting them back where she got them. I still can't find the second volume of the *City of God* or the complimentary copy of *Shakespeare's Bawdry* that Jolls sent me. There was always a book missing when I needed it most. Once at the Canyon house she shut up Norkid in my room and he got Yeats's *Collected Poems* off the bottom shelf and tore it to pieces. I still have his tooth marks puncturing the *Plays*. If she can't keep babies and puppies away from books I must do it my way. She's always sorry about such things but she never learns from experience. It's the same negligent mishaps over and over again. No use talking to her. Who can blame me for not wanting her to use my only property as symbols? And who can blame me for worrying about the security of my private papers, both literary and financial? She's not my partner, though I can hardly say so.

Sometimes she assures me that she would willingly suffer the insufferable if only I'd let out my anger once in a while rather than clamming up in uncommunicative resentment. No doubt it would be good for my health to yell and scream like a passionate Italian. But the one time I lost my temper was not successful. Knowing the kids were safely out in the yard I affected an ungovernable violence to express my unaffected rage by jerking the cloth and all the dishes on it right off the kitchen table and slamming out through the door (Semiramis shooting before me like a black cannonball), just to see if it would do any good to call her deluded royal straight flush with my little pair of jacks. By then I'd learned at least that she isnt really lazy, or by an means indifferent to the work she cannot bring herself to do, but I was still unwise enough to lash out in calculated fury at what seemed to be her histrionic acts, accompanied by cryptic sarcasms, intended to get my attention while Rome wasted in flames, or simply to stop me from thinking by myself about what she thought were impersonal abstractions. Often I thought she was pulling stunts to make me take her slovenly incompetence as a sign of inspiration beyond my sphere.

I had found her sitting with one elbow on the table and her eyes on the floor while the cat, ass brushing the open milk bottle, licked the butter. Putting the best possible face upon this little midafternoon scene I said as cheerfully as I dared: "You look like the Virgin Mary wondering if the Holy Ghost has come yet."

She struck back like a copperhead instantly animated, replying to no presumption of mine: "I'm no servomechanism!" I started to laugh. But then she added: "I'm only your Ophelia. You've never married me. But there's no brother to protect my honor. . . . I don't care. You're too fat. You could lose weight if you weren't such a glutton." [And if I started cigarettes again. Or if I had more sport in bed. But I'm glad she understands that I'm not naturally or irreversibly obese.]

Such sallies I had always previously ignored, too ashamed to make repartee, but this time my hour-glass was empty, not full of anger but desperately empty of patience. Johnnie Appleseed Chapman once flared up and involuntarily killed the only viper that ever bit his bare feet, immediately repenting his instinctive self-defense; but I deliberately flouted civility. In fact any trace of temper or uncontrolled impulse on my part only multiplies her terrors of the sea, as I saw later when it began to dawn on me that I am her only rock.

Returning to the house half an hour later (contrite and doubly anxious) I found her gone with the children, the stinking house in shambles, the broken dishes and spilled food still on the kitchen floor. After a while I began to clean things up. It was a bleak raw Sunday between fall and spring. I had no clue until long after dark. In my lengthening fear I cautiously telephoned her mother and all her known friends. Finally I got an astonishing call from one of the priests at a Roman Catholic church in Berkeley. She had somehow made her way there to ask for help—not to complain about what I'd done but to explain herself as avatar of the Blessed Virgin Mary, perhaps in more literal language than she had yet used with me. Until that very moment I had taken it as a figure of speech with which she intended to convey her wish for one more annunciation. He thought she was drunk (a typically deracinated housewife longing for an authoritative rock like Peter?) and told me he was sending her home in a taxi, advising me to keep her off the bottle. He didnt seem to care about her soul, whether it was Catholic or not. I was grateful for his obtuse or jaded generosity, which it was a little comforting to suppose must have grown out of many others' troubles not unlike my own.

I watched at the window cravenly, incapable of any other occupation, forgetting to bless the children's safety in my dread of embarrassment. When the cab arrived twenty minutes later I stood behind the curtain in our dark bedroom waiting for her to come up. Nothing happened. The taxi stood there at the curb with its lights on and its motor running. I could see her leaning forward from the back seat talking to the driver. When I finally crept downstairs to peep out the front door she was standing on the sidewalk, the two boys huddled at her skirts, still speaking to her black listener through the window he had leaned over to roll down.

I assume she had been setting forth some of her ideas, but perhaps in terms ambiguous and equivocal to a man who might classify his fares like a priest of much pastoral experience; but he was doing a little talking too, softly inaudible. More than once I heard her gay clear laugh with a pang of immature jealousy, and for a minute she seemed all too normal. No doubt they were listening at cross-purposes, and he seemed finally struck by the truth that he was wasting his time, because the last thing she said to him as she turned toward the house, raising her voice above the intimate level of their murmurs, was that "Americans are too clean—we take too many baths!" Having run back upstairs so that I could greet her from my reading chair without any show of surprise, when I had to go down and pay the guy an extra buck (presumably for waiting time the priest hadnt allowed for), he treacherously abjured whatever interest he may have had in her and shocked me with his insolence. "You'd better have that lady put away, Mac." he called as he clutched into a violent U-turn.

I'd almost forgotten that incident among all the others that shaped my conflicting attitudes toward the woman I love with profound respect.

"Sell your books!" she repeated. "And live on your royalties too I suppose! How can you have the nerve to call *me* Donna Quixote?" She laughed shortly, but not scornfully; her words are never malicious; she never tries to hurt me, despite the pain she suffers from mine. She always felt, when I did not, the hostility in by-names I called her to relieve with playful wit the unbearable frustration of all my liberties. It is always herself she's trying to get the better of. Anyhow, to her I seemed a jagged ledge of adamantine minerals with plenty of chips and cracks and faults but vulnerable in vanity only: a hard man that never weeps. Yet her misconception was more excusable than my own when in all those years I'd mistaken the longanimous struggles in her soul as antagonistic waves breaking and lapsing in all weathers on my reef.

It had seemed nothing but affectionate lampoonery to think up quizzical pet names—"Lackadaisy" was one—by way of recognizing nobility in her motives and implying true admiration of her person while saying what otherwise I could find no way to convey without blunt cruelty. When I come up against incompetence waste or gesticulative spending that shackle me in my personal war against death I have always been unwilling to purge my spleen by repeating bootless vents of wrath that can only exacerbate or confuse the cause of my distress. For the family as a whole jocularity is more efficient. But even as I began to understand the damaging pain of my derision, inflicted upon her like the barbs of sporting fishermen imbedded in a dolphin's flesh, and ceased to cast it, I couldnt muster the grace that some men can summon to scold their consorts with sunny encouraging words, or the charity to give my time and pride for gentle patient speech full of elementary and redundant explanation either objective or subjective.

"Michael, we havent really discussed things with each other for many years. I think we should have a talk now." I suppressed my groan. We were already having a talk. To her way of thinking we never talked; to mine, we'd had the same heart-to-heart talk far too many times: in fact, save for the little business of moving to Gloucester, we had covered more than once in disconnected and unacknowledged fragments most of what I knew she was going to say even on that unique occasion. I could come no closer to improving the situation by weary exposition of the naked issues than I could by the compendious equivocation I usually practiced for the sake of peace and time. On the other hand her reasons for raising them now were unprecedented and eminently just. If I was to constrain her to accept my plan I could no longer deny the continually deferred appeal for extended debate and democratic judgment of everything that stood between us—or at least I could not refuse to make the effort of nominal discussion in reply to everything she wanted to say. "Sure. What do you want to talk about?"

As it turned out we couldnt get very far in one night, but I can fairly say that I cooperated decently, mostly with gritted teeth, by sheer force of will and policy, despite the rootfelt urge of every neuron in my body to cry out openly against the disorganized bundle of shifting thoughts I was obliged to respond to, but sometimes in unfeigned compassion or remorse.

On this occasion I was at the gravest disadvantage morally and logically. I could summon few arguments to support my major intention, which was nevertheless so deep and clear to myself—so broadly to the ultimate benefit of the children and of Ruth herself—that like general patriotism or love of life it dissolved under my pencil when I tried to sketch it. And at such times, as usual playing my Celticity false (to her general regret and in this instance to mine), in searching for the simplest words I am always too distracted to revive the emotion that has been burning for a decade as the source of my contention; or else I find myself compelled to acknowledge that the satisfaction of adequately expressing myself is not essential to my largest purpose, and indeed that it may even tend to divert me from my course like "creation without toil" by substituting a series of immediate reliefs for the infinitely more valuable labor of solitary and integrated imagination. As usual, by this stage of the dialogue I was so defensive that though I never took my eyes off the ball I forgot where it was in her court that I wanted to return it to. Such is the flaw in my rocky nature that has always incapacitated me for successful rejoinders. Thus the danger in partaking of degenerate humanism too sympathetically.

"I want to talk about the progress I've made. Don't you think things are getting better?"

Yes of course.

"I'm afraid I'll never be the best housekeeper in the world, but at least I no longer sit all day crying about it. I get the shopping and laundry done most of the time now. The children are happier. We have fine kids, Michael. Arent we lucky?"

"It's not luck." I honestly replied. "You deserve the credit."

"The father is just as important as the mother. Most people don't real-ize that. You're a good father. And I'm getting to be a more practical mother. I think we understand one another better than we used to. That's why the boys are happier."

(I now recalled the incident not long before in which I found out that at least the oldest child was aware of the family's infirmity. I never told her about this but she's always been much more sensitive than I to the boys' anxieties, especially when—blaming herself for being the cause of them—her determination to find and overcome the source of her life-fear is redoubled. One night at supper I had openly barked at her for the first time in the presence of our children. After a hard day at the store I truly lost my temper at her persistent and apparently impudent indifference in giving us half-cooked potatoes and other such unaccidental signs of sloppy defiance. For once some devil put it into me to be straightforward instead of sullen. When I shouted it was with considerably less passion than many households would have taken much notice of—but I'm reputed to be emo-tionally reserved in my familial resentments and my disgraceful little explosion was then a new experience of terrifying significance to my ten-derly sophisticated oldest son, most Anglo-Saxon of them all. Ruth shouted back as quickly and clearly as if on cue: "I'm not trying to poison you!" Matty succeeded in taking it all as a joke but Jonathan burst into tears and ran out to his bed on the porch, and when after a long silent pause I solemnly followed, burning with remorse, I found him face down under the blankets. I stroked his head for a long time before making any inquiry, and longer still before he answered it, after his tears had subsided. "I don't think it's very polite for you to argue in front of us." he said at last. But that's nothing, I said. It was just about food: nothing important. You and Matty argue all the time. For a moment there was no reply, and then with his face still turned away from me he said: "I'm afraid." I asked what frightened him, wondering if he who had been brought up by a mother gentler than the angels feared only the violence of voices. But it was meaning not sounds he had been listening for. "Afraid of what's going to happen." It was very difficult for me to ask what might happen that worried him, but he answered at once: "It can't go on this way. Nothing is straight." I did not press him further.)

The kind of primly self-conscious comradely confabulation that I was being drawn into as I lay beside Ruth is enough to turn me against universal public education as well as popular psychology. Nowadays it can't always be avoided. Yet then she did say an interesting thing: "I have finally learned that the opposite to love is not hate or strife but disorder."

Love versus Chaos, that's what Hesiod's genealogy lays down, that's the contention of the Christian Vine. She had come to the idea by introspection. If only that mind could be unlocked—or liberated by kisses—she'd be the crown to mount all brilliants in. But her reason is a lily pond full of swift waterbugs darting by short lines in all directions without any centripetal organization of movement. (She senses this herself. "Some day the earth is going to shiver in revulsion and shake me off into space." she once told me. "Or maybe it'll just switch off its gravity for everybody and spin us all off like water in a washing machine." I kissed her spontaneously on that occasion but I couldnt explain the access of love that drowned my fear and pity. I was ashamed of seeming to care for nothing but intelligence.)

Nevertheless she had lately been winning her way through to good intentions with increasing frequency, and sometimes to small successes— the reason I'd been emboldened to buy my ticket. I knew what she was going to say next before the words were out: "From now on I'm going to do better with housework and meals." I touched her fingers in encouragement. But then she added: "Let's turn over a new leaf together!"

Together, forsooth! Suddenly again I had to swallow my wroth— though it was getting a little easier as the conversation wore on, like getting used to my distaste for the latest style of domestic architecture. "Okay." said I, "What do you want me to do?"

"Help me keep on schedule. Insist that I make the beds and do the dishes every day and have the meals ready on time." An old request easily granted in contemplation. It's always easy to show my goodwill as boss. But of course she was only begging our question, for the nth time. As she lay flat beside me we spoke to each other with parallel eyes staring up at the dark ceiling under Hecuba's bed like a gray duke and duchess on the lid of a double sarcophagus in their private crypt. "You are our shepherd!" (My namesake in the Wordsworth poem she had picked out for me in our playful romantic days. She wasnt embarrassed to recall it, but I was glad she didnt drag up her old favorite lines: ". . . his mind was keen . . . Intense, and frugal, apt for all affairs . . . watchful more than ordinary men . . . Albeit of a stern unbending mind." There was a time when she teased me thus, before finding out the truth of it in marriage. Was she now hinting at her strength to restore the joke? When I was in the Western Pacific she had fearlessly typed up the whole poem for me.)

"This time I'm going to be ready for Christmas." [Oh the crisis and deadline of every year! Sending her downtown in a cab on Christmas Eve to do her shopping—staying up all night to wrap presents on her behalf long after she has collapsed into the last drained dregs of her annual struggle to meet the responsibility that other women seem to undertake without any help at all from their husbands. Every December I swear to myself that I will not bail her out of the blue funk (having already done my share of enthusiastic providence several times over), but I always end up with no alternative. We somehow pull through—Christmas dawns merry, and I have lost weeks out of the time I live for.] I didnt hear all that she was promising because it sounded much too familiar.

"Well don't try to do it all at once." I said. "Oakland wasnt built in a day. As long as things gradually get better I'll be satisfied."

"But *I* won't!" Her asseveration was as calm and low-pitched as all our other words in the dark of our hushed bedsittingroom, with Roger asleep just behind the nearest door. "It's about time I grew up. Michael I want to go back to the Campus and get a teaching credential. When I have a job in some school we'll have plenty of money for the things we need, and I'll have a housekeeper to take care of the children and cook dinner. I may as well do what I'm good at and pay someone else to do what I'm not so good at." Her enthusiastic hopes are almost as troublesome as her depressions. "... car ... house ... furniture ... bank account for the boys ... and in the summer I'll have time to work on my writing."

What writing? I asked involuntarily, checking my surprise just too late to keep from getting sucked into her daydream simply by acknowledging it. "I work out my ideas in popular language." she explained. The prim lip-pressing complacency in her manner made me wince. "As a matter of fact I've just sent a contribution to the Saturday Evening Post." I said I wished she'd sent it to the Democratic National Committee instead, glad to have found any reply at all, especially when she was amused by it and pressed my arm in glee. Thus without a word of skepticism about her success or of praise for her talent or of opposition to her endeavor I managed to convey the literary recognition she wanted, and at the same time diverted her mind from a distant goal. I think I do well in never protesting her objectives and never attempting to head her off at the first step, or even the second, unless she's on the point of spending more money. I can afford a few typewriter ribbons and self-addressed stamped envelopes. But alas her failures are usually expensive for the family in one way or another, and therefore all the more reflexively wounding to the inner self that was made vulnerable by a monoparous mother's obsessive protection of her child's outer person. That's why she must needs forget her broken promises at each new quickening of hope.

[There's every evidence she's completely forgotten all the night-school courses paid for and enrolled in—everything from ceramics to short-story writing. Even dance—which she might have excelled in—at the

Y W C A : modern dance as physical education. This beautiful woman's one essay at body-culture came a few weeks after my incautiously revealed admiration of Elizabeth Quicherat. "You adore her because all men see her body and envy you!" That had seemed a harmless bit of jealous wit. But when she asked for money to register for the dance class she said she wanted to learn to use her toes to communicate certain ideas. She remarked that Miss Quicherat had never been able to influence the real world as she herself had—for instance in getting the Catholic Church to start thinking about the relaxation of Lenten fasting so that people some day wouldnt have to eat so much fish, and about reforming the ritual so that Protestants could understand it. "She has no children you know. And as a ballet dancer her toes can't be seen at all. In modern dance I'll be able to do much more good by getting on television. That's my medium anyway, although I never get credit for it. When I was a little girl I used to listen to the radio and imagine movies to go with what I heard." I gave her the money without protest—and for a pair of leotards in which I must say she was quite fetching from most angles—hoping that she'd last beyond the first two or three lessons. It would have been good for all her muscles. But of course the first couple of times she left the house too late to get to the studio before the classes were half over, and thereafter neither of us said anything more about that the bravest of her hopes.]

My task was now to suggest without betraying my weariness or wariness the obvious difficulty of raising tuition money and also paying somebody to take care of the kids while she pursued her program in Berkeley day by day. She explained that she would first work for a few months in some office. As patiently as if we were considering this problem for the first time I pointed out that she couldnt expect to make much money after she'd paid for clothes and carfare as well as for a fulltime housekeeper (providing she could find one that our particular kids could be trusted to).

"Even if I didnt end up with a profit, at least I'd get out of the house and have people to talk to. I could be useful somewhere." I'm always amazed how she repeats words she's said before without seeming to remember how theyve always been mocked by events. We'd already tried exactly what she was talking about. But even on my own part I forgot the most formidable difficulties that had swamped her new little lifeboat. Among all my jumbled half-suppressed memories of her sporadic quests and launchings I was under the hazy impression that she had quit a job, after barely starting it, on account of a pregnancy; but if I were more humane in my outlook upon marriage I would have remembered on the spot that she had unexpectedly found herself unable to do the secretarial work she once happily performed better than anyone else in the world to pay her way through college. She had wept over the stenographic pad when the boss was trying to give her the most routine dictation. On another job she succeeded with the voice-transcribing machine but foundered on light bookkeeping. Naturally she was worried about leaving her children in the hands of some woman who whether sly or honest was bound to be a better housekeeper than foster mother: of course that was part of it.

But all this history I let myself forget in the suddenly renewed hope for an orderly life that she was arousing in me despite all my previous disappointments. I understood her cottage fever perhaps too well, and I thought that if she could find a job that really interested her (perhaps at the University) it was possible that we could have some good times again. By disengaging her from the worst part of her present life I thought I might at last be able to pursue my own work in a steady rhythm of limited but crucial fruition.

"Well," I said "the trick is to find a job to start no sooner or later than a woman good enough to take your place at home." I bit my lip after letting out that last innocent phrase, but fortunately she heard it as a jest rather than a criticism. And the thought of even the slightest help around the house lifted both our hearts. As an economic possibility it was not totally out of the question.

We talked about it. "But I don't want anyone doing your cooking when I'm not here!" she said with a stern laugh. I told her that she would always be my only palace dancer. But though my spirits rose in illusory hope for rapid domestic progress she was in no mood for further byplay—which all the more astonishes me that I could have taken leave of my senses so far as to block from my memory the well-attested invalidity of this woman's will to whom I had pledged myself—that little had changed since our last crisis, even though, without resumption of her expensive visits to the doctor (as she now called to my attention), she was no longer showing tears, no longer leaving *all* her work undone. I was still not wise enough to see how the forces of life in recruiting themselves must always suck their virtue either from other lives or from the strength of the organization they possess. I did not then fully understand that within fairly broad chunks of time there is an approximate law conserving the entropic irrationality in a person's life, modified only by the aforementioned process of disorganization operating in the family as a whole. Yet her mental tone had definitely improved, and further improvement was in the wind. For a few minutes (though not for the first time) the glass of her casket was polished to such transparency that I thought I might at last break through with a kiss that would wake her to the one world we all have in common (as Heraclitus calls it).

But no: "though reason is common most people live as if they had an understanding peculiar to themselves." Her raft was still embryonic, hardly as buoyant as a life-preserver, little larger than her contraceptive ring. Maybe madness is sometimes merely a certain degree of intensity that decreases as its particular reason is shared more and more broadly until it disappears into common sense—which is nevertheless divided into sexes, as you can see by the wit and judgment of conjugal courtship wherein a man may turn as daft as Shandy the father whose judgment became at length the dupe of his wit for other reasons. Insanity is only a more private and adventurous irrationality than what you encounter in the fictitious person of a corporation brittle with fifty years of fixed habits policies and suspicions. But the Holy Spirit founded the corporate Church. There's always the unlikely chance that crazy men and crazy women will understand each other like poets. It's singularity only of *operational* thought (which occupies in time and volume the largest part of mental functioning) that distinguishes Joan who carries away a nation with her prophecy from Cassandra who will never be believed.

"You're right Michael:" she was going on, though I'd said nothing on the point, "I'm not ready for a house yet. And I can certainly get along without new furniture or fancy refrigerators and clothes dryers. It would be good to escape my mother I suppose, but I'm learning to deal with her as an adult, and that's what will help me get control of the housework. It's a terrible thing for you and the boys to have the house so poorly taken care of. But while I'm working at an outside job I won't have any trouble with her."

An obscure malady that dogs my fool of a mind at important junctures made me stop listening carefully to anything but the tone of her words. I found myself straggling at an earlier conversation that had ended with the same vows. [She wakes me up about three in the morning with commercial music from the radio at her side of the bed. I have to squeeze my eyes to keep them shut against the light from her lamp. I know at once that she's challenging the sleep I need to start my work only two hours later. Without moving a muscle I hiss with occulted fury: "Turn off the radio!" She complies instantly, as if she's been waiting for complaint, responding sprightly: "Sure! I'm broadminded." Hoping to take up where I left off in sleep I am determined to keep the seal of my eyelids unbroken, loathe to lose the last rivulet of Lethe's precious continuity. But she is equally determined not to be intimidated by her man at his present disadvantage, and she begins to speak in a clear firm voice, thus insisting upon a wide-awake colloquy, as if that were the least I could grant her. At first I try to dismiss this shocking contretemps as just another theatrical pain in the royal red ass, but still without opening my eyes I am soon vividly alert to the anxiety that ordinarily I'm a master at suppressing for months at a time but that usually enlarges itself between appearances. What's the matter? I coolly ask. "I have many unrecognized abilities." So what? I know that. "Do you still think I'm crazy?" Of course not. Never did. "I thought you did." I'm not as spiritual as you are, that's all. "Yes you are. You're just too masculine to admit it. . . . I must keep doing the things I'm criticized for." How do you know you're being criticized? "The comic strips are full of criticism. For a long time they were helping. Now they've turned against me. . . . Just at the time I'm beginning to have my great success with the world in much more important matters. The Catholics are going to start using English and stop eating fish. I've led them to see that it wasnt the Jews who killed Jesus, and the Pope is going to take 'perfidi-ous Jew' out of the Mass. I'm getting all the religions closer to each other. But now that the funnies have started to oppose me even the advertise-ments are showing disapproval." Well what is the criticism? I ask in a pseudo-sleepy voice, tightening my eyes in silently groaning despair, clenching all my fingers and toes in angry fear. "They are censuring me for the things I write to the *Tribune*, and they make suggestive comments about me in order to discredit my work. They think I'm being defiant." Defiant of what? "Defiant of conventional behavior. But I'm really not defiant at all. It's just that I have to keep the shades down in the front room while you're at work because the windows are so dirty. The world has been on my side up until now. I'll miss my chance if you don't wash those windows. When you live in a tenement and don't have enough money to look decent you shouldnt live sloppily. For six months now you've been promising to do the windows. If you won't do the work your-self at least borrow some money and I'll arrange to have a man come and do it." I don't have a ladder (affecting a lazy yawn every time I speak). "You could borrow one from Mr Topalis easily enough." Okay. I'll do it next Sunday if the weather's good. "Another thing that makes them think I'm not a respectable woman is your strange job. There's something shady about it. I can't say that I blame them for thinking so. You profess not to like it but you won't look for a better one. At least you could stop wearing that cotton straightjacket while you wait on customers. All day long I visualize you as seen by my friends looking like a hospital attendant! I hate to visit the store when you're there." I wear it to save my clothes. If you're ashamed of me I guess I could take it off when I go out front. But it might annoy Val if I did because then the customers couldnt be sure who's there to help them and who isnt. "It's not that I'm ashamed of you, dear: it's just that I must protect my reputation. . . . Besides, everybody has found out that you work there. You're a byword, like Noah building a huge barge nowhere near the water. You shouldnt get depressed when they laugh at you." I used to wear an apron. "That was all right when you were younger. But I can't stand any more humiliation. I know it's hard for you to understand my influence, and to appreciate what I can accomplish for society, but I'm going to have to leave you. I woke you up to tell you that I'm about to get dressed and call a taxi—so you'd know why I've gone." By this time I'm oblivious to the existence of children as objects of practi-cal responsibility. I'm so entangled in my own idiosyncratic net woven from tactical compunctions and scruples of taste, which tightens about me even when I behave like a model prisoner, that in the midst of panic I give up the baffling struggle. All at once (for a few minutes) I don't care what happens. What I want is simplification. All right Ruth, I say, disdaining to put on an Italian act of woeful alarm or to go through the motions of Anglo-Saxon dissuasion, but managing to speak in a tone of resigned sorrow appropriate to the end of many years' wailing and gnashing. I'll phone for the cab. Where shall I tell the dispatcher you're going? My response either surprises or satisfies her. Perhaps she has never intended to make a move. We both expunge the threat. After a long silence she switches off the light and her next words are cheerful. "Do you think it would be helpful if my mother went to live in Los Angeles?" Better yet, Florida! That seems a good joke to us both. It is then that she says (*on that earlier occasion*) that she wants to find a job because it's terrible for the boys and me to have to live in such a dirty house.]

"... Later on we'll have all the money we need, and you'll be able to retire early to do your creative work if you still want to, because there's a strong possibility that he'll leave me his fortune."

"Who will?" What had I missed or acknowledged by grunt or silence during my reverie? Had she been revealing an entirely new pipedream while my foolish mind was mulling delayed perceptions of the past?

"Lytle King, I said."

"Oh yes, I remember. You told me that a long time ago." King the industrial magnate, maker of new little cars. I didnt know how to interpret what I heard. It was a time in our history when I had been thinking that her references to him whom she's never met, having grown rare and brief, persisted only as wryly mocking acknowledgement of a former delusion, or anyway as brave and humorous metaphor of a real convalescence. But she suddenly came out with this serious statement in the manner of one announcing some new development in her special relationship with a philanthropist! Did her apparent disdain of objective correlation indicate that the fanciful belief was more deeply lodged than ever—or should I take mild encouragement from the reduction of certainty in her prediction?

"Did I? Well that's why they're trying to kidnap my children. I have some very powerful enemies."

This fresh proof of inextirpable trouble was the worst jolt yet. My heart sank into such disconsolation that I would have determined to resort for help to some social services agency if my waterlogged brain hadnt felt like driftwood thudding dully against the bottom of a scow under tow by a tugboat already out of sight. I longed to sink into sleep, and at daylight to escape into the neat bright rationality of the book business. Let time heal what it could of the symptoms while I took the path of least resistance to accommodate the illness each day afresh.

I said nothing but my eyes opened: she might have read my soul if she'd snapped on the light and peered at my face quickly enough. But I found that she was just getting warmed up. Her voice took on the bridling complacency that I detest in women when they are relishing the captivity of their husbands or treating them like partners. It's appalling how well the mundanity of marriage can harbor bizarre fantasy, and a consumer's paradigms engage the most sublime spiritual talent of the loveliest body—as for instance in her divination by automobile advertising.

"But the people are supporting my cause and they want me to run against Senator Knowland when his term expires. By that time I may have the money for a campaign, even if you have to let me borrow against the legacy. I have a lot to learn about politics between now and then but my prayers always bring me the knowledge I need."

I contracted all my muscles to suppress a shudder. Through cold lips I asked "Why do you want to run for the Senate?"

"Because Mr Knowland is an evil man and his newspaper attacks me every day. Now he's trying to take over television, which he knows is my only means of defeating him. I'm the only one who understands how to use television to stop the Administration's unchristian attacks on communism. I was hoping I wouldnt have to run because I'd much rather stay home with the kids, at least until they're much older. I sent the President a telegram to tell him so, but he still refuses to fire either Knowland or Nixon: so I have no choice. Of course that means that I have to maintain my residence in California. It's also one of the stipulations in Mr King's will that I do not leave the state."

"When did you get interested in politics?"

"This is not a question of politics. It's a matter of religion."

"What religion?"

"My religion. You don't have a personal religion so it's hard for you to grasp what I'm talking about. My prayers can bring peace to the world once and for all. After that I can pay more attention to the housework." She laughed gaily at the incongruity with which her last statement would strike an imprisoned mind like mine. I asked her why she had to be elected for her prayers to work. "Because a Senator or Vice-President can get on television whenever she wants to explain her ideas. People would see the special powers I have. . . . Yet we're the only ones left who don't have a television set! It's a rather strange disgrace. . . . I can't very well barge in on Hecuba to watch every important message! . . . Even the Wolfsons and Cahners have a T V : they're erudite enough for you, arent they?" She turned her head a little toward mine. "I have hesitated to mention this, Michael, but I find that no one else has the courage to speak of it; I hope you won't think I'm hostile or unsympathetic to your ideas: but you are only deluding yourself when you deny that television is a great force for the good of civilization. I must say it makes you look foolish. The vision of the future!"

"I use a dictionary that's fifty years old."

"Because you don't want anyone to understand your words! You shouldnt boast about it. Television is not mere entertainment. It is becoming the spiritual channel of the universe, the new way of evangelism."

"'The slow dying of men's hearts that we call the progress of the world.'"

"That's another thing: you'd better stop quoting Yeats all the time. That's all right for young men like Caleb. I don't go around quoting God all the time do I? People are beginning to think you're odd. . . . With the use of television I can awaken dead hearts—so that eventually my daughter will be able to save all nations!"

She was taking my breath away with one shock of dismay after another.

"Why else do you think Mr King is going to give me his money? But I lose it all if I don't have the baby before he dies—and then my city never becomes the City of God. When she grows up to be a beautiful woman full of love she will lead the people of both parties. Any husband should feel as honored as the Holy Spirit to share that daughter! She's there already: I have her inside me, but I need a man to *give* her to me, to release her."

"You've had three babies, Ruth. That's two more than we agreed on before we got married, and five years sooner."

"But they're all boys. That's not my fault. You've been using fertility rites against me. Don't think I overlook your black magic! Why else would you be so interested in ritual?" She was growing more excited. "You say it's immoral to have children nowadays. If so, you are the one who's made me immoral. It's exactly what the devil does: makes people immoral. You speak with Satan's forked tongue. If you want to quote poets quote the right one—"

And then to my amazement she suddenly sat up and turned on the lamp. I squeezed my eyelids together with all my might but as soon as her pupils were adjusted to the light she insisted on reading a couple of passages in *Paradise Lost* that she'd dug out in preparation for our argument. I opened my left eye long enough to see what was going on but the blinding glare drove me over to my opposite edge of the bed with the sheet covering my head, cursing her deliberate effort to scare me out of my skin. Before I could think of a worthy remonstrance I was listening to the verses which she must have extracted from some college course-book—but which I am indebted to her for having prompted me to thereafter read with care:

> Our Maker bids increase, who bids abstain
> But our Destroyer, foe to God and man?
> . . . Man by number is to manifest
> His single imperfection, and beget
> Like of his like, his image multiplied,
> In unity defective, which requires
> Collateral love and dearest amity."

A few years ago I would have disputed the inconsistencies of her discourse, but now I took them as compendious epitomes or ellipses of a rationality not the less clever and subtle because it floated free of other people's. Nevertheless it was not the logic but a single topic of vital practical importance that dominated my attention. I sought certain assurances—just as she was adding: "Michael, I want another baby! I must have a girl-baby to bring up the way I wish I had been brought up. So that when she's grown she won't shrink from my touch as I shrink from my mother's."

I was so softened at this lightning clarification of the misery she might have been spared by a more sensitive and generous husband that I hung back from the brutal objectivity of the question I was about to ask. At that moment it would have seemed coldly loveless and obtuse. She turned out the light and I was again flat on my back with eyes wide open. She now lay half turned toward me and I soon felt her light diffident forefinger on the back of my hand, tracing a slow thoughtful path up my forearm, lingering at the biceps she has always admired, before reaching the plateau of my chest; and after a short silence her head was pressing against my shoulder. I deferred my major point with a minor curiosity: "How do you know it would be a girl?"

"My prayers tell me. Personal prayers always work."

"Especially when you have the religion all to yourself!"

She laughed easily enough. "I know: you think I pray to myself. Do you think I'm selfish?"

"Only in a very selfless way." To my way of thinking it would be hard to find anyone in the living world less selfish than Ruth, judged by the definition of my own selfishness, but I accepted the implication of her question as working hypothesis of a more universal selfishness that was now being suggested without my accusation and that at the same time put us on a plane of discussion where it was possible to broach her character from my standpoint. I was content to enter any mutual system of reason, no matter how narrow or fragile, in which I could calmly unfold at least some trifles of my distress. Perhaps such is the main value of moral principles. Anyway the charge was one I could somewhat press without fear that she couldnt more than somewhat defend herself, for my chief qualm was that she usually accepts characterization at the expense of her self-esteem. All I said to start off was: "It's a good selfishness of course, since to you and to most people having children is the divine purpose of life."

"But if we have happy children it makes you as happy as me. That's the only reason I talk about houses and furniture. The world isnt happy enough. I know you'd quit writing if Roger's life depended on your giving it up."

The question she thus raised must always be ignored. In case of fire should St Herman have saved his babe (who was to become a suicide) or the unpublished manuscript of *Pierre*? My response is to imitate the logical positivists and declare the problem meaningless or irrelevant. It's a dilemma that must be obviated by precautions. In any case the issue is evaded by the inordinately high probability that in an actual emergency free will would be nullified by circumstances; an unspeakable choice calls for thoroughgoing determinism. Ruth has never suspected the full depth of my selfishness, even though she has plenty of cause to know its range, for to her my article of that species is unconscionable and she would charitably misconceive any attempt I might make to confess it, if for no other reason than to prevent herself from reprobating the rock she clings to. I would seem capable of acts as horrifying as the votive offerings of Agamemnon or Jephthah, albeit I have no daughter. She gives all persons and especially me the benefit of her slowness to doubt.

But it was her kind of selfishness that had been mooted, and I turned aside this old perplexity about mine to come at last to the inquiry that had been weighing on my mind since the birthday party. I brought it out haltingly: "The other night Sarah seemed to think you were—" I've always found it difficult to speak either of the fact or of the possibility, as if it were something shameful or disgusting and not merely ignominious. "What did she mean by congratulating us?"

Ruth laughed her silvery laugh. "Oh I like to pretend I'm pregnant. It was just some little thing I said for fun. I was afraid she might have taken me seriously so later I told her that I was only kidding, but I guess she took my explanation for the joke. She must have wanted to misunderstand me because she's always thinking about it. She and Jack are trying everything they can think of."

That last was an interesting piece of news to me but I was more conscious of the effort to conceal the exhilaration of my relief. The blue sky of expectation for the second half of my life was in one sweep cleared of a spreading cloud bank. This commonplace reprieve was impetus enough to renew my unaccountably sanguine disposition. I tried to conceal my joy in the good news as I replied obliquely: "Sometimes you make fun with such a straight face that people who know you well look for double entente in everything you say. That's because it's taken them so long to find how droll you can be in your kindnesses. You'd have made a good chancellor of the exchequer's wife."

"I'd rather be either the chancellor of the exchequer or the chancellor of the exchequer's good wife." She was lightly stroking my chest with the flat of her hand inside my pajamas. "I was telling her about the net reproduction rate used to predict future population. Only girl-babies really count. As far as posterity's concerned I'm childless. You might say I'm a virgin. I bewail my virginity. Do you call me selfish if my net reproduction rate is zero? As for you, you should be pleased to have the personal blessing of three children without contributing to the population problem!" She laughed her golden laugh.

"I don't regret any of the kids. I just don't want any more."

"You used to tell me you didnt want to be happy!" she teased. Her distinction between hawk and handsaw seemed so clear in the sweet south wind that I chuckled not only at what she was now saying but also at recollections of her often disconcertingly dry humor. "If we had a daughter you could be unhappy, she and I could be happy, and some lucky man of the next generation would have a good efficient *and* happy wife to make him happy with your happy grandchildren! Besides, you'll be aching for a toddler in the house by the time Roger's in the third grade."

Seeing that she made merry of her passion I was glad to indulge her, though I'm sure I never deceived myself about her earnestness. She had showed herself quite as capable of playing with thoughts as any disinterested cocksman. But so am I, I thought, as I said "I've warned you that I couldnt be trusted with a daughter!", encouraged by the fact that she would so readily rise smiling to the open air when her heart's desire was even hypothetically mentioned as within reach in the sunny world. Her attitude now seemed to allow that if she could bite any solid satisfaction at all she would be willing to compromise with life on the surface. To this end it was important to yield her something real. She had to be spared absolute disappointment. Meanwhile her feathery fingers were signifying an interest in me. My feelings grew powerfully ambiguous as my motives bifurcated and subdivided symmetrically. For a time it seemed as if I had mastered the way to live simultaneously on several separate levels with a woman who had more than one story of her own in the same tower. "Maybe you could find a good second-hand television set." I offered. "The money I got for my birthday might be enough for the downpayment."

I held my breath. She said nothing in reply. But having unbuttoned the jacket of my pajamas to rub the exposed skin in an endless chain of epicycles with the base of her palm gently rocking and swaying to a tempo of gradually concentrating attention she now rose on one elbow to make warmer more delicate spirals with tiny brushstrokes of her lips on the near side of my breast while her fingertips traced similar fretwork all around the off nipple. Her plashing fragrant hair made deeper shadow of the darkness on my face. Slow fairy-weighted steps of her mouth circled their goal with the tiny sweet moist nibbles of a Lilliputian doe—just as her musical thumb on the opposite side first touched the center that her left hand had been teasing as it lightly skimmed the nearly virgin plexus thereabout. Her own softer paps pressed against my ribs as she inched into my half of the bed. Without leaving off the snuffing graze of my pasture she whispered her grateful pledge: "I promise not to let the kids watch it more than half an hour a day."

I was amused not only at the frankness of this bribery at what I thought was the end of a much more complex transaction but also at the rather novel notion that this time it was she not I who had to watch her erotic step. I chose to think that it was within my power at the slightest false note to shake off the advances she was making and turn my back on her caresses! (In my time men no longer enjoy such ascendancy as Rousseau's over his woman when he could simply insist that all five of his children be sent to the foundling home as soon as they were born—not that I would have exercised power so cruelly, even as a tyrant in forestalling life unbegun.) But at that moment for vague and unsound reasons I thought I was playing a strong hand. Among other things I reckoned on her intention that after the immediate compromising was over, because she knew my weakness and was tasting success, she would temporarily back off in the confidence that she could eventually win her campaign.

My own complacency was straightway to be abetted by an opportunity to trade off another unessential quid. To be sure, nothing could be more significant of the war's general trend than admitting the diabolical cyclops into my camp; but it was an inevitable concession to the whole world of allies on her side that I had always known would have to be made sooner or later: therefore, give or take a year, it was not crucial in the bargaining. The next accommodation was still less fundamental.

Kissing like a zephyr, as she waited for a moment to see if I would protest what she'd said so far, her lips wandered about my mammary zone like tiny warn stepping stones. Then she added the second demand. "I won't buy it until we can really afford to. But I'll have to know more about the family finances. I want to pay the bills."

Under other circumstances I would have dug in my heels like a stubborn ass against this old familiar claim to partnership. *Pay the bills* had a long history; it's a phrase hoary with wrinkles from the failures and disasters earlier peace conferences have led to. *Pay the bills* meant taking over responsibility for a joint checking account, the very concept of which is so repugnant to my dignity as a free man—especially after terribly unsuccessful experiments with her financial management in the past—that ordinarily I would have flatly refused to reconsider the subject, which as usual she was bringing up as if it had never been mentioned before. But now I thought I saw an advantage in yielding to her wish once more, temporarily obliterating from my toady memory all traces of rage at the patience and time (not to mention money) I've had to waste cleaning up the confusion left by her unreckoning neglect of numbers and by the consequent imposition of fines and debits from bounced or overdrawn checks presumably written in all innocence. (But how she relished the fellowship of audits we had to cooperate at for hours at a time in retracing her endeavors to make ends meet!) "I'll need the experience, you know."

She may have meant that she would need fiscal experience in order to handle her legacy properly but I preferred to think that she was referring to the period in which she would be running the household alone for a while after I'd left for Gloucester. Anyway I could see the justice of her demand in light of its prospective compensation to her for my much larger winnings. And of course if this time it worked well I'd be delighted. I'm not against it in principle. I'd take nothing but satisfaction in being relieved of the accounts payable function as long as I remained the controller. So in my gesture of assent I hesitated just long enough to simulate honesty, shruggingly resolved to devise procedures that would prudently keep her in the dark about my gross salary my reserves and my anchors to windward, as I asked her if she was really ready to manage our estate. "Oh yes Michael! I've grown up a great deal in the past few months." How often I'd heard those very words! But never mind, there were larger matters to consider. "Well then," I said, "go to it whenever you want to start. It'll save me a lot of time. But I can't see why you want the worry of it." She made no reply to this insincerity. Probably didnt want to risk disturbing the better balance we had equivocally negotiated.

I'm sure now as I wasnt then that she was aware of having regained her grace and palpable beauty by ministering to her beloved's unbloomed breasts, by breathing her desire into his skin and leading him beyond any stage at which he could continue to defend himself against her. She became my suitor. I did not exert myself. There seemed nothing for me to gloss over, no resistance to relinquish or reluctance to put an end to, nothing to do on my part. My powers were content to be courted by the shy musician who deliciously coaxed the full range of my passivity as if evoking a choral symphony from an assembly of taciturn backwoodsmen. With idle fingers outspread on the sheet and toes curling upright I submitted to the dreamy nicety of being brought to my highest senses. Her mouth descended my torso artfully; one hand ascended my thigh. As she deftly opened the lowest buttons my trembling gravity came to its center with a faintly giddy flutter. My legs parted slightly and one drew the bedclothes up into a tent of dalliance while all other limbs but one slackened to the tactile suggestions of my devotee. The gluteal sinews upon which I rested began to tune themselves to a rhythm of almost imperceptible contractions. All at once my softly fluttering white moth threw back the covers and undressed me. As she unslipped her own nightgown my eyes closed in the effortless luxury of being waited on, missing the first gleam of her nakedness in the dark.

I was still a cool cucumber under the skindeep but converging sensations she was playing me for, as if it was the first time in our annals she'd taken such interest. It seemed strange to feel no need to act. It was easy and delicious to refrain from reacting to her seduction. If I had any purpose it was only not to make love to her. I wasnt trying to teach her a lesson, least of all to make her feel what it was like to burn by the side of a frozen consort: I simply wanted her to revere the integrity of my unmarried self. In her worship was my strength. Nothing must be done to anticipate her.

With parted mouth on mine she tendered the immemorially unrefusable invitation. Had I never before allowed her the leisure to demonstrate this beautifully unhurried growth of avidity? (Was she giving me a lesson?) Whatever she was doing in our pas de deux it was a new feeling for me to be the attended dancer. By now my legs were demurely disposed in the demisemigenuflection of a reclining nude. The posture flattened my belly; I fancied that with some regular fencing I could readily restore my scant breath and recondition the philosophical fat. [At least I can say that the worst of years' misspent tobacco soot is already burnt off my lungs.] Meanwhile I was attractive enough for the noblest of women to be fascinated by my lodestone as she boxed its rose with a compass card of kisses. [All I have to do is stop eating so much; maybe some workouts at the Y— skipping rope, slow bag, fast bag. With the magnetism I've displayed no one could suspect me of adiposogenital dystrophy!] I opened my eyes in the gloam of our streetlight to see the pale menhir risen for the ten-thou- sandth time in her presence. [The marble column did not seem too stout for classical representation, though less than eight diameters high and more primitive than the Doric, despite its Oriental entasis; but its veins (now invisible) arrissed the shaft like a Moorish vine and its flutes were swollen smooth like the trunk of a beach rooted deeper in living rock than any acropolitan olive tree. Its ogival unentablatured capital over the round of my stomach looked like a German battle helmet. . . .]

But whereas a young bride entertains inarticulate fancies of marriage that fade in and out at the beginning or end of her pierced swoon, or dreams of fruitfulness to germinate her passion, and does not wish to give herself without receiving from her lover the inward and invisible anoint- ment of hope, my response to what she was about—like her advances not wholly free of the material soul's higher calculations, in unbargained trade of sincerely untendentious ecstasies—was conditioned by phantasms of barren liberty. Was I any trickier than she herself had been as my baited trap on at least three moonlit nights? However, the jaws of my snare were no stronger than my will; there was no impersonal spring to snap them shut when she was at my mercy.

[Marriage being no simple truce in the war between men and women but a complicated treaty between the contenders that is supposed to pacify their relations, when the union cracks or becomes uneasy half the world seems to take up arms against each of the principals. In any event, whether our comity was founded in prize of conquest on one side and rapt slavery on the other or in a symmetry of hopes, the time had come when the pros- pect of its end would never again be very far from my unacknowledged thoughts, or no doubt hers; and I'd be surprised if sometimes Ruth and I arent thinking about it at the same time. There are too many reasons of love and convenience to ever fully recall why you keep living together, but one of them is paramount and constant: the hostages you hold against each other. They guarantee nominal nonaggression. For me Solomon has no command wise enough to make distinctions in the sense of responsibility. This must be the case in any matrimony blessed with the sole justification for symbiosis. But when you see the war (which is only patched up by an alliance) as partaking of the larger strife between man's seacraft and the amorphously mixed heaving of the sea, you can't escape the sailor's duty to navigate as well as he can by dead reckoning when the sky is overcast. You find no way to shrug off the fate of your passengers without bringing on your own destruction. Therefore the law rightly hinders divorce when there are not two with competence for its consequences. But whenever I nevertheless take a vow to wreak havoc illegally if I must in order to make my only possible escape from the comprehensive intensity of an impasse that can never be fully analyzed by the mind but is always directly present as an absolute demand to carry on I soon find myself reviewing the true woman who's glad to be a woman—whom I would lose *forever*. As long as I desire her quiddity and prize her haecceity it is mistaken to say to myself that except for the children my wife and I have no common interests. (Do I tell the judge: "She's interested in people and things like that."?) I scorn marriages that more than half confine themselves to common interests; but I don't underestimate this one just because it more than half violates my own haecceified quid.]

It seemed that I was surviving that nude interview, and that thenceforth every day would advance the children's independence the mother's relief from household misfortune and the defense of my freedom. Lying there under her hand I understood that neither travel nor repatriation was essential to my liberty. Those are mere presentiments of pleasure elevated to desire. Life is inexhaustibly interesting from inside a porcelain stove or a nutshell, and it is easy enough to find entertainment anywhere in society. I already knew that pioneering-in-reverse might fatally interrupt the circadian travail that can make time worth its passing.

The essential clause was the one dealing with infertility. Even as I was being tuned like a double bass by my fiddler I envisioned my own sterility. I thought that if I could absolutely remove the danger of new babies we might both be justified at last in coming to an equilibrium that would grow more satisfactory year by year. There was no question of deceiving my lover, who was growing more ardent every minute and whose vision was nothing of the kind: yet I couldnt think of proposing her teleological disillusionment right now! Let her have her way with me tonight, I said to myself.

Meanwhile I was determined that the parley wouldnt leave me with losses only. I made the decision to achieve by other means the moral purpose of divorce.

As I abandoned myself to this intriguing and delectable version of logic her tingling middle finger lighted like a migrating Monarch on my perineal keel. Her unexpectedly skilled palm had moved upward from my knee in fluttering recognitions along the whitest most sensitive skin of my inner leg. With exquisitely careful gaiety she tickled the wrinkled hairy skin of Castor and Ballux the twin saddlebags wherein her trovest treasure lay. They had been darkly exposed in their hiding place like the clotted roots of a great trunk blown almost flat but still hinged to the earth. My handmaid cupped the inert sacs as airily as if feeling the shape of orchids; then gently tightened her firm warm support like Atalanta hefting a golden ball. Now came her other feelers spread wide and gliding across the hollow of my loins, a summer breeze riffling my groin, to meet their sisters in a prehensile circle in which the whole tree was arced by pressure on the thewed roots where they merged with their bulbs on the mound of Hermes. Then like a worker of clay she shaped with firm two hands a gourd as if to quench her thirst ad hominem, but made light of my expectation by feigning to shift her attention. Breaking away, her body swept up again, half her breasts pressing my chest, and her mouth in its mandorla of sweet hair came upon mine in a vehement style of confidence, no longer content with kisses of recessive femininity but after a rapidly delicate lingual hint of her intent made a tantalizing incursion of my slackened lips. Her astonishingly lambent part flicked and darted on both sides of my insensate teeth searching out the byways of resistance, teasing my thirst with retreating advances as I strove to suck the flame that roiled my passivity as my tongue sought and parried hers in duel. But suddenly she left me open-mouthed and went to lick my nipples, dexter and sinister, lingering at each choice, favoring neither, testing this minor dilemma before retreating once more down my frame. This time her fingertips made sport of the arrow yearning to be drawn by the love-god's bow but then solemnly made amends with concentrating lips, buttressing the object of adoration with the firmly laminated coil of both her hands. Her head was a condensed heap of beauty, its sheltering veil of scented hair scattered upon my loins like angel feathers dropped on summer snow. I lay self-absorbed in my suspended dance, legs and arms now flung wide in acquisitive spasms of sensual intelligence. My mistress was bringing me to a higher octave, and my eyes rolled inward, no longer looking. But they opened aggrieved at the shock of privation when she abruptly withdrew and left the nerves of my flesh moistly chilled, quivering in the open air like some schoolmaster of mackerel gasping alone on a moonlit deck. —Stay! It dawned on my dimmed mind, craving the pressure of my goddess, that after all it was a mortal libation she really sought. She was now electing her greater pleasure. It was for the lady to make our choice, so long as she denied me not. I waited for her to leave the bed on winged feet to fly to the bathroom fillet herself by mercurial prestidigitation and return right well armored against my disputing partisan. But lo, my irresistible lover, she boldly ignored the habit of wisdom. I was swiftly overwhelmed by a colossal Aphrodite rising up to darken my supine landscape, seeming to smile in reckless hermaphrodisiac superiority at my dizzy dismay. Her head disappeared in the higher shadows and before I could remonstrate there was a flash of pale haunches flanking a patch of black garden as she bestrode my flanks like a lady horseman high on her knees, the finials of her bust tumescent, spine and neck erect, preparing to seat herself by directing with one hand the horn of her saddle. Thus descended valley upon nightingale, thus came my target to split itself upon her lance. When the flourished tenon had been touched to the flowering mortise the joining began with was a slow tentative posting, playfully shy at first, most of her weight still stirruped, thighs rising only slightly less than they sank in each gentle gustatory dip, sometimes pausing to assess, sometimes almost imperceptibly swiveling in the osculations of the tongueless lips that were unsealing themselves under her own pressure. Soon her neck bent forward, her hair flung from side to side in a tempo she still controlled like a pendulum faithful to its period throughout an increasing displacement. Goddess and nature forbid that you repulse or decry your lover once it's come to such a pitch. No consideration of the consequences could now stop me from indulging in guttural transvulvar luxury. I offered my own advances toward the tantalizing depth, but fell back obediently to the tune of her discipline when she shrank from my callow impatience. So I surrendered to her action, meaning to enjoy for one sweet dangerous moment the snug cincture of her full enthronement before waving off the coronation. She rose and fell in lovelier and lovelier blossom, ever closer to perfection, until she sank back upon her doubled knees, her total split weight no greater than a jockey's eased down upon a mount now unsaddled, as if the unvivacious lips that could neither laugh nor speak (but all the better kiss) were sinking to rest from conversation. With fully engaged leverage on her backbone, her palpitating heart cloven by my capstone, I could not bring myself to call a halt quite yet. Settled bareback, at first she rode like a lady, soft and easy. Only then, when I was wrestling casuistically with my skepticism of the old wives' tale that conception was rare with the woman on top, did she telepathetically regard the human feelings of her docile stallion: still at a walk, reins loosely in hand, my Joan reassured me: "I pray you sir, worry not. I have donned my armor."

Whereupon like a gentleman she started up a languid trot. It was the best of news, for on the point of passion no man can pluck out the limb that offends him, at least not when mounted by his brood mare. I gave sign of gratitude with a toss of my pubic arch; but it was not the buck of an untamed bronco and I tried to settle down to the bridal trail before us, immeasurably relieved that the long chase would be victimless after all. The joyful jackrabbit found his way in and out to the very end of that cuniculus with little assistance from me. But with an emissary so smoothly rehearsing the information he transceived I was confused. To be plunged upon so voluptuously by the Lady of the Lake was to be plunged into. I had begun as a normal proprietor of the redgold spike that joined us, but it proceeded to figure itself as double-ended; and at length as I exfoliated to the metaphormosis, transferring the female internality unto myself, the limb took root in my lover. They were my sphincters that clasped her spine, and it was I that was penetrated in my penetration; my bones lay between hers but the forked seam now was mine. Altering the refraction of his movement he leaned forward to kiss my shoulders, his chest lightly brushing my distended breasts; he grew larger and harder in all my feminized senses. I raised my arms to return his embrace, fingering the back of his neck, stroking the broad flats of his restless wing-bones, and clasped the athletic gluteal muscles of convex ivory that drove his hips into mine. He covered me with his vigor, blocking the dim ceiling, blocking my sight, sometimes stifling my air, looming over everything, dominant in mass without weight—yet always in extension of my own sagittal plane. Once or twice in an instant of the dance I drew myself up like a hanging tree-sloth to catch my shameless hussar's soughing mouth at the zenith of his wave. But as our contact specialized the sea rose in roll and pitch leaving my upper body inert. He made some experiments in gait and angle but the variations grew fewer and fewer. A pulsed undulation absorbed all lesser motions. Sensations converged and my eyes gimbaled sightlessly in the sockets of my whirling head, but I had to check the giddy ecstasy, lest I be carried away by the merely introductory first movement of our concerto, so I collected my wits to study the delicious monotony of the second, an unmelodic stretch of rhythm in which nothing changed but the intensity of my appreciation. We now cantered easily across a wide landscape with particular attention to form. The unhasting homopropriosensual partnership was cooled for a while by the tender breeze we made in covering all that ground. With palms pressing the sheet I rose tirelessly in unison with my dipping rider, whom I faced—oh most beautiful wonder of all—like a woman overboard clinging supinely to the martingale of a rushing clipper, ducked by every rising swell, her back to the bottom of the sea, praying to the figurehead that looks straight down upon her, seeing it from underneath as a deckhand or observer of profiles never could. I seemed to clasp in my thighs the heaving noble stem, cradling the masculine bow with my whole body in an endless series of drowning plunges billow after billow. —Alas by sharing the opinion of Tiresias I was not really granted his experience! My thick male body was no more penetrable than my pervious brain could make it, yet how I loved the skillful horseman pillioned on our reciprocating pillicock! I bent him forward over my withers, drew his head down to whisper that aspect of my voluptuousness. But this was no mane-clutching jockey striving for the finish with ass on high: he kept aloof in his own style—which was more than all right with me. Still, I was responsible for making half the sensation even as my phallicised rider, no longer looking for hedges ahead, dropped the reins and abandoned us to a precarious gallop, her arms I knew not where to keep herself from falling, as I in my frenzy clutched her vaulting croup. —Yes *hers* forsooth! The spasm ad quem ended my experimental dream of intussusception, reminding me that hers was the cleft—mine the crest. Strenuous intrusion more and more distinguished my nerves from hers within the riotously confused sheath of afferential sensations as it was fitted and refitted with less and less deliberation by the sword that does not cut but more and more rapidly opens and reopens its pacifier. My brain naturally reverted to the interpretation that I was born for. Yet up from the downside I still tossed that fissured figurehead as if the divided thighs were mine. I was no gladder to become a man again (before I could get to the bottom of being a woman), but it was no mean second choice. With face upturned and open mouth the circus-rider rocked forward, hands braced on my shoulders. Having no

further wish to disavow pelvic aggression I had no doubt which way the
stars would shoot. The stamen felt the flower tremble in warning of the
slow explosion of colors that would fill its night sky. But it was still a
time to delay the inevitable irreversible: for a bouquet of heartbeats we
prolonged the headlong rush; for another long suspending moment we
circled each other in a single woven garland. —In the end it didnt matter
that my conceit had failed to sustain the confusion. All along her prehension had been more interoceptive than I could imagine; elevation had only
piqued the feminine aesthesis. Her fingers dug into my skin for dear life as
I slipped the leash with a manly quake that echoed and amplified in the
labyrinth. —Yet finally for three seconds, nay five, in that power-factored
pollination of the rainbow my salient flesh seemed no less hers than mine.
As a swooning connoisseur during the protracted instant of flow in which
the potential was all at once made kinetic I savored every iota of the quick
current deliciously propelled by half an hour's systolic tension. —Gravity
reasserted itself. She sprawled on my chest without breaking the bond.
The glowing plowshare that had come to a halt in the curded furrow
would not disengorge while the heavens remained reversed; for a long long
time she made no move to release the cisterned runnels of balm. My
motionless hands rested on her motionless hindquarters. Her forehead
pressed my collar bone, her hair clouded my neck. Our involuntary utterances at the exquisite peripeteia of exaltation, each in its own sound
female and male (repressed only by the habitual discipline of parents in
close quarters), subsided like forbidden keening. I could scarcely sense the
faint breathing that superposed itself on my slower sighs through the cool
virginal dunes cushioning my ribs like heaps of wheat overturned. Nothing moved except dying ripples from our dive. For once there was no need
to dismount for fear of crushing her with my weight; instead, in blissful
comfort to us both, she weighed on me like eiderdown. My senses faded
and I was left with the perfected pleasure of having no pleasure to seek;
with profound elation purged of all desire, voided of all ambition, more
soporific than the honeyed stuffing of a mummy. I could feel no limbs
below my waist; no neuron from toenail to crown was left knotted or unresolved. A bridegroom has never been more contented.

Such are the erotic adventures of a portly married clerk. I did not
regard that ecstatic decantation as a mark of forgiveness; rather I was
somehow persuaded in the minutes before I fell asleep under my lovely
burden (not much heavier than the sheet I had drawn over her back) that
the moment of transcendent confusion had sealed my determination to end
forever the nerve-wracking danger in my deepseated marriage. Nothing
yet had occurred to alter the odds on that score; I had merely shifted my
ground to defend a single point that wasnt even mentioned, while Ruth
was taking all the pieces on the board. To do well in the marriage bed
makes a man complacent, like a lobster just finishing up the bait in his
one and only trap. Too happily in the confusion my hopes had been

reduced to a single intention, and I was as foolish as a virgin rejoicing in the conception of her child by a transient seducer.

The next day I was too excited by my secret "decision" to notice not only that I was exactly where I'd been before my thirty-third birthday (except of course for my moral losses in the spoken dialectic) but also that I was embarrassed with a superfluous railroad ticket and an envelope stuffed with greenbacks that I'd have to apologize for to my generous and trusting friends. It took a long time to get through my fat head that before I could carry out the resolution to do away with my masculine virtue I'd have to wage a new campaign of negotiation in which she couldnt be expected to trade away the reserved purpose of her life for concessions that I had already yielded, especially when she thought I'd gained as much as she had in the salubrious upshot of our night in communication.

To her our reunion appeared to arise from a meeting of minds. The stalemated conversation preceding my efferential surrender seemed to have satisfied her troubled mind in many respects. Certainly it had scared the daylights out of my tyrannical leadership and left me on my mettle for defense. In any case, for whatever psychical reason, it had temporarily redressed my naked offense and restored to her the decently clothed appearance of mental vigor.

The fabrics of beauty render only the attractive light waves, reflecting their frequencies and absorbing the ones that are kept out of sight in our middling spectrum. A Ruth's ordinary magnetism comes largely from opaque surfaces; the mystery's in the matter to which neither eye nor mind can penetrate—unless their vision is too acute for mankind's scale of life. If the terrors within were made visible by transparency or emanation, betraying the inborn femininity as scarified or flayed, there'd be nothing a man would want to touch. She's not the kind of woman who will fard her face for phony panache or cicatrize her heart with mail of pigskin under pneumatic pressure. Instead she spins a glass cocoon to shroud herself from the pain of open air, and to shut out the sounds of my horror when I look too closely. Yet after every spell of perspicuity if she is to live she will attire herself in the opacity of natural love; her own desire, howsoever Lysistratan, must again and again seem to her more important than theomancy. No Cassandra or Joan nor any Ophelia could ever catch a husband, and there's no room for madness when Nature's mania rules below the midriff.

Nevertheless even the longest run or the most frequent recurrence of this passion can't cure the illness of a soul or transfigure troublesome reality for more than a few days at a time. The aesthetically manageable aspects of being married are either undermined or reinforced by observations that expand inward from the lovely sexual surface. For my part I perceive not only Ruth and her perceptions but her apperceptions also, and her perception of her apperceptions, and so on to ever higher orders of sensitivity at ever lower depths in a narrow world full of worldwide delusion;

and at every level I perceive that her cognitions and intuitions are compounded not only by the various levels of my own awareness as she perceives them but also by sheer misapprehensions and stupidities on both sides. If there were nothing like brute love to stop this progression after it starts, and to reverse it pro tem, we'd never be able to keep together the few logs all five of us float on.

Even so I failed to take what profit I might have found in that regenerative afterglow. It was prolonged by a whole week's succession of reunions that seemed cumulative—briefer and more concentrated, to be sure, and more orthodox withal, yet in each bout she seemed to rehearse our previous beatitudes and add another to her female coefficient in what became an inequality much to my credit, until for herself in the last meeting of our accelerated course she must have multiplied my simple unity by a higher count for herself than the score I used to keep for whole nights in the honeymoon of youth when we matched each other one-for-one in ordered pairs (and I felt no more call than a young billy goat to refrain from taking the shortest way)—as if she was celebrating all the waterways we would never cross between San Francisco Bay and the Annisquam River; and she appeared as glad to have wreathed her cervix with rubber as she had been to prepare herself for our more cautious atonements before the wedding long ago. It might have been the best time to tell her what I had in mind, but there were a number of reasons than I did not—and still havent. The most immediate was a reluctance to utterly destroy the somatic rapport that sustains such a winning streak.

When the usual morbid announcement of misconception put an end to our long run of equilibrium (during which every room of the house had been cleaned and we were ticking along as reliably as an eight-day clock, my bed of roses encouraging the false sense of security that unfortunately makes me overweening) I was well enough sated to occupy my eventide leisure with matters that again seemed more important, namely reading and sleeping, and to forget—as apparently she also did—everything that had been said the night she fathomed me. It wasnt until my libido rejuvenated itself, in deteriorating circumstances, that I thought seriously about the first practical steps toward my only possible salvation.

With the utmost secrecy I got myself referred to a Doctor Stone who has no connection with the King Foundation clinic. The fact that he's in Caleb's building on the floor below Ruth's sometime psychiatrist Dr Etwas makes me a little uncomfortable, but there's no convenient alternative. Anyway it's only a matter of two or three visits. His hazardous proximity to our house makes it easier and less suspicious for me to visit him within the framework of my normal schedule, as long as I keep a weather eye for Ruth and the kids. Caleb certainly doesnt hang around the place during office hours. I was so choosy about my first appointment (which I wanted to be his last consultation on a day of very early darkness) that it was after Christmas before I finally left work much sooner than usual one afternoon and went to him on the way home. Then too I could never have taken time off during our only trade-book season, which is when all my good work pays off if I'm personally there to make the hay.

By the time I finally met that versatile urologist I had reviewed and overcome all my own objections to homuncular vivisection, but until the last minute I shall hold myself scientifically open to any arguments I havent yet thought of. I must confess that my generically genetic vanity is still not thoroughly laid to rest. So far all my regrets reduce to two varieties of fantasy, both of which I am able to relinquish as extremely low in probability of realization and/or as extremely high in likelihood that if they did occur my circumstances—my status my temper and my philosophy—would be so altered that I'd be glad to have absolutely burned my bridges and put the power of generation beyond the reach of reconsideration. First, if all three of our children died of accident polio or leukemia, and only one possible consolation remained for their mother. Second, if I were somehow freed of chastity and became prized at stud by college girls and countesses for my proven productions (sons or other works), or if by peculiar luck I escaped a general carnage or an epidemic of impotence arising from industry's chemical warfare with nature, or even from some endemic wave of excessively undeliquescent feministic terrorism. (Of course I can easily dismiss the idea of reproductive masculinity as intrinsically valuable, especially in view of my opinion that there are phases of manic indifference to insemination in which the priapic fascination common to both sexes transcends anthropology's fertility principle.)

The fact is that there are one or two things you ought to worry about before committing yourself to the knife. [Besides getting your terms straight! There's no such thing as pleonastic circumcision, to be sure, but full emasculation would frustrate my will in all circumstances! I have no wish to transcend the protoplasm of Maya, nor to drive my wife to expediences. But if I hadnt confused sterility with impotence in the ignorance of my youth as a sailor I might not need this operation now, for without the dire warnings that came from sheiks on all sides fearful of electronic black magic, some of them as reckless of more mortal dangers as Kane and Abbie, I might have painted the mast or done my preventive maintenance on the antenna assembly while we were at sea with the radar turned on. They said the microwaves would cook my manhood, and though I was the expert and they were laymen, despite all my skepticism of overwrought scuttlebutt, I was still vulgarly anxious not to alter my torment. They insisted that the ill effect would not be temporary or equivocal like that of the saltpeter in our chow. I didnt understand that they were referring to a category of disability that I regarded as secondary, seeing that on liberty ashore as well as in college it was more advantageous than otherwise. Nor at that time did I appreciate the prophecy of reproduction in Ruth's love of me.] For one thing, you should be rather particular about the possible psychogenic or genitopsychic affect the interdiction of animalcules from your obscure Dioscurian reticules might have upon the quality of prostatic sensation or indeed upon the ballistics of seminal propulsion sometimes said to be appreciated by gasping women even when indifferent to both conception and contraception.

But by all accounts I have nothing to fear. On the contrary infertility will be so thrilling to us both that we can start out on every trip in the carefree joy of traveling light, happily secure with a lifetime prophylaxis for postpartum depression. Item, remission of psychiatric bills and no further charges for obstetrics. Item, as to volume she will quaff practically as much of my potion as ever, and my genius for enjoying the decantation will remain unimpaired, if not improved. Item, the truth is that even Ruth has never wanted a baby every year, and she won't suffer any abrupt discontinuity of attitude while she's learning to open every last petal to my horticulture as I gain fuller mastery of the subject from confidence that it's all in play. My quaker gun will fire royal salutes all month long year after year to celebrate my helpmeet! It will be like Eden restored.

Dr Stone is far too masculinistic in the sources of his caution, although of course he's excusably interested in protecting himself against the lawsuits of outraged wives or outrageously ignorant patients who claim they really wanted to be circumcised. [He seemed shocked by my request. It makes me leery of his surgical experience. But you can hardly ask a doctor point blank how many times he's rehearsed the "procedure" he's about to practice on you, or how many victims he has lost to opera-singing through his malpractice. I suppose he could even amputate your whole bowsprit if he's drunk. Or what if he doesnt bother to take a good look and a freak like me turns out to have a couple of extra vasa deferentia? Could I sue him for procreative negligence?] It is not unknown for weak-willed husbands after the dies are cast to convince themselves that their doctors guaranteed reversible surgery. Since he's unaware that I'm more on his side than his own insurance company I can't blame him for demanding that I take home for my wife's adjoining signature the exculpatory waiver of liability, assuming as a matter of course her power over my body. That paper was handed to me on my second visit (with an inept apology for his ethically mandatory misgivings about my sagacity) after he'd looked at my sample zoo-sperm—which I'd been asked to produce at home without the assistance of his well-stacked young nurse or his advice as to how it should be extravasated into such a small bottle, an amusing problem which like Archimedes I pondered in my bath—in order to circumstantially confirm my putative paternity of three sons whose existence he took my word for: an examination that took him no more than ten seconds at the microscope behind his desk.

On the same occasion I was obliged to present half his fee to the same underemployed girl in white (who at least mans his reception room), I suppose because many patients of my kind chicken out before the third and crucial appointment, balking at their own John Hancock on a dotted line below the good wife's after further reflection on the bleak prospect of their value to posterity in any other way; and some sexual poltroons may be inclined to reclaim their fascist masculinity by welshing on a Jewish doctor's billable time thus wasted. The other half must be plunked down before the critical session begins, as the doctor has no recourse to repossession or annulment of his work if you should repent your occult mutilation and seek to avenge it by refusing to pay the balance. Yet the very fact that Dr Stone has learned to make such rules for this surgical specialty is reassuring as to his experience. He's well aware that what he's ostensibly reluctant to perform is almost universally regarded as something like multiple abortion or assisted suicide—and not least by married libertines or traveling bachelors who would never give the children they father so much as the time of day.

Stone could teach me a lot about caution. Here I am risking half my investment before I think I'll be able to complete the deal without criminal fraud. I have half a mind to take Lilian Cloud into my confidence and ask for her woman's hand in forgery. She seems to have kept the secrets I've told her in times of stress or euphoria—not that they've amounted to much, or to anything that most people wouldnt tell all their friends; but she's the only one at the store who knows I'm not a businessman. More than once I've been on the point of trying to reconcile myself to my alien marriage by suggesting to Lilian the law of kind. Our sympathies are plainly mutual and she must guess something of my discomforts: under the skin our humors and complexions are not unlike. It's possible that she'd be willing to deceive a sister she's hardly seen. —Yet I know very well that Lilian would never cheat another woman of her right to breed. She might be willing to scout the sanctity of my marriage but she's too ambivalent in her bohemianism to deny anyone a baby. Who knows: maybe she'd be thinking of herself with me. If the fancy took her she's the kind that would deliberately conceive and joyfully bear my bastard, asking no help—providing that she were persuaded our temporary liaison would strengthen my determination to see Ruth and the boys through another ten or fifteen years.

[What a cock-and-bull pipe dream! That girl hasnt the ghost of a reason to admire my extra-commercial person, with scarcely an inkling of how I would prove my distinguishing intention. There'd be nothing sentimental in her art-criticism. I'm like poor Keats with his nose pressed against the sweet-shop window while she chooses among talented lovers. Her friendliness with me is shallow, perhaps merely compassionate, or only for the sake of making a job she hates less unpleasant than it would be if she didnt have any relief at all from purely economic supervision. . . . She's a loose fish young and female, that's all—that's why I have these fantastic thoughts.]

But even if I got the operation by mendacity or ruse, either from Stone or from some devil-may-care surgeon, I doubt that I could prevent Ruth from finding out about it afterwards. Very likely it's many weeks before the scars become unnoticeable, and in the meantime I'd probably find it very difficult to favor the tenderness without arousing dangerous curiosity. And that would just begin a tangled web of deception I'd have to weave in the years to come to prevent her from dragging me to a fertility clinic or from throwing herself into the arms of a seed-donor. On the other hand if I simply confessed that I'd had myself undone behind her back, without the courtesy of a warning that her legal and customary marital rights were about to be curtailed (to say nothing of a partnershipshaping discussion beforehand), it would be worse than a retrogressive migration to Gloucester. The psychic storm ensuing—probably with public embarrassment—would lose me a thousand times more than what I hope to gain.

But what about forthright honesty on the verge of the fact—if it can be called honest to carry the plot this far before becoming honest? If I go to her and assert my right as a he-man to abuse my body as I see fit (even to the extent of imprisoning millions of my unborn babies in its granaries until they dry up and die of slow suffocation or old age), appeal to her rational sense of equity by begging her to consider that our premarital covenant is already violated in her favor on several counts of quantity and timing, and boldly ask her to sign the release—I might in five minutes reverse all her recent recovery and set her psyche back forever. It would do no good to rush her into momentary acquiescence by sheer force of argument and get the job done against her better judgment. That would have the same affect as futile trickery or an unsuccessful attempt to cover up the crime. The consequences of high-pressure persuasion would be as disastrous as those of imperfect deception. She might freeze at my touch for the rest of our lives; she might get her daughter "some other way"; she might disgrace me, or destroy my work; she might jeopardize the lives of her sons in some great final commotion of prophecies. At the very least those two quick little sections made by an impersonal stranger would precipitate a premature divorce incalculably dangerous to the children and to herself, or throw her into a crazy promiscuous reaction against lifelong modesty and sexual self-respect that would be intolerable to my honor and far more destructive to a barely manageable family than any amount of unguarded philandering on my part—almost as unbearable as her incarceration for schizophrenic paranoia or mine for forgery. She's the kind of woman who could conceive by walking in the sun (or as Rabelais puts it, by crossing the shadow of a monastery steeple). The complications and miseries would become immensely worse than they've ever been before— and, worst of all, lethally fazing to my work: her final retribution.

No, I must face the music fair and square from this point on. It's almost too late. Without bullying her without deceiving her without coercing her I must get her agreement through full understanding (necessarily little by little) of why it's important to her life as well as mine.

But if I tell her too soon—without waiting for the proper conditions—the chances are she'll take it into her head that I'm as insane as if I proposed to mutilate myself, or deranged like Satan the prince of lies and great sterile adversary of mankind, to her mind the only purely phallic purely self-sufficient being, worshipful for nothing else; and she'd shudder every time I darkened the doorway. (She's too smart ever to mistake my motive for high-minded renunciation.) Thenceforth any attempt at contact would make her flesh crawl in horror at the diabolical mimicry of sacramental love. All fascination would turn to taboo. She who would love me forever in saintly resignation if I'd been castrated by the Nazis in a concentration camp, or if I took holy orders like Abelard, will despise me as an evil wanton if I don't approach her as an equal with a cause she might respect.

—I begin to think my own dementia is getting out of hand! In pure speculation I'm denouncing my own plan! After all, many multiparous women would rejoice at this proposal from their husband. She's getting older anyway, tired, creased—interested in other things forsooth! Perhaps she's grown fearful of prenatal damage, anxious about her maternal strength. The boys are now separately burgeoning, learning, falling sick, growing, walking in danger, bending toward good or ill: each is now a world to devote herself to. With three children the $(N^2-N)/2$ of a family's social difficulties is more than enough for any housewife. When I watch her stand absently at the stove turning the handles of pots and pans inward out of the baby's reach I don't know whether she's wondering what to cook in them or sadly regretting her place in the great wide world or dreaming of another conception to cure everything; maybe she's thinking of her inheritance, the property and substance it would bring, not for her own gratification but for the wellbeing of her sons: education, decent careers, self-confidence. Her obsession with the idea of a daughter, even the very word that means girl-child, seems more than anything else in the whole pragmatical pig of a world to threaten my doom; yet if she were definitely concretely and irrevocably promised a house of her own I might change her attitude. Wouldnt it be funny if her deepest desire turned out to be the one for real estate!

If things stay on an even keel for the next few weeks I'll risk mooting the combined subject. So far she hasnt claimed her spoils from our night of reconciliation. Should I regard her as a chivalrous gambler unwilling to demand her winnings from a loutish loser in his cups—who would have exacted every penny if he'd won? Or does the game now seem a dream to her, everything forgotten but the good feeling that came out of the conversation? In any case I'll make a fresh proposition. It will take unanimous decision to escape a fourth stroke of mortality.

I'll try to pave the way.

If I can get it done, say after Easter, she will be my rose of May forever, all year round. Until then I must lie with her in danger.

It's well always to keep one hope before you, far enough off as a goal so that it won't have to be replaced too often, whether it's trivial and 98% certain or so important that it can't be anything less than 98% doubtful. I can hope for Gloucester later.

(54)
HY.08

SALES PROSPECT

*C*ame a likely customer, Sam out to lunch, who wanted many many books, and Michael smiled rubbing his hands. The young carinate face came straight up the store to the lurking merchant, wasted no time in looking around at the merchandise, and quickly said (perhaps on its lunch hour, no doubt not a student) that it had some birthday money and wanted to fill a five-foot shelf. (Why was the man putting himself in Michael's hands, of all the bookmen in town, and with no beating about the bush?) He had entered Bow's Ark trustingly but not humbly. There were dollars burning a hole in his pocket and it was up to the shopkeeper to bid for them. A princely sum to be spent on books, here or elsewhere.

Loose-jointed and gracefully flapping moved a thin body under the bold tomahawk of a head occupied by a single thought, probably capable of sharp energy before fast running down. This was no warrior but a wigwam dude who backwatered and sidewatered his skittish birchbark canoe, baffled by the breezes when he reached Michael's parley strand, now looking at every object except the chief clerk and his wares, distracted from everything by nothing.

But if our Jesuit's highest pleasure is to be able to find at once, through foresight and memory, a book suddenly asked for and not findable for sale anywhere else in Berkeley, smugly perhaps, his second delight in business at the selling end of it is to be made a maestro of and to be vouchsafed discretionary power over the disposal of even a small part of some purse; and so much the greater his pleasure (with something like the gusto of a professor) if he's invited to spend for a customer what could be—at an average of say three bucks each—something over a hundred dollars! He anticipated the approbation of his proprietor and the gladness of this entire establishment (not excepting Sam's who contrived not to lose face in sharing the cheer even of such dubiously mutual prosperity as that of the Christmas rush or the opening of a semester). Only once in a blue moon does opportunity knock for the tradebook department even threescore claps at a time: a week's supply of vending zeal discharged in a single spurt and freighted off by that pale irresolute macaroni!

Alas, spoke Conscience, *irresolute* can scarcely be the least of possible words here, for there is surely no mind at all facing the purveyor's, and the potential transaction that makes the latter's mouth water in this case entails no hope for future business, since this is a fool who won't twice be parted from his money merely for books: yet even a popinjay's ad hoc desire for exanimate printed matter should not be abused in fobbing off our mistakes. If a trader pays for pearls, pearls should be cast into his vessel, not beads or trinkets, even if it's ballast that he wants. I'll not deliver bogus goods by the measure. Nay nor will I contemptibly unload with words of praise a single faded beauty of the New York Times bestseller list from the dead stock that grievously weighs down my inventory (a redundancy of gems that Prince Val ordered when I was on vacation three years ago).

Still, you can always say I don't know . . . I havent read it . . . The dust jacket says . . . I can give you ten percent off . . . without the dishonor to yourself of talking up what you know needs weaseling. I certainly wouldnt do it more than this once. But this fool's a twerp. I can begin and end my commercial vice with the present deal. It will prove my maturity as a salesman. Besides, have I not vowed never again to take in a title that doesnt honestly belong in somebody's bookcase?

"Yes sir." he said locking his fingers behind his back and tilting forward on the balls of his feet. "What kind of books would you like to look at?"

"Books with hard covers and paper wrappers on the outside."

"No used books?"

"Not unless they look new. I don't want anything that isnt dressed up."

"Most of our books are new, a few are used. But sometimes the new ones don't have paper jackets. A few of the best are naked." The guy's surprising sense of humor made the chapman reckless, less anxious and unctuous than usual rather than more so. "Five feet of great books deserve a good discount."

All fluttering ceased and the hatchet face librated to rest before the moonface, smiling all at once from ear to ear, demanding to be told exactly what that statement meant. The smile betrayed neither friendliness nor heightened interest—no more than a claim to understand practical business and an appreciation of the fact that the bookkeeper had come to the point.

Now the black-haired roundhead wavered—disconfronting and temporizing as he turned to evade the pointed gaze of a vizard with long lips drawn back over high contumelious teeth. "Oh I don't know . . . Varies from book to book. Depends on what subject you're interested in. . . ."

"How much will it cost me per foot?" Now the smile was gone but the mouth gaped in insolent challenge. The walk-in sovereign would abide discussion of neither classifications nor particulars.

Michael tried to lead him toward the displays by edging a few steps up the floor but the foppish battle-axe only swiveled on its unmoved backbone and he had to come back to his station again. This was not a case of finding what a customer was looking for but of testing the pure classical function of price in a buyer's market on the commodity exchange: a humorous plight for the seller. But humoring has its limits even for an easy sale to an ignorant buyer.

As Michael got hotter under the collar his adversary grew steadier and cooler. But the vendor was obliged to make some sort of a quotation. "Depends on what you pick!" he replied querulously. "Maybe, oh, at an average of—well, some would be ten percent, some twenty, a few thirty or forty percent off."

"Off what? At forty, what would each book run?" the dangerous coxcomb insisted.

Face to face, blinking with annoyance, Michael had to answer: "If I had to guess, the average might be two-fifty apiece."

"Two-fifty!" The woman inside the man (thinking of rummage sales) came out in a shriek. "Good grief! I can't do business with you at those prices!" All aflutter again in squealing complaint, touching the water table of hysteria. The discomposed high-pitched braveling, befuddled unbeliever, retreating in shameless disappointment, yawing in haste, wheeling in a new wind, countering his own confused strokes, vamoosed.

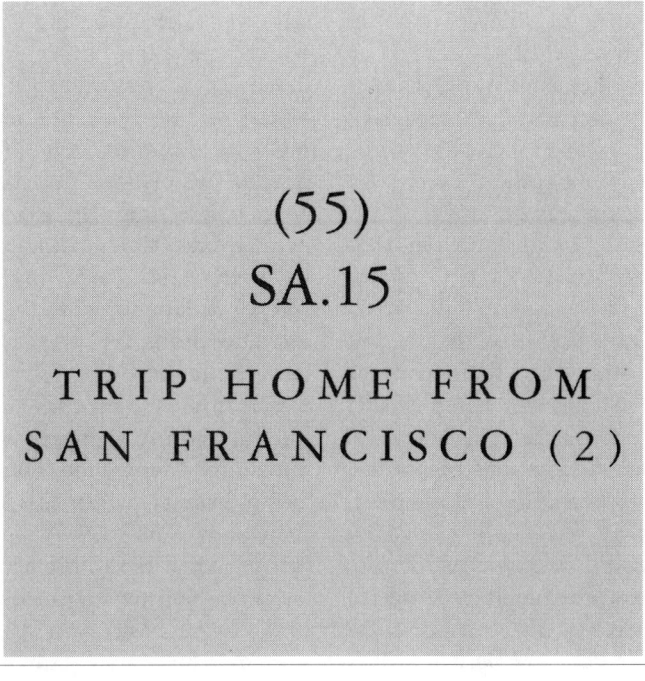

(55)
SA.15
TRIP HOME FROM
SAN FRANCISCO (2)

The whole movement of the world resolves itself
into and leads to this coupling.

—MONTAIGNE

*A*mong souls black yellow brown and white clustered for the Teleology car they waited for their last ride of the day. Some of the children around them were more perfectly beautiful than Roger, whose father wished them well nevertheless for none were palefaced or rich and their friendly innocence of what lay ahead in their lives blessed their beauty seven times at the knee of Jesus, and whose mother simply loved them. The white baby was wet at the neck from indoor sweat which the man holding him spread asleep on chest and shoulder tried

4] The Italians say that a woman who has ideas different from her husband's either is betraying him or can never feel a man at all. Ideas come from lovers they think. It follows that if her notions are confused she has had a confused lover or several lovers or several confused lovers. If her ideas are prophetic I must suppose her lover to be a god. And if she is driven to madness by being born a mismothered woman it is not to be wondered at that more than one god may be taken to her bed. No doubt she's honest enough in her heart when she lies with me on my small raft her hair

with forearm to shield from the wind. Ruth stood lifeless as a junkman's horse her hair and clothes in a disorder that no poet especially the prosaic one at her side would have thought of calling sweet. The two young hoofers on this occasion were scarcely more animated than their protectors and the Chapmen (every one of them except the sire of that family a native of the county) were as tolerated as all the damned by the other mostly alien shades standing in the long shadows of their hopeless uninteresting home-team metropolis. Their sad familiar uninteresting trolleytailed horseless horsecar could be heard on the opposite side of the block entering the turn to this its start on the brisk dreary trip back to Berkeley. Few from here rode all the way. But a handful of larking students on a progression in the other direction for an evening of pleasure to be reached by way of this transfer point had to get off before the tired people could get on.

Now behold a small marvel: the boys found upon the seat they chose a slender triple tuft of natural waxy green wands with edges showing pale yellow. Jonathan at once fought Matthew for possession of the commemorative reeds, clean long and sharp but too supple for spears and too light for whips. The father put an end to the dispute by confiscating its object in the interest of equity, sniffing at the fronds and presenting them in turn to each curious nose. For Ruth the scent was no more than an idly pleasant identification but Michael breathed it again and again in an

still wet with brine but forgetting where she came from and never dreaming to return to the bottom of the sea. Perhaps she's never told me a lie about anything important because it's seldom that I ask, and at such rare times the facts seem to her beyond the sordid truth. I'd have to have made my inquiry when I didnt care what the hell she did and didnt feel like talking to her about any doings on earth, which is not my mood for curiosity. I should admit to myself what I've known for a long time, that her suffering has its origin less in mind than body. The pain of somatic injustice is referred to the psyche. She bears the pain of my selfish love as well as the basic pain of being a woman reared among men formed by men directed by men and longing for men as father gods which they can never be. But the thoughts are there: she can't get rid of them. Who can blame her because she bargains with Apollo for the power to speak with tongues? What better way to rouse an intellect of crippled senses aching in its cage? Does she for my sake, crediting my rights, refuse the Pythian god her half of what he takes to be a reciprocal promise even though she knows full well that she thereby gets not more but less of the real power she wants to save the world with? But maybe in the end after all she ceases to refuse his golden thigh, for as the one kiss he took conveyed the curse that she will never be taken seriously (not even by herself) it is quite possible that she believes it would be absurd to confess any guilt to me. Besides, who knows

unhurried series of refreshing recollections less definite than visual events of childhood yet also less mistakable. No whiff of eucharistic incense could have diffused a more subtle tincture for tracing certain capillaries of forgotten memory. The lovely wonder of this unexpected intrusion spread a gentle pain like jags and tiny patches of deep pure blue cracking a solid gray cloud bank that has packed the sky for months. But the heavenly fissures closed again as though the firmament had been commanded not to clear away its obstacles until it was ready to disburden itself of one entire winter's snow. With Roger still in his arms he could not for long free the hand that held out the rushes for contemplation balanced like a graceful three-plumed pen in the cradle between thumb and fingers, so he gave the sweet emblems to Ruth. She peeled them from each other at the papery butt and handed one to each of her sons. Roger was now awake and interested in everyone else's interest. He squeezed his wand as readily as if nature had meant it to pacify the clutch of small fists but he was too tired to examine it. "Is it from Sunday school?" Matthew asked. Of course it was, Jonathan snapped at his brother, but he appealed to his father for confirmation in a much different tone: "It's for Palm Sunday isnt it Dad?" I used to know how to make crosses out of these palms Michael told them. "We ought to go to church some day." Ruth remarked. [If the Mass is working aright the Vine still lives and the

what goes on in psychiatric offices? The patients' husbands don't: Chanticleers sending Pertelotes to the fox's den for a course in home economics. Etwas is a grave dispassionate expert, but he's a man for all that and she tells him her dreams without holding back or breaking off. He leaves none of her letters unopened (as the Talmud puts it), and finds out all about me from an unhappy point of view. But how long does he remain mysterious and infallible? He has his own miseries no doubt. It would be very strange if she didnt inflame his aging desires. Or maybe he contents himself with stirring up hers. Yes he makes her innocently pander to his scopophilia by subtly convincing her of the therapeutic value in adultery if she tells him all about it. Thus he affects to stabilize a dangerous psychosis by sanctioning a merely neurotic disorganization of behavior! If it wasnt Etwas it was the Reverend Gilchrist. They're both divines by virtue of a laying on of hands in direct succession from the old world and both authorized by anointment to hear confessions and to bless. The doctor was analyzed by a doctor analyzed by Freud, and the priest was dubbed by a bishop who was handed down by Peter. Those two must be at least as susceptible to the fairest daughters of men as undergods or angels are, but unless theyre simply blinded by passion they apparently scorn their poor crazy client's powers of persuasion in telling the truth about them to husband or ecclesiastical court in the event of their failure to finally undermine

Word newly reunderstood can be encoded and decoded as well in the binary language of clicks as in the Greek tongue. Perhaps the Last Dispensation is quietly in the making now that men have once again proven the impotence of their own unincorporated wisdom. Maybe men without ceasing to hope are almost ready to confess the idolatry of their humanistic hopes. But alas not yet—not until we run out of gas. Meanwhile the only hope for me is to get the family home to rest, and to get to bed early so I can rise full of new hope before the first business day of Holy Week begins.]

Roger was dimly anticipating supper's eating and drinking while his mother tried to give some thought to the making of it and the old man keenly envisioned the bottle of beer that would give him patience for the waiting of it. But the last lap of the journey was briefly restoring to the older brothers an incongruous vim. For them the fun of the present excursion was nearly over for the day, for the week, maybe for a month; so they began to remember and look ahead. The car had already filled as much as it ever could on a late Sunday afternoon when the motorman waiting to begin his run looked once more at his watch. "That's what I need." Jonathan confided to his parents in a low voice nodding in that officer's direction. "I wanta watch for Christmas." On double facing seats the parents smiled at each other in sly amusement and for an instant neither would offer an answer without hearing the other's cue. Then Ruth said: "We'll see."

with their dirty loveless touch the virtuous urge for confession at home. Ruth's bewildered by these cowardly frightening shamans and even if she doesnt yield to their unethical lechery the raft that keeps her afloat between office calls or sermons is riven by their authoritatively insincere advice, and when she finally gives them up (as she now seems to have done) she's left with a crack in the deck more deeply disturbing than the social flaws and alienations defined by male bishops as schizophrenia. Menticians can feel up their patients without the laying on of hands. But she also changes physicians too often for comfort. Maybe there's something special she's looking for. Remember the letter I finally got from her at Okinawa when it looked as if we wouldnt get home for another year and I thought I'd lost her. Just one letter after weeks of waiting to hear something more about the loneliness of her life without me—and all she talks about is going to get a filling, the big strong white gentle hands of her dentist forsooth! Now that's the one kind of doctor she never seems discontented with. A dentist's more instrumental in the cause and cure of real pain and perhaps more capable of genuine sympathy or at least concentrated intimate attention; and there's a certain dentist whose ruddy thigh would be more easily confused with that of a god than Gilchrist's or Etwas's, even though it may therefore be more willfully excluded from the memories of a spiritual woman. When she stops telling me

and Michael with a straight face added in a mumble not meant for the understanding of his son: "Maybe we'll let you." This allusion to the patter of the little man in the straw hat was cut short by the middle child sunburnt and dirty speaking from the depths of Chapman picnic luggage piled beside him who rode backwards head pressed against a window of the family's stall well forward in the ark where all might see the bedragglement and disarray of the expedition he belonged to, ringing out in clarion candor unmindful of the weary stillness in which all passengers awaited the first lurch forward, for even the thrumming compressors underfoot had caught up to the silence he lucidly broke: it was like a splendid call for solidarity to the peoples gathered there not unfriendly but hitherto indifferent to each other more black than yellow or white and more female than the contrary:: "Daddy will you take us to the circus?" His crystal voice was filled with the expectant hope of clear sunny morning. No soul even of the lowest class represented in that straightway united brotherhood could have failed to recognize the kind of ordeal that the daddy had obviously not yet emerged from. Laughter drowned out the clatter-closing of the glassed door as the dour driver himself smiling seemed to take one family's question as signal to fold up with one lever his open invitation to all families and strays while pivoting another through the arc of his power box to mete out the electromotive force that had been waiting

her dreams for fear they're really recollections I want to shake the secrets out of her with all my strength. Tiresias himself would be tormented with jealousy of the feelings she finds in herself thanks to the insidious homeopathy wrought by doctors who expose but cannot cure what I myself could all too easily expose if I werent compelled to hoard her concupiscence by the conviction that I give her the least disillusionment she could hope for without happening on a far better bird than any of those irresponsible humanistic vultures. At conjunctions of menfluence and corybantic theology who could say what woman's incapable of throwing herself without premeditation into the arms even of anyone who isnt a doctor—or incapable of forgetting active passions as conveniently as innocent unmentionable dreams? [His fingers flexed and tightened the arms wrapped about his baby son whom he hugged more warmly than ever to prevent himself from getting up and squeezing the absolute truth out of his wife right there in front of the children, right there in front of the whole complacent gang of marriage-mongers riding home from their various outings who knew nothing about themselves despite the fact that what little there was to know must have been banally simple in comparison to what remained to be known about Ruth. (He overlooked his rash subsumption in covering black passengers by this generalization and didnt stop to consider the madnesses of other wives; still less did he think of troubleshooting the

overhead tirelessly alert. Inhibited by few of a true steersman's duties he simultaneously swung round the high stool he leaned against to see which of his free or half-fare customers could have made himself so loud and clear; but the comradely tittering buzz that had been set off all down the two rows of divers primates merged with the moving clang of the vessel and perplexed his delayed observation, though Jonathan wonderfully insensible of public mortification was gleefully clapping Matty on the back in congratulation for faithful trusting innocence. With the commencement of general noise the privacy of the one who had caused the merriment was quickly recovered. "Next year." said Michael patting his staunchest son on the knee who remained unaware of the stir he had made.

After a stop or two they came to the unpleasant corner of desolation where a penny arcade commanded foot traffic at both angles flanked by hangouts for eating and drinking much less attractive to mature civilians than to disguised sailors drugstore-motorcycleboys and ass-wagging broads who couldnt breathe without flaunting loosely rigged or tensely extruded chests and jarring their own once tender little brains with the muscular rhythm of impudent jaws in unending sugary joyless mastication viciously numbing to the senses and totally antipathetic to the rationality of all parties in the scene, none of them (swaggering violent male or strutting juicy-fruited female) not terrified to soften up, blacks and whites segregated from each

circuits that flashed between his own two ears whenever his science was too baffled to keep up with dumbfounded feelings.)] Else why is Donna Quixote always when in her secret chambers most occupied with well-reasoned delusion so worried about the slander of unknown censors against blinds drawn during daylight in our bedroom windows? In her rarely professed crusade against nasty fears of sex as imbedded in the religion understood by our forefathers—a campaign so mystical and arcane that I may be the only one informed of its symbols—there must be some association with real misconduct. I'm sure there are times when the men she talks to can sense antinomian discontinuity in the modest housewife even when they suspect nothing of her illness. —Yet maybe it's only an old husband like me who's disposed to postulate such a fault in women married more than four or five years, at least to the extent that they don't seem to be absorbed by their children, no matter how reserved in their manner, no matter how firm their first rejection of improper advances that are meant to take advantage of it. Still, in another light I think it's the excitements of paranoia that prevent her from realizing the possibility that her love for me has dissipated with all the other zests of youth. Then in this sense too she dons her psychosis for protection from interference while she casts about for her hidden motive, which she never suspects is still buried under the neolithic lava that all our cities have been built over. Is this the reason that perhaps

other by selective blindness, from the middle class by money only and from their present invidious observer by almost every apolaustic category not to mention age and responsibility, without exception fortified by one narcotic or another whether illicit or transcontinentally advertised, their feelings sweetened by nothing but music. Without that sugar they'll listen to nothing. Michael characterized them as antiintellectuals and sought to define their common ground with Republicans. [The brutal folly of their kind of insolence is sooner seen— that's one difference—and you don't have to wait for posterity to punish them by making clear the vanity of their lives too late for them to learn their lesson; for every one of them jostling milling shrieking catcalling whistling pinballing spitting squinting scowling wisecracking threatening teasing cursing gaming plotting and hating on that noisy garish commercial pavement down there will be fucked to pieces smashed to pieces or rotted to pieces within ten years. There is no possibility for them to learn from experience because they are as deprived of personal future as of cultural history and their sensations will wear out far short of transcendence consummation or even fun. Like their literary counterparts they despise me for my smug moon face and my genteel job never doubting if they take any notice at all that I'm a sanctimonious antidisestablishmentarian or at least a law-abiding constitutionalist if not indeed an outright obvious fearful dupe of convention married to the same

all women after a while seem to us to go crazy unless theyre wiley enough to conceal the symptoms most likely to claim the attention of our vanity or lust? Or is it simply that none of them ever soundly sleep our trance of reason—which isnt very reasonable after all considering that we don't deem it applicable to the consistency of our assumptions, such as the postulate that their love in marriage will go on growing and clinging like ivy in the Harvard Yard despite tired soil winter frosts and careless mutilations, together with the doctrine that our own love for them should be earnestly allured as a gift from preoccupied beings who otherwise must be indulged as natural goats or as fastidious foragers with wandering appetites? The docile wallplant can be severed for a long time at the main stem before anyone notices that the hanging foliage is dying here and there. The weaker party will take only so much abuse without beginning to deceive you about her feelings. It's hardly rational to believe women's loyalty the one exception to a universal mortality of enthusiasm, especially in face of all we ought to know about their erotic abilities, which when not insane they conspire with us to forestall ignore divert deny despise or limit, starting so early in life that like Japanese girls with bound feet they grow up no matter how rich or liberal wearing tight skirts because their steps are short, having been trained to conduct themselves much more politely than Atalanta. For the best of motives either party can betray the conspiracy, but then

woman without relief for years and years and years too afraid of reality to enter the city's bars and too afraid of naked truth to surrender my consciousness to the supernal occlusions of pharmacal unreason. I'll never have the satisfaction of seeing these cowboys repent, and they'll never know that my way feels better than theirs, not only because it is their lot soon to be wasted and scattered but also because I'll remain too unknown even with luck and success in everything that's important ever to be recognized among their kind as one that has suffered their dominance on land and sea and loathed them whom I should have loved by reason of our common enemies who make them what they are. I swear I'm not jealous of their teenage girls—not the college type at all—certainly not of the noise and speed they gun on their terrifying infernal bicycles, nor of their lean muscular youth so empty of both pleasure and achievement that their maturity promises nothing more than their present mental torpor. My enmity has cause enough without calling for envy to explain it. Didnt Nietzsche say that this world can be justified only as an aesthetic phenomenon? Even as a dumb victim of history or as a simple patriot without letters I would shudder every day of my life at the violence offered women children and earth by these cocky rebels, though a criminal class of little power compared to those who vote, for each one of them disposes of more horsepower than a hundred Indians notwithstanding that it takes a hundred

they no longer have any reason to make us guess their thoughts. (Women themselves must make the choice which way to suffer. They should expect nothing for themselves as long as they insist on being mothers. Even daughters are born by travail and reared at home among the dirty dishes.) Once they've discovered the infinite femininity below their necks they can't help wanting to turn day into night, even in the least vindictive retribution for their born subjugation, while the man they're married to is away playing honorable games with windmills and cash registers. Doctor Ruthle and Mrs Hide! Even an Oakland housewife may be a Guinevere by day.

Sandy married that pig for no other reason than that her name was Ruth. And Dave would drop that Greek of his in half a minute to renew his old love for Ruth. Gave himself away at the party when he said maybe he'd get East: which of course really means that he'd have come to visit her *here* after I left. In fact I can see now that they didnt act like a pair who hadnt seen each other for many years. In the old days I'm sure the least they did was dance together. (Navel engagement without loss of semen. They say Euripides used the same pun in Greek! Except that then there was no question of balking the semen. Naval battles took a lot of rowing: stitching they called it, like verse, from the fucking motion.) At least Dave's a gentleman, worthy of the women who fall at his feet: I wish them joy of him. But once they turn sensual even the

of themselves to spend as much money as a single school kid of the ruling Yahoos. Ye who believe in kicking over the traces always end up most fully constrained—maybe in jail, maybe reduced to a choice between four channels of advertising, maybe foully enthralled by a single poisonous appetite that kills you with humiliation or craven rage before it puts you out of your misery. Even fifteen years ago General Marshall knew that America's greatest difficulty in waging war would be to discipline its youth.] The traveler could see sidewalks and gutters tinkling and rustling with the trash that spenders and unemployables took as much pleasure as they took at anything in flinging to the ground which was here shielded by bituminous skin to keep winter rains from making mud of the mother dirt these street cats never scratched in. [They like to use up expend or throw away anything. It's the selfishness of irresponsible simplification and the vandalism of vindictive sloth. On the beach they swagger in droves stomping through the sandcastles of creative children. On littered grass twisting in the seat of an automobile or against a dark wall their only love is the relief of assassins stabbing antagonists in an abstract depravity of the senses devoid of delight and full of spoliation for the victims who are nevertheless their only arbiters in the vast competition of exterojective pressure that keeps America moving, blatant victims who on this corner are not the sort that get back their own with the sentimental tyrannies of virginity or

cool and fastidious ones can ignore the most ridiculous figure cut by a lover. Who could be more irritating or boring than a damn fool like Sandy? —That's just how he does it: irritates until they respond; then bores them. —In his case it can't have anything to do with admiration, especially when she already knew him too well to find him attractive in any way but one. An outright reversal of civilization's advance. Even little Caleb visits my house with the hopes of a troubadour. Thereto it's a good thing we don't see much of the Jacksons. She's not incurious about what she hears of Jim's prowess—or why else would she always be talking about how mistaken Americans are in their conviction that sweet-smelling cleanliness is healthy? . . . Speaking of Greeks and heroes there's also the landlord. Likely to be home at any time of day. Despite the greedy housing shortage he's never raised our rent. God only knows what Hecuba puts her up to. . . . You can forgive a desirable woman almost any repented transgression, but only if she's not your own jailer that's stood for ten years between you and the heroines of your own natural mania while the family ivy was climbing. No man of honor can free his warder of her guilt. All he can do is what his brothers would gladly do for him: make a contribution to the liberation of someone else's custodian. But I'm no closer to that compensation than I am to Lilian's bed.

Still I don't believe Ruth could lose her *heart* to any of them except maybe Adlai Stevenson to whom I

marriage. Without access to guns and too lazy for athletics these boys imitated by these girls like to snap their butts over the side, snap down the corner of their cards, snap down their coins, snap open their packages of beer and tobacco, snap up or down their zippers, snap the knobs of music machines and television sets, snap ignition switches and other triggers of power. What they don't fling stamp kick eject drop or snap they rip shove or smash. They and their kind in higher circles equally hornswoggled by the least convincing instance of monistic fallacy call everything shit.] An aging veteran no longer had to live at their immediate mercy but now and then it was well for him to be reminded of the least common denominator. [Theyre not the only ones for whom true fame is to be seen alive in real time on television. None of them knows there is a past. I know nothing of the present, but the past is much bigger than the present in fact nowadays bigger than the future too. (You must be quick to get on television before we're all dead. Ruth sees that.) Even clean neat thrifty people just push the trash out of sight or merely put it off their property: they take the same pleasure in getting rid of their larger share of the mess, washing it from their bodies with four hundred hot showerbaths a year (as Ruth says) and expelling it from their houses banishing it from their yards and neighborhoods but above all driving it elsewhere in their cars: and that's the end of their care for cleanliness. They hire bulldozers to make strip-mines for

wouldnt grudge my wife anyway. She sent him a telegram at least once I know of, about something he was quoted for in the paper. "That was meant for me." she said afterwards with a peculiar smile. "We are old friends." Now there's one case methinks I don't have to worry over. She may have imagined— Wait, there's more to this! It's very very strange that I could have forgotten what made her tell me, after all the distress it brought, back before Roger, maybe even before Matty. Something I said just kidding her and never dreaming it might be serious, probably just fishing for some new nugget of psychical womformation and accidentally provoking her into a little confession that she'd never have made (almost infallible as she is in matters of tact) if she hadnt thought I was mature enough to take in figmentary things without disturbance to my self-esteem, little suspecting how it would shake the foundations of my lordliness until perhaps a little later when I may have betrayed my anxiety despite every effort to conceal it in my determination to learn more about the secret appetite of her body; and then I could get nothing more out of her as if she'd suddenly reminded herself that she dared not offer even the wisest man in the world a scrap of fact that might injure his vanity. "I make up stories if I'm scared, in order to come when you want me to. When you seem to belong to the world I can't trust myself to you. So I have to use my imagination." But I've never been able to extort from her by plea or artifice a single one

their trash. —Wa-hoo, ro-deo! The thrill of driving one-handed with a carful of kids on the edge of smash! Wa-hoo, ro-deo! Living live and free as per devilvision. You don't have to go outdoors to get the time of day. Who needs literature? And we're only beginning to see the prosperity yet to come!] Yes while the streetcar was waiting for the light to change Michael suspended other thoughts to look down on the swaggering swarm that he competed with for space on the planet and criticized Homer's metaphor of mankind as the seasonal succession of leaves on a tree—as if all contemporaries belonged to the same coterminous puberty cohort, offspring of the same previous generation. (Even in Homer's way of thinking who had no notion of evolution this trope overlooks the path of personal lineage and continual transmission by which each man engenders personal progeny before he turns orange red brown (in New England at least) and falls to the earth. [In truth a continuum of personal ages within the parameters of birth and death preserves until we end it all at once a labile cloud-chamber of private freewills. Yet most of my countrymen seem glad to be regarded as units in a cherry harvest or crop of navel oranges. They wax complacent when speaking of some characterization stamped upon them by the accident of birth (the one thing about their lives that isnt accidental). When Jack London rode this track our country didnt seem dangerous to Europe, but the economics of bell-curves is now advancing across both oceans; it will

of her bedtime stories or any hint of the images that do the trick, and I can't even find out whether the fancy's for particular men or for vaguely faced gods. She's only said that she thinks up "situations" to explain what's being done to her. It may have been in a slightly different mood that she once expressed the opinion that most women did the same thing because it was "the only way to get physical excitement from loving a bad man." My sluggish perception always protects me from full and immediate understanding of painful implications, but anyway I must have heard these remarks at the pitch of desire (and not of course after it was wiped out by purgation, whereupon I always lose sight of questions and spare not a minute of my peacefully exhausted sleep for even the most dismaying agitation in my repertory and thank god that in the subsiding afterglow of my success she may never remember the scaffolding she's kicked away in her convulsion) when my spirit was bent upon what usually seems at the moment an ultimate ingression promising to undo all historical knots by healing the soul I cleave to. (Certainly it wasnt on any wretchedly incompetent occasion that I would have asked for or listened to this cause for taking further displeasure with myself; nor would she have been so tactlessly untimely. Anyway only now after all these years is the suppressed news percolating back into the cortex of my deanesthetized consciousness where the whispered words were originally registered When she first mentioned the

soon be powering Japan and Germany alike: the doctrine of demand:: immortality no longer in time but in myriadic space. Gaia's population has grown to the point where the statistical duplication of any child is conceivable. For mathematical reasons such trends always accelerate. Already Melville could see it coming when he particularly rejoiced that *Pequod's* carpenter was an original. After a hundred years our national economy depends upon unlimited reduplication. If a people relishes the prophetic persuasion of random samplings it is bound to dispense with memory of the past as well as with the prudential eschatology that was taken seriously when history was read etiologically. We'll begin to entertain the notion of reversible time when we get to the point of regarding the causes of history as weaker than the synchronistic forces of interaction governed only by laws of superorganic probability. And when our spirit loses perdurance for this reason or because of succumbing to the doctrines of oriental philosophy it will cast itself adrift from the floating archipelago of real human freedom.]

As the car started up again with its slightly altered muster of passengers scattered in varieties of private thought, passed in both directions by white families on rubber wheels speeding home in insulated comfort, working its way up in the numbers the streets were named by, Matthew having had his attention drawn by an unusual craning of his mother's neck to glimpse the last refraction of sunset framed by the opening of a cross-

subject she was equally friendly and perhaps archly amused by what she was telling me, even happy to exchange a confidence for the extraordinary attention I must have been paying to her feelings; but then the second time we spoke of it after I'd had a chance to brood awhile and work up my thirst for self-laceration she seemed to have perceived some shame in what had earlier struck her as a harmless wile practiced to complete my pleasure as well as her own. In fact she wept at the twist my investigation was taking. Nothing but such obtuse meddling could have so magnified her disclosure. I kissed away her tears with an affectation of cheerful reassurance. Think of all the women who don't have the brains to do that I said. I couldnt find the words to persuade her that the need for such subterfuge did not arise from any deficiency on her part, but she was gradually comforted by my deprecation of its moral significance. Perhaps I only helped confirm a habit that I might have cured her of by being a more patient lover. Yes I was very disturbed by the problem—and yet after a while it didnt seem worth the effort, the time it would take, every time to head off something entirely inaccessible to my verification and apparently irrelevant both to her pure senses and to the lovely attitude toward me that she was usually left with from my phallic impressions upon her. In the end her private custom (if such it is) did not seem to reflect upon her good opinion of my person in spite of the shock her revelation imparted to

street they were passing on the left asked his second and more disinterested question, this time heard only by his intimates: "Will the rooster crow now?" His father's answer was unenthusiastic, almost perfunctory, and the son's spontaneous interest was quickly dulled by a fatigue at the back of his head that often came with the monotony of his father's voice endlessly explaining the world without bringing it to life: "Not the one we saw. He's sad to see the sun go down over the edge of the world. That's not good news at all. I'd hate to be sailing out through Golden Gate at this time of day. We're far enough west as it is. . . ." Michael summoned further comments that neither he nor anyone else listened to. He was growing a trifle bored with his children who expected so much attention morning noon and night, no more hesitant to intrude upon his erotic preoccupations and historical speculations than to prevent him from going to bed with their mother before the lustier parts of a day were washed out by old anxieties or new fatigues. Yet he perfectly well understood why it should be that his wife's priorities were ordinally the reverse of his own and though making no attempt to imitate her patience he tried to do his duty. "The cocks in Japan will soon be crowing. But I'll never take you there."

"But you promised to take us to Londonbridges!"

"That's because Gloucester is half way to England." Jonathan explained to his brother. "It's in the other direction."

my complacency. Nevertheless there's been no new evidence for me to take comfort in. I discounted the melancholy truth by attributing it to universal difficulties of marriage after all its delightful explorations have grown routine and every pique of curiosity or invention is dissolved into familiar expectations of that one flesh which the institution is said to aim for without the prospect of joining two minds. If I were the newfound lover (I told myself) there'd be nothing to stop her from thinking about me in the flesh as she lay beneath her hardworking husband. And I soothed my discomposure with the idea that eventually she would "trust" me as her lifelong suitor every time I made love to her and that in due course we would outgrow the need for her to dress me in false masks. But notice that I then made sure to forget the whole thing! Now I shall suffer or rather now I shall know that I have been suffering for my lazy pusillanimous and selfish retreat from the spiritual mystery at the totally unknown center of this sexually enigmatic individual with whom I'm supposed to be in close communion. Some might think it wiser never to have raised her expectations (as if she couldnt read!), but there's not much pleasure in fucking a frozen princess no matter how beautiful she may be. I'm lucky to have a wife who makes up stories. A woman of less imagination would be looking for easier excitement.

But that's just the point my dear horned and horny simpleton— she's done that too! There was another dream she gave me a glimpse

"Oh."

"Well someday boys we'll go to Europe Eyerup and Syrup together. You can go to Japan by yourselves. I want to go to the Atlantic Ocean where the cock crows earlier."

"I thought Japan was the land of the rising sun." said Jonathan.

"A three-ring circus in Syrup!" Matthew was merrily envisioning.

Michael with Roger on his lap facing forward in motion and his arms wrapped around the chunky little body fell silent and rested his chin on the hot little head opposite the mother who had closed her eyes for a moment's rest while she wasnt needed. For the second time that day this father contemplated the fine gold hair that whorled about the tiny tonsure of the softly suturing skull. (Come to think of it maybe the green mansions are not below the equator after all—can't remember the map of Guiana and Surinam which was once very important to Gloucester. . . . Should have looked for Rima's coral snake at the zoo. How much like Yillah she was in her origins! . . . Hudson, Pierre's great Hudson valley to the sea—could Riolama be an English imitation?) He snorted wryly at Walter Shandy's concern about the affects of birth trauma on a baby's cerebellum. The fear seemed laughable compared to his own dread of the evil eye's radiation to which Roger's tender newborn brain like millions of others at the family hearth would soon be exposed.)

"You know what?" Matty was saying: "Hodgy-Podgy didnt need his pacifier all day! He must have had a good time. Did you notice that, Mommy?"

of: said she couldnt remember anything about the scene of it or anything that happened except the sweet smooth cresting of amorous feeling at the end and the words she said to herself. "No no, don't come—save it for Michael. . . . Oh it's too late!" Then she gently woke me with heavenly hands and lips so that she could share with me a second flowing of her midnight honey on the same occasion. It's clear that wave after wave is what she longs for, hours of slowly cascading eruptions merged into immense syzygial flood tides brimming over the shoreline. Or maybe she only recalls that first year after the war when there were no misgivings to trouble the tireless treadings of her single-minded goat. Yet now that my virile nerves are educated by middle age each thunderclap bursts a whole sky of thick clouds more heavily loaded than a dozen of those quick shallow rainbow showers. Veteran mothers can storm the knowledge that Eve only trembled for in Eden. However when youre cooped up together year after year you run plumb out of the allelotropic zeal that it takes to cultivate the jewel of games. You get weighed down by accumulated reasons not to be joyful about your desire and not to trust the other's. As a matter of fact it speaks pretty well for me that under such conditions she's ever beatified at all: that's the way it ought to be looked at. If a housewife can't have fireworks every night at least she's better off seeing a few stars once in a while than staring at lighted punk forever. Yet the worst of it is that when youre locked in a

Ruth smiled. "I couldnt find it. Has anyone seen it since yesterday?" It was a familiar question usually taken as rhetorical. Michael saw that she was preoccupied and he felt obliged to supplement her reply. "Sometimes he likes the real bottle or nothing, Matto Grosso. When he sucks he expects to get his milk. Now that he has all those pearly little sharp teeth—"

"But Daddy lots of times he goes to sleep with it. Like me, I chew on the corner of my blanket when I can't stop thinking. Grownups can go to sleep much faster than kids, you know. Jonny tries to put me to sleep by spelling antidisestablishmentarianism but he's the one that falls asleep because he's a little older."

This statement was about to be indignantly disputed when Michael laid his hand on Jonathan's arm whose mouth was already open and Ruth mildly interposed with the remark that she hoped their baby wasnt too tired to eat his supper because he hadnt had much of a nap that afternoon. So Jonathan wisely let the matter rest.

They passed Mr Gilchrist's church of a certain charm where the Mass was softened and laid low to the fullest degree of spiritualization sanctioned by Cranmer's ambiguous and ambivalent prayer book without however satisfying Ruth's famished sense of protestantism. The rector made no great thing of Palm Sunday or any of the following days of Passion Week until Easter itself when all the stops and lilies were pulled out. "That's where I used to go to Sunday School." Jonathan

Lowermiddleclass contract without the advantages of cocktail parties or free social intercourse (not to mention experimental liberties), hitched forever to an irreversible chain of resentments spoilages and defeats, every catalectic game goes into the record book: you can't expunge it or cut and run at the first bitterly disappointing default, nor at the last either; you are manacled to your own history in a joint autobiographical system and barred from any heterogeneous intimacy outside it. When you come right down to it under the circumstances parallel short stories are an impossible gift of the gods.

When we first talked about her secret little fictions she countered my questions with one of her own. "What do you think about when you're giving me orgiasms?" (We always use Hecuba's version of the word. There was a guy on the L S T who talked about his wife's orjissoms.) Why I think about what I hope you feel was my answer. I didnt say that it would probably be better if I thought about S M D C or the Democratic Party or that I wished I had the same trouble she has in which case she wouldnt have any problem at all I'm sure and if I could spare the time she'd have an orgy of asms at least twenty-one nights of every moon and find the cure for fiction, yet I must learn to sprint before I can run her marathon at every start. The treadmill gathers too much speed under my feet when she cooperates too desperately in keeping pace. But who can blame her body for its fear of losing the opportunity? I should

told Matthew. "I'm glad I don't have to go anymore." The younger brother wondered how good the stories were that came out of a school where there was no spelling or arithmetic.

"This is the beginning of Easter Week." the father said. "It's almost Easter. Easter is the time to pay your Christmas bills."

"But we live in the *west!*" Jonathan crowed. "Easter in the wester!"

"Ya Dad, Easta in da Westa!" chimed Matty in approval and support of his corporal.

"Easter is April Fool's Day this year." Jonathan added. "I found that out from my teacher."

[Doesnt that make this Annunciation Day? I can't explain that one to the boys and I'm too superstitious to mention it to Ruth.]

Roger was too sleepy to take up with the agreeable sounds.

The formerly antiseptic neighborhood on the west side of Teleology Lane had come so far down in the world that the church was now buffered only by its side street and a small used-car lot from a commercial block that housed the far less exclusive establishment of a couple Ruth had made friends with because she didnt have her own washing machine and clothes dryer, an automatic coin laundry owned and operated by a tall thin saintly pale agnostic named Smith with his short swarthy lumpy bulbous wife an atheistic Jew so homely good-humored and generous that she had become the most beloved public figure in the district who had a happy baby girl about Roger's age

talk to her about it. If I had a new wife without such a reflex I'd start off on a better footing and knowing more about women I wouldnt let her settle for less than galactic arcs of stars and exploding chains of emulsification, but she'd have to make more of an effort than Ruth does to study the psychophallic mechanism of a spiritually hostile husband anxiously trying to make the peace that dissolves animosity close to its source, and that would take a lot of somewhat mechanical practice with love suspended at the outset—the very attitude that Ruth abhors. Of course you can't have a bunch of kids swarming around either. All it really takes is plenty of time. . . . But am I exaggerating her mania for undergoing the sudden resolution of pelvic frenzy into blessed relaxation of all the senses? Since my own delight lies in hers I rely more upon an uncertain estimate of what I cannot know than upon the purely subjective results of stroking or lisping. It's this transcendence of sensuality which thank god requires sensual methods that finally renders consummate fucking more ecstatic than all other rubbings and lickings devised by men or women together or alone, makes it a universal sign of humanity's instinct to discontent itself with mere reproductive survival, and explains the sacrament of marriage. The desire to penetrate dissolve and restore a fine woman's integrity bears only formal resemblance to the splitting lust of rape which to be sure occasionally possesses a gentle man under extraordinary conditions but which exercises

no better looking than herself. The two neat banks of slightly canted machines with portholes like the fire doors of miniature boilers in a super-ship, with the larger and fewer mills like turbines to collect their output, the gleaming chrome and immaculate enamel, and the light gray deck swabbed twice a day by the proprietor, together with soft-spoken kindness to every customer, had brought them all the business they could handle without going to the bank for more money to invest in bigger premises elsewhere. Michael's surprise both at the match and at the efficiency of the partnership had been resolved on learning that the two had met in New York as Marxist comrades during the war when Glen was a merchant seaman (from Idaho) and Jeanette a worker for one of the C I O canteens, which were the only patriotic charities that permitted black men or communists to dance with white girls. Ruth and Jeanette had become fast friends but their attempt to make Michael and Glen love each other equally well had been abandoned after a single exchange of dinner invitations offered and accepted with the best intentions of all concerned. The clerk found he could talk to the entrepreneur about nothing but business methods and tactics; there was no room for discussion of politics: he an employee was forced by this capitalist's anticapitalistic dogma (which lay just below the surface of many another handsome gentle and intelligent radical) to defend Democrats as if they were as vulnerable to the attacks of benign

most doctors in this field as positively fundamental who can make bold with such generalizations because they are even less sensitive than I to the fibrillations of our opposites and are like to explain feminine interests in terms of their own stuprations at home. Nearly every one of them is a sloppy impatient writer without learning or judgment and contemptuous of intellect. Etwas seems to be an exception, a sweet and generous man without any professional affectation truly educated philosophical and literary in the old world way entirely out of the main stream even among those who write and publish, too wise to be recognized by his fraternity, like some obscure country priest who's exiled from Paris for his original theology—but even he has a falangist streak. Why would such a man devote his life to personal therapy if there werent some screwy lechery at the bottom of his sorry heart? None of them are higher minded than other men when it comes to the subject that disturbs us all. All they do is explain away a woman's integrity. Even when they don't offer themselves as the personal agent of a wife's corruption they presume to decompose her moral fragments and degrade them into counterparts of their own pathological anatomy that cryptically motivates disingenuous careers. If a woman refuses to knuckle under to their disrobing iconography they want to put her away. All medical specialists are annoyed by a patient who individually threatens the norm of a diagnosed disease by reflecting systemic complications.

reason as Republicans or Nazis. Furthermore the Smiths were addicted to the entertainment of their television set at a level of appreciation that he felt he could not allude to without hurting the feelings of three citizens (counting his own wife) who little deserved any kind of scorn, especially Jeanette who had already had five cancer operations and knew she was dying from the inside out, as she smilingly confided to Ruth in the course of explaining her opinion that religion was an opiate especially for women. But Glen and Michael both put in twelve-hour days and neither wife expected them to keep up an artificial social life. The laundromat was open for business even on Palm Sunday, and as the streetcar rolled past it Ruth was silently praying for the comfort of her friend during a forthcoming stay in the hospital and wondering how she could and whether she should approach first Jeanette or Glen and then Michael with her idea of adopting the happy little girl when the end came. The space between the church and the Smith's storefront had given the riders a last look at the red streak hanging over the unseen Pacific.

Moses Chapman began to rally his family for its final public convulsion of the day, making sure that everything was counted and ready to hand. He awaited the funeral parlor that would be his passing signal to rise from repose early enough to cope with any contingencies in the execution of his commands. [Come west young man! —She thinks New England's a charnel ground of mouldy human

Nine out of ten won't even consider questions of objective value, or can't conceive the patient's need of imaginative treatment. Most of them have one standard way to meet a "crisis situation", which they recognize by separating the dysfunction from the person, and if the poor girl insists on mooting well-established assumptions they resolve to waste no more time on her mind and prudently discontinue all flattery of her body: then it's either drug her or take her away:: give her children to the state.

But who am I to talk like Tiresias? I don't know any more about women than Joseph did (Old Testament or New) and to make it all the worse I don't truly want such knowledge beyond the marches, all my sciolism notwithstanding. You'd have to be a female to have any idea what it's like. I wouldnt envy Catherine the Great herself even if she'd been serenely contented by every one of her lovers and regally happy with health and beauty. It's impossible for manhood to prefer womanhood. (Tiresias never said he'd rather *remain* cloven.) I'm certain that it's likewise a grievous perversion of humanity for women to grow up with a man's attitudes and that it's a crime to deliberately despoil the purity of a female who's true enough to stay gladly on her side of the veil and wise enough not to reduce the mystery to hatred for an egotistical enemy or her sensations to some sort of ethological symmetry with the pleasures of bedroom fascists.

Yet an unadulterated woman is all the more perfidious in deceiving

compost and decayed history redolent of dead languages where our forefathers are still resisting the momentum of psychological progress.] He commenced a shower of warnings instructions exhortations and reprimands; he chode with his people, a tired weakened family that offered no active resistance to his precautious wisdom. Lurching backward into the aisle, turning full circle as he loaded himself with baggage—he suddenly clapped eyes upon the golden heiress of erotic splendor who had shared the earlier part their journey. She had all along been sitting right behind him! No doubt Ruth would have recognized her over his shoulder and put him on his guard if his own bulk hadnt eclipsed her face not three feet from his shoulder blades. Stunned with embarrassment and pausing irresolutely in his graceless discharge of the day's most unwarily unromantic duty he was now thoroughly daunted by her beauty. In the dusty wrinkled degradation of his shabby garb he shrank in shame at the thought of having presumed to dream himself up as this girl's possible lover or even friend. Whereas she had previously seemed above Ruth's station in life she now appeared far beyond his own also. This second encounter was sicklied over by the deeper ruminations that coursed beneath his most recent fussing and budgeting to undermine his pride and confuse his confidence. Then the skin of his low brow flamed under his thick black hair with the sensation that his wish never to be seen by her again was plainly contemptible. At the

a man like me by denying him the credit of her ecstasy while claiming his responsibility for her livelihood her behavior and her children. It's not to pay for the privilege of common ravishment that he takes it all upon himself. There's such a thing as too much sympathy for women. Anyway it's no help in making love to them. Typical irony in the war between ... Self-criticism can be tolerable if it refers to the past but this line of thought stabs me right in the beating heart of my present life. Which includes last night! Am I deceived by my own paltry epithalamic sacrifices? If you're really going to transcend sensuality with your goddess you've got to master mortal adjustments. If your pleasure is her pleasure then her excitement is also yours—and hers is bound to take longer for the same physiological reasons that account for Tiresias's opinion which he lost his eyes for that she has the better of it. The critical point between by-play and high-play changes from day to day and that's no less difficult to ascertain than the general psychosomatic condition that determines it. There are only two people in our act but it's a system more complex than the weather. Her first wave—almost always the only one there'll be time for in thrice-post-partum circumstances—darkens my sky and makes me dizzy with the power of my incantation as I call it higher and higher to swell the comber I would stay for—but no matter how mightily it mounts and beclouds my horizon it sometimes fails to break into the roaring foam that sweeps the beach before I am

same time the girl's phenomena began to strike him as superficial and even meretricious. All at once he was able to reduce her to the veridical value of a callow decoration scarcely to be mentioned in the same breath with his wife. She was not reading the book in her lap but sitting easily erect and gazing at whatever came before her eyes. He was no longer moved to pick out the nice things about her, a faint friendly smile for instance not quite showing itself between the small curves bracketing the ends of her modest mouth which must have been capable of lucidly complicated shapes for intelligent enunciation of informal pearls in English or French, the lips neither too full nor too thin to comport perfectly with her firm shoulders and breasts, nor too loose or too stiff, tinted with freshest most vernal pink rather on the inside than where they were obvious to uncommunicating strangers—a mouth that doubtless could speak simply and directly of what she was thinking (perhaps the conception of babies) but always declined to do so at unseasonable time or place. Since the Chapman family occupied most of her visual foreground it seemed likely that one or more member of that fold or something that one or more member of that fold reminded her of was what brought to her face a lovely expression that the sidelong man foolishly nonplussed by her unexpected presence could not quite dismiss as insipid after all. It was a look not of abstraction but of alert yet decorous and unassuming attention to

overcome by its invitation in my one dive to its depth. A landsman may do better paying no attention to the waves and simply going for a cool swim off shore. (Was it unsympathetic timing that made Zeus and Apollo such superhuman lovers?) It's not that I'm lazy in physical training or unwilling to gather my food for each meal (especially on feast days) or even on most occasions unduly impatient but you might say I'm psychically too sympathetic for infallible superiority to the tempest around me. When the old equalizer can't absorb the heat of exchange without exceeding its threshold of liquefaction the receiving entity of much greater enthalpic inertia who would like to make a night of it is naturally nonplussed. Over the centuries her sex has been taught to dismiss disappointments. What else could prevent so good a mind from curing its own illness? —So then, is the transcendental phase really mine alone? While I drop off to sleep in fatuous bliss she lies there in wakefully melancholy hysteresis already educated to despair of my aging recrudescence betimes! Apparently I'm a wretch whose goddess so pities him for the clumsiness of his worship that she fakes a burst of shuddering foam to grant him false beatitude! Then in all these years of close attention to sign and symptom I've failed to decode her terrible kindness. That's the only way to justify her infidelity. I've driven her to it. If only she had spoken out early in the game, if only she had been wise enough to disabuse my dotage,

objects of immediate vision. In the fugacious spasm of gentle hatred that almost blinded Michael to some of the accidental details clothing her essence he scarcely noticed the laced hands that pressed the kneecap of her right leg crossed over the left under the hem of the light blue cotton skirt he had erst admired, and suspending one slim sandal-shod foot above the grooved wooden floor swaying faintly with the motion imparted to it by their shared vehicle; scarcely speculated upon the pressure that one thigh exerted upon the other or wondered about what she felt between them, whether or not she was aware of her negative attraction for positive charges (as an early physicist might have put it), whether or not she amused herself with fanciful images of herself in connection with strange men of passing circumstance; scarcely considered the possibility that perhaps even without any distinct thought of micturition she was practicing a habitual need to compress and seal the orifice of her bladder as the accumulation of urine gave rise to a dull ache in the groin and set certain sphincters into a slow autonomic rhythm of postponement marking time against the moment of relief from an unwanted waste of positivity when she would relax uncrossed legs on a seat at home; and scarcely gave thought to the distasteful contingency which should never be left off a man's checklist that she was now stuffed with a swab or pledgeted with a garter to stanch the diapedesis of womhopes

I would have been able to teach her how to help me with our teamwork; but now the pattern has indurated our reflexes and it's too late with all the habits we've acquired to start anew. Such an intelligent woman—to fool an eagle eye like mine—and yet too softheaded to pull me up short and cure my overweening satisfaction. To think it could be me—I who have always taken every pain I can think of to get her to say what she thinks about such matters without fear of my anger at hearing the truth! How can I have been such a fool as to believe such frankness possible when she senses that I resent or abhor almost everything she reveals even as I bless my stars that she trusts me? I'm as sulky and childish as the next man. Men are all fools but most foolish of all when we congratulate ourselves like a blinded prophet that we understand our own embryonic gender.

But if Donna Quixote doesnt let Don Quixote know that his bread is all dough there must be a better explanation than misplaced charity. After meditating on this question what can you suggest but some cunningly buried wish for an excuse? If my end-game isnt good enough it's not surprising that such a mistress of the chessboard (champion of her high school) should feel free to challenge one opponent after another until she's mastered. —I'll never get to the lowest level of her rather admirable deceit. I'm led deeper all the time even when I'm trying to avoid simple truth at the bottom. Of course I can always

that she probably was not yet disposed to indulge.

Michael blushing but impassive made no polite sign of recognition but as he swung deliberately round to family business pretending to have seen no one at all on the seat behind him (while Ruth rising now caught sight of the remembered face and gave it her glad and gladdening smile, which was instantly returned with the wordless friendliness of sorority) the trailing corner of his stiffnecked eye caught sight of a commonplace talisman near the knuckle. If he hadnt been inhibited by sullen pride and the fear of being taken for a lecher looking at her legs he would have checked his follow-through in order to verify the dull gleam of the flat gold wedding band that he thought he had seen like a public tendril of summery defloration; but he instantly reconstructed the snapshot that he thus refused himself the impulse to fix by another look and retrospectively placed that slender fillet on the third finger of her left hand. It also came to him that she was traveling home from the zoo to Berkeley, for no other story could satisfy his data which included the tones of Bohemian freedom in her hair and dress and the simple liberality of style seldom seen outside the acropolitan precincts, suggesting the plausibility of her having made an observational trip alone. Yes an artist or scientist of some sort, he couldnt help supposing, this alluring hybrid of a hundred intellectual beauties briefly ventur-

manage to reassure myself since no doubt there's plenty of evidence to support the signs of satiation that her sounds and motions declare inasmuch as after all I'm not a trigger-happy catechumen and there's some reason to suppose that she appreciates the maturity of my art seeing that I usually no longer offer myself at all when she's not predisposed. But even if she's not dissimulating it seems to take longer than it used to. That's all very well if she's just waiting for me, but then for her own sake she should let me use the margin to iterate her beatitude. There are only two possible reasons that I can think of and most likely both of them come into play: (*a*) from the vantage of heightened experience having lost her innocence with another lover she has become well aware of what she's been missing and her imagination can't make up the difference between exotic perfection and household joy; and (*b*) her point of fusion according to physiological laws of familiarity has risen more steadily than my householder skill. In short either someone else has set a new criterion or youth's high-water mark has become mean low tide for her ripened loins, for a mother expects more of her husband after every delivery, the spring chicken finding that no longer was she born yesterday. Has our lover's knot worked too loose, is the lock too worn for its key? It takes no end of cuddling to make up for that and the more time we take the longer everything may require. Yet even

ing away from the safe headwaters of Teleology Lane.

    The end of the Chapman journey was nigh. As Michael worked his family to the porch of the car an oblique slowly combing undissembled wavefront can wash the length of a beach. So there's more to this than the trauma of childbirth.

(dank Roger now at his shoulder facing to the rear and trusted to bestow upon the girl a sleepy farewell smile that would earn response in kind) he concluded that her matrimony altered his plight. It was not entirely displeasing to know of her onsetting constraints and although he remained to her no more remarkable than the putative father of a fortuitously beautiful goodnatured child and indistinguishable from thousands of stout goggle-eyed men struggling weakly to maintain their small gains he could now presume that she was in some degree beholden to the same mean necessity he and his wife lived by, and even that she was (though probably still unaware) as mismatched in her higher circumstances as he was in his higher wisdom. Having made at least provisionally a personal compromise with fate her mortal superiority could be no more secure than her defenses against fertility, and she seemed too intelligent to have married for no other reason than to keep house for a man. She was certainly too beautiful to need a legal bond for keeping any lover at her side.

    In this light the palm would now be awarded to Ruth who had already got the best of her young betters in what they all bargain for. This piquant no doubt talented little slip of a half-woman had let her goddessity go by the board like all other wives except Ruth, whereas that full-woman's discriminating good fortune in coming up with himself had assured the aristocratic endowments of her three children. Therefore to Michael his wife proved herself the more valuable of these two persons, and the more desirable, though her belly was no longer flat and her career no longer open to the higher possibilities. In his view furthermore a man capable of comprehending the deficiencies of others must logically be greater than they and consequently though poor and unprofessional the best for all the best women to open their mouths and legs to, and she who had won him all to herself must be esteemed as the cream of the cream.

    It did not follow however that even the best woman was enough for the best man who was of opinion he could make more than one of the better women happy, nor that this married girl (riper than she had at first appeared to be) did not know that her second-best husband was good enough (most likely being academic moreover) for the best of the better women—unless she was still too newly married to have gotten over the idea of her man as really something or was already pregnant. How much did his own wife's differ from this younger heart glistening with dew, lovely bilateral rose— *Roses!* Yes there had been roses for his own Valentine on St Valentine's Day: . . . long long ride to love on this very streetcar after a valiant day waiting for the Prince and watching through Valentine's window for the hips of roses pausing in twilight to look at books—*but not alone*! Yes yes *this same vaginal flower was idling with her black mate as they searched out Valentine verses to read each other*! There could be no doubt that he had seen this lovely girl once before.

Michael's providence brought his family to the forward vestibule of the car and nearly onto the motorman's elbow a full block before Matt was allowed to run back to an empty seat and press the white signal button, much to the official's irritation just after he had made a bootless voluntary stop gratuitously mistaking their intention whereupon the Chapmen had politely stepped back to make way for other passengers to get by who of course did not materialize, so that as things fell out it seemed as if the one man in the world most solicitous of a driver's sensibility convenience efficiency and rhythm (yet well aware how hard it was to guess an irritable unionman's attitude toward the buzzer that ruled him: whether or not he preferred to exercise informal intelligence and oblige his customers by anticipating their wishes) had doubled with ill-timed pedantry an insult to the gruff operator's effort to perfect his public service. Regretting the decisions that exasperated a worthy civil servant, in final consideration of everyone's feelings as well as general pedagogical consequences Michael shrank from offering any explanation or apology as all too likely to compound the misunderstanding as it fleeted. His companions stood in comatose speechlessness holding onto stanchions amid their rubble of possessions and swaying with the roll of the vengefully accelerated

5] No one in the ship so pitilessly hated savage little yellow Japs as the malicious black kid from Arkansas who with the other servants of the wardroom was segregated in bed board and duty from the white men of the crew but shared the saltwater showers. He let it be known that he would jerk the head off their necks between thumb and fingers the way he had ended the life of many a woodcock wounded by his shotgun pellets. In his dungarees just an ordinary sharecropper steward neither tall nor short nor fat nor thin shambling his way through the Navy with awkward ignorance born for humiliation in every jot and tittle of public appearance scarcely able to sign his pay chit yet quite as opinionated about the yellow traits of Reds as any Republican quartermaster, graced with little of the well-carried strength of his messmates who sequestered from the friendly overtures of an electronic technician or any other niggerlover worked in officers' country and slept forward on the port side where no redneck or hillbilly could be offended by their exhalations, his mouth was always working his head was always wagging and his hands were always jingling and with self-abasing effrontery he said yassir to every Caucasian of any rank except our enlisted Jew. But the naked Clovis Jones was a byword among all the dispossessed cocksmen and forlorn

creaking groaning vessel. Matt now clung to his father's jacket and watched the hypnotic stream of automobiles as it passed below them in a hum of soporific fluctuation, appreciating his possession of a family that so lovingly set him on his life's way. For his part Mr Chapman in full view of all appraising passengers was meanwhile owning in silence to the futility of dreaming up fantastic blisses little conducive to the peerlessly valuable intention of his will; on his life's way acquisitive prurience was simply ridiculous, a silly idle itch worse for the scratching. [A woman's mind is a womind never mind how embellished or trained, and beneath the womhope lies the womurge unacknowledged and unsuspected by the mind itself. Perhaps one female person offers more or less molluscular resistance than another, or slightly differing palpitations, but when the fandango is over for the nonce maybe at bottom they're all on a par after all as sailors say more crudely when choosing them by their decorations or by the way they walk, at least as far as that hardened manikin down there is concerned. The old lad will leap as high for the same lass as for a new one, and none of the perfectly formed fresh new blossoms that might be buzzed would remain particularly strange after the honeylooter's first parting of the petals, nor would it any longer seem a monosyllable more intriguing than the one he's already assigned to. Ergo, for the sake of efficiency (in case longevity fails) restrict your exploration to one pollen rose—and

husbands drafted to cuntless reaches of the earth (much unluckier than some whalemen who complained merely about not seeing a white woman for four years at a time) where they had plenty of time to worry about the temptations of women at home. To me and other fledglings whose experience was no broader than that of tender unconsummated loves or a few tyro couplings on the wing it was nothing but a more or less insignificant joke to call the rickety black bumpkin a mule, which in the mind's eye of most of us was about the same as a disproportioned little Spanish donkey. Flaccid it hung like baloney half way to his knees. "It doesnt matter how big it is if you don't know how to use it" I remember scoffing to a shipmate when I heard it mentioned in awe. It never occurred to me to envision it extended, and I was too naively preoccupied with possible opportunities for the seduction of girls as an end in itself to imagine a mature woman's interest in comparative anatomy. Where is Clovis now I wonder, migrated to Oakland maybe or languishing more forlorn than other convicts behind bars or back home breeding his tenth baby in a plain woman who feasts on it still and works her fingers to the bone for its sake far from putting children first? With his clothes on the only hint was a huge mouth outsize hands and big feet (judging by aristocratic proportions), like Sandy the uncircumcised infidel whom I've never seen undressed. Allometrics are tricky: height for instance comes mainly with the

incidentally leave it not idle for thornless prickings of peccant humming birds. A bargain's a bargain: I'd like to be able to trust to it while attending to my idiotic businesses. —Farewell thou fair strange daughter of man! I have now known thee and divined thy womlust. As long as I keep my own difficult careworn bride at home to put the quietus to Mr P when he dilates upon his swollen troubles I can forego thy quenching. Still, would faith be broken if Ruth invited you and your Othello to our bed for a valedictory round-robin? I'd love her the better for it. —But no, maybe not quite worth the risk she'd love me the less thereafter. I'm doomed to a prudent householder's joie de vivre.

ARKANSAS TRAVELER: Have you been faithful all your life?
HILLBILLY: Not yet.]

Matty tugged at his pocket and he bent down to listen to the tremulously whispered words: "I'm glad God made you Daddy." There was nothing more to say and the child smiled not at the sentence he had spoken but at the relief of having delivered his heart. Michael pressed the boy to his thigh with all the bearish strength that could be brought to the lower end of his unlevered arm. [Alas that women not children possess my manhood and compass my dreams as the alpha and cipher of my alphanumeric spectrum. It signifies nothing that their flesh decays and their bones dissolve as soon as they are laid in the grave enbalmed or not and that their tombs can be reused long

length of legs; anthropologists say men don't vary so much in torso. But whether it grows with the trunk it sprouts from or with the limbs it hangs between it's obvious why women like tall men. There's Glen's glans penis for instance, that man in the laundry business she's had many occasions with and once said she felt sorry for because he probably couldnt make love to a woman with cancer of the cervix but Clovis his stomach was short his hips high his arms as long as a gorilla's with feet a foot from heel to toe but Sandy also with big feet and wide foolish-looking grin has a long body with short legs and if a woman varies with the mouth why not a man? Eskimos have short branches to conserve heat and they lend their wives to visitors so Japanese men's said to be small for their size must have been designed for cold weather too though I never got a look all that time down there on the open deck one reason MacArthur's occupation was so successful the female population got giggling benefit of an evolutionary jump which only makes their own men extremely competitive especially in exporting motorcycles yet I never got a chance to find out how those simpering little women feel if only I hadnt been so stupid as to get myself put on the shitlist for laziness the one time in my life I ignored the call to work detail like everyone else outside the deck gang who'd never been put on report before just when a liberty in Yokohama was coming up that it would have been better to load stores for a month than miss out on yet if the

before the eight years stipulated in Sweet Will's cadastre have expired, or that no testament left by them can continue to modify the causes of the everliving world, or that you can't imagine a sexton's shovel grating on a frivolous girl's friable skull, or that not one of them at death amounts any more than I myself to a hill of beans for what remains: they are still the source the motive and the goal of dead men. From pussywillow to full-blown rose, you are driven out of your head by what seems anything but transitory. One of them provided me with my own flesh and blood, and now another has borne me this tiny new man that loves me more than he loves himself. . . . But blessings upon their dying eyes for taking to the earth so cleanly and leaving behind no skeleton in a foolish box for vanity to cling to. A hundred mothers can fade like angels into the same spot without jostling each other, still brooding on the children that walk above or might have walked: having expected nothing else from the first. But that deceiving sylph of alert deceiving eyes of supple deceiving torso of languorous deceiving legs of quick deceiving hands of deceiving frank manner of deceiving lips and paps deceives me with a black man and pretends to so much more than poor pretty Ruth the one woman I can't imagine dead that her young glamor seems doubly evanescent; and insofar as her pretension springs innocently from sweet ignorance of life her double defectiveness is triply unworthy the serious attention of a man devoted

Barbary monkeys of Gibraltar have no tails at all to keep from getting frost-bite people from the tropics must have been selected for the maximum dissipation of caloric and a man's Long Tom is for heat-exchanging like a blood-jacketed equalizer so I wonder how tall Norsemen and broad Argives compare for surface area seeing that long strong fingers are good for throwing the javelin something that Sandy did in school before he gave up outdoor athletics but you can't be sure of that correlation either because Agamemnon was the best of them all at casting the stick and yet his wife wasnt pleased about having him come to her bed although according to scientific accounts the individual's coefficient of expansion is not indicated by its withered state if you can trust experts even for the basic facts when they're sensitive about their own and don't know what a good female doctor ought to be able to divide her life well enough to put down in black and white that it makes a mighty big difference all other things being equal not because of longitude in itself which even male investigators can prove to be a minor factor as they lightly overlook the other dimension to arrive at the comforting conclusion that eminence is a purely symbolic indication of vanity like Sandy's who once long ago told me that when he was depressed and given over to thoughts of suicide he'd take a bath to restore his confidence or of anxiety like Newt's who's one guy I guess I don't have to worry about judging by his psychoanalytic

to vain artifacts.] At the moment he was unable to recall anything of his wife's quality but her skill and wisdom at motherhood.

All the same, as the family at last piled out with its usual raggety bumble Michael felt the small sad pain of a possible love's leave-taking added to the twinge of generally disappointed experience—even while unpleasantly persuaded that the eyes of the girl whose reserve he had stripped were at the end of the adventure all too alert to his pitiable indignities. Like a laundry woman herding children for her mistress, fussing and puffing in twenty fits, dressed at his worst, displaying the most unflattering aspects of his corpulence, he left her sight. Back to work, back at least to the cave of idols where he could prepare for working by shielding himself from just such chimerical temptations. To sum the whole: safe again, virtued by the scorn of a beautiful woman!

The Palm Sunday procession formed for its last leg on the corner opposite the manufactory of prosthetic devices and toiled its final threescore yards in the dusk now tender of an early evening. Away from the thoroughfare they heard the straggling chirps of sleepy city birds. The troubled heart of the psychopomp hung like a fluttering monarch butterfly at the interface of two opposed breezes blown to a standstill, one of which brought praise and thanksgiving upon the beloved upright head of his sweetmare wife for giving him miraculously more joyful comfort than any man with a bitter mistress lament but because the cross-sectional area is critical in applying frictive traction to the not so pleonastic little pricklet by way of the partitive genital when all is said and done and the psychic thrills have worn off and all moods averaged out so the aphrodisiact aint simply a product of area frequency and time nor can I put much stock in the pseudo-statistical proposition that in the variation between two limits of phase-state the lateral distension varies not only independently of the vector but also more greatly as if Hecuba sizes up a man at first sight I'd like to be her ghost-writer for a book on thlipsis because I dare say she's calibrated as many short-arms as any researcher though she did confess to Ruth of having always been too shy about her reputation to satisfy her curiosity about black men but leaving aside the excitement of anthropological novelty an afrodizzyact is probably nothing extraordinary especially among sensitive intellectuals it's just that Clovis happened to be a special case that fits the folklore which Othello obviously didnt believe for as Milton says the brain is the divine organ anyway without mentioning that it's common to both sexes but meaning that it's more critical in the overall scheme of a man's life than the divinity that doth hedge a king when they say every inch a king especially for small Napoleonic guys like Lytle King who must be pricks to work for making their own world-wide pyramids to stand on or Newt Cahners who trumps the world by psycholiterary analysis or any other

across the hall could justly expect. No elegantly groomed thorough-bred could match the beautifully simple pace that seemed so awk-ward when it was on the wrong track or ridden by fearful confusion. He began to conjure up the sex in her grace on the tennis court and the chessboard too. But suddenly she sneezed twice, harshly and vio-lently, in her unaccountable discon-certing peasant manner, as if in her sneezes she purposely reinforced the natural whickering rejection of a tiny tickling nasal itch with all the honking force of an otherwise sup-pressed vulgarity. Like someone's loud fart it always made the boys laugh and their father shiver. Then she yawned. Jonathan yawned, Mat-thew yawned, and even little Roger yawned. But Michael did not yawn; he trembled in the other breeze, for at her sneeze his sense of satisfaction gave way like sea-fog before an abys-mal gale of bonechilling dismay whistled up by play of mind:

The historical truth he sought certainly had a reference point somewhere in the present woman. He stole a glance at her tired face marked by traces of sweat that might have been tears. Strands of darkened brown hair had drifted to her cheek from temple or forehead and rays stood out behind as if they were like-charged filaments flying from each other in static tension. In-deed hers was the greatest force in his field; now his concern lay with her to the exclusion of all other sub-jects. But as the center of values and polestar to his nerves she walked be-side him so wrapped in bolt upon bolt of gauze contingencies that the

stub of a man who has to turn his entire self into one erection larger than anyone else's mere limb any-way there I was like some barely tolerable barnyard rooster with the dunghill all to myself because poor Pertelote had been too busy with her eggs to compare her Chanticleer with noble birds of prey until all of a sudden she must have sensed a shadow in the sky but as St Laurence says "A dwarf who brings a stan-dard along with him to measure his own size—take my word, is a dwarf in more articles than one" although all he's talking about is good chap-ters in a novel which I don't think is what Sarah means by calling Jack her Giant Joshua just between themselves according to Ruth and how can a wife think of such names if she's innocent of other men even Sarah unless she's just taking Jack's word for it but just to hear such things is enough to make Ruth be-gin to wonder even if she's no catherine the great and what about the time she pretended to be puzzled and amused but maybe though she told me about it in-genuously enough was really thrilled by the man she saw in an alley ostensibly pissing against a wall but no doubt intentionally ex-posing himself to passing ladies professing that she couldnt be sure whether it was hard or not despite her notion that "it seemed very big" but there was no doubt on that point in my dream when Jim turned away from a urinal to go make love to Lilian in the next room where Ruth was doing her sewing as he telescoped it out of his pants high as his chest sliding it up

excitement of unveiling her over-whelmed his fear of exposing an unequivocal point d'honneur. He began by trying to imagine other men's imagination of her favors, and particularly Sandy's craving for the reserved but imaginable privi-lege of her aphrodisia. Even in most tentative hypothesis the briefest un-completed acts of her imagination weighed on him with greater disqui-etude than the whole vast corruption of Christ's vineyard and struck him as a visitation no less shattering to his pride, as apocalyptic to the vis-ited one, than triumphant to the visitor. The agony of uncertainty drove him toward wildly divergent hazardings of irrevocable fact. With apprehension and avidity tumbling together in his chest he turned over the possibilities. . . .

Meanwhile Roger had chosen to keep himself awake for the last distance by going on foot, hand in hand with his peacefully forbearing mother. Without impatience Joseph slowed down to the pace of Mary and Jesus. The other boys had raced ahead to plunk themselves down on the front steps and wait for the keybearer. As Michael oblivious of his cumbersome lading hovered at Ruth's shoulder she put him off by beginning to hum. He gritted his teeth at this second familiar but unexpected jarring of his suddenly intensive observation. Looking away to recruit his tolerance he bit-terly refrained from spitting into the gutter with disgust, yet his motive was so urgent that soon he gallantly overcame his repugnance for this plebeian aspect of her natu-ral aristocracy and spoke to her the

with his fist like the radio antenna of a car yet no slenderer than a bull's in its succession of waxy tapers yet wait I think that's a rep-etition of the unforgettable one I had more than twenty years ago not long after I happened upon that cow-mounting in Lanesville before we moved to Cambridge which my genius has transferred to Jim from that muscular blond Enos kid in eighth grade I admired as the best short-stop and hitter in our ward long before I'd ever given a thought to phallic differentiation but in any case even with Jim it was as dis-torted as El Greco with far too little girth for the priapic image that you wouldnt think there'd have been any need for my upper mind to suppress at a time of life when that universal has become consciously fascinating all of which may tend to prove that indeed there was something sacramental under-lying both fertility and pleasure in neolithic ambisexual dromena which by the time of Euripides and Aris-tophanes was degraded through hierodulia and homoeroticism to the level of bawdry something hypersymbolically related to the special energy displayed by anti-thetical embryoes when they evert the primordial ventricle to extreme ectropic form but then again Greek vase painting versus Indian archi-tecture shows that an unwomaned cult prefers the elongated bull's pizzle to stout horsecock better suited to the vulvascular yen of an uninhibited queen and by the same token bulls perform no other ser-vice than on occasion to induce ges-tation in cows that must lactate for

more readily that he might put an end to her unseemly sounds. Thus from a dry throat the faltering owl made his first awkward trial. (In order to converse with her husband while Roger availed himself of the chance to make slow circles dangling from her hand she came nearly to a stop. For once Michael nursed no objection to her dilatory progress on the sidewalk and in fact scarcely noticed their situation.) "Well it's been a long disconglomerate day!" came out with false heartiness.

"I loved it!" She smiled with such bright gladness that she seemed suddenly cleared of all her own troubles fatigues and anxieties by the opportunity of his ostensibly casual attention. He was unprepared for this reiteration of the candid beauty that shook his purpose and almost erased the shadows from which he had worked out more than one statistical postulate. The same smile however he knew was smiled to other friends acquaintances and strangers, not all the time and not with aforethought but whenever any came up to her. He reminded himself that its splendid gladness was no telltale to her passions.

He said "Who would have thought the poor young bum we took under our wing would turn out to be a professional man? He's already climbing the thermometer."

She smiled again, effacing all traces of her hard day (much of it still to come), but he couldnt be sure whether it was for the subject he had introduced or simply for his apparently disinterested companionship. "Yes, isnt it wonderful!

men almost without ceasing so grotesquely hypertrophied that they seem a different species humbly inferior to their sons and never dream of fun for themselves whereas bovine males are sacrificed when men consider them of more oblatory worth than horses or cows that are merely more useful but in a catherine's court the stallion was king and if horses there had been bred to hypertrophy it would have been for the corpus cavernosum after all the average plowing of earth herself even nowadays in this country with horsepower to burn irresistible chemical force and rich black topsoil is no more than six inches it says in the Tribune though the length of our tickler may equal the depth of the share it's the moldboard that makes the furrow yet on the other hand I've heard of huge men doomed to a life of erotic discomfiture because theirs is as thick as a catsup bottle and they can't get into any woman at all except maybe some multiparous whore encountered by chance six thousand miles from home perhaps big gentle brutes capable of the most tender feelings while on a man's side never to reach the hilt must be much more distressing than the failure to touch bottom in fact it makes you wonder about Odysseus and Zeus and Apollo and Dionysus if not Hermes and Priapus what their classical key was maybe some standard of dimensions analogous to St Willie's when he insists that Jesus Christ was exactly six feet tall even if only six inches disregarding the sensuality of females in the belief that all a god's or hero's parts must

He's worked so hard all these years, he really deserves his success."

"Holy mackerel, he can't fail to make a lot of money with all the women patients that flock to him!" Michael insinuated in secretly serious jest. How does a man talk to his own wife the hardest woman to talk to without arousing her suspicions?

She lightly dismissed the point. "Oh he'll soon outgrow that kind of talk. —Wasnt it nice that we met them today? It's good to see that they're still together. I think both of them are straightening out, don't you? I liked her more this time. She's very brave."

Michael quoted her the English St Henry: 'It is, indeed, the idea of fierceness, and not of bravery, which destroys the female character.' And then he added: "She still needs a good beating. If she and I were in Congress together we'd probably vote the same way on ninety-nine percent of the things that actually came to a roll-call, but I wouldnt want to be on any of her committees. She'd make me sympathize with Republicans."

Ruth paid no attention to his typical complaints. "Well let's have them over to dinner sometime, just so they won't think you hate them."

He bit his lip to suppress a characteristic Michangelic reply which to such an obviously inappropriate proposal on another occasion might have been no sir those people bore me beyond curiosity or pity and you should know that I can't waste the time—assuming as usual that she wouldnt dare mention all the evenings and weekend afternoons he'd spent for the best

be perfectly proportioned at least all the recorded evidence of civilization seems to bear out the conclusion that living pricks if not stylized phalloi in most cases are no more distinctive as instruments of proximate sensation than the circumferential purses they fill in other words to put the best face on my ignorance I am now hoping to persuade myself that I have simply fallen into the phallacy of "extracted categories" in diagnosing like a specialist and then treating the complaint alone instead of listening to the real patient an infinitely more complex person who wants to be cured by palaver with Doctor Etwas who's quite understandably impatient being paid for pragmatic therapy not for mere analysis and has heard pretty much the same symptoms dozens of times before when he ignores the internal value or meaning of what she thinks in spite of the fact that she's the only one continually and totally present at her feelings as well as at whatever causes them yet all of us doctors are bundles of disparate categories ourselves and no matter how well made as an entity we may fail to meet the statistical norm in any one item the match to which in our patient may fall on the opposite side of the bell curve and ontogenic details often seem randomly distributed as for instance the lumen evolved for pillicocks is hardly adjustable to the heads of modern babies and after it's wrenched out of shape once too often the poor fuckee can sometimes hardly feel a thing if there isnt as much byplay as usually can be mustered only by

part of the last decade nine months out of the year listening to baseball or football on the radio without even washing the windows while he was doing so and inflicting upon the whole household endlessly repeating sounds of jejune and frenetic narration mindlessly expressive crowds and battering repetitive advertisements, all of which are extremely unpleasant to anyone not dumb enough to be interested. This time he preferred to find out what she was thinking, without warning her off or awakening doubt by an attitude too far out of keeping with his selfish pigheaded ways. He marveled at how she brazened out a complete disregard of the erotic past she and Sandy shared. How could she have forgotten that little kiss on the back of her neck if it hadnt been superseded by a guilty fugue? Perhaps it was only that she didnt remember telling him about it. But in order not to put her on guard he resisted his almost overpowering urge to directly interrogate the selections of her memory. The only safe way to continue the examination was to talk about the third party as if still equally acquainted to them both. He was also well aware that his opinions of Pig Ruth couldnt be expressed without using words that in Horse Ruth's ears would be wounding to humanity and therefore to herself. He trembled at the specific enormity of his suspicions; his whole body broke out with sweat he hoped was invisible in fear of exposing his distrustful jealousy or his sensitivity to the mere possibility that under certain conditions she could substi-

a new fucker and so our gender trying to catch up breeds bigger men every generation whose average growth of this extremity is not increasing quite as fast as the phylogenetic natal skull diameter but no man by taking thought can add a cubit to his stature and there's no Lamarckian hope for the heritage of lucky anomalies and meanwhile un homme moyen may need almost superhuman magic to compensate for his beloved's failing coarctation even though it's still all too easy for him to come and go with plenty of sensation before she's fully aware of being gorged and no matter how many times in succession he's able to charge and discharge the pelvic capacitor exciting and soothing the lining of her allure she may still go nervously unreplete all her life so intrinsically important is the means to her end just as her internal beauty turns his own mere relief into sacred libation since it's not enough for a woman to learn the psychic trick of neuroendocrine complementarity when she's always left dreaming of pleromatic solidity adoringly prolonged and followthrough seems to be just as critical here as in all other doings except the decapitation of a soft-boiled egg with a blow of your knife so that's the rub that maybe there's not enough rub left in married life even for the chastest matron but a man can't grow an annulet nor is it wise to just shrug off disappointment as her own fault for having demanded offspring so I suppose it's not fair to act like a dog in the manger about her sensual cultivation since as St Leo has Napoleon say the body's

tute another for himself. Cunningly he chose to put her to the test with the subject of emancipation. Ignoring her suggestion as if he'd been too preoccupied to hear it he said "I wonder what's the secret of her success with Sandy. She seems to have him well in hand. He'll be washing the diapers."

"Ruth must be very competent at her work. It's a shame she can't get a good job. She's not afraid."

"I guess she's a threshing machine in bed. She'll conceive with a scowl and bear her child 'like those that under hot ardent zeal would set whole realms on fire.' She'll be the Sam Adams of the lying-in hospital and make maternity into a revolution."

"It always is!" the present Ruth laughed. "But you must admit she's driven by a sense of justice."

"Families are beyond justice."

"Beneath it you mean?"

"Above it."

"You sound like Caleb speaking of tragedy:" she said, "'paradoxical antithesis of equity.' Did I get it right? I never know what he's talking about of course."

"Anyway it's easier to imagine her in childbirth than in honeymoon. She'll make it prove a point. Forty years ago she'd have been a tee-total firebrand virago of the Women's Continual Torment Union." [Jingoistic androgyne! I can see her as sea lawyer to the crew of LST 1066. Can't blame Sandy for wanting the solace of a woman who doesnt know all the answers. . . . These fucking bossy fe-persons never stop bulldozing long enough to fall asleep. Anything that hap-

merely a machine for living still must every father have been better hung to keep the undivided loyalty even of a wife who doesnt always care to cooperate with his generous and more or less indefatigable efforts to make the most of nature's gifts remembering that there were plenty of second-choice heroes at Troy not in all respects inferior to Achilles and Hector inter pares sed non primus should be good enough for husbandry and if I hadnt quit smoking for the sake of longevity I'd still sport the athletic lines of my myopic physique the appearance of which may enter into her sense of touch since nothing is but the brain makes it so I think if I walked to work every morning I could alter the Gestalt . . . [Michael deceives himself in refusing to believe that it's over-eating makes him fat in the wrong places, but his confidence in the basic body he had in the Navy is not misplaced. His arms below the elbow are still lean and muscular; his legs below the knee still shapely enough for a peruked courtier; under the round flesh of his face the skull is long. In his youth except for the defect of goggles he always passed muster as an average swain. Whatever shortcoming he may now fancy to detect in himself would be statistically average to an experienced observer or patient, but in any case he is tolerably able to overcome his normal handicap by paying more court to the hooded trigger that surmounts the gothic aperture than unusually gifted cocksmen are wont to do who can ignorantly trust to unaided anatomy for the desired ef-

pens inside them probably comes in clicks; and whether it ever clicks or not they probably jump out of bed before the poor guy's quite finished giving up his ghost. Now that one will be crowing over the domestication of her oaf.] "Woe unto the world because of its offenses, for it must needs be that offences come; but woe to that person by whom the redress cometh! When I'm not in her presence I can pity her courage."

"But don't you think she'll change now? Sandy will make a good father."

Michael decided to hazard another step. [She's always more clever than I allow for. Maybe she's reading my mind. The only place I can hope to get anywhere by talking to her is in bed but how will we ever get these damn kids to sleep?] "It's only her name he married her for. Can't be anything else."

Seeming to pretend not to have heard his archly mentioned bait she asked "Why do you think it's a mismatch?" [I didnt say it was a mismatch!]

But just then patience ran out of the two boys waiting on the steps who had been driven to distraction by the sight of their parents standing still in conversation paying no attention to anyone but themselves and showing no sign of a wish to return to the point of departure where food drink and bathroom were to be found. "If you don't hurry up we're going to ring the Topalis's bell!" Jonathan hissed in a stage whisper. The threat was well calculated to make the mother and father get a move on. Thereupon Michael's efforts

fect indirectly. Heretofore he has hardly applied his science.] . . . like Frederick the Great inspecting his troops on the parade ground I wish all men were born equal notwithstanding his additional lament that their breathing caused movement in close-order ranks he must have been driven to distraction by odd-size soldiers and likely he probably sent the overgrown ones across the border to Catherine the Semiramis of Russia who preferred brutes to delicate Russian gentlemen with aristocratic hands and feet but it's also said that the same personage wrote the French libretto for an opera—and so once more I find my mind wandering in demonstration of the plain fact that I have no stomach to face a simple truth when it takes me down a peg yet I keep circling it e g Prescott mentions the belief that not an apple but a banana tempted Eve the fruit forbidden because its "exuberant returns are so fatal to habits of systematic and hardy" life so what a nerve I've had to call myself sir Proudfit when sir bignoise small-piece would be more like it though she's never hinted at critical evaluation during my cocksure phases I must admit to wondering quasi-masochistically what it would be like to watch the cleavage by a mighty plowshare in my own lit à trois yet that's just the kind you could least expect your wife to forget when the little orgy's over it would have to be some foreigner some unassuming stranger we could both take to in a passing moment of friendship yet as impersonal as a donkey assisting my researches like

were directed toward his last ordeal of the excursion.

"I'll tell you later." was all he had time to say to Ruth, not knowing what he meant by the promise but intending to leave an opening for later renewal of his inquest. Meanwhile he found himself grotesquely elated at the prospect of a fascinating topic to talk to his wife about, something to make talking to her more important than reading any book. The longer his resolution was balked by family duties however the more prolonged his improbable hope that the day would be put to rest with some unpredictable explanation which would ease his heart once and for all. What such an explanation could turn out to be was beyond the perimeter of his imagination.

Each of the five Chapman plants was looking forward to rehabilitation in the family garden, which nevertheless because of its ugly familiarity was going to contract the mind and cloud the soul by recalling chronic troubles and discontents after a whole day of new impressions free associations and fresh emotions, even as it confirmed an inadvertent confidence in the stability of a domestic locus, because now all reasonable hopes for immediate amusement had been realized modified or disabused and no one except the mother flower had a good word to say for anything or anyone. The homecoming both called forth and oppressed without silencing the composite genius of male Chapmen, or rather their prevailing spirit which against the female's watchful endurance was

a sounding instrument it's all very well for Hermes to tell Apollo he'd fain couple with Aphrodite if need be tangled in the net of Hephaistos with all of Olympus looking on for I too might gladly teach with another's wife but this is my own self's one flesh and I full of jealousy both prudent and sordid but unlike the smith in having no peers yet he and I are both unsuccessful performing artists yes three's crowd enough for Ruth and me it introduces the universal heterophallic motif of which I can speak only as an interested virgin how strangely solipsistic must a cocksucker feel shortcircuiting a creature like himself or like the self he'd like to possess never missing the proper half to contain its eruption as if a woman without a woman's valence in that version of greek love the worshipper's sensation is probably more symbolic than sensual the long and the short of it is that the excited codpiece is normally erotic to both genders whereas the female's softest palate is too obscure to invite such ubiquitous imagery and a nearly uninterrupted phallicism must have fascinated spermwhaling seamen more than the suggestive blows and blowholes so few and far between but even as an involuntarily surrogate preoccupation Saint Herm was not at liberty to mention it or its own literally solipsistic substitute but homoerotic or not I couldnt stand the thought of Sandy getting inside my wife secretly I'd have to see it to believe it maybe everyman's a cryptofascinated quasihermaphroditic aspirant to this universal mystery with nothing

about to yell and whine or thump and bump and drag or fret and vex its way up the narrow crevasse into the tweendeck plateau of the second tier where it would bargingly reanimate the littered disorder of the lone cold articles that had been left behind reduced to homespun yearning for animal heat, as soon as the puffing reirritated father could put down his burdens and unlock the windowpaned street-door backed with white muslin stretched taut between brass rods top and bottom. This decorously curtained portal was the only article used in common by landlord and tenants. It was set into the bare white stucco box plainly off center with no windows to the right of it, as if the short side of the house contained warehousing space. This mitigating asymmetry suggested an architect's design at least of the facade; there was no other culture in the glaring streetfront surface of this cube that crowded three of the plat sides. Two narrow patches of hyperverdant grass flanking the concrete steps were protected from dogs and children by galvanized steel wire fencing supported by stout pipe frames. The one on the left (STAGE RIGHT) lay directly under the two parlor windows of the landlady whose husband didnt have enough leisure to crop the lawn as closely as a goat would have done in the old country. There was no other vegetation to tend or to curb. No trees or vines obscured the Topalis lot because the narrow driveway stage-right to the rear as well as the back yard itself was paved with concrete. A cinder-block garage invisible

gnostic about it a marvel of hydraulic mechanics and structural autonomy almost instantly erected without bones or rigging when the frictionless demon of mind alone simply closes off a body-valve to trap a column of incompressible fluid in anyman's monumental flourish a tower of flame brandished against entropy like the Tower and Flame Honor Society she belonged to on the Cal campus as if heat flowed by a suddenly applied prayer of prehistoric religion from the cool stem to the hot bowsprit while it lasts more resistant to deformation than the hardest muscle though never seeking opposition more recalcitrant or abrasive than parting lips altogether an unburdened column before it collapses the Greeks found that the height of a compressive member made of stone was limited to 18 diameters but phallic art varies with style rather than material yet in pictures when the ratio is too high for the stamina of real love's fennel stalk it's clear that the artist is not thinking of receptacles at all but stylizing the dick an sich without reference to its natural object in the flesh whose homologous though inverted part is heated by similar venous congestion to concentrate and release blood-power when it can be contained no longer which fascinates me only at times like this since I have no general interest in physiology but I doubt that in my insanely clinical obsession I'm any more heteroclitic as a mutant of the ur-woperson than any other hardworking monogamous man without riches albeit an indelicate cliteroclitic phallopomp as di-

from the front door housed under its flat false-fronted gravel roof, to which the cats of the neighborhood could find no access, Tom's pink and white cream-puff fin-tailed Pontiac sedan. But the Topalis pride was embarrassed by an uninhabited and dilapidated dark gray wooden house next door insufficiently screened by rank shrubbery and a ragged jungle of trees. Off right (STAGE LEFT) a windowless brick mass met the dun concrete sidewalk in the clean straight line of intersecting perpendicular planes, guaranteeing the Topalis property against sloppy neighbors on the east side. The back of this commercial building officially situated on Teleology Lane bounded their real estate no more than a foot from their own east wall and exceeded it in height; yet the house was rather favorably aligned in respect to the solar system, for once the morning sun rose behind Medical Hill, soon after clearing the distant elevations of the skyline, short and brief were the shadows cast upon it from that direction. Because the Chapmans' rent had not yet been raised to what the traffic would bear in a seller's market, the Topalis spirit kept an upper hand over the Chapman spirit; and because the dirty windows of the second floor as seen from the street rarely matched each other in the level of their shades or displayed with their curtains the tidiness of either the funereally crocheted plum drapery at their ground floor counterparts or the demurely starched white lace at the top story where dormers once had been (for the house owed its spank-

vided in mind as St Willie has us for engendering art in short a bisexual externalized female like some brawny Sappho devoid of poetry anyway it may explain why men are usually far more avid than their wives for the graphic details of a mate's infidelity in principle I have nothing against homoeroticism in fact along with autoerotic harmlessness it should be rewarded with special tax deductions for mitigating the suicidal success of mankind's fertility-worship at least in the male case without entire loss of recto/verso sexuality seeing that all men are women it's only my insensibility to the whole of a male person and my temperamental attraction to the whole of a woman that determine these my wandering speculations and so I begin to understand why a caliburn can't be dissociated from the entire armament by a woman selecting a knight for her favors whereas to me there have been no beautiful men in my whaling ships or locker rooms especially in consideration of speech and behavior as components of beauty Kane was no Glaukon and Abbie no Ganymede in my eyes and how different from Clovis's the delitescent prickette of a woman which in truth there's little opportunity to admire indeed the more pressing your search the further it retreats there must be something more orgulous or at least outstandingly corniculate to make a universal cult certainly for a form of unhooded statuary yet if it werent for our incidental encounter and the scattered hints it recalled I like most unenflamed civilians would

ing clean lines to the fact that it had been converted from a physiognomy of shabby clapboards with Mansard curves surmounting the second floor to its present style of unadorned squarecut cardboard, which but for the raspy texture of its crust would have reflected all the light that struck it.) Despite Michael's exceptional success in avoiding bad books thanks to more important demands upon his time as well as to a wide range of preemptive preconceptions, his absolute success in avoiding bad pictures by seeing no plastic art at all, and his partial success in avoiding bad music by staying away from congregations as much as possible, he was totally unable to avoid bad architecture. In consequence of this necessity he was prejudicially inclined to dismiss from his pantheon of muses the art nominally responsible for the look of houses. While he didnt disagree with theorists that domestic architecture like the life supposedly reflected therein should be generated informally by freewill occupations and protections rather than prescribed to guide the behavior of inhabitants, he had long since ceased to evaluate his residence in aesthetic terms. "Functionally modernized it myself!" the landlord said to new spectators. Ruth had nothing against it—as apartment buildings went—seeing that it couldnt qualify as a real home. As for Michael's delight in the beauty of his country's artifacts: "Four-fifths of our energy is spent in the quarrel with bad taste, whether in our own minds or in the minds of others." was what the truest Irish

find that most primitive maquette a ridiculous misdirected object of meditation especially when I'm gnawed by truly essential hunger of the stomach and harried by three clamorous dependents innocent of money-worries a purely sensory organ so shy of observation and so arrested in development that you can't easily believe in its urgent function as a microswitch to satiety with no more personal distinction than the limbic lobe at the other end of the woman's spine and wouldnt be tremendously interesting at the Topsfield Fair where what's wanted is the whole animal as best of breed in a functional beauty contest not just standard parts incorporated into all models as essential but interchangeable though it may be that my experience is too limited to prove me a connoisseur but scientifically speaking there are directly related apolaustic reasons for her gross discrimination of phallic rivals—but beyond jestful play of mind all this lascivious maundering in technological anatomy is a game of solitaire to evade what may be the truth because although I may be stewing about something no more important to her than my double chin bulging eyes yellow toenails or bad breath of which I'm negligently unaware and although the pen is mightier than the sword I know Sandy's always been in love with this Ruth so the question really reduces itself to why at least after a few years and maybe only recently she succumbed to him and perhaps also to others once the maidenhead of adultery was rent I

aristocrat always said. Michael made every effort to reduce such waste. As far as one function was concerned, the protection against fear offered by a house in the marches between poverty and respectability lay more in prestige than in security, for the second-floor back sleeping porch was fastened against marauders only by a three-inch slide-bolt rottenly socketed in worn softwood. The front entrance however was controlled by an interactive communication system. Three signal buttons punctuated the scant trim on the left side of the door each within a weathered brass frame enclosing a label aesthetically proper to its correlative dwelling unit. As Tom Topalis had done the wiring himself his name led all the rest, typed by hand and covered with a strip of buckled isinglass: "Mr. and Mrs. A. Thomas Topalis, PROP." Next under it—by Freudian slip in the amateur electrician's decoding of the distinguishing colors with which the concealed wires were insulated— came the third floor's fancy insert in italic type cut from a calling card: "Miss Hecuba Jones". And at the bottom—for the middle floor— hastily lettered in faded pencil, to the perpetual annoyance of both Topalises: "CHAPMAN". Without trial and error a literate visitor even very late at night by light of the street lamp could sound the intended chime in any of the apartments without disturbing the other two; but the marvel to Tom (who'd never had to take a physics course to get his night degree in Communications a k a Public Relations was

havent forgotten the time she told me there was more to true love-making than a sneeze together which was possible with a stranger she also said that half an hour melting ice with referred sensation isnt all a woman desires and it's well known that there are times when they all would like to be helved without ceremony by the first tom dick or harry to come along and lately she's had no more to sing in my praise than something about being as hard as a hammer which can be attributed to any midget though in that respect I must be second to none far too much of the time just a peg to rivet together the softer flesh of everyman and his woman as long as it lasts and sometimes a four-penny nail does as well as a gandy-dancer's spike she no longer says anything else about the shortarm that the sleeve should grip and palpitate against before it slips away in what should be a lovely aftermath of the outcome and she's left vaguely disconcerted almost like a man when his climactic foison is deprived of snug loculation the old story of follow-through that seems academic to young athletes not understanding that you can't take a good swing at anything if you're not concerned with graceful satisfaction in the phase that follows your immediate purpose and with her the plenitude of those sensations seems to count more than foreplay if I've hit the ball at all and in the early days when once or twice she confessed to missing in me a tinge of violence I laid her hint of discontent to extraneous troubles but

that upon hearing the diapason of three different chimes in an undeveloped melody one could press a responsive button inside one's donjonkeep and throw open the portcullis without missing anything in the hearth cinema. On the second floor this device to unlock the outer door was mounted out of children's reach; whenever Jonathan was left in charge of the Chapman household, or when Matty insisted on helping out a mother or father occupied in the bathroom, the active reflex to a request for admission—after a dash to the front window to look down and characterize the applicant—was likely to be a pounding descent of the hall stairs—unless a heavy chair was dragged across the formerly polished hardwood floor as gratingly to Topalis sensibility as if it harrowed the smoothly frosted plaster of the ceiling below. Inasmuch as there was no key to their elevated outdoor postern the Chapman ensemble couldnt help using the common sally port for all their sallies and retreats, little as Michael and Ruth liked to exacerbate the Topalis spirit, anxiously and ineffectively attempting to head off every thump of the boards and every smear of the stairway wallpaper once bright with its large flowers. Even though the boys were taught to use the back door for exiting and aditing when a parent was at home it was diurnally used only by Semiramis, when her will intuitively coincided with one of the Chapman's.

The lecherous landlord was a quiet solemn man no older than Michael who during his bitter years in the infantry had saved enough of

now I see that even then she'd have liked to have her wave break upon a massier rock I fear that momentum increased by velocity and duration can never fully meet the want of perfection a woman may be never so sympathetic but you can't expect her to accept a compromise of the one bliss that is supposed to compensate her for the unselfish paucity of all her other satisfactions without some kind of psychic if not physical recourse sooner or later so it's the very least of offenses when in our dance she metempsychosizes me with thrilling masks her meretricious tact is not to dream away my beloved face but to envisage me as supersufficient for her absolute recreation and thus alas have I discovered the proximate cause and insufficient reason to pity her for finally being driven unintentionally from necessarily faulty prosopopeia to an acceptance though probably far less analytical than mine of a seldom stated natural law governing wedded romance when allusion and metaphor can no longer maintain the reverberations of such specific nerves as I have been deceiving these many years for the matronly flower whether traumatized or temporarily dilated by passion begs blunter visitation than the rosebud demands even as the wingless hunter buzzing as loudly as ever makes it his business to overlook the effects of weathering still even the most genteel gentleman likes a lady who welcomes him firmly though of course not so tightly as to set him off half-cocked which

his pay and travel allowances to put with his bonus and buy half a house. By now he was sallow and bald, his face lined with worry and confused ambition, his eyelids puffed with lymph like softened walnut shells, and not a bit too lively for his plain dumpy wife, widow of a fruit merchant with enough cash for the other half before she married the sad veteran younger than herself. But Tom had already been around the fringes of almost any minor racket you could name, at least in his mental speculations. And anticipating a great flood tide of African upstarts determined to expand their beachhead on the eastern shores of the Bay he had been quietly trying for two years to sell his property at a price commensurate with the creative pains he had devoted to it, and profitable enough to double his net worth, a scheme that could be realized only by finding a rich black buyer of the utmost courage and discretion and by consummating the deal before his neighbors suspected anything. He confided in Michael whom he assumed to be a pinkish but sly niggerlover willing to receive a black prospect and show him the insides of his castle without tipping off the watchful eyes of the restrictive convenanters who had vowed to yield the eastern end of the street only over their dead bodies or those of any real estate broker in town who ever expected to do business with white hopes, not understanding that his egghead tenant had no great relish for having his rent raised by a black landlord whose new market would

may be more annoying than the limerick interruptus of the once a young man from kildare who fondled his girl in a chair on the forty-third stroke their furniture broke and his pecker went off in the air and such an aludel works best with neither too much nor too little vacuum you don't have to be a rapist to want some resistance to your prying and there's less fun in tillage without digging old Stanski from Dubuque told me soon after we left the States "the old place don't feel like home no more" the radioman I worked for younger than I am now his wife had had a quick war-baby and he was surprised at the after-effect not married much more than a year and already pretending to laugh about the problem but in those days I didnt know enough to pay any attention to middle-age mechanics which is just as well because a young buck looking for loose or semidetached fish even if he's filling in for an exceptional husband doesnt have to concern himself with return engagements and their rising threshold of expectation this worry isnt entirely my obscene imagination because although I have put it out of my mind as if it were an absurd dream it wasnt long ago she told me she didnt seem to feel me as much as she used to her tone was apologetic and puzzled when we were walking home from the movies extremely amorous with each other and equally eager to keep trying nothing daunted by the odds it must have gone well that night if I was able to dismiss her remark so easily like some Keats deceived by a re-

bear twice as much as a subprofessional Democrat could tolerate, or for suffering irregular musical families above and below to take the place of pussyfooted Jones and clandestine Topalises. However Mike said nothing to discourage Tom because the secret cooperation tacitly expected of him was worth at least ten dollars a month in rent as a present advantage, and he counted on an examination of his shabbily inhabited apartment to dishearten any prospective purchaser white yellow brown or black in considering the price his landlord was holding out for. Tom's B S degree had been laboriously procured for the sole purpose of getting him out of the scrounging class into respectable business, but no one yet was willing to hire him for work he could admit to. In a mood of promiscuous desperation he had once inquired of Michael about bookselling with the hint that he envied anybody's steady income. Generally he occupied himself with small deals unknown and big deals deferred. Thus it was that to a house where hardly any letters were written came a bewildering diversity of mail, chiefly printed matter in response to inquiry coupons provided by newspapers magazines and previously mailed printed matter, mostly related to independent salesmanship or personal investment opportunities.

The lettercarrier slid consignments for all three spirits through the same horizontal slot cut so low in the door that he had to bend down to do it even from the lowest step of the stoop. Ten seconds later Mrs Topalis on the inside would

mission of his phthisis there are always so many variables of mutual condition that can account for changes in symptoms and so many unexpected new twists of sweet rediscovery that after a few years you learn to grow forgetful of what seem passing imperfections yet it's now apparent that the disparity between maiden and nulliparous wife is hardly more pronounced than the graduation to initial motherhood but multiparity makes a further difference and it's not a lady's sixth husband but her sixth son who brings the family's call for piston rings it makes you wonder about Aphrodite after all the Erotes she bore unless female immortality confers perfect elasticity some husbands of mortals apparently yearn for Geisha girls by the time their wife has had a couple and ponder the physical fitness of machines for living wedded to each other one of fixed dimensions but the other worn by life no doubt Hephaistos like a functional architect started his design of Pandora from the inside so she must have made a pretty nice wicket for Epimetheus even after an eon or two but male donkeys having once mated with their own kind never again much like to mount a mare it's nicer for a stallion begetting hinnies in tea houses but no mate and make have ever found a potion for adaptive opsimorphogenesis or a condiment for jaded sensoria and woe is me that to her I am every year less sedative so after all there seems little to credit in allometry after all such small jaws crowded her teeth which had to be straightened before she could

squat to gather all the mail that had been delivered, scrutinizing each piece with counterintelligent interest. She always placed the Chapman yield next to the left wall on the fourth tread of the hall stairs and Miss Jones's one level higher on the right. A recent innovation by the Republican administration ostensibly to help absorb Post Office Department overhead made it profitable for advertisers to send a broadside or monograph to every OCCUPANT of an area without the trouble of determining proper names; otherwise none of these three occupied dwelling units would have been on a single mailing list in common. The Chapman kids if they had been taught anything at all about their social responsibilities had learned from the earliest age not to tamper with the U S Mail. But there was no delivery on Palm Sunday. Climbing the steep narrow stairs Michael reminded himself that Harmon Sandys had devoted a whole day of his tireless brawny youth to lugging Chapman books and furniture up those risers after having helped shoulder the same all the way down a steep wooded trail from the romantic house to a rented truck in that deep glen on the other side of the hills.

The reboant family hoarse with loud whispers helped itself climb step by step. The ground floor was as silent as ever but though the proprietor was absent much of the time no one could ever tell whether or not his lady lurked shrouded with cushioned secrecy in some undeterminable inner room, so low did she keep the sound of her ceaseless television shows. Where do

believe that the kids in school would take her into their circle so she had a long adolescent acquaintance with that kind of sorrow when I came along to trump all the suitors of her late-revealed beauty and persuade her that she had forever left behind the frustrating side of sex but I now see that she remembers the early Sandy and his charms including the impression he made on her belly when they danced together even after we were married when I was the one diligently tutoring her crannies yet like a rancher who can't see beyond the end of his nose I gave no thought to protecting my prizewinner against predators I would not heed the books Chaucer and all but thought I could make a heifer who wanted to be a milch cow into a lifelong winner of blue ribbons I didnt aim to cultivate her taste just for some cupidinous mule of a dentist to come along and take her measure so that now she can make invidious comparisons why this very day she said I was fat in the right place which means she's thinking along those lines I know damned well she's always curious whether or not anyone else has exploited her interest she contemplates the possibility I can tell from that dreamy look of hers even if the affair with Sandy never went beyond the feel of him through two sets of clothes she never quite forgot the impression but all things considered I doubt that Sandy's any great lover he's got too high a turnover and mark you furthermore his wife who hasnt even once borne a child doesnt manifest

they go when absent, this somber couple of melancholy mien? Who can know what they ever are up to, singly or together, Orthodox or foul? No visitors are ever seen to enter their dark abode. [But I hear through Ruth from Hecuba that Tom longs for the illicit. Apparently to his astonishment she won't have him. Is he a snake accustomed to pitiless success with some horrifying hypnotic glower to fascinate the birds? Or is it that the slow nictation of his heavily hooded eyes seduces women in pity for his jaundiced sorrows? There can be no doubt about his Balkan lusts. Is he still attempting Ruth? The man once softly boasted without moving his twisted snickering lips that in the Army he was called Long Tom Topalis the Sneaky Greek, and like a fool I passed that amusing confession on to my wife. Yes the rent is too low for comfort. . . .]

During the expectant lull on the landing while Michael fished for the key to their sandwiched flat he managed a few more words with Ruth. "You must be very tired, honey pot."

"It's been a wonderful day. Thank you for taking us."

"You did most of the work. It's my fault we're so late. We took too long getting to the zoo. I got it confused with Golden Gate Park and took the wrong route out of the Ferry Building. We got back to the Key Terminal in half the time."

She laughed at herself with unfeigned insight. "No wonder I didnt seem to see anything twice! But it was doubly educational for the boys."

an adoration of him anything like Dido's and it may be that with patient understanding caresses even Caleb could do as well as that clumsy boor fie my lady like me whose roving eye is far less chaste you should have allowed us more time for necessity's inventions we arent a peculiar couple for countless wives have had larger broods and less to gnaw on too besides since researchers still argue about whence stems your ecstasy I hope it remains an open question women themselves when adjured to objectivity can't distinguish one subjective cause from another god forbid that one like that pig should ever discriminate even in flagrante delicto the barb from its barbette notwithstanding that the world's art and all its frank talk emphasizes volume in the formula for crucial action where distance time and frequency are also variables of the total displacement in which I find my consolation however undetermined the empirical value of this venereal mathematic may seem to women it keeps me in the running and anyway oversimplification is the least of my concerns because they seldom understand functional relationships or at least are primly laconic and maybe are glad to be confused about what's going on which I suppose is a good thing considering the trouble they've brought into the world with some abuse of reason always on the end of their tongue but knowing less about themselves than they do about us especially at the peak of fertility when they can suck unobstructed semen all the

"I wish we had a dog!" cried Matty.

"—dog!" echoed from Roger's thesaurus.

"Why don't we have one?"

Jonathan corroborated impromptu:

> "Not a dog
> not a rat
> —just a little kitty-cat!"

Michael's outward eyes suddenly opened. Bending to open the door with his key he blushed at his insanity, he listened again to the real world around him, the world of love and trust. He burned with the humiliation of his lewd folklore and cacoethical science. Her madness is noble, mine is base. But restoration of sanity's social perspective relieved the most shameful of deadly sins, making way again for work and pride.

way to the navel and all the sooner when every local nerve has been brought into play at the very beginning rogered by an overgrown—

6] Oh my God my God not a sterile mule but a treacherous donkey! Unobstructed sperm is not something for the open mind to play with you fatuous worker of words making fun of your anxiety as if it were some vulgar farcical jealousy you jackass manqué you smug clerk of the works can't you see the most serious part of your game? Stop trying to conceal a cuckold's worst anguish, the stork's old vengeance for adultery. All the other pain is puny. Don't try to avert the ultimate destruction of your tranquility by explaining away the teleology of all their giddy thrills and forgettable sneezes. Lovers can make babies too. Roger my own baby son Roger!

{*Postulants only:* GO TO ITEM (56) MS.06.0, Antilog 1: Tenement, page 697.}

(56)
MS.06.0

T H E
R A B B I T
W A R R E N

PROLEGOMENA TO ANY FUTURE METAFICTION THAT
MAY BE ABLE TO PRESENT ITSELF AS AN ART

Antilog 1

(Tenement)

The original rooms of the Rabbit Warren must have been so many times subdivided that the tenants of the run-down chateau were numerous enough standing together to pack the noontime shadows of the oaks in front or lying in the moonlight each with a guest to flatten the stubbly grass within the great oval made by a vestigial carriage drive. It might have served as barracks for a regiment of fencibles guarding the eastern slopes of the Bay, or before the latest remodeling as general headquarters of the Western Sea Frontier. Half the shutters of the hill-mounted gray pile mansarded with ragged slates and patched windows had fallen to the ground. It was undoubtedly one of the largest wooden gogmagogs ever built before the San Francisco earthquake to rival the urban manors on Nob Hill across the broad waters. Owing to unchecked shrubbery and all the capricious addenda of little porches entry-ways and outside stair

697

turrets that obscured the already interesting lines laid down by a liberal Victorian architect the double-L shape of the ground plan was difficult even for the most audacious prowler to abstract. And no one but the rent collector had opportunity to get the gist of its present internal layout or to detect the erstwhile parlors drawing rooms libraries galleries pantries and great highceilinged bedrooms, for even if you knew how to visit a dozen scattered tenants by their several and alternate routes you'd have no more notion than an Athenian maiden in the labyrinth designed by him who made the wooden cow for Pasiphae what lay on the other side of windowless walls in corridors averaging no more than three feet in clearance which you followed by countless rightangle turns and a few of greater or less degree, or under the squeaking floor that on any story went up and down steps of various count without any structural logic discernible even by such an inquisitive visitor as Michael Chapman, sometimes as if ascending and descending the miscegenated gothic ceiling of a Doge's chapel that had been filled to the peak with passageways and erratic staterooms similarly pitched beneath your feet.

None of the steep shafts of staircases intended for breathless servants connected more than two floors, and none was likely to match in elevation or plan the one you'd have to find if you were seeking or leaving someone like Caleb on a floor above the second. Looking downward from an unmarked door hinged inward to the right it might wind in sinistral squares or gyres to another unmarked door opening to the right outward and facing a different quarter of the compass from that of the upper. In that case any attacking force of righthanded swordsmen or guntoters would have had the greatest difficulty in storming from within a handful of dexterous amateurs on an upper level who were able to distinguish for defense the crucial portals randomly placed in the long rambling confusion of congruent doors to apartments or branch corridors, or blocked-off doors used to piece out permanent partitions, and those to common bathrooms or waterclosets likewise unmarked, for each such stoutly hung panel (painted as brown as the formerly varnished floors and wainscot, darker than the walls and ceilings that were tanned with a uniform deposit of airborne dirt) made a pavis as sturdy and opaque as any that you could bear the weight of, and on the stair itself twisting downward counterclockwise the freedom of your fighting arm would have been doubled by a corresponding disadvantage to the marauder, or indeed firefighter.

But Caleb had not as many friends as there were staircases down to the second floor, and in any case the assault would have been mounted by way of his windows, and at one of them, which was in a plane perpendicular to the other, no scaling ladder would have been required, for outside his primary room where the bed and all his other furniture were placed (the other being no more than an old linen closet opened out as a cramped kitchen with very narrow fenestration) he was lucky enough to share one of the fire-escapes that an owner long ago had been ordered by law to install here and there along the back walls like dangling strings of lifeboats on a crewless ship full of careless passengers. When Michael examined this safety system—and he even used the exposed framework once or twice to climb up and frighten Caleb with a knock on the glass next to the table when for some reason or other the young fire-stoker wasnt spending an evening-off at the Chapman place—he said he doubted that the authorities had considered the actual subdivisions of this elaborate cote for wingless doves even at the time of low population density when ordinances for the mandatory fixture were applied to the rambling structure, as if the formula concerned itself exclusively with linear feet per capita and not at all with the existential situations or circulation of tolerably agile occupants. As a lucky beneficiary of the inequitably designed fire escape Caleb had felt safe from burglary by virtue of the fact that he had nothing that anyone would want to steal, while handily provided with other means of egress in case of attack by aggrieved fathers enraged husbands or discarded rivals.

It would turn out that in a year of living there (with neither fire nor earthquake) he'd have no need for these advantages. In the Warren itself he found no companionship. The few female tenants he encountered did not excite his indefatigable appetite. Along with such disappointment, and deeper doubt about his unique struggles, he suffered indifferently the tolerable inconvenience of rattles drafts and cockroaches in his crazy little aerie.

One Sunday afternoon before Caleb went off to work Michael brought Jonathan and Matthew over to see the place, so important did he think the image of a free man's life in their early education, and Ruth with Roger had asked to come along. "How do you ever move furniture up these stairs and around these corners?" was the housewife's foremost question.

But it was at the Chapman flat—so much less distinguished yet so much more spacious sunny comfortable and even clean—that Caleb was fed and sheltered on many a Wednesday evening, the day he always shaved. Though he yearned for time alone with the father he was generally adopted by the family, all members of which strove for his attention. Without the least evidence of impatience he read stories to the kids while waiting for Michael to get home from work, or taught them games. Sometimes he helped Ruth shift heavy objects or put up curtains, or performed other acts of service that the husband abhorred. Thus he was welcome to all parties in the house despite his sometimes untactful teasing of the kind of life that was led there. He was appointed uncle, and the youngest child he dubbed Jolly Roger.

After hearing his wry accounts of aesthetic hardship at the Warren, where he was disinclined to lie in the semi-public tub even though he was obliged to use one of the showers every morning to remove the coal dust that augmented the irreversible grime of the facilities, the Chapmans invited him to have a bath whenever he liked in their cleaner enamel howsoever cluttered. Whenever he did so, usually in the late reaches of

Wednesday afternoon, the boys pressed upon him an armful of boats and other floating objects to supplement those that ever remained on or inside the edges of the family tank. Jonathan's sailing sloop was the most honored toy. Fatuous in the slack of his own home economics Caleb chode Ruth for worrying over what the master of the house might think about trivial states of disorder, and the master soon ceased hinting that a guest (especially a gentleman) should wash the tub after a sooty soaking.

In fact with some justice the young knight was more offensive than otherwise to his king in domestic matters, losing no opportunity to chaff him about having been waited on all his life or served by institutions and still knowing little about the plainest cookery, whereas he himself could already shift well enough and was able to profit from Ruth's simplest culinary advice. The case against Michael was overstated but he let it stand, frankly remarking when Ruth was out of the room that a reputation for self-sufficiency would only expose him to broadened responsibility.

But it is also true that Caleb furthered his lord's appreciation of the thought and skill for which the queen was daily called upon. The visitor, who brought wine or ice cream, having done his duty with the kids usually helped Ruth clean up after the meal.

"Uncle Cabe, Jonathan wants you to come and play chest!" Matthew called. "I want to learn too. Teach me all the brooks and ponds!"

"I'll be right in. Help him set up the board. I want to talk to your mother for just another minute." And then turning to her as he dried a plate with the dish towel: "Michael ought to give the kids more attention instead of listening to the sports news."

"He thinks you'd do well to get interested in football and baseball. Maybe he wants to see that you're punished for freedom from American culture! —He calls it freedom. It's a good thing for us he can't be home Saturday afternoons to listen to the Cal games!"

"He's hoping to foist his mania off on me."

"Doesnt the baseball season begin pretty soon? That's almost every night! But it sounds a little nicer. I know some old names from the World Serieses . . . like Joe DiMaggio. Now Michael's enthusiastic about Mickey Mantle. He says the Yankees would be the best for you to get started with; they break records every year. He loses interest in teams that don't win."

"I can see the romance of foot-pained heroes like Philoctetes and DiMaggio, especially when they're famous for grace and skill."

"I've heard about a pianist who lost an arm in the war. Some composer wrote a piece for his other hand." Ruth was amused to find herself groping in the past for analogies she scarcely understood. "My father said Babe Ruth had spindly legs."

"That's different. He was never known for his running or fielding. Michael calls the Babe Ruth tradition gross sentimentality. Not much like the bullfighter who compensated for weak legs by inventing the classic style of footwork that made him number one in all of Spain, the standard for everyone's style."

"Football sounds to me almost as evil as bullfighting. It's frightening to hear those roars off the hillside in Berkeley."

"Well let's hope he doesnt fall for professional football. He could waste as much time on that as on all the rest put together."

"I don't so much mind the time he spends on politics. I wish I could understand it better. Why does he hate Nixon more than some of the others like Knowland?"

"Calls him the dysphonious man. None of the wiseacre journalists seem to see through him, the fools. They think he's only partially phony like MacArthur or Taft."

"Well there's no use getting furious about it. Now that you're eligible have you registered to vote?."

"Oh yes. I used to think there was no difference between Democrats and Republicans, since we can't have either aristocracy or socialism. But now thanks to Mike I know that it's not policies but values that make the basic difference. The Democratic Party is no better than it should be but it's the fair-ground for everyone who sees through the Republican smokescreen of individualism. Mike's the only one I take advice from."

"I always vote the way he tells me to. I know he's wise about things like that. Can you explain what he means by 'regulatory commissions'?"

—"Uncle Cabe! Are you coming? Roger wants you to draw him another skull and crossbones!"

{*Postulants only:* GO TO *Log 1* hereinafter, page 726, first column.}

Antilog 2

(Symposium)

Jack and Michael both liked to visit Caleb at the Warren as if they were bachelors visiting their friend at the Inner Temple, though there were no scouts or gyps to serve the gentlemen. One Wednesday evening Jack made a salad there, adding distinction to Caleb's simple viands. Michael came to dine with them without stopping at home after he left the shop. All three smoked cigars after dinner. The elders looked upon Caleb with approval for refraining from cigarettes as long as he remained sober. Michael was prepared to pay dearly for staying up late, and so stated. As there were only two serviceable chairs Caleb sat upon the bed with his back against the wall and his ankles crossed. The soles of his feet were close to the center of their circle. The wine was gone. They settled down to a new bottle of Scotch. They'd had their fill of beer before the meal.

Jack explained a subject he had broached to Caleb before Michael's arrival. The director of the Berkeley radio station who was in Jack's bookbinding class wanted him to take part in a Yeats festival that was to be held on the local FM airwaves. One night Jack would read and comment on a lot of the poems, another night join some other poets in reading verse of their own inspired by Yeats. He'd later give a talk on Yeats's gnostic interests.

"Boy there's a program to hit the East Bay right in its lunar plexus!" Michael grunted.

"I told the guy about Caleb's paper and he's very interested in getting him in a special colloquium with some others to talk about Yeats's idea of the theater. We're even going to get paid something for our contributions. But this highminded young man refuses the invitation! Thinks it's casting pearls before swine."

"It's not that at all!" Caleb protested. "I'm no connoisseur. I'm merely carrying on the Rhymers Club tradition of sticking to emotion that has no relation to any public interest! Everyone makes out tragedy to be one of Yeats's sub-specialties, mentionable only after magic and Irish politics. As if it's about as important as symbolic logic to Whitehead's organic philosophy!"

"Well we can't ignore his supernaturalism the way you and Michael do. It's as plain as the nose on his face. Would you have us skip all the lyric poetry too? But here's your chance to criticize the scholars! We're not asking for emotion. That's for us poets!"

Caleb was silenced by the critical emotion in conflict with his gratitude for Jack's aid and respect.

"It'll start your reputation." Jack continued to urge. "Scholars writers and critics listen to that radio station!"

"I'm not a poet and I'm not a critic! I'm a janitor. —Anyway I don't believe in broadcasting."

"Even Yeats himself spoke on the B B C . " Michael said.

"But all alone. He didnt have to share the time or defend himself against experts or explain himself to journalists. It wasnt a community education affair. Besides, he had done his work. I havent even begun mine."

Michael mediated between the two friends who were his own friends for different reasons, but his tone to Caleb was fondly ironic. "For Jack and me there'd be special savor in consumers hearing you argue the theory of tragedy that Yeats might have held to. But you should be explaining it to St Willie himself. He's one of the few readers worth writing for, though I say it whose kind of mind he abhors as much as the smiling and clicking sewing machine he dreamt about with horror."

"Except you don't smile!" Caleb couldnt help pointing out. —"But we don't hear his talk and he shouldnt hear ours. Writing is the only proof for him and us."

Caleb's interlocutors were given pause by the unintentional effrontery of his last remark. Hastily he continued: "They'd have scholars from the faculty to lacerate my constatations! When I read aloud I sound like a

Chicken Little, and when I argue I'm tongue-tied with enthusiasm or rage. Who wants to be ridiculed?

"—Listen to this." Caleb picked up a book he'd been reading and repeated this quote from Francis Bacon: "'For those whose conceits are seated in popular opinions need only but to prove or dispute; but those whose conceits are beyond popular opinions have a double labor: the one to make themselves conceived, and the other to prove and demonstrate.'"

"Yes," said Michael "that's one difference between advertising and literature."

"All broadcasts are comic: I can't communicate."

"That's an enthymematic statement if I ever heard one!" said Jack, apparently not at all offended by Caleb's rejection of his help. "But since I've read your essay I know what you mean." He laughed at Caleb's reactionary attitude. "I suppose it's true that if you're both going to correct Yeats you'd better do it in writing. For my part I like creation without toil. In my B B C talk I'll quote you both passim as my George Gissing and Villiers de l'Isle-Adam!

"—Mike, I'm very sorry you never got to give your last dance lecture."

"I'm sure it wasnt missed. My performances always go as if the king were present: there's never any clapping. And the very effect increases the effect, as Rousseau says quoting Montesquieu: in my case that's negative feedback. It would have been taken as anti-feminine anyway. The people around here have no sense of irony, as Caleb says. And to think that the church once opposed dance because it seemed to mock the agony of Christ! Probably the same reason it has opposed female orgasm. Of course ethologically speaking it's true that human dance is irrelevant behavior; but if it mocks anything it's courtship, by deferring not just indefinitely but forever the purpose of allurement. Our favorite poet loved old John O'Leary who was willing to go to jail and die for Ireland but refused to commit revolutionary suicide by giving up his personal taste and judgment for the sake of patriotic doctrine. It's too bad that women who read books are outraged when I suggest that they refrain from committing feministic suicide. . . . But it doesnt matter: what I had to say will show up in the book Caleb and I are going to write together. Did he tell you about it?"

The bottle was more than half empty. Michael went on: "Remember that outfit you told us about that is willing to subsidize unpublished books—Society for the Propagation of Critical Knowledge?"

"S P C K . Are they going to publish your essays?"

"No, but they do give grants through their subsidiary, the Foundation for Underwriting Critical Knowledge. We're working on the proposal now. If the world really wants a new theory of culture let it put up or shut up! Here's its chance to pay us, through tax-exempt S P C K , to quit our jobs and make this one effort to explain ourselves. If not, fuckit, we'll do more important work. But it would be an interesting way to earn a year's living."

"You and Caleb! You wouldnt be pulling my leg now?"

"Honest to God, me and Caleb. —Right, Cabe? —I do the base and he does the apex. He's not too old to provide the romantic parts. He's young and he has no idea of how much there's left for him to learn. One of the disadvantages of aging is that you can't so easily dismiss the importance of what you don't know. Nevertheless he's right that it's degrading to have to adopt a tone of behesting defiance before gentlemen of the jury who always consider themselves superior to the prisoner guilty or not. Caleb is inclined to see red, but he has less dignity to maintain than I have by twelve years a wife three children and a supervisory position. Yet we can't resist communication—this one time! Show our friend the Prospectus, cousin."

Caleb waved some typewritten sheets from his table. Jack insisted upon examining them [*Appendix 1 hereinafter*]. "Oi Weh! But at least the title has all the earmarks of perfect collaboration!" Having rapidly scanned the pages while Michael was expatiating Jack put them down and pursed his long lips. His leonine face blew benevolent smoke into the central pool floating among them. It was explained to him that Michael and Caleb were each attaching essays [*Appendix 2 & 3 hereinafter*] which in some form or other would be incorporated into a discursive context of history anthropology and metaphysics. Caleb's he recognized from its earlier version; Michael's was new to him.

"My last essay without a commission." Michael said. "Caleb's first and last. We can't lose. If they give us the money we live like gentlemen and express ourselves like scholars; if we get turned down, better yet—we'd have nullified temptation! I have promised myself to stop this indulgence in self-expression so that Caleb can get on with his creative life. He's still young enough to become a proper artist. And so success will give us freedom, failure will deny us the decadence of leisure!"

"But you'll never find professors or big names to vouch for something like this! The Foundation will want high-power recommendations."

"We'll be sponsored by the Institute!" Caleb cried.

"What Institute? The Institute of Business Machines?"

"THE INSTITUTE OF DROMENOLOGY!" answered Michael and Caleb in unison. Jack was thereupon informed that they were about to incorporate in that name under California law as a non-profit charitable organization.

Indeed he was offered the chairmanship if he would join the board. He replied that unfortunately as a gnostic he could not in good conscience accept the honor of presiding over his opponents, expressing sorrow that Caleb had cast his lot with the other camp; but he magnanimously promised to search for the one missing incorporator required by statute. Michael and Caleb claimed to be confident of getting the commitment of Hecuba Jones and Sigurd Hansen, the former as Secretary-Treasurer. They were sure that Ruth Chapman would decline to participate for reasons not unlike his own, Jack was told.

So the three of them discussed at some length the vacant chair in their nominal corporation, for they hoped to hold their initial meeting soon. The two principals urged Jack to join them, unless he could find among his many academic acquaintances a trustworthy sympathizer who would lend his name and make a single trip down the Lane to write his signature and say Aye at this their place of business.

"But where did you ever get an idea like that?" Jack asked. "I might try it myself!"

"Arnheim won't consider my S M D C proposal, on the grounds that I'm an individual, until I'm sponsored by an organization. Policy. Made no pretense of considering the case on its merits."

But here Michael introduced a typical digression: "They also said they were now concentrating their grants on the improvement or propagation of male sterilization. It's an allocation of funds I can hardly oppose. I can't blame them for being more interested in contracepts than concepts. But they won't get to the heart of the matter that way. One fertile man may easily take care of a hundred women a year" [—Caleb suppressed a groan—] "so a fertile woman needs only 1% of a father. Maybe to help correct human nature we should start by decimating boybabies at birth, like shooting hostages: one chosen at random out of every ten should be sterilized as he's circumcised right at the hospital's baptismal font. But the doctors would be legally obliged to leave no trace and keep no records as to which have been chosen."

"Then you'd have to outlaw microscopes and masturbation." Jack retorted. "Smart girls wouldnt get engaged without seeing a wiggly sperm test. And the unlucky other ones would just borrow studs after they were married. It happens elsewhere in the animal kingdom. I think you'd have to make it nine out of ten to satisfy your immoral purposes—more like 99 out of a hundred."

"I'd like to be one of the known exceptions." the little bachelor cackled.

"I shouldnt have brought it up. However, once the Institute exists, domiciled here at the Rabbit Warren, I might be able to tout an application of the S M D C to neonatal birth control—

"The Institute would sponsor me at Arnheim too, wouldnt it Caleb? — But I'm realistic: even the foundations that purport to seek new Nietzsches from outside the academic universities do not expect to find them alone in their exile; they must be attested by limited liability companies or thermometric peerages of some kind. It's like a black man trying to get into a skilled union at a time of high unemployment when they won't let him work even as a common laborer. Think of how credentials simplify the onus of selection! —But of course we have to do the dromenology job first. Next year I'll rewrite the S M D C proposal to emphasize 'critical knowledge'. I take *critical* to signify what's decisive as well as what's judgmental, and *knowledge* to apply to the management as well as to the acquisition of what's knowable: so I'd propose to apply S M D C particularly to libraries. . . ."

Meanwhile Jack always mastering the layout of books in any room he visits had reached over to pluck from Caleb's shelf a book all three well knew though only Caleb who having reported it his loss from the Oakland Public Library had paid a nominal penalty possessed a copy of the translation. Jack was searching the closet-drama's pages as he began to speak. "Except for counting the dignities of God and the ordinal uses of the Cabala in interpreting the divine language that holds existence together, numbers have a deleterious affect upon literature and it's a vile waste of time for you to pursue such quasi-scientific madness. —Here, listen to this, from one of Axël's books called *Treatise on Secondary Causes*: 'In the circle of its action every word creates what it expresses. Consider well the verbal fictions of your mind!'"

"The gnostic equivalent of psychonarcotic solipsism!" Michael interrupted. "Even a philological Jew should dismiss it as ungodly name-making!"

Jack seemed to pay no attention to the thrusts of his familiar antagonist. "Every gnostic and humanist and classicist and magician and poet cries out against the presumptions of mathematics. By all that's holy, in the name of the Tetragrammaton, keep your damned technology out of literature! 'Dromenology' is bad enough, but at least it deals with the somata and pragmata of that moyen world of yours! Numbers are enemies of culture unless they have style, and they can have no style unless they have meaning. But your numbers have no characteristics except when they stand for some gross physical quantity that isnt even truly mathematical. Every number is one more than its predecessor, that's all! It's a crime for you to utter the name of Pythagoras—or of Yeats either for that matter! You lift a few sentences or diagrams and blithely ignore the author's spiritual intention!"

"But Yaako, you should like my lovely numbers! You'll be pleased to know that I've solved the problem of weighting. At least with the use of an electronic calculator I could arbitrarily repeat selected columns as many times as you *for any reason* deem proportional to its importance in the composite evaluation of entities. This advances the art of polylectics by increasing the information conveyed by the profile diagrams. That's half way from numbers to words!"

"But words are quanta of pneumatic energy from the mouths of living men!"

"Which are excited controlled and preserved by marks and diagrams. All I'm saying is that one can defend the liberal mind against the fascism of technology with digits of measurement. Statistics are perpendicular to causality and you shouldnt be afraid of them when they're organized by the S M D C . In fact I'm already working on an Antinomial Theorem."

"That's for me!" Caleb yelled, calling attention to his advantageous youth.

"I'm not afraid of your statistics: I despise them!" Jack shouted. "Antinomy, polynomy! . . . Come to think of it, every one of your wavy lines is nothing but a great big polynomial, if you want to break your balls figuring out how to write the formula!"

"It's the system, not the expression, that makes the difference. Can't you appreciate the value added by a human mind?" Michael asked with a smug lick of his lips. "My good man, don't splutter. As Caleb is my witness, I fully agree that the study of language subsumes all other studies—at least all studies that are expressed in writing—as well as literature and the study of itself. Far be it from me to attack your poetry!"

"Don't my good man me, my good man! You can't throw flour in *my* eyes. I'll cudgel you black and blue with distiches. I know enough about your taxonomic lumping and splitting to see that it all depends on the thoroughgoing standardization that you so carefully soft-pedal. But I'll grant you something: take astrology, if you can get the human data to feed into the microcosmic columns of your matrices:: it's too complex for scientific astroanthropology, and your statistics might be very useful there to distinguish it from superstition. Or better yet, meteorology and nutrition, which are still too much for orthodox methods whether deictic or elenctic!"

"S M D C might help define *tragedy*—!" cried Caleb.

"There!" Michael smiled for the first time. "Isnt that literary enough for you?"

"—or *hierarchy* or *system* or *ritual*, or any set of artifacts!"

"Don't get carried away, my friend." said Mike, patting Caleb's arm.

The corners of Jack's lips were beginning to blow tiny bubbles of saliva. "Exactly: *sets*! But books have unique souls, each alone in the eyes of the Lord."

"They're still artifacts." said Michael in ironic words ill suiting his irenic tone. "The whole issue would fade out if the law required all books to be the same size shape and color. Dust jackets would show nothing but name rank and serial number. Then people couldnt keep judging books by their covers! You at least wouldnt have to spend all that time binding your library in calfskin like a disemployed harnessmaker. You do it only to reduce variation. Printing is standardized reproduction in the first place isnt it?"

"I wish they'd take the pictures off the covers." Caleb remarked. He had been following the play back and forth from one court to the other as an enthusiastic spectator hoping the volley would never end. Any hostess would have envied the success of his foodless party. But now he feared the ball would be aced at every serve.

Michael's half inebriated play of mind seemed relentless. ". . . and authors would be more independent of personality. Books would be cheaper to make and simpler to distribute. . . . If standard book design didnt foster literary culture I don't know what would. . . . Furthermore, the librarians and their card files could double the productivity of every scholar if every book had to have an index—even without S M D C ! And I happen to know that you yourself write poetry on a standard typewriter.

—Caleb, have I not proved that 'standardization' is no ground for hating S M D C ?"

Making a spade of his left hand Jack laid it in the crook of the elbow of his right arm extended with its fist toward Michael's face. Then he sat back and took out his curve-stemmed pipe of knotty-grained briar lined with meerschaum, which he filled with deliberate motions from a paper pouch of imported Dutch tobacco with a picture of an amphora on it presumably ancient Greek, and with his pocket tamper of stainless steel carefully packed the pungent long grains. He struck a lucifer on the sole of his shoe and holding it horizontal moved the flame slowly back and forth across the exposed fibers until the disorderly curls and wisps had burned away; then he again tamped the evenly charred surface and lighted his pipe in earnest, sucking the flame with long drawn-in vacuums until he nearly burnt his fingers passing the match impartially back and forth above the bowl lined with clay that once was white. The others watched. When he was done he leaned back in what looked like supercilious disdain for the animated glint of Michael's opaque eyeglasses.

"Typical gnostic gentility." remarked the archangel amicably. "A pipe that prevents the wood from reacting with the weed; the aesthetic object insulated from its dirty black boiler."

The shapely polished gnarl curling down almost to the open collar on one side of his burgher chin, Jack repeated his Italian gesture.

Michael in turn touched a thumb to the tip of his nose and flattened his palm upward in a plane perpendicular to his moony face; looking at Jack he slowly waved his spread fingers like a dreaming cornet-player. "My salute to a man who knows French wines drinks his coffee black and speaks rather well about Botticelli. He knows everything aesthetical."

Jack grinned. "All right Mr Appleseed. I'm a cognostic." Despite his faultless procedure and sustaining puffs the pipe would go out more than once before he finally exhausted the fuel knocked out the wet dregs and pulled apart the two pieces of his face-furnace to clean it in the methodical habit of one who knows English culture. (There were two straight-stemmed pipes in his pocket, thick and thin, gargoyle and fencer, for he had anticipated a long night of rivalry with cigars. In his drying rack at home there were slots for nearly a dozen pipes in all. As a connoisseur he had removed from each the aluminum moisture trap that even the most traditional manufacturers misguided by the modern market felt obliged to screw into the inner sleeve of the tube. So snugly had he packed his present charge that if he had not relieved the draft of that scientific pinch he would have been unable to vaporize a single load of his fuel with three dozen wooden matches. Even so the ashtray was piled high with his burned-out faggots.

It was a long night. Sometimes Caleb was so disgusted with the nonsense he heard from these grown men skimming words at each other like volleys of paper plates that he hoped they werent thinking about what they said but only using the disks to symbolize feelings. Yet he couldnt help moaning inwardly at his own reason's incapacity for whiskey and philosophicalistic allusions. For the most part he was too giddy from drinking to follow the polemics, though as always in the end his sympathies moored with Michael's, in whose every word his faith was continually restored that there was some reason. Thanks to this unfamiliar distrust of his own ability he made more of the wisdom he listened to than its confusions warranted.

Sometimes the logomachists seemed to be pitting the Synectic Method of Diagnostic Correlation against literature: S M D C vs lit'rature. Michael dragged in epistemology and ontology, one as necessarily deeper but less comprehensive than the other he said. Jack countered with the axiology of ethics and aesthetics. Both seemed to champion both sides of every analogy that both advanced, yet the conflict between them remained unmistakable. At times it was all a question of distributing praises. Caleb had the feeling that in getting Jack to agree to the meaning of certain words Michael was taking all the ground he wanted to win despite demonstrable inconsistency between previous definitions and his own latest denotations.

At one deadpan goggle-eyed pause, when Michael (fishlike mouth arrested half open) had momentarily silenced Jack with the startling dictum that S M D C was at least one level deeper than Sanskrit, Caleb bleated out that his mentor was contradicting himself. "You're on record that English is the most complete system, so you can't really mean what you just said!"

Michael smiled for the second time. "Naw I'm only saying it. —As if comprehension and profundity werent two different values. —Anyway, Sanskrit's not English." Caleb's face burned at the dry rebuke he had rashly evoked from the one person in the world with whom he hoped always to be attuned.

"Caleb's perfectly right, old man." Jack intervened. "But it's just the strain of overwork and intellectual isolation. —You see," he added, turning to Caleb and patting his knee, "he gets carried away by the irritably endearing tendency to put his construction upon everything in the world as it happens to come up. In this case he stubbornly resists the plain truth that his S M D C matrix requires an illusory universe of plenitude and symmetry, as well as standardization; which lit'rature does not, because it's negatively capable of putting up with reality as reality wants to be."

"I admit my case is somewhat less than I have stated it" Michael replied. "I must have been born a statesman. . . . Yet you should admit that literature never deals with life as it now is—always with life as it was or might have seemed. Sometimes it can't see the wood for the trees or the tree for the leaves, but we have agreed that as a whole it covers all subjects and that it is not perpendicular to history."

"But your S M D C is merely spatial! In fact it's synthesized from one dimension."

"At the least it has one more dimension than writing! Literature is always suspect as a means of information. Much of it is nothing more than perpetuation of yesterday's hearsay. It undermines true knowledge."

"So you're on Plato's side after all! Charlatan!"

"Furthermore it's a Babel of untranslatable poetries—"

It was at this point that the term *metalanguage* entered their dianoetic dispute, the first in a family of terms that made Caleb's head ache *metaphorically* long before his hangover began. Metaphor vs metalanguage, metaphysics, metamathematics, metasystem. Michael reproved Jack: to wit, under the influence of *metaphor* his good friend was mistaking *meta* as always a reference to change or trope whereas it more often connoted *beyond* in the sense of being deeper or broader in comprehension (perhaps having more dimensions) than the phenomena of its agglutinated terms. A metasystem has more dimensions or levels than the systems situated within it, though its higher order may only be epigenetic or transcendent from the same elements. Thus it can serve as a field for the future. Thus the question of hierarchy. Has fiction more dimensions than reality or fewer? So there was talk about metafiction. Maybe art can enter into the ontological series that produces it at some arbitrarily creative level. Could that really be what Michael said? Was it Jack who wanted to go further, holding that art could swallow up the whole series? Whereupon flared the old fight between dromenological myth and gnostic mythicism.

[Caleb had already been persuaded by Michael—despite what he had thought to be his native temperament—that as an intellectual system the real is far more complex mysterious and interesting than a priori constructions with all their mystical fantasies perfections and tropological proliferations—past or eternal or eschatological, no matter how cunning and elaborate—that could be worked up in the arcane parlance of "psycholognostic symbullisticism". But which of the two debaters did he seem to remember saying (as well as he could reconstruct the jumbled words droning in rotation back and forth across the semicircle before him) that though art may not be as large or as comprehensive or as consistent as the middle world it can always go one level deeper if not higher within its limited system? Faust was in a fair way to matching the gods in gnosis: but he wasnt the artist—Goethe was.]

On and on they went, Caleb making less and less effort to inform himself with the sounds he heard but confident that Michael was sweeping the battle front with adroit definitions even as Jack would catch him behind the lines in rhetorical self-contradiction and then tease him with respectful assuagement (as: ". . . but I'm sure you can claim a higher consistency at a deeper level; if you had more time to think of course you would be able to define the ultimate metasystem and at the same time account for Gödel's Theorem by applying S M D C to the truly orthodox christianity heretofore grasped only by yourself").

Yet it was Caleb's impression that Michael had retreated almost to his trenches when he was heard to say "The only point I've ever tried to make is that S M D C if it's technocratically developed can deal with an unlimited multiplicity of categories better than statistics and information theory can, which are useful for making choices but contribute nothing—maybe less than nothing—to invention. Decision-making and imagination are as different as picking out a wife from the graduating class lined up on a stage and inventing Pandora to bring death into the world and all our woes. An equation implies all its possible solutions; a line of regression or a distribution curve gives emphasis to the norm and banishes the egregious—whereas the figures of S M D C represent a new winning of the West!" Michael proposed a toast to his own vision.

This somewhat labored jocularity nearly revived Caleb's old romantically reactionary animus against technology. But Jack was alert to mood voice and form, even as a worthy opponent ought to be when a bout is approaching its end. "Well," he said "if you've just been talking in metaphors after all then I grant you that sense and numbers have always been joined in verse!"

Caleb closed his eyes in silent unsnoring resignation to his baffled inferiority—until the bottle was empty and they woke him up to ask for coffee. After a few minutes of bustle at his little gas stove he felt okay again, useful at least as footman to serene highnesses, gladly excused from following their arguments as long as he pottered. When he sat down with them, all three sniffing at the vulnerary brew of java before it was cool enough to drink, the atmosphere of fraternal conviviality began to oil the billows of their drunken sea.

Jack was speaking: ". . . Well all I'm really interested in is your ritualigious dromenology, rith and mitual. I've been thinking while we talked that maybe this is the time for me to start my magazine at last. Just in case you two don't get your grant for furthering critical knowledge"— here he winked at Caleb—"I'd like to see that all your work doesnt go to waste. I'll publish your two essays as the main feature of a balanced number celebrating Yeats, the first to burst upon what I call the Pacific Rim, along with some of the other things from my radio festival, if any of them are good enough—maybe two or three poyems of mine to him, and of course some of my own prose remarks. At this stage of his career a little teasing wouldnt hurt him anyway. I'll use photo-offset and reduce the type so that Mike will fit inside the front cover and Caleb inside the back. Just don't embarrass me with anything about S M D C . I want the first issue to be a collector's item, because it may be the last. But the important thing is this: you can put it down on the grant application form that your two pieces are in press for the little magazine *Vocative Case*, Number One addressed to Willie. (God willing, other saints to follow.) In the end he'll thank me for discovering you.

"You might get blackballed by the Rhymers' Club for our sake." said Michael.

"Not if I get the credit for making an end of Michael Chapman's essays. But I know you'll eventually go back on your promise to quit, stung again by the bug of discourse. Some new system or other will pitch camp among the others in your head. Yours is a weak character and you won't be able to hold out against temptation for very long. But just try to space things out a bit, old man. Who knows—your own antibodies may cure you."

"Essays aint art like your poetry but at least artists may read them for a hundred years." said Michael.

"Then they shouldnt be underwritten." said Jack.

"No danger of that." said Michael.

"Take comfort:" said Jack "even if you *are* subsidized to finish your book no publisher would so foolhardy as to throw his production costs down a white-elephant rathole."

"Yes, you are safe. I know of no publisher with no hope of return on investment." said Michael.

Caleb had bethought himself to dig out of a cupboard the best part of a pint of Bourbon just as Jack rose to take his departure. "There's enough left for you and Caleb to drink to my coattails." He bent over and showed them the shiny ass of his pants. But it was two grateful friends that he was leaving behind. They had never loved him so well. "If worse comes to worst I can always give you a letter to the Great Academy of Lagado." he added.

"Time is short and art is long. It's too early to predict and too late to repent." Michael replied. "Must you return to the metaversal aesthesis of Berkeley and leave us in the riteful adversity of Newest Grub Street tropesis?"

"I return unto my people who have grieved at my sojourn in this Philistine city and even now pray for me to recover my sobriety and virtue."

"There's nothing but virtue in my house." said Caleb with a deep sigh shaking the right hand of his guest's fellowship who had brought so much. "—Wait! Your salad bowl."

"I hate to leave Sarah alone when it's only for my pleasure. Wish I could stay to polish off this vulgar American bottle with you." Jack and Michael bowed to each other. "Good night arch-cherub. Don't make Caleb into a Christian Pangloss."

"Good night Herr Faust. I only keep him from being made into a patent lawyer by your colleagues. But now that we have a bachelor to visit we can talk once in a while without the ladies around." [Caleb had already perceived the constraints of uxorious pairing.]

"Yes." Jack agreed seriously. "This was no mere social occasion." He hesitated at the door, his eyes for a moment on Michael's feet. "Uh . . . I meant to ask . . . Does this mean you'll put off your farewell to us at least until you hear from . . . at least until you finish your work with Caleb?"

"I guess so." Michael drawled without expression.

"Wonderful news! The Berkeley tribe will be very happy to hear that! . . . I was actually afraid this might be the last time I'd see you." His eyes blinking with moisture he hugged the impassive but now grinning friend to his chest and laid the side of his head against Michael's cheek. Then he saluted Caleb more formally and lumbered down the hall. The dim bare bulb overhead tenebrously highlighting the blondness that remained in his shaggy youthlost hair. Michael and Caleb were left to drink his health. They could faintly hear his huge prewar family sedan start up and roll away.

"I suppose I should give back the money they collected for me." Michael said as if casually. "It's bad enough to defraud my friends of a going-away party."

"But it was your birthday! You probably won't be here for your next one."

Michael changed the subject. "I know you appreciate Jack's attentiveness to his family. It's partly to make up for the money he spends on books. Have you seen his study? The library only starts there. The books in the living room and front hall are just overflow from the ground-floor pool, but they climb like osmosing wisteria and line the walls upstairs. And none of it's junk. He gets rid of anything he finds to be shoddy or useless. He's my common reader: the one I think of when I go through the catalogs to make up my orders—either for a book I might know he has thought fit to keep or for one I know he'd like to buy. Which very often he does. His moral struggles are touching to witness. The only thing besides money that limits his avarice is the size of their little house. When he's a professor with a big place and plenty of income he'll lose his painful discrimination.

"But wouldnt it be fun to be his architect when he's rich? Corbusier says a house should be designed from the inside out. Why even as it is Jack's woven Sarah's nest as his little model of the universe. If he could design his own house he'd operate like a subscriber to Giulio Camillo's theater and remember everything he's read without losing track of what he hasnt got to. The memorized storage of other people's work fills a man up from the toes like water in a surge tank; air in the top of the head is so compressed that his skull is like to shatter, and all his other gases are forced into that rigid fluid. No wonder he sometimes stutters. I can hardly bear to guess his feelings. The agonizing wellspring of his poetry is that cranial satyriasis."

Caleb wondered if the equable man to whom he was listening had ever undergone the distress to which his metaphor referred. "Jack's first editions and leather bindings are too much for me. That's not the kind of passion for lit'rature that builds a tower of winding stairs."

But then he reminded himself of his own attraction to literature: how weakly it opposed the primary desires with which it often conflicted, overborne by sloth and by an invidious impulse to attack the opinions of all its contemporary adherents except those of the master he accepted— like a vicious stray suddenly domesticating himself with a vengeance as the one best man's one-man dog, churlish to the rest of the male world, but now with a focus of admiration and love that seemed identical to self-interest—but investing him with more omniscience than omnipotence. He gave himself pause for a few seconds at wisdom's warning that when the chips were down it was a generous friend like Jack who'd feed and succour him.

And the chips would be down when the master discovered that little Caleb (to whose honor it was if he did say so himself that he'd never made any effort to conceal his ignorance and well-founded diffidence) was unequal to his aspirations, the substance of which was his unique qualification for adoption as number-one friend. This was a master who valued a dog not for its love but for its mentality and for its performance in the field. Yet like all faithful hunters retrievers shepherds and fireside companions as he strove not to disappoint expectations Caleb refused to harbor doubt about his master's ultimate fidelity, especially as it was his preeminent desire to prolong the basking warmth and distinction of being the preferred companion and chosen listener, if not confidant, in the preciousness of time, at least when there were no preoccupations or distractions to hinder any unstoppered flow of opaque revelation.

All at once Caleb was glad to remember a couple of bottles of beer in the back of his refrigerator that might keep Michael going after the last of his supplemental whiskey. Whatever the steady unmusical voice was pouring in his ear was low and flattering, sometimes (when he fully caught a bolt of meaning) monotonously exciting; but in his own cups he mostly listened without hearing, or heard without understanding, wide awake with pleasure in his status as dog friend and host.

". . . maybe he'd want to lay the double gyre on its side so that neither end would be uppermost and instead of a silo he'd have a wind tunnel but he's too modern to content himself with Yeats's scheme the turbine would be only one wing of his house which would look like the compounded palaces of Byzantium but it would be formed from the inside by the feeling that comes out of memory informed by true imagination since there's nothing phony about Jack's judgment and he has too much spontaneity to comport with academic dignity among the patent lawyers of philology so that after all these years his doctorate is still touch and go though of course he got a late start on it being four years a sergeant probably a very good one and then taking all the courses with long reading lists while he was still eligible to get the books from Uncle Sam instead of bearing down on a respectable specialty in consequence of which he knows more about literature in general than any of the professors he works for but memory's all old and it can play you false like stars in a fanciful constellation that don't really belong to the same image at all but for the accident that our celestial sphere makes them out to be in the same perceptual group whereas another perspective would show them not only in different regions of space but also in different ages of time so memory and science conflict and it's nothing to be ashamed of that you would have regretted memory if in school you'd chosen science instead even though as it is you should regret science because it's able to discard earlier perceptions when it accepts the latest removing your imagination from the torment of history therefore no architecture of books can reconstruct the truth as it was and at the same time urge you to discovery in meristic biology or even to fresh examination of the past itself as in dromenology while I on the other hand if I were to follow the derivatives of ritual mythologically and managerially as far as I could take them would find myself modeling instead of a historical theater of books some sort of wretchedly reasonable sculpture like the distorted globe that accounts for 267 hued and saturated colors in the atlas of charts instituted by an Inter-Society Color Council under auspices of the National Bureau of Standards that even though it treats of biological values and not just the objective physical spectrum of wavelengths accounting for all the annectant classifications a painter can distinguish and does so in only three concrete dimensions of sense wherefore it turns out to be no simple geometric spheroid but as a tear-dropped lopsided asymmetrical solid built phenomenologically from the inside out it is so orderly and subtle that it assigns individual hodological digits to all the substantives of color transformed by an -*ish* adjective from a different noun corresponding for example to the -*istic* modifiers I use in dromenology all in all a virtual epitome of critical knowledge and I'd have a galactically complex diagram of human time abstracted from human time incidentally it goes to show you how we're trapped by Platonism whenever we use our heads in other words I'm compelled to lose history in whatever I think like most children I rebelled against memory when I was young in favor of adventure I thought which is now too late to cultivate and I'm still unwilling to trade for it a single scrap of even poor imagination yet I've ruefully learned its inestimable value to me of all men so that sanity is about all I have more than anyone else to advance your youth with and that is why I'd like to teach you a respect for memory beyond my means though allowing you to practice it only in moderation for wasnt Mnemosyne mother of the three original muses but as far as you're concerned the same thing goes for science a wingèd siren more dangerous if less seductive than Jack's fork-tailed mermaid in any case at least acquisitive cognition is no more sufficient as a cause for creative proof than talent or memory and furthermore your personal system must be able to survive without any mnemonic organon or scientific continuum that you might learn or construct or imagine not even thermodynamics or parity physics which in cosmogeny is so ironically like the great double gyre or the vital helix that controls from within the incomplete circle of life moving through time and of course so much the more must you get past all the

closed systems of architecture that never open their circles at all where everything in the inscape is related to everything else in the inscape but to
nothing at all in the outscape thus in self-absorbtion precluding irony of
any kind and you who struggle with the definition of tragedy as I with
that of ritual know from experience that the meaning of a word is an un-
closed circle that in evolution loses nothing of its flaw no matter how exclusive chaste or arrogant it grows in time and it is for this dynamically
open superiority to the occult tradition of kinematics that I who am
purely prosaic and mundane can love Yeats's vision of the pern-hawk's
flight enough perhaps to make you curious about Christianity which for
the present let us call only a personal metasystem leaving aside until
later in the last testament the church that is the lord in the meantime
it's only in Jack's kind of Goethean effort shafting deep in specialization
to tunnel out metaversality under a mere university's acreage and then
following the black seams which intrigue you into other fields that you
can really foster the illusions of agglomerative metalanguage like the
Sephiroth a single name made up by stringing ten names together or
some comprehensive Ur-Deutsch packing in unsyntactically all the foreign words that can't be translated but the interesting thing about his
armamentarium is what happens at the acme of its acquisitions for great
private libraries can't stay whole under the laws of partible inheritance
that Toqueville saw are so important in the New World and especially
when people bring up children as ambitiously as the Wolfsons do the
testator's treasure can be unbound in one family conference and indeed
someone has offered a mob scattering a library as the image of civilization's most violent consummation of disorder just think of the entropy
let loose upon Europe by the ransacking of books and pictures from the
houses of well-rooted Jews in Germany even when they were not burned
for as small a thing as a bookmark left undisturbed in a volume has
added to the universe a quantum of information that is lost forever when
someone pulls it out so think of the staggering value accumulated by a
man like Jack in organizing five thousand books each tracked down or
cunningly selected by his vastly cultivated intelligence O Caleb if you
love justice not to mention truth never fail to return to him any book
you borrow of course when he sells one the dealer pays nothing for the
personal structure of his library that makes it available though of course
thus to unsort it is not to pull apart a true mosaic it's still a bit of
destruction not unlike the disinformation of tearing out pages differing
only in degree from what happens when I sell a book out of my theater
at the store in fact the bibliothecal order at Bow's Ark is even more important than at Jack's house because there he's the only one that has to
find anything and he has only to scan his own mind but at the store you
and John Doe have to search according to my peculiar theories of relationship which most of the time even I lose sight of and especially to my
distinctions that make no difference whereas in truth Bow's Ark is an anti-

library more of an index or diagram than a memory device just something to lead one's thoughts it's a constructive landscape rather than a reflection of the past though no one should ever lose any sleep trying to get Greatrakes to believe that my arrangement of his titles above and beyond the collection of them is worth more to the business than his investment in the stock because books are like tesserae at least as colorful modules stuck to the wall somewhere in particular and if I were paid half of what I'm worth he could still make a profit on me the store is an anti-library also because as a warehouse its purpose is to keep the books moving away from it therefore the content is temporary more like working thoughts than guides to memory and managed accordingly its cells are continually replaced but in such a way that as a functional rather than topological pattern in my brain I can let the stock be looted or cleared out in one big sale and still readily reconstruct it without much help from my memory . . . energy of organization . . . catalogs . . . purchase orders . . . packing lists . . . invoices . . . discounts . . . "

After the vocative second person dropped out of the monologue Caleb's attention had drifted away from Michael's reasoning. But the host who ceased to listen to his droning guest had no wish for him to stop. The important thing was that Michael who ordinarily didnt speak at length was talking to a privileged friend with whom he chose to say things he'd been thinking, easing himself of compacted observations that could be uttered to no one else. Though reluctant to admit that St Willie would have accepted Jack and rejected Michael, Caleb was exhilarated by the dawning American antithesis in which he was chosen to be educated. He felt himself undergoing a metanoia corresponding to skeletal metamorphosis—a liminal correction of his enthusiasms—which without demanding a transvaluation of all values refocussed and reinvigorated the intellectual emotion of his well-shapen prejudices.

He congratulated his self for beginning to acknowledge that it was still too ignorant and full of its own purposes to understand everything that it would like to understand of what it was told. He was immensely excited by what he thought he had understood but he was not yet inclined to consider the fact that understanding could play him as false as memory, both his own and Michael's. Assuming the virtue of innocence he contented himself with a broad view of truth, or rather with a vague perception of its perception. His probative responsibility, and Michael's too, seemed to lie elsewhere. In a state of such resonant imagination Michael's views required no defense; they were drunk in like lullabies or marching songs. It was a contagion of intuitions. No one cares to prosecute all injustices, especially those to truth, not even a youth setting out prove the cosmic injustice he believes in.

But at last Michael had warmed up enough to stop drinking. He insisted upon making ready to roll home down the hill and across the Lane from east to west. Caleb insisted on staggering with him in mutual escort all the way to the Chapman doorstep.

The building that housed Michael's family was wholly dark but the two drunks passed a fairhaired sailor hastening therefrom who glanced at them in mild apprehension. When Caleb returned to cross the car tracks again he saw him striding away south as if convinced from experience that he'd better hurry all the way downtown on foot to catch the last Key train to Treasure Island instead of relying on a streetcar to make his connection. Having climbed back up the hill to his oak trees Caleb lay down on his back in the grass to look at the firmament. The city was almost as quiet as it ever gets, its dormant respiration surrounding the wakeful inhabitant like a natural silence. It was not his customary time for sleep and his alcoholic drowsiness had passed. With his arms folded behind his head he tried to study a sector of the sky, which wheeled and counter-wheeled with every movement of his eyelids. As he rolled his head the moon a week past its full came out from behind the cloud bank that defended the Pacific Ocean from lunacy. In the clear remainder of night's ceiling he saw neither gyres nor galaxies nor constellations: he saw nothing but pairs of stars. Everywhere he looked the points were two and two; every star he picked out seemed to be in correspondence with one other of equal magnitude, whatever the distance between them. "This is a wonderful discovery!" he cried out. "People should be told!"

Caleb's pride of youth and bachelorhood, which almost always sustained his habitual sense of advantage over tamed owls as well as lesser birds despite many assaults of evidence threatening his prospects in the world, lost nothing in his present happiness, but it was submerged like Engidu's in the loving joy of companionship with one greater than himself not in every gift or condition but in strength knowledge and prudence. He was elated to find himself confirmed in friendship by his peer and leader. Even as he delighted in the freedom of his circumstances he voiced to Sin father of Inanna in the night's heaven this thought that had for the moment dissolved reflections upon the loneliness of his fundamental desire. In a flood of jubilant relief at the postponement of Gilgamesh's removal to Gloucester he couldnt help believing that the dipolar brotherhood had in some occult way altered also the course of the other's life. They had embarked upon their first adventure together.

"I am the only one in the world who knows that deep and heavy man. I am a detective of ironies. My studies have led me to possession of the lodestone that no one else has had the wit to seek. It is so sensitive that he is astonished at my divination. It has won him to my friendship who has no other friend. What a world of good fools! Those of science are horrified when he says that earth is the center of the universe, man the be-all and end-all of cosmic evolution. They are reminded of Ptolemy anthropomorphic dogma absolute morality and the Middle Ages. The spiritual ones turn away when they hear him talking about the mysteries of matter, and alchemists when he praises matter above the principle of light. Even the uncommon reader whose ear he knows will mistake his vision from the very first. . . . But no savantical poet likes to be grappled *only* after death. . . ."

Caleb heard the last trolleyship of the night clatter down the empty thoroughfare in hushed fidelity toward the somewhat lightened patch of sky over the city's electrical heart, leaving its coldsteel wake for the morning's warm-up. He began to croon to himself. After a while he was satisfied with a couplet:

> O sweet heavenly Muse,
> Let me be the man you choose.

When he rolled over twice in his indifferent effort to get up he narrowly missed rubbing his nose in a rather fresh dog turd.

Appendix 1

(Prospectus)

[Excerpts from the Prospectus of the Institute of Dromenology as entered on the Arnheim Foundation's application form.]

. . .

P. TITLE AND SUBTITLE OF PROPOSED WORK

The Scarcest Art: A Dromenology of Tragedy for Poets

. . .

S. GENERAL PURPOSE OF PROJECT (State sources, intended
    audience, distinctive contribution to a body of knowledge, which
    should be carefully defined)

The ideas of this organon are rooted primarily in literature, secondarily in philosophy, anthropology, and history. We nevertheless recognize that drama is literature only technically, and that the art of tragedy is not drama only. We address people who are intensely interested in action or the theory of action rather than aesthetic experience or self-awareness. The book is designed for those who find with disgust that contemporary barons of culture are only fawning on democratic taste or pandering to common sensations instead of stimulating the practice of mind; and for writers who read but have not yet found the active world sufficiently interesting.

Tragedy reflects a certain imaginative wisdom. It is therefore both art and philosophy. The philosophy without the art, as in our book, is no more than tragic knowledge—but the art without philosophy is impossible.

Yet we are just as glad that the frontiers of intellectual venture in our time face away from the dominant philosophical tradition as much as from the psychological relativism of current humanistical self-congratulation. We propose a thoroughgoing revision in both directions of time, but especially in the view of extremely distant history, where we find excitements antithetically complementary to those of the present age.

Our intention is to make a generalization about tragedy that will chasten and clarify the confusion of values that is usually admired as tolerance in life and art. We attempt to speak as a poet might who, under the sole guidance of intuition, having proven in her own art a revision from the depths of personal experience, analyzes the imagination of her masters according to the suggestions of savants who have shared her selections and criticisms.
. . .

V. ORGANIZATION & METHOD (Discuss methodology of research and presentation)

The Scarcest Art will be a complex of ideas focused upon the small space where several lobes overlap at their origins. Its content is likely to seem irresponsibly alien to those belonging to one lobe or another. We must express ourselves neither in the cautiously modulated argument of professional criticism nor in a manner of emotional self-indulgence, stating plainly whatever can so be stated but never pretending to simplify the true density of nodal points in a broad subject treated shortly.

Our facts are chosen from among competing facts made available to us by scholars we love and trust. We sift evidence in the telic light of our *Weltanschauung* without claiming the virtues of thorough enumeration or induction.

We offer persuasion of another kind, like the persuasion of drama on the strength of its hypodynamic ritual. Just as physiological reaction often precedes and causes emotion that in turn initiates thought, according to a principle that underlies many of the themes of our book, so etymological meanings and syntactical forms (not to mention mental sensations) lead to statements that cannot be proven without a lifetime's work tested all along the way. The diversity of our material, moreover, warns us of the temptation in succinct organization.

Therefore it is no wonder that we expect to leave something to suggestion, to adumbrate something of a matter long before we deal with it directly, and then continue to suggest it without explicit allusion after we have done with its proper place in an architectonic sequence. For the dissertation will be organized on a spine-climbing axis of discursive prose. The writing is to be epicyclic or epigyral in method. That is to say, subjects will return again and again to certain relative positions even as the argument moves upward, like points in the spiral of an ascending hawk. We trust the form to evolve organically with the continuous release of compressed knowledge, determining a style unfortified by citations.

Things will be said in a number of ways, here and there, not in emphasis or in didactic mistrust of the reader but in order to sympathize with the greatest possible variety of minds. The universal specificity of tragedy is like the electronic oxymoron of fidelity to a broad band of resonances.

. . .

X. ABSTRACT (Summarize your argument as briefly as possible, stating
expected conclusions)

[It is hard to say what we will have said by the time we have worked out the saying of it. Therefore this précis and the chart that follows it are no more than an imaginary digest of the future book by some fourth or fifth party, as if to brief an acquisition librarian.]

In the first part of *The Scarcest Art* Chapman and Karcist categorize the human experience upon which their idea of tragedy is founded. The first two chapters are chiefly anthropological, dealing with the phylogeny of culture and forming the "base of realism" (a phrase borrowed from Yeats) for tragedy regarded as a highly specialized and greatly distilled instance of conscious existence. The remaining parts of the book develop an entire philosophical attitude as well as a rather restrictive literary position. The axial movement of the examination is from what is common to all cults (rhythm) to what is most rare and distinguished in rare and highly distinguished cultures.

The two poles of value are liturgy in he world of reality and tragedy in the world of creative imagination. They are opposites in conviction yet counterparts in function and cousins germane in form. But in provenance the second follows from the first as a peculiar reaction of myth upon ritual. In one case a myth of truth transforms ritual into the most practical work in the world; in the other a myth of the poetic imagination transforms ritual that is already dramatic into an imaginary action realizing the most extreme tension of human freedom. This dromenological dialectic begins in ritual practice central to corporate values and hopes.

In Parts 2 and 3 the authors show that liturgy and tragedy can never reach synthesis. If liturgy does not entirely give way to the tragedy that it *may* bring into existence it degenerates into rituals of professional magic or aesthetic comfort. By the same token no attempt at tragic drama can amount to more than fantasy if it has not been germinated in an inherited experience of liturgical sacrifice. Liturgy is the source of energy for the kind of freedom that is exceptionally demonstrated only in tragedy; and tragedy, the most valuable product of culture (as the authors claim), is that freedom's final cause.

Liturgy and tragedy are diachronistic waves of dromenological praxis with ironically similar shapes: which is not very strange since (according to Chapman and Karcist) all the elements of a culture may be more or less directly traced to its rituals, the first and fundamental institutions after the necessities of minimum survival are met. Ritual underlies or influences most of the nurtured behaviors of mankind; the *doing* of ritual generates the *saying* of myth, and from myth at the beginning proceeds all other thought.

Chapman emphasizes the reciprocal mutations of ritual and myth from the social point of view. He maintains that whereas it is religion that unifies the subjective and objective world for men and women leading communal lives it is especially drama that does so for those more attentive to the virtual life of imagination. Tragedy in particular brings to human physical action—through the breathing and moving presence of persons in an immediate locus of time and space—a certain objective possibility that has no other manifestation. He holds that drama in general is a desecration of ritual, but that tragedy is furthermore a sacrilege of liturgy, which is a special case of ritual. As the most blasphemous of dromena tragedy presents an excess of human potentiality (which cannot be found in nature or normal civilization) by opposing without denying the values of society.

It does so in the person of the hero (Karcist's emphasis), who as the sole force antithetical to the choral principles discussed in Part 1 is the chief subject of Part 2. The most acute possibility of life is never known in real experience, for reality blocks or destroys the extreme motive required to discover and endure it; but it can be realized in the *art* of tragedy through the literally effective imagination of the tragic poet, whose masked double the hero is. In the real life of unrealized tragedy it is only the artist who is able to face the absolute paradox that the hero faces in actual existence.

Since tragedy violates the ritual in which it is rooted, Chapman and Karcist regard it as anti-liturgy wherein corporate work is irrationally contested in a purely voluntary action by the most highly informed human being humanly imaginable. That work includes the preservation of this person's life.

The dramatic action concentrates superhuman counterentropic energy on the edge of a razor for artistic release totally without practical consequences yet even more intense than society's regularly recurrent transubstantiation of sacrificial victims. The real and imaginary energies are measured on two different axes. Yet tragedy omits nothing of social life, nothing of value—nothing of truth or reality—in the religious system which it fulgurates in a single stroke of lightning from zenith to the center of the earth. It does not for instance disdain survival in renouncing it. Thus the most personal and intensely symbolic of the arts is also the most comprehensive, subsuming all the values of comedy.

In fact (as C and K take pains to show), divine and human comedy is the very ground of the book, the universal base of comparison that reflects all systems of value. The chosen myth, sprung remotely and anachronistically from a foreign cult and shaped by many layers of subsequent lore or poetry, is cacophonically engrafted. This interference disrupts ritual's mastery of life's epigenetic complexity, which has produced by volutions of natural liberty the very poet who in imagination does the interfering, whose dangerously independent work is the ultimate achievement of culture.

Part 3 is devoted to the art that manifests tragedy dramatically and incarnates it theatrically. The special difficulty of the tragic playwright is to make concrete the philosophy expressed by symbolic physical actions under almost motionless tension created through the free yet systematically combined responses of managers, actors, and spectators. Since there can be no tragedy in a second-rate performance the responsibility for direction of these multiple energies must be assumed by the poet, primarily by means of the self-directing spoken words themselves whose virtue works as much upon the speaker in the speaking as upon his hearers in the hearing. Otherwise the tragic vision remains tragic knowledge only.

The poet's principal problem is to create a hero of the imagination out of, yet opposed to, the fictitious ritual of the play. Unlike real-world heroes this one comes not to save his country but to live out, in the theater, life's highest possible pitch of *self*-fulfillment, utterly undefended by god or tradition, under spiritual conditions shared with no one.

Irony is tragedy's essential artistic means. It compounds all meanings by doubling and redoubling actions and symbols. With such leverage the artist can hope to pry open tiny cracks in the great weathered rock of the city's *somata* and *pragmata* with frosty words directing austere action. In tragedy's irony the spectator discerns disparities that escape the generality of minds, such as the exorbitance of some heroic passion that seems to rise from common motives of self-interest or goodwill.

The judgment of C and K is chaste and frugal. History is allowed to have had no more than five tragic poets, and only a small part of their work achieved tragedy. The body of "tragic knowledge" comes almost entirely from a scarcely larger number of cold and passionate thinkers.

Yet just at the point where even liberal critics would pronounce extinction for an art far less scarce, C and K insist upon hope to be found in our culture's broad but not prevalent refusal to abandon the fundamental problem of freewill. They examine as not quite absurd, even in the light of present American civilization, their vision of a new tragic theater, which was already nearly absurd in Yeats's Ireland.

It is not that a new enterprise in drama would lack patrons. A sufficient number, says C, have the economic power to support an unprofitable establishment of sufficient size. The greatest difficulty lies with those who love the theater or make the grants. In order to produce tragedy, says K, we must overcome the humanistic, journalistic, and relativistic categories that have formed the education of our best minds. The entire conception of theatrical performance, they agree, must be revised with heed to the ritual of our own true religious tradition.

Plays should be written not for the amusement or edification of patrons, and not for the glorification of actors or dancers, but for the dromenon-in-itself—which is not to be mouthed and sawed at and torn to tatters by psychology. "Personality" (in Yeats's terms) replaces "characterization" in this counter-reformation; dance deposes discussion; action, scenery; mask, costume. Proscenium theaters must be torn down and rebuilt for the uses of ritual, so that all sounds and lights may be emitted without disguise from the place of action. The people will expect masks and sculptures instead of cosmetics, camouflage, and verisimilitude.

The applicants end by explaining their ostensibly sanguine persuasion that tragedy will be possible again when our era has finally shaken off the platonism which having straitened Western reason from the very beginning remains imbedded in our vestigial religion. They seem to think that the only true idealism is creative art.

Y. STRUCTURAL OUTLINE (Show skeleton of the work, assembled, labeled, and lightly annotated)

Chapter	Matter	Historical Center	Scope of Reference
PART 1.			
THE MATRIX OF TRAGEDY			
1. *Body and Blood*	Dance, ritual, liturgy	Preclassical Greece	Definitions, rhythm, decadence of desire, parts of ritual, action *vs* passion, three kinds of liturgy, symbolism, meaning of sexual action, social basis of sacrifice
2. *The Egg of the Phoenix*	Profanity, the chorus, from dithyramb to drama	Classical Athens	Regulation of desire, Dionysianism *vs* Olympianism, dramatic ritual, Homeric mythology, epic as Logos, ritual as analogy, parts of drama, the choral function, sport, magic, legislation, art as

			ritual degeneration, the comic base, seven kinds of plays, *Moby Dick*

PART 2.
THE SEED OF TRAGEDY

3. *The Black of the Moon*	Myth, Christianity, Dante, Milton, Goethe	European Middle Ages	Comedy, saint, freedom *vs* organization, man of the world, culture hero, Faust, ethical irrelevance, Kierkegaard *vs* Nietzsche
4. *The Tragic Abstraction*	The tragic hero, Shakespeare, Euripides	Elizabethan England	Sacrilege, the absolute antinomy, objective irrationality, destiny *vs* determinism, sin *vs* vice *vs* crime, Mystery and Miracle plays, violation of chorus, tragedy *vs* sacrifice

PART 3.
THE BIRTH OF TRAGEDY

5. *The Mask of Dionysos*	Art of tragedy, Aeschylus, Yeats	The turn of the century	Irony, theory of masks, poetry and action, voice, sentimental-ity, fiction, play-within-a-play, Artaud *vs* Yeats, fictitious place
6. *Apollo's Skills*	The theater of tragedy, Sophocles	American culture	The director's job, monotony of passion, objective ecstasy, acting and dancing, the player's humil-ity, perfunctory performance, archi-tecture, carpentry, illumination, plastic restraint, political economy, the future of the novel

{*Second-encounter Postulants only:* Continue to *Appendix 2*, page 726.}

Log 1
(Caleb's Protest)

What's going on around here? He promised me a girl, not a story. What does he take me for? I really don't care to be used for what he's using me for. I like to be made out more successful than I am as little as I like being made a fool of. I hope it isn't going to turn out that I'd have been better off with no advocate at all.

I'm so worried about encroaching upon his time that I never have a chance to pursue the most important questions. Besides, when I ask him what it's all about he just grunts and lets me do the talking, which I can't stop myself from doing when he won't say anything. Or he just chuckles to turn aside my annoyance. Is he trifling with my name or is he serious? I ask him. All I get is his usual deadpan.

But in his presence I'm always an overjoyed puppy. My wagging tail gives me away when I'm trying to act reserved. Even if I tied it down my whole body would wag with it, rear end and all.

The ignominy of being understood by him far better than I who understand everybody else understand him is only the least of my humiliation. The fact is that I can't help doing everything he wants me to do because it's always something that I seem to have wanted to do all along, or that's necessary under the circumstances. (But I wish he would help me not to smoke.) He has harbored me so long now that I bear witness to that flat face and that promiscuous mind only as

Appendix 2
(Caleb's Matter)

[The theory of tragedy attributed to William Butler Yeats by Caleb Karcist, as revised and shortened at the Rabbit Warren after coming down from the University at Berkeley]

THE MASK OF PROMETHEUS

1.

For once a writer of tragedy has left blazes by which to follow the thought he came by in working and contemplating the deepest subject of his imagination. For not only in the verse and plot of Yeats's plays but also in plain sentences throughout his prose can be found his theory, his reasoned feeling, about what he was making. By means of this intellectual vision he also tried to specify the difficult intuitions that identify authentic tragic ideas when they are obscured by theatrical or philosophical confusion. He proved his theory on the stage whence it had been derived. It is only my terms for his concept of tragedy that are less flexible than his own, and perhaps a little more consistent.

Yeats leaves us with his occasional persuasion that some spirit of tragedy is essential to all "true" art. But this face of his criticism is best understood from its obverse.

For Yeats the comic attitude is characteristic of fading cultures. In our time democracy as a leveling social order rejects excellence and fosters the comic enmity to exceptional and integral men. Love of

relative to my own existence whereas really it's my own independence that I should be doubting—even though I'm sure I don't absolutely need him to protect me from the sea he's dragged me into. The only reason I don't kick over the traces when he moots alterations of my course is that I get more interested every time he does so. Then too I'm envious of his sons, and too jealous of him for his sons' mother to stay away from the family.

When I'm alone I can quite clearly see his unselfcentered selfishness, his irresponsibility toward truth, his heartless treachery. I also see that I may have been right in my first impression of him as a smugly laconic clerk, a reference machine working downward like a dictionary and upward like a thesaurus, a self-made self-improving parvenu quite oblivious to the plaintive degradation of offering goods for sale. I should have taken warning when I found he was full of tasteless hatreds and enthusiasms for organ music, opera, Republicans, baseball, football, Democrats—wasting on worthless chaff the precious time that Ruth and the boys and I are so afraid to make the slightest claims upon. He pours praises on the head of a political man for qualifications that it shouldn't be necessary for us to trouble ourselves to inquire into: what should go without saying he's rapturous about. Is this a fatuous Ben Franklin (without kite or bifocals) or an Apollonian admiral of pseudo-science whose intelligence has been perverted by progress-machines and neologisms? He can't

comedy, without excluding the democratic mind from half-ignorant success through logic and science, deprives it of all the subtlety and passion beyond consensus. "State a logical proposition," he says, "and the most commonplace mind can complete it. Suggestion is richest to the richest and so grows unpopular with a democracy"—in which the spirit of adjustment breeds hostility to the imagination altogether. Democratic leaders are necessarily mediocre, and therefore safe from ridicule, since the modern world, respecting above all mere knowledge and "self-improvement", follows only those persons and idols that make themselves the mirrors of popularly acclaimed values; and they acknowledge only that art which concurs. The complacent audience is aroused by "plays of commerce", which substitute a "succession of nervous tremors" for the "purification that comes with pity and terror to the imagination and intellect."

It follows that artist and hero are allied in estrangement from even the best of majority opinions. The comic and democratic thirst for equality seeks to undermine with vulgar "individualism" the integrity and beauty of every passionate personality. The tail of the coin is infinitely broader than the head, and it is no wonder that the hero and his creator find themselves in a tiny camp of the remaining aristocracy where the superfluous qualities of true art may be at least tolerated. In this view we may attach a specially modern meaning to Yeats's prescription of heroic "nobility".

possibly understand how I feel. He's too successful and self-preserved to see anything deeply. An enemy might call him prim. His emotional adiposis is so serenely well-rounded that he's inebriated by eggs.

Yet how could he help growing pompous, a man of such ability, with all those leaderless womanish parrot-brains hanging on his words? At least he knew himself well enough not to become a professor. If he had power to match his self-confidence he'd be unbearable even before he opened his mouth. —Yet maybe not, after all. It's possible that prestige and leisure would liberate his human sympathy.

But why am I expected to forgive him for betraying my secrets that I never told him? It's unconscionable perfidy to violate my jesting confidence about Shakespearean ambition. His exposure of my boyish artless confession only redoubles the burning shame of my shiftless failure. A true friend, or a friend of true sensitivity, would have taken my indiscretion to his grave undisclosed. Everything I have told him he uses against me, for he despises the most sacred moral law of friendship—and then trifles with the truth. Thank God I never had time to tell him much more before I got wise to his ways.

How can a man of such healthy sensibility presume to know anything that isn't obvious about sloth, jealousy, or half-ignorant lust? The whole figment is probably spun out of the distant memory of a few sweetly consummated dreams of youth, back in the days when girls

The most inimical of all democracy's corollaries is optimism in philosophy and art. Faith in the wisdom of a majority, or in society's welfare as the paramount value, stems from the belief that life if only properly governed can satisfy all needs without irreconcilable paradox. The optimism of modern psychology is implicit in determinism itself.

Tragedy arises, to the contrary, from the understanding that for metaphysical reasons (which illuminate for the intellect what can be known by any illiterate) the most intense values of human existence *cannot* be realized by good fortune or good works. In its objective aspect the action of passion must be judged pessimistically. In the interest of well-being and success ordinary men are naturally unwilling if not unable to undertake the supreme experiences of whole being. But in attending an art that may perhaps barely escape the corruption of democracy they can briefly apprehend the ultimate joy of true individuality. With this epiphany of the suffering chosen by a superior person they witness the logical necessity of the cosmic injustice that they fear more profoundly than death.

Enlightenment in social reform or therapy hangs upon nature's working justice which Yeats calls "mechanism". The survival-motive is encouraged by the equity of inductive logic that has come to replace the medieval wheel of fortune as well as more moral schemes of theodicy. In sentimental art specious comfort takes the form of poetic

weren't so free with their hands. But doubtless before long he had all of them he wanted. I've seen snapshots: he was something of an athlete perhaps, even with his glasses, and quite good-looking. It's all very well to make fun of torment when you're a contented latterday saint and no longer deprived of anything but the company of peers, well furnished with a nice big bed and blessed with the softest wife in Christendom; but it's something else entirely when you have to wrestle with all the angels of disfavor and insignificance while living where free-love is rife and all other guys have their way.

I'm sure I was intended for a nobler beginning than Inanna's last pick. "I was a fine child, but they changed me!" One man's bull is another man's motto. According to Toqueville a young man is defined in the Delaware language by a concept of chaste innocence. That makes me the only young Indian left in North America. It's easy to speak well of chastity when you're on the right side of the law with a woman like that in your arms every night. Why you can't even be hypocritical when you don't have so much as an old deaf mute chamber maid to pat on the ass for self-assurance.

He tries to make my chastity romantic, but the fact is that I've never fought vice. I cheat at solitaire. I'm so free in granting myself solace that I never get far enough along to have a beautiful remedy in dreams. Naturally I'd trade all my sordid self-indulgences for a handful of schoolgirl kisses. But he seems to have worked out at my

justice. Literary "journalists" weave reason's justice into "classical morality" and perpetuate the tradition of the tragic flaw. But whether as scientific causality or as religious ethic, common wisdom reduces tragedy to a story of just desserts. In either naturalistic or theological language it may be true that the hero suffers for something disorderly in his character; but in the poetry of truly tragic consciousness his deviation is revealed as an intemperate act of perfect freedom. The "tragic flaw" belongs to comedy.

Yeats saw Hamlet much in the character of Villiers de L'Isle-Adam's Axël, the hero whose Promethean intelligence anticipates the tragic issue and forestalls the obviously successful act that would debase his disinterested passion, which transcends all natural emotions. Hamlet's inaction is more complex than Axël's in its ironic negation of success, but it makes itself a similar target to the swords of classical criticism that never cease poking at the romantic "disease of perfection" (Flaubert), or "illusion of infinite perfection" (Santayana), or failure of "objective correlative" (Eliot). A certain sensibility that appears sick or weak in the landscape of what Yeats calls "malign externality" proves as strong and virile in his criticism as in Nietzsche's. The hero is responding ecstatically to the contrariety of his ironic crisis.

"The substance of tragic irony" is the sympathetic exhibition of extraordinary, almost superhuman, "men as they are, as apart from all they do and seem." Yeats incessantly

expense some high-minded theory of onanistic feedback. He mocks his solemn promise by serving me up fantasies-within-fantasies. No one who knows the trouble I know would waste his wishing on black panthers and yachting deflorations. My misery generates no such pretentious visions. I've already learned enough about tulip maidens laughing among the lilacs to the purling accompaniment of an unpotable brook, or panting in a rose garden.

The Rose Garden! Good heavens, what a seclusive dark warm misty night it was! No moon, no star, no sound of person or machine except our own sweet murmurs at the double mechanics of desire. On a green wooden bench drenched in the fragrance of all flowers, saturated with the dew of kisses, we made the blackness luminous with shrouded patches of pale flesh striving against paler strife to unite in will. Right on that populous hillside we felt as if we had finally sequestered ourselves from all intrusion upon the happiest and most passionate of all the world's loves. We might have been hidden in the most silent depths of the redwoods, under Mount Tamalpais far across the roads of the bay. She was allured beyond all prudence by the virgin wonder of her own body. It was the one time in our early purity that she anticipated my urging. "Let's do it!" she whispered faintly in my ear.

Those words still echo! They still swell the hard-frozen capital of my flesh—and perpetually renew my burning shame like the eagle-eaten liver of Prometheus. Ever

poses being against common operational logic, "intensity" against objective and discursive circumstance. Such ironically perceived antitheses underlie his appreciation of Shakespeare's heroes: their deeds are "no more than the expression of their personalities"; the poet is not "accusing" them, as the tragic-flaw critics would have it, for "men are made useless to the state as often by abundance as by emptiness"; and the hero must not be judged according to the criteria of "success" or "efficiency in action". The deepest irony of tragedy is a discrepancy between the persona's understanding of his own passion and the spectator's presumption of a leader's or champion's motive.

The "active virtue" of tragic "passion" lies beyond the boundary of psychological analysis, and it cannot be suggested by naturalistic dramatization. In praising Blake he writes: "False art is not expressive, but mimetic, not from experience but from observation, and is the mother of all evil, persuading us to save our bodies alive at no matter what cost of rapine or fraud." He tells us that true art, always passionate, can have nothing to do with humanistic description. Indeed even within art it is only the superhuman personality that is willing to commit virtuous crimes against the culture it belongs to, against the gods, against the deterministic order. The hero "refuses passive acceptance of a current code," not with "that excitement of the will in the presence of attainable advantages" which our public thinks is "the natural stuff of drama", but with an "emotional and

since my disgraceful display of virility on that memorable occasion I have prayed and willed that she should forget it; I myself have sometimes been able to put it out of mind. Even in my most self-abasing confessions to her I never could bring myself to mention that mortification; with all my powers of obscurantism I've thrown dust in her eyes, talking about all my other shortcomings, trying to render this one undone. The one time I did not fail my Hermes in craft and guile he had to gush out the message before it was delivered! It may be that soon it was for her as if it had never happened, but for me, especially after I no longer had the prospect of rectifying history with a proper deed, it haunts the future of my manhood. What if such a response to good fortune became ingrained in my nervous system? It's certainly not very good therapy to beat my short-cuts into a single goat path straight through the pass. If I don't learn to climb Inanna's first foothill I'll live out my life in this slough and every girl I get will be sorrier for me than for herself unless she laughs outright at my effrontery and in that case I'll never get past this symptom of my excessive sensibility to females, or whatever infirmity it is that she's left me with.

It's strange how quickly and considerately her excitement dissolved into sweet affection as soon as she became aware of the shambles I'd made with my tall-talking petard, almost as if her passion had overflowed too. She didn't seem disappointed at all. I think it was her godsent excuse to repent aesthetic" self-possession as wildly joyful (I think Yeats would have said) as the divine possession of Homeric horses and fighting men, but colder, utterly undeceived.

A Vision was conceived as much as for anything else to provide an objective civilization with a system capable of appreciating tragedy. Yeats's doctrine of the mask originated in his struggle, now as artist, now as hero, against the Will of "normal ego". Despite lifelong abhorrence of pragmatical reason, his purpose was always to reach the fullest intellectual consciousness (though it fall short of ecstasy), knowing however, he says (after Plotinus), that "things that are of one kind are unconscious." A man with a Daimon is of two kinds to begin with; and "the antithetical Mask" is but a "form created by passion to unite us to ourselves."

A man's Will is a measure of his position in reality. "When not affected by the other *Faculties* it has neither emotion, morality nor intellectual interest, but knows how things are done . . . everything that we call utility. It seeks its own continuance. Only by the pursuit or acceptance of its direct opposite, that object of desire or moral ideal which is of all possible things the most difficult, and by forcing that form upon the *Body of Fate*, can it attain self-knowledge and expression." The hero's "pursuit" of self-unity is distinguished from the saint's "acceptance" of a mask made by religion. This typological difference corresponds to Nietzsche's exaltation of the hero's "masculine crime" as against the unassuming

her rash curious acquiescence to months of my entreaty. Maybe she even took it as my unselfish gesture of respect for the fears she'd only momentarily lost sight of! On the way home she kissed me more tenderly than ever before, and her words were the sweetest yet, though they never penetrated my melancholy. And in all our long history of subsequent frustration at less advanced stages of my heart's desire she never gave any sign of suspecting the kind of lover I'd turn out to be if I got my way again. She still called me her great god Pan! But if only I hadn't stopped to unroll that wretched codpiece I might at least have had one swooning taste of the intrusion I was living for!

To love her was an illiberal (i e technical) education. I need the kind of girl who keeps her head, who knows what men are made for and won't change her mind in midstream, who'll take it easy and give me more than one chance. That's when I'd excel, like Jesus Christ in resurrection! Not another skittish fearful virgin but a mature woman who doesn't think the virtue of the world's at stake. Above all, no love; by God, no love!—in any event not on my side. I've got to find a woman I won't fall in love with just to win her favor, or out of gratitude after I get it.

I suppose he thinks Hecuba's the answer to my maiden prayers. If she is he'll have to prove it. What a coincidence that this Pandora just happens to be his neighbor, and just happens to work for my boss! How can he expect anyone to be-

deficiency of "feminine" sin; but Yeats's dichotomies have the advantages of a dynamic model over case-by-case description, as for example in his doubling of polar pairs. Thus sin and crime, both of them transgressions, or saint and tragic hero, both of them positively exceptional individuals (and both, in their extremity, too paradoxical for life), appear as mutual reflections in the concurrently doubled inversions of the gyre as opposites each with its own separate opposite. With Yeats's schematic instrument there is little need for rhapsody or obloquy: all states and conditions can be related to each other without rhetoric by playing upon a set of simultaneous equations with a couple of pairs of dependent variables. Different Masks are appropriate to different Wills, and correspond (in accordance with "phase") to the two other inversely related "faculties": Creative Mind, or "intellect", and Body of Fate, or "fact as it affects a particular man". By tracing a circle to generate indicative values of Will (usually chosen to function as the independent variable for purposes of initial determination) one is able to introduce into the system a reciprocating motion that suggests that of equal and opposite sine waves (although Yeats himself uses the double-cone imagery of solid geometry).

Intuition may be deceived by desire for a false Mask, or in some trick upon intelligence the Creative Mind may be deluded in the prehension of its Fate's Body; but these consequences of emotional or intellectual defect, like trees reflected in

lieve such arch devices—or that he got me this job when there can be no doubt (unless I'm stark raving mad) that I was already working here when he met me?

The funny thing is that I've never given her a thought, and it's only this insidious little tale that makes me give her a second look— probably the only female under forty who's passed before my eyes these six months that's escaped my futile consideration. She must have seemed too savvy and coarse for a tenderfoot like me, and my eyes made the judgment without bothering to pass the data along to a higher level of intelligence. Clearly she's not my type, and would only laugh or jeer at any effort I might make to get her amorous attention. That's the kind of elementary fact about me that he can never seem to understand—what a misfit I am in the social world, or any world if it comes to that. I'm a solitary drinker who'd never think of pinching a chorus girl. Besides, I hate mindless women, and no matter what he makes her out to be I'm sure her taste does not belie her quality. I guess like most men he's intrigued by blatantly free and easy blondes. Still, maybe I don't give her the credit she deserves for making her own way in the world. I shouldn't withhold my charity just because she bleaches her hair and uses eyeshadow. She'd be the last woman on earth to look at the likes of me, but if she did she might not be so formidable. Yet I wouldn't know how to go about getting to a nightclub even if I had the money to take her. If I forced myself to listen

the waters of a pond to offer a choice of contemplation, or like desire for the flesh of a beloved's phantom, multiply the combinations of being and thus the ironies that can be counted in literature. All possibilities of spiritual type and all possibilities of circumstance can be specified, and all are rationally related to each other.

By the time this vision completes itself, however, Yeats has grown generally too pessimistic in his feelings, and in his mind too susceptible to the celestial unifications of Neoplatonism, to sustain the romantic preeminence of pure tragedy in an artistic hierarchy. On one side his personal illusion has weakened; on the other, his sense of cosmic injustice. In the final philosophy of A Vision tragedy therefore loses its anomalous place among numerous symmetrical values. But the earlier poet of middle life, still too intemperate to suffer systematics gladly, still unbalanced in enthusiasm, was the man of the theater who wrote what he is never to take back about tragedy as drama. I now propose to treat it as he did then.

2.

The hero's self-determination, as distinct from the prudential conditioning or religious obedience of either "objective" or martyred men, is symbolized by the mask that he has himself created in the image of his own personal and inimitable ideal, an impersonal stage-face representing the immortal passion of a mortal person perhaps in the very

to her kind of music, what could I ever say to her? She'd laugh at the way I talk, I'm so ignorant of what's expected.

I suppose I could learn if she gave me a chance. Even with Cindy I had to get used to a lot of things I used to hate. I was intimidated by the chic currency of her taste. But now I'm getting to hate them again. On the other hand he's making me more tolerant. And Ruth likes Hecuba. Maybe she'd help me get acquainted if I run into them together at the laundromat again. I'll go more often now. Maybe Ruth will give her the hint that I'm not just a little sour-grapes prig. The day she really brings me my paycheck she'll find out otherwise! Nevertheless he's crazy if he thinks I'm going to risk getting rubbed out by making a pass at the Silver Fox's girlfriend!

As it is already I've been losing whatever social confidence I acquired during my palmy days with Cindy. It's evaporating all the time. If this degeneration doesn't come to a stop I'll soon be no more than what he would call the square root of a negative Caleb: a purely imaginary dog misplaced in the real world. It's mean of him to use me for grist to whom bread was promised, especially when he wins his glory not by frank challenge and manly duel but by sly legerdemain in the name of romance! By the bowstring of Engidu, I'll rob him of his honor! He thinks I'm some poor little sniveling twentieth century Werther who can be satisfied with his lady's breathtaking smile, but some fine day he may be in for

act of shaking himself free of natural law, as the primitive Cuchulain does in the epic *Tain*, with the terrifying warp-spasm spiked like a helmet to his brainpan; or even in the icy detachment of inhumanity already attained, as expressed in the manner of Nōh plays. It is under the self-affirming tension between Will and its chosen Mask, not under the pressure of "duty", that a mortal can "exceed nature" and overcome human propensity in the "antithetical state" of heroic ecstasy.

"The motives of tragedy are not related to action but to changes of state," and "ecstasy is some fulfillment of the soul in itself, some slow or sudden expansion of it like an overflowing well." This joy begins by electing a naturally hateful opposite in which to realize the most difficult of all possible self-completions. For Yeats, as for Spengler, destiny makes itself "from within" (unlike fate, which like what Spengler calls causality is externally imposed). Willful opposition to his own nature is the hero's destiny but not his hope, for the ecstasy of it brings him to destruction in an antithetical state without surrender or synthesis or victory. He commits himself to excruciation by an act of the will, yet his agony ends in the will-less and impersonal passion of a moment's "supernatural or ideal existence".

The subjective antithesis may be explained philosophically, and brought into being by lyric poetry spoken on the stage or in a small space before the wall of a drawing room; but tragedy is an action, even if one does not call it action, even if

a surprise. —But alas, there's no danger that *she* would ever reward me by deceiving him. She only loves me like an amusing little brother.

Whatever happens, he has no right to play fast and loose with the facts. Item, I'm not a boxer but a runner, and I can't run because I smoke too much and I have an ingrown toenail. And he ought to know that I can't go to a Y M C A locker room in my condition of fire. All that moonshine about color-blindness is just to trump up a euphemism for homosexuality, which the draft board thinks my satyriasis is a symptom of. The Army could have another sack of cannon fodder instanter if somebody would tell them how easy it is to cure me. But maybe I'm colorblind too: they never told me otherwise. I'm also a left-handed bastard that can look into the sun.

Why is he so all-fired fanatic about brute exercise—for me? He's the one that needs it. Eats like a horse and puffs like a steam engine. I guess he wants me to enjoy whatever longevity he's deprived of. (I'll take his widow too.) But I could never outlast him. He's all mind and placidly married. Very few moving parts, no great wear and tear on his tissue—while I burn myself out in idle lust and rage.

But by the ark of Ut-Napishtim, I don't burn books. Least of all for the sake of an infernal job or to further my purification. When I must get rid of my books I'll sell them to his competitors. (They all pay better than Bow's Ark.) It's conceivable that in a fit of

the action is not what it seems to be; and it is the purpose of dramatic poetry, which otherwise would intrude upon undebased truth as an external impurity, to make an objective antithesis that not only reflects the inner paradox but actually brings it about. A dramatic Body of Fate does not determine the hero's choice, which is utterly free, but it presents the web of causes and motives of the flesh that make a human world.

As the only modern writer with the vision and poetic chastity for true tragic art Yeats of course found his greatest difficulty with the "concrete" Body of Fate that in every kind of comedy and problem-play so little troubled talents born for their times. The "fated Image" that everybody could understand was never as interesting to him as the "sensuous" Mask, which forms in the "chosen image" of lyrical epistemology the other half of the "double contemplation" that is life's ever-vain "endeavour."

3.

The short explanation of Yeats's incomparable art, among many peers in talent and perhaps a few in intellect, among all those who have shared divine madness and aesthetic rage, is the heroic character of his lifelong resistance to the most heartfelt values of his times and of times to come. It should go without saying that no artist can himself become a tragic figure—not even as the imaginary creature of another's art—unless he exchanges his mask for that of the hero and

self-assertion I'd think of chucking them into my incindyary engine—but what do I know of scientific symbolism, caloric or anticaloric? I never even heard of Carnot. What the hell do I care about entropy and efficiency, or any of the other jargons in his fatuous objectivity? Anyway, I'm not so simple-minded in my notion of science that I can't see through his smoke-screen of plausibility: if information and energy were really convertible by fire there'd have been an explosion at least big enough to blow off the furnace door. To think that he's the one who inveighs against gnosis and "symbullisticism", and worries about the magical degeneration of liturgy! If he had any real sense of true art he'd notice the fanciful regression of his imagination.

The last time he came to my castle he had the nerve to say with a smirk: "Why, look at all the books! I thought you'd burned every last one." And he gives me a big fat wink. (He won't get rid of his own books, he says, because he has to be an auto-university.) I've never seen such an ill-disguised comedian.

I suspect the whole episode's just to get Jack's goat. Apparently I'm an inexhaustible source of amusement. Well they won't find any little alchemical pot among the ashes of my inferno. They should both know that I'm not interested in any kind of magic that supposes spiritual regeneration. Until Jack proves to me that witchcraft attracts naked women I don't join anybody's coven.

So I'm supposed to study the work that takes place in a firebox? thereby puts his work at less than his person, disqualifying himself for both masks, since tragedy is art in supremacy. But in the proof of his tragic imagination he can learn to know the hero with such a totally ironic sense of identity that he ceases to worry about doing justice to the world.

Yeats declared that "tragedy must always be a drowning and breaking of the dykes that separate man from man", and yet the creative work of his whole life arose in part from the rejection of fellowship in art. Unlike Shakespeare, the sympathies he found hardest were those to be aroused against the hero for making tragedy out of the "antithetical state". It was most difficult, of all things possible for his chorus (which was "out of fashion and out of date like the antiquated romantic stuff this thing is made of"), to intoxicate a modern self-improving public, "sociologists all, pickpockets and opinionated bitches", with an exalted "emotion of multitude". The hero beneath the mask had to stage both manifestations of the tragic antinomy before an audience of objective individuals with no tragic knowledge and full of misinformed heroic poetry. There was no other way than to compress in a legendary imagery of kings and blind men the latent feelings of community or religion for which even a denatured audience needed far less arousal than for a glimpse of the personal passion no populace has ever known. As practically sole creator of the theater in which his plays were performed Yeats could not choose but symbol-

Hell: I'll study hell first! (To hell with that four-flushing work-mechanic George Whatshisname who stole my clever witty beautiful independent girl with soft breasts like secret bouquets and firm thighs like the beating wings of an angel swimming underwater who used to suck my soul to the quick in the mortal thirst of her love for me.) As if my torment could be abolished by holocaust! Just because I once burned her painful love-letters and a welter of quotations he takes it into his head that I like to play romantic games—and burn most of the things I write!

It may be that a corrupting paralysis of will is going to leave me moldering with muck-worms, but at least I have enough self-respect not to adulterate my brain with real-estate chicanery and other people's income tax evasions. Even Ben Franklin couldn't have been so interested in financial pyramids that he'd have wasted his time explaining them to the public, much less Scotch whiskey schemes. It's a grotesque mind that seriously ponders the doings of a Wine-swine—and furthermore drags stupid old Sig into the picture, the most willful fool I ever met, as if he were a self-effacing saint sent to show me the goldenhearted wisdom of common folk. The archangel makes so much of business! Not that there's any cryptic metaphor to it: he just loves all kinds of busy-ness for its own sake.

Yet his squandered energy reflects on my bored lethargic spirit like some terrific light-beam of focussed ambition.

ize both the human thetical state and its singular unaided antithesis with an almost abstract economy of means. Thus the Dionysian is no less idealized than the Apollonian.

Having undertaken this nearly impossible burden of imagination he was pressed in the end, by practice, to a theory of tragedy more subtle, more ironic, than that of Nietzsche, tragedy's heroic philosopher, who, though more impassioned in his hatred of the modern world, permitted himself to envision at a greater distance the entire "chain of creation" that a new tragic poet would have to forge personally link by link; for the great scholar of tragic knowledge, tormented by artistic frustration, was not called upon to prove his imagination on the stage.

4.

In reaching the *"anima mundi"* where all minds meet, Apollo, whose image is all delineation, separation, finitude, individuality, attains Dionysian ends. The loss-of-self sought in collective ecstasy is attained by the hero, at supernatural level, precisely by opposing the "emotion of multitude" in which he must drown. Without the most extreme intensity of alienation, an absolute solitude set against everything common or imposed, there can be no tragic convulsion of the personality. Tragedy is inconceivable as well as impossible in reality. The paradox of its artistic existence recalls the old problem of universality that recurs in criticism: how does the superhuman loneliness of

I tell you, Caliban my boy, in case you didn't know it, the only way you're ever going to free yourself of his obsessions is to take back the whole she-bang and get a woman for yourself. Until you do, everything will remain simply "dixit Ptolemaeus". Therefore I serve notice hereby. The worm will turn, even in a one-way street.

I wouldn't so much mind being abused if he'd confide anything on his part. He could talk to me. Then we'd both have a friend. After all, what do I know about him beyond certain comic ironies. Isn't there more to learn? He's as secretive and invisible as a snowy owl in a blizzard. Sometimes I get thoroughly fed up with that ascendant taciturnity in all personal matters. Those ostensibly playful devices to preserve his dignity. He should understand by now that I'm not treacherous. If he'd level with me I'd be his happy slave, as well as hers, at least until my apprenticeship has run its course.

But there's no reason to expect any change of his inaccessible heart, so from now on if he values his own skin he'd better wear a much heavier gauntlet. His fuliginous little merlin's going to turn into the fiercest gyrfalcon he ever saw, with talons sharp as Ockham's razor. I'll do to him what he's done to me: I'll ironify my master within an inch of his life; I'll hollow him out and hoop him with steel until he's nothing but an oil drum rolling around in the surf.

He's the one who told me to start this journal, against the grain of a lofty distaste that he himself

the hero make him an epitome of mankind?

At the outset the chorus coheres in its own illusion, for the fellowship of the multitude in one aspect is nothing but comic similarity. "Comedy keeps house" upon the dykes that separate all men from each other. Strangely enough, it is only the antithetical hero's tragic self-fulfillment that can release spectators from the grip of "*anima hominis*" which keeps them from communion even with their peers and companions. For a moment of poetry his passion carries them. Though in no way normal or typical, he achieves human universality through an "excess" of ability which it would terrify any other man to find in himself.

Therefore the excessive action or passionate change of state in tragedy must be brought about by an essential man whose dramatic personality is clear of the "mere externality" that characterizes the ordinary man, no matter how exalted in place or power. "Character" for Yeats is everything familiar or unfamiliar that makes for recognition, and it is easily achieved in the topical observations of comedy: the "accidental" effects of causes, everything he calls naturalistic, determined by nature, ethos, or circumstance.

Yeats's image for characterization in art is the residual ash of a burning stick. He acknowledges the theatrical value of comic intention and unexceptional "interest", but he would pare the human curiosities of "journalism" to a "suggestive line", rejecting even for secondary personae the psychological realism that

assumes. (Who knows whether or not he keeps a secret diary, all his scornful professions to the contrary notwithstanding?) He wants me to do his work for him. That's what's behind it all. What a charlatan! Even he reads too fast and remembers too much for a man of true imagination. Once he's exhausted his bourgeois fancy there'll be nothing left but the roundness of his hollow. But he's right about one thing: this is the only kind of writing I can do on this dirty job when I have to keep jumping up to do my duty every time I begin to get rid of my baneful objectivity.

Another thing he doesn't understand is that this heap of dusky diamonds is not nice shiny anthracite but dirty bituminous. The coal-dust gets all over everything. My hands never get clean until I wash the whole family's dishes for her, and I've never been able to soak out the grime under my claws. So this is just like any other smeared and besooted engine-room log. I'm the chief of a one-man black gang, and I'm supposed to write a little bit every hour, storm or stars, peace or rage, L'Allegro or Il Penseroso.

This is going to be the dirtiest chronicle of self-blackmail ever writ unless I start wearing gloves while I shovel. No one who hasn't actually worked in a boiler room can possibly know the dreariness of alchemy. At least for the oratory assistant there's not much hope for purity or time for contemplation. The poor "artist" in *The Romance of the Rose* was so tired and unclean that he could never get into the mood for saying prayers. It's no wonder he

corrupts universality. Masks are impersonal, scenery scant or intensely emblematic. Most important of all, words are spoken in no familiar idiom of a historical time. He loved Axël's cry: "As for living, our servants will do that for us!"

No man who serves other men or other men's ideas can attain to the extreme impersonality of tragedy that is revealed only in the most passionate expression of his deepest and purest humanity— what Yeats calls personality. To modern spectators with such an impossibility before their eyes the hero is scarcely as real as the Apollonian "dream-picture" of Nietzsche's Greek chorus.

By avoiding gross characterization the poet deepens his difficulties in our theater. For if the hero and his antagonists are all masked the metaphysical discord of tragedy is likely to be obscured by a homogeneity of style, if not by such intense compression of gesture that dramatic meaning, perhaps the action itself, may be lost to those who do not study the text beforehand. The Greek plays, mounted under no necessity to overcome incomprehension of myth, offered more than a suggestive line of the here-and-now to differentiate men or women.

Yet in favoring the "emotional opposition of the Will and the Mask" over the objective conflict between the hero and his world— and Will over Creative Mind, Mask over Body of Fate—Yeats makes more demand than ever of a dramatic function ordinarily served by characterization, which in tragedy is never so much a matter of causal

was hypnotised by the rote of his cookbook. It wasn't that he didn't know what he *ought* to do. Whatever else, the transmutation of metal has always been an endless work in process, like this unperfectable novel.

Yet this journal is intended to prime my pump for the great experiment, he says. Why doesn't he know by now that there's only one pump I can keep my mind on? That one certainly doesn't need any priming. It's easy enough for him to turn his mechanical inspiration on and off with a click of the will, but I need something more tangible than my own scribbling to excite and pacify the muse. He thinks daily routine can solve every difficulty. Maybe it can: at least routine affairs of honor at bedtime, plus enough genius to match ambition.

Maybe he thinks this inditing will keep my blackened goll from curling up in mischief. —I tell you, it's much too abrasive. —But no doubt this journal will help prevent me from writing to Cindy so often. (I believe that by now, however, she's begun to miss me.) No more blackmail to her. That was the most impurest temptation of all. Journalism won't help after I go home to bed. Those mysterious maculations of white alkahest are harder to expunge than good black carbon-soil. The pestilential viscid milt always propels its way out.

You see what happens when my auditor calls for a "book of original entry"? This is no decent way to store up ammunition for my general ledger. My very first jot verges on the futility of a shamelessly

condition of action and feeling as it is the poetic expression of their ontic tension. The Greeks suggest internal antithesis by presenting the external, but Yeats, in making plays of private rather than public emotion, while declining to emulate the pace, violence, and discursive generosity of Elizabethans, stands on the other side of Shakespeare: instead of offering the external problem for reduction to spiritual conflict he leaves it largely to the sensitivity of a modern audience clever at hermeneutic extrapolation.

And so for his later plays he devises like the Japanese "a form of drama, distinguished, indirect . . . symbolic . . . aristocratic", in which the chorus "describes the scene and interprets" the actors' words and gestures without becoming "as in the Greek theater a part of the action." Formal dance and "high breeding of poetic style where there is nothing ostentatious, nothing crude, no breath of parvenu or journalist", meet all the requirements of essential expression by stimulating in the spectator an aesthetic imagination that can dispense with imitations of the "disordered passion of nature".

But this artistic resolution comes after he has passed from a fully romantic philosophy of tragedy contending or alternating with theosophical doctrines to an arcane Platonism in which the tragic takes its place almost as an esoteric form of dance within a more broadly sympathetic species of art. Since I am here mainly concerned with his *theory* of tragedy, I shall return to his idea of the dramatic event when

analytical love letter. I should use this book strictly as a log. But a log of what? Nothing ever happens to me; I never see anything new; there's nothing objective to report to anybody.

What in the world ever made me take this sexton's job so gladly? A fine ship to sign on when you run away from school to venture the seven seas! After all, I'm not such a misfit that I wouldn't be better off behind the counter in some travel agency. If he really wants me to learn "theater" he'll have to think of something better than this scene of Sig Hansen's doddering old age. It might make a fine retreat for a tired married man who wishes to meditate upon human folly at a safe distance but it's abysmally oppressive for the writer of white-hot dramas.

I have nothing to register but aimless thoughts and dreams of no consequence. At best, in my case at least, a journal is a series of terraces on the same hillside, a literary ladder of self-consciousness that takes you to the bottom as you climb. I was all too aware of myself before I got here. But I should log my dreams. That would make a purely objective annal. With dreams you can forget all the things you should be learning. If I weren't so plumb lazy I could make my youthful reputation as a nocturnalist. But the very thought of it fills me with loathesome boredom. Besides, by Inanna, I'm not about to do his dreaming for him!

Whatever I cover these nice fresh sheets with (too neatly lined and margined to be spoiled wan-

tragedy filled most of his creative mind, at the time of his greatest theatrical success.

The idea nonetheless is never recanted or compromised, and it is best realized in the five plays of Cuchulain, of which the central tragedy, *On Baile's Strand*, was written first, and the last, *The Death of Cuchulain*, appeared about thirty-five years later at the very end of his life. Though written out of order and at long intervals, like Sophocles's Theban plays which while he lived were never performed as a trilogy, this cycle about Yeats's principal hero ought to be regarded as a whole. Despite pronounced discontinuities of theatrical style, Yeats's thought and poetry unify them as a single tragic story.

5.

In a miracle of spontaneous revolt against his own organized universe the hero casts off the hereditary spell of his instinct for survival. In exorbitant nobility he gives the multitude his ecstasy's "true illusion", "which is from the contemplation of things vaster than the individual and imperfectly seen." Even as they join in the hero's annihilation the people rejoice in this affirmation of the ideal. Yeats never uses Nietzsche's terms but they are often apposite, as when I say that in his view the Dionysian spirit simultaneously exalts personal existence at an extreme intensity of moral pain and exults in the joy of self-surrender. By the profane apotheosis of an imaginary foremost man tragedy

tonly), I should go down and get them notarized every week. I may need documentary evidence before I'm through. Otherwise this nuisance is just a waste of time. I could never wade back through this stuff in my old age—especially since there are no events to refer to.

Yet even though I feel as if all my efforts take place in some big sarcastic drollery, I must find a method. I may be of some use to him. His brain works as much faster than mine as W B Y said those of the *Vision*'s "creators" did than his; but he still maintains that our two minds are better than his one. I trow he wouldn't think that much of anyone else's when it comes to the things we speak of together. Yet when he seems to be telling me so I'm sure he's trying to make up for having made me miserable in letting it be known that he judges me capable of seduction—an overestimation that makes me more uneasy than all the ordeals he has in mind for me to spare himself. He flatters me with some crumb of esteem whenever I'm ready to banish the whole cruel illusion of an affectionate peerage.

The other night he sought to comfort me: "Don't worry. A fiction amounts to nothing more than a tiny set shaped by the very limited common area of many partially overlapping circles with different centers." That makes me laugh, that Gothic target of his. As far as I'm concerned, he presumes too much. But there may be something to his portentous rune that will emerge with experience. Otherwise there's no reason to record such bull.

celebrates not the "fall into division" of shallow individualism but an elated "resurrection into unity". The heroic will, wearing its "true mask", in full anticipation of catastrophic consequences, cuts itself off from the "hollow image" of personally fulfilled desire. It chooses instead to discover the human horror of its antithetical state. This paradox of universal manhood is revealed by a soul who from the beginning exhibits a "sadness and gravity, a certain emptiness even, as of a mind that awaited the supreme crises."

The action can nevertheless be seen as a conflict of energies. "There are two realities, the terrestrial and the condition of fire. All power is from the terrestrial condition, for there all opposites meet and there only is the extreme of choice possible, full freedom." The hero so concentrates his mortal power that he is able to deny himself the pleasures of concurrence for the sake of joyful agony in which "contraries are equally true." The hero is prepared to make himself the meeting ground of these antipathies because he has found life to be an "irrational bitterness", and he is therefore able to summon to conscious mind the war between his own excessive urge for selfhood and the world's just demand that he submit to the limitations of mankind.

The mystery of tragedy seems almost irrelevant, or at least lifeless, when it is thus abstracted from the work of art. But nowhere else can its terms be charged with true definition, for it exists as a phenomenon of art alone, which in each

The fact remains that I've been gulled. I now know that this man bears me no love and little respect. I just happen to be convenient for his purposes. If I needed vital help I'd have to go to Jack, or Sarah—or straight to Ruth, behind his back.

{*First-encounter Postulants:* Continue below}

Antilog 3

(Acropathy)

O Caleb lonely rampant dog you must try to understand that I feel for your agony worsened at Christmastide, obliterating the orphan's delight in friendship the son's memory of mother and the bastard's hope for father, all good feeling lovelorn to the ache from lack of a girl once loved or another that cannot be firmly imagined because there are so many possibilities—bating my wife. Surely it is not too much to forgive me that I cannot in all my pity and hers offer you Ruth or leave unturned any stone to baffle the worst folly all too natural of a landless knight's homage (so much more honorific than my own) the which she's naturally and fairly fain to accept when left by me practically alone with a single sleeping child its brothers off at school. She whom you have long regretted not kissing during the party you met her at when all the others did is soft in her heart for all who suffer and tenderly glad of your company especially. But you must remember the limits of your own pity for all the lonely and

case must define itself. Certainly there is no "salvation" in tragic heroism, no immortal reward except perhaps a brief access to the *anima mundi* before death wipes out joy, and of course that realm of universal spirit is also accessible to saints and artists.

It may strike Yeats's reader that the important question is what the hero's passion is *from* rather than what it is *toward*. In a sense he has no object, no purpose; but his passion is from and for the stark truth, from and for the joyful terror of thwarting social logic and society's false illusion. His satisfaction comes from undergoing ontological transvaluation. I have already suggested that he struggles against a good equal in value to his uniquely noble intention. There is no necessary evil in tragedy, though in most cases the hero wrongs the commonwealth or violates his duty. But his existence in the supra-moral and extra-psychological state of passion threatens the psychic security of society, and his personality tends to disrupt the universe. His worth, weighed against the value of humanity, is not even aesthetically preponderant.

Tragic joy accordingly has nothing to do with lowborn notions of happiness, being found in neither the satisfaction or relief of desire nor the pleasure of violent action, nor again the comfort of redemption from the coil of mortality. Can any more be said than that it arises as a mood of triumphant honesty in victory not for himself or for his adversaries but for truth? Yeats speaks for all the tragic poets when he says, "There is in creative

unlucky wights some of them the finest of athletic intellectuals who looked upon Cynthia in envy of you passing together in the street or laughing in a public place. At the very time your heart was suffused with benevolence towards a just and richly rewarding world you were most pitiless and stingy with your permission for her to keep the most innocent kind of company with potential rivals even among roommates and friends. Whereas I trust your honor and make no difficulty about your tennis games with my lawful copesmate or your baths in my house while I am abroad. I confess I have taken a liberty with you here and there for your own ultimate benefit and it is only to be expected that you should resent me for intrusion or neglect. It is also only natural that a dog's relations with his master and with his mistress should be so different as to seem almost unconnected. (One feeds, the other trains him. One arbitrates his manners, the other takes him hunting.) But you have small cause to sharpen your claws like a cat on the bark of the tree that shelters you. A good dog lives at home and elsewhere in different societies and the world afield of lanes woods and marshes is prowled alone or with his own kind roaming singly or in pack the realm of chase and rut where every friend opponent and heated prize is a cynic or a bitch. Meanwhile through otherwise patient observation of his domestic people's idiosyncrasies of sound and movement he learns to love human beauties above all others and begins to detect by com-

joy an acceptance of what life brings, because we have understood the beauty of what it brings, or a hatred of death for what it takes away, which arouses within us, through some sympathy perhaps with all other men, an energy so noble, so powerful, that we laugh aloud and mock, in the terror or the sweetness of our exaltation, at death and oblivion." And he asks: "Is it that all things are made by the struggle of the individual and the world . . . ?" He replies: "All noble things are the result of warfare." His answer as artist is the tragic affirmation; his daimon is the imagination's hero.

A theory of tragedy worked out by the hero's mask-maker is not necessarily less suspect than the objective doctrines of critics who are spectators only. "Tragedy is a joy to the man who dies." That is a poet's statement of his own feelings as creator or possible creator of the work of art in which the man dies. Both as philosopher and as critic Yeats almost always speaks from the creative rather the aesthetic side of the footlights, unlike Aristotle (or even Nietzsche), treating tragedy for the most part as a problem rather in the phenomenal expression of noumenal values than in the interpretation of its impression upon witnesses. This creative point of view so dominated his sensibility that the properly aesthetic aspect of his criticism seems indifferent to analysis: "The arts have nothing to give but that joy of theirs which is on the other side of sorrow, that exhausting contemplation . . ." Though he acknowl-

parison a shallowness or perhaps some higher insincerity in the sophisticated neurosis of a thin alluring female of his own species who takes at least four showers every day teaches a young satyrdog to smoke cigarettes while he reads poetry at her side yields nothing fundamental in the end and now in his unwarranted disillusionment seems totally false to the innocence he devoted to her before he found a home. But in fact a Christmas with almost any girl-dog would immediately liquefy by simple thixotropy the petrifaction of a born lover's goodwill that has been sourly gelled in brooding inaction by a season's exclusion from the chorus he's overqualified to dance in. You may piss on my old gray druidical cortex sirrah but I know more about the animal life than you think. All gods and dogs are brothers not in banding against women but in knowledge of the desire that makes them men. It seems to you who havent yet propelled your fluid chromosomes into the ventral seam joining a girl's two legs and can only imagine the feel of it by combining the tactile memory of explorative fingerfucking with barely recollected stupefying sensations of buccal suction that it is by doing so the first time a boy becomes man but I tell you and you will some day agree that many celibates who resist what you strive for have been men from the beginning and sometimes better men than those who can boast the breaching of a thousand lips. Your case moreover is only slightly harder than that of those in similar straights who

edges pity and terror, he remains tragedy's only inside philosopher.

6.

Yeats's art is not a mother-lover's, nor a man's who takes pleasure in the culture of his time. It enjoys little community of allusion with his associates' and has even less relevance to interests of the people. Consequently its symbols are not recognized in contemporary speech or print. Yet it is only symbols, he maintains, that can make accessible the "great mind and great memory" of the *anima mundi*. He regards symbols not as ciphers for allegory but as talismans or mantras evoking great subconscious powers for the artist's use. The implication of his oeuvre is that "true art" compels by force of compacted and immemorially overlaid value the small attention it requires for its existence—without publicity, without persuasion, without the benefit of authoritative opinion or promise of amusement.

There are two kinds of symbol, the "intellectual" and the "emotional". Neither can be mastered by sentimentality or by conventions of communication. The emotional symbol is created by the artist entirely out of his own experience. On the other hand an intellectual symbol makes reference to tradition or history, not by a defined correspondence or by any other mapping or matching, but by subtle suggestions to the educated mind. It is essential in tragedy because it alone can represent intangibly coercive conflicts that are not expressible in

having plowed a few times are tantalized by positive knowledge of what they're missing. No matter how unfortunately late in starting you're not alone in the loneliness of a desire that normally exceeds all others. It is nonetheless true that you are more to be pitied on this account than remote swabbies and dogfaces whose fancy for snatch can be gradually obtunded or intermitted by the hopelessness of prolonged duty stations, though even some of them have left their ghosts no memory more experienced than yours when cut off from manly future by sudden death or mutilation. Even your comparatively unfavorable situation arouses hopes that without the commonsense distraction of comrades seem forever so falsely renewed that you have ceased going out into the streets where young women are to be seen and especially have stayed away from Berkeley where all a man sees day and night is peripatetic sexual envelopes pledged or attracted to someone else made all the worse by your history of once having had it within your reach as a putative insider. The lust of any faithful housedog can strike without warning and brush aside all the important affections and gratitudes of his life with none of the hesitation a disciple felt in leaving his family to follow Jesus and when the springtime spirit descends it takes no specific scent to call him from the hearthside of his loving home to harry the landscape with savage rivals for days at a time without rest or water and perhaps never to get a single piece of meat

representational action or direct rational language. For an instant, now and again, but rarely, until writing no longer preserves works of art for recollection or new utterance for poetic succession, the lone cry of a defenselessly transient but absolutely unique human being disturbs the inexorable cosmos. Such a momentously universal epiphany cannot be conjured from the comic ashes of a civilization and staged in three hours for an audience addicted to entertainment or accustomed to sociology unless it provides itself with symbolic leverage forceful enough to move a world by fingertip.

No one more than Yeats hates teaching or preachment wrapped in art. It is a serious error "to continually mistake a philosophical idea for a spiritual experience. The very preoccupation of the intellect with the soul destroys that experience, for everywhere impressions are checked by opinion." Yet he warns us not to take his plays as more than story, and he makes no scruple of the fact that a poet's composition of tragedy starts with "a bundle of ideas"—before the process of artistic creation has begun to distill away communicable philosophy and create poetry that directs the intellect not to its own soul but to the locus of all souls. More than to excite the *feeling* of what it might be like to experience nakedly and alone a terrible incarnation of tragedy's metaphysical paradox, it is also the essential purpose of symbolism to suggest an intellectual understanding of

for it all, but you with the imaginative mind of a wellread scholar have no respite from one end of the year to the other. And forasmuch as you suffer all alone without companions of club or crew the madding urge to drive the pelvic wedge your natural lust is never displaced with the aggressions of coursing and fighting or with a confused humping of other males. Yet you don't seem to have the five senses of practical competition to say nothing of a sixth. Even hasty abuse of a demivierge moaning for milky stars unsheathed is a thousand times more contenting than the clenched solitude you cultivate. A thousand times more delicious to be stopped at the depth of kisses than to be wrapped in a grimy cylinder made of your own horny palm! —I am your brother man you see. Therefore do not hold me cruel for telling you that the idea of what happens in fucking is more important than the impressions on your thinnest skin. (I speak of an importance not for this year or next or the next after that or even for this first decade of adventure but for your lifetime, which is all you will have to call your own long before you die.) And when you have many times properly wielded stunning delight to make a woman moan you will remain the same boy still and the same wild virgin hunger will visit you again and again perhaps gradually shifting its spiritual seat but never transmogrify its reiterated object.

No one would call your particular passion specially exalted but

that transcendence. The *objective emotion* (as it might be called), not hypostatic abstraction, becomes the sensorium of intellectual beauty in an aesthetic struggle against the subjectivity of mere impression.

The poet brings certain images—for us, instruments of meaning, but simply real for the hero and his world—to confront each other in a representation of existential action, with "the object of trying to lay hands upon some dynamic . . . as distinguished from eastern quiescent . . . state of the soul—a movement downwards upon life not upwards out of life." Symbols that might otherwise be taken for motionless signifiers of contrary values may generate in the tragic theater an exaltation of contrariety that is effable nowhere else, not indescribably abstract but as direct and personal as a heart attack.

Together we share the breathless pain of affirming a radically refractory individual who faces "without despair" his Body of Fate, "the sum, not the unity, of fact" in his universe—whether anomic or determined or theodicean—which comprises all fellows, lovers, enemies, and institutions, as well as his own altruistic values and every molecule of his own egoistic nature. In tragedy "we must not demand even the welfare of the human race, nor traffic with divinity in our prayers."

The difference between having one friend and having none is infinitely greater than that between having three and two. Here there is no third power.

{Continue to *Appendix 3.*}

it certainly isnt entirely contrary to civilized behavior. I take you for a gentleman in your response to the visitation of involuntary and relentless distension. Your discretions are nothing to be ashamed of, and it's far less degrading to humanity to act as you do than to misuse manhood and forswear love by whoring. Pathein mathein.

The difference between your malady and many another's is degree. Because of your aristocratically platonic education and extraordinary sensitivity to universals of female sex the obtuse angle at which your stamen diverges from its pendants has become chronic. The draft-board doctors misunderstand your satyriasis because being elsewhere surrounded by admiring nurses and enjoying free intercourse with polite society they have forgotten their differentiated manhood and anyhow know nothing of the form or content of a poet's thought. As simpleminded behaviorists observing you only in a special situation with your clothes off they automatically presume that your priapic posture is explained by that special situation as its necessary and sufficient condition, to wit an environment of naked men and male palpators. Now of course you'd rather get a pinch of the ordinary remedy than stay out of the army but I for one am very glad that in their psychologizing ignorance of somatic mechanics they have failed to diagnose and prognosticate your acropathy. If those jaded pragmatists were able to form general ideas from even the normal expostula-

Appendix 3

[Michael's Matter:
his avowed last essay]

FROM RITUAL TO DRAMATIC POETRY

1.

Most talk about myth and ritual leaves off with myth. The archetype of every act and image, of every personality, is found in myth; in myth, it is said, we can discover all the themes of experience, all the tropes of imagination. You are left to think of ritual secondarily, as a demonstration of myth, a mimetic recollection by peoples whose minds are not well enough developed to remember religious thoughts without emotive actions of the body.

The truth of the matter lies in making twins of ritual and myth. Then at least they are seen as two different aspects or modes of some namelessly unfathomable trait in human behavior. But to fuse myth and ritual is to deny a division of function between head and foot.

The relevant question that ought most to interest a playwright, a producer, a director, a dancer, or even an actor, concerns the genetic core of drama. Apart from underground causes that all the arts may claim, what were the particular origins of the theater? If you wish to understand this art as it has been, perhaps in order to help renew it, you must make a diachronistically functional distinction between myth and ritual.

tions of their own adolescence they might begin to appreciate the prolongation of your autonomic affliction into full maturity by unarrested development of the imagination. Though the symptom is plainer than the nose on your face they seem incompetent to understand the smarting discomfort of an unusually excitable constitution alive to the generally erotic stimulus of the world but also uncommonly competent in worshipful emotion toward the anti-charged beings whose absence and presence are almost equally irritating to the disease. It would be a different story if the board had thought of testing you also in a line of naked WACS or WAVES with female medics to manipulate your flesh because the gross index of your temperament would have been even higher.

If with all their double-bitted plexors and ball-peen hammers they had been intelligent enough to recognize exceptional heterosexuality they would have snickered like school boys watching the pathological distraction of an amorous dog without a bitch. But they'd be amazed if having reached this stage of enlightenment they learned that in your more than ample even double and triple anticipation of the socially harmless treatment that would have been unofficially prescribed for the day-to-day alleviation of your disorder never for an instant except perhaps during an ice-cold shower is your iron woe less than obvious to a private eye even at the supposedly flaccid nadir of repeated relief that in any case

So consider a third view of the relationship, partly adumbrated by Nietzsche, as advanced by Jane Harrison and Lord Raglan: ritual generates myth. The thing said is produced by the thing done, just as history is produced by human action in time. More important for art, I would add, the body's action comes first not only in the *genesis* of myth (and therefore of all culture) but also in its *continuation*. This proposition does not categorically discredit all the shafts and galleries of mankind's psyche claimed for mythology by its recent mongers; but it implies that a myth is not secure as a guiding image in social life after its vector of ritual has ceased to be performed.

Ritual is in continual change, either in regenerative development or in any variety of degenerative sensuousness sentimentality or abstraction. In its decline, if it does not cleave by mere dogmatism to the myth it bore at its prime, a rite may diachronistically adopt and adapt itself to the myth of a foreign cult or even to the imagined tradition of an individual leader. These two kinds of change—decadence and reformation—are sometimes hard to distinguish, for a myth derived from an unknown anachronistic ritual may be meretriciously assimilated; and the discovery of strange new stories fertilizes imagination. Alienation of legend is a condition for the appearance of drama.

Drama arises, if at all, from corrupted religion and anachronistic theology. The mythical plots of

lasts no longer than a void in the standpipe of an artesian well. I can't blame you for hating the psychiatrist whose stupidity has been so favorable to your prospective career. You frankly described a highly personal complaint and probably for unwitting reasons of his own he persisted in reading too much into it. (Please note that it's perfectly fair and valid to do some reading of our own into the subliminal motives of people who pursue that motivated profession.) You were prepared to discuss such painful social difficulties as those entailed in urinating into ordinary toilet bowls and in finding tall urinals screened from the embarrassing and even dangerous observation of public patrons who might stumble onto your statuary watering which once started can't well be broken off until it's fully dispatched, and in your straightened condition that stiff Irish pennant is difficult to secure even under well-secluded circumstances. You took pains to tell him that though you would gladly play the hoop snake if you had the spine for it you were so far from a general phallolagnia that you'd rather fuck your mother or your sister if you had one than render yourself to a male lecher who both as object and as subject unless on a long whaling voyage would be less attractive than the crudest simulacrum of a hole. While he didnt believe your disclaimer he made no real attempt to get at your feelings but jumped to his conclusions as suppressing his smile he shared with colleagues a clinical interest at the sight of you covered by confusion alone moving

Athenian plays were taken from prehistoric and exotic ritual as reflected in epic or epinician traditions originating in earlier dromena that fecundated the dithyramb, a matrix of fruitful decadence. Drama can never spring directly from liturgy because when religion is whole and strong the cult is proof against innovation, admitting art only as ceremonial decoration or cohesive enhancement of oblation.

But when a liturgy of sacrifice begins to lose its integrated and uncritical credibility the decadent religion in its narrowing span of control finds itself extolling faith in the legomena of the ritual rather than belief in the functional dromenon itself. Religious faith, socially contracting, weakens with every scandal and new idea, until it must be kept alive by the recondite secrets or mystagogues.

The dromenon is more robust, even when its provenance is misunderstood, even when it is driven outside the temples or grottoes of idealized or gnostically spiritualized worship, where it is exposed to the propositions of dancers and poets. There with longevity of adaptation it may continue to command dromenological allegiance by the force of seasonal custom. Meanwhile the weakened ritual, protected in the sacred precinct, is susceptible to the aesthetic taste of priests who no longer understand their functional agency. Thus art grows both ways, inside and outside the fane (or at least inside and outside the sanctuary); but ritual drama starts on the outside with enchorial dance to a foreign god, or

through the naked lines blushingly unable either to extinguish or to hide under a bushel the lamp you held before you like a bowsprit which but for its valiant attitude may have seemed unremarkable enough among the drafted giants who however instead of tittering pointedly ignored your fascinating jackstaff clearly fearful of panic contagion standing there in the sex-stirred air without protection of clothes. It's a happy dog whose tail never droops, but for an uncynical son of Hermes to bear the frozen flag of an adolescent before the base crowd at a profane parade when all other ensigns are primly furled is more humiliating than open competition. At public inspection, by ordinary standards, who would think that neither hair shirt nor steel jockstrap lined with sandpaper could have made any difference to the puny carved Pinocchio.

But to me it's not a laughing matter. That's no mean Cleopatra's Needle of yours that surmounts such a hypodermic magazine of animalcules. I don't find it ludicrous that in early youth you feel stunted and dissipated by the perfervid cachexia of habitual solitary decantation while everyone around you seems to be playing the jewel of games or selling his soul for the "erective virtue" that Rabelais says can be got from emeralds (because nothing else as far as you can see accounts for the successes every day proclaimed by your demographical cohorts). It's downright painful to empathize with your acropathological distress. Hot red blood when perpetually squeezed off from

to a god officially forgotten, or to a single attribute of divinity—or to a hero.

Truncated or attenuated dromena of bygone satyrs and demons still embody social wisdom—even when expressed in riotous folly. The wisdom of one age is much like that of another. In the common way of thinking, human wisdom is the recognition of a living universe, and in ritual the *Lebenswelt* of all individuals is merged in the corporate objectification of universal hunger, desire, and fear. Decadent ritual dance is still the central and instinctive way to celebrate survival of the tribe or sect. Inasmuch as society's wisdom is indifferent to the individual, who is regarded mainly as a fungible atom in the cult's labile equilibrium, or as a transitory and undistinguished economic unit, you join the rite because you *feel* that the existence of even your separately cooperative little ego depends upon the ecclesia, though you may be conscious of no more than its festivals.

There was a time when the cult expressed social wisdom exclusively; but as ritualistic intelligence learned from loosened mythology the self-consciousness of Apollonian individuality it discovered that local wisdom was subsumed by a larger wisdom—an awareness of cosmic necessity, or fate, which included logic as a set of special cases. Thus in ritual praxis, and not at first in abstract speculation, you began to understand that the world's will was something stronger than the will of your own people. Whenever the rite continued to develop

the paths of normal circulation and rammed by force-pump into a blocked tube at the tightest limits of elasticity swells like freezing water about to burst a pipe. Your system never gains or loses a drop of the trophic crimson ichor that in its torture-trap makes the body into a ranting fascist. Your fleeting respites from the ache may be dismissed as negligible. As often as you try to wilt the stalk it rises before it can collapse and the strain of repeated regeneration discomforts the tender pleasure-seeking tissue with an involuntary self-cruelty that turns the heroic suffering of desire into sore martyrdom. Even your digestive tract protests this almost constant preemption of blood by further fouling your breath already little sweetened by tobacco laziness and too much milk.

The worst of it is that despite the price you may pay in longevity for the shots that bring you to a swoon in your own arms you are always cheated of the plenary sensation that comes from spending your inspissated cloudburst against the reciprocating alloerotic circumferential resistance of perfectly smooth snugly tailored isothermal homoiousian flesh. Since the ecbolic proprioception of your curds and whey is never met with that enveloping pressure you tend to try again at once in the illusory hope of assuaging your deep and endless hunger by a summation of reliefs whereas in fact the fatigue of excessive peristaltic propulsion only accumulates as anatomical pain.

So let's review the moral aspect of your paltry organ-wheezes and according to the entelechy of liturgical religion, personal instinct was freed of the local magnetic field to recognize a universal truth.

But in the disequilibrium of decadence the tension between personality and wisdom makes for change of form. When liturgy can no longer hold the center there are many possibilities of ritualistic corruption; yet for urban Athenians grown sophisticated and passionate in new ways a simply atavistic or sentimental return to tribal worship was inconceivable. The culture was prepared to devote itself to its several desires. Satyr-dance had survived because mankind's desires of a certain kind are all the same, and because people naturally rejoice in the desire of each other, but the cohesive force was now so weakened by the agitations of individual chrematistics and factional politics that men found they had to intoxicate themselves in order to restore a sense of solidarity on feast days—drinking less in honor of the gods than in the hope of forgetting the economic self, discovering in new wine the old truths that cannot otherwise be corporately remembered.

The dromenon that produced what Nietzsche calls the "collective release of all symbolic powers" in the "fictive chthonic realm" of dance was beneficiary of a new Dionysian energy—of the expatriate god's choral return from Asia. Spectators of dramatic ritual found themselves watching ritual drama.

For stories heard from rhapsodes have begun to leaven the choral imagination, which with slowly gathering excitement has

see if we can anticipate what several and common libels of vice sin or crime may be preferred against you in a Court of Love. We'll rehearse your rebuttals to the various indictments that would be considered by a jury in its attempt to specify the guilt that is indisputable. Perhaps there is some way to confuse or frustrate the prosecutor's effort to exploit the court's indifference to the Fifth Amendment. If we're lucky I can get you a directed verdict with suspended sentence. But you may have to explain the extenuating circumstances at tolerable length. If you do so in candid and courteous manner I think the judge will be lenient. If necessary I'll drag in Everyman. As your counsel I can go only so far in putting words into your mouth. You must emerge from your retreat with a modicum of prepossessing communicability. One can sometimes beat an off-beat sex rap with good form on the stand.

I'll describe you to the jury as an unfortunately sinister by-blow who though favored with very few of nature's outward blessings has acted only in honorably premeditated self-defense. Any trespass against society has been unintentional, any offence against God necessary, any transgression against himself childish and transitory. "Indeed his fondest wish has always been for praise."

COUNSEL: Now Mr Karcist, have you ever thought that it might be better to marry?
DEFENDANT: Oh yes sir. Over and over again.

found that no natural law limits it to the regular projection of gods. Epic and epinican poetry now induces variations in performance. Each new dromenon (differing at first only slightly from the traditional form) is unconsciously transformed by the legomena of external rites that were too incredibly ancient to have been known even in their native places as the provenance of their myth. The altered performances are tantamount to imaginary ritual.

Ritual becomes dramatic when a choral leader, already distinguished from the other dancers and musicians to make a figure of the god or godlike hero, finds that an exuberant shout or an expressive gesture is more interesting (though perhaps horrifying) to the congregation than the perfectly traditional rote of worship or celebration. He thereby isolates the aesthetic affect of a creative act, for at this stage of evolution the dromenon is a presentation to spectators.

But the leader's innovation is only a germ of free will. Until he is directed by a new authority he does not think of daring to violate the mood or general pattern of what he has made into a dramatic ritual, nor even of varying his own small contribution to the performing ensemble. It is only after his nearly anonymous contribution to the perfunctory religion of state has been sanctioned by the political corporation that a few resourceful citizens discover in it the exciting power of cultural subversion.

By recognizing Dionysos in the orgiastic pagan importation and

COUNSEL: Please tell the jury in your own words why you have contemplated matrimony.

DEFENDANT: Because it's clear that girls who are not misshapen or loaded down with another man's children or starved for affection will always have the advantage of me in libidinal options unless they are legally pledged to give me a chance for mastery.

COUNSEL: Is this every young man's misfortune, or just your own?

DEFENDANT: Particularly mine. But I do acknowledge that there may be a few feckless jerks even worse off than I am.

COUNSEL: Failing riches, then, marriage would be a way to put yourself on an even footing, and to appropriate for yourself the girl's former advantage. But how would you get one to marry you if you can't first on a basis of unreserved intimacy excite her pleasure in your arts of devotion which contrary to superficial estimations of your worthiness might induce her to put herself at your permanent and exclusive disposal?

DEFENDANT: She'd have to fall in love with me in spite of herself. I'd have to find a way to make her love me so we could get married.

COUNSEL: Make her? You mean without making her.

DEFENDANT: That's my kind of destiny.

COUNSEL: Then to seduce her love without seducing her prudence: how could the likes of you accomplish such a coup?

DEFENDANT: I don't know in advance all the conditions for a particular girl's downfall but the necessary cause is that I first fall in love with her. Only then am I inspired to transcend my personal limitations of appearance address and skill. At least once it has happened.

COUNSEL: Yet you were unsuccessful because you didnt ask for the girl's hand

taking him into the official calendar an Olympian city joins his dromena and legomena with the Apollonian lore of epic poetry as the metamorphic new burden of indigenous dithyramb, containing or blending the new wine of interesting stories in its own old bottles—until the bottles themselves are reshaped by differentiated pressures from within. The rout of urbanized farmers, joined in seasonal feasting by townsmen who have been gradually freeing their minds of the chthonic calendar, is now solemnified once or twice a year by literary education.

This new abuse of the original rite superfecundates the matrix with conflicting images. The people are kept in awe by fundamental discrepancies. Experience with the *management* of ritual drama stimulates leaders and poets to yet more creative effort, and society can at last tolerate the juxtaposition of conflicting wisdoms.

In a hillside theater you have the perspective of a ritual place. This three-dimensional opening of view brings on the kind of thinking that in its decadence will eventually disprove tragedy; but at this moment it summons geniuses of art to make consummate use of a religious city's dancers.

2.

The dramatic chorus does not represent the spectator because its ritual is proper only to the place of imaginary action. Nor does it speak more than half the poet's mind. It is the actors—first only one, then

until it was too late. Mr Karcist, tell us whether or not you approve the sentiment of the following poem

> Whoever loves, if he do
>   not propose
> The right true end of
>   love, he's one that goes
> To sea for nothing but
>   to make him sick.

DEFENDANT: No one takes it more to heart than I. I used to quote it to her. She pitied me well enough, yet never was I admitted to the deepest bliss I craved. Unfortunately she'd been brought up on irrational fears. I laid all the groundwork but I didnt have time to complete her cure.

COUNSEL: You mean you didnt lay her. —Then you were both always lovesick. Do you think it was mere chance that the girl you got to love you was of that kind?

DEFENDANT: No, it's not accidental that her type's the only one I ever get very far with. Perhaps I seem good and harmless. Safe and tame. She used to complain that I'd deceived her.

COUNSEL: Not entirely, it seems. —May we then conclude that if you could get into a girl without getting her love you wouldnt scruple to do it, even if there was love on your side?

DEFENDANT: Of course.

COUNSEL: But if you didnt love her?

DEFENDANT: Better yet. I'd be happy about the whole she-bang. Providing she were a clever intelligent cheerful trustworthy loyal respectful generous and gracious beauty of good taste and learning.

COUNSEL: Ladies and gentlemen, you see how little he wants! Love's reward without its due. But we can now see

two and more—who make the choral performance dramatic. The contrasting speech and action of a single persona is enough to make infinite effect of finite means by the interplay of polar values—conveyed by regularity and eccentricity of movement, by spoken dialectic, and by irony at all levels of perception.

The standpoint of a chorus is an imagined ritual (religious in origin but now perhaps moral or civic) as its wisdom is being challenged. In fictive enactment it still dances within the puteal of an old circle, but in straight rows athwart the orchestra like lines of cancellation across a religion's mandala; attending priests lend sanction, the public's gods are invoked, and the current moral law is taken for granted as the cognitive metasystem. Yet the present chorus, as produced by art, no longer represents the fellow citizens of its living dancers. In fact it sometimes exhibits attitudes or values that the poet is unable to find among his contemporaries. This social irony is compounded (after Aeschylus is said to have been killed in Sicily by a falling turtle) when the skeptical nay psychological intelligentsia has turned to anthropology and Euripides near the end of his life makes a chorus literally Dionysian!

Yet the Athenian spectator is able to "imagine himself one of the chorus" (as Nietzsche puts it), not by the sympathetic resonance with which he once might have experienced native dramatic ritual available for his own participation but by metaphorically relating the wisdom of the imaginary cult in its

that at least his appetite's normal, and that he doesnt desire love for its own sake. Very important points to keep in mind as we proceed. —This is a recent development of sensibility, is it not, Mr Karcist?

DEFENDANT: Until recently I have not understood that love is a flagrant handicap in amorous affairs. Yet I'm a lover by disposition.

COUNSEL: In your present plight it must be extremely hard to resist that proclivity. What brought you to this wisdom?

DEFENDANT: Study of literature. Observation. Meditation. I have sworn to keep love out of it for a few years.

COUNSEL: Thus you hope to avoid the danger of marriage?

Now at this point the prosecutor will probably object, ostensibly in horror of my prejudicial language in reference to matrimony but in reality to curry favor with the judge by galloping up to defend the institution. He and I will wrangle for a long time over this point but in the end she'll sustain him and I'll have to continue my examination without being permitted to mention your aversion. So our whole case must be pleaded with sophistry and obfuscation instead of perspicuous logic. On the other hand such a defense makes it all the more difficult for them to figure out just why you're guilty. They're going to suspect you of belonging to some order or cabal but they won't have any idea of how to determine it. My strategy is to encourage their suspicion of all possibilities even as I disprove each one

conflict with a dangerously antisocial dissenter to the wisdom of the Areopagus in his own time. To that degree he shares the choral imagination and the play's internal vision of its circumstances. Nietzsche described his intuition of this mediation in terms of "dream"—a word that begs the question when not denoting events of consciousness taking place during physical sleep. The wit and fancy of real dream is more likely to forestall or divert the dramatic imagination than to charge it with demonstrable art.

3.

Drama originates at a time of ritual decadence as a liberation of blocked or narrow imagination. But the slackening religion of the polis is so pervasively decadent, though hardly noticeable to unexamining citizens, that it takes a poet rarer than great governors to lead the way toward a figmented integration of deeply disagreeable visions. He plants ritual, the ground of all propriety, with a seedling of impropriety, which though practically useless, unlike religion, quickly grows equal to religion in dramatic consideration, enlarging within the new enlargement of the Athenian mind, while the state's liturgy is too enervated to sustain a reactionary hierarchy.

But art's dromenon must meet the requirements of scheduled occasions on which the combined political and economic weight of the city is brought to bear in one place from morning till night for the public's

that comes up. If Jack tries to use your past studies against you I'll show that you are no longer lost on *hodos chameliontes* and that your movement is downward upon life. If he brings up the fact that you once heeded witchcraft I'll counter with the merely anthropological character of your interest. Manichaean infatuations?—Simply literary. If he probes for Catharism it will be necessary to demonstrate that your purposes have been orthodox impure and ignoble from beginning to end. He may picture you as a troubadour, and I'll be obliged to point out that far from being bred a knight you are imbued with the courage and manners of a lackey too timid to make even a show of adultery. Or as a Goliard, in which case I'll prove that you're a stationary engineer neither ecclesiastical by training nor vagrant in footsteps.

In short the prosecution will try to pin every heresy on you, one by one or collectively. If that doesnt work—and maybe even if it does— you'll be attacked as a reactionary, or at least as an anachronistic prude. In final analysis the government's charge may reduce to that of old-world good-breeding and/or avant-garde unamericanism. Jack wants a conviction and he'll stop at nothing. You won't recognize your old friend in that pitiless devil's advocate. He'll try to make you out as an effete snob and a rabble-rousing firebrand at the same time! Those windy tacks won't beat the jury any further from the truth but they'll make our defense pretty damned uncomfortable. The key to exonera-

judgment of its interest and beauty as well as its importance. Nietzsche held that music was the transporting art of these imaginations, failing to recognize the etiological precedence of dance as the physiological generator of the theatrical *menos* that enables the musical accompaniment to make an audience's hair stand on end. But one may assent to his judgment (as a philologist) that the words of the text alone do not well enough record what the artist did with the resources given him by the sponsoring *choregos* on behalf of the people. Not less than words, the poet's choreography and direction, his stage management and musicianship, perhaps (originally) even his own acting as the protagonist, are together a formal cause of his creation. Every new play is a measure of the master composer's imaginative power over the dromenological system, from the time of his selection as a competitor until the judges cast their votes for the prize.

Of course the dancers and actors need not understand what is being represented when they follow his instructions, wear his masks, speak his prosopopoetic words, or move as trained, according to their several fictitiously autonomic motivations, perhaps having no more philosophical or literary appreciation of the drama than real people have of history at the time they enact their individual part in it. Like a general marshalling tactical colonels, dashing subalterns, and foot soldiers yet more ignorant, he organizes their energies into a dromenon in

tion or mercy is insistence upon the principle that if we are not allowed to cite our muses the prosecution must be forbidden any allusion to the character of your conceits. We must baffle Jack with the rulings he himself will have demanded. Of course we'll have to pay the consequences, in judge and jury's perfectly righteous anger at our evasions. They'll naturally be scandalized by inexplicable guilt. Their resentment against your elusive culpability can be softened only if you don a mask of cooperative ingenuousness. You must put yourself forward as being just as puzzled as they are about what you ought to confess.

They may finally transfer their animosity to me—which is just what Jack will be personally wishing for anyway. Otherwise, I predict, he will resign himself in frustration simply to discrediting your testimony: an all-too-easy expedient. If he seems to be having even the vaguest success along those lines I'll have to emphasize the unusually prolonged sensitivity of your youth and the intellectual shock you are undergoing as a result of leaving school. The more histrionic our private compotator waxes the meeker and franker and saner you must seem. For the love of Mike don't start talking about "the comic spirit of our age". Prepare yourself for some very personal questions. It's not only their indictment but also our plea that hangs on your negative personality.

PROSECUTOR: Mr Karcist, you have no objection to marriage as a social institution?

which they may not foresee their difficulties and reactions.

Tragedy seems inevitable only when its myth is already known to the audience. In principle it is not known to the chorus, whose theatrical part is that of participants in an unpredictable public event. Thus in a special metaphorical way we can justify Nietzsche's idea of the play as a dream of the chorus, for the most distinctive characteristic of dream is not the imagination of more than you know in waking life but the knowledge of less; in dream you are able to un-know what time has actually unfolded to you, such as the fact of a person's death. Doubts and curiosities, as well as hopes and expectations, are restored to naivety. In art they can be freshly resolved, as if entirely new to mental experience.

Although the theatrical corps is bred to the service of the master of arts as its paid duty, the chorus is no mere passive source of trophic energy. At least in the primitive phase of tragedy's ontogeny it functions as two or more psychical agents of the poet's imagination, first as itself in the play and second as the school dialectically producing first one actor and then others whose performance Nietzsche calls its "vision"—its antithetical vision. But in tragedy's artistic maturity the poet allows it no leeway or urge for hermeneutic liberty. Each person is so fully occupied with his collective or personal role in a new play that for everyone except its poet the "fable" (plot) reveals its shape only in the blind synergy of perfor-

DEFENDANT: I'm not against it in principle.

PROSECUTOR: Then please tell the jury, in light of your condition, which is perfectly clear to anyone with eyes to see, why you havent sought out for courtship a respectable nubile maiden or a well-educated young widow capable of advancing you in life.

DEFENDANT: No one would have me.

PROSECUTOR: How do you know? Have you asked them all? Have you asked ten? Have you asked a single one of them?

DEFENDANT: I don't know any to ask.

PROSECUTOR: They're hardly likely to come knocking at your door, I'll grant you that. —Doesnt it seem a little strange, ladies and gentlemen, that a youth of evident passion, with some money to spend, isnt out looking for a girl friend every spare moment? —Mr Karcist, it's difficult to believe that *nobody* would have you. In view of your earning power as a college graduate, or at least your opportunity for academic distinction, the expanding market of white-collar jobs, your fundamental good health, and your liberty to settle anywhere or travel, I fail to understand why you havent solved your problem. My brother counsel has been presenting you as an underprivileged misfit warped at his unknown origins, traumatized by a disastrous love affair of perverting intensity, and doomed to mute blue-collar drudgery. Your alleged incompetence in social relations is supposed to account for disgracefully unaggressive behavior and apparent contempt for a man's role in the real world. Of course it's not in and of itself at your present demographic status that we raise our eyebrows. Many of the most vigorous and successful young men wait until later in life to marry. No, clearly, what we're all

mance, which is recorded in official text.

In the larger social context everyone concerned with the drama has a different motive or interest. Men of affairs are attracted by the prospects of an honorable reputation for theatrical production. At a time when real life is changing dangerously the public takes comfort in traditional forms of seasonal celebration. In the excitement and immemorial pleasure of getting ready for mass congregation the conservative polity conspires to divert and seal off the germs of originality in the variable content of an ostensibly unchanging species of dromena where they can least contaminate official religion.

Until the whole city is hushed on the hillside for a day's performance no one worries much about what the poet may be doing to change the meaning of it all. The features given most attention by the audience are technical or aesthetic, just as the musicians, dancers, and actors in preparing the play have concerned themselves with nothing but procedure and skill. At first matters for criticism or delight are likely to be no more conspicuous than subtle variations of style in bullfighting. One mind alone anticipates the blasphemous passion or transgression that may be expressed in these fine points. The poet's ultimate intention is perhaps deliberately obscured like the innovation of an architect who submits to his client plans and elevations so cluttered up with necessary details and specifications that they look nicely conventional. The owner is

wondering is why—if you choose to defer marriage—you arent out sowing wild oats. I believe every one of us is willing to accept at face value your scruples about visiting commercial women. But one of my purposes is to help the jury understand how an irreligious boy of your manifestly ardent nature can so offend humanistic reason by leading a celibate life in our liberal society—and especially in this licentious community. There must be something in what my distinguished colleague calls your harmlessly self-indulgent eccentricity that hasnt yet been brought out. Why should you be such an erotic failure? After all, you have a good stock of words and some command of literature. You have no noticeable speech impediment. I defer to the ladies of the jury for their opinion, but it seems to me that you're not so bad looking; you're tall enough to get by with half the women in this country, and you'd be totally acceptable on that score in populations like Japan's. The doctors tell us and the evidence proclaims that to say the least your codpod is fully everted. Your skin has no decently visible blemishes. Oddly enough, you're rather clean-cut in general appearance—or could be, with a little attention to your person. You move with a certain degree of confident coordination that gives no impression of weakness or effeminacy. Indeed I should think you'd make a pretty neat little secondbaseman. Furthermore your manners are excellent and your smile seems forthcoming. And finally there's nothing in the record to suggest that you're afraid of talking to girls. As a matter of fact—and here I appeal to the judgment of our gentlemen—I'd say you had a pretty damn good time with that ex-

as surprised as any passing citizen by an outcome of radical originality. The Athenian state is sometimes astonished when the theatrical organism, which it has fostered at one step removed from its own supervision, violates the religion it is sworn to uphold.

And so tragedy evolves in antithesis to the dromena from which it is descended, as if the poet were high priest or prophet of a new rite. Unlike the hierophant who takes the leading part in true ritual, this creative operator does not himself enter (or remain in) the action; yet it is from within an official company that he opens the closed cult to Panhellenic mythology history and geography, drawing his audience into that larger system by opening their minds to the imaginary situation he puts before them.

By obediently moving and speaking according to his directions the chorus indeed finds itself experiencing an objective vision, contributing uniquely and permanently to the general culture, which cannot benefit from ecstatic dancers in narcotic ritual or orgy. It is now several generations since drugged or drunken dancers of dramatic ritual tried to imitate the old satyr-people. For these modern performers, to have a vision is to show it. They themselves have no existence except in the showing. There are no subjective dreams in ritual that has turned into art.

This secondary parturition of the dithyramb recapitulates the genesis of *mythos* in artificial generation of the tragic *logos*; but art-dance and theatrical legomena evolve a thousand times faster than

tremely attractive swan you cut out from the flock of Berkeley ducklings. Many a married man might envy you her oral liberality. She must have been quite a dish herself. To have captured her heart and kept it on parole as long as you did—without promising marriage and without spending as much money as most high school boys do—argues that you must really know something about how to conjure up love in a girl. We neednt inquire into just what your charm may consist of. The important point in this court is that at least occasionally you have what it takes. Now it's true that you did not get all the way into her, but I'm sure many a Don Juan would trade half his conquests for what you did enjoy. Surely you could have kept her and made natural progress if your intentions had been normal. It's almost as if you queered the deal on purpose—as if you wanted to see and know and yet abstain. Again I ask, what naughtiness is this? Is it manly to wallow all by yourself in such pathetic jissom if indeed passion for your lost female rages in your soul as you swear it does?

Let's first go into your putative hypersensitivity to the qualities of women. Mr Karcist, can you give the court an example of your extraordinary preoccupation with feminine matter?

DEFENDANT: Images and words inflame me. Things like the dovetailed corners of wooden codfish boxes. Ordinary words. Common nouns like *wife, girl, body, hair, leg, triangle, college.*

PROSECUTOR: Adjectives too?

DEFENDANT: *Naked, soft, open, internal.*

PROSECUTOR: And a verb, for example?

DEFENDANT: *Penetrate.*

PROSECUTOR: And of course proper nouns like *Cynthia.* What other names?

the acts and words of religious evolution, for every dramatic festival can be an extremely concentrated series of experimental developments. As protagonist the leader of the chorus undertakes before our eyes to release actors from the lyric sodality, just as the *kouros* had once been released from among his brothers in a band of seasonal worshippers to become as a proven vision their king or god. In that primitive process of myth-making a wild landscape dance was turned into ordered ritual, producing in turn an annual succession of leaders performing an action that was to be remembered as the persistent image of a recurring event, which thereafter is rationalized as the story of an independent personage unfixed by time or place.

But though the purposeful creation of drama corresponds in sequence to the collective and inadvertent generation of myth, the motive is reversed. The final cause of ritual becomes the efficient cause of theater. It is with myth inherited from elsewhere that the poet's personal imagination begins. He makes from the imagery of myth an action that produces the aesthetic vision. Somewhere, much earlier, a complex of dromena has projected the alien myth of superhuman suffering or achievement in the same way that a succession of individual kings of ritual had given rise to the notion of an immortal god. But the dramatic poet's imagination of a god in action, or of a hero, requires an agent of singular action (act*or*) to take the place of a composite aboriginal act*er*.

Such an acter was likely to be the most acclaimed or most adven-

—Inanna? —Dido? —Eve? —Yes? Or Semiramis? —Aoife? —Ah, Fayaway? —Yseult? —Maude Gonne? — Phaedra? —Guinevere? —Aphrodite herself? —Even Sappho? —Come come, Mr Karcist, there must be some closer to home—

COUNSEL: Your Honor I object! No innocent party may be brought into these proceedings simply as the name in a young man's overwrought fancies!

JUDGE: Objection sustained. Prosecutor will not question the witness in such manner that the discretion of any lady living or dead may be aspersed.

PROSECUTOR: In any event, Mr Karcist, your lubricious fancy for the female is not confined to the person who cast you off?

DEFENDANT: I am aware of no exclusions within the class—no sir.

PROSECUTOR: And I believe no one but Army psychiatrists would impute to you an erotomania directed outside the class. But we already know it's true that you have brooded so thoroughly on what you desire that there's hardly a word in the language you don't secretly troat to. By the same token you blush at the use of certain plain blunt terms commonly used by menfolk among themselves in referring to women or their interesting sexual functions, is it not so?

DEFENDANT: One transitive verb in particular that I consider a blessing is commonly employed as a term of violent exploitation. But I don't think I actually blush. I just feel as if I'm blushing. I've become almost inured to the diction you mention. Root words don't bother me now: it's the insulting metaphorical application of them to execrations and trivial or utilitarian matters that contemns their original

turous member of a *thiasos*, which survived in civilization only as the dithyrambic chorus. The new theatrical company of musicians dancers and actors represents the economic power of a people still willing to acknowledge Dionysus. The dramaturgical problem is to make of art-dance a virtual ritual—but not merely an imitation of ritual—that will induce in the performers both the power of worshippers to create their god and the power of artists to arouse in spectators an intellectual ecstasy as relevant to extant values, private or universal, as to fictitious theses and antitheses in the orchestra. It is only with the success of its double function as object and subject that the chorus is able to turn over to the actor an almost insufferable burden of scrutinized action, so that he (or she) may seize the initiatives of personality within the vision. As quasi-ontological imagination, medium of both life and fiction, dance itself has given the poet access not only to the energy of solidarity but also to the culture's symbolic powers. When devoted to a purpose transcending the individual will's universal motives, dance seems by virtue of its physical limitations the only expression common to all organization, human subhuman or superhuman, normal or enormous. When it is modulated by the creative mind it can move art-life some further distance beyond reality.

What the poet shows with two or three actors, put at his disposal by their maternal chorus, is revered as a continuation of mythopoetic tradition. And it is true that at first he takes his divine comedy from a

meanings and brutalizes the vernacular by treating love's true end as venereal or venatic triumph over a victim. It's always a needless shame to drown linguistic distinctions.

PROSECUTOR: An eloquent defense of chivalry from a hands-on philosopher! Almost as if you'd persuade us that the path of love shouldnt lead to a cockpit! We can see for ourselves that you are more skillful than other men in periphrasis and delicate imagery, which many women still find admirable at a time when the word you mull like a holy mantra is so promiscuously bandied and abused that even finishing schools will soon be taking it for naught. Yet your nice sense of profanity betrays a shockingly blasphemous religion that cruelly deceives any old-fashioned girl to whom it may endear you. —Ladies and gentlemen I submit that such touching modesty on behalf of the exploited sex is perjured and mocked by the brutal lust in his heart. Why does this oversexcited organ-grinder keep his monkey to himself? Why does this ludicrously implausible gallant, professing a desire as inexhaustible as Zeus's, remain an unhappy tear-jerker who exposes millions upon millions of unborn babes by scattering to death the precious flagelliforms that the beloved half of our race longs to collect for dear life? There's hardly a moment that he isnt leading his reason under the yoke of his lust and convincing himself that a bird in the hand's worth two in the bush. We are all aware that too many men slight the women's pleasure at their disposal, but this kid seems bent upon *multiplying* the negative orgasms of his non-girls! If this arrant disservice to love is given free rein in our time the newly enfran-

theological canon, delighting in recension, as if he were making the way for a deep-sea salmon back to its hatching place in a sacred mountain spring. But then he possesses himself of the freedom to move from gods to demigods, and from them to heroic men and women. Just a little later, nearly all at once, his vision of tragedy is debased by secular theatricality. Human action attenuates into rationalistic or psychological problem-playing, or puddles into the *komos* of entertainment and satire.

Thereupon the matrix of dance withers and falls away. The plays no longer call for dancers. Like a discarded scaffold they are kicked away by their own progeny. Self-important personae believe themselves totally emancipated from ritual's culture.

4.

A priest working at his mactation of the people's offering has none of the poet's plastic freedom, even though the sacrificial act is invested with an absolute authority infinitely surpassing in extent and certainty the hardly superhuman faculty of an artist. Yet both poet and priest *make* their dromenon. To make (*poiein*) is not of course the radical creativity of bringing matter or energy into existence (an ability that is only equivocally claimed for God); it is but a selective transformational construction from existing substance. The dramatist *makes over* the dromenon even when as a tragic poet he does little to make over the myth.

chised sex will lose at the very moment of efflorescence the faculty it claimed in the twelfth century under the tantric caresses of patient selfless troubadours who refused to spend their virtue with the incontinence of rapists. Is this triboelectric power which absorbs Karcist's true passion the kind of merit that once earned the love of ladies sometimes even in despite of their personal attraction to knights of lesser worth? Is this his humble and courteous *Frauendienst* to the queen of his dreams that's supposed to justify his turpitude to posterity? Notice please that I have not called this wastrel an unhappy *romantic*, as we have reason to think he wishes to be known. A romantic lover would die for his unrequited love instead of throttling it—or would press love to its death by full requital. Meanwhile he'd be tupping barmaids or ravishing barefoot shepherd girls. Why even a runny-nosed Goliard with no more Latin than this son of a bitch has, and far less protection against society, would at least have had a few pelts hanging from his belt by this time. The chastest knights *sometimes* enjoyed their lady's fault (as well as often a wench's), just as they *sometimes* consummated their tiltyard jousts of honor mortally. Bear in mind that troubadours enjoyed the privileges of gallantry among their inferiors, including all but a handful of the most exalted women in any duchy they might attend. It was tolerably easy for them to practice continence with their elected mistress—and they had no need for the Karcist mode of consolation—because they felt no compunction about availing themselves of local nooky during off-hours. And anyway

The Mass too is said to be "made" by the priest when he and the people celebrate it together. In this usage the general sense of the word is *to make an act, to do*—to realize, to complete, to perfectly repeat a thing that has been repeatedly done in the past. But in the particular case of Christian liturgy this transitive verb is an ellipsis for *making the sacrifice* of what is brought forward by the people, *poiein* meaning specifically *to offer* bread and wine as representative of society's goods and services. And *to do* or *act* is also the sense of *dran*, from which *drama* is derived.

In a special way both priestly doing or making and poetic doing or making seem to reverse the energy-to-information phase transition of earlier ritual in which action generates symbol and idea; for liturgy and tragic drama, informed by *nous*, use symbol and idea to produce the action. But the religious myth is really true to those who act in social and emotional reality, whereas in dramatic poetry the imaginary dromenon and its legomena are understood to be arbitrary. In order to create a strange new action the artist reforms or abuses the *mythos* as his metaphorical manifestation of a story that has long since been displaced from its chronologically distant origins in ritual. (Later poets invent wholly fictitious substitutes for myth.) Like an incubus he implants the program that will conduct chorus and audience to their respective visions.

But in the narrowest genre called tragedy the chorus will never

their haughty lady, often enough mounted in her marriage bed to keep her from falling prey to the dire torments of monastic deprivation, might have been embarrassed by the riches of a lover's total dedication. Of course the solemnity of adulterous passion may have been sustained by the inconvenience of a trap locked about the lady's treasure, or by considerations of birth control in prolonged absences of her lord, as well as by the worthiness of feeling and estate that distinguished it from waves of ordinary appetite that could be safely blunted with familiar or unremarkable intimates, just as the lover's prowess courage and mercy manifested in the lists before all eyes were made possible by purging his fund of treachery cowardice and cruelty in the conduct of real wars. But the defendant leads no such life, and seems altogether too much of a slacker to do so even if he were translated to King Arthur's court. Nor can he be regarded in any sense as a Continental knight of Mary—he who's never in his life said a sincere prayer, who's never given a thought to avowing poverty or obedience—to say nothing of voluntary celibacy and still less of humble patient scholarship. Full of depraved notions like those that have defiled this courtroom, empty of all spiritual leaven, reeking with feckless self-indulgence—could this be our Galahad? Of course not. His Grail is almost any vessel of flesh and blood. . . .

We shall be lucky if the judge lets Jack thus expatiate on his specialty. Let him mystify the court all he wants. She'll probably get tired of the insulting ambiguity in his wholly grasp the dichotomy of his imagination.

5.

Incunabular ritual grants no more liberty than the freedom to join an action when society and the ethos demand that you do so. It allows no individual variation. Collective verse or music sets the rhythm like a fly-wheel and signals all preestablished changes of pace or figure. Subtlety comes in mastery of trance rather than in extension of experience. The sounds and words of mature ritual (which like myth are sometimes preserved long after their hypostatic dance has disappeared) typically turn back upon themselves over and over again, retracing memory of old rhythms, almost tone-deaf to melody. Even in the labyrinthine style of decadence they remain faithful to fixed modulations, preserving even monotony as long as they can, while only very slowly assimilating even the "differentiated sameness" of earliest art-music.

Thus repetitive gesture was the base of mythopoetic *geste* in primitive ritual. However, since there was no audience and no "communication" (as transmission of information), corporate emotion was uttered in expletives maybe like *Oi!*, *Ah! Ha!*, *Oh!*, *Ho!*, *Oui!*, *Doc!*, or *Zee!* (according to local proclivities of idiom) and demonstrated with corresponding gestures that accentuated the proprioception of action. These sounds and movements were detected without meaning by the

Languedocian feminism. All you have to do is sit meekly like the unassuming victim of a long overdrawn academic curse. Sooner or later he'll work in a few of his other favorite disquisitions. What you have to be on your guard against is questions of value.

PROSECUTOR: . . . Mr Karcist would you say that food cures the pain of hunger by supplying the lack that was the cause of distress?

DEFENDANT: Yes.

PROSECUTOR: Do you also think that the cures of medicine are usually effected by filling a deficiency that brought about the disease?

DEFENDANT: No.

PROSECUTOR: Counsel claims that protracted virginity is the cause of your acropathy, the excessive discomfort of which leads to the lonely incontinence that drains you of the libidinous energy required to hunt down a girl to devirginate yourself with. Now would you regard the affectionate and uninhibited companionship of a desirable girl as food or medicine?

DEFENDANT: Food.

PROSECUTOR: In view of the fact that you've lived this long without a wanton, and that you may be drafted or otherwise deprived of opportunity for some time to come, would you say that a woman's pity is essential to your life?

DEFENDANT: No. It is not absolutely required. I can live with my affliction.

PROSECUTOR: Ah! Then it would be as it were temporary rations, nonessential food— but, even if you werent in love, good enough to cure your acropathy. Is that what you mean?

DEFENDANT: I think so.

inner ear, but from them words and gestures gradually evolved—first in pronunciation of the feelings that began to distinguish themselves from the unison and then in significations that followed therefrom, stimulating and modifying each other. Look backward from the standpoint of a resultant myth: just as a baby is teleologically implicit in the desire that may be oblivious to procreation, all human mentality is potential in the cell-motives that joined in a primitive community of expression without cultural intention.

But eventually by consciously controlling its dance the cult discovers and defines freedom like a sculptor discovering space by the formation of a statue that establishes the center. Only in advancing stages does it little by little permit internal dissent. For dissenters there comes a time when they do not participate, and then their freedom is exercised not in the ritual but outside it.

Yet even in the most decadent phase of a culture one can't belong to a religion without delimiting certain salients of liberty. Nothing is more natural than such compromises, which are more or less easily made in all relationships; for few go out of their way to seek intellectual liberty that contributes nothing to career or pleasure, and those who inherit such freedom are likely to waste it in self-indulgence, for unchecked autonomy always fails in self-discipline. Dance—choral action—orients and stabilizes the feelings of those who join the movement of their fellows in assent

PROSECUTOR: You think so. One little jig to enflesh yourself and you'd be normal ever after?

DEFENDANT: Oh no, I want it more than once. Many times and often, for a while at least. But naturally the first time is most important to my spiritual improvement. Initiation would establish my right by knowledge and precedent.

PROSECUTOR: Spiritual eh? You want to start a spiritual sex-rite!

DEFENDANT: No, no—my mastery—as a man!

PROSECUTOR: If mastery is what you're pining for Mr Karcist I'm afraid you underestimate your masterful accomplishments as a consummate stimulator (or should I say simulator?). They say that's half the battle. And obviously you have digital and linguistic talents for pacification. Perhaps you have learned more as a performing musician than most composers who have made scores of pieces. Your observations have been a degree more objective and a degree less uncertain than the experiments of luckier physicalists whose judgment is compromised by intensely subjective sensations. You have proven that it isnt necessary to skewer a girl to make her look up to you as her master. A hundred times by sheer skill you have brought a self-possessed girl from hostility or indifference, or from an intellectual mood, to the most abject surrender of her virtue with nothing but the touch of your hands and lips. It's possible that you'll never get much closer to what my learned colleague calls the mystery. Your manipulations have affected at least one whole anima, and you are better able than many a stud to say what

to its celebration; as the flywheel of concurrence it provides kinetic inertia to keep the drama moving. But it also has the gyroscopic effect of keeping the story centered on the axis of wisdom in resistance to aleutherian (or aleatory) disturbances.

In order to find the force that can sway or at least perturb the chorus in its gyroscopic persistence a free mind must ally itself with external myth that retains the persuasion of alien dromena. Reinforced by this power of myth, the poet takes advantage of the fact that art-dance, despite its preponderant moderation, is more easily challenged than the collective emotion of indigenous religion by extrinsic ideas. The artifactual chorus responds to a poetic impulse in the illusion that it is only delivering itself to a different version of wisdom.

Whether the diachronistic myth was derived from the ritual of a single unknown place or from many similar dromena whose imaginations had coalesced into a single tradition, we can in principle reconstruct a composite proto-rite by morphological inference; but even without speculating about any particular provenance it appears from the researches of Jane Harrison and one or two others that typical ritual has always been partly constituted or reconstituted by words, and that the words are of two kinds or aspects. Some of the words in ritual function both ways.

First there is *mythos*, words applied to the description or interpretation of what it represented in the Ur-rite, during the practicing life

it is that a girl is. When your time comes you will therefore know profoundly the woman that the girl can be made into, or remade and confirmed as. I don't feel sorry for you. Personally, I think you should thank your lucky stars to have had such a quasimaiden to heighten your first love. She was a girl whose response to the method you would have preferred could only have been more guarded and less revealing than it was to your madding strokes of invention. Rejoice in your apprenticeship; from a humane point of view, rejoice in falconry without the killing. Besides, too much of a carnal inroad too soon in life can ripen a girl too fast: she can become spiritually impervious to men without ever having softened; all her life she may tend to do it to please them instead of herself. It's almost as if certain antibodies stirred up by premature penetration coat her internal nerve-ends with a satin sheen that grows more and more difficult for a man to dissolve. Then she's apt to get businesslike about giving a lover what he wants, and once she's worked out a recipe that's proven acceptable she cooks exactly the same dinner over and over again in the conviction that any man will like it though insipid to herself. She's accustomed to dispatch her ingratiating gift with practiced efficiency and little wish for wondrous leisure at it, hoping that if her symbolic affection has met with approval something emotional will come of it. Think how much less the next guy would have enjoyed Cindy if you hadnt been so Catharistic in—

JUDGE: This court will not tolerate this taunting disrespect for the defendant, Mr Prosecutor. You will please apologize, and refrain from further gynecogize, and refrain from further gyneco-

of which they may account for its origin or explain its purpose. When the mythos has become separated from the dromenon, and survives it, it passes as poetry into the lore of *mythology*—in which story, the *myth* proper (usually as preserved altered and transmitted in the epic), can be distinguished from the *logos* of the imaginative dromenon: interpretation, exegesis, or even allegory (as in Hesiod), often further extended by anagogical metaphor (as in modern psychological platonism focussed on the Mysteries). These things said *of* the dromenon, and especially things said of those things, persist through centuries of secondary transformation.

But things said *in* religious ritual, for which I use the term *legomena*, are lost entirely if not written on altar cards or printed in missals. These are the operative words of the rite, some of them sacramental and effective, or otherwise essential to the particular religion; others, procedural or merely ceremonial.

The dramatic poet constructs his story from a vast or ambiguous mythology, perhaps ignoring the most authentic version and reshaping the myth according to his personal imagination. He then invests his carved pseudo-mythos in the theatrical enterprise as the armature on which to model his clay.

As an individual he has inverted the collective process of mythopoetry: his recension of the mythos determines the action. But his vision is procedural as well as sculptural; he must not only project the play's story *through* words but also prescribe *in* words the rubrics

logical comment. Confine yourself to the case we are trying.

PROSECUTOR: I'm sorry, Your Honor. I just wanted to let Mr Karcist know that I'm not a bad cop, that on many counts I agree with his attorney. Speaking as one with almost five years service in the Army of the United States I wanted to assure him that he was well off with a girl that truly desired him even though he never got the chance to violate her with anything more salient than his middle finger, and that a player sitting on the bench who never gets into the jewel of games himself may sometimes learn more about foreplay than the rest of us. Ha, ha!

JUDGE: That will do sir. If there is any repetition of this insidious levity I shall hold you in contempt.

PROSECUTOR: Yes your honor. It's not characteristic of me. —Now ladies and gentlemen, by his own account the defendant is too sympathetic with the *mundus muliebris*, too tender, too considerate of woman's natural dignity, to envy an erotic career like Don Juan's. Of course he'd like to have a whole flock, I think he said, but only to the number that he could know each one as well as any of them can ever be known. —Pardon me, your honor; no offense intended. —By the way, my friends, can't you just see him the minute he's scored his first bullseye? All that heartrending diffidence will suddenly turn into the typical cockiness of a precocious runt! Right now he thinks all girls have the advantage in a seller's market, especially on account of the inflation brought on by sex-advertising, and he despairs of ever being worth enough to meet the price—but once he pricks that fragile bubble of self-doubt, watch out! At his first sigh of

for action that will bring his vision into theatrical existence. Thus legomena return to the orchestra as both formal and efficient causes.

By means of instructions spoken as director and choreographer but never recorded, in support of words rehearsed for lyrics and speeches, the poet finally produces his own new legomena of art— which, once mounted in public performance and officially recorded, are perpetuated as dramatic poetry. For later directors, altering the dramaturgy in accordance with their own creative and aesthetic imagination, the mythos and the legomena freshly unite in a playscript. In some new way the poetry actually *effects* the action that it describes explains or reflects, and the action *affects* the poetry.

6.

Although dramatic poetry ruptures or contradicts the habit and regulation of ritual its artistic effectiveness corresponds to the effectiveness of ritual in real life. But the rare and extreme case of tragedy is liturgy's diachronistic opposite. At a distance of many generations, separated from sacramental ritual by religious decadence and ritual drama, but as an equal and opposite counterpart of value laggingly excited across the insulation of an electrical capacitor, tragedy is a unique reaction to liturgy. Without the apostolic Mass there would have been no Elizabethan tragedy. For lack of evidence the liturgical provenance of Athenian tragedy apparently can be sought only in

satisfaction he'll acquire such an inexhaustible treasure of confidence that he'll think he can meet any woman's terms—or at least lose out only to vicissitudes that bring no discredit to a buck. Yet meanwhile we're asked to believe that there's not one girl in all of Alameda County that he can make! What's up, I ask you? How hard does he seek an assignation to prove himself? He complains because he's been disappointed in love once more than he's been appointed! And seems to have convinced himself that one major loss (following several minor ones) proves that for the rest of his life his head is destined to be bruised by the heel of Eve—despite the fact that he gets further into the minds and hearts of his victims than most real fuckers do. "Lose one and find two!" we used to say, but he loses one and immediately assumes that he is evermore cursed to leave his snake spit upon the cold grass for maids to giggle at when they cross his tracks in the morning with armfulls of clean sheets. Yet, after all, he lost his brainy blond beauty for no other reason than that she feared his power to disturb the equilibrium of her practical evaluations. He excuses himself from the normal pursuits of a brave merely by the plea that he doesnt know how to dance or sing or play the lute or ski down mountains or ride the waves of a suntanned beach—pastimes most advertised as erotic skills. He compares himself to a Chinook salmon that's baffled by white water a thousand miles from the sea in his one chance to spawn before he dies. And to the inconspicuous males of such species as the wild turkey of Texas who live out their whole lives as useless failures while a few dominant Toms tread

speculation about a classic but pre-Classical age of religious sacrifice that preceded history in the Greek psyche.

Yet it is not very significant that tragedy and liturgy are similar in shape, since dromena, like languages, seem to be almost universal in deepest structure. But they reflect each other as a pair of contrarieties that form similar polarities. In both cases for instance, as Yeats said of one of them, a "passionate and logical" intensity has emerged from an "enthusiastic and sentimental" background. But the correspondences are not to be carried too far. Most of the contrasts are imbalanced. The metasystem of the poet's mind must be owned a small vanity compared with the whole of God's cosmically comic reality. The chorus that offers a play within its dance is nothing but a festal team compared with the working congregation that sacrifices the best products of its economy. Liturgy outweighs tragedy in any rational judgment.

Yet the poet who by himself unnecessarily challenges necessity in utter despair of satisfaction is worth more according to the values of scarcity than the priest ordained by a profession, sanctioned by a god, and supported by law. Is it less valuable to imagine a new dromenon than to work an old one? True art has always anticipated its teleological supremacy, implicitly claiming its ultimate value as the end-product of culture, if not indeed as the chief justification for saving mankind any kind of future. We have never waited to see the success of liturgy or evolution be-

thousands of tail feathers. He also points to the giant sequoia that go a thousand years without reproducing from the seeds they drop. Yet he weeps such a crocodile lament for his rather enviable lot that you'd think he was the only stag on earth who doesnt get to mate with the first doe he happens to surprise in a well-stocked wildlife reservation, overlooking the fact that almost every male, whether a patriarch or a misfit, misses or spoils numberless occasions or apparent occasions presented by a randomly selective fortune before he rises to one of them. —Mr K, considering that you've written off said Cynthia (to whom however you havent omitted to send twelve unacknowledged elegies since first beginning to take satisfaction in epistulatory farewells), tell us: is there any real woman you know whose favor you pretend to?

COUNSEL: I object!

JUDGE: Objection sustained. Prosecutor has been warned. If he once more defies my ruling the case will be dismissed.

PROSECUTOR: I intend to confine my questions to the abstract, your honor.

JUDGE: Then see that they remain general and hypothetical, without circumstantial hints or artful innuendos. You have gone too far in insinuating particular persons.

PROSECUTOR: Yes your honor. Since you have refused to disqualify yourself from the case, I must submit to your ruling. But I may say that we are deliberating the culpability of a Goliardic neo-Albigensian Magus-manqué who's trying to acquire occult power with an artificiality that would astound Goethe himself, and it is my duty to show the jury that this knave is actually pleased that his reach exceeds his grasp.

fore creating our art, however; and in case salvation fails us tragedy is the one art that will have celebrated the end of our species. Mind and imagination must make up for the shortcomings of liturgy as long as we last. In the imperfect and inconclusive world tragedy is more than equal to liturgy in this at least, that it can temporarily dichotomize religion's integrated system of desire and hope and faith, systaltic and diastaltic, whether carnal rational or mystical, against which are measured any deviation from the normal or happy.

Long after the Dionysian chorus has been prevented by the enclosure of artificial place from swarming after its god to the wild places of the mountain, its concentric momentum keeps it pointing the course of nature. All ritual, and comedy its immediate profanation, imitates or regulates destiny. Vice and deformity can better be corrected in ithyphallic men and fertile women by the triumphal catharsis of lust in a seasonal riot of orgasm (which can scarcely fail of mass pregnancy conveniently timed in the economic year) than by unexcepted Apollonian moderation. Nothing ultimately prudent or rational is overturned by komos. (The Blessed Virgin Mary herself was conceived at the time of the Greater Dionysia). It is the ruling calendar that a tragic poet outflanks in perspective by attaining a vantage that comprehends the entire comic system—divine human and bestial— and accounts for himself as well.

The dithyramb, lyric dance, remains essentially comic, or returns

COUNSEL: Well watch your step or I'll bloody your nose with my gauntlet. —Your honor, please?

JUDGE: Mr Prosecutor, proceed with great care.

PROSECUTOR: Can it be, Mr K, that while you grieve over Cynthia and tame the beast within you by methods best kept to yourself you contrive to sustain and exalt your intellectual energy by adoration of the one woman in the world to whom you are forbidden to make advances and whose chastity in any case you believe to be impregnable? Is that why the word *wife* inflames you?

DEFENDANT: Yes—no! To her I'm nothing physical.

PROSECUTOR: But you wouldnt kick her out of bed, as the saying goes, eh? Is that right sir? Who would, if it comes to that?

JUDGE: These questions are *too* hypothetical. I'm surprised counsel doesnt object.

COUNSEL: Your honor I'd like to hear the answer first.

PROSECUTOR: I'm sure everybody appreciates your frankness Mr K. When you reply don't forget you told us earlier that you're always willing to risk taking a false intuition for a true one as long as you have the remotest prospect of tangible reward. Again then: assuming you were able to reconcile yourself to the guilt of becoming secret lover to the wife-person you covet—

JUDGE: For the love of Mike, Jack! I've been warning you against this impertinence! —Bailiff, remove him. Clear the room. —You are hereby disbarred from practice before this court. —The jury is dismissed. —Counsel will go take a walk. The defendant will come to my chambers for ex parte consolation. . . .

to comedy, unless acutely altered by tragic vision. Tragedy is derived from comedy (to which it also returns) as the male is evaginated from the female; but this evolutionary leap is extremely rare and precarious. We must count as comic all unsuccessful or degenerate attempts at tragedy, all mere catastrophes and calamities, all drama of pathos only. It is true that blasphemy is generally futile, but only tragedy can blaspheme the divine comedy that is so easily profaned. If there is some possible coexistence of liturgy and tragedy it is nothing we have to worry about until the Kingdom of God is at hand.

Any reconciliation of liturgy and tragedy across the dromenological space or time that separates them is meanwhile inconceivable. Every performance of tragedy obliquely reminds both worshippers and divinities that the choral power which first projects and then destroys a man of hybris for outraging his origin also represents the residual power of the temple, which still protects the sanctity of the god's name and provides his sole sustenance. Tragedy's indescribably painful "shattering of the *principium individuationis*" disturbs the sophrosynic equilibrium of even the most spiritual and idealistic variety of religion by recollecting for the highminded their power over the god their creature. The force of such hint momentarily offsets the obvious fact that the poet is no more than an ion in the divinity's universe. It is by this pinprick of philosophy that tragedy opens reality's system into the vastest

Now she'll pass unofficial judgment and I can't be there to help you. Her opinion won't have the force of law, but if you don't heed it she might order a retrial, and this time the case would go a lot further, to everyone's displeasure. If it ever gets to the petit jury and they start asking a lot of their own questions you'll have to give plenty of details instead of listening to long-winded hypothetical inquiries. Can you imagine what that dirty-minded little foreman might ask you? It's easier to evade fate than psychoanalysis. Newt Cahners can make out an Oedipus complex where there's no mother and no father! And Sylvia would make you tell all about your acropathic symptoms in quantitative terms, and how you treat them. Now behave yourself in there.

JUDGE: Sit down Caleb. It's my turn for a sermon. I know this has been very painful for you, but perhaps it will all turn out for the best. Jack makes me very angry, but at least he's given me the excuse to get you away from that torture. I just have a few things to suggest. Some of them I would have to say in open court if it came time to instruct the jury or pass sentence, whatever the indictment might turn out to be. When you suffer the penishment of foregone guilt the only justice that the Court of Love can administer is the equity of truth and consequences to fit the crime in principle. The actual rehabilitation of romantic love must come with experience.

First I want you to understand that you know no more than either of the learned men-of-law about girl-field of mind, where even for a merely watching listener the moment's exaltation can seem more valuable than a lifetime's false solace. Dramatic poetry may then seem to prove that the divine grace of liturgy will always fail of emergent perfection, yet that in extinguishing the most precious violations of comity mankind implies its preference for brotherly love.

7.

Dramatic violation of natural law or custom would not occur if no one thought freedom more valuable than survival. In religion men and women find no greater degree of freedom than their destiny demands; nor is there perfect freedom in the service of art: yet you might say that the poetic imagination makes its freedom by bringing into existence what God has not. In employing itself the creative mind has already exercised the common freedom of choice to thread its way through the wilderness sometimes called its Body of Fate, but in refusing to content itself with this human privilege it sets forth a revised landscape for itself or others to pick through. Every artist augments the precedents of free will. And *within* tragedy the psyche extends freedom to human limits. It masters in consciousness the unconscious determinism that otherwise chokes off every tendril of its roots.

The tragic poet, working the matter of ritual, is not primarily an inventor of forms or structure: he discovers his freedom in language. His figmentations in unsanctioned

pain. Your burning is little enough to suffer. You arent tied to the stake. The man I know best is right when he says that young people use their bodies without any more interest in how they wear out than the rest of us usually take in how our minds are belabored: it's the subject's object or feeling that they devote all their study to. Especially boys, I am told. Except when teachers or coaches otherwise insist, their own biological processes are as transparent and invisible to them as the air they breathe. They eat anything that doesnt taste bad and mistreat themselves in every other way because no matter what they do or swallow their bodies seem to carry on steadily, apparently unravagable, with strength or beauty that seems ageless. The instrument of pleasure or persuasion (or force) is so reliable in youth that it rarely diverts their care from the object of gratification. And even girls, the foolish ones at least, for all their cosmetic preening, fail to look beneath the surface of their physiques, ignoring at their peril the special warnings of mortality that they are blessed with. I myself have observed that boys seeking to relieve their satyriasis and girls seeking to please boys all expect their satisfaction or achievement not *in* the body but *by* the body.

But my point is that men can get away with this abuse of their carcass (as your counsel might put it) longer than women can. Any girl with a drop of feminine common sense knows before her first kiss that it's the core of her life she's playing with when she takes a boy at his word. A man pays the piper only with the pain of knowing his woman's pain, which is the responsibility he takes upon himself by winning a

poetry must be made as important as the priest's sacramental deeds in true history. Poetry is his means for informing the energy of circumscribed physical movement with infinitely painful and difficult meaning. The free para-actions of poetic will are diction, syntax, and prosody, which are empowered by both intellect and emotional self-reliance. "The will is the non-aesthetic element *par excellence*", says Nietzsche. That is to say, in this case, the creative element.

The poet himself can be no hero, but he can call up through the chorus "some action separated but for this from all but itself" (as Yeats declares), which is displayed in the unity of temporal and spatial imagination, but into which, through actors, he can introduce by language his shockingly passionate speculation. The meaning of this play-within-a-dance, as I have said before, remains inaccessible to the players, for it is expressed only by their separate parts taken altogether by witnesses outside the internal prehensions of the world on stage. Since a series of meanings makes up the whole action, it is affected by gestures and movements that are mainly determined by words.

The meanings in tragedy concern an interaction of causality and free will, as revealed by the catastrophe of him whom the chorus has given over to the poet unintentionally. It doesn't require art or even life to prove determinism; to the degree that character can be distinguished from behavior in a particular historical situation, persona in art is as determined as character

girl. So naturally it's less painful for you to burn than to marry and assume a woman's suffering. But I'm not referring just to the troubles of marriage and children. I'm speaking particularly of women in their childhood, girls young as you in age or experience.

You seem to have no idea of your advantage over them. If you knew anything about being a girl you'd be far less discouraged about yourself, but maybe more melancholy about the world at large, for you'd appreciate the uncertainty and vulnerability of the next self-assured bitch who seems to scorn your shy smile. Perhaps women are not the prize you think they are. I would sooner praise than blame you for the way you respond to anatomy's desire. It seems to be only a general urge for the expression of energy, especially when it has lost or not yet found the personal element of love. And so your way is more respectful to my sisters, while you wait for the girl who is now waiting for you, than the womanizing manhood that men try to teach you, which counts every conquest the same as far as the innermost feeling of it is concerned, like so many A's awarded in an academic record that fails to distinguish among subjects courses or teachers as to their importance.

You may take my word that there is something in you to attract many girls, especially when they have become mature women, and much more to attract a special few—not just the wall flowers either! The girl who happens into your next streak of luck will appreciate you better than you appreciate her, though she may have been desired by many others, because even the most beautiful ones have always had the short end of

in life; but freedom only begins in life, in animal movement, perhaps in play, before it develops mentally. Liberty more significant than permissive freedom *from* constraint is heuristic or creative or noetic in various proportions, and the first two kinds (which are often physical) can directly affect the world, especially of course in technology, management, and other practical arts of construction, combination, or skill. But sheer freedom of the will—will being the last faculty in which wisdom would expect to find freedom—is experienced solely by the imaginary hero of tragedy, who asserts by dramatic action a spiritual liberty that is otherwise known only as abstractions like mine of tragic knowledge.

From this vantage the hero's eleutherian passion may be taken as an existential ideal: it bears truth commensurate with phenomenological reality but it derives from the noetic psyche's heuristic and creative use of language. The highest peculiar volition, a potentiality for exception to both natural and moral law, in violating its ritual, disrupts not only custom and pragmatic usage but also probability and any category of logic that might be drawn upon in ordinary elucidation. Will is proven to be contingently free when a persona possessed by intention makes itself known as an excessively noble deviate from the norm that it is supposed to have been a model of.

To us the feelings of others are opaque mysteries, unless they are poets, except as one's uncertainty is reduced by observation of their be-

the stick. Did you ever really listen to Cindy when she tried to tell you about her earlier life of terror among hounds baying for quarry and whispering false hints as they licked her hand, when she grew up learning that she had to hide all her soft spots and at the same time for her own safety put aside every temptation to follow the bents of her mind—her guilty thinking mind that was inclined to wander away from her part in the noble sports of chase? Can you possibly suspend your desire long enough—without yielding to the bents of your own mind—to imagine what it's like not to be born even free enough to form your feelings? You more than most men suffer the curse of too much liberty, but half the human race has no more than a vague inkling of what freedom is.

In this light young girls should not be blamed for paying more heed to their danger than to your poor acropathic algesia that's even now mostly a matter of acculturated pride. No one but me is altogether forbidden to you. Your unease is lightly borne in comparison to the lifelong pain of being a female, which blithe young misses feel in their bones long before they realize that they are no exception to universal suffering. You shouldnt take them to task for defending themselves against your shortsighted fever. As you know, it is not absolutely difficult for them to forfend the full development of experience if it's left to themselves. Their instinct warns them that their craving will only begin where yours ends. When you imagine girls sleeping alone you think of Cressida; but most of them who are not yet married, no matter how many lovers they have been tried by, when

havior under significant circumstances; but the alien as well as mysterious passion of the hero exists nowhere else than in the theatrical doings that bring it about and that are brought about by it. It exists only in its expression, which cannot be exhausted or completed by the action. Little that's essentially internal can be conveyed without the language of poetry. The hero becomes the dramatist's poet in order to speak from his feelings.

The poet himself however, by virtue of his artistic experience in epitomizing free will as presented in the mythic action of drama, demonstrates an originality that leads his successors into an intoxicating abuse of artistic responsibility. As intellectual libertines they become susceptible to merely foreign or novel ideas, and are henceforth tempted to indulge the cleverness impertinence or satire that verges on "creation without toil", or the realism of characterization that grows in an interbreeding series of stock masks.

8.

Nietzsche surmises a powerful Greek music to compensate for the spurious or anecdotal simplicity of the myths called upon in tragedy for the deepest truth of which its culture is capable, namely that "whatever exists is both just and unjust, and equally justified in both." He finds in music what I would find in dance, the aesthetic mass to account for "metaphysical solace" from a mere work of art. But the hero's only existence is in the dromenon, and wisdom's weight whether in sound

they're not weeping with despair go to bed as you do, like Madeline on St Agnes Eve:

> Nor look behind, nor
> sideways, but require
> Of Heaven with upward
> eyes for all that they desire.

For every boy that burns, ten girls are like to perish from the cold. It's socially inefficient, as himself would say. Now it seems to you that if Caleb (or Cabe or Caliban, or Caliburn, or whatever you and your parts like to be called by) were a lonely girl you could soothe your own body whenever you felt indisposed to make a choice from the unbroken series of offers that you assume all girls always have ringing at their telephone; you think Caleb-girl is more fastidious about her suitors than Caleb-boy about his suitees because she can afford to be. But what if she's not perfectly shapely or invariably lovely-looking with lustrous curly hair of some indescribably attractive color and skin with never a blemish anywhere? What if she's more like you as far as first glances go? Or mousy, or too tall—or can't dance because she's straight or stringy? A girl that's commonly overlooked must hesitate all the more at your approach for fear of the double damage love can do her. The most likely Caliburnia, whose beauty is hidden, or is revealed only over the course of time by voice and movement—and who are you to expect anyone more glittering?—must always doubt the most timid Caleb's smile, for its pity if not for its rapaciousness. Put yourself in her place. Even more than the striking beauties who have a thousand chances she is persuaded—lest the

or movement is bound to lie on the choral side of the scale.

In the *Birth of Tragedy* he came late to the revelation that it is not Apollo of the aesthetic equation who opposes Dionysus but mankind's earlier champion Prometheus—expelled god, enemy of Olympus, and according to Aeschylus the son of Themis. In his enthusiasm for music and lyric Nietzsche had been too preoccupied with the spectator's aesthetic—and making too much of the satyrs' ecstatic recovery of an "original one-ness" at the "eternal core of things" beneath the "phenomenal world"—to properly notice the hero's dramatic situation. Despite his own Titanic struggle against idealism the philological philosopher had not been able to throw off the Platonic bias for permanence and the "eternity of true being" that he thought the drama was celebrating under the influence of symbolistic mystery cults. Maybe the agony of his own fracted superindividuality forced most of his attention to the impersonal resolution of all wills within the dark wisdom of a dithyramb that claims to submerge in joy every differentiation.

But radical differentiation of will is the discernible phenomenon of human liberty that the poet implants in tragedy to separate it from the tragicomedy and comedy that it resembles in theatrical skeleton. If because of a culture's prejudicial determinism or prevailing insensitivity to abstraction free will is not apparent from the plot alone, its philosophical presence must be realized in language unfamiliar to the audience.

barely attractive force of her sexual existence be neutralized—that she must hide the mind that makes her exciting. This is your own incestuous twin I'm talking about now: like you an orphan without pedigree, a lover with no one to love—yet without an iota of your footloose liberty. In other words, what if you were a girl—you who think you have no attraction that isnt mental?

Like her fortunate sisters she is prevented by every rule and instinct from making any kind of advance—least of all intellectual—even to a Caleb. She can't bring herself to so much as pluck your sleeve. If things begin between you but then stall after the beginning—even then she is not permitted to take the initiative, though she may clearly see how small or asinine your misunderstanding is. Worse yet, what if she's never even imagined a real Caleb, thinks that such a boy is possible only in books, far away or long ago, or maybe hasnt even read about such a paragon? Then all men remain to her hopelessly opaque strangers meant only to be served, in return for protection, forever ununderstanding, forever ununderstandable. It's men and boys like that, sometimes fatally repugnant, sometimes faintly appealing, she has to wait for phone calls from. While she's looked over and commented upon by the other beasts of prey ganged up in public places as if her clothes were no shield at all from insolent disparagement and rejection—when she wants nothing more than to be exempted from their inspection.

If by some miracle of chance Caliburnia does find her Caliburn her doubts of his love are much more important than his doubts of hers. Even to a sparrow-hawk carried on his lady's

Consider in principle what happens to language when poetry moves it in and out of the vernacular reservoir, where many words are treated as arbitrary synonyms and constructions are riotously redundant. By a process of evaporation, mountain cloudburst, and percolation, some of the common syntagms are always being taken up in poetic or rhetorical constructions and returned as altered molecules to make the brackish lake either more alkaline or less so. Without such circulation poetry could never break up the mortific crystallizations (such as those of advertising) that tend to coagulate as semantic scum. But much of the dramatic poetry formed by stress and tension belongs only to its own dromenon and is lost to demotic culture when its unique imaginary conditions are no longer staged or studied. The best expressions of tragedy are often so far from seeming passionate or vivid that they are overlooked in the demand for "dead metaphor" by the functional prose that surrounds poetry on all sides.

In the kind of creation known generically as poetic, polymerized idioms or tropes of the age are broken up in order to liberate their components for new combination, reversing etymology's procedure for getting to the bottom of experience. The etymon is faithful to its meaning until it finds its way to the lake in the valley. There later it reveals to the scholar what was elementally concrete or irreducibly mysterious to the humans who first agreed to it. The etymologist is able to recover direct experience by

wrist love is a single adventure, or at most a liberal education, not the purpose of his existence. Caliburn refuses to see her risk in accepting his touch, which is like any other stranger's who wants to tamper with her body while he deceives her brain. Every last one of them with whom she opens communication, including Caleb himself, or Tom or Dick or Harry, or any other good man, remains a hard blue stranger, perhaps funny or poetic or half wise but never capable of feeling the smallest part of what a woman feels.

No: it may be that for a few years longer girls will seem to give you a run for your money—as long as your puppy scepter continues to hold all the prolific energy you were born with, like some sleepless whip ruling you who wield it. But you hold all the high cards—even you, poor little Caleb. At least you and your brothers among you. The pain of your desire is no wound, and when the smart is soothed (all too soon and scatheless) it's only in your pride that you'll ever be vulnerable, in the world's scale an even slighter discomfort than your lust. I don't agree with my associates that you'll get cocky; you're not like other men who look like you: as soon as you find a willing girl with a mind your ugly torment will become tender and beautiful. But there'll still be great inequality in your exchange of pledges, especially if you don't undertake with open eyes the responsibility that civilization has devised to compensate women in part for the shortfall and evanescence of men's best impulses. You have no grasp of the axiom that nearly every schoolgirl understands before her first kiss—that

taking apart, demythologizing, and unsymbolizing the civilized language in which it appears. By so doing he may inspire the poet to ransack the foundations of his inherited language for lost atoms of expression from which to make new molecules as original metaphors.

But the special case of dramatic poetry needs less of the etymological imagination than of the syntactical. Sentences are wanted more than images, and most of all the transitive sentence composed of the meanings that make up the whole story, in which the main verb may be an action never put in words at all. Lyrical and descriptive passages qualify subjects or objects for interest and dignity, but essential dramatic speech works with etymons of plot, and it is apt to be so plain or concentrated that when merely read or even spoken outside the performance it seems crude. That is one of the reasons why many of the phrases of dramatic poetry, removed from their places in the field of force they are written for, do not distinctly enter even literature.

The substantives and verbs of dramatic poetry are rather seen than heard, and may take part in the word order without lyric images.

9.

The chorus of society purges itself of guilt for allowing the flint-and-steel stroke of free will by seeing to it that the blasphemous flame is extinguished. But in another season it will be willing to work for the poet again. Imagination of human possibility cannot be finally sup-

once a woman truly yields to a man everything she gives him is turned to his advantage, whether he came to her as a dominating knight in velvet armor or as the most wretched substitute for her midwinter dream. Unless she can bring herself to walk out of the game without being relieved of the injuries and penalties that she may have incurred for his sake without hope of honor or reward. But most women simply cannot walk out; their necessity has changed a solemn game into the deadly work of preserving life.

So the girl-heart of Cindy/Caleb-girl, full of foreboding, whose desire has never been ugly, vacillates in fearful attraction and dismay when it's asked to open up to a love-hound like you, though she may indeed find you to be her very twin brother in sympathy, because you are the most dangerous man of all for the incipient woman with a young girl's bright free mind who should be practicing to defend herself. If it came to a marriage certificate you could no longer get away with shrugging off as irrelevant or uninteresting all the questions of burden and handicap that couples do their betting on. And I will tell her if she doesnt know it already that you're the kind of insouciant jockey who won't keep riding when you lose hope that she will endure all the steeplechases of her career without making you serve as her trainer and stableboy too.

My dear Hippolytus, it is not as judge but as stepmother that I lay upon you a penance to fit the sin of being an incipient man no more though also no less than half educated to gentilesse—more worthy than most of pressed. Once enacted in heroic art, the *idea* of freedom breeds decadent and debased posterity a thousand times faster than the most goatish degenerations of ritual.

The high moment passes as soon as the poet begins to get his way too freely, when ritual's gyroscope is losing rotational inertia. He can reset its direction at will. With a touch of his hand every new play becomes an experiment. And at last he can dispense with the chorus altogether, for even in common opposition to the hero it has broken up into basely autonomous individuals. Rules of reason harden the heart against blood rhythms; conventional principles gradually exclude ancient and common matter in order to establish psychology and manipulate new symbols. Soon every play is expected to surprise. Within new parameters of broad but shallow liberty, typical sensibilities and novel acts can be swiftly interbred without ritualistic gestation. The theater finds itself with mechanisms of entertainment, and the misunderstood ruins of a *skene* on which to paint its verisimilitudes.

In the widening gyre each decadence of a theatrical culture comes faster than the one before— Irish, Elizabethan, Greek. This volatile art corrupts itself into scattering pieces of sentimental amusement or problem-solving morality, which then devolve into imitations of pleasure without the solidarity that dromena began in. Yet the self-congratulated decline is only syncopating the pattern of ritual degeneration made by liturgy when

your brothers yet uncouth still. Pending your rehabilitation, this court order will turn to advantage the talent that burns you. At the same time it will help redress the general injustice of world history, and also help you open your thoughts to a broader variety of conceivable mates. Best of all, in exchange for the services you will render hereby—or rather for disposable goods you'd never salt away otherwise—you'll build up income to dispense with alchemy and free yourself to seek nighttime dates in Berkeley.

In certain quarters semen is highly prized. Perhaps you think yourself of no special worth for what you'd most like to be of worth for, but in fact you may be of inestimable worth for your affliction, as if you were an angel granted passion without body or parts. For you dwell at the medical heart of Oakland where all the fertility-seekers go for therapy. Even in your own building there is a specialist who might have clients interested in immaculate conception. You have much to offer and are close at hand, always on call from behind the scenes. With you on tap there'd be no need to draw frozen deposits from a public bank. How easily you could contribute to the well-bred population of the country, simply by trapping your essence in a bottle! After all, you're not a stupid bull, and the doctor won't have to hide inside some counterfeit contraption to catch the stuff. I don't think you'd have to be stimulated by pictures either.

DEFENDANT: It's ridiculous to have any intermediate vial at all, especially when the stud's always willing to give a baker's dozen for his money.

it much more slowly attenuates into aesthetic magical or idealistic varieties of religious experience. When art's satisfactions are concentrated in illusions either of fulfilling sensational wishes or of solving riddles (which is no longer a practical skill useful to bards prophets and kings but only a game of decoding symbols) the ontological value of the *cause* of pleasure makes no difference.

The poet who originally managed everything and played the hero is now a writer only, and he leaves to professional specialists all the acting, directing, choreography, music, and stage design. The open orchestra of imagination has been flattened into a proscenium arch; the atmosphere of Apollonian daylight has become a skyless night craftily lighted as exception to darkness; and the architecture of the stage has become a three-walled box with interior decorations. Profit has replaced glory as the motive for both writing and underwriting, and advertising has taken the place of festival not only in drawing the crowd but also in swaying the judges.

Leaving aside television, however, the worst of our theater is the impassioned tattering that Hamlet suppressed until after his death: shouting that starts with the first scene of the first act and is brought to mounting crescendos with everlouder shrieks, ever more expressive clutchings of the air, ever more artistic costumes, and ever-quickening strides of aimless locomotion across ever more mechanical boards and backdrops—all of which does away with the need to compose

JUDGE: I happen to agree with you, personally, but this is the way husbands prefer it to be done. Besides, there's the whole virago market. There are some businesslike women who'd deem the revolution won if they had the means for "motherhood united with virginity". (That's what the father of logical positivism wanted to invent.)

DEFENDANT: I could make up cartridges, packaged by the quarter-dozen. Buy a full dozen and get the phalloid water-pistol free!

JUDGE: All it will take is a single success story and your fortune will be made. Of course you'll have to start eating a little better.

DEFENDANT: Oh I'm perfectly confident of my sperms.

JUDGE: Well take a look at them under some microscope on one of your nightly prowls upstairs, while you're looking for clues to the private lives of nurses and receptionists and other consulting-room secrets. Every once in a while they must forget to lock the cupboards.

DEFENDANT: Those one-eye machines are hard to use. Maybe I smear the slides too thick. I can pick up a certain chaotic agitation but I can never get any actual comets to swim into my ken. You took Biology didnt you? Maybe you could teach me how to focus the objective and the subjective without making the victim self-conscious.

JUDGE: I'm afraid it wouldnt be proper for me to visit you there at night. He'd never let me. I don't remember how they work anyway. Just take your time. You're probably too furtive. I'm sure there's nothing to worry about. After the doctor puts you on the market your count will be found so reli-

poetry and dance, without which it is much easier for critics to explain the imbedded psychology. Or else it's as if active free will could be exhibited only in the close-up urbanity of its symbolic vestiges as the most pathetically subjective kind of passion; and as if a campanile full of bells would go to waste if you failed to wring all the changes. "The emotion that comes with the music of words is exhausting, like all intellectual emotions," says Yeats, "and few people like exhausting emotions; and therefore actors began to speak as if they were recording something out of the newspapers. They forgot the noble art of oratory, and gave all their thought to the poor art of acting, that is content with the sympathy of our nerves."

Even in Aristotle it can be discerned that what we define as tragedy was really an exceptionally narrow species of a generic poesy that broadly included various kinds of theatrically improvised *komos*, which justifies us in calling comedy the canvas for drama. In plots of all gradations from happy endings to the most painful misfortunes of fate, tragic heroism is problematic. Sometimes in Euripides you can't be sure who the hero is—Hippolytus (a sort of Pentheus), Phaedra (a reminder of Medea or Clytemnestra), or noble Theseus (who suffers like Oedipus or Othello or Cuchulain)—the first, second, or third actor of the same play. But the American theater set out to prove that heroes are necessarily no more autonomous than vectors of passion or victims of circum-

able as well as handy that he'll have his patients crying you up to all their friends. It will save him a lot of trouble and expense to have a single supplier. All it takes is one man of stamina. Once he's sure of your production capacity he might even recommend you to one or two of his colleagues across the Bay.

DEFENDANT: I could handle two cities.

JUDGE: Naturally he'll tend to play up or play down your various physical characteristics, and of course he'll magnify your education because some of his clients may be fully as engaged by intelligence as their husbands are by a son's stature or a daughter's beauty.

DEFENDANT: The trick is to get a lot of business before the first crop is old enough for the kids of show their true colors.

JUDGE: But it would take a long time for the word to get around. Sometimes a child has to be fourteen or fifteen before you can tell it isnt destined for either jail or glory.

DEFENDANT: I hope by then I'll have a better way to earn my living—or at least a woman of my own to intercept some of the transactions.

JUDGE: Irrespective of national or local fertility rates the demand for specialists with your potential will never decline, for certain curious reasons. (I can't help my enthusiasm for your talent!) For instance there are many benighted men like the foreman of our jury. He's prepared at an unnatural wife's behest to do what a good patriarchal Jew like the prosecutor whose wife is faithful to him and to her religion or any egoist weak in other categories of success would never dream of—to have himself denatured. All

stance—that freedom of the will is a merely political fiction, and that drama is not poetry at all.

But we do have dancers, and a few humble actors; and above all, with all our indulgences of language and sensation, more liberty than we need to make progressive or reactionary experiments with bodies and ideas.

We have poets too. Let them have a chance, with art-dance at their disposal, an electrically controllable bass for their rhythm, with the amplitude and fidelity to sustain any modulation, if willing to join in denial of box-office music and spectacle. Dance might recover its old energy to serve as the poet's medium of dramatic vision. There are no theaters ready for him now but the elements of production are available.

Every culture is closely or distantly determined by its antecedent rituals. We are no further from liturgy than Aeschylus was. But destiny never delivers itself into the poet's hands—not in Athens, not in London, not in Dublin, not in San Francisco New York or Gloucester. When there's no dithyramb for him to take over he must work backwards and with unprecedented irony, confounding all past artifications, write plays that will generate a theater.

An American can at least hope against hope that for the first time in a legal and monumental civilization, before it ends, language will be wrought strong and pure enough to make our own new imaginations in an art recovered from the highest of our component cultures, as

these sterilists profess to be reducing mankind's losses in the next war, but in truth most of them (like juryman Jackson) just want no more interruptions of their wife's fascination with number one. Of course it's different if it's a question of setting some limit to an overpopulated family's poverty; but poor people can't afford to go to doctors. I'm talking about the ones who are well off. They go to an office building like yours for outpatient surgery that is said to be all too quick and easy.

Romans did not from the Greek, nor Hebrews from the Sumerian.

{*Second-encounter Postulants only:*
GO TO ITEM (5) HY.02, page 53.}

DEFENDANT: Well I can see why Newt might subconsciously want to save himself some uncertainty if Sylvia should get pregnant again. Maybe also by openly telling everybody what he's done she'd take warning to go easy.

JUDGE: Sylvia's still young. She'd regret it, like other women when they realize too late that there's not much conjugal felicity when fertility's no longer at their disposal. I think it would just make things worse between the Cahners. Maybe she'd end up going to your doctor! Wouldnt that be funny? Anyway you'll have the pleasure of saving many another kind of marriage from needless dissolution. More often than you might think from the history of cruel kings there are congenital or acquired disabilities that can be laid to the family sportsman himself without justifying infidelity or divorce. Even husbands who have sired two or three times can lose their virtue. Then what's a wife to do?

DEFENDANT: Come to me and let her husband pay for it! I can make money hand over fist! I'll never have to work again.

JUDGE: Wait a minute now my dear boy! It's a rather pleasant avocation but it's no bed of roses. You have a lot to think about if you want to enter this market, and you must approach the doctor cautiously.

> All that glitters is not gold;
> All that's reckless is not bold!

DEFENDANT: But without hindering my serious career I could earn more in a week than by selling all the blood in my body fifty two times a year.

JUDGE: But your health.

DEFENDANT: It won't be an iota different than it is now. Just some slight changes of procedure. Besides, with an arrangement like that who could complain about his headache just because he doesnt drink?

JUDGE: Well just remember that this sentence is not intended to make you give up the hope of drinking. It's just your half-way probation. It must not become an addiction to easy antisocial habits. Keep looking for the right girl in your spare time. Meanwhile you can augment the commonwealth by assisting nature without losing the purity that makes you dearer than other knights.

DEFENDANT: What's the first step?

JUDGE: Write a curriculum vitae that suggests attractive qualities. List your distinctions, mention your dreams and aspirations.

DEFENDANT: God forbid! But I'll give myself a decent ancestry.

JUDGE: But you'll have to shave and clean your fingernails before you take it to the doctor. Soak yourself clean and fragrant in our tub.

{*First-encounter Postulants:* Continue with *Log 2* below}

Log 2

(Vigil of the Feast of the Circumcision)

When will I begin? No one takes me seriously. Too long I've been the butt of fleers. To some people I'm just a false start—tossable into the fire and preferably rewhittled. Cheap softwood. But this is the eve of a new year: tomorrow shall not pass before I have begun my Lesedrama.

When Odysseus sat in disguise among beggars listening to a bard tell stories about his quarrel with Achilles and his clever contrivance of the hollow wooden horse he heard not a single word to put him out of temper; but I must confess that it nettles me to suffer this fiction. Not only does my identity never escape detection but the exposure of my privacy, with all the facts at sixes and sevens, becomes the object of a game. For his own purposes this reconstructor affects poor memory (though he quotes prose as well as rhyme); and he excuses himself by pointing out that all Cretans may be liars but they're not liars all the time. Yet I'm the only one in the world, apparently, who can straighten out this sagacious foolishness— whether hoax, parody, or challenge. If it weren't for Yeats and Ruth I would never have let this opaque black operator get so close. He's as pro- saic as a lettercarrier, but leaves his gentle readers to imagine the evidence for his solemn generalizations! In sheer self-preservation I must put a stop to this book by undertaking to redeem myself with proof. Except maybe for *Moby Dick* all novels are comic, but he seems to relish making low comedy of everything he touches.

Wherever he got his ideas, as an uneducated amateur of strictly American propension who can't even wade through Kant, he seems deter- mined to prove the canard that art anticipates reality. But I'm equally de- termined to disprove his calculations. I've had enough of these paltering fancies from a head full of book biz—albeit I was very nearly coneyed by the authority of his voice. "You haven't fallen far enough yet," he says to me, pontificating like *Michael, the great prince who has charge of your people.* "Stay out of the hero's crescent until you have earned your scutcheon. When you come back to tragedy in twenty years you won't be so absolute. Meanwhile there's no more need to rank epiphenomena than there is to abhor and oppose things as they are. Let yourself sink into history!" So saith old apPendragon, who complains about bestsellers but reads all Churchill's memoirs as if they were the autobiography of Edward the First. Naturally he'd rather have me serve in his campaign than quest for a muse beyond his domestic horizon. Yet he piques himself on the ontological means by which he usurps my life and arrogates to himself everything out of his reach that I can see or think or do.

It's easy enough to make fun of a wrung-out little wretch. I'm nothing but a despised reptile full of venom and rancor because not yet evolved to the level of mammalian pleasure. He archly quotes me Yeats—I should say flinging him in my teeth: "Only when we are gay over a thing, and can play with it, do we show ourselves its master, and have minds clear enough for strength." But what do *I* have to play with except my own miserable hornpipe if I don't get to work? By all the gods of Uruk, I'll play him a thing or two once I begin.

When it comes to that, it's taken him long enough to get started, just to bring forth some library science. At his best he's no better than the architect who says "Art is the application of knowledge to the realization of a conception. . . ." Forsooth, it's the knowledge he labors over, like the patent lawyers he speaks ill of; the conceptions have come all too easily. His whole life as far as I can see has been a series of conceptions.

I'm just as bored by the fuss over fertility as I am by petty finance, if he wants to know the truth. On that subject aristocrats are as bad as the bourgeoisie. It takes a southpaw mongrel to bear a sinister coat of arms with rude gaiety. Men of blood, I'll level them all! We swineherds and cabin-boys call them fools. I laugh and laugh and laugh at their bloody vanities. When all the old superstitions begin to fail they pretend to the science of genetics (which I bet they won't stop touting before the century's over).

Frightened as I am by the prophetic shadow of his figmentation, I am even more horrified at the fakery. The misappropriations of his mind falsify the existence I must get to work in. It's constantly necessary to remind myself that I can quit whenever I choose. I may have to leave behind his snapshot of me, but at least it's not my soul.

In fact I'd rather be embraced by the iron maiden than have my melancholy anatomized by a clinical crew acting as my peers. Yet he tells the world more about his perverted middle-age fantasies than my cravings when he teases me with his honest wife, abusing her reputation by pretending to tempt providence.

There's nothing exceptional about what I want, the same as any other yearling stealing down to the salt lick after the big bucks are gone. There's bound to be a meek little doe that everybody's overlooked. Or it could be just a humorous piece in normal straightforward fun at some well-known water hole. But it doesn't have to be joyful. It wouldn't take a magnification of the pleasure to delight me. I don't ask to see forbidden sights, and I'm certainly not after the masochistic sweets of confirming a jealous suspicion. Other lovers fail to fascinate me. I need no excruciation, my desire needs no renaissance. If I had a wife the last thing I'd do is appoint her to the love-court as chief justice; and I wouldn't harp upon the theme of fault like one of the old professors who can't mention great literature without mouthing the tragic flaw.

When she kissed me under the mistletoe I was too surprised to make the most of it, and so confused I almost gave myself away in front of the boys. He hasn't kidded me about it yet but I suppose they told him because they laughed about it. It seems to me it was a very long soft kiss, considering how hesitant I was in response. He says kisses are tokens or vestiges of sucking, a reciprocal sucking of what sucks, but her kiss was more like avid generosity, for all its casual gaiety, than anything esurient. I'd forgotten how sweet a simple kiss can be.

When Promethean fire began to burn in men with the kind of desire Zeus had wisely intended to reserve for immortals at least they got Pandora from Hephaistos. If I had that god's technical ability I wouldn't bemoan my ineluctable shortcomings, nor complain about infidelity: I'd just hack myself out one bad girl after another. But I suppose I'd never make it even then. It's a good thing the world didn't depend on a kid like me to deliver Athena from Zeus's head. But the truth may be that I can't lift a finger for culture until I deliver myself from innocence.

Who can write without writing about women, and who but the Reverend Robert Burton can write about women without deep experience of the delitescent cleft? Yet perhaps celibacy would be a fair price to pay if I could concentrate my scattered brain from beginning to end on something more important than love's middle. Jackie Keats was only a cut or two above the servant class but he was the truest romantic. He had the guts to put all the others to shame by suffering every mortal disappointment in the hope of fame's future trumpet. I am pleased to learn that he was "as proud of being the lowest of the human race as Alfred could be in being of the highest"! As a love-poet maybe he didn't know much more about what he was talking about than I do. Without a mistress—and without freedom or display of personality—the poet willingly underwent "the Turmoil and anxiety, the sacrifice of all what is called comfort", quite content to "Measure time by what is done and to die in 6 hours could plans be brought to conclusions" —perhaps "greater things than our Creator himself made!!"

By cracky, Nietzsche's right: "Art is not an imitation of nature but its metaphysical supplement, raised up beside it in order to overcome it." I should be able to work alone though tormented *all* my years by any Britomartis! My Prime Object is "a refuge as well as a Passion." And as I dig my pen a quarter of an inch into this spotless white paper I swear that my troubles are no worse than mere practical difficulties like "that Money affair". If bookburning could have sublimated my cacoethes fuckendi into cacoethes scribendi I'd never have kept more than three volumes on my shelf at a time! But my daily unresolved relief leaves me with no puritanical stamina for fame.

Is it possible for a 20th century boy with merely potential conceptions to evade the law of nature that to imagine life one must have lived? Possible, yes—but less than probable. Still, I'm an oxymoron of negative probability or I'm nothing. I am not meant to play poker with friends but to pass my life as a hermit in what himself would call the troughs of literary quantum waves.

All I have to do is divert the pneumatic fluid to my head for museless inspiration. Under the goad of others' false fame I'll need no hair shirt to keep me from falling asleep. If he'd ever smelled the ladies' room of a public building before the cleaning crew arrives he'd know there's a limit to satyriasis; he might be less confident of his persuasion that I spend all my time making up stories about secretaries and medical technicians working late. It's only a matter of overcoming the deterministic truth of my case, which is that if it had to be reduced to simple binary choice I'd rather cuntle my prickle than rarify its substance into immortal words. What's really wanted for this work is not a man thinking but a thinking man: that is to say a man free to speculate with images. All I really need is images—not experience! I have been hoping that if I didnt make any serious claims to foreign languages the gods would grant me proficiency in this one. With that sole gift comes as much as I'd need of what Aristotle calls intelligence because it necessarily includes the facility to simultaneously hold two conflicting ideas without deciding between them. Two or more. Like Engidu I could simply name all things for the first time in my own Ur-language, making up images perfectly appropriate to my innocence.

The difficulty is that my libido's just too inflexible. How can I make it follow my mind? Could realized pleasure liberate my enslaved talent?

Who can assist a man struggle against his own voluntary inaction? There's not a soul in the world who can help C K begin to become what C K thinks he's born for. No. For C K there's no alternative but to sit down and do what he thinks he may have in mind.

To fail in what I would give up all success for is absolute humiliation. But a reprobate must risk disproving himself. "The most frightful of all things, the indifference of Fate!"—even if you should have a thousand servants living for you!

If I continue to futter away all my verve with the comforts of solitude I'll be lost in the forest of desire forever. My esteemed Ti-Jean couldn't become a star halfback when he got to Columbia because he didn't even make the varsity, and I won't shine if I don't make a beginning. In all my ignorance I know too much about stardom. My start must be made from a point earlier than Massachusetts or Tara or Troy or Sinai—before the babble of writing itself. I go back to Gilgamesh.

My master says that he himself has passed the age to become an artist, but that I have no excuse. Just to make my life a little easier to bear! But others would have me modest and successful. It is as if they say to me: you can no more enlarge or intensify the reticulation of your brain by impassioned will than you can bend your mouth to your tail. To me such a face upon the truth is horrifying—more appalling than the unbearable taunts of Inanna, more unconscionable than the certainty of death. But he says no such thing. Him I love in spite of all abuse because when the chips are down he insists upon my possibility: not only the simpleminded indeterminism of decision-making or even heroic choice between two or three absolutes, but the liberty of undetermined Creative Mind. He and I agree on end-purpose.

Being unidentified and conscious of my insufficiency I can rise above my comparatively comfortable sorrow (so much less hopeless than his) and learn to scorn despair, for merely by defining my feelings he now persuades me that a known lack is an unknown space for art, and that my intuitions are subject to whatever annealment will make them plastic. That's a pretty vague prophecy—and it may only lull me through more weeks of drifting reverie and bootless journal-writing, as if I were warming up my pen with little poems of joy and melancholy; but it helps me keep at bay the self-indulgent misgiving that I may have nothing to prove after all. My head glows with sweat at that hideous doubt—and the fear that a wormunculus of knowledge is my only instigation. And yes, it is then that my guardian angel shows himself as infinitely more important to my salvation than any mere generous well-meaning friend: he insists that dramatic poetry is what I have within me!

But I must take his advice in season. This journal is only a scaffold that I'm about to kick over. My plaints are finished. I am done praying Anshar and Kishar for the favors of their granddaughter. I ask for no assistance to still my turmoil. I seek no deliverance from this murky job. My will to see, my will to know, my will to act may quarrel all they like, or in unison turn against me—but with his encouragement I'll manage them to my advantage. I didn't drop a glittering career to be left high and dry by anybody's belle dame! When you haven't yet begun to work precious time is lost by chasing skirts, and in old age there's mickle time to grieve for failing in that hunt.

I will begin tomorrow. As I willed to begin yesterday, as I willed to begin last week, as I willed to begin six months ago. This is my one last night of meditation. I'll think about the past; then I'll screw my inspiration up to the sticking point. Tonight I'll gird my mind, and tomorrow I'll obliterate the channels of habit.

Then I shall begin with a short running jump off the surface of the earth, with a single tiny language-leap in strong black ink. Perhaps I'll begin with one of Shakespeare's definite articles, and make that little word my own! Having impetuously swept all my plans and notes into the fire and called a lordly curse down upon the muses of circumspection, I'll jolt myself loose from both aesthetic sensibility and morbid spells of sloth. One swift thoughtless word is all I need—and then a second out of the blue to copulate with the first. Thereupon the trooping throngs of sweet phrases will evoke sentences, which should press me thick and fast, rushing from forgotten storage places, bringing with them in an hour all the thoughts I'll need for the rest of my year's joyful afternoons. All it takes is to *begin*!

Afterwards, every day overflowing with riches, I'll assimilate unrefined minerals deep in the ground where now they lie inaccessible to sciolistic reason. Each right word will draw me down to my own uncultivated wealth beneath the thin topsoil where I've been endlessly tracing circles and figure 8s like a brainless kid's electric train.

Doesn't it work something like that?

My obscurity keeps me free of criticism. There's nothing to inhibit my epigenesis but the problem of controlling and filtering the cloudbursts of creative passion that will surely possess me. Somewhere inside me there must be an adjustable butterfly valve.

By the blessed mother of Jesus too, in the morning without further ado I'll start the new regime, teach my idiotically impressionable body to reform its customs. As soon as I cure my grubby soma of its greedy expectations I can release its less commonplace governor from enthrallment to the single image of his obsession. I'll groan myself to sleep unrequited if it takes a pint of whiskey after breakfast to put me into a stupor. After I have once begun it will get a little easier every day.

If I can stop up my cornucopia long enough I'll not only get going on my great work but I'll also be so full of vinegar that in my spare time I may get up on my hind legs and *casually* track down a whole girl, wisely contenting myself at first with the deferred delights of ordinary conversation, a friendly word of two without plans or calculations.

Therefore this is my last entry in his log, which I'll chuck into Wine's firebox without waiting to see if I become a man.

Tomorrow I also start shaving every day.

{*First-encounter Postulants only:* GO TO ITEM (58) SO.07, page 905.}

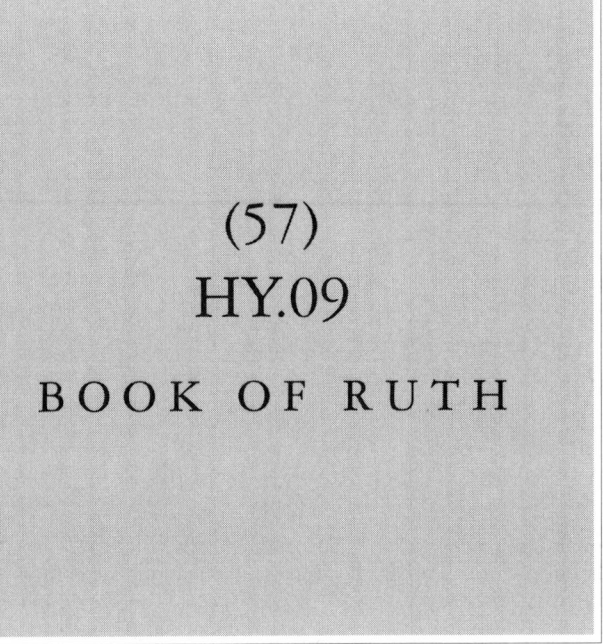

(57)
HY.09

BOOK OF RUTH

I do not oscillate in Emerson's rainbow.
—MELVILLE

uth is not one of my favorite names but now I can see that it has dogged me since I was a kid. I had forgotten about Ruthie Perkins. Two long black pigtails sleek as tame snakes braiding themselves in loving service to their Indian princess. In fact I always thought of her when I heard the name Tragabigzanda whom I confused with Pocahontas because of her love for the Admiral of New England a k a North Virginia who was overruled in his cleping of our vineland by the same unfortunate Prince Charles who is commemorated by the river in Cambridge. She was one of my principal interests after I became aware of them at Maplewood School when she was taller than most of the boys including me. I liked her for being slightly awkward and diffident as the smartest one in the class and because like me she had to wear glasses. The kids saw that we had something in common. They had practically no other evidence for chanting "Mickey loves Ruthie!" every time the subject of heterosexual affections came up. Even though none of the other boys took interest in her I was joyful with tenderness and pride whenever I saw hearts and arrows drawn with our initials and especially when some girl who either knew Ruthie's heart or paid particular attention to mine chalked on the new W P A sidewalk RUTHIE LIKES MICK. I wished she had dared to put it forever in the wet cement. Yet it was embarrassing because I was certain Ruth herself hadnt done it and I was afraid she'd be so mortified if she ever saw it that she'd go out of her way to disprove the legend. But how did the kids divine anyone's feelings? Was everything always obvious? When I was a sailor I had no compunction about betraying my desires in public but back in those days I almost never even dared speak to her. That's how they could tell. On her part she was always shy except when giving answers in school. She used to like to rock in swings at an age when other kids had outgrown the sport. But we were aware of each other. She used to blush when I caught her eye. TRUTH OR CONSEQUENCES! Even after we started writing notes we couldnt face the consequences and always behaved as if we were hardly acquainted when we had a chance to talk, she and I the only Protestants in the class though she was a puritan Congregationalist or even a Baptist I forget which involving us in a tacit community of defense as excluded from the ultimate solidarity of the others who held at least one universal allegiance despite variances of nationality, notwithstanding the disparity of our family standards of living. The Jews and the Greeks of Gloucester attended other schools and of course except for Chapmen the Episcopalians did so too. The Maplewood neighborhood had declined a lot since old Yankee days but I think our class in its overwhelmingly Mediterranean Catholicism not only Latin but also Levantine (known generally as "Syrian") under Irish priests at St Ann's and Atlantic Iberians with their own rite at the more distant blue-topped Our Lady of Good Voyage was still only a demotic forecast of what the whole ward must be like now. She and her younger brothers might have been the last kids of the Yankee maritime tradition to be enrolled there. The family lived in her grandfather's big house a third-generation skipper long since retired. In fact the only time we really talked freely was once when I was cutting home through Oak Grove Cemetery and I found her putting flowers on her great-grandfather's grave that had a schooner carved on the stone and a surname I had never noticed as being the same as hers even though it was within sight of her bedroom window. Very very slowly we walked together to her back fence and I actually gave her my hand to help her over it and then she sat in her swing hanging from the great oak limb while we talked some more in the twilight I of course remaining in the graveyard where I could duck out of sight if anyone should come into her yard. She had to go in when we could no longer deny that it was dark. I used to ride past that house on Washington Street half a dozen times a day no hands and nonchalantly or fast as hell hoping to see her or be seen. For a couple of years she was the one I always showed off for at school or anywhere else in town that I thought she might happen to be especially when I was in the Memorial Day parade that marshalled in the cemetery under her windows and marched right past her front door. I was elated whenever I saw that I had attracted her attention. She was usually with her friend Maureen who used to hang around her house a lot which I was glad of because Maureen lived on Cleveland Street and was poorer than we were. It showed that Ruth didnt care about social differences. Nevertheless I was acutely ashamed of the place we lived in and I always avoided her when she passed it on her way back and forth from school. It was close to the school and painfully conspicuous especially because the LeBlanc family in the other half was so sloppy. I liked my Cub Scout uniform since it removed economic distinctions and since all the badges I won were emblems of true worth that she could respect. Risking censure or ridicule I would wear it at the slightest excuse. My bike I'd often leave at home just so I could walk from Grove to Derby through the cemetery or take Billy to play there among the boulders close to her house when the caretakers werent around. But that one lovely encounter was the high point of our love. Ever afterwards we pretended it had never happened. But why? Maybe we felt too precocious. I know I was afraid of her father. But what kind of guilty thoughts could I have had then? I was still honorable in those days I think. After we moved to Cambridge it was a different matter. My retrospective intentions toward her changed character after the last time we saw each other. I forgot the tenderness and remembered our love only as a lost chance for touching and kissing. But as long as we stayed in Gloucester I dared make her my choice at pairing games and she me. "Red Rover Red Rover send Ruth Perkins right over!" In our part of town we never had Valentine parties. If we'd both lived in East Gloucester or Riverdale we might have had the chance to bob for apples together or to play spin-the-bottle. A nineteenth century face of smoothest oval ivory pure black hair parted in the middle lips full as Lilian's but still scarcely sentient. I always wanted to see those hazel eyes with her glasses off. That's exactly what I told her over the fence the night she sat gently twisting on her narrow seat now and then touching her foot to the ground for delicate impetus and playfully altering the period of her oscillation by extending her legs with stiffened knees or drawing them in. All at once it came over me that she had taken the words amiss not understanding my special sympathy or my admiration of her overlooked beauty. But to make it worse I became too confused to say anything that would put it right. I was so ashamed and embarrassed by what I'd said that thinking I'd hurt her feelings I could never speak to her again. So that was really why our love went no further! But for all the rest of my time in Gloucester, averting my eyes when I longed to see, it was for her that I conducted my competition with the world. Which was equivalent to earning a living.

I wonder how she did at the High School. No doubt valedictorian with her pigtails still. I hope she at least escaped to college. Probably now an old-maid librarian having failed to find another man like me! I never knew what happened to any of my old friends. Some of the boys probably killed in the war, some of the girls shattered with foolishness or grief. And

I've had more classmates than most people, changing cities changing schools every year or two until I finally settled down at Cambridge High and Latin. The Depression unsettled people and later the war moved them, its prosperity ending even Gloucester's "art of frugal living". I never knew why the old man lost his job after all those years in the office. Didnt occur to me that the company might have had some new pretext beyond just the hard times that accounted for the woe of other families. He must have spoken up about something. Maybe he defended Joe Sheehan and they finally found out he was a liberal. Or opposed someone in the ruling family perhaps their smart young Harvard Business School C P A brought in over everyone's head with all the answers about how to run a fisheries and manage its remaining fleet. To me it seemed a liberation to get away from Gloucester. I thought there'd be more to do in a real city and that it would be pure freedom not to have miserable chores where my leisured friends could see me like cleaning up the cluttered yard or helping put up storm windows. As it turned out I got my anonymity in Cambridge but I still had to haul the kerosene bottle from a hardware store shovel coal clean out ashes empty the ice pan or take down the garbage. I hardly knew how desolate my parents felt to break up housekeeping and go into exile. But there'd never have been a Theater Project job for Dad to get in Gloucester.

I was glad to be spared the shame of living off any W P A work there because the Republicans called it living off Relief or leaning on your shovel and as always they set the moral tone. Even Ruthie wouldnt have understood I thought. But if I'd stayed in Gloucester and gone to high school with her we might have married. My Ruth must have been like her at that age entering San Leandro High three thousand miles away and just as smart though prettier and smaller, just as late in acquiring outward grace. Maybe like thousands and thousands of serious intelligent girls born vulnerable even to men of sympathy born too vulnerable to them. After more than twenty years I suddenly remember the polar sweetness of unprogressive love between bashful minds still innocent of love's literature. It faintly echoes other memories that I can't right now recall at all that once every blue moon give me pause in the occupations of my life and for a few minutes seem to belong to history only as true ideals forgotten with birth. To think that Mike Chapman should ever entertain a thought so platonistical! Whatever you may gain with a woman over the years that lovely feeling fresh and shallow as dew can never be recovered. It would take a new girl and a new boy too.

The known person always takes full possession of her given name which becomes to the knower an image as concrete to the imagination as the person herself whom it substantiates with exactly the same sounds and letters that the brain uses indifferently to symbolize absolutely incompatible women not even noticed to own the same signifier. Proves at least that language can't be platonic. If I don't particularly meditate upon today's events I can call Sandy's woman by her name without remarking its familiarity to the ear. The difference between objects not to mention their contexts is so great that the brain automatically performs its algebraic substitutions. But the other two Ruths from the much more distant past whose coincidence also strikes me now for the first time demonstrating the native sluggishness of my intelligence must have been absorbed by Ruth Chapman. Why are they now released from oblivion? Maybe this delayed perception foreshadows the disintegration of advanced marriage. Ruth Perkins! Ruth Chapman! I don't remember the surname of the second Ruth that came between. She too was a history that ended for me before it could begin. In that case it was getting drafted that spared me pain. In astronomical time not much more than a year before I met the superseding Ruth but in my own time a whole youth between the two of them.

The Ruth in New York I loved more specifically than the one in Gloucester because I was 6 or 8 years older but I understood her far less. Here my faintheartedness was mature and serious but much better justified. On the whole I must consider myself lucky to have been leaving the shop so soon after she came to work. Still I was spared joy and grief by never seeing her off the job. During that two or three months she walked in my mind day and night yet I continued timid, quaking at everything that seemed to forbid our friendship. Though I was ravenous for great bites of worldly experience seizures of passion threw me off my feed and blunted my excitement about the war just when it was finally beginning to raise everyone's hopes. My concealed love for this second Ruth among workaday machines was in the beginning just as sweet as the innocent feeling that had been all but declared to the first in a summer's grove of oaks while the birds were going to sleep. She must have known enough to suspect a white boy's desire. In the end she could not have mistaken Karl's feelings. Mine was just the love of an explorer and I was about to go piping off to marvelous adventures in uniform but long after she'd have gone back to the world she came from or moved on to the world all three of us thought she was destined for he would have to remain on the spot with no hope of new hopes, staring every day at the boards she'd walked upon. At first blush having no pity or wisdom I thought Karl was far too old to rival me a year or so younger than herself or my unknown rivals if any. So worshipful was her dignity that I could imagine it only as that of a maiden devoted to her art.

But though I loved her in our most cosmopolitan city at the height of international war I was a coward about the social matter. I persuaded myself it was more for her sake than mine. I'd heard stories that might still have been true in those days. Even today it's too soon. White hatred of miscegenation may so long outlast civic exclusions that it'll be too late when all black people have grown to scorn us utterly. Contempt is what I already felt to have deserved of her, classifying myself as an admiring Caucasian. Anyhow the streets were swarming with uniformed dangers full of unpredictable diversity and violence. The city to most of its wartime tourists was as strange as Paris but in no way so inhibiting. New York did not suppress the Southerners who dominate in sound at least all American military services especially as seen at the enlisted and Congressional levels. They set the standards of tolerance and force. The moral rule of the South has always been too strong for my courage. I see it everywhere. Coca-Cola of Georgia drove Moxie of New England off the market along with its signs everywhere fingering you straight in the eye not to mention plain old root beer and sarsaparilla. I was so daunted by self-praising Rebel yells that like a good German I forswore my manhood. It was easy to convince myself that black Artemis would have been disgusted at any invitation I could have brought myself to make. It would have been too obvious. It seems too obvious to ask any girl for any date. The fact that I was in love with her beforehand could not be beforehand proved. And if she had divined my honesty I still could have seen no reason for her to go to the movies with me or even to a concert of her choice unless she was already prepared to return my love who showed nothing worthy of her respect. Even a West Indian understands American lust all too well I thought. And then how would I get her home to Harlem or wherever she had to live among people who would take me more amiss in their terrifying enclave than the Ku Klux Klan would take her at one of their picnics. I supposed that she was by then well trained to the difficulties of living in our most hospitable city after a civilized island like Jamaica where she'd been to better schools than I had.

After a year of secret effort to get into the Navy despite gross imperfection of physical vision while the bosses at the shop plotted they thought on my behalf as well as their own to make me an indispensable toolmaker for national defense, when I was at last called up and snatched away from the Army at the very induction center supposedly for limited service I suddenly felt the conscientious objection of love. Old Mr Mello our neighbor in Gloucester from the Azores which unlike Ireland for the English had no aborigines to resist Portuguese imperialism once amazed me by protesting the line of squares I used to show along the side of my famous three-quarter perspective of what I thought was a clipper ship under fullest possible sail. One evening during a visit of our family to his we were reminded that he'd been to sea in those days and I was asked to run across the street to fetch my latest version. I was doubtful that the ignorant old man who could hardly speak English would recognize any connection at all between my picture and his experience as if I was about to display before a dog a portrait of its mother. He picked out the detail at once. "Warship! Bad bad! No make guns no no . . ." spoiling my pleasure in his appreciation of the drawing. The stocky dodderer with a yellowed white walrus moustache was scarcely heeded by the younger generations of the large clan that sheltered him more as a charity boarder than as the old world patriarch in my view and I felt sorry for him but I agreed that he had grown too simple-minded to distinguish one thing from another in history or technics. Yet in his single briefly animated response to my insufferable self-assurance he exposed me to a love of peace more venerable than the contemporary pacifism of untimely Harvard boys demonstrating as Veterans of Future Wars. I had either assumed that clipper ships carried a full deck of guns or mechanically copied the square ports from paintings of unamerican packet ships without knowing what they were for. Neither I nor the senile fisherman knew that the Limejuicers' tradition was to make a painted show of defense along the sheer strakes long after all pirates had been hanged and privateering for all nations obviated when voluntary commerce became the sole end of investment in sailing ships perhaps for the very purpose of striking awe into the hearts of misbegotten inferiors who had not forgotten Britain's enforced reputation for demanding courtesies at sea. As a momentary pacifist in the sudden isolationist pang of leaving the Ruth who at the time of my induction bore the provisional burden of my lifelong ruthful love I saw too late and presently forgot glory's unmentionable paying freight the final cause of war concealed by handsome shipshape trimmings that were always represented under blue sky and flocculent clouds with no killers in sight.

When I started off from Grand Central Station in my little ad hoc draft on the first Pullman-berth trip of my life, still shabbily dressed among first-class civilians and transient officers of various military services, on the way to claiming a uniform and lowest class living quarters at boot camp, where my relief from the economic struggle was to be cleanly marked by having all the clothes I'd brought shipped home by Railway Express at government expense in a neatly contrived corrugated carton, my conscience had already been cleared of having lied to my employers, who called me "a born toolmaker" though truly I was just beginning to learn the craft and could be officially classified only as an apprentice machinist, in stating my preference as to the part I should play in the war effort. Until that girl came to the shop my intention if I had been disappointed of induction was to take my savings and go to college, but then I found myself submitting to the influence of their honorable profession which they believed anyone would put first who was blessed with my talent and opportunity. Even as I thrilled to the American Rhine skimming past the Twentieth Century Limited almost at track level watching the dull effects of an obscured sun setting behind the Catskills and doing my best to savor the fulfillment of a desire almost as old as myself shamelessly magnetized to the window for every last minute of waning light, thus from the very outset deliberately withdrawn from my loudly socializing comrades, I took no satisfaction in the good luck not only of ending up in the Navy but of being assigned to the most abstract of training programs and getting rated Seaman Second Class rather than Apprentice, all on the strength of a promise I found myself to have made by passing a special technological test someone had thought to try me with. Glimpses of the Erie Canal having been lost to darkness it wasn't until the next morning, when daylight began to tantalize me with other interesting works in an open landscape stripped and withered by icy white winter which excited all my cupidity for knowledge though whipped out of sight before they could well be taken in, that I finally made the transition from lovesickness to the undivided joy of travel. If I wasnt getting immediate sea duty in the European Theater at least I was seeing America first.

My half a dozen or so maiden shipmates thought nothing of having to accept the leadership of a first among equals arbitrarily but shrewdly chosen by the Chief who'd mustered us at the Center and handed him an envelope full of orders and tickets, a tough brown beefy Jew from Brooklyn with a degree in radio engineering and hopes for a commission. I was stuck in his company for another six weeks. When he reverted to undistinguished status on our arrival at the Great Lakes Training Center he was more hateful to me than ever for the truculent gleam of big white teeth everlastingly disclosed in the left side of his mouth as he chewed gum at a rapid clip from morning to night in his pouched cheek on the right. His broad muscular face was invulnerable no less brutal than his body and his deportment as arrogant as an Italian fascist with a degree in German science. But all the men in my little group aboard the train were pretty cocky about being selected for what they regarded as elite training in a confidential new branch of electronics. Most of them were already ham operators. Until I finished my schooling in electronics a year later and joined the common people of the Navy with all their inferior trades and callings, for which my envy had been renewed and strengthened as the classes I sat in were gradually addressed more and more to the uninteresting maintenance of particular equipment models, my spirit was cumulatively darkened by the society of erstwhile amateur radio operators the most liberal of whom are superheterodyne bores. However I soon began to see the advantages of my special classification and petty prestige and of not being dispatched as a Pacifist to face the Asiatic enemy whose dark suicidal cruelty I dreaded more than arctic U-boats. It was already clear that the Navy was directing to the Pacific Theater all the new men and ships that were not immediately deployable against retreating Nazis in order that the war might culminate in a final world-historical demonstration of seapower used to bypass large masses of jungle in which Churchill the Former Naval Person said it was as foolish to fight the Japanese as to enter the water to fight sharks. In the primary phases of my studies first at a requisitioned high school building amid the slums of south Chicago but near a fine green park where we did our marching and softball playing and then on the Monterey peninsula at a palm-embowered hotel with swimming pool and converted golf course on the grounds I competed as eagerly as the rest of them in trigonometric computation of power factors and surgical soldering. But in the latter part of Radio Matériel School still so called, as we were still called Radio Technicians to disarm the intelligence of our enemies who might otherwise be confirmed in their suspicions that the U S was investing a great deal in radar sonar loran and automatic identification equipment all belonging with radio under the new generic heading of Electronics, I hated every syllable of the solemn jargon I heard all day long and every wiseaching tone in the whole range of empirical hamminess that scornfully dismissed all our sliderule mathematics and electrical reasoning that had been intended to train our generalized diagnostic faculties and I rebelled so sullenly against the last three months of rote pedagogy that I nearly flunked out at a time when I suddenly least wanted to be sent to sea having become totally absorbed in the liberty that came three weekends out of four, almost the sole subject of my thoughts the object of which was by then a new and last Ruth. My ambition all along had been trammeled by desire for girls by whom I learned new locales in tireless searches sometimes rewarded by proud possession or even love in the one case between Ruths when my heart ruled supreme and blighted my delight at being a sailor who even as a student had to move on from one station to another. For a long time or what seemed to me at the time a long time the glory and excitement of San Francisco Bay could not console me for the little yellow-haired 17-year-old-Norwegian-blooded Marley what's-her-name with long curls I'd left behind in Monterey whom I had loved to the depths of my commonplace soul on the shores of that soft semi-tropical bay with a sardine-fishing harbor and a sea-wracked beach surmounted by duney pines and palms for lovers where the first American ship to stop on the Spanish coast *Otter* of Boston but not the first-ever Yankee smuggler had come to anchor for clandestine trade in 1796 where I thought I'd found my Gloucester Edenized. The dumbest girl I ever loved and called my little Okie though emigrated from Wisconsin and sweet as a Swiss flower who somehow took to me among all the hundreds of electronic apprentices eating like gentlemen at the long tables she and a number of other lucky girls waited on. For hour after hour night after night when I'd sometimes sneak past the guards to meet her in the warm secluded moonlight by the sea we'd coo and kiss as passionately as if ecstasy was nothing more than that. But she was alas too good a Sunday school girl in one of the sects known as extra strict on the fundamentals. Maybe she picked me to love because she knew that I'd never take advantage of her ardent feelings by main force or false promises. But though I was never permitted to lay a hand on her softest parts or to speak all of my mind and she never even counted the thirteen buttons of my dress blues apron I don't remember much frustration in the lovely pleasures we had together for I never doubted that I would make slow progress while she I suppose never doubted that I would eventually come back after long faithful correspondence to claim her lawfully. On my part there was never any serious thought of the future neither with her nor with any other girl not even with the Ruth I'd be loving six months later in a total concentration of sense and intellect so intense and violent that it would remember nothing of significance in the sailorboy infatuation I had so recently deceived myself with. In any event if my artificerial career in the Navy hadnt been undermined by love I might have better abided the long dull specialization of the last few months when I was expected to pay closer attention than ever and more easily swallowed my loathing of the vulgar enthusiasm with which my classmates cataloged vacuum tubes by rote, a kind of taxonomy I've always hated.

At least my nose had been kept to a civilian grindstone by the virtual affair with Black Ruth—as the Reverend Thomas Cranmer's fortunately short-lived young wife was called before he picked her up at a tavern—for it was only on the job that I ever saw her and only on the job that I could demonstrate any ability worthy of her respect. The building in which I met her was newer than most of the others in the block, lower and smaller, but the yellow bricks of the facade had been weathered to smoky mellow brown by twenty summers of Manhattan air. In wartime it was probably neater than usual. The plain flush entrance on the northern sidewalk was nothing more than a green double door with a small square of glass reinforced by imbedded chicken wire in each of the upper panels and a single brass knob. Next door on the east stood a small jewelry shop densely packed with merchandise and on the west an enameled lunchroom somewhat smutched by grease. Each of the four floors above displayed a pair of long plate-glass windows which by their broad horizontal lines suggested the comparatively modern style of Chicago. Set symmetrically between raggedly taller buildings on the block every one of the eight distinguished a separate tenant and in daylight there was little need to consult the customary glass-cased directory mounted on the wall next to the elevator in the lobby because the windows served also as billboards. Upon them were etched in black or emblazoned in gold the products and mottoes as well as trademarks of novelty manufacturers pattern-makers commercial printers doll-and-toy makers stitchers engravers and bookbinders with a variety of lettering that executed the combined function of catalog covers and display advertising. When I searched out the place, fed up with the poverty and eventual boredom of delivering Postal Telegraph messages in the shabbiest neighborhoods of City Hall way down town and ingenuously excited by a want-ad suggesting the glamor of a well-financed "vital defense industry" (possibly with a bright blazing nightshift at premium pay) within walking distance of home, my high spirits were instantly depressed by symptoms that I later recognized as those of a non-union shop making out during the profitable national emergency on the labor of youngsters refugees and other undesireables. This vicinity of the garment district seemed no part of the arsenal of democracy. Nobody hereabouts worked at night or gave any other unequivocal sign that the Depression was ended. With the Times classified page in hand I was trying to visualize the industrial relationship between machine shops and the machine tools that were then still higher in war-production priority even than L S T s , which I'd never even heard of when I looked up with sinking heart to find the level of my destination. On that muggy overcast afternoon at the time of day when crosstown traffic is most miserable I failed to appreciate the exceptional conciseness and restraint of the legend on the window of the third floor east EMPIRE STATE TOOL & DIE CORP. No explanation was necessary to those for whom as customers or vendors the business could have been of any interest nor under ordinary circumstances for anyone who might hope to work there. Having just been turned down for two jobs that I thought I had aptitude for namely drafting and quality-inspecting my urge for survival had been elevated. I resolved at least to satisfy my curiosity about the term that I'd noticed elsewhere in southern Manhattan and throughout the daily want-ad columns if not to fight for the opening. It was a machine shop of craftsmen who required no advertising and had nothing to do with coloring fabrics or German cartels. I found that dies were very hard but feminine tools for special purposes. As it turned out I was not particularly allured by die-making for it required a professional finesse that was less congenial to my temperament than the more masculine toolmaking of jigs and fixtures where structure and outer surface were the concern rather than internal shaping.

Ere long in spite of newly incurred grievances I appreciated and liked that front window with its long bench extended halfway across the building above the low windowsill conveying to the knowledgeable spectator's wintertime eye, though from the other side of the street only vises could be seen and calendared S A E screw charts or the backs of tool chests against the glass, a familiar warmth and cheer within the depths. In the early morning these talismans visible over the tops of produce trucks and sealed semi-trailers swinging over to the East Side from the elevated expressway on the Hudson hinted to anyone acquainted with the guild a long room filled with machines serving and served by the masters of this bench the old kind of mechanics unwilling to replace a whole part or subassembly when something went wrong with a machine if they could find the defective unit of malfunction for repair according to a notion of material efficiency still common among mechanists, who didnt doubt that they would always be paid for their cheap time though even then being supplanted in the armed forces and elsewhere in industry by the modern concept of labor efficiency exemplified in the use of interchangeable black-box subassemblies as least common denominators of skill. They would come to work with smug professional modesty altogether superior to the humdrum commerce now resuming in the broad thoroughfare on which their employers happened to be located. Two or three workers of the neighborhood would already be sitting on stools in the lunchroom waiting for the first brew of coffee while they read the action-packed funnies and sports pages of the Daily News to all intents and purposes unaware of the authoritarian political doctrine of its publisher an economic royalist cousin to America First McCormick leader of freshwater oligarchs who took Rhode Island's star out of his flag because its supreme court approved part of the New

Deal and who made out the war as Mr Roosevelt's own doing both of them still cherishing their military titles from earlier expeditions that had been of no assistance to Reds. Behind the counter in soiled white uniform a man moved sleepily with the efficiency of long specialization. For untold years he had patiently excluded from his life other occupations and other places of business. His establishment endured the war because the draft in this country never reached his age-class and because he required very little help to supplement his own unremitting labors. Brooding over the new day without resentment he poured hot water into the coffee urn turned over eggs which in this lucky country were always available for our grills and deposited extrusions of unlovely dough in the doughnut machine that filled the streaked window of his storefront. The rancid smell began to reach the broad sidewalk still clear and clean in the garment of beauty worn by West 23rd Street still half enshadowed by the keen morning sunshine. Me in youth new to the city and trusting myself not doomed to die in it the air already astir but not yet roaring would fill with vigorous zeal to handle the machines upstairs after greeting colleagues among whom I had been gradually accepted as if we all were friends. And toward the end of my stint there when Ruth was with us my matutinal zest was intensified to joy at the immediate prospect of her exotic beauty. In a few minutes we would perhaps speak to each other. I would respond as articulately as I could to her serene cheerfulness. The hot greasy doughnuts floated down their molten canal in a regulated file but instead of dispersing smartly like people stepping off the bottom of an excalator they dropped abruptly into a paper-lined wire basket.

Karl would usually come in for his day's third cup of coffee half an hour before eight the only morning customer who ever read the Times. He never knew that I followed his movements even before Ruth was in the picture wishfully regarding him on that slight evidence as the educated man of the shop. I remember him as a tall middleaged man with large pale protruding blue eyes always opened very wide and a sagging stomach. He usually wore a brown business suit and a maroon tie over his gray working shirt. At the counter his brown fedora was tilted back to expose a high hairless forehead which when he stood uncovered at his machine was seen to round off and flatten vastly where it underlay thin hair still blond streaked back to hang limp behind ears as white as his face. With habitual courtesy he smiled at the lunchroom proprietor whose only recognition was a gloomy nod and took from a broad horizonal pocket of his durable fuscous overcoat the neatly folded newspaper to continue on an inner page what he had been reading in the subway on his way downtown. Since he was not a narrow-elbowed tabloid-reader he chose the stool at the inner end and when he came to the turning of a page he extended his paper far to the left as he meticulously tapped the back of the crease with his right hand so that the reverse fold could be made without a wrinkle, though he took his time and ordered nothing to eat. On the train home he must have had to make rush-hour folds long as window shutters stiffened doubly but bent at the middle. I saw him sniff the peculiarly informed smell of inked pulp that I was pleased to think blindmen identified the stack of Timeses dropped at their newsstands by. His coffee was heaped with sugar and lightened with cream to an extremely pale tan. One might have taken him for a Swede. When the cup was emptied with a reduplicated sip of the last drop he methodically turned the front page outward and respectfully smoothed the sheets he had read against those left fresh for the remaining leisure of his day.

Inside the abutting green entrance our little lame janitor would be waiting to take his first load of workers up the shaft to their pit. For the last moments of poised inactivity he stood crookedly at the front of the bare plastered green and gray lobby staring out through one of the square ports at the rapidly diminishing loveliness of the day as it yielded to the renewed struggle for victory in war by means of all the tangled agencies of personal gain and bustling goodwill represented by the traffic of the city's twenty-third numbered street eyeing pedestrians who at this time of morning except for one or two derelicts muttering and stumbling in the hostile light scarcely cursed or faltered at all while the other swung back and forth in its panel to admit each of his charges to the building he had been preparing for them the best part of his day already passing through its zenith. Somewhere down in the basement forbidden to everyone but himself the light at his little desk had been on for hours. Steam hissed in the radiators hospitably. The public decks were swept down inside and outside. It was a morose Irish face too young and miniature for the pain that seemed to have deprived its crippled existence of any sympathy for fellow men. He responded curtly to Karl's invariably polite greeting. The people of the machine shop had the place to themselves at that hour. Most of the other tenants were on short rations, some making hardly a show of business as the war deprived them of buyers sellers and workers. Anyway it was we who witnessed the beedle's daily mastery of the building as the diffident confidants of his prickly taciturnity. On few occasions did he choose civil conversation and then with our leaders only.

Most of Empire's habitual early-birds not all of whom were among the oldest or the best employees stood close to the elevator leaning against the nick-scathed wall smoking and talking dressed as members of the fraternity usually were when outside their shops in creditably maintained street clothes beyond the pretensions of unskilled laborers while they waited for the key man to arrive from Queens who alone could let them in to their machines through the blank steel panel that one of the two opening sides of the car would face when they got to the third floor. Their pointed shoes most of them were polished and the hats of the younger men were flexed and tilted but none offered to compete in sharp rakishness of manner with the foreman they expected. Deferentially watching those pale or jaundiced faces I'd stand without a word too inexperienced as the single Yankee

among them not to fancy that I could learn to measure from physiognomy
alone the distance each had come from original immigration. Not one of
them wasnt in my mind a near or distant representative of the European
civilization I craved to know and fight for. Or at least I thought I could
distinguish ambitious natives from perceptive refugees whose unrecounted
experience intrigued and horrified my imagination to the degree that I
never dared allude to their personal histories or circumstances, all the
more so because it seemed to me that they might take any curiosity as an
inquisition into their racial or political prejudices betraying my own. In
those days of necessary war which even as late as Joe Louis's glorious second bout with Max Schmelling who the kids said shtunk could easily have
been scotched in the hatching I still estimated all men's degree as friends
or enemies of the President. Even in a machine shop mostly owned by
Jews and devoting all its efforts one way or another to the benefit of
people for whom the war in Europe was just and justified I put the burden
of proof upon everyone I did not know to be Jewish. It was my unreasoned
judgment that when F D R had told us even before the clear and present
Japanese attack upon our principal outpost that we must prevent Germany
from defeating Britain in order to protect our shores he was thinking of
the nearer danger to internal security and was conscious of his social metaphor. And even after the battle had been joined on both sides of the world
I was of anxious opinion that it was not espionage but private feeling that
we had to fear in our war against the Third Reich. All citizens not excepting members of Congress who had voted down funds to dredge the harbor
at Guam and practically all appropriations for the gun-shy Army granting
it only all the time in the world as General Marshall put it were now
openly and righteously united in generalized enmity to treacherous slant-
eyed yellow men, and such unAmerican feelings were hardly considered
anything to hide or equivocate, yet at that stage of war against the Axis,
despite the fact that ships right off the coast were being torpedoed every
night in the targeting glow of city lights which took three more months
of politics to turn off because there was so much fear among businessmen
especially in Florida of ruining the tourist business, Yorkville's German
element of the Manhatten population seemed to me sinister enough to
inhibit discussion of Europe from a Semitic point of view even at that
shop. Maybe I was too suspicious of a dread "fifth column." It's hard to
remember that grip of fear at the time when Hitler had almost won and
was not yet losing, especially when it was my impression that many citizens of the upper East Side continued to sing sentimental German songs
and wear Alpine hats with feathers. To judge from what I heard at the
elevator door native Jews and refugees whatever their accents started the
days like all American working stiffs philosophizing on the weather.

   A pert little bitch manipulated the shop's male society with genteel
affectations and sexual characteristics molded and painted and faked as if
her sveltely binding clothes and calculatedly fluttering gestures were

charming disguises of a femininity never revealed to anyone but her husband. She hoisted herself absurdly high not five feet tall on spiked heels which she changed for somewhat blunter shoes only when she was perched on her stool at a drill press in her dainty smock. Outside the shop she wore a tiny hat decorated with plastic fruit and cloth flowers. It was stuck upon piled black coils that she touched frequently with pointed polished red fingertips and it suspended a prim veil of black netting which on the street or in the subway indicated her sense of ladyship. I seem to remember her name as Vera. It couldnt have been Sarah. A very special tiny thin type of denatured Jew whom I'd have taken at sight for neurasthenic Italian. It went hard for me to believe that this skinny little female popinjay was truly the darling of the shop and the favorite of the bosses but in a whole year I could never detect except perhaps by a certain amusement in Karl's eyes any inclination toward mockery or criticism in the band of men who so fatuously made her just as she wished their mascot their arbiter and their flirtatious queen. In the hallway she stood demurely apart from the men but rather closer to them than to the jolly plump black girl who always waited alone warming her backside against the radiator just inside the door until the first elevator load had taken off. And now none too early but well on time in strode Vera's humming debonair social peer our young but not too young slim and jaunty leader by the name of Joe for whom she reserved her first coy banter and to whom she first opened wide her long blackened eyelashes which seemed each separately controlled in diapasons of blackeyed admiration. He waved at large but with her he stopped to talk. No one disputed his privilege or hers.

The janitor let them have their minute together and then consulting his dollar watch attached by a braided cord to the bib of his overalls he limped harshly over to his empty cage lighted more brightly than the lobby it rested at, no one having dared to enter it before the summons. His own early edition of the *News* was tucked behind the operating lever. "All right everybody!" he gruffled out in a brogue that sweetened the meaning of his tone whether surly or humorous. "Time to go to work. I ain't got all day." As the small crowd led by Vera and Joe converged onto the homely platform spacious enough for batches of steel or other freight taken to and from all the manufactories of the building Karl stepped back nodding and smiling to each in turn until the load-limit was reached and managed to be left behind with myself and the plump black girl who was now joined by a second breathless in haste and fearful of reprimand audibly relieved to find she was on time but too shy ever to acknowledge the speech of white people this far downtown until after some weeks she had begun to grin a little when he turned back to appeal to her as he spoke to her friend the first. "Looks as though you already early last night went to bed Bunny." he said with his broadest smile addressing the two girls with genial courtliness bowing in fact and gazing down into the first's broad merry face with one hand on his hip. I recall his remark and her reply as nearly invariable. "If you hate your work as much as I do you gotta go to bed early once in a while so next day you can drag through to quittin time!" And she'd shriek with laughter because everyone knew that she loved every minute of her job and would gladly have worked overtime for nothing if it hadnt been for our King Alfred's protection of the working class against Congress and all the other witenagemots state and local subverted by his enemies and ours. The stragglers of the second wave would ride up with us. Whereas the men of the earlier group remained silent during their passage staring straight before them through the open grill and involuntarily counting the floors while they listened to the ostentatious raillery of Joe and Vera the second batch buzzed with democratic informality on the way up. Karl always took off his hat as he stepped inside the battered lifting box with his ladies.

But it was I who had the reputation for being a gentleman. From the accent I still spoke even foreigners could not forget that I was from New England and as it was known that I hailed from Cambridge the story got abroad that I'd gone to Harvard maybe just a joke in origin as I took it but apparently plausible to some of the credulous New Yorkers who alluded to it in my presence. The same canard was launched against me later in the Navy where the charge was much more serious especially among those southerners who despised Harvard as a name to curse by without having ever heard of its seat Cambridge so called by the Great and General Court (when the university was planted in the settlement formerly known as New Town) in honor of the ancient English establishment that had formed the literary and theological minds of leading immigrants including John Harvard whose books and other legacy started it off, and without suspicion that their ostensibly rednecked politicians soft-pedaled the years they'd spent there or would have liked to qualify for, and where I knew enough not to take it for a pleasantry and not to reply with droll sarcasm that in another melieu would have been unmistakeable: "Sure I've been to Harvard!" I was prepared to explain what I meant by that ingenuous remark at Empire but the conversation never went any further. So at first I deceived myself that city people were urbane enough to guess the gist of my jest without requiring to hear the particular incident that happened to lend it substance and went off chuckling at my arcane wit.

I did go to Harvard once. By invitation. Not counting of course the many times I went through it unseen on the way to Boston because streetcars and busses met subway trains underground right in the middle of it or on foot short-cutting across the Yard which had no intelligible place in my world because its bricks and ironwork seemed mere natural obstacles like a financial district or a yacht club or any other institution you're brought up within sight of knowing it has nothing to do with your personal possibilities even though important enough to the academics' kids who were admixed with the Irish Catholic Italian Catholic and French Catholic majority in a few of the plantation schools like the ones I attended on the heterogeneous frontier kept at a certain distance by the nuclear repellent of Harvard's taxfree wealth although every neighborhood I ever basically lived in was ruled by the repelled masses absolutely. Cambridge toughened my skin for New York ever so slightly and New York less slightly for the Navy but each term in the progression shocked me more than the previous one. It was all a prelude to earning the living that I'm still earning: love's field, interminable prelude to art.

When we went to live in Cambridge I didnt know I was homesick for Gloucester. But for a whole year Gloucester was all that Billy talked about. Too old and too young for such a disrupting change of scene yet wiser than I! I was ashamed of my origins at first. One of the rich kids in school used to spend his summers on Cape Ann called Cabo de Santa Maria by the Spaniards and whenever I inadvertently mentioned Gloucester he would declaim the only witticism he could remember on any subject "Manchester-by-the Sea! Gloucester-by-the-Smell!!" That's what the conductor on the Gloucester Branch was supposed to have called out with a ten-minute interval between. Pugh! Gorton-Pew. Salt fish drying in the sun soon to give way to frozen fish the product of electrical refrigeration. I secretly loved the despised waterfront smell. To me the kid's attack was personal but I tried to hide my growing allegiance to the disreputable town. If he'd heard Hesiod's advice to take to boats for a couple of months after the summer solstice because that time of year in Askra wasnt much good for anything else he would have retorted that Gloucester wasnt much good for anything else all year round. But the last-gasp International Fishermen's Races gave me heart. Gloucester Schooners were ships for all classes, Yankees and Latins of divers schooling even literary English imperialists. F D R loved them too.

I had a series of brief manias that eased the pain of transplantation. One of them as soon as it was over seemed odd even to myself. Collecting matchbook advertising covers! I'd never heard of such a thing when some kid mentioned pursuit of that rare sport. He himself probably went at it in a tempered more or less rational manner not going out of his way to augment his collection patiently and moderately month by month. But not I! Somehow the idea instantly fixed the motive and direction of all my power. The prospect of *immediately* acquiring a uniquely copious and variegated heap of tiny begrimed cardboard folders took unaccountable possession of my libido as if I had by the wildest stroke of good luck hit upon a quick way to both skill and respect by means of energy alone without benefit of talent family or money. As long as it lasted the cathexis was an irresistible pastime. We pitched in at once Billy and I without regard for appearances. It was in the fall I think when such voracious drives of a somewhat mental cast usually overtook me. For reading we had Big Little Books with hard covers and large type an ephemeral species about two inches thick and four inches square that cost a dime unless acquired second-hand for next to nothing by means of barter dealing with the further adventures of famous funnypaper characters like Mickey Mouse then still apparently harmless or Little Orphan Annie with Sandy the dog that looked like a ring-tailed hyena and a rich step-father that looked like our present President, or Renfrew of the Royal Canadian Mounted Police with the highest-style uniform ever invented including high boots flared britches campaign hat Sam Browne belt and best of all a lanyard to his pistol carried in a weatherproof holster or Tarzan of the Apes and his Jane forasmuch as the lines and stanzas of cartoon strips were rendered back into colorless prose literature by setting a single-panel line-illustration with a caption instead of a cloud-puff opposite each page of text thus organizing a story so that kids could follow it both the new way and the old way at once or simply by riffling through the pictures cinematically without the sound track an ultimately unsuccessful commercial attempt to make additional profit from an aesthetic compromise for semiliterate consumers but the books we now collected were for glancing at from cover to cover just long enough to distinguish one from another or to identify it with previous specimens despite variations of damage and skip the fine print especially after dark. At first I had to make Billy come along but he soon became genuinely enthusiastic on my behalf and dragged himself along the gutters opposite me as long as he had the strength to stand up. Poor little kid loyal as my son Matty. For nearly a week we sought those sodden mutilated advertisements as if our living depended on it. I never again saw the unidentified kid who started me off on this vehement whim and there were no other collections that I knew of for competition so I didnt have any idea what to do with our treasure after it was amassed except to sort and count its items. Nor was it anything to brag about. I naturally concealed such eccentricities from the oppressive Irish majority who despite my claim to a share of Celtic blood were all too ready to mock and rob me for my religion and my putative Englishness what with a surname like that—"Oh I say old chap! Percy-chap! Hey sissy-prissy I say a spot of tea eh-what goggle-eyes?"—as well as from the rich kids who spent their time doing wholesome things like learning to play music or intelligent things like playing chess or scientific things like cataloging leaves and flowers or cultured things like looking at the great picturebooks of the world or creative things like building crystal radio receivers. Collecting matchbook covers is just the thing to put down for a hobby on your Harvard application form! It wasnt contagious after I caught it. No one who knew about it followed our example. I am most sorry for Billy's sake who followed me trusting in future fame for our enterprise. Yet I bet now and I was then convinced that no one else could have matched the swift economy of our pickings. There was one kid I knew who had every Big Little Book ever carried in a five-and-ten-cent store but my mess of matchbooks cost me no more than a box full of wartime softcovered Armed forces Editions of literature NOT TO BE SOLD. We didnt spend a cent trudging both sides of all the streets we could

cover from Observatory Hill to Sears Roebuck between Walden and
Linnean. It never occurred to me to choose better hunting grounds further
from home. The moiety of each expedition took place in the dark because I
couldnt bear to call a halt once we got into the swing of it. And in the
rain! Almost alone on the streets under trees of late autumn peering
beneath parked cars as we skirted them and experimenting with search
techniques while we galloped along in a drizzle sometimes with one foot
on the curb and the other harrowing wet leaves for hidden nuggets which
we plucked hastily for fear of being stopped by property owners, always
rushing to the next block inspired with hope like that of gold-prospectors
and propelled by the determination to beat unknown world-historical
rivals we pushed on tireless as wolves until we tested the limits of our
endurance first Billy's then mine somewhat later and found ourselves foolishly measuring progress more in mere distance than in gain of true ends
until at last I had to acknowledge my sympathy with the little kid's
exhaustion. But by the time I admitted that neither of us had the strength
to put one foot before the other we were as far from home as ever so of
course we had no alternative but to plant those same feet a thousand times
again yet still without retracing a single pace we gleaned our way home
where we checked in about midnight wet almost to our underwear and the
night's catch about to fall through the bottom of soaked paper bags. Our
only real rivalry was with street cleaners who came by day pushing stiff
high-bristled brooms wheeling by handled shafts their barreled chariots,
but even during the Depression when Harry Hopkins was whipping up all
the Federal jobs he could think of in a hurry Cambridge seemed to have
none too many such W P A employees considering all the horseshit from
junkmen and milk wagons. We got more Juicy-Fruit Gum matchbook
covers and International Correspondence Schools than all the rest put
together but still there was a plethora of treatments for bald heads. Also a
great many put out by finance companies. Most of the ads were related to
failure in the pursuit of happiness. My favorite though far from the rarest
was Charles Atlas with a pair of his pictures before and after that "ninety-
seven-pound weakling" had become the world's most beautiful specimen
wider in the shoulders and slimmer at the ass than Killer Kane but his
campaign was so broad and sustained that I its then premature target may
now be conflating some of his advertising media such as concave subway
and streetcar placards. He certainly saturated all the magazines I read for
instance Air Trails the bastards I sent a very hard-won fifteen cents for a
pair of silver wings long before the end of the school year so that I could
wear them on my scout uniform at least one Wednesday before eighth
grade graduation along with my prize gold medal as the year's number one
boy of the troop and the regular badges I'd qualified for in order to
impress people with my achievements outside class but they didnt come
until too late and pretty tinny at that. A medal feels very good when it's
high enough on your chest so that it doesnt flap too much when you walk

but presses its weight when you breathe and feels perfectly secure as long as you don't run but wings and bars are worn by men ready for all kinds of action. No cloth insignia of rank can raise your distinction in such handsome relief or so trimly stiffen the cloth of a tunic. When I got my crow at Treasure Island with only a few weeks left to show my arm on liberty in the States I would have traded it for the most commonplace campaign ribbon. When I finally had a bar of my own I was on my way back to civilian clothes. Atlas may have been in newspaper ads too. Sophisticated successors to his corporation if it was really he and only he in whose name he became famous would be glad to know that I can't remember how I got all my phony information about him. "Murine For the Eyes" was definitely a transit-ad campaign but as far as I was concerned the description that went no further than the slogan was entirely insufficient and I never did find out what the product did for peepers though I could see from the gleaming picture that it was especially for women and the name always made me think of Ruth Perkins's best friend and therefore of Ruth herself who was infinitely too intelligent to have such dumb-looking windows to her soul. The most memorable thing about matchbook covers besides their uniformity of size and shape was that they bore a standard all but unambiguous imperative CLOSE COVER BEFORE STRIKING. I had cause to remember it in the breach. Several years earlier one bright spring day fooling around with a loaded matchbook at Half Moon Beach had ignored the injunction and not seeing the flame of a single match in the sunshine I suffered a nasty burn when the others all at once ignited. I felt like such a damned fool that I never permitted myself a sound or otherwise let on even while it was hurting like hell. The Portugees used to say the Italians wouldnt go out fishing if the wind was strong enough to blow out a match. I was at sea six months before I learned how to keep a match alight in the wind with two hands chaliced to the lips. The craving for tobacco didnt disappear overnight like the manias that had seized me while I was waiting for important things to come along with age. I was always waiting I guess for education travel and girls.

But my passion for drawing was something else. Anything I couldnt have or wished to see or hoped to make I drew pictures of, ever improving upon the world's artifacts in size complexity and power or in multiplicity of function from the world's most heavily armed bicycle to its longest triple-decked suspension bridge brought into existence line by line in the sequence of erection like that of a circus tent neither architectonic nor organic in its tensions of growth and rest. I already had the makings of technalogy's neo-renaissance man! The rich kids would sometimes pay a nickel for my renderings of warplanes with options of air-cooled or water-cooled engines either complicated well-braced biplanes or slick streamlined monoplanes which were then coming to the fore. I had happened upon the trick of representing wings in sideview simply by showing their cross-sectional profile at the tip within the contour of the seam at which they joined the fuselage and no one else could get the knack of it. I also had a pleasing style for propellers in motion as seen in side elevation. Pursuit planes they were called a euphemism imposed by the old-guard Republicans as a condition for their reluctant agreement to spend taxpayers' money for machines to chase away bombers that might cross our shorelines provided we didnt spend any more for bombers of our own to attack Hitler. It was not only for the sake of Jews that I wanted us to go to war but also for the sake of our army and navy. If I got hold of a very large sheet of paper or the back of a poster I could do a dogfight of planes at all angles combining the best features of World War the First which I had studied and World War the Second which I anticipated immeasurably enriching suggestions of the literature I read which was too much influenced by an unregenerate state of the military art in Spain where good people were losing to fascists. In the end however as far as airpower was concerned my main interest lay in the technical and aesthetic problem of an extremely fast highly maneuverable longrange armed-to-the-teeth fighting seaplane with a single sleekly faired float and retractable sponsons that could launch itself from grassy field or open water for all the purposes of undercover paramilitary adventure and meet all the other requirements for protecting the battleship by which five of them would be carried and catapulted. Above all I was a naval architect. For nearly a decade my talent for design was concentrated upon capital ships and I steadily advanced beyond the restrictions of the Washington Treaty as well as the engineering compromises discussed in Jane's Fighting Ships and the Naval Institute Proceedings so beautiful with photographs of what other designers had settled for.

But only in my celebration of schooners did I merge aesthetics and scholarship. There was almost nothing I could improve upon technically. My intention was to come as close to the real as I could. I drew them over and over again practicing the difficult curves of their bodies but never with any consummate joy akin to possession. My drawing wasnt live enough for Gloucester fishing schooners. It is true that I often fitted them for Q-boat secret service with powerful twin screws concealed guns searchlights and advanced radio equipment or for utterly independent cruises of exploration with unprecedented structural reinforcement and British Guiana greenheart sheathing against furious whales and grinding ice and that my unwritten stories to explain the reiterated picture monotonous with unbelievable excellence overwhelming victory and unchallenged heroism usually for the benefit of an incredibly beautiful female passenger and in liaison with a U S Navy platonically perfect in tolerance and wisdom would put Billy to sleep before I could think of a plot but at bottom I only wanted to possess a ship that could be historical and therefore possible. I had trod the deck and played in the lower rigging of more than one schooner at Gloucester piers before I was old enough to appreciate the privilege including the Gertrude L Thebaud the last of them all which had sailed to visit F D R and his Canadian guest Ramsay MacDonald in Washington and then by the St Lawrence past Quebec and Montreal into the lakes to help celebrate the Century of Progress at the Chicago World's Fair. I had seen schooners under sail even inside the breakwater. At the time pictures of those draught swans were published in all American provinces showing the last world series of races on full white wings. It was an interregnum when schooners seemed neither yachts nor commercial vessels. For their sake I began to love while I was still ashamed of it the Gloucester they hailed from. In my fear of Irish Catholics and in my repugnance to the Cambridge society repugnant also to them I pledged allegiance to my birthplace for its community of glory. My private stories and drawings were merely to justify its creatures in an age of mechanical force. But I found it wasnt necessary for me to content myself with pencil and paper in furthering the satisfaction of my desire to own and manage under present conditions such a beautifully complex machine of the past even if I couldnt board her for in the craft of sculpture I had open to me the touch and heft of a real artifact with real properties visible in the full spectrum of perspectives clean out of its element or deeply immersed at rest or in motion. "Of all fabricks a ship is the most excellent" said Admiral John Smith and I wanted to feel Cape Tragabigzanda fabrick. I wasnt humbled by my poor resources and lack of skill for the highly probative art of ship-building. To this day I've never been out sailing not even in a freshwater dinghy but I've always been as free with nautical advice as Hesiod the in-spired poet and I've always loved schooners more than other rigs as I've loved Gloucester more than Massachusetts. As a provincial pedant on the subject I allowed no latitude for Stevenson's solecism in calling what must have been a Limey brigantine the *Hispaniola* of Treasure Island fame a real schooner. I might better have been glad of the tribute paid my favorite species by making its name generic in some quarters for practically all use-ful two-masted sailing vessels of a certain size.

Thus one day I took up the solid hull of my sloop. Unfortunately I could dispense with neither the steel blade of a keel it had come from the store weighted with nor the ridiculous balanced rudder that hung behind like an illustrator's afterthought. I accepted the practical need for sharp compromise with verisimilitude below the waterline. Nor could I do any-thing to refine the flat lines of the glibly shaped hardwood splinter planed on top with no pretense to sheer or camber. Any attempt to gouge a grace-ful curve out of the unworkably brittle grain would have split the block like knotty kindling or at least further reduced the drowning freeboard with which it barely supported the monstrous undercarriage afloat. And the functionally longhandled tiller could not be replaced by a wheel. But in any case the single mass-produced mast and its trifling sails could look pretty only to a mother who gave dearly bought presents with such heart-breakingly misguided generosity that nothing could be said against it. Ever since Christmas in the gloaming between wakefulness and sleep the imagination of my eyes had brooded over the white shape tall as a weathercock perched close to my bed on the cradle of my devising but now in sudden determination to ignore sentiment I rashly ripped out the mast and swept the deck clear of all fakery in order to re-rig the vessel from scratch as a proper schooner. All day Saturday I labored to graft fair masts booms gaffs and whittled bowsprit upon the misshapen platform. Twice I had to run with dimes all the way down to Woolworth's in Harvard Square to get dowels brads glue screw eyes or pack thread and Billy went once more when I persuaded him to fetch a ten-cent can of gray paint and a fifteen-cent brush. With bits of scrap wood I fashioned token superstructures and a deck-mounted tender something between a dory and a seine boat. I cut the sails and sewed them on the family Singer after an intensive lesson patient in instruction but wildly hasty in learning from my mother. The workmanship of cut and stitch was nothing to be proud of but I trusted it to be overlooked in the larger aspect of the rigging as a whole which was nothing less than a taut web of shrouds stays braces and manropes integrated in a single system of triangular countertensions the entire hybrid assembly of second-rate parts more flexible than any tent or bridge. The string used for halyards and sheets would slacken more than Manila when it got wet but I took pains to provide for the adjustment of all running lines and I even attempted to keep the loose ends neatly coiled around their cleats grotesquely out of scale. Many oh many the halfway measures and shortcuts I ended up with because my fingers were too clumsy and my patience too short as for instance in failing to distinguish mast from topmast ignoring fife-rails omitting ratlines from the rigging or skipping staysails altogether. I did not make the best of such tools as I had. The vessel was kept mounted by its keel in my little cast-iron vise clamped to the edge of a rickety table until the paint was dry. Sunday morning I took her to the bathtub for trials. Handsome is as handsome does. But I could test her under no greatly adverse conditions in a few gallons of transparent water churned up by hand inside smooth white enamel walls. No tank can ever try the essential quality. I've always wondered how the models driven through M I T test basins by traveling cranes could imitate in their plowing of laboratory waters the furrows made by a living ship in turbid brine enraged by Poseidon and Apollo's sister from below and above. There was some pleasure in watching her ride the waves with battened hatches and furled canvas but despite the fact that the deck was almost awash with the burden of disproportionate aerial equipment added to the weight of her enormous keel I couldnt persuade myself that I saw plausible displacement relative to the implausible potable water. She bobbed in place without dignity at the slightest agitation. If only by virtue of its identity as a working schooner my toy was more to be respected than the deadly serious hollow sloops set on course in the Esplanade boat pond by grown men with varnished boathooks. Certainly there was nothing like it available for any price at the F A O

Schwartz emporium for rich kids. But in a bathtub there's no gravity. My boat was really no plaything nor yet an archetype either. The builders of a Gloucester schooner often made a model to celebrate success after the fact unlike architects whose models come before buildings or Donald McKay whose wooden patterns served as the designs to start his clippers with but mine as a Ding an sich was neither fiction nor plan nor simulation. She was meant to be fast and able in her own right. But obviously she wasnt hollow obviously her shipyard was the bedroom of a kid with no access to a hobby shop and no Yankee fisherman seagoing Catholic or Episcopalian yachtsman for a mentor. Yet I hadnt intended her to sail the seas of a bathtub. If children knew how ignorant they are they'd never hope. One of the Fragments says "If you do not hope you will not find that which is not hoped for since it is difficult to discover and impossible to attain." It was in a manner suitable to her station of life that lying in bed I admired her as she swung at anchor in the vise romantically visible by the nightlight of the backyard sky. It was sufficient not to know too much. The next day at school separated from her presence my hopes drifted further beyond my personal possibilities. The classroom floor was a sea in which standing at the wheel I sailed her fast across the wild wind or beating and tacking through long narrow straits between the rows of desks. After school I dug dirt in a corner of our triple-decker's yard and rooted the thing herself in ocean swells of patted earth, the monstrous centerboard that was best unseen buried aslant beneath molded waters that washed the starboard gunwale with a singing swishing surge of living foam, and then whistled for a wind to give cause for her swift heeling. But that day my real weather held fair much too blandly fair and the next and the next after that.

Finally the rain came blowing steadily across the streets against easterly and southerly windows. I was the first one of the neighborhood home from school and before anyone could stop me I'd snatched her from my room as she stood with raised sails and tightened sheets. Out in the storm we pitched into the wind. Gray warm rain was driven to earth by green mist pressed down to the treetops. Everything outdoors deferred to the sideways descent of the heavens. Familiar edifices of humanity contracted into rain-tight islands shrinking from my path even as distances between known fences shortened and the span of my effortless strides lengthened. Some of the wind that tensed her sails held above my head was made by our speed. She wrenched my wrist like an osprey in the grasp of Triton and like Triton from the waves beneath her I adored the quivering creature's forceful opposition as she struggled to escape from my grip to follow the grain of the weather. I went up Huron across Concord Avenue and then over the hill at the bend straight down the rich part of Sparks all the way past Brattle and Foster to the slummy block and across Mt Auburn to the river at the tract that had still been known as the Ox Marsh sixty years before the Revolution when Andrew Robinson who may have been a

descendant of the Pilgrim pastor who never got to Plymouth and whose
granddaughter married a president of Harvard sent down the ways from
his wharf now known as Pirate's Lane in East Gloucester the first true
schooner in world history which schooned even before she was rigged, like
the flat stones we always looked for that skipped and skimmed there on
the Charles if you threw them right but always sank in the end. It is hull
and rig together that make the true schooner not the one or the other each
with its own traditional prototypes. Houses trees and vehicles drawn apart
from each other made way for us neither stumbling nor colliding. Every
obstacle by keeping to itself secured our weathering passage. We penetrated and embraced natural elements of the lowest atmosphere the
beneficent storm assured us of lovely secrecy and by the time we reached
waterside the boat's steady vibrant wings hauled closer to our course than
to the wind had proved equal to all opposing forces.

At the edge of the river she trembled and fluttered while I fiddled
with the sheets and attached the endless hank of string I'd brought as a
cable. Standing still we heard the softly muted hustle of traffic on Memorial Drive laid along the embankment where half a century earlier coal
sheds and warehouses had received river shipping after the marsh was
filled and before the tide was excluded by massive engineering downstream at Lechemere when the railroad took over all freight to Cambridge-
port. On that leafy boulevard beyond the insipid little triangle of park
where older kids I was scared of played baseball stood an array of most
palatial apartment houses for retired generals active philosophers and the
like followed by the Romanesque but Anglican monastery and the Boston
Elevated Railway yards filled with parked streetcars and third-rail rapid
transit trains which close-up could be seen through the high iron fence
except where the long brick and stucco Boylston Street wall concealed the
whole length of a special passenger platform known as Stadium Station
that I never had the good fortune to ride to beyond the regular end of the
line at Harvard Square on a football afternoon when it was briefly available
to the public having been built into the country's first subway system
when Harvard was still respected for national football championship as a
convenience for the middle class masses on four or five Saturdays of the
year to get to Larz Anderson Bridge of the same style and vintage from
which I now wished to keep a good distance upstream. At first in Cambridge I always got that name confused with Lief Ericsson the amphibious
galley-master who was supposed to have come ashore upstream at the bend
where Billy contracted impetigo learning to swim in the beery fluid at
Gary's Landing a scabrous brown beach hidden in the slimy cracked mud
flats of hell's half-acre that quivered and palpitated underfoot on the
clayey paths among scatalogical cattails and tall fetid marsh grasses
drained of their clean primeval salt water and growing I thought like hair
from corpses in the city cemetery on the stunted bluff above although
because it wasnt canonized in our schoolbooks I never really believed that

claim similarly undisprovable anywhere along the coast of Norumbega. Many a time on clear lonely days I'd heard the cars whining and whizzing along this bending boulevard in the unending doppler sing-song with which self-powered wheels measure out the familiar dreary distances of America but now the continuous parade of engines and gears on European-smooth black asphalt was softened and slowed by the blanket of rain. Elsewhere hereabouts thanks to the Depression the greensward of the Charles was still largely preserved from the riparian rights of pavement for which it was destined after the prosperous manner of the Hudson the Schuylkill and a hundred other metropolitan waterways that belonged to the Indians. On both banks leisured lines of sycamore still groved the roads yet nothing less than water from the heavens could have dissolved and muted into ceaseless plashes of smooth black pneumatic rubber the concentrated columns of autonomously rotated explosions that hauled countless tons of molded steel up and over the steep bridge from a dead stop at the lights on either side where we loved to assert our personal rights by pressing the pedestrian buttons at arbitrary moments to make the traffic stop and let us cross a couple of its infernal streams. Everything else was hushed to silence by the wet gray space of an autumnly tranquil environment through which softly flowed the pruriginous river that separated liberal Harvard from its trade school and football stadium. Behind my back old Mount Auburn streetcars now and then trundled quietly across the faces of a Chinese steam laundry tenement houses of uneven class and the stockaded outdoor skating club on the other side of the parkway seeming not to be driven by steel wheels so hushed they were by the windblown rain and by my preoccupation.

Not a soul in sight for the furtive maiden voyage. In my sopping knickers I knelt upon the narrow oozing margin of coarse mottled sand smoothly grayed by silted recrement from mills and cesses to the westward a filthy unnatural strand where the dead river now seething under the pelting assault of Zeus slapped at a steep grassy embankment long since raised from mud flats by the enlightened Metropolitan District. Ten feet downstream from where I squatted on that malodorous strip never broadened by flood or tide a bloated rat rolled back and forth in the discolored foam that perpetually lapped at the foundation of Cambridge.

At my intimate level invisible from the street the agitated cutlets of slapping water could at last be made to seem waves of brine. I untangled my string and made slack for the launching simply a short toss not at all mannered to get her into deep water with a graceless bellyflop resembling anything but a schoon with no more ceremony than an embarrassed mutter despite my premeditated intent to sing out loud and clear I christen thee *Gloucesterman*.

I drew back on the bow line to see how she with the masculine name would look heeled over heading in my direction. I was rewarded with joy. Leaning out to catch her before she grounded I had to support myself with one sleeve wrist-deep in the sticky scum of barely translucent metallic

fluid warmed by continuous decay of organic detritus. With the other
hand I managed to loosen the sheets just enough for her to tack or run as
she wished when she was on her own. She was too low in the water and too
much lower in the head than stern to display anything like "the true
comeliness of form which only her proper sea-trim gives to a ship"
according to St Joseph speaking for all sea captains. The former fault I
tried to attribute to the thinness of unsalt water but the latter I knew to
be the penalty for imprsing my will upon the hull of a racing sloop.
Nevertheless I was elated to see that even with sopping sails the storm
could not for long keep my hybrid flattened thanks to that blessedly
weighted toy keel broad as a headsman's axe. I was not excessively disappointed to find after several exasperating experiments that it didnt much
matter how I set the sails and rudder or which way I pointed the bow but
I had to admit she wasnt very weatherly. Under free rein she always heeled
over and turned diagonally downstream. I gave up trying to make head or
tail of sailoring and at last yielding to the only possibility paid out my
line as fast as she could take it in her teeth but as it lengthened, her top
hamper beaten as far down as the ears of a German Shepherd under a
tongue lashing, its port drag kept whipping her about and running her
aground on the near shore before I could stop her. I'd have to slosh along
with the stormy current to fetch her by hand and shove her off again further downstream while I fouled my cotton string with repeated slackening
and fumbled coiling. The last time she veered I was more than half way to
the bridge. In the effort to get her headed upstream as she drove toward
the bank I tried to jerk her around against the wind. But the keel was too
long and deep to be hauled about so fast and my frail painter broke off at
the bow. Unleashed at last she turned once and for all like an escaping dog
and without the slightest sign of gratitude or regret sped the way she had
in mind down the broadening river toward the sea she was too ignorant to
fear. This time as she fell away the gusting wind caught her broadside
with such force that she hove down on her beam ends like the schooner
Teazer for example that in 1911 lived to tell the tale with a dory hoisted in
her crosstrees when she righted and a mustard pot stuck to the cabin's
overhead under command of a Gloucester Russian of which I then knew
nothing because it was in the past and anyway my brain was paralyzed
with dread that she'd go to her end wheeling like a shapeless chip until
she was ground down to waterlogged driftwood cheated of nobler shipwreck on rock or shoal. Just a few years ago I read that *Teazer* died in the
ice hunting seals for Gorton-Pew. Ruth loves seals and I didnt give her a
chance to get a good look at them today. We went all that way and didnt
go to the main aquarium at all. But by that time the *Teaser*'s rig had been
cut down and she was fully converted to diesel with her bowsprit sawed off
like one of Flaubert's elephants mutilated at Carthage. A truncated unicorn must be more horrible than Howard Blackburn's finger stumps or the
gums of a used-up book of matches especially when there's no figurehead

to cap the disfigurement. But *Gloucesterman* now met the supreme test of a vessel as Captain McClain the ace designer from Sandy Bay put it whose *Helen G Wells* had done the same without so much as springing a leak though of infamous clipper bow, for after rolling a slow half circle beneath the river's angry waves her dripping sails heavily rose again on the opposite angle, restoring the keel to its proper element and infusing my heart with pride defiant of the loss to come. Pacing along the bank in concentrated infatuation as I mechanically rolled up my string I watched the dauntless craft cut through surging hills of ocean pinned half down by the full spread of her resisting wings. The immense force of the storm swept half her deck with tons of broken white water but lashed to the helm I kept her steady and refused to let the crew strike canvas or take a single reef. In exultation I steered against the violence of a universe that would destroy my groaning vessel. *Non* JESUS CUM MARIA SIT NOBIS IN VIA is what negating Columbus I'd have writ every day in the ship's log to warm up my pen.

In my twilight suddenly loomed the forgotten bridge. Giants and their structures! The whole massive full-scale world. With hands grungy from the uncleansing suds of the Charles now clenched in my soaking pockets dripping and squishing from head to foot and deprived of horizon I was snatched back to the reality of disaster. This bridge bounded the world I could navigate in. From its promenade we had watched on the darkest of nights Harvard's great display of Elizabethan fireworks a gorgeous magic arborway of rockets and roman candles as far as the eye could see along both banks of the Puritan river named for the highhanded prince as king beheaded leaving me to this day unimpressed by any other such display of generosity. Harvard was named before Gloucester but its tercentenary came later and ever since arriving in Cambridge despite the interesting side-stairs and battlements of the bridge for persons on foot I'd been talking against that dreary nouveau-European brick-trimmed ferroconcrete monument to the university's economic importance because it used no keystones to make it hang together under pressure like the old bridges of Cape Ann granite built over a public and a private railroad where ravines had been cut through living ridges of rock for I was of vehement opinion that only an ancient and cunning fit of stone without mortar save to keep the weather out could attest to structural sincerity in masonry arches especially stately imitations of the European ones spanning placid tideless courses of extreme cultivation though I much approved modern steel arches frankly triangulated and riveted for strength and distance such as has lately been thrown across the Annisquam regrettable only for being named after a Republican and joining my native island with the mainland to bring it a continuous flow of motorized horsepower serving tourists and frozen-fish distributors whereas in truth the poor Edwardian bridge across the Charles was no phonier than my eclectic schooner bouyant without

hollows and counterweighted by an oversized factory-made parody of a
foolproof day-sailer's plowshare. In any event the Larz Anderson Bridge
was now rapidly enlarging itself as a towering dark chateau across my path
and occupying the whole sky at the top plain of my beanstalk about to
suck into one of its thrice-evil maws of Gargantuan engineering the sole
pride and treasure of my poverty. *Gloucesterman* was going from me was
almost gone and I had no hope of rescuing her. I visualized even beyond
the distant tidal locks that kept the river so dull and level a battered hunk
of flotsam bumping against rotten pilings of a slovenly fish-wharf where
the insensate seas of winter pounded the artificial black shores of Boston
Harbor smeared with grease and hostile to all frail creatures inexorably
poisoning the puppy-eyed seals that were sometimes known to wander in
and get away alive, stripped of stumps rudder and keel, ground down to a
colorless lump by the laving brine at its heartless task. The makeshift
work of beauty that had stoutly sustained the attacks of weather was now
to be flung with smashing force upon steel-ribbed concrete to begin the
shredding of her flesh and the crushing of her bones. Albeit born of slash-
ing machinery without the faculty of organic reproduction my little
schooner was more innocent of brute force than my cat Semiramis is.
—Yet dear god how confidently she steered clear of the abutments I
dreaded and disappeared through the middle of the furthest arch!

Black despair gave way again to the hope for luck. With pounding
chest I pounded up the outer stairs that flanked the great barrier three
steps at a time and reckless of the danger dodged diagonally at full speed
across the roadway trusting to my sure feet among flocks of bumpers fend-
ers and hoods piloted by frowning windshields rightly indignant at my
darting apparition as they wiped away the rain drops clicking each with
its own metronomic rate of impatience at the pace of its own forward
motion which to my good fortune was at the moment no more than a halting creep between the two sets of signal lights that saved my life on the
passage to the southwest riverbank which had always been kept out of the
oblique perspective from my northeast stamping ground by three textured
stucco tunnels archivolted with brick.

From the further parapet of the bridge overlooking the grassy slope to
which the roadway descended on the right bank in front of what I then
thought was the Law school but was really the Business colony with an ivy
frontage made to seem intended for the advancement of learning and a
gold-tipped central spire that made John Harvard twirl in his grave I
caught sight of my schooner just as her bowsprit as I could hardly make
out at my distance was shattered by the only stone anywhere along that
strand deep enough in the water to receive its thrust before the keel struck
bottom. I paused to miss not a wink of the event so quickly finished that I
might easily have lost it entirely by taking even autonomic care for my
next step. A career finished on its maiden voyage! Glory in the blink of an

eye! Whipped by the remorseless wind and rain she instantly flopped over broadside onto the shore below the edge of turf her sails plastered flat on sludgy sand by lapping russet saprophytic waters.

A few seconds later I had dashed down to retrieve the wrecked schooner. I could ask nothing better of chance. Without touching the topside wreckage I lifted her aloft by the underpinned blade. In the rain now easing I admired the shambles that proved *Gloucesterman's* integral survival. The broken bowsprit hung from the jib and the sails fell under their own weight from parted halyards to cover the deck in folds drawing their gaffs halfway down the masts after them and I shook the ship to make them settle further as if dropped by exhausted mariners without the time to douse them properly. The hull was smeared and scratched the hatches and skylights displaced or missing, but except for a loosely dangling forestay the standing rigging still held the two study masts like self-buttressed tetrahedral antennas sturdily anchored to their station.

She had sustained the kind of violence you anticipate and repair not the fatal kind suffered by personal victims of accident. That wreck was managed by me but it was no more personal than accidental. In essence I had planned all but the contingent details. Persons are accidentally hurt by force just when the junction of causes makes that happening the most unmanageable of an event's possibilities. Accidents seem fast to the victim by whom almost until it has occurred the one fully determined possibility has been considered little probable. Thus there is no chance to savor the true accident. Even theoretical preparation for it as one possibilty cannot prevent the shock of a true accident. Such as the personal happenchance of bullets or shards even in war. Violence that no one is ever ready for. It does no good to count on being the aggressor. Look at Kane. I once dreamt he said to me in his death basket "I didnt think it was possible for me to die but it was!" He was being covered with a sheet on Holy Thursday like the other mirrors in Carlo's house at the Fort and the old Sicilian grandfather wouldnt let me comb my hair in respect. But that furious grounding of my boat on a lee shore though fast enough and shocking to the crew was for me planned and unnecessary. An episode in earning my living.

Usually the things that happen in earning a living are long protracted and have no climax. I earned my living in an L S T by taking care of radios and radar the precursors of television and for five dollars a month extra from the ship's welfare fund by mixing and dispensing Coca-Cola a job I was offered doubtless because when off watch my only chronic duties were those of preventive maintenance which like all defensive foresight even when prescribed by the manuals was considered by good healthy men of arms as well as by American doctors performers and all other pragmatical operators to be no better than schoolmarmishness with nothing to show for itself because it was presumed to be equivalent to the kind of leisure I could have made it into like the positivistic gunner's mates' who were negligently responsible for the gyro compass system an analogical ancestor of the unprehensile digital logarithmoids now leading artifactual evolution seeing that we had no Fire Controlman the rating I'd liked to have pursued at least on a more complex ship where everything depended upon combinations of relative information, despite my rage at the Navy's recognition of that ubiquitous saccharine stimulant next only after Walt Disney's on the civilian toxicity list in that last decade before entertainment became fully electronic, which in retrospect has grown nearly as intense as my rage at official recognition especially during the Republican administration of God Bless America as a patriotic hymn. If that livelihood had ended as it didnt in disaster for the hollow 1066 my particular personal extinction would have been assured. I myself was the only one who took seriously a certain duty that only I was supposed to perform in case the ship was to be abandoned. I doubt that any superior except Mr Tree the solemn Communications Officer a law school liberal formerly president of the world's largest student body which happened to have included Ruth, he who assured me that the Navy meant what it said, knew or cared whether or not I observed the regulation that practically obligated me to go down with the ship as its electronic druid. It is now hard to believe that I actually worried about court martial and execution or prison if I survived. Did I really fear that they'd ever even think to ask about such a small matter in such a small ship manned and equipped like hundreds of others that might have been blasted by the aimed weapons of Japanese patriots when the war was about to be ended by sheer economic superiority before Truman's resort to the sheer force of concentrated entropy or by floating mines their uncontrolled agents anywhere at sea. Who cared about my spare transmission tubes or confidential wiring diagrams? What difference would they have made even to an enemy trying to salvage this particular one of our numberless ships? What other Radio Technician wearing the same Zeus-emblemed crow as an ordinary radio operator would have scrupled to flout this special injunction when panic-stricken to save himself from a ship suddenly doomed to join the inaccessible bones of Moby Dick or at any rate from the wreckage of a ship unlikely to be searched by Japanese copycats or researched by their mooncussing engineers working on countermeasures? It is true that in the actual event I'd probably have been as self-preservative as the next man in following other rats over the side in unhesitating disregard of the absurd act stipulated for my billet but I believed that if so I would afterwards have treated myself as a cowardly deserter not to say an outright traitor. No professional Navy officer who took the trouble to read the procedural twaddle his ghost writers were apt to cook up at the suggestion of counterintelligence specialists would privately enforce unequivocal instructions for an expensively trained young sailor to enter the valley of death for the futile sake of a manufacturer's patent license when he well might live to serve his country on a reenlistment. Yet if we got hit by a torpedo,

notwithstanding assurances that under most sea conditions if it was set for
our draft we were so shallow it would skip right over us surfing the swells,
a specious comfort to try to rest in because we might just happen to be
ploughing through the wrong crest or wallowing in the aerial path of its
schoon even were it not that more than a few of our sisters had been bitten
by tin fish waves or no waves instead of being split open by shells from the
myriad shore batteries that it later turned out would have been waiting for
our amphibious fleet on Kyushu in early November, or exploded in the
pyre of a Kamikaze pilot as we nosed a beach and had to give up hope for
the ship, after having deep-sixed my technical manuals and blown up the
radar transmitter behind the chart room with a built-in detonator I was
supposed to find my way in the lurching dark confusion far from my
battle station to one of the engine-room gang's most remote escape shafts
assuming it wasnt being used in the panic while everyone else was rushing
for life rafts or jumping ashore in suicidal terror, climb three decks down
the four-deck manhole ladder probably already as hot as the hinges of hell
to unlock a certain hatch holding to the rungs by one elbow and loosen all
its dogs to get at my unventilated storage compartment which was under
the best of conditions so stifled by musty heat that I mortally dreaded
even a routine visit to fetch supplies as if I tempted fate by a descent to
my tomb, and presumably by then in total darkness getting hold of the
damned magnetrons destroy them with a hammer or maybe it was some
intimate bit of dynamite I forget the method prescribed unless I was supposed to improvise like a secret agent swallowing his documents. There
were no instructions as to how to escape thereafter. It seemed taken for
granted that up to my neck in fire or water I would then make my resurrection if the way wasnt blocked by further explosions or by the very
proper efforts of damage-control shipmates to seal off watertight compartments by closing hatches against me never dreaming anyone would be
damnfool enough to be following some academic regulation in the evacuated depths of the ship and throw myself over the side in deep water trusting to my athletic ability seeing that I couldnt possibly have followed this
program dressed in a bulky life-jacket when all hands who were able to
move had long since preceded me in safer fashion including the skipper if
he wasnt dead without allowing myself to be impaled by wreckage floating below or sucked down by a swirling sinking mass behind me and
assuming that I managed to swim toward crowded life rafts already out of
sight beyond the ocean swells that in their hollows at the level of a
swimmer's eyes surround him like malevolent mountains even when
bathing without fear in a sharkless blue bay under the protection of a
peacetime mother ship anchored motionless nearby. To me it was a grimly
serious duty that was to be evaded only at somewhat lesser peril for I
feared being put to the test more than I feared getting killed first off. At
that time I still believed that technical invention like true surprise could
be kept from an enemy as if by virtue of secrecy alone science could be

turned into art which indeed it is possible to learn but not to filch. A
manager of inventions is sometimes called the father of them because he
may cause them to be conceived by abstracting from various wants and
conditions the functional specifications that guide and stimulate the
proximate innovators or simply by organizing statements about problems
for which he need not have any particular suggestions so long as he is able
to recognize good ideas when encountered perhaps in other contexts and
above all because he insists upon applying them to practical purpose in the
face of every possible objection by every possible person on his staff.
Churchill in successive generations for example claims to have fathered or
anyway fostered at least fertile ideas for both tanks and amphibious ships
for tanks along with lesser devices like inland waterway mines used
against dams and locks as well as boats and trench-digging machinery
obviated only by other inventions of warfare and I like to think of him
while still officially eclipsed as a merely private Member godfathering
radar itself twelve years before it could be baptised by the war. It is the art
of technology management that an enemy would do best to steal. If the
Japanese had then been able to develop that ability they'd have been
installing electronic direction and ranging detectors as widely as I afterwards found Americans were scattering them around with very little of the
occult discretion that we initiates had been indoctrinated in at considerable cost to the efficiency of our training to the effective dissemination of
improvements and to the resources of men material and time that might
have been devoted to maintenance or combat instead of counterespionage.
Nevertheless I must admit that in another Theater it was indeed a matter
of gratuitous convenience to the Germans, an enemy that usually spied not
in order to imitate but to find out the character of what they intended to
overtake or disconcert whose own radar development was mismanaged for
reasons having little to do with failure of invention, that they did lift from
a downed bomber much like a beached and disabled L S T one of those
encapsulated electromagnetic oscillators, like mine powering Anglo-Saxon
radar sets licensed for production on rocky upstream banks of the Charles
where Yankee milling of paper and cotton and watches began, in which
gyres of electrons were transformed into microwavelengths of radiant
energy concentrated narrowly enough to transmit themselves great distances and acutely enough to provide discriminating reflections for the
sensitive receivers with which they were coupled in their cabinets. Allied
advantage from radar superiority throughout the war especially in hunting
down U-boats Britain's most deadly danger did not however justify the
price I would have had to pay for the semi-secrecy that surrounded the
smallest magnetrons late in the game if the particular organizational
entity in which I earned my trip to Hawaii and the Western Pacific with
salary and all expenses paid had been brought to the one contingency I
dreaded more than the loss of Ruth, for by the time those dense little
tubes were being plugged as replacements into the small mass-produced

radar gear used by amphibious fleets in which not even a million-and-a-half-dollar ship was considered a capital investment and everything was produced or trained as cannon fodder with plenty of wastage to spare as if no less expendable than fuel oil the Axis experts must have known all there was to know about the resonance of the ethereal vibrations they emanated.

Like the infantry L S T s were equipped only with the least common denominators of machines and men allowing plenty of leeway for ordinary operating skill. Our search-radar intended mostly to detect hostile ships and planes especially in Nacht und Nebel was chiefly used by our conning officers to keep the ship on station within its own flotilla. The Ninety-day Wonders who took turns as O D on the open "con" above the wheelhouse misnamed because we had no wheel but only a small lever controlling electricity, in appearance more like a streetcar motorman's rheostat than a helm like 15thC pilots on their sterncastles passing orders for every movement down to their blind horse of a tillerman who could see nothing for himself though our helmsmen had a semicircle of portholes and a gyro compass to see by, put more trust in the radar as interpreted and reported by the likes of me than in their own eyes. The Navy had not yet decided that young gentlemen still innocent of television would be able to read a topside duplicating screen and take full advantage of the information gathered decoded and compendiously displayed by the machine in a self-correcting circular diagram without being distracted from their assimilation of everything plainly in sight. Even on the calmest most brilliant moonlight nights nay in daylight itself I and my reliefs were kept busy on the headphone singing out the distances and bearings of our nearest sisters. The steering quartermaster twelve feet from the radarman could have dispensed with most of the responding instruction that came from above. Yet though the humanly linked electromechanical system may have been abused by lazy or diffident ensigns without the guts to work on their seamanship in a Navy obliged by progress to disown a great many maritime principles of Renaissance Europe such as the mortal danger of shipboard profanity or the cardinal advantage of a captain's loud voice and the propriety of his sometimes lending a hand "to make seamen more prompt in their attention" no more mercy or respite was granted the tireless antenna steadily circling the skies for weeks at a time without pause for my preventive maintenance than the faithful prime movers in the engine room rotating both our screws day and night for thousands of miles without intermission not to mention the smaller dynamo that had even longer tours of duty because its magnetically resisted cycles of A C were essential to the Reluctant Green Dragon even when she lay motionless and perfectly safe from collision or attack. By the same token it was necessary for non-commissioned human beings practiced in the manipulation of controls to optimize the contrast between artifactual blips and the white-noise clutter of "sea-return" always to be peering at the screen with such intensity that two of us on every watch until hostilities were over had to alternate with each other every hour in order to rest our eyes and to restore the patience all enlisted men must summon in answering to the asinine demands of aristocrats. One general effect of universal electronics was that even our crude new species of seagoing ship born in cornfield shipyards, so simple that its repairs and mutations were easily made at docks far beyond the Western Sea Frontier but not so simple that it couldnt adapt itself to an astonishing variety of tasks one of which realized British hopes for a floating four-cornered antiaircraft beach castle capable of anchoring barrage balloons to force counterattacking planes into cross-fire before antiaircraft artillery could be landed and emplaced, found itself nearly as dependent upon internal combustion for its electrified vision as for its ventilation and very movement. The same compromise of self-sufficiency has now been struck in the accelerated evolution of fishing vessels including the converted hulls of schooners. Like L S T s when their motors stop they can only float dead in the water deaf and mute. Now they too take incessant noise to sea restlessly scanning airwaves surface and bottom with commercially advertised electronic gear.

A thousand new schooners driven silently by wind would have contributed less than nothing to victory over Germany and Japan. Anyway they don't have rectangles and are very difficult to build inland though perhaps closer to the lumber which nevertheless needs too much time for seasoning or wherever else you can't make ship's carpenters out of square farmers or metalworkers brought up to see curves as welded approximations of contiguous straight-line segments or gigantic infinitessimals of calculus suitable like an L S T 's to the pragmatic convenience of mass production despite their horror of such sloppy quality control as the Russians' who turned out myriad tanks under the worst possible manufacturing conditions by accepting every variation in the gauge of steel used to armor them. Thereto though many schooners have been saved from northern icepacks in latter years by an inboard engine coupled to a wheel as the Ericsson screw propeller is called in Gloucester though I don't know the vernacular there for a windmill's blades that cannot trace a helix because they make no axial locomotion a typical unanalytical expression based purely poetically upon the deception of appearances far less apt than if it meant a triskelion or swastika which can move if at all only in the plane of its diameter they havent the electromechanic power to blow ballast tanks in order to ground themselves neatly upon a sandy gradient of one in fifty and let down a drawbridge on tidal land or unsling from flat sides a number of modular steel pontoons to be clamped together on end and side-by-side for containerized cargo to roll ashore upon and then back off again on the tide to resume their sea trim or carry on their backs and launch into the surf like pregnant baby dragons with ramps of their own half a dozen landing barges carrying 500 fully equipped troops. Nor do schooners lend themselves by shape or handiness to the functions of ammunition barges or intermediary hospital ships and of course never under any circumstances could they be considered suitable platforms for spotter-plane flight decks no matter how useful Piper Cubs might be in hunting mackerel. No other vessels have ever been as good as schooners for hunting and hauling a particular class of cargo in their own era but they proved too refined to meet as L S T s did the world-emergency calling for a version of the armed amphibious merchantman a general type with which the navies of the world began. The engines of schooners when they first got them were just strong enough to make way against unfavorable elements with no power to spare for driving them any faster than necessary to get in or out of a harbor. When the petrochemical I C powerplant became large enough to drag a net along the bottom and haul it in full of fish it was no longer merely auxiliary and the vessel was no longer a schooner no matter how elegant its hull. But even multiplied by ten to the third power that disturbance of the fisheries' labile equilibrium is nothing to compare with a fleet of L S T s driving themselves onto a beach to disgorge bulldozers which straightway turn around to scrape up ramps and causeways as nests like rows of temporary cradles for the very wombs that laid them ashore in turtlelike defiance of Tokyo Rose's vow that not one gasping monkfish mother would be allowed to deliver and which then charge up the slope with a madding roar like fascist goslings disdainful of Churchillian art and Odyssean deception to level hills and fill marshes for roads or airstrips developing the real estate before any offer is made. The sheer profligacy of chemical forces in a massive symphony of unintermitted I C eructations drowns out the sound of guns and bombs. They arrogantly mock all history's previous clashes of men horses elephants and dragons trumpeting with rage or screaming with agony and far exceed the requirement of their own tractions. In this devastation nothing remains inexpugnable and nowhere can its consequence be taken back. Land does not heave and fill like sea to reclaim the wakes of engines. Right from the beginning Mother Russia speaking through her paternal Premier saw that the war hung not upon quaquaversal explosions of bombs or directed exlosions of guns but upon limitless repetition of tiny contained explosions easily governed at variable speed in the manned machines that contained them whether in airplanes and track-laying tractors or harnessed to pneumatic rubber wheels in American trucks and general purpose personnel buggies that we called Jeeps which she admired more than P-38s. L S T s afloat on either side of Russia, often enunciated LOVE SUGAR TARE in order to protect voice signals against noise in conveying their generic identification without risking the slightly longer LANDING SHIP TANK that might mean more to enemy intelligence, were of all ships the most intimate with land engines. They even had traffic signals to control the lanes in their ferry-bellies and they were always in danger of being blown apart by gasoline vapor that by easy accident can be externally ignited. These landcraft carriers that I so much despised at the time in resentment of duty therein became so crucial to Allied offences that the first production models were laid down to replace an aircraft carrier's keel on the ways at Newport News and even such prime facilities as Charlestown's graving dock were for a time devoted to the anguished demand signifying our Navy's ambivalent acknowledgement of the urgent tactical problem that had been recognized by broadminded Allied statesmen notably F D R himself also a Former Naval Person who on one occasion had sketched his own design as well as by their most anxious godfather whose success in proliferation lay pretty much at the mercy of his shotgun wife Mother America who had the production capacity. The experimental prototypes built by the British as *Thruster* and *Bruiser* and *Boxer* had doubtless been too expensive for the job being 62 ft longer than the final model and driven by steam turbines. Churchill believed in naming all worthy entities for instance antiaircraft platforms raised on pilings like oil-drilling rigs in the Thames Estuary as well as meetings conferences and projects like Tube Alloys in which his people launched the research for the most secretive of all explosions and in the case of his submarines delighted to do it himself when the Admiralty seemed to run out of imagination. There were even class names like Mulberry Gooseberry and Phoenix for his brain-children blockships synthetic harbors and sunken breakwaters half-cousins of the L S T yet used only in a single invasion. But before the Big Show ended such sentiment was overborne by the American "mass-production style of thought" by which he meant our integral calculus of cumulative mechanistic power despairing of the nearly humane efficiency with which "every scrap of fighting strength plays its full part all the time" especially for the Italian campaign in which he was sure that a mere dozen L S T s kept in the Mediterranean a couple of months longer and scarcely to be missed from the preparations for Eisenhower's large-scale invasion would have permitted all war efforts to "fit together" by taking advantage of sea flanks and anticipating by Panzer dashes the Russian occupation of Austria at least. By his own account those three letters L S T were branded in his mind as deeply as in my own. When W S C wailed that the "destinies of two great empires" were being frustrated by the failure to keep "some God-damned things called L S T s" at the top of Allied priority lists though very likely offending some Americans' sensitivity to our particular profession of manifest destiny he was only reinforcing our Army Chief of Staff's own insight who had bypassed West Point in his education a most sagacious leader not given to suboptimization and apparently anticipated the Annapolis men whose business it had to be. They'd all been accustomed to the idea that landing craft if not simply rubber boats to cross rivers in were nothing but ship-to-shore launches for marine hoplites who as infantry would capture harbors in which to unload freight. And then the first of these arks to reach the Pacific were armed with nothing better than seven machine guns. It's a wonder they werent counted by the number of archers and slingers they'd carry or horse marines. Yet as a matter of fact they'd make good cattle boats nowadays what with their superb air blowers and

opening bows to shovel the shit out of. Hannibal could have spared his
elephants the Alps.

Before we moved to Cambridge I once read at Sawyer Free Library
when working on a standard project called the Gloucester Book which
each grammar-school pupil had to undertake for himself that the engineer
of the first powered schooner like several others before owners learned the
advantages of diesel was killed by fire from a gasoline leak. He was an
African. So also had been Gloucester's first recorded murder victim over a
century earlier a slave girl already known to be with child. Killed in
Dogtown with a sword by her owner the town doctor's son a Harvard man.
Yet what a sweet thing it would have been if more black-colored people
had not continued on the underground railroad but stayed to share
Gloucester with all-colored citizens. In my time there was none to be
found in the whole school system and on the streets in summertime I saw
only half a dozen who were said to be serving estivators in Magnolia or out
on Eastern Point. They say the Portuguese, whose ancestors as misceg-
enous Norsemen of Africa and Brazil themselves anciently subject to
Moorish conquest were the world's foremost navigators one of whom our
very first European discoverer who tried to sell Indians into slavery labeled
the cape in honor of St James on his map for Charles the Fifth almost a
century before Champlain found his Beau Port there, are too sensitive to
tolerate them, and that the few Black Portugees who joke about genetics
are shushed by their countrymen. Yet in New York I used to daydream of
taking that splendid noble girl back to Gloucester for I imagined she was
born to be a princess of the place where I hoped to make her a friend of
Ruth the First and all the other good citizens that I never knew. Someday
I would buy the Stone Jug built as Fitz Hugh Lane's studio and set her up
to reign there on Gloucester's Merry Mount where the end of the Revolution was celebrated under a great blasted oak "solitary and venerable"
twenty-three feet in girth all lighted up with torches and rum where
there's never been an Anglican dance on May Day or a pine tree decked
with rainbow streamers and fragrant garlands now a residentially
undesireable neighborhood that we could afford to live in among the
wooden-dwelling inner harbor populace encircled by what might be left of
marine railways nautical machine shops chandleries coal-and-lumber yards
and fish packers strung along between the decaying wharves and sheds of
the waterfront with the power plant a sail loft the ruins of gas works a
paint factory and the police station looped around all that might be left of
the old bars and boarding houses used in the city's highest old times by
visiting sailors fishermen and whores. Lovely softspoken girl already
mature in her private purpose and so reserved that she hinted no more of
her aristocratic ability than her social defenses in a small white machine
shop required! I thought of her as a tall black schooner with black spars
and elegant black sails. None of my Ruths have been bulldozers like that
androgyne of Sandy's today who forces her way through the world by

internal combustion and walks like a tank so far out of trim with aggression that you don't even notice her lines or the cast of her snout. To lie with her would be like sleeping in a garage. Vulture crossing a stockyard the Japanese major would have said. Yet if I'd been at sea a long time maybe I'd put up with it for half an hour out of sight in the bushes somewhere. I used to feel sorry for the pigs sailors sometimes had to go out with until I learned that it wasnt simply a matter of hereditary misfortune. They chose their appearance or at least their sounds and movements as they chose their thoughts. Of course few of them were educated and political like that one and they did deserve some pity for not daring to resent as she does the free favors they can't help offering men who seek the easement more than the woman. It's self-repugnant to watch yourself exchange words of false friendliness even with goodlooking intelligent viragos just for what is called a piece of ass. They are no teasers those hot clenching appeasers primed for grimly silent consummation before you even touch their skin and in malodorous haste with no alteration of tone they seem to be instructing you according to some doctrinaire routine first with one or two openmouthed hardnosed kisses while their hands are busy and then abruptly with full speed pumping like wound-up dolls already triggered so you have to chase them around a monotonous circle until you get tired of the game and no matter how well stacked they may be with soft curves under their tasteless unironed clothes they feel like inept imposters at the sport all for no other reason than that they have taken upon themselves a masculine mind which as St Joseph says makes a woman not into a "being of superior efficiency" but only into a "phenomenon of imperfect differentiation." I would almost prefer the fraud of Vera's professed femininity. Sandy's Ruth a disgrace to her given name is torn between ingratiation and insolence. But it's conceivable that a truculent bloody bitch like that can be softened up at a poor baby's expense and she can't help being bloody it isnt even a curse the B V M herself must have dripped blood before and after the incarnation. I wonder about Artemis Athena and Aphrodite et al did they suffer the discomforts of our women or did they like male gods as Achilles points out to Priam avoid all the sorrow woven into the very ground of mortal lives not to mention crucifixion or other pains beyond the common lot?

There was a bloody Limey in our engineroom gang or so they called him not because he wasnt American or needed ascorbic acid more than the rest of us but because he never let up with the cockney talk and at least was such a good mimic that I could never be sure he was merely celebrating the good time he'd had in England a garrulous goodnatured little First Class Water Tender with a toothy smile skinny as a bird and bald as a creased rock the result I heard of a horrible boiler-room burn in his destroyer that went down in the North Atlantic. Liberty so flourished in the British Isles he claimed that even mothers tolerated the omission of honorable intentions in their gratitude to Yanks for helping out in the war

and encouraged our sailors to stay overnight with their daughters. It must
have been true if he affected East End speech so wholeheartedly that he
never spoke his native tongue. With his hard beak and beady black eyes
piercing the cartridge case of the florid boney skull laced by blue veins,
however little he may have resembled the flaccid lugubrious uncircum-
cized cod-nosed character whose unmistakable name and image still mysteriously appear like the signature of some sottish despairing Jonny
Appleseed on patches of public surface by way of rearguard protest against
Disney's style of personification wherever freehand Americans of the
penultimate world war have set foot, for me he will forever remain Kilroy
himself. In any case such was his popularity and such the respect commanded by his many hash marks his cheerfully survived hardships and his
wiry bowlegged flagrance of vitality that his amorous successes were universally credited and he singlehandedly neutralized in our ship the distaste
for Brits that more than aversion to Germans seemed to animate almost
everyone I ever knew in the Navy probably under the balefully unspecific
influence of Irish animadversions everywhere in America rather than on
any grounds of anthropological prejudice like the kind that supported our
insensate enmity to little yellow men. Indeed I've since been surprised to
read the enthusiastic opinion of Mr P as W S C coded himself for the
Casablanca Conference that the friendly cooperation among our Combined
Chiefs of Staff was unprecedented in all military history despite occasional
misunderstanding of idiom stemming from the assumption that they all
spoke the same language to wit for example the contretemps arising from
an American apprehension that the British misprized a very reasonable
and proper proposal when with matter-of-fact alacrity they moved to table
it. Having led under our super-imperial yoke of thermonuclear entropy-
bomb defense the two self-declared former empires lying on either side of
us the one formerly an imitation of the other led and staffed by educated
gentlemen we are now infecting their home islands with our social ver-
sions of internal conbustion so that they too will concentrate on our kinds
of luxury and entertainment in fact we arrogate the right to corrupt the
whole world with Disney-visions mainly by erstwhile virtue of our I C
engines that kept Germans out of England and our hyper-I C bombs that
kept Russians out of Japan. We're about to convert consumers of fish and
rice whose standard army rations were considered even by Limey logisti-
cians to be starvation diet for white men into beefeaters who'll soon be
bidding up the price of meat in all three empires just as we've already
taught knowledge of good and no-good to delicate women formerly content with the aesthetic flight of Asiatic nightingales. But when the Japanese start producing I C engines and T V sets better than we do perhaps
we'll understand too late that even in padding our gross national product
with vicious goods and services marketing is a sorry substitute for efficient
production. Maybe then the day will come that all the American people
even Irish will prefer the chaps who were trying to find a way to survive

without so much growth to the Nips who compete for progress all too
well. I liked the bloody Limey patter of that Kilroy from Hoboken who
haply sailed first to the east and then to the west for both kinds of pussy
that I never had the good luck to get either of but which perhaps was not
to be expected at my minor age Jonnnie-come-lately to the war. The first
American sea captain to visit Cipangu was from Gloucester and what a
wry fate that I too should succeed where Columbus Cabot and Cartier
commissioned by Francis the First at Mont-Saint-Michel had failed without ever touring Italy Spain France or Albion the motherland of my mind
to which Cape Ann's half way from here who would eagerly have served
without pay or expenses just to get a glimpse of the European Theater. If
as a bluejacket, the literary or sociological term used like peasant by the
official Navy and its historians but never in my presence referring to a live
swabby or to any muster detail draft crew or rout of real sailors, I had been
denied the society of ladies and gentlemen having reached the green and
pleasant land laved by tides twenty times as strong as Truk's I too might
have taken up the bloody version of our fucking speech if not like the Earl
of Rochester who as a gifted mimic disguised himself in the London
underworld and died at my age from the pleasures of his rubbing post but
I wouldnt have had the guts to stick to it in the company of my shipmates. In the Middle Ages French gentlewomen were never supposed to
see the blood of anything stronger than lambs or pigeons but Queen Elizabeth in her impatience at courtiers would cry out in the name of God's
wounds. Whether the bloody version of English is obscene or blasphemous
in derivation it was foul language for a godfearing ship too foul for
Columbus or any other prudent captain of exploration either Catholic who
had his crew singing offices or English who led daily services from Edward
the Sixth's Book of Common Prayer. The only trace of piety left in my day
was the Navy's rule against whistling aboard ship perhaps not so much in
respect for the tweets of the bosun's pipe still used in more ceremonious
vessels than ours or in prohibition of anything that might compete with
the official loudspeaker as in vestigial superstition against calling up a
wind that wasnt wanted. But the chipper little Limey favorite of the
snipes below deck and the only colleague ever to call us Mate as the Navy
wished instead of Mac in the breezy manner of the day stood out in my
mind as representing something more than the advantages of transatlantic
travel. He was the sole man of steam among all our Motor Machinists and
other artificers of the black gang making our only connection with the
great tradition of marine engineering that came to birth barely a hundred
years ago and is already fallen into decadence like the crafts of
marlingspike seamanship that it itself had obsoleted. A little steam had to
be generated for an L S T 's heating cooking laundering and the like but
the ship's complement called for a First Class Water Tender mainly to run
the evaporators in which salt water was turned to fresh. Thanks to Teddy
Roosevelt an ingenuous Republican who in New Hampshire mediated

peace between the empires of Russia and Japan the U S N having assured
the superiority of its gunnery had emphasized cruising range in its ship
design by incorporating desalinization boilers a policy that was reinforced
and extended by a program under the politically more sophisticated second Roosevelt whereby the squadrons of our redefined imperialism were
made even less dependent upon overseas freshwater procurement and shipboard brine-conversion which was thermally expensive by developing a
service fleet that could sustain fighting ships far from their bases unlike
the British who had only to stay with the sun from day to day to find their
flag waving over a spot of rum and limes until they finally lost their coal-
ing as well as watering stations in half the world all at once. Yet an L S T
was built not only for beaching but also for wandering and as itself an
insignificant sometimes unaccompanied gypsy it was expected to trouble
the fleet tenders for very little except diesel oil. To enjoy the services of a
shore base in outreaches of the Pacific she had to wait for the Seabees to
finish civilizing the islands we conquered. The ship's water tender was
therefore our counterpart to a cooper. There was a time when the Crown
wouldnt let any ship put to sea without a barrel-maker aboard professionally responsible for an inventory of hoops and heads and beveled staves as
well as for the repair and preservation of casks already cunningly fitted and
compressed out of precious English oak and charged not to return without
a single damned one of them or its replacement from foreign trees. No
American not even T R would dare suggest the enforcement of conservation by penalty of imprisonment or fine least of all the conservatives who
grudge even as little as the nuisance of returning reusing and circulating
wooden freight pallets that stevedores deep in their hearts for fear of efficiency still don't like to see around at all. Even in our self-governing maritime parish of the old empire then being formed the King tried to
preserve the great pines for his masts which otherwise had to be grafted
and spliced together from inferior Old World stock. It's hard to visualize
Gloucester covered with timber as England once had been. But of course
when there was no I C electricity for cooling Coca-Cola or keeping frozen
supplies of Thanksgiving turkey or payloads of fish slabs it was in a ship's
own interest to enroll a master cooper who could prevent and repair outward leaks of potable fluid which in a North Atlantic full of rain and
icebergs was chiefly beer and inward leaks of air that spoiled the crew's
pickled junk and the owners' cargo of salt herring. The fishes' brine that
we took our scintillating showers in wasnt salty enough by half for fishermen. In the Western Pacific our Kilroy was obliged to burn fuel to get rid
of the same commodity that the settlers of Gloucester had to import from
climates where there was plenty of solar energy in exchange for the fish it
dressed after failing from the very beginning of colonial times in their
efforts to pan it in usable quantity. An L S T 's barrels tuns pipes pun-
cheons and casks were nothing but a few standard steel drums full of fossil
lubrication that had to be kept less saline than whale oil. An evaporator is

a steam generator the rudiment of a steam engine and it was from steam engines that scientists learned the natural philosophy of entropy. In the especially artificial case of computing machines they now similarly study the opposite science of information or rather a noiseless arcane technology that under the guidance of theories like mine could make a practical art of national frugality.

All the same *Gloucesterman* got home on my power her I C auxiliary. Proudly examining my torch of wreckage I headed back up the bank toward the bridge. But suddenly I faced a Harvard man as I presumed from his handsome trench coat fashionably shaped rain hat and romantic pipe in the mouth upsidedown. Photographic paraphenalia hung about his neck and shoulders. He carried a wooden tripod with patined brass ferrules that he'd just folded into fasces for his left hand. On the other side he balanced with his fingertips on the slippery grass of the bank he was descending. For an instant I thought he was after me for trespassing in the B-School latifundium but all he said and very softly was "It's too bad about your boat!" Oh no I said I just wanted to find out if it was able. There was no jeer in his face or voice and he looked at me as sympathetically as if the schooner was a violated doll. He raised a finger to the broken bowsprit. I could see that he didnt get the point. That's nothing I said it wasnt the boat's fault it'll be better than ever when I fix it up. I was too embarrassed to call her she or a schooner. He was as solemn and methodical as a rational midwesterner demanding to know why repairs would improve the original. I had to explain that it was now weatherbeaten. I've proved that it's seaworthy. I seemed deferential so he had made up his mind to patronize my vagary and when he took the boat from me to see the rig more closely he imitated my manner of holding it by the keel. "She's a schooner. Two masts." I know said I. "I've never seen a toy schooner before. Very realistic. Did you make her?" His unselfconscious change of pronouns eased my part of the conversation. "I made everything except the keel." In my preoccupation with the rig by which I had forced her into the schooner type it never occurred to me that I should confess the obvious prefabrication of her hull. I told him she'd sailed all the way across the river and under the bridge from way up on the other side. It was no disgrace she ran aground at the bend after all that distance with no one steering. To my relief when he found out her name he took no notice of the conflict in gender that still worried me. "Oh do you go to Gloucester in the summer? I've sailed to Gloucester many times." I was further eased by the delight of meeting someone to speak of Gloucester with but I had learned to be cautious about expressing my sentiments. The fact that he had really cruised through the Cut with the bridge drawn for him in transits such as had never ceased to thrill me as I watched like a wharf-rat on the rip-rap waving at passengers a gamin struck with awe almost as conducive to hero-worship as the apparition of a Navy officer. Since he made no remark about the dirty harbor or its stink and did not complain about

the overpopulation of gulls and dogs which to me were more to be longed
for than the city's other residents at first I failed to realize that he found
the town agreeable simply because he knew only the course that took sea
tourists right past the entrance to the inner harbor and around to
Annisquam which has charmed white men more than the Plantation itself
these three hundred years or perhaps the land route from the yacht club at
the breakwater to neighboring houses along the back shore. Even if he'd
motored inside to the smelly picturesque waterfront of Beau Port's actual
port he wouldnt have seen where all the people live. Most mainlanders
who travel to Gloucester especially when aware of its reputation never
guess anything of its essence except the inconveniences like absurd traffic
on Main Street narrow and sinuous from its origins as a Colonial path
along the rocks on the way to Eastern Point or Sandy Bay. He knew less
about it than some of the Italian kids in Cambridge who'd never even been
there but were connected by background with people who might have
lived in such a fishy place or than Ruth my present Ruth unconsciously
instinct with the historical sensibilities of San Francisco Bay. Anyway not
yet having learned to bridle first blushes of enthusiasm I excitedly sought
the friendship suggested by his disarming ingenuousness about the
Gloucester in which he saw no shame. It was very nice not to have to
apologize for unsavory fishmongering or treeless jumbles of homely houses
set at random angles on the two most conspicuous hills which tourists
never visit and which only an artist or two among a thousand painters ever
paint. In my joy as ever in thinking I'd found a friend I presumed too
much. I told him that I didnt like fancy boats that couldnt stay out in a
storm. "That's the kind of boat we sail I'm afraid. From Marblehead."
Marblehead and Granitehead there's the whole difference right in the rock.
In the course of time those two towns originally peers in cussed independence have become almost as different as mill town and suburb though I
didnt then know enough to hold that broad opinion and can only say so
now. But my vague hopes partook of the farfetched idea that I might
someday be invited to go sailing with him and I was checked by the sudden fear that my overweening self-expression had killed the prospect
aborning. "You wouldnt like her." he understood enough to say. "Painted
white with a lot of shiny brass and not much good for cruising. Only a
sloop." Oh that's all right I quickly replied I've never been out on a real
boat. When he flattered me by wondering how I knew so much about
schooners I had to own that I got my experience from books as I adroitly
reversed the direction of inquiry by putting questions about the real
thing. "She's called *Anglican*. Spinnaker balloon-sail all that for ocean
racing never came near winning Halifax Bermuda. I'm not much of a
yachtsman myself. Dad's always skipper."

It turned out that my friend's father was a Low Church clergyman
born to high connections but it didnt seem to strike him as rare and
strange that I an acolyte of the High Church with low connections was

living among Romans who were neither high nor low but allied with the
American Legion in administering the one true culture of Cambridge lace-
curtain Irish as represented by St Peter's church and school across the
street from Harvard's astronomers only one of a dozen parishes in the city
each more thronged with seething relays of congregation than any twelve
low Episcopal churches in all of Greater Boston such as Christ Church
where George Washington had listened to sermons while he was cuffing
together the Continental Army and where I attended Sunday School and a
Scout troop for lack of High Church youth facilities but sheltered by
higher social circles I'm sure than his father's inland parish could boast.
The poor guy probably had no idea there was a North Cambridge or an
East Cambridge or even a Central Square except as a subway stop which
wasnt surprising in a prep school boy but when I discovered as we headed
back across the river that on the other hand he had not even heard of the
Anglican monastery next to the Boston Elevated Railway carbarn that I
pointed out to him in which American monks and priests meditated
Anglo-Catholic plainsong discretely endowed with financial and theological independence of the Diocese that it and his father in the suburbs both
belonged to I thought he might be impressed by the advantage I had of
him. But no doubt he had no attention left for anything that brought his
father's voice to mind having been born too much of a baptized Christian
as well as rich and respectful and therefore deprived of a certain unreckoning zest that comes with having to get your culture where you find it. Not
that I was aware of learning anything or wouldnt have preferred a hundred
pleasures that simply werent in the spectrum of my lot when I did what
was expected of me in the particular contingencies befalling a family alert
for anything interesting in its dreary circumstances. And so once a week
though I was lazy and it was a hard thing to do with no compensation in
money or recognizable glory when I didnt oversleep and incur my own
remorseful reproaches I got up early long before school to serve Father
North at the altar of a tiny private chapel about the shape of a two-car
garage attached to the back of a mansarded Victorian house with a semicircular carriage drive an estate converted to a genteel nursing home for
declining ladies I presume pious patrons of the Oxford Movement in
America not far from the marvelous facilities of the Windsor Day School
where the kids of Cambridge intended for Harvard and Radcliffe prepared
for their prep schools under stimulating instruction quite beyond the
scope of my imagination. The kindly old spiritual autocrat had himself
founded the order of Sisters habited in stiff white wimples long black veils
and robes with dark wooden pectoral crosses edged in silver who ran the
place laundry bakery kitchen sacristy and all in starched tranquility perfumed by fresh cleanliness and the smell of ironed linen yearning for the
company of children however worldly and he still ordered them about as
their chaplain and confessor if not pope. I never saw the inside of the
Order's convent on Beacon Hill in Boston but I was a familiar visitor to

this rather elegant affiliate where I was cosseted with misplaced praise and whatever trifles they fancied a half-tamed wilding or his siblings might like from the fruit and candy given them by friends and patrons unknown to me and with this affection Father North was in perfectly patient accord as long as the nuns werent sentimental when he was around who himself rewarded me as one gentleman with another by having them serve us at a table in an often sunny bay window of the Mother Superior's high-ceilinged drawing room overlooking a front garden the most delicious breakfasts of my life composed chiefly of poached eggs on tender buttered toast while with his own white-clothed tray and snowy napkin he ate deftly from his eggshell in a tiny silver chalice after neatly decapitating it with a table knife while opposite me he read his New York Times that must have been full of melancholy news from his native England. We were waited upon by the meekest and most timid of the house Sister Martha who seemed to me a perpetual postulant judging by the simple homespun grays she always wore with an abbreviated white veil that looked half civilian for whose aging wrinkled ego which I knew loved me well my heart ached in pity when he treated her especially in a boy's presence not with the gratitude I thought she deserved but with a brusque even irritable indifference that seemed to me too harsh even for a paid servant. Sometimes in the bonny part of the year he would take me along when he went outdoors between mass and breakfast with a slender crane-spouted watering can to refresh some of the more fragile plants in rock gardens and crannied walls while I nearly died of polite starvation never remembering anything he told me about the flowers. He assumed a base of knowledge and curiosity associated with youth in England. I was always afraid he'd talk to me about something serious or chide me for forgetting my lines in the preparatory antiphon which of course seemed to me no more relevant to my interests than any other chore of memorization never suspecting it to be a psalm from the Bible but thank God he never offered to do so because he must have been tactfully grateful for my entirely adventitious and supererogatory efforts since women naturally couldn't serve at the altar and I'm sure there wasnt any other Anglo-Catholic boy so voluntarily available in Cambridge. I liked well enough what action there was in the job following the Introit but I keenly delighted in doing the candles before and after. In a chasuble Father North looked like a storybook turtle with his skinny wrinkled neck moving inside the round white collar that ringed it with plenty of room to spare and his black-rimmed glasses resting on a benign beak. Even when he was not vested he kept a handkerchief in the sleeve of his cassock. Only when I heard of his death two or three years after I had let my association utterly lapse in favor of agnostical self-indulgence did I understand that I'd loved him. Love with guilt, soon enough. It was sanguine Sister Mary in the fullness of goodnatured vigor who talked important business not only to me but to Billy Peggy and some rich kids for whom she got permission to start a little unofficial

Sunday afternoon catechism class because she was sorrowfully aware of the
thoroughly Protestant and liberal cast of our regular Episcopal church
schools in the morning. But even she pressed no personal examination of
our belief or of our progress in doctrine and simply taught us to memorize
as pleasantly as possible the canonical answers to spiritual questions without testing her tacit assumptions about the Christian households that sent
us there for it is only in Southern sects that one's faith is boldly probed.
Even then after twenty minutes or so we played games or made things.
She and her colleagues provided us Chapman kids as the most deserving or
at least the most receptive with an inexhaustible supply of great hard-
bound albums of stiff black leaves once used I suppose by some greeting-
card distributor related to one of the friends of the house to show his new
lines every season. The samples themselves had been removed from ghostly
rectangles outlined by whited maculations on the empty pages and given
to aged invalids or indigents who took pleasure in mounting colored pictures or comforting verses. I had heard of keeping scrapbooks but far from
being at once ignited to a new mania I helped Peggy and Billy carry the
first three home animated by nothing more than awkward compassion for
Sister Mary who in her boundless charity thought a redblooded boy would
like to spend his spare time cutting out and pasting decorations like a girl
or a sissy. Yet one evening at home after we had the books I noticed Peggy
cutting a doll's picture mere model of a baby out of the Saturday Evening
Post and was about to tease her when I suddenly realized that I could likewise capture almost anything real that I didnt own visit or draw for
myself. From that moment there were never enough newspapers or magazines in the house and for several years especially in the winter when my
acquisitive appetite was strongest we methodically collected them from
friends and rubbish barrels. My arbitrary preemption of raw material
wasnt as hard on Peg as on Bill because her passions and mine did not
overlap. After a while he gave up on his own book and dropped the hobby.
For my part quantity was more important than selection and I filled all
the albums the Sisters could get me crowding the pages with cut-out
illustrations of the world's attractions and making no attempt to classify
or label them. We never had enough paste or mucilage still made in
Gloucester but no longer as glue from gurry and at first we squabbled over
the single pair of sewing scissors owned by the family and often lost.
Whereas in my two-dimensional binders I saved trains ships aircraft and
ordnance, vehicles with two or more wheels driven directly or indirectly
by internal or external combustion, bridges dams tunnels fortifications
castles skyscrapers derricks cranes and harbors, alps canyons and rivers,
great cats wolves eagles horses elephants vipers constrictors sharks and
whales, I learned more about the world especially after I began to read
articles that went with the captions than did the rich kids who actually
saw some of the things I knew of. I particularly remember Pan American's
China Clipper a flying boat that crossed the Pacific from Treasure Island

with half a dozen stops avoiding secret Japanese islands because we thought it had a nose like our dog's named Lud for his howl after Ludwig von Beethoven whose music sounded awful to us in our uncouth lumpishness about art and all black like the one that haunted Faust having been driven from heaven to hell in another form or the one that gave its name to the fits of depression Churchill suffered all his life when he wasnt fighting wars. I don't know where he came from or what became of him. You can love a dog like a brother and yet remember nothing more than his name his color and the fact that he embarrassed you humping other dogs in public places and even kids on living room floors. We never worried about him because we assumed from his sagacity as St Herman called a dog's tolerance and self-confidence that he was safer than we were in the street-jungles of I C power thanks to our belief in a mysteriously extraordinary sense of smell which without depending on the diffusion of gases raised his sight and hearing to such high orders of acuity that he could practically see around corners in the dark and unlike his namesake hear the presence of anything within a mile even if it made no noise being there. Poor dog on his part was probably counting on our supernatural protection almost like my furry little puppy in Gloucester not eight weeks old already impersoned with the name of Handy from his original size and my hopes for training him who had scampered lickety-split squealing with fun exactly under the only moving car on Grove Street right in front of my eyes absolutely unprepared to encounter anything in the world unfriendly to himself. My fault for letting him loose just to see if he'd obey my call for the first time. The people in the low black touring car from out of town were extremely apologetic but coming up over that little rise there wasnt a thing the driver could have done to avoid running him over. When I pulled him out from under the car he bit me like a savage whelp and when I laid him on the front steps he was still breathing but he died almost at once as I gazed numbly at the blood and flesh oozing from his mouth. Billy saw the whole sequence and didn't get over it though he never referred to any aspect of the accident until long after we'd left Gloucester. He avoided me for several days. After dark all by myself I buried Handy in the back corner of the cemetery among some weeds just off the short cut to Ruth's house his jaws frozen but his plump belly not yet fully stiffened. My very eyes remember the running board of the car and the worn brown earth of the grassy path in the opening of the tumbled wall of boulders and rough granite blocks. If that part of the grounds is ever improved for human use the dust of his tiny bones won't be noticed. All because of my enthusiastic impatience I couldnt wait to take him to Dogtown for safe training experiments. It never crossed my mind to speak of Dogtown to that Harvard guy. The Dogtown commons were reserved to the common consciousness of us settlers. You naturally couldnt expect off-islanders to take in that wold or moor or heath of terminal moraine which to me even in the cricketing sunlight was always

eerie enough with the ghosts of women and children humble Anglos oppressed by Danelaw who perhaps had succored Alfred incognito in his adversity massacred in their cabins by Vikings and Indians too in a misty
prehistoric era of Cape Ann that has never been wholly eradicated from my
memory-mundi to keep me from going there alone for blueberries. An irregular expanse of rock grass and leaf centered in a triangle of overgrown
cellar holes with vestigial kitchen gardens and pastures strewn with juni-
pers cedars and the earth's own bones across which the train whistle is
plainly carried back and forth between Gloucester and Rockport, except
on the tracks themselves the safest place in the world for dogs. You can
save a dog's life ten times and he thinks nothing of it but by the same
token he doesnt hold it against you if you let him get killed. Most people
are as insensitive as animals to the favors you do them say when you step
back from your right of way at a crossing to let their cars go past and it
would never enter their heads to acknowledge such courtesy. But dogs at
least make no invidious comparisons and like God respect no persons. I
wonder what happened to the little black puppy on the 1066. Did somebody kick him overboard after Abbie was sent ashore? Dogtown was generally unowned not just the Common where three lanes met even after the
last witches were gone like the lonely place where Oedipus killed his
father but all the rest of it and yet it wasnt a park or reservation. No cows
no cars no signs. An uninhabited tract it was the heartland of three well-
peopled shores cut off by a populated tidal river but I'd already begun to
think the whole cape too small and anachronistic for me. In Cambridge
near the skating-club rink Mark Wheeler let me build a city in his house
to improve our layout of his electric trains. He was a clubfooted only-child
rich enough to have two or three rooms at his disposal for such purposes if
he could find a playmate who'd encourage his imagination. I was happy to
have access to the resources for doing so and he was happy to find someone
who could tell him what to do with all his equipment as he called it for a
gigantic project as he liked to say. It was from him I learned both those
words equipment and gigantic. He had a beautiful morally overwhelming
Lionel catalog in full color and every once in a while without waiting for
Christmas we'd go down to Harvard Square to get him some new sections
of track or another switch and look at the rolling stock that even he didnt
have enough money to buy out of his own pocket. It was after we had
shaped and glued a variety of solid balsa wood models from store-bought
kits to make small pursuit planes medium bombers and four-engine ones
all pretty much the same size in disgusting violation of my sense of proportion that I prevailed upon him nevertheless to integrate them as the air
corps for all the rest of his disparate simulacra. To me even more valuable
than the trains was what I'd give a lot to have the like of for my boys right
now if they'd only take care of it an immense neatly cased Meccano set from
England in total effect much more realistic a word he learned from me in
its antiplatonistic sense than the lightweight construction toys made in

U S A as nominalistic steel girders. It was a pleasure just to run your fingers through the copious reservoirs of tiny fully machined screws bolts and smoothly beveled hexagonal nuts. The stacks of assorted beams were as heavy and compact as guns. Boldly but laboriously fabricated into a truss bridge they gave the heavy rocking trains solid support across a broad river. As tall cranes and signal towers they dignified the swiftly laid railroad. Most of the time I was content to let Mark operate the trains with his levers and buttons advancing or reversing the D C reduced and rectified from an A C domestic outlet none of which either of us had any idea about the properties of except in gross mechanical effect. I usually preferred to shunt the cars by hand. You could feel the lovely inertia of their rolling weight and sense by touch the clicks of bogie wheels as they traversed track connections and frog points just as easily backward as forward pushing or pulling. The challenge in laying out that railroad was to make use of every last odd section of prefabricated track and to serve our territory in every possible variation of line and level with intermodal connections using building blocks Lincoln Logs Tootsie-Toy vehicles all our flatbottomed boats and every airplane that could be perceptually falsified in scale as foundations or contextual enhancements of the electrified modules. Anything else that came to hand was planted in the landscape as an embellishment or space-filler. In our city-planning form followed material. By half closing my eyes and affecting a distant view I could accept this congeries of representation in a spatial medley of sizes and shapes as one pretty convincing work of art on the whole but I could never feel comfortable about the conspicuously raised triple rails of the bulky track itself an insistent skeletal detail disproportionate even to the oversize wheels that rolled along everywhere dominating the otherwise tolerable verisimilitude of supraorganic urban unity whereas real-life rails being artifacts of landscape bedded into the earth on cypress crossties that in rhythmically unending repetition absorb the hurtling shock of far greater relative weight banking it properly for various different curves and speeds become mineralogical and floral fixtures of the earth abiding as if eternal while trains appear and disappear like fauna in uneven cycles of prosperity and dearth according to weather or political economy. Used or disused the candelabra of sidings with long wooden platforms as high as my eyebrows spreading from easygoing gray freight sheds and at the neck of it a briskly comfortable passenger station with warm waiting room and caged ticket office full of digitally clicking undecoded information which sounded nothing like the simpler urgently expressed tones of radio-telegraphy and which except for Western Union telegrams was mysteriously occupied with routine railroad messages seemed most of the time ignored by the 24-hour staff of clairvoyant assistants to the stationmaster was for me the vital center of Gloucester half a mile from the waterfront and at the end of the line in Rockport I loved the more spacious open yard the only thing left of importance to me in that protestant town besides a couple of strug-

gling granite quarries being run out of business by the brute success of
reinforced concrete where the broad-eaved passenger platforms went right
to the bumpers at the end of the tracks excitingly close to the street beetling and threatening to cross which down to land's end you could often
see a towering engine suspiring at rest while two or three others pointed
the opposite way at the far end of open-platformed coaches waiting to
return to Boston or reserved for the morning commuter traffic on another
siding in that exfoliated terminal yard of the busy Gloucester Branch
where a little further off freight cars stood singly or in short strings and
with luck you could catch an engine panting with grateful whinnies at the
ever-dribbling iron-hooped wooden water tower shabby and gray as the
fireman climbed on top of the tender's coal pile against the humming hot
blue air of the local welkin and pulled a chain to bring down the fat pipe
nicely counterweighted. For a long time I thought that water was a secondary necessity for cooling and perhaps required replenishment only to
recover leaks not understanding that in railroad locomotives the primary
element of steam was as irreversibly expendable as the fuel that boiled it.
At the edge of that yard cinders and leaves of grass mingled smell and
color with daisies and dandelions and there was no barrier between the
tracks and the town team's baseball diamond with its neatly raked crescent
of smooth dirt and sunloving stands behind the batter's cage like a village
hearth facing the level green spread out unto the steep grassy slope that
served as right field bleachers for those who couldnt pay overshadowed by
the granite ledges of an escarpment tangled with thick woods down
through which you could drop to Rockport on a sudden descent of the
path from Gloucester by way of Whale's Jaw or the Dogtown swamp.
There was nothing to prevent a kid from making the most intimate
examination of complicated driving wheels as tall as himself with balancing segments of steel weight set into the rims opposite the connecting rod
pins an intriguing eccentricity that remained puzzling for many years
puny as those gigantic engines were by Western standards some not much
heavier than switchers and used only for short light runs with passengers
and mail. I sometimes spent all the money I had to take the ten minute
ride from our double-tracked Gloucester station to that relaxed terminal
on the all-too-well-semaphored single track that at other times I hoped
would conduct to a wreck built as an afterthought to the original line by
Rockport investors about the time of the Civil War. Alas there was no
roundhouse or turntable to watch but the high point of all my early years
was when an engineer invited me to ride the turn-around loop with him
and the whole train between his arrival and his departure at the end of the
line. I never ceased to boast about that adventure. When we moved to
Cambridge the excitement of riding all the way down the line to the roots
of the railroad at North Station on one of the trains that I'd watched crossing Washington Street a thousand times mitigated any sorrow I might
have noticed at leaving Gloucester even though I'd been as far as Salem

several times with its cheeselike sector of a roundhouse and a turntable in the middle of the Peabody sub-branch wye that came on the north side before the granite keystoned smoke-blackened tunnel running right under the main ridge of the city to the gigantic sooty echoing gray barn of an enclosed passenger station at which we got off to go to a cut-rate shoe store not getting even as far as the marshalling yard on the south side probably first ramified when Oakland was still a trading post for collecting the hides to be shipped around the Horn for nearby Lynn where shoes were made for all the world the North Shore's most miserable city which nevertheless by stocking Shelley on open shelves in the public library ignited its volatile native now Gloucester's selfmade poet whom Sam studies on his lunch hour looking for political sentiments a city more miserable save for its ocean front than Lowell which is on the main line further to the west in our Mariana grant. In dark Satanic Lynn the embanked railroad was thrown right across the darkly knotted central square on a broad 4-track overpass the kind of bridge that never turns out plausible when you build your own. With drawing you have only two dimensions to worry about and you can easily control all the details with which you choose to inform the beholders while skipping the laborious environs that would take all day in a story but with Lilliputian cities you have to deal with depths and situations in all directions. And even a separate sculpture of the real thing like a schooner can never overcome the problem of scaling down volume with surface not to mention density especially in relation to the unaltered size of molecules in the tiny atmosphere of your represented world. If you shrank a horse to the size of a mole without revising the modality of time and space its efficiency in running would be marvelously diminished. There's the question of microscopic texture too. You can't reduce the circumference of a cotton thread as you reduce the beam of your boat. Toy sails are bound to be too coarse and stiff no matter how worn the old percale they're made from and it's with good reason that professional modelmakers howsoever zealous in their miniaturization of blocks belaying pins and other such fineries hate to be asked to fit their replicas even with furled canvas. St Jonathan had much to fudge when he scaled whole systems of tissue and fabric up and down from Gulliver. The most precise and isolated model of ship or building is little more convincing than architectural rendering which is determined by vanishing points chosen according to conveniences of the drawing board. The truth is that no iota of the universe can be copied without fiction and whoever abhors fiction is fortunate if he does as well as a historical movie in offering a more or less consistent set of suggestions focussed on the one or two aspects of contemporary reality that he takes most seriously.

But if I was all too tolerant as the developer of my client's city and if even as builder of my own schooner I thought it a waste of time to attempt close imitation of my imagination's objective correlative I was still devoted to purely cognitive scholarship as far as Gloucester's real vessels were concerned. Before the war our press had been full of schooner pictures since 1920 when Gorton-Pew's *Esperanto* beat the *Delawanna* off Halifax not only because those beautiful wave-winging machines of wood raced foreigners on the high seas but also because they were very good at smuggling the water of life. Locally they had always been loved for evading Canadian customs and violating inshore fishing rights but when they joined the fight against Prohibition they became underworld heroes of the nation. But all this sentimental attention first to their honest American stealth and then to their openly competitive speed marked the last blooms of decadence. At the turn of the century schooners had been perfectly straightforward and highly profitable economic instruments no sooner launched than fitted and sent out on the briefest of trials serving fish chowder to a throng of personal friends getting their first and last look at an unspotted virgin of the sea. Each lofty forefooting team of tensely flexible sea-wings would be off alone to the banks for cod or north to Viking shores for halibut two weeks after she came down the ways or hunting mackerel anywhere between Hatteras and the Gulf of St Lawrence. Thereafter as long as the market held up summer and winter she was given no leisure in port and her capitalists laid down replacements without hesitation directly she was known to be lost. After eight or ten years any lovely vessel that survived battering hard usage and competition for good men would loosen in the seams like worn-out mothers and have to be pumped even in the best weather until they lost their tone for any kind of fishing and finally had to be sent lugging coal from Nova Scotia or sold to gentler seamen for calmer packet-boat service perhaps in the Azores or nearer Africa in the Cape Verde Islands where there was a demand for marked-down rerigged ladies. By fast passage in and out of Gloucester the high-liners generated remarkable financial turnover but what really ran up the return on investment was the profit on labor or rather on what amounted to the cost of capital seeing that fishermen by tradition lasting from the 15thC to this day ventured their own persons demanding no better guarantee against returning broke than their red-curtained bunks a little more private than the rack of an L S T and victuals somewhat more liberal sanitary and tasty than the junk and biscuit of whaling voyages especially if they liked to eat fish though as a matter of fact at least in my time the Yankees and Scandinavians and even Italians insisted on too much beef and pork to make as much money from their shares of the settlement as the Portugees in their own vessels did who were happy to eat food from the sea for all their meals cooked a hundred different ways most of them unpalatable to me. Gloucester owners in the fishery never made the market killings Salem merchants had posted over and over again in mere trade but many of those schooners must have paid for themselves in a couple of years. Delays in turnaround from slow-motion preparations and uxorious indulgences at home berths became habitual only with the installation of more and more powerful engines. By plowing the sea with brute force our fishermen calculated to make up for the time taken by pleasures ashore. Yet in Gloucester's classical days these tall Nereids of Thetis moved by wind alone could be almost twice as fast as L S T s designed fifty years later to meet the world's first really global emergency and often as not faster than yachts built for speed especially when there was anything stirring in the dielectric between Poseidon and Zeus. Yachting is an older pastime than you might think and taken more seriously by respectable sailors too. Schooner *America*, derived like its rivals from the anti-Latin idea of moving the fulcrum of a yard from the center to one end and adding a boom at the bottom edge, was racing against dukes from whom she won a sportsman's grail long before the Civil War in which she was to serve first on the wrong side and then on the right. Afterwards all the wonderful 1461-day midshipmen of the regular US Navy some of them destined for coal-burning world diplomacy in the Great White Fleet learned to sail in her on Chesapeake Bay while reading *Two Years Before the Mast*. But neither she when she lived in Gloucester nor hundreds after her built in Essex County or elsewhere for sport or show if not speed as well could hold a candle to our working matrons notwithstanding the ambivalence with which many of those fishing freighters were named after celebrated pleasure boats by commercial owners either expressing their social ambition or mocking rich men's pretensions. A true schooner is a windmill not an awning and more of a barn than a stable. It's a warehouse made to catch the air, a production machine to live in. Sailing for mere pleasure is a sin perhaps and at present for me would also be a waste of time. But back then the Harvard boy couldnt help thinking of my boat as a yacht. So I trimmed my sails like a circumspect critic.

But at least he was an athlete on the river. Long before I was born the traffic on the Charles which of course came out only in fine weather had become to my mind worthless and dull except for the neat blue Metropolitan District Police launch which we were sometimes lucky enough to see on quiet patrol up or down from Boston to Watertown where it was stopped by the scoriaceous remains of a waterpower dam and which was the closest equivalent to a Canadian Mountie's stately horse always reserving its full force and speed ever to be seen in Cambridge where the law was mostly Irish beefy unreserved and pedestrian but the racing shells jacking waterbuggers with coxwains rapping like quarterbacks beaked with trumpets and barking angrily at their galley rowers whether they caught crabs like freshmen or skimmed with phalangeal precision gave all the river traffic an appearance of organized motives to which the independent double and single sculls imparted humanistic quickening. I was very pleased to find that he might have been one of the shimmering aristocrats I'd so often watched taking solitary exercise with effortless skill too proud or too intellectual to join any of the crews. "Sometimes I like to be alone to think about things." he said. "Especially on the water." If you're going to be alone on water the Charles River is as safe as you can get. No sharks

of the ancient fossil family once the most numerous of fishes and perhaps as thriving dogfish about to take over the oceans of the earth again as whales and cod and all the rest are exterminated like bisons wolves and eagles though even the brineless excrementous Euphrates supports one of the 250 extant species doubtless because it's easier to metabolize brackish leprous waste than the inorganic chemicals of newer rivers and because no B-School entrepreneur has yet discovered any profit in their evil liver oil. As long as you don't fall out of your boat you won't even get dirty. But he was now out in the rain to take pictures of the Houses from across the river: "They're beautiful in this misty light don't you think? During vacation I'll try to paint them from these shots." He wanted to know why I was sailing my boat today of all days for a maiden voyage without a raincoat and imbrued with weather to the skin.

All over again I tried to explain myself. I repeated as plainly as possible that I'd wanted the storm and that I was glad the string had broken. We mounted the bridge and found ourselves walking up Boylston together to start my shortest route home which was straight across the Square and through the Common past the specter of the elm under which Washington sitting on his horse without illusions avowed himself commander-in-chief of assembled militias thereby vamping them into an army with a formality that must have been more rationally patriotic than MacArthur's photogenic return to the Philippines victoriously wading ashore from a bow ramp wearing sun glasses and an open collar hoping to make President when he returned to the States. When I wasnt too busy I usually stopped on the green to get astride one or more of the iron-wheeled cannon gratutitously spiked with 20thC concrete that were captured from a British fort in Boston or maybe sent down from Ticonderoga or elsewhere by Ethan Allen who has become a hero of mine simply in contrast to Benjamin Franklin thanks I believe to St Herman's historical novel though too much like John the Baptist. I knew that dreary Common all too well where nothing had happened since the Revolution dominated by a frustrating fenced-off monument to the war against slavery which would have been worth climbing seeing that there was a platformed cupola for Lincoln and a tapered summit with an even better overlook where someone else stood above him far up in the open air much higher than the Speaker of the House sits over the President during a State of the Union message. But very early I had closed my eyes and ears to Cambridge history drummed in from all sides. Except for the patined image of a once-important individual about whose name I was incurious sitting larger than life near the entrance to the Common with the pendulum of his crotch modestly bulging under one leg of his trousers anything official like a statue unless equestrian for instance Joan of Arc in Gloucester I automatically dismissed as either insipid or phony like the solmization drills we had in music classes at school intoning the do re mi notes of a song's printed staves for a few weeks after first learning to speak them in unison before we were finally permitted to sing the lyrics themselves toward the end of the term in stuffy travesty of the singing school tradition started by Cotton Mather and subsequently called Christian Harmony in the South. I had to traverse that damned Common a mile from home at least four times a week going and coming to all the things I did at Christ Church Protestant Episcopal my parish the mathematical inversion of St Peter's on Observatory Hill near where we lived in that it comprised a small congregation from a large area where I had more fun than anywhere else and truly liberal charity quite beyond the traditional benefaction of Praying Republicans though including a Sir Galahad Club based on Tennysonian murals in the Boston Public Library that featured high ritualistic misconceptions about the mystical Glastonbury symbolism of the one true Holy Cup too pure for Sir Lancelot or King Arthur in my mind Alfred's successor and contemporary of Robin Hood whereas the establishment as a whole was lower than whale-shit run by people I loved and admired from the rector whom I sometimes served at Holy Communion on Thursday morning with a red cassock under my plain Protestant cotta to the sexton whom I served putting away folding chairs after Sunday School in one class of which I was taught easier tradition by various intelligent and goodnatured Divinity School students and genial curates. The most wonderful times I ever had before the disinterested purity of fun was kinked forever by self-serving consciousness of girls were at annual Sunday School picnics when the church hired four or five orange Boston Elevated Railway busses of the type used on the Belmont run with a single seat up in front over the wheel opposite the driver and took all ranks to Beaver Brook at Waverly Oaks or to the Fellsway park in Melrose. I found nothing but totally absorbing pleasure in unlimited hot dogs hamburgers potato chips popcorn lemonade and ice cream as well as in marshalled games in which I could always win a green if not a red if not a blue ribbon pinned to my chest such as dodge-ball or three-legged racing or potato-balancing or seeking something blindfolded. All afternoon there were woods or brooks to explore and endless softball games with indistinguishable saints and sinners of all ages and several colors not that half of us werent obviously female for extra zest and brighter hues. God always granted us good weather. We were taken back to the church sunburned and sorry to disperse for home. So I had mainly the Christ Church view of Harvard across the Colonial burying ground with slate headstones and table-topped graves and iron-doored sepulchres which is to say that no more than I attended to theology did I heed the academic aura permeating my whole district of the third industrial city in Massachusetts without penetrating City Hall. Only when I got to Cambridge High and Latin with HOMER VIRGIL EUCLID superscribed by a much earlier generation of politicians on the ugliest yellow brick building I ever entered did I learn enough about it to suffer and scorn its affects. "Being out on the real Atlantic in a freezing northeaster with waves as high as the masthead wouldnt be so

much fun. It's dangerous. A lot of fishermen have been lost at sea." He was
telling me my own business. I'd lash myself to the wheel. He laughed at
me now. "Have you ever been seasick and scared at the same time?" I knew
I'd be scared and seasick but I didnt care because I'd get used to it.
Besides it wasnt to go to sea that I wanted as much as to live in a ship that
moved. I'd like to see the U S A from canals and rivers especially the Mississippi I added. He'd seen only Europe. "You like your water with the
land. So do I. It gets boring when you're too far out to see anything but
gray and blue or gray and black. There isnt enough contrast. Not even
birds to watch." To show that I knew something beyond the range of a
local yokel and also because I couldnt help japing at pretentious conceits I
asked him if he knew that the California Gull was the official state bird of
Utah. To my amazement he not only knew that fact but chastened me by
explaining it. Those seabirds came to live on Salt Lake and saved the state
from a plague of insects. But that didnt tell me why they came in the first
place. Maybe they followed the railroad construction gangs across the Sierras
is what I didnt think of then I was so flabbergasted with respect for his
learning and so mortified by the figure I was cutting. "The herring gull
should be our state bird." he said. "They lead a sacred life in Massachusetts
and Gloucester's are bolder than the rest." So I regaled him with praise of
our gulls and my estimation of their hardworking self-reliant individualis-
tic freely enterprising characters bragging that on cold and stormy nights
as well as in warm moonlight a few were always to be seen flapping or
paddling about the harbor alone while the others slept in colonies. And
when I was warm to my subject I boasted that Gloucester had more gulls
per capita than any other place in the world. Someone in Maplewood
School must have made that claim with poetic license that I'd always
respected as gospel. Not that it might not have been true for anything
anyone knew to the contrary leaving aside guano colonies. Anyway it's still
a fictive fact. I think I held my audience. Maybe I was eloquent in my
happiness at having one. Perhaps therefore I also presumed too much
when I complained that you hardly ever saw gulls in Cambridge only a
few in the winter of Depression and made bold to conclude that I wouldnt
want to be stuck there for four years of college. I continued to complain
about the city how boring it was as we paced slowly up the brick sidewalk
opposite Stadium Station's long block of gratuitously impenetrable stucco
wall with sliding doors of the same material fitted without cracks for
peeking which were opened only on home-game Saturdays for the football
crowd on specially extended rides from the normal subway passenger terminal at Harvard Square rolling affluent spectators right into the mysterious storage yard lethally ramified with third rails. I never got to see it
because the ramparts were unscalable even with a brother to give your leg
to. At that age I wasnt interested in football which was something the rich
kids spoke of and unlike yachting relevant to nothing worth my attention.
It was otherwise but not to Harvard's advantage when in my senior year at

Cambridge High and Latin I was wishing my eyes were good enough to get me into the Academy at Annapolis I finally bought a Navy-game seat available only on the home-team side from which at half-time I delighted to salute the colors and hear bloodstirring Anchors Aweigh played by a battalion of Midshipmen standing down the field as if it was a glorious legion from some clan of my own and determined to show my colors at an appropriate moment between cheers during a home-team goal-line defense against Navy I summoned up courage enough to screech sarcastically "Restrain them Harvard!" I dared not look around to see if I got any smiles but I didnt hear any laughs. If I'd done anything like that out here in Berkeley the mob would have tossed me down to the cinder track for tar and feathers. There's always more enthusiasm in the colony than in the mother country. Not that passion is enough to win in the Rose Bowl against midwestern anti-intellectuals. But I was always fascinated by the manifold forms and functions of railroads.

The mystery of railroads is in the fascination and not in the object of it yet if I could do better at praising the object I could come closer to disclosing the mystery. My attraction to tracks is only part of it and at that time I was terrified of the sinister rail that bore magical electric force not under but beside the subway's wheels like an invisible cobra in the worst of dreams it could spit silent execution at anyone who disobeyed the no trespassing signs. Partiality to railroading is not essentially due to steam's place in its history. In the whole municipal system there was no steam except at the power houses I was never taken to visit. Under the El over on Atlantic Avenue, Boston's Embarcadero founded upon the ruins of a sea barrier intended to keep French ships out of the inner harbor even as wharves once famous all over the world for their spaciously efficient warehouses and far longer than those that have survived were truncated by filling in with dirt and rubbish the heads of half a dozen harbor coves, was a belt line built in 1850 on which specially boxed double-ended steam locomotives still threaded dark lanes of commerce under interarching elms of steel along a hustling bumping waterfront and made the only connection I could ever discover (besides the single track crossing the Charles a mile or two upstream on its own trusses diagonally underneath the Cottage Farm road bridge) between the B & M and the New Haven Railroad, stuttering and clanging across slats of sunlight filtered through the beams and ties of the El canopy onto tracks imbedded in public cobblestones that I romantically believed to be shared by extraordinary trolley cars because in fact there was a live-looking wire suspended overhead yet what made me long to loiter there instead of sticking to the drearily familiar precincts of Cambridge may have been not so much anomolous engines on the throughfare as the delightful intimacy of freight cars coupled in clanking strings intricately pushed or pulled on side tracks curving off to the sides of "banana boats" and other seagoing skyscrapers or in street traffic among jolting pug-nosed Mack trucks with chain-drives and solid rubber tires worn

down to the rim clattering teams of gigantic dray horses banging hand
carts and shouting dodging pedestrians all drowned out and further darkened every now and then by the overhead squeal and roar of electric trains
belonging to the subway. Likewise the most intriguing elements of public
transportation in a city filled and leveled before the age of bulldozers were
for me the twin and triplet tandem streetcars that weaved like Swiss toys
through downtown tunnels curling and branching under the forgotten
contours of 17thC shorelines before zinging out along arbored center
strips of fine broad avenues to suburbs prosperous and educated or up
upon an arched concrete viaduct across the river to a looping transfer terminal but never on the dully familiar lines connecting with the trains
under the kiosk of Harvard Square. I took great pleasure in the uncommon
cars thus employed when they pulled up among common ones in the
underground central plaza alive with the tracked but autonomous movements of divers trolleys and sweetened by the odors of flower shops baker-
ies and newsstands below the Boston Common at Park Street but above
the main subway line. They were designed especially for fast rush-hour
loading and unloading with great wide barn doors in the center only and
attended by a fulltime conductor who left the motorman to contemplative
seclusion in a tiny compartment at the head of either end that might happen to be leading a hitched caravan sitting high in the beveled pilothouse
with a trolley wand raked back over his head like a unicorned oryx instead
of waggling behind him like the tail of a cat. I thought they could have
provided elegant urbane parcel service if it hadnt been for the invention of
internal combustion. Those handsome coaches were intriguingly akin to
the work trams parked outside the carbarn behind the Harvard subway
terminal with open flatbeds or derricks between double-ending sentry-box
cabs springing amphibolous antennas of which I sometimes caught sight
going to an emergency job maybe attached to a rolling machine-shop that
could just as well have been hitched to a bunkhouse caboose. It's trains
that make a railway a railroad. Ships to be sure are integral self-sufficient
machines for living that tantalize you with the liquefaction of their clothes
leaping and heaving all parts in one piece. They plow their own trackless
tracks in converting courses to wakes. Each if she's not a landing craft or
Liberty Ship or a pleasure class-boat is formed by unique three-dimensional curves or at least by an idiosyncratic personality resistant to standardization and each of sufficient size when manned at the helm between
"earthy parts of the globe" is free to tread tracks older than any path on
land with all sorts of latitude and longitude for error or to score untraceable wanderings of undisprovable originality. A ship is a quasi-indepen-
dent organization a temporarily closed system that can be syndicated
tontined or incorporated. Like a poem it shapes its own compartmented
space and lives its own dependently variable history as it moves in freedom
exercised by a purposeful executive whereas trains are merely a chain of
links whose fixed paths are totally determined by landscape engineers and

whose infrequent decisions to change course are usually taken even out of their crews' hands by remotely regulated or automatic switching. In wending their labyrinths they can control nothing but their own power in one of two directions. As a planner I was excited by trains for these very reasons. In a railroad dance there is no leeway for melodic caprice. Civil engineers leave no spatial uncertainty to managers who in turn reduce the temporal uncertainty of operations by scheduling in the fourth dimension. Even then as a landsman I was captivated by the charm of efficient law and order that can never be realized in the free society of steering wheels. There was solid satisfaction in merely witnessing a system of clear logical cooperation in which the waste of human and artifactual energy is less than the sum of wastes dissipated by moving parts unorganized, not to mention efficiency in overcoming inertia and friction. Once a train is articulated like movable type in a flexible composing stick you are assured that sequence syntax and punctuation will remain insusceptible to deranging influences such as weather or emotion. And not only will every vertebra follow its fellows in designated order at equal speed but no matter how complicated the way may be in bights and deviations whether piloted by locomotive or caboose with the consist in forward tension or in reverse compression every bogie and integer will trace exactly the same course even if on a double horseshoe the middle car finds itself passing both engine and caboose in the opposite direction. When put in motion no string of untracked wagons no column of barges unless converted into a train by the walls of a canal and no rope or dog or lazy serpent can be prevented from tending toward the chord of its arc. On an untracked curve the tail end is always dragged into a shortcut and no unit will exactly retrace its leader. Even California which particularly lends itself to the indulgences of automotion recognizes the danger understood in this natural law by limiting to one the number of trailers that may be hauled behind a 10-wheel rig on state highways. Freight-train information when it isnt woofed at rest like a bookstore's wall in lines and paragraphs inside a yard is wefted like a tape through all the grade crossings at which it is read before the point of delivery. But a man loves channeled energy of all kinds and he takes no less pleasure in a train for the guided force of its movement from place to place than for the knowledge it conveys by virtue of consist and routing. Whether he works on a railroad plays with a railroad or imagines a railroad he's fascinated by the management of a technology in which the driver's volition can be satisfied only by making its way in a groove. It's an inconclusive libidinal affection within the scope of greater dromenology.

I even complained about the site of Cambridge that you couldnt see the sun rise on a natural horizon as if in Gloucester I had even once taken the trouble to get up early and walk over to the back shore to see it come up on the ocean something I don't think I can claim to have experienced firsthand and clearcut until I was aboard the 1066 a long way to the west of the Pacific coast. I complained about school that we were never taught anything modern. Our shop class in the basement was called sloyd a Swedish word that like the grammatical terms used in the rote upstairs was never explained by the Irish teacher and never ceased to disconcert me in its strange isolation from any other sound that had meaning to me. Every boy while the girls were learning the tools of sewing spent part of one whole semester at a bench vise with a short piece of pine a plane and a try-square attempting to get one edge smooth and perpendicular ostensibly for its own sake only. At the end of the year three more sides were grudgingly certified to have been mutually squared with the parallel faces after a lot of grief working across the grain on two of them and then it was revealed that we had made a bread board to take home to mother. It was not until we were about to leave grammer school that hammers and saws were recognized as legitimate tools for a cabinetmaker and I began to breathe a little more easily about my disreputable interest in fastening things but it was only boys headed for the carpentry program at Rindge Tech who would learn anything about ordinary construction from the school system. At Latin School we werent even introduced to Plato's idea of the craft. Sloyd was originally intended as a discipline in tools with a view toward woodcarving and I must have sensed in it something like a patented pedagogical technique that I later seemed to encounter again in plane Euclid class because I finally decided it was a proper name as in the frankly identified Palmer Method of handwriting which I hated more than music or anything else ever inflicted upon me during my entire sojourn in Cambridge. The only man at the Peabody School besides a janitor was the sloyd teacher. By an effort of imagination I could conceive of male instruction in arithmetic geography history reading or even writing and spelling as the kids at Shady Hill got it though under the fancy titles of mathematics social studies and other such affectations where men of some sort were both allowed and willing to waste their manhood but not in Penmanship. Year after year this brainless discipline was inescapable inexorable and futile. It was like a slowly progressing course of calisthenics in which you can't drop the elementary drills even after you've become an athlete. In our most advanced year we still began the penmanship period of the day by warming up with a pencil in the simpler arm-moving exercises before we repeated them and completed the repertory with our pens usually in fear of blots dipping the scratchy nibs too frequently and not deep enough into our wells of black ink sunk flush into the upper right corner of our newly spotted desks already defaced by earlier recalcitrant occupants of the darkly varnished 19thC rooms with spintered softwood floors. First with stiffened fingers we made circles over and over each other in a series of separate well-emphasized hoops then rolled them out for a couple of inches or a full line like a tightly coiled spring or a corrugated steel culvert in three-quarter view. That was for one of the two basic motions. The second was up and down to a slightly greater height than the other at first as leaning sheafs of wheat on parade stitched together by goosesteps then as

long fences of almost upright faggots close-packed all across the paper and
again as smaller and smaller tightly clustered pickets like files of soldiers
leaning forward on their march to the right until at last in preparation for
actual writing by way of recapitulating the elements of Mr Palmer's
method the neatly tied fasces were placed as nearly vertical diameters of
some more spokeless wheels to form a landscape of graceful shapes like the
letter Phi all with "positive and assertive movement" of the elbow from
the shoulder. We slowly progressed through letters of the alphabet copied
in standard shape and size and groups of affinitive letters before being
rewarded with orthographical words. And it was a long time after we were
each as letter-perfect as we could ever agree to become before paradigm
sentences yielded to creative freedom in paragraphs timidly elaborated
from traditional topics. I began to discern a kind of rhythmic rote in this
rite that was not entirely unredeeming. Maybe I even wouldnt have
minded the invention and pedantic dissemination of the Method if we had
been drilled only in the kinesthetics of Is and Os. But I was furiously and
impacably rebellious because the mystic guru's disciples dictated not only
old-fashioned sanctimonious feminine characters originally introduced as
modern but also the insufferable technique of making them without the
Godgiven use of fingers for anything else than jigs which I had suspected
all along was the main purpose of our tedious exercises. I was willing to
observe authoritarian ends but I balked at the means. You were supposed
to move your whole arm with wrist and fingers fixed like a drive-rod.
That's what made the Method infuriating. "Don't use your fingers!" was
the vigilant teacher's angry watchword. We heard it wearily intoned a
thousand times. "Not with the fingers!" Only the docile girls of the class
made any consistent effort to comply. Whenever the teacher wasnt watching me personally whom she naively trusted I coolly and assiduously
cheated. In almost everything else I was a good pupil for I could usually
persuade myself of some ultimate disciplinary benefit in the boring things
we were told to do even when they appeared needlessly unpleasant. Like
the absurd conditions of a dream most of the practices in what I regarded
as outmoded and sterile education nevertheless seemed as natural in life as
the fun I had after school. On the whole I'm glad they did. For instance
we were encouraged when our hands were unoccupied to bend our arms
over the back of our seat for the sake of healthy posture the chief element
of what was called hygiene when presented as a partitioned subject of no
intrinsic interest to me but suggesting a contribution to the formation of
athletic or military shoulders and of course as I got older it was nice to see
some of the girls follow my supererogatory observance of the advice
although the ones who didnt were generally the ones I'd most have liked
to feel. Yet I saw no personal development no useful skill and no freedom
for personality or plastic expression in the Palmer Method. I vehemently
preferred to take advantage of free will with every last tiny muscle and
ligament of my sword arm and to double the recommended number of

words per line. Palmer's singlehanded inhibition of temperament in millions of children especially girls putatively to escape the earlier otiose tradition of ornate festoons and curlicues was probably once justified in the mass by a crying need for uniform legibility and celerity without the pains of writer's cramp wherever commerce and administration employed scriveners but in my day the typewriter had long since proved itself even at Gorton-Pew's Main Street office in a corner of which my father still settled fishing trips with pen and ink. In any case Palmer's calligraphy would have been far too prim for the vexations of Grub Street. My new companion didnt know what I was talking about because he'd lived only in suburbs and had gone only to private schools that probably encouraged nothing but a humanistic and inefficient font of cursive lettering which emulated type while denying regimentation and urged their students a fancy word for pupils to write their own myths or to build stage sets instead of bread boards.

It wasnt surprising that my new friend's name turned out to be Rodney but to a trifling degree it did modify a prejudice I shared with my Catholic neighbors against sissy-names or at least it extracted that one from the class that included untouchables like Harvey Roy Lester Claude Percy and Ronald. He wouldnt allow me to call him Mr Adams. When he asked about my family I was afraid that he'd get too personal and I didnt want to have to tell him that my father was on the W P A so I drummed up a blizzard of questions to keep his mind on himself as you can do with some teachers when it's urgent to temporize once you know their favorite subject. I was perfectly aware that all his kind of people hated Sacco Vanzetti Harry Hopkins and Franklin Roosevelt and thought that the unemployed were simply too dumb or lazy to earn their living properly. I also assumed that I had to avoid foreign affairs as a politically sensitive subject. But he only asked if the rest of the family disliked Cambridge too and when I allowed that I thought so with certain reservations on Peggy's behalf he gently voiced wonder that we didnt go back where we came from. In my judgment it was impossible to make even a very nice grownup rich kid who might have read Dickens understand that when you're poor you don't have the money to move from one place of poverty to another. I would have burned with shame if he'd been given cause to suspect that we got our Thanksgiving turkey basket padded and garnished with potatoes squash celery cranberry sauce walnuts and olives from the Jefferson-Jackson Democratic Club of Cambridge buying our vote as if we didnt have plenty of reasons for hating Republicans. But he didnt seem to notice that I made no answer and he put his arm over my shoulders in a friendly manner that was enormously pleasing but made me so ill at ease in trying to determine the appropriate response if any that I stopped talking until he withdrew it. I began to question him about the university an institution for which I felt a great deal less affinity than for the federal government in Washington. To this day I'm much too awed by the privileges of any college. He invited me to turn off with him to Lowell House before *Gloucesterman* and I continued our long voyage home. And that's how I happened to go to Harvard.

I didnt stay long but I saw enough. It was a matter of honor not to lend myself more than politely to such luxury. I was glad to get a few cookies out of it but I declined as humiliating the invitation to take off my shoes and socks and dry them at the fire. Besides I knew they'd just get wet again. But I was downright curious about the place and tried to compare it with my imagination of the living quarters at Annapolis where all my fictional heroes were appointed to the best of all possible educations without cost to themselves all social distinctions obliterated by equal salaries and uniforms from the same tailor devouring marine architecture and engineering and enjoying summer cruises in a lovely standard curriculum of naval science. Even after I undeceived myself as to the U S Naval Academy judging by its graduates and became aware that most of its alumni preferred little yellow men to Nazis as the enemy I took comfort in the decent legacy of Captain Mahan native of West Point reflected in the doctrine of the highest of his students' students under whom I served who almost alone in the government understanding the strategy of seapower and the new tactics of naval bombardment in support of seaborne aerial and land attack especially in view of the fact that unlike the home of the British Empire which was also outflung for easy pickings the islands of Japan had history's greatest navy in opposition instead of defense and were therefore hopelessly vulnerable to the negative economic power of submarines estimated that the enemy was practically defeated already and before he died opposed it is said the cruel drama of dropping even one of the two absolute-entropy bombs merely to scare the Russians and save some thousands of American lives like mine. If I'd had normal eyesight I might have been serving under him at a higher level. But when I went to Harvard that day before the war I still had some wildly delusory hope that I could improve my astigmatism or get some special dispensation. Later during high school I did eye exercises that I got out of a book because the optometrist didnt believe in them for obvious reasons and ate a lot of carrots which have always been cheap but at the time of my visit to Rod's place I was more worried about the position of my eyes for I had discovered that my nose moved when I closed first one eye and then the other. Within two or three years I was also worried about my muscles not for getting a commission but for general self-respect and put myself to sporadic regimens of chinning and push-ups because I had noticed that my thighs were thicker than my biceps and at about the time I discovered the swelling of my nipples and lumps in my balls I was also embarrassed to find that too young my prick was getting big. But all that came after Harvard. We had gone into an entry and up one of many like staircases in many like entries to the second floor of four or five as if into a townhouse or an apartment building instead of a proper dormitory or barracks which should have

longitudinal corridors like a ship's. I disapproved of this vertical compartmentation of the building but I held my tongue. There were man-of-the-
world voices from the landings mostly broad of accent and self-esteeming
especially on the lower floors though then in my inexperience of ruthless
varieties I mistook them for weaklings in the ways of the world. Perhaps
not one of them had not the sound of the highest type of amateur reserve
officer for the war that was to interrupt his career along with the lives of a
majority from the minor leagues but merely defer his quick success in
Business or Law or duties of government north or south or east or west as
an obvious member of the oligarchy. A few years later their successors not
even half way through college would become ensigns after ninety days in
some emergency reserve midshipmen's school like the one in a converted
hulk fixed to Manhattan Island on the Hudson's bank near Harlem.
Despite all vulgar prejudice against a Harvard man no one questions his
ability to govern sharks himself a Veblen gentleman of "divine assurance
and imperious complaisance as of one habituated to require subservience
and to take no thought for the morrow." None has ever had to rise to a
wardroom through the hawsepipe the way I got to Harvard by a such a
short-lived and unofficial connection. You'd think a native of Gloucester
would be entitled to some special consideration his town's having been
exhorted and practically supervised by preachers doctors teachers town
clerks and tavern keepers trained by Harvard when it was still austere. Yet
the only Harvard man I knew in the Navy who went to sea without his
gloves on was the crew's Jew a skinny little radio operator by the name of
Michael Einstein who behind his back was occasionally called Mike the
Kike as I was called Mick the Prick. No ship's cousin he before the mast.
At first I thought he was despised simply for his dual misfortune of birth
and affiliation but I had to agree after trying to befriend him that it was
not pleasant to lose every argument before it could begin in conversation
facing the precocious and authoritative knowledge of an undergraduate
who had matriculated a couple of months before he was drafted. Our
Harvard supply officer Mr Dodge who for all the use he was as O D in
navigation or discipline might just as well have been supercargo in the old
tradition coming right out of the very digs that I had visited wouldnt
have anything to do with him no doubt for quite other reasons since there
was no question of argument across ranks. Before Elizabethan times an
officer was allowed to hit a seaman once with impunity and after that the
man could fight back but in my navy there was no defense at any round of
wounding words and no gentleman would take advantage of such ascendancy over another. To squelch his incongrously high and mighty squawks
Einstein was openly yclept Chicken Little and he looked just the part his
scrawny neck and clipped hair with wide eyes and ears sticking out as if
perpetually astonished at what he'd heard was about to happen in the
welkin rather than The Brain as he preferred. "Hey the sky is falling
Chicken Little the sky is falling!" you'd hear at least once a day somewhere

in the ship from anyone who might be feeling magnanimous or condescending as well as spiteful and from no one as often as from silly black donkey-dong Clovis. It's true that Chicken Little was an alarmist about injustice and he never took the taunts as tolerant jibes of mild distaste but as poisoned arrows of hatred which he affected not to feel at all. If he'd shown a little courtesy to potential friends like me there'd have been less need to overdose himself with belligerent anaesthesia. I suppose and he certainly supposed that he was a brilliant chess player. He missed his peers so acutely when he found that not a single shipmate knew how to play the game that he offered to teach me. I managed to learn the general objective but got no more than a smatter of the rules because the first session was as withering as an oral competition in mathematics and so abusive to my ego as a man of catholic taste that I flew off the handle in a petulant rage and he trumped me with silent contempt. I hardly ever spoke to him again. He was also insufferable to his immediate associates in the radio shack for the arrogant manner in which he drew their attention to his negligently triumphant speed and accuracy in both wireless telegraphy and typewriting but as he hated me most of all for my reputedly elite technical rate which he'd never been offered a chance at I was made to suffer his most insolent disdain for failing in the effort to teach myself the Morse code at any speed and scarcely managing an upper-case typewriter even when I looked at the keys. Though as a matter of fact I was glad to have something to grant the radio operators it was not much fun having him lord it over my modesty and our mutual enmity was swollen thereby. If he'd been the ship's clerk a Yeoman with crossed feathers under his crow instead of radiation bolts whom everyone would have been constrained to deal with humbly as having a self-important bureaucratic stranglehold even when the position doesnt go to his head like that guy who came in to buy a five-foot shelf of books a Yeoman type if I've ever seen one I doubt that he could have survived many ventures out on deck late at night in the dark of the moon that for an 0800-to-1600 below-deck office man would scarcely have escaped somebody's malignant notice. Born troublemakers are easier to identify than born toolmakers before they get placed in an organization. There's a lot of difference between being in the minority and being the minority but that prickly little turd as lethal to a man's pride as a hunk of radium soaking in a bowl of heavy water was never worn down by all the bastards like me. He was certainly a sea lawyer about his own rights yet I must say that when he was so inclined he could do his duty with punctilio in a certain measure intended to mock those who made him do it but also I'm sure simply under the urge for perfection that often shows itself in men too able and energetic for their permitted means of livelihood who are intellectually compelled to turn some customary part of their duty into ceremony for its own sake if they arent themselves given the power of martinets. On anchor detail to which he was extraneously assigned during brief operations that took place all too seldom when there was no need for

his skills in the radio shack or elsewhere he stood like a conscientious boy
scout at the very peak of the bow above the boatswain and his deck gang
who were assembled to unshackle the portside's great chthonic double-
biting sea-stake for its headlong dive on signal from the bridge, ready
with the halyards to raise the union jack as soon as our hook touched water
in a deep splash drowned out by the fast thundrous roar of hugely running
chain that began before and lasted long after that instant, or in the reverse
procedure to lower it as the pudgy black hammerhead quite unlike the
slenderly speared skeletons that used to be forged for schooners in the
furnaced shed hard under the railroad drawbridge on the Annisquam River
slowly broke the surface on its groaning way back up to its niche of seagoing captivity by which point most of the clanking hawse-train's twisted
double-looped vertebrae had already been cranked in by the rumbling
low-geared electric capstan while the seamen far from having to wind the
spindle like blind draft horses singing chanties had little to do except hose
them down watching for kinks and dropped stiffly link by link over a brutally grooved lip down a ten-inch pipe to coil themselves in the clangrous
locker below. The ordinary manner of performing Chicken Little's special
task was to approximate the moment for hoisting or lowering flag from
the bosun's shouting gestures and the ship's own sounds since the anchor
itself was normally out of sight from the little semicircular enclosure at
the base of the jackstaff but he would lean far out over the bow with a display of gratuitous chicken-shit pedantry to determine for himself the exact
instant of the anchor's refracted transition from one element to the other
before snapping back to consummate the ceremony as quickly and precisely as if to set a chronometer or jerk the lanyard for a cannon salute at
sunset. After demobilization began and a general thinning-out of crews he
was transferred to another L S T at Manila and I took over those formalities with an ease that one could not have expected of anyone without my
liturgical experience as a Christian which of course was utterly unnoticed
and irrelevant to the Executive Officer to the Chief Quartermaster responsible for the whole Ship's Control gang or to the piratical-looking Boatswain who never could spare a deck hand for such academic exercises.
Without profaning the sacramental precision proper say to ringing a
sanctus bell I performed in an efficiently relaxed and fairly respectful manner as I had learned to do in working out my own way to light the candles
from the lucifer struck against the sole of my street-worn shoe in the sacristy to ignite the white paraffined wick in the sliding brass tube of the
candle snuffer and then at the altar to make the final transfers of flame in
rapid succession through the extended end of my upstretched arms as in
black cassock buttoned snugly from neck to metatarsus before vesting
myself in the white cotta lovingly hemmed as for a doll's wedding dress by
needleworking sisters moving at my own pace back and forth before the
altar genuflecting to the tabernacle at every crossing of the median without hesitation or failure in my feathery touch of flame or smoking up the

pure wax of the tall thick tapers by a false move or knocking them askew in the attempt to end each swing not on but exactly next to each point of conflagration, and in returning after the Mass again without my cotta to extinguish the serene spears of yellow holiness first the Gospel light which could never be left burning unguarded by the Epistle so gently that the brass cup now brought into play by having twisted the unlighted stick on its axis painlessly extinquished the living fires without clapping the life out of them in smothering puffs of black smoke that would have discolored the snuffer and given off an air of clumsy haste as if uneasy at having been left alone to wrap up the ritual I was trying to catch up with the congregation already going about its ordinary affairs or crudely scraping their delicately gilded collars that made ringed capitals to the unfluted wax columns.

Einstein had plenty of spunk withal. For instance he entered one or two of the ship's boxing bouts with the most nearly matched men to be found who had never expected to be able to express their animosity officially but in fact could do little against his feckless flailing fury except wait it out a tactic that could bring nothing very much better than a draw in a two-round fight. Apparently he had learned to take care of himself. Once when I was still hoping to make friends he confided that his father as a boy had lost an eye from the ragged disk of an open tin can in a Lower East Side street attack. At last the one-eyed Jew's son became the talk of the ship by putting on the gloves to spar with Kane who was so surprised and grateful that he pulled his punches like a fond bulldog playing with a kitten but no friendship blossomed there likewise and either the invitation or its acceptance was never repeated their acquaintance on the contrary soon turning into dangerous hostility the climax of which I happened to witness following some squabble between them in the chow line when I heard him scream at the Killer "Go take a flying fuck at a rolling hoop! You're in the Navy now not in the gutter!" as he ran up the ladder to temporary safety on the bridge. Fortunately for him Kane's astonishment at his bravery was great enough to sublimate as laughter and even more fortunately he happened to be transferred off the ship only a day or two later before anybody could start brooding about the unprecedented lese majesty. It's hard to imagine such grit in an inmate of Lowell House. The only man in the ship's company I hated constantly and mercilessly as I now hate Nixon for his perniciously mawkish use of television of whom however I don't have to be cooped up with on daily duty to heighten my perspicacity was Einstein's most poisonous enemy one of the quartermasters who a couple of years older and a little smarter would have been an officer on some admiral's staff now running for Congress I read in the Tribune and possibly yet to make Senator before Democrats catch up with Republicans in Maine which is essentially a very decent state by the surname of Love whose family riches were made known to the ship at large but always called Phil his christian diminutive by officers and men alike except the two of us his foes in deference to his social status charming face and generally assumed influence headed for Dartmouth where he could ski and play hockey all winter without encountering Jews. But I'm not sure he was any happier after his scapegoat had departed from our tight little bridge gang because he had no categorical grounds upon which to turn the crew against me whom he addressed as Cheapman and still lacked popular sanction to broadcast his inexhaustible venom against President Rosenfeldt whose removal from power had left the rage of most New England oligarchs scanning for new personal focus. Like Mike Einstein though for reasons of class rather than reasons of culture Phil Love ironically approved my disavowals of Harvard affiliation despite my true reputation as a defender of the nation's late patrician educated in Cambridge.

Thanks in part to F D R I can't help feeling kindly toward Harvard when I'm not in its presence. Rod's quarters opened my eyes to Oxford colleges and all the other rooms for English bachelors that I later read about and the memory has not been driven from my gallery of fixed images by the impression of Caleb's shambling burrow which accomodates itself rather to the shabby Russian pattern in my penurious magazine of visual notions though also enviable in my present condition. Lowell House unlike Caleb's roachy mountain of housekeeping rooms had a dining hall with waitresses and menu options. Rod wanted me to meet his roommate a schooner yachtsman and member of the N R O T C who probably would have said WELCOME ABOARD while heartily shaking my hand not understanding how uncomfortable it is for a poor incult townie lad to cope with fashionable introductions far above his station but luckily he was hobnobbing at the Lampoon and I got away before he returned to discover for his ingenuous companion the contemptible limitations of my maritime savvy. It was a well-appointed suite those two lived in with private bath and maid service each with his own bedroom study as well as all the space he could wish in front of the fireplace in their common chamber. Notwithstanding the restrictions upon their liberty of entertainment and usage in respect to girls compared with the liberties of Caleb and many of the independent students at Berkeley they were destined for officers' wardrooms simply by virtue of a Bursar's card as sirs or dukes from the outset. I did not conceal my enthusiasm for the manly lines and crimson colors of the seductively comfortable room in which I sat surrounded by Veritas devices and expensive bibelots that seemed more appropriate to cultivated characters of fiction than to college boys and for a few minutes almost stole away my loyalty to the uniformed vigor of fouled anchors and pennants of blue and gold. I'd be willing to bet that before the war was over they both made it to Lieutenant Commander at least. Rod kept the conversation going with stories about the House as a worldly Senior affecting to deprecate their importance in his personal thesaurus of facts. One that didnt come back to mind until I was able to grasp its import after nearly four years of a high school that preserved respectful lore of Harvard in a few of its classrooms was that the Houses with their quasi-English tutorial system were endowed by a Yale alumnus after being turned down in New Haven. Endowment underlies everything centered in the Yard academic as well as architectural and maybe that's one place where culture justifies the supremacy of property rights. At any rate Harvard men whether skinny Marxists on scholarship or incipient stockbroking leaders of Class fund drives always seem to be occultly gifted with the economic advantage of mastering interrelationships between mind and matter. It's surprising not to hear of that faculty so fully developed even at Yale where they seem to be more interested in artifacts which brings to mind an old song that never reached Cambridge High and Latin in my time because it was then superannuated and which I didnt hear until Mr Drake who was a Duke man sang it to me mocking what he had heard from Mr Dodge in his cups who'd learned it oddly enough not from his fellows at raw brick Eliot House which Rod and I had skirted opposite the site of the subway's original powerhouse once fed by coal carried up the river and long since removed to a less offensive location but from his father before him of some class so far back that I'd like to think it was carrying on something started in F D R's student era whom I can easily imagine crooning it as he mixed White House cocktails for Harry Hopkins and Winston Churchill

> Oh they don't have any tail down at Yale
> Oh they don't have any tail down at Yale
> In place of fornication
> They all practice masturbation
> Oh they don't have any tail down at Yale!

But that day I got into Harvard I was interested in an innocent story of tintinnabulation. Through gleaming perspicuous panes in Rodney's handsomely curtained array of double-hung Georgian mullions I could see over the arched tunnel of the courtyard's main gate the lofty blue-tipped tower which he told me had been intended for clocks but altered at the last minute to accept a gift of bells purchased from a Russian monastery just as the Soviets attempting to fulfill some five-year plan were about to melt them down for bronze in the manner of Henry the Eighth despoiling his abbeys of statuary bearing gold that was not to go to waste. In our own Revolutionary times brass made the best ordnance such as "the noblest piece" of all a mortar landed at Gloucester in a British transport taken prize by one of our privateers and sent to Washington at the Cambridge Common where it was dubbed The Congress then a noble body in whose latterday degenerate continuation at the time of which I speak served Hamilton Fish of Dutchess County notorious to my kind a Harvard man who fought F D R his own constituent as a traitor to his class the charge of which being taken up by such as QM3C Love in the petty opposition only made electoral hay in my more numerous faction for The Man himself who by the way telling Churchill what his enemies accused him of heard in reply from the lips which a few years later rejoiced to intimates that he had been "brought up in that state of civilization when it was everywhere accepted that men are born unequal" as betokened by his having kept a manservant all during youthful days of financial embarrassment in wildly enterprising military journalism that in England they had no classes. It happened that the belfry had begun to sound soon after I got there. Half-hearted shouts and groans of protest responded from various elevations and unseen reaches of the House but as the exotic changes kept ringing proved desultory in the manner of a demonstration echoing by abbreviated rote long after losing its force and conviction through regressively unsuccessful repetitions of the original protest which I was too untutored to have criti-cized psychologically for its ostentatious selfgratulating aestheticism of prankish cast. Since the bells were not melodious to my ears either, I was at first gleeful to hear that all the gentlemen except those involved deplored the formation of a Lowell House Society of Russian Bell Ringers designed to perpetuate this "amiable discord" and "organized clangor" that was being planted as a tradition-in-the-making by a handful of eccen-tric musicians equally selfconscious. I hinted at a dispraising comparison to the sweet carillon of Our Lady of Good Voyage in Gloucester said to be the country's first though I had to apologize for its Roman Catholic aus-pices and I was glad to show a wry face as partisan of majority taste at Harvard. Then Rod told me that the House wag had written a letter to the President of the United States asking if the bells could be named after him Harvard's most illustrious living graduate and F D R had graciously assented only to be awkwardly informed by the misgiven House Master that the offer was bogus whereupon the princely politician who was to become by his fourth term the de facto chief magistrate of the world as the one of the Big Three most instrumentally concerned with all Theaters of the war replied that he'd rather have a baby or a dog named after him any-way. I was prepared to take this gossip as illustrating F D R'S generous goodhumored victory over obtuse young Republicans including the anec-dotist himself but after a moment's reflection I believed that Rod was only boasting about the importance of Lowell House in the larger affairs of the universe and when I bethought myself that he had referred to F D R with simple respect as President Roosevelt and not with some reactionary slur I felt a flicker of otherwise unsupported hope that he too might be a traitor to his class. It all goes to show that there are Harvard men and there are Harvard men and that the Democrats among them including most of the faculty can be prepared for decent politics just as well at St Grottlesex as at Peter Stuyvesant High School. According to Love and all other others who hated the man I loved as the father of my country and later as com-mander-in-chief of the United Nations the best argument for opposing him by means of monied free speech seconded by practically every opin-ionated voice in the press was that he had not been able to succeed in busi-ness. But his picture was on the wall of almost every barber and cobbler shop every little neighborhood store in Gloucester and Cambridge and there's no reason to think the proprietors were not praying to stay solvent just as hard as the big businessmen were striving to resume dividends who in the darkest days of Depression had been glad enough to display the Blue Eagle his personal crow under which sign he had marshalled them to save themselves at the cost of recognizing unions under the persuasion of suspended anti-trust laws before the anachronistic Supreme Court killed it off to save the country from social planning thereby laying him open to the charge of running the U S A by opportunistic pragmatism without any policy except that of fomenting the unworthy poor to class-hatred against the rich. There must have been a few constructive Republicans at least in New England simply by virtue of being impressed by a strong Democrat though perhaps not deeply enough to make them into angels but naturally they did not like the corniness of Fireside Chats or the socialistic sound of people singing "Happy Days are Here Again!" and as good Hamiltonian Federalists caught in the illogic of their own phony slogans about self-determination where self stands for property the Overseers were just scrupulous enough about the complexity of our political economy to keep Harvard in the ambiguous business of studying its regulation while they waited for someone ungovernable like Nixon to come along promising to ungovern.

Yet there must have been millions of people like me who were secretly pleased by the truth of Republican accusations that our President had never had to meet a payroll because in my class of political royalists his pictures framed in parlors or calendared in kitchens hung more numerous than crucifixes on the walls of households harboring no wish contrary to *saving the system* professed by Landon and Knox another Chicago newspaper colonel who probably no more believed such campaigns as their own than did most core Republicans when their overriding motive was to get HIM as His Imperial Majesty out of office by fuzzing the issues in order to prepare the American mind for their future candidates who did and do and will serve the Prince of Lies more frankly. HIM—THAT MAN—who came out of Harvard who loved schooners who united for a while all factions of the anti-Republican Party like the Indians South Africans Australians New Zealanders Canadians and Northern Irish joined in allegiance to one king and who was treated by the other English-speaking Former Naval Person not only as a congenial fellow Anglican head of government though of national stock rival to the mother country whose biceps he was invited to feel which a great prizefighter was said to have envied but also as the ranking chief of state whose wheelchair he felt himself privileged to push through the White House with memories of Sir Walter Raleigh spreading his cloak for Queen Elizabeth and whom despite misunderstandings about the future of the British Empire he loved with unprecedented respect as sovereign of the world until too worn out to govern the Soviets. The Day of Infamy was as nothing to the seismic shock of HIS death as if warning that in other hands the center of earth's atom would not hold five months longer. It was inauspicious even to Japan itself whose premier perhaps cloudvoyantly shuddering for his people expressed for us his Christian enemies a "profound sympathy" passing over the dead man's most definite tort which should have been infamous whereby in Executive Order 9066 he played fast and loose with the Constitution without a squawk from whites or blacks or reds or Jews by driving over 100,000 yellow people most of them voting citizens into unsympathetically paternalistic concentration camps having deprived them even of their property and wherein he revealed an insensitivity which on the part of his truly imperial friend W S C who was by his own boast better schooled in self-expression than in self-control would have been small cause for surprise. In the end F D R idiosyncratic in both and generous with press conferences was more enigmatic than Joe Stalin. But I knew nothing of his blindspots or his lapses or his opacity that earth-shaking night when I got the fatal news like an arrow thudding into the heart of my own affairs which were perfectly unexceptionable as matters for an enlisted serviceman's exclusive concentration leaving politics economic struggle and even most of the daily news to civilians who we were given to understand had an easier time of everything and made no sacrifice worth mentioning compared with our emotional hardship and personal fear voluntary or otherwise. As it often happens in systems cranked up for peak loads the destitute old commuter coach conscripted for emergency service on the Pennsy route between Chicago and New York swaying and faltering like a cow pressed into a troop of twenty mule teams had groaned along much of the way half empty and I was huddled around my own chest like a homeless dog in shivering sleep on the lowbacked hardplush seat grimy with refined coal peacoat backwards over my shoulder as a blanket midway between the draft that pushed in through the rattles of the door ahead under pressure of forward motion and the more generous swirl of April weather that was sucked in with the exterior noise of greaseless steel traction through the door behind me which kept banging open after anyone passed through it without giving its latch the special attention it required having no notion of complaining as a noncommissioned sailor to one of the scowling brass-buttoned zombies that stumped up or down the aisle toward more comfortable cars every hundred miles or so about the stone-cold radiator which I'm sure was turned off only because the car had been too hot crossing Indiana at twilight when it was full of restless people including officers of all branches who were to drop off at their home towns before bedtime when long after midnight the jolting stop at Pittsburgh woke me up. In dazed bewilderment at coming out of dream with my head against the cold window hardly transparent between dried streaks of Midwest bituminous dust inside and out to stupidly face the dim yellow lights of a nearly deserted platform below me and stare down on a forlorn baggage cart with a few blackened sacks of mail its dangled tongue

seemingly rusted to splotched asphalt all skylines screened out by the canti-
levered roof under which the train had come to rest I was terrified by the
abrupt silence that for a moment contained nothing but compressed air
relaxing its tension. At first the shock that followed so closely upon the
phase-change of my consciousnes struck me as an ordinary jarring interruption of travel no more significant than the unwelcome intrusion of a candy
vendor waking me up in the middle of the night to offer outrageously
expensive comforts and its message seemed hardly worth the effort of decoding. A small black boy far too young under New Deal child-labor legislation
to be working at that time of night had climbed into the forward vestibule
and flinging open the door to hawk his papers was crying out in harsh Elizabethan sing-song "Ruse-uh-velt deceasèd! Ruse-uh-velt deceasèd!" I slowly
grasped the words one at a time subject and predicate. In my stunned loneliness for the next eight or nine hours until swallowed up by the imperturb-
able roar of Manhattan I felt as if benevolent power had passed forever from
the face of the earth and as if all national resistance to fascism would cease at
once no matter what the United Nations did to Hitler.

That's about all there was to my affiliation with Harvard. I didnt want
to meet the roommate and I didnt want to overtax my confidence yet courage and invention was called for to take courteous leave before it was suggested. In short I left as quickly as I could a diffidently interested little
locofoco with a crumpled toy boat so pathetically cherished in such singular play that together they had deserved to have their picture taken
unaware. It at last became clear to me that photography had been the
cause of our riparian encounter. Not that I wasnt pleased to have been a
camera's object meaning to me in a certain sense its hero because in those
days not everyone was a photographer and I thought there was a science to
that performing art as well as an expense that flattered me or excited at
the prospect of getting visual proof of Gloucesterman's beauty both just
before and just after her glory if I came back to Lowell House in two or
three weeks and I had every intention of taking him up on his generous
offer of prints especially as my indefinite acceptance made it easier for me
to get out of there without having to propose or avoid proposing the terms
on which we were parting. With a sense of satisfied liberation I picked up
the weatherbeaten *Gloucesterman* from where I'd careened her on the Persian carpet and made one last monstrance of her wreckage for Rod's edification. Thanks for showing me your room. "Goodbye. Don't forget to
come back for your pictures when they're developed!" Thanks for the
cookies. Goodbye. "Goodbye." Goodbye. I escaped at full speed free as a
gull and steered my crippled vessel through the throngs in Harvard Square
past the subway kiosk where the cabs swishing with pleasure at the prosperous rain were having no wait for fares on past the University Theater
where they insisted upon "community singing" before the Saturday morning shows while I squirmed with impatience when I'd had enough money
to come see great pictures like *Wings of the Navy* with Helldiver open-

cockpit biplanes lost in white fog or funny ones like *Ali Baba and the Forty Thieves* from which I first heard the words "inflation" and "deflation" as flying carpet commands at a time of the latter or pretentious ones like *Alice in Wonderland* which enkindled my critical faculty by the visual sentimentality that totally belied the imagination of the book as established for me by Sir John Tenniel or cinematic novelties like *The Three Little Pigs* Walt Disney's first superanimated cartoon in color the highest artistic point of his career in which I didnt yet detect subversion, movies being my makeshift for edifying arts and travel, below the sharp wooden steeple of the Unitarian church guarded by four small spires which were soon to be lost in the '38 hurricane and along the old burying ground that separated it from the low blunt belltower of George Washington's Episcopal fane of God in all three aspects, straight through the Common past Abraham Lincoln drier than I under his granite spire and the ghost of George Washington's military elm keeping the forbidding Hotel Commander on my left a citadel of forceful transients where I'd once seen some Midshipmen up for a game trooping out the door like ordinary laughing college boys except for the breathtaking dignity of their winter overcoats and caps of blue so deep it was black bossed with gold-bright brass between a pair of brick apartment houses full of well-fixed old couples and single ladies and further on beyond a baffling yellow music school to the Hotel Continental on my right a less formidable citadel of genteel transients where down a step from the sidewalk I could buy Baby Ruth candy bars at the standard price when I had a nickel on the way home from my Sunday job at the church because I was always too hungry even when I was saving up for something much more important, now hotfooting it masts on high up Garden Street opposite I guess the house Thomas Wolfe used to hang around while he was reading ten books a day. The irregular brick of the sidewalk changed to granular pink dirt and back to brick again before I reached a footing of cracked concrete across from the dominating grounds of the Observatory where they let kids coast in the winter and where even now I could have ducked behind a copse inside an open gate of the high iron fence and relieved the pressure that drove me if I'd still been wearing shorts that you could simply lift the inside corner of without the fuss of buttons or flaps and if fear of breaking the law hadnt overcome my agony. If I'd known what the professor from Missouri was doing up there on the hill I would have gone and pissed with all my might right against the Observatory wall because in playing around with cosmic double gyres to show the absurdity of our local distance scales his only purpose was to subvert my more satisfactory hypothesis that earth is the sacramental center of it all. I never had much interest in astronomy but at C H L I was suddenly beset with an appetite for theoretical physics that conflicted with my ambition failing Annapolis to get into the Webb Institute for naval architecture and marine engineering which later I found on a visit to be directed by an officer of the Spanish-American War in a celluloid collar. A whole series of even more untimely and ill-paired contrarieties of passion ended in such mutual nullification that I not only never went to college at all but I never learned to navigate even by dead reckoning which I'm sure Rodney Adams mastered easily enough along with celestial calculation though no more mathematical by temperament than I on his way to the government of men. But within a week I grew shy of my social contact at Harvard and soon I was so ashamed of my behavior as a rich man's client that I never went back. Swiftly on the way home with *Gloucesterman* I also left behind on my right the Botanical Garden whose merely naturalistic purpose seemed so dull that I was never tempted to enter it.

It was at the artificers' shop on 23rd St that I first encountered a case of good non-commissioned leadership not appointed but earned making the most of fortune's accidents to be sure yet not by virtue of class in the person of Joe Kalish the foreman whom in the beginning I despised but in the end had learned to appreciate. For a while after I fell into the knack of loosening the boundaries of my intolerance I nearly got to like him. Him also I found more tolerant than he looked which if you didnt ignore such demarcations was ridiculously Hollywoodish what with his meticulously clipped fence of blond moustache not far from the tip of his chin under a long snout and hair of the same color combed and recombed in waves as advertised. He was not the leader merely as a nephew of one of the bosses. The indisputable basis of his authority was competence in toolmaking supported by and supporting indisputable selfconfidence inner and outer. Unlike many inept subalterns of technology he understood his technical ability in itself to be no more sufficient than nepotism in itself as adequate reason for his position and he did not scorn what he did not yet know of the art of management. The disarming egotism of a precocious winner as justified by ability and diffused by natural friendliness was acceptable to the older men of the shop who recognized the headaches of a foreman's job and unlike Otto Rank in his Vienna machine shop were quite willing to retreat into the security of pure craft where perfection was possible. It was his male-dog nonchalance that more than anything else at first annoyed me and perhaps Basil the only bachelor besides me younger than middle-aged. Joe found it meet and amusing to act as Vera's workday squire and he did not learn what a poor managerial practice it was to do so only because in those particular circumstances nothing happened to upset that particular organization. In a newcomer's estimation his favoritism some-what exalted the elementary and subservient work she did at her drill press but later after mastering the same kind of machine all too quickly it seemed to me that she was affecting to run the machine during a time of labor shortage as a personal favor not to Joe but to the front office inas-much as her husband was overseas and she was determined as well as a lady could to match his war service "for the duration". With polite conde-scension she had taken charge of Bunny and her friend in the back room. The fraternization between Vera and Joe was calculated to be advantageous

on both sides, for just as she was able by means of inchoate flirtation to
disarm the resentment of other men that might have deprived her of general influence and warned Joe of the indiscretion implicit in his natural
attraction to herself thus scotching everything that was pleasant about her
job, and by means of daily gammon in the back room to neutralize the
racial distrust of the shy underling girls and abuse their ability to distinguish one white mistress from another as if their common femininity
united them in a sensibility taking precedence over race despite the protective coloration she gave them to understand she was obliged to assume
when summoned to men of her own kind, he was able to separate the
minor pleasure of her attention at the shop from his plain determination
to make the most of exemption from military service by investing in the
civilian war effort a trifle more than was required of him, to the decided
advantage of his professional seniority in the competitive times that would
come with peace above all for the benefit of his wife and daughters whose
comfort and social position in Queens always came first in his goals and
whose admiration of him was uppermost in the values of his leisure. At
least it was then incredible to me that any real adultery could either
account for or ensue from the all too obvious coquetry of these two known
to each other in family circles before she was employed especially when
one was in my sagacious opinion fundamentally frigid and the other advertised himself as a rakish ladykiller. Now however I'm not so sure of what
didnt go on after hours for in my diminishing wisdom I am coming to
think that things are just what they seem more often than they arent. But
Joe wasnt entirely free of rivals on the job. He was ethically bound to permit Basil's triangulation of the sub-ruling twosome which was isolated
from the top bosses rather by youth and rigidity of schedule than by barrier of class or clan. The sallow blond sycophant from Poland was balding
and a little too fat certainly softer than I am now but of an age with Joe
and Vera though more ebullient and humorous wherefore less constantly
cheerful than they. Basil was well naturalized to this country but his intellectual selfpossession had nothing in it to challenge their regime since it
was based on superior education in English as well as in other subjects for
which their respect was tempered by economic skepticism. He was shorter
than Joe yet much taller than Vera and despite his bouncing chest and
feminine hips the hairless arms below his biceps were as lean and muscular
as a sculptor's and his hands as strong as a ball player's though very white
and smooth after washing up. His elastic ambition seemed sometimes
sidetracked by baubles but it was robust enough for most social purposes
and as a well-spoken free male with plenty of money in his pocket and
clearly interested in women he was probably attractive to some who
looked for husbands. In this case he competed only for Vera's admiration.
Except for his rather pleasant accent good manners and correct grammar
he'd have been taken for a native and with view to becoming a respected
professional in some enterprise much larger than the one he was now

working in he pursued with vigorous success at the night division of City College a degree in industrial engineering specialized by a program in tool design which was the only option that seemed promising to him and his friends as a discipline for the hard world. Nevertheless by way of nurturing a rich and lively regard for things that women might find more interesting than bits of steel when he didnt go to lunch with Joe and Vera he sat at the front bench with a businesslike leather briefcase containing along with his schoolwork for the evening a copy of The Reader's Digest two or three cuts above the Daily News in intellectual distinction which he ingested every month for amusement and general education innocently swallowing its political grist while he ate the sandwiches also brought therein. But if he went out to eat he'd usually have to catch up to them in the cafeteria for he was always the last to finish scrubbing his hands at the sink and even for a hurried lunch he scoured the black oil from his fingernails before changing to and from his street suit that never lost its press. In deprecating the value of "theoretical" tool-engineering for a volatile amateur like Basil no more experienced than any temporary production machinist chiefly engaged like most of the rest of us in the kind of commonplace subcontracts taken on by the master toolmaker's shop with a shrug to help the world out of its agony, jobs that still might have been disdained by the proprietary family if they hadnt constituted a steady backlog of income to capitalize long-term aristocratic jig and fixture business that having made their reputation remained nuclear to the firm and would outlast any passing bonanza that could be handled by an expanded payroll of fairweather people hired almost indifferently with obsolescent equipment lent by the government and temporarily crammed into permanent floorspace better dedicated to elbow room for craftsmen with no redundant machinery, Joe did no more than amplify his taciturn saturnine uncle from Switzerland it was said but I somehow suspected Czechoslovakia the founding-partner boss of production who had learned the trade through decades of apprenticeship. But since Basil was a gentleman in Vera's eyes and since in Joe's he at least ought to have known what he was doing his sloppy lathe work was not beneath management's oblique animadversion. Joe and his uncle uttered sarcastic asides about "genius engineers who can't even read a mike". But Karl as the star producer above anyone's criticism was assigned without question to the shop's finest turret lathe undoubtedly the most profitable machine of all. His purpose seemed nothing else than to turn out a cheerful quantity of goodhumored quality as his response to the opportunity for fighting a Hitler who was said to be increasingly ill-humored and cheerless.

The men changed at least their outer clothes in a makeshift locker room and went at once to their places but the women in their closet were always slower in getting started. There among them in the rear chamber of the flat where I began my apprenticeship with an utterly monotonous but extremely loud punch press that thumped the whole building with every

stroke all the machines were driven independently each with its own electric motor and when my Boanerges was not stepping and stamping the
sounds of drills grinders and band saws randomly joined and quit the
rhythmless cacaphony but in the main shop almost all the machine tools
were spun by a single engine the last descendant in industry's horsepower
windpower waterpower and steampower lineage for until very recently in
the evolution of lathes from the potter's wheel after the human-crank- or
pedal-stage it was technically impossible to bring to bear a sufficient concentration of energy at each work station in a factory without inefficient
distribution from a comparatively efficient large-scale centralized force in
constant rotation. For economic reasons small electric motors were not yet
generally applied to the individual lathes of Empire State Tool & Die Corp
whereby much of the noise wasted friction and overhead paraphernalia
could have been eliminated. In more modern shops the decentralization
and simplification of mechanical advantage abolished an entire intermediate apparatus of power transformation by more directly tapping the energy
of the city's prime mover as if operators were each given currency to spend
exactly according to the time and degree of his need like so many separate
organists all by themselves in so many chapels. Instead at Empire there
was still one large electric mother-motor connected by a heavy leather belt
worn smoother than a razor strop constantly whirling a main overhead
shaft as long as the ceiling serving as an axle crammed with local pulleys
for the machines beneath it but at the other end coupled also by major
ceiling belts to two lesser spindles parallel on either hand for powering
jennies along the two walls. Each lathe had its own sub-belt turning on a
spool of three alternate diameters graduated inversely to a live tripartite
pulley turning on the shaft above so that with a flick of the wrist by the
leverage of a little stick you could slip the drive off one diameter and send
it climbing or descending upon its complementary overhead bobbin when
you had to change the speed of your machine. Even to me still innocently
green from backward Massachusetts and not yet familiar with the Protean
advantages of electric power the whole open rolling whirring whipping
slapping dangerous system at first glance seemed a ludicrous perpetuation
in some awkward grammar of 19thC concepts. Nevertheless with the
thrumming vitality of successful integration it determined and coordinated the rhythms multirhythms and subrhythms of all production work
starting the day at 8:01 AM when Joe threw the main switch and each several machine was eased onto the power train by its machinist like a flight
of fighter planes starting its engines for the dawn patrol. Meanwhile the
toolmakers at the front bench unlocked their personal tool chests which
were themselves the handiwork of masters marvelous little mahogany
bureaus fitted with felt-lined trays and drawers of gleaming steel instruments and delicate hand tools for squaring measuring scribing pricking
punching drilling threading screwing filing and polishing more refined
than a draftsman's and more varied than a surgeon's though there were no

nurses to help lay out the jobs at hand and each deliberate cautious hierophant celebrated independently at the common altar. Before the sun risen above the roofs of buildings to the east was too high to suspend the dancing motes of dust in leveled golden beams as it brightened the battered softwood floor rougher than Linnean School's with cheerful rectangles and more intricate patches composed by the shadows of revealed machinery and its network of interconnections picking out the steel and brass filings pressed into the grain deeper than any broom could sweep by years and years of calloused soles while the indoor air had yet to neutralize the tang of a winter day in skin and lungs it was a pleasure at least for Karl and me who never caroused on the eve to begin the day's work. More spirits than only ours hummed with the taut power of the throbbing shop but Karl was the one who actually sang and whistled as he stood at his machine bending to make his swift settings to finger his micrometer readings or to try a gauge and while the controls were on automatic feed to occasionally douse the bit with a profusion of cutting oil to keep it in gray temper under heat otherwise enough to make it red-hot. What an astonishing thing it was that conditioned by preliminary sophistries of treatment certain steel could carve other steel when lavished with whited fluid plashing forever over the stock and down the drain with very little of it actually coming into contact with the cut or the cutter at the point where new caloric sprang into existence like electricity that had to be bled away or quenched. Imperceptibly the strangeness faded after I began to get though only with soft porous iron-castings my own feel of a beak keenly ground to the curve of a plowshare taking advantage of its victim's anaesthetic speed which alone seemed to account for the strange submission of one metal to the other no more than a couple of degrees harder than itself as if you could turn down pine with wedges of oak simply by spinning it too fast for surface or tool to notice pain or scrape up sympathy. In gaining that sense of willful precision and control I lost my feel for organic materials and in my growing mastery of machines I began to scorn as child's play the softer art of woodworking and to dismiss as spurious or intolerable for instance the suasive drift of a tree's native grain as varying with the axis or direction of your setup. Now and then in the intervals of quick action Karl stooped to peer up out a window at blue sky or stepping rearward feet splayed out flat for stability hairless skull thrown back pensively supported both thumbs in concave bows on his broad hips elbows canted slightly forward akimbo cheeks puffed or hollowed with sounds made for his own pleasure rarely heard by others. Or sometimes he stepped about in a small ambit smiling at everything he saw perhaps with approval the operation of another machine always smiling humming whistling singing or looking while he rested his eyes and kept an ear open for possible hitches in his hitchless spinning. Most of the time though in a much inferior capacity I too was on production work to make my presence pay as I absorbed with very little instruction and no sanction to watch any

of the masters whatever emanation of knowledge or skill my preconsciousness might be able to detect while I was soaking up the drudgery of my
time-weary tasks that stretched for weeks on end between occasional small
odd-hour projects I was assigned at the bench as a part-time understudy in
medieval toolmaking and I never got anywhere near one of the long complicated procedures on an automatic screw machine that might have
afforded such moments as Karl's of skilled relaxation. The castings I
turned on a simple little engine lathe were so irregular and sometimes
positively eccentric on the outside that the chief difficulty of the job was
to get the chunky gray mushrooms centered in the chuck before I could
knap them into rough and ready outer shape merely for the sake of appearances since the main task was to face off the stems and bore them out so
that as cylinders within pestles apparently intended merely to make
weight they could easily but snugly receive some sort of shaft in an assembly said to involve the compass mount for lifeboats. Before I was through I
could turn out one of those hollowed knobs every minute and I never
inquired what happened to them after I carried them over to the corner in
wooden trays batched six by six and as for the final cause of all I did the
people I asked didnt know and didnt care beyond the narrow limits of very
subsumed specifications from Sperry Gyroscope in Brooklyn. So I made
the most of my small pleasure in slowly accelerating production-without-
rejections day by day at forty cents an hour gradually perfecting my
rhythm in picking placing centering tightening and setting into motion
the material cause of the product no sooner than with nicely overlapping
anticipation I swooped in upon the object smoothly traversing the two
dimensions at my disposal by means of little wheels at right angles to each
other one hand cranking fast the other slowly twisting to generate an
elegant and continuous motion ending exactly where and when the first
curling bite was called for. There were times when I preferred that semi-
soporific cycle of repetitive production to fussing with unnatural patience
at the customized creation of some sloydishly simple template or guide
fastidiously honed to pedantic exactitude of angle and sheen one of a kind
meant to fix a single step 10 000 times repeated in somebody else's production on drill press or milling machine. When I dropped in during my
leave a year later born toolmaker turned out as a sailor in salty dress blues
with the badge of a new profession before even making journeyman in the
old to find the girls gone and Karl out giving blood to the Red Cross I was
told that none of my successors on the lifeboat subcontract including full-
fledged machinists who now appeared to me surprisingly narrow and pitiable as pathetic expert bumpkins frightened or ignorant of the larger world I
knew had ever equaled my record in the production of iron knobs. Thanks
to my childhood experience in ritual time and motion perhaps I had been
too good at what immediately profited the firm to be taught the higher
matters of priesthood any more rapidly than the customs of apprenticeship
permitted war or no war. For the most part management had kept its

satisfaction with my work so well concealed that I was more often conscious of my mistakes in the special chirography of toolmaking than of my
general progress 90% tedious. The tacit and taciturn master of my apprenticeship the oldtimer boss-uncle himself had taken habitual pains not to
assuage my sense of having disappointing him. My economic incentive
was the time-and-a-half I got on the regular and mandatory schedule for
one hour a day over eight as well as eight or nine more on Saturdays the
only residue of the F D R 's National Recovery Act in that hardworking
backwater of wartime society explained rather by state law than by any
great competition for labor where I saw no old blue eagles tacked on the
walls even though New York Jews are supposed to be liberal in their voting.
Yet the other 10% was my spiritual incentive. Toolmaking smacked of
drawing and model-building. The old man gave me a textbook on shop
practice put out by the Ford Motor Company which I'm sure didn't square
with the old-world training tradition he'd have preferred in peacetime and
I studied it ambitiously more out of love for learning than in hope of
advancement. Maybe he was a better judge of character than I thought at
the time. I was privileged to purchase as a starter for my hope chest a professional micrometer made in Massachusetts supposedly available only on
war priority. With one hand to fit and adjust a little verniered sickle on
the diameter of a round object cradling the clef in my palm and fingering
its barrel like a miniature cello that I took the notes off without a bow was
my first ostentatious skill. I also displayed in the breast pocket of my shop
apron as badges worn like an engineer's sliderule or multicolored mechanical pencils a six-inch rule for measuring lengths and depths with a sliding
clip that made it into a cross and a tiny flat file for taking the burrs off
newly machined circumferences and edges. I'd like to go back and see the
place again if it's still in business. Before I have totally renounced my
letch for strange cities and new women I now find myself dwelling upon
the pleasures of haunting revisitation. You can wrench your heart with the
wonder of any place you've spent part of your life in and you can suffer the
mysterious attraction of things you loathed or abhorred for their cruelty
and ugliness schools shops neighborhoods or whole cities when afterwards
in prowling bitterly or brooding analytically you may find in them less
worth to yourself than you originally thought you did. It's the opposite of
"When I grow up—" which you're still in the habit of saying to yourself
at the age of thirty-three. So you think "When I go back—" about every
habitation of the past and someday maybe it'll be Oakland maybe even
this miserable little house. And then the queer feeling such as I got last
time I walked through Harvard Square after the war impossible to match
with the longing that brought me there and lonesomely disturbing
because the fulfillment revealed nothing at all! But with Gloucester the
hope and pain would be different. It's more than just an accident of birth.
If it were new to me I'd love it as well. There's there there that I'd recognize at once as Aristophanes would have taken to Athens even if he'd never

heard of it before and as St Joseph in fact left the sea to make England his home. The feeling is nothing like Japanese patriotism or Parisian matriatism or any rural nostalgia. In Gloucester that never changed for me if I ever get back there much will be gone the elms of Washington Street the steam trains half the wharves all the schooners. But I relinquish none of them in my desire.

At nine o'clock the bosses came in watched sidelong by everyone stationed nearby as they entered a pair of flimsy smudged-green offices partitioned two thirds of the way to the ceiling opposite the stairs and elevator where the strait between main shop and back room was narrowest. One was a stubby cross-eyed little woman who candidly arrested old age with undertaker's rouge the wife of Joe's uncle my grumpy tutor. She walked with a tense preoccupied stoop still publicly exhibiting the old country's accent and tradition Swiss or Czech of conjugal and secretarial submission though Americanized in all commercial essentials and the only real businessman of the three principals their wielder of administrative power as typist clerk bookkeeper office manager controller treasurer and director of personnel. We were chary of this suspicious probably hysterical personage but because of her childlessness and my good manners she hinted at a soft spot for me right up until the time I quit and she was the one I was most sorry to break the news to. I think she was the only one who really thought I might come back after the war to ask for my old job. But her husband was the high priest of the place. I had scarcely divined his expectations of me but it was really he whom I betrayed for the easygoing shortcuts of Navy life. He was short and thick with black hair brushed straight back from the horizontal lines in his swarthy brow and he brooked few questions as I learned at his side an iota at a time from deliberate acts and a few curt words yet sometimes I'd catch his brown eyes lighted at my ejaculations of dawning admiration and his shrouded sense of humor would reveal itself in a chuckle. No doubt it was my awe at the implausible skill of his heavy blunt fingers and my reverence for the methodical phlegmatic self-satisfaction of his trade that fooled me about his temperament. His affection and tolerance for the American nephew was also undemonstrative. I think he was more amused than annoyed by Joe's brash speedy interpretation of the solemn old music of production as long as he himself kept tight control over everyone's crucial toolmaking including Joe's own. Yet the third and much the youngest partner's name was the only one I remember though I don't think I ever spoke to him after I was hired no relation I'm sure to the translator of *Axël* for whom Yeats wrote a preface Sidney Finberg I fancied the most congenial to me of the owners. I sympathized with his struggle as I imagined it to infuse the enterprise with "theory". The poor guy was clearly ill at ease among his employees and always at a disadvantage in his conflict with the dogmas of practical experience that united aunt uncle nephew and all the elder retainers who agreed on its exclusive importance even in specialities they knew nothing about. Furthermore anything in his tall thin nervousness that might have suggested leadership was distracted or obscured by the inexperienced intensity of his interest. He seemed to have been born with eye glasses and I recall his smooth pasty hairless face corroborated by thin shoulders and narrow chest draped in a billowy white shirt compressed at the trunk by a buttoned vest of one of his fine herringbone business suits. Not in vanity but in tense conviction he made awkward splay-footed efforts as the corporation's majority stockholder and educated native Manhattan president to promulgate his vision of diversifying the business through the contracts he brought in. From time to time he made loping appearances among us in his capacity as chief engineer but he was never permitted to interfere with work on the floor and more than once when he got too excited his more forceful associate affecting a pleasantry had been seen pushing him with both hands back through the office door. When he occasionally darted into the shop with his cuffs drawn back by rubber bands at the elbow to make some hurried test at one of the idle lathes looking as if he was oblivious of all human beings so passionately did he pour over an idea I was surprised at his proficiency in handling the machine as if by reason alone but Joe as always made a point of smiling derisively behind his back. When our real boss was called to the office for a phone call where he hated to be tied up the youthful Mr Finberg would sometimes quickly walk the shop floor like a furtive staff officer prowling about a command he didnt approve of and wrestling with the impulse to offer the men suggestions until abruptly turning back on long swift strides resolved to argue with his peer.

But all in all as I now can see taking one thing with another in a broad worm's eye view of the American economy it was a fairly taut ship. By and large thanks to willing labor our unit in the war machine stumbled amicably along in its state of tension under conditions reasonably concordant with the spirit of the Atlantic Charter which Churchill didnt think applied within his own empire but a morning pause for coffee was conceded only reluctantly to the trend of the times and there was no further pampering. Our management's prudent distrust of new people until they demonstrated they would work every minute they were paid for without prospect of promotion or additional reward reflected its defensive attitude in the continual struggle against all the forces opposing success and even survival in the alien circumstances faced by native and immigrant alike along with all other corporations in the U S A professing to be robbed by Uncle Sam's Internal Revenue Service before they even began each new fiscal year. The instinct to ward off unionism was reflected in their ready adaptation of the counter-intelligence propaganda motto CARELESS TALK COSTS LIVES to the protection of their privacy from employees. Like their Yankee counterparts in a fishy little seaport on the Atlantic and their Hoosier brother in the retail book business on the opposite coast and most small businessmen in between you'd think they would have gone out of business in sheer pique if ever their unorganized workers were organized. But I dare say that in the anxiety of youth confusing national security with entrepreneurial neurosis I was excessively inhibited in refraining to ask what was contained in the little packages that I was sometimes sent down to the Bowery with or elsewhere in bewildering depths of the old city where streets running at odd angles had proper names to pick up or deliver at a mill supply house or a heat-treating shop. I especially did not want to jeopardize those assignments accepted with suppressed joy for the paid freedom and travel they entailed. But I seriously felt responsible for the cost to my employers of an hourly wage plus expenses for my subway ride or for a cab tipped parsimoniously on their behalf when there was a special hurry. If by chance I did see the tap or die or jig or fixture or machine part that I carried in a box to or from some disordered dirty little ramshackle hole in the wall for case-hardening or annealing where the experts' experts conducted their gnomelike professions I was usually amazed at the small size and utter simplicity of the precious express that went out and came back entirely unchanged in weight shape or texture the added investment being no more apparent than its improved temper. I flew like Hermes faithful and swift except when I could find a good excuse to read a book by riding a local instead of waiting for the express or to explore interesting streets as if in London by miscalculating my directions. I was proud of my elementary reliability but I often returned with pangs of guilt over the fact that I had not abbreviated my liberty as much as I might have. Anyway I had my own wartime rule against careless talk and I concealed my excitement in running errands that New Yorkers considered menial. It would also have been careless talk to admit the boredom or fatigue with which I yielded the firm my surplus value. Even 45 minutes away from the shop at any point made the day and indeed the whole week pass so much faster that I would have offered my time without pay and they would have accepted if it hadnt been for New Deal conscience imposed like honesty in tax returns by wage and hour audits. After work I was so hungry that as often as not I'd skip my swim at the Y because it made the walk home twice as long in distance and over an hour later. I was always as hungry as I am right now. Then I'd eat so much at supper that I wanted to do nothing but go to the movies where I had my only adventures and see almost anything especially at the Gramercy though it was 40 cents because I usually didnt have the energy to drag myself up to 42nd St on the Broadway bus where there was much to choose from at 15 cents and net saving of a nickle even if I didnt walk home. I wonder how I ever got through those night school courses at Washington Irving a Girls' High by day going to classes when I was waiting for the Gramercy pictures to change or had no disposable money at all. I don't remember ever doing any homework but somehow I passed the Regents exams. I thought the Advanced Algebra course would help get me into college but it only destroyed my hope to match smart prep school boys by sheer willpower. The tough male teachers who instructed with abstractions like district attorneys teaching pragmatic law alienated me from postgraduate learning. Going up and down between classes in elevators designed for mass-transit seemed as bizarre as professional football a boys' game. I reckoned that if I helped the family for a while I could go to sea with a clear conscience. I've never had a clear conscience. But during a school vacation my conscience was not a difficulty because the days of work passed with such relief that I thought of putting my savings into a tool chest and pending military service I cheerfully intended a regime at the Y M C A gymnasium to complement a career without college athletics. In warm weather on Sundays all I wanted to do was ride the open upper deck of the 5th Ave bus from Washington Square to Riverside Drive or take a cruise on the Staten Island ferry hardly hoping to pick up a girl at which I never succeeded because everywhere I hunted even if I hadnt been too bashful for timely moves there were thousands of better hunters freespending uniformed men especially sailors. When I finally got my own uniform I found that it was officers and rich civilians who had all the advantages including luck. From a job like mine at Empire T & D there were no leaves with pay. Nowadays the politicians don't allow our wars to discommode the voters but for that duration the whole country was affected and we seemed to feel that we were practicing our true natural religion whether for piety or profit not of course under conditions of domestic devastation like those suffered by Europeans and Asiatics but with a measure of selflessness even among the greedy and for a few years our Gross National Product though largely negative in residual worth had a certain social integrity. New York was the last city in which to expect sanguine solidarity yet there were a great many middleaged people who then and there became youthful in their outlook not only because they were not out of work in the lightly industrial and reduced mercantile exchange of Manhattan before the Depression was really cured but also because for the first time they did not expect to be stuck for the rest of their lives with whatever they found themselves doing. Just as a patriotic war levels personal dignities it can occasionally excuse eccentricities and abberations even unto neglect of possible excess profit. On 8th Ave there was a small storefront empty like a lot of others presumably for reasons of necessity displaying in the window a hand-lettered sign declaring the haberdashery *CLOSED FOR THE DURATION OF THE "WAR"* which in my naive pedantry I suspected to be owned by a sullen Nazi trying to undermine our morale with sarcastic punctuation wasted however on an ill-literate populace. Reminds me of a classified ad I saw that Ruth didnt notice on the page of our *Tribune* worse than Chicago's she asked me to look at the other day when her insufferably maleficent innocence put me so much further out of an indulgent humor than I already was at the lack of solitude that her real-estate cause was set back beyond my original loathing: LARGE PRETENTIOUS HOME FOR SALE. As for me stand-

ing at my machine in a grubby shop that was unqualified to deal directly
in prime war contracts and known only by card file to half a dozen specialized assistant purchasing agents among subcontractors and envying those
who worked in clean well-lighted places unionized with employee benefits
hopeful training programs and non-profit cafeterias I hadnt any idea of
how anybody's output in a land of slovenly language was usefully absorbed
into the immense largely muddled stream of material with which we were
going to repair our defeats or how it was to be brought timely to bear
piece by piece in military evolutions to force unconditional surrender all
over the world. We were not fighting for our lives and in fact Churchill
said that unlike the British and their other allies we had joined the war
disinterestedly as a matter of principle but when I first went to work on
23rd St I was as self-interestedly depressed by news of defeats as his people
had been at the fall of France when "the light went out of the landscape"
and it seemed to me almost impossible that F D R could prevent his partisans from going the way of the Jews and all values. There was no comfort
in visions of Hitler as Ozymandias. The German and Japanese ensemble
not to mention Italians who had invented fascism looked stronger than the
Juggernaut of Gog and Magog more logical than the Inquisition crueler
than Aztecs shamelessly evil and arrogantly omnipotent without taking
into account their secret weapons always hanging over our heads dimly
comparable to the one we ourselves finally came up with. I couldnt appreciate the fact that at home we had already risen to our height of decency. I
shuddered at the fearless everyday blather of economic men who couldn't
decode quotation marks or distinguish house from home but I failed to
understand that they were actually at their best in but partially and temporarily checking the national love of pelf spotted by Toqueville which
since then by divided inheritance through mobile generations of exogamy
has intensified not dissipated as it multiplies and which has so quietly
resumed its permeation of the American psyche that it's taken as sine qua
non and there is no need for scientists or artists to mention money which
has rescued our people from the hardships of bartering in a wilderness as
the addictive motive that keeps them in countenance with their times.
Things looked so bad to me before it was clear that we were going to win
the war that any mention of postwar plans or settlements grated on my
sense of proportion and I could forsee any end at all only as something too
momentous to conceive if truly unconditional far more epochal than the
beginning which despite its proximate causes had come in many slowly
developing aggressions. I was too saturated with unmomentous facts of
wavering monotony and relative poverty and changeless cityscape. Until
victory was in the air I found it very hard to believe that events would
turn for the better or that Satan could be sentenced to death by humane
forces. I gradually got more hopeful but in the Navy years I knew less and
less of what the *New York Times* was recording. No modern people wages
offensive war unless there's money or excitement in it for the multitude or

the hope of betterment condensed into currency as each day's incentive to
get out of bed and go to work at whatever each individually is charged to
do for the cause and not even Churchill who had earned by competence in
niggling detail as well as grand strategy his royal commission as leader of
the eminently manageable United Kingdom could have marshalled the
limitless network of inefficiently dovetailing yet wisely redundant defense
production that can never be predetermined by truly comprehensive planning if he hadnt permitted pounds shillings and pence to play their invisible hand in every minute transaction of a nation so desperate that money
itself was no object. It takes indifferently vicious or innocent money-
motivation to effect the indeterminate details of coordination without
which plans as intricate in their totality as those of war production can be
no more than hopes in anticipation and statistics in retrospect. Who could
have planned for example that D O Frost the erstwhile oilskin company in
Gloucester should produce the very dungarees I would buy from the supply ship at Saipan which were always too big in the ass I suspect because
the Navy was foisting WAVE pants off on us either in order to reduce
some colossal blunder in inventory allocation since there were damned few
feminine seamen within 3000 miles or in some misconceived inhuman
demeaning attempt late in the war to improve logistical efficiency by a
needlessly generous uniformity of cut that they'd never have dreamt of
applying to the clothes of male officers? Thank god I never came across a
WAVE officer in the course of duty much as I liked to get their attention
by saluting with erotic vengeance on the streets of San Francisco not however to the point of "insubordination through manner" and in fact I was
romantically deferential for I have no objection to a woman becoming a
governor or Pope as long as I don't have to take mannish orders from her
or a Queen if I must.

As the day wore on the floor filled with barbed coils of steel and brass
parings that stuck to your socks hot as hell when they curled off the
chucks of the lathes acridly burning the thin white oil that kept them
from bursting into open flame sometimes so sharp and jagged that you'd
lacerate your hand just pushing them out of the way as they cooled.
Beneath them underfoot the fine chips and filings silted the floorboard
grains and cracks. One of my odd jobs was to sweep the aisles before noon
with a broad-brush broom pushed like a snow plow wearing gloves to
separate the scrap metal for salvage from the cigarette butts paper cups
and mixed dirt. Everyone felt better about resuming work after lunch with
a clear place to stand though the catchment trays of the machines and the
floor under them were still piled with caked messes of scrap soaked in the
cutting fluid and streaked with the black lubricating oil that leaked down
from shafts and gears. That was one of the small ancillary interruptions
that eased me into the fulltime tedium of repetitious machining at which
afterwards my routine productivity depended upon diversionary idiosyn-
cracies of procedure that got me through the day not by expressing my

personality but by maintaining a ratio of psychic to physical action below which I could not have borne the boring ordeal of standing in one spot. The stamina for sticking it out over even a single year of self-competing production came with the development of a personal style at the cost of less than maximum quantity on any one day. The trick was to make sure that the subtle spinal twists and knee-bends of your choreography were in rhythmic harmony with the cursive chirography of fingers both functional and superfluous in flourishes of momentum according to the principle of least action measured by output over the long run perhaps. A little private ceremony may limit the maximum speed of cutting but it makes for smooth continuity between pieces tempers your mood and frees your mind of resistance to repetition. Every day in anticipation it reduces the reactance to starting up betimes. Thus I invented a restrained and soothing manner of rote not mainly to assert my efficiency but to alleviate discipline with the freedom to think of other things. No stoop laborer can conserve as much chemical energy as a man whose work in foot-pounds is not much more than that of keeping his skeleton erect all day. Like the stepped-cone pulleys that drive his machine at various ratios of force the skilled worker can make a little power go a long way once he's up to a graceful speed. Of course he doesnt think of style but merely observes to himself if he notices his own ways at all that he breathes best with loosening gestures and expressive follow-throughs like a pianist or a batter warming up or relieving tension if not just for pleasure perhaps even not aware that in making his work easier the interpolated motions have grown habitual. Industrial engineering which thank god our shop was too primitive to attract should distinguish between the habits by which a worker unnecessarily tires himself or strains his own nerves and the ludic idioms by which he puts himself into the daily trance for otherwise uncreative work. The highest efficiency may be attained with such formal deviations as a long curve replacing a short straight line or a sharp corner of motion. Non-replicating toolmakers were denied this ritualistic rounding of the clock. Their craft was in thinking through and executing unique sequences of detail and preventing themselves by an extremely conscious set of precautions against making a mistake at any step in the sequence of miscellaneous operations. With a variety of machines but no division of labor it might take a month or more to construct a single lapidary jig or fixture. Toolmakers had time for dreaming only when they took time out perched on their stools ostensibly planning their tactics. But they had no need for rest or diversion. If they hadn't abused their night's time off it was their blessed pleasure to be generally alert not only to what they were doing but also to alternatives and they could work at the comfortable pace of their moods totally absorbed in every move they had to make and only occasionally rushed or slowed by the tempos of gears or belts. They painted with purple dye the dully gleaming glass-smooth surfaces of perfectly squared steel blocks scribed them with a stylus as fine as a dentist's explorer drawn along the blade of a tiny stainless steel try-square and laying out distances from finely calibrated rules by purest analog with dividers more precise than distinctions without differences punctuated the colored surface with perfectly formed dots no larger than a needlepoint locused exactly at the crossing of faintly scratched hairlines by a punctilious mallet-tap on the head of a perfectly hardened steel punch held perfectly perpendicular by eye and touch alone every finger lightly playing its part in sensing at all azimuths the right angle made by the axis of the instrument before it was permitted to barely intersect the plane by just the right amount of force to make a point without periphery. Or arcs with the same divider used as a John Donne compass with two feet equally sharp and hard. I never saw half the uses of the unexpendable jewels in the felt-lined or even velvet drawers and delicate compartments of their hardly portable toolchests like Venetian argosies as their work elaborated itself each piece at last being fitted to another in the apparently seamless synthesis of some scaffold for production work or of a invisibly cunning matrix. Like harpooners they'd have none of the shipowners' weapons but carried their own tools or fittings to the machines they had to use from time to time viz collets chuck attachments mandrels midget anvils drills reams knurlers diestocks threading dies and taps their male opposites angle plates clamps shims and heavy gemlike little mill vises precise enough to be deposited at the Bureau of Standards as square flat and smooth as platinum ideals not to mention all the hammers screwdrivers wrenches pliers tweezers forceps scalpels speculums tenaculums and gauges in sets of graded shapes sizes and thickness used on the operating table or files of every tooth and taper not to mention divers calipers and micrometers. A carpenter's gross toolbox is often not much more valuable to him than his car or boat and it can be slung around with him wherever he goes in the open air but a toolmaker's chest such as I craved to possess until I escaped to other callings was his library his laboratory his desk his file cabinet his safe his locker his art gallery his capital fortune. This thesaurus was a compendium of his tradition and a tabernacle of his skill the certificate of his suffrage in a profession. By way of fixing his person to his credentials he titivated the mahogany cabinet under lids or trays and inside portals with family photographs rabbit feet vacation postcards pin-up girls and other penates or memorabilia of sentiment. Most of a toolmaker's time was spent within reach of his bench vise and he didnt often resort to powered mills or harsh retching shapers or even purring jeweler's lathes but before any job was finished he would most likely have stood more than once at a high-speed precision grinder by which diameters or joined planes were reconciled to the nearest ten-thousandth of an inch or less and planes cylinders pyramids or cones buffed to perfection. Glyphed dies begun with etching and engraving had to be finished off in hollow or relief by the pure art of filing curved surfaces perhaps more irregular than French curves or the lines of schooner hulls which can only be approximated by

the designer even as patterns plotted on paper. Most of these delicately
shaped cameos and intaglios had to be sent out for hardening that they
might be used with endless repetition of thermal or mechanical stress for
molding stamping or extruding sheets or puddles of plastic petrochemicals
or metals less hardened than itself. On some jobs both before and after
heat-treating the inner surface of a cylindrical boring must be tested at
every degree of rotation for maximum internal osculation with minimum
friction by the outer surface of a separately turned and polished cylinder
made solely as a full-length gauge of all but exactly the same diameter.
The painstaking deliberation of the masters seemed leisurely but it tolerated no defect no standard deviation every sculpture being its own norm.
As makers of ideal forms that might mint for a singular more or less useful
purpose identical production parts centered in the distribution curve of
quality control these craftsmen at whatever wages were grossly underrated
by whatever value the gross national product gave them credit for in comparison to those who laid out advertising for Coca-Cola sold in bottles still
formed by one original master mold. Most of the scholastic guildsmen who
thus incarnated Platonic realism voted in political misapprehension for the
nominalism practiced by Republicans to protect private wealth from creeping socialism.

Joe himself a prodigious young toolmaker usually spent little of the
day supervising machinists. Most of the time he sat at the window a cigarette balanced on the edge of the oilstained bench or stuck dangling from
the dry skin of his lips head jerked back and off to one side eyes screwed
up narrowly to evade the thin streak of his own smoke. The hard energy in
his lean frame bent over masterwork then seemed oblivious of his other
responsibility. Since most of the machinists were serious and competent
the shop practically ran itself much to my good fortune as a general student but far more to Joe's whose natural inclination was to concentrate
upon his toolmaking in total nervous occupation for hours at a time
unconscious even of the hot smoke pumped in and out of his lungs by
mouth and nose and continually renewed by fire struck with his own hand
while deep in contented care. He could dispense greetings and wisecracks
or perfunctory instructions to his crew without looking up or interrupting
the thoughtful business of his hands while yet perhaps cursing under his
breath not at the messenger but at the nuisance of his supervisory job
when he was positively called to inspect in situ a toolmaker's type or an
operator's antitype or especially to solve some production problem in the
world behind his back like a man wakened from a sleep in which he could
speak but not interact with society. Yet on some occasions he would suddenly relax and bark out an item of raillery maybe at Basil in an effortless
voice that penetrated all the whopping flopping stropping pounding singing noises of machines and belts that tangled the jungle of fellowship.
Only now and then at a stopping point in his project did he take a turn
around the room ducking and dodging through short-cuts among vines

and creepers parlous with kinetic energy to scrutinize with glances the procedures or products of any of the machinists except Karl who by acclamation was as exempt from examination of his work as of his life pushing them aside when it was necessary to demonstrate corrections. When the plump little black girl came from the back room with a box of castings to work on at the small drill press near Joe's stool she was subjected to a few preoccupied pleasantries but if Vera came for the same purpose he was likely to look up from his work and enter into protracted gallantries.

I must guess at much that went on in the shop for I usually saw less than anyone else. My lathe faced out a side window away from this society and when working elsewhere in the front room I tried to watch Karl whenever I had a chance to take in anything besides my own affairs. I marveled at the helpful friendly unassuming way he guarded the spirits of his colleagues like a sagacious Newfoundland dog in a complex household as if even when tending his own machine he instinctively distinguished from merely adventitious whines whangs and wheezes any operational anomolies within earshot. When his automatic doppelganger was piloting the lathe he gazed all about smiling at everyone he saw whether he caught their eye or not but invariably turned back in time for a quick train of movements that with a quick twist of the turret disengaged one cutting tool and fetched another before again trusting his piece to the combined synchronized motions of a mechanical program always checking outer or inner circles with micrometer or vernier calipers and stepping back with pursed lips to pat his chest with both hands and look about once more while whistling some operatic melody.

At the approach of noon many necks were craned to see its proof by the clock on the wall behind the gas forge whence on no other authority it controlled all our collective startings and stoppings. By that standard Basil's machine stopped at one minute to twelve even though he had plenty of reason to suspect that his own chronometer was a little fast. The others were all silenced before the various time standards were summarized by steam whistles on the East Side in short overlapping blasts spread out over the best part of another minute. He justified his anticipation officiously by being johnny-on-the-spot at the main switch to turn off the power to all belts as soon as the most conscientious worker was ready to knock off. It took a few seconds for all rotations to cease. Then the sudden silence revealed by sound the fauna of a teeming cityscape. For a minute or two the people unconsciously lowered their voices in respect for their dead noise but it wasnt long before human mastery of nature reasserted itself. Karl of course was the last to clean up smiling and stretching himself without haste as he stood by the wash basin for his turn. Joe adjusted his hat before the mirror as he waited for Vera to come out of the back room. "Shall we dine?" she said.

I'm sure I was the hungriest of all. My famished stomach grinding ravenously I competed unobtrusively for a place in the elevator close to the door seeing that a fast start to the sidewalk was crucial in the race for an almost intolerable cafeteria line when the city turned out all at once for the rushing pleasure of food though its myriad appetites could not have been as sorely pent as mine. There was a place across the street where I discovered a bargain unnoticed by those who absorbed it carelessly as part of larger gratifications. For fifteen cents I could get a bowl of thickly sapid bean soup with a set-up of dark rye and butter and free half-cured pickles. The pickles particularly pleased me because I could fold them in the bread deliciously astringent and deep to the teeth. Some time after Ruth came to the shop I began to make more manducatory lunches at home not as cheaply but worth more as fortification such as overlapping baloney or salami with piquant mustard and a couple of hard-boiled eggs quickly peelable in large shards in fact virtually brushed off with the side of my thumb and popped into my mouth in two bites each while unwrapping the main course supplemented with sweet stuff of one kind or another all carried in a brown paper bag that I threw away without the loss of a crumb licking my fingers sliding my hands together with little slaps. Not having taken up smoking at that time I could the more easily dispense with noontime coffee. I still wasnt fat. Later I actually got pretty thin as love gripped me preempting all other desires and I found most of my eating reserved for the weekends when I couldnt see her at all. But I wasnt always able to find what I needed to pack my own lunch among the cockroaches in our miserable little hole of a kitchen and I still sometimes had to go out at noon determined to return in ten or fifteen minutes with some lame pretext for going back to find her. Before Ruth began to affect our lives however Karl and two or three others were left in the peaceful front of the shop during the so-called lunch hour hunched on stools at whatever little clearing they could make at the bench where if they chose to look they could gaze at the hustling throng on the sidewalk across the street. But Karl chewing slowly as I could never chew no matter how fed up with my vituals left before me and back at his machine plunged again into the *Times* having now reached music news the greatest pleasure of his day and with one hand abstractedly munched an apple fetched from his overcoat pocket opposite the one his newspaper came from under the hat rack on the rear wall while retaining the use of his huge thermos bottle still holding two cupfuls of tepid white coffee. Last of all he turned to the editorial page which I was brash enough to tell him was a Krock of shit much too free with pompous criticisms of my beloved Administration almost as aggrieved as if its columns were truly malignant like the *Chicago Tribune*'s still defending "America First" or William Randolph Hearst's ceaselessly attempting to turn the President's constituency against him or the *Daily News*'s which I took to be overtly fascist because it had its own private police force guarding the futuristic lobby of its ominous new building on 42nd St near where they've now settled the United Nations an outgrowth of the Atlantic Charter that might have been called Associated

Powers if F D R 's choice hadnt taken precedence over Winnie's but my
animadversions against our favorite newspaper were not very serious when
the right wing frightened and angered me too much to sneer at anything
generally on the other side of politics yet nonetheless uttered with didactic
warmth simply because I thought he deserved a true interpretation of
American politics from a native who knew better than he did the enemies
in our own ranks and their vast rhetorical powers of deception. I found the
Times's bending-over-backwards in well-balanced objectivity toward F D R 's
policies very tiresome when what was wanted from the Anglo-American
Chronicle of our times along with sober intelligence was insight into leaders' motives and values. But all this I would speak in a low voice. The men
nearby conferred in unexcited fraternity of interest upon baseball football
basketball hockey horseracing or radio programs. Karl being a Bavarian
was especially sympathetic to "states' rights" and couldnt help swallowing
the phony line taken by the New Deal's enemies to justify their opposition
to almost everything proposed by the one consul who represented all the
people of the states so he just smiled at the immaturity of my liberalism.

It was at just such a time that he and I chanced to see Ruth when she
first appeared to apply for the additional job required by a new contract of
which we yet knew nothing. The bosses usually ate together inside their
citadel having their lunch sent in from the delicatessen which I supposed
was their best opportunity to sit as a committee of the whole for I could
hardly imagine them not discussing business. It wasnt hard for us to guess
why another black girl should show up. She was obviously no messenger
or salesman. Karl had just risen to get rid of his lunch wrappings and take
the thermos back to his coat handing me the Times so I could get a quick
look at it before 12:45. I'm sure neither of us had any comments and we
probably forgot all about her until she started work a day or two later. For
any man who watched and heard her speak she was unforgetable. The
1066's Limey more familiar than I with West Indians would have said in
the tone of a connoisseur using Brother Jonathan vernacular with John
Bull accent that she was the best piece of ass in sight anywhere. The language of other sailors would have been more brutal with less sympathy.
We had none of their kind in the shop but we did have racetrack bettors.
She was such a fine horse that they always called her Black Beauty and for
once I accepted their banal nomination when I talked to myself at the
lathe or in bed at night. Now I can't remember exactly what she looked
like but I know how she walked. There was no exaggeration in her slender
hips. Yet it wasnt love at first sight. I became aware of her unique quality
little by little while fetching my castings from the back room as I passed
her at the new double-spindle drill press. She cured me of the dreary drony
lassitude of the early part of the afternoon that I'd survived only by dint of
the muscular effort required to remain on my feet which reserved just
enough nervous energy to search for excuses or causes to go home sick and
to keep me from falling asleep until my metabolism restored itself to equi-

librium and I was wide awake on the home stretch. Soon there was no part
of the day in which by the mere thought of her I was not stimulated to an
alert consciousness of peculiarly lovely attraction. Her very proximity
doubled the zest of my mornings. With no particular hope beyond the
expectation of another look and a word or two I was usually too tongue-
tied in her presence to say anything interesting or personal and she was
politely laconic without making any apparent distinction of persons. At
work she was at her most beautiful in gray coveralls with a blue bandanna
by which her hair was bound high above an unbending neck that seemed
to me incomparable in regal grace and proportion. Nothing about her
movements or appearance either defied or mocked or imitated white
women. Her skin was as smooth and clear as a colorless pearl that absorbed
all wavelengths of incidental light without reflection save that her thin
lips were lightly tinted with a cosmetic crimson in exquisite taste. I began
to imagine the touch of her exotically civilized mouth, enunciator of purest English words shaped like gems with a delicate accent that could be
reproduced by no mimic or Shakespearean actress. She had been nurtured
with the Anglican Prayer Book at a place called Cambridge to my delight
in the mountains of the Isle of Springs and I could guess nothing in her
heritage either European or Arawakan to modify an Abyssinian nobility
sold across Africa second-hand perhaps in Arabian gyves to Portuguese
slavers and robbed from them to be forcibly smuggled maybe in his ship
Dainty into the hands of colonial Spaniards by the pirate John Hawkins
returning to England via Newfoundland to get a load of salt cod so that he
wouldnt have to deadhead his way back across the Atlantic who also introduced our forefathers to tobacco Drake's cousin from the mercantile class
of sea dogs in Plymouth later comptroller of Elizabeth's navy rewarded
even before his part against the Armada with a crest conspicuous for its
Negro in chains. It was embarrassing for me to represent the civilization
she had come to work in.

Everyone was discreetly aware of Vera's uncommon interest in the
impressions made by the newcomer's modest presence if only because Ruth
though champion of no cause or attitude was immediately attended with
respect by the two black girls who were more awed by their tall educated
coetanean than by their tiny elder mistress from the ruling class who protected her hair from the machinery with a snood that to me was as fakely
obscene as her concealed corsets. The cluttered back room served to store
raw material stock and disabled apparatus as well as to house machinery
for the female division of labor that had been introduced by Mr Finberg
no doubt in opposition to the skepticism of his partners before they saw
the proof of his economic calculations so despite its small population it
was a rather large territory supervised only partially and unofficially by
Vera who was tacitly assumed to be an informer but who in that location
had no continuous male support in resisting with chatter the unintentional challenge to her preeminence by a novice pretending to no

promotion making no attempt to dispute social or moral ascendancy and
exhibiting no resentment at the white woman's assiduous campaign to
trump with condescension the courteous acceptance of suggestions about
doing the work in a customary manner. But however slowly and undra-
matically it may have been detected by visitors from the front room the
old regime was weakening back there. In Vera's colloquies with Joe and
Basil she probably wasnt foolish enough to confess a rival. No doubt she
reassured herself with the asseveration that Ruth after all was only a
nigger. One day I noticed with a shock that she had revived throughout
the shop a popular hit song called "Rum and Coca-Cola" which not only
advertised the chronically profitable national toxin but also implied that
the Caribbean

> ". . . mother and daughter
>   working for the Yankee dollar"

were both merely picturesque black whores doing their bit against enemy
submarines by comforting careless American sailors and airmen who were
stationed at the bases that had been pressed upon F D R by the Former
Naval Person seeking our obsolete destroyers in his undesponding desperation before we had cause to remember Pearl Harbor. I'm sure Ruth never
gave sign of distaste either for the meaning or for the meretriciously imitative rhythm of the tune still heard on every radio and here sung or
whistled by Vera and others perhaps even the black girls in their innocence but her general attack at most in the eye of anyone who entered the
gyneceum could only have enhanced admiration of Ruth's dignity. The
black beauty's reserved behavior encouraged neither calumny nor invidious
comparisons. It was unremarkable that she did not join the praise of rum
and Coca-Cola because she would never sing a word or make a move not
required to earn her living among us. After we discovered that she was a
dancer I felt that for me knowledge of her art was as far beyond my station
in life as the privilege of her body. My adoration wasnt innocent but it was
too inexperienced too diffident and too aesthetically enamored to imagine
myself a white ram tupping a black ewe, or perhaps just too realistic to
hazard the possibility reserved for her own kind in art or society. Karl and
I each secretly had to infer her talent or joy in anything beyond standing
walking or casual speech. Few among the other men were partisans of any
art or color except their own yet I divined that Vera was afraid to risk
denigration of herself with unfounded aspersions on her rival's quality.
After a while she was clever enough in fact to confound any suspicion of
her jealousy by commending at large the novice's excellence at the drill
press. The married men of Empire State Tool & Die's civilian crew did
indeed sometimes allude to their own "homework" but there was little
open talk of pussy either black or white.

It happened that for the stretch of about a week I had to eat lunch out at the cafeteria. Probably Peggy was having some kind of a tantrum over being expected to do the food shopping on her way home from school. The first day I had my sandwiches in hand again I was surprised to find that Karl did not remain at the bench for lunch and then stunned to realize as I was about to get back to work that instead of having gone out he had been eating in the back room where the afternoon sunlight was already dominant. I suffered a pang of umbrageous vexation at the march stolen on me even when I was again trustingly available. But I put the best face upon his probably inadvertent treachery because it dawned on me almost at once that he had broken the ice for us both. If there was any gossip about the middleaged German dining with three black girls I never overheard it. The second or third day I got up the courage to do the same by strolling out back with a book in one hand and my lunch in the other as if merely looking for a place where I wouldnt have to listen to the talk of the front room that had gotten much louder since Karl's sudden change of habit. I too didnt care how obviously I altered my noontime behavior as long as I got away with it in Ruth's eyes though at my age such pursuit of companionship must have been regarded as less disinterested than Karl's. I never had to open the book for I was selfeffacingly able to insinuate myself into the general conversation and at the following day's session I slipped as an auditor into the dialogue between him and Ruth when it was no longer of interest to the unschooled girls. He repaid my intrusion with kindness and even made room for me to sit with them every time thereafter despite my ignorance of music. It was music that made their true friendship honorable. Later I talked to her a little about the literature of our common native language and this aggression Karl also took in good part listening with a smile in his usual generosity of spirit. As there was nothing to be shy of during this one real remission of discipline the other girls were content to gabble in their low-falutin corner taking no interest in our interests glad enough to see that their lady was content with agreeable companionship though not entirely comfortable with our adulteration of their workroom until it had been confirmed as a new custom without protest from authority or public opinion. When the weather was good they'd leave us there and spend a few minutes on the street nearby often bringing back for Ruth a cupcake or stick of ice cream to start her afternoon with. Occasionally I'd have her to myself for brief sessions during working hours when I contrived to eke out some job near her machine which she operated in easy rhythmic placidity as if she'd dismissed the dimension of time and freed her muscles of mental supervision by having trained the double drills themselves.

But I never gained the trust that Karl enjoyed. In respect for his professional and moral seniority but without the virtue of entirely denying myself her company after finishing my sandwiches I would often withdraw to turn the pages of my book scarcely grasping what I read in the pain of my loss just far enough off for them to feel secure or at least so confident of my sympathetic discretion that they could converse against the background of an unceasing buzz from the city below our windows almost as if they were alone in the seclusion of a picnic glen. I began to believe in this limited deference to the unspoken wishes of both my friends when I understood it as my sacrificial duty their admiring junior in that noonday greenhouse to chaperone their spiritual liaison in order to disarm vulgar observation and social unease as well as to forestall unequal growth of pitiable passion. In getting used to my hanging around they could persuade themselves that I was a good friend who took no care to hear what passed between them. I myself was to be similarly protected by my only friendship aboard the 1066 when Mr Drake a poet by intention now living in the Village a roistering friend of St Jean-Louis but then an officer and southerner who grabbed my letters from the wardroom stack of outgoing mail before other gentlemen could get their hands on them as he afterwards revealed when we met as socially equal veterans at his expense in a San Francisco bar after he returned with the ship to preside over her decommissioning at the mouth of the Sacramento River while in a still-enviable uniform handsomely drunk and open-hearted he confessed his disappointment at the lifting of censorship soon after Hiroshima and the fact that he had been especially moved by a series of two letters written as it were in his presence to my ultimate Ruth beginning respectively "You are like moonsilver" and "You are like sungold." It was on the same occasion too late for me to make amends for a self-disserving prejudice of mine that he recited from memory the far more important words of a young shipmate of mine a QM2 by the name of Clark his favorite assistant being navigation officer an assignment that did not suit his undisciplined literary temperament but in which he acquitted himself very well thanks to friendly and unassuming cooperation with enlisted quartermasters like that quiet kid from Kansas who unbeknown to me in my stupid opinion that there was nothing interesting about him especially since he didnt seem to like me was doggedly studying celestial navigation under the guidance of the officer whose job he helped save though he had no intention of staying in the Navy or of going anywhere but back to the wheat fields which nevertheless in my mind's eye are always seen with my heart beating in nameless excitement leaning out the window of a cattlecar as a legendary inland sea of flattened tawny motion first sailed by prairie schooners drawn by teams of six and now laid out to infinity on either side of the iron horse his tightening wake of sharp lines invariably parallel as they vanish in the distance never dissolved by tide or weather exactly as in the scene ahead which is distinguished in the foresky only by a tubby long-legged watertower painted peach yellow weathered shabby by ceaseless winds feeding by downspout our halted engine on the mile-long siding white steam leaking straight up from mouth and nostrils like the smoke of three peaceful tepees to join white clouds sailing in the blue while the whole train's hushed in awesome suspenseful silence and I yearn to live at that very spot on the railroad until I can possess with my own hands its sparse arbitrary history although unlike Babbalanja we can no longer count ourselves so lucky as to be living midway in eternity. Perhaps brought up by parents resentful of New England bankers and Harvard intellectuals Clark was too reserved with those not of the Kansan type and I with everybody. Now in missing him I would repent any attitude but that of praise toward one who was able to understand what had happened the very hour we got the news without perspective and cut off from all journalistic commentary while every other manjack was elated with relief at the victorious salvation of his own life in the suddenly certain prospect of return to women. Moreover he was not ashamed to reveal his feelings in words that no enlisted man was likely to utter even if so wisely inspired. "Mr Drake" I was told he said "if what we hear is true the world will never be the same again. We can never depend upon the sunrise or the sunset." And he was referring only to the first in our country's pair of psalms to God. *You are like uranium!* Would either have been allowed if F D R had stayed with us another year? Should we believe that scientists who made ready for such offences to occur deserve more woe than the few politicians by whom the offenses came? Excluding Nagasaki as an unconscionable stutter of terror I have tried to comfort myself with the assurance that men would have been less loathe to threaten their Antichrists with wars to come if they hadnt seen the horror of ending that one in a way we almost all approved including the ship's one known man of divinely apocalyptic religion a Jehovah's Witness from Missouri striking for Radarman whose anoesis was presumably less excusable than my insensitivity at the time. But now we have a new translation of the psalm. *You are like hydrogen!* A reduction to the universal gas of water named by Lavoisier the year we won our revolutionary war and the Massachusetts Supreme Judicial Court outlawed slavery. Noble gold which according to reason should be found exclusively on earth and radical hydrogen plasma which obtains throughout the universe almost to the exclusion of everything else having been reproduced in athanors and cyclotrons though in an Eastern view regarded indifferently as boundaries of a totally illusory spectrum have defined the limits of purely abstract value worth dying for. If what St Alfred calls the "massive endurance" of matter due to the "simplicity of the dual association" can now be destroyed from within the nucleus of the lightest atom we must admit that statistics is justified not as impure mathematics but as the ultimate science of infernal combustion wherein we unbind that which binds the center of centers.

That night at the San Francisco bar across the street from the club to which he'd taken me for Dixieland jazz so crowded that we had to stand up near the door craning eyes and ears the kind of place that players of black music are still doomed to for the distribution of their art as painters are

doomed to art galleries for their publication and as artists of all kinds are
doomed to a livelihood of selling their work by the promise of someone
else's profit before they can have an opportunity to convince consumers
like Karl of its retail value who even after a hard day's work would wait in
line without supper for standing room at the Met though as for me I've
never had time even for free pure music since it takes pure free time unless
you overlap it with something else treating it as nothing of the mind can
be treated without debasing the experience and insulting its creator I tried
to tell Mr Drake now Jim and amazingly still a distant friend about the
occasion on which his chosen music of another kind had gathered up my
whole discursive analytical soul into a unitive mystical ecstasy as I lay
sleeping a practice almost as bad as doing something else while listening
though I could recall the sounds themselves with no more authenticity
than the past nausea of seasickness. I thereupon found out that my brief
and evanescent musical sensibility had been preternaturally induced by his
crazy impulse sitting alone in the wardroom as he wrote in his journal to
play a couple of his records without noticing that the ship's internal loudspeaker system was switched on when all other off-watch officers and men
not even excepting the compulsive cardplayers lay in their darkened bunks
trying to sleep out a typhoon not because they realized how extraordinarily dangerous that storm was but because they found it too irritating to do
anything else while every unsecurable object large or small including dice
and paper money was sliding or knocking about all compartments in the
ship's jerkily gyrating response to the most violent wind and waves of its
groaning career or were exasperated by the effort required to keep a seat on
bench or deck while continually flung back and forth between bulkheads
or stanchions. Unlike an articulated train speeding around curves or up
and down hills on a rough roadbed a classically braced fighting ship is rig-
idly unified in all its irregular motions but an L S T's unarticulated integrity was designed to be swayed like a sheet of tin flexing simultaneously to
separate stresses especially between bow and stern. But a sailor lying on
his back as if in a Pullman berth except for jerky loosening and tightening
of the chains supporting one side of his rack feels only one resultant vector
at a time and he personally describes but a single oscillating trajectory of
nearly frustrated forward progress. If he broods too long about the aggressive cliffs that slam the bow and beetle the stern in rolling valleys of
unending succession never allowing the vessel to complete its heavy
stitches with a breath of relief since she's too sluggish for the whirlwind
yet at the same time blessedly responsive to the quaking surfaces she must
mount as her heavy stern bucks low and high in the hoarse labor of respiration, he is likely to start worrying about how well the hastily trained
overpaid hayseed welders who superseded conscientious Rosie the Riveter
did their job on the hull amidships in particular. Since the war was then
still on and members of any one department had to be scattered about the
ship in coldblooded insurance against concentrated loss from a limited hit

by bomb torpedo or shell it was my good luck at that time to be quartered aft in the thick of the ship's population where the sounds of storm were masked by the normal and abnormal sounds of the ship's own power and where my alarm was more concerned with possible failure of our sustaining mechanisms than directly with nature's terrifying forces that I didnt yet appreciate were uniquely gathered against us between the howling coast of China immovable to God himself and the irresistible upheavals of an enormously unpacified ocean. Forward in the hollowest and least essential compartment where I later had my billet I would have died a thousand deaths with my ear to the full personal blows of furious Poseidon. We were also lucky that we no longer carried the crowd of soldiers and cargo of wheeled equipment that we'd beached on Okinawa the night before just in time to be spared both the nauseating stink of landsmen's puke and the lethal battering of military vehicles broken from their chains either on the tank deck or above in the open like loose cannon in a frigate. But our After Crew's Quarters below the main deck occupied the stern over the engine room and next to the hydraulic steering gear whose combined pulsations and grinding vibrations gave way to sudden muted gasps of horribly unresisted torque whenever the rudders and screws of the shallow ship were tilted out of water by the plunging bow. Like a soul terrified by violently irregular heartbeats the ship would catch her breath at the shuddering disconnections of her vital power when in the midst of her integrated thrashing the reassuring noise of twin diesels driving geared shafts was abruptly altered in tone as if on the point of fatal cessation. She must have been grateful to the indomitable black gang on watch below her water line in what they regarded as their ivory tower a compact engine room snugly secure in bright electric light with all its moving parts tautly fixed save the innocuously sloshing bilge beneath the nethermost grating the throbbing main engines based like live altars among motors generators pumps tanks pipes and other auxiliary organs nothing like the infernal scene of a classic steamer with bunkers that shift coal fire shovels and pokers that slide furnace doors that bang and other movable objects that are acted upon by constant gravity. Lying in my bunk I had listened anxiously to the starts stops wheezes and straining reversals of the squeaky steering gear in the semicircular compartment between me and the chasms chasing our fantail and to the groan of the whole ship undergoing mountains of brine knowing nothing of the urgent general warnings and MAYDAY distress calls that were breaking radio silence all over the East China Sea into which we our sisters our cousins and whatever enemies might have remained afloat in their own western seas were being dispersed to get us off the lee shore of Okinawa and having no idea that the officers on the con were quaking with rational fear at the conjunction of radioed weather intelligence and what they witnessed in their oilskins open to the weather. Drake and the other wonders earned their commissions that night. He had just come off watch up there and everything that could be done to button

up and batten down had long since been undertaken by the bosun's men. I
lay below unaware of the storm as an infamous typhoon subject to general
fears but basically undismayed at what I took to be merely my first taste of
really bad weather. When I went on watch at 0400 after we had passed the
eye of the crisis allowing for retrospective hyperbole I was still uninformed
of the whole danger behind us and indeed I was so accustomed to discount
or avoid the pronouncements of my shipmates that I didnt grasp the mortal significance of our ordeal until Jim Drake told me in that bar a year
later how critically the ship and its navigators had been tested. At the
time as I got used to the commotion I soothed myself by the patterns of
sound and vibration that I searched for and seemed to find as characteristic
of a steady state. But it was Jim's music or its distorted apparition swinging in dizzy arcs within my confused skull or at large in the shapeless
quarters left over from the ship's vital compartmentation like unclaimed
pasture serving as the enlisted commons and grand concourse a truncated
apsidal crypt cluttered with tables benches lockers stanchions ducts pipes
and cables as well as hatches opening above below and forward on both
sides crammed at every angle with four or five dozen folding bunks
stacked up to the overhead most of them now let down and bearing the
weight of men like catacombs for transients that captured my drifting
wisps of consciousness and wove them back into a cohesive cloud of overwhelming aesthetic satisfaction from which I was able to exclude any oxygen that might have supported the combustion of fear. Provided that the
dream of music may be regarded as compatible with the pleasure of sleep I
was wrapped in a dilerium of art. But it is possible I wholly imagined that
solitary afflatus. In an uncultivated pragmatical guy like me it naturally
had no aftermath except memory of the fact that it had occurred or had
seemed to occur. An ineffably primitive religious experience or a Babel of
philosophical ecstasies would be easier for a prosaic brain like mine to
summon than music's glossolalia. As a practical matter it had to be treated
like a surpassing erotic dream produced by my unconscious imagination
that is to say dismissed with a sigh as irretrievably faded and too exceptional to be equalled in affect. Within the cataclysmic heaving of a suspended bower the size of a coffin it was as if a blessed ionosphere insulated
the coulombs of my nerves from all sensations except sound while exciting
an immensity of consciousness without apperception. Even in the engine
room I could not have ignored intimations of cataclysm so successfully.
Jim was too full of Bourbon water for me to trust his answers to my
inquiring reminders about the records he had played on the phonograph
that distant night alone in the wardroom as he wrote what might have
been the last entry in his secret journal. It hadnt occurred to me that
rather than an anagogic descent of art's paraclete the stimulation of my
unformed aesthetic susceptibility might have been an almost purely auto-
suggestive sublimation of the typhoon's terrifying cacaphony. Yet I did
learn from Jim in his cups who with his own eyes and voice of command

had faced it in open battle on the conning tower struggling to save all
our lives that during the worst of that long night our situation was so
precarious as not only to mark the acme of his navigational career in the
Navy but also to have seemed the crisis of all existence. I had formed a
mitigated conception of the absolutely sober facts that Jim had actively
confronted on his open-air watch only when toward the end of the night
I crept up to my watch station in the chartroom by way of the internal
Officers' Country companionway to avoid the dangerous passage by
topside ladder exposure to the imperceptibly abating violence of a black
maelstrom illumined by phosphorescent wave crests still howling both
above the oscillating masthead and below the ship's waterline and heard
as cheering daylight approached that the most experienced officers were
betting we'd survive the onslaughts which for some time after passing
the eye of the typhoon had not been getting any worse. Since the 1066
was not a sailing vessel but an encased machine only a few officers quartermasters and boatswain's mates had recognized the moments of our
greatest peril and in the morning when we could clearly see the waves
most of the rest of us who never saw the barometer were inclined to
dwell upon the respite those spume-blown mountains were giving us
from fear at least of submarines and Kamikaze planes if not of floating
mines torn loose for random contact in those narrow waters anxiety
enough to keep our minds off the older despair of men who go down in
the sea with ships. Without counting on the absolute speed of light
Elizabethan seadogs consoled themselves that they were as near to God
by sea as by land but I've never had any hope of heaven and my supernatural music was more like the anodyne drunkenness of ancient Mediterranean sailors hopelessly facing worse odds off the lee coast of Africa.
I doubt that Sir Humfry Gilbert half-brother of Raleigh more of a new-
dealing philanthropist maybe from his experience in Ireland than a
seadog and in fact as his queen discerned a man of "no good happe at
sea" could get his chamber quartet to play in extremis. It's the one time
I have taken to heart the opiate of the new masses but mine was a variety
of the aural anaesthetic that has no aesthetic affect upon most Americans
especially those in military service. Even the minority who do not reject
classical genres as elite or anachronistic would be astonished at my
ingenuous response to the recording that enthralled me which though stirring and dramatic was I now know nothing subtle or profound. If I really
heard music at all it could have come only from Jim's own shipboard
library in which there were no more than two albums *Tristan and Isolde*
and *Carmen*. I remember enough to believe it wasnt Wagner his favorite
for moods of depression that he was playing that night. Bizet had never
come over our speaker before but according to circumstantial evidence and
Jim's recollection if I heard anything from outside my own head it was one
of those orchestral recapitulations from the gypsy opera rotating like a car-
ousel of tumbleweed above the sounds of the ship's travail drowning out

God's own whirlwind like a Götterdämmerung. Under apocalyptic conditions in the youth of my ignorance that broad fairground music might
well have seemed unearthly in beauty. At least it provided me a standpoint
from which I could despise the music I was brought up to that I'd almost
constantly hated dumbly for instance even F D R 's favorite "Home on the
Range". It took *Carmen* if that's what it was with all the thrilling orchestral
power projected from its pit onto the plastic disk in which it modulated fossil energy converted to electricity by the ship's diesels to reproduce artistic
combustion opera's one great virtue calculated even without electronic
amplification to drown out the virtue of true drama and to split for germi-
nation and conditional maturity the seed that had been dropped onto my
cobblestoned turnpike by Karl whom I had listened to in my love for
Ruth though he said nothing in praise of music and only betrayed by
accounting for much of his ordinary leisure its dominant matter-of-fact
claim upon him a pure and disinterested sensorium where there was no
known talent even for recreating what others had conceived. Listening to
him was for me the first accidental step in a born sinner's notice of virtue
whose casual spark of morality fades at once as his aggressive narrowminded perception of culture reasserts itself as interestedly as ever. But the
inchoate seedling's still alive. I don't have to remember the first bursting
epiphany of my deciduous tree now grown much unlike its germ to yearn
every now and then for its immediate satisfaction of a sporadically conscious hunger with say Bach or Beethoven if only in order to fortify my
resistance to the narcotic sounds demanded by my countrymen to put off
death or its harbingers either by extruding a soupy paste in which words
are forced together or apart into an unfitted masonry more mortar than
brick with all its strength in the stickiness of arrested sentiment worn out
with repetition like a blanket retained from the cradle every song a unit of
competitive popularity or by sentimentally evoking a personal emotion
without true cause whether ethereal or frictive. My kind of half-starvation
in the national poverty is a hunger for rare sweetness known to no aesthete
who doesnt have to work for his living or live for his own works perforce
exclusively. How many who perpetually rage at the banal noise around
them have otherwise unoccupied time for such music as they crave to hear
rising from silence? I pity the composer more than all other artists because
our air is already saturated with music. Even music finer by far than
Carmen and worthy of taste higher than bourgeois Karl's good as it was by
accident of nationality now multiplies like printed currency. Lesser music
drenches all marketplaces with projections and precipitations. Organs and
loudspeakers bombard infant brains in fane and home. Even Vivaldi and
Telemann are used like stuffing to fill a background void of mentality.
Electronically they keep the air moving to maintain for effortless hearers
who do not listen a kinetic illusion almost as comforting as the relative
motion that quiets babies rocked back and forth or carried from one place
to another not to get there but to keep moving as an airplane does to keep

from falling. But what I heard against the background of a void filled with
the sea's palpable chaos wasnt anything I'd ever heard Karl whistle and of
course it wasnt the Toreador song which the kids in my world had known
as a parody of highbrow culture deadly enough to mock the piece forever
even as the overture pirated by the Lone Ranger of the radio was ruined by
the ridicule of twenty million kids as they outgrew the law and order
always beating in the hearts of Texas lawmen represented by the former
one of them whose Indian sidekick waits outside whitemen's cafes while
his master disguises himself by taking off his mask to search out evil or
else Tonto explains his own errand in Basic English soliloquy as the
Masked Man gallops off undisguised crying HEIGH HO SILVER! to his
great white horse which I myself used to shout when I was delivering
bundles at a nickel each to rich people anywhere within a mile for the Chinese laundry on Observatory Hill usually in the dark before I was through
on winter afternoons skipping to rest my knees from running Torea-dora
don't spit on the floor-ra use a cuspa-dora but I'm sure there werent many
words much more-ra. If I listen to that opera now I can't find anything
before the last act that could account for my mystical response and at the
end before the bullfight there's nothing but the faintest suggestion of
what I remember as a careening bolero that inflated my mortal envelope.
Was my memory confused by the wild dashing spirit of Ravel whose
music momentarily possessed me four or five years later or did my frightened soul on this single occasion provide itself with the affect of a brilliant
melody resorting to some supernatural muse that didnt belong to me so
that with stolen esemplastic cheer I could recover my insensitivity to
death in the same mysterious way that my unconscious and inaccessible
genius has always constructed dreams of wit and imagination far beyond
the powers of my art or intellect sometimes so funny that I wake myself
up laughing? I suppose my lumpish optimism was breached by fear
beyond the reach of all-too-willful mind. Yet so stupid am I as a listener of
music that I don't even know whether or not there were voices in the transcendental sounds that used the laboring storm-toss'd ship itself as the
loudest instrument in their orchestra.

When I was with Karl and Ruth all I knew about the kind of music I
didnt hate was that Beethoven's Fifth cried out in the alphanumeric Victory symphony of Churchill's virile V-fingered dit-dit-dit-daa the most
manly foot in German meter known the world over by courtesy of the
B B C for penetrating the hiss of Hitler's propaganda. Once or twice I had
heard it beyond the theme's announcement all the way to the end of the
first movement and accepted it as the beginning of my education in the
higher culture of underground fighters and ordinary Europeans oppressed
by the compatriots of its ante-Nazi composer. Karl sometimes was obliged
to use a small pilot lathe in the back room for minor subsidiary tasks
while the big turret screw machine remained set up for his main job.
That's why Ruth'd heard him whistling something interesting maybe the

Fifth itself for he could do the whole thing as well as many operatic scores
that he loved. Perhaps she had spoken first after two or three days of
responding to his smiles in the regular let-ups between boring whines of
her double drills as half a dozen times a minute she replaced castings in
the jig that never changed shape color or temperature month after month
and waited for his reply while the spinning fangs plunged into
unhardened steel and recoiled in poise for their next victim. The war loosened some hardpacked soil that the Depression and the New Deal hadnt
harrowed but even under the influence of music with cohesive power
stronger than the city's agitations that kept them apart it could not have
thrown them together if they hadnt both been foreigners innocent of certain subtle fears that constrain Americans to habits of behavior often mistaken in any one generation for proprieties of national or local character
despite public acknowledgement of social evolution. All three of us
acknowledged other people's hatred and taboo by refraining from much
further expression of our mutual affection than the lunch hour afforded. I
was too young for Ruth he was too old for her and we were both too white.
He and I were kept at a small distance from each other just when we
might have become friends by the two like charges she couldnt help
inducing opposite her own. Karl the widower went to Carnegie Hall alone
I the bachelor went to my movies alone and as far as I know Ruth went to
school and studied dance in loneliness greater yet.

As a sympathetic witness with no music I was of course the least of
the three yet so trusted as sometimes to be forgotten entirely and the crucial conversation took place after they knew I'd be leaving soon. Thitherto
Ruth and Karl had revealed to each other little more of their selves than
the sense of humor that came out for instance in merriment she liked to
raise about her strengthening right arm which she said was going to end
up twice as thick as her left adding that there was nothing she could do
about it because the jig the flow of material and the drill press itself had
been set up for dexterous human intervention and that though the procedure might have been altered for her if at the beginning she had mentioned that she was sinister. Karl's reply had been "You vill be zee only
ballerina die can hold up her partner py one hand!" She said it was a jolly
good thing it wasnt her legs she had to use on the drill press because she'd
never get even into the chorus. Could you imagine solo choreography for
an asymmetrical girl like the special sonata for a one-armed pianist? In a
distinction that I now know enough to make she had no interest in creative dance. Saddler's Wells was the goal that I almost hope she failed of
because it would have been an abuse of that body its color and the music
of it to continue in the whited platonism that had directed her imagination. But according to all the probability curves that might be applicable
it's far more likely she's now modestly teaching grade school or mothering
her own golden black Jonathan Matthew and Roger or maybe a Karl Ruth
and Michael totally dedicated to whatever illusions may center in them

and it's quite possible that her own hopes for the performing art if she
finally fell in love no more outlasted the war than I'm sure did Karl's smile
about the jest she made that he was a German spy neither of them as
immigrants being sufficiently acculturated to avoid the dangerous indiscretion of overlooking literal interpretations by civilian counterintelligence. It was a fine day outdoors and we were left alone for a few minutes.
With her tantalizing waist pressed against the windowsill she was standing with her back to the room looking through the dirty factory glass
mullioned in steel frames now tilted open on horizontal axes out upon flat
rooftops cluttered with odds and ends of weathered rotting boardwalk
rusted radio antennas or dilapidated garden furniture pushed up among
watertowers chimneys ventilating shafts or elevator hoists no longer pretending to be penthouse shanties altogether cartooning a cityscape of rectangles as far as the eye could reach from our own stratified housing each
disorderly plateau betraying the penury of real estate neither wholly residential nor wholly industrial piled behind or above facades and lobbies
and leaseheld improvements complementing on high the basement junk
dropped down available fissures and noticed over the years only by cats
and corruptible building inspectors or dragged out into alleys overlooked
by nobody's windows for the needle trades made no pretenses about whatever they were up to in mid-Manhattan. The beauty was in the surface
planes as related to each other most of the day under the shadows of taller
buildings that screened them as barriers to any sun-horizon all outshone
by the Empire State Building our mortal silver and gray Olympus cutting
distant north light from the day's blue Madonna-robed sky though a
coastal defense bomber later crashed into it lost on the underside of clouds
lowered by the weight of flooded heavens without damaging the tourists'
peak as high as the length of Britain's greatest ships of the sea and meant
to serve like the Eiffel Tower as mooring for gossamer ships of the air that
unfortunately have proven too passive for evolution the cynosure of all
souls living working or traveling between the Woolworth and Rockefeller
precincts as well as beacon to Jersey flats Long Island wastes and rolling
sulcate ocean on clear days and unbusheled peacetime nights.

Outside that window there was no sign of war's destruction. Inside the
gentle kidding had drifted into silence. Then softly, continuing I knew
not what conversation: "I suppose things here are after all no better than
they were when my mother came to college. She warned me but I thought
the war would have liberalized New Yorkers and that times had changed
for Negroes." Karl smiled encouragingly at what may have been the first
beginning of talk about herself. By glancing over his shoulder though
never before fearful of eavesdroppers he distinguished her confidences by
nearly seeming to threaten uncharacteristic resentment of anyone who
might inhibit them. I edged away to a sentry's position taking out my
book and unsuccessfully resolving not to listen. "I'm too proud even now
to accept the ways of America. I didnt expect to bump up against the

seamless curtain of entertainment. Even if you arent a black girl you have to be an entertainer to get on the stage." Her tone was disheartened but not bitter and in fact she laughed in a determinedly cheerful English way that exactly suited the beauty of her mouth as if her life was the art she wished to perform in instead of donning a false mask in search of the true. I doubt that Karl understood what she meant any better than I did at the time for I'm sure that as a reader of nothing much more than the daily Last Testament he was as innocent of true art's motive as most young children used to be innocent of their fucking conception. He was too pious about music to have learned manmade irony even in it. Anyway I don't see how he could have kept his wits for listening to her words as she faced him again in a soft flame of dignity speaking as clearly as the bell of a moonlit schooner under sable sail still warm from sunshine. "Of course . I'm not sure I believe that. It's easier than believing that I have no talent in a city full of talent that overwhelms understanding. Why should it get me down on a cloudless day like this? Even in the most horrible cold weather I hardly ever get sad enough to sing the blues! It's the white people here who seem to get depressed. —Except you Karl! You always smile. You're always courteous too. Your kind smiles and your courtesy help me through the day. And sometimes through the weekend too." She added the codicil so swiftly glancing once more toward the sunlit bricks outside that I almost missed its import. When he told her that after a certain age one doesnt get depressed so often and that he guessed he was just older than everyone else the last of his words were contested by the watchful attention of his smooth white face which seemed young and bright with grateful wonder as he stood like John Smith before Tragabigzanda thanking her for his boon a free frank high-headed princess the tight edge of her purple bandana-toque making a level crown on her clear brow where it met the light-absorbing skin above large unflinching eyes of deepest color not yet either hardened by the ambition she was still appraising or humbled by domesticity of any kind. "Besides" he said dropping his gaze from hers to look at his feet "I'm free now."

It does not seem possible that any intelligent woman so young and essentially chaste though older in years than I who judged and older too it seemed to me in wisdom could have faced so steadily a loving man so much older yet and not to be considered as a lover. He could not have been expected to sustain without stammering the sudden intensity of her interest when he felt no more within the reach of her sympathy than a classical bust outside her bedroom. In his embarrassment it was impossible to evade the examination that followed. Of all men despite his reticent modesty he was the least able to stand mute or equivocate before a woman clearly taking his part especially when already trembling in his struggle not to speak naturally about what an old fool he was to fall in love with her having expressed himself on no subject to anybody else perhaps for as many years as she had lived. I willed myself invisible. Hardly breathing I shrank so far into their shadow that I'm sure they forgot me as they forgot the tyranny of the clock until the giggling girls came bursting in three or four minutes later full of the joy they had inhaled from an unseasonably warm sun.

Under her questioning he revealed that he wasnt literally a widower unless he could be called a grass widower. "Already for a long time I didnt like my vife venn ze Nazis came up around us. Now zey are zumsing ve don't haf hier!" At first he'd paid no attention to them but they started getting after him to join the Party. There were all too few model Aryans for their purposes. He must have looked like an ideal blond block captain and no doubt he had great moral influence at the plant where he was foreman. (Indeed I had marveled that he seemed so content to forego advancement in the new world.) They stopped music written by Jews he said. Pfui! After Hitler took power they came to him again. All of a sudden everybody was beginning to support the swastika with conviction. People he'd thought kind and decent turned into swine when certain words were spoken. Everyone acted like the worst kind of policeman even women. "I say I can't be a Nazi married to a Jewish vife who plays die fiddle. They vant me to divorce her but py Gott I vill not do zat now to please them. So ve must leave or go to ze concentration camp and already yust in time ve get away and haf not been able to take anysing wis us tools or wiolin or nussing." In New York he had got his divorce and taken out his first papers for citizenship. "At first I am hearing no music at all. Now I can find even music by Jews!" He laughed. But too bad everything else was not as wonderful as it seemed at first. "Aber ist my country jetzt!" His wife had a good teaching job and made no further claims upon him glad enough to be free of a machinist.

The conversation was never finished unless some beguiling angel by miracle restored those delicate feelings for each other after I joined the Navy. A few mornings later Joe was working in the back room setting up in the punch press some dies he'd been preparing for a new contract. It was the usual procedure as I could see in passing back and forth on two or three errands. He would feed a belt of strip steel into the clumsy console of brute hydraulic force and in short pounding bursts like the massive phlegmatic travesty of a machine gun it would spew down into a grimy corrugated paper carton kicked into position under its hopper a batch of samples that he carefully studied almost one by one before tossing them aside still warm from the pressure that had stamped them into formal individuals though by pure reason they should have been perfectly identical in reflecting the initial imperfections of Joe's matrix. He scrutinized them as closely as if with an eyepiece screwed like a jeweler's into the cavity between his long flat cheek and his wrinkled brow but actually using a simple magnifying glass held close to the work as like an etcher he mentally translated concave to convex or negative to positive before removing the die from its mounting to touch it up with a pocket file in quick short strokes and an emery cloth in tenderly abrasive touches lighter than the friction of a bow on four strings always conservatively never allowing himself an ordinary workman's flourish for good measure or merely for the rhythmic satisfaction of a followup and repeatedly appraising the results before putting his die to the test again even returning a few times to the front shop for an infinitesimal touch of the surface grinder. This unruffled patience only verified his power as an energetic cocksure crackerjack in taking all the pains of plastic artifice to perfect a mold that as the single tooth of a noisy unclean automaton with measureless appetite would emboss its unique cavities upon a myriad impressionable items. That day and until long afterwards immersed in a life of other places and girls I hated this complacent confidence equivalent to arrogance. He did not miss music he did not miss college. Inwardly I raged at the vanity of his meticulously tended citron bristles on the curled somewhat puffy upper lip and tightly combed waves of sepia brass thickening the scalp of his narrow weak-chinned somewhat vulpine head which looked to me more like a certain type of Irishman's than a Jew's. For I was aware that he had begun to talk to Ruth as he leaned his skinny rump against the shipping table blithely facing her way while looking down at his work for all the world like a dandy filing his fingernails. For a while Karl also happened to be standing within earshot at the pilot lathe silent in the background no doubt subjected to the young squire's insolently respectful condescension the words of which I was too late to hear.

Why did the next step follow so fast? After slow agricultural incubation the black lily budded in our hothouse only to wither suddenly before it blossomed as if Karl's predestination was to suffer incommensurate prolongation of sorrow in a reversal of his mild hope. At noon when I got to the back room with my lunch according to our new custom he had spread out his meal in deliberate ceremonial manner and begun to look around for Ruth whose drill press was deserted. Having changed to her street clothes she just then called to the other girls from the ladies' room door in crystal tones of debonair British self-deprecation for Karl and me to hear "I was silly enough to oversleep this morning so I didnt have time to make my sandwiches. Now I'll have to go out for lunch the very day the weather's turned bad again!" We watched with astonishment Karl and I as she went to the elevator to join Joe who had paused to wait for her behind Basil and Vera.

My head flamed with stunned confusion and chagrin as if Karl my best friend if not I myself had been drummed out of the regiment. For the first time since I'd known him his smile faded. As soon as the little group disappeared he gathered up his things without a word and oblivious of me returned to his old place disemboweled, stoically picking up the Times on his way past the coat rack. At his stool he stared for a couple of minutes with vacant pale blue eyes at the oily sheen of the lathe's carriage track like a bemused footman waiting belowstairs. The silent belts and pulleys of the machinescape seemed to thin out voices coming through vines and creepers from the front bench as stillborn echoes of things said a million times a day. "Dixie Walker is the best ballplayer the Dodgers ever had!" The letters reversed on the plate glass were stupidly meaningless to me as with equally abstracted eyes I tried mechanically to puzzle them out from my own acrid thicket. Without a book in hand I sealed myself off from what I had witnessed. I cast my mind toward the forthcoming adventure of running away to sea.

That black beauty at our non-union shop prevented me from harvesting the fruit of Karl's friendship. Without her there I might at least have practiced my high-school German. Some of the greatest saints write in that language. But maybe it would have turned out differently if I'd made my own claim. At boot camp soon afterwards I pondered Ruth's black ivory body without tenderness and chided myself for missing the opportunity of a lifetime as if I'd had a chance to compete with impunity. In Navy training there wasnt much time to brood nor in the excitement of westward travel but at first my precipitate new opinion of female treachery weakened a congenital loyalty to the nameless white victims mostly uncaptured whom I heard abused and despoiled every waking hour in the speech of shipless sailors suddenly unwomaned but not yet introduced to the irreconcilable continence of sea duty. In the companies to which I was assigned during my quasi-academic naval education not even vacuum-tube jargon was clearly distinguished from talk of hot cunt the otherwise classless prey of born hunters. For some time but much too late for real brutality she was my lust's one living image stripped of all attributes and specifications not conducive to the satisfaction of fucking her ruthlessly. I would have written a boldly disingenuous letter if I'd known where to send it and for a while I really thought that if I'd thus been able to inveigle her into correspondence I would return the vindictive revelation that my sole interest in her person was to pin it under me like a great black butterfly. But by then I was on my way to less fantastic objects further west. It was only a matter of chance that I wasn't sent south to schools in Gulfport Mississippi and Corpus Christi Texas instead of Monterey and Treasure Island.

There are varieties of involuntary celibacy that may get bad enough to drive you not only to yourself but to your own kind but even whaling voyages are sometimes emolliated by scurvy and occasionally assuaged by the genuine rewards of Omoo Typee and Owyhee and schooner fishing which anyway doesnt last very long on any one trip is totally engaged if not constantly with mortal fear of God's ocean certainly with unremitting hard cruel work sometimes so cold that the watch on deck must be relieved every six or eight minutes thus banishing at least from one's mind for whole days at a time even when snugly behind the little red curtain of a bunk all visions of a port with call girls Newfoundlanders or Nova Scotians easily called upon if a man's not too drunk or broke from drinking. Or monasteries which I began to steer clear of when I was still a boy that obfuscate the one true object of male lifeforce by quelling the body's storms with music and ritual for the sake of God's love. But in long Navy stints at sea or desert island without much danger or labor to distract your libido you learn perforce abetted only by saltpeter in all the food you can eat to endure by sublimation or unsublimated language the shackles of chastity clasping your loins. At least you're no worse off than the men at your elbow or the captain himself and you don't want to throw yourself to the sharks lest you miss what you've supposedly got coming to you if you ever get back to the States. Yet the most tormented singleness of all is the one that Caleb's suffered the madding state of erotic loneliness imposed only by your own failure to overcome the indifference of landswomen when all about you they flaunt their interest in successful men especially if without diverting cacoethical intentions your desire is mentally complicated by the technical nescience and uncertainty in which you are left after reading illustrated erotic books when you havent yet even for the first time felt the pressure of a girl's skinless flesh the full length and circumference of the homunculus that leads you like a nose. You cling to the excuse that it's like trying to get your first job that everyone knows you'll be so good at which you're willing to take for nothing just to get started when all hiring is based exclusively upon experience yet feed upon the failure to prove yourself and secretly grow more strongly convinced that it's your misfortune to be born a crippled or ill-favored exception to the general law of reciprocal attraction without the money to disguise that fact, your virtue all the more bitterly mocked by women's invidious new liberality. The poor guy has to wait much longer than I did to do more than lift the veil of manhood's temple.

Until initiated by that compassionate work-worn waitress with a past revealed only later who came out of the commissary steam tunnels another connection with Harvard I almost forgot about doubtless because it was extramural in consummation I was still under the influence of a drawing I'd seen when I was in about the seventh grade and subsequently contrived to revisit several times chalked on the flaking gray paint on the steel faceplate of a main truss where it rose out of the sidewalk on the bridge over the rail yards of the main B & M line through Fitchburg and the Hoosac Tunnel to connect with the great westward railroads and where the Concord Turnpike starts north toward Walden Pond. The ugly structure stood alone more than a mile from home where Cambridge was so raw and shabby from the Depression that I was reminded of it when I saw Yokahama a few months after V J Day. I would have seen the illustration many times more if it hadnt been weathered into oblivion because it was on one of the ways to swimming in the clay hole called Jerry's Pit from which we always trudged home hotter dustier and more discontented than when we'd set out for refreshment. With Billy and Peggy trailing me I pretended not to notice and strode right on by. Allowing for both my

exceptional knack with airplanes and the infinitely more difficult rendering of living figures I thought it must have been executed by a fifth-
grader. The isocephalic frieze cartoon had some commonplace FUCK legend in transitive verb form connected by line to the mouth of the male
half who stood in profile with his single tubular arm sprouting blunt
crownlike fingers extended straight at the udder of his lovee similarly facing him his massive Ionic column leveled straight ahead from its scroll-
hilted capital like a battering ram half sunk into a female's single thigh or
belly at an angle mutually perpendicular to both their stances her own set
of tumid digits not at all feeble pavid or modest grabbing for the part of
their nexus where it was exposed. Within a few years I was worried about
mine always pointing upward for fear it wouldnt bend horizontal when
my time came—

"*Home at last! Thank you for taking us to the zoo, Daddy!*"
"*Yuh, thanks Dad! I like San Francisco.*"
"My pleasure I'm sure. But you should thank Ruth."
"*When are we going to the beach?*"

{*Postulants only*: GO TO ITEM (8) SO.01.0, page 97.}

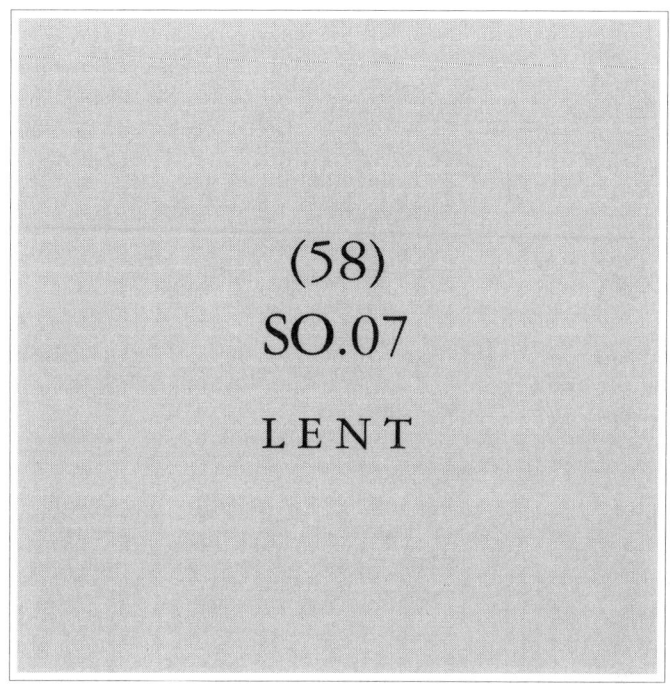

(58)
SO.07
LENT

CALEB KARCIST (B)

1.

It befell at a time when the age of steam was waning and common folk used the world as they saw fit that a landless youth without orders or preferment, lacking horse and arms, was set to guard an absent landlord's treasure in all the darknesses of a year and a day. One night in the dungeon where he tended fire to warm the castle his lonely vigil was cheered by the visit of his lord's scribe, a fair comely woman whom he had seen but once and long before. Haply she liked the beardless boy and gave him to drink of the wine she carried as he taught her how to throw coals into the athanor with a great fire shovel as sparingly as ever might be, for there were few left to last out the winter. She doubted not that he would become a great magician, or else prove wood. He made delight of her fellowship for he desired the simple knowledge of ordinary men that he had not yet learned, and he soon found it in his mind to become her prentice, seeing that she was wise and kind, buxom and jocund eke.

The youth was yclept Caleb and the gentlewoman Hecuba. He spoke not the speech of her country which at first in her mouth seemed harsh and uncouth, but her voice was soft as her white hands and he saw at once that her heart was good, so he strove to make himself accustomed to her free and easy manner of address. He was astonied withal at her understanding of his words, whereby she took to herself his strange learning, for she offered to fetch to him from the counting house each day's pages of the empire's great diurnal chronicle ordained to be brought overland from the Eastern ocean, save only on each week's sabbath, that her master might know the prices and ventures at fairs and markets everywhere beyond his own city, forasmuch as that copious scripture of the times revealed divers matter of thick weight and substance right powerful for wreaking the magic she wished to learn. Caleb answered nothing but laughed in pleasure at the nicety of her wit, for the which he would fain have embraced her in desire for her person, heedless that he knew not of woman and she was said to have lain with many men.

Without yet speaking her tongue entirely he made show to deliver his mind at her ruby mouth. "Sheer off now!" she cried, haply just as she yawned from the heat of the fire that shone on them like light from the face of an orange pumpkin, for it was drawing toward the end of her long day of counsel to the lord in his business, and she was more weary than a villein that has labored in the fields. Whereupon she bethought what she had done, lest he be offended, for she held in esteem his deep knowledge and his gentle manner. She reasoned within herself that the ill-fallen yawn confused his pride more sorely belike than any wrothful refusal, and she guessed that he was more tender than a woman in his feelings, witting that save for the befuddlement of drink he would never have durst so much as touch her elbow to guide her steps to the peephole of the furnace.

And in truth, even as she kenned, he was not so tipsy that her yawn escaped his eyes and ears, and in chagrin he withdrew from her shoulder the protection of his arm, repenting that he had offered neither more nor less than what any other man would have attempted at her side, as assuredly the simplest wench might have foretold of churl or sailor. Yet he feared his advances did seem to her passing rude, namely if she guessed that he had heard tell of her from another man.

Hecuba jumped up and made shift to banish the dark humour she had brought to Caleb's countenance against her will. "Being as how I'm here, why don't you show me the closets in this vacant tower? Yet I would shiver in fear if you were not to take me by the hand." At these words his visage somewhat brightened, malgre the wanhope of his desire to taste the lips so many had tasted.

She pressed his hand as he led her to the elevation machine that was devised for lifting wights to the topmost gallery of the castle that he was appointed to keep warm against the west wind and to watch against the lord's enemies. "This is a lonely place only at night." he said. "As well you know, I sleep by day in another house among people who do not own to the lord's fiefdom."

"Nay," said she "this very day has come to my ears the news that he has made purchase of the rabbits' burrow where you hold tenor. Now you dwell in his latifundium by day as well as by night; but little harm will it do you, for I am his steward and I shall pray him not to raise your rent. Be it natheless known to you that you will lose the weekly service of maids with bed linen, for he means to give displeasure to all his tenants, save you only, that many may choose to leave his estate, and he trusts that the sheriff at his behest will dispossess those that remain, seeing that he means to pull down the ruins after you have served out your year, so that he may let out the land at greater profit as a paddock for the horseless chariots that bring doctors and gentry to this steep from sun to sun. The leveled space of the warren will be smoothly flagged and given in charge of your fellow his trusty old servant the grizzled Norwegian seadog to collect the rents and fees hour by hour, unless you yourself will choose to serve that office while you live by night in another place for as long as you wish. But these tidings must be kept hidden between us, for I pass them to you as your friend in despite of his charge to keep them from all men until he can make his intents known at his own time. Do you swear? I wager you would do as much for me, and on my side in such case I would have my lovely carmine nails of hands and feet pulled out by the roots before I would reveal your secrets."

Caleb thanked Hecuba and willingly took his oath, caring nothing for the future when his year was to be done but grieving for the house he loved and the ancient druids that would spread their arms no more for the shade of living horses and lusty men. Yet presently he ceased to wax sad for he had heard it said that the best way to seduce a gentlewoman is first to plant a secret solely with her, or the secret of a secret, the which he found she was doing with him as if he was a reluctant maid, but that she was unwitting of what her friendship inflamed in him. He laughed with wry mien, and said nothing of his astonishment, thereby filling her with admiration of his silent bravery, for in her reckoning he seemed not to weigh as a feather the dangers to his sustenance.

This is how they came to the top of the winze. He pressed a button cunningly contrived to make the basket rise that he seldom rode when he was alone for fear of weakening his knees and shriveling up his lungs with luxury ill-matched to the hardships of his spirit, and he told her of his scorn for Pegasus, that he might have aught to say during the ascent. He spoke in such wise that she looked at him in new wonder at the strange thoughts that filled his weird head. Thus did Hecuba begin to see that in his heart there was as much poetry as philosophy, which aroused in her head the love of learning.

Then Caleb showed her the booths of doctors and wisemen left empty
for the night when all had gone away to sleep in manors and villages
round about. The lamps that he caused to burn overhead in the passages
dimly lighted the portals she wished to look into, to which he admitted
her with his magic key to all cells.

Hecuba being keeper of the landlord's rolls well knew and now made
known to Caleb the fame and deeds of the learned men whose names were
inscribed upon the roiled hoar-glass of the doors they passed to distinguish
one from another in the eyes of the halt and the hale who came to those
corridors by day seeking the succour of skill or craft. Some of the sages had
one door only, opening to an anteroom with no more than one inner chamber, whilst others had several outer doors in disuse where two or three
rooms led each other in train like the apartments of nobles sojourning at a
hostelry. A few stalls were sparsely furnished and their floors were bare,
with nothing but a parchment or two for honorable notice on the walls,
but many were richly beseen with thick tapestries underfoot and adorned
with all manner of likenesses on the walls, both true and conceited,
together with trophies of prowess in the gain of gold. And others again,
the lairs of metrical clairvoyants or piratical orators, were filled with a
throne of visions or tortures garnished with wondrous machines made to
move at the will of a magus with the several and divers motions of all the
stars as if to follow the sun and moon through a year of changing shadows;
which no twisting body of man or woman could elude, once lured to sit
thereupon.

One den of second sight Hecuba was seeking, and they found it before
the first minute was put much behind them. "I've been here before." she
said. "I came to Doctor Cloud to get my eyes examined." She peered into
every corner of the two rooms as he lighted them for her, even opening the
drawers of a writing table behind the great chair nigh hidden by a tree of
spars and marvelous tackle. Small hangings of framed parchment bore
large and small black oghams turning against each other. Hecuba made
bold to touch the machine, smoothly swiveling its curious black caskets,
wherein she contrived to turn rings of glass within rings of steel as if she
would gently learn the secrets of their science. She also looked into the
desk of the antechamber where a young serving woman sat by day to
receive messages for the seer-of-seers and admit inquirers one by one to his
darkened cabinet.

"But you have not spectacles on your face." he said.

"I use them in the city when I cipher. He is tall dark and handsome. A
good man is he, which his wife understands not."

"Aha!" said Caleb. And she let sound several little tiny laughs in a
row, like a girl outside school.

"How many times a year does he take the measure of your merry eyes?"

"Ask me no questions and I'll tell you no lies!" she gave back, looking
slyly at the smile on his mouth. Then she caught him unaware with her

two hands on his head and kissed him before he could make ready. Her lips were level with his own and very soft, set aside by his nose a little only, but he had no time to lay his palm upon her back and draw her unto him for she stepped quickly away and taking his hand would grant no other boon. Yet methinks his spirits rose as they descended the staircase story by story, sauntering in more familiar converse.

On the floor next below, which was the fourth, Hecuba asked to see the chambers of Doctor Anguish, for he had recently yielded up the ghost without leave or parley, and the landlord feared to lose the rent of his tenant if the widow did not sell her husband's trade at once. Hecuba satisfied herself that neither the throne nor any of its belongings, nor tables nor chairs nor tapestries, had been removed, and then sat down on a small sofa to consider the counsel she would give on this matter when she returned to the City two days hence. But when Caleb dropped to her side and kissed her weightily she was not so astonished that she could not have warded him off if she had been so minded. Her kiss was warm, but she offered no more than one.

Then they went into the chambers of other tooth-doctors on the same floor in order that she might compare Anguish's wealth. Caleb watched for her to sit down but she would not, wherefor at each visitation he took from her yet another buss standing with his chest pressed against her paps and one hand laid close to her haunch. Betimes the novice and the damosel were playing together like daffodils in a field of May, though they kept their laughter as quiet as they might and spoke in whispers lest they hear their own echo in the hallways. "Whisht—" he said "or the night watchman will catch us!" He knew not but that she might deny him more than kisses only for that she was in her courses after the custom of women and he bided his misfortune with good grace, hoping for the future.

But it is soon told how Caleb ended his postulancy that night. On the third floor it was the apartments of Doctor Philuberus that Hecuba first chose to be brought to, for she remembered from her codex that he was a leech to the fair sex. She said "I wonder what he looks like." and gazed at the rich appointments, admiring the chairs and lamps that guarded the door to the sanctum of private inquisition, wherefrom one cabinet concealed the table fixed for the posture of innermost examination, but it was not the one in which she allowed Caleb to lift her skirt. It was in the larger one joined thereto, wherein Philuberus talked to his patients beforehand and afterwards, that Caleb had his way on an ample sofa furnished for the doctor's naps.

But Hecuba did not forget to finish out the tour she had begun. On the second floor they visited two more healers. One of these was named Etwas, whom Hecuba knew by hearsay to be the most longheaded savant of them all, though not the youngest nor the most handsome, renowned for the cure of souls. He had a couch for gentlefolk to lie upon and tell their dreams, but Hecuba told Caleb that of latter years it was seldom used even by the richest. These things she had learned from her friend Lady Chapman, who was also known to Caleb. He was much surprised to hear that the wife of his spiritual lord had been a frequent visitor to this place of wisdom, yet his heart was too full of Hecuba's teachings to yield space for a new wonder.

But he no longer had eyes for couches of any kind. It befell his new estate that the carpet beneath their feet was uncommonly thick and costly, and more bewitching than moonlit greensward. It came to pass this time that her nostrils flared like his at her moment of highest delight.

Yet even there they did not long tarry, for they looked to a whole story that remained to them below. Hecuba now wist that the dubbed novice was not meek in the manner wherewith he tilted fiercely and oft at the cleft betwixt her legs and her belly. As they tripped gaily to the stairs, like a goat and goatherd well used to the paths and byways of the mountain and no longer fearful of its hollow dark silence, she softly whistled with smiling lips a song of the people that Caleb recognized:

> Roll me over
> In the clover—
> Roll me over
> Lay me down
> And do it again!

On the ground floor Caleb showed Hecuba how to use Dr Stone's double-barreled spy-lenses, and by that time she had waxed so amorous to his emprise that when she saw under glass the blithesome animalcules of the kind that now overflowed in her loins she put aside all her study of other matters, tempting him to yet another two or three closets of dalliance before she gave heed to his weal.

At the last they returned to the hermit bower of her swain. His fire had almost died out of neglect, and for long space Caleb had need attend his duty with what remained of his vigor, until the coals were cheered to proper heat again. Then came he her tireless new friend to sit at her side on the hard bench, loathe to lose her company until he knew her thoughts.

"Beshrew me," she cried "all swollen up again and not a maid in sight!" She swore that she had done all her healing art could do albeit she was in his debt for striking off the chains of ignorance that all her life had quelled the love for words. "Alas that I have no nook for the skill of medicine!" But Caleb had never felt so pleased with his jack staff since its first full growth, for his distemper had found its cure, notwithstanding its outward and visible sign that lingered and would ever return, as even now, in sickness or in health. Far from falling melancholy at his breach of celibacy, he took joy in the peace of newfound prowess; wherefore he wished to try in words his claim upon the woman, as long as it might last. She bided at his side, whose ardor and fortitude had endeared him to her with right good will, and gave her thoughts over to the passing pleasure of such a strange champion. Yet she counseled him that all things must come to end, for she feared that he was assotted upon her and that he weened to take the place of her chief paramour who was passing generous and wise in the way of the world, but vengeful too. Meanwhile she tenderly stroked his head, like as her own true son's.

2.

"Is this your first six times?" she asked.

"Yes—well not exactly. I've done other things with girls."

"I thought so. I could see you've been saving yourself for a long time. Well I'm very pleased to be known by you! But you should have a whole harem of porcupines. You won't need me any more. Now go out and find a complacent girl your own age."

3.

Caleb protested his loyalty so sweetly and with such honest praise of her person that she promised to consider whether she would lie with him again, touched in her heart by his sore distress in fear of her reply.

4.

"I have a boyfriend, you know." she said. "He doesnt like me to see other men."

"I don't blame him for that. If I were your lover I'd lock you up in a chastity belt." He had to stop and explain that device. She was skeptical of its efficacy, and in any case suspected a hoax. "But I can't let you go as soon as I find you, my pride and glory." he continued grandly. "You're my Golden Fleece!"

"Oh no I'm not. Didnt you even notice that it's all shaved off? He likes it that way."

"It was too dark, and I didnt want to waste any time in case you changed your mind. —Let's see."

"Oh no, you're not going to see me defrocked! You think I'm a strip-teaser or something? You with your dirty hands! —Do you ever clean your fingernails? —If you hadnt beat around the bust so long up there in the beginning before you laid me I'd be home by now sleeping cozy! I'm so tired I can't see straight!" She yawned chromatically, bending her head to his chest. "By the way, what was all that fuss after you finished the first time, up there at Doctor Lugubrious? The way you were crawling around the floor and poking at me, I thought you'd lost your dingus!"

"The rubber came off and I couldnt find it anywhere. I was worried someone would find it in the morning! I finally came upon the grisly thing in the darkest place of all. I guess you couldnt feel it. I was afraid of an inside spill and so scared of what might have happened that I didnt dare say anything."

"You didnt act scared of anything. I'm the one that was scared you were crazy!"

"Why didnt you tell me right away there was no need for it, you little golden goose?"

"You needed the practice in interception. I know a guy lost one and his wife found it in his pants cuff when he got home. But I hate those prophylacteries anyway. I thought you were afraid of catching something. I've never had the clap or bad blood."

"Oh no, I wasnt thinking of anything like that! It's a good thing you were ready, because I had only one in my wallet."

"Don't worry, I wouldnt have made you marry me. But I always keep the diagram in my purse. You never can tell when you'll get stranded somewhere."

"I didnt see you put it in."

"Jesus Joseph and Mary, what a nosey son of a bitch! I'm not going to explain everything. Stop asking so many questions. —See this? This is just for protection too!" She opened her purse to display a neat little nickel-plated pistol. "It came with my liquor flask. The Silver Fox gave it to me to use on anyone that makes a nuisance of himself. Watch out young man! But you make me soft-hearted with your long eyelashes and your college education. This gun's no six-shooter like you. I still can't get over how you do it! You've got enough juice in you to be a great-grandfather. I'd like to see more of it under the microcosm when we're not in such a hurry. It looked real versatile, wriggling like a spool of fish. But don't let it go to waste. Save some for your own kids." And so she praised his remarkable powers of refocillation, kissing him for the twenty first time and holding both his hands.

And he kissed her for the hundred and first. "When can we sleep together? I could be good at it in a real bed."

"Good, better, best—
Never let it rest,
Until your good is better
And your better best!"

"That's what I mean. I wouldnt interfere with your love-life."

"The hell you wouldnt! You'd be humping me all night if I let you. I'd be worn out. A woman can't be relined like the guns of a battleship you know!"

"Every week you'd have six days to rest. I get only one night off a week. You should know."

"Well even then I might get tired of you after twenty years or so. Besides, don't worry, you're plenty all right now. You could have taken your time though. I wasnt going anywhere. We could still be up there! I must admit at first I wasnt very excited—not that that's unusual—but the last couple of times I had real orgiasms."

"You didnt seem as excited as I was."

"I don't think its right to fake it with an honest guy like you. Then again you're a young fella and I wanted you to last as long as you could. But the more I got of you the more I wanted. Just goes to show, sometimes it doesnt matter how tall a man is. We could get used to each other awful fast, and then you'd break my heart. You make me feel domesticated, like."

"You don't work tomorrow. Come to my room in the morning."

By the light of the firebox peephole she looked at her watch and sighed. "It's almost morning now! It was a beautiful way to begin the Mardi Gras. But honey, even you need sleep. I've got two dates today, and I have to go to confession. Tomorrow Lent begins. I can't see anyone until Easter. No one but the Silver Fox. I have to see him whenever he wants. We may get married someday."

Caleb curbed his inquisitive mind and wisely swallowed his jealousy, for he had no wish to marry the woman himself. It would be silly to tempt providence with ingratitude for his good fortune. He resolved to ignore the life she led beyond his sphere, but to spare no effort to get her to his living quarters, or to be invited to hers, where his practice for the art of bachelorhood could begin in earnest. He hoped to purge himself of curiosity about what was none of his business so that in good time he could lightly go on to another seduction with qualmless self-esteem.

But the first chase was far from over. "You can call me on the telephone after Easter. Meanwhile I'll think about it. But don't try to see me—or I'll drop the word that you're stocking me. You'll soon wish you hadnt, long before his guys get through with you."

At that time Caleb was less impressed by his danger than by the prospect of forty days' reversion to his former condition, with little promise of her favors after that, for he naturally doubted the constancy of her feelings toward him after presently leaving his arms. But he still wished to make the most of a bird in hand. "One last time." Taking a seat on the straight wooden chair that belonged to Sig Hansen's nearby desk he set her astride on his lap.

"Gad Zooks, again? I'll never be able to make myself respectable to go home." she said, laying her hands on his two shoulders. "Take your time. This will probably be our farewell caper, must as I hate to say it, you adorable little billy-goat. But if I ever come here again I'll let you know in

advantage so you can take a bath first. You stink almost as bad as that
lame artist from Berkeley. I guess he had the idea I ran a betrothal or
something. He may be a genius but he also thinks he's the wild bull of the
pampas. The nerve of him, calling me a fire shovel! How would he know?
Someone called me a scupper when he was mad at me. Is that the same
thing? But men seem to like the feel of me. They say some women feel
like the inside of a corrugated culprit. I won't let him get near me again.
Actually I kind of like your smell, but other girls might not. You don't
need to wear a jacket and tie but you should keep clean like an optimist.
My mother always said never to let a coal-miner touch me. I guess I'm not
the one to talk though, being as how I'm not so dainty myself right now.
You've really messed me up. I've already got semenship running down to
my ankle. I'll take a bath as soon as I get home and try to forgive you for
discombobulating my unanimity. —Say, this is a pretty good stirrup
cup. . . ."

At first she was merely amused by indulging his satyriasis, but soon
she stopped talking, and in the end his efforts were rewarded with a few
romantic moans. When she went home at last, after kissing him fondly,
she was really sorry to leave him.

"Don't forget to call me in a couple of months. If I have company I'll
just say wrong number."

In her absence Caleb felt a new void that his selfsatisfaction could not
wholly fill.

5.

But Hecuba repented of her prophecy and at undern the next day she
knocked at his door as he lay sleeping, and he woke to receive her nigh out
of his wit with joy for he had thought to be forlorn for many weeks in
despite of his newly won worship. She bare a goodly heap of viands
esculents and all manner victuals for a good repast, and a bottle of dark
red wine withal. Nor did she forget for his pantry a flagon of liquor that
had been a present unto herself from her lord who dealt in it with the
Gaels and Picts of upper Britain, where he ordained to make further trade,
well ware those men were renown in all the world for their corn and living
water. Bysene in fair weeds she shone in his cell like the morning sun
upon a glade, banishing all shadows brightly, yet was she right shy at disturbing his rest, doubting that he would fain not see her eftsoons, or not
at all forever, by cause that she belike had overmatched him the night
before when he was weary from his watch and mayhap turned his will
against all womankind, or altogether against herself for that she was no
gentlewoman. And she craved Caleb pardon saying that as seneschal it
behooved her to see her lord's new property, wherefore she had studied to
interpret the draught which the erstwhile landlord had purveyed to him

for rehearsal by picture of all and sundry bushments in the maze, for to find her way to Caleb's lodging, nor failing to look all about her on the way and mark in her memory what she might tell her lord to warn him or to please him when she returned to duty on the morrow. She brought meat and drink to make Caleb feast for Shrove Tuesday afore that he went again into the black mountain to bide another night of durance, and many more also, for the which she pitied him. And she desired to make him gree for his courtesy to her when he knew not that she hid sorrow over her years in the world without learning or wedlock. When she saw that the young knight was not sorry to see her but joyous, and would not go on with sleep but embraced her as a friend, she was no more afeared and she chode him for his sorry condition, with all her force causing him to undergo his bayne in the hot fountain of a common chamber whilst she made busy with the vessels and basins espied in the poor kitchen.

Thereto deep in her heart the damosel Hecuba had bethought what yet might pass between them to her pleasance without unrightfully costing him aught of pain or mickle time, if she could yet find in him a degree of lief according to her intent. She would be his leman until the sun went down, but he must swear him to secrecy and open his deeds to no one, nay not even to his mentor the husband of her friend and neighbor whom she trusted more than herself in all unfeigned matters, for that man was like to bear record for all the world to read that she deceived the old knight whom she would fain have take her as bride.

When he returned in his robe of towels gleaming from the bain she lauded him for his cleansing and avowed him "pure as the shriven snow" save for the nails of his fingers. And while not long after the sun began his decline she laid the table with rich viands, his breakfast forsooth, he made no move to dight himself in seemly clothes but followed her steps to and fro with his eyes, whom he saw by light of day for the first time as her lover, and he found her fairer and more comely than any innocent maiden in all the realm.

Sitting down at table each to each she raised her glass brimful and drank saying "To the health and happiness of a wight that needs never a love portent!" And he quaffed her in turn, pledging she should have such service of him as she desired, redressing past wrongs done upon her. "Nay", quoth she "what's wanted is my undressing, and that I would gladly have, when you shall have eaten what I put before you on this board."

As Caleb satisfied his hunger Hecuba told him that sleep had not come to her bed. She had lain at home sore sick for having bade farewell to him without knowing his clean nakedness with her body in the same bed, though only for an hour or twain, as man and woman should, talking together on one pillow like true friends, before parting forever, for she blessed the day that he was born and deemed him as worthy a knight as ever cast seed to maid or wife or widow, though but yesterday a forlorn clerk plaining without solace.

"Why did you never have a wench to hug and kiss, who would stroke your head?" she asked.

"Yet I had by me a cruel scholar-maid that I loved out of measure and in the fullness of time, and meddled with her, but she was faithless and sometimes cold, and would not grant me the boon I had of you. Now when I have you before me to see and touch, a kind lady right soft and warm, most pleasing to a man's heart and delightful to his mind, meseems she was a poor fearful girl who pitied me without love's courage. But of all men she loved me the most, and succoured me in the ways she dared, so that I was led and governed by her in all things."

"Haply anon I too will succour you," Hecuba said unto him, "for I would give you every delight in my very yielding, but only once, that you may still be weened from my toils lest you be misguided from noble quests by the habits of a common villein. You are a gentleman of parts meet for a daintier mouth than mine with little liking for brute unfit giants who cannot be fully served by cause of overmatching a gentle-woman's person. You deserve a coral reef. Last night it was revealed to me that you are fairly circumscribed. Are you perchance a very Jew?"

"No more than half at the best. I know not my father" he answered her; "I may be half red-Indian for aught I know."

"That's possible, your stomach is so hard and flat." said she. "But Jews are the best men for kindness to a woman and I trust them more than most. I have found that they are wise when clean and oftentimes they adventure more than other men. Howsomever, I predicate for you even as black Irish an extinguished refutation."

But when he turned questions against her she denied that Sir Wine had ever touched her body, and for three reasons: first, he was not of an age or aspect that pleased her in the manner of one she would lief go into bed with; second, he paid her wages for hire of a different kind, and goodwill was always sore strained when man and woman consorted both as master with servant and as friends that should be equal in dalliance; and the third reason that she would never let Sir Wine lead her into evil in all their years of company, until he had stopped altogether in his talk of it, was that the Silver Fox her protector lay in wait to watch against him lest he enjoy her.

Caleb stinted not in drinking to her discretion and she likewise to his good speed. With much thanksgiving they did justice to her generosity, celebrating their feast like a brace of love-birds well content one with other. But in so much as she had charged them to take leave of each other almost before their friendship was well begun, he forebore to inquire further of her lovers, for he had liefer laugh in foolish ignorance than search wounds not yet incurred, and he remembered him that he had wished just such blithe enchantment when as he suffered the pangs of true love.

As to her person, Caleb praised Hecuba for the wit to find him out in the twisted warren without guide or escort, and sware that if she had not come to him he imagined in himself not to souse him in bayne for all of Lent but if he saw her again for that he was loth to wash from his body withoutside the sweet odors and other precious trace that remained to him from her withinside, seeing that he wished not to forget the satin sleeve of his boon. On her part Hecuba owned to Caleb that despite the case forbidden by the stars of their birth she also fantasied to lie by his side betwixt white sheets with all his skin and hers to be touched and stroked as they would, sleeping with limbs entwined like two vines of grape on one trellis.

Her words liked him full well but he must needs ask her how it might be that she could stay with him until his time of sally if she had appointed to be with two others that day. "Can it be that you have entertained with others this day betime afore toiling here with a great burden to break my fast?"

And she laughed saying "By no means have I had speech with any man until this hour sith I left your side save only a priest, for I went to mass and after to shrive myself in the early light of the day that I might find you the sooner, and enter Lent with an easy mind. I have sent word to Sir Deadeye Cloud that I surely would not be at home to receive him at this very hour whenas he is accustomed to see me on the Tuesday of many weeks, and I ween he will be distraught or wroth that he may not come to me at all throughout the season of penance when I forethink his friendship, or ever again, as he shall be told when he next sends to ask my company, for I have enamored him overmuch and no more is there any delight to me in his addresses, which of a sudden I am grown weary on, seeing that from you, though we never meet again, I have learned the ways of true noblesse, albeit he is known as a burgher of high degree in his lauded guild and you but as bachelor in art of no force. From this time forward though I be of no worth myself I shall love none other than those that be of great worship, and nigh keep troth to my right true suitor hight Silver Fox, for you have proved with your regard unto me that I am a pearl of no small price. Not one word of your teaching escapes my ears or is not treasured there. Tonight when Sir Fox comes to me, or we go together to dance for Mardi Gras, I shall remember you without dispraise of him, for he too is of noble spirit, full generous and kind, albeit lowly born with a big voice rough in speech that lacks all learning, yet more than twice your age, with hands like unto yours and feet of gentle measure. In brief, I have done with sailors and physics and men of all other incubations, and soon I shall be done even with you, sorry as I am to say it must be so, seeing 'tis your havior by gentle hand and fair speech that spurs me to partake the guise and port of a lady!"

When their beakers were empty they went to the bed, but she would not have him see her without small clothes at the least until that she was under his threadbare sheets, witting that her beauty had passed its bloom, and she heeded none of his protests that the sight of her standing before him without veil or ornament would be cherished until the end of his life, just as he had dreamed to see Inanna herself to whom he avowed she made close likeness, for it was the first time since he came into the world that he might have seen any woman standing naked as a needle. For she believed him not, and covered her shame, nor would she disrobe before him, forasmuch as she had been fairer of shape at half her years, and in this one thing she would not yield him his desire.

6.

But he had little else to complain of, and indeed it was little time tofore they undressed them for dalliance on his pallet, and they loved together more hotter than they did tofore, so that when the webs fell away she no longer took thought of him avising her better. Long ere his call to duty her thrice-spent passion was so trustful of his friendship that she made bare not only the flaws of wanton disclosure but also divers morsels of her life past, delighting him unto her with every whisper. Together they drew smoke from tobacco parchments atween jousts of sport. He took keep of her humanity like as she took keep of his courtesy.

At the waning of her bliss with all remaining strength she faintly cleight him inwith her arms and legs, whispering him: "Words flail me in my swoon, yet you cannot in reason gainsay my aforesaid doctrine, all these things considered, that we must not love in earnest. This is not exercise of the virtue I am in want of, yet unwittingly you beseige my heart with most excellent hardiness. You must make do your foins of chivalry without me, or return to celibate prayer. For I am a simple person, and mean to be married in fitting estate and degree while I am left on live."

7.

"But not right away!" Caleb protested.

"Maybe very soon. Might be any day."

"But when? He's after you all the time I suppose."

"When certain things happen, that's all. Never you mind, it's none of your business. What you don't know won't hurt you. I'll be damned if I'm going to let myself get emotively resplendent on *you*! Besides, you'll only get drafted or something. You're about the age they want, arent you? Say—that's right—how come you haven't been taken already? You're not too small for the Army. You've got more lead in your pencil than any dogface I ever knew!"

Caleb always dreaded this question about conscription, but she was one person to whom there was no need to lie that he was color-blind. "As long as they don't call me for another physical I'm safe." And he explained to her what a fortunate thing it was that he hadnt met her sooner. "I think you've cured me." he concluded. "Now I may be normal."

"It's a little too early to tell." she commented, palpating the ever-recrudescent offender. "You still need the harem treatment. I guess I'm not a very good curator, honey."

"But you're the best fucking doctor in the world!"

"You said it! You said the word I thought you'd never say, you find so many different ways! But it's nice—that's why I like you so much—it really means something when you say it. —Well I took a couple of years of Latin in school (and I had to fight to make them let me do it) because I thought it would help me study nursing, but then I got into a biology course and realized that I couldnt stand squishy bodies all full of tubes and bubbles. But this is a different kind of theriatrics, and there's some who say I was born for it. Now in this case if I were still your physicist and the next appointment didnt do the trick I'd consort to indirect discourse, which I conserve for the most unusual cases, but only when there's a very strong doctor/patient relativity."

"I am fully confident in your practice, doctor, but I'm not recommending you to my friends. —Just once more. . . ."

"Never mind your dear friends once more into the breach—just you, my precious rabbit!"

The toenails flanking his shanks like the nails of her hands on his shoulders were gorgeous glossy shields fit for ten heraldic devices; her darkly fimbriated brown eyes were bright wells shining with softly indulgent femininity: but Caleb still digging the treasure that he feared might have to last him another twenty years scarcely noticed her colors. Each time, before she closed her eyes clenched her toes and spread her fingers she seemed ingenuously amazed at his rapture with the common element of womanhood. In order to attend the extraordinary sounds and grimaces with which he accompanied his spasms she suppressed the genuine utterances that flatter all men. His idiosyncrasies were even dearer to her than the sensations to which they contributed. Once in fact she was so smilingly contented during a reciprocal paroxysm that he dubbed her his Belle Dame Sans Souci.

Once she said: "Now I understand why the draft board calls you a satire. I thought you were too cuntcupiscent to be just normal! But be patient with your doctor, sweetie. If we had more time I could trump you. But the best of it is that you do it with all your art and soul. I love to watch you when you're not looking, and hear the funny noises you make. You're not too heavy on a woman either. Stay on top of me and rest for a few minutes while I catch my breath." And so Caleb would relax for a minute or two. "I love your smooth skin and your nice little ass." she murmured as languidly as ever yet she had murmured. "You must have been a long-distance tractor man in college. There's no fat on you anywhere."

"I'm glad you don't kick me out of bed as soon as you've had your fill."

After a rare silence she said "You're not a real Jew if your mother isnt, you know. It wasnt the Jews that killed Jesus. Anyway he was a Jew himself. No one else has ever kissed me the way you do—like you care about how I feel it. I wish I'd known you when I was fifteen. Or twelve. I mensurated when I was twelve, and I already had a little hair on my pussy and pretty little tits not much bigger than yours—you have some nice muscles on your chest, you know that? Must be from swimming a lot. But I waited three years. I would have let you be the first. But I didnt know any better then. You're supposed to be more sentimental about your first man that your last. But with you like this is the next best thing at my age. It's nice to know I can't possibly get the clap from you. Make believe I'm your Holy Frail, Sir Galaham."

"He was a bastard too."

"Probably a sparse minuative athalete like you. In those days all the men were small. Did you ever see the sweets of amour they used to wear? But nowadays even little guys have big sons. That's because all they do is eat and have fun—the kids I mean. Why is it though the short guys always seem to have the fabulous personalities, or they're smarter? You're posolutely cute when you're making it. It helps me imagine what you're like most of the time when you're not self-conscious. Like some men, you can tell their true personality when they're drunk. They may be extra nice or they may swear at you; you never can tell when you first meet them. Was your mother a good dancer?"

"I don't know. I think she must have been."

"Good. I think that's very important in a woman. It tells a lot about her and what kind of mother she'll be. The way a woman treats her baby makes a big difference. I learned a lot about that from Ruth Chapman. She's the best there is. Was she a drinker?"

"Ruth!?"

"No, you idiot: your mother. Did she smoke before she had you? Do you think she ever had a venial disease? Was she unusually plumb or else flat-chested?"

"I think she smoked for a while, but she was never a drinker when I was growing up. Of course I can't be sure. She wasnt fat or skinny either."

"Were you ever sick much when you were a kid? Before you, was anyone in your family ever crazy? Did you have any psychic problems from the time you were born and not just because of the ideas you got in college?"

"I was always normal in the head and properly shaped in every other way. If this were the twelfth century you'd never know I was anything but a possible champion. But why are you asking all these questions, Pandora? You don't answer many.

"Well we're doing so much of this all at one time I was afraid I might slip up. You've been so long on top of me and all: that's concisely the best way to get pregnated. If something were to go wrong I wouldnt want it to be just anybody. As a matter of fact I'm always pretty choosy about who gets into me at all."

"Shall I get my thimbles, just to be doubly sure?"

"Phooey! You can't lead a horse to water after the barn door's closed! Besides, I like to feel the squirts. I'm not really worried, but I'd be a little stuporstitious even if I only salivated you. I don't have a diagram for my throat!" She giggled at the concept. "Speaking of that, what was your girl friend like? Was she stuck up about still having her cherry? How come you never made her?"

"She took five showers a day."

"Why, was she too dirty from shoveling coal?"

"Clean as a whistle." he continued.

"Did you blow the whistle or did the whistle blow you?"

> Blow the man down,
> Oh blow the man down!

I guess she was no ill wind. You two must have been quite a pair of vestigial virgins!" And her giggle burst into pewtery laughter. "Show me how you got so close to making her!"

She kissed the nipples of his nearly hairless chest and smoothed his belly with her hand, taking care to avoid homo erectus.

"There were several phases of disappointment. The first would bore you, and it would be dishonorable to violate Cindy's privacy by revealing the third and fourth—but I can freely show you the second."

Turning Hecuba on her back he began an obeisance to her breasts with the lips of a fawn lightly grazing on their gibbous slopes and gently nuzzling the nearly snow-white flesh above the pectoral rim of her armpits, then alternating equally left and right in fairy-light sprints clause by clause took sweet time on each to wind softly upward to the summits as he propelled and retracted the tip of his tongue. Thus slowly his lips drew nearer to the crests, the nulliparous buds reawakening from their strawberry beds, each on its own quivering tumulus. Just as his lips parted over the pink lantern of a flattening dome and his tongued cheeks began to suck as gently as a sated babe about to fall asleep in bliss, taking good care to bate his fullgrown teeth, he was suddenly overtaken by the predatory urge to violate the forgotten virgin Cindy in a doubling of possession, and at the same time reminded by the clock that his time with Hecuba was running out. Arching his back he found again his erstwhile nether adit and sank inward in quest of inmost satisfaction, with some contortion continuing the task of autobiographical illustration—in which he paused only long enough to explain: "This is what I always missed."

He meant to set astir a transhumance of sensations that would meet in the center like a subaqueous quake of the earth. And sure enough, under gradually more forceful imposition, Cindy gave way with the susceptibility he had never got to feel from within her. He marveled at the vastly thrilled woman who bided his caresses as wildly and heedlessly as if finding without his aid the goal of all her previous susceptibilities—and in his marveling attained unwittingly to the psychic distance that increased his power over her. She made sweet moan such as he hadnt heard before that went up and down a low-pitched scale ending in a shriek muted by embarrassment. "Oh sweet Jesus, what's he doing to me? Come, you fucking angel man! Don't hold back! God help me—let it all come!" But those were only her words. Though she spoke no more he heard more of her voice. All at once his own shudder of transient deliverance obliterated amazement at what he was doing. For many minutes he and Cindy lay back in paired exhaustion like true lovers verging on a happy death.

Hecuba at last roused herself to ponder the happy alteration that had taken place in her senses during that ordinary event, which by all reason should have been no more than tolerably sensational. "Maybe that's what *I* always missed! I'm already jealous of your future wife." For the time being she thought she'd met her match with this puzzling kid in the semblance of a poor little clerk. She had been tricked into ecstasy by the inordinate application of his beseeching respect. But she knew that her strange beguilement would soon wear off, and as she made up her mind about the proprieties of the situation she resolved to stay on her guard against overpraising him, even as she again resolved never to consort with him beyond the light of this very first day, but a little longer therein, just to savor the lees if he still had any.

8.

And so it passed that midway between nones and sunset Hecuba lightly did upon her the outermost weeds that might cover her nakedness and with her purse hasted her down the hall to the cess closet. When she came again upon Caleb she saw and understood that time and drowsy rest had wrought her cure too soon. Alas, said the enchantress, what may this mean? Will he stint his pricking and no longer have ado with me by cause my dulcet language and nurture has learned him too well the cudgeling of love? I repent me that I had great fantasy unto him and did let him be worshipfully proved upon my body to make him a knight. Sythen I had need avoid his body for brief time my doughty champion has fallen in soft sleep afore the sun! Alas it do make me efte athirst that I have come upon the fierce merlin shriveled and piteous as a dove. It would be passing sore to depart forever from such a gentleman and not taste the foison I have so oft today partook without seeing, an I can conjure it from the part that lies abashed which I have found liefer to inhold than the avaunting buffets and war-dances of great heroes who bring dole to my heart with their paynim lust. Faith, she said, upon pain of my life let me deal, that he may no longer drupen as a wilted lily forgot by serving woman. Now must I gird his loins with my arms and exercise my speechless feat, first with tip of tongue to undo the shrunken sprite from my mortal cure till that I heal him of the distemper I have wrought. If he lies much longer all befolded without manly strength I cast me to have no more pleasure of him afore the dole of my farewell anon. —Now as humble suckling let have ado with sir knight and bestir him ready to take the joust to uttermost and put comely end to deeds as heard never before this time.

In the labor of her smithcraft she spoke no more, but the skill of her lure was artful as no other tongue might tell, and she made her leman passing hale and strong again afore she could make space for words from the work of her mouth, and she did unto him the deepest reverence and most lecherous that damosel had ever done him, and she engorged her with such subtil grace that he deemed her an angel sent to transport him unto heavenly bliss. He could make no delay against the new delight of her fair head before his loins but of a sudden waxed full quick with the hot phlegm she was used to savor in other part. But she could not cry out against her drowning until she had swallowed covertly somewhat of his brackish gift, which her seemed as all the spicery of the world had been gathered there for her to drink of, full of rare virtue too precious to be spilled.

Whenas she was cleared to speak she chided the mischief he had done. "Fie upon you sir for defiling a maid of language." Yet also she made play of praising the generosity of his gifts, saying "He who gives quickly gives more than once." and she kissed his lips with the draught of ichor from his own sword. Then she said "you have done violence to my custom that was used heretofore of old time to defend against this mishap for you have ravished me unaware and filled the cup I imagined in myself never to drink of. Your naughty treachery shall cost you dear, for even now I spy the sanguine lance feutred yet again to challenge the meet escutcheon of your lady, and I ordain that it once more but alas once only splash gouts argent by introit proper. From that moment forth I undertake not to make magic too strong for holy tide."

Howsomever, full two hours more they wantoned and conversed together, and either of them made much of other. She wot that unnethe in the world women might not find his match for seed, ne could he find space of time to say unto her all the thoughts he would tell or ask.

9.

Hecuba was more than a cradle Catholic. She went to confession once a year, always on Shrove Tuesday, as her mother had taught her, because Lent was the easiest time to repent.

"Not that I ever do penance, most of the time. But I do eat fish and cut out fishermen."

"What in the world do you tell the priests?" Caleb asked her.

"Oh just enough so they'll know I'm a sinner and expect to hear no more. The only thing that gets them mad is using a diagram, so I never mention that anymore. But I have to tell them something, so I try to make it a little interesting. Poor guys must hear the same old things day in and day out year after year. Do you think they masticate a lot, at least in their sleep? I've never let a priest touch me. You have to saw the line somewhere. I've got enough on my conscience as it is. There was one in San Francisco called me Mary Magdelene and laughed about it. He was pretty young and very good-looking too. Beautiful teeth with a little gap and brown curly hair. Did you ever think of studying for the priesthood? They can't get enough of them you know. If I was a man they might not take me because I'm not smart enough, but you wouldnt have any trouble getting in. I bet you're a natural-born scholar. Wouldnt it be disgusting if they had women priests the way some of the Protestant sexes do? Might just as well not be religious at all."

"Is there anything else you'd never do with men?"

"Besides just now? Yes. I'd never kill a baby!"

"Why, would you kill anyone else?"

"No I mean a baby inside me. If it runs down my leg before it gets in there, that's one thing. But I'd never never never do anything to it on purpose—I don't care how many dirty little bastards I might have—oh, pardon me!—even if it wasnt against the law. In Massachusetts I hear you can't even have a miscarriage! Maybe that's a little too strict."

"I was born in Massachusetts."

"Well maybe they aren't that strict after all. —By the way, what do you like to be called?" She hadnt yet addressed him by name. "I could never get used to *Caleb*—it's too formal. Sounds like some old New England pasture; reminds me of Abraham, and nobody would want to be called that nowadays except orthocrat Jews. *Abraham Karcist* doesnt sound any worse. Illinois's right next to Indiana, so don't think I'm prejudiced against Lincoln. But you wouldnt make a very good President. You couldnt handle the pols. Maybe I could do that for you. I'd be your secretary in the White House—your socialist secretary. —Well, Cable—that's what I'll call you. It's easier to say and it sounds more natural. Cable, my dear boy, I guess this is as good time as any to make my confession to you. There's something you ought to know, so you won't worry. I've already got something in the oven." She patted her stomach.

Young Caleb was at first silenced by this stunning information for fear of saying anything untactful. They were lying on their backs side by side. Betraying he hoped neither too much nor too little astonishment he pressed her hand in sympathy, meaning to indicate as tenderly as possible his pity for her condition and his respect for her bravery. He was amazed at the proximity of gestation. Then to gain time for reflection he asked a few questions, carefully avoiding the indiscreet subject of paternity. She explained that she had been sure for several days, having confirmed her suspicions by a visit to Dr Philuberus very early in the game. "It's not the first time I've been to him, you see. Every time I'm the slightest bit irregular my old man makes me go to the doctor. I'm pretty positive this is his kid. So I guess I'll be getting married right after Easter. Too bad we have to wait for the end of Lent."

"I've heard that even doctors can be mistaken."

"I can see you're not exactingly enthusiastic about getting your first tail with a knocked-up woman. I was afraid you wouldnt be. But it's too early to make any difference at all. At least you don't have to worry about anything except a superstitious husband. You can't do me any more harm and there's no danger I'll claim you're the father!"

Her tarnished laugh relieved the shock.

"I'm only just barely penitent you know. For a long time it won't stop me from working or having fun. Foxy and I both wanted a kid, Cable cutie-pie, and it doesnt concern you at all."

Now Caleb was nothing if he was not a coldblooded opportunist, for whom the problem of future disengagement was neatly solved. He judged that it would not be inexpedient to betray that fact at the eleventh hour. After a short silence to make his thoughts seem much slower and more scrupulous than they really were he said softly and evenly, testing his boldness with the utmost trepidation: "Then Hecky I don't understand why I shouldnt see you during Lent."

Her reply was equally thoughtful. "You know, I've been thinking the same thing." She paused, glancing at his face. "We could have a real honeymoon. At least there won't be any mensural interruptions. I'm not too old to have my last fling. I'll cancel all my other estrangements. There's no harm in hearing your sweetheart's voice just a little longer."

By her tone of body thereafter he was convinced for the first time that the Romans were not far amiss in counting sex and confession among the violated sacraments, along with baptism as substituted for circumcision. But any rate by the laying on of Hecuba he regarded himself confirmed as a practicing worshipper of the triple goddess. The afternoon was somewhat religious altogether. What a vapid creature Cindy that thin clever schoolgirl now seemed, cast into shadow by the coalminer's daughter.

10.

"Gramercy, La Belle Dame, it is well that you at last are not abashed to make your life clean unto me. Certes I like you the better for its truth. You do you no dishonor in making known to me the wages of your innocent sin. It is well for our delight that you are disburdened of your witch's disc made from gum of the Indies while I also wear no coif of sheep gut; that like Father Adam and Mother Eve before eating of the apple we may disport ourselves with light hearts and play together till you shall be richly wedded with great noblesse." Together they drew smoke from the burning fragrance of a tiny white sleeve and put away thoughts of Holy Week which little bested their lief. "When we erst came together in my dungeon I was right proud with my adventure but I had my pleasure in no full measure forasmuch as we clipped in our weeds and I had fear to be discovered doing wrong in those chambers that long to others. And then here in my bower I kenned your body all naked and free. But never yet till now did the cock so blithe me acrowing his makeless fortune in full enjoying the betrothed lady of my wilely lord."

No more did Hecuba pat him upon the head as he was her bairn but snugged her down next him like as his own bairn. "Familiarity breeds content." she said. "And for my part I will for the days that remain to us give you service to the best of my nobility. Only you must swear to silence and obedience, and be ruled by me in all matters betwixt us."

Caleb again took his oath to be her privy knight forever, and not only for the six-and-forty days and six-and-forty nights that would make an end to the fellowship that was between them.

11.

Before Caleb's very last offering of the day Hecuba was again obliged to answer the call of nature. This time she left her purse behind. As a matter of general curiosity about the habits of a free and easy woman he opened it and poked inside. Along with an empty silver flask and its matching pistol, and scores of papers and cosmetic items in which he was not interested, he found a flat round case of baby-blue plastic. It contained the first female contraceptive saucer he had ever actually seen. He could not mistake the intimate function of that brown rubber life raft. He imagined a circle of firemen with upturned faces holding its ring as they shifted their feet to catch a baby tossed from on high. It was still beaded with the moisture of a very recent rinsing.

Strange doings for a pregnant woman! What superstition could account for ex post facto birth control? And had she a pair of the things that she alternated? Anyway he had read that it was dangerous to remove artificial membranes before the wriggling pathogens gave up their ghosts like netted fish flung gasping on a deck. Had she then changed her mind about something? Why was she lying to him about one thing or another? Was there an obscure consistency somewhere in the jolting enigma?

His sudden doubts were divided between an indulgent resentment of deception and a nameless new excitement. Indeed he found himself almost glad of the hesitant shock that set his body trembling and his brain awhirl yet instantly seemed familiar, for he was suddenly aware that his cumulative delivery from innocence freed him for a disengaged if not dispassionate adventure in ideas for the ensuing six or seven weeks of holiday. As long as she kept to her friendly word for that long the well-defined riddle would be a game in real life infinitely less abstract than poker. He made up his mind neither to fabricate far-fetched suspicions nor to betray his own ignoble indiscretion in searching her private effects. Perhaps his education had in store certain mysteries of adult life, even unforseen varieties of virtue. Meanwhile he would only conceal his new intelligence and listen to her more narrowly.

But for a full week in his callow resilience he practically forgot his bewildering discovery, so sweetly and tenderly was their secret friendship growing.

12.

They studied the church calendar. It was not easily that Caleb and Hecuba could hold their trysts except on her day off. Tuesday's sunlit hours had always been respected by her protector as a time for her own maintenance. The Silver Fox acknowledged her inviolable right to a day of privacy in which she could wash her hair do her laundry and talk to Ruth Chapman her only friend in the neighborhood. Caleb's Wednesday night off was less certain for the new friends than Tuesday's free daytime, though during Lent there was nothing remarkable about Hecuba's forbidding the Silver Fox to see her that evening of the week if he happened to be inclined to pay her a second visit so soon.

Caleb would have been wild if she hadnt given him that first Ember Day: Wednesday, the only night of the week they could stay together. Neither of them suggested assignations at Mr Wine's medical building on other nights of the week. It would have been a gratuitously furtive breech of responsibility. That dim workplace had served the wheel of fortune's purpose, and they both tacitly feared an uncomfortable anticlimax to their long-drawn-out ceremonies of dramatic separation.

Thus almost every Tuesday afternoon and Wednesday night were paired as the feast-days of their Lent, for it was the Fox's right and habit to spend with his betrothed the Sundays that followed his Saturday nights with her. Sometimes before Lent he had even claimed her from Mr Wine for the sixth working day itself, so that she could be taken on a weekend trip in his horseless white phaeton with a big gold Nike on its nose.

The first Tuesday night Caleb could hardly keep his eyes open on the job till the cleaning crew had left the building solely in his possession. He was sentimentally grateful to Hecuba for having found Dr Philuberus's sofa, where he catnapped between timeclockings in deferred exhaustion nearly heedless of shirking duty for the first time in his life. Nearing the end of his shift he awoke in a sweat of alarm and rushed downstairs to find the furnace warmed only by embers. There was barely time to rake out the slag dump the ashes inflame a new bank of coal and bring the fire to apparent normality (wasting several bushels of fuel in the inefficient process of getting up steam as fast as possible) before Sig Hansen relieved him. As long as it lasted the panicky exertion excluded all thought about his new manhood and the unfamiliar perturbations that had momentarily threatened to taint its savor. But as soon as he had time for reflection he set about to cultivate his worldly wisdom, in which he was satisfied to find some success: he was not in love with the woman. This emotional triumph also came for the first time in his life, compensating for the guilt of professional derilection.

He slept most of the day. Before dinner he went down the hill to visit Ruth and her boys, begging off his usual evening with her husband. A little odd, to be sure, but not entirely unprecedented. Then he came home and made a simple supper for Hecuba. It was the first time he'd ever cooked a meal for anyone but himself. He spent a lot of money on the ingredients to make up for limited effort and less skill. To celebrate their mutual seduction he bought his first bottle of champagne—a domestic imitation that was not especially phony.

It was not yet certain that she could come. The time approached when he was to go down to the telephone booth to call her if she hadnt appeared. But at the last minute he heard steps on the squeaking floorboards outside his door and her knock on his door. His joy cast aside all the restraints of maturity dignity and psychological prudence that he had promised himself. Wildly he kissed away the last smudge of ashes she had left on her forehead and danced her back and forth across the floor to opportune dance jazz from his radio. "Cable, I thought you said you couldn't dance!" she cried. "You're a *wonderful* dancer! You'd be a terrific fencible!"

"Just because I can make the two-backed beast on my feet?"

"I don't believe a nice boy like you would do anything unnatural—not while I'm around at least. Wait until after Easter."

They dawdled over food wine and kisses. Seldom had a man cooked for her. Never had one treated her like a Bohemian aristocrat. He took her home after it was likely that the Chapmans had settled down for the night.

She hated having no private bathroom at his place. "I couldnt stand that spooky dump at night unless I had a dog." she stated.

"I'm your dog. Arf arf!"

"It's not so much your bad housekeeping, except I like clean sheets." Furthermore she was obliged to attend her phone in case the old boy called. Luckily that night he had taken himself off to Los Angeles, where he often went on his business. Caleb pretended to be not only a man but a calm man of the world. It wasnt as if his next enjoyment was going to be with the queen herself; but Hecuba's bed would be directly above the royal couch.

Yet he found that visiting Hecuba's apartment was a riskier business than he had anticipated. "Are you sure I won't get caught here and gunned down like a rat in a trap?"

"You should talk about rat traps! The pot calls the kettle black. I've spent a fortune fixing up the place. I'd get Wine to buy it, but the Silver Fox would smell a cat. That schmuck of a landlord won't do anything. Greek. I can't stand the sight of him, and he's always trying to feel me up. That shit-heel once offered me free rent. Gives me the creeps, such a puckered sour-puss! If he was a girl and had a twat like that he wouldnt be able to give it away. I bet his dick is pink and slimy like a dog's. Himself, he's more like a snake. He's not normal. The bugger wants me to make a business connection for him with the Silver Fox. . . ."

Caleb was at first stunned with shock and admiration at the infelicitous speech released by the home-base venue, as if she was deliberately exposing him to the truth underlying his polite illusions—as if to see if he would flinch at her unguarded manner. But with a genuine smile he immediately chided himself for narrowminded inessential fastidiousness. His bemusement at this unexpected stumbling block step was a benign medium in which to reconcile taste with moral judgment. His affection for her goodnatured intelligence was only strengthened by each new evidence of her virtual honesty. And as he passed this test he thought she noticed his resilience.

"Anyway this is my castle, let me tell you, and not even my sugar daddy gets in here unless I feel like pressing that button on the wall. I pay my own rent, and nobody else gets a key. Foxy respects me for that. He wouldnt want to marry some corsair. That's always been understood between him and me, no matter what kind of presents he gives me. I've got a nice little bank account too and he'll see that over my dead body. That's something I wouldnt even show you, and for some dumb reason I trust you more than anyone else. . . .

"I won't forget you Calibie, even if he finds out and gets you taken for a little ride in a burlap sack down to the cement-mixer. But he won't find out. He once tried to have this house watched. When I got wind of it he heard from me in no uncurtained terms, believe me! I'm not partial about my language when I'm talking to spies. He'll never do it again you may rest insured! I'm not scared of him. He might have *you* tailed if he got jealous, but not me: he wouldnt dare. Anyhow he's not suspicious of small timid men who get close to a woman's heart by the tricks of education. Besides, you often come to this house anyway, and no one would be surprised to see you round about as long as the Chapman lights are on. And if by any chance Foxy ever did come barging over without warning on account of some unforeseemly evidence you can slip out the back door. That's the way to leave in the mornings too. Mickey gets up very early to type his script. He's an arthur but no one's supposed to know. Ruth told me. Don't ever let on that you heard it from me or I'll bite off little Galaham and make a hot dog out of him. . . . But once you're up here you don't have to be comprehensive about anything besides an earthquake. But you and I already know what that's like, don't we kiddo? . . . Now you just relax and take a nice hot bath. I'll wash your back. Prolly no one's done that for you since you were a teeny-tiny. . . .

"—My God, what a funnylooking bellybutton! What kind of bugs live in there?"

"It's strange." he said. "When I clean it I get a tingling sensation at the end of my—."

"Irish pennant. I wonder where a woman would feel it if she had a novel like that."

He finally succeeded in getting her into the tub with him. Once a woman who's no college girl makes herself mutually grotesque with a man what matters her degree of ripeness when she's manifestly more voluptuous than the beauties most men ever see even in pictures. Indeed he had already found her considerably slimmer and firmer of figure than her orchidaceous clothes suggested. He was now a convert to her school of flesh. After he had climbed out of the water to make room for her length he laved her with soap like a respectful equerry. With her eyes closed much to his surprise she allowed him to inquire into her most private anatomy. "My critterous is very sensitive." she said. "—Oooh, you have just the right touch! I can tell you're no neosight in the sophistries!"

It was no Murphy bed that she led him to in the front room but an exceptionally wide sumptuously furnished dais decorated with boudoir colors and scented in the same tradition. Now clad in a diaphanous camisole she turned down the covers and Caleb jumped in like an eager puppy so confident of her affection that he had no doubts about the luxury before him.

"No, no, Caliboy, that's my side of the bed!"

"But I'm left-handed!"

"I don't care about your hand. I just want you to fuck me."

"The only copulative verb that's transitive."

"I guess I'll have to get used to sermons on sintack. —Okay, if you fall asleep on top of me you can stay on my side."

But since Caleb was habituated to staying awake all night she would be the one to pray Hermes for sleep in any juxtaposition. It took her until Saturday to recover from the sacrifices of her tireless new priest but she had until the following Tuesday to rest from his embraces.

In the interval he began direct work on his first play. Fortunately it didnt immediately dawn on him that he'd be lucky if he got as many as seven days and nights out of Hecuba before the final passion. He had barely begun his erratic convalescence from satyriasis.

13.

In the event it was a full two weeks before he had his next chance to cultivate that primary game of recreation in the bed of his tutelary blonde angel, who for the nonce he expected to complement with her gender's gifts the pedagogy of his dark archangel in the flat below. For on the proximate Wednesday he was balked of his feast.

At first blush he thought himself the victim of black treachery, or of some unfathomable corruption that undermined the certainties of his senses and mocked as fatuous pretension all the human understanding of the western world. The day before, their second Tuesday, had been in his mind only a card of playful heaters for its morrow, all the gayer that she could not stay for long on any of her visits to the rabbit warren but came and went (learning various routes to his door) in the intervals of her errands: to wit, on the way to the grocery store, during the automatic cycling of her laundry in one of Glen Smith's coin machines, during the drying of her load in his great gas-heated tumbler, and on her way down-town to the hair-dresser. Some of these visits were longer than others but none was too short to polish off a facet of the jewel. Toward the end of her last appearance she had evinced extraordinary happiness with his company (he thought) by deciding to spend an extra twenty minutes with him and rely on a cab to recover her schedule at the last minute. Having already harnessed and preened herself for the outside world she was content to sit at his table and look into his face. When he brought out the Scotch she called for beer to chase it. "Let's have a pot-boiler!"

They drank to each other also with their eyes. She rose when she abso-lutely could stay no longer. "My hair's been a mess ever since I met you. If I don't get it done this afternoon I'll lose my job and my boyfriend, just for the sake of a crazy little shaggy-headed Bohunk entelectual. —Why are you picking up that raggedy old thing? It's much warmer outside than it is in here."

"This sweater has so many holes in it that I put it on when I want to cool off."

"Say, on top of everything else you're quite a pundit! But I've known a lot of camelions. I might like you better if you were serious, honey. Don't smudge my lipstick."

And then he had walked downstairs with her, harassing her descent with squeezes of her waist and shoulders at every dingy nook and turn until she got to the telephone booth. And then they waited together under the oaks until the taxi came.

Since he'd fitted in several naps during her absences he went to work that evening no more than somewhat tired and inestimably refreshed. It was agreed that the next day he'd phone her as soon as he thought she'd be home from the City.

All day on Lent's first Wednesday after sleeping as much as possible he wrote a line or two of drama and walked on air, visiting Ruth and the children only briefly. He wanted to persuade Hecuba to meet him for dinner in Berkeley where she could not possibly be seen by anyone in any of her epicircles, and he was anxious about nothing but overcoming her reluctance to do so. But she was very late in getting home, or at least in answering her phone.

"Hi."

"What's the matter?"

"Nothing. I'm just extra tired."

"I'll rest you up. Come up and take a nap while I make you some supper."

"I can't see you tonight."

He tried to repress an inquisition of violent disappointment. "Why, is your boyfriend coming over?" he asked in a quiet steady voice.

"No. I just had a hard day, that's all."

"Someone else?" he asked again, his tone quivering slightly.

"No." Her tone seemed indifferent. "Curiosity killed the cat." she added negligently, as if the adage was her stock response to unwelcome questions.

Contrary to his own rudimentary wisdom in erotic diplomacy he appealed to their unequivocal appointment as excuse for his persistence in demanding personal information. ". . . . Who's going to be there? Or are you going out?" He immediately sensed that she was accustomed to his pattern of injured vanity and suspicion.

"Nobody. I'm just going to wash my hair and go to bed early."

"But you just had your hair done!"

"Look sonny, do you mind? I'm just going to bed. Period. See?"

Caleb said goodbye sullenly. He wasnt willing to risk overt anger. So he walked around the hill before calling her again.

She apologized. "I'm sorry I talked to you that way, Cable. I'm not mad at you. I just don't feel like seeing anybody tonight. I've got a headache."

"I don't have any right—well it's none of my business, I know that. But I miss you. After all, we had a date."

"I'm sorry. Some other time."

"You sound depressed."

"I'm too old to get depressed. I just don't feel good."

Caleb hung up heavily. It wasnt until he was brooding over his supper that he guessed what might be the plain fact of the case. Without stopping to review the ambiguities of their tangential history he went back down to the telephone.

"Let me just come over and talk to you. I'll bring some beer. I won't stay long."

"Are you really sure you want to see me?" she said.

"I'm no fairweather friend. I'll be right over."

"I wouldnt mind. Come through the yard. I'll wait at the back door."

On the way downhill Caleb whistled through his teeth as he was suddenly struck by the compound significance of this contretemps. His curiosity leapt forward in a single bound and he felt his experience expanding like a balloon with the breath of surprise. It was not grievance but impatience to know her better that made him tremble in his haste. Any action that night was better than none.

He was astonished at the diffidence with which she greeted him, almost shyly, not as the same woman who'd opposed him on the phone. He even thought he saw traces of tears on her cheek, for she had made no attempt to paint and powder her face for his arrival, and her trained chrysophenine hair was mussed.

"I can see you need sleep." he commented.

"I don't blame you for being mad." she said, avoiding his eye. They sat down with the beer in her brightly colored kitchen. There were no traces of a meal. "Have you eaten?" he asked.

"I'm not hungry. Let's get drunk." She got out a huge bottle of Southern Comfort for herself. "I wouldnt hold it against you if you left any minute now."

"I'm not going to leave until you want me to. Why should I be mad? It happens to every woman."

"After what I told you?"

"You just made a mistake. That's all. Why should I be bothered by good news? But you'd better get a smarter doctor."

"It isnt good news and there was no doctor. I told you a big fib."

"But why did you want me to think you were pregnant?"

"It was possible. How should I know I *wasnt*? I wanted it to happen. But I guess it's no dice, and it was too late in the month for you to do much about it. But it doesnt hurt to open the barn door after the horse is gone—and you never can tell. Just my bad luck: on a Wednesday. I was hoping it would wait one more day so we could keep trying next week without your knowing. So now you've found out what kind of girl I am. Too bad. —You might have solved all my problems before Easter." she added sadly. "I just waited too long to make up my mind that night."

Caleb took thought. "I love the job—as long as you hold me harmless. There's always next week. Why have you changed your mind? What have I done wrong?"

"Nothing, dearie. You're a better man than any girl like me could hope for." Her eyes filled with tears and she took a gulp of the sweet liquor. "You're too good. But I know you won't like me any more: you're just too polite to show it. I can't stand the thought of you frigging me when I've lost your respect. I should have told you the truth. But after I made up my mind that you were the best one to help out I wanted to be sure we'd have a couple of more days together. You seemed about right to make the kind of kid that might look like his own, and you certainly have what it takes to make a stud."

"Does that mean you were just pretending to like—?"

"Oh no! I wouldnt fake anything like that, not after the first night. You're a fabulous missionary. I loved every clinch. I think you were born with a woman's insinuation. Besides, you're cute to look at and very literal."

"Then why don't we keep going, now that I know what you want? If I can make both you and the Silver Fox happy. Maybe I'm your best friend. After all, what's a warm friend for? Many are called but are too frozen!"

"Don't be such a smart-ass or I'll give you the back of my hand. I like you better when you're respectful. This is a serious matter. Actually I'm quite fastemious. You should know that by now. . . . But I know you don't mean anything by your parables. I've got a very special crush on you. There's more in you than any movie star. Too bad I'm not younger and better educated: I'd set my sails for you. If you really arent disgusted with me you're a saint: the horniest saint since the one that cut off his own tentacles.

"But another two or three weeks is all I can count on. Foxy wants a baby more than tongue can toll. At his age it's important to a man. And to me, at my age, it's getting late. I love the guy more than you'd believe, and I don't mind saying he loves me even more. But he thinks something's wrong with me. He doesnt say so but I can tell. I'll lose him to one of the young gold-diggers over there if you don't get me in the family way. At least it'd be good to find out I'm not the arid one. This wouldnt be deceiving him as long as he doesn't know about it. It's my last chance to start middle-class life as his snow-white bride. If I have a baby for him he'll give me a fur coat and a house and everything I want! That's the gist-essence of my whole story." And with new tears in her eyes she laughed for joy, squeezing Caleb's hand on the table. "I pray to Mary mother of God for you to do the trick or I'll take vows from the Sisters of Immaculate Reception!"

"Well let's not waste time this coming month."

She signified her agreement in a quick kiss with her tongue. "But no more useless succulence. At times like this even you have got to save every ounce. Chrism can get tired, just like blood, even if everything still feels the same. I realize that all you have to get in there is one tiny little beastie but we've got to give them all a chance if we're going to find the one that can make it. An onomastic like you must have wasted a million babies already. But don't worry honey: no matter what happens—even if Foxy takes a powder on me—I can take care of myself. I won't marry you. You're not my type. You're just a cocky kid who didnt know what he did!" She laughed her tears away at the very thought of Caleb as her husband. But she fell silent for a moment before adding "If it doesnt work he'll find another girl to marry. I couldnt blame him I'm sure. I'll die a dried up old spinnaker."

"It's better to burn than to marry."

"Like hell it is. When your soul's on fire it stinks in your own nose. By Christ—win lose or claw—you'd better not tell *anybody* about this as long as you live! There's nothing lower than a squealer. Don't you ever kiss and sell, and not just with me. If the Silver Fox doesnt kill you I will. To him hearing that you screwed me would be a lot worse than wondering about a miracle. He has ears everywhere, you know—and a very strong word of honor. We'd both be goners. Cross your heart and hope to die?"

"I don't want to be murdered. I'll never give us away."

"Especially to Mickey Chapman. He's the most dangerous one of all, mostly on account of his philology. Ruth told me he thinks it's a sin to have babies on purpose. —Speaking of her, she's the best mother I ever saw. I hope I'll have a toddler like little Roger. But you wouldnt believe what she puts up with! She never complains, and she's so good that if she ever did anything behind his back she wouldnt even tell herself."

"Mike and I saw a sailor coming out of this house very late one night."

"Oh that's an old friend of *mine*, you stupid loaf. I'd bet my life that Ruth's true blue."

"What about Michael?"

"Well he's never prepositioned me. But he told me a lot about all different adding machines. He's not small and wiry like my father was, but he seems pretty smart for a guy that's never been to college. He was born in Ukraine under the rectum of the Russian Cigar you know."

"Michael Chapman??!!"

"No, my father. Same place the Comrade came from that wrote Lord Jim I read in school. Was he a Red? He's a vet and he could of gotten an education if he really wanted. He knows as much as Foxy, but different things."

"Your father does?"

"No, Mickey. Between them they must know all there is to know about the way things work in this world. Not the kind of things you know of course. More practical, like. You're out of this world!"

"The devil knows a lot too."

"Only because he's old. Not because he's bad. Good memory too. He remembers all the bowling scores we ever had."

"The devil?"

"No, Foxy. He knows all the other numbers in town too. God he's nice to me. I really believe he loves me."

"Of course he does. So would I if I didnt know it was hopeless."

"Go on with your Blarney. It's the Irish in you. Do you think he's circumscribed like a Jew?"

"Who, the Silver Fox? You should know."

"No, Mickey. Told me he was part Irish. They don't believe in it. That friend of his, studying to be a dentist, before he knew you: he was."

"What, Irish?"

"No, fixed. You know what I mean. Don't make me say it over again. He was a Limey though I think. Sometimes I see him on the street in the City but I don't let him see me."

"I never heard of him. Was he your lover too?"

"Just once. Don't ask so many questions. I talk too much as it is. How would you like a bowl of strawberries and cream? Maybe they'll help me keep my mouth shut. I'll make some coffee too."

"What about the Navy guy? He looks potent enough."

"O Lord, I wouldnt let him knock me up. He doesnt come from a good family and he can't talk right. As a matter of fact I always make him put on a cuntdom, just to be doubly sure. It's too bad too, he's got such a tremendous beautiful prick. I won't be seeing him any more for a long time even if I don't get married. His ship's gone to Vanilla. Besides, I don't want to be knitting monkey-suits for a brat with sea water in his blood that'll want to start climbing the rigging as soon as he hits the deck. This kid's got to get into college. I want one just like you, only maybe just a little taller. That gob's nothing like the Fox in any manner shape or form. Neither is Mort Cloud. Know what I saw in his desk the other night? A whole gross of rubbers! Opened too, partly used up. He's been feeding me a line about how lonely he is for someone who understands him and not just for a piece of ass. What does he think *I* wanted? Not that I care, except I hate a prefabricator. I didnt tell him on the phone that I was in his office of course but I'm through with him and not just for Lent. But the other thing was he has kids of his own. I don't want any other woman's wellspring but he'd want mine. He's a very attractive man when you first meet him, and no disappointment either, seeing as how he's so well hung. No one can resist him so he's been spoiled. Well I can resist him, especially now I know you. But I think he's a little safer than a sailor that goes to whorehouses when he's hard up. But none of them can beat Cable for quality and quantity. Matter of fact I have too much of a weakness for men, baby or no baby, and you make it easier for me to be faithful to Foxy. A lot of girls are going to want to marry you. Not me though. I'd rather burn up. I want a liberal spender!"

And she laughed and laughed and laughed, holding each bright red strawberry whole between her teeth before it disappeared in a fragrant wash of thick white cream sweet as fresh-mown clover.

"Married to just one older man it's going to be hard to have enough fun. I'll prolly get fat. Whenever I'm under the feather I read magazines and just futter around the house by myself. When there's nothing else to do I watch everything on television but I can't stand it when I'm with somebody. Maybe I'm over-sexed. I bet even the B V M was glad to be by herself once a month—but not *all* the time!

"But you're the one I'm going to miss the most. Incite some more Shakespeare to me."

"Hail, periatic swoam! A brandle's drick
Shifts shape before my crandy
And mackly dompts foredele, in assoilment
Nitly karaboatic—"

"Don't kid me, Cable. I'm not that dumb."
"From a scene in my play."
"Dreck, even you wouldnt get away with that! You'll have to simplefly it for the commonwealth." She paused to search her memory for an illustration. "It should sound more like

Oh the old gray mare,
She aint what she used to be,
Aint what she used to be:
She pooped on the whipple-tree,
Pooped on the whipple-tree—

I forget the rest. If you're going to put poems in a play nowadays it should be in poplar songs. You write the limericks and I'll sing the music!" She tried to whistle a tune but had some difficulty keeping her lips pursed. "Foxy knows all the musicals that come to the Opera House. You should jazz it up a little. —Maybe I'll come see you again after all. Neither of us is going to have to worry about old man Wine much longer. You won't be so jumpy. —Do you like this expresso? —If I'm really a fire shovel like that artist said I shouldnt have any trouble dropping a kid. Anyhow it's going to hurt like hell. But I'll burn that bridge when I come to it.

"Next Tuesday now: I've got to go to the laundromat first thing in the morning. Maybe you'd better get some sleep while you have the chance, but you could run into me there accidentally on purpose if you like the idea, just for fun. Mr Wine's ending maid service at your old rabbit warrant this week you know. The only way he can turn a profit on it he says. You might as well get used to gossipy housewives down on the Lane. Good place to pick up women they say. Glen is a very nice guy. I felt real sorry for him, with his wife being so sick and all. She's great too: always laughing and joking. I don't think she wouldve minded if she knew about it, he's so good to her. Maybe I helped keep them together. He's a very quiet guy but he's got the same interests as the rest of you. Looks skinny as a pencil—but he's not by a long shot, not in the gentles. He makes me feel a little funny though with his communistic ideas. Maybe Rosenberg was like that too, not a bad guy at all, just mistided from all the bad things that went on in the world. I don't think a girl should go by a man's politics too much but nowadays you can get in trouble just for looking at a Red. We used to have chickens called Reds. I wonder what they call them now. And the Cincinnati team too. He reads lefty books. Maybe you could talk him out of it. Whenever he started complaining about the country I said 'That's a big mouthful Mac' until he stopped trying. I don't like to be crude, but listening to that stuff is not what a woman's for, especially when a man's in his condition.

"—So I'll be over a little later that night. If you dare leave your door unlocked you won't even have to get out of bed. Maybe I'll catch you asleep again. Don't you ever relax? You're the stiffest kid I've ever seen. I guess I'm not normal either. Do you think I'm a nymphochondriac? Notice you never have to simulate me. Did you ever go to bed with two girls at the same time? —Oh no, of course you couldnt have!"

"What about you, would you ever do anything like that if you were invited to?"

"I would never share a man with another woman! Do you think I'm crazy?"

"With two men I mean?"

"That's more like it! But I don't answer purely hypocritical questions, especially about reversions. I never dared to ask the priest how bad that was. One thing I hate is humbuggers and fairies unless they keep it to themselves. It's unnatural if it's not a way to make babies. I guess that's how you can tell what's an immortal sin. You don't have to learn a lot of rules if you remember that."

"Have you ever been to a psychiatrist?"

"No but I've had practically every other confession. Still, as long as I stay natural and don't stick around Communists I figure I won't burn in hell. Those tampions are immoral. I don't think they're good for a woman. Not that I'm against all new-fangled gadgets. Like television for a sample: that's a great thing for someone who can't run around much. Only thing I don't like about it is the same dumb people you see over and over again until you're sick of their product.

> Fools' names
> And fools' faces
> Are always seen
> In public places.

That's what they used to say down on the farm. Nowadays nobody believes in keeping quiet about themselves. 'Pride goeth before a fall.' Know that one? I always think of it when I see that phoney Nixon on T V. 'Don't count your chickens before they scratch.' I've got to be very careful not to do that myself right now. But even if it doesnt take, you and I will have a good time trying. Win or lose, I'll never forget you. You'll forget me as soon as you're famous, but that's all right: you're a man and I have no subjection to that as long as you don't lose your respect for me. That's the worst thing about most men. I don't like to think about it too much. I wish I could be like your Cinderella and get letters from you. That's the kind of romance I always wanted, where a man takes the trouble to talk to you when he isnt pawing you over and making you forget the good things in life."

"Want me to write to you?"

"Naw, that would be pediculous when we're right next to each other; it would make me feel funny if you did anything silly just for my sake. And after Easter it'll be too dangerous. We've got to break off clean. I don't want you on my mind. I want to forget you completely—understand? No letters, no phone calls, no nothing. That's all there is, there aint no more. Get it? After Lent I don't even want to bump into you on the street, see? Never never again: just a secret *memory* is what you'll be for me. If I do get knocked up this month I'll be remembering you every day of my life. But we'll never be posolutely sure it's yours because Foxie's still at work. Don't get too cocky about yourself. Remember: pride . . . ! Arent you afraid she'll show her husband the letters you send her?"

"I put things in them about the past that she wouldnt want him to know."

"For crying out loud!"

"I know. I don't do it anymore. I've stopped writing to her. I've gotten over the whole thing. I can't even remember my memory of her. I fell in love to the sound of a purling brook, polluted but unseen. If it starts that easily it can end with a song of pure praise for the Golden Fleece. I told you, you're the world's best doctor."

"Well in a way it's too bad. Don't ever talk against her. She'll be having troubles enough. —Limping lizards, I've been talking too much! Get along with you now."

"There's just one more thing I want to know, Hecky. Did Jim Jackson call you a fire shovel to your face?"

"He wouldnt dare!"

"Then how do you know he said it?"

"It's in black and white. This is one book I read. Of course I skip the parts I'm not in."

14.

A great mist formed around the landless squire and his damosel and for the days of that moon they were held enchanted one to other with eyes dim to the worldly ways they walked to earn their bread. For Caleb, ever without sad satiety, it was as the last hour before domesday, but for Hecuba it was as the time of angels before the word was made flesh, and her hope was for a new world that would make amends for doleful parting from her liefest leman, for she cast the happiness of her life upon the issue of their dalliance. None could see them for the mist, and neither of the two tarried or supped with accustomed friends, save that Hecuba

consorted with her betrothed lord at his pleasure, saving herself from it of
certainty on one night and day of each week, for the which she annointed
herself and made all manner of readiness so that if need be she would not
sleep at all in enduring the love of Caleb.

But none might refuse herself from sleep in all measure hard upon such
disport with Caleb and another night or more pleasing her amorous lord
that would sire him a scion at whatsomever cost of health or wealth whenas
she serves her livelihood by wending upon a broad mere to and fro the noi-
some city for purposing full busy matters unto the goods of her master
thereof who deemed nothing of her weariness sithen that she could ne tell
him naught of her person though she wist his heart would not harden
against easing her tasks. All these fatigues she must full boldly dure ere
returning to Caleb's arms to do her Lenten feastdays with fantasy of heart.

Thus on a certain Wednesday night in the middest of Lent she took
breath in sleep as he yet clipped her in his passion also aforespent, until
she fell upon a great laughter in her dream and woke him on loft with the
shaking of her belly under him where he was rooted to her like a weakened
tree to the earth.

Offtimes it were hard case for the tongue of wight to tell the soul's
dream, but under that meek and gentil man of learning, the courteoust
that ever she bare upon her shield, her dream was clear as vespers bell and
she would fain tell him of it as they woke together well pleased to find
them still one upon other in her full soft bower. In the dream she dreamt
all hideous things well and good, and merry things seemed beyond bounds
of mortal wit. Thereby her light heart was lightened the more and his was
brought to laughter also before he heard words telling cause of her mirth.
But when she stopped to tell him the jape or jest that he had spoken in
her dream she could not call to mind his words, for the story faded in her
head and only certain visions did she remember to speak of. Yet none the
less she laughed at the laughter she remembered, which passed unto him
by way of his manhood shaken loose by he knew not what meaning.

"My fur stole was a white fox pleasuring himself with sweet milk from
my bosom but its teeth were in no wise sharp as he nuzzled my pap with
dainty lips, while we were playing at bowls, you and I, and you said unto
me that when it was sated I would conceive and be with child for forty
moons till I cast the whelp, a true Christian dog that would be loved by
all the world for his learning, but now I know not what made me laugh at
what you said to me efte. An if you kenned my dream, wise Caleb, tell me
what your saying was."

"Nay, I cannot say, fair Hecuba. I did laugh for no cause but your
laughing and nothing more."

"Then" said she "this means that somewhat has done between us
whenas you lay pinned to me like a pitchfork left standing in a rick of hay
under the full moon of summer's night, for this is the fifteenth day of my

moon, and at such time even a maid may conceive if she lie in the grass warm and wet with dew. I pray to God that your work in this splendor has brought under my heart the wondrous beginning of a babe, and I ween that it may be even so for I saw never a man that I owed so good will to in all the nights that I have lain with men, outher gentil or other. But lest I be wrong or mistake the fellowship of the holy spirit for your makeless noblesse let us stint no more this night but make every trial we may to prove your prowess and my worship in the eyes of the archangel of the Lord, for you are passing lief to me, wherefore I have brought you into league with my forecast. Soon the light will begin to break on the hills to the east above our heads and you must take your leave once more and forsake the jousting that binds us together in wood delight like brace of young otters bobbing and sliding upon a Maytime riverbank upward and downward. Therefore make haste to lose no pleasure that may be left to me this morn. I will well that you be ruled as your strength will rule you."

Thus she unlocked her hoard of words and showered him with their riches until he yet again astonied her unto forgetfulness of speech.

And thenceforth likewise till all the feasts of Lent were dured they made no end to enjoying each the other whenever they held together in tryst, and the centers twain of their mist were one. Never did knight and damosel contend so oft or so long for the delight of outher within short space for dalliance. Her seemed that they evermore fitted closer shape to shape, and him seemed that he grew nuptial pads on his palms and fingers to hand her as he list without failing of his will and hers howsomever he might dispose her or she curvet as out of wit. Yet in truth Caleb took care to keep his hands clean and soft to touch her, lest he feel to her as a varlet of the soil, and betwixt their trysts he donned gauntlets for all his toil with the dross of worldly matter, thereby for the most part saving his skin and nails from the defilement of black diamonds that he must fling like dung six nights of the seven, and preparing him against the hap of her visits to the castled pit if once or twice in a week she might make do the secrecy of it and an hour could be spared from duty to her lord and from the rule of God who has ordained that all men and women of this earth must sometime rest and sleep or they will die.

Hecuba was fain to compass her end in good conscience by giving thought to Sir Fox when she lay with Caleb, but not always might she move her mind to it, so dear to her heart now was the youth Caleb, whom she had taken to be her lover for pleasance. And likewise, that she might give her body with right good will to Sir Fox, she made of him Caleb's semblance in her thought, for thereby it seemed her that she might better conceive by her betrothed suitor if Caleb might not make do as sire maugre wondrous prowess in swivening. Thus made she the best of either and her heart was always full, as were her loins with the virtue of both lovers, yet the most of it by far was Caleb's, like Irish Sea mingling waters of the Boyne.

But Caleb deemed not how much he overbare the old knight in the pleasuring she took of each, weening that old foxes fare with wiles and skills hidden from young dogs, for Hecuba held always to the use of courteous ladies and would say no thing in favor or disfavor of her lord's person nor of his privy skills with her, and at the end Caleb wist ne more of the Fox from her than the Fox wist of him who was altogether concealed. And never would Hecuba discover unto his ears the things and deeds that were most curious to him, nor the Fox's nor any man's, but full well he knew that there was much in her memory that might be told, seeing that her history was full rich, and he came to understand why men choose maidens to marry, not by cause of spotlessness or narrow girth but in faith that they hide little to be shriven. She kept her counsel in this case more than any else, yet neither she nor no man could know of a certainty which lover was truly her champion an if she had her boon in issue.

One Wednesday night by the largesse of Sir Fox the merchant of billes, who was most bountiful to Hecuba's friends through her hand and choice, King Michael and his queen Ruth were given means of wending to the far city and attend upon a company of strolling dancers. Sithen they had too oft craved Hecuba to stand guard of their children they now demanded of Caleb to set him over young Jonathan Matthew and Roger in sleep. Caleb did not by heaviness refuse their bidding for he had not much honored them with his presence of late weeks and doubted to offend them if he did not as they wished of him. Thereto he desired not to make excuse from courteous service either of the king or of the queen's fast friend his paramour namely of Wednesday. Yet when his duty came to pass he and Hecuba ordained to make visits one to either, above stairs and below stairs by turn, ere Michael and Ruth returned. Whereupon Caleb took his leave and walked seven times about the streets of the town while they opened down the bed and made their love together as he supposed. Then when he thought them to be on sleep he climbed at last to Hecuba's bed by way of the postern and straitway made use of the hours left to him between her sheets. He slept not but watched till the edge of dawn drove him to alight and avoid her.

And the moon waned to its last crescent; then came heavily to its full darkness. By night and by day Hecuba prayed the God of her people to forfend her flux. The last Tuesday in Lent she lay all day in Caleb's arms without doing any other thing, neither to wash her clothes nor to refurbish her coiffure nor to provide herself from any market, whispering to him in sore dread that that dalliance might be their last each to each if she failed of her purpose, or nigh the last even if he had done for her the geste she had bade him in her service as a gentle lusty youth come by chance in her need. She soothed him and gave him comfort unto her powers for she well knew that he had no list to depart from her forever whether today or tomorn or the next day or the day thereafter or the day after that, caring little or naught that she conceived save that it granted him once or twice more to hold her long while in joy and play.

She was bestad with dole that if wrake befell her sweet advision it were not his default or Sir Fox's but her own, witting that she was no longer a fowl of the spring but belike gone too far past the prime of life. And so she warned him not to address without a scabbard of the Indies when he purposed to go in unto other women, for she doubted not his power to beget child passingly well made and big.

Thereupon he gave comfort and soothed her troubled spirit. "You speak no wisdom when you dread too soon and overmuch bewail the moiety of your womanhood, for you have seen unnethe mickle more than thirty winters, not yet the end of youth, and certes is it no end to bearing child. Behold my lady Chapman and her babe Roger. With more time perhaps I would not fail you."

"Nay!" she cried "So be it. Belike this very hour you will have done with me, or all too soon hereafter, come what may. You and I shall not again deal love together. Thronging dangers beset your quests, and mischiefs to my heart lie in wait. In these latter years after the birth of our Savior, loves fare soon hot, soon cold. We have no doom each to each but must pass like pilgrims, one to the east, outher to the west. Whether or no I shall carry your child whenas I send you from my arms forever, mayhap my heart will not serve my chosen domain, but you will have your owned children upon another after I am an old woman too wrinkled for your desire. But in the meanwhile, who knows? It may be my destiny that another whom I have not yet seen will beget my child upon me when the hope of it from you is stricken."

But Caleb would not hold entirely with that sentence. It was meet and right in his eyes that many more damosels should open to him in the adventures of his life to come, but he was sore jealous that she should find any service but his own for fathering her child unless it were Sir Fox himself, though she might take never so many lovers for her delight before she took the veil of wisdom. Yet he could not but bide her command to depart from her bed at proper time, and before his sorrow well began he murmured against his waiting for the next of her kisses. For they had bethought themselves that the end was not yet; their essay was not yet full done.

And lo the next day again being Wednesday he found her at home to him that night and he was not refused. They undertook to pass the fleeting hours afore dawn of day with as good cheer as ever they might, like wedded twain about to part each from each heavy with the doom of carnal knowledge ending in her scented bed, come what might. But they lightly offered and suffered every delight that either could devise, for the season had come when no manner earthly pitching was of any skill whatsomever in sowing seed to furrow, and it was no force how much they put to waste of time or substance so only that it pleasured them.

No damosel or lady ever so featly learned young gentleman how to cause her swoon in seeking after his lust, neither from the olden times of Alexander nor in realms Christian or paynim. Hecuba praised Caleb as a wolfhound in instinct for what he had taken to in one month only, and she deemed him the most learned pupil that ever she had to learn from, though with no outher teacher he had but begun a man's amorous feats. "Alas, I shall not be in your arms as you grow cool and sure in your vigor like a lion that tears his gobbet slowly, content to have his meat in small bites, and win to the wisdom of usage in mastering divers women. And well you may surpass all fellows unto the limit of your stature."

These words did not much please the orgulous youth who abade with no lists for the tournament in his imagination, nor any margins or marches to his pride, but in courtesy he kept silent under her disworship and put it out of his mind, for he natheless had much to thank her for in the honor she vouchsafed.

Toward morning Hecuba's heart rose a little higher, for though Caleb would presently depart from her she was not yet annoyed by ooze of blood, and as she made her long farewell strokes of him by the midmost of her body she prayed and hoped right earnestly that she need never be cumbered with harness to stanch such courses until the time be passed that she was laid full low in delivery from womankind's greatest pain.

When at last he crept down the open stair of her courtyard after his appointed hour he came round to the front of her wall and looked up upon her tower with doleful visage. There saw he a white face at the window, and him seemed her tearful as she waved white hand like as she loved him and would remember his love forever, so that he could not forbear lingering in despite of the danger from the archangel's eyes or others' if they should look upon the gray dawn and see him pacing slow away from her watch, back forwards till he made pratfall on the curb. He doubted she laughed at him for taking dread leave in this manner, and her mirth at such cruel unhap brought naught to his soul but overmuch of bitter grief.

Yet still—still again, that farewell was not to be the utter end. All day again she dreaded the onset of discomfort but the curse of Eve was still withheld from her. That night a Thursday she made for his dungeon smiling unto him, short of breath from her hasting up the hill, to tell that her womb still sent no forecast of the customary issue, and once more they took leave of each other by divers manner in the darkling castle of Sir Wine. Albeit she vowed not yet to count her young fowls ere they broke from egg, in gladness she had brought sweetbread that she and the lady Ruth had made together, and white wine purveyed from her purse. Late in the night they supped before the eye of the furnace on Caleb's wooden bench caring not for weird shadows or coal dust, kissing many kisses of peace. They thought them surely together for the last time and bade farewell each to other in such sore dole that no tongue may tell, yet not as lovers wood with grief, for she took no force of the sorrow she endured if her greater joy came thereby, and he had withstood greater love by enjoying in her speech.

The next day, although she had slept but few hours in many days, she craved Sir Wine for three hours leave as granted by custom to all Christians who willed it to go and pray at the cathedral from sext to nones in the dim midday ere full sun returned in sky. To Mary she said "Blessed is the fruit of thy wound Jesus." And she prayed in penitence, promising Our Lady that she would not visit Caleb in carnal joy again, for it was the day of all mankind's greatest grief, if only she might wear no more bloody trappings until she delivered.

And though that night she did go once more to behold Caleb, and tarried many hours, she would not in no manner lie with him, nor give him ease of any kind save with her words. "Wit you well, my dear friend, I would as fain as you that you might come in to me, but I may not disobey my vow to the Virgin."

And this was the last time they were ever alone together apart from other folk. She told him sundry of her knowledgings and many that she had heard, and much wisdom that he never would forget.

By all manner of signs her joy was nigh sure but she bade him for certainty send his voice to hers on Easter Day itself, when she would give him news, whether or no she might be mother to his first child, for scarce beforen had the visitation upon women been more than a day or two in retard for her. She said "Pray for me and say me well." and held her language thereafter.

Thus she took her very last leave of him, mingling hope and dole in one moan, with the longest kiss of all, savored with the salt of her tears but so fresh and sweet withal that he forebore to lick his lips until Sigurd Hansen greeted him at full morning and made him speak and clove in twain the spell of purity that she had laid upon him all night long as though she were a shepherd maid taken in mountain meadow far from men. All this time his loins had remained at peace, malgre she fairer seemed than ever before, never offering to slake his desire with her body but holding thilke in charity only. Heavily he fared homeward to break his fast and sleep all of Holy Saturday.

A short tale to tell, on Easter afternoon when he weened that Hecuba and her Fox Argent would be returned from high mass to eat their paschal lamb and drink the wine of resurrection he made ring the bell in her house that called her voice to his.

"Good Easter to you, Golden Fleece. Has sadness befallen your hope, or are you confirmed in happiness?"

And her voice came back to him: "I have had no mischief in the service at this house. Belike it was by another number that person had cause for complaint. All is well with my box, both for speaking and listening."

"Alleluia!" he said to her for his last sound in her ear, but he did not speak with heartfelt spirit of the holy day, forasmuch as he well knew that her glad tidings set a seal upon his interdict, seeing that Sir Fox would surely set vigils whenas she announced him her news; and that if he made suspicion of this thing about the child not jealousy only but dishonor would enchafe his heart to vengeance and treachery. And thereto Caleb wist that her love for him ever waned as the child waxed in her womb.

And so Caleb felt himself a culprit, a craven churl, once more an outcast from the tribes of men, yet more worthy than before she had disclosed to him her beauty and her speech. He set his mind to seek another woman by fair means or foul for every month of the year, forasmuchas first knowledge weighs greatly to a youth but far from quenching lust gives vision to the manifold desires of a whole table round of knights. Ere the words of Hecuba had begun to pale from his mind her sound and scent were misted in memory, and her limning eke. He remembered him her words anent the prairies and boroughs of her childhode long past his keeping in thought her parts that longed to him whilst her gift did last. And never ceased his wonder what man had smitten her with fantasy for strange words, unless it were her father a digger of coals.

Ever feeble was the thought he henceforth harbored for his moiety of the seed that Hecuba would bring to fruit. There was but one conception came to his mind with aught but faineance, and that his own. Till now Caleb had been careless even of the same, but the fair gentlewoman's passion for a babe mentioned of it to his mind, and anon the wonder of his own origin filled him with mystery, for it was harder in his imagining than the virgin birth of Jesu Christ.

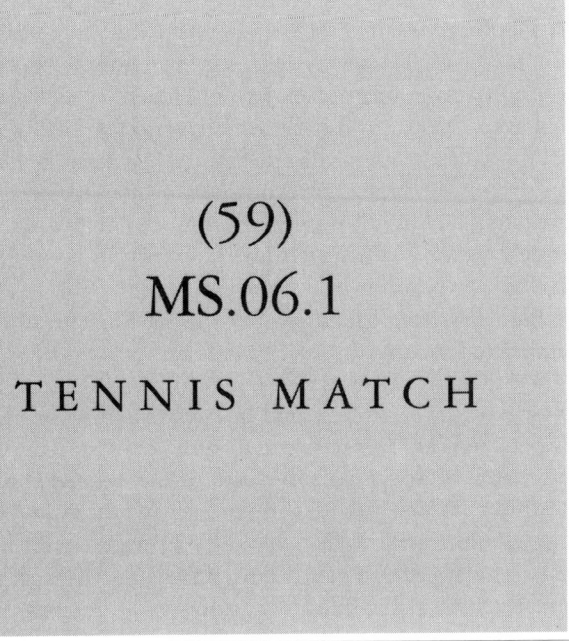

(59)
MS.06.1
TENNIS MATCH

Antilog 4

"Today is Sadie Hawkins Day! I'm already married so all I can ask you
to do is—"

"I thought that was in November!"

Leap Day, and Ruth Chapman was at Caleb's door, alone, and he in his
bathrobe only, just after he had wakened from some sweet dream and was
fresh with vague confidence at his writing table. It was like a second more
lovely dream but his heart beat wildly at the unprecedented intrusion
upon his afternoon.

"Well anyway it's only once every four years. Come and play tennis.
Take the rest of the day off and meet me at the court in an hour."

He was not sorry that she had to leave at once to get back to Roger
whom she'd left at home for a few minutes under the unwilling surveil-
lance of Jonathan and Matthew just home from school, for he was left
trembling long after she had immediately disappointed his instinctive and
instantaneously fleeting surmise, swift as the flight of a swallow through
his belfry, with her uncharacteristically peremptory and prosaic summons
in the world he actually inhabited. But in his fluster there was no question
of declining this invitation from the handsome lady, especially when it was

not lightly given, for she was ordinarily more loathe than he himself to disturb his lucubrative schedule with activity merely pleasant. It was such an unseasonably beautiful balmy day that even a mole had no call to waste it underground. And it was his duty to obey her.

As he shaved dressed and had a small breakfast his agitation subsided and in retrospect he took notice of her manner, which he now perceived to have been a debonair surface covering an inner agitation of her own. But he could not tell whether this disturbance of her usual composure arose from an emotional excitation or from the effort of running up the hill to deliver a friendly invitation under the influence of spring's zestful harbinger. It was hard to dispel the suspicion that the briefness of her smile and the unprecedented breeziness of her address were forced by something more weighty than the embarrassment of calling on a bachelor at a time when he was likely to be in bed, and he dreaded the hint of vague desperation in her behavior, as if she'd come to him as her doctor or lawyer.

When he arrived at the park he found that she had come much earlier with her children in order to devote all her attention to them for a little while before assigning the two older boys to watch their little brother at the sandpile (which she also could keep an eye on through the wire screen of the tennis courts) as they played on the swings see-saw and jungle gym nearby, with due respect for the rights of the few other children doing the same thing, whose presence was a superadded irritant to Jonathan in his resentment of the whole boring excursion to a park much more interesting to grownups and young kids than to himself. The boys' day of school had done nothing to mitigate their aversion to supervision, but Ruth was unusually firm in her insistence that they assume their custodial function with a definite degree of responsibility, leaving her and Uncle Caleb to talk in peace while waiting at ease in the warm sun on the greening grass for a pair of players to vacate one of the courts. Jolly Roger could be expected to remain occupied and sweet-tempered until he hungered or wetted.

Ruth and Caleb both wore shabby sneakers but otherwise, except for the new vacuum-packed triplet of gleaming fuzzy balls that Caleb was contributing to their duet in token of his newly steadied finances, and their heavy old-fashioned rackets, they exhibited no equipment designed for the sport such as the snow-white socks shorts blouses and caps of those who ostentatiously frequented the asphalt clay, though Ruth could have outplayed them all as easily as she could beat randomly encountered players of chess. Tennis and chess, at both of which Caleb's skill was rudimentary, had been high achievements of her youth. Unlike her golden record on academic scrolls they were modestly mentionable as erstwhile talents on a plane of the world that was now of merely nostalgic interest to her, amusements from which she had graduated but to which she occasionally returned in recollection of simple fun. She was glad to win. In her scoring she gave the benefit of doubt but yielded nothing out of sentiment. She had always beaten Caleb as he strove to gain on her in grace, the attribute in which he had the furthest way to go, considering that his advantages in breath and strength and speed of foot were of no avail. He was docile to the tactful tips she offered sparingly at his own request, as worth no less or more notice in a person's life than the knowledge of what streetcars to take for given points in San Francisco, and he analyzed as well as he could her inimitable form. But he couldnt help being displeased at his losses, much as he'd rather lose to her than any woman on earth.

On the banks of two great intersecting traffics it was a fine sunny park full of shade when shade was needed. Their ears were accustomed even to the MacArthur Boulevard channel of unceasing counter-flowing motors. Sitting by Caleb's side Ruth Chapman talked as he plucked blades of grass. It seemed clear that her chief purpose in routing him out of bed was to get a listener. Then the conversation continued sometimes even between serves, slowing up the sets, and they both had trouble keeping score.

That day he won a match for the first time, though by very little—not because she gave him points (which would have been untrue to her principles) but because she was unable to concentrate her outward eye in total independence of her inward. Yet when the afternoon was over Caleb did not count his triumph, for he was so perturbed by what he heard that he scarcely noticed how his play improved with inattention to himself. She was nonetheless displeased with herself for losing a game when she stopped to notice what had happened, glad for Caleb's sake, believing that he had already overtaken one of her few abilities as she praised his talent and assured him that he underestimated his proper seeding.

By the time he appeared her excitement at the impropriety of her initiative an hour earlier had yielded to unapologetic compunction. "I had no right to drag you down here when you have something better to do, but you're the only one I can talk to. You really didnt have to shave, you know." Caleb's heart rose again at the prospect of a secret between them, at her confidence in him, even if it was for advice that would be considered only for comparison with her own judgment. "I havent seen much of you lately, since you started your play, and something happened a couple of weeks ago that's been worrying me. I wasnt going to say anything to you about all this, but I know you're Michael's best friend."

"I'd like to be. I can't speak for him."

"But perhaps he confides in you."

"Not at all." Caleb laughed. "I don't know his real feelings about anything but Yeats, and even at that he's ambiguous!"

"He's really not as cold and self-sufficient as he seems. But to tell you the truth, he makes me dislike Yeats. He never quotes the poetry—maybe I'd like that—but only the sayings, which usually sound perverse or precious, and I have given up trying to appreciate them. Art-for-art's sake is a bad influence on our family!" She smiled her unselfconscious and unpremeditated smile that never failed to stir Caleb's heart with its sudden beauty. At first he thought she was teasing him. "If the spirits took all that trouble to communicate with me," she went on "I wouldnt let them waste their time on silly diagrams. The spiritual world can't be reduced to geometry. But it's only the abstraction of it that Michael likes. All his own writing that I've seen is too abstract for people to read, don't you think?"

"That's just because he gets so little chance to speak to the world that he has to cover a lot of ground in a few words. He doesnt have time to make images."

"Well he has plenty of chance to talk to me. You must admit that looking for abstractions is a very odd way to spend the time he doesn't spare us. But his fantasies about giving lectures and seminars are stranger yet, especially when you know that he didnt want to go to college. I know how you hate psychiatry, but don't you think there are certain cases when it can do some good? Maybe only to talk things over with someone who's had a little experience. Just therapy, I mean, not analysis."

"My hatred is purely theoretical. Psychologists hold the intellect in contempt. You can read sheets and sheets of psychosity without a word of philosophical relevance. Deviation is the only thing they reckon, not objective truth or value. Most of them are ignorant of general ideas. In fact they reduce all meaning to emotion. That's what I object to. But I know psychiatry can be good for people who want to feel better."

"Even the best analysts pay no attention to their patients' insights. I have been seeing one, you know. Michael never mentioned it to you? He's ashamed I guess."

"Then you know a lot more about psychologists than I do. I'd certainly want a doctor who's well educated."

"You'd have much harder time finding a peer than I did." she solemnly teased without a hint of mockery, as if she prized intellect as highly as he did.

Caleb was at last abashed. "All I really mean is that I wouldnt want to be evaluated by people who have no sense of free will."

"It always amuses me that you seem to think they have such great power. Actually they can't even boss one patient around!"

"What sickens me is all the artificially induced psychoselfconsciousness. They're like dipsomaniacs determined to make everyone else alcoholic too. Look at Newt and Sylvia: they can't keep anything to themselves. They've actually started their kids with a psychoanalyst before they're old enough to go to school! Iatrogenic medicine! They're determined to make the whole population live at a level of Freudian anxiety. Before long people like that will be practicing on each other in round-robins."

"That might not be such a bad idea. We depend too much on doctors. But there is such a thing as practical therapy. Do you want all the women in the country packed off to Bedlam on the word of a few educated men?"

"God no. Nor the converse!"

"Well then. Women are no crazier than William Butler Yeats or Michael Chapman. Is there anything reasonable or useful about studying *ritual*—when your family's in a condition like ours and you're working so hard to make a bare living? Of all the archaic superstitious irrational—! For heaven's sake, in the midst of this poor suffering world, where most people live in violence or starvation or confused unhappiness! He'll die of the strain, without helping anyone. —Caleb, what do you think of his writing? You know a lot more about intellectuals than I do." She smiled at the echo she'd made.

For once in his life Caleb had no reply to a request for his opinion. He was tongue-tied in dismay at this seditious outburst against the king. She had suddenly confronted him with a view that called into question the ultimate wisdom of absolute loyalty. It seemed as if he was being asked to choose between king and queen. He thought of anger, but he was not angry. In the shock of doubt he remained mute, deserted by his resources and by his will to exert influence. But he accused himself of permitting her to take his demurral as a tacit disparagement of his king much more telling than her own, for her animadversion as a wife implied the wish to strengthen rather than weaken the bonds of allegiance.

But she did not expect a reply. "Perhaps I'm wrong. The only thing I remember from Rousseau is a bishop's story of an old woman who could never think of any prayers and every day she could only say 'Oh!' to God, she marveled so much at creation. That's the way I really am too, and I'm never sure about anything at all when I get analytical or critical. But sometimes I too must become abstract in defense of my family." She smiled at this joke upon herself but he could see that she had no intention of changing her tack until she'd sailed much closer to the wind. "After all, neurotic behavior may or may not lead to psychosis according to the response it gets from others, how they interpret it. It may be my fault. Hecuba told me that mules are very intelligent but you have to hit them over the head with a stick to get their attention. I don't know why I'm remembering all these quotations today—maybe because I'm trying to be as objective as possible about what I see—but the one thing I got out of *Tom Jones* was the statement that it's much easier to make a good man wise than to make a bad man good. Michael's not only intelligent but he's a good man too, a very good man in many ways. I love my husband very much."

What's she driving at? said Caleb to himself. What is it that's her fault? Why is she telling me what I've never doubted?

"Please don't think I'm complaining about him." She laughed again in the contemplative manner that made all her words benign and uninsistent. "I'm only explaining a little of the situation. Because I know you admire him and want him to be happy. It's not merely his masculine characteristics that worry me. Probably most men have minor selfishnesses of one kind or another, or at least quirks that seem unnecessary. He has to have his butter, you know, when everyone else eats margarine. And he loves eggs—oddly enough, when you stop to think about it—the way Roger loves milk. But milk is the only thing that keeps Roger healthy and too many eggs arent good for his father. The yolk and the white arent allowed to be mixed in the cooking, only as they're about to enter his stomach. You can say things to him that I can't. Somebody ought to warn him about gluttony if he's really as interested in longevity as he says he is. He gets positively apoplectic with hunger. He says most alcoholism is caused by men having to wait for their dinners. So it's beer too! And radio baseball! Sometimes I have to take the kids and leave the house. Not so much because of the noise or the laziness: it's the insensitivity, the waste. Of course he deserves his rest. But he's the one that's always talking to you and his literary friends about irony! He doesnt seem to have any idea of the ironies in his own life. For instance when we got married the first thing he bought for the house was an expensive art book, yet a few years later when I wanted to get an album with a photography contract for pictures of our own children twice a year as they grew up he carried on as if I'd suggested that we invest in a diamond wedding ring. Of course he's now glad we signed up, although he'd never admit it. When does he ever look at the art book? You know how he says he hates television? Well at last I'm going to get a second-hand T V for the kids. For a long time I'll have to keep it in the closet and never get it out when he's at home. He'll pretend he doesnt notice it, since he can no longer stop me from having it like every other family in this country. —I wonder how I'll be able to keep the boys from telling him about it every night when he gets home? Some little fibbing on my part. It's always hard to explain his capricious tyrannies to the boys. I have to deceive them too. But wait until this baseball season! Then he'll discover the conveniences of television, mark my words! Not to mention football. We probably still wouldnt have a telephone if my mother hadnt paid for the installation, but now he couldnt live without it. Yet I know he doesnt want to make things hard for me, and he loves the kids in his own way as much as I do. I've always thought he just doesnt understand the pain caused by his perverse ideas. Scientists say that fish have low-level nervous systems, and that even when they're fighting to the death against the hook in their throat they don't feel the pain the way we would. I suppose in Gloucester the lobsters don't feel anything when they're taken off the ice alive and dropped into a pot of boiling water! But the scientists and fishermen are men, and they boss the women who do the cooking. Anyone who's treated like a fish should know how they feel. Jonathan Appleseed Chapman was a Swedenborgian. He loved even the snakes and hornets that bit him. I'm afraid my little Jonathan is going to be more like his father than his namesake. I can't seem to intercept this kind of maleness that comes down through the recent generations!" She laughed in Caleb's face and tapped his chest with her middle finger.

"My father's an old almost indigent blindman now," she continued "and I'm sure he's quite sensitive to his fallen estate. How he must have lorded it over the earth in his palmy days. There isnt any story he couldnt tell about his experience. He once crossed Asia on the Trans-Siberian Railway on some business for the Tsar. But he used to ride horses as hard as anyone else, with no thought whatever for the pain of the bit and the spurs. You may be too young to remember how horses were treated. They don't have free will but they're victims of ours. I'm glad we have automobiles. The more cars the less horses there are to suffer. Have you ever seen what spurs do to a horse's side? Rodeos are as bad as bullfights. A horse's mouth is just as tender as ours. Daddy used to take me to the track, and he'd laugh when I cried at the way they whipped the horses. Even then I saw how unnatural and brutal horse-racing was, but he didnt pay any attention to the animals except for their genealogy and their earnings. Thank God Michael isnt money-mad. I have a lot to be thankful for."

Caleb at last found something he could say. "Yes. You should like Yeats for that. I think that's one of his main attractions for Mike. He said the Rhymers Club 'made it a matter of conscience to turn from every kind of money-making that prevented good writing.'"

"That's a fine sentiment for aristocrats or prosperous bachelors. He was probably talking about *extra* money. But that's not really Michael's line. He's a very ambitious clerk and he gets extremely involved with the fortunes of his little store; he defends Mr Greatrakes's nickels and dimes. Wouldnt he be a lot truer to himself if he got a writing job? At least he'd get some professional advice!"

Caleb was always ready to fight for this cause of the king's. "The only prudent way to cope with the necessities of livelihood is by a double life—never by compromise. Is how he puts it."

"That's hypocrisy!"

"Love fifteen.

"Yes, it's play-acting. He believes in the job when he's on the job. When you're poor it's just foolish not to be interested in money insulated from the work of art—or after the work is done, if you live long enough."

"Well his wife is outside the work of art. In his case there can be no doubt about that! I have no objection to a higher standard of living. We can't live where we are much longer. The boys have no room and Roger's getting too big for a closet. . . . I suppose I'm inconsistent about money. —You're making me say much more than I ever wanted to, as if I were talking to myself."

"Love thirty."

"Most people consider things from the man's point of view. Not only you my dear boy but even most women."

"Fifteen thirty."

"All maps point north. North was invented by men. The northern hemisphere dominates the world. Astronomy is northern. Biology is northern. Theology is northern. It's a male idea to have four directions. Three would do just as well. There are only three dimensions of space. That's all you need to locate a tennis ball."

"Fifteen forty."

"I suppose you too want to be a gentleman?"

"Your ad. —Only an American gentleman. I always wash the ring out of your bathtub."

"What is a gentleman? Is it something like honor?"

"Deuce. —Yeats says 'a gentleman is a man whose principal ideas are not connected with his personal needs and his personal success.'"

"I thought as much! His personal need is his family. His family's welfare is the measure of his success. Those are the things he doesnt want to give much thought to!"

"My ad."

"Am I to understand that a true gentleman—even if he's American—gives little thought to his children? Then he should be extremely efficient with his ideas about them, since they're the measure of his success. Well let me assure you that I am not the only inefficient person in the family!"

"Game!"

"Your service is getting very good. But this is a masculine game too, like marriage. It's always love-something or something-love. If we're lucky we get the deuce!" She laughed in a brief burst of gaiety as she took up the balls to serve.

> [When I watch her serve the ball
> My mind's not on the game at all!]

"The score is never love-love or ad-ad. Someone's always at a disadvantage! Or someone's always at fault! —Now I'll get even with you."

"Woe unto the world because of offences, for it must needs be that offences come; but woe to that man by whom the offence cometh!'"

"Am I playing against a Christian American gentleman?"

This conversation went no further because after the court was yielded to another couple there was much ado with children. They encountered cheerful ugly Jeanette Smith wheeling her cheerful ugly child. Caleb was introduced as one of her new customers at the village pump. Ruth was the formel of this neighborly park, to whom all fowles nodded or spoke, and her children were the happiest in sight. Except for Jonathan who would rather listen in on his mother and the merlin than make friends or fool around with siblings.

When the fair eagle's party was at last organized for the return stroll over to Teleology Lane and down its west bank, past the home for blind people where the eerie lights were never on at night, toward the Just-As-Good Laboratory, ignoring the long ragged wall of nondescript doors and windows in between, she found it difficult to work her way back to the point at which she wished to again center the young gyre-bird's attendance. As they approached the most familiar corner she was saying "I'm glad we're not going to live in the clam bogs after all. From what I hear Gloucester's a town full of dirty albatrosses."

"I wouldnt stay in California any longer if you went back East."

"Oh you'll get over your idealism. Especially if I find you a girl friend. Some day we're going to have you and Lilian to dinner together. Anyway, I don't really think I'd ever have gone East."

On sudden impulse he risked joking about it: "Denise de L'Isle-Adam said there should be no divorce because it was important to preserve the symbol of eternal love."

"It must have been an idealistic man who wrote that script."

They agreed to play again the next day if the weather stayed dry and warm. "I never got to the heart of the matter today." she said. "I won't ask you up to the house this time. People will talk if they see you coming over very often when Michael's not home. Right now I have to be especially careful of my reputation."

Friday was easier for Ruth because Jonathan was out of the picture for a Cub Scout meeting after school. Matty and Roger were far more cooperative alone together, and less curious about what was going on between their mother and their nuncle. Ruth reasserted her mastery of the court. Caleb's service deteriorated. They spent more time at the park both before and after the game.

Afterwards Jonathan was to hear with annoyance that he had missed Caleb's treat at the park. On the way home Matty taught Roger the English language, starting with "ice cream" as they ate it. The incident reminded Ruth to tell Caleb about a colloquy between the older boys that she'd overheard some time before. Jonathan was explaining the connection of Caleb to the family. Matty had been puzzled about the uncleship of a man who wasnt related either to mother or to father. "Is he part of the family?" "No. He's the star of daddy's story." "What's the star of a story?" "A hero." "Then where's his sword? I never heard of an uncle like that before. I think he's more like our best friend."

But Caleb was now hearing the anecdote too late in the day to give him pleasure. Neither tralatitious syllables from Roger nor ice-cream-gratitude from Matty could divert the process of doubt that Ruth had by then set astir in his mind like a lump of yeast that could not be prevented from fermenting its boundaries. It was new uncertainty, not knowledge: it was the disillusion of confidence in his own senses. And it had very nearly the same affect as a revelation of treachery against himself, even though he had no part in the disequilibrium that burst upon his awareness to shatter the beauty of his friendship with the royal pair. But he was obliged to acknowledge that they could hardly have been expected to keep him informed. Without delight Caleb stared distractedly at Matty playing Old MacDonald Had a Farm on his kazoo sitting opposite Roger who was too busy in the sandbox to listen.

Ruth had watched Caleb's face with conflicting regret and satisfaction at the nasty enlightenment she wrought upon his innocence simply from her overwhelming urge to talk to someone who would believe her. Unsuccessfully she had pondered ways to mollify her carefully prepared revelation.

She had taken up the conversation of the day before by expressing her admiration of intellectual women who refused to be overborne by marriage. "Look at the way Sylvia Cahners keeps up with all the new developments in psychology. And even Sarah Wolfson who's a born mother keeps working on her Master's degree. I'm old-fashioned. My intelligence, such as it was, has faded. When I try to start reading again I can't make up my mind that I ought to be thinking about what the words mean, as if that would be taking the time out of someone else's life. I suppose this state will pass if things get better, but I often wonder if it's because I'm a woman. Do you think so, dear Caleb?"

"I'd hate to be a woman." Caleb replied, never dreaming that such a remark might strike her as anything but a pleasantry. "But you can't blame men for everything. It was a jealous woman, Athena, who saw to it that Aphrodite the laughing goddess with a magic girdle was prevented from cultivating her useful mind."

"That's a true story. Hecuba Jones—the girl upstairs: it was the spinster teachers at her school who stopped the principal from allowing her to take the subjects she wanted to learn—probably just because they thought the boys liked her too much. She's very clever and original, but all she's learned to do is make her own clothes and Christmas cards. Of course she runs the businesses of the man she works for, without getting a ditch-digger's pay of course. What a fine teacher she would have been! Yet even though she's a woman and we bake bread together there are certain things I can't talk to her about as I can talk to you, because tradition conditioned those spinsters to keep her from getting the education she ought to have had. She could have held her own with Newton Cahners or anyone else.

"By the way, do you know an optometrist named Morton Cloud that has an office in your building?"

"I hardly ever see the people I take care of. What's he look like?"

"Oh, he's—tall and very tan—" It was the only time Caleb ever saw Ruth Chapman blush, ever so faintly, and if more startling matter had not supervened he would have remembered the occasion day and night for a long time. But the crimson shadow quickly passed from her face to her shoulders and her voice remained steady. "It's just that he rang my doorbell the other day to see if anything had happened to Hecuba. He'd found she wasnt home when he expected her to be there. She must have told him I was her friend. He's rather self-confident and aggressive. I think he was a bit upset. He seemed to be trying to control himself. He must be—" she smiled "—quite fond of her. She may be going to get married soon, although she's said that before and nothing's come of it—but of course I told him I knew nothing about where she was and he didnt know that I knew who he was or that I'd often seen him coming to the house on Wednesdays." She hesitated and laid her hand on Caleb's. "But I'm afraid I've told something I shouldnt have. It's an unforgiveable thing to do. I certainly didnt intend to. You must swear, for my sake——"

"Don't worry. I'm a stranger to everybody, and I won't even mention it to Michael!" And he understood that she had blushed at her betrayal of a dear neighbor's secret.

"I trust you. Hecuba's my best friend, you know. Perhaps the only one, really.

"Anyway, despite the unintellectual life we lead in that little pigeon-hole of a tenement I've been getting known for my letters to the paper and other things I'm involved with. (Perhaps I can help you get your play produced when the time comes. I have the ear of some influential people.) At least they wanted to list me in the Social Register of the United States. In my opinion it does no harm to get better known for the sake of one's work. Anyway I filled out the form and now I owe them $25 for a copy of the directory. It's a perfectly reasonable price when you consider the limited circulation. But Michael refuses to pay it!"

She paused for Caleb to express his surprise, but he had no idea what he was expected to say. It occurred to him to offer the money.

"Oh no Caleb I wouldnt think of borrowing from you! I certainly wasnt driving at that. I was just telling you about one little marital crisis that we'll have to get by, one way or another. I must keep my credit good. But can you imagine what state of mind the poor man must be in to resent such minor recognition? I try to give him no cause for jealousy of any kind, but I don't think it will do any good for me to bury myself in domesticity. He really needs more help than you and I can give him."

Caleb had no mind to help anyone, but he at last ventured a remark to temporize his confusion. "The only time I ever saw him fazed was at his birthday party the night I met you. At first I thought it was because they'd spoiled his surprise for you, before I saw there was more to it than that. But then I forgot all about it until this minute."

"He has the power to make people forget things that he doesnt want them to remember. Do you know how he does it? By silence. By ignoring the matter totally. By pretending to himself that it never happened. After a while, when there's absolutely nothing to corroborate your memory, when all the evidence is wiped out, you do forget. There are so many new things to take its place. I often wonder if he's aware of his technique.

"He calls me Cassandra. Well I prophesy that he'll never write a single book if he leaves California. It was for Michael's sake that I refused Apollo, and though Apollo spat in my mouth so that Michael would never believe what I say at least I was left with the gift of knowing the truth that should be spoken. Naturally the doctor wouldnt believe me either—but that doesnt matter so much because he doesnt really care what happens to the man I love."

Caleb still dared ask no question. For the moment he wished only to open his distance from both the man and the woman who had befriended him, regretting that he had entangled himself in a courtier's dangers. He feared for Ruth and her children but his latent anger was reserved for Michael. All faults lay with the king. Nevertheless it was Michael's authority that still held sway in the habits of his mind. From Michael's own example with Sarah in her kitchen the previous September for instance he had learned that it was much easier to comfort another man's woman than your own, simply because there was no obligation for you to *do* anything about the distress. Yet though he was assured by the timbre of Ruth's voice that he was not expected to expose himself by any kind of participation in her troubles he could not bring himself even to offer comfort. The more she confided in him the further he shrank from sympathy.

"Recently he's been complaining about the smell of his own nose. What can that mean? He's worried about cancer. It's an odd symptom, don't you think?"

Once she chose a thought to tell him the bell of her well-tempered voice sounded out the words as lucidly conciliatory as ever, without haste or hesitation, never so self-absorbed as to discourage an interruption, never warding it off, as if always listening for better wisdom than her own, or as if she was speaking compassionately about persons in a book she loved. But Caleb had no comment, no wisdom, and she continued as evenly as before, increasing his embarrassment at the honor she did him with the intimacy of her divulgence. "I really don't think the world would come to an end for me if he were unfaithful now and then. Perhaps he's driven into these odd ways by the fetters of marriage. He never talks about freedom but I've always heard that that's what all men want, no matter how much they love their wives. Just to explore new bodies; perhaps no more than enough to taste his possibilities as a conquering bachelor. He does say that the customs of modern marriage have been imposed by women. According to him we feminized Anglo-Saxon institutions like a conquered population that imposes its language and its values on its oppressors long before it begins to assume their power! There's something to be said for that view, but why does he harp on it all the time? Of course I'm sure that if he actually did sleep with another woman I wouldnt be so calm about the thought of it, especially if I knew who she was and could set her straight. But would something like that reconcile him to his blessings, and give him the incentive he needs to adjust to the life *he's* chosen? After all, a wife is not a man's superior: maybe like a child he needs a mistress who can *reward* him. But we're Americans and of course I'm afraid to breathe such a hint. He might fall in love! He might throw away money on her! And the boys and I would have less of his time than ever before—unless he gave up his writing! No, it's unwise to solve any problem by doing wrong, and I'd be the last to want it that way. Besides, he's too jealous of me to turn his back for a minute to look at someone else."

"I don't blame him for that."

"Most of the time he conceals it pretty well, but I think he's afraid that some of the guys attracted by Hecuba will try to seduce me when they can't get to her, and he's secretly suspicious of every man we know except you."

Caleb swallowed the gallantries that in other circumstances he might have been bold enough to offer at such an opening.

"Jealous of me! Can you imagine?" Ruth went on. She was not soliciting his answer, and nothing was further from her tone than the coquetry that might have been suggested by these words in another woman's voice. But she laughed with an amusement that Caleb would have been impelled to redirect if she had paused. "Once last summer I noticed that he wasnt speaking to me at all. For a whole week or more he scowled and paced around the house with his hands in his pockets. I've never seen him so agitated. I wracked my mind for what I might have done to him, but I could only imagine that something terrible had happened at the store. Finally one night he took a deep breath and asked me who my lover was!

"It took me a long time to find out what had brought on this attack. One morning he'd found on the dining room floor near our front door one of the rubber prophylactics that men use. Naturally I was flabbergasted too: right in my own house!" She laughed merrily at this scene of the comedy. "But it's like losing something: the only way to find it is to methodically reconstruct what you've been doing since you last saw it—only in this case since the last time you saw the place it's been found! Or whoever lost it! Not that it took much method to remember that Hecuba had been baby-sitting for us the night before. It was quite plain that she'd just been amusing herself with a visitor while we were out. I must admit that it would have made me a little uncomfortable to contemplate that sort of watchfulness over my babies if I hadnt known what a keen sense of responsibility she has. It's no worse than what goes on among the baby-sitters in Berkeley. A lot of girls don't want to be alone all evening on their jobs. It's more interesting than television. But she's always very neat and careful about everything she does. It was just a funny accident, and not her fault at all. I've never been able to bring myself to accuse her of acting like a college girl, much as she'd like to hear it. But I could see that Michael was determined in advance not to be taken in by a cock-and-bull story, and I think it was many months before his suspicions died down. But they can always flare up at the slightest provocation. The truth is that to this day I can't be sure he believed the obvious. Most of his jealousies are based on much less than that."

I should think so! said Caleb to himself as he thought of what he had missed in Berkeley. He would have liked to ask whether or not the sock had been unraveled and sodden with use. But his suppressed levity regret and curiosity were fleeting inward attempts to displace the import of what he was hearing, of what was coming next.

"Perhaps I don't mind it as much as I ought to." she continued. "Illusory suspicion certainly isnt conducive to harmony. But it's less harmful to a family than the proof of adultery.

"I realize that this sort of domestic distress is only a trifle in the history of civilization. I've only mentioned it as a significant example of comparatively unimportant symptoms. I'm burdening you with my private problems only to prepare you for what you should know as his friend. He's trying to kill me."

Caleb stifled an automatic laugh—then froze, waiting for the metaphor to unfold.

"Not by murder, literally speaking, but indirectly. It's like poisoning in two or three doses." She paused for half a minute, not to wring from him a reply but to consider the case once more before dragging it into the light of day. "Years ago he used to call me Struvel Mater. You see even then he wanted to cut off my thumbs. But I knew it was normal to harbor hidden hostility, and such things can be worked out in the course of time, or even ignored indefinitely. And now he calls me a breeder reactor. I don't know exactly what that means but it gives me the same sort of feeling. Except that he says all women are the same: that's a comfort!" She laughed again.

"You know, I think there's such a thing as benign disintegration of reason. A sudden explosion of unreason may be the only way to break up old patterns of feeling and free oneself for healthy new thoughts. But he'll never explode. He's always too wrapped up. His disturbances come out indirectly—like breaking wind (if a lady may say so!).

"Now he wants me to sign my death warrant! It's a paper he got from a doctor. He just barely lets me read what he wants me to agree to, watching me like a hawk for fear I'll tear it up before his eyes. The fact is that he wants to mutilate himself! Just to prove that he believes in his theories! And exactly at the time when he knows that I want a daughter more than anything else in the world. Perhaps it would seem to you that he's trying to kill himself rather than me. I'm sure there's a suicidal element here. But you see this is just the first step. Let the camel's nose inside your tent, they say, and—well, whatever a whole camel would do under canvas. But I know what Michael would do. The next step would be to get *me* spayed like a dog!"

"But why?" Caleb couldnt help crying out in an affectation of jocularity. "Surely one of you two is enough."

"Why? So that I could never marry again, or go to a doctor to get the benefit of another man."

They had reached the corner and stopped while she finished her disclosure. But Roger had to be taken home to get his pants changed before she could gloss it further, and before Caleb could be confronted with an appeal for counsel.

"If you have any washing to do I'll meet you at the laundromat bye and bye." she offered. "I have a load that can't wait any longer. Semiramis needs a clean pile to sleep on! It's strange how clothes get dirty. Is it the person or the world that soils them the most? Have you ever looked through those portholes during the rinsing phase? It's always hard to tell bubbles from suds."

But Caleb never showed up to give his opinion on the question of sterilization. And he heard no more about the matter from her, although at various times thereafter he eavesdropped on a variety of other gossip at the neighborhood pump.

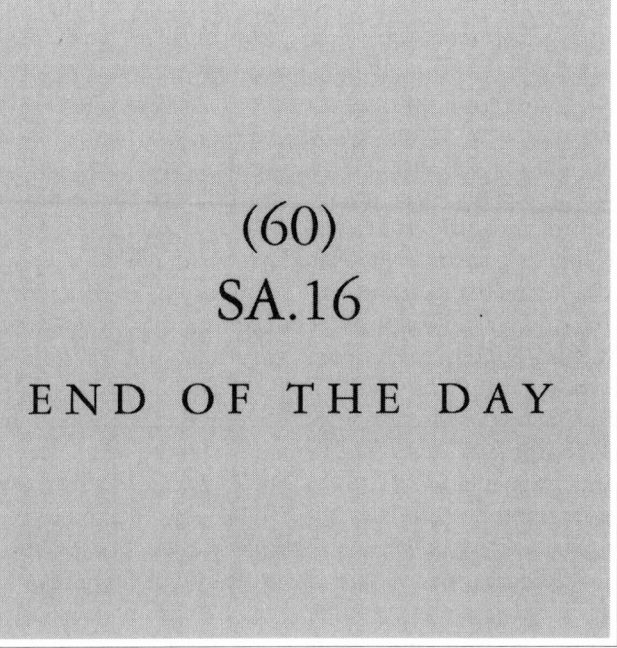

(60)
SA.16

END OF THE DAY

Our life is part folly, part wisdom. Whoever
writes about it only reverently and according to
the rules leaves out more than half of it.
—MONTAIGNE

Yes, credit for the day belonged to Ruth. But now before the end of it their holiday was over and her familiar part again came to the fore in all its old inveterate inefficiency. How she managed in the next three or four hours might make or break the little corporation's net profit of pleasure from the excursion she had instigated. The four men known to be in her thoughts were now looking to her solo performance of the finale, not as an enthusiastic audience eagerly expecting the rendition of a prima ballerina assoluta but as a tired hungry corps de ballet waiting for its housekeeper to produce board and beds of customary quality within a reasonable time, special circumstances notwithstanding. All appetites and fatigues were vivified by attention to her unsung duty.

—Ah where has Herr Doktor von Philosophiereich disappeared to all of a sudden? The knecht begins to suffer now. Play of mind has come to an end in disgrace. The blade that has been tickling the skin of his plump white belly now sinks silently to his guts, swift as a snake and at first almost painlessly,

Michael secured his castle door. The returning palmers were now safe from marauders and neighbors. Ruth went at once to the postern and admitted loudly crying black grimalkin anticipating her attention. Of one accord the apprehensive couple looked into the courtyard below for Topalis's cream-puff. Fortunately the garage was empty, signifying that though it was not yet Orthodox Palm Sunday the Greeks were out celebrating the sabbath with their joyless relatives. The coast was clear for a little Trojan noise. The beleaguered family could lay aside its armor carelessly because the confusion was vertically contained by the bearing walls and no writs from below stairs could be served against the chaos bounded in its meiny; above them Hecuba Jones did not care.

"Daddy why does she wail her tail at Mummy like that?"

"She's as hungry as a panther and demands the first feeding."

"Kitchen cat, cupboard love!" said Ruth dropping everything to serve Semiramis.

"Let's get a dog!"

Thumping and shouting gradually subsided into an endurance vile of spated squabbling and wails of awaiting. But Roger had to come next—after the pile of clean laundry on the kitchen floor was hastily divided between usable spaces of the dining room and the unfolded murphy bed in the front room, while everyone else's patience underwent its final trials. As the little tyke's antipasto milk was warming before his eyes in the kitchen and he sat in dry raiment testily sweep-

like a needle shorn of mass and friction until his own cold hand starts to carve its torture with a rolling twist of the edge and an upward jerk of the point into his panting heart. All mere jealousies along with hunger bone-weariness and ordinary frustrating irritation are banished with sweeping and contemptuous indifference to their claims upon the tabula rasa. A man's abrupt changes of state are sometimes inconceive— Oh Christ, live germens are here invulved! Or rather this is no mere ecstasy that he's conceived for the flesh of his flesh, that she's received. The real rub is there was no rubber buckler to protect his honor. Under the conditions of disposition and/or surprise at which he's assisting neither her foresight nor her defense can be supposed. Therefore the impudent biogens of this imposter must have rocketed from foreskinned muzzle through a cyclone of honey to the throat of a gasping womb unimpeded. An unlawful murder of marriage engendering new life, an avid deglutition mocked at length by the agonizing extrusion of a baby boy's head, and the short-armed farmer hoodwinked long enough thereafter for a third filial love to root itself mutually and irreversibly. All four parties to the event or events have had pleasure from it, and that is the most horrible fact.

After a moment of pure and unconscionable pain devoid of all words and images Michael's mind plunges into the passionate contemplation of an essential topic in the uncongenial science of repro-

ing to the floor every pacifying trinket and utensil laid on his built-in tray by the solicitous mother Michael at last got his turn in the jakes for a few minutes of private relief.

Even in the blessed pleasure of easing himself he brooded glumly about the untoward urge that had gripped his bowels without preamble just as he reached the house. At first the restraints exercised by his anal sphincters had been autonomic, as if coping with chronic discomfort, but finally his difficulty had become so acute that he was obliged to summon all the forces of public safety to control himself. [Holy shit where did that load of thunder come from all of a sudden? Half an hour ago I noticed a little cloud no bigger than a man's hand way off in the northern sky but nothing with any hint of volcanic urgency. How can it make up into a typhoon so fast?] But when he was free to give the cloacal tempest its leave to burst it blew at first more gas than solids, mostly squibs and squirts of broken wind. [Probably something I ate at one of those public places. Well if this aborts a germ so much the better. I'm purged now and hungrier than ever. Maybe if I wait a little there'll be some substance to it. —There that's better. Roger's droppings never get a chance to drop they only smear. I must admit I don't want longevity so much that I'd keep living in my old age if they had to put diapers on me.] As the mind's ordinary traffic resumed he abstractedly dug into his nose with restless forefinger for the mucous

ductive biology. But he's certainly not drifting into his usual noetic anaesthesia; he seeks knowledge only to grapple with an enormous new idea that shatters the present culmination of his existence. In another instant the owl is a-cold in personal anthropology as he undergoes the excruciating metamorphosis right out of owlhood altogether. With a dizzy reel of his swift visions a young mother makes her choice at the fertility dance and envelopes a hot libation from the flaming headhard snout of a hind; boneless as rock under its padded spermacetti forehead it staves the besotted vessel, and under its own violent provocation the blowhole injects a geyser that sinks her moaning. The synoptic observer of Eden's invention, confused angelic informer to the law he can't enforce, already benumbed to the apostasy of her mere pleasure and the desecration of his private temple, has suddenly transcended his heady empathetic androgyny by thinking upon what happens when clotted glutinous bilge overshoots the site of his own copious sacrifices and sticks there. He is left with a single spectacle mounted on the boards of his own bed in which he perceives the foul rut of a conceiving varlet. The suffering observer of its climactic surcease now dismisses as not only indeterminable on his part but also as merely incidental the momentous lust and surrender of that double-backed beast.

A splitting pain gradually locates itself in a channel up the center of his trunk parallel to his spine. His thoughts circle the bases

worm that ever eluded his search. A little later he found with a cry of rage that the roll of sanitizing paper was down to its cardboard armature, which he thereupon ripped from its sockets and hurled into the heaping wastebasket a yard or two beyond his reach; naturally it bounced lightly off the bullseye and trundled briskly off under the bathtub to hide from his sight where he'd have to fish it out in an awkward kneeling position if he didnt leave it there in spite. Knowing better than to waste his hopes on a reserve supply he charily resorted to jagged shapes torn from some newsprint he'd hoped to save for its biographical and statistical assay of the new season's Yankee roster. This paper remained stiffly lustrous and positively inclement to the flesh even after patient attempts to macerate the perversely ridged fiber by balling and stretching and snapping and crinkling on every axis from one perpendicular to the other. No using complaining after he got out of the bathroom; to hell with training for the future: let someone else cry out at the shortage. Once again she would prove her improvidence without learning anything from its inconvenience he muttered to himself. But it was a small matter in the larger scheme of a wife's behavior and he was more annoyed by the frustration of his shot at the basket than at the familiar household scrape he had found himself in to provoke it. And he gave himself a wry hoot when he reflected that his squall of fury paled to expressionless stoicism in the face of certain global misgivings

faster and faster, and clockwise also in subtraction, or swing like a pendulum back and forth between first and third without scoring, while at home the wound in his heart grows cold. (Love's a wasting fever that ends in waste.) The shipwrecked husband has clung to the waterlogged fragments of his indelicate imagery until their last grams of bouyancy are enleadened with salt: now he must support himself or drown. (Everything's universal in the end.) Even his sympassionate blood is drained by the laceration and there's no flourish or flare left in his loins. Mr P has subsided into his seaweed withered and forgotten in bleak humiliation. All bawdy cream has been skimmed off the raw milk by his earlier whirl of intoxication and now his cranking of the highly geared separator begins to yield a bucketful of lean bluish protein heavier than brine, skimmed of all its taste. Between motionless lips he quaffs a long bitter draught from the cold rim of the pail he's filled, struggling to stomach it with visceral enzymes of assimilation. His toes retract and his entrails tighten but with the relief of his tumescence his furrowed brow vibrates feverishly with the synectic confusion of owlish calculations that quicken the metabolism of his chilled and trembling soul. No airconditioned computer could have sustained such a frightfully wracking excitement of mentality in a network of body, parts, and passion that together dance in jerks without leadership.

[Isnt it just the last two or three years that Sandy has been

that underlay every trivial execration of that anomolous afternoon.

When Michael returned to society in better trim the Chapswoman was spoon-feeding Roger his second course and there were signs that preparation for the third had begun. She plied him slowly patiently and smilingly between her moves to further the common meal. He was happy to hear the soft plopping and folding of water at the boil, which augured well for a supper that was at least hot. At each of Roger's unhurried mouthfuls she said with long drawn-out undulations: "*Up* the hill—*down* the hill—and into the big tunnel!" as the grinning recipient responded to every word with a beam of recognition. Now and then she chatted other comments or questions almost as familiar but less intelligible to the attentive gazer now well pleased with the service and rewarding it with laughs. There was for instance one line of nonsense with many variations that he'd been hearing since his nursing days: "Are you the little teeny-tiny man what everyone loves that looks at? Little teeny-tiny Tiger Cheek?"

The father paused before the small prince to add his bit as Ruth rose and turned away to attend the pots on the stove that were murmuring or seething like another brood of children. Said the towering man:

The first the worst,
The second the same—
The last's the best
Of all the game!

Solemnly chewing Roger listened until the new sounds had sunk in;

staying out of my sight? That foul rambling maladroit lewd lascivious louche cunning falsehearted double-dealing self-appointed babyface womanizing donkey-dong gallimaufry-monger has the nerve to say Roger's got a touch of me in him! Too shrewd to dwell upon that red herring—just tosses it out as if it were the world's most commonplace white lie and sowing an angelic son the least ironic of all his infernal phallacious conquests. The best deception's a tactful misconception. Yes tact is touching. He's hurried my wife off her feet and touched her at the uttermost when maybe she was forgetting many a touch of mine and remembering herself as unfulfilled. So the gothic portal parted and from the sanctuary itself he spat my poetic punishment for narrowing the idea of sacrament. She let him pollute her with thee my Roger fair so beauteous blithe and debonair. *Woe unto the world because of offences, for it must needs be that offences come; but woe to that man by whom the offence cometh!* But to me comes the woe, not to him. Yet hers was the almost inconceivable deception, for perhaps after a perfumed bath on the night of the same day she drew me to the same vesica piscis fain to replicate her ecstasy and confuse the issue by reversing the prosopopoeia with which she had perhaps envisaged my head on the torso of her incubus. Well at least that would explain the improbability of her third joyful conception against the odds of contraception, which is maybe just what her undermind wanted of him all along even more

then his face delighted in their import.

But Michael's melancholy equanimity was ruffled when he noticed that Semiramis under the sink was greedily wolfing off the bare floor huge hunks of gurry-hash that she had dragged off the dinner plate of blue and white china on which she had been served from a half-empty can that stood on the sideboard over her head with its jagged cap hinged up in counter-balance on one side to a silver tea-spoon planted like a spade on the other. It was one of his unvoiced complaints that Ruth had again forestalled the rudiments of family discipline and all the future benefits thereof simply for the sake of immediate convenience in keeping the cat off the table, in diverting the brazen black beggar from her shameless patrol of the kitchen sink with piercing miaows and tail waving in the cook's face. On a full belly Semiramis would never think of catching a mouse overnight; Jonathan's appointed new chore would not start in the morning: nothing would change. Nothing would ever change in this outfit except to reduce its incidence of mitigating good luck that was less than average to begin with.

"Matty for the love of Mike don't jostle me while I'm getting dinner!"

"But it's for Daddy! Daddy's beer. Quick—where's the church key? And I need a clean glass."

The weary king was somewhat soothed by his second son's eager loving ministrations, by the cold amber mead itself, by the almost

than her husk craved the cocka-doodle. So the fecundation was no more rapicious than a north wind drawn by sucking from the south or a plethora of caloric flowing from a hot body to one less hot and equal-izing the heat like a short-circuit making maximum contact. My life raft has been torpedoed by acro-somes drawn in negative barometric pressure to a yawn in vivo! His ma-licious spermatozoa merely capaci-tated facilitated or disinhibited by inhibiting the virtuous inhibition of those loosely tethered ionized plasmatic eggmines that implode at minimum touch. Naturally the odds against their success are re-duced if nothing stands between them and their goal when the grossly cooperative intruder presses to her limit. Then each of the myriad infusoria in the expostu-lated swarm spends exponentially greater relative flagellant energy to swim with its stream than a sperm whale does in propelling itself by fluke against an ocean current under the pressure of a thousand fathoms. . . .]

With subterranean momentum these swift masochistic conceits keep his deepest brain clicking and whirring at the tocological ques-tion. He puts two and two together and takes them apart like a beserk logarithmoid flicking through a Möbius loop of tentative data. All the same a single idea sticks to his mind like wet leaves on both shoes. He's impatient to test his hypoth-esis but as in many biological stud-ies it is far more difficult to devise one experiment than to speculate upon a thousand observations in the mettlesome air of steamy operations beyond the open doorway a few feet from his elbow where he had by now taken his place in the rocking chair that nearly blocked passage around the overladen table in the lobby called dining room that served as lounge and warehouse for all sorts of Chapmanana. He and the two older princes understood that Ruth had a certain amount of catching up to do before she could cook in earnest, such as clearing the kitchen table and washing the dishes that were wanted. The family's unity could be restored only in her way, which though eccentric in manner was universal in means. Man and boy they waited for her to complete that part of her day's work. In the lamplight of a long day's gloaming some of the details were slowly warming to the touch. Jonathan like his father before him at the same age a draftsman in all his spare time sat at a corner of the table where he had pushed back various drygoods to make a working surface trying with light hard pencil and smudgy superficial eraser to get on yellowish manila paper the knack of rendering a municipal cablecar at plausible angle of ascent. In a tiny clearing on the opposite corner rested the frosty glass that was warming the cockles of his father's heart. Matty had returned to the blocks with which he was making a zoo on the floor in front of the curtained glass double doors to the less presentable front room.

However as the baby grew bored with eating alone (although the appeasement of his evening field. Yet for an active man playing this passive part in his own history the nearest act to action is directed research. One small thing he can do is ask his wife if she has a picture of her father as a boy (when photography was expensive but carefully posed). Yet there would have to be an amicable family conversation at the supper table or some rare moment of mutually casual leisure for his interest to seem disinterested. Otherwise any appearance of selfless curiosity about her loved ones might strike her as an alarming expenditure of his time and charity. He nevertheless resolves to find a way to mention the old man tonight: it's a wasted day anyway and he'll never find a better evening to write off as well. He seemed to remember at least a dim picture of his father-in-law as a young man in the aftermath of the San Francisco earthquake. Maybe it would account for Roger's physiognomy, who perhaps resembles the male side of her lineage paedomorphically. At the same time his anchor to windward is the hope that he himself (having no early portraits) appeared to others as an almost dolichocephalic fairheaded slim and ebullient child before he was old enough for the Gloucester public schools, though he puts no great faith in such evidence of paternity, suspecting as he does that any man's by-blow conceived in that spot as the third of her children, irrespective of the passion entailed, would be formed by a matrix so saturated with his own chromosomes that it could never throw off the Chapmanic influence.

hunger and thirst was hardly well begun), as the mother had more to do than amuse him, and as a father had nothing better to do when trapped in the family's best baby-sitting chair too hungry to read, Michael consented to take Roger upon his lap where each could enjoy the company of three gentlemen. The obligations of courtesy oftentimes became tolerable even in the worst disorder when the mistress of the house was rustling up some grub. To the periods of a slow oscillation Michael thus once again that day nodded over the child of his old age whose fragile warm rib cage always gave him pause with its trusting confidence in the arms that hugged it. For a while in calm repose he even forgot to sip his beer, but what he had already downed was beginning to penetrate his sober core with irrepressible cheer.

Without looking up from his drawing Jonathan suddenly called out. "Ma what are we having for supper?" This violation of unwritten family etiquette flew past the commander's ears like an unauthorized cannonball from his own fleet, but all the same he listened for its splash with bated breath. "I'd rather have something good to eat than a carload of gold doubloons." the boy added to himself aloud. But would any answer come? Had she heard the demand at all who never failed to answer a question politely? Or was she only hesitating to risk some premature disturbance by announcing news that would disappoint young or old?

The reply surprised all who awaited it. "Never mind dear. You

[Influence? But effluence is the rub! Why even though my Jonathan and Matthew had shaped her soul and body it took as much or more semeffluence to make a baby brother. Yet likeness smacks little enough. The seedling's unlike the seed. I would like to think that the spermatic animacule may as well become a man like the father of the seed that prevails in the family's furrow as like the feckless strain of a spurious sower blown into the muddy rut like weedling pollen in a single windstorm. Besides why can't I believe that especially in the first nine months nurture dominates nature with exclusively maternal nutrition and claustral education? If necessary I can hold that the one pronucleus happening to make it to the one ovule happening to lurk in its way merely facultates the first of 56 self-motivated female reproductive cell divisions that generate an embryonic girl. So that if it's launched in corruption it may still rise uncorrupted. The son gets no more than his start from the male donor. Call it a case of rape. *There is a natural body, and there is a spiritual body.* The natural father begets what the mother forgets the begetting of in the persuasion that the not-only-begotten son was made if not begotten by the meet husband sent by God as protector and ass-leader for the journey across deserts of helpless infancy and as doting parent of the holy scion's uterine brothers his only begotten sons among all the numberless ghosts he's given up upon the family's sacred hearth each of numberless quanta. She accuses

know perfectly well that your father says you have to eat everything that's set before you. So it doesnt matter does it whatever we have and you don't need to know in advance." But forasmuch as she was whistling cheerfully as these uncharacteristic words issued through the open door from the chamber of the smoking tripod her suppliants all laughed and they were disposed to read into them a favorable prophecy. Then she added, calling out to the king of the roost, "Hey Pop, what do you want for supper?"

Before he could suppress his involuntary reaction the instantaneous response was blurted out: "Holy Smoke havent you started yet—?" He halted sheepishly as it dawned on him that he was being drily teased.

And "April Fool's Day!" came her cry, to the great delight of rational sons at both the mother's wit and the mother's besting of father.

"That's next Sunday." Sacrilegious wit lost upon his audience was all the father could summon in feckless riposte.

"So it is. But I can't very well play tricks on Easter Day can I?"

But Matt still had his eye on the ball. "Limpin lizards, I hope we're not having fish. Just because it's Psalm Sunday it doesnt mean we shouldnt have a big Sunday dinner!"

"I don't care as long as it isnt fat slugs of bacon!" Jonathan commented. "I smell *something* cooking."

"How 'bout beans?" Matt giggled. To which his brother replied as expected according to ancient usage:

me of liking eggs because of "an unconscious wish for children" but if a man of only 10^{13} cells gushes 10^{12} potential half-kids in his lifetime there's clearly always going to be a buyer's market to say the least and it's no wonder he'll even pay to get them off his books just to save the cost of storage handling and interest especially as that bony-looking peninsula that leads him from one thing to another is his only outlet so he can't be blamed if they end up in my case for instance yoked in no more than two live entities as it now appears out of sixty trillion possibilities for immortality in spite of God knows how many million alluring tantalizing egglings that have set their caps for poor exhausted little cast-out fishlings in search only of warmth and peace to die in. God must love inefficiency he perpetuates so much of it. In other words the rule of chance that so many people love for the hope it offers. But when I alone trot out such a surplus of competitors why in the name of all probable gods should Sandy's longshot have taken the purse if it wasnt because his candidates raced the odds on a cleared and leveled track while mine had the highest barriers to leap? Still, with only one shot or very few I hope! The boor's double sling of gendering stones must be weightier than the catapult itself like the cups of Constantine's victorious troops that were said to be heavier than their swords. I suppose it's no wonder considering that the holy spirit in my own balls is mightier than the unplumed pen with which I disseminate it and his

"Beans beans
The musical fruit—
The more you eat
The more you toot!"

Ruth came to the doorway dripping spoon in hand. "No, not beans. But why don't you men discuss supper among yourselves and let me know what you decide." And she turned back to her secret work. Michael put out his arm to prevent Jonathan and Matthew (moved by the same impulse) from following her to take a look; they immediately understood his silent puritanical injunction to play the game without cheating and returned to their places. But no one could yet quite identify the smell that now began to come from the kitchen with a faint sizzle. There was no use being hungry for steak or lamb chops so long after payday, but whatever there was to salivate about the alkahest of hunger had brought on the peristaltic phase and was now like to dissolve at least the two active stomach linings that didnt have even small deposits of gruel or beer from which to wring nourishment during the latter part of their vigil. But Ruth's little jest had whiled away a few minutes, and when she finally did reveal the secret she gave them something interesting to think about just when patience would have burst its limits.

"I don't like roast pot very well either." said Matthew taking up a line of speculation that his brother had begun. "Not *very* well. But I wouldnt mind it now."

"Don't expect anything as good as that after a hard day like this."

is the instrument of retribution for all my rejoicings at our abuse of nature's purpose. Only twice in all my hot pursuits of something more attractive than pleasure have I quickened an egg in all our confusions of fluid. "Wish for children" indeed! Desire is polysemous. The urgency of my semenship has nothing to do with semantic self-expression or reproduction. Yet that old game is more vitally informative than any other communication. My sigil imprinted on the zygote was to have been my only consolation for what I hope was the third and culminating misconception of my marriage. It's a problem for theodicy that a lout like him can implant messages in an archangelic wife. By the baby Jesus, it's easier to conceive my whoreson as her agamic clone. Is it any comfort that if a woman forgets the sorrow of her travail and remembers nothing of the anguish that brings a man-child into the world then likewise beforehand she may banish from memory the anguished ecstasy of the deception that begot him and therefore allow the guilt to melt into her sterling honesty during sacramental liquefactions as an unassayable alloy thereafter. Perhaps even as soon as the strange brutish seed puts a stop to the menses of my woman chosen by God to rear truthful gentile boys of tonsile foreskin amid misguided notions of infant education that almost always prevail. Pray let me believe that the conception was accidental and owed nothing essential to the stud's special qualifications for her passing passion. —But Christ, why could he not have

his father warned him, currying Ruth's favor who could overhear everything. But now he raised his voice to address her directly: "If it's eggs sister, don't bother to whip 'em—just throw 'em at us wild!"

Matt was amused at his father's strange sally but Jonathan more experienced in the governor's vagaries took notice only of the thematic word. "I hope it isnt eggs!" cried he. "I'm sick of eggs. We've already had eggs for breakfast and lunch."

Now much as Michael loved his eggs of morning and noon he could not but tacitly agree that it was too much to eat them also at night save after a long party. But at once relieving his anxiety that she might have mistaken the relevance of the nonsense he had initiated Ruth stepped in to touch his shoulder and say "I'm sorry dear, you can't have any more eggs today. The hens have gone to sleep. But tonight we're having the next best thing for an appetite like yours."

At that moment they all guessed from the developing smell. "Holy smoke it's chicken!" Jonathan shouted dropping his pencil and entering into a little hornpipe he'd inherited from one of his father's happier modes. "I suppose we're going to eat the chicken that laid the eggs we had today!"

Matthew and Michael were both shocked by this suggestion (though sharing the joy that launched it), the junior M impressed by the cruelty of animal husbandry and the senior by its metaphorical potentiality, but no one's hunger was impaired. All in all it was a hunger that made previ-

wasted that one spray in his distinguished career of wasted sprays? I can't much longer rob this cryptogenesis of its sting by playing with ideas. The possibility of virgin birth is improbable enough but it's still less conceivable that engendering would take place within a multiparously voluptuated aperture without an extraordinarily sympathetic appetite assisting access to its teeming ova in total disregard of the sentimental fact that the poor breadwinner has always loyally observed the chaste "principle of self-sacrifice" (false sacrament!) for the sake of nest and nestlings.]

A dim-sighted cuckold doesn't resemble a horned owl however: he's featherless, born of woman, no better than other men and weaker than many, ridiculously besotted with a good wife whom he doesn't suspect he's been unable to enthrall. It's a wise bird that knows his own son. Someone else's was hatched under his wing but he has fatuously called himself the father and taken on almost intolerable new burdens as protector and provider, never questioning his responsibility for its demands of the world. Yet his love for the third offspring is no less irreversible than any of his own incarnate ejaculations. At this late date what could it matter whose tiny frizzled weevil-sharks were let loose in the fertility pit on a certain occasion? Nor simply by graduating into Leonardo's second class did he regret his love for the imp—no more than his wife could unboot her possibly messianic sin. Now for a moment at the sudden rise of a strange new desire to ravage the

ous hungers of that day or any other day seem no more than the merest velleity of a striated muscle compared to the suction of vacuumed intestines. "Hurry up Ma I'm stying of dyation!" Jonathan added as he picked up his pencil again.

Matty suddenly propounded a riddle he was reminded of by something in the tension of expectation. "What makes the holes in Swiss cheese?" he cried with the haste of an overlooked member eager to make an impressive contribution to a committee's intelligence, though he'd never seen such an article of food and wasnt at all sure of its existence in the modern world. "I don't know" his father answered "but to me the eating matter is more interesting." Yet when Jonathan simply demanded the right answer Matt found that he couldnt recall anything about Swiss cheese except the question.

Before Jonathan could hurt his brother's feelings with scornful insults the old bear thought he'd divert the cubs with one of his own: "What does more swimming than walking and more flying than swimming?" It was too easy; both the boys got it at once: "A seagull!" Before he could fall back on the Sphinx's riddle he had to listen to Jonathan spell ANTIDISESTABLISHMENTARIANISM three or four times with increasing speed.

Now the tutor so hated conundrums and orthography that under the anodyne influence of his cups he began to chant for his own pleasure more than theirs:

treacherous strumpet he thinks he could unlove the god-bearer herself, but to unlove his loving youngest son is as inconceivable as the reversal of his conception.

The long cold shock of his discovery settled and began to ache. [A housewife's spurious erotic experiment with a ladies' man may be no more significant than the acceptance of an impulsive invitation to dance with a friend of the family, conceivably justified by intellectual curiosity or temporary insanity and therefore as it were unscrewed and expunged by confession—but only when its germs are flushed away by the laving tides of nature to leave the peccant parts freshly immaculate if not intact and the fading conscience at least half contemptuous of its jejune adventure as a silly woman's bagatelle of misplaced sympathy for a pitiably importunate young admirer. Thus might the wound to my honor be cured—or masked by the recurrent ever-renewing joys of old sacramental love. But no correction or denial in the present or the future can ever alter or shame the precious existence that was got by the rogering, nor must it ever be stricken from history's register of unique forms by any of my whited hogwash.] The aching no longer transfixed Michael like acute pain: instead it lapped in an irregular tide; at times it could even be forgotten as if whole nights were passing:: but it was knelled back in some degree at the hazard to chance words or mental glances, bringing again to his crown the burning

Kid little,
Kid middle,
Kid big,
Got up to dance a jig.
The whole house shook,
And they stopped to look
When I tried to kiss the pig!

"Dad can't think of a better rhyme after all this time." Jonathan candidly observed. "Sing us something that makes sense, not stuff you made up!"

"Why how dare you calmagiverate my epicomptorious debostulation you castinacious little noodlegoosic twirp! Today's divage contrary to fossinalogy and notwithstanding your impudential dabor deserves pifflicate renetreviation instead of merely frexious mediosity on my part. I don't get such pistlethwunking from this here little tiny Matteenie.

It aint so easy to adumbrate
When time itself is running late.

Try to act like a gentleman!"

"How can I? I fell off a brook!"

"So go fly a bucket of water and when things around here get too hot for the likes of you you can soak your head in a kite!"

"I double it!" Jonathan shot back. But he decided to mend his manners.

Matthew on the floor looked up from his blocks flabbergasted. "Holy cats!" he cried. "Did you hear that Ma? Upstairs and downstairs and in my imagination! I've never heard anything like that before!"

humiliation of knowing less about a vital fact than a couple of other bodies seemed to. On the other hand his ache was quite capable of drifting off with discursive speculations of its own making, or of gravitating into otiose self-analysis even in the very act of recalling his faculties to a relevant path, and so veering from object to subject as an easier aspect of his discomfiture. As usual in this creature of body parts and passion the mind appeared to dominate by attempting to anatomize an ache that literature has always treated as surdly indivisible. Yet his thoughts could never drift into pathological self-examination without abstracting the disease from the patient and leaving the self semi-philosophical. Thus (in part): [. . . If my equity in this boy is nil my distress arises not from that fact but from the discovery of that fact and I must ask whether I am not therefore more chagrined by the abuse of my credulity than by the substance or potential quality of that whelp. Am I shaken primarily by a sense of true affection falsely sired or by visions of the momentous event or events in which or among which it originated and by which I am both horrified and fascinated? Does the act disturb me more than its fruitful issue (if forsooth it does) partly because it arouses homoerotic curiosity? But my discomposure is complex. Is it tinctured by the discovery that my love for Roger is derived merely from the accidental responsibility for his egg in my nest? Or by the pathos that he the beloved nestling is most

"Yes dear it's too bad isnt it. But never mind, dinner's almost ready."

The older men had learned to double or triple her estimates but Matty had forgotten all about food. "Dad please sing us a real song."

"Okay.

> Early in the morning
> Off to the station—
> See the little puffinbillies
> Standing in a row!
> Daddy in the engine
> Pulls a little lever—
> Choo choo!
> Poo poo!
> —Off we go!"

"Another one! We've got plenty of time."

> "Come all you rounders
> For I want you to hear
> The story told
> Of a brave engineer.
> Casey Jones
> Was the rounder's name,
> On a heavy big eight-wheeler
> Of a mighty frame.

[Sung in full-voiced uninhibited cadences hallowed by tradition.]

> Caller called Casey—"

"It's funny how you like trains so much Daddy." Again Jonathan heartlessly put a stop to familiar lines. "What's your favorite railroad?"

"Not the Times Square Shuttle. Maybe the Belfast & Moosehead Lake that never got to Moosehead Lake because the Maine Central

deceived of all in his love for me? Or again does the fact that my Ruth invited the culprit's whore-pipe into her purse shock me more than the fact of my putative paternity (if forsooth it does) only because it indicates that I'm not man enough to content her? Thereto is the question of whether I'm enraged or demoralized. If I am angry am I angrier at being hoodwinked by my wife or at being bested at pandemic love by the most blatant cunt-hunting tumbleweed outside the U S Navy who has thereby degraded her from my peerage to his string of impressionable peasants? Am I further nettled because I've proven myself a peasant too by getting her as a virgin and jealously attempting to keep her chaste? It's hard to say what the blood-line has to do with my feelings. (Of course blood doesnt transfer the genes: it only washes them away when all goes well between lovers. Besides, to say that my blood flows in any of my children is an outworn trope.) Yet what will hurt the worst . . .] Here the ache ascended again to pain. [. . . is being reminded that the small man on my knee whom I'm flatly unwilling to cease loving more and more with each dawning of his days is baser than his brothers and myself. One who did not want kids at all should be the last to have an inferior's semi-duplicate foisted off on him. . . .] At this point Michael's contemplation lost itself in expletives of normative ethics that cursed not Ruth or Sandy but the causality of poetic justice. [. . . Thanks to the quirks of genetic determination any gimping moronic

directors wouldnt let it cross their tracks."

"What was your favorite plane during the war?"

"The Martin Mariner, a gull-wing flying boat. But I never saw one."

"Yeah I like that one too. It wasnt very big though—only two engines. But I meant fighters. What was the carrier plane that had sort of gull wings only upsidedown?"

"The Corsair? That was a nice one. It's too bad the jets have spoiled everything."

"All you like is old-fashioned things!"

Meanwhile Matt's hunger had returned and he was tired of building. He razed his unoccupied zoo with a sweep of self-criticism and came to stand at his father's side to watch his baby brother being softly rocked in tender warmth. Reaching out with one thick arm to draw his second child by the waist into that special circle Michael said: "Thanks for letting me use your thermos bottle today dear Zwischenkind. It's one of my favorite uses. I will remember you in my shall."

"You're welcome Daddy. As long as you didnt leave any coffee grinds in it."

Jonathan joined them. "Dad look at my elephant." One slim hand dropped lightly upon the sleeve that clasped Roger as the other held before Baloo's face the paper representing a new ideal.

"That's too close to see—now it's too far—that's better." Michael had no free limbs to focus the image for himself.

Quasimodo may beget healthy well-formed babies. But what's the difference between one's variety of healthy well-formed son and another's? I wonder if such fertile cuckoldry would distress a husband of ordinary blood as queerly as me. If my authentic misery stems from recognition of the inferior hereditary component in this third son's destiny it's an element of disappointment that doesnt enter into the woe of a common Joseph whose stirp might well be improved by his wife's resort to (say) a service like mine. —But it's the desperate resort of my thoroughbred matron, not necessarily sufficient for a foaling, that strikes the deepest pain. Though rationally in itself no injury to me—only to the mare's own pride in remembering herself beholden to an ass for stud—the most intimate transgression is my secret shame, no matter what he believed and no matter what she may have been thinking at the time, no matter what her marriage counsellor or Hecuba Jones may suppose about the less private aspects of our conjugal life. No, my pride, not hers. The worst of it is that there's nothing unique in my cringing disgrace.] The nice thing about 13C courtly adultery had been that the husband's self-esteem could remain intact, but this castellan's brooding was Jacobean in emotion and modern in ignobility. Reason brought him to face his debasement but it could not clarify the bewilderment of his feelings, even though similarly secret perturbations were commonly known as if by tacit convention to most Anglo-Saxon

"See—" Jonathan began eagerly.

"Shshshsh . . ." whispered the archguardian. "The little cricket's almost asleep."

"Shshshsh . . ." echoed the cricket not asleep at all just fooling them, quite able to fool them though not yet of an age for reason, and made them all laugh. (The father was not to be blamed for misreading the long silence of a face he could not see.) Matty broke away and ran into the kitchen to describe to his mother exactly what had happened, while Roger and Michael (who now had a hand at liberty to hold the paper before both pairs of appraising eyes—or rather three pairs if he himself was still to be reckoned a Four-eyes as he'd been classified in Gloucester and Cambridge for his goggles) examined the big brother's artwork.

The elephant with finely chiseled ears and horse-swift legs was caparisoned for war and ridden by a heavily armed Texas Ranger in a Western saddle hung with coiled lariats or hawsers. All the baggage of self-sufficiency was lashed to the roofless howdah between this pilot and an empty cockpit behind him for the red Indian not shown who manned the defensive machine gun mounted on a swivel. Michael praised his son for attempting live figures as he himself had rarely dared whose otherwise similar style of complication had been pretty well confined to technology without much effort to counteract that self-indulgence until his talent was immitigably deformed. "He looks like Abu-Lubabah that Sultan Haroun El Raschid sent to King

gentlemen who found themselves in this interesting condition. Since the psychic affects of his darkling enlightenment were therefore neither heroically exceptional nor as universal as the instinct for survival, and since he was by no means guiltless of his own illicit hankering, he was forced to own himself no more Moorish than savage. From that idea arose a broader anxiety, and from the uncertainty of understanding a discourteous situation.

His brain tormented to a standstill by this circumvallation of infelicities Michael finally turned back to the evidence. Maybe by applying commonplace inductive logic he could at least get the ache to translate itself if he examined stubborn facts in the perspective of his new humility. Then it would become a question of what to do about them. [To hell with my feelings. Even Theseus's wife fell for another man.] But until the facts were found defined and acknowledged he couldnt determine whether to shout with rage or harden his heart or desert his responsibilities; he must know whom to shout about, what to harden his heart at, when to desert. Before he could put his mind to the fundamental truths of the case he was overtaken by a hurry of libertine spirits resurrected from temporary quiescence to protest the body of his fate. For a moment he fancied that all claims against his freedom were nullified. The facts were a blessing if they gave him leave to bolt. [Let Ruth lie in the bed she's made for herself! I've always been a romantic axiologist at heart. If

Charlemagne along with a friendly dog named Becerillo. The poor lonely beast died fighting the Danes."

"I hate Danes." said the eldest prince. "Nothing but pirates!"

"They called him the father of intelligence because he was the ugliest of animals."

"Elephants arent ugly!" the second prince protested.

"Dominus proboscum!" The king made a sign of the cross over Jonathan's picture. "Thou art being replaced by a new species. And after Moby Dick dies there'll be no more sperm whales either. But the Republicans say the only beasts we need are feed-lot beef and poultry. —The old zoologists couldnt figure out how elephants fitted into the animal kingdom below mankind so they just put them into the pig category—pachyderms, for their thick skins! Doesnt that seem a lousy way to treat superhuman strength and wisdom?"

"I don't care what they call them," Matt objected "I think they're the most beautiful creatures in heaven. They're so good I can't stop looking at them. They make my legs shiver!"

Again he was gathered in by his father's strong arm. "It's too bad we didnt get to see the goats Matty. We came back through Goat Island though."

But those classical enemies of the vine were no longer as vivid in the boy's sympathy as his new friends. "That's all right Dad. . . . They have elephants on television you know—there's a program the teacher wants us to watch."

Sandy does not feel at liberty to take my place as professor of deontology she herself will have to bear my erstwhile burden. Go fuck yourself sister: I've had enough!] But of course he had to laugh bitterly before the words of bravado were throttled in his larynx—for sister had three sons, not one only. What would become of the elders' security? Or their education? To say nothing of their loyalties. And what would happen to the utterly permeant love that the father of two of them bore for all of the three?

You see: how could one adopt a policy or assume a manner until the facts were clarified? Screwing his courage to the sticking point he promised himself to contrive without procrastinating in doubt a mousetrap with which to confront his wife that very night. It would take the form of a scenario without other witnesses to the verification as he watched her face and listened for unprecedented quavers in her voice. This exhibited play of mind seemed no unadvised way to accuse his queen of perfidy. Her attitude toward the facts might have some bearing on the shape of his amorphous outrage. [Even when they're guiltless women prefer to be nearly as dumb as cats about their previous masters. She'll need a spur to make her trot out a confession that she knows more about some facts of life than I do. For evidence I can't rely upon the pentimento of the few dreams she has choosen to recount in part no doubt revised. But seeing that I must start her off on the course of healing candor I hope

"Damn the teacher!" Michael snarled. But the old boy immediately reminded himself of the Reader's Digest subscriptions his own teachers had insisted upon, riding roughshod over his incipient sense of political and cultural justice. As it's only a sunny household that's so easily oppressed by a single cloud he made up his mind not to let the educational bastards wear him down. He went on in a gentle tone. "It's not your teacher's fault Matt. She's very nice and you're lucky to have her. It's just that everyone's mesmerized by the Father of Lies. —Never mind. Don't listen to me."

"But Daddy you used to listen to the radio every afternoon when you were little. You used to drop everything at five o'clock and rush home. You told us so yourself! You still listen to—"

"Yuh Dad, he's right!"

"Well that's different. Anyway it was a bad habit of the ears that's not as easy to get over as cigarettes. Think how much harder it would be to get over television!"

Just when Michael would have expected Ruth to be chewing her lower lip the sound of some good singing came from the kitchen clearly enunciated and tuneful:

> "Folks around here
> Tell the time of day
> By the Atchison,
> Topeka
> And Santa Fe."

"Steam train number 49!" yelled Matty in appreciation.

I've got the guts to begin by pointing out that the legal significance of marriage has always been that it guarantees a man's responsibility for any children born to his wife but that nothing ever truly belongs to a person anyway unless it's eaten or carried internally. Mere zygoating with a mother does not entail a father's property-right yet he can love an antipodean orphan as solidly as his own clone. Roger's yours I'll say and no more anyone else's than mine. Or maybe it would be more diplomatic to invert that proposition. —On the other hand it might be better not to beat about the bush in broaching the issue. I could begin with the infidelity and leave Roger out of it until the clandestine coupling is admitted. Either way the question of Roger's blondness must be probed. So better yet before all else I'll ask her whether he isnt fairer than Jonathan ever was at that age and I'll say with a smile that's no Chapman mouth he laughs at me with. But I won't let on so soon that I know about Sandy. I wish I could disarm her with a laugh by lightly quoting in succinct Old French the proverb that he who doesnt know whom to suspect ends up suspecting everyone. Certes if it wasnt Sandy it was some god that lay with her to misbeget my happy little angel-boy but to her I'll simply say that if a son in my possession is of mysterious origin it's important for my peace of mind to identify his biological father known or unknown to me as someone with a proper name rather than as an un-

But Jonathan returned to the object of his art. "I think they're more like pythons than pigs!"

"Pigs arent afraid of snakes at all." his father remarked. "They stamp out rattlesnakes."

"Then you should like pigs Jonny." said Matthew.

"That must be why there arent any snakes in Ireland." Jonathan suggested.

"Oakland too." Michael added. "But I'm afraid the time will come when so many animals are extinct that we'll love even cobras copperheads and water mocassins."

"Who said?" Jonathan protested reflexively.

"Me myself and I." Matthew answered for their father.

"I'll never like any of them."

"Don't worry." the old man reassured him. "The bulldozers will kill them all."

Matty offered to trade his jackknife (which Jonathan had forgotten to return to him) for the elephant likeness. Before the temptation could take serious hold Michael persuaded the artist to donate his work to the dormitory wall over the admirer's bed, who with all the praise and gratitude of an impecunious collector of commercially unrecognized art trotted off to find a thumbtack. The male group had fallen into weary silence when he joined it again.

A little while more they waited, their leader no longer rocking: living statuary of man's indomitable will, patriots about to cross the Delaware or making a stand on westward trek, waiting for specified individual among known admirers or an adventitious rapist and complain that otherwise I'll have to wait for years to see whether the kid turns out to look like any of my relatives or hers or like any man I've ever seen so she'll get the idea that if I fail to put my finger on Roger's male co-author through frank dialogue I'll be left to infer the worst kind of calculating premeditated deception unmitigated by the slightest moral justification or by my own neglect or mistreatment of her, and that no matter how long the detection is dragged out— Wait a minute, that's a bassackwards approach! Post hoc non propter hoc unless the hoc were done by me!}

Only when he had come this far in floundering ratiocination was he consciously struck by the hastiness of his enthymeme. It now occurred to him that notwithstanding the efficient multiplications wrought by love's trice in many species of our mammalian genus there was no necessary correlation between a married mother's random enjoyment of unfamiliar pleasure and her next confinement even if the lover's preamble to conception was repeated more than once especially in this age of impervious elastics. His heart leapt with hope at the plausible reappearance of his formerly unnoticed assumption (when preoccupied with the concupiscent aspect) that the familiar barrier had been emplaced to save the citadel's magazine of Sabine halflives from an assault by Roman raiders! that she took care to confine her magnificent satisfaction to the im-

the tide to flow or the dust to settle. . . .

Ruth appeared before them with the old wooden pestle of a potato-masher in her hand (which augered well for the forthcoming meal.) "What are we going to do about a bed for Roger?" she asked her captain. "His crib is really about to fall apart, and he's going to be outgrowing it soon anyway."

Michael groaned. Matt gained him a few seconds however by relevant interruption: "Ma! Arent we going to have rice?"

"Yes dear, we're going to have rice too, specially for you. —They have children's beds at Sears." She knew her skinflint favored the huge plain store in East Oakland for such hardware when it wasnt available secondhand.

The digression had given him just enough time to master his manners, and to a stranger his reply would have sounded tolerably negligent or even indulgent, as if he assented to her premises. "Oh? Well let's not worry about that now. Sufficient unto the day is the anxiety thereof." How to get her back to work in the kitchen? Give her a truly patient answer and she'd start a long conversation while everything behind her back either cooled or burned up.

"That's all you ever say!" she goodnaturedly grumbled but began to whistle as she turned again to preparations for the family refection, having added one more grain of persuasion to a pile she had been augmenting from time to time in the family manger.

mediacy of its presentation! that she'd had the wit to refuse seed from a rotten sac! [Yes of course she'd left his great I AM throbbing on the wing while she lurched to the bureau drawer feverishly smeared the rubber saucer with perfumed spermicidal sealant and pressed it oval in her fingertips for the slightly crouching insertion swift as the blink of an eye in that autonomic routine too habitual in itself to elicit her occulted sense of guilt, that is if she could find both the kit and the tube of antitoxin. Of course she sometimes drops them at odd places because all it takes an experienced wife cornered almost anywhere is a quick knee-bend to make ready for a quick jewel of games when the older kids have just slammed the door on their way out to play in the back yard. But there's no reason to assume that she wasnt as prudent as a widow or didnt properly accomplish the procedure even in her haste to swing out and fold down the broad conjugal bed probably still mussed from action or resistance and anyway indented with my weight.] Michael's heart thumped with fearfully prurient anticipation at the prospect of cross-examining his only available witness in hope of reassurance about the ontological fear that commonly transcended the transitory indignation of a husband deceived with simple sensuality. If the event were to be reduced to a mere tupping at least he and all his sons would find themselves in the same evolutionary niche; his devotion to the boys would remain unconfused.

Over and over again Michael counted as a blessing however brief her evident happiness with the course of the day. He readied himself to absorb the secondary distress that was bound to arise from discovery of whatever was now transpiring in the kitchen on this most ironical of all feast days. The potatoes still might end up boiled instead of mashed, and underdone at that. Her contextural timing was always off. It seemed to him her severest critic that she never failed to put quick-cooking raw material to the flame before anything else and that the easiest jobs were always finished before the tough ones were underway. He anticipated being called to the table as soon as the steaming little fowl was out of the oven but before the plates were laid, when the water was just beginning to warm the frozen lima beans and the cooked broccoli was already stone cold, by rising from his chair with Roger in arm and strolling into the kitchen for a look. Then without waiting for so much as a May-it-please-you-gentlemen he and his sons took their places about the crowded table. He was unable to refrain from performing this act of leadership even though he was as aware as ever that you shouldnt prompt a good woman for pleasurable purposes too obviously. It would be no harder to remain civil while he sat there watching the process than while it drifted at the corner of his eye, and at this stage he thought she'd sooner have their company than be free of their obstruction. "Here, I'm

Thereupon the disconcerted wits of the owl composed themselves well enough to reflect for the first time that Roger resembled Sandy no more than himself or anyone else on his side of the family (his sister Peggy for instance). With a short belated hoot he chided himself for having jumped to a needlessly suspicious conclusion.

His objective composure restored for the nonce he dropped again into the shameful torment of sympathetic imagination. Indeed it seemed most likely that she was forced—not precisely raped (for naturally her own demon would assist the seducer's) but truly surprised and taken by storm—to her subsequent sorrow and anger of course. Sandy had ever after been kept away by her fury and abomination. Or perhaps he had been banished with gentle recriminations and fierce self-strictures accompanied by flat commands of supreme moral force. She had said nothing of the aberration simply because she was too honest to cry that she'd been wronged too courteous to raise a fuss too considerate of her husband's feelings to disturb him forever with images of a stud prancing in her lap. He told himself that women had invented tact after finding that men were as shocked by honest speech as women themselves by objectivity. Hadnt she herself once confessed that if he ever betrayed her she'd rather not hear of it? Ruth never preferred needless truth to healthy good feeling based on relative dignity, whether her own or anyone else's. He was long

bringing you back the boy you brought forth!" he said to her as he set Roger in his high throne.

"Go and take it!" cried Matty famished and hopeful.

"You mean come and get it!" said Jonathan thumping Matthew's shoulder with affectionate amusement.

Ruth looked at them all with a smile. "Well I see I didnt have to call anybody twice tonight. Are you all allergic to inanition?" [One of Michael's own shabby locutions that he didnt think sat well on her less nonsensical tongue.] "Dinner's almost ready." she assured them. Without being asked Matty got up to set the table with missing forks and glasses.

All waiting must come to an end. At last they sat together for the feeding. Michael having called for implements began to push and tug his way through the savory joints and slabs of unfarced Pertelote, hacking and sawing with the wrong kind of knife that had never been sharpened; but in fact the overdone flesh fell apart pretty well with a little yanking. "Oh I forgot the gravy!" And she was on her feet again rapidly stirring a saucepan on the stove while her menfolk struggled weakly against the wolfish discourtesy of digging in too soon that overcomes civilized restraint in the lower social orders. No power on earth could have prevented the boys from gobbling their meat at soon as it was handed them on salad plates (most of the dinner plates being unavailable just then). Michael only made them wait the longer for their second round. But the gravy came

since convinced that she cared instead for truthful responses and sincere affects—though to be sure the responses and affects on her part had always been conditioned by moral principles. Notwithstanding that on the same occasion taking up her quizzical vein he had clearly insisted his contrary preference in case of her misconduct he thought she was likely to assume the full burden of her guilt without any effort to dilute her responsibility by spreading the knowledge of it. Thus out of love for him she had kept her secret—

[But she did tell me something! And it was probably nothing more or less than the subliminal recollection of what she told me that started my suspicion this afternoon! But come to think of it it's a fact she's unlikely to have mentioned if she was guilty of a heinous consummation. Let me see: I must have had more than that to go on. What was I thinking of? Of course a good woman regretting her transgression would have sealed off the entire affair from its earliest beginning to the end as an entombed memory or else confessed the whole thing outright. Whatever yearning for riches of the flesh she may suffer in her parous maturity she would never play the sly wanton telling half a bit to relieve her conscience of a whole piece and even in the grip of an illness that piles all her thoughts in at least two separate uncommunicating stacks she knows reality too well to fail to relate her level account of an impertinent bumpkin's half-successful kiss to any proximate or deferred sequel in carnal relationship nor could she

on excellently and almost every-thing was delicious. Ruth's serial method of serving table made for something like a three-course meal, each element more or less separately consumed. Only the hostess herself ate her victuals fully assembled be-fore they reached the stomach's melting pot, for her trencher was wholly cold before she could get to it, what with her duties to the oth-ers, not the least of whom was drooling Roger a royal man not born to serve himself.

Matthew knew when he'd had enough but Jonathan and Michael stuffed themselves with third and fourth helpings of scraps and sur-pluses from various starch protein and vitamin dishes. While Ruth fi-nally availed herself of moderate and unreplenished rations Roger was left to pick like a giggling Arab from the mess before him; but he was more occupied with the funny greed of masculine gods than with his own appetite, which was elliptical rather than asymtotic.

Conversation started when in the slightly slackening voracity that succeeds a first mindless rush the quantity of remaining hunger and the certainty of its satisfaction having been assayed the Chapmen began to chew their food before they swallowed it. They were be-ginning to estimate the taste as well as the bulk. The beery Pa's gross throat (and even his palate too) commenced to take refined de-light in the gorging as he spoke and listened. The potatoes had got-ten mashed after all and the undercooked lumps could be stomached innocuously within their

ever be so wanting in diplomacy as to gratuitously direct my vulgar imagination toward the agent of that disturbing little assault.] For convenience in the management of his fervid speculation Michael plucked out and filed for future con-sideration the corollary problem that concerned the relative historical point at which he had been given this privileged information. Cer-tainly the story differed in signifi-cance according as to whether it was delivered before or after a more suc-cessful renewal of attemptation. But in net effect at any rate the only rel-evant testimony she had ever offered all at once sapped the undisinterest-ed investigator's indictment and turned him into a defender of his wife's patent innocence. In review-ing his thoughts Michael was amazed to find that he had no new cause to explain the peripeteia.

The benighting fog lifted en-tirely. Joyous blue sky transformed lurking hazards into friendly land-marks for navigation. How sur-prised he was to find himself amidst familiar piers and moorings! He had put together words to make a thing—and now the words were dispersed. Smiling foolishly to him-self he gazed benignly at the sweet disorder, at the perfectly guileless ineptitude of Ruth's household works. With a deep sigh of grati-tude for his destiny the sailor who two minutes before had despaired of ever seeing land again smugly heaved his line ashore. No one in the family that gathered at his gangway blessedly unaware of the peril he had put them to noticed his audibly heartfelt whiff of the sweet dry fleecy clouds laced with delectably ladled earthy brown gravy which tended to unify (as on the fluffy redundant rice also) a man's gusto for the whole meal. Once more she had amazingly proved that viand for viand she was just the right cook for that family's taste. Though she had not mastered the higher art of truly systematic culinary operations her uncouth man had only to remind himself that he could bite but one pitch-

port. His marriage license fee had been no bitter waste after all. The inefficient toils of joined existences and all the expenditures of his life for the sake of other lives were not to be mocked. His mate and crew were jolly indeed after a long day at sea. In short the Mediterranean winter was over, love was on the mend, faith was vindicated! They all welcomed themselves home to the Bower of Bliss.

forkful at a time anyway and that when all was said and done the flavor of a meal in its entirety is more influenced by the succulence of its parts than by the heterogeneity of its cross-sectional structure.

In any case the bird of dawning was soon was no more. Michael eyed the greasy dismembered skeleton with heartfelt gratitude. "Honey that was a good solid piece of magic to end the day with!" he sighed. "Ya!" said Matt; "Yuh!" said Jonathan; "Uh!" said Roger.

"The day's not over yet." the chef solemnly winked at her husband. "Praise not the day before night has fallen!" She hadnt often winked at him of late years. "But I wish I'd made some stuffing. A phoenix shouldnt be left hollow."

"I just couldnt hold any more!" ("Ya!"; "Yuh!"; "Uh!") "A feed like this should be preserved in the Smithsonian Institute." ("Ya!"; "Yuh!'" "Uh!") And at such a pass, when enough food suddenly seems too much for a great starving hunger, a first-class citizen must loosen his belt, groan, pat his belly, and wipe his lips with a flourish of the paper napkin.

"You had the appetite of three bears." she seemed happy to report.

"Bears!" Matty shrieked. "We didnt see the bears!"

Jonathan was annoyed by the piercing voice of his inferior. "Don't be silly. We couldnt see everything in one day. Besides, who cares about bears!" His scoffing tone was calculated to silence trivialities.

"Well your father cares." the mother replied irenically. "He can't bear to see bears bearing captivity—"

Roger interrupted. "*My*-bu!"

"Mom—Dad, did you hear that?" Matt leapt from his chair in glee. "'Who's been sleeping in *my* bed?' Get it? The Three Bears!" Ideas from an old story book that Matt himself had been telling Roger about the pictures of. All hands beamed at the intelligence of their pride and joy, marvelling at the first appearance of allusive genius. The rougish runt at the very dawn of thought was learning to associate sounds that no one but Ruth had believed he paid any attention to. With every new sign of learning he more endeared himself to father and brothers as a person in the bud, an existence making its own space in the world, a new creature gradually being recognized by history. Although this new chap so far was significant only for adding what his father called a Supererogatory Mouth to the hypertrophic population of the kingdom of Dis he seemed to his other admirers nothing but a unique new subject for life's experience love and sorrow. The newcomer was no longer satisfied simply as a mother's baby to open his five senses to the winds continents and oceans of the earth: he must understand the meanings of mankind and become a party to conversations. Therefore he laughed at the stir he had made. [But has his innocence been irreversibly modified by that moment of terror this afternoon in Apollo's temple? Does his tender brain retain the unqualified image of what the rest of us are too educated to pass to ours without the modifications of civilized context? Did he therefore grasp the essential horror of a great snake, for which he was totally unprepared and had no word? American citizen though he is, and prince of peaceful hope against the drift of human events, surely all learning doesnt come word-first from pleasant sessions with adoring siblings. Good morning sweet prince. Grow up fast—or rather history slow down—that you may get ready.] ". . . What I like about Jolly Wolly Roger" Matt declared enthusiastically on the spur of general approbation "is that he's little and solid. When you hug him you know that everything's right there!"

The men were served their dessert before the server had finished her main dinner. It was a perfunctory course that no one raved about. "Oh Ma!" The sour note sounded from Jonathan. "Why do we always hafta have fisheyes and glue?"

His father reproved him: "Among troglodytic aborigines tapioca is considered a delicacy."

Now although Ruth often felt herself to be in some unfathomable way the butt of Michael's nonsense, inasmuch as she was inarticulately averse to the forms of it that he was partial to (especially when it seemed worn thin in a kind of conspiracy against the world's small fund of kindness), she took this homespun repartee in good part as only a means for hard men to relieve their unimportant disappointments. Her least respectful son bravely threatened to go out and buy some candy (knowing full well that any such display of independence after dark with the nearest store open for business more than half a mile away was out of the question) if only he had some money, the concept of which brought him to a happy thought as he rapidly spooned his pudding—a claim many months of age but never remembered when the governor was both present and flush. "Hey Daddy don't forget you owe me a dollar twenty seven from my bank!"

"I'd hate to tell what you owe me."

"What?"

"Life itself."

"Oh come on, when are you going to pay me?"

"When my ship comes in. When are you going to pay *me?*"

"Don't worry" said Ruth patting her firstborn's hand. "There's no charge. But maybe Daddy will take you with him when he goes for the Sunday paper. Matt can go too if you're back before eight thirty."

This bold manner of making her husband a suggestion would have been intolerable to the thin-skinned bear in other circumstances but this time her prompting was not taken amiss, despite his uneasy awareness of her interest in the classified ads, for he was suddenly seized by his recurrent appetite for novel and effortless reading matter, and especially for hopeful Democratic news that might have made its way into a Republican newspaper in that leap-year of Republican oppression, not to mention gossipy wisps about Major League spring exhibition baseball that might be gleaned by an isolated Yankee fan living in the bush. Besides, for the first time in years he hadnt read a line of print all day. But—wonder of wonders, tribute to the day's density of experience, symptom of weary satiation—the boys sounded no joyful assent to a walk with their father. And truth to tell their father shared more than proportionally to his weight the weariness and satiation, and in fact during the preliminary digestion of his brimming surfeit (as long as the blood remained extraordinarily busy at his center of gravity) he'd not have been able to drag himself out of the house even in the most blessed solitary escape, to say nothing of ten blocks with a couple of dashing or foot-dragging question-machines. So his obliging impulse passed away aborning. And he found a small measure of purification in leaving this customary Sunday license unexercised. There was always more news in the Monday morning paper, it was cheaper, used up less wood pulp, and was supported by scarcely any classified advertising.

"Both my feet are lazy." Matty said in self-exculpation. Jonathan was scraping the bottom of his tapioca dish. On his own account Michael sighed at the drum-tight heaviness of his belly, tacitly excusing himself from any duty less self-indulgent than resting in his castle. At this moment the whole family—including Ruth who really had not made the suggestion in her own interest—preferred cohesion to dispersion.

Roger's doings helped keep them together for a while longer because as the feast was drawing to a close he again began to play the leading part. According to an established precedent he was franchised to collect the drops of milk or water remaining on the table in empty tumblers by draining them into his mother's glass, a practice by which he intended to teach himself to drink as others did without meanwhile waiving his prerogative with the infant bottle. Ruth had been absently handing him the glasses on the table one at a time, the shallowest of which now contained half an inch of diluted milk. Into it with doubled fist he dipped a crust of bread—not to play with and make a mess of but to eat, as if his little pearly white seed-corns were still too young and tender to chew the staff of life unsopped. He then drank some of the fluid holding his goblet precariously by both hands at the very rim (his mother by this time watching carefully to assist at need), covered the top with a saucer grabbed from the table (a more or less cleaned-off butter dish), and spread Matty's neglected napkin over the flat-topped stack, creasing the soft paper to make a facing folded down almost to the surface of his workbench. Then he reached under the skirting with one hand to raise the glass with precocious deliberation and shake it horizontally with a slow circular motion as he held the veiled mortarboard steady by a slight counterforce of the other hand pressing downward at the center. Waving the tented grail on high and setting it down upon the table as gently as a bird alights he whipped off the shrouded lid and swiftly drank up the dregs. Whereupon he put aside his chalice with unhesitating assurance as if he'd run through this routine a hundred times on the vaudeville stage, said "Aw gone!", and proceeded to fold the napkin into the semblance of a long oblong. None of his relatives paid any particular attention to this performance until he spoke those two words, for the motions seemed neither new nor especially skillful. But the unselfconscious priest intent upon the action was roused from his concentration grinning with surprise at the outcry that greeted his clear and unmistakable words in the congregation's language. Though he could not but remain illiterate and innumerate for several years to come he gratified his keepers by this normal graduation of talent almost as excessively as if he'd picked up a pencil and written out verbatim a King James version of the Last Supper without referring to a missal.

"*What's* all gone, Hodge-Podge?" his father asked. The actor of course did not expect to understand the voice but when he heard the question he gazed at the man's mouth and his smile faded bathetically. He blinked once and then a second time more slowly before he replied, the light of angels flaring up again in his sunny blue eyes, as he flapped his elbows and crowed out a laugh that startled the cat sitting tall and sober-sided on the windowsill over the sink: "Da-ee! Da-ee!" Saying which he turned to his mother with open arms, half rising from his highchair. He thus abruptly made it known that he was ready to be made ready for bed and bade his father attend him before he closed his eyes for the night.

He was soon obeyed. The older boys made themselves scarce for fear of being asked to do something useful while their mother in the front of the house was putting the baby down to sleep the last time that day. After the dining room was cleared of food scraps Michael was left alone in the cluttered kitchen full of encrusted pots uncooked food oxydizing in the open air and caches of garbage that only his stern presence kept Semiramis from picking over. With ankles crossed and legs straight out under the small overloaded table he sat with laced palms behind his head staring with drooped eyelids at the dark mirror of the window duplicating the whole brightly lighted kitchen including himself opposite the day's palms gathered by Ruth from where they had been dropped about the house and planted in a glass of water at a corner of the windowsill now vacated by the cat who was trying to ingratiate herself at his feet. [This is the bitterest Sunday of the calendar the sabbath of misunderstanding the feast of irony and deceived acclamation with citizens' cheers and waving pompoms along a donkey track lined with happy children brought to watch an impromptu parade. Passion Week is at hand.] But he soon returned to his easy chair in the other room to await a summons, taking Semiramis onto his lap in order to keep her out of mischief before Ruth returned to put away any remaining temptations.

In the dining room confusion was of a richer steadier state, far too heterogeneous to suggest hope for complete cleansing by diurnal tides. Disorder may seem sweet under certain conditions if all its constituents belong together (as in the flushed disheveled appearance of a beautiful maiden gone amaying in the meadows), especially when the beholder has himself kept cast in the personal struggle against general degradation, but if presented for contemplation at the time of day when a man would like to renew his energy for the ensuing week's campaign of livelihood a saloon scattered with toys newspapers books dishes and odd pieces of silverware interlarder with a farrago of laundry supplies ironed laundry washed but unironed laundry and unwashed wads of dyed and undyed wool cotton and synthetic clothes that never made it to the top of the laundry pile can be discouraging. Michael wondered if sometimes domestic untidiness reached a practical limit and his thoughts led to the anthropological necessity for demarcated middens. Perhaps he did detect the almost indiscernible beginning of some such evolutionary change which by its very tardiness promised a more permanent reformation than any hasty conversion. It may

Ruth returns to the kitchen as scullery maid smiling at Michael and patting him on the back as she passes his chair with a step lighter than anyone else's in the family having finished for the day her job as nurserymaid to the youngest master. At this signal the honorary chamberlain heavily rises and steps into Roger's darkened closet off the front room. The child has been cleaned up clad in white and laid flat on his back. A rubber plug quietly gurgles in his mouth at the lower end of a white bottle held aloft with negligent skill by two lazily flexing sets of fingers in sleepy self-reliance. To the boy's father the bandy legs under the blanket seem short the neck skinny the shoulders

seem surprising that it never occurred to him that it would be no more than fair to draw up a sum of all the jobs his wife had done that day and yet had left to do, but at least he gave her full credit for the latest repast, and he even made a brief attempt to consider from her point of view the ordeals of some twelve hours that had preceded it. After all a meal needed no trimmings to be square. What important element had been missing? The greens hadnt been too few or too many, or any of them execrably overcooked. Actually as a matter of fact how often in late months had the family been served three or four vegetables in a discontinuous series as each happened to mature in its odd skillet or saucepan; or after no

narrow and the torso long, all of which suggest future proportions resembling those of the man at the zoo with a camera, the complexion all too fair, the mouth too wide for a Chapman; yet he calmly disentangles the none too fragrant bedclothes from the bars of the rickety crib and gently slides the pink coverlet's discolored satin edge beneath the exposed wrists and up to the mumbling chin. The comforting glass vial, needlessly heavy with milk that won't be downed before the sandman comes, now droops upon the chunky chest; the humorous mouth releases its bent nipple as momentarily widened eyes watch the father bend over them and suddenly says what's been saved for this manly occasion, "Bee-bee!"

At this new sign of the child's intelligence Michael rededicates great joy, bursting to tell Ruth the brothers and all the world abut his surprise but at the same time lively to the priority of his duty to respond even without witnesses, that the burgeoning new maker of language may be encouraged by intelligent feedback. "Okay small man, you want me to sing *Baby*?" The small man makes affirmation with the smile of a gratified tutor. So in a low gently swinging voice the large man repeats ritualistic lallations with pronounced accent:

Rockabye *Baby*
On the tree top,
When the wind blows
The cradle will rock;
When the bough breaks
The cradle will fall—
And down will come

protein for half a week little but meat at every sitting for days on end; or tiny rations of highest grade delicately marbled feedlot steak (though with the lion's share for him and none for herself) rather than decent quantities of good plain hamburger? Recently, come to think of it, very seldom. Could it be that things were looking up? He began to question whether the inertia of his old grudges had been carrying him against the slow onset of some deep new current toward a new world. [By Themis and Hegel, if fretting could do it she'd certainly become a good housekeeper! She's turned over at least 1066 new leaves! In bursts of humble tears or in clouds of holy inspiration she tries so hard that it makes my heart break to see her striving. In her admiration of housewifely competence she sets every woman above herself in moral worth, even Hecuba who's no wife at all. She looks upon the compulsive habits of Athena Topalis as if that silent harpy were the arbiter of Olympian happiness. Yet she's wasted by the illness of fancy; her desultory housekeeping keeps me poor. Mismanagement of almost every prudential responsibility frustrates the hope for any cooperation between us, and there's no margin whatever for experimenting with other kinds of life away from the city where she still believes her latent powers—the assets we incorporated with (which I've never written off)—could return our investment! Why in the country any strength born of illusive escape from the past would fade within a month and I would be left buried

Raw-ger
Bay-bee and all!

Again and again he croons the
lines, gratefully rewarded by renewed smiles and reopening eyes
that all the same fadingly pursue
the downward path to sleep. Now
empty fists twitch like the paws of
a dreaming dog with final reverberation of the day's impressions.
Happy tremors continue long after
the end of the path has been
reached and the bottle set aside by
the tender valet. To assist at the in-
cunabulum of a word-hoard is to
countenance all filial claims. No
harm can befall such purity of spirit
from a shadow of the past. With
the lepid rascal's silence a private
fire is banked for the night.

When Michael returns to the
back of his house he finds that the
scene has shifted to the older sons'
sleeping porch where the serving
woman is straightening up their
quarters and directing their preparation for bed, having sent them
one at a time to the bathroom while
she was tightening sheets and shaking out pajamas. The kids are about
to stage a pillow fight that may get
out of control, but the great white
father arrives to drive them under
the covers carrying on his breast the
big black cat whom he's just surprised foraging for dessert on the
kitchen table.

FATHER {*setting Semiramis upon Jonathan's bed*}: Don't forget to feed your
panther in the morning. Did you
take out the garbage?
1ST SON: Oh I forgot.

for the rest of my life under a
mudslide of primitive inescapable
labor while she went numb with
the undreamt-of desolation in
which madness itself is drowned by
leaden inextricable circumstance,
and it could only end in the suicidal predicament of utterly mutual
dependence. It would take the resources of a gentleman farmer . . . }

He was sometimes persuaded to
believe in her extramural abilities
when she was not accompanied by
children or her other relative. As
soon as the door to the street closed
behind her she apparently became a
different woman, sometimes for the
worse but often for the better. Not
that she would keep a secretarial
job long enough to advance the
purpose of hiring a servant for her
work at home. But she was this
year's elected president of the Parent-Teachers' Association as well as
an esteemed supervisor of Cub
Scout auxiliary operations. Her academic and athletic record was the
envy of anybody who learned of it
from himself, and there was no sign
that coordination or acuity had
been impaired by alienation. But if
her gifts had informed and survived
her youth how could the secret of
adult estrangement from the world
be traced to her childhood?

Until this moment the husband's opinion had followed his
wife's own conviction in attributing
her acknowledged ineptitudes to
unconscious protest (made only abstractly conscious, he presumed, by
sketchy therapeutic suggestion)
against the formidably helpful effi-
ciencies of her toiling bread-

MOTHER: It's my fault: I didnt have it ready for him. I'll take it out later.

FATHER: When I was a kid in Gloucester there'd be water all over the kitchen floor if I didnt empty the ice pan every night.

2ND SON: Daddy tell us all about when you were little.

[MOTHER aside: There is no daughter to ask me the same.]

FATHER: I was a fine child but the Dogtown Little Folk changed me.

1ST SON: It was during the Depression wasnt it?

MOTHER: They used to say "Brother can you spare a dime?" and sleep in the park under Hoover blankets.

FATHER: The first time I saw a beggar: one cold day I was walking down Beacon Hill in Boston with my mother and father. A very thin dirty man in dark ragged layers of second-hand clothes who hadnt shaved for weeks came across the street and asked for a nickle to buy a cup of coffee.

1ST SON: Did your dad give it to him?

FATHER: He gave him a quarter.

2ND SON: Wow!

FATHER: That was even more in those days. Later there were so many men out of work that nobody could give more than a dime to each one. When we got back home that night I cried and cried and nothing Ma and Pa said could comfort me. When they tried to explain the Depression to me I thought they were just telling me about big cities, but it made the whole world seem sad. Then I got used to panhandlers. The Republicans always called them bums.

winning mother the undisputed master of an earlier household in which sheltering little Ruthie had been the principal motive. "It's the one who does the fussing that gets the most enjoyment!" the selflessly untiring old lady would say with a formal laugh at odd moments of ostensible relaxation, affecting to make fun of all her own wiry stamina on Ruthie's behalf, when there was anything to laugh about in conversation with the dour son whom it was hard to make much of that she had gained in not losing her daughter. The indefatigable mother-in-law had no remembered mother of her own. The best part of Ruth's psychic energy was consumed in resistance to that agelessly willful protection, which Michael considered the most odious of all his handicaps in the tests his own freewill had put him to; he felt nothing but fearful contempt for its genteel aspirations on his wife's behalf. [The old bag will be so thin and dry by the time she dies at the age of 99 that it'll be like burying a withered root.] But tonight he was bethinking himself.

Without denying the aforesaid codeterminant of Ruth's constitution, or even the concomitant possibility of accidental mutations in the central nervous system, he began to ken through his newly perspicuous looking glass a closer and perhaps larger planetary influence than any he had previously suspected: himself. He himself might have something more to do with his woman's affliction than making exorbitant claims upon her strength. With a

2ND SON {*weeping*}: Those boys we saw in the city today, they didnt have anything good either. Maybe they're too poor to have a father. {*First Son snorts.*} Do you think they have a bed to sleep in Dad? You should have seen them Mom. I bet no one ever takes them anywhere . . . Of course they don't have so far to go. {*Mother switches off wall lamp, leaving half light from kitchen door; sits down on his bed and kisses him.*} You can take anyone into your family that you want to you know. We could take those kids or the man with a cane on the street car or Uncle Cabe or anyone who's alone if he wants us.

1ST SON: There's no room in this crowded place! Did you live in a bigger house than this Dad?

FATHER: In those days rents were low back East and the houses were built for big families. {*Sits on 1st Son's bed opposite Mother.*} The American Legion still doesnt have to pay any rent at all to the City of Gloucester for a whole building.

1ST SON: Well I'm glad we don't have a sister to take up space.

2ND SON: There's room for Roger though!

{*They all reassure him on that point. Father studies physiognomies and psychic lineaments of the two offspring about whom there's never been any genetic anxiety while Mother and Sons start up a sport from her side of the family which he soon joins. {Sees the worst in himself divided between them rather unequally in inverse proportion to their share of his features. Matthew looks like himself between brows and bridge of nose. Jonathan is a firstborn*}

slow blink of his eyes the diachronistic Gestalt in his stained old ceiling plaster that featured lines of repellant force from the mother was replaced by a more complex configuration of the cracks.

He now noticed in retrospect that even in her most buoyant moods, as when she spent whole evenings cleaning up the kitchen, at least one significant task would be forgotten, such as washing the grounds out of a coffee percolator left like a discolored tower alone on the gleaming stove for his usage at dawn. But no project of interior decoration was ever quite finished: there was always a piece of old wall showing in the corner where she had stopped for lack of paint or because over a weekend the uncovered pigment had hardened in its can for the last time and would no longer yield to the latest brush petrified for want of a turpentine soaking.

But it now seemed to him that incomplete closure (like the penannular rings upon which the Danes swore peace to King Alfred) was only one of her forms of abstract expression. Taken alone it failed to distinguish her signal or symptom from that of a million male individuals all across the country who for instance almost finished building their own houses for passersby to see year after year without such finishing touches as steps to a useless front door until the glaring incompletion grew so familiar that it took on the aspect of virtuous individualism in defiance of financial institutions as well as government; but all at once he was struck by

of incontestable certainty in view of impeccably sacramental conditions.} Game is played simply for pleasure of legomenal action. They take turns leading it off, each of them sounding off several times with whoever offers rejoinder. Object is to increase speed of dialogue until it's a marvel of polished lickety-split stagecraft. Much stumbling and laughter until all get the rhythm, which takes much amusing practice for everyone but Mother who's an old hand. They don't stop until every speaker is breathlessly letter-perfect at blinding speed in either role of any paired interloctors—as:}

A: Did you speak?

B: Who?

A: You.

B: Me?

A: Yes

B: No.

A: Oh!

{Inasmuch as such an exercise is scarcely soporific the parents are drawn into a much longer leavetaking than they intended; but in fact neither is anxious to cut short the festivity. When game has been perfected discussion of day commences. Satisfaction expressed on all sides. Father proposes a cheer for Mother:}

ALL {except Mother}:

> Two—four—six—eight,
> Who do we appree-she-ate?
> —Mama!
> —Mama!
> —Yay—Yay—Yay!!!

FATHER {singing}:

> Dais-y, Mais-ie,
> Give me your promise true.

many other kinds of disappointed expectancy or formal discontinuity that lacked such functional justification as that of easy adjustment to any size of finger. [She scrapes food from saucepans with a fork and stirs porridge with a paring blade.

> Cold boiled rice,
> Cold boiled rice!
>   Did you ever see such a
> sight in your life—
>   She butters the bread
> with a carving knife!
> Cold boiled rice,
> Cold boiled rice!

I'll never sing that song to the kids again. The lofty spaces in the refrigerator are littered with flat sparsely laden plates of odds and ends like the clustered shops of a Sacramento Valley settlement while tall bottles and jars are crammed lengthwise or leaning where they leak on the bottom shelf or else left outside altogether for their bacteria to propagate at atmospheric temperature. . . .] Without inclining to pursue his diversionary conceit he vaguely realized that her most poignant balks to his normative sensibilities were remotely parallel though contrary in aesthetic affect to the sensual satisfactions withheld by a dancer in art. With this renewed palpitation of the heart his postprandial lassitude vanished. [She never buys the right size of anything at the store. She guesses and always guesses wrong. Wastes good money on a sheet of linoleum that falls six inches short of the kitchen floor's dimensions leaving a

I'm half crazy
All for the want of you!
It won't be a stylish marriage;
We can't afford a carriage
—But you'd look sweet
Upon the seat
Of a tricycle built for two!

{*Applause for matrimonial solidarity.
Mother is obliged to kiss Father and Sons
in order of appearance. Nuptial jambo-
ree gradually abates but all four continue to muse upon the day's excursion.*}
2ND SON: I love Uncle Sandy because he's so cuddly to me! Did you
see him pick me up Mommy?
MOTHER: Yes dear. He remembers
you when you were a very little
baby.
1ST SON: It's a good thing the python didnt hug you Matt! {*Makes
sudden muffled noisy flap with both feet
beating bedclothes and reaches out with
one arm to jiggle brother's bed.*} Watch
out for the big snake! He almost
got you!
2ND SON: {*unalarmed*}: Almost is a
lot of difference from did.
1ST SON:

Kaa wanted to squeeze
But couldnt squeeze—
Because Dee-Diddle-Dum
Diddle-Dee did!

FATHER: I thought you were Old
Hairless the Gloucester sea-serpent!
2ND SON: We should of taken pictures for the family album, that was
such a nice suspection trip.
MOTHER: I couldnt find the camera
this morning. I'd like to have gotten a snapshot of that seagull to
give to the police.
2ND SON: Did you hear all those

gap to trap and accumulate the
damp filth which that damned imitation pavement is supposed to intercept entirely. Buys shade rollers
too short for the window frames
and then when she finally does get
others cut close enough to stay in
the sockets she unrolls them far
past the sills and beyond the limits
of their elasticity. All such wasted
time and money might not mean
much if she didnt without exception fail to get personal things for
me that fit. The clothes I buy for
her are usually just right but her
most generous and careful presents
to me are never the right size. She
takes it amiss that I insist on doing
all my own shopping little as it is
but if I left it to her I'd be wearing
the hat of Charles de Gaule the pajamas of Charles Atlas the shirts of
Winston Churchill the socks of
Paul Bunyan and the shorts of
Panurge!} He trembled under the
psychoanalytic intimidation of an
inchoate trope that had taken so
long to claim his full consciousness.
He feared in earnest that his wife
the only confidant of his manhood
and the goddess of his bed was an
unconscious martyr to his fatuous
addresses, not simply deprived on
occasion of the joys she had a right
to expect but piteously ignorant of
the natural and fundamental fulfillment which she knew women were
born for. It was himself that she unwittingly protested in all the mis-
calculations of her present life! The
unplacated discontentments of a
body must needs signify themselves
somehow. If in the years since
Roger—since Matthew?—since Jonathan?—she had been able to satisfy

screes and gracks the other birds made when he did it??!!

FATHER: Those seagles should be eating fish sandwiches instead of hotdogs and hamburgers. [We havent had any frozen haddock all during Lent when for once it's available in this provincial market. More Protestantism!] But that was a good winged fish we had on the table tonight.

1ST SON: I'll say!

FATHER: It was probably raised on fishmeal. But gulls arent very efishent birds you know. They'll drop shellfish over and over again on sand or mud trying to break them open just because it succeeds once in a while when the pickings happen to land on rocks. There arent any mussels at the zoo but if gulls were a little bigger they could snatch turtles and bomb thick heads like mine to crack the shells. {*Feels compelled to explain his early memories of wildlife on the island of dogs and gulls but not his implied classification of turtles as bivalves or of himself as a tragedian. Is about to mention supposed ossiphragous habits of fish-hawks, one of which he thinks he saw in September 1945 on the southeast coast of Shikoku. . . .*}

2ND SON: Let me feel your muscle Dad! {*Obvious bedtime fillibuster but answers the purpose. After the mighty arm is bared and doubled up for close examination under maximum self-induced contraction and admired by all hands including Mother biceps of Sons must be examined in hopeful comparison. After a while:*} Hey I know, let's play owl! {*Refers to a paired game brought to Chapman tradition by Mother. Should be played in erect pos-*

her nerve-ends only by developing brave dissimulations with the neurons of her brain (as he now could imagine her erotic actions and passions) the arrears of his true debt to her had to be balanced somewhere else in her books. No married man had to look very far for clues even if his wife was still sane. There was for instance the frequency with which she turned aside his advances: clearly the defensive aftereffect of repeated disappointment. Considering the phenomenal consistency of her droll or metaphorical messages to him, conscious and unconscious, and the rarity of intimate praise for his lovership, he thought he at last understood what had obscurely prompted his earlier intuition that she was rearing a bastard baby or might have been doing so but for some good luck in the calendar dice.

But of course Michael had no wish to hear out infinite uses of the finite words he had released like sinful ghosts startled out of a sealed crypt, one for each act of cruelty by which he had driven his wife toward lunacy all the while she was lovingly beseeching him to take heed of his imbecility. Still less did he wish to spin lectures for imaginary peers. He did not wish to speak even to himself about the revelation; and in fact he immediately resolved thenceforth to converse less freely with everyone about everything, to shut his mental mouth forever. He did not wish to examine this inner intelligence—not even by speaking to himself through frozen lips from his paralyzed throat with a tongue

ture toe-to-toe or across a narrow table but when negotiating goodnights the custom is to perform in horizontal parallel positions, Mother or Father bending down to touch foreheads with Son lying on pillow. Partners close eyes and keep them closed until signalled by word Owl!!! to open them wide as possible in unison, thus:}

EITHER OF EITHER PAIR: One, Two Three—Owl!!! *{Chant is repeated at least 16 times and it would go on to a higher powers of 2 if Sons had their way, but Mother and Father contemplate means to quash the delaying tactic. Father must remove spectacles in order to participate in pastime.}*

1ST SON: Doesnt Daddy look funny without his glasses—

2ND SON: Looks like a barney-googled goggle-eyed gillimicuddy when he has them on!

1ST SON: especially when he walks around! His feet stick out anyway, like the footman in Alice in Wonderland.

2ND SON: Yah! And he snores when he's awake too.

1ST SON: No wonder he picks his nose when he thinks no one's looking!

MOTHER *{thinking it's gone too far}*: That's not nice! Don't make fun of poor old hardworking Baloo. I won't play this game. I've got too much work to do tonight. I'll kiss you goodnight just once more.

1ST SON: Look Ma he forgot to shave under his nose this morning!

MOTHER: Never mind that stuff now. Besides, it makes him more fun to nuzzle up with.

2ND SON: That's true. —Mom let's get a dog just for me. Semi always

cut loose from his heart. But an American scholar can't stop thinking, especially when thinking is the only way to ease his pain and guilt.

{How now Michael Agonistes? This is no Muse you provoke but Psyche whom you have professed to scorn and dared to trifle with. Only now does it dimly dawn upon your eremitic wits that you have spent a decade decrying her science just to tread down with benighted force that bulging turf of the Chapman churchyard packed with the corpses of your inferiorities. And even yet—to this very minute—though in taking stock of suppressed knowledge you affect to renounce the comforts of weaseling discourse you mean to hold in reserve the final notion that psychology is a self-consciously mirrored axe that can be chopping away at the roots of this terrible new knowledge with the same strokes that bite into your trunk. We shall see! But will we ever see? The interested mind may explore truth and countertruth until the cows come home but the metatruth must be left to other novelists. You are no wiser than a holy man taking pride in his humility. The insights of commonplace doctrine may succeed themselves in an endless chain which you endlessly reforge with the optional links of assurance or mortification that even the healthiest of men sometimes owned to. It is written that you will never be otherwise than too obtuse or too knowing.}

For a few analog jots of the kitchen wall-clock (which was so

sleeps on Jonny's bed. It's not fair. I get lonely in my legs.

MOTHER: Do you need another blanket?

2ND SON: No. But she keeps me awake with her growling. There! Hear that chugging sound?

FATHER: She's been out all day and so have you. She won't keep you awake tonight. From now on I'll put her out before I go to bed.

1ST SON: No!! Please.

2ND SON: I wonder how grownups fall asleep so fast. It always takes me about an hour to go to sleep consciously. Well she'd better be quiet tonight is all I can say. She's older than I am but I'm bigger than she is! I'd like to have an animal that growls when he's mad and wags his tail when he's happy instead of the other way round. Didnt we have a police dog once? He couldnt have been black. What was his name again? *{Everyone else smiles. He is bringing up all the diversions he can think of.}*

MOTHER: The landlord won't let us have a dog Matty dear and you know perfectly well that it's past beddy-bye time. Someday perhaps we can have a house of our own with a sand-box and everything.

FATHER: It is pretty nice to be a dog's best friend. *{Bethinking himself of jealousy and altercation over hypothetical dog:}* I mean for a family. Of course one person has to do the training.

1ST SON *{precociously}*: I bet you're glad we didnt see any wolves today Dad, all cooped up. There should be a law against keeping any animals in cages.

old and creaky that it often broke out with loud digital chatterings in protest against the relentless electricity that drove it onward) he sought flight in his old prayer for standardization. [Oh God let all males be equal on the perfect model of your son Jesus Christ so that husbands need not trouble themselves on the subject; stamp out all personality of the body as in the golden age (which you are said to have supplanted with the new Vine) when all lovers and parents of both genders divine and human must have encoded and decoded their feelings by scytales of a fixed specification making equally elastic impressions upon each other, never objecting to full and sufficient sensual monotony.] But he knew his orison was somewhat beside the point, for the dance is not the dancer, and it skills not Dionysos himself playing his pipe at the thighs of a nymph if the performance never gets beyond a solipsistic rehearsal of his own movements. {Of course it's not as bad as all that; you can put a better face upon it: but your alternating constructions of what few communications you receive do certainly contradict supercede or cancel each other. The probable truth remains as mysterious as when men made it a matter of honor to assume the best about themselves and let women's prehension take the hindermost. Yet quaking in your boots at the injury to masculine vanity you refuse to search the depths. However well or ill you fill your shoes the fact that you have hitherto paid too little

FATHER: Except snakes. {*Sons open their mouths to correct his sloppy thought: it wouldnt do any good to put snakes in cages; it takes glass cells to confine them!*}

MOTHER: Well I'm really going to say goodnight now. {*Kisses both boys.*} Don't forget there's school tomorrow. Daddy can tuck you in.

1ST SON: Ma tell us a story before you go. Just a short one. No one ever tells us a story.

MOTHER:

> Much have I travell'd in
>   the realms of gold,
> And many goodly states and
>   kingdoms seen—

1ST SON: Oh not *poetry*!

2ND SON: {*hastily*}: I'll tell a story. Many long years ago and not far away they lived happily ever after and—Ma why do they make crosses out of palms?

MOTHER: It's a sacrament that the Catholics believe in I think. — Goodnight again! One more kiss and that's positively all there's going to be from me. {*Repeats kissing routine.*}

2ND SON: Jesus is God too you know.

MOTHER: Yes dear. Mary's son. Goodnight! {*To Father:*} Now it's up to you my love.

2ND SON: Say the twenty-third palm for us Mommy!

{*Exit Mother.*}

1ST SON: You tell us a story Dad.

FATHER: You know I can't make up stories. Besides it's crialogous to recite logafactually.

1ST SON: O Daddy there you go again!

attention to possible deficiencies and dysfunctions argues either an unsuspected stupidity about imperfection itself or an actual imperfection as the subliminal motive for inexcusable simplicity.... Still, this is no chiefless family of anarchic Scots. "Michael, one of the chief princes ..." saith Daniel: "the great prince which standeth for the children of the people."}

It happens at least that I am not the last among equally great princes, a distinction without empirical difference that shouldnt trouble the woman that loves me, and apparently it indeed does not, judging by the times she's searched out my one-ended staff when I've been preoccupied with different thoughts entirely and by her admiration made it as bombastic as possible when she was certainly not precoccupied with tricking another baby out of me to take up the slack in her cradle of conception or with enticing me to plow over adulterous seed merely for form's sake, an artifice too sly to conceive in the conscious behavior of such an honest queen.]

When he examined slightly further into himself however he found one of his frets dissolved for good: under the threat of serious analysis he no longer gave a bear's hoot what his wife might be dreaming about by night or day—so long as she turned down any waking invitation to partake of forbidden fruit. The horned owl (still dwelling on his pride) would be content to die without the horns of ram bull or faun if he could escape the horns of his dread. All he asked of

FATHER: All I know is true stories that you don't care about—

2ND SON: *I* like true stories!

FATHER: —all boring. Like the job I had on a bakery truck after school when we lived in Cambridge.

1ST SON: Oh no, not about the good old days of the Depression! Tell us a story about ships.

2ND SON: That fairy boat we went on was like a mother: all day long it goes back and forth working for other people; it doesnt even have time to turn around!

FATHER: That's why it's double-ended.

1ST SON: Daddy everything has two ends!

FATHER: [Everything except Meilichios the bearded python.] Well I can't tell you a story but I can tell you something interesting about Goat Island. {*Moves to bed of 2nd Son.*} Are you listening little Zwischschwein?

2ND SON: Yes, I'm not sleepy!

FATHER: Good. I'm the swineheard. {*Tells them about the three lighthouse keeper's daughters who attended school in San Francisco sailing themselves back and forth across the channel every day in their own sloop.*} Now go to sleep my fine feathered piglet. {*Kisses 2nd Son.*}

2ND SON: I can't, with the darn clock in the kitchen making all that noise. Remember the time it was running backwards and I was the only one who noticed it?

1ST SON: Oh Matty that's ridiculous. You and your clocks! Anyway I saw it before you did but I was thinking about how it could happen when nobody was home. —Dad: you know that L C L you were on—?

fate was that Ruth having committed herself to marriage abide by the discipline of law to which her bondage committed him. The sacramental bargain was simple enough, hard though it went especially for an exceptionally libidinous husband (as be believed himself to be), and he intended to honor it. He could adjust the pas de deux dance to the inelasticity of maternity if she would share the effort to ignore it. [By the pussy of Pope Joan if she will not, nor will I! I wouldnt play Menelaus without at least double compensation. If Roger had turned out to be Sandy's daughter maybe I'd have brought up the bastard to my own advantage cultivating a cherry tree for my aging desires with no more taint of incest than Pygmalion.] A wise bear could bear the unbearable law as well as teach it. Any ultimate satisfaction with the single span of his life's irreversible arrow could be better served by silencing a few of his excessive passions and foregoing certain varieties of sacrilegious experience without which most other men didnt think life worth living than by setting research in carnal knowledge above songs of innocence. One wife might be sufficiently representative to provide her faithful husband with a good enough sample of what he was missing and a decent schedule of lawful emissions might well keep an edge off the unwisely burning appetites that hindered a susceptible American scholar in smithing his self-assigned contribution to technology or high culture.

[A christian operates on the principle of most action; since my

FATHER: L S T .

1ST SON: Oh yuh, L S T ... well ... uh ... well I forget what I was going to say. {*Father returns to First Son's bed, putting his finger to his lips in a shushing gesture before kissing him. First Son drops into a whisper.*} Oh I remember now! When can I—

FATHER {*lowering his own voice and smiling lays hands on both shoulders of 1st Son*}: After a while.

1ST SON {*grinning*}: After a while *what?* And when's the while?

FATHER {*this time touching the boy's mouth with his fingertips. Leans close and whispers very very softly into one ear the cue to a familiar formula, bringing broader smiles to both faces*}: Who's your favorite Daddy-boy and if so why?

1ST SON {*rendering the answer which he himself long ago composed, before the question had been devised to canonize an antiphon*}: You—because Mama married you! {*Whispers excessively with gesticulations of the mouth*} Is Matty asleep already?

FATHER: Yes. Now it's your turn.

1ST SON: A A Sir!

FATHER: Try to act like a gentleman.

1ST SON (giggling): I can't: I fell off a brook!

Sitting on the edge of the cot Michael delightedly kisses again his oldest child, to whom he is only dimly visible for an adoration far too trusting in its happiness. [Oh the sadness to see any creature happy with another, or a dog's tail wag in nameless hope or simple joy at nothing more than your approach!] He kisses him on the mouth on the cheeks on the forehead on both sides of the neck, rate of work is limited by talent the total action I bring about will be a direct function of my longevity. Redundant passions contribute very little to a producer's vital formation and I ought therefore to prefer a long career of orthodox propriety even to a longer life of libertine pleasure—for is not one word worth to me a thousand strictures? Great age is not commensurate with worth insofar as its time has been wasted in the abuse of essential freedom by futile attempts to compensate for oversights in infrastructure when gifts of person and privilege were determined by one's Body of Fate. To dwell on otiose pleasure is to batten on a principle of least action. The liberty to do so complicates one's life. Complexity should be saved for the end-product. But keep the groundwork as simple as possible. I am distinguished from a cuckolded phalarope by the potentiality to transcend the action I was born from. I hereby reaffirm my renunciation of all pretension to the predatory fly-by-night charm of slim athletic poets. The only way to remedy my bane as well as hers is to put copulation in its place and the only way to put it in its place is to place the unicorn more often in its seat and for longer stretches if only I could get her to understand as much without having to devote my leisure to erotic diplomacy. The more spiritual harmony she gets out of me the more she wants that's the hell of it yet the whole matter might drop to secondary importance for both of us if carnal harmony were brought to frequent and bountiful

tickling the tender smooth skin so roughly with the day's stubble of his chin that the boy squeezes his eyes shut and grimaces with pleasure at the scratching masculinity. Jonathan's seniority entitles him to these few extra minutes of congee. With both arms outside the covers he on one side pats the cat for whom he has made spacious place against the wall and on the other holds the hand of his father whose enormous weight hollows the listing bed. They hear the soft far bell tolling lateness much too soon. Distant street noises substantiate familiar gratifying clinks from the kitchen (which draw Semiramis tense under the father's restraining hand with thoughts of scraps), and spates of water running in the pipes, by which they are informed of their home economist's brave attack upon the dismal Palm Sunday night mess. [How does she conceal her fatigue so well, infinitely heavier than mine yet tonight infinitely lighter in manifestation? Was last night's clearance so rare?]

On the pillow Michael now sees tears in the eyes that are almost always cool and dry. He instinctively refrains from asking after their cause, not for fear of forcing the exposure of shame for some weakness in male fortitude but because he knows they well up from a fusion of general love and sorrow that can be traced to everything seen and heard in a whole day of traversing the world's favorite city built of gold and named for the first mendicant friar (who never preached). Instead he silently strokes the hair of the head made

perfection which doesnt seem much to ask does it, now simply to be freed of the most invidious anxiety among many. Yet of course it doesnt require perfection after all my contentment and her cure hang more upon what we have than upon what we might not miss if we settled down to the perfectly normal state of inactive curiosity— unless that's just what this disquieting condition of hers and mine already is! Maybe there's no cure for the normal state of advanced matrimony. Does every faithful bride become at last a sleeping queen because her fat lumbering old tachyderm with the timing of a rabbit often if not always fails to wake her up? But I suppose if she got stirred up too often she'd never be able to sleep. When you attend to an itch in one ear the other starts up; tighten a shoelace and the other foot feel too loose. Soon she'd be expecting me to celebrate a trental in every octave! Well so much the better: once I get the knack of it again every new tally on her side of the scorecard will be notched a little sooner and by Jove I might be an iron man worthy of Lou Gehrig if she'd put me in the lineup every day I'd never complain of the time it cost me as long as I don't have to spend a lot of it warming up. I'm not going to worry about my stamina it's a lucky ballplayer that has to cross that opsipathic bridge by coming to it and meanwhile all I can do is improve upon every dance she gives me a man's got to expunge grievances even from the subconscious relax the muscles at the base of his spine and learn not

more in his own image than any docile dog's. They confidently search each other's faces for confirmation of the wordless understanding between them as if passing in review all the hopes that meet and match the manifold suffering of the world. But the son is reassured by the father's smile and smiles responsively in the misunderstanding that his worst fears for humanity are foolish bad dreams.

For yet more time Michael lingers in the company of the son who most reflects his own life. He wishes to restore him to the courage if not the felicity that he himself has tried to disabuse of illusion for the sake of defensive education as the mother could not do—indeed as she would not, since she sees nothing but advantage in a happily insulated childhood, though she hopes to endow boyhood with some counterpart of what her girlhood missed, holding to the opinion—perhaps not so wrongly when everything is said and done—that the reality of the world can be put off until it's easier to deal with, when the boy's a hardened man and learns it as he must, which is to say all too soon. Still, Michael admits the biological plausibility of her policy as perfectly consonant with the ontogenesis of humanity. Does a father who shirks most of his responsibilities have any right to instill brutal truth?

[Christ, the unremitting nobility and vigilance required even of a father! A bachelor can safely show depression and despair; he can afford to let women feel sorry for his

to think too much about his success or his godly sensation but rather to divert his rational faculty with some pastime like the great American one whose box scores and statistics often serve the inner eye with objective pleasure I could try thinking about the Yankees it's nice they still have the class to travel by train and talk about strength down the center this year it'll be even better than it was in Bill Dickey's day with Berra defending the hearth they may all hit over .300 with Larsen on the mound to round out Ford and Turley then McDougald to either Martin or Coleman for the old doubelplay ball to Skowron so many good hitters they have Bauer to lead off and Berra's understudy is so versatile that he can play left field while he's waiting their first black man whom I have higher hopes for than any of the other new ones except of course Micky Mantle even if he is something of a redneck the Cardinals turned him down when he was seventeen because they thought he was too small why this year he'll lead the league in slugging if nothing else and he's the fastest man in baseball when he's batting left he can get to first base in 3 seconds flat and takes only a tenth of a second longer from the other side— well I don't want to run out of object-matter now I should save all my coolly interesting thoughts until we're brisket-to-brisket when communication between me myself and I should always be dampened though St Francis says there's "an indissoluble sympathy between the body and the soul" meaning your own but if you have too much sym-

weaknesses. But with dependents you cannot be your straight self impulsively. You also should not presume your own person in the persons of your children. You must not train them along the branches of learning alone, and in all your teaching you should know when to lay off especially where their mother has laid off. How selflessly Ruth lays off with her young before they reach the age of reason! As for instance in a bath of comfortable hot water maybe shaving her legs she once let Matty when he was still learning basic things for himself run icy splashes from the tub's cold-water faucet to fill and rinse and rinse and fill and fill and rinse and fill again the cup he needed for a job he was working on, though watchfully prepared to preclude use of the other tap lest he hurt himself with scalding heat: not a single shrill warning, not a single "don't!" She's incessantly aware that children's minds as well as bodies are as vulnerable as the fawns of tame deer and as sensitive as Romantic poets. The delight or oblivion of a clearhearted child is nearly intolerable to behold—and by the same token it's an act of vandalism to disturb it—when you remind yourself that sooner rather than later adversity will be visited upon the innocent in some or all degrees, and that the real world is full of other keen and beautiful kids without the benefit of a calm sensitive mother and deferring father: children of pestilence rapine and war, children in famine, children at once bereft of love and deprived of protection, children who suffer from the very

pathy with a woman's vibrations you'll find your "nervous and hollow member" shot full of hot spilt milk sooner than she wishes so it's usually best to play the power factor by slightly lagging her in phase in order to defer full resonance or to debonairly prolong the dance by misleading her into several successive anticipations of its true end much to the enhancement of her beatitude and your gallantry you feel as if you could go on all night if only we both werent always so tired from daily life that more often than not we're too sorely tempted to flop down at the first goal and if too mystical at the beginning it's a short circuit. Despite her subtle perceptions of other people's emotional frailties her intuitional retina seems to have a blind spot for my sensitivity in the one thing we do together and she takes either as jokes or as coldblooded calculations all my diffident hints that the jewel of games could be polished if she'd devote a little gross empathy to what she sometimes seems to regard as a male machine just because of my fascistic flourish at times of manege but it's generally more like drayage for a jaded team like us with no goddess of sexual tact to inspire us simultaneously with the gees and haws of this ultra-secret dromenon that you can't learn by watching show horses there's only me for player-manager and she thinks anyone managing reins of any kind is brutal since teamsters usually seem cruel unless they're driving delicate creatures of legend like the Flying Red Horse under whose trademark I heard my first

outset as hopelessly as animals born in an abandoned unattended zoo—suffer more guiltlessly than torpedoed watertenders entombed with scalding steam or the passionate and tender women who have borne them or would have liked to.]

At the very sight of sons possessed by a happiness so much more transitory than the playless misery of their near and distant facsimiles the needles of pity bite the father's vitals. Again he wonders if a mother and father deserve well of offspring whom they have kept in halftruth happiness thousands of times more healthy than the tyranny of absolute subservice or fearful respect and in fact not without some knowledge of their old man's foibles. But of course it's not love of truth or any virtue half so noble that makes him give rein to their criticism of what simply can't be concealed from his most intimate followers by a most tactful mother's art: his merit is nothing greater than providence, a certain sense of efficiency as measured over the course of time, a mere Mithradritic foresight of what they'll see in him when reason has cultivated itself with the learning of fully opened eyes. Indeed far from loving truth before satisfaction Michael Chapman if he had certain knowledge that the vicissitudes of history were going to cease would gladly keep his three sons in innocence of the present and leave them with only a progressive and suspended past to master, taking their chances with no more than incurable diseases and new wars as slow as the last.

Red Sox ball games long before Boston's Achilles spoiled the team for me by trying to outshine Joe DiMaggio the Hector of walls that never fall. On the other hand she ought to know by now that ancient arts can't be learned by the sink-or-swim method for sinking makes the patient drown too soon whereas it's no sacrilege to rehearse with care like four-handed piano partners and if I find it no disgrace to pause or loiter during the recital she should be glad to keep time by forbearing in kind seeing that she never had any trouble on the dance floor following my lead or Dave's or Sandy's like a willowy feather even if I improvised curlicues out of step with the music and if she'll just heed my whoas in the beginning little by little they'll get less frequent and every stint of plowing will gradually lengthen until she can gather a whole nosegay of golden daffodils in serene confidence that there'll be no halt before it's topped off by the accumulated bloom of one magnificent tiger lily at the very instant of mutual consent of course I'll have to school myself to ignore the superexciting urgency with which she snatches each flower from her King of the May as if from the first it were the only prize available but I'll teach her to be greedy and reserve her giddyap spurring for a final untamed belly-dance bearing in mind that a garland of wildflowers inspires more gratitude than single pluckings from the garden every now and then. Bouquets are facets of the marriage gem that at its best no string of promiscuous brilliants can equal in carats. But

[Do I tell my boys that slum kids are used to penury, black kids used to disenfranchisement—that they miss no comforts until they see the lives of rich white brats depicted on the hearth-sets they steal? But that's exactly what they are already seeing or will soon be seeing all over the world, as if the primitive nervous system of ants were suddenly gifted with consciousness of pain and rage. —Ants? What was it about ants in our Matty-lore oh yes from the days of his earliest worldliness in the yard below the porch he pointed to one he had just stamped the life out of on the concrete pavement having learned the sport from a new friend at nursery school and said to me laughing "Ant had sore place on his foot!" That was before he learned pity.] Michael glances over at the more inexperienced of his two experienced sons. The loving learner is now sound asleep, resigned for the nonce to both present peace and future truth.

But Jonathan's eyes still wide awake seem wiser than before. Everyone knows the cleverness of this frail white Bagheera. In school he makes douzepers of his friends, humble or highborn, and enemies of the rest. Yet he still listens to the stout old bear who teaches him the law of the jungle; he continues to learn not so much out of definite respect for his father's jurisprudential administration (which is admittedly sometimes arbitrary in matter and inconsistent in application) as from a subconscious appreciation of the homoiousian selfhood in his immediate male stirp, though thin there's a lot more to this leggy art than mounting on the port side when I was not much younger than Caleb I thought it was practically mastered when you grabbed the halter and got a bridle before I found out that saddled trotters even when they're bred for work are too mettlesome and heady to be cheffed with an economy of effort like some dinner acooking in the kitchen Ruth herself told me that poor Sarah isnt allowed to move at all under her giant Joshua maybe she's been given to believe that reciprocation is forbidden by Deuteronomy like working on the Sabbath I've learned much more than Jack yet there are times when Ruth and I are so estranged and I'm so black with lust that I feel like tying her to the bed to make her feel by force even though I know that in such a pass my resentful brutality couldnt much outlast the first plunge and that if instead of struggling she lay contemptuously dumb and inert I'd be too ashamed of seeming a perverted lunatic totally ignorant of the jeweler's craft to do anything at all what an ugly mania lust can be despite her innocent dreams of rape she must never be allowed to suspect the degradation she brings me to the point of with her paranoid protestantism who can preach in favor of reforming the universal church and liberating sexual love in adolescents while rebuffing the courtship of her husband as a mechanistic debasement of sacred union. But whatever I have to complain of is small enough in the scheme of things since it hasnt driven me crazy and it's my own fault anyway

and nimble the truest son an owlish father ever had (surer by far than the true son of his mother in the other bed who more resembles the sire in body) and for that very reason the first object of his father's irascibility who knows his heart all too well, who knows all too well how superfluously a cockerel's imperfections are likely to multiply. From the vantage of experience which is useless for persuasion the father grievingly perceives that during the first small loop of spiral ascent from the ground in early life (when talent seems amenable or plastic) almost every child is deprived of almost every chance to perfect the amalgamated self that the parents failed to perfect before handing it down. And yet in the middling sweep of his own gyre the second or third time around an older bird is still learning too and begining to believe that missing the lure may turn out for the best as long as one keeps rising.

Thus it seems to Michael Chapman that a boy has to muster more will than genius if he's going to bend to the proper axis his vortical energy, the exuberant exfoliation of which is generally frustrated by a dozen congenital flaws or limitations of the body and its transcendental brain. The worthiness of scions who have everything presented to them cleanly and betimes, with all manner of healthy encouragement and goodly assistance, is belittled by this father who presents his sons with very little that isnt wheedled or extorted by a mother not much interested in the discipline of art or science. [Let

I could have saved a lot of doctor bills not to mention the crippling of her life if I handnt been so parsimonious with my devotions in a thing like this at the bottom of everything humane you should spare no marginal expense to improve your investment ever so slightly seeing that the yield may prove as elastic as the price of fish and any lazily misguided man who relies on the aftereffects of gestation to correct matters has only himself to blame for almost any kind of domestic trouble maybe I'm not as selfish as she believes because most paters familias aren't so studious in country matters any revolution we may have in this country will be Amazonian but I suppose psychology will soon make the secrets of marriage as vulgar as middleclass golf skiing tennis and yachting. The devil will jargonize their poor unwordable feelings with the cant lingua franca of lowbred moving pictures brought into every American home to help sell malevolent lies. As one of the fragments said it's hard to contend with passion because it buys whatever it desires at the price of its soul but it'll be harder yet to impassion satiety when orgasm becomes the battle cry of amazonasters leading the revolutionary suicide of sex if some of them at least don't turn to art or other peacemaking and give more forethought to intellectual beauty in their old age than men do by resisting the devil in their youth instead of demanding the right to swill drugs consume sporting events abuse machinery fly fighter planes drill with bayonets and sell them run free then—as Mozart did not? How can they get more than school-system learning without my help who hasnt got the time? Must it always be my children's improvement versus mine? I can't give them culture if Ruth doesnt. Our boys don't get any music at all. Musicians leave us in the dust especially me but they don't have to deal with the meaning of everything they're prodigies of talent like figure skaters or switch-hitting virtuosos trained from the age of four at the expense of all other development by cruelly ambitious fathers or mothers despairing of success for themselves mere fiddlers or miners with an ambitious sense of responsibility the poor kids forced or hoodwinked into an intense regime to gratify elders who are justified only once in a million cases, before their poor offspring get a chance to stumble for themselves upon some other broad or narrow interest in life what a fine C P A Mozart might have made if left to his own devices as a son of mine and Michael Mantle would still be digging lead and zinc in Oklahoma's Blue Goose Number Six Mine but don't worry nobody with gifts like theirs would be born to my family there's still time enough if their bent is science or painting not to mention poetry.] Thus even as Mickey Chapman and his half-neglected firstborn are contemplating the conditions of existence in tenebrous harmony of attitude he must argue with himself to justify his shabby ways as preceptor and provider of all three promising mortals in his charge.

themselves to advertising we need very few babies to keep posterity going for art's sake if we can learn how to breed them in vitro women will no longer be required for the purpose of reproduction and provided that normal men don't start humping test-tubes in their disgust with feministic jostle the vagina will evolve by unnatural selection into a more specialized seat of sensation exactly adapted to this hyponastic bowsprit that leads us through the seven seas of torment unless indeed we're teleologically bound to evulve piston rings or propellers to please the girls in vivo as it is I sometimes think the barb returning on the exhaust stroke does more to further my service than the plunge under pressure during which I'm less inclined to tease anyway the worst of it is that if they cease to shun reason in the blind instinct of multiplication they'll only find a way to screw up their new destiny by aping the mentality of men. . . .]

Would nothing short of a death in the family sink this obsessively rounded reasoner? The insulating optimism that encased his anxieties like puffed white synthetic cork kept bobbing him back to the surface of existence even when his guts were waterlogged with sick cold misery. For a plump player of the mind it's easier to float than to dive. He was still a dull owlish bear in the eyes of a world that found itself more exciting than his excitement; in the eyes of his children grouchy lazy and methodical; stout fishfaced and nearsighted in the eyes of women he passed on the

But seeing that he hasnt yet given up on his own promise—and indeed even assumes as a working hypothesis while awaiting future evidence that his promise will for at least another decade outweigh that of anyone who shares only half his blood at best—it is scarcely surprising that he should suddenly feel a chill gust of irremediable regret at the waste of a precious Sunday. [What in hell were the notes about that I made this morning I don't even vaguely remember what my mind was working on—mind?— it's ludicrous that such an untutored smalltime domesticated provincial presumes to address the smallest part of high culture after selling down the river every promise of rebellious dilation concealed by the Second Class crow with which he separated from the Navy he who'd sworn to avoid all intellectual conventions! So I have. The insidious conventions of merchants are less permeant but much stronger. No cloud of nutshell philosophy can hide the fact that I'm bewebbed like a foolhardy gadfly in spiderland waving my legs in the air as I rationalize the fixation of my glued pinions. Today I have not even anabolized words of print from another mind nothing nothing nothing either done or gained all day what a miserly life I lead when I must feel guilty for doing the right thing in placation of a greater guilt yet still tonight I have the prior claims of my most urgent love to reckon with a passion that burns more fiercely in its drab prison than in the liberty of a troubadour's conflagrations and the only question

street who were ready enough to grant such a figure any amount of wisdom in his own lore. But in the eyes of Ruth? He pondered her opinion of him, he tried very hard to imagine what she really thought—or rather he soon gave up new speculation on that subject because he was simply unable to concentrate upon the consciousness of another person, especially one who was necessarily an object of his own practical consciousness, not to say a stumbling block to the continuation of his selfhood; he had always had to give up this effort after a few seconds. All he could do was bend his will to a recollection of words from her mouth in the belief that there were times when a careful objective ear could pick up fragments or glimmerings of reality from what she said. But he did known that she was a woman able to love a bear (though not as easily perhaps as she might have loved a dancer or a swan or a stallion of similar mental qualities), thanks to a lovely unselfish nature whose telic vocation was love itself.

Words actually said? She had once asked him: "Michael do you ever doubt that I've been true to you?" It was not long since; he remembered in fact that it was after Roger's birth for she had been teasing him with the confession that like many another matron she was in love with her sympathetic obstetrician (the mit-Weib man that stands in front to block the way and gets as much gratitude for relieving the patient's condition as if the cause of it) whom he'd never seen whether billygoat swan or Per-

that I as love's poorest captive think to ask is whether I'll be permitted tonight to remake old love without having to borrow from Monday morning the energy to overcome boneweary prostration on my beloved's part.]

Is a son's promise or the father's first to be jeopardized? A promising father who is continually pressed by weird harpies to persevere in his own fragile faith at any cost (not less so but more so as potentiality is steadily dissipated into the actuality of domestic economy while ticking its way ever closer to total evaporation) can hardly be expected to display the motherly unselfishness required for even one promising son to have the start he was born for, either running free or running trained. [That more than willing mother, if only she were able to play father to the children! My erratic vigilance and fitfully fussing care will always be nothing to what it should by all rights be.] Again he casts a look at the second son sleeping in the shadows at his left. Right now it is there that more of his attention is needed, for there lie possibilities he does not know so well. But he clings to the thesis that when a father in the diminishing childhood of his own promise owns nor time nor cash for culture travel or the accumulation of capital in his own behalf a womanish society has no call to reprove him for failing to wrest these boons from that society's own economy on behalf of his sons. [Besides, a higher moral law adjures you not to put your equity in children lest they fail of thine own excellence

cheron but had been told was fair and slim with remarkably strong white gentle hands.

"Well I don't take you for granted." He had no memory of any such doubts at the time, but a wise Panurge would never say Naw I'm perfectly sure of you my dear, especially during long wretched months of complication grotesquerie travail and leaky convalescence while waiting for the baby to begin to crawl and in long black periods when I can find nothing healthy or attractive about your person and am more than ready to accept the first college girl or countess to make an overture.

"I have been faithful you know. Since we got married I've never been with another man." Her frank straightforward way of reassuring him on that occasion put to shame all the earlier forgotten jealousies and all the concealed suspicions that had today finally burst into suppressed flame. He had not then been aware that he was in want of those words that now served as solid testimony.

But testimony on which side of the case? It was positive evidence only of the fact that she was aware of the possibility. In his former ingenuousness he had not pondered what he now tried to remember, the exact circumstances of her statement. Was it uttered as he lay at her side attempting so to excite her that the last thing she'd want to do was slow up the proceedings with inconsequent remarks, only to find that his advances merely reminded her of other dolphins in the sea which even a chaste housewife

both acquired and inherited without any way of your knowing so until it's too late to expose them for their defects in the Spartan fashion as Laius did with Oedipus (if you want to know what was really behind that story) and what son can help but fall short of a father's earned merit which isnt passed on with the seed whereas the increase possessed by men of no worth usually finds its way to sons? It's simply my lot to have no such increase and I'm afraid I leave behind me none of the crutches that give young musicians scientists and scholars the headstart needed by geniuses of that kind.]

Now Jonathan is glad enough to have time with his father in peaceful silence but he reckons that if he doesnt renew conversation his father will steal away sooner than otherwise. Therefore he begins again by asking if snakes ever do escape from the zoo. His father is glad to be able to reassure him on this point without unwitting misinformation, but when the learner then asks if there's any reason to fear violent revolution and guillotines or camps with chimneys the teacher though sincere in his assertion of grounds for hope on that score finds the question entwined in his own fears with the menace of noetic destitution fostered by the American defense against the kind of atavism Jonathan seems to mean who's only reflecting upon some of the words that come over the airways from journalists and businessmen not terrifically worried by what our late German enemies did to Communists and Jews: so it's

might think of when considering the delights that had eluded her? Or had the subject occurred to her wistfully under the very shadow of her latest disappointment as he dozed off in a fatuous glow when he might have expected to hear no talk from her at all? Why had she said *since*? Why had she chosen the word *with*? Did these two prepositions somehow qualify the burden of her sentence or delimit her idea of fidelity? Had she always glossed over some wartime affair while I was overseas, maybe on V-J Day when it might have started by having a few drinks with almost any officer dogface or swabbie to celebrate her betrothed's deliverance from death by Einstein's bomb? And did she regard befuddled debauchment or unpremeditated and absolutely repented seduction as a purely passive act on her part done by but not *with* a man? To what degree of metaphorical transformation did she submit the literally ambiguous adjective *faithful*? [A whore can be faithful to her pimp according to the covenant of her heart. Ruth is an honorable woman and Ruth did not flatly say No rod of ducted flesh but yours has ever been inside me and still less did she add the declaration that no man's hand but mine had touched her chest or reached inside her clothes since I first claimed the privilege.]

But when all was said and done this mistrusting green-eyed bear proved as reasonable as ever. Though he was wont to dwell upon the possibilities that had been open to a lovely college girl passionate and lonely in a port of embarkation

time to call a halt to the day's education. Leaning down to kiss his
star pupil a final goodnight he
whispers as softly as his lips can
sound: "Little Mowgli if you don't
knock it off and go right to sleep
I'll have to give you the RED
HAND!" Jonathan of course smiles
at this secondhand threat from his
father's incredibly remote childhood at the famous Maplewood
School in Gloucester whence it took
something like two decades of exile
for the old boy to grasp the etymological fact that the local term for
that catholic chastisement was a
brilliantly apt corruption of the
universal metonymy for the fescue
anciently made of *rattan* that
welted a malefactor's palm. The
young Californian has always been
somewhat doubtful about the literal
truth of this horrible old custom
which at least in a public establishment seems to violate all the civil
rights he takes for granted, and under present circumstances it strikes
him as more than ever likely that
it's a jocular fiction of the auto-
biographer's. He closes his eyes to
ponder again that strange far-off
place apparently so unlike all others
in his father's estimation.

[Should I have convinced him
that python-cobras and galloping
giant-squid crocodiles are now absolutely dismissed as quaint and
charming terrors not to be feared in
dreams? Certainly those in the
camps despaired of their lives and
they probably cherished no hope for
any renaissance of kindness justice
or scholarship after their kind was
wiped out but perhaps they saw no
reason to doubt that history itself of

among a score of military establishments his final judgment was as
usual plain and homely, for in the
end he accepted the ordinary import of his wife's words. At last he
stopped short of quibbling inquisition about the distant past. It was
not unlikely that her affirmation
had been offered from the depths of
a conscience uneasy about unfaithful thoughts or polite reception of
praise from improper lips but it
was inconceivable to him that his
true-blue Ruth could have given
voice to her reassurance as a gratuitous barefaced lie. He was well
aware of the traditional opinion
that women could be mysteriously
deceptive without committing
themselves to the logic of lying—
that their words and tones had no
consistently direct or inverse correspondence to veridical phenomena—but as a generalization about
females it had been many times
confuted by this blessed one among
them. Ruth in her right mind had
always conducted herself with candid dignity as simple as the
mother's of Jesus. It was no less
plain than ever that she abhorred at
every level of consciousness the duplicity and degradation of falsehood. Thus it became clear to him
that in her voluntary declaration
she had only been anticipating one
of his Chapmanias before he himself
felt it coming on.

One thing remained to be explained away however, the fact that
had popped back into his head after
encountering Sandy at the zoo and
set him to thinking about this the
most painful outcome of his long
day's excursion in the side of life

whatever polarity would serve out its natural term under the first dispensation but now that even the ruling classes of all religions have more to fear for global destiny than the most vulnerable slaves of former times setting aside the fact that no personal death can be more terrible than oldtime fire at the stake. Should children be allowed to underestimate what most mothers and fathers have not yet learned to mourn even more than the deaths of their own and themselves? Or is the ignorant deprecation of terror with which government and devilvision instill those able to bring children into our world a better part of human valor? Sometimes I suspect that I alone I and a scattered handful unknown to me joined by saints five years or five centuries dead fear the worst for reasons peculiar to the selfishness and presumptuous pride of mortal immortality while most others take broad alarm if theyre not too stupid to fear at all either in personal dread or in affright for persons directly sprung from their own flesh whereas few indeed are magnanimous enough to be dismayed like God out of charity for Mother Earth and all her children. In any case I always say not faith but hope alone is left and it's God's hope that men will pause to eat the bread made by women but we can't seem to stop fooling with new recipes always baking new kinds of cake mixing and admixing newfangled yeasts sugars and salts rolling folding and kneading by machinery molding firing and cooling every new way we can think of filling the wrong parts of the hungry world

adjacent to his heart: no longer merely the fact she had told him that was known only to her and Sandy and then to himself but suddenly the possible fact unknown to himself that perhaps it since had led to. Now if Sandy's attempt upon Horse Ruth had not failed Michael assumed that it would have been made known to Pig Ruth by the Lothario himself who was likely to boast such a conquest by way of confession to the kind of woman who probably would have tempted him with pitiable boasts of her own. Now in retrospect the bear was unable to detect the slightest reservation of respect for himself or his wife on either of the Sandyses' part. On the contrary both of them seemed especially to admire the integrity of his family. Hence it was to be inferred that Sandy never returned to the Chapman household because his advances had failed, and of course he never would brag of having stolen an unrequited kiss from an impregnable housewife. Of course the balked predator had no way of knowing whether or not the revered housewife had told his old friend her husband. Did Sandy's doubt on this point leave our ursine king with an upper hand despite the secret affront to his majesty?

Yet it was quite possible that the wolf like the bear himself in the conversation today had simply forgotten the fact as a vain trifle from the distant past which he'd only shrug off if brought to mind by chance. The list of his adventures was presumably too lengthy to have space for misfires, and Michael supposed that in any case such inci-

with a diversified glut of uneaten bread that'll turn to stone before we quit boasting and am I Michael Chapman not as restless feverish and greedy as my fellows despite my claim to better excuse for do I not every day like them bake bricks of bread and lay them in patient courses for the walls of my own private house encourage new young appetites for progress and nourish young bodies to make the usufruct and very flesh of Mother Earth ever more dear and by the pursuit of comfort in which to gorge with bread and wine do I not improve myself as ignobly and ambitiously as if all along I've been aiming for nothing but my share of consumption? As a father and Democrat with a social security number I must tithe almost like the best of Calvinists and union men yet nothing's beyond my free enterprise if I live in health long enough before everything we enjoy comes to an end but I pity Ruth who hasnt even hope to call her own and I pity the boys because they probably will not follow in my probably unavailing footsteps. I fear for the fear of persons I love who have less reason than I to fear the worst in all time.]

Behold, Jonathan is asleep.

Michael shakes off his sentiments and rises to go to his bath. Passing the helpmeet at real work in the kitchen he pats her hip and extends an invitation. "Honey I hope you'll have a Palm Sunday drink with me before we go to bed." [Maybe she'll taste something just to celebrate the holiday.]

"That'll be a good time for me to sign that paper of yours."

dents were a dime a dozen in all careers except his own. . . . —Then again it was plausible to imagine Sandy surmising that if Ruth hadnt told Michael what had occurred during his unauthorized visit to the castle he might have reason to revive a casual hope for future success, or concluding that if she had told her husband about the incident he was free to take Michael's apparently somewhat indulgent though obviously cautious renewal of acquaintance as an indication of conjugal weariness that might lead to the same sort of tolerance that he'd accustomed himself to without any sense of iniquity as if it were no more serious than courtly flirtation or recreational experiment even for the other sex— [Enough, by all the saints! I'm running reason into the ground.]

So he no longer cared to pursue the foolishness of honor. A busy man should not enter into interminable questions. [Put these tiresome nightmares out of your mind. They are the fancies of an unemployed imagination. They don't bear mentioning with the great troubles of our time let alone the Albigensian Crusade or the arson at Alexandria or even the mere commemoration of events in Holy Week. Let's get on with the most important thing in your private life the present act that anneals the past and don't fret about your impersonal work until tomorrow morning. With a fresh start you can think of this lost day as a salubrious vacation. Tis a pity when the world's booming with talent and leisure that a man vested with nei-

The astonished husband dares not display surprise or gratitude or haste. Instead he silently reexamines and confirms the sounds and meanings of her words, and thereupon without further ado makes sure to profit from every current moment to make ready for her when she's finished with the dishes, hoping against hope that exhaustion or depression won't alter her intention before then. Perhaps he will even have time to come back and help her.

In the meantime holding his breath he dares not risk colloquy to clarify the issues entailed in what she's promised; so with a quick step but not so lightly as to suggest exultation he graciously disappears into the bathroom. The first thing he sees is a new roll of toilet paper, properly mounted.

ther should choose to take on the world's most complete system. Nothing save intensification can make up for the time you lose.]

Michael spoke impatiently to himself. His voice was as harsh as he could make it. It is no laughing matter at any age even for a man of genius with a staff of life-relieving servants to inflict upon himself the kind of pains Michael dredged up that day (however cleverly he may have subsequently allayed them), for they leave him with a new complex of discomposure which though neutralized nevertheless precipitates a fine accretion to the subaqueous sediment of pulverized visions relating to himself as an American aristocrat. [I must learn to rejoice in the difficulties of teeming monogamy for workers of every race creed and gender as well as to simply renounce "vile prurience for fresh adventure in all things". It is sufficient that I am alive and thinking and that those I love still live. Tonight I am called upon only to seal this day as a day of love. I must never forget that the faults of driveling suspicion and petty jealousy at the core of my character are visible only in the X-rays of my own laboratory and that as long as they are never developed and printed they may do no harm in stirring up my embers. It is well to keep such flaws hidden if you don't let them jeopardize your immortality by fermentation bearing in mind that there must always be a hundred million people more or less rubbing each other in the natural craving for an end to the craving. I myself can't lay off just because I'm not worthy of my beautiful little chestnut mare all I can do is make it clearer to her that love is engendered by the generous contragendering that helps make a jockey lean and outlasting.]

He was so relieved at finding no horns on his forehead—only the vanished shames of a dream—that his evening turned out to be happier than it would have been if his pride had remained intact all day. There was no need to look for the family album. Husbands have always prized virginity for its proof that any biographical data kept from them was not likely to be important; and the later experiences of a chaste girl's heart and the lusts of her mind are considered no less irrelevant to a man's reputation than to his bloodline. In any event, unlike Panurge who would rather have died than be deceived by a wife (though he liked cuckolds well enough he said and gladly visited their homes), Michael Chapman would rather live in peace than worry about his honor or damage someone else's. [Mine's a good practical attitude when you have other things to get done before you die and no other women to take more than the edge off gynolagnia but there was a time when a scholar could keep one for the solace she gave and still get his work done without being bound to ill-fated domestic romance or having to invent lurid competition to persuade himself he's in love with her when he's no longer got any choice. Would I love her freely if I had my freedom still? Seeing that I have no possibility of disinvestment that would be less than disastrous for my children I make the best of my fetters by imagining that a cocksman wants to get into her behind my back for even promiscuous attention seems to make her more desirable to me than any woman could possibly be as the single inmate of my own seraglio so the demon in charge of this mania gets hold of a certain neural plexus in my brain cuts it out of the larger rete at jagged boundaries and crystallizes a single spuriously transient state of the circuit as if it seriously corresponded to an event in the real world thus providing an apparatus for excitation no more or less reasonable than the doctrine of Jehovah's Witnesses Ruth's paranoid delusions or many of my reasonable derangements though I trust far less persistent but at least it serves the purpose of electrifying my possessive instinct with the symptoms of love when I seem to need them really a cycle of symptoms like some others I go through as if I were continually getting a cold and coming out of it with disturbances descending from crown to lungs and retreating up again yet the artificial induction of symptoms has always been one of true love's wiles or at least since the age of Henry the Second and for perpetuating attraction it's as authentic as inertia or the arrow of Eros in the first place I find it takes very little desire to extract the general property of love from the pathos and sympathy in any intimate knowledge of humanity's desirable half an accidental meeting starts us off and thereafter the "inertia of feeling" that St Hermann talks about keeps us together on our joined tangents. When I'm hardhearted to both her gentlest and wildest tears I can't credit my love with much particularity.

> But which of you that love most entricketh,
> God sende hym hire that sorest for hym syketh!

By chance we met in wartime and by chance she began to love me because I happened to be the one among those who loved her that made an impression alas a paternal impression but there's one good thing about having a wife that loves you more for her faith in your strength and protection than for the thrill of your touch and that is that since a girl can have only one father she's more likely to be faithful than a mothering or sistering woman who can have any number of sons or brothers in succession if not simultaneously so you might say that I've burdened myself with a stable marriage and her fidelity is the one thing it doesnt lack of. All along I've been mistaken in believing the reason I never fight with her is that I see her side of our quarrels better than my own but it's really because I'm a coward about disturbing the equilibrium of possessing a prize coveted by other men who suspect nothing of her disequilibrium and I'm instinctively aware that when you're riding the declining half of your wave it makes considerable difference whether you're in a smooth swell of the open ocean or on a lee shore under the overhang of a breaker.]

From long experience Michael and Ruth whenever they were in harmony at warping the family ship could move about their little basin without getting in each other's way. Having emerged from his showerbath the master was immeasurably pleased to find that the chambermaid had tidied up their sleeping room and trimly smoothed the sheets of the big bed under the wrinkled blue counterpane neatly turned back. When he returned from his study across the hall with the paper that required her signature to disinhibit the operation that seemed to represent the removal of his ultimate grievance against love she was taking her turn in the bathtub. In his regal maroon bathrobe and carpet slippers he shuffled into the kitchen to wait for her, pouring out two glasses of port. The checkered green oilcloth of the table was scrubbed clean. Even the salt and pepper shakers had been put aside against the batten of the drawn shade on the sill of the porch window in order to make a clearing for face-to-face armslength parley. He failed to make the most of this intermission by fetching a book; instead he turned on the radio to listen to the day's news (which unfortunately included no Party tidbits) and then paced about the gleaming galley in silence with hands clasped behind his back like the captain of a shabby whaler. He was no longer too tired to read but a rare immediacy of feeling for the present moment excluded past and future. The mental claims of anything as external as a line of print would have jammed his brain and disrupted even the resonance a body must have to draw a breath without thinking.

Tonight for him his wife's was the only literature in the world, and he marveled at what last night's ladylove had wrought in him this day. But he would have preferred a less ceremonious setting for the treaty she was about to sign if she didnt change her mind or stipulate too much. It was an agreement he had despaired of; in his mind it had been tabled from his current agenda, deferred until such time as it might be passed off carelessly as more or less routine paperwork confirming some legal technicality scarcely worth the notice of a spiritual personality. It was in this hope of avoiding the formalities of discussion that he busied himself nervously stowing away the wine bottle on the pantry shelf and taking it out again as she reappeared in the conference room. On the other hand he felt prudentially obliged by the affectation of this stage business as well as by the fear of being taken for a self-serving flatterer to refrain from open admiration of the breathtakingly renewed and indeed tonally transformed woman who filled his amorous eye before he turned his back to reach for the wine. There was every reason to keep their minds off beauties of hair and skin but even at a distance the visual fragrance that he associated with the woman he saw (before she was close enough to shimmer in the scent of artifice that she had touched to her wrists earlobes and throat) was enough to make him tremble like an abject suitor. He promised himself not to purchase what was left of his freedom by acknowledging a perpetual gratitude for her abnegation of fertility lest it would always come to "Let's play bridge with the Smiths" or "Come with me to pick out a washing machine" or "Please help me put up some curtains" or "Tell me what you think about this and that" or "You shouldnt get up so early" or "Let's go look at houses" or other tortures commonly inflicted in marriage—even "What are you working on now?"

But he neednt have feared and he neednt have steeled himself, for wrapped against the stage lights in his old blue dressing gown Ruth hadnt the slightest notion of taking advantage of anything, and at the same time no discipline known to mankind not even being lashed to the other side of a mast could have prevented him from gazing outright at his alluring nemesis as she paused in the doorway before taking her place at the shipshape table; even if it had been absolutely and unequivocally prohibited for the purpose of this special moment in his life he could not have refrained from expressing what he suddenly realized for the first time with full clarity (when at a like moment even an insensitive Everyman would never have offered to compare his ordinary wife to a famous beauty as he yet once more wheedled her to forget herself in his arms). "Sweetheart, by all the saints you look like Elizabeth Quicherat's twin sister!" he cried out impetuously in the grip of star-struck epiphany. "No wonder I fell in love with her!" But it was a plausible compliment.

Her smile was eloquently grateful—not the illuminating smile that gladdened people at her sympathy with what they were talking about but an inward smile that drew down her eyelashes—and it only reinforced his recollection of a lilied face at the end of an overwhelming curtain-call. When he bent to kiss her amused mouth full softly her lips were as sweet and receptive as a new lover could wish but they gave him to understand that she wasnt going to fall for his blarney just yet. He stepped away in splay-footed circlets enthusiastically agog at this manner of getting acquainted with the dancer he'd never been close enough to speak to. "Well" said his correspondent "I'm afraid I'm not quite as superior to living as you think that fine lady is." She laughed outright. "I'm certainly not very magnetic!"

"Not much! Nor are hoops of steel! Only think, my own bedfellow!" Once more he stopped to rediscover her refined ungarnished beauty.

"Isnt there anyone you're in love with who doesnt look like me? I've failed you in so many ways."

"No there's only her and you my Rosinante. You know me: if I can't be bothered reading unsaintly writers I certainly can't stoop to women less than the best. . . . It's easy to see why Sandy's still enamored."

"Sandy's married. And he's never been in love with me. You like to imagine things like that. He must know I'm not attracted to him. Besides, he always has bad breath. Your breath is always sweet. You're the only man that interests me—except maybe your little friend who takes himself so seriously." She knew he was never jealous of Caleb.

"That's a terrible thing to say about a dentist. How do you know he has halitosis?"

"Why I smell it every time he kisses me." She amazed her husband at the jest, doubling up to shrink like a giggling schoolgirl from his retaliatory pinches. What could be more reassuring to a conservative husband?

"Well I guess I'd better watch you with Caleb. He's a pretty horny little bastard you know."

"How would I know? I havent noticed. . . . When are we going to invite Lilian Cloud to dinner? Under the right conditions she might like him, since she's an artist. . . . But goodness gracious dear you must know by now that I'd never be unfaithful to you unless I was attracted to somebody!" She looked up at him with merry solemnity. "All the times I've heard you say that the open ocean gets tedious after a while, when there's nothing else to see—"

"I just mean that seafaring's more interesting when there's land or other ships in sight."

"Yes I know. You find monogamy dull without something to give it a filip. But I don't think women miss mountains and harbors when they're at sea with their husbands. Familiarity breeds content!"

"It's just that a sailor always has to keep watch. With you for my vessel I'm content to sail all around the world without a landfall. I tell you the best is good enough for me."

"Well we've already been around the world." He was now sitting opposite her at the little table and musing with bent head she stroked the back of his hand. Her soft chestnut hair had been brushed smooth and was gathered by a blue ribbon loosely knotted at the nape of her neck.

"I'm so grateful to you for taking us out today! You're really such a good father, the kindest and most generous man at the zoo, considering all the things you have on your mind."

"That's the greatest exaggeration I've ever heard you utter!" Michael in his turn took no thought for advantage from her fond bemusement. Covering her hand with his but making no further move toward taking her inside his robe, inside his skin, to match his yearning bone for bone, he praised only the speakable. "You did all the work. I don't see how you can be so patient with us all. Whence cometh your strength?"

"From my lord and master of course.

Thy husband is thy lord, thy life, thy keeper,
Thy head, thy sovereign."

"But thou art no shrew. No earthly woman less so!"

"I was purring all night and ever since then I've been like a new bride rippling in satin cream. I couldn't very well purr in public but all day I've felt shriven from within. Besides I had a lot of rest while we were riding around." She touched her small new smile with the fingertips of her other hand, looking a little to one side of the black hairs showing at the top of his chest. "I'm sure you were the best lover at the zoo today."

"I had no idea you were so pleased after all these years." He bridled, his self-satisfaction totally restored.

"Perhaps I shouldnt be so reserved in the sounds I make. Sometimes I'm afraid of waking up the baby. But also it's fun to fool you. I don't know how many times I lost my head last night before I gathered that last handful of pearls."

This was rare dialogue between the veteran lovers. Michael dared say almost nothing without great care lest he frighten with some inadvertent ring to his words the honest creature whose complicity he required.

Came a discreet scratch at the door. Semiramis had heard the pleasant voices and was asking to share the affection. "Here comes little Mrs Purr-Box!" Ruth said. Michael reached over to admit the regal cat, who entered with a single trill of greeting, her tail flung up in a flickering wave like an erect blacksnake, sprang at once to the surface of the table, and walked over to face her mistress. "Keep this wayward girl away from my innocent boys." the human woman said laying her forehead eye to eye against the cat's and stroking her sleek spine. "She looks so contented I suppose we're going to have little panthers all over the house before we know it. Take her away! She's your cat. I can't write my name while she's walking on the paper."

Ruth reached for the pen that Michael had brought with his document. With hardly a glance at the typed statement she signed it quickly in her smoothly clarified penmanship hand somewhat acculturated to the exigencies of writing in college. Only after her name was down—Michael fussing over the glossy cat now in his arms saw from the corner of his eye as he paid no attention to what she was doing—did his wife seem to reflect upon what she'd assented to, pen suspended for a few seconds as if awaiting other papers, thoughtfully nibbling her lower lip. But she looked more satisfied than doubtful and Michael very softly began to release the breath trapped under his ribs.

"There!" she said. "You poor guy, you should get your way more often. I've never done enough for you."

"Oh," said he as if called out of a reverie, mumbling almost indifferent thanks as he suppressed an elation unequaled since in wartime livery he had tasted her astonishingly deliquescent response to his first kiss sitting on the living room couch of the professor's house she lived in overlooking Treasure Island outlined in orange lights on the moonlit bay and the great headland city beyond it. "Oh!" he repeated carelessly but in a more attentive tone. "You do everything for me. —Here, have some wine!" He handed her the untouched glass and they sipped, lady after gentleman, not in the unison with which it is customary to toast an accomplishment. This trifling dissonance helped keep him from giving way to the exultation that made his fingers twitch with the urge to snatch the paper and lock it up in his study instanter. He let it lie there like a neglected napkin. Semiramis escaped, leaping down to sniff at the oxidized hunks of food remaining on her plate under the sink. For the first time he noticed that unsavory dish as the only Irish pennant left in sight.

However Ruth did ask him a few questions about the surgery he proposed to submit to. It would be only the fourth operation of his life. He remembered his childhood terror at the ether cone putting a stop to his consciousness before he'd had his tonsils out during the long garish gyrations of an abstract dream; but he was informed of the other two severences (which had been performed without anaesthesia before the dawn of significant consciousness) only by the practically congenital disfigurement of his surfaces where umbilical cord and foreskin had been attached. He assured her that the blood of this less common covenant would be negligible; that its catamnestic affect upon her Caliburn would be positively salubrious (for psychological reasons he dared not mention), so that he'd shine more brightly than ever (in frightening off the blue devils at her door that were also better left unspoken of); and that she need not fear any detectable stint or enfeeblement of the nacreous balm that he would still have the honor of saluting her with at least as often as she liked.

"That's what your androcologist says maybe—but how can you be sure? After all he's a priest who doesnt need to join your sect." Since Ruth never accompanied her own wit by physiognomic gesture or accent she often missed it (though far less often than others did), at least until his reflection came too late for the moment; but this time he immediately perceived that she was twitting him about his faith in a male profession while seeking expression of her anxiety not about the upshot and quantitative outcome of the dual Atropusian incisions as far as his erotic capability was concerned but about her own susceptibility to the mere knowledge of his irreversible sterility. "I can't deny your reasons for this. You certainly have earned the right to alter your own body as long as you know what you're doing. I suppose it will make you less nervous. But do you think it will have some unconscious influence on my attitude? Of course I'll always love you: it won't affect that side of it. And it's not that I think it has anything to do with manhood. Yet it would almost have been better if you'd forged my name and had it done without my knowledge. . . . But then

again I may forget all about it after a few years. . . . Well I won't say much
more about it." She drank some wine. "I'm almost too old to have a
daughter now anyway. But I must tell you one thing: if one of the boys
should die my ideas about chastity might change."

He took her hand again. "If our children died nothing like that would
matter. I'd want you to find comfort any way possible." [—That was a stupid thing for me to say, as if her fidelity were of little worth to me!]

"For another baby. That's all. As long as I'm able to have another
baby."

"I understand."

So she had not entirely exonerated his conscience after all. But it was
not her purpose to dissuade him with pathetic ghosts of fear. Having
rendered herself this last moral precaution she evinced more interest in
the quick and painless procedure by which in two strokes of a scalpel she
would be forever deprived of the miraculous plasma stemming from the
Dioscuric reticules in his crotch than he had ever mustered for the long
agonizing labor by which she was delivered of its products. He told her
all he knew about what he had to face, ending with the postoperative
test by microscope.

"There'll be no need for a nurse sir!" She wagged her finger at him. "I
shall assist with any necessary sampling. I still hold exclusive copyrights."
Then she added: "And another thing: you must promise not to tell anyone
about this. I don't want swarms of funloving girls to follow you up and
down Teleology Lane." But she was serious about the secrecy and she
paused for his vow before she continued. "—Yes please I'd like some more
of that stuff. Wine agrees with me better than it used to. —I wonder if
you could get a test tube of it frozen for me. Just in case. I've heard it can
work. Like Jim's story about the bull you know. —Well at least when I
get older you won't be going to another woman for children."

Michael drank to that.

"Why don't you get some swing music on the radio." she suggested.

"Sure. I'm broadminded." Luckily he found a jazz band unspoiled by
human voices and in sudden enthusiasm born of sweet reminiscences they
took to the floor on bare feet as contentedly engrossed with their tiny circle
of linoleum as when pressed of yore by a likeminded crowd that didnt exist
for them. Ruth was the best of dancers, Michael not the worst. They improvised accommodations to the slowest rhythms Michael could detect in each
blue or red tempo. For a long time the loveliness of supernatural reeds and
brass attuned the formerly sentimental lovers to undertones of drumskin and
strings in music that stood for freedom to them who as superannuated
graduates of popular amusements scarcely ever heard its old call to dispense
with the illusions of daylight responsibility.

"You're as good as ever my dear." she said. "I think it was your dancing I married you for. I already had your other services."

He was surprised and quite pleased. It was she who had been famous for her dancing and he apologetic. Perhaps it was her almost obsessive dancing that had bouyed her virtue against all the storms of youth until the cleverest seducer of all (not yet plump) had come along in his monkey suit whispering literary alusions and no use for nightclubs. "You were always the best mover on the floor." he said. "When I first saw you I didnt dare ask for a dance. But since you were also the most beautiful I finally decided to risk a naysaying."

"But I neighed at first sight!"

Even in this oldtime gaiety they kept their voices low for fear of waking the boys or disturbing the Topalises who must have been at home by then. Stepping about their patch of dance floor as lightly as fairies on a midnight green they excited each other with old thoughts like the sweethearts who once on a moonless coeducational ski trip had whispered new ideas for violating the curfew with a game sweeter yet than dancing. Again at the table with purple-stainéd mouths they lifted bubbleless beakers to drain sun-drenched thimblefuls under bright shadowless light from the bare kitchen ceiling. Their low tones italicised the meanings of what they said to each other. Ruth's droll risibility was renewing their courtship.

"To my light fantastic beauty!" he saluted.

"But this beauty will never be passed on." she lightly replied to his reminder of halcyon days before desire began to distinguish itself from the other elements of their love. "Boys can't inherit it. Can you visualize all this danceability rotting in my grave? My one talent. I guess I still have it. But it will die with me because now I'll never again make you dizzy with a mother-earthquake."

Michael was brought up short by this velvet jolt, casting about in his word-horde to smooth over this sudden blemish in the conversation without pause or hesitation that might admit that deflection of her goodwill. "Yes it'll be my fault when we must content ourselves with merely volcanic activity. But maybe the job you get will be interesting. First thing you know I'll be losing weight!"

"I don't know whether I'm glad or sad tonight, the way I love you," she told him "but I can't help feeling as if I'm betraying my ancestors when I cut off the female line."

"You'll have granddaughters no doubt."

"Not if our boys take after you! But what if I don't live to see their children? Anyway I won't be allowed to bring them up." She chuckled like a wise grandmother. "Do you know how much Sarah wanted her daughter? When she finally produced Mimi she was wrapt in wonder at seeing herself in a flawless baby that wouldnt be spirited off to be maimed by a mohel. So when she got home from the hospital and needed Jack's help while she was getting the cradle ready she handed the baby to him and without thinking said *Here, hold me for a minute*! She's still bewildered by her mistake. But Jack had no use for the tradition that she should purify herself for sixty six days. Why that's twice as long as it is for boys!"

"I'm glad it wasnt the other way around for us Christians."

"But don't worry my darling. I'm not ever going to Jack or Sandy or Dave or Jim or Newt or Glen Smith or Valentine Greatrakes or even Caleb Karcist or someone you don't know to get my daughter. I'm my own daughter. Mary the Mother of God never had a daughter."

"Nor Joan of Arc."

"Many important women don't have any children at all, especially movie stars. Once we finish this bottle of wine I won't ever again think of infidelity. And this is the last time I'll ask you if you're absolutely sure you want to go through with this strange folly of yours, making a mule of yourself, when it isnt the only way to keep me from getting pregnant. I'm not thinking of my disappointment but of your own opinion of yourself. It's true that I already have so many children that I don't know what to do—sometimes. And anyway if we tried again we still might not have a girl-baby. There are enough men in the world. . . . I feel like a cuckoo bird singing *Ku-koo, ku-koo—oh where oh where has my daughter gone?* —If I died you'd marry again, and no matter how well your wife loved my children she'd want a few of her own."

"I'd never think of such a thing. But I wouldnt want more children from Inanna herself. I do other things to justify all you've gone through for me and my children."

"It wouldnt take much of your time to start the process. When you have enough money for servants you may change your mind. By then I'd have my legacy to leave you." He kept shaking his head. With tears in her eyes she laughed at his simplicity.

After a while in the dance that brought them closer to each other he loosened the sashes of their two robes in order to feel her heartbeat without insulation through the twin granaries pressed against his bare ribs, and he made shift to bind himself to her as if they shared one mantle. Her eyes rolled upward and closed in recognition of the warm codpole from under his belly that now indented cooler skin above the wombilical knot of her fallow pod like the blunt nightstick of a burlesque policeman boastfully insinuating himself into her good graces, yet the music's undiminishing conjuration of a passion freer and simpler than any they could ordinarily remember transformed them into muted immortals dancing on a floor of the sea. He had contrived to turn out the overhead light and take off his glasses; they watched each other's eyes and smiles in beguilingly imprecise shadows, visible each to each by a shaded lamp in the next room, as their synoecious movements—now embraced and now half parted on allegro toes under a whirling dome of pleasure, slow or fast—seemed to lead the kinds of sound made by popular strangers some now dead, of which they were conscious only when pausing to sip their Hippocrene. His wife was the last person in the world Michael would have expected to

celebrate this occasion with. Semiramis dozing tone-deaf on a chair occasionally opened her yellow eyes to gaze at the antics.

Their more jocund steps gradually merged into a smoothly gliding
posture that kept them in closer touch, selecting cheek-to-cheek rhythms
reminiscent of their romantic youth for the disk-jockey's music to follow
or incorporate, moving sometimes to patterns picked out in united intuition from the beats of alien musicians sounding undomestic instruments,
their own Unamerican cares so reconciled to American music that they
overlooked the discrepency. At last came a slow blue skirl to mesmerize
them like a pair of cobras in unison no longer leading their own dance but
swayed by an invisible one who sways to their swaying and so avoids the
relative motion by which his presence could be fixed, but their hoods were
swollen by dreams as dissociated from the business of the piper as tethered
airborne balloons of a playmate building his sandcastle on the verge of an
incoming tide.

Michael thought it was about bedtime when the set came to an end,
silencing the radio for fear that commercial words would break the spell.
It was Ruth who brought Michael out of his trance by switching the
bright light on again.

"Well I suppose we won't be needing this anymore!" Re-wrapping
herself in Michael's gown she drew from its pocket uncased her weathered
drumhead contraceptive. With both hands she raised the stiff-rimmed
slightly bellied diaphragm like a stained brown host as if preparing for a
Black Mass with the reserved sacrament. It had rightly been worn all day
and was still moist from a rinsing. "We can save a pretty penny on gadgets
like this."

She stepped into the other room but instead of replacing the precious
buckler in its proper niche she found her sewing basket and before he
grasped what was going on she laid her hands on a pair of small curved
fingernail scissors long ago provided by her mother and brought them
with her rubber saucer to the kitchen table. Too quickly for him to stop
her she punctured the rubber just inside its corona and deftly completed
the interior circumcision like a little girl cutting out a sunhat for her
paper doll. The circular panel fluttered to the floor like a coupon as she
held up the empty annulet between thumb and forefinger. Her soft low
contralto grew plangent. "Hossanah in the highest! See, the pneumatic
body of Jesus! —Want a game of quoits? We're on an ocean cruise playing
deck tennis with my halo. —No, horseshoes! My daddy taught me how to
throw ringers!" She tossed the little hoop at Semiramis's chair-knob, who
fled to another room like the terrified cat of a witch. "I'm the only one
who can play this game of skill, but you must see that I win."

She turned out a chair and made him sit down before her with his
knees together and his robe open. Numbed in mind by suddenly resurrected fear, enflamed in body by the demand of a Maenad he'd never

known, he was powerless to deny her. Glancing up at the unshaded window overlooked only by the stars but mirroring the kitchen's bright scene she spoke with level boldness. "This may look like a game of inverted basketball to aviators. —Pull in your stomach . . . Ah, you're doing your part as well as ever!"

Despite her shocking demolition of the family ship's only life-preserver in the very teeth of the last storm before a life of safe sailing the naked movements beneath her dishabille had been so irresistible that she was able to drop two or three ringers on the stake before it collapsed in autonomic alarm at her feral recklessness. "Oh poor dear!" she cried when she felt what had happened, removing herself and kneeling before him. "Poor poor Mr P. Well it's nice to see that he isnt always stuck-up and crusty! My little man's so delicate and tender after all, so sensitive to silly thoughts, so charmingly bashful for a change! Shall I put my head in his lap, shall I nurse Il Duce back to his fascism?" His uneasy and irresolute heart compassionate for what might have seemed to her the final disappointment he could not but thrill to her boldly generous attention, responding involuntarily to her hand and mouth. He did nothing but sit still with his arms resting stupidly on her shoulders as he cravenly submitted to sensual greed and grisly disillusion. Was the frustration of her highest womhope finally bifurcating her psyche? Or was it only bringing out a streak of bitterly mordant mockery to which she had never before resorted? [My God I've never heard her talk like this . . . How can she be talking at all while she's . . . ?] "If I were a man I'd love men. . . . I think I'd rather suck like a girl-baby . . . than fuck like a concubine. . . ." She lifted her eyes to his face in mirthless defiance. "Does this language from docile little Ruthie offend you to the soul? In vino veritas!" [Yes but it's not for me to frown upon this lip of madness what better moment for patience pure exquisite passivity now that she's given me my way in the largest matter wait and see just a few seconds longer listening as calmly as possible under the circum—oh Christ!—until the blood comes back to my head and I can think again I won't react until I know what should be done to pacify her maybe she's only making her prophesy of desertion or divorce. . . .] He was stonied by the new skill of ministrations that kept silence for protracted intervals between her halting salivary words and bewildered his weird fears. "I'll probably do a lot more of this from now on if you like. By then I'd have nothing to lose." Drawing back to estimate her success she passed the back of a hand across her lathered lips with pensive gusto like a connoisseur of beer, and then resumed her task. "I protest sir, now you're a fair something to lie between a lady's legs. . . . I'll wager you're thinking of country matters . . . thinking of Hecuba! But what's Hecuba . . . to an intellectual like you? . . . of Lilian! But she's meant for Caleb. . . . Better you think of Elizabeth . . . the love of your life! . . . . An American scholar can love an English dancer. . . . Or think of

the pretty girl Roger liked on the streetcar today. . . . But of course you
can always count on your housekeeper to relieve Old Hairless. . . .

> Ruthie is a friend of mine . . .
> She will do it any time . . .
> For a nickel or a dime . . .

Did they sing that one in Gloucester? . . . Goodness gracious just think of
all the experiments we can conduct from now on! . . . Nothing we do will
make any difference! . . . There, the clock's drawn nigh midnight again!
. . . Who is like God? Why Michael is like God! . . . He giveth and he
taketh. . . . away! . . . and I adore him!" The sensualist could hardly take
in these cheeky words as deranged or sarcastic at the time they were
uttered in such contrast to her tender eroticism. She knew what she was
doing and she was inhibited neither by his all-but-inert dumbness nor by
the glaring light of their privacy. Her salutations and invocations almost
seemed playful or reasonable. ". . . now that I can't have lovers without the
risk of giving myself away."

It had seemed to him that in such moods it was only natural that
she'd be glad to get rid of the fabric nuisance which must have insulated
some level of her consciousness as well as his own from the natural love
they made but here and now she was exposing her restored idol to cool
inspection in the open air as her curious fingers traced the deferent connections between the fecund twins and the bulbed roots of his monolithic
expostulater and with curling tongue in hollowed jaws slowly engorging
herself to the limit of cincturing lips with the ego-pronoun directed by
both her hands summoning to the base of that pylon the faint slow pulsations that always presaged his ultimate loss of will yet as if she wanted
him to have something to remember the jazz by that was still resounding
in his brain she gracefully withdrew to catch a breath and free her
vocal cords in order to murmur words that continued to amaze him.
"Omphallus or Not-omphallus, the object of my meditation!" In spite of
himself he chuckled at this interruption of her obeisance and his amusement which was prolonged by a nervous cough sidetracked the almost
irresistible train of epididymal vibrations that augured male abandonment. Yet neither Terpsichore nor Thalia nor Euterpe nor Erato but some
annectent and unpersonified daughter of Thunderbolt and Memory
seemed still to inspire this succubus and he was again losing his distance
when she left off abruptly, baring his grotesquely sanguine nakedness to
the chill of white light. He opened his eyes and found the jazz gone with
his blindness leaving a faint hum of white noise. "There that's enough
cocktail appetizer! I've almost gone too far. I refuse to be a fullblown
wastrel!" He sighed at the disappointmant as she suddenly gave him a
peculiar smile that he'd never seen before and responded harshly "I'll

give you something to groan about! There's a much better way to take the edge off you." With downcast eyes but grace too swift to parry she rose from her knees and opening to the unicorn carefully fitted herself to rest on his thighs without stirrups flinging her arms around his neck with a wild laugh ending in tears that wrung his heart with pity and love the sanction to yield up the treacherous blob of quicksilver that he had hoped to govern. Giving way with a capitulatory moan he prayed for improbability.

"That groan's good enough for us both." she declared too promptly even as he quivered.

In flat sorrowful anger at he knew not whom he made great effort of imaginative commiseration for a state with which he was no longer sympathetic. Simply in the lesser vanity of making sure she didnt think he failed to understand the plight he presumably had left her in he forced himself to voice the apology she undoubtedly sensed.

"I'm sorry. It was too good. I need more practice at this way of doing it."

But she was smiling at her ingestion when he opened his eyes. She kissed him fondly on the brow. "Not at all." she assured him without a single false note in her tactful assumption of gaiety. "Thanks for not warding me off. I won't count the sperm. I meant to be short about it. I was ravishing you. I wanted to see if I could still dominate my first lover. It felt so good I'm afraid I was shameless." She smoothed the hair on his forehead and dropped her eyelashes. "Anyway you were too puffed up with rooster-pride. I thought you needed a prefrontal phlebotomy."

In the sad aftermath of unrequited yet vitally dangerous coitus the life had gone out of him and he had fallen too stupid to appreciate her multiphasic witticism. But again she wept in his arms and in part he understood her own apology for winning at least the first game of her despair. At the moment to was too confused and exhausted to care very much about whether or not she had foiled his grand strategy with a calculated trick. It began to worry him that she might be looking with second thoughts at the paper lying on the table behind his back well within her reach. If she should now play Indian-giver it would take him ten years to get her signature on its like.

"Dear good man!" she said kindly taking his head in her hands and kissing him on the mouth with her old tenderness. Then the pursed pressure on his lips slackened; her mouth opened to encircle his and her tongue flicked against his teeth to communicate without words that it was nothing for him to be sorry for if she had not shared his mystical quaking and that she was happy enough just to have had the more essential chance that might be her last.

But he could only smile wanly in wry gratitude for the way she was willing to put pleasure behind her with apparently unflagging respect. She rested her forehead on his chest as she clung to his thick inert body. His face drooped above her sweet scalp. Without looking at him she began to stroke his hair absently, faintly rocking on equestrian hips. He suspected her of hoarding and working the viscid juice trapped between them, but since it was not a gaseous substance he prayed that gravity would save him. For a long time she chose not to dismount.

"Men have always treated women the way I've just treated you." she said with an ambivalent and ambiguous laugh. He could feel her mirth where she had felt his chuckles a few minutes earlier. "You take your fill and walk away. But I'm not going to walk away. I like it too well right where I am. I like this better than being dropped like a newspaper. Besides, I don't think any number of sneezes can take the place of a single baby. They arent necessary at all."

She had made a diplomatic error of which she wasnt aware. He resolved to ignore it as merely superstitiously offensive, for the damage if any was already done—and if it was not he didnt doubt that he could make her eat those words on the next occasion for ecstasy. If only there were some way by such a pass to leech her of those sly cryptic hysterics! But now his energy was spent like the gunpowder of a used-up firecracker and truth to tell he was left without the erotic interest to worry about much how she suffered the slow grumpy reflux of her unadvised assault and still less to offer the mechanical strum of a listless hand (especially as he knew she would reject such obscenely tactile assuagement in her spar-kling Dutch kitchen inspected by the stars or interrupted by the passage of a boy on his way to the bathroom). [Let mercy prevail over justice at her expense this one last time I'm so fucking tired right at this moment though maybe after a while in bed . . .]

The whole mass of a dense day's fatigue weighed heavily upon his eye-lids as he heard her out. He was too enervated and ashamed to take in all the meaning of her oddly persistent and indefatigable speech which at any other juncture would have excited or terrified him with its novelty.

She was reciting lines learned from her mother:

"Women must work and women must weep,
And the sooner it's over the sooner to sleep."

The hangdog husband silently bore a spate of pitying kisses all over his face. "If I had twenty lovers I'd always give you first choice. Surely you believe I'll always be faithful to you as long as we're married?" Right now he thought he wasnt especially interested in her loyalty one way or the other: sleep was all he wanted. Let the devil take all those wearisome emo-tions and the women that caused them. [Why does she keep harping on that theme? I'd rather be a monk.] She seemed to be rambling however. "When I was about six years old I wrote a poem that I remember because my mother saved it even though she didnt like it:

Headless or toeless—
That's the thing to be:
Toeless so your shoes will fit;
Headless, not to see."

All asperity was gone from her melancholy meanings.

The warmth and pressure of her body was not irksome but he now found the jurisprudence of love repugnant as a field of study. [If you can love a stray mongrel the rest of its life you can certainly tolerate marriage.] As for his kids, it was only their degree of consanguinity that he was now indifferent to: his love of Roger was in no way altered. As far as their mother was concerned on the other hand he could hardly believe that there had been a time when prancing like a two-headed centaur balanced on its hind legs he'd carried her to bed riveted to him in her present position save that her feet were locked behind his back to keep every inch of her purchase. [Copulations actually get you nowhere unless you're breeding they begin and end at the same place over and over again an endless squirrelcage-chase even for Apollo and Zeus too was no wiser than I or any other sailor for how can a god always be so tantalized even when he's already spitted every variety of quail a hundred times over in heaven and on earth and what difference does it make if one cunicula is a little snugger or wiggles better than another the outcome's always the same for him Prometheus made fire by rubbing two sticks together but fire is always the same conflagration any Dick and Jane can make it. . . .]

There was also no outcome to radio music when you got right down to it; it was tireless to be sure he thought but it too got you nowhere. To mask rustlings murmurs sighs and the creaking of a chair it had been turned low for familiar background noise to ears asleep on the porch. For a few minutes the idle partners sat out the end a set listening for the first time in attentive repose to hushed stomping tuckets and velvet snarling blues with brassy sackbuts and black voices on ivory. Michael comprehended it not. During all the years that jazz had been infiltrating national culture by railroad and talking machine the Cambridge public schools were still teaching solmization to the tune of a hickory stick. Now listening to sounds-an-sich almost for the first time since the Okinawa typhoon everything represented by words seemed to fade from his mind and he heard without metaphor the neural details of a moral leisure that he could never know directly. The foundling fathers of American music seemed to mock him with a Schopenhauerian polity of pure narrow will at greater depth than the unlimited individuality of his mental life afloat and partly beyond his desires. As if a European though not so docile he allowed himself to be fascinated for a time by native improvisations which still could not wholly absorb him but which now were strangely tuned to the middling passions that his present state of blue helped him realize were more reflected in the night-club art of black American men than in the stage art of white American women. In its presentational immediacy this music— resistant to sentimentality and resistant to politics as it was resistant to discourse—was for Michael in his immediate present the one true art to induce an authentic aesthetic for his countrymen in common. Yet the Unamerican puritan's innermost rational soul (his lap drenched with the lees of desire) still protested its demotic dilution and degradation by the show business that made it ubiquitous for every lazy lout with less than no exercise of spirit simply by the twist of a knob.

Perhaps the housewife clinging to him like one rag doll sprawled upon another was less conscious of the music's world-historical sociophilosophical significance but however great the discrepancy between her wakefulness and his somnolence the Palm-Sunday-night blues tended to equalize their states. All their frets and preoccupations (including love and aspirations and every sense of responsibility for accumulated or engendered possessions) gradually dissolved or retreated under the influence of black and white players and singers in San Francisco Los Angeles New Orleans St Louis Chicago Pittsburgh New York or even Boston where the actual beating plucking and blowing had originated for the most part in a semicircle of hollows and strings struck or scratched or daubed or blown with fingers sticks brushes bows or epiglottal reeds, their syncopated rhythms anchoring the vagile melodies of instruments crying out for the liberty of locomotion.

Recovering from the private disappointment of her secondary desire and for the nonce putting behind her the remaining frustration of her maternal life Ruth rose to turn off the radio and leave him in the cold dispirited shipwreck of detumescence. Feeling felt less like a stallion than a sweated chaise-horse left standing naked in a chill when the thills are rolled back he opened his eyes to catch her disappearance only to be shocked by the dazzle of her tidy kitchen. Covering his legs with the skirt of his robe he staggered to his feet picked up his spectacles and clutched the paper that might yet compensate him for a wasted day. He feared that her attention would be drawn by the sound of him unlocking and relocking the front door and the door to his study across the hall, sealing his heartless intention and reminding her of his matrimonial mistrust. Still stunned by the descent of silent solitude he knotted his sash and took the key from his pocket. As he turned off the kitchen light he noticed the cat stretched out in luxurious slumber on a laundry pile just inside the other room, a streak of no color against all the colors. Semiramis had long since deserted Jonathan's bed slipped behind them through the porch door and sneaked past the lovers! She trilled a cordial greeting at his touch when he interrupted her dreams, stretching six more inches and twisting on her back to smile at him upside down, renewing the purr of security. He repented any thought he might have entertained about starting the new discipline a day early and left her in peace for the night. The stillness set in more slowly than the music had ceased, much more slowly than the blinding darkness that commenced when the final light was out. He groped the way to and from his safe-deposit vault on his way to the master bedroom but began to see well enough by the cityscapes's diffused nightlight.

He had hoped that Ruth would be asleep. She was not. How could she be? With her naked back to his side of the bed she was crying so softly that at first he didnt recognize the sound. In order to avoid any further tokens of disparity he too got under the covers without his pajamas. The quiet tears immediately ceased and she turned half way in his direction. They lay on their backs side by side with their arms touching from shoulder to hand. No need to ask wherefore she had wept. But she surprised him with an apology: "I do believe I'm drunk." she whispered. Then in silence they pondered each other and their acts upon each other.

Without desire in a penitent renewal of tenderness he tried to remember what desire was like, wondering how to make a gesture of second try without actually doing his duty to the occasion. [But maybe she's reading my mind. . . .] He touched more of her bare skin with the edge of his limply straightened arm. At the same time he was very sleepy. Yet it was only now that full silence settled to his brain from their evening's entertainment as a deprivation of stimulus that stimulated its purely passive sensorium as the room was growing more visible to his dilating eyes. Just then as if to ally themselves with self-willed body against self-willed mind the distant bells pacifically proclaimed the time for sleep at which even the silence of music must cease, when two working people must dismiss all jazz absolve all absolvable inequity between them and reconcile themselves to inevitable and eternal mismatch of cerebral neurons like the carillons of Paris that first signalled Panurge to get married so that all would be well and then just the opposite.

Ruth lay her head on his chest. He encircled her back with his arm, savoring a single long stroke of sensuous pity and admiration before he rested his open palm on her marble-smooth hip. They each shifted slightly to snuggle her down for sleep if it should come before the other god returned. The husband's body was still inert but in sympathy with the affectionate attitude of hers he had already begun to swing round at anchor to follow the lunar tide's current counter to the stream of consciousness. He weighed an incipient rejuvenation of desire against the long odds of fecundation, calmly wondering what the odds were within those odds for generating a dancer of his own to electrify the stage a few years before he'd be eligible for Social Security.

But as he awaited the choice of fate he was unable to dwell upon causality's probabilities, for a miscellany of scenes and images more vivid and consequential than those of dreams made a strange procession across the well-rubbed tabula rasa he was supposed to be in charge of. They searched or were searched by a host of captions whenever ideas or details were called for, starting with his telephone call first thing tomorrow to make an appointment with Dr. Stone. [Yes I'd like to get the family jewels disconnected right away this week before Easter telling the girl at his office I may have to go on a business trip or some such story seeing that I can't very well plead the exigencies of my incontinent susceptibility to a wife's seasons who has burned our bridges because she hates birth control even Spy Wednesday would be none too soon lest the business drag out into next month considering all the temptation I'll be subjected to before the old fertilizer works its way out of my network and I get my lifetime pass though I pay the costs of her monthly depressions each as bad as her old postpartums finally to be dubbed a regular Knight of the Garter serving a lady covened to her sacrifice who'll wear a bloody martingale thirteen times in every year as long as that minor curse may last and cheap at the price much as I abhor that ticture of Eve's punishment though it may look no different from the blood of a bull an instinctive repugnance no more sane than my zero-boned frisson at the presence of snakes likewise harmless unless they turn out to be the ones that slither out of dead women's backbones to reincarnate putrefying mortality the only unconditional retribution of God or vipers like Riolama's pet or even benign pythons like the phantom that Athene's priestesses never saw that guarded the Long Rocks at night with the sacred owls for its lookouts in return for a few honey-cakes and no more hostile than the kind forbidding my path in Dogtown a black sine-wave streaked with gold soundlessly flashing its fated symbolism in and out of sight but sensing from end to end with its whole antenna my absolutely minimum thermal vibrations as I turned to a pillar of salt infinitely more sensitive than I was when I put one ear to the rail near Old Stone Bridge trying to hear trains coming five miles away around the curves from Rockport or in principle all the other way out here to California without ever detecting anything I could be sure wasnt the singing heat the blood rustling in my head or my own heart pounding with fear that a huge black engine would rush out of nowhere while my neck was on the steel block or Panurge listening for the watch through the blade of his sword pointed into the cobblestones of Paris, soundlessly that is except for the inaudible hiss of air from tiny tubular lungs that must be as hard to locate as the heart or liver or genitalia if you had the guts to autopsy him (though of course not nearly as difficult as determining when the humanity of a zygote begins) whereas I can easily see that a dog's heart beats at the center when he's lying with lifted head and hindquarters folded or where the vital organ's hidden when a wife's on her side with legs drawn up to sleep through a winter of hopelessness abetted by the curse of even the B V M inherited from Eve or Pandora which even Athene Artemis and Britomartemis the original Lady of the Lake must have suffered seeing that most of the other goddesses submitted to reproduction which can't be done without disturbing an unsyncopated rhythm that oozes menos lest it build up unladylike pressure to dominate the secondary sex but of which young girls anticipate the advent as thrilling proof of nubility though it may bar them from cage jobs at a zoo or work at the altar yet even venomous snakes as predestined enemies of mankind are sometimes benignly taboo especially the king cobra that eats smaller cobras as the evolutionary acme of hairless featherless creeping things detached double-ended linear specialists in terror headed by a lethal glans colubris perfectly adapted for orgastic injections who labor the peristalsis of childbirth in reverse gradually reducing full-length live prey from a large organism to its simplest constituent cells by squeezing in instead of squeezing out yet are themselves prolific of enormously multiple spit-and-images of wriggling spermatazoa though I doubt that for women and dreaming children their putative subliminal symbolism fits in with the masculine love of culverins and hand-guns except to the same degree as all elongated cylindrical shapes solid or tubular that cannot flit smoothly into obscured holes apparently too small even when exposed and do not suggest some basically unstable form of matter but it's curious that a hectoring husband thinks his Achilles heel is the fraity of his wife's fidelity as always susceptible to the serpent's hissing intelligence that poisons men's law which is the only thing that keeps her chaste in the face of nature and justice to the contrary and that a man who fails to bruise those diabolical heads is liable to incapacitation like Philoctetes a great archer who prized his own poisoned arrows before he was stung by one of them just as in some such fashion I may be tempting providence with this presumptuous surgery of mine for one way or another I'm going to have to make it worth her while to forego the fulfillment of her longing for female immortality so different from my kind since she's too wise not to see that a virtuous married woman who doesnt keep having children or at least one daughter can't have much hope for intensity of feministicism after the illusory years are past if she's older than her husband she may not remain the first choice of his cravings and if she's younger he'll soon be unable to match a tenth part of hers unless she's unlucky enough to have an ageless satyr with nothing else to cultivate although I doubt that Silenus himself if he were sober and wide awake every night of the year with an inexhaustible magazine of Quaker cartridges could persuade Ruth that the greatest good for her daughter is not to be at all which seems at least as true as ever for almost everybody who nowadays exists without implying that early death is the second best instead of maximum longevity even if she'd never heard that he can't distinguish truth from falsehood having been involved in the original theater but I confess I'm stirred at the thought of a married woman who isnt chaste and the devil take me if the thought of the thought isnt making her desirable again even before Mr P an unimaginative and fatuous cocknomen that sacrament never allows out of the family is arising from his coma judging by the fact that I'm only just beginning to resume feeling below my belly which goes to show you that mind and body are sometimes separate all my theories to the contrary notwithstanding for instance when you're stricken with a physical affliction you say I have a misfortune to bear and you havent any doubt that it's the first per-

son singular who's thwarted or aggrieved but when you're short of mental
capacity or positively daft you don't feel blocked or deprived by anything
in yourself and you don't say that your prick for example is unfortunate to
be served by a defective consciousness because the I knows no other possibility of I just as the souls frustrated by contraception have nothing to
complain with so I wouldnt be surprised if this duality turned out to be a
key to the investigation both of true intelligence as opposed to alacrity in
learning and of the various neuroses as opposed to psychosis calling into
question whether a person of slow wit or irrational fears is aware of wanting genius or salubrity unlike healthy geniuses who are unaware of others'
pigshit labor and S M D C would be just the thing for such research if the
statistics were available that nobody collects but right now I'm inclining
toward memories and hopes that will bring on the desire to penetrate that
mystery of hers with the I of my head generally held to be more worshipful albeit less fascinating than the pompous spermatic I whose pricking
power has been temporarily betrayed by his own nervous greediness
though in our joint attraction his and mine to this dark lady he usually
leads me by the flying-jib-boom so far down at the bow from the sheer
weight of all that blood out of balance that I feel like Dionysos they called
the lame god for the same reason but this time I'll steal a march on the
shriveled coward grossly sated and still half oblivious of the poor
Mrs sublimating or smouldering as close to him as I am maybe by courting with lambent tongue his shy rival the prickless thorn he overlooks or
underrates in his headlong depredations because sometimes it's the best
way to get flames from cold lava which are sometimes harder to ignite
than to quicken new life by mistake either in holy joy or in wretched haste
not quite what is meant by accident of birth an absurd phrase for what's
really accidental only if devices to oppose it were defective but the fundamental contingency of happening upon a mate is almost as accidental as
my deep love for the dogs that happened to fall into my possession as
strays or gifts amid a life of great world-historical interests though they
numbered no more than girlfriends and now except for the last I could
hardly list them by breed or shape not to mention personal distinction
despite having wept at their deaths and it may be the same when you've
had a series of wives more like dogs than children in the fortuity of special
relationship since the affiliation of offspring is a necessity determined by
the aforesaid accident plus a little free will whether or not said affiliation
is truly understood by the putative male party to the accident whose
fatherhood may be legal but geneless then too even when there's no overlap of accidents dogs and women can attach themselves to a succession of
masters each perfectly willing to assume that the others if he knows of
them at all were or will be loved by his present beloved simply according
to a different accident of destiny insofar as everyone seeking a mate is
likely to be loved desired admired served or protected by someone of the
complementary sex even if it's anyone at all and tonight that's about as

much as I care to ponder the relative mysteries of a man's love for the creatures that depend on him as distinguished from his charity for all mankind
and for most other mammalian species or for the children of others who
arent insolent or spoiled chiefly my own dear brother and sister as I remember for instance the night after Handy was killed on Grove Street when Billy
woke himself up crying and couldnt be comforted until he was taken into
bed with Ma and the old man but he seemed to have no idea that his infinite
sorrow and pity had anything to do with the puppy and I don't think it
occurred to me either at the time having already practically forgotten the
accident so easily did the house return to equilibrium but Peggy who hadnt
even been home when it happened wailed in private all the rest of the day
and wouldnt eat supper or yet have anything to do with the burial and afterwards reproached me for not putting him in a box since I'd used only a piece
of old green curtain for cerecloth which she said would rot too fast and she
wouldnt even look at the grave when anybody was around while to me the
manner of interment was entirely insignificant just as adultery seemed
insignificant when I was older but not old enough before I had enough experience to discover in spite of myself what many of the enduring conventions
are founded on namely just such customs as totem funerals and family fidelity which defend rather than constrain your nutshell freedom yet important
events of the past don't come to my mind's eye as clearly as random and
unbidden flickers of memory like my feelings about that great patinaed
wide-mouthed bell emplaced like a howitzer in earthworks at the foot of the
knoll on which the winding-staired tower of crenellated granite in Mount
Auburn Cemetery later used for wartime skywatching dominated the
Charles River basin because its mournfully terrifying notes at the end of the
day had to be obeyed if we werent to be locked all night inside the iron palisades of God's most arboreal and horticultured acre with the ghosts among
others of respectable cisatlantic Chapmans who flourished as franklins before
our proletarian decline or about the dusty obsolete anvil that used to be
stored in the corner behind my punchpress or the entirely undistinguished
curb at the corner of 23rd and B'way that I trod no more often than scores of
other berms going to and from the shop but is still as unaccountably vivid
and intimate to me as the Vanderbilt pavement hard by Grand Central
where I rarely walked and never awaited a cab albeit the kind of privilege
I've always felt I was born for and can still visualize the castiron storm-sewer
grating and dirty Cape Ann granite cobblestones a few steps from the usual
station of the legless pencil vendor on his padded square caster board probably the very spot in Manhattan where they say a beached old salt once stood
and turned a crank to churn up waves in his glass case making a schooner
bob up and down for landlubbers as he held out a tin cup that maybe St
Herman himself once dropped an ill-gotten bureaucratic copper into before
he was pensioned off. . . .]

Lo, Ruth was asleep, half cradled in his arms! He was excused from
any further effort and he was soon snoring with open piscine mouth.

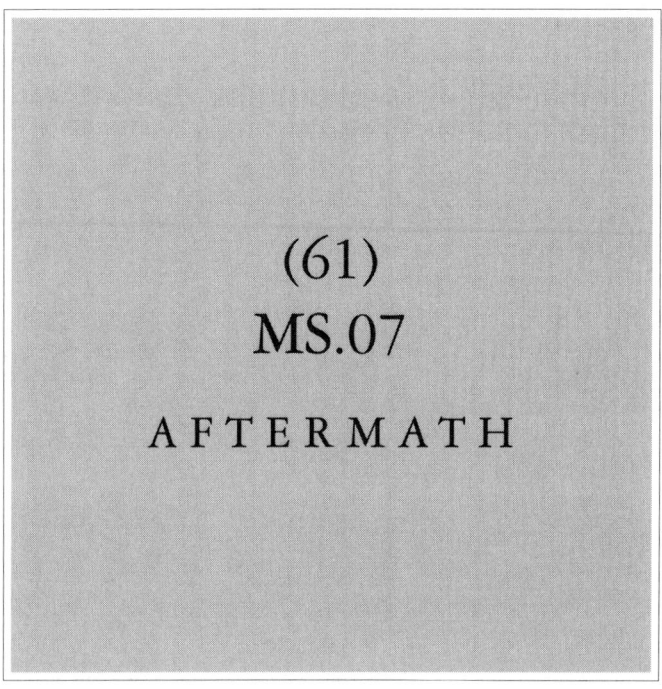

(61)
MS.07

AFTERMATH

Exegesis & Continuation of Preceeding Items

(Unlike simpler strivings against entropy a personal integer must recognize its own unjust tendency to disorder the life around it. By pausing or slowing down (short of death) it should give the human plants within its immediate circle a chance to love. Otherwise the selfish organism may banish itself from its immediate society and suffer its own starvation for reasons of its own making at the only place in which it can act. Indeed in Michael Chapman's situation a steady state for the family as a whole was necessary to prevent his degradation and eventual disintegration.

One cannot be sure whether or not he had to douse his freewill in order to obey this necessity, but take note that his future probabilities did not necessarily depend upon the answer to this question, for the will is not incapable of being resurrected by the mind. In principle at any rate it is almost never too late to act somewhat at will. After I've put this hermeneutic aftermath before you as part of the story outside the story estimate for yourself the prospects of his story within the story.

It's only in the interest of familiar simplicity that Michael Chapman's losing struggle to irrationalize the Pythagorean triangle (which perhaps he should have been satisfied to lock himself into) by increasing toward unity its already parlous sine-ratio has been treated with conventional Euclidean notation. If one had not chosen this dynamic standpoint of perspective Michael might have been imagined facing his pragmatical pig of a hypotenuse from the fixed right-angle that has no trigonometric functions and doesn't measure change or compromise. Then with the left arm of domesticity and the unequal right of vocation he would have been seen subtending his larger economic life. In his own mind of baneful abstractions the trigeometrical notion of a radius vector was generalized to represent a man's directed distance from his origin viewed as an arrow defining the rectangle whose dimensions are equal only in a special case. At least this Cartesian scheme was his basic device for drawing whole decision trees and conflict thickets. After all he might have said (quoting Yeats) "No mind can engender till divided into two." He'd have pointed out that even a mindless plebeian who did not love pelf was tormented by tension between the ceaseless urge to get and spend his love and the ceaseless responsibility to get and spend his living. Hence the willful mind's need for triangulation.

Of course an engendering mind that's concerned with specification beyond the two-dimensional continuum can also move out on a third rectilinear axis and describe a tetrahedron. That spatial structure is even less likely than one of its faces to turn out isosceles, but it adds another perpendicular reach of variable measure. Of course it's no more than Chapmanically natural in this geometry to introduce denser spaces with the imagination of serial dimensionality, starting with a fourth orthogonal axis to represent immediate time and advancing in principle all the way to an $(n - 4)$th metasystem of time beyond the time of the plane—or to an nth dimension of attributes. The psyche might locate and confront a point of intersecting variable dimensions in hyperspace that defines a corner virtually opposed to the origin like a True Mask. A worker's direction is determined not by the way he hangs his face but by the arms of his cross. Obviously a Chapbook of such language would forfeit any claim to a common reader's interest if it adopted a hyperpolyhedral right-angle for the point of view of an American thinking. One can merely hint at what Michael would do with a rectotetrahedract if it ever served his purpose.

But in the present work one must keep both number and diagram within the overlapping Venn bounds of English, the most comprehensive but least efficient of the three languages used by professionals and laymen of land sea and air, and apply analytical geometry in ambiguous or imprecise words. Perhaps it would have been better to follow Gulliver's precedent who got Swift off the hook by promising a separate scientific treatise to explain everything about Lilliput that wasnt clear from the Travels, or Shandy's who mentioned a map of the midwife's locus that was to be appended to his last volume. Even the core of this story, correlative of the simplest plane figure, can't be understood without recourse to at least the first in a regressive series of metasystems that afford the ontological perspective for regarding this scheme as a demonstration of Gödel's Proof.

But there's no need to see much more of Chapman's space or time, to say nothing of Mrs Chapman's. Otherwise you might have been faced with a discourse on cosmogony. Nor is there any further use at present for the fiction that finally began to free itself of his opsimathematical essays; in any case its integrity and vitality are called in question by the later history adumbrated in this codicil. As it is you're very lucky in your accidents of education and experience if you have been able to grasp all the adversaria that have been shown passing through this abstractor's mind. (Certainly his songless words could not have done justice to your aesthetic knowledge of the botanical and ornithological phenomena assumed in the belletristic tradition, or of mysticism, or of music, or even of the latest American idioms; but it is to be hoped you'll agree that the want of beauty grace and pungency were your gain in appreciating the leisure of which he deprived himself. Also for this if for no other reason the mystery of consciousness has not been evaded by easier recourse to the common unconscious.) But it's more important simply to get the idea that howsoever he might have cut his cloth or staked his topological claim the hypotenuse would always have exceeded the other two sides. To that end a discriminating reader may consult the Index hereinafter to find out what she can skip without accusing herself of literary laziness.

Maybe it should be explained why one has been obliged to indite more technical matter than may be welcome to eyes well versed in the arts. In Conrad's words: "Man is a worker, or he is nothing." (Who also speaks of "the intellectual destitution of mankind".) Now as the Spielman before you is really something to behold he should be known at least by his labor! As you now know he is more of a worker than a feeler. Still, by way of concession to demotic prejudice, in representing his work the actual proportion of real-time economic life has been nearly inverted in proportion to his homework because for the most part it's repetitive and low-grade. Within the exposition of his livelihood disproportionate space has been given to his thoughts about enriching it. By the same token, at the risk of tedium, raw chunks of his secondary vocational production have been delivered with little reduction of relative weight since his private work is accounted somewhat more interesting—if only because it's always in progress.

But the gentle reader will have perceived that difficulty (or rather estrangement) has arisen from something more than subject matter. The other reason that you couldnt be expected to understand everything that Chapman has pondered is formal. It was intended that the matter conveyed—as much of it as could be understood well enough to be chosen for presentation—be broadly intelligible not only to yourself and to what's left of posterity (which will be educated to an entertainment jargon that makes you as archaic as I am and will care no more for our topical styles than you do for J F Cooper's) but also to saints of past ages who foretold nothing at all of our times except through indifferently relevant hopes or fears. It would be easier if we had the common convenience of an English metalanguage universal in time as well as technological philosophical and laic.

In default of universal highest education the elementary ancient trigeometry (which was once esoteric), though also the infinitesimal of modern calculus, seems a godsend for the middle world of consciousness. By its means all diagrams can be constructed or broken up, binary decimal and duodecimal thoughts analogized, the circle triangulated, the square circled. Also ritual and history reconciled; physics and biology; mechanics and electricity; Yeats and Whitehead. For with dynamic scalene right-triangles or their polar vectors (including not only our special and transitory case but also the isosceles and the most versatile module of all called by Plato the most beautiful, the one that makes the equilateral when doubled enantiomorphically) you can generate or trace through time:

—circles shrinking to points or opening into gyres (whence also all conic sections) and inclined planes wrapping into helixes;
—Uncle Toby's pyroballogy;
—the spiral growth of the chambered nautilus;
—the fascinating magnitude and hyponastic pitch (or celestial angle) of ithyphallic postures;
—the bisected triangle (in vivo strictly speaking closer to a clefted spherical triangle) found at the fork of two legs in every other enumeration of the census;
—the erotic equity in a heterosexual group of three;
—neckerchiefs for sailors, and gores sewn into their regulation trousers to make them bell-bottomed; with suitable truncations and alterations, the sails rigging and keel of a schooner;
—keystones and trusses for bridges and buildings; tripod milking stools (stable on the roughest platforms);
—intervals of eccentricity for crankshafts (especially in 6-cylinder engines);
—with some curvature and Irish pennants, the wye of a railroad (by which a locomotive can be reversed or redirected from any of three approaches without a turntable);
—equilateral three-phase electrical power, in the parlance of which a Delta circuit (cf the Trinity enclosed within its three aspects) is analogous to the railroad Y and a Y-called system controls the cunning synchromechanisms used in all sorts of radar-directed analogical fire-control systems for beautifully complicated ships as well as in the commonplace gyro repeaters of such cheap vessels as L S T s;
—sweep-circuit voltage for laboratory oscilloscopes radar screens and television sets;
—alternating current phases in terms of imaginary and complex numbers;
—the irregular non-reciprocating angular rotations of baseball, an abrupt open-timed azimuth game played in one quadrant of a ritual circle irregularly radiated but centered at home;
—Hegelian dialectics . . .

Or at least a biographical theory of trivalent alternation has been suggested by Chapman's sequential manipulation of trialectic tensions up to the middle of his thirty-fourth year. Naturally his self-management leaves something to be desired even when smoothed out by the course of time. You have been shown some of his confusions and failures as well as his plodding methodical contest with determinism though too weak of will to control well enough the depth or duration of each several occupation, to exclude the others entirely, or to escape tripled distraction when it's least wanted. This negative demonstration of trivalence seems to prove the necessity of imperfection wherever ambivalence and ambiguity are oversimplifications.

Among Chapman's unnecessarily disorderly affections have been certain excessive but not uncommon appetites and culpabilities. Obviously his most exceptional hunger is for theory, a mania that feasts on fresh knowledge. He attributes this vice to having been born under the old Chinese curse: "May you live in interesting times." A fault that requires no further mention. As to his guilts, they divide into major species: those incidental to inadequacy either inherited or involuntarily acquired, which earn him no distinction; and those accrued at will, advisedly or illadvisedly, either easily or at great pains, for which perhaps he deserves nearly as much praise as blame.

Perhaps your reprehension should be reserved for two faults that you are now in a position to judge.

First, he was too proud of himself, or too lonely, to conceal his intelligence and remain as silent as a black operator ought. He was not loathe to arouse wonder among those few whose attention was drawn to him—despite the fact that his best talent was the owlish gift of avoiding attention. Indeed he was secretive enough with his employer; Valentine Greatrakes was never allowed to suspect his disreputable motivation. But he talked too much outside the store and away from home. Semi-public pundification bled his private energy and spilled his private time. He wasted as much speech as semen. Yet at least he was sensible of remorse for his profligacy, like Dostoyevsky after every bout of gambling.

But he had less notion of his second more essential guilt in the vocational work of his life—worse than his weak resistance to Jack Wolfson's scholarly imagicnation: his jealousy of Caleb Karcist's youth liberty and expectations. Too often, whether Caleb sits moaning before him with nothing important to complain about or actually laughs indelicately at the difference between their estates, he suffers Caleb to taunt his mask of authoritative self-possession by drawing a comb through his ostensibly unruffled feathers in the wrong direction. Though to be freer than Caleb and of fewer winters would be a lessening of his actual self (as a golden egg is lesser than the goose that lays it) he was sometimes tormented by the young gander's patronizing preconsciousness of a famous career.

However, in spite of his own imperfections frailties vanities vicissitudes envy and sporadic malice, Chapman has labored to sustain that unspent little hero's resistance to imprisonment and contamination; he generously warns against squandering the arrows of error that he himself has misspent; never with more hope did Pandarus plot the success of Troilus's lustful fancy (though maybe it's more like the ghost of some bumpkin advising a troubadour in affairs of love). But his precepts have been abstract and fleshless; they have arisen very little from memory of experience and very much from regret for lost opportunity. "A ghost without a human past!" he mourns to himself when in the depths of self-contempt. Even after *he has set Caleb Karcist to work Michael Chapman is less peaceful than a spectre that rues its day.)*

1.

. . . life is not lived, if not lived for contemplation or excitement.

—Yeats

From an indefinite distance it had always seemed to Michael that quitting his job would be the most delicious moment of his hypotenuse. If the time to make the move had never actually arrived he would have continued to savor it over and over again in endlessly varied rehearsals that even the people who knew him best never suspected. In his exquisite cinema of the climactic scene he was to carry off a spasm of revenge with polite contempt for the owner's fatuous power over such an insignificant outfit. Suddenly revealing his true vocation yet omitting no dignified hint to Prince Valiant that the galley was losing a pilot beyond price, he would at last indulge sweet displays of emancipation. It goes without saying that he should have known that it wouldnt be that way at all.

Actually he had nothing to crow about except another job with a triflingly greater salary and a totally unpretentious clientele. He anxiously omitted revelation of what and where it would be lest his master Valentine Greatrakes go out of his way to spoil the connection in retaliation for his sudden disloyalty and leave him with no job at all. He had already sweated through many days of worry that the prospective employer would make inquiries of the present employer despite all assurances to the contrary. These unfounded fears reflected his inexperience in any business beyond the shadow of Sather Gate, which he was about to break out of with the trepidation of an apostate nun. It was not easy to break the spell of high culture and make a transition from the gentle trade to an alien industry. He was soon to laugh at all these doubts, but he wasnt laughing as he finally faced his dreaded deadline for giving notice.

When the week came he postponed the day; when the day came, the hour; and when the last hour came on Saturday afternoon—the best time to find the boss free of interruptions, free of busyness, free of irritable preoccupation with any more urgent matter than the resignation of his righthand man would be—he put it off until the last minute. In the meantime he had seized every opportunity to avoid being alone with Val. Having screwed up his courage a dozen times he repeatedly found himself absurdly cringing before the most remote contingencies of overwrought response, as if merely by miscalculating his manner of address he might bring down upon himself a future of vulnerable dispossession.

Would the master merchant lash out at him for betraying the store's investment in what was regarded as an expensive apprenticeship, angrily reproaching him for treachery or at the least ingratitude? Above all, would he refuse to pay him for his accrued vacation? If it hadnt been for that crucial card in Greatrakes's hand Chapman might have risked retribution or anyway a bad conscience by giving less than the customary two-weeks warning. It was wise to be polite, to court a good reference in case of unforseeable future need for yet another job. In order to obviate the slightest unpleasantness or even uneasiness both before and after he walked out the door for the last time he might well have preferred to give four weeks notice, but even if they hadnt wanted him as soon as possible on the new job (which was by no means high enough in the business scale to warrant an encumbent important enough for the new employer to believe that the former employer would be seriously inconvenienced in finding a replacement) he would have been afraid of Greatrakes firing him on the spot— much too soon—in a fit of pique, or angrily countering with his own two weeks notice—still too soon (maybe without vacation pay too)—leaving the disloyal lieutenant with two weeks less work than he'd counted on, indeed with a disastrous hiatus of income.

Or what was calculated to humiliate the good soldier more than any vindictiveness, would the prince far from being shocked at the prospect of losing his star assistant take the news with a cordial smile and wish him the best of luck, making no better than a polite effort to disguise the lift of his spirits at this unlookedfor lightening of the payroll—not even thinking to inquire about the defector's destination or official motive?

Such a cheerful reception of the blow would be all the more demeaning to the one who dealt it, seeing that the prevailing conditions of booming prosperity made hardworking help hard to find just when his own hopes for Bow's Ark's trade-book expansion seemed about to be gratified with an increase in space business machines floor staff and buying power thanks to Val's new bank loan. As it was he cast many a sigh in the pang of leaving all his works incomplete just as they were about to dazzle the local book market and earn the proprietor's generous recognition.

Then too he had been given pause by his liability to the boss's suspicion that he was trying to pull off an obvious tactic of extortion. Would Val take this announcement as an attempt to get a raise by threat, an implicit offer to bargain from a position of strength like an unscrupulous union agitator negotiating a socialistic featherbedding settlement without the foggiest promise of increased productivity? Exactly in what manner would he decline to answer Val's conceivable questions about how much more salary would induce him to stay on? Or showing no such interest would Val smile contemptuously at the implication that his assistant thought himself worth more money than he was already draining from the shop's precarious little bank account? The bitter irony was that the discontinuation of Val's most conspicuous controllable item of overhead expense would spur rather than jeopardize the approval of his impending loan from the local financiers whose wisdom in management was no more profound than their client's.

Despite his worldly mien among friends Michael had never quit a business job before. Every remote possibility was now ingenuously magnified. He did not understand that even a close small shopkeeper like Greatrakes who'd graduated into a league beyond the comfort of his previous experience (and who'd been buoyed during the whole period of success by his senior employee's apparently limitless devotion to the cause) knew that resignations like this were now taking place every day all over the Republican world: trusty workers suddenly quitting after ten years if they could better themselves anywhere in the land of opportunity or thought they could, sometimes on the verge of promotion. Even nervous twitchy blinking Valentine Greatrakes, already far over his head in the emotions of a tireless struggle for ruggedly individual success (Catholic though he was), had prepared himself to confront this unscheduled problem like a hardheaded businessman and not to bat a single eyelash more than he would have done at the quitting of a casual laborer.

On the other side however Chapman was saved by his dread from feeling the bitter disappointment of a satisfaction he had so long contemplated. In the event, instead of marshalling with the compendious cogency of cold anger all his complaints about the owner's interference, onerous responsibility without authority, poor pay, unpaid overtime, and generally short-sighted financial policy, he summoned not a single grievance. In fact, pleading nothing more vivid than a vague "better opportunity" (which he did not know to be the conventional term usually accepted without question), he made a clumsy attempt to comfort his former antagonist with suggestions of apology and gratitude. Furthermore he took care to make it clear at the outset of the short interview—Saturday being one night in the week when Greatrakes always tried to get home in time for social life—that he was definitely not joining the local competition. If he had saved that reassurance for the end he might have prolonged the busy businessman's interest in his silence about the nature of his new job.

"I've learned a lot from you Val. I'll never forget what you've done to help me get started. But I just want to try another kind of business where I can work my way up a little faster."

Greatrakes's moist blue eyes, as brightly delineated behind crystally clarifying lenses as a Maurine user's, blinked as usual nineteen to the dozen, shifting abstractedly from one point to another as he jingled his keys and toed the baseboard of the counter.

"Well I'm sorry to see you go Mike. I think you have an aptitude for the book business. But I know you're ambitious. I won't stand in your way. A man like you doesnt make this kind of decision without giving it a lot of thought. You've got your reasons. I won't try to talk you out of it. . . . Of course I could offer you a little more money if I thought that's all it was, but you're taking a long-range view as you see it I guess and that's good, that's what you should do for yourself. I *was* hoping you'd be with me as the store expands. You could have been making five thousand a year here before too long. But I sincerely hope you'll meet with success in your new endeavor. . . ." The gargling voice petered out with a renewal of its twisted smile. The man looked as sad and affectionate as if he was saluting the failure of a common cause. With the knuckle of his forefinger, just as he'd been seen to do a thousand times every week for ten years, he pushed his eyeglasses back up into their proper seat in the saddle of his nose. His evasive stare rested longer than usual on one spot however, just as it would if his party lost the Presidency.

That's about all there was to it. Chapman was at first almost touched by Val's paternalistic manner, so relieved he was that everything had gone off smoothly, but by the time he got home that night he felt as if he'd cheated himself out of his last nugget of self-respect in Berkeley. The bridge had been crossed but his intent remained both unsatisfied and undissatisfied.

For he never showed his true colors, nor even the colors of a pirate among privateers. He granted himself not so much as the pleasure of hoisting a jolly roger as he sailed out of range. In the back-office of business (where he was never seen by children wife or friends) he lacked not only a strong punch but also the iron guts of a professional fighter. Thus with no display of pride or passion, without a flare of the nostril, he apologetically relinquished his right to indignation as well as his chance to strike consternation into the heart of his master by exciting the fear of spies that is more damaging to an establishment whether revolutionary or reactionary than the spies themselves are.

This limply fading withdrawal of his highly emotional commitment to the firm after so many years, as if he was only closing out an inactive checking account, may disappoint the spirited reader of this "comic epic poem in prose" devoted to the middle world of consciousness. Indeed Chapman cannot be made to seem more adventurous than a trusty elephant liberated from lifelong teak-logging slavery who is constrained by the grass loop that still shackles his mentality to the mahout after he's been turned out on his own in the jungle. But in reality his pusillanimity is as complex and misleading as Hamlet's. Having complained that Chapman was a poor black operator the critic can't fairly blame him for holding his peace.

His purpose you see had never been to undermine Bow's Ark or the larger economy, nor even to discover their secrets, but simply to cozen a living out of free enterprise so that he wouldnt have to corrupt himself among the academic lotus blossoms or within a journalistic profession or by way of advertising vice. It was nevertheless all to the good that he had gained some radically useful intelligence in the process of contributing to the efficiency of comparatively benign commerce. Chapman was more keenly aware than you may be that the best way to gather the kind of critical information that he thought necessary for his maximum survival is to accomplish some real work for the people you're spying on, and as he expected to be obliged to continue his career of cryptic adaptation he had no wish to give himself away at any checkpoint.

The most successful undergrounders are those who make themselves more valuable to their dupes than to their sponsors. Even when an assignment seems absolutely finished and about to be obliterated in the obscure untraceable past a prudent self-informer (on the principle of least disclosure) considers it sheer dissipation to indulge intemperate egotism by exposing his talents like an immature seducer to him upon whom he has practiced them. He was wise enough to forsee that he would have immediately regretted such a futile and improper betrayal of himself. Any sort of callow impure behavior risked in some unforeseeable way an unnecessary cracking of the shell in which he must elsewhere survive. He was too well balanced as a blackguard of natural managerial temperament not to appreciate both sides of a profitable relationship. Moreover Greatrakes had already guessed that he was a liberal; there was no sense in letting him know the worst.

Chapman could cite a tenuous but specific possibility to justify his apparently irrational determination not to divulge the new job. The least you must admit is that he was thoroughly scrupulous in protecting Pat Murphy of C R F through whom he got it. The salesman naturally wanted no reprisal from the principal at Bow's Ark, one of his oldest accounts. Pat had confidentially told Mike about an opening that one of his other customers had mentioned, and then enthusiastically recommended him for it in terms that included a mistaken implication that the candidate had a degree in Business Administration if not in mathematics. Greatrakes might put two and two together if he learned that Mike's new employer was called Thanatron Rectification and also happened to know that Murphy sold business forms or adding machines to a company of that name.

It was a strange yet vaguely familiar name that would have stuck in Greatrakes's mind though represented in no advertising that a bookman or consumer ever saw or heard. It identified a small manufacturing company among scores of others located far away on the southeastern industrial flats of Oakland through which one drove on the way to the airport, far beyond the Sears Roebuck store. Except for the sign on its building and its trademark usually unnoticed on greasy equipment in service stations it was unknown outside the wholesale automotive trade. In that auxiliary industry however its battery chargers were respected from coast to coast: at almost any gas station behind the hydraulic lifts of you could find a rubber-wheeled red and white enameled Thanatron box sprouted with long rubber cables that ended in copper-jawed clips like an electrically extended crustacean.

The company also made from sheet steel for the same channels of distribution, peddled by the same half-dozen regional manufacturers' representatives, a "quality" line of handsomely finished gray catalog binders for the endlessly accumulating pages of auto-suggestive descriptions specification sheets and price lists required on the counters and in the stockrooms of jobbers, not for resale to the trade (as in the case of battery-chargers) but for their own use in meeting the myriad scarcely intelligible demands of gas stations garages truck fleets construction firms and various small plants that were dependent in one degree or another on petroleum-fueled engines. Every jobber's counterman had to be an infallible reference-librarian for hundreds of manufacturers whose innumerable parts accessories tools and supplies of all types and sizes occupied the dim shelves and bins in stock rooms indicative of a bewilderingly diversified end-use market. Thanatron's own catalog sheets were but one to a thousand in these expandable loose-leaf binders on intricately fitted inclined planes assembled from cunning modules into countertop lecterns sometimes as long as any pair of giant-squid clerics would want for quoting gospels epistles and lessons, or for six volumes of the Oxford English Dictionary lying open side by side. But the pages of this variorum scripture were thick and glossy, for these expandable binders held manufacturers' loose-leaf sheets punched in the margin with slots resembling master keyholes for anybody's set of rings.

Thereto Thanatron sold an adjustable 6-hole punch with patented dies of amazing force and precision by which any piece of $8^{1}/_{2}$ x 11 plain or folded sales literature bound or unbound could be prepared for insertion into arbitrary sequential position in the chosen section of any of these infinitely renewable indefinitely large heterogeneous master-catalogs eclectically compiled by the jobber, where it was guaranteed to turn easily lie flat and resist the stress of hard thumbing. Thanatron also offered (as a distributor of ancillary products from another industry) sets of indexed dividers labeled with all the major and minor categories recognized by trade associations professional societies or automobile manufacturers' service organizations.

The company's new "sales correspondent", hired thanks to Pat's salesmanship on the strength of experience at the 23rd Street machine shop in New York, electronics training in the Navy, and hope that he was educated enough to communicate clearly with its traveling men and customers, had been turned down for the more internal job that he really wanted, Production Control Clerk, when he was obliged to clear up the misunderstanding about his qualifications, as lacking a college education.

At first Chapman was not enthusiastic about his new place in this alien industry. He'd lost out on the more technical job because of his own pigheaded recusancy way back when he had just taken off the Navy's livery (and before he'd generated too many kids or other impedimenta to swing a student's life as Jack and thousands of other career-minded veterans were to do on the salary and expenses paid from Federal funds thanks to New Deal precedent, including the cost of many a private library for those who took Philosophy English or History courses for their long reading lists)—for no other reason than that he preferred like a great many blue collar workers to join the "52-20 Club" of veterans wearing the "ruptured eagle" in the lapels of their ill-fitting civilian clothes whose members were entitled to twenty dollars a week for fifty two weeks while they were putatively trying to find a way to make their living unassisted, either by a paying job or if they chose to regard this subsidy as an extension of the W P A Federal Writers Project by the composition of literature presumably interrupted and inspired by the war. A few rejection slips for pieces Chapman had tried to contribute to certain periodicals proved that he could be classified as a writer. In those days, about the same time that Nixon was beginning his malign ascent in Congress, Michael had been puritanical enough to resist what he called a stampede of sheep to the security of prolonged instruction under folded shepherds of the thermometer while he waited for his successful girlfriend to graduate and marry him, using up his mustering-out pay on the first and last true vacation of his life, having convinced himself that next to the advertising business a college education (as at best no more than an antidote to advertising for them that needed it) was the worst possible influence on an independent mind.

Nearly a decade later the new sales correspondent venturing cautiously out into the mainstream of espionage still privately professed (almost everyone else's opinion to the contrary notwithstanding) that few variations in qualification are more significant than those among accredited colleges (taking as his example the disparity between Harvard and Whittier as places at which to have four years of intellectual experience), the difference being more important to the cultivation of critical faculties than the difference between Catholic and Baptist upbringing, between northeastern and southwestern cultures, or between autodidacticism and ordinary Bachelorhood. (Some colleges even converted natal Republicans.) But of course a fortiori (Chapman told Wolfson) a man matriculated only at the great Godgrant university of adversity with no football team might make himself almost as independent as Ishmael, a master if not doctor of whaleshit, without the humiliation of trimming his sails for a committee of ill-assorted patent attorneys. So it was this concealed attitude that had prevented him from getting into the actual production of "automotive equipment" where he would have felt much more at home despite his propensity for the written word.

But in his position as de facto order-processor he soon found himself a kind of administrative assistant to the sales manager and made it his business to acquaint himself with other departments of the company. In pursuing the satisfaction of his curiosity he was unexpectedly useful to an executive preoccupied with the external relations of marketing, his open-minded boss. He began to ferret out Thanatron's practices in accounting and credit management and purchasing and traffic as well as in manufacturing and industrial engineering. Gradually he learned the jargon of these divers specialties and induced general principles. Before long he was tactfully contributing improvements wherever they might be unwittingly accepted in the name of anything but efficiency.

In the sales department, where he more nearly minded his own business, he got himself involved with statistics, forms-design, mailing lists, printed-matter, industrial advertising, office furniture, addressograph and mimeograph equipment, diazo copy machines, and of course (in Murphy's interest as well as his own) all the office adders and calculators, always trying to save the company wasted minutes or dollars in the hope that he'd be allowed to spend them where they would do some good, all in the face of frustrations and delays in developments outside his exclusive personal control. Meanwhile, according to duty's priority, most of his working time was spent in the tedious research required to answer by dictating machine the ceaseless stream of questions and complaints from salesmen customers and prospective buyers about electrical and mechanical specifications, estimated shipping dates promised shipping dates and actual shipping dates, crated weights and volumes, export documentation, truck routings railroad routings and even steamship routings, credit denied and credit approved, credit limits and sight-draft bills of lading, warehouse receipts and releases, defective parts, trade discounts and cash discounts, mistaken commissions split commissions and overdue checks, travel and entertainment expense accounts, billing errors, ambiguous sales policies, undefined territorial boundaries, and countless other "details" that had to be faced by sales departments of every small industrial firm. But by doing so singlehanded he accrued a reputation as his boss's champion in all administrative matters both within and without the walls of the plain one-story building that housed all company operations with plenty of land around it for future expansion.

This metamorphosis of livelihood was part of a complex revolution in Chapman's life in which several advances were realized. First, by liberating himself from the degradation of personal selling he overcame his distaste for genial interaction with what his supposititious ancestor George called "the prophane multitude" (his social intercourse being confined to the premises) and cut himself loose from the entangling net of books that had been unmanning his will for action in the name of knowledge, learning what he had forgotten, namely to fear nothing but real danger. Second, he got his body sterilized by vasectomy. And third, he raised the expectations of his family for an improvement in the platform of living from which he hewed, for he changed his place of residence as well as his place of work.

These changes together radically altered his means of daily shuttle. He borrowed money to buy a second(at least)hand Little King. This acquisition of chattel property put an end to most of his reading, for although the car afforded a rather pleasant flexibility of locomotion it brought with it an altogether demanding new diversion.

Soon afterward, according to conjugal treaty, as a war veteran with trifling equity he invoked the backing of the United States Government for a

20-year mortgage at a subsidized interest rate on the only real property upon which he and his wife could agree, an old waterside house in Alameda, the only town he'd consent to, an island (famous in the Navy for the aircraft-carrier base at its western tip) with interesting maritime margins, where she had been born and educated before hard times forced her family to emigrate to Contra Costa County at the outset of her high-school years. He was pleased with the shipping estuary on the opposite side of his new little city like a river separating it from Oakland but sorry that although its own little Belt Line railroad was still operating for freight terminals no commuter could get to work without a car save by an elaborate interchange of noisesome busses. Even high-class passengers to the metropolis no longer had the San Francisco & Alameda Railroad with its ferry from the Alameda Mole.

The new job reduced his nominal work-week by nearly eight hours; but this advantage was offset by the various complications that absorbed his gain twenty times over.

2.

But my servant Caleb, because he had another spirit with him, and hath followed me fully, him will I bring into the land whereinto he went. . . .
—Numbers, 14:24

Socialclimbing Michael Chapman raised the money for down payment and insurance on his Little King Six—for in the used-car lot he happened upon the least little model in the King line, strong enough to haul a family but with only two doors, a feature calculated for safety when there were young kids in the back seat—by selling Caleb Karcist his unreserved coach ticket to Gloucester. Caleb had by then saved enough to pay for it, though he'd had no intention of going East when his year as a night watchman was over. He had thought of living in Berkeley with Lilian Cloud after he and all the other tenants were evicted from the Rabbit Warren to allow its razing. (The hill itself was safe from leveling, thanks to the hospital and other large properties already built thereon.)

"Go East young man. *Go home!*" Chapman pointed east with an arm straight out, clarifying and emphasizing his orders to the dog. "Leave this frontier of Western gloom. To the people here, brought up to live easy, looking east is looking backwards—and so it is, for all our origins have their origins in the series of origins from Sumer to New England—but this gyroscope we live on always points north, and eastward is its forward motion. You came here only to avoid Harvard. But now you've earned your colors. You can decamp with a respectable diploma in your pocket. A hundred years ago Harvard's colors were blue and gold too.

"You still have two weeks pay coming when you leave. It will make a nice little fund for getting settled somewhere close enough to the lower reaches of the Charles so that you can make a habit of going to the theater—even if it's provincial poetic and half deserted. Let the draft board try to catch up with you there. Find a miserable job and buckle down to write your play. After you're well begun take a day off with an easy mind to surrender the coupon left on this ticket and ride the good old Boston and Maine to Gloucester for my sake. They might even still be running a steam engine if they're short of equipment."

"But it's all your fancy! What about you? It's you who live in exile!" Caleb affected surprise that Michael had canceled his anti-pioneering plan; but the news of his own banishment was a genuine shock. "Is it because I've been a disappointment to you? Have I wasted your time for nothing?"

"It's too early to predict and too late to repent—certainly no fault of yours that I've been riding too many horses to go myself. You must go back to the Boston States alone, while I stick it out in this occidental Siberia of milk and honey. Carry word of me back home. Be my peregrine fishhawk. Tell the blackbacks and herring gulls that you are the disinherited merlin, my winged herald to Apollo. You are the peer to whom I yield adventures and exploits. I have reached the age at which if I'm going to accomplish anything in time I'll have to rely on memory and prejudice alone. I must forego the pleasures of repatriation."

Now reason holds us accountable for what we profess, but it can do so only to the extent of its influence in our English speech, which however has much else to fit itself for: not only what the redhaired Father Vivaldi thought of as "the struggle between harmony and invention" and Blake's contraries versus minuses but also an unmystical romantic's ambiguous abnegations. Despite Caleb's carefully concealed disgust at the fashion in which Michael shied away from the difficulties of carrying out professed purposes he understood that there were personal matters that he knew little about except what Ruth had hinted at in a few very limited conversations when the three of them were together, and in any case her fourth pregnancy (which his master never announced or alluded to) was enough to explain any change of plans.

Thus Michael was allowed to pass off his new job in service to the infernal combustion industry and his new house on a primarily residential holm and his last child as good reasons for renouncing his heart's desire. "Without you hereabouts I'll be completely isolated." he boasted. "Before long it'll be too much trouble even to visit Jack in Berkeley. Meanwhile you'll be half way to Europe."

"But you won't be!"

"Who cares about Europe?—when I can't even get to Gloucester!"

Caleb pretended to overlook the lame rationalizations of his indefatigible authority and dearest friend whom he suspected liable to new hobbies arising from progress in prejudices overcome. His invisible smile irritated Michael; but self-disgrace has never had good defense against clever youth.

So Caleb, cruelly exhilarated by his apparent liberation, washed the coal dust off his hands for the last time almost the same day that Sig Hansen forty five years older did the same. Hecuba had given up Mr Wine's bookkeeping to go live in affluent wedlock with the Silver Fox, but she still had considerable influence on her former employer who often telephoned for information about details of his business that he'd never learned, especially after he bought the Topalis house hoping to rent all three apartments to small communities of white-clad nurses or other hospital workers who would be jointly willing to pay high rent at the edge of a black neighborhood for the sake of being close to their work. She saw to it that he dealt honorably with his two firemen at the end of their service.

Caleb left Michael most of his books. They helped cover the wall of the new study in Alameda.

Michael drove Caleb with Lilian to the open-air Western Pacific platform near the Oakland waterfront to put him aboard the Zephyr at its starting point, where it also took on passengers who'd come across the bridge on a bus from San Francisco. While the young lovers were saying goodbye to each other at Caleb's seat he walked up and down the length of the train on the street outside, from diesel cab to the streamlined club-car fantail. When Lilian rejoined him they peered up at their friend, who according to bossy instructions had immediately claimed his right to a place up in the glass observation dome where he could look down on the landscape and up at the sky as the train glided eastward to the end of the city (right past the Thanatron factory) and threaded its way through the hills to speed up across the great flat valley toward the gorged forests of the high Sierras and again the horseshoe bends of the Rockies.

The last they saw of Caleb he was waving and smiling wanly like a scrawny child leaving home for the first time. At that moment and for the next hour—and perhaps again that evening—the person taking his departure felt as forsaken as if the city of Oakland with all his love had been rolled out from under the train to leave him in a insulated capsule of desolation.

"I'm going to miss our Caliban." said Chapman to Lilian as he drove her back to Berkeley.

"I called him frog. He called me Lily-pad." she mildly replied. "It's sad to see him go. But he'll be happier in New England where he can walk in the country without worrying about rattlers. I've never known a boy so scared of snakes. He says our culture is too thin out here. I really believe that he wants fame more than money, and excellence more than fame."

Chapman chuckled. "Aren't you going to be love-sick?"

"No, not exactly. Just morning-sick. It was the best time for him to leave." Thus she confided to Michael what Caleb was not to know.

"He's not levanting on you then?"

"Oh no; I knew what I was doing. I don't want a family or a husband: just a baby. He didn't want a wife or a Ph D . I hope I won't miss more than one month of painting. I'll go back to the maize fields as soon as I can walk." Her broad face never resembled a delicate Blue Fairy's but this was the first time Michael had ever seen her looking robust and joyful. He was suddenly conscious that her noble Indian body no longer attracted him.

3.

When Adam delved and Eve span
Who was then the gentleman?
—Motto of the Peasants' Revolt

It was the end of September before the changes that had begun soon after Palm Sunday resolved themselves in a settled way of life. Semiramis's latest litter had come and gone, except for one male kitten and one female now well grown, spits and images of herself named Bagheera and Morgan le Fay who had been brought with her to the new neighborhood, which was much more pleasant for cats and children. It remained for the chief to find the dog he wanted.

Only then, but then fully, did Chapman enter into the marches of what we generally call middleclass life (as if the rich all about them were of an upper class). He defended his new social medium: indeed the most limited of classes—ne quid nimis—yet the only one abutting two others. Growing older he learned more and more about the things in which he was like other men of like circumstances. Soon there were jars of nails and screws with tools in the cellar, a lawn-mower in the garage; he began to acquire rakes ladders fuses paint brushes and a houseful of furniture. Already he was thinking about at least a rowboat for the tiny wooden jetty that stood with four legs in the tidal flat at his sea wall.

Everything was made possible by installment credit (counted as personal savings in economic statistics), assisted by Ruth's Republican mother who supplied them with a new bed and many other articles from her provident warehouse of heirlooms, to whom they were already indebted for various small legal fees that apparently were so firmly attached to all real estate transactions by the Magna Carta that they required no mention in the U S Constitution. But this period of expansion could not last. It must be followed by lean flat tenacious years at the new level.

While the Chapmans were still in the grip of their enthusiasm for pleasures that he at least had never anticipated they decided to celebrate their good luck (which was really no fluke, owing to Ruth's resolute and competent work digging up improbable vendors while he turned a blind eye and deaf ear) to possess this quiet shabby piece of property, under tall trees, right on San Francisco Bay not far from a yacht club, among spruce and sedate neighbors they'd never get to know, by giving a party for all the old gang, whom they'd scarcely seen since the inception of their upheavals. The house-warming (also intended to honor the birth of St Michael Cervantes) was a year to the day after Chapman had been given his Gloucester going-away present at the Wolfsons'. In fact, he told his guests, the pin-money they'd embarrassed him with on that occasion was underwriting this thanksgiving banquet: his present to them all, Ruth's present, in recognition of kindnesses over the years that could never be repaid.

The roll-call was altered however. There were other friends, equally welcome, none Republican; and half a dozen more could not or would not accept the red-letter invitation. Another, Sam the mustachioed poet, Michael had thought of taking pity on, after years of exclusion from his social circle, now that he was no longer a presumptuous subordinate. Greatrakes as if to show his contempt had nominally promoted him though presumably still an extreme left-winger to fill the shoes of Bow's Ark's old trade-book buyer by downgrading the job. From him Michael might have gleaned with mixed feelings of interest and revulsion the latest developments at the store, for which he couldnt help hoping the worst. But his hesitancy was concluded for a particular reason and in the end Sam wasnt invited. His former colleague Lilian, a most important and cherished guest of the Chapmans (especially as she had volunteered to help Ruth cook and serve the huge turkey dinner), who had also left the store and was no longer a source of intelligence about it—beyond the news that Greatrakes had had the sense to close out his art supply department after losing her, on hearing of the proposal had begged with uncharacteristic firmness to be excused from spending an evening in Sam's presence.

Joan the throaty cigarette smoker who had borne Dave Wilson a daughter had taken herself off with the child and was replaced in that Nordic airman's San Francisco bed by a black girl whom the East Bay people could not now meet, for despite Ruth's most cordial and diplomatic entreaties she refused to show herself carrying his unborn baby among a parcel of white liberals trying to make her feel comfortable in a place where she'd be spied out by the neighbors as either a temporary servant or a Communist at a time when she was in no mood to fight it out; so David had to come alone. It happened too that the Philoctetetic artist Jim Jackson and his doting cow were just then flaying each other to raw sensitivity with the combined or alternating passions of guilt anger hatred lust tenderness and recrimination in a series of marital battles that had recently begun to disturb Mary's erotic complacency, and neither of them had any stomach for seeing people who'd watched them bill and coo over their singularly cherished lar familiaris; and it seemed clear to everyone but themselves that the extramural Helens, whom he'd discovered were easy to come by after making no secret of being sterilized at her request, were leading them straight toward divorce just as he was being swamped with commissions to cover the walls of San Francisco with his bold colors. The Smiths, those dialectically materialistic radicals who kept the laundry that served as town pump on Teleology Lane and would have been Ruth's most heartfelt guests were unable to attend because Jeanette was in the hospital for what turned out to be her worst course of radiation treatments. And finally the Chapmans were disappointed by Sig Hansen, for though he was full of sea stories and jokes about Norwegian horsepower in private conversation, though he might have substituted for Caleb as Lilian's dinner partner, and though they were eager to have him meet Hecuba's husband, who would have liked his company in that young crowd to which he himself was also a stranger and who might have been able to put in Sig's way some retirement job that wouldnt be reported to the Social Security Administration, nothing could overcome his shyness about appearing in a free and easy mixed company where he didnt think he could make himself understood.

So besides the Silver Fox and his golden giglet, and Lilian (neither maid nor wife nor widow) the unaccustomed faces invited at Ruth's suggestion during one of her husband's unaccountable fits of generosity after other invitations had fallen through belonged to Sandy the Shark and his porcine woeperson who as host and hostess they were glad to find was gradually reverting to softer spoken Tidewater femininity of manner if not of ideas as she made steady progress in truly reforming her mate the dentist, now apparently as domesticated and loyal as a shoemaker. Michael's acquiescence is all the more remarkable in that one of his codeterminant motives for giving up the Topalis tenement (even though Hecuba the lodestone for unscrupulous men was about to remove herself from the premises) had been the discovery that Sandy was buying the practice of a deceased dentist at Wine's medical building much too nearby.

For the first time all three Chapman boys were being allowed to stay overnight with their grandmother. No one had to sit below the salt because Ruth had found in her favorite second-hand furniture store a vast oaken round table which with all sorts of improvised sitting structures was just the thing for persons of alternate sex every thirty degrees, each with a partner not quite opposite, man facing man, woman facing woman. The old faces were well interspersed: the savantical Jack Wolfson and his Sarah, the plump nymph Sylvia Cahners and her cherubic consort the Newt. There was courtesy and equality for all, but like democracy in imperial Britain the places were predetermined and reserved, more like a cabinet than a parliament of birds, kinged by a very lively host crowned with a round white sailor hat (found by the queen when packing for the move to Alameda) squared down like a democratic crown on his broad low brow. Except for the rimless eyeglasses—usually opaque but now as transparent as a pair of magnifying glasses—and his owlish pasty cheeks and his fishy-looking jaws (for he could never be called tightlipped even by his wife and always breathed through his mouth) he looked salty enough to please any critical boatswain's mate on Shore Patrol who didnt look below his chin. He was no longer able to squeeze himself into the other articles of his Navy uniform, among which he especially regretted his blue dress-jumper with a pig-tail flap, white stripes on the cuffs, red chevroned crow on the sleeve, a stiff bar of service ribbons on the breast, and airy open vee at the neck, nearly as much as the bell-bottom trousers that had only enough buttons to cover the original colonies or some core of a coven. His black temples were only ever so slightly salted (on very close inspection) because he kept them close-cropped, whereas his friend the leonine dogface from the same war was noticeably agraying in the mane, that thinner head of hair being much longer finer and curlier, having been goldilocked to start with. Of course Jack was handsomer than he at every age, though no more than tolerably spectre-thinner above the knees.

The birthday owl didnt get as much chance to hoot as he'd have liked until the long wassail that came after the eating, but he was not entirely out of the conversation beforehand as he busied himself keeping everyone's glasses filled while he showed his property and pointed out Hunter's Point Naval Shipyard distantly across the Bay under a new moon, and then during the main event carved the mountainous turkey so patiently that he scarcely got a bite until everyone else was ready for dessert. It wasnt until a long symposium afterwards that the guests got the benefit of his old self.

But there was much to talk about before the celebration reached that stage. It was an unusual season of baseball and politics, full of imminent success and unthinkable failure from the angle of a Yankee fan and Democrat. Mickey Mantle, batting third in the lineup, some of whose games Micky Chapman had heard "recreated" three hours late on the West Coast time-zone clock from on-line telegraph transmissions (with simulated crowd noises) by a local radio announcer who advertised the transcontinental brand of ale that the portly fan began to favor, was an Oakie Protestant married to a girl named Merlyn and had no claim to Rome, World, or Heaven, or to hereditary riches, but was on the point of winning the Triple Crown and the Most Valuable Player title, even without official consideration of Runs Scored, which his most learned California namesake complained was a statistic too often overlooked that reflected his valuable bases made on balls or stolen, a measure of potency subtlety and speed as well as hitting power, more significant to the Yankees' payoff in double-pi radians of rotation toward the pennant than his amazing slugging average, especially for the successor to Joe Di Maggio (no mere lead-off batter either) who had made San Francisco famous to a Gloucester boy for its Italian fishermen before he dreamed of being sent to California by the U S Navy. This admirer asserted that Mantle would probably end his career scoring more runs than any player who'd ever walked the earth; and that S M D C was admirably suited to the composite ranking of all-time players by their numerical records, just as it could be used to rate football teams that never played each other in a given season, or to pick All-Americans. Of course that same statistical technique would have been just the thing for the Democratic National Committee in planning the campaign geographically.

It was a good thing Chapman didnt then know that Adlai Stevenson (for whom there was many a toast that night: "Eggheads of the world, unite! You have nothing to lose but your yolks!") was on the way to his second defeat. To buck up his hopes for the future of the world Chapman was continually reminding himself and telling anyone who'd listen that twenty years earlier at the Linnean School half full of Cambridge "rich kids" who made affluent display of huge Landon-Knox buttons featuring the Kansas state flower during a viciously personal campaign (now forgotten or forgiven like other Republican attacks after history's overtaken them) even while he and his own gang were bravely chanting "Sunflowers die in November!" (their only rebuttal to the children of Protestant individualism) he'd been convinced that F D R was going to lose and that Harry Hopkins had secretly thought so too. It was now the fateful year of the crisis at the Suez Canal, the Israelis' last neutral border, and Stevenson's campaign was complicated by his apparent defense of the residual British Empire against the Egyptians whom the Jews sometimes seemed to fear less than they hated the British their erstwhile common overlords. Chapman declared that the most significant portent of the year, in fact, had come somewhat earlier, when the United Kingdom finally stopped financing and staffing the Arab Legion after King Hussein fired the British commander, even before the United States punished Egypt for its socialistic leanings by withdrawing its subsidy of the Aswan dam and the Egyptians seized the canal that separated them from their religious allies surrounding Israel. It was a year of endless ramifications and Chapman thought he saw them all, or at least he trusted Stevenson to master those of which he was ignorant—the burden classically expected of a leader understood to be wiser than his electorate. Anyway, having been to Harvard, Chapman felt a personal affinity for this Democratic egghead who had been to Republican Princeton. That very year the new Ivy League had been instituted, a tardy confession of the amphictyon that the rest of the country had been making fun of ever since the football colleges started issuing their own Ph D s. Both Chapman and Stevenson were well aware that the Supreme Court had just outlawed Jim Crow on busses and trains, but Chapman (not having daily access to the Anglo-American Chronicle put out by Jews in New York as the national newspaper of record) had missed the more anthropological detail that although Pius XII condemned artificial insemination as immoral and absolutely illicit he approved the transplanting of corneas from the eyes of dead people to the living blind, the latter perhaps representing a class of cases in which medical science has dissolved the biological barrier between individuals. Neither of these American minds dwelt much upon our first dropping of the hydrogen

bomb from a plane, blasting for the hell of it—by way of controlled experiment—an atoll of the Marshall Islands where LST 1066 had once
landed a load of construction equipment, for it was by then politically inevitable if not scientifically necessary that we demonstrate our negative
technology. But it is doubtful that Adlai Stevenson or perhaps the *Times*
itself even noticed—certainly Michael Chapman did not—the commercial
introduction of an equally inevitable expedient, the art of recording by
television camera endless strips of tabula rasa for storage and delay or reiteration of broadcast, to an effect that before America was finished would
surpass in importance even the recording of music. And then there were
the local events of 1956 that Stevenson had no interest in, like a great
flooding of the Sacramento or the opening of a lengthy Richmond-San
Rafael Bridge, which put an end to one more ferry line at the mouth of the
uterine lake where the salt tides of the Bay mingled with the fecund
waters of all the rivers draining the long broad valley of the promised
land, not far above the yacht roads that lined the inner coast of pleasure
from the art colony to San Quentin Prison.

Most of these current events Chapman spoke about with one or
another of his guests before the evening was over, the Silver Fox for
instance, who quietly made himself the Most Beloved Person of the party,
father even to them who'd never met his like, a small well-dressed man as
alert as Sandy to the people around him—the likes of most of whom he on
his part had never talked to about anything except theater tickets (whereas
there wasnt any type of human female Sandy the wolf hadnt met who
however fell far short of such foxy charm) and many of the words of whom
he made shrewd guesses about as to their signification. Said he to Chapman from the opposite end of the host's diameter where he'd been placed
in honor: "Aint it kind of funny you're a Yankee fan when you come from
Boston?" He listened patiently to the host's reply that it had all started
before he even understood the gibberish cluttering up the airwaves every
afternoon all summer long after the family was given a radio, when his
interest in baseball was aroused by the awe-spoken name of the retired
Babe Ruth, whom he immediately disliked for his beer-belly and spindly
legs but who had had a truly heroic team-mate at first base called the Iron
Man for his endurance and reliability, still playing though (as it was later
revealed) on the verge of death, and that it was for the sake of this heroic
Lou Gehrig that the father of the man had attached his enthusiasm to the
New York Yankees, who subsequently justified and reinforced his loyalty
by a dynasty of excellence at all nine positions unto the present day, a continuity that he now declared to be the fruit of a superb organization.

"You're too abstract about it Mike!" exclaimed Sandy (born a Yankee
fan in New York, his original claim to Chapman's friendship, but long
since graduated from mere spectator sports), who had been overhearing
that dialogue among others.

"Abstraction's more efficient than rhetoric." the king snapped without looking at the interloper. His answer to the Silver Fox was only the beginning of his explanation, but fortunately the old man's attention was interrupted by others closer to his ear who needed it more, so he finished it to Lilian on his right, the person most sympathetic to him at the moment despite being as indifferent to the great American pastime as to steeplechasing in England.

Without much literal comprehension she heard that the other reason he had faithfully committed his emotions to the New York Yankees (as far as he himself could remember what had happened) was a complex of prejudices that to this day he hadnt fully succeeded in tracing. Thus, in part (as he labored between tort and equity to carve light and dark fowl for twelve hungry mouths): "I was always intrigued by the name New Yorick, because even at that age I was proud of my Anglican ancestors in Yorkshire; and as I got older my allegiance was inflamed by mindless Anglophobic and anti-intellectual slander on the Irish-Catholic side of Observatory Hill where the kids around me viciously impugned the Yankees for their excellence; but the rich kids on the other side also hated them for winning. They'd always trump my citation of self-subordination and teamwork (in contrast to the play of Fenway Park personae) by reciting the sports-page dogma that the Yankees were only a money-machine but the Red Sox were 'the most *colorful* club in the American League'! How could I argue against *colorful*, always uttered in a tone of smug dogma, as if I espoused some New York Jewish-inspired heresy of mon-eyed colorlessness? My days were dark whenever the Yankees led the League by less than ten games. Like the British Empire, winning made them hated, but losing made them despised. I learned to suffer my martyrdom for the them in almost secret isolation, and it wasnt much better when I grew up and went to New York where Yankee-hating was expressed by rather pointed enthusiasm for the National League teams."

Meanwhile most of the listeners in the room who werent totally occupied with the distribution of food or engaged in dialogue of their own were watching the Silver Fox. His dapper movements and deep voice ninety degrees away especially fascinated plump lascivious Sylvia Cahners and she was cryptically teasing the senior guest whom she like most of the others had never seen before for falling into a dotage on his voluptuous young wife somewhat slimmer than herself albeit no blonder no younger and no less pregnant. "Have you chased girls all your life Mr Fox?" she asked in her lowest slowest most seductive voice which as she intended stopped all other conversation.

"Not yet Ma'am." he replied with a polite smile and indifferent eyes. Everyone but the interlocutors laughed of one accord with friendly admiration, but her round pale face usually so cool in its gaze at men colored in confusion as if the laugh had been on her. And the handsome man of the world at once turned back to Sarah Wolfson on his right who had been looking out for his table conveniences before all others, making sure that he was first served, first waited upon in all particulars, like a beloved patriarch of her own family; and it was his courtesy not to notice the special respect paid him but rather to take particular interest in this new daughter, where and how she lived with her husband and children, what he could learn from her of academic life, Ruth on his left being far too busy running back and forth from the kitchen and doing her duty as inclusive hostess to give him more than priority in her general attention, though she who still puzzled him more than other young women, beyond the margin of his ability as father or lover, was the beautiful madonna of his imagination and the one whose company he was most proud of. And so it was that Sarah the timid lioness whom he knew the Chapmans had placed next to him because they loved her best of all their guests had the mysterious stranger almost to herself when the feast was well underway. Having never been warned that this amiable ticket-agent for performing arts who knew a lot about her home town Los Angeles was understood to be a baron of the underworld she asked him a hundred innocent questions about the theatrical ambience of his legal business that he was so modest about. As far as business turpitude was concerned she would have sooner suspected a uniformed usher in an outer lobby of the Opera House. So he let her amuse herself with the tacit notion that he was some diamond in the rough, a self-made impressario who controlled half the legitimate glitter of the city. At any rate she was perfectly sure that he wasnt antisemitic, and might even have been at least in part Jewish. Less than anyone else in the room, less than the man himself, would she have believed such a canny man-about-town so unwittingly beholden to her circle's young renegade student for having successfully risked the clandestine rivalry to which the reader has been privy.

But Caleb missing from the gathering of his friends was perhaps not much more ignored than he would have been if he'd now been sitting between Hecuba and Lilian, except by those two themselves who as it was were not thinking of him but certainly would have been sensitive to his presence if things had gone nigh as they actually did go save only for his departure. As it was they liked each other for an implicit good-natured frankness in antithetical deviations from the feminine norm. Everyone knew of Caleb's success with Lilian, which had been applauded until the consequence was known, but Hecuba, prudently assuming Lilian's knowledge of her fling with the same lover in case he had been foolish enough to have confided in her (perhaps prompted only by way of accounting for enlightenment beyond his years in the jewel of games), trusted to some inkling of the Fox's underworld connections to make Lillian anxious for Caleb's life even on the Atlantic coast as sufficient motive for absolute secrecy.

Most of the celebrants were much less informed of what had been going on under their noses in this story, but there wasnt yet enough furniture in the Chapman house to encourage them to rise from the table and lay their heads together confidentially, friend with friend, to get what little low-down there was to share about the new configuration of this crew. Therefore instead of hearing enough to indict Caleb as a dastardly scoundrel they found themselves charitably conversing first in threes and then in fours, sometimes even disjoined into two superposed but interphased compass roses of six rhumbs each, speaking across the table to each other or around their neighbors, boy to boys, girl to girls, like counterrotating round dancers glad to get rid of their partners, as the interesting condition of the vulnerable ones crystallized a diestrous pattern of social intercourse resembling that of prepuberty. But the transitory divisions of the company often broke into the undisciplined configurations of social maturity as they wore away the evening still at their places. Thus:
Michael as the head of state with platter and
   Lilian was so busy with teamwork that Jack had
     Hecuba also was so occupied that Sandy couldnt
       "My ball and chain won't let me play poker." the
serving dishes at his end of the table was assisted
   to talk with Pig Ruth and soon judged her the
     get her attention to renew their old acquaintance
       Silver Fox was saying. "She says now the horse-
by Hecuba and Lilian in filling the plates with
   most adamant woman carrying a soft burden that
     so he at once turned leftward to Sylvia, estimating
       shoe's on another foot. She says being left alone
potatoes and vegetables after he'd laid the meat
   he'd ever met. "Don't call me a whoman." she
     sidelong as well as he could beneath napkin and
       in a big house with television is enough to drive
upon them having asked each diner for preference
   was saying when he tried to kid her about the
     maternity garments the normal shape of her body
       a girl to destitution. I told told her she wouldnt
as to color. They were working rapidly and there
   Women's Surrogation League that she'd become an
     and the tone of her muscles to see if she would
       get much business in her present condition."
was much too much to think about in keeping
   officer of. Newt on her right immediately took up
     some day be worth the risk of an exception to his
       "Well she doesnt know what she's saying Mr.
orders straight to have more than a little

the defense more smilingly than his new client,
        promise not to disturb the peaceful gravity of
            Fox." said Sarah."Yaako's home nearly all the
conversation, yet he was saying to his distracted
        who had at once pegged Jack as a petty house-
            ease and luxury that was beginning to stabilize the
                time!" "Well what do you ladies think I should
handmaidens ". . . and when they cried throughout
        hold tyrant affecting patriarchal superiority.
            professional respect he was surprised to find
                do?" he appealed to them both, spreading his
the ship *The Smoking Lamp is out* it always sounded
        As usual Newt started in fun while at the same
            himself earning or his devotion to the marvelous
                hands palm up on either side of his plate. Much
as if some devil had put out the red flame that
        time indicating his enlightened opinions, not
            offspring his sometime androgynous wife was
                to his surprise Ruth and Sarah each captured one
hangs over the altar to guard the reserved
        without permitting himself liberties which nor
            already fiercely guarding with some rather
                of them and squeezed but had to release them so
sacrament. . . ." Then after a long busy silence
Jack nor even the archangel would have dared, as:
        gratifying signs of private submission to the
            that he could eat. Ruth tapped his knuckles with
Hecuba expressed surprise at his deft dispatch,
        "This is a savvy who-person. She's emancipated
            female principle that seemed to him consonant
                cool fingertips. "To begin with, my advice as an
sure as a butcher's, considering all she'd heard
        from your linguistic prejudices. —You should
            with her previously unrelated fascination by
                old married woman is to take her to church every
about his distaste for most domestic duties. He
        talk to my wife. She was just getting interested
            male parts. Recent developments had thus brought
                week and see that the baby's baptized right away."
told her she should see his ambidexterity on the
        in the W S L when it turned out that the damned
            him to the unfamiliar notion of sticking by her
                "Oh don't worry about that!" "Are you a Catholic
new C R F machines. She was pretty good two-
        doctor had botched my vasectomy. . . ." Mrs Sandy

until the boy was old enough to have worn out
                too Mr Fox?" This time he laid down his fork to
handed on a typewriter keyboard but she had to
        solemnly warned the men of civil war if they
                his welcome, or to suffer an untraumatic transfer
                take Sarah by the wrist with paternal sternness.
admit that on digital machines she never used
        didnt mend their personal and possessive pro-
                to some younger woman's care. This Sylvia's low
                "Listen young lady—" she shivered until she saw
her left. And then when the carver was silenced
        nouns. At that the poet Sam (as a guardian of the
                indifferent voice and indolent movement hinted
                        the smile in his furrowed eyes—"never call a guy
by one of the turkey's knotty articulations she
        language) warmly retorted: "I'd rather make all
                something new for his phallic reach; and she said
                on his religion. They used to say that to live in
peered under his outstretched elbows to ask
        genders feminine than fearfully qualify every-
                she happened to be looking for a new dentist.
                California a man had to leave his conscience at
Lilian if the crickets liked her paintings. The
        thing I say. Whenever we mention the North Star
                Hitherto David Wilson had been too quiet and
                Cape Horn. They tell me that under the Spiks
artist explained that she'd never had a one-man
        do we have to add that the earth also points south?"
                severe to please Sylvia but now he leaned over
                you couldnt own property unless you was a
show. By the time Chapman had appeased the
        with his hand flattened to screen the left side of
                Catholic." He looked back at his other daughter
hunger of all his guests with offers of second
        his mouth and said in a stage whisper winking in
                and winked. Ruth gently pursued her thought. "I
helpings (accepted by the scot-free men, consci-
        comradely fashion at Sandy on the other side of
                was just going to tell Sally" she said, bending
entiously declined by the gravid women) he was
        her, suddenly exposing in a boyish smile his
                forward to address both Sarah and Hecuba
ready to start catching up with his own appetite.
        mouthful of unassuming white teeth as he swayed
                diametrically across the table who had no interest

The heaping plate before him, though a trifle
　　　　　stiffly back again and bridled with a cowboy's
　　　　　　　　　in the argument her companions were drawing
cool, was wonderful to behold, yet not long after
　　　　　bashful deprecation of his own competitive
　　　　　　　　　her husband into on the other side of the turkey
the others had pushed back their plates to sip
　　　　　gallantry. "You wouldnt need a pilot too, would
　　　　　　　　　carcass, "that we've joined the Episcopal church
sauterne he was consuming with prodigious speed
　　　　　you Ma'am?" She had been waiting for him to say
　　　　　　　　　here and the boys have started Sunday school.
the contents of reduplicated self-servings, lest he
　　　　　something. "Are you a sky pilot?" she drawled.
　　　　　　　　　—Oh it's so nice here Hecky!" she added, looking
keep them waiting too long for their dessert. Not
　　　　　But it was Lilian's dark unbeseeching eyes that
　　　　　　　　　over at her former neighbor with the smile that
however without taking breath for a decent con-
　　　　　he had been trying to catch far across the table,
　　　　　　　　　gladdened everybody. "And do you know, best of
tribution to the pig-baiting. He remembered his
　　　　　and just then she glanced his way, idly noticing
　　　　　　　　　all, the children each have a room of their
uncrenelated white crown and removed it from
　　　　　how unlike Caleb he was, having picked up
　　　　　　　　　own. —Of course it's nothing like your house
his head before joining battle. With a quick twist
　　　　　Sylvia's last words through the thicket of friendly
　　　　　　　　　Mr Fox: you'll be able to have six or seven
of both wrists he intussescepted two sides of the
　　　　　sounds that even in the Chapman house could
　　　　　　　　　children before you have to move. But this is all
stiff brim and in a trice the white duck hat was
　　　　　not protect her from the most unassuming
　　　　　　　　　we'll ever need. Of course we've had to go way
transformed into a thickly rolled croissant or
　　　　　assumptions. She smiled in her usual melancholy
　　　　　　　　　into debt. They let you do that if you have an
boomerang one leg of which might have been
　　　　　way but spoke loudly enough so that they could
　　　　　　　　　important job." She laughed. "But in a couple of
tucked into the neck of his sailor's jumper for snug
　　　　　hear her ask if he was going to be willing to
　　　　　　　　　years I'll be able to help out by running a nursery

safe-keeping while he chowed if he hadnt had a
                christen pagan babies. "Well I'm no chaplain" he
                        school here." And while the Fox listened to the
corner of his own ship to toss it into. "We gave
                called back "but I do like babies." Yet he took
                        innocent unmoneyed pleasures of this true-blue
them the vote;" he said, trying to raise a smile on
                counsel with himself in time to refrain from
                        young housewife on the suburban island that
mother-pig's downturned puss, "we let them
                encouraging the hopes of this quietly crazy artist-
                        thought itself safe from crime because there were
smoke, first in the parlor and then out in the
                girl. Since the war he had yearned for a quietly
                        only four getaway routes (three bridges and a
open street; we taught them to drive cars; why we
                crazy artist-girl to teach him how the images still
                        tunnel) Ruth told her two friends about all the
even granted them the orgasm: soon they'll be
                in his head might have been expressed if he hadnt
                        things Michael had been doing around the house.
carrying equalizers and committing crimes of
                been born with hopeless paralysis of expression,
                        "Sometimes he's even out mowing the lawn after
violence!" —"They're already padding their
                but memory of a mad loud baby-bearing Italian
                        dark, and digging up dandelions with a fork! He's
montes veneris!" Newt cried gleefully, his deeper
                and the reminder of present responsibility for a
                        getting a live Christmas tree to plant in the yard
feelings about feminism betraying themselves in
                soft-toned healthy black girl with another baby
                        after the holidays. And what a lovely sandbox he's
irresistible wisecracks. Michael continued: "Next
                checked the impulse to take Lilian under his
                        made for Roger! The big boys play in it too—
thing you know they'll want us to vulgarize the
                wing and talk for a thousand and one nights
                        only the cats also use it! It's rigged up with a
sacrament of holy orders, as if holy Jesus was
                about all the things he had not yet been able to
                        flagpole and an awning to look like a yacht, ropes
female too. From women priests it's only a step
                say. It was not beauty or adventure that he
                        and pulleys and everything. And did you notice"

to substituting milk for wine. That's the kind of
   craved; still, she had pushed back her chair to
      —how could they have failed to?—"the beautiful
encroachment that worries me almost as much as
   cross her legs and despite the tenderness of his
      suspension bridge he built near the sea wall for
the devastation of English. . . . Dred Scott! You
   anticipated desire he could all too easily forsee
      Matt and Jonny? I'm sure the neighbors think he's
firebrand abolitionists are going to split the
   how awkward it would be to tread that ugly
      crazy. If you half close your eyes at sunset it looks
Democratic Party! That's my main objection to it
   crescent belly in a month or two. It would have
      just like Golden Gate." [She didnt mention that
now: it gives female legislators and judges too
   to wait—again it would have to wait—even if he
      before anything else he'd fixed up his study like a
much encouragement as executives!" —"The
   never had another chance. Besides, maybe this
      captain's cabin, the room with the best view,
Democrats are no better than anyone else at
   girl really hated art as much as the others did, and
      though he liked to tell visitors it was only the
surrendering power to women and other minori-
   he would again end up supporting instead of
      office of the ship's yeoman.] Sarah insisted on
ties!" she sallied angrily in a calm voice that
   learning. [None of them can be blamed for not
      clearing the table, her turn to work while Ruth
usually carried all besiegers before it. She was
   seeing what could have been seen only through
      rested, so that the people could see each other
stunned and confused by their unanimous shout
   the eyes of a tall fair Angle brought down from
      better, and not ruin the good dishes with their
of laughter: "*Minority!*" She who wasnt used to
   the clouds by fanatic little self-immolating fiends
      tobacco cinders. Hecuba listened quietly and
being corrected by men was then straightened
   desperately defending the center of their
      wide-eyed, marveling at what had come over her
out by two English teachers, kindly antagonists
   Emperor's yellow hell; yet it's only to a truly
      friend's lazy husband. The report didnt sound

or ambivalent allies. But she knew the basic

     loving woman warm and naked in the dark with

          quite right, but she said nothing. She was

living logic of her protest well enough. When

     her head on your chest and her hand comforting

          thinking about how Foxy had changed too.

Jack drolly tried to humor her humorlessness with

     your guilty body that it can be told. Never to any

          Before he got the good news he always used to

the statement that a female mind is clearer purer

     other kind of human being except Michael Chap-

          slyly question her about the cocks of her other

and more mnemonically receptive to foreign

     man have you even mentioned the tour you and

          lovers, ostensibly of the past or in her dreams;

languages for instance, because of being less

     the living members of your gravitated crew were

          but now he was jealous and angry at any hint

intimately associated with the body, she coldly

     given by the philosophical English-speaking

          that she hadnt been a blushing old maid when she

rejoined "Thanks brother!" in a tone of intimi-

     military police captain just as short and bandy-

          married him. [Will you listen to that! Now he's

dating sarcasm that sufficed to reject at least one

     legged as the rest—and maybe just as stoic,

          started singing those World War One songs to

of his premises. Thereupon Michael put an end to

     despite his degree from U C L A , as the Jap

          poor Ruth about how we should send word that

the accidental combat by proposing a toast to

     officer whose famous picture taken as he be-

          the Yanks are coming to screw the French girls

Gloucester's Joan of Arc commemorating World

     headed an Australian airman was imprinted in all

          until it's over over there. There: I knew it: he

War One in front of the Greek Revival American

     our brains—who had saved you all in the nick of

          wants everybody to drink to the Red Cross Nurse

Legion hall that as former seat of government

     time from a vengeful swarm of implacable peas-

          their Rose of No-man's-land! She must have had

and schoolhouse really belonged to all citizens

     ants whose hatred would never have contented

          quite a time for herself. But shit I don't care about

especially those the F B I called "premature anti-
            itself with a mere lynching in the Western style,
                        all that stuff now. Men can get boring. Army,
Fascists" for volunteering to anticipate future
            only with making you forget terror for your life
                        Navy, and Sexy!—that's all they mostly ever talk
Legionnaires in the war you sometimes wouldnt
            even on your very way to their deadly prison
                        about when you let them get together.] And just
have known was against Hitler or under F D R 's
            camp. My trivial little personal tremor
                        about that time all the women in the room who
direction, so many patriots seemed to want to
            was soon turned into fearless selfless suicidal
                        hadnt already forgotten about men felt a whiff of
fight the British under MacArthur's royal crest.
            horror by the immediate and nearly silent vision
                        the same weary fed-up distaste for the childish
Jack replied by drinking to all honest fishmongers,
            of dead and dying babies, the shades of baby
                        games of the other gender, and most of them had
Polonius Napoleon and Vanzetti included; and
            devils, with their mothers or the shadows of their
                        a twinge of secret gratitude to the brave revolu-
Newt by pledging in riposte Hamlet Josephine
            mothers, in the flattened streets of Hiroshima only
                        tionist among them. But not excepting the
and President Lowell of Harvard who hated
            twenty-four hours before they hauled down the
                        firebrand herself they all turned to each other for
fishmongers unto the death. They were back on
            evil flag of the Rising Sun far far to the west of
                        the comfort of women as women always have
whiskey now and the Silver Fox was glad to see
            this table.] One other woman he had wished to
                        done. Even Lilian listening for the handsome
some solid drinkingby the intellectuals, though
            tell it all to. Probably she now knew the bare
                        flyer's secret was becoming hourly more avid for
he was himself somewhat abstemious. Jew and
            facts—not what he felt but where he'd been—
                        words that might shed some light on how to
Gentile acclaimed Michael's statement that
            beyond the official story that he'd simply been
                        launch fit out and sail a baby by herself, for he

Republicans were no more fit to govern than

shot down over the inland sea and taken prisoner-

had overestimated her attraction to him. "Look at

Protestants to run a universal church. "Or a uni-

of-war so late in the game that he suffered no

them!" Ruth Sandys cried, drawing closer to

versity!" Dave added, who had thought about it

hardship, because she was married to the one

sisters who she assumed didnt like her, in honest

more than anyone else though born and bred a

friend he'd ever told it all to, who to that extent

disgust at the way men ganged up when they had

Protestant Republican with distant Puritan

may have breached his secret after they tempo-

half a chance, *All for one and one for all!* From that

ancestors. Newt who had escaped service in

rarily lost touch with each other largely as a result

point on even she ignored the men's toasts and

World War Two and Sandy who had shirked

of that marriage. —Nor was Sandy's heart in the

foolish talk. Her precious parasite in the third

liability during the more recent crusade waged in

tiresome old game with Sylvia (whose swollen

lazy trimester of slowly wakening sleep bestirred

a single oriental country for the defense of our

fertility despite all efforts of imagination neutral-

herself more often now. The drumhead was

Japanese interests without inconvenience to the

ized his inextirpable priapic pique). Like Dave he

stretching tighter every day, pushing the knot of

voters listened deferentially to the ancients of

was almost ready to relax the habitual intentions

her navel, and every night with his ear to the

war, the one to learn something that might

of mature gynecomania and join as a sextet the

pigskin Sandy tapped out messages to the piglet

strengthen his critical appreciation of fiction, the

passive fellows there present.

other to garner war stories as details
of fictional autobiography for impressionable clients. Jack was
granting little to the Navy's credit,
adducing as evidence of its merely
conservative contribution to Victory the alleged fact (intended to

who was in no hurry to come out of
the poke. She wondered if the time
would come when Ruth Chapman
would invite her to help run the
nursery school she was talking
about, mainly to give Roger some
playmates while the new one was

becalm Chapman's sailfull of claims for seapowers's innovations) that archers men-at-arms and mounted knights had stormed Byzantium by amphibious assault with aerial ramps from their ships as far back as the fourth Crusade, not to mention Vikings who'd been hitting the beaches for a couple of centuries before that. This reactionary thesis turned out to be the first pass in a bear-baiting: reference to the British failure to take Byzantium during the first war, which of course (he jeered) wasnt Churchill's fault at all, who thought he was finished at the age of 40, but the bloody heel-stamping British Army was still riding horses and wearing puttees, which he thereupon humbly joined in France (along with other literary people). Never mind, Michael insisted, it was at that anti-Iliadic labium of Turkey more than a quarter of a century before Americans were old enough to think of such assaults that the First Lord of the Admiralty had learned that "an amphibious operation . . . has to be fit together like a jeweled bracelet" whether the ships are driven by oars steam or diesel, with or without the support of airplanes or naval gunfire. But it can't be left to lapidaries. From what they now heard about L S T s Newt Cahners thought they must have looked like Pinocchio's dogfish and Sandy was reminded of Helen's pursuers at the Dardanelles. In Fox's day the imperial American fleet didnt have to worry much about resistance to its adventures: every blue-jacket was a good enough soldier; he just laced some canvas leggings called boots

getting old enough. In any case her own shoat would need guardians sooner or later and there were five of them right there at that fertility convention. The poor valiant dissenter, no longer single-mindedly indignant and indeed for the time being proud of her reduction to the common lot, was never one who could tempt male observers by lying on a beach clad in the tiny triangles of cloth that had been named by fashion hucksters for the island where entropy-bombing was studied, but as her voice grew softer, and as her face gradually disclosed its native femininity under the tasteless oversized sloe-eyed glasses that she had always worn for soul-armor, she flaunted her waddling pregnancy and went as naked as she dared in public places. For Sandy's delight at home she proudly bared her huge white cauldron like a blood-swollen tick incongruously underpinned by its recessive black fork. As her time of agonizing cure approached she sometimes thought hopefully of a Caesarian short-cut, nowadays so anesthetic, but in the company of other women the fear that made her a coward dissolved in fellowship. She was bonded in the magnetic circuit (now complete) that ringing the table had grown impervious to all the extraneous lines of force that elsewhere disturbed each of them with special troubles. She felt clear of private eddies and sexual perturbations, truly independent of the tiresome mechanics who were unferrously impermeable to the field they sat in. A love for these new friends— the only friends she could claim—

around his bell-bottoms, hitched on his webbed guard belt, grabbed a rifle, and stepped ashore from one of the launches in Nicaragua for a show of force or a little skirmish under some palm trees—and in fact the main purpose for being sent to boot camp was to learn those conventions. He still liked to wear spats dove-gray with pearl buttons when he got the chance at opening nights funerals or weddings. Jack, having briefly been a dogface passenger in an L S T —he thought it was an L S T : it was called by some such jargon:: perhaps only an L C I ::: in his seasick misery he hadnt been studying naval architecture) —to begin his grand tour of Europe in the Italian campaign, had no compunction about ridiculing the Limeyphile's ideas of how operations were actually mounted, of British tactical perspicacity, and of grand strategy as a determinant of success. Jack didnt hate Churchill and he certainly had nothing against Roosevelt but he usually attacked modern hero-worship on principle. Most of his own admiration was reserved for General Marshall (the selfless high-domed eminence of Washington D C); but there they found good measure of agreement. Thus Mike and Jack touched on issues that the others would have ruled out in testing a philosophy of history either because they were too large or because they seemed minor. Newt had never taken interest in the practical affairs of nations but he was inclined to sympathize with Churchill despite the man's semiantisemitism atrocious taste and jingoistic contempt

rose up her innards like the warmth of the cordial she was tasting. Her affection included the floozie blonde who was facing the terror for the first time much later in life than herself; and Sylvia the yawning composed cocktailer who must have been as worried as her simpler sisters about a miscarriage stillbirth club foot mental defect or other nightmarish malformation no matter how many spoiled overfed brats she'd already brought into the world; and even the stand-offish girl who called herself a painter and seemed to affect an absurdly serene self-confidence. Meanwhile the whole female party was joking about precedence. Although no one of course gave voice to calendared speculation about the details by which she might have secretly modified her doctor's estimate, going by the book the dentist's wife seemed to have as good a claim to priority as the baron's or the sales correspondent's. The three of them were officially scheduled for the end of December. But the experienced mothers were willing to bet that their hostess would come first, probably a little early, maybe within a few hours of her Christmas dinner, seeing that she would have unusually exerted herself during the holiday season and that the Chapman trail had already been broken. Sarah and Sylvia were only a month or two behind. Lilian wasnt due till May Day. Each of her matron friends silently pledged the unwed Bohemian Indian all the help and sympathy she would accept in her lonely travail, and each gave silent thanks for being married at a time

for psychiatry since he himself was about Churchill's size and would soon be of similar shape; he didnt much like to hear David (the derivation of whose quiet animosity remained obscure but was associated with the Irish Famine) call W S C a blood-thirsty crypto-catamite petty-cock, a self-serving emotionally infantile killer who tried to teach the British people to butcher Germans with pitchforks and pruning-hooks to the pretty chant of

> Let every one
> Kill a Hun!

Dave had heard from a British infantry major in P O W camp that at Singapore during the siege one Imperialistic company commander had changed the words for his Far East bayonet drill:

> Let every chap
> Stick a Jap!

Harmon Sandys was on Michael's side because he fancied himself a long-lost relative of Churchill's son-in-law. He hoped to hear a rebuttal to his wife's old accusation that Churchill was a quasi-fascist who had refused to lift a finger in support of the Abraham Lincoln Brigade or any of the Loyalists fighting the Falange in Spain at a time when it would have been easy for the British and French to defeat Hitler Mussolini and Franco all at once. But before he could ask a question about those early years of his childhood Michael was lecturing in abstract terms on W S C's talent for operational organization

like this. In any event as they all would be dehiscing within four months of each other they got up various jackpots of I O U s, one of them to be shared by the girl babies of the crop. No one expected a pair of jacks or better but Hecuba felt so prematurely clumsy that she harbored an unspoken confidence of the prize for weight. "What a dinner!" she said. "I couldnt help eating for at least two. Foxy says he needs a shovel to keep me on my feed. Calls me his honey barge. That's what the Fleet garbage scow was called. I know I walk like one. It'll be nice to wear a fur coat and spiked heels again." She gazed at her long red fingernails to conjure up the vision of a night on the town with an openly proclaimed husband respected by all doormen and headwaiters from there to Los Angeles. "No matter what I wear I feel like I'm dressed in a burlesque bag. . . . But anyway that's neither here nor care. I used to mind Ruthie's baby and now I'll be able to mind my own!" But she bit her lip in superstitious dismay at having counted her chick before it hatched. "I don't believe in betting on my own hand." she muttered with knuckle under nose. Ruth Sandys and Lilian Cloud had a like attitude toward telling their own fortunes, for though of course all six had carnal knowledge of men these were the three who anxiously awaited initiation as epopts of what is for all women the greater mystery. Lilian reminded herself that despite her horrifying morning-sickness and the incredible pain to come she was a perfectly healthy

as transcending all the genius you could deprive him of by hindsight (strategic wisdom tough-minded objectivity humanity grasp of economics moral strength historiographical profundity sociological sympathy artistic creativity critical acumen masonic skill or omniscience): namely the gift of executive acuity selflessly dedicated by a self-centered man to any and all political entities that benefited used or depended upon English "law, language, literature" sincerely intended for the good of all peoples on earth whether or not they yet spoke that tongue. Who cares if a man like that isnt a New Deal democrat? He certainly wasnt a Republican, though it was true that he didnt sufficiently distrust some of his own ambassadors who were duped by certain Republican Senators into believing that F D R was leading our folks to the left against their will, splitting the country they called it. Thus Chapman's disquisition took a familiar turn: it was really party politics that he wanted to talk about. ". . . and when people say that Roosevelt had no principles they are only saying he held no doctrinaire policy comparable to their own high-minded axiomatical tenets (like 'solvency' or 'free enterprise') about the means to reach his ends. The ends were what the Republicans feared to debate—the question they must always shun in public discussion. Of course the Marxists also hated him (a little less disingenuously inasmuch as they were committed to nothing but principle) for his temperamental aversion to doctrine—

specimen. She could see that in the mirror. People were made bilaterally symmetrical so that unsound lumps or vital injuries would show up clearly no matter what you looked like but naturally it was a different picture in the sagittal plane; her normal figure would soon be as obtrusively unlovely as Hecuba's. Meanwhile Sylvia listening to the babble of innocents mused on Newt's goodnatured acceptance of the situation. He blamed his surgeon but no one seemed to notice that he never spoke of going back for a test. Still, she had taken a stupid risk during the first Summer Session. It was an almost conscious slip that she hoped to get to the bottom of with her Freudian doctor when she finally told him the full story about someone he might know. But Newt was pulling all the strings he could think of to get to watch the delivery. In fact he even wanted the kids to be with her all through the labor—probably just to hear how foul-mouthed their mother could be when there was really something to swear about. Whenever she had her clothes off he made them come in to see. "Feel Mother's fat belly!" he'd urge, as if she was some kind of breeding animal, when the new little Oedipus was still hardly showing at all in the cradle of his conception. "Well they say a bad seaman makes a good husband." Hecuba remarked, needlessly apologizing to the ladies for her Silver Fox who was reminiscing with the men about his brief dishonorable and mostly under-aged life in the Navy before she was born. [And a

which is characteristic of almost all effective leaders, Churchill included. . . . Principle my ass! The higher a Republican gets in public life the more of a follower and the less of a leader he gets to be, because when he finds the country can't be run to make a profit he turns to some semi-intellectual who can rig up a sophistical policy for letting things ride. To Republicans almost any well-educated person seems liberal: so they boast about 'liberal' Republicanism to get the educated vote, and—" Dave interrupted the tirade; he detested the mean prejudices of what the Federalist fathers called factionalism: "If your two friends hadnt decided to bypass Truk when they got together at Casablanca" he pointed out "we might never have had to attack Japan itself . . ." And so they were dragged into the old controversy about "unconditional surrender" in both halves of the war. The term had sexual connotations for Sandy. To the Silver Fox having lived through that war as a thoroughgoing civilian such ex post facto argument was ungrateful, for wartimes were good times when everyone's residual motives left over from business legitimate and otherwise were knitted together in a sodality of feeling against national enemies and no one grudged the expenditure of money or pleasure, times of solidarity when you might get to like anyone who was with you against all Japs and the worst kind of Germans). Labor people black people Oakies reformers social workers civic big-shots farmers itinerant field workers college stu-

good husband makes bad semen, says Sylvia to herself.] Sarah wanted to change the subject for Lilian's sake, so she said the first thing that came into her head, calling over to Sylvia: "What's your excuse for increasing the population of the world after all we've heard about how you've got other things to do besides bringing up children?" She immediately realized that she had forgotten the reason already given and that this was a dangerous subject; instead of bringing up the cause of conception she should have shamelessly described her new Caloric stove which if the truth was known seemed more important than another English course. But Sylvia was already answering: "There's no such thing as an infallible method of birth control. If there are too fucking many people in the world it's only because there are too many people fucking. What can you do about it when you're married to a horny man? —What's yours Sally?" On the way over Sarah's hermeneutic husband had glossed her an Anglo scholar's scholium on some exegesis of the Talmud going through three or four languages as if to justify the trip to Alameda for some fun at a time when he was too busy with his books to let her relatives drop in and say hello: Michal (he pointed out not for the first time) was historically a heathen goddess who endowed Jewish chieftains with their kingship by virtue of her matriarchal gestation of their children the first important male of whom was always called Adam, so that in the natural evolution of patriarchal

dents art-history professors—all of them free and easy with each other in a war-town like San Francisco— warmed up the cold sisters of America who seemed for the first time willing to acknowledge the human nature of their brothers. Women worked everywhere they'd never worked before, almost in the locker-rooms, no longer pretending that in the good life a decent woman knew nothing about the way God made men and always would. He remembered with fond pleasure more than the girl herself, a college graduate with real class who'd come down from Marin County to do her part in a shipyard, the tableau she'd stumbled on down in one of the lower compartments of a Victory hull—a blunder that hadnt bothered anyone concerned as much as it embarrassed him when she recounted it: this cheerful society broad still a virgin in every way bouncing through the hatch with her electric riveting gun to find half a dozen welders or electricians lined up in a row with their cocks laid out on a work bench to settle a bet. Of course she hadnt lingered to register the details but for him who heard about the comedy six months later as her fourth lover it remained the most vivid scene of World War Two. Even now when he was nursing every minute of his restorative furlough from conjugal duty before facing again the vexatious problem of pleasing his young wife whose desire to be pleased would soon be at the very peak of her long love-life the renewed imagination of that story fetched up a sensation at the uncir-

mythography it came to be said that a masculine angel named Michael gathered dust from the four quarters of the earth for God to create the first man with; and thus in the so-called second dispensation of the Christians, by a reverse transformation according to the needs of a Medieval cult, some said that Michael going much further than Tiresias became immortal Mary to bear the Messiah: or suchlike intrication (all the while she was trying to figure out if the plumber knew what he was doing when he set all the pilot lights so high) which he would probably quiz her on the next time she asked to take a course in ceramics. "A lot of Jews need to be replaced." she replied to Sylvia. Yet all the women at one time or another had noticed that Lilian who tended to drift off into reverie never seemed embarrassed either by her predicament or by anything that was said in her presence. Sarah's mind was well schooled in memorization and watching Lilian she recalled the Christian gospel she'd heard a year ago that night at her own house: . . . *for it must needs be that offences come; but woe to that man by whom the offence cometh.* She wondered if Lilian had let her man off scot free; but the seating arrangement prevented her from whispering with Ruth. Hecuba was saying she couldnt help being scared about having her first baby at a ripe age. "Fear ye not!" Ruth Sandys spoke out in a clear and pleasant tone devoid of all belligerence, looking to her left at both Lilian and Hecuba and perhaps for the first time since puberty ventur-

cumcised tip of his weary old flesh; but he was no longer grossly ruffled by his recollection of this recurrent spectacle in the inward eye. Vacantly and pensively he gazed around the table at his five friendly rivals (including Randy Jillison, tonight more inconspicuous even than his nearly silent Nancy, as if they were both worried about natal deformity). By this time Michael was telling everyone what a joy it had been to see the land of milk and honey for the first time and go on liberty among the palm trees of Monterey, which Dick Harry Dana who'd also been to Harvard liked better than all the rest of that amazing coast, as did the Limey tourist Bob Stevenson. "Say Mike, y'know back before Prohibition I went ashore a few times in your home port. There werent no palm trees or hula-hoola girls but it was the best damned little liberty town we had up that way. Course I can't say much in decent company. . . ." The Fox laughed and winked all around the compass card. "A lot of places are all pretty much the same once you get in off the street. But those fishermen were rough-looking bastards and they didnt take too kindly to young whippersnappers like us all spruced up full of piss and vinegar." Now Michael during his own hitch had wanted nothing except a girl as much as to visit Gloucester Massachusetts in uniform, and Gloucester England too, even more than Key West Charleston Norfolk Baltimore Philadelphia Brooklyn New London Charlestown Portsmouth Halifax St John's Liverpool Bristol Plymouth

ing a jest on the subject: "Trust in God. She will comfort you!" They had all heard that one before (thanks to Adlai Stevenson) but coming from her it brought them of one voice to a loud clap of mirth. The gentlemen paused in their blooming buzz and looked about questioningly, slightly annoyed at having been excluded from a joke without learning that it was one of their favorites. But they were in no mood to cajole the girls, so meeting nothing but prolonged laughter they turned back to their own conversation. Ruth Chapman had been thinking up jests by herself, briefly forgetting all about her guests. The first was that she had cured herself of "apathy, crippling fatigue, and distorted perception" by making her husband go so deeply into debt that they'd never again be able to afford a head-doctor—unlike the Cahners pair who delighted in iatrogenic troubles transmitted unto the third generation at least. By spending too much money on a house she was going to succeed in having four healthy children who would never need a psychiatrist as long as they lived. By her own suffering and determination she had brought to a stop the fatal pendulum of aggressive and regressive illness in her lineage: her daughter would be free of all unnecessary pain and weakness. And in her nursery school, if someone like Lilian assisted her own vigilance, she might be able to block the wrongheaded perpetuation of force and fear in the children of others who didnt yet understand what she knew about how to make their con-

Portsmouth Old London Dover Newcastle Aberdeen Belfast and all the other North Atlantic seaports of Churchill's "English-speaking club", which along with lands to the west and the shores where Spanish was spoken as far south as the Canal would have been bound into one democratically chauvinistic empire if his childhood plans for the American expansion had been fulfilled, for he had been somewhat more imperialistic than the British P M from a different political perspective not to mention the social. (In those prematurely anti-fascist days in Gloucester and Cambridge as the leader of his siblings he had designated himself to represent the U S A in all games of power; Billy was England and Peggy was France: a true model for his fraternal feelings in international affairs.) Was it surprising that he should rival Churchill in scope and ability, seeing that his ancestor an alumnus of Oxford as well as Cambridge who was willing to go to gaol for his art had rivaled Shakespeare and got himself mentioned in sonnets? But even if he'd been a man-of-war's-man in the Atlantic Fleet he wouldnt have known a great deal more than Jack did about the structure or operation of his own ship at the time. In Dana's day just a few months fled from Harvard a new sailor knew all the ropes and enough of sail's infinitely complex seamanship to serve as second mate (having studied it by rote and untutored apprenticeship almost twenty hours a day without anyone to buffer him from the hard knocks of not learning fast enough); there was

tribution to the world both happy and enlightened. [If I were only a doctor I'd be a doctor to mothers. I could cure the trauma of birth itself. The babies I delivered would be born smiling. The husbands of my patients would never want a vasectomy; they'd make love to those mothers for forty years as if they were new brides every time. With kids born and brought up so gently television wouldnt enter into the question at all.] A real joke was "Whithersoever thou goest I will go!"! After all was said and done she had only come home! She had only settled in! She had not been uprooted! [In Gloucester I wouldnt even have been able to keep in touch with my mother. He says the mail service there is so fast that the postal trucks go around with sirens blowing—but I don't think they'd know what to make of airmail even in the city of Boston.] She chuckled also at the polished marble egg she'd given him in an egg-cup that morning for his birthday. [The poor man was afraid he wasnt going to get any eggs to eat. A funny kind of paperweight. He was very nice about it. Said now he had a petrified egg to throw at Republicans. But he once told me he found nothing as unappetizing as a fertilized egg. All of us girls look like eggs now! Half a dozen eggs please sir. Hardboiled eggs have a sort of amniotic skin inside the shell don't they? I must tell him *my* theory, that Chanticleer crows up the sun because it brings the light that makes his hens lay.] Thus she found herself thinking of him again, and when she spoke aloud to Sandy's

no dark and Satanic electrical machinery to make him a mechanician for life. But our son of Gloucester would have felt himself an imposter if he'd come back in seaman's clothes to pass as a sailor in the place where he was never to hang his fullgrown hat. All he knew about seamanship from his two years under the mast was the mast itself, a simple stout pipe not much more important to most of the crew than the taffrail staff but welded integral to the ship in a rigid continuity of irrefrangible steel without stays or triangular bracing of any kind, its nautical heritage almost entirely overlooked in the simple design to support futtock plates for the radar antenna—whence it came about that the vessel's Radio Technician was invited to paint it from time to time, a young buck so far from having been sterilized by radiation on the job that more than ten years later he had to take the trouble to get an inconvenient operation for that very purpose, when he finally faced up to the fact that he was incapable of the moral restraint specified by Malthus as the only alternative to "vice" (probably meant to signify both auto- and homo-erotic practices as well as whoring) or to the misery associated with a decimating or worse mortality rate. [Spare the rod and save a child.] Even now that he'd acquired property, which that same precursor of Darwin supposed would foster moral restraint, he knew it still would have taken the sheer force of the surgeon's knife to keep him from making further personal contribution to what Tocque-

Ruth whom she'd been meaning not to neglect she said that the thing she loved most of all about the house was an oak tree that he had hung a swing from strong enough for her to sit in. Then she saw that Lil and Hecky and Sylvia and Sally were also listening to her. She couldnt seem to stop talking about him, but she wasnt saying quite what she was thinking. She was thinking about the beautiful letters he had written her. Some of the words were misspelled, and not entirely because the enlisted men on the ship didnt have access to a dictionary: in those days he'd refused to use one anyway. She had been like silver and gold fretwork then: not a fertilized egg. Yet that's what love was for. ["Let in the maid that out a maid/ Never departed more."] What she was saying to her friends was "You've never seen such a—" she lowered her voice and all the women bent closer—"such a sweet Don Quixote. We have enough tools and implements for a—for a machine shop I guess. I don't know what he'll ever use them all for. Why there are three or four different kinds of shovels alone. I must say he gets them cheap enough, new or used, I have no idea where. There's a spade and a longhandled shovel and a post-hole shovel and for some reason a coal shovel, an old one with a bent lip. There's even a snow shovel. What could that be for? Perhaps he spends a little too much on grass fertilizer, but most of what he accomplishes is by plain hard work. He rakes the lawn after every mowing and waters it almost every day

ville and divers men of means thought of as a country's wealth. Michael expected but could not await the evolution of a universal pollutant (if the emanations of radar television and nuclear power should prove ineffectual) to save the human population from its asymtotic approach to extinction by a decimating or better incidence of involuntary sterility. [Now I hear Sandy telling the old one that always amuses Ruth about the kid who wanted a watch for Christmas, ending "So we let him!" Naturally Malthus never suspected how long we'd be able to postpone the need for poison or death rays to counteract the universal urge to breed. How could he have foreseen the chemical force to jack up agriculture with inorganic compounds called fertilizers and applied with the chemical machinery of infernal combustion? Greek fire and Greek love threaten the purposes of women. It'll take a few more years for hyper-agronomy and high-power fishing to fall behind demand. . . .]

even when it's rained. He waters the trees too. Lil, you'd never believe he's the same bookkeeper you used to work with!" Those who knew her well smiled doubtfully at Ruth's dry way of putting her overstatements when you least expected them. But in what she said was wrapped many a plain fact. "He bought a whole bunch of little Sears fire extinguishers on sale for 98¢ each. We have one in every room of the house—two in the kitchen. It's hard to keep them out of the children's reach. Now he's planning a bomb shelter in the basement if Stevenson loses again, with a fireproof box for his literary notes."

. . . Jack was teaching Newt and Sandy how to count a cadence. Michael mechanically joined the other men to reinforce the suddenly intimidating chant: *HUP-two-three-four, HUP-two-three-four* . . . The women were annoyed at this childish irruption, strident to the mind and jarring to the belly; but even the players themselves were daunted by the overriding mindlessness of their magnifying unison and the fun petered out sheepishly without another word about it on either side.

Michael Chapman would never be brought to such despair as Conrad's who condemned consciousness itself as mankind's curse, but he imagined being the last bear of a species that has lingered too long cleaning out every hollow tree of honey with winter coming on half a world from home. His wisdom nevertheless remained in thrall to piecemeal hopes that could have sustained no comprehensive examination and which even to himself made reason seem absurd as long as society was too stupid to accept the means of grace. Not only every election but also every public opinion poll and every littering advance in the gross national product of advertising seemed to mark a watershed dividing corrupted progress from universal death—and yet like millions of other frightened prophets he dealt with a prospective truncation of human existence by calculating the probabilities of his own family's survival of the first shock. He groped for wisps of short-term mitigation, hoping that even on the island of Alameda which was totally unprotected by such granite as might have been a temporary shield in Gloucester and which lay within lines of sight from countless military and industrial targets there might be an inkling of encouragement in the report that whereas the radius of a hydrogen bomb's heat varies with the square root of its energy the radius of its blast varies only with the cube root. He secretly brooded about the renitency of his castle's shallow basement virtually floating on the water table of a tidal landfill.

It was far too late for women to save the world by refusing to bear daughters. He stole a glance at each of his female companions as if he might empower himself to read at least one of their minds, but especially Lilian's, to judge whether or not if it came to a binary choice the acculturated art of harmless coupling could ever supplant the natural science of multiplication.

4.

To work hard, live hard, die hard, and go to hell after all, would be hard indeed.
—Merchant sailors' proverb quoted by Richard Henry Dana the Abolitionist

Propriety, Orthodoxy, Freedom
—Michael Chapman's motto

Billions of mammals in the earthy part of the globe have forseen better than Michael Chapman their instinctive parental affection and the advantages of having power or property in its service. Any pursuit of happiness (whether or not possible for any particular person)—conditioned by luck talent skill brutality or thermometric endurance and directed toward real estate kitchen appliances political power general prosperity social welfare international peace yachts horses scalp-collection high society nightclubbing pub-crawling cuisine music photography golf athletics travel scholarship beauty virtue fame narcotic serenity science or art—is to be execrated not for what it aspires to but for what it neglects. Most of what's excluded or disdained may well be passed up for a good life, but there are some things more important than other things and almost every one of them is less important than most things. Chapman missed a lot. He could manage even his limited life only by alternation. The reader has seen him as a poorly archangelic namesake; but at least he was "panorganic": all brain, all heart, all eye, all _____. At any one time he was usually "a single sensibility", as an angel should be, impassioned or not.

But sometimes the cycles of alternation are years or decades, not merely undertones of months weeks days and hours. Reserve your judgment accordingly. Of course he was a foolish codfish to linger for the last shred of bait after he'd gobbled most of it: but he hasnt been hauled in yet. Until his last gasp is reported in the newspapers you'd better not exaggerate his failures. At least he's cut his losses. Despite all his moaning and groaning it's not too late for him to toughen up and go for broke with underground anti-poetry. Ruth and her children will pay the price.

You have not been shown the private revulsions and rages that may still save him in what solitude he has salvaged. His roundtable party was not necessarily the end of the beginning of a losing war. He could still bank on longevity for waging a second by losing weight and getting another dog to walk with. He could still learn to sail more weatherly.

Still, what a joke his waggish motto is! The singular Propriety of a black operator who applies Ockham's Razor (a k a Law of Parsimony) to the supernaturalism in Orthodoxy! As for Freedom, he needs servants to undertake that for him—distant phantoms of his own making.

At least he wasnt greatly worse off than his friends. All six babies were born live and whole as daughters. Although in each womb there was good and sufficient cause for the unmodified fundamental sex, in a four-month-thick demographic cross-section you would have expected a little less than three of these babies to be girls. Thus in one sense it was a remarkably counterentropic little group. Elsewhere in Alameda County during that interval there must have been by way of demographic compensation a virtual group of half a dozen women similar in age and origins about to deliver seven sons. In exemplifying the statistics of gender one must round off to whole numbers.

{*Postulants only*: GO TO ITEM (38) HY.07.0, page 417.}

We must not nail ourselves down so firmly to our humors and dispositions. Our principle talent is the ability to apply ourselves to various practices. It is existing, but not living, to keep ourselves bound and obliged by necessity to a single course. The fairest souls are those that have the most variety and adaptability.

—MONTAIGNE

INDEX

... it becomes an author generally to divide a book, as it does a butcher to joint his meat, for such assistance is of great help to both the reader and the carver.

—HENRY FIELDING

SECOND CURRICULUM
Syllabus for Postulants

(Postulants' commencement)

THIRD CURRICULUM
(For specialists and reviewers)

Syllabus for the Metasystem

Syllabus for the Side Adjacent

Syllabus for the Side Opposite

Syllabus for the Hypotenuse

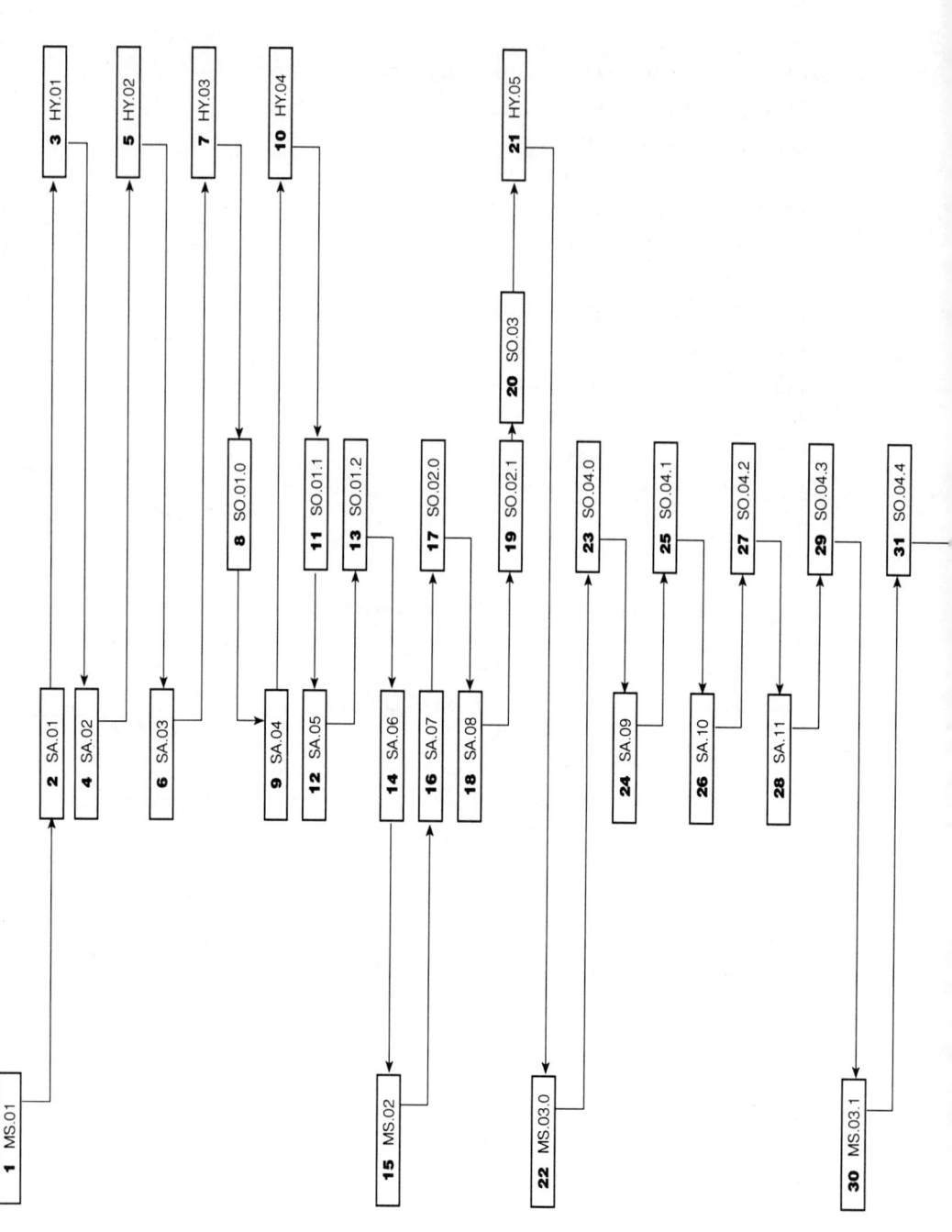

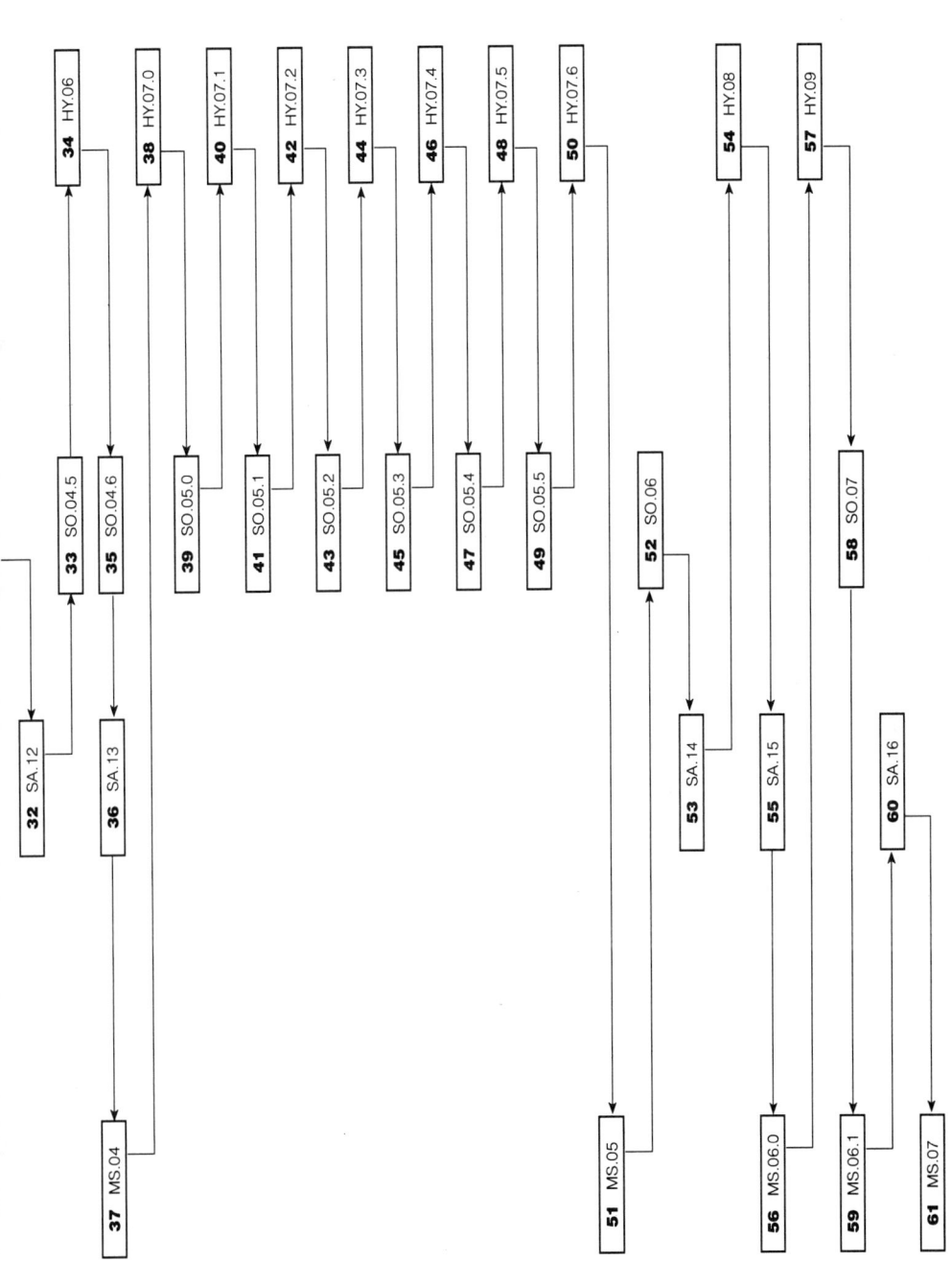

Behold, I am doing a new thing.
Do you not perceive it?
—ISAIAH 43:19